THE ENCYCL(

SIXTIES MUSIC

COLIN LARKIN

IN ASSOCIATION WITH MUZE INC.

Dedicated To Ronnie Lane

First published in Great Britain in 1997 by
VIRGIN BOOKS
an imprint of Virgin Publishing Ltd
332 Ladbroke Grove, London W10 5AH

A catalogue record for this book is available from the British Library

ISBN 0 7535 0149 X

Written, edited and produced by
MUZE UK Ltd
to whom all editorial enquiries should be sent
Iron Bridge House, 3 Bridge Approach, Chalk Farm, London NW1 8BD

Editor In Chief: Colin Larkin
Production Editor: Susan Pipe
Editorial and Research Assistant: Nic Oliver
Copy Editor: Sarah Lavelle
Typographic Design Consultant: Roger Kohn
Special thanks to Trev Huxley, Anthony Patterson and Paul Zullo of Muze Inc.,
and to Rob Shreeve of Virgin Publishing.
Typeset by Fast 'n' Bulbous Studio
Printed and bound in Great Britain by Butler & Tanner Ltd, Frome and London

INTRODUCTION

The 60s music boom has been continuing for more than a decade, so much so that it is not going away. The influences cited and heard in dozens of today's groups and artists is monumental. Never before has one decade produced so many major musical figures. Never has one decade been so chameleon-like as it wove its way from American pop to British beat at the beginning of the decade, to psychedelic pop and acid rock as 1969 ended, choking on its own marijuana smoke. Smack in the middle we had the glorious soul music from Atlantic, Stax and Motown. The sight of Otis Redding at the Monterey Pop Festival highlighted, more than any other event, the way the music of the 60s became united and defragmented. The audience, stoned and bedecked in kaftans and mom's beads, had experienced music from an even more exotically dressed and completely stoned bunch of artists. Otis stepped onstage in a three-button, blue tonic mohair suit, white shirt and tie. He looked like a fifth string on a bass guitar as he addressed the 'love crowd'. Yet this man knocked down every musical barrier as he delivered a breathtaking set and arguably united every music fan present in the one decade when everything came together.

I hope I have represented it well with this selection of entries, if not, I know you will let me know, as you have done in the past.

ACKNOWLEDGEMENTS

We lost John Bauldie (*the* Dylanologist), who tragically died in a helicopter crash in 1996. Love and respect to him wherever he is. His contribution to our appreciation of Bob Dylan is immeasurable. To Johnny Rogan, who continues to be a rational ear and sounding board. He was the first person to hear of my proposal for the original Encyclopedia and agree to be involved. His great attention to detail shaped the original editorial stylesheet. John Burton continues to send his never-ending supply of newspaper obituaries.

Our in-house editorial team is even smaller than before, such is our super-efficiency. The Database is now a fully grown child and needs only regular food, attention and love. Thanks to Susan Pipe; reliable and trustworthy as ever. Nic Oliver 'the new boy' is shaping up pretty well, and Sarah Lavelle is our brand new quality controller. Our outside contributors are further reduced in number, as we now write and amend all our existing text. However, we could not function without the continuing efforts and dedication of Big John Martland, Bruce Crowther and Alex Ogg. Brian Hogg, Hugh T. Wilson, Spencer Leigh and Robert Pruter continue to supply their specialist knowledge. We also received some entries from our newer contributors; Salsri Nyah, Tim Footman, Christen Thomsen, Essi Berilian and Jamie Renton, while Lloyd Peasley sent some important corrections free of charge.

Other past contributors' work may appear in this volume and I acknowledge once again; Simon Adams, David Ades, Mike Atherton, Gavin Badderley, Alan Balfour, Michael Barnett, Steve Barrow, John Bauldie, Lol Bell-Brown, Johnny Black, Chris Blackford, Pamela Boniface, Keith Briggs, Michael Ian Burgess, Paul M. Brown, Tony Burke, John Child, Linton Chiswick, Rick Christian, Alan Clayson, Tom Collier, Paul Cross, Bill Dahl, Norman Darwen, Roy Davenport, Peter Doggett, Kevin Eden, John Eley, Lars Fahlin, John Fordham, Per Gardin, Ian Garlinge, Mike Gavin, Andy Hamilton, Harry Hawk, Mark Hodkinson, Mike Hughes, Arthur Jackson, Mark Jones, Max Jones, Simon Jones, Ian Kenyon, Dave Laing, Steve Lake, Paul Lewis, Graham Lock, John Masouri, Bernd Matheja, Chris May, Dave McAleer, Ian McCann, David McDonald, York Membery, Toru Mitsui, Greg Moffitt, Nick Morgan, Michael Newman, Pete Nickols, Lyndon Noon, Zbigniew Nowara, James Nye, Ken Orton, Ian Peel, Dave Penny, Alan Plater, Barry Ralph, John Reed, Emma Rees, Lionel Robinson, Johnny Rogan, Alan Rowett, Jean Scrivener, Roy Sheridan, Dave Sissons, Neil Slaven, Chris Smith, Steve Smith, Mitch Solomons, Christopher Spencer, Jon Staines, Mike Stephenson, Sam Sutherland, Jeff Tamarkin, Ray Templeton, Liz Thompson, Gerard Tierney, John Tobler, Adrian T'Vell, Pete Wadeson, Frank Warren, Ben Watson, Pete Watson, Simon Williams, Val Wilmer, Dave Wilson and Barry Witherden.

Record company press offices are often bombarded with my requests for biogs and review copies. Theirs is a thankless task, but thanks anyway, especially to Alan Robinson of Demon, Sue and Dave Williams at Frontier, Tones Sansom at Creation, Trisha Coogan at Essential, Mal Smith at Delta, Darren Crisp of Science Friction, Julia Honeywell at Ace, Murray Chalmers and Laura at Parlophone, Pat Naylor and Nicola Powell at

Ryko/Hannibal, and Dave Bedford at This Way Up.

Press offices in general at: 4AD (Colleen), A&M, All Saints, Alligator, Almo, American Recordings (Louise), Arista, Beggars Banquet, BGO (Andy Gray), Big Cat (Sharon), Blue Note, Che Recordings, Chrysalis (Iona), City Slang (Wyndham Wallace), Coalition, Cooking Vinyl, Deceptive, Dedicated (Paula), Domino, Duophonic, East West, Echo, EMI, Epitaph, Fire, Fontana (Tina Mawjee), Geffen, Grapevine (Jane), Greentrax, Gut, Carol Hayes, Hightone, Hit Label, Hollywood, Dorothy Howe, HTD, Hut, Indigo, Indolent, Infectious, Island (Deborah), Jet, Jive, Junior Boys Own, Koch (Pat), London, MCA (Ted Cummings), Mercury, Mushroom, New Note, No. 9, Nude (Ellie), One Little Indian, Park, Pinnacle, Poole Edwards, Poppy, Qwest, RCA (Sharon), Savage And Best, Silvertone, Sire, Strange Fruit (Jo), Sub Pop, Superior Quality, Telarc, Tommy Boy, Transatlantic, Trauma, Virgin, Warp, all at Richard Wooton's office, and Zoo.

I wish the press offices at Columbia, Epic, Polydor and Warners would take us more seriously; phew, talk about blood out of a stone.

Thanks for the enthusiasm and co-operation of all our new colleagues at Virgin Publishing under the guidance of Rob Shreeve, in particular to Roz Scott who is always reassuringly efficient. To our new owners at Muze Inc., who oil the smooth running of the UK operation and are the business partners I always knew I wanted but never knew where to find them. In particular to the conscientious Tony Patterson, the scrupulously garbed Paul Zullo, Steve Figard, Bill Mullar, Marc Miller and the prodigiously tactful Trev Huxley. And lastly to my tin lids; the smile you send out returns to you.

ENTRY STYLE

Albums, EPs (extended play 45s), newspapers, magazines, television programmes, films and stage musicals are referred to in italics. All song titles appear in single quotes. We spell rock 'n' roll like this. There are two main reasons for spelling rock 'n' roll with 'n' as opposed to 'n'. First, historical precedent: when the term was first coined in the 50s, the popular spelling was 'n'. Second, the 'n' is not simply an abbreviation of 'and' (in which case 'n' would apply) but as a phonetic representation of n as a sound. The ' ', therefore, serve as inverted commas rather than as apostrophes. The further reading section at the end of each entry has been expanded to give the reader a much wider choice of available books. These are not necessarily recommended titles but we have attempted to leave out any publication that has little or no merit.

We have also started to add videos at the end of the entries. Again, this is an area that is expanding faster than we can easily cope with, but there are many items in the videography and further items in the filmography, which is another new section we have decided to include. Release dates in keeping with albums attempt to show the release date in the country of origin. We have also tried to include both US and UK titles in the case of a title change.

ALBUM RATING

Due to many requests from our readers we have now decided to rate all albums. All new releases are reviewed either by myself or by our team of contributors. We also take into consideration the review ratings of the leading music journals and critics' opinions.

Our system is slightly different to most 5 Star ratings in that we rate according to the artist in question's work. Therefore, a 4 star album from the Beatles may have the overall edge over a 4 star album by Des O'Connor. Sorry Des.

Our ratings are carefully made, and consequently you will find we are very sparing with 5 Star and 1 Star albums.

★★★★★ Outstanding in every way. A classic and therefore strongly recommended. No comprehensive record collection should be without this album.

★★★★ Excellent. A high standard album from this artist and therefore highly recommended.

★★★ Good. By the artist's usual standards and therefore recommended.

★★ Disappointing. Flawed or lacking in some way.

★ Poor. An album to avoid unless you are a completist.

PLAGIARISM

In maintaining the largest text database of popular music in the world we are naturally protective of its content. We license to approved licensees only. It is both flattering and irritating to see our work reproduced without credit. Time and time again over the past few years I have read an obituary, when suddenly: hang on, I wrote that line. Secondly, it has come to our notice that other companies attempting to produce their own rock or pop encyclopedias use our material as a core. Flattering this might also be, but highly illegal. We have therefore dropped a few more textual 'depth charges' in addition to the original ones. Be warned.

Colin Larkin, July 1997

A BAND OF ANGELS

Formed in 1964 at Harrow Public School, England, A Band Of Angels consisted of Mike D'Abo (b. 1 March 1944, Betchworth, Surrey, England; vocals/piano), Christian (John) Gaydon (guitar/vocals), John Baker (guitar), David Wilkinson (bass) and James Rugge-Price (drums). The group made great play of their 'upper class' origins, wearing matching sleek suits and straw boater hats in publicity photographs. They signed to United Artists Records in 1964, and recorded 'Me' and 'She'll Never Be You' for the company before switching to Piccadilly Records. 'Leave It To Me' was issued in 1965 and a year later the group completed their last, and finest single, 'Invitation'. A strong beat and nagging chorus led to its becoming a favourite on the northern soul scene of the 70s. D'Abo replaced Paul Jones in Manfred Mann in 1966, while John Gaydon became a successful entrepreneur in partnership with ex-A Band Of Angels manager David Enthoven. Together they formed EG Records, home of Roxy Music, King Crimson and Brian Eno.

A.B. SKHY

This San Francisco-based quartet included Dennis Geyer (guitar), Howard Wales (keyboards), Jim Marcotte (bass) and Terry Andersen (drums). A seven-piece horn section supported the group on their debut album, a blues-based set modelled on B.B. King and Bobby Bland. Following the departures of Andersen and Wales, the remaining members continued with newcomers Rick Jaeger (drums) and James 'Curley' Cooke (guitar), the latter being a founder-member of the Steve Miller Band, and a former colleague of Geyer in an earlier group, Tim Davis and the Chordaires. *Ramblin' On* was produced by the notorious Kim Fowley. This informal collection showcased the group's instrumental muscle and featured cameo performances from guitarist Elvin Bishop and pianist Ben Sidran. However, the band failed to secure a commercial success and broke up during sessions for a projected third album. Founder-member Wales later enjoyed a brief association with the Grateful Dead, and recorded the experimental *Hooteroll?* with the latter's guitarist Jerry Garcia.
●ALBUMS: *A.B. Skhy* (MGM 1969)★★, *Ramblin' On* (MGM 1970)★★.

ABYSSINIANS

Formed in 1968 in Jamaica, the Abyssinians consist of the lead singer Bernard Collins, along with the brothers Lynford and Donald Manning, who had both been members of their brother Carlton's group, Carlton And His Shoes. The latter's 1968 recording, 'Happy Land', strongly influenced the Abyssinians' first record, 'Satta Massa Gana', a Rastafarian hymn sung partly in the ancient Ethiopian Amharic language, recorded at Coxsone Dodd's Studio One in March 1969. 'Satta', which has been covered by dozens of artists, is a classic reggae roots song, its plangent, understated rhythm and the group's cool harmonies providing the template for the roots music that dominated the following decade. Dodd apparently saw little potential in the song at the time, however, and 'parked' it. Eventually the group saved enough money to buy the tape and release it on their own Clinch label in 1971, and the song became a huge Jamaican hit. In the wake of the song's success, Dodd released his own DJ and instrumental versions. The Abyssinians' second hit record, 'Declaration Of Rights', which featured Leroy Sibbles on backing vocals, is similarly notable for its militant lyrics, close harmony vocals and hard, rootsy rhythms. In 1972 the trio released two more singles on Clinch, 'Let My Days Be Long' and 'Poor Jason White', both recorded at Dynamic Studios, as well as a version of 'Satta', retitled 'Mabrak', which featured the group reciting passages from the Bible. Their next release, 'Yim Mas Gan' (1973), was recorded for producer Lloyd 'Matador' Daley and was released in the UK on the Harry J label. The group continued releasing tunes on their own label throughout the 70s, including 'Leggo Beast', Bernard Collins' solo on the 'Satta' rhythm track, 'Satta Me No Born Yah', Big Youth's DJ version of 'Satta' called 'I Pray Thee'/'Dreader Dan Dread', Dillinger's 'I Saw Esaw', and Bernard, solo again on 'Crashie Sweep Them Clean', backed with Dillinger's 'Crashie First Socialist'. Records for other producers during the same period included 'Reason Time' (*c*.1974) for Federal Records, 'Love Comes And Goes' (1975) for Tommy Cowan's Arab label and the Amharic 'Tenayistillin Wandimae' (1975) for Geoffrey Chung. *Forward On To Zion* was released in 1976 after being pirated in the UK, and further singles appeared on Clinch, including 'Prophecy' (1977) and 'This Land Is For Everyone' (1979). However, internal rivalries threatened the group's stability, and *Arise* was recorded under stressful conditions. Eventually relations worsened and the group went their separate ways. Little was heard from any of them throughout the next decade, although Donald Manning, as Donald Abyssinians, released an excellent single, 'Peculiar Number', in the early 80s on his own Dahna Dimps label, and an American record company, Alligator Records, released the *Forward* compilation. By the 90s, however, the members reunited to release two excellent singles, 'African Princess' and 'Swing Low', as well as making available much of their classic back catalogue.
●ALBUMS: *Forward On To Zion* (Different 1976)★★★, *Arise* (Front Line 1978)★★★.
●COMPILATIONS: *Forward* (Alligator/Clinch 1980)★★★, *Satta Massa Gana* (Heartbeat 1993)★★★.

ACADEMY

This UK rock quartet comprised Richard Cobby (guitar), Damon J. Hardy (vocals), Polly Perkins (vocals) and Dick Walter (flute). Formed in the late 60s, the group's sound was dominated by the dual male/female vocals of Hardy and Perkins, with Walter's woodwind contribution helping to establish a distinctive sound that clearly incorporated elements of progressive, folk and jazz rock. In 1969 the group released its sole album, *Pop-Lore According To The Academy*, and the single 'Rachel's Dream'/'Munching The Candy'. Neither secured any mainstream interest, however, and by the early 70s the group had disbanded.

● ALBUMS: *Pop-Lore According To The Academy* (Morgan Bluetown 1969)★★.

ACKLIN, BARBARA

b. 28 February 1944, Chicago, Illinois, USA. A vocalist in the style of Dionne Warwick and Brenda Holloway, Acklin first recorded under the name Barbara Allen. In 1966, following a spell as a backing singer, she worked as a receptionist at the Brunswick Records offices, and submitted some of her own compositions to producer Carl Davis. One of these, 'Whispers', co-written with David Scott (of the Five Dutones), was a major hit for Jackie Wilson, who returned the favour by helping Acklin secure a recording deal with Brunswick. 'Love Makes A Woman', her US Top 20 pop hit from the summer of 1968, was followed by 'Just Ain't No Love' and 'Am I The Same Girl' (a UK hit in 1992 for Swing Out Sister), while a duet with Gene Chandler, 'From The Teacher To The Preacher', also charted. Meanwhile, Barbara began writing with Eugene Record from the Chi-Lites, a partnership that resulted in several of that group's finest moments, including 'Have You Seen Her' and 'Stoned Out Of My Mind'. The relationship continued despite Acklin's departure for Capitol Records, but in spite of her early promise with 'Raindrops' (1974), she was dropped from the label in 1975 and has barely recorded since. *Groovy Ideas* collects the cream of her Brunswick recordings.

● ALBUMS: *Love Makes A Woman* (Brunswick 1968)★★, *Seven Days Of Night* (1969)★★, *Someone Else's Arms* (1970)★★, *I Did It* (1971)★★, *I Call It Trouble* (1971)★★, *A Place In The Sun* (Capitol 1975)★★.

● COMPILATIONS: *Groovy Ideas* (Kent 1987)★★★.

ACTION

Formed in Kentish Town, London, in 1965, this respected group consisted of Reggie King (vocals), Alan 'Bam' King (guitar), Pete Watson (guitar), Mike Evans (bass) and Roger Powell (drums). For two years prior to this the quintet was known as the Boys. As such they recorded one single, 'It Ain't Fair', for Pye, and served as a backing group for up-and-coming singer Sandra Barry. Rechristened the Action, the band established a reputation as one of the best Mod groups on the booming London circuit and became the subject of a BBC2 television documentary that examined the travails of life on the road. The Beatles' producer George Martin spotted their talent and supervised their recordings for his newly established independent company, AIR. He bestowed a crystal-clear sound on a succession of excellent singles: 'Land Of 1000 Dances', 'I'll Keep On Holding On', 'Baby You've Got It', 'Never Ever' and 'Shadows And Reflections', which combined a love of soul music with a growing awareness of US west coast harmony styles. Watson left in 1966, but the group persevered as a quartet until the following year when Ian Whiteman joined. He, in turn, was replaced by ex-Savoy Brown guitarist, Martin Stone. The Action failed to secure a hit and a proposed album was duly left unissued. Several completed masters appeared belatedly on *The Ultimate Action* CD. During their final months the group took a new name, Azoth, before reverting to the Action, but the departure of the charismatic Reggie King brought this period of indecision to a close. He later recorded a solo album while his former colleagues, with Whiteman back in the fold, embraced progressive rock as Mighty Baby. Although credited to the Action, *Action Speaks Louder Than* consists of Mighty Baby demo recordings.

● COMPILATIONS: *The Ultimate Action* (1980)★★, *Action Speaks Louder Than* (1985)★★, *Brain - The Lost Recordings 1967/8* (Autumn Stone Archives 1995)★★.

AD LIBS

This US vocal quintet evolved from New Jersey's the Creators (formed in 1962), and consisted of Hugh Harris and Danny Austin, plus Dave Watt, Norman Donegan and lead singer Mary Ann Thomas. Under the aegis of the swing-era veteran John T. Taylor (b. Morristown, New Jersey, USA), they had a hit in 1965 with 'The Boy From New York City', which was composed by Taylor. Their compelling performance blended contemporary R&B with doo-wop, but the group was unable to repeat the single's impact. Although a subsequent release, 'He Ain't No Angel', was a minor hit, the Ad Libs struggled to sustain any momentum. 'Giving Up' entered the R&B chart in 1969, but this commercial reprieve owed little to the charm of their heyday and proved equally short-lived. The memory of that lone hit was revived in 1981 when Manhattan Transfer took their version into the US Top 10.

ADAM, MIKE AND TIM

This trio from Liverpool, Merseyside, England, was formed in the early 60s and went on to release a succession of singles for Decca Records and Columbia Records without ever recording an album. Comprising Tim Saunders, Mike Sedgewick and Peter 'Adam' Sedgewick, the trio's vocals were supported by studio musicians as the occasion demanded. They made their debut in 1964 with 'Little Baby', a song written by Les Reed and Barry Mason. After 'That's How I Feel' and 'Little Pictures' in 1965 they moved to Columbia from Decca, but neither of their releases in the following year, 'Flowers On The Wall' and a version of Paul Simon's 'A Most Peculiar Man', brought any sort of breakthrough. After the expiry of the group's contract, Mike Sedgewick recorded an unsuccessful solo single in 1968.

ADAMS, CLIFF

b. 1923, Southwark, London, England. As a boy, Adams was a chorister at St Mary le Bow in East London, but yearned to become involved in popular music. After studying the piano and organ, he played in dance bands before joining the Royal Air Force in World War II. In the late 40s he arranged for several name bands, including Stanley Black and Ted Heath, and in 1949 formed the Stargazers. They became one of the top UK vocal groups of the 50s on radio and records, their hits including the novelties, 'Close The Door (They're Coming In The Window)' and 'Twenty Tiny Fingers', plus two UK chart-toppers, 'Broken Wings' and 'I See The Moon'. In 1954 Adams formed the Adams Singers for Cyril Stapleton's BBC Showband. This led to *Sing Something Simple*, a half-hour programme of 'songs simply sung for lovers', featuring the Singers, piano accordionist Jack Emblow's Quartet, and a piano solo by Adams. It made its debut as a 'six-week stand-in' on the BBC Light Programme in 1959, and celebrated its 35th Anniversary with a special programme on BBC Radio 2 in August 1994. Adams also composes music, and his work for television commercials has included 'For Mash - Get Smash' and 'Fry's Turkish Delight'. He had a UK Top 40 hit in 1960 with his 'Lonely Man Theme', which was used in the memorable 'You're never alone with a Strand' cigarette commercial. In 1976 he composed the music for the West End musical *Liza Of Lambeth*, an adaptation of Somerset Maugham's novel, which featured a book and lyrics by William Rushton and Bernie Stringler.

●ALBUMS: *Sing Something Simple* i (1960)★★★, *Sing Something Simple* ii (1962)★★★, *Sing Something Simple '76* (1976)★★★, *Sing Something Simple* iii (1982)★★★, *Songs To Remember* (1983)★★★, *Sing Something Silver* (1984)★★★, *Sing Something Disney* (1985)★★★, *Sing Something Country* (1990)★★, *Single Something Simple To Victory* (1995)★★★.
●COMPILATIONS: *Sing Something Simple - 100 Golden Greats* (1983)★★★, *All The Very Best Of Sing Something Simple* (Pickwick 1995)★★★.

ADDERLEY, CANNONBALL

b. Julian Edwin Adderley, 15 September 1928, Tampa, Florida, USA, d. 8 August 1975. Cannonball Adderley was one of the great saxophonists of his generation. His fiery, blues-soaked interpretations of Charlie Parker's alto legacy brought jazz to many people hitherto untouched by it. In the 60s he launched a new genre whose popularity has survived undiminished into the 90s: soul jazz. Cannonball was derived from 'Cannibal', a nickname earned at high school on account of his prodigious appetite. He studied brass and reed instruments there between 1944 and 1948. Until 1956 he was band director at Dillerd High School, Lauderdale, Florida, as well as leader of his own jazz quartet. While serving in the forces he became director of the 36th Army Band, an ensemble

that included his younger brother Nat Adderley on trumpet. Persuaded to go to New York by legendary alto saxophonist and R&B singer Eddie 'Cleanhead' Vinson, Cannonball created a sensation at the Cafe Bohemia, playing alongside bassist Oscar Pettiford. In 1958 he signed to Riverside Records and over the next six years released a series of albums, many of them recorded live, that laid the foundations of the soul-jazz genre. As well as his brother Nat, Adderley's first group featured a superb rhythm section in Sam Jones and Louis Hayes, supplemented by pianist Bobby Timmons, who also wrote the group's first hit, 'This Here'. From 1957-59 Adderley was part of the classic Miles Davis Quintet, an astonishing group of individuals that also included John Coltrane (tenor), Bill Evans or Red Garland (piano), Paul Chambers (bass) and Philly Joe Jones (drums). As well as playing on the celebrated *Kind Of Blue*, Cannonball recorded his own album *Somethin' Else* for Blue Note Records - Davis guested on the recording, a rare honour. After leaving Davis, Cannonball re-formed his own band, with Nat still on cornet; in 1961 Yusef Lateef joined on tenor saxophone and stayed for two productive years. This band nurtured the talents of electric pianists Joe Zawinul, and then George Duke. It was Zawinul's 'Mercy, Mercy, Mercy' - recorded live at the Club Delisa in Chicago - that provided Adderley with his next major hit: it reached number 11 in the US charts in February 1967. The title is indicative of the band's fondness for gospel-orientated, black consciousness themes. Their last hit was 'Country Preacher', again a Zawinul composition, which peaked in early 1970 (29 in the R&B charts). Straight jazz never again had this mass appeal. When asked about his inspirations, Cannonball cited the swing alto saxophonist Benny Carter and, of course, Charlie Parker - but his understanding of blues distortion also enabled him to apply the *avant garde* lessons of John Coltrane and Ornette Coleman. His alto saxophone had a special immediacy, a welcome reminder of the blues at the heart of bebop, an element that jazz rock - the bastard offspring of soul jazz - too often suppressed.

●ALBUMS: *Presenting Cannonball* (Savoy 1955)★★★, *Julian 'Cannonball' Adderley* (EmArcy 1955)★★★, *Julian 'Cannonball' Adderley And Strings* (EmArcy 1956)★★, *In The Land Of Hi-Fi* (EmArcy 1956)★★★, *Sophisticated Swing* (EmArcy 1957)★★★★, *Cannonball's Sharpshooters* (EmArcy 1958)★★★, *Jump For Joy* (EmArcy 1958)★★★, *Portrait Of Cannonball* (Riverside 1958)★★★, *Somethin' Else* (Blue Note 1958)★★★★★, *Things Are Gettin' Better* (Riverside 1958)★★★★, *Alabama Concerto* (1958)★★★, *The Cannonball Adderley Quintet In San Francisco* (Riverside 1959)★★★, *Cannonball Adderley Quintet In Chicago* (Mercury 1959)★★★, *Cannonball Takes Charge* (Riverside 1959)★★, *Cannonball Adderley Quintet At The Lighthouse* (Riverside 1960)★★★, *Them Dirty Blues* (Riverside 1960)★★★, *The Lush Side Of Cannonball Adderley* (Mercury 1961)★★★, *African Waltz* (Riverside 1961)★★★, *Cannonball Enroute* (Mercury 1961)★★★, *Cannonball*

Adderley And The Poll-Winners (Riverside 1961), *Cannonball Adderley Quintet Plus* (Riverside 1961)★★★, with Nancy Wilson *Nancy Wilson/Cannonball Adderley* (1962)★★, with Bill Evans *Know What I Mean* (Riverside 1962)★★★★, *The Cannonball Adderley Sextet in New York* (Riverside 1962)★★, *Cannonball's Bossa Nova* (Riverside 1963)★★, *Jazz Workshop Revisited* (Riverside 1963)★★, *Nippon Soul* (Riverside 1964)★★★, *Cannonball And Coltrane* (Limelight 1964)★★★, *Domination* (Capitol 1965)★★, *Fiddler On The Roof* (Capitol 1965)★★, with Ernie Andrews *Live Session* (Capitol 1965)★★★, *Cannonball Adderley Live* (Capitol 1965)★★★, *Great Love Themes* (Capitol 1966)★★, *Why Am I Treated So Bad* (Capitol 1966)★★★, with Ray Brown *Two For The Blues* (1966)★★, with Nat Adderley *Them Adderley's* (Limelight 1964)★★★, *Mercy Mercy Mercy Live At The Club* (Capitol 1967)★★★, *74 Miles Away - Walk Tall* (Capitol 1967)★★, *Cannonball In Europe* (Riverside 1967)★★★, *Things Are Getting Better* (1968)★★★★, with Milt Jackson *Accent On Africa* (Capitol 1968)★★, *Cannonball In Person* (Capitol 1969)★★★, *Planet Earth* (Riverside 1969)★★, *Country Preacher* (1970)★, *Experience In E, Tensity, Dialogues* (1970)★★, *The Price You Got To Pay To Be Free* (1971)★★, *The Black Messiah* (1972)★★, *Inside Straight* (1973)★★, *Phenix* (1975)★★, *Spontaneous Combustion* rec. 1955 (Savoy 1976)★★★, *What Is This Thing Called Soul* rec. 1960 (1984)★★★, with Wynton Kelly *Cannonball Takes Charge* (1988)★★, *Cannonball In Europe* 1962 recording (1988)★★★, *In Japan* (Blue Note 1990)★★★, *Radio Nights* (Virgin 1991)★★, *Dizzy's Business* (Ace 1993)★★.

●COMPILATIONS: *Cannonball's Greatest Hits* (Riverside 1962)★★★★, *The Best Of Cannonball Adderley* (Riverside 1968)★★★★, *Cannonball Adderley Collection Vols 1 - 7* (Landmark 1988)★★★, *Best Of Cannonball Adderley The Capitol Years* (Capitol 1991)★★★, *Quintet Plus* (Ace 1992)★★★, *Portrait Of Cannonball* (Ace 1993)★★★.

ADDERLEY, NAT

b. Nathaniel Adderley, 25 November 1931, Tampa, Florida, USA. The younger brother of Cannonball Adderley, Nathaniel was a singer until his voice broke and he took up the trumpet. In the early 50s he served in the army with his brother and played in the 36th Army Band. His professional break came in 1954, when Lionel Hampton asked him to join his riotously swinging, R&B-inflected big band; he stayed for only a year. Later he played with Woody Herman and J.J. Johnson. In 1960 he released *Work Song*, a brilliant amalgam of the soul jazz for which he is celebrated and a more 'cool' style, chamber music instrumentation (including cello and guitar, the latter played by Wes Montgomery). Throughout the 60s and early 70s he played in his brother's band and since the latter's death in 1975 has kept alive that special brand of warm, rootsy bop, both on

his own recordings and in other contexts, such as Nathan Davis's Paris Reunion Band.

●ALBUMS: *That's Nat* (Savoy 1955)★★★, *Introducing Nat Adderley* (EmArcy 1955)★★★, *To The Ivy League From Nat* (EmArcy 1956)★★★, *Branching Out* (Riverside 1958)★★★, *Much Brass* (Riverside 1959)★★★, *That's Right* (Riverside 1960)★★★, *Work Song* (Riverside 1960)★★★★, *Naturally!* (Jazzland 1961)★★★, *In The Bag* (Jazzland 1962)★★★★, *The Adderley Brothers In New Orleans* (1962)★★★, *Little Big Horn* (Riverside 1964)★★★, *Autobiography* (Atlantic 1965)★★★, *Sayin' Something* (Atlantic 1966)★★★, with Cannonball *Them Adderleys* (Limelight 1966)★★★, *Live At Memory Lane* (Atlantic 1967)★★, *The Scavenger* (Milestone 1968)★★, *Comin' Out Of The Shadows* (1968)★★, *You, Baby* (A&M 1968)★★, *Natural Soul* (Milestone 1968)★★★, *Calling Out Loud* (A&M 1969)★★, *Zodiac Soul* (1970)★★, *Soul Of The Bible* (1972)★★, *Double Exposure* (1974)★★★, *Don't Look Back* (1976)★★★, *A Little New York Midtown Music* (1978)★★, *On The Move* (1983)★★★, *Blue Autumn* (1983)★★, *That's Nat* (1985)★★★, *Blue Autumn* (Theresa 1987)★★★, *Work Songs* (Fantasy 1987)★★★, *Talkin' About You* (Landmark 1991)★★★, *We Remember Cannon* (In & Out 1991)★★★, *The Old Country* (Enja 1992)★★★, *Working* (1993)★★★.

●VIDEOS: *Nat Adderley Quartet* (1988).

ADLER, LOU

b. 1935, Los Angeles, California, USA. Adler emerged as a potent force in Californian pop as the manager of Jan And Dean. and co-writer of their second US Top 10 hit 'Baby Talk'. At this time he also managed and produced Johnny Rivers and formed a songwriting partnership with Herb Alpert. As 'Barbara Campbell', he co-wrote 'Only Sixteen' and 'Wonderful World' for Sam Cooke. Adler was subsequently involved with the Colpix and Dimension record labels, where he came into contact with several staff songwriters, including Carole King, Steve Barri and P.F. Sloan. The latter pair formed a successful partnership at Adler's publishing house, Trousdale, and supplied material for his several protégés. In 1965 Adler founded Dunhill Records with Jay Lasker and Bobby Roberts. This influential label became the natural outlet for several of the entrepreneur's discoveries, including the Mamas And The Papas and Barry McGuire, and had major hits with Richard Harris and the Grass Roots. The company was later sold to the ABC Records group, whereupon Adler set up a new venture, Ode, and had a huge international hit with Scott McKenzie's summer-of-love anthem 'San Francisco (Be Sure To Wear Flowers In Your Hair)'. In the same year, 1967, Adler was a director of the highly successful Monterey Pop Festival, which served as a world stage for the emergent west coast scene. Ode's subsequent signings included Spirit, Cheech And Chong and Carole King, whose 1971 release, *Tapestry*, which Adler produced, was one of the decade's biggest-selling albums. Adler then became increasingly involved in films and theatre, where his work included

Brewster McCloud, The Rocky Horror Picture Show and *Tommy*, and his subsequent diversification into night-clubs emphasized his disparate interests.

AFTER TEA

Formed in The Hague, Holland, in 1967, After Tea evolved from the beat-based group the Tea Set. The revitalized quartet - Hans van Eijck (keyboards/guitar/vocals), Ray Fenwick (guitar/vocals), Rob 'Polle' Eduard (bass/organ/vocals) and Martin Hage (drums) - scored a Dutch hit with 'Not Just A Flower In Your Hair', while a follow-up single, 'We Will Be There After Tea', secured airplay on Britain's pirate radio stations. The latter song was subsequently covered as 'After Tea', by the Spencer Davis Group, whom the English-born Fenwick joined in 1968 on the expiry of his work-permit. Ferry Lever, also ex-Tea Set, replaced him in After Tea, which continued to enjoy popularity in its homeland. However, the departure of chief composer van Eijck in 1969 robbed the band of its individuality as Eduard, Lever, Duitser Uly Grun (organ) and Ilja Gort (drums) revoked flower-pop affectations for a heavier direction. The group broke up following the release of *Joint House Blues*, but Fenwick and organist Hans Jansen joined the final line-up for a one-off single, 'Mexico', in 1975.

●ALBUMS: *After Tea* (Ace Of Clubs 1967)★★, *National Disaster* aka *Bubblegum Beat Party* (1968)★★, *Joint House Blues* (1971)★★.
●COMPILATIONS: *After Tea* (1978)★★.

AITKEN, LAUREL

b. 1927, Cuba. Of mixed Cuban and Jamaican descent, Laurel, with his five brothers (including the veteran guitarist Bobby Aitken) and sisters settled in his father's homeland, Jamaica, in 1938. In the 40s he earned a living singing calypso for the Jamaican Tourist Board, as visitors alighted on Kingston Harbour. By the age of 15 Aitken, like many of the early Jamaican R&B and ska singers, including Owen Gray and Jackie Edwards, entered Vere John's 'Opportunity Hour', an amateur talent contest held on Friday nights at Kingston's Ambassador Theatre. He won the show for several weeks running, and his success there led to his establishment as one of the island's most popular club entertainers.

His first sessions were for Stanley Motta's Caribbean Recording Company, where he recorded some calypso songs, the spiritual 'Roll Jordan Roll' and 'Boogie Rock'. The latter was one of the first ever Jamaican R&B/shuffle recordings. In 1958 he recorded 'Little Sheila'/'Boogie In My Bones', one of the first records produced by future Island Records boss, Chris Blackwell, using a Jamaican saxophonist and a white Canadian backing band. It emerged on Blackwell's R&B imprint (where it spent over 12 months in the Jamaican chart), and in the UK on Starlite and, some years later, Island. Between 1958 and 1960, Aitken made a number of recordings in the pre-ska shuffle mode, including 'Bartender' and 'Brother David' for Ken Khouri, 'Judgement Day', 'More Whisky', 'Mighty Redeemer' and 'Zion' for Duke Reid, and 'Remember My Darling', 'The Saint', 'I Shall Remove', 'What A Weeping'/'Zion City Wall' and 'In My Soul' for Leslie Kong. On the strength of the popularity of these records in the UK, Aitken came to London in 1960, where he recorded a number of songs including 'Sixty Days & Sixty Nights', 'Marylee' and 'Lucille'. These were released on the entrepreneur Emile Shalett's new Blue Beat label, created to handle Jamaican music exclusively in the UK, one of its first releases being Aitken's 'Boogie Rock'. Aitken returned to Jamaica in 1963 and recorded 'Weary Wanderer' and 'Zion' for Duke Reid: these, too, were released on Blue Beat.

Back in London, he recorded for Graeme Goodall's Rio Records, which released around 20 titles by Aitken between 1964 and 1966, including 'Adam & Eve', 'Bad Minded Woman', 'Leave Me Standing', and 'We Shall Overcome', other titles appearing on the Ska Beat and Dice labels. In 1969 he enjoyed great success on Nu Beat, a subsidiary of the Palmer brothers' Pama group of labels, writing songs for other artists, including 'Souls Of Africa' for the Classics. He also recorded 'Guilty' by Tiger (which was Aitken under a different name), and enjoyed great success with his own exuberant reggae songs like 'Woppi King', 'Haile Selassie', 'Landlords & Tenants', 'Jesse James', 'Skinhead Train', 'Rise & Fall', 'Fire In Me Wire', and the notorious 'Pussy Price', in which he bemoaned the rising cost of personal services. During this period Aitken's popularity among Britain's West Indian population was matched only by his patronage by white skinhead youths, and it is mainly with successive skinhead and mod revivals that his name and music have been preserved.

The emerging trend towards cultural and religious (i.e. Rasta) themes among a new generation of young British (and Jamaican) blacks in the early 70s sharply contrasted with Aitken's brand of simple knees-up style. It was probably not to his advantage that he spent so long away from Jamaica's rapidly changing music scene, where producers like Lee Perry and Bunny Lee were coming up with new rhythms and ideas in production almost monthly. Aitken spent the 70s in semi-retirement, gave up regular recording and moved to Leicester, performing the occasional club date, his show-stopping act undiminished despite his advancing years. He has recorded intermittently since, almost scoring a Top 40 hit with 'Rudi Got Married' for Arista in 1981, and riding for all he was worth on the 2-Tone bandwagon. UB40's *Labour Of Love* featured a cover version of 'Guilty', but since this time Aitken has largely disappeared from public notice.

●ALBUMS: *Ska With Laurel* (Rio 1965)★★★, *High Priest Of Reggae* (Nu Beat 1969)★★★, with Potato 5 *Potato 5 Meet Laurel Aitken* (Gaz's 1987)★★*Early Days Of Blue Beat, Ska And Reggae* (Bold Reprive 1988)★★★, *It's Too Late* (Unicorn 1989)★★, *Rise And Fall* (Unicorn 1989)★★, *Sally Brown* (Unicorn 1989)★★.
●VIDEOS: *Live At Gaz's Rockin' Blues* (1989).

AKENS, JEWEL

b. 12 September 1940, Houston, Texas, USA. Akens sang in a church choir as a child and moved to Los Angeles in the late 50s. There he worked closely with Eddie Daniels as Eddie And the Four Tunes, before making his recording debut with him as Jewel And Eddie for the local Silver label. Akens went on to make records in the early 60s with the Four Dots and the Astro Jets before he linked up with the Hollywood-based Era label in 1965. There, Akens had his moment of glory with the novelty song 'The Birds And The Bees' in 1965. It was composed by Herb Newman under the name of Barry Stuart, co-owner of Era and was both a pop and R&B hit (numbers 3 and 21, respectively) in the USA. The song was also very popular in Europe, reaching number 29 in the UK. The follow-ups, 'Georgie Porgie' and 'Dancing Jennie', were too similar to succeed, although he did record credible versions of 'Little Bitty Pretty One' (Thurston Harris and the Paramounts) and 'You Better Move On' (Arthur Alexander and the Rolling Stones).
●ALBUMS: *The Birds And The Bees* (Era 1965)★★.

ALEXANDER, ARTHUR

b. 10 May 1940, Florence, Alabama, USA, d. 9 June 1993. Despite his own interpretations, Alexander's recordings are often better recalled for their inspirational quality. 'Anna (Go To Him)', a US R&B Top 10 hit, and 'You Better Move On' were covered, respectively, by the Beatles and the Rolling Stones, while 'A Shot Of Rhythm And Blues' became an essential British beat staple (notably by Johnny Kidd). Although 'You Better Move On' was recorded at the rudimentary Fame studios, Alexander's subsequent work was produced in Nashville, where his poppier perceptions undermined the edge of his earlier work. Later singles included 'Go Home Girl' and the haunting 'Soldier Of Love', but his fragile personality was particularly susceptible to pressure. This problem bedevilled his move to another label, Sound Stage 7, and although a 1972 album for Warner Brothers Records was promising, the singer's potential once again seemed to wither. A pop hit was secured on Buddah Records with 'Every Day I Have To Cry Some' (1975), but the success remained short-lived. For many years Alexander was out of the music business; he was a bus driver for much of this time. Alexander began to perform again in 1993 as a renewed interest arose in his small but important catalogue. *Lonely Just Like Me* was his first album in 21 years and indicated a revitalized performer. He signed a new recording and publishing contract in May 1993, suffering the cruellest fate when he collapsed and died the following month, three days after performing in Nashville with his new band.
●ALBUMS: *You Better Move On* (Dot 1962)★★★, *Alexander The Great* (1964)★★★, *Arthur Alexander i* (Dot 1965)★★★, *Arthur Alexander ii* (Warners 1972)★★, *Arthur Alexander iii* (Buddah 1975)★★, *Lonely Just Like Me* (1993)★★★.
●COMPILATIONS: *A Shot Of Rhythm And Soul* (1983)★★★, *Soldier Of Love* (1987)★★★, *The Greatest*

(1989)★★★, *The Ultimate Arthur Alexander* (1994)★★★, *You Better Move On* (1994)★★★, *Rainbow Road - The Warner Bros. Recordings* (1994)★★.

ALICE'S RESTAURANT

Folk singer Arlo Guthrie avoided military service during the 60s owing to a conviction for illegally dumping garbage. He later immortalised the events surrounding this in a lengthy monologue 'Alice's Restaurant Massacree', which was the lynchpin selection on his debut album. Arthur Penn, director of *Bonnie And Clyde*, took charge of this 1969 film, based on that particular song. Although humorous at intervals, the feature fails to match the wit Guthrie brought to his famed composition, despite his starring role. Instead Penn concentrates on an picturesque view of hippies, accentuating a charming, but naïve, world-view, rather than producing an incisive statement. Pete Seeger, friend and fellow activist of Arlo's father, Woody Guthrie, makes an appearance in this rather disappointing film that in some ways diluted the positive aspects of the song inspiring it.

ALLISON, MOSE

b. Mose John Allison Jnr., 11 November 1927, Tippo, Mississippi, USA. Allison began piano lessons at the age of five, and played trumpet in high school, although he has featured the latter instrument less frequently in recent years. His music is a highly individual mix of blues and modern jazz, with influences on his cool, laconic singing and piano playing ranging from Tampa Red and Sonny Boy 'Rice Miller' Williamson to Charlie Parker, Duke Ellington, and Thelonious Monk. He moved to New York in 1956 and worked mainly in jazz settings, playing with Stan Getz and recording for numerous companies. During the 60s Allison's work was much in evidence as he became a major influence on the burgeoning R&B scene. Pete Townshend, one of his greatest fans, recorded Allison's 'A Young Man's Blues' for the Who's *Live At Leeds*. Similarly John Mayall was one of dozens who recorded his classic 'Parchman Farm', and Georgie Fame featured many Allison songs in his heyday with the Blueflames. Fame's nasal and understated vocal was similar to Allison's, as is Ben Sidran's style and voice. In the 80s Allison saw a resurgence in his popularity after becoming a hero to the new, young audience hungry for his blend of modern jazz. Ultimately, however, his work is seen as hugely influential, and this has to a degree limited the profile afforded to his own lengthy recording career.
●ALBUMS: *Back Country Suite* (Prestige 1957)★★★, *Local Color* (Prestige 1958)★★★, *Young Man Mose* (Prestige 1958)★★★, *Creek Bank* (Prestige 1959)★★★, *The Transfiguration Of Hiram Brown* (Columbia 1960)★★, *I Love The Life I Live* (Columbia 1960)★★★, *Autumn Song* (1960)★★★, *Ramblin' With Mose* (Prestige 1961)★★★, *Take To The Hills* (Epic 1962)★★, *I Don't Worry About A Thing* (Atlantic 1962)★★★, *Swingin' Machine* (Atlantic 1962)★★★, *The Seventh*

Son - Mose Allison Sings (Prestige 1963)★★★, The World From Mose (Atlantic 1964)★★★, V8 Ford (Columbia 1964)★★★, Down Home Piano (Prestige 1966)★★★, Mose Alive! (Atlantic 1966)★★★, Mose Allison (Prestige 1966)★★★, Wild Man On The Loose (Atlantic 1966)★★★, Jazz Years (1967)★★, Mose Allison Plays For Lovers (Prestige 1967)★★, I've Been Doin' Some Thinkin' (Atlantic 1969)★★★, Hello There (1969)★★, Universe (1969)★★, Western Man (1971)★★, Mose In Your Ear (1972)★★, Your Mind Is On Vacation (1976)★★, Ol' Devil Mose (1976)★★★, Retrospective (1976)★★★, That's Jazz (1976)★★★, Ever Since The World Ended (Blue Note 1983)★★, Middle Class White Boy (1982)★★, Lessons In Living (1983)★★, My Backyard (Blue Note 1990)★★★, Sings And Plays (Fantasy 1991)★★★, The Earth Wants You (1994)★★.

●COMPILATIONS: Mose Allison Sings The Seventh Son (1988)★★★, Alison Wonderland The Mose Allison Anthology (1994)★★★, The Best Of … (Sequel 1994)★★★★.

●FURTHER READING: One Man's Blues: The Life And Music Of Mose Allison, Patti Jones.

ALLISONS

John Alford (b. 31 December 1939, London, England) and Bob Day (b. 2 February 1942, Trowbridge, Wiltshire, England). The pop duo played the rounds of coffee bars and youth clubs before being spotted by impresario Tito Burns, who became their manager. He saw their immediate potential as Everly Brothers lookalikes. Under the guise of brothers John and Bob Allison, they became overnight British sensations when their self-composed 'Are You Sure' became Britain's entry in the 1961 Eurovision Song Contest. They received a big wave of publicity when their song became runner-up in the competition. The record, produced by Jack Baverstock and arranged by Harry Robinson on Fontana Records, went to number 1 in the UK charts, sold over a million copies in Europe and narrowly missed the US chart (Billboard number 102). The latter fact was significant, as British acts rarely crossed the Atlantic and entering the Billboard Hot 100 was a major feat. The duo, who were backed on stage by the Hunters, and who toured with Larry Parnes' stable of acts never returned to the UK Top 20. Their only other chart entries were their next two releases 'Words' and 'Lessons In Love' (a song from Cliff Richard's film The Young Ones) in 1962. They have occasionally resurfaced over the years as accomplished writers and record producers but have had no further chart success.

●ALBUMS: Are You Sure (Fontana 1961)★★.

ALPERT, HERB

b. 31 March 1935, Los Angeles, California, USA. A trumpet player from the age of eight, Alpert proved an exceptional arranger, songwriter and entrepreneur. In collaboration with Lou Adler, he wrote Sam Cooke's hit 'Wonderful World', then turned to production, scoring successes with surfing duo Jan And Dean. After a short-lived partnership with Lou Rawls and a failed attempt at acting, Alpert teamed up with promoter/producer Jerry Moss. Together they founded A&M Records and launched Alpert's own hit recording career with 'The Lonely Bull' in 1962. Backed by the Tijuana Brass, Alpert enjoyed a number of instrumental hits such as 'A Taste Of Honey', 'Spanish Flea', 'Tijuana Taxi' and 'Casino Royale'. A regular in the album charts of the 60s, he cleverly cornered the market by signing and producing his easy listening rivals Sergio Mendes And Brasil '66. In 1968, a rare Alpert vocal outing on Burt Bacharach's 'This Guy's In Love With You' became a US number 1. Meanwhile, A&M flourished and by the end of the 60s had ventured into the rock market with signings such as the Flying Burrito Brothers, Joe Cocker, Carole King, Cheech And Chong and Leon Russell. It was the easy listening, soft rock Carpenters, however, which proved the label's most commercially successful act of the early 70s. In spite of Alpert's record company commitments, he sustained his recording career and earned his second US number 1 with the instrumental 'Rise' in 1979. One of the most successful music business moguls of his era, Alpert finally sold A&M in 1989 for a staggering $500 million. In 1994 Alpert and Moss started a new record label, this time with the even more imaginative title of Almo. Alpert returned to recording in 1996 with a slick jazz/AOR album Second Wind.

●ALBUMS: The Lonely Bull (A&M 1962)★★★★, Tijuana Brass (A&M 1963)★★★, Tijuana Brass, Vol. 2 (A&M 1963)★★★, South Of The Border (A&M 1964)★★★, Whipped Cream And Other Delights (A&M 1965)★★★, Going Places (A&M 1965)★★★★, What Now, My Love (A&M 1966)★★★, S.R.O. (A&M 1966)★★★, Sounds Like (A&M 1967)★★★, Herb Alpert's 9th (A&M 1967)★★, Christmas Album (A&M 1968)★★, The Beat Of The Brass (A&M 1968)★★★, The Brass Are Comin' (A&M 1969)★★, Warm (A&M 1969)★★, Down Mexico Way (A&M 1970)★★, Summertime (A&M 1971)★★, America (A&M 1971)★★★, You Smile - The Song Begins (A&M 1974)★★★, Coney Island (A&M 1975)★★, Just You And Me (A&M 1976)★★, Herb Alpert And Hugh Masekela (Horizon 1978)★★★, Rise (A&M 1979)★★★, Beyond (A&M 1980)★★, Magic Man (1981)★★, Fandango (A&M 1982)★★, Blow Your Own Horn (A&M 1983)★★, Bullish (A&M 1984)★★, Wild Romance (A&M 1985)★★, Keep Your Eye On Me (A&M 1987)★★, Under A Spanish Moon (A&M 1988)★★, My Abstract Heart (A&M 1989)★★, North On South Street (A&M 1991)★★, Midnight Sun (A&M 1992)★★, Second Wind (Almo 1996)★★★.

●COMPILATIONS: Greatest Hits (A&M 1970)★★★★, Solid Brass (A&M 1972)★★★, Foursider (A&M 1973)★★★, Greatest Hits Vol. 2 (A&M 1973)★★★, 40 Greatest (A&M 1977)★★★★, Classics Vol. 20 (1987)★★★★, The Very Best Of Herb Alpert (A&M 1991)★★★.

●VIDEOS: Very Best Of Herb Alpert (Polygram 1992).

ALTAMONT FESTIVAL

6 December 1969, Altamont, California, USA. The free festival at the Altamont Raceway was the first major musical event since the peaceful 'happening' at the Woodstock Festival earlier in 1969. Altamont tarnished the reputation of the new music revolution. Until then, all events had been free of violence and had allowed the older generation to reluctantly reappraise their perception of pop music and its cultural trappings, even although the conventional press still regarded Woodstock as a disaster. The festival spirit died when Meredith Hunter, an 18-year-old black spectator, was beaten and stabbed to death by a group of Hell's Angels, while the Rolling Stones were onstage. Mick Jagger, only yards away, was oblivious to what was happening at his feet. When he finally realized what was happening and called for help, it was too late. The Angels had become involved in the festival after being recruited by the organizers to keep the peace as 'security' guards: their fee was as much alcohol and drugs as they could consume, and consequently, it was later claimed that they were not in control of their horrific actions. Tempers had earlier become frayed when Santana's performance had been interrupted by a scuffle. Jefferson Airplane, who followed, had their singer Marty Balin knocked unconscious by a blow from one of the Angels when he tried to stop another disturbance. Although the Angels were ultimately deemed responsible, they had themselves become victims of appalling organization. David Crosby defended their actions in a lengthy *Rolling Stone* interview. Mick Jagger has been the focus of a great deal of resentment from particular Hell's Angels groups who accuse the singer of shirking any responsibility for the incident and quickly shifting the blame towards them. It appeared that Jagger did not act responsibly by continuing to perform, but over the years he has established his position: he was not aware of what was going on. Jagger has received numerous death threats and apparently there is still a 'contract' out on his life. Other artists appearing in front of the unmanageable crowd of 300,000 included Crosby, Stills, Nash And Young and the Flying Burrito Brothers. Although the Grateful Dead were members of the organizing committee, they ended up not performing. The film *Gimme Shelter* ends with the Altamont tragedy and is an interesting, if gory, piece of celluloid rock history.
●FURTHER READING: *Altamont*, Jonathan Eisen (ed.).

AMBOY DUKES

Originally from Detroit, Michigan, USA, the Amboy Dukes - John Drake (vocals), Ted Nugent (b. 13 December 1949, Detroit, Michigan, USA; lead guitar), Steve Farmer (rhythm guitar), Rick Lorber (keyboards), Bill White (bass) and Dave Palmer (drums) - achieved notoriety for their rendition of 'Journey To The Center Of The Mind', which added Ted Nugent's snarling guitar and reached the US Top 20. The brashness of their version of Them's 'Baby Please Don't Go' set the tone for the group's subsequent albums on which Farmer's rather pretentious lyrics often undermined the music on offer. The band

were highly competent on instrumentals, however, such as the evocative 'Scottish Tea'. Frequent changes in personnel (Drake, Lorber and White were replaced, in turn, by Rusty Day, Andy Solomon and Greg Arama), made little difference to the Amboy Dukes' development, as the group increasingly became an outlet for Nugent's pyrotechnics. He unveiled a new line-up in 1974 with *Call Of The Wild*, the first of two albums recorded for Frank Zappa's DiscReet label. The guitarist then abandoned the band's name altogether and embarked on a solo career.
●ALBUMS: *The Amboy Dukes* (Mainstream 1967)★★★, *Journey To The Center Of Your Mind* (Mainstream 1968)★★★, *Migrations* (Mainstream 1969)★★★, *Marriage On The Rocks* (Polydor 1969)★★, *Survival Of The Fittest/Live* (Polydor 1971)★★, as Ted Nugent And The Amboy Dukes: *Call Of The Wild* (DiscReet 1974)★★, *Tooth, Fang And Claw* (DiscReet 1975)★★.
●COMPILATIONS: *The Best Of The Original Amboy Dukes* (Mainstream 1969)★★★.

AMEN CORNER

Formed in Cardiff, Wales, this R&B-styled septet consisted of Andy Fairweather-Low (b. 2 August 1950, Ystrad Mynach, Cardiff, Wales; vocals), Derek 'Blue Weaver' (b. 11 March 1949, Cardiff, Wales; organ), Neil Jones (25 March 1949, Llanbradach, Wales; guitar), Clive Taylor (b. 27 April 1949, Cardiff, Wales; bass), Allen Jones (b. 6 February 1948, Swansea, Wales; baritone sax), Mike Smith (b. 4 November 1947, Chesterfield, Derbyshire, England; tenor sax) and Dennis Byron (b. 14 April 1949, Cardiff, Wales; drums). After hitting the charts with the classic 'Gin House Blues' in 1967, Fairweather-Low became a pin-up and the group swiftly ploughed more commercial ground with a succession of hits including 'World Of Broken Hearts', 'Bend Me, Shape Me' and 'High In The Sky'. What the pop press failed to reveal was the intense power struggle surrounding the proprietorship of the group and the menacingly defensive tactics of their manager Don Arden. After all the drama, the group moved from Decca to Andrew Oldham's Immediate record label and enjoyed their only UK number 1 with 'If Paradise Is Half As Nice' in 1969. Following one final UK Top 10 hit, the energetic 'Hello Suzie', they split. Ironically, their pop star career ended on an anti-climactic note with the inappropriately titled Beatles cover version 'Get Back'. Lead singer Andy Fairweather-Low formed Fairweather and then went solo while Blue Weaver found his way into Strawbs. His keyboard work on their *Grave New World* was particularly noteworthy. The brass section became Judas Jump.
●ALBUMS: *Round Amen Corner* (Deram 1968)★★★, *National Welsh Coast Live Explosive Company* (Immediate 1969)★★★, *Farewell To The Real Magnificent Seven* (Immediate 1969)★★, *Return Of The Magnificent Seven* (Immediate 1976)★.
●COMPILATIONS: *World Of Amen Corner* (Decca 1969)★★★, *Greatest Hits* (Immediate 1978)★★★.

AMERICAN BREED

Originally known as Gary And The Nite Lites, this Chicago-born quartet was a popular attraction throughout America's Midwest prior to achieving national fame in 1967. Gary Loizzo (b. 16 August 1945; lead vocals/guitar), Al Ciner (b. 14 May 1947; guitar/vocals), Charles Colbert (b. 29 August 1944; bass/vocals) and Lee Graziano (b. 9 November 1943; drums) enjoyed a US Top 30 hit with 'Step Out Of Your Mind', before securing a gold disc for 'Bend Me, Shape Me'. Here the group's tight harmonies were perfectly offset by arranger Eddie Higgins' purposeful horn arrangement, but this excellent single failed to emulate its US success in Britain, where it was overshadowed by the Amen Corner's opportunistic rendition. The American Breed enjoyed further success in their homeland with 'Green Light' (1968), but their amalgamation of pop, bubblegum and soul failed to retain its appeal. Kevin Murphy joined in 1968 to add keyboards and Al Ciner, who was also briefly with the band, evolved into the first version of Ask Rufus, later truncated to Rufus.
●ALBUMS: *American Breed* (Acta 1967)★★, *Bend Me, Shape Me* (Acta 1968)★★, *Pumpkin, Powder, Scarlet And Green* (1968)★, *Lonely Side Of The City* (1968)★.
●COMPILATIONS: *Bend Me, Shape Me: The Best Of The American Breed* (70s)★★★.

AMES, ED

b. Ed Ulrick, 9 July 1927, Malden, Massachusetts, USA. Ames was a member of the very successful 50s vocal group, the Ames Brothers, who disbanded in 1959. In the early 60s he studied acting in New York. He appeared in several stage productions including *The Crucible, The Fantasticks* and *One Flew Over The Cuckoo's Nest* before playing an Indian, Mingo, in the popular US television series *Daniel Boone*. He returned to recording in 1964 with an album of Broadway songs for RCA Records, and one of the tracks, 'Try To Remember' (1965, from *The Fantasticks*), became the first of seven US hits for him in the 60s. His biggest solo record success came with 'My Cup Runneth Over' (from the musical *I Do! I Do!*), a US Top 10 hit in 1967. Ames also had a Top 20 hit with 'Who Will Answer?', a protest song, which seemed quite out of character for the MOR balladeer. He continued to work successfully on the supper-club circuit after the hits dried up, and settled in Los Angeles.
●ALBUMS: *More I Cannot Wish You* (1966)★★★, *My Cup Runneth Over* (1967)★★★, *Time, Time* (1967)★★, *When The Snow Is On The Roses* (1967)★★★, *Who Will Answer? And Other Songs of Our Time* (1968)★★, *Apologise* (1968)★★, *The Hits Of Broadway And Hollywood* (1968)★★★, *A Time For Living, A Time For Hope* (1969)★★, *The Windmills Of Your Mind* (1969)★★, *Love Of The Common People* (1970)★★★, *Sing Away The World* (1970)★★, *The Songs Of Bacharach And David* (1971)★★★.
●COMPILATIONS: *The Best Of Ed Ames* (1969)★★★.

ANDREWS, CHRIS

b. 1938, Romford, Essex, England. Originally lead singer in the early 60s band Chris Ravel And The Ravers, Andrews found greater success as a songwriter. Signed by manager Eve Taylor, he composed hits for her artists Adam Faith ('The First Time', 'We Are In Love', 'If He Tells Me', 'I Love Being In Love With You', 'Stop Feeling Sorry For Yourself', 'Someone's Taken Maria Away') and Sandie Shaw ('Girl Don't Come', 'Long Live Love' and 'Message Understood'). He scored chart success in his own right during 1965-66 with two catchy, upbeat numbers, 'Yesterday Man' and 'To Whom It Concerns'. Although he occasionally recorded additional solo singles, no further hits were forthcoming. He subsequently continued his career as a songwriter.
●ALBUMS: *Yesterday Man* (Decca 1965)★★, *Who Is The Man* (1977)★.
●COMPILATIONS: *The Best Of* (1993)★★, *Swinging Sixties Hit Man: The Definitive Anthology* (Repertoire 1996)★★.

ANDREWS, JULIE

b. Julia Wells, 1 October 1935, Walton-On-Thames, Surrey, England. After singing lessons with Madam Lillian Stiles-Allan, which formed her precise vocal style and typically English delivery, she made her professional debut in her parents' variety act at the age of 10. Two years later she performed at the London Hippodrome in the Pat Kirkwood musical, *Starlight Roof*, and the following year appeared in the Royal Command Performance. On BBC radio, she was Archie Andrew's playmate in *Educating Archie*, while appearing on stage in the title role of *Humpty Dumpty* at the London Casino at the age of 13. Her big break came in 1954 when she played Polly Brown in the Broadway production of Sandy Wilson's *The Boy Friend*. Having insisted on only a one-year contract for the latter show, she was available to star with Rex Harrison in one of Broadway's major musicals, Alan J. Lerner and Frederick Loewe's *My Fair Lady*, later repeating her performance in London before returning to Broadway as Queen Guinevere, with Richard Burton as King Arthur, in *Camelot*. Although passed over in favour of Audrey Hepburn for the lead in the film of *My Fair Lady* in 1964, ironically, she won an Oscar for her performance as the 'flying nanny' in the title role of Walt Disney's *Mary Poppins* in the same year. Since then, her career in film musicals has taken her from the blockbuster heights of *The Sound Of Music* to the critical depths of the Gertrude Lawrence bio-pic *Star*, *Thoroughly Modern Millie* and a gender-bending role in *Victor/Victoria*, in-between. The latter film, and her straight roles in movies such as *10* and *S.O.B.* which were directed by her second husband Blake Edwards, have sometimes seemed a direct effort to counter her life-long cosy, old-fashioned image. Nevertheless, she has been a major film star for over 25 years, and in 1989 was awarded BAFTA's Silver Mask in recognition of her outstanding contribution to the medium. She was less successful on the small screen with her 1992 ABC comedy series *Julie*, which was poorly received. It was a different story back in the 60s when she and Carol Burnett starred in the multi-Emmy Award-winning television special, *Julie And Carol At Carnegie Hall*. The two actresses were paired in similar shows at the Lincoln center for the Performing Arts (1971) and at the Pantages Theatre in Los Angeles (1989). Also in 1992, Andrews sang the role of Anna in a CD recording of *The King And I*, amid general amazement that she had never played the part on stage; British actor Ben Kingsley was her regal partner in the studio. in 1993 audiences flocked to see her in the Off-Broadway Stephen Sondheim revue *Putting It Together*, her first appearance on the New York stage since *Camelot* (1960). The critics were not so enthusiastic, and they did not care much either about the stage version of *Victor/Victoria* which opened on Broadway in October 1995, although Andrews' name on the marquee guaranteed nightly standing ovations until she finally bowed out, being replaced by Racquel Welch, in June 1997. Andrews won Drama Desk and Outer Critics Circle Awards for her sterling performance, but controversially turned down the 1996 Tony Award nomination for leading actress in a musical because no one else connected with the show had been nominated. In 1996 she was also inducted into the Theatre Hall of Fame, and a year later released an album of songs by composers such as Kurt Weill, Frederick Loewe, Burton Lane, and André Previn, all with lyrics by Alan Jay Lerner.

●ALBUMS: *My Fair Lady* Broadway cast (1956)★★★★, *Camelot* Broadway cast (1961)★★★, with Carol Burnett *Julie And Carol At Carnegie Hall* (1962)★★★, *Mary Poppins* soundtrack (Disney-Vista 1964)★★★★, *The Sound Of Music* soundtrack (RCA 1965)★★★★, *A Christmas Treasure* (1968)★★, *The Secret Of Christmas* (1977)★★, *Victor/Victoria* soundtrack (MGM 1982)★★★, *Love Me Tender* (Peach River 1983)★★, *Broadway's Fair Lady* (Columbia 1984)★★, *The Sound Of Christmas* (1987)★★, *Julie Andrews And Carol Burnett At The Lincoln Center* (1989)★★, *Love Julie* (1989)★★★, *The King And I* studio cast (Philips 1992)★★, *Broadway: The Music Of Richard Rodgers* (Philips 1994)★★★, *Victor/Victoria* Broadway cast (Philips 1995), *Here I'll Stay* (Philips 1996)★★, *Julie Andrews Sings* (Philips 1997)★★★.

●COMPILATIONS: *The Best Of ...* (Rhino 1996)★★★.

●VIDEOS: *Julie Andrews Greatest Hits* (1990).

●FURTHER READING: *Life Story Of A Superstar*, John Cottrell. *Julie Andrews*, Robert Windeler. *Julie Andrews*, James Arntz and Thomas S. Wilson.

●FILMS: *Rose Of Baghdad* voice only (1952), *Mary Poppins* (1964), *The Americanization Of Emily* (1964), *The Sound Of Music* (1965), *Torn Curtain* (1966), *Hawaii* (1966), *Thoroughly Modern Millie* (1967), *Star!* (1968), *Darling Lili* (1970), *The Tamarind Seed* (1974), *10* (1979), *Little Miss Marker* (1980), *S.O.B.* (1981), *Victor/Victoria* (1982), *The Man Who Loved Women* (1983), *Duet For One* (1986), *That's Life!* (1986), *Tchin-Tchin* (1991), *A Fine Romance* (1992).

ANDROMEDA

Andromeda evolved from the final line-up of UK flower-power pop group the Attack. John DuCann (guitar/vocals), Richard Sherman (vocals), Roger Dean (bass) and Keith Hodge (drums) provided Andromeda's first incarnation which dissolved within weeks of formation. Mick Hawksworth (bass/vocals) and Ian McClane (drums/vocals) then joined DuCann in the line-up that recorded for RCA Records. Although their sole album has become a cherished example of British progressive rock, it was not a success and the trio broke up in 1970 when the guitarist joined Atomic Rooster. Hawksworth subsequently formed the much-lauded Fuzzy Duck and collaborated with Matthew Fisher (ex-Procol Harum) on his solo album *Journey's End*. The bassist latterly appeared in Ten Years Later, a half-hearted conglomeration led by former Ten Years After guitarist Alvin Lee.

●ALBUMS: *Andromeda* (RCA 1969)★★.

●COMPILATIONS: *Anthology 1966-1969* (Kissing Spell 1995)★★.

ANDWELLA'S DREAM

Formed in Northern Ireland and originally known as Method, this melodic rock band initially comprised Dave Lewis (guitar/keyboards/vocals), Nigel Smith (bass/vocals) and Gordon Barton (drums). They took the name Andwella's Dream upon moving to London, England, in 1968. *Love And Poetry* featured the assistance of jazz musician Bob Downes (saxophone/flute). This impressive set captured the transformation from psychedelic to progressive styles, notably on 'The Day Grew Longer' and 'Sunday', which feature excellent guitar passages. Lewis, who composed all of the material, then recorded a privately pressed album on Ax in 1970. *The Songs Of Dave Lewis* included new versions of two songs from *Love And Poetry*, as well as other impressive selections featuring simple piano and guitar accompaniment. Dave McDougall joined the group for *World's End*, by which time they were known simply as Andwella. Here the tracks were more mainstream, with orthodox brass and string arrangements replacing their previous inventiveness. Dave Struthers (bass/vocals) and Jack McCulloch (drums, ex-Thunderclap Newman) augmented Andwella for *People's People*, which echoed the style of its predecessor. Unable to maintain their early promise, Andwella split up in 1972.

●ALBUMS: *Love And Poetry* (CBS 1968)★★★, *World's End* (Reflection 1970)★★, *People's People* (Reflection 1971)★★.

ANGELS (USA)

Sisters Barbara and Phyllis 'Jiggs' Allbut began performing as the Starlets in the USA with Linda Jansen and Peggy Santiglia. The quartet became the Blue Angels in 1962 but dropped the prefix prior to securing two minor hits with 'Til' and 'Cry Baby Cry'. By this point Jansen had left the group and forged a lucrative partnership with the Feldman/Gottherer/Goldstein songwriting and production team. Their relationship peaked with 'My

Boyfriend's Back', a lightweight, but irresistible example of the girl-group genre. Despite further excellent releases, the trio was unable to repeat this million-selling smash, particularly as their mentors were distracted by several other projects. The Angels grew unhappy with prevailing business practices - a fourth vocalist, Bernadette Carroll, appeared on several of their singles - and in 1966 they tried to relaunch their career as the Halos. This venture ended unsuccessfully, and Jiggs Allbut and Peggy Santiglia later resumed work as the Angels with singer/guitarist Stan Sirico.

●ALBUMS: *And The Angels Sing* (Caprice 1962)★★★, *My Boyfriend's Back* (Smash 1963)★★, *A Halo To You* (Smash 1964)★★.

●COMPILATIONS: *The Angels Sing 12 Of Their Greatest Hits* (Ascot 1964)★★★.

ANIMALS

Formed in Newcastle-upon-Tyne, England, in 1963, when vocalist Eric Burdon (b. 4 May 1941, Walker, Newcastle, Tyne & Wear, England), joined local R&B band the Alan Price Combo. The Animals comprised Alan Price (b. 19 April 1942, Fatfield, Co. Durham, England; piano), Hilton Valentine (b. 22 May 1943, North Shields, Tyne & Wear, England; guitar), John Steel (b. 4 February 1941, Gateshead, Co. Durham, England; drums) and Chas Chandler (b. Bryan James Chandler, 18 December 1938, Heaton, Tyne & Wear, England; bass). Valentine had previously played with the Gamblers, while Burdon had played trombone together with Steel on trumpet, in college jazz bands. With their raucous and exciting stage act, they quickly attracted the attention of several music business entrepreneurs. R&B legend Graham Bond recommended them to his manager Ronan O'Rahilly. The group became stars at the legendary Club A-Go-Go in Newcastle. On one occasion they performed with Sonny Boy Williamson (an album of this explosive gig was released many years later). By the end of 1963 they had moved to London and became an integral part of the fast-burgeoning club scene. After signing with producer Mickie Most they debuted with the energetic 'Baby Let Me Take You Home' (a version of Eric Von Schmidt's blues standard 'Baby Let Me Follow You Down'), which became a respectable hit. Their next release was to be both controversial and memorable. A pop song about a New Orleans brothel, lasting four-and-a-half minutes was at first resisted by their record company Columbia as being too long for radio play. Upon release, this record, Josh White's 'House Of The Rising Sun', leapt to the top of the charts all over the world, and ended up selling several million copies. The combination of Valentine's now legendary but simplistic guitar introduction and Price's shrill organ complemented Burdon's remarkably mature and bloodcurdling vocal. Over the next two years the Animals had seven further substantial hits on both sides of the Atlantic. Their memorable and dramatic version of a song Nina Simone popularized, 'Don't Let Me Be Misunderstood', featured the autobiographical 'Club A-Go-Go' on the b-side. Their choice of material was exem-

plary and many of their hits contained thought-provoking lyrics, from the angst-ridden 'I'm Crying' to the frustration and urban despair of Cynthia Weil and Barry Mann's 'We Gotta Get Out Of This Place'. Their albums contained stirring renditions of classics by Chuck Berry, Sam Cooke, Jimmy Reed and Burdon's hero, Ray Charles. During this time Price departed (supposedly suffering from aerophobia), and was replaced by Dave Rowberry from the Mike Cotton Sound. Burdon still maintains that Price's departure was because he had taken ownership of the lucrative publishing rights to 'House Of The Rising Sun' and was therefore financially secure. Steel left in 1966, replaced by Nashville Teens drummer Barry Jenkins. The new band scored with the brilliant 'Its My Life' and the adventurous 'Inside Looking Out'. By 1967 Burdon and Valentine had become totally immersed in psychedelia, both musically and chemically. This alienated them from the rest of the group (who preferred good old-fashioned alcohol), and led to its disintegration. Chandler went on to discover and manage the Jimi Hendrix Experience. Burdon, however, retained the name and immediately reappeared as Eric Burdon And The New Animals. They found greater favour in the USA where the band was domiciled. The band courted the west coast sound and the school of bands from that period. 'San Franciscan Nights' perfectly echoed the moment, with the lyrics: 'Strobe lights beam creates dreams, walls move, minds do too, on a warm San Franciscan night'. He further encapsulated his reverence in the song 'Monterey', cleverly eulogizing the epic Monterey Pop Festival of 1967. A number of interesting musicians passed through various line-ups of the New Animals, notably John Weider, Vic Briggs (formerly of Steampacket), Danny McCulloch, Zoot Money and Andy Summers. The tamed Burdon was now writing introspective and thought-provoking lyrics, although many of his previous fans could not take the former raver seriously. Long improvisational pieces began to appear in their live performances, with watered-down versions to be found on the albums *Winds Of Change*, *The Twain Shall Meet*, *Everyone Of Us* and *Love Is*. They disbanded at the end of 1968. Interestingly, the original line-up regrouped twice, in 1977 and 1983. On both occasions new albums were released to an indifferent public. For the 1983 revival tour it was reported that Valentine had become so rusty on the guitar, that a lead guitarist was recruited. The Animals' contribution to the 60s was considerable and at times their popularity threatened even the Beatles and Rolling Stones. 'The House Of The Rising Sun' gave them musical immortality, and will no doubt continue to be re-released at regular intervals. Valentine and Steel are still gigging on the pub circuit as Animals II.

●ALBUMS: *The Animals* (Columbia 1964)★★★, *Animals On Tour* (MGM 1965)★★★, *Animal Tracks* (Columbia 1965)★★★, *Most Of The Animals* (Columbia 1966)★★★★, *Animalization* (MGM 1966)★★★, *Animalisms* (Decca 1966)★★★, *Eric Is Here* (1967)★★★, *Winds Of Change* (MGM 1967)★★★, *The Twain Shall Meet* (MGM 1968)★★★,

Everyone Of Us (MGM 1968)★★★, *Love Is* (MGM 1968)★★★, *In Concert From Newcastle* (1976)★★, *Before We Were Rudely Interrupted* (Barn 1976)★, *The Ark* (1983)★, *Rip It To Shreds* (1984)★★, *The Animals With Sonny Boy Williamson* (1988)★★★.
●COMPILATIONS: *Best Of The Animals* (MGM 1966)★★★, *Best Of The Animals Vol 2* (MGM 1967)★★★, *The EP Collection* (1989)★★★★, *The Complete Animals* (1990)★★★★, *Trackin' The Hits* (1990)★★★.
●FURTHER READING: *I Used To Be An Animal But I'm All Right Now*, Eric Burdon. *Wild Animals*, Andy Blackford. *The Last Poet: The Story Of Eric Burdon*, Jeff Kent. *Good Times: The Ultimate Eric Burdon*, Dionisio Castello.
●FILMS: *Get Yourself A College Girl* (1964), *It's A Bikini World* (1967).

ANNETTE

b. Annette Funicello, 22 October 1942, Utica, New York, USA. Initially billed as 'Annette', this singer/actress rose to fame under the aegis of the Walt Disney organization. A one-time Mouseketeer, she enjoyed several hit singles between 1959 and 1961 which included two US Top 10 entries, 'Tall Paul' and 'O Dio Mio', as well as the enduring 'Pineapple Princess'. During the 60s Annette starred alongside Frankie Avalon in a series of 'quickie' beach films, including *Beach Party*, *Bikini Beach* (both 1964) and *How To Stuff A Wild Bikini* (1965), which combined slim plots, teenage themes and cameos from often-transitory pop stars. *The Monkey's Uncle* (1964) drew its appeal from an appearance by the Beach Boys and musical contributions from their leader, Brian Wilson. The latter assisted songwriter/producer Gary Usher in creating material for *Muscle Beach Party*, Annette's strongest album, which also featured back-up from the all-female group, the Honeys. Funicello later appeared in the Monkees' cult film *Head* (1968), but was unable to sustain thespian and recording successes.
●ALBUMS: *Annette* (Buena Vista 1959)★★, *Songs From Annette And Other Walt Disney Serials* (Mickey Mouse 1959)★, *Annette Sings Anka* (Buena Vista 1960)★, *Italiannette* (Buena Vista 1960)★, *Hawaiiannette* (Buena Vista 1960)★, *Dance Annette* (Buena Vista 1961)★, *The Parent Trap* (Buena Vista 1961)★, *Babes In Toyland* (Buena Vista 1961)★, *The Story Of My Teens* (Buena Vista 1962)★, *Teen Street* (Buena Vista 1962)★, *Muscle Beach Party* (Buena Vista 1963)★★★, *Annette's Beach Party* (Buena Vista 1963)★★, *Annette On Campus* (Buena Vista 1964)★, *Annette At Bikini Beach* (Buena Vista 1964)★, *Pajama Party* (Buena Vista 1964)★, *Annette Sings Golden Surfin' Hits*, (Buena Vista 1964)★, *Something Borrowed, Something Blue* (Buena Vista 1964)★, *Walt Disney's Wonderful World Of Color* (Disneyland 1964)★, *The Beast Of Broadway* (Disneyland 1965)★, *Tubby The Tuba And Other Songs About Music* (Disneyland 1966)★, *State And College Songs* (Disneyland 1967)★, *Thunder Alley* (Sidewalk 1967)★, *Annette Funicello* (Buena Vista 1972)★.

ANTHONY, RICHARD

b. Richard Anthony Bush, 13 January 1938, Cairo, Egypt. He forsook higher education in Paris to become a singer but was obliged to make ends meet with a variety of jobs and as a session saxophonist. He signed to Pathe-Marconi in 1958, but his debut single, 'La Rue Des Coeurs Perdus', fared poorly. However, he became popular with his native reproductions of US smashes such as Buddy Holly's 'Peggy Sue' and Lloyd Price's 'Personality'. He came into his own, however, with the twist craze with 'C'est Ma Fête' ('It's My Party') and an untranslated 'Let's Twist Again' established him as a rival to Johnny Halliday (the Gallic 'answer' to Elvis Presley). After a million-selling French cover version of Peter, Paul And Mary's '500 Miles Away From Home', he secured UK chart entries in 1963 with 'Walking Alone' and reached the Top 20 with 'If I Loved You'. His admirable revival of the Everly Brothers' 'Crying In The Rain' narrowly missed the charts. Concentration on this market adversely affected his domestic standing, until 1966's 'Fille Sauvage' (the Rolling Stones' 'Ruby Tuesday') brought him in from the cold. Both on tour and in the studio, he was backed for some time by the Roulettes, who impressed him with their playing on a French version of 'Concrete And Clay'. Anthony's career continued its ups and downs and his total record sales exceeded 12 million.
●ALBUMS: *Disque D'Or* (70s)★★★.

AORTA

Formed in Chicago, Illinois, USA, in 1967, Aorta initially consisted of Jim Donlinger (guitar/vocals), Jim Nyholt (piano/organ), Dan Hoagland (tenor saxophone), Bobby Jones (bass/vocals) and William Herman (drums). In February 1968 Hoagland left to join the Chicago Transit Authority, later known as Chicago. The remaining quartet was then signed to the local Dunwich production company who leased Aorta's first single, 'The Shape Of Things To Come', to Atlantic Records. The song, which provided the theme to the film *Wild In The Streets*, was originally recorded by Max Frost And The Troopers. *Aorta* revealed a group fusing rock textures with melody, drawing comparisons with fellow Chicagoans H.P. Lovecraft. This stylish blend was equally apparent on the now-dated *Aorta 2*, despite the defections of Herman, who joined the New Colony Six, and Jones. Michael Been (bass/guitar/vocals) and Tom Donlinger (drums) were featured on this second selection, but Aorta broke up soon after its release. Unsurprisingly, given their common musical styles, Jim Donlinger and Been quickly resurfaced in a revamped H.P. Lovecraft, now known simply as Lovecraft. Been formed several subsequent bands and during the 80s led the Call.
●ALBUMS: *Aorta* (Columbia 1969)★★, *Aorta 2* (Happy Tiger 1970)★★.

APPLEJACKS (UK)

Formed in Solihull, West Midlands, this early 60s UK pop group comprised Martin Baggott (b. 20 October 1947, Birmingham, England; guitar), Philip Cash (b. 9 October

1947; guitar), Megan Davies (b. 25 March 1944, Sheffield, Yorkshire, England; bass), Don Gould (b. 23 March 1947; organ), Al Jackson (b. 21 April 1945; vocals) and Gerry Freeman (b. 24 May 1947, Solihull, England; drums). Signed by Decca A&R representative Mike Smith, they found Top 10 UK chart success in 1964 with the memorable 'Tell Me When'. The grand follow-up, 'Like Dreamers Do', was a song taken from the famous Lennon and McCartney Decca audition tape. It barely scraped the Top 20 in spite of its pedigree and the next single, 'Three Little Words', did no better. Always capable of finding a first-class demo, the group turned to the Kinks' catalogue for Ray Davies's moody 'I Go To Sleep'. Its failure effectively signalled the Applejacks' doom and they duly returned to the northern club scene.

●ALBUMS: *The Applejacks* (Decca 1964)★★.
●COMPILATIONS: *Tell Me When* (Deram 1990)★★.

APPLETREE THEATRE

Brothers John and Terry Boylan created this highly imaginative unit in 1968. Their sole release, *Playback*, was completed with the aid of several session musicians, including Eric Gale, Chuck Rainey and Larry Coryell. An original, and indeed pioneering, concept album, the set balanced memorable songs with experimental sound collages, wherein the duo's soft, ethereal harmony work enhanced a spirit of adventure. Although *Playback* became a cult favourite, it was not a commercial success and its protagonists later embarked on contrasting solo careers. Terence Boylan completed a series of well-crafted albums, the latter of which were redolent of Jackson Browne, while John became a highly respected producer for the Eagles, Linda Ronstadt and, in 1991, for the cartoon 'group', the Simpsons.

●ALBUMS: *Playback* (Verve Forecast 1968)★★★.

ARCADIUM

Miguel Sergides (vocals/guitar), Robert Ellwood (vocals/guitar), Alan Ellwood (keyboards/vocals), Graham Best (bass/vocals) and John Albert Parker (drums) were a short-lived, but inventive, group, active in 1969. *Arcadium (Breathe Awhile)*, released on Middle Earth Records, captured their highly original style, particularly on 'I'm On My Way', the impressive opening track which features inspired, emotional guitar work. The remainder of the set, all of which was composed by Sergides, combines introspective lyrics with densely-packed arrangements, resulting in a sense of tense claustrophobia. Despite undoubted promise, Arcadium split soon after the album's release.

●ALBUMS: *Arcadium (Breathe Awhile)* (Middle Earth 1969)★★.

ARCHIES

Created for mass consumption by bubblegum-pop genius Don Kirshner (the man who gave us the Monkees), the Archies were the ultimate manufactured pop group. They existed on television and on their record sleeves as pure animations, based on the comic book characters of the same name. The voices behind the singing cartoon characters were vocalists Ron Dante (b. 22 August 1945, New York, USA), Toni Wine and Andy Kim, who were later called upon for touring purposes. Kirshner was astute enough to employ solid commercial writers of some standing, including Jeff Barry and Ellie Greenwich. After several minor successes, the group released one of the biggest selling singles in the history of RCA Records. 'Sugar Sugar' became a transatlantic number 1, hogging the top spot in Britain for over two months. Back in the USA, where the television series was extremely popular, the group enjoyed another Top 10 hit with 'Jingle Jangle' before suffering the sharp plunge into obscurity common to animated creations.

●ALBUMS: *The Archies* (Calendar 1969)★★★, *Everything's Archie* (Calendar 1969)★, *Jingle Jangle* (1969)★, *This Is Love* (Kirshner 1969)★, *Sunshine* (1970)★.
●COMPILATIONS: *The Archies' Greatest Hits* (1970)★★★.

ARDEN, DON

b. Harry Levy, January 1926, Manchester, England. After attending the Royal College of Music as a singer, Levy changed his name to Arden in 1944. He worked as a compere/comedian on the music-hall circuit and switched to promotion during the 50s. As well as bringing acts such as Billy Eckstine and Eddie Fisher to Britain, Arden was also heavily involved in rock 'n' roll. During 1959, he compered Gene Vincent's first UK tour and went on to manage the uproarious Virginian. Their rocky association lasted until 1965, when they parted amid much acrimony. By that time, Arden was moving away from rock 'n' roll and taking advantage of the beat group scene. After promoting the Rolling Stones during 1963, he became agent for the Animals and claims to have introduced them to producer Mickie Most. Arden lost the group following a fracas with their controversial manager Mike Jeffrey. Undeterred, Arden wasted no time in signing the Nashville Teens. Several hits followed, but the group failed to sustain their original promise. A far more lucrative acquisition for Arden was the Small Faces. He later claimed to have helped their first single 'What'cha Gonna Do About It' into the UK Top 20, along with other singles from his short-lived Contemporary Records roster. Among these was his own recording of 'Sunrise Sunset', which failed to reach the Top 50. After a series of regular hits with the Small Faces, including the chart-topping 'All Or Nothing', which Arden produced, the entrepreneur lost the group to his managerial rival Andrew Oldham. Arden continued to thrive with his agency Galaxy Entertainments, whose roster included such acts as the Applejacks, the Action, the Attack, Neil Christian, the Fairytale and the Skatellites. His next major find was Amen Corner, whose management he inherited from agent Ron King. By this time Arden was already notorious as an intimidating character and, as during his association with the Small Faces, threats against rival poaching managers were commonplace. Amid the drama, Arden lost the group and a similar fate befell his next find, Skip Bifferty. The 60s ended for Arden with the inheritance of the celebrated Move, but this proved another unhappy association involving a serious dispute with manager Peter Walsh.

By the early 70s, Arden at last found a near perfect manager/artist relationship with the Electric Light Orchestra and various offshoots like Roy Wood's Wizzard. With the formation of Jet Records, Arden increasingly spent time in the USA and found his niche in stadium rock. Among the acts he oversaw in the 70s were Black Sabbath, Ozzy Osbourne (who married his daughter, Sharon) Lynsey De Paul and Air Supply. Despite his many successes as a promoter and manager, Arden's career has been punctuated by countless legal battles and tales of intimidation and alleged violence. In 1987 he stood trial at the Old Bailey for allegedly falsely imprisoning and blackmailing his own accountant. The jury found him not guilty and he left the court a free man, after which he set about reviving his record label Jet.

●FURTHER READING: *Starmakers And Svengalis - The History Of British Pop Management*, Johnny Rogan.

ARNOLD, P.P.

b. Patricia Arnold, 1946, Los Angeles, California, USA. This former singer in a church choir and talented session singer first came to notice in 1966 as a member of Ike And Tina Turner's backing group, the Ikettes. Relocating to England, she was signed to Andrew Loog Oldham's Immediate label, and was backed on tour by the Nice. Her exceptional version of the Cat Stevens ballad 'The First Cut Is The Deepest', was a UK Top 20 hit in 1967 and she enjoyed a second major hit the following year with Chip Taylor's 'Angel Of The Morning', which was arranged by future Led Zeppelin bassist John Paul Jones. Highly regarded among her musical peers for the sheer power and clarity of her voice, her first two albums were produced by Mick Jagger (the second in conjunction with Steve Marriott). Arnold repaid Marriott's production work by contributing some powerful vocals to the Small Faces' hit 'Tin Soldier'. Never quite hitting the big time, Arnold increasingly concentrated on acting, appearing in such musicals as Jack Good's *Catch My Soul*, Tim Rice and Andrew Lloyd Webber's *Jesus Christ Superstar* and Lloyd Webber's *Starlight Express*. A session singer for many artists ranging from Dr John to Nils Lofgren and Freddie King, she returned to the UK charts in 1989 fronting the Beatmasters on 'Burn It Up'.

●ALBUMS: *First Lady Of Immediate* (Immediate 1967)★★, *Kafunta* (Immediate 1968)★★.
●COMPILATIONS: *Greatest Hits* (1978)★★, *The P.P. Arnold Collection* (1988)★★.

ARS NOVA

This unusual, but enchanting, sextet featured former students from New York's Mannes College Of Music, at the time one of America's finest conservatories. The ensemble comprised Wyatt Day (guitar, keyboards,

vocals), Jon Pierson (trombone, vocals), Bill Folwell (trumpet, bass, vocals), Jonathan Raskin (bass, vocals, guitar), Giovanni Papalia (guitar) and Maury Baker (percussion, vocals). They were discovered by producer Paul A. Rothschild, who signed the group to Elektra Records, declaring them 'the most exciting thing since the Doors'. Ars Nova's debut album was a curious hybrid of medieval styles and contemporary rock. Although some of the results were lightweight, others, including 'Pavan For My Lady' and 'I Wrapped Her In Ribbons (After Ibiza)', were genuinely moving. However, this line-up fell apart following a disastrous performance at the Fillmore East and the group was dropped by its label. Pierson and Day secured a replacement contract and found new colleagues in Sam Brown (guitar), Warren Bernhardt (keyboards), Jimmy Owens (trumpet), Art Keonig (bass) and Joe Hunt (drums). A major piece in *Life* magazine celebrated their imaginativeness, but a second collection, *Sunshine And Shadows*, lacked the inspiration of its predecessor and Ars Nova broke up soon after its release.

●ALBUMS: *Ars Nova* (Elektra 1968)★★, *Sunshine And Shadows* (Elektra 1969)★.

ART

Although formed in London, England, in 1967, the origins of this excellent act lay in a Carlisle based R&B band, the VIPs, who recorded three singles before December 1966. When three founding members then left the line-up, Mike Harrison (b. 3 September 1945, Carlisle, Cumberland, England; vocals) and Greg Ridley (b. 23 October 1947, Cumberland, England; bass) regrouped the VIPs around ex-Deep Feeling and ex-Hellions member Luther Grosvenor (b. 23 December 1949, Worcester, England; guitar), Mike Kellie (b. 24 March 1947, Birmingham, England; drums) and Keith Emerson (keyboards). Emerson left to found the Nice following the release of 'Straight Down To The Bottom' and a French-only EP, after which the remaining quartet rechristened themselves Art. Aided by maverick producer Guy Stevens, they completed *Supernatural Fairy Tales*, which blended R&B, pop and psychedelia in a genuinely innovatory manner. Harrison's gritty vocals and Grosvenor's blistering guitarwork are particularly of merit. Stevens was also involved in a concurrent project, Hapshash And The Coloured Coat, which featured designers Michael English and Nigel Weymouth, who were responsible for *Supernatural Fairy Tales'* distinctive sleeve. Reciprocally, the group supplied accompaniment to the trio's experimental album debut. Stevens was also instrumental in suggesting Art required another keyboard player, and, having added US singer Gary Wright to the line-up, the band became known as Spooky Tooth.

●ALBUMS: *Supernatural Fairy Tales* (Island 1967)★★.

ARTWOODS

The collectability of the Artwoods' rare recorded works has increased considerably over the past three decades. This competent UK-based R&B band had a brief moment of glory during the early 60s British beat group club scene. The band comprised Arthur 'Art' Wood (vocals; brother of Ron Wood), Keef Hartley (drums), Jon Lord (organ), Derek Griffiths (guitar) and Malcolm Pool (bass). Their only album contained workmanlike cover versions of regular R&B songs such as 'Can You Hear Me?' and 'If You've Got To Make A Fool Of Somebody', alongside bolder arrangements, including Jimmy Smith's 'Walk On The Wild Side'. Lord demonstrated the seeds of what became a powerful organ style with Deep Purple. Hartley, a technically brilliant drummer, found limited success with John Mayall and his own unit, the Keef Hartley Band. Leader Wood disappeared from the music world.

●ALBUMS: *Art Gallery* (Decca 1965)★★★.
●COMPILATIONS: *The Artwoods* (Spark 1973)★★★, *100 Oxford Street* (Edsel 1983)★★★.

ASPINALL, NEIL

As personal assistant to the Beatles, Neil Aspinall (b. 13 October 1942, Prestatyn, Wales) is one of many to have been dubbed the fifth Beatle. He has certainly known them longer than most - ever since he moved to Liverpool and met Paul McCartney and George Harrison at the Liverpool Institute. When the embryonic mop-tops started gigging regularly, Aspinall bought a van and became their driver. While they were in Hamburg for the first time, Aspinall helped Pete Best's mother, Mona, run the Casbah Club, and on their return he became the group's official road manager. Along with Mal Evans, Aspinall accompanied the Beatles around the world not only as personal assistant but also as a friend. In 1968 he was put in charge of the Apple Corporation and despite the break-up of the Beatles, and the subsequent mess in which Apple found itself, he continues to run their London offices.

ASSOCIATION

One of the most attractive pop/psychedelic harmony groups of the mid-60s, the Association comprised Gary Alexander (lead vocals), Russ Giguere (vocals/guitar), Brian Coles (vocals/bass), Jim Yester (vocals/guitar), Ted Bluechel (drums) and Terry Kirkham (keyboards). After releasing two singles on small labels, 'Babe I'm Gonna Leave You' and a folk rock version of Bob Dylan's 'One Two Many Mornings', they found success with Tandyn Almer's evocative 'Along Comes Mary'. Its ascent to the US Top 10 coincided with allegations that it was a drugs song. The Association's image was ambiguous: genuinely psychedelic in spirit, they also sang ballads and appeared in smart suits. With their strong line-up of singers/composers, they largely wrote their own material for albums. Terry Kirkham gave them their first number 1 single with 'Cherish', while their debut album, *And Then ... Along Comes* (1967), produced by Curt Boettcher, displayed their harmonic talent to extraordinary effect. Singles success followed with another US chart-topper, 'Windy', and a number 2 with 'Never My Love'. Their smooth balladeering was consistently balanced by aberrations such as the genuinely weird 'Pandora's Golden Heebie Jeebies'

on their second album *Renaissance*. Never candidates for the hip élite, the group failed to attract a devoted following and by the late 70s their sales were dwindling. Gary Alexander left briefly for a trip to India and returned with a new name, 'Jules', while their long-standing producer Jerry Yester, brother of Jim, replaced Zal Yanovsky in the Lovin' Spoonful. Soldiering on, the Association continued to release accomplished singles such as 'Time For Living', but soon lost ground and major label status. A soundtrack for the movie *Goodbye Columbus* (1969) and a reasonable 'comeback' album, *Waterbeds In Trinidad* (1972), brought new hope, but the death of founder-member Brian Coles from drug abuse accelerated their eventual move onto the revivalist circuit.

●ALBUMS: *And Then ... Along Comes* (Valiant 1966)★★★, *Renaissance* (Valiant 1967)★★, *Insight Out* (1967)★★, *Birthday* (1968)★★, *The Association* (1969)★★, *Live* (1970)★, *Stop Your Motor* (1971)★★, *Waterbeds In Trinidad* (1972)★★.
●COMPILATIONS: *Greatest Hits* (Warners 1968)★★★★, *Golden Heebie Jeebies* (1988)★★★.

ASYLUM CHOIR

This short-lived duo comprised Leon Russell (b. 2 April 1942, Lawson, Oklahoma, USA; piano/vocals) and Marc Benno (b. 1 July 1947, Dallas, Texas, USA; guitar). Although the latter was relatively unknown, Russell was an established figure in the Los Angeles session hierarchy through his work with disparate figures such as Phil Spector, the Byrds, Frank Sinatra, Herb Alpert and Gary Lewis And The Playboys. *Look Inside The Asylum Choir* received enthusiastic reviews, but when its marriage of psychedelia and white R&B was not a commercial success, the duo's label refused to issue a follow-up album. Russell later purchased the master tape and released the set on his own label, Shelter Records, in the wake of his fame as a solo act. Benno also embarked on an independent career and played guitar on the Doors' album, *LA Woman*.

●ALBUMS: *Look Inside The Asylum Choir* (1968)★★, *Asylum Choir II* (1971)★★.

ATKINS, CHET

b. Chester Burton Atkins, 20 June 1924, Luttrell, Tennessee, USA. Atkins is one of the most influential and prolific guitarists of the 20th century, as well as an important producer and an RCA Records executive. The son of a music teacher and brother of guitarist Jim Atkins (who played with Les Paul), Atkins began as a fiddler in the early 40s, with the Dixieland Swingers in Knoxville, Tennessee. He also played with artists including Bill Carlisle and Shorty Thompson. He moved to Cincinnati, Ohio in 1946 and his first recording session took place that year, for Jim Bullet. In 1947 Atkins was signed to RCA, recording 16 tracks on August 11, including a number of vocals. Atkins first performed at the *Grand Ole Opry* in Nashville in 1948, working with a band that included satirists Homer And Jethro. He toured with

Maybelle Carter in 1949 and recorded as an accompanist with the Carter Family the following year. At that time he made a decision to concentrate on session work, encouraged and often hired by music publisher Fred Rose. During this period, Atkins recorded largely with MGM Records artists, such as Red Sovine and the Louvin Brothers, and most notably on 24 of Hank Williams' tracks for the label. He also recorded on several of the Everly Brothers' Cadence Records hits later in the 50s. In 1952 RCA executive Steve Sholes, who had signed Atkins for session work, gave him authority to build up the label's roster, and Atkins began a second career as a talent scout. By the mid-50s he was recording his own albums and producing 30 artists a year for RCA. Atkins' first album, *Chet Atkins' Gallopin' Guitar*, was issued in 1953, his discography eventually comprising over 100 albums under his own name. Among the other artists with whom he worked at RCA were Elvis Presley, Jim Reeves, Don Gibson, Charley Pride, Waylon Jennings, Hank Snow, Jerry Reed and Perry Como. He is generally regarded as the chief architect of the 'Nashville Sound'. His trademark guitar was a Grestch, which was later manufactured as the 'Chet Atkins Country Gentleman'. George Harrison endorsed this instrument, and this led to a huge increase in sales for the company during the 60s. During this decade Chet recorded the first of a series of guitar duet albums; including works with Snow, Reed, Merle Travis, Les Paul and Doc Watson. Atkins was named an RCA vice-president in 1968 and remained in that position until 1979. In the early 80s he left RCA for Columbia Records and continued to record for that company into the 90s. He has won several Grammy awards and was elected to the Country Music Hall of Fame in 1973. In the 90s he collaborated with Suzy Bogguss and Mark Knopfler and went full circle in 1996 with a true solo work, *Almost Alone,* which contained tributes to the aforementioned artists.

●ALBUMS: *Chet Atkins' Gallopin' Guitar* (RCA Victor 1953)★★★, *Stringin' Along With Chet Atkins* (RCA Victor 1953)★★★, *A Session With Chet Atkins* (RCA Victor 1954)★★★, *Chet Atkins In Three Dimensions* (RCA Victor 1956)★★★, *Finger Style Guitar* (RCA Victor 1956)★★, *Hi Fi In Focus* (RCA Victor 1957)★★, *Mister Guitar* (RCA Victor 1959)★★★, *Chet Atkins In Hollywood* (RCA Victor 1959)★★, *Teensville* (RCA Victor 1959)★★★, *Hum And Strum Along* (RCA Victor 1959)★★, *Chet Atkins' Workshop* (RCA Victor 1960)★★, *Down Home* (RCA Victor 1961)★★★, *The Most Popular Guitar* (RCA Victor 1961)★★★, *Christmas With Chet Atkins* (RCA Victor 1961)★★, *Caribbean Guitar* (RCA Victor 1962)★★, *Back Home Hymns* (RCA Victor 1962)★★, *Our Man In Nashville* (RCA Victor 1963)★★★, *Travelin'* (RCA Victor 1963)★★★, *Teen Scene* (RCA Victor 1963)★★★, with Hank Snow *Reminiscing* (1964)★★★, *Chet Atkins Picks On The Beatles* (RCA Victor 1965)★★, *Play Guitar With Chet Atkins* (RCA Victor 1966)★★★, *It's A Guitar World* (RCA Victor 1967)★★★, *Chet Atkins Picks The Best* (RCA Victor 1967)★★, *Class Guitar* (RCA Victor 1967)★★★, *Solo Flights* (RCA Victor 1968)★★, with Jerry Reed *Me And Jerry* (1970)★★, with Merle Travis *The Atkins-Travis Traveling Show* (RCA Victor 1974)★★★, with Les Paul *Chester And Lester* (RCA Victor 1975)★★★, with Floyd Cramer and Danny Davis *Chet, Floyd And Danny* (1977)★★★, *A Legendary Performer* (RCA Victor 1977)★★★, *Me And My Guitar* (1977)★★★, with Les Paul *Guitar Monsters* (1978)★★★, *The First Nashville Guitar Quartet* (1979)★★, *The Best Of Chet On The Road...Live* (1980)★★, with Doc Watson *Reflections* (RCA Victor 1980)★★★, with Lenny Breau *Standard Brands* (1981)★★, *Work It Out With Chet Atkins* (1983)★★★, *Stay Tuned* (RCA Victor 1985)★★★, *Street Dreams* (Columbia 1986)★★★, *Tennessee Guitar Man* (Pair 1986)★★, *Sails* (1987)★★★, *Chet Atkins, C.G.P.* (Columbia 1988)★★★, *Country Gems* (Pair 1990)★★★, with Mark Knopfler *Neck & Neck* (1992)★★★, with Jerry Reed *Sneakin' Around* (1992)★★★, *Read My Licks* (Columbia 1994)★★★, *Almost Alone* (Columbia 1996)★★★.

●COMPILATIONS: *The Best Of Chet Atkins* (RCA Victor 1963)★★★★, *Solid Gold Guitar* (1982)★★★, *Guitar Pickin' Man* (1983)★★★, *20 Of The Best* (1986)★★★★, *Best Of Chet Atkins And Friends* (1987)★★★, *The RCA Years* 2-CD box set (1992)★★★★, *The Collection* (1993)★★★, *The Early Years 1945-54* 4-CD box set (1993)★★★.

●VIDEOS: *Chet Atkins & Friends* (1991).

●FURTHER READING: *Country Gentleman*, Chet Atkins with Bill Neeley.

ATLANTIC RECORDS

The Atlantic label was founded in 1947 by Herb Abramson, a dentistry student, and Ahmet Ertegun, the son of a Turkish ambassador. The New York-based company's early releases included R&B and jazz but by the early 50s it became established as a leading outlet for all facets of black music. Ruth Brown, Joe Turner, the Clovers and the Drifters were among its most successful acts during this period. Jerry Wexler, a former journalist with *Billboard* magazine, joined the flourishing label in 1953 as a partner and shareholder and became their greatest producer. Abramson, meanwhile, was drafted, and although he returned to the company in 1955, events within Atlantic had overtaken him. Ahmet's brother Nesuhi was involved in building up a formidable jazz catalogue while Abramson became responsible for the newly formed Atco subsidiary. His wife Miriam also became a key member of the board, looking after the fast growing accounts department. He grew increasingly unhappy with his role and sold his share to the company's three executives. Atlantic's success continued unabated throughout the 50s with hits by the Coasters, Bobby Darin and, crucially, Ray Charles. This gifted performer provided the natural stepping-stone between the R&B prevalent during the decade and the soul of the next, by which time the label had grown into a major concern. As such, it began lucrative distribution deals with independent outlets, one of which was Stax. This Memphis-based label/studio was instrumental in shaping Atlantic's 60s identity through hits for Otis Redding, Sam And Dave, Wilson Pickett and Carla Thomas. However, tension between its owner, Jim Stewart, and Wexler, latterly soured the relationship, and the two sides split in 1968. In the meantime Wexler had entered another fruitful period with Rick Hall's Alabama-based Fame studio following success with Percy Sledge. It was here that Aretha Franklin recorded her first major smash, 'I Never Loved A Man (The Way I Love You)', which began a long, critically and commercially rewarding relationship between the singer and outlet.

Despite continuing its work with black music, Atlantic was increasingly drawn towards white rock. The Rascals, a blue-eyed soul quartet, and Sonny And Cher were successful singles acts, but the floodgates to the album market were opened when the label secured with their Atco subsidiary the American rights for Cream's releases. New groups, including Vanilla Fudge, Iron Butterfly (whose second album, *In A Gadda Da Vida,* was for many years the label's biggest selling album) and Crosby, Stills, Nash And Young, furthered a process culminating in Atlantic's commercial triumphs with British acts Led Zeppelin and Yes. This period was also marked by a lucrative marketing deal with the newly inaugurated Rolling Stones label. Atlantic retained its black heritage during the 70s with the Detroit Spinners, Roberta Flack and Blue Magic, but its autonomous position ceased following its acquisition by Warner Brothers Records. The newly inaugurated WEA group was itself taken over by the Kinney Corporation in 1969 but this brief renaming was soon superseded by Time/Warner. Although the label continues to forge success on several musical fronts, Atlantic no longer boasts the individuality which made it such a potent force during its first 25 years. Ertegun, however, remains one of the most important ever figures in popular music and now shares the presidency at Atlantic (since January 1996) with Val Azzoli, a 41-year-old Canadian.

● COMPILATIONS: *This Is Soul* (1968)★★★, *Atlantic R&B* (1986)★★★★, *Atlantic Blues* box set (1987)★★★, *Atlantic Jazz* 15-album box set (1987)★★★★, *Atlantic Soul Classics* (1987)★★★★, *Atlantic Soul Ballads* (1988)★★★★, *Great Moments In Jazz* 3-album box set (1988)★★★★, *Classic Rock 1966-1988* (1988)★★★★, *Atlantic Rhythm And Blues 1947-1974* 8-CD box set (Atlantic 1991)★★★★.

● FURTHER READING: *Sweet Soul Music*, Peter Guralnick. *Making Tracks: The Story Of Atlantic Records*, Charlie Gillet. *Atlantic And The Godfathers Of Rock And Roll*, Justine Picardie and Dorothy Wade.

ATTACK

This mid-60s mod-influenced UK pop group was signed to entrepreneur Don Arden's agency Galaxy Entertainments in the hope of emulating the success of his other protégés, the Small Faces. Their first single, on the Philips label, was the amusingly titled plea 'Please

Phil Spector'. In spite of several further singles on Decca, they failed to chart but became embroiled in a war of words with Jeff Beck after recording a cover version of his hit 'Hi Ho Silver Lining' in 1967. That same year, the Attack folded but their talented guitarist David O'List later found a degree of fame as a member of the Nice.
● COMPILATIONS: *Magic In The Air* (Reflection 1990).

AU GO-GO SINGERS

Evolving from New York group, the New Choctawquins, this nine-piece vocal ensemble came together in Greenwich Village in 1964. Heavily influenced by the New Christy Minstrels and other commercialized folk aggregations of the period, the Au Go-Go Singers sang in an off-Broadway musical, toured the southern states and recorded one album before fragmenting in 1965. Among their alumni were Stephen Stills and Richie Furay who formed the hit group Buffalo Springfield the following year.
● ALBUMS: *They Call Us The Au Go-Go Singers* (1964)★★.

AUTOSALVAGE

One of the more enigmatic groups to emerge from New York's post-folk/rock circuit, Autosalvage consisted of Rick Turner (guitar/banjo/dulcimer), Thomas Danaher (vocals/guitar), Skip Boone (bass/piano) and Darius LaNoue Davenport (vocals/oboe/piano/drums). Skip was the brother of Steve Boone, bassist in the Lovin' Spoonful, one of several groups influencing the above quartet. *Autosalvage*, the group's sole album, was released in 1968 to universal critical acclaim. Traditional themes were mixed with jugband music, while the adventurous, quirky compositions blended shimmering guitar with textured instrumentation. Commercial indifference doomed their continuation and by the end of the decade Autosalvage had broken up.
● ALBUMS: *Autosalvage* (RCA Victor 1968)★★★.

AUTUMN RECORDS

This teen-orientated label was founded in San Francisco, USA, in 1964. Co-directors Tom Donahue and Bob Mitchell were disc jockeys on the local KYA station and owners of a club, Mothers. Autumn's second release, Bobby Freeman's 'C'mon And Swim', reached the US Top 5 in August 1964, but it was not until the following year that the company enjoyed more consistent success, thanks to the Beau Brummels. Although early releases, notably 'Laugh Laugh' and 'Just A Little', owed a debt to the Beatles, the group's later work was more folk rock-influenced. Subsequent label signings included the Tikis, the Vejtables and Mojo Men, but sales were restricted to the Bay Area. This did not reflect the high quality of Autumn's recordings which surpassed contemporary independents. The producer Sylvester Stewart, later known as Sly Stone, created a clear, resonant sound and played on several sessions. He also completed two solo singles for the label, 'Buttermilk' and 'Temptation Walk'. Although Autumn was already in decline as a commercial proposition, Donahue and Mitchell launched two subsidiary outlets, North Beach and Jest, in November 1965. 'Someone To Love' by the Great Society was issued on North Beach but it drew scant attention. Paradoxically, the song, retitled 'Somebody To Love', later became the smash hit Autumn required when Great Society vocalist Grace Slick introduced it to her next act, Jefferson Airplane. Autumn Records failed to connect with the emergent 'San Francisco' sound - Donahue recorded, then rejected, the pioneering Charlatans - and the label folded in 1966. Existing acts were sold to Warner Brothers Records while master tapes, including a considerable number of unissued titles, were leased to the Los Angeles label, Vault. Interest in Autumn's output has nevertheless remained high, and there have since been numerous compilations.

●COMPILATIONS: *San Francisco Roots* (Vault 1968)★★★, *Dance With Me: The Autumn Teen Sound* (Big Beat 1994)★★★.

AVALON, FRANKIE

b. Francis Avallone, 18 September 1939, Philadelphia, USA. The photogenic 50s teen-idol started as a trumpet-playing child prodigy. His first recordings in 1954 were the instrumentals 'Trumpet Sorrento' and 'Trumpet Tarantella' on X-Vik Records (an RCA Records subsidiary). In the mid-50s, he appeared on many television and radio shows including those of Paul Whiteman, Jackie Gleason and Ray Anthony. He joined Rocco & The Saints and was seen singing with them in the 1957 film *Jamboree* (*Disc Jockey Jamboree* in the UK). Avalon signed to Chancellor Records and in 1958 his third single for them 'Dede Dinah' reached the US Top 10. It was the first of his 25 US chart entries, many of which were written by his hard-working manager, Bob Marucci.

Despite the fact that he had a weak voice, he quickly became one of the top stars in the USA and managed two chart toppers in 1959, 'Venus' and 'Why', which were his only UK Top 20 entries. He has had an astonishing 25 hits in the USA, astonishing because his musical talent was often in question. He had to wait until his 21st birthday in 1961 to receive the $100,000 he had earned to date, and by that time he had passed his peak as a singer and turned his attention to acting. His acting career was also successful, with appearances in many films, including a string of beach movies alongside fellow 50s pop star Annette. He also appeared in the highly successful 1978 film, *Grease*. He later recorded with little success on United Artists, Reprise, Metromedia, Regalia, Delite, Amos and Bobcat. Apart from his film and occasional television appearances, Avalon still performs on the supper-club circuit, and in 1986 toured in *Golden Boys Of Bandstand*. Alongside his fellow Chancellor Records artist Fabian, he is often dismissed by rock critics, yet remains one of the American public's best loved 50s teen-idols.

●ALBUMS: *Frankie Avalon* (Chancellor 1958)★★, *The Young Frankie Avalon* (Chancellor 1959)★★, *Swingin' On A Rainbow* (Chancellor 1959)★★, *Young And In Love* (Chancellor 1960)★★, *Summer Scene* (Chancellor 1960)★★, *And Now About Mr. Avalon* (Chancellor 1961)★★, *Italiano* (Chancellor 1962)★, *You Are Mine* (Chancellor 1962)★★, *Frankie Avalon Christmas Album* (Chancellor 1962)★★, *Songs From Muscle Beach Party* film soundtrack (United Artists 1964)★★, *I'll Take Sweden* film soundtrack (United Artists 1965)★★, *I Want You Near Me* (1970)★, *Bobby Sox To Stockings* (1984)★★, *Frankie Avalon* (1987)★★.

●COMPILATIONS: *A Whole Lotta Frankie* (Chancellor 1961)★★, *15 Greatest Hits* (United Artists 1964)★★★, *Best Of Frankie Avalon* (1984)★★★, *Frankie Avalon: Collection* (1990)★★, *Venus And Other Hits* (1993)★★★, *Venus: The Best Of Frankie Avalon* (Varese Vintage 1995)★★★, *Greatest Hits* (Curb 1995)★★★.

●FILMS: *Jamboree* aka *Disc Jockey Jamboree* (1957), *Beach Party* (1963), *Bikini Beach* (1964), *How To Stuff A Wild Bikini* (1965), *Beach Blanket Bingo* (1965), *Grease* (1978).

AVONS

Sisters-in-law Valerie (b. 1936, Willesden, London, England) and Elaine Murtagh (b. 1940, County Cork, Eire) originally performed as the Avon Sisters. After being discovered singing at the 1958 BBC Radio Exhibition, they signed to UK Columbia where they recorded with producer Norrie Paramor. Their debut was 'Which Witch Doctor' with the Mudlarks and their debut solo release was a cover version of 'Jerri O' - both songs failed to chart. They added Ray Adams (b. 1938, Jersey, Channel Islands), whom they spotted singing with Nat Gonella's Band and then changed their name to the Avons. Their first single under the new name, a cover version of Paul Evans' 'Seven Little Girls Sitting In The Back Seat' in 1959, gave them their only UK Top 20 chart entry. The light-pop trio had three minor hits and last charted with a cover version of 'Rubber Ball' in 1961. In 1962 a song they had written, 'Dance On', became a UK number 1 instrumental hit for the Shadows and it returned to the Top 20 the following year with a powerful vocal version from Kathy Kirby. They recorded for Decca in 1963 and Fontana in 1964 but had no other hits. Valerie continued to have success as a writer and is still a well-known behind-the-scenes figure in the UK music business. Their only album is now much sought after, fetching high prices in the collector's market

●ALBUMS: *The Avons* (Columbia/Hull 1960)★★.

AZNAVOUR, CHARLES

b. 22 May 1924, Paris, France. Premier vocalist/songwriter Aznavour's parents fled from Armenia after the Turkish massacre, and his composition 'They Fell' shows the bewilderment felt by all Armenians. He declares, 'I am Armenian. Everybody figures out that I am a Frenchman because I sing in French, I act like a Frenchman and I have all the symptoms of a Frenchman.' Aznavour's father had a small restaurant but Aznavour himself was preoccupied with music. When aged only 15, he wrote a one-man show. In 1942 Aznavour formed a partnership with Pierre Roche and they had success in Canada between 1948 and 1950. Aznavour's first hit song was 'J'ai Bu' for Charles Ulmer in 1950, the year he also became a solo performer. He comments, 'I was small and undistinguished, so I had to become rich and famous.' Aznavour often opened for Edith Piaf, who recorded several of his songs, including 'Il Pleut', 'Le Feutre Tropez', as well as a translation of 'Jezebel'. 'When I gave "Je Hais Les Dimanches" to her, she laughed in my face and told me to give it to an existentialist singer,' he recalled. 'I took her at her word and gave it Juliette Greco. She said, "You idiot! You've given my song to that girl. Now I'll have to record it to show her how to sing it."' Aznavour has written numerous songs about ageing, notably 'Hier Encore', which was translated into English by Herbert Kretzmer as 'Yesterday When I Was Young'. 'I wrote my first song about being old when I was 18. The songs I wrote many years ago haven't dated at all, although my way of singing them, my interpretation, has become sweeter.' 'The Old-Fashioned Way' was an antidote to rock 'n' roll, but ironically in the film *And Then There Was None*, the character he played was poisoned after singing it. His film appearances have included the title role in François Truffaut's meritorious *Shoot The Piano Player* (1960), and he has been featured in popular films, including *Candy*, *The Adventurers* and *The Games*. Matt Monro made the UK charts with the maudlin 'For Mama', while Jack Jones recorded a tribute album, *Write Me A Love Song, Charlie*. In 1974 Aznavour had a UK number 1 with 'She', the theme for the ITV television series, *The Seven Faces Of Woman*. Although small (5 feet 3 inches), slight and with battered, world-weary features, he is nonetheless an imposing concert performer, acting his songs with the ability of a leading mime artist. Aznavour starred in the 1975 Royal Command Performance, and he has been parodied by the Goodies as Charles Aznovoice. He rarely records anything other than his own songs and his inventive compositions have included 'You've Let Yourself Go', in which his woman is overweight and argumentative, 'What Makes A Man' about a transvestite, 'Pretty Shitty Days' about an English word that amused him, and the hilarious account of a disastrous wedding anniversary in 'Happy Anniversary'. He says, 'Songs mature inside of me and then take their life on paper. A song may take me five minutes to write but it also takes 40 years of living.'

●ALBUMS: *Charles Aznavour Sings* (1963)★★★, *Qui?* (1964)★★★, *Et Voici* (1964)★★★, *Aznavour Sings His Love Songs In English* (1965)★★★, *Charles Aznavour '65* (1965)★★★, *Encore* (1966)★★★, *De T'Avoir Aimée* (1966)★★★, *Aznavour Sings Aznavour, Volume 1* (1970)★★★★, *Aznavour Sings Aznavour, Volume 2* (1971)★★★, *Désormais* (1972)★★★, *Aznavour Sings Aznavour, Volume 3* (1973)★★★, *Chez Lui A Paris* (1973)★★★, *A Tapestry Of Dreams* (1974)★★★, *I Sing For ... You* (1975)★★★, *Charles Aznavour Esquire* (1978)★★★, *A Private Christmas* (1978)★★, *In Times To Be* (1983)★★★, *Guichets Fermés* (1978)★★★, *Comme Ils Disent, Aimez Moi, Face Au Public, Hier Encore, Il Faut Savoir, Je M'Voyais Déjà, Je N'Ai Pas Vu Le Temps Passé, La Bohème, La Mama, Le Temps, Non, Je N'Ai Rien Oublié, Paris Au Mois D'Aôut, Plein Feu Sur Aznavour, Reste, Une Première Dance, 1980 ... A L'Olympia.*

●COMPILATIONS: *You And Me* (Angel 1995)★★★, *She, The Best Of* (EMI Premier 1996)★★★★, *Greatest Golden Hits* (Angel 1996)★★★.

●VIDEOS: *An Evening With ...* (1984).

●FURTHER READING: *Aznavour By Aznavour: An Autobiography*, Charles Aznavour. *Yesterday When I Was Young*, Charles Aznavour. *Charles Aznavour*, Y. Salgues.

B. BUMBLE AND THE STINGERS

This short-lived act was one of several US groups formed by pop svengali Kim Fowley as an outlet for his production/songwriting talents at Rendezvous Records. Their 1961 release, 'Bumble Boogie' (featuring Ernie Freeman at the piano), an adaptation of Nicolai Rimsky-Korsakov's 'Flight Of The Bumble Bee' reached number 21 in the US chart. It was, however, the following year's 'Nut Rocker' (with pianist Lincoln Mayorga), which brought them lasting fame. Although it only reached number 23 in the US, this propulsive instrumental, an irreverent boogie-woogie reading of Pyotr Ill'yich Tchaikovsky's *Nutcracker Suite*, fared much better in the UK where it soared to number 1 and, 10 years later, again reached the Top 20 on reissue. The group - B. Bumble (who at this juncture consisted of R.C. Gamble, b. 1940, Spiro, Oklahoma, USA), Terry Anderson (b. 1941, Harrison, Arkansas, USA; guitar), Jimmy King (b. 1938; rhythm guitar) and Don Orr (b. 1939; drums) - completed a UK tour in 1962 that year. Although only compilations are available featuring variations on the same theme, 'Bumble Boogie', 'Apple Knocker' and 'Bee Hive', their one major hit remains: 'Nut Rocker' - it is set for immortality.
●COMPILATIONS: *Best O'B Bumble* (One Way 1995)★★, *Nut Rocker And All The Classics* (Ace 1996).

BACHARACH, BURT

b. 12 May 1928, Kansas City, Missouri, USA. As a composer and arranger, Bacharach is rightly regarded as one of the most important figures in contemporary pop music. Although his father was a journalist, it was music rather than lyrics which were to prove Bacharach's forte. Raised in New York, he was a jazz aficionado and played in various ensembles during the 40s. He studied musical theory and composition at university and served in the US Army between 1950 and 1952. Following his discharge, he worked as a pianist, arranger and conductor for a number of artists including Vic Damone, Steve Lawrence, Polly Bergen and the Ames Brothers. From 1956-58, Bacharach worked as musical director for Marlene Dietrich, a period in which he also registered his first hit as a composer. The song in question was the Five Blobs' 'The Blob', a tune written for a horror b-movie. Bacharach's co-composer on that hit was Mack David, but a more fruitful partnership followed when Burt was introduced to his collaborator's brother, Hal David. In 1958, Bacharach/David enjoyed their first hit with 'The Story Of My Life', a US Top 20 for Marty Robbins. In the UK, the

song became an instant standard, courtesy of the chart-topping Michael Holliday and three other hit versions by Gary Miller, Alma Cogan and Dave King. Even greater success followed with Perry Como's reading of the engagingly melodic 'Magic Moments' which topped the UK charts for an astonishing eight weeks (number 4 in the USA). Despite their chart-topping songwriting success, the Bacharach/David team did not work together exclusively until as late as 1962. In the meantime, Bacharach found a new songwriting partner, Bob Hilliard, with whom he composed several recordings for the Drifters. They also enjoyed minor success with Chuck Jackson's beautifully sparse 'Any Day Now' (later recorded by Elvis Presley). It was during the early 60s that the Bacharach/David team recommenced their collaboration in earnest and many of their recordings brought success to both USA and UK artists. Frankie Vaughan's 'Tower Of Strength' gave them their third UK number 1, as well as another US Top 10 hit in a version by Gene McDaniels. The highly talented Gene Pitney, himself a songwriter, achieved two of his early hits with the duo's 'The Man Who Shot Liberty Valence' and 'Twenty Four Hours From Tulsa'. Other well-known Bacharach/David standards from the early/mid-60s included 'Wives And Lovers' and 'What The World Needs Now Is Love' (successfully covered by Jack Jones and Jackie DeShannon, respectively). From 1962 onwards the formidable Bacharach/David writing team steered the career of songstress Dionne Warwick with a breathtaking array of quality hit songs including 'Don't Make Me Over', 'Anyone Who Had A Heart', 'Walk On By', 'You'll Never Get To Heaven', 'Reach Out For Me', 'Are You There (With Another Girl)', 'Message To Michael', 'Trains And Boats And Planes', 'I Just Don't Know What To Do With Myself', Alfie', 'The Windows Of The World', 'I Say A Little Prayer', 'Valley Of The Dolls' and 'Do You Know The Way To San Jose?'. Interestingly, the songwriting duo maintained a quotient of number 1 singles in the UK, thanks to first-class cover versions by Cilla Black ('Anyone Who Had A Heart'), Sandie Shaw ('There's Always Something There To Remind Me'), the Walker Brothers ('Make It Easy On Yourself') and Herb Alpert ('This Guy's In Love With You'). Looking back at this remarkable series of hits, one notices the strength of Bacharach's melodies and the deftness of touch that so neatly complemented David's soul-tortured, romantic lyrics.

Since writing the theme song to *The Man Who Shot Liberty Valence*, Bacharach/David were popular choices as composers of film scores. The comedy *What's New Pussycat?* brought them an Oscar nomination and another hit when the title song was recorded by Tom Jones. Dusty Springfield recorded numerous Bacharach songs on her albums throughout the 60s and together with Warwick, they were arguably the best interpreters of his material. Further hits and Academy Award nominations followed between 1967 and 1968 for the films *Alfie* and *Casino Royale* (which featured 'The Look Of Love'). Finally, in 1969, a double Oscar celebration was achieved with the score from *Butch Cassidy And The Sundance*

Kid and its award-winning standard 'Raindrops Keep Falling On My Head'.

Although there were opportunities to write further movie material during the late 60s, the duo were determined to complete their own musical, *Promises, Promises*. The show proved enormously successful and enjoyed a lengthy Broadway run. Although Bacharach's reputation rests mainly on his songwriting, he has had a sporadic career as a recording artist. After a minor US hit with 'Saturday Sunshine' in 1963, he outmanoeuvred Billy J. Kramer And The Dakotas in the 1965 chart race involving 'Trains And Boats And Planes'. Personal appearances at such prestigious venues as the Greek Theatre in Los Angeles and the Riviera Hotel in Las Vegas have produced 'standing room only' notices, while television specials based on his songs proved very popular.

By 1970, Bacharach seemed blessed with the hit Midas touch and the Carpenters' beautiful reading of 'Close To You' suggested that further standards would follow. Remarkably, however, this inveterate hitmaker did not enjoy another chart success for over 10 years. An acrimonious split from partner Hal David broke the classic songwriting spell. A barren period was possibly exacerbated by the concurrent break-up of Bacharach's marriage to actress Angie Dickinson and the loss of his most consistent hitmaker Dionne Warwick. Bacharach's desultory decade was alleviated by a series of albums for A&M Records, which featured his own readings of his compositions. Although the late 60s recording *Make It Easy On Yourself* and the 1971 *Burt Bacharach* were chart successes, the curse of the 70s was once more evident when *Living Together* sold poorly. Worse followed when his musical *Lost Horizon* emerged as a commercial disaster. His succeeding albums *Futures* and *Woman* also fared badly and none of his new compositions proved chartworthy.

It was not until 1981 that Bacharach's dry run ended. At last he found a lyricist of genuine commercial fire in Carole Bayer Sager. Their Oscar-winning 'Arthur's Theme' (co-written with Peter Allen and singer Christopher Cross) returned Bacharach to the charts and in 1982 he married Sager. Together, they provided hits for Roberta Flack ('Making Love') and Neil Diamond ('Heartlight'). In 1986 Bacharach enjoyed the level of success so familiar during the late 60s, with two US number 1 hits 'That's What Friends Are For' (an AIDS charity record by Warwick and 'Friends' - Elton John, Gladys Knight and Stevie Wonder) and 'On My Own' (a duet between Patti Labelle and Michael McDonald).

In the late 80s Bacharach collaborated with Sager on film songs such as 'They Don't Make Them Like They Use To' (for *Tough Guys*), 'Everchanging Time' (with Bill Conti for *Baby Boom*), and 'Love Is My Decision' for *Arthur 2: On The Rocks*). He also wrote the score for the latter film. In 1989 the American vocalist Sybil revived 'Don't Make Me Over', Warwick's first hit with a Bacharach/David song, and a year later the UK group Deacon Blue went to number 2 with their *Four Bacharach And David Songs* EP. In 1992, some months after Bacharach had announced that his nine-year-old marriage to Sager was over, he and David finally reunited to write songs, including 'Sunny Weather Lover' for Dionne Warwick's new album. In the following year, Bacharach extended his publishing empire in collaboration with veteran publishing executive Bob Fead, and was subsequently reported to be writing with Will Jennings, John Bettis ('Captives Of The Heart'), Narada Michael Walden, and Elvis Costello ('God Give Me Strength' for the movie *Grace Of My Heart*). He was also said to be exploring the possibilities of writing another stage musical, with B.A. Robertson. In 1994, a musical revue entitled *Back To Bacharach And David* opened in New York, and in the following year, BBC Television transmitted a major film profile, *Burt Bacharach: ... This Is Now*, which was narrated by Dusty Springfield. Naturally, she was represented (with 'I Just Don't Know What To Do With Myself') on the 23-track celebratory *The Look Of Love-The Classic Songs Of Burt Bacharach* (1996), which also contained other significant versions of the composer's immortal melodies, such as 'Walk On By' (Dionne Warwick), 'Raindrops Keep Falling On My Head' (B.J. Thomas), 'This Guy's In Love With You' (Herb Alpert) and 'Make It Easy On Yourself' (Walker Brothers). That album, along with Bacharach's *Reach Out* (originally released in 1967) and *The Best Of Burt Bacharach* (on which he plays instrumental versions of 20 of his hits) were issued in the UK in response to a tremendous upsurge of interest in easy listening music among young people in the mid-90s. Suddenly, Bacharach is considered 'hip' again. Noel Gallagher of Oasis is reported to be a great admirer, and leading figures in contemporary popular music such as Jarvis Cocker of Pulp, Michael Stipe of R.E.M., and Paul Weller have all covered his songs. Welcomed by many critics as 'a backlash against the hard rhythms of the dance/house stuff', the phenomenon has also dismayed others, one of whom groaned: 'And to think we went through two Woodstocks for this.'

●ALBUMS: *Hit Maker - Burt Bacharach* (London 1965)★★★, *Casino Royale* soundtrack (RCA 1967)★★★, *Reach Out* (A&M 1967)★★★, *Make It Easy On Yourself* (A&M 1969)★★, *Butch Cassidy And The Sundance Kid* soundtrack (A&M 1970)★★★, *Burt Bacharach* (A&M 1971)★★, *Living Together* (A&M 1973)★★, *In Concert* (A&M 1974)★★, *Futures* (A&M 1977)★★, *Woman* (A&M 1979)★★.

●COMPILATIONS: *Portrait In Music* (A&M 1971)★★★, *Portrait In Music Vol. 2* (A&M 1973)★★★, *Burt Bacharach's Greatest Hits* (A&M 1974)★★★★, *The Best Of Burt Bacharach* (A&M 1996)★★★★.

BACHELORS

Formed in Dublin, Eire, in 1958, the group was originally known as both the Harmony Chords and Harmonichords and featured brothers Conleth Cluskey (b. 18 March 1941), Declan Cluskey (b. 12 December 1942) and John Stokes (b. Sean James Stokes, 13 August 1940). The Dublin-born trio initially worked as a mainstream folk act, all three playing harmonicas. In 1961, they were discovered in Scotland by entrepreneur Phil Solomon and his wife Dorothy. After a further period of struggle Solomon introduced them to Decca's A&R head Dick Rowe who recalls: 'They all played harmonicas and sang folk songs. They weren't an act you could sign to a pop record company. We went backstage afterwards and there were these three boys who looked at me as if I'd come from heaven and was going to open the door for them to walk in. I said, "God be with me at this moment", and I meant it.' After signing the trio, Rowe suggested a name change: 'I said, "What do girls like, Philip? . . . Bachelors!".' With producer Shel Talmy, the group scored a UK Top 10 hit with a revival of the Lew Pollack and Erno Rapee song 'Charmaine' in the summer of 1963. After three unsuccessful follow-ups ('Far Away', 'Whispering' and 'I'll See You') they struck again with a string of easy listening pop hits including several revivals suggested by Rowe: 'Diane', 'I Believe', 'Ramona', 'I Wouldn't Trade You For The World' and 'No Arms Can Ever Hold You'. In 1966, they revealed their former folk roots and completely outmanoeuvred Simon And Garfunkel by taking 'The Sound Of Silence' to number 3 in the UK charts.

Working primarily with agent Dorothy Solomon, the Bachelors achieved great success on the cabaret circuit with a line-up that remained unchallenged for 25 years. However, in 1984, a dispute arose between the members and John Stokes was asked to leave. He duly took legal action against the brothers and the company Bachelors Ltd. During the hearing, Stokes' voice was likened to that of a 'drowning rat' but he received compensation and left with plans to form a duo. He was replaced by Peter Phipps who was inducted into the second generation New Bachelors. As Philip Solomon concluded: 'The Bachelors never missed a date in their lives. One of them even had an accident on their way to do a pantomime in Bristol and went on with his leg in plaster and 27 stitches in his head. That is professionalism.'

●ALBUMS: *The Bachelors* (1963)★★★, *The Bachelors Second Album* (1964)★★, *Presenting: The Bachelors* (1964)★★★, *The Bachelors And Sixteen Great Songs* (Decca 1964)★★★, *No Arms Can Ever Hold You* (1965)★★★, *Marie* (1965)★★★, *More Great Song Hits From The Bachelors* (1965)★★★, *Hits Of The Sixties* (Decca 1966)★★★, *Bachelors' Girls* (Decca 1966)★★★, *The Golden All Time Hits* (Decca 1967)★★★, *Live At Talk Of The Town* (1971)★★, *Under And Over* (1971)★★, with Patricia Cahill *Stage And Screen Spectacular* (1972)★★.

●COMPILATIONS: *World Of The Bachelors* (Decca 1968)★★★★, *World Of The Bachelors - Vol. Two* (Decca 1969)★★★★, *World Of The Bachelors - Vol. Three* (Decca 1969)★★★, *World Of The Bachelors - Vol. Four* (Decca 1970)★★★, *World Of The Bachelors - Vol. Five* (1970)★★, *The Very Best Of The Bachelors* (1974)★★★, *Focus On The Bachelors* (1979)★★★, *25 Golden Greats* (Warwick 1979)★★★★, *The Best Of The Bachelors* (1981)★★★, *The Bachelors Collection* (1985)★★★, *Bachelors Hits* (1989)★★★.

●FILMS: *It's All Over Town* (1964).

BAEZ, JOAN

b. Joan Chandos Baez, 9 January 1941, Staten Island, New York, USA. The often used cliché: the queen of folk to Bob Dylan's king, Joan's sweeping soprano is one of popular music's most distinctive voices. An impressive appearance at the 1959 Newport Folk Festival followed the singer's early performances throughout the Boston/New England club scene and established Baez as a vibrant interpreter of traditional material. Joan's first four albums featured ballads drawn from American and British sources, but as the civil rights campaign intensified, so the artist became increasingly identified with the protest movement. Her reading of 'We Shall Overcome', first released on *In Concert/Part 2*, achieved an anthemlike quality. This album also featured Dylan's 'Don't Think Twice, It's All Right' and Baez then took the emergent singer on tour and their well-documented romance blossomed. Over the years she interpreted many of his songs, several of which, including 'Farewell Angelina' and 'Love Is Just A Four Letter Word', Dylan did not officially record. In the 60s she founded the Institute for the Study Of Nonviolence. Baez also featured early work by other contemporary writers, including Phil Ochs, brother-in-law Richard Farina, Tim Hardin and Donovan, and by the late 60s was composing her own material. The period was also marked by the singer's increasing commitment to non-violence and she was jailed on two occasions for participation in anti-war rallies. In 1968 Baez married David Harris, a peace activist who was later imprisoned for several years for draft resistance. The couple were divorced in 1972.

Although a version of the Band song, 'The Night They Drove Old Dixie Down', gave Joan a hit single in 1971, she found it hard to maintain a consistent commercial profile. Her devotion to politics continued as before and a 1973 release, *Where Are You Now My Son*, included recordings the singer made in North Vietnam. A 1975 collection, *Diamonds And Rust*, brought a measure of mainstream success. The title track remains her own strongest song. The story of her relationship with Dylan, it presaged their reunion, after ten years apart, in the legendary Rolling Thunder Revue. That, in turn, inspired her one entirely self-penned album, *Gulf Winds*, in which her songwriting continued to develop, often in new and unexpected directions. In 1989, she released an album celebrating 30 years of performing - *Speaking Of Dreams*, which found her duetting with her old friends Paul Simon and Jackson Browne and, surprisingly, with the Gypsy Kings in a rumba-flamenco cover version of 'My Way'. However, she has preferred to concentrate her energies on humanitarian work rather than recording. In 1979 she founded Humanitas International, a rapid-response human rights group that first persuaded the US President Carter to send the Seventh Fleet to rescue Boat People. She has received numerous awards and honorary doctorates for her work. In the 80s and 90s Baez continued to divide her time between social activism, undergoing therapy and singing. She found a new audience among the young socially aware Europeans - 'The

Children Of The Eighties', as she dubbed them in song. She retains a deserved respect for her early, highly influential releases. At the end of 1992 *Play Me Backwards* was released to universal acclaim; this smooth country rock album put Baez very much in the same bracket as Mary-Chapin Carpenter. Baez sounded confident flirting with rock and country and in the mid-90s she began to dally with African rhythms and sounds. By her own admission, in the 80s and 90s she underwent therapy as she had discovered that she was a troubled soul. Baez appears a relaxed individual, although still capable of being a prickly interviewee, especially if the subject of Dylan is broached. She remains, largely through her achievements in the 60s, a giant of folk music.

●ALBUMS: *Joan Baez* (Vanguard 1960)★★★, *Joan Baez 2* (Vanguard 1961)★★★, *Joan Baez In Concert* (Vanguard 1962)★★★★, *Joan Baez In Concert Part 2* (Vanguard 1963)★★★, *Joan Baez 5* (1964)★★★★, *Farewell Angelina* (Vanguard 1965)★★★★, *Portrait* (Vanguard 1966)★★★, *Noel* (Vanguard 1966)★★★, *Joan* (Vanguard 1967)★★★, *Baptism* (Vanguard 1968)★★★, *Any Day Now : Songs Of Bob Dylan* (Vanguard 1968)★★★, *David's Album* (Vanguard 1969)★★, *Joan Baez In Italy* (1969)★★★, *24 July 1970 all Arena Civica di Milano* (1970)★★, *One Day At A Time* (Vanguard 1970)★★★, *Blessed Are* (Vanguard 1971)★★★, *Carry It On* (Vanguard 1971)★★★, *Sacco And Vanzetti* (Omega 1971)★★, *Come From The Shadows* (A&M 1972)★★★, *Where Are You Now My Son* (Vanguard 1973)★★, *Gracias A La Vida (Here's To Life)* (A&M 1974)★★, *Diamonds And Rust* (A&M 1975)★★★, *Live In Japan* (Vanguard 1975)★★, *From Every Stage* (A&M 1976)★★, *Gulf Winds* (A&M 1976)★★, *Blowing Away* (Portrait 1977)★★★, *Honest Lullaby* (Portrait 1979)★★, *The Night They Drove Old Dixie Down* (Vanguard 1979)★★★★, *Country Music Album* (Vanguard 1979)★★★, *European Tour* (1981)★★, *Live Europe 83* (Ariola 1983)★★, *Recently* (Gold Castle 1988)★★★, *Diamonds And Rust In The Bullring* (Gold Castle 1989)★★, *Speaking Of Dreams* (Gold Castle 1989)★★★, *Brothers In Arms* (Gold Castle)★★★, *Play Me Backwards* (Virgin 1992)★★★, *No Woman No Cry* (1993)★★★, *Ring Them Bells* (Grapevine 1995)★★★.

●COMPILATIONS: *The First Ten Years* (Vanguard 1970)★★★★, *The Ballad Book* (Vanguard 1972)★★★, *The Contemporary Ballad Book* (Vanguard 1974)★★★, *The Love Song Album* (Vanguard 1975)★★★, *Hits Greatest And Others* (Vanguard 1976)★★★, *The Best Of Joan Baez* (1977)★★★, *Spotlight On Joan Baez* (1980)★★★, *Very Early Joan* (Vanguard 1983)★★★, *Rare, Live And Classic* 3-CD box set (Vanguard 1994)★★★★, *Diamonds* (Polygram Chronicles 1996)★★★.

●VIDEOS: *Joan Baez In Concert* (Old Gold 1990).

●FURTHER READING: *Daybreak: An Intimate Journey*, Joan Baez. *The Playboy Interviews: Joan Baez*, No editor listed. *Joan Baez, A Bio-Disco-Bibliography: Being A Selected Guide To Material In Print*, Peter Swan. *Diamonds And Rust: A Bibliography And Discography Of Joan Baez*, Joan Swanekamp. *And A Voice to Sing With*, Joan Baez.

BAKER, GINGER

b. Peter Baker, 19 August 1939, Lewisham, London, England. This brilliantly erratic drummer was already a vastly experienced musician when he formed the legendary Cream, with Eric Clapton and Jack Bruce in 1967. He had drummed with trad-jazz bands, working with Terry Lightfoot and Acker Bilk before sitting in with Alexis Korner's Blues Incorporated and enlisting in the seminal Graham Bond Organisation. Following the unprecedented success and speedy demise of Cream, Baker joined with Steve Winwood, Rick Grech and Clapton in the 'supergroup' Blind Faith, followed by the ambitious Airforce. Ginger then left Britain to live in Nigeria, where he cultivated an interest in African music and built his own recording studio (Paul McCartney's classic *Band On The Run* was recorded there). He briefly had a Nigerian band, Salt, and recorded with Fela Ransome-Kuti. Baker reputedly lost all his money on his Nigerian adventure and returned to Britain and formed the Baker Gurvitz Army in 1973. Following their break-up he spent much of the next few years playing polo, an unlikely sport for a working-class lad from south London, but one at which he became most proficient. Baker's solo outing *11 Sides Of Baker* was justifiably panned in 1977. He returned with Energy in 1979 and briefly joined Atomic Rooster, Hawkwind and his own Ginger Baker's Nutters. In 1986 he played on PiL's UK Top 20 hit 'Rise'. Since then he has been unable to make any major impression and is openly bitter at the phenomenal success of Clapton. He remains, mostly through his work with Cream, one of Britain's greatest rock legends; a temperamental man who at his best showed astonishing ability on drums. His rolling polyrythmic playing laid the future foundation for heavy rock drumming. In 1994 he joined with Jack Bruce and Gary Moore and, as BBM, they released an accomplished and satisfying album, although friction within the group led to an early parting of the ways. Baker has since returned to his first love, jazz, and has recorded some excellent material with his trio (currently recording with Bill Frisell and Charlie Haden). Those who perceive Baker as the wild man of rock should investigate the excellent *Falling Off The Roof*.

●ALBUMS: *Stratavarious* (Polydor 1972)★★, with Fela Ransome Kuti *Fela Ransome Kuti With Ginger Baker* (Regal Zonophone 1972)★★★, *11 Sides Of Baker* (Mountain 1977)★★, *From Humble Oranges* (1983)★★, *Horses And Trees* (Celluloid 1986)★★★, *The Album* (ITM 1987)★★, *No Material* (ITM 1987)★★, *In Concert* (1987)★★, *African Force* (80s)★★, *Middle Passage* (Axiom 1990)★★★, *Unseen Rain* (Daylight Music 1993)★★, with BBM *Around The Next Dream* (Virgin 1994)★★★, *Going Back Home* (Atlantic 1995)★★★, *Falling Off The Roof* (Atlantic 1996)★★★★.

●COMPILATIONS: *The Best Of Ginger Baker* (1973)★★★,*The Alternative Album* (1992).

BAKERLOO

Originally the Bakerloo Blues Line, this late 60s power-blues trio from Tamworth, Staffordshire, England, were briefly compared to Cream. Ironically, the band's leader Dave 'Clem' Clempson found himself singing Cream numbers many years later as a member of Jack Bruce's band. The original Bakerloo comprised Clempson (guitarist/vocalist), Terry Poole (bass) and Keith Baker (drums). Their self-titled album is a collector's item, both as one of the initial Harvest fold-out sleeves and for the music therein. The extended 'Moonshine' gave each member the opportunity to show his musical dexterity. Clempson was soon tempted away to join Jon Hiseman's Colosseum, and Bakerloo was terminated. Keith Baker re-emerged in one of the early line-ups of Uriah Heep, later teaming up again with Terry Poole in May Blitz.
●ALBUMS: *Bakerloo* (Harvest 1969)★★★.

BALDRY, LONG JOHN

b. 12 January 1941, London, England. Beginning his career playing folk and jazz in the late 50s, Baldry toured with Ramblin' Jack Elliott before moving into R&B. His strong, deep voice won him a place in the influential Blues Incorporated, following which he joined Cyril Davies's R&B All Stars. After Davies's death, Long John fronted the Hoochie Coochie Men, which also included future superstar Rod Stewart, who later joined Baldry in Steampacket (featuring Brian Auger and Julie Driscoll). After a brief period with Bluesology (which boasted a young Elton John on keyboards), Baldry decided to go solo and record straightforward pop. Already well known on the music scene, he nevertheless appeared an unusual pop star in 1967 with his sharp suits and imposing 6 foot 7 inch height. Composer/producer Tony Macauley and his partner John McLeod presented the perfect song in 'Let The Heartaches Begin', a despairing ballad which Baldry took to number 1 in the UK in 1967. His chart career continued with the Olympic Games theme 'Mexico' the following year, which also made the Top 20. By the end of the 60s, however, the hits had ceased and another change of direction was ahead. Furs and a beard replaced the suits and the neat, short haircut, as Long John attempted to establish himself with a new audience. With production assistance from former colleagues Rod Stewart and Elton John, he recorded a strong album, *It Ain't Easy*, but it failed to sell. After a troubled few years in New York and Los Angeles he emigrated to Vancouver, Canada, where he performed on the club circuit. In the early 90s his voice was used as Robotnik on the Sonic The Hedgehog computer game. After many years a new Baldry album was released in 1993, subtly titled *It Still Ain't Easy*.
●ALBUMS: *Long John's Blues* (United Artists 1965)★★★, *Lookin' At Long John* (United Artists 1966)★★★, *Let The Heartaches Begin* (Pye 1968)★★, *Wait For Me* (Pye 1969)★, *It Ain't Easy* (Warners 1971)★★, *Everything Stops For Tea* (Warners 1972)★, *Good To Be Alive* (GM 1976)★★, *Welcome To The Club* (1977)★★, *Baldry's Out* (1979)★★, *It Still Ain't Easy* (Stony Plain 1991)★★.
●COMPILATIONS: *Let The Heartaches Begin - The Best Of John Baldry* (1988)★★★, *Mexico* (Spectrum 1995)★★.

BALFA BROTHERS

The Balfa family name is legendary in Cajun music. They grew up in abject poverty in Bayou Grand Louis, near Big Mamou, Louisiana, USA, where their father, from whom they gained their musical interest, worked as a share-cropper. The music offered a means of escape and relief and in the mid-40s, brothers Will (b. c.1920, d. 6 February 1979; fiddle), Harry (b. 1931; accordion) and Dewey (b. 20 March 1927, d. 17 June 1992; fiddle/harmonica/accordion/guitar and sundry other minor instruments) began to play for local dances. In 1951, they made their first recording on home recording equipment, but during the 50s Dewey frequently played and recorded with Nathan Abshire. He also appeared at the Newport Folk Festival, in 1964, playing guitar with Gladius Thibodeaux (accordion) and Louis Lejeune (fiddle). In 1967, Dewey was joined by Will, Rodney (b. 1934, d. 6 February 1979; guitar/harmonica/vocals), daughter Nelda and Hadley Fontenot (an accordion-playing local farmer) and the unit toured extensively both in the USA and to Europe as the Balfa Brothers. (Incidentally, Will always preferred to spell his name as Bolfa.) In the late 60s, they recorded for Swallow and their recording of 'Drunkard's Sorrow Waltz' was a best-selling Cajun single in 1967. In 1968, they appeared in Mexico City at music festivals run in conjunction with the Olympic Games. They played music for and appeared in the 1972 film on Cajun life *Spend It All*. Dewey also formed his night club orchestra which comprised himself and Rodney (fiddle/guitar/vocals), Nathan Menard (accordion), Ervin 'Dick' Richard (fiddle), J.W. Pelsia (steel guitar), Austin Broussard (drums) and Rodney's son, Tony (bass guitar). In the mid-70s, they made further recordings (with Nathan Abshire) for Swallow and Sonet Records and appeared in a documentary on Cajuns. On 6 February 1979, Will and Rodney were killed in a car accident. Dewey continued to perform and record as the Balfa Brothers with other musicians, including Tony, his daughter Christine (triangle), Tony, Ally Young (accordion), Dick Richard, Mark Savoy (b. 1940; accordion), Robert Jardell (accordion) and Peter Schwartz (bass/fiddle/piano). (The latter, who first played with the group in his early teens, being Tracy Schwartz's son.) Many of the Swallow and other recordings made by the Balfa Brothers have been reissued in the UK by Ace Records. Dewey Balfa later ran a furniture business but remained active in music until his death on 17 June 1992. After his death his daughters, Christine and Nelda, continued the family tradition by playing and recording with other Cajun musicians, including Mike Chapman, Dick Powell and Kevin Wimmer, as Balfa Toujours.

●ALBUMS: *Balfa Brothers Play Traditional Cajun Music* (Swallow 1967)★★★★, *Balfa Brothers Play More Cajun Music* (Swallow 1968),★★★ *The Cajuns* (Sonet 1972)★★★, with Nathan Abshire *The Good Times Are Killing Me* (Swallow 1975)★★★, *Cajun Fiddle Tunes By Dewey Balfa* (Folkways 70s)★★★, *Dewey Balfa & Tracy Schwartz Traditional Cajun Fiddle Volumes 1 & 2* (Folkways 70s)★★★, *J'ai Vu Le Loup* (Rounder 1977)★★★, *The New York Concerts* (Swallow 1980)★★, *Dewey Balfa, Marc Savoy, D.L. Menard: Under The Green Oak Tree* (Arhoolie c.1982)★★★, *The New York Concerts Plus* (Ace 1991)★★★.

●COMPILATIONS: *Play Traditional Cajun Music Volumes 1 & 2* (Ace 1991)★★★★, *Dewey Balfa & Friends* (Ace 1991)★★★★. Balfa Toujours: *New Cajun Tradition* (Ace 1995)★★★.

BALL, KENNY

b. 22 May 1930, Ilford, Essex, England. The most successful survivor of the early 60s 'trad boom', Ball played the harmonica and bugle in a local band before switching to the trumpet. Having previously played alongside Charlie Galbraith for a BBC radio broadcast and deputized for Britain's leading dixieland trumpet player, Freddy Randall, Ball joined clarinettist Sid Phillips' band in 1954 and formed his own dixieland-styled Jazzmen four years later, between which time he had worked with Eric Delaney, George Chisholm, Terry Lightfoot and Al Fairweather. The Jazzmen did not record until the summer of 1959, resulting in the single 'Waterloo'/'Wabash Cannonball'. Signed to Pye Records, his first hit was in 1961 with Cole Porter's 'Samantha' originally from the Bing Crosby/Frank Sinatra movie *High Society*. This was followed by the million-selling 'Midnight In Moscow', number 2 in the UK and US charts, 'March Of The Siamese Children' from *The King And I*, 'The Green Leaves Of Summer', 'Sukiyaki' and several more throughout the 60s. Ball featured alongside Chris Barber and Acker Bilk in the compilation album of the best of British dixieland/trad jazz, *The Best Of Ball, Barber And Bilk*, which reached UK number 1 in 1962. The band made its film debut in 1963 in *Live It Up* with Gene Vincent, and appeared in *It's Trad Dad*. In the same year Ball was made an honorary citizen of New Orleans. For three years, 1962-64, he received the Carl Alan Award for the Most Outstanding Traditional Jazz Band, and in 1968 the band appeared with Louis Armstrong on his last European visit. Throughout the 70s and 80s Ball extensively toured abroad while maintaining his UK popularity with regular concerts, featuring guests from the 'old days' such as Acker Bilk, Kenny Baker, Lonnie Donegan and George Chisholm. Ball claims his career peaked in 1981 when he and the Jazzmen played at the reception following the wedding of Prince Charles and Princess Diana. The early 90s Jazzmen include founder-member John Bennett (trombone), Andy Cooper (clarinet, ex-Charlie Galbraith and Alan Elsdon bands), John Benson (bass/vocals, ex-Monty Sunshine Band), John Fenner (guitar/vocals), Hugh Ledigo (piano ex-Pasadena Roof Orchestra) and Ron Bowden (drums, ex-Ken Colyer; Lonnie Donegan and Chris Barber bands).

●ALBUMS: *Kenny Ball And His Jazzmen* (Pye 1961)★★★, *The Kenny Ball Show* (1962)★★★, with Gary Miller *Gary On The Ball* (1962)★★, *Midnight In Moscow* (1962)★★★, *It's Trad* (1962)★★★, *The Big Ones - Kenny Ball Style* (1963)★★★, *Jazz Band Ball* (1964)★★, *Colonel Bogey And Eleven Japanese Marches* Japan only release★★ (1964)★, *Kenny Ball Plays For The Jet Set* US only release (1964,)★★★, *Tribute To Tokyo* (1964)★★, *The Sound Of Kenny Ball* (1968)★★★, *Kenny Ball And His Jazzmen Live In Berlin Volume 1/Volume 2* German releases (1968)★★★, *King Of The Swingers* (1969)★★, *At The Jazz Band Ball* (1970)★★★, *Fleet Street Lightning* (1970)★★, *Saturday Night With Kenny Ball And His Band* (1970)★★★, *Pixie Dust (A Tribute To Walt Disney)* (1971)★★, *My Very Good Friend ... Fats Waller* (1972)★★★, *Have A Drink On Me* (1972)★★★, *Let's All Sing A Happy Song* (1973)★★, with the Johnny Arthey Orchestra and the Eddie Lester Singers *A Friend To You* (1974)★★★, *Titillating Tango* (1976)★★★, *Saturday Night At The Mill* (1977)★★★, *Way Down Yonder* (1977)★★★, *The Bulldog And Kangaroo* Australasian only release (1977)★★★, *In Concert* (1978)★★, *Kenny In Concert In The USA, Vols. 1 & 2* US only releases (1979)★★★, *Soap* (1981)★★★, *Ball, Barber And Bilk Live At The Royal Festival Hall* (1984)★★★, *Greensleeves* (1986)★★★, *Kenny Ball And His Jazzmen Play The Movie Greats* (1987)★★, *On Stage* (Start 1988)★★★, *Dixie* (Pickwick 1989), *Kenny Ball Plays British* (MFP 1989)★★★, *Jazz Classics* (1990)★★★, *Steppin' Out* (Castle 1992)★★★, *Strictly Jazz* (Kaz 1992)★★★, *Kenny Ball Now* (1990)★★, with Chris Barber, Acker Bilk *The Ultimate!* (1991)★★★★, *Lighting Up The Town* (Intersound 1993)★★★.

●COMPILATIONS: *Best Of Ball, Barber And Bilk* (Pye Golden Guinea 1962)★★★★, *Kenny Ball's Golden Hits* (Pye Golden Guinea 1963)★★★★, *Golden Hour* (1971)★★★★, *Golden Hour Presents Kenny Ball 'Hello Dolly'* (1973)★★, *Cheers!* (1979)★★★, *Golden Hits* (1986)★★★★, *Kenny Ball's Cotton Club* (1986)★★★, *The Singles Collection* (1987)★★★, *Images* (Images 1990)★★★, *Kenny Ball - The Collection* (Castle 1990)★★★★, *Hello Dolly* (Spectrum 1995)★★★.

BALLARD, FLORENCE

b. 30 June 1942, Detroit, Michigan, USA, d. 22 February 1976. In her teens, Ballard formed the vocal group the Primettes with schoolfriends Mary Wilson and Betty Travis. Diana Ross completed the line-up in 1960. The following year, the Primettes were signed by Motown, who renamed them the Supremes. As the group's acknowledged leader, Ballard was the featured vocalist on their early Motown singles, but label boss Berry Gordy insisted that Diana Ross become the lead singer in 1963. Thereafter Florence was allowed few opportunities to take the limelight, either on record or in concert. Unhappy with her diminishing role in the Supremes, she repeatedly complained to Gordy and his executives, and the resulting friction led to her being ousted from the group in 1967. Throughout the drama, Motown maintained that she was retiring because of the strain of constant touring.

The label annulled Ballard's contract, and she signed with ABC, for whom she made two singles under the direction of ex-Satintone Robert Bateman. Florence was legally barred from capitalizing on her glorious past with the Supremes, and while her former group went from strength to strength, her solo releases flopped. Her deal with ABC was terminated. Other labels were wary of offending Gordy by signing her up, and Ballard became an increasingly embittered figure, ignored by the Detroit music scene in which she had played such a central role. By the early 70s, Florence was living in extreme poverty on a Detroit housing project. Her reliance on a lethal cocktail of alcohol and diet pills had weakened her health, and in February 1976 her tragic career ended when she suffered a cardiac arrest. Ironically, her contribution to the success of the Supremes has now been recognised, and her fate has been described as a telling verdict on the way in which Motown handled its more uncompromising artists.

BANKS, HOMER

b. 2 August 1941, Memphis, Tennessee, USA. A former member of the Soul Consolidators gospel group, in the late 50s Banks worked as a clerk in the offices of the Satellite Studio in Memphis, hoping that the emergent label, later to become Stax Records, would recognize his talent as a singer and songwriter. At first his talents went largely unnoticed at Stax, although Isaac Hayes and David Porter were instrumental in setting up Banks' own solo recording debut for the Genie label in 1964, and in 1966 they wrote one of his early songs for the recently reactivated Minit label, '60 Minutes Of Your Love'. Banks cut five singles for Minit between 1966 and 1968, including the self co-penned 'A Lot Of Love', the strident riff of which would later be borrowed by the Spencer Davis Group for their hit 'Gimme Some Lovin''. Meanwhile Banks, still a Memphis resident, had maintained his connections with Stax Records and, by the 70s, was writing many hits with regular collaborators like Raymond Jackson, Carl Hampton and Bettye Crutcher, including 'Who's Making Love' for Johnnie Taylor, 'Be What You Are' and 'If You're Ready (Come Go With Me)' for the Staple Singers, and 'If Loving You Is Wrong (I Don't Want To Be Right)' for the Koko Records artist Luther Ingram, a 1972 million-seller, later covered by Millie Jackson, Isaac Hayes and Rod Stewart. Banks also co-wrote Shirley Brown's 1974 hit on the Truth label, 'Woman To Woman'. After the demise of Stax, Banks went on to write for and/or produce artists on labels including TK, Sound Town, Parachute and Malaco. He also formed a Memphis-based partnership with Lester Snell called Two's Company, which has released albums on the

Platinum Blue label, including 1993 sets from J. Blackfoot and Ann Hines.

BAR-KAYS

Jimmy King (b. 1949; guitar), Ronnie Caldwell (b. 1948; organ), Phalin Jones (b. 1949; saxophone), Ben Cauley (b. 1947; trumpet), James Alexander (bass) and Carl Cunningham (b. 1949; drums) were originally known as the River Arrows. Signed to Stax, the Bar-Kays were groomed as that label's second string houseband by Al Jackson, drummer in Booker T. And The MGs. The Bar-Kays were employed as Otis Redding's backing group on tour, and the tragic plane crash in 1967, which took his life, also claimed King, Caldwell, Jones and Cunningham. Alexander, who missed the flight, put together a new line-up with Ben Cauley, the sole survivor of the accident. The latter musician soon dropped out, leaving the bassist at the helm of a frequently changing line-up. Primarily a session group, the Bar-Kays provided the backing on many releases, including Isaac Hayes' *Shaft* and several of Albert King's 70s recordings. The group pursued a funk-based direction on their own releases with the addition of vocalist Larry Dodson, but while 'Son Of Shaft' reached the US R&B Top 10 in 1972, consistent success was only secured on their move to Mercury Records. Later singles, including 'Shake Your Rump To The Funk' (1976), 'Move Your Boogie Body' (1979) and 'Freakshow On The Dancefloor' (1984), were aimed squarely at the disco market. Since 1987 the group has featured Dodson, Harvey Henderson (tenor saxophone) and Winston Stewart (keyboards).

●ALBUMS: *Soul Finger* (Stax 1967)★★★★, *Gotta Groove* (Stax 1969)★★★, *Black Rock* (Stax/Volt 1971)★★, *Do You See What I See* (Polydor 1972)★★★, *Cold Blooded* (Stax 1974)★★, *Too Hot To Stop* (Mercury 1976)★★, *Flying High On Your Love* (Mercury 1977)★★★, *Light Of Life* (Mercury 1978)★★, *Money Talks* (Stax 1978)★★, *Injoy* (Mercury 1979)★★, *As One* (Mercury 1980)★★★, *Night Cruisin'* (Mercury 1981)★★, *Propositions* (Mercury 1982)★★, *Dangerous* (Mercury 1984)★★, *Banging The Wall* (Mercury 1985)★★, *Contagious* (Mercury 1987)★★★, *Animal* (Mercury 1988)★★★.

●COMPILATIONS: *The Best Of The Bar-Kays* (Stax 1991)★★★★, *The Best Of The Bar-Kays* (Mercury 1993)★★★, *The Best Of The Bar-Kays Vol. 2* (Mercury 1996)★★.

●FILMS: *Breakdance - The Movie* (1984).

BARBARIANS

Formed in 1964 in Provincetown, Massachusetts, USA, the Barbarians consisted of Jeff Morris, Jerry Causi, Bruce Benson and 'Moulty' Molten. They made their recording debut with 'Hey Little Bird', issued on the local Joy Records, prior to signing a contract with Laurie Records. In 1965 the Barbarians enjoyed a minor US hit with 'Are You A Boy Or Are You A Girl?', a brilliant garage-styled single about long hair fashions. It was succeeded by 'Moulty', a monologue from the group's one-armed drummer about his disability, interspersed with a call-and-response chorus. His story enshrined forever, Molten left the Barbarians in 1967. The remaining trio moved to San Francisco, California, USA, where they formed Black Pearl.

●ALBUMS: *Are You A Boy Or Are You A Girl* (Laurie 1966)★★.

BARRETT, SYD

b. Roger Keith Barrett, 6 January 1946, Cambridge, England. One of English pop's most enigmatic talents, Barrett embraced music in the early 60s as a member of Geoff Mutt and the Mottoes, a local group modelled on Cliff Richard And The Shadows. He acquired his 'Syd' sobriquet while attending Cambridge High School where his friends included Roger Waters and Dave Gilmour. Gilmour joined Barrett on a busking tour of Europe where their folk-based repertoire was peppered with songs from the Rolling Stones. Barrett then took up a place at London's Camberwell School Of Art, alternating his studies with a spell in an aspiring R&B act, the Hollering Blues. Waters, a student of architecture at Regent Street Polytechnic, had meanwhile formed his own group, at that point dubbed the (Screaming) Abdabs. In 1965 he invited Barrett to join his group, which took the name the Pink Floyd Sound, at Syd's suggestion, from an album featuring Georgia blues musicians Pink Anderson and Floyd Council.

Having dropped their now-superfluous suffix, Pink Floyd became a lynch-pin part of London's nascent 'underground' scene. Barrett emerged as their principal songwriter and undisputed leader, composing their early hit singles, 'Arnold Layne' and 'See Emily Play' (both 1967), as well as the bulk of *The Piper At The Gates Of Dawn*. Syd's child-like, often *naïf* compositional style was offset by his highly original playing style. An impulsive, impressionistic guitarist, his unconventional use of feedback, slide and echo did much to transfer the mystery and imagery of Pink Floyd's live sound into a studio equivalent. However, the strain of his position proved too great for a psyche dogged by instability and an indulgence in hallucinogenic drugs. The group's brilliant, but erratic, third single, 'Apples And Oranges', reflected Barrett's disintegrating mental state. During a 1967 US tour he refused to mime on the influential Dick Clark Show - 'Syd wasn't into moving his lips that day' - and, on a corresponding programme, Pat Boone's vacuous repartee was greeted by stony silence. Dave Gilmour was drafted into the line-up in February 1968, prompting suggestions that Barrett would retire from live work and concentrate solely on songwriting. This plan did not come to fruition and Barrett's departure from Pink Floyd was announced the following April. The harrowing 'Jugband Blues' on *Saucerful Of Secrets* was his epitaph to this period.

Within a month Barrett had repaired to the Abbey Road studios to begin a solo album. Work continued apace until July, but sessions were then suspended until April 1969 when, with Malcolm Jones as producer, Barrett opted to begin work anew. Several tracks were completed with the aid of Willie Wilson, former bassist with an early Gilmour group, Joker's Wild, and Humble Pie drummer, Jerry Shirley. On one selection, 'No Use Trying', Barrett was supported by the Soft Machine - Mike Ratledge, Hugh Hopper and Robert Wyatt.

Dave Gilmour had been taking a keen interest in the sessions. In June he suggested that he and Waters should also produce some tracks, and the rest of the album was completed in three days. These particular recordings were left largely unadorned, adding poignancy to already haunting material. The resultant set, *The Madcap Laughs*, was an artistic triumph on which Syd's fragile vocals and delicate melodies create a hypnotic, ethereal atmosphere. It contained some of Barrett's finest performances, notably 'Octopus', which was issued as a single, and 'Golden Hair', a poem from James Joyce's *Chamber Music* set to a moving refrain. In January 1970 Syd began recording a second album, again with Gilmour as producer. Sessions continued intermittently until July, wherein the 'best' take, featuring Barrett on guitar and vocals, was overdubbed by a combo of Gilmour, Shirley and Pink Floyd keyboard player, Rick Wright. Released in November that year, housed in a sleeve sporting a Barrett painting, *Barrett* was largely more assertive, but less poignant, than its predecessor. It did include the chilling 'Rats', one of the singer's most vitriolic performances, but Gilmour later recalled that Syd seemed less prepared for recording than before. 'He'd search around and eventually work something out.'

Barrett then completed a session for BBC Radio 1's 'Sounds Of The Seventies', but despite declaring himself 'totally together' in an interview for Rolling Stone (December 1971), in truth he was slipping into the life of a recluse. The following year he did put together a group with bassist Jack Monck (ex-Delivery) and former Pink Fairies/Pretty Things drummer Twink. They supported Eddie 'Guitar' Burns at King's College Cellar in Cambridge and, although reportedly 'chaotic', the same group, now dubbed Stars, subsequently shared a bill with the MC5 at the nearby Corn Exchange. Syd failed to surface for their next proposed date and ensuing shows were cancelled. He remained the subject of interest and speculation, but a disastrous attempt at recording, undertaken in September 1974, suggested that the artist's once-bright muse had completely deserted him. He gained a high profile when Pink Floyd included a tribute - 'Shine On You Crazy Diamond' on their best-selling *Wish You Were Here* (1975), but Barrett's precarious mental state precludes any further involvement in music. *Opel*, a 1988 release comprising unissued masters and alternate takes, enhanced his reputation for startling, original work as evinced by the affecting title track, bafflingly omitted from *The Madcap Laughs*. Barrett pronounced his approval of the project and was last rumoured to have returned to painting.

●ALBUMS: *The Madcap Laughs* (Harvest 1970)★★★, *Barrett* (Harvest 1970)★★★, *The Peel Sessions* (Strange Fruit 1995)★★★.

●COMPILATIONS: *Opel* (Harvest 1988)★★★, *Crazy*

Diamond 3-CD box set (1993)★★★.
●VIDEOS: *Syd Barrett's First Trip* (Vex 1993).
●FURTHER READING: *Crazy Diamond: Syd Barrett And The Dawn Of Pink Floyd*, Mike Watkinson and Pete Anderson. *Syd Barrett: The Madcap Laughs*, Pete Anderson and Mick Rock.

BARRON KNIGHTS

Formed in Leighton Buzzard, England, the Barron Knights rose from comparative obscurity following their appearance on the bill of the Beatles' 1963 Christmas Show. Duke D'mond (b. Richard Palmer, 25 February 1945, Dunstable, Bedfordshire, England; vocals/rhythm guitar), Butch Baker (b. Leslie John Baker, 16 July 1941, Amersham, Buckinghamshire, England; guitar/banjo/vocals), 'P'nut' Langford (b. Peter Langford, 10 April 1943, Durham, Co Durham, England; guitar/vocals), Barron Antony (b. Antony Michael John Osmond, 15 June 1940, Abingdon, Berkshire, England; bass/vocals) and Dave Ballinger (b. 17 January 1941, Slough, Buckinghamshire, England; drums) scored a UK Top 3 hit the following year with 'Call Up The Groups', a parodic medley of contemporary releases by, among others, the Rolling Stones, the Searchers and the Dave Clark Five, based on the Four Preps US release, 'Big Draft'. Two similarly styled singles, 'Pop! Go The Workers' and 'Merrie Gentle Pops', reached numbers 5 and 9, respectively, in 1965, but the group failed to emulate this success with conventional releases. The group were also the subject of one of the most bizarre high court actions in pop history when their original drummer, who had been hospitalized, sued the Barron Knights for engaging Ballinger. The Barron Knights pursued a lucrative career on the cabaret circuit throughout the late 60s and early 70s, before reviving the pastiche formula with two further Top 10 hits, 'Live In Trouble' (1977) and 'A Taste Of Aggro' (1978). A slick, showbusiness professionalism had now replaced the quintet's original perkiness, and they closed the decade one of Britain's most popular MOR attractions.
●ALBUMS: *Call Up The Groups* (Columbia 1964)★★★, *The Barron Knights* (Columbia 1966)★★★, *Scribed* (Columbia 1967)★★★, *The Two Sides Of The Barron Knights* (1971)★★, *Live In Trouble* (1977)★★, *Knight Gallery* (1978)★★, *Teach The World To Laugh* (1979)★★, *Jesta Giggle* (1980)★★, *Twisting The Knights Away* (1981)★★★, *Funny In The Head* (1984)★★.
●COMPILATIONS: *Knights Of Laughter* (1979)★★★, *Barron Knights* (1982)★★★, *The Best Of The Barron Knights* (1982)★★★.
●FURTHER READING: *Once A Knight: History Of The Barron Knights*, Pete Langford.

BARRY AND THE TAMERLANES

Barry And The Tamerlanes were a Californian trio consisting of leader Barry DeVorzon, Terry Smith and Bodie Chandler. Best known for their upbeat 1963 US Top 30 single 'I Wonder What She's Doing Tonight', the group recorded the song only after another one-hit group, the Cascades ('Rhythm Of The Rain'), turned it down. DeVorzon had previously experienced some success as a songwriter, penning minor hits for artists such as Marty Robbins. Later in his career Barry wrote songs recorded by Glen Campbell, Dorsey Burnette and others. DeVorzon's greatest successes came in the 70s, however, when he co-wrote the Grammy award-winning 'Nadia's Theme' and 'Theme From S.W.A.T.', the biggest US television theme song of all-time, recorded by Rhythm Heritage. As for Barry And The Tamerlanes, they never returned to the charts following their first brush with success.
●ALBUMS: *I Wonder What She's Doing Tonight* (Valiant 1963)★★.

BARRY, JEFF

b. 3 April 1938, Brooklyn, New York, USA. Barry began his music career as a singer, completing several singles for RCA and Decca Records between 1959 and 1962. He also enjoyed concurrent success as a songwriter, most notably with 'Tell Laura I Love Her', a US Top 10 hit for Ray Peterson and a UK number 1 for Ricky Valance. In 1961 Barry was contracted to Trinity Music for whom he completed over 100 compositions and gained valuable experience in arranging, producing and recording demos. Although Jeff collaborated with several partners, his relationship with Ellie Greenwich would prove to be the most enduring. Together they wrote for Leslie Gore ('Maybe I Know'), the Four Pennies ('When The Boy's Happy') and the Exciters/Manfred Mann ('Do Wah Diddy') and, as the Raindrops, recorded a US Top 20 hit, 'The Kind Of Boy You Can't Forget'. However, the couple, who were now married, are best recalled for their classic work with Phil Spector which included the joyous 'Da Doo Ron Ron' and 'Then He Kissed Me' for the Crystals, 'Be My Baby' and 'Baby, I Love You' for the Ronettes and the monumental 'River Deep Mountain High' for Ike And Tina Turner. Greenwich and Barry also wrote, and co-produced, releases on the Red Bird label for the Dixie Cups, Shangri-Las and Jelly Beans. It was also during this period that the duo 'discovered' Neil Diamond, whose early work they produced, but despite this professional commitment, their marriage ended in 1965. Barry then resumed his recording career with singles for United Artists and A&M, but achieved a greater degree of success in partnership with singer Andy Kim, writing, producing and performing for the Archies' cartoon series. The work with Greenwich has rightly stood the test of time having reached the pinnacle of stylish pop music during the 60s.

BARRY, LEN

b. Leonard Borrisoff, 12 June 1942, Philadelphia, Pennsylvania, USA. Barry began his career as the anonymous vocalist on the Bosstones' 1958 single 'Mope-Itty Mope' before joining the Dovells between 1961-63. As a solo artist, his white soul vocals were best exemplified on the scintillating chart topper '1-2-3' and the similarly paced 'Like A Baby'. With his sharp suits and clean-cut image, Barry seemed a Philadelphia teen idol chronologically cut adrift in 1965, and his contention that long-haired groups were on the way out caused a few ripples in the pop press. Although he enjoyed another minor hit in the US with the *West Side Story* anthem 'Somewhere', the song had already charted in the UK courtesy of P.J. Proby. During the psychedelic boom in the late 60s, Barry went out of fashion and gradually toned down his lively stage act for cabaret purposes. By the end of the decade and through the 70s, he moved into production work.

●ALBUMS: *1-2-3* (Decca 1965)★★, *My Kind Of Soul* (RCA Victor 1967)★★.

●COMPILATIONS: *The Very Best Of ...* (Taragon 1995)★★.

BART, LIONEL

b. Lionel Begleiter, 1 August 1930, London, England. The comparative inactivity of Bart for many years has tended to cloud the fact that he is one of the major songwriters of 20th-century popular song. The former silk-screen printer was at the very hub of the rock 'n' roll and skiffle generation that came out of London's Soho in the mid-50s. As a member of the Cavemen with Tommy Steele he later became Steele's main source of non-American song material. In addition to writing the pioneering 'Rock With The Cavemen' he composed a series of glorious singalong numbers including 'A Handful Of Songs', 'Water Water' and the trite but delightfully innocent 'Little White Bull'. Much of Bart's work was steeped in the English music-hall tradition with a strong working class pride and it was no surprise that he soon graduated into writing songs for full-length stage shows. *Lock Up Your Daughters* and *Fings Ain't Wot They Used T'Be* were two of his early successes, both appearing during 1959, the same year he wrote the classic 'Living Doll' for Cliff Richard. Bart was one of the first writers to introduce mild politics into his lyrics; beautifully transcribed with topical yet humourously ironic innocence, for example: 'They've changed our local Palais into a bowling alley and fings ain't wot they used to be.' As the 60s dawned Bart unconsciously embarked on a decade that saw him reach dizzy heights of success and made him one of the musical personalities of the decade. During the first quarter of the year he topped the charts with 'Do You Mind' for Anthony Newley; a brilliantly simple and catchy song complete with Bart's own finger-snapped accompaniment. The best was yet to come when that year he launched *Oliver!*, a musical based on Dickens' *Oliver Twist*. This became a phenomenal triumph, and remains one of the most successful musicals of all time. Bart's knack of simple melody combined with unforgettable lyrics produced a plethora of classics including the pleading 'Who Will Buy', the rousing 'Food Glorious Food' and the poignant 'As Long As He Needs Me' (also a major hit for Shirley Bassey, although she reputedly never liked the song). Bart was a pivotal figure throughout the swinging London scene of the 60s, although he maintains that the party actually started in the 50s. Lionel befriended Brian Epstein, the Beatles, the Rolling Stones, became an international star following *Oliver!*'s success

as a film (winning six Oscars) and was romantically linked with Judy Garland and Alma Cogan. Following continued, although lesser success, with *Blitz!* and *Maggie May*, Lionel came down to reality when the London critics damned his 1965 musical *Twang!!*, based upon the life of Robin Hood. Bart's philanthropic nature made him a prime target for business sharks and he was wrested of much of his fortune by trusting too many people. By the end of the 60s the cracks were beginning to show; his dependence on drugs and alcohol increased and he watched many of his close friends die in tragic circumstances; Cogan with cancer, Garland through drink and drugs and Epstein's supposed suicide. In 1969, *La Strada* only had a short run in New York before Lionel retreated into himself, and for many years kept a relatively low profile, watching the 70s and 80s pass almost as a blur, only making contributions to *The Londoners* and *Costa Packet*. During this time the gutter press were eager for a kiss-and-tell story but Bart remained silent, a credible action considering the sums of money he was offered. During the late 80s Lionel finally beat his battle with booze and ended the decade a saner, wiser and healthier man. His renaissance started in 1989 when he was commissioned by a UK building society to write a television jingle. The composition became part of an award-winning advertisement, featuring a number of angelic children singing with Bart, filmed in pristine monochrome. The song 'Happy Endings' was a justifiable exhumation of a man who remains an immensely talented figure and whose work ranks with some of the greatest of the American 'musical comedy' songwriters. In the early 90s his profile continued to be high, with revivals by the talented National Youth Theatre, of *Oliver!*, *Maggie May* and *Blitz!* (the latter production commemorating the 50th anniversary of the real thing); and the inclusion of one of his early songs, 'Rock With The Caveman', in the blockbuster movie *The Flintstones*, in a version by Big Audio Dynamite. In December 1994 Lionel Bart's rehabilitation was complete, when producer Cameron Mackintosh presented a major new production of *Oliver!* at the London Palladium, starring Jonathan Pryce. In a gesture rare in the cut-throat world of show business, Mackintosh returned a portion of the show's rights to the composer (Bart had sold them during the bad old days), thereby assuring him an 'income for life'.

●FURTHER READING: *Bart!: The Unauthorized Life & Times, Ins & Outs, Ups & Downs Of Lionel Bart*, David Roper.

BASS, FONTELLA

b. 3 July 1940, St. Louis, Missouri, USA. The daughter of gospel luminary Martha Bass, Fontella toured as keyboard player and singer with the Little Milton band during the early 60s. Simultaneously, she made several solo records, including one for Ike Turner's Prann label. When Milton's bandleader, Oliver Sain, left to form his own group, he took Fontella with him, and teamed her with another featured vocalist, Bobby McClure. The duo was subsequently signed to Checker, on which 'Don't Mess Up A Good Thing' and 'You'll Miss Me (When I'm Gone)' were hits in 1965. 'Rescue Me', a driving song, gave Fontella success in her own right that same year with an R&B number 1 and a UK/US Top 20 hit. Other solo hits, including 'Recovery', followed, but by the end of the decade she had moved to Paris with her husband, jazz trumpeter Lester Bowie. When they later returned to America, Fontella recorded a series of fine records for the Shreveport-based Ronn/Jewel/Paula complex. She has also worked with Bowie's *avant garde* group, the Art Ensemble Of Chicago. In Milan in 1980 Bass recorded a real 'back to basics' gospel album in the company of her mother Martha, her brother and fellow soul artist David Peaston, and Amina Myers. In 1985 she had resumed working for Oliver Sain in St. Louis.

●ALBUMS: *The New Look* (Checker/Chess 1966)★★★, *Les Stances A Sophie* film soundtrack (1970)★★, *Free* (Paula/Mojo 1972)★★★, with Martha Bass, David Peaston *From The Root To The Source* (1980)★★, *No Ways Tired* (Nonesuch 1995)★★.

●COMPILATIONS: *Sisters Of Soul* 14 tracks Fontella Bass/12 tracks Sugar Pie DeSanto (1990)★★★, *The Best Of* (1992)★★★.

BASSEY, SHIRLEY

b. 8 January 1937, Tiger Bay, Cardiff, Wales. A thrilling, highly emotional singer, whose career has spanned some 40 years. Her early jobs included work in a factory's wrapping and packing department, while playing working men's clubs at weekends. After touring the UK in revues and variety shows, Lancashire comedian Al Read included her in his 1955 Christmas Show at London's Adelphi Theatre, and his revue, *Such Is Life*, which ran for a year. Her first hit, in 1957, was the calypso-styled 'Banana Boat Song', followed by 'Kiss Me Honey Honey, Kiss Me' nearly two years later. With her powerful voice (she was sometimes called 'Bassey the Belter'), the unique Bassey style and phrasing started to emerge in 1959 with 'As I Love You' which topped the UK chart, and continued through to the mid-70s via such heart-rending ballads as Lionel Bart's 'As Long As He Needs Me' (Nancy's big song from *Oliver!*), 'You'll Never Know', 'I'll Get By', 'Reach For The Stars'/'Climb Every Mountain', 'What Now My Love', '(I) Who Have Nothing', George Harrison's, 'Something', 'For All We Know', and an Italian hit with a new lyric by Norman Newell, 'Never, Never, Never'. Her singles sales were such that, even into the 90s, her records had spent more weeks on the UK chart than those of any other British female performer, and 29 of her albums registered in the UK best-sellers between 1961-91. In 1962 she was accompanied on *Let's Face The Music* by top US arranger/conductor Nelson Riddle. In live performances her rise to the top was swift and by the early 60s she was headlining in New York and Las Vegas. In 1964 Bassey had a big hit in the USA with 'Goldfinger', one of three songs she has sung over the title sequences of James Bond movies (the others were 'Diamonds Are Forever' and 'Moonraker'). In 1969 she

moved her base to Switzerland but continued to play major concert halls throughout the world. The American Guild Of Variety Artists voted her 'Best Female Entertainer' for 1976, and in the same year she celebrated 20 years as a recording artist with a 22-date British tour. In 1977, she received a Britannia Award for the 'Best Female Solo Singer In The Last 50 Years'.

In 1981, Bassey withdrew to her Swiss home and announced her semi-retirement, but continued to emerge occasionally throughout the 80s for television specials, concert tours, and a few albums including *Love Songs* and *I Am What I Am*. In one of pop's more unlikely collaborations, she was teamed with Yello in 1987 for the single, 'The Rhythm Divine'. In the 90s, with her provocative body language, ever more lavish gowns, and specialities such as 'Big Spender', 'Nobody Does It Like Me', 'Tonight' and 'What Kind Of Fool Am I' - together with more contemporary material - the 'Tigress Of Tiger Bay' has shown herself to be an enduring powerful and exciting performer. In 1993 she was also awarded the CBE, and a new cabaret club named 'Bassey's', was opened in Cardiff. In the following year her 40th Anniversary UK concert tour attracted favourable reviews, even from some hardened rock critics, and in 1995 Shirley Bassey was named 'Show Business Personality of the Year' by the Variety Club of Great Britain.

●ALBUMS: *Born To Sing The Blues* (Philips 1958)★★★, *The Bewitching Miss Bassey* (1959)★★★, *Fabulous Shirley Bassey* (1960)★★★, *Shirley* (Columbia 1960)★★★, *Shirley Bassey* (1962)★★★, *Let's Face The Music* (Columbia 1962)★★★, *Shirley Bassey At The Pigalle* (1965)★★★★, *Shirley Bassey Belts The Best!* (1965)★★★, *I've Got A Song For You* (1966)★★★, *Twelve Of Those Songs* (1968)★★★, *Live At The Talk Of The Town* (1970)★★★, *Something* (United Artists 1970)★★★, *Something Else* (1971)★★★, *Big Spender* (1971)★★★, *It's Magic* (1971)★★★, *What Now My Love* (1971)★★★, *I Capricorn* (1972)★★★, *And I Love You So* (1972)★★★, *Never, Never, Never* (1973)★★★, *Live At Carnegie Hall* (1973)★★★★, *Broadway, Bassey's Way* (1973)★★★, *Nobody Does It Like Me* (1974)★★, *Good, Bad But Beautiful* (1975)★★★, *Love, Life And Feelings* (1976)★★, *Thoughts Of Love* (1976)★★★, *You Take My Heart Away* (1977)★★★, *The Magic Is You* (1979)★★★, *As Long As He Needs Me* (1980)★★★, *As Time Goes By* (1980)★★★, *I'm In The Mood For Love* (1981)★★, *Love Songs* (1982)★★, *All By Myself* (1984)★★, *I Am What I Am* (1984)★★★, *Playing Solitaire* (1985)★★★, *I've Got You Under My Skin* (1985)★★★, *Sings The Songs From The Shows* (1986)★★★, *Let Me Sing And I'm Happy* (1988)★★★, *Her Favourite Songs* (1988)★★, *Keep The Music Playing* (1991)★★★, *Sings The Songs Of Andrew Lloyd Webber* (1994)★★, *Sings The Movies* (Polygram 1995)★★★, *The Show Must Go On* (Polygram 1996)★★★.

●COMPILATIONS: *Golden Hits Of Shirley Bassey*

(1968)★★★, *The Shirley Bassey Collection* (1972)★★★, *The Shirley Bassey Singles Album* (1975)★★★, *25th Anniversary Album* (1978)★★★, *21 Hit Singles* (1979)★★★, *Tonight* (1984)★★★, *Diamonds - The Best Of Shirley Bassey* (1988)★★★, *The Bond Collection - 30th Anniversary* (1993)★★★, *Classic Tracks* (1993)★★★, *The Definitive Collection* (Magnum 1994)★★★, *The EMI/UA Years 1959-1979* 5-CD box set (EMI 1994)★★★★.
●VIDEOS: *Shirley Bassey Live* (1988), *Live In Cardiff* (BBC 1995).

BATTERED ORNAMENTS

Formed in 1969 by poet and lyricist Pete Brown (b. 25 December 1940, London, England), this innovative group was initially completed by Graham Layden (vocals), Chris Spedding (guitar), Charlie Hart (organ/violin), George Khan (tenor saxophone), Butch Potter (bass), Rob Tait (drums) and Pete Bailey (percussion). Brown's early intention to play trumpet rather than sing ended on Layden's departure, but the leader's gruff, untutored delivery added considerable empathy to the unit's excellent debut single, 'The Week Looked Good On Paper', and their subsequent album, *A Meal You Can Shake Hands With In The Dark*. This eclectic set drew its inspiration from Graham Bond, jazz and oriental modes and included 'Politician', Brown's acerbic view of parliamentarians also recorded by Cream. However, strained relations between Brown and Spedding culminated in a disingenuous *putsch* when the former was fired on the eve of the famed Rolling Stones' Hyde Park free concert of 1969. *Mantlepiece* had been completed prior to this development, but the original vocal was wiped and replaced prior to release. Brown then formed the highly-regarded Piblokto!, which included Rob Tait, whereas the Battered Ornaments split when Spedding embarked on an independent career.
●ALBUMS: as Pete Brown And His Battered Ornaments *A Meal You Can Shake Hands With In The Dark* (Harvest 1969)★★★, as the Battered Ornaments *Mantlepiece* (Harvest 1969)★★.

BEACH BOYS

The seminal line-up comprised: Brian Wilson (b. 20 June 1942), Carl Wilson (b. 21 December 1946), Dennis Wilson (b. 4 December 1944, Hawthorne, California, USA, d. 28 December 1983), Al Jardine (b. 3 September 1942, Lima, Ohio, USA) and Mike Love (b. 15 March 1941, Baldwin Hills, California, USA). When the aforementioned three brothers, one cousin and a schoolfriend formed a casual singing group in 1961, they unconsciously created one of the longest-running, compulsively fascinating and bitterly tragic sagas in popular music. As Carl And The Passions, the Pendletones and Kenny And The Cadets, they rehearsed and played high school hops while the elder brother Brian began to demonstrate his songwriting ability. He was already obsessed with harmonics and melody, and would listen for hours to close harmony groups, especially the Four Freshmen and the Hi-Lo's.

One of his earliest songs, 'Surfin'' (written at the suggestion of keen surfing brother Dennis), was released on a local label and the topical name, Beach Boys, was innocently adopted. The domineering father of the brothers, Murray Wilson, immediately seized on their potential and appointed himself as manager, publicist and producer. After his own abortive attempts at a career in music, he began to live his frustrated career dreams through his sons. 'Surfin', with Murray's efforts, became a sizeable local hit, and made the *Billboard* Hot 100 (number 75). His continuing efforts gained them a recording contract with Capitol Records during the summer of 1962. In addition to the developing group's conflicts, Nik Venet (the producer at Capitol) became embroiled immediately with Murray, and their ideas clashed. Over the next 18 months the Beach Boys had 10 US hits and released four albums of surfing and hot-rod songs (each cover showed the photograph of neighbourhood friend, David Marks, who had temporarily replaced Al Jardine while he attended dentistry college). The Beach Boys' punishing workload began to affect the main songwriter Brian, who was additionally writing similar material for fellow surf/hot-rodders Jan And Dean.
In 1963 the Beach Boys phenomenon reached the UK in the shape of the single 'Surfin' USA', which mildly interrupted the Merseybeat domination. The predominantly working-class image of the British beat group scene was at odds with the clean and wholesome west coast perception blessed with permanent sunshine, fun and beautiful girls. During 1964 a further four albums were released, culminating in the *Christmas Album*. This represented a staggering eight albums in just over two years, six of which were arranged and produced by Brian, in addition to his having written 63 out of a total of 84 songs. In America, the Beatles had begun their unmatched domination of the charts, and in their wake came dozens of groups as the British invasion took place. The Beach Boys, more especially Brian, could only stand back in amazement. He felt so threatened that it drove him to compete against the Beatles. Eventually Brian gained some pyrrhic revenge, when in 1966 the Beach Boys were voted number 1 group in the world by the UK music press, pushing the Fab Four into second place.
Wilson's maturity as a composer was developing at a staggering pace with classic hits like 'I Get Around', 'California Girls' and 'God Only Knows'. The overall quality of albums such as *Summer Days And Summer Nights!!* and *Today* was extremely high. Many of Wilson's songs portrayed his own insecurity as an adolescent. Songs such as 'In My Room', 'Wouldn't It Be Nice' and 'Girl Don't Tell Me' found a receptive audience who could immediately relate to the lyrics. While their instrumental prowess was average, the immaculate combination of the members' voices, delivered a sound that was unmistakable. Both Carl and Brian had perfect pitch, even although Brian was deaf in one ear (reputedly caused through his father's beatings). In private the 'musical genius' was working on what was to be his self-intended masterpiece, *Pet Sounds*. Released in August

1966, the high profile pre-publicity proved deserved and the reviews were outstanding. The music was also outstanding, but for some inexplicable reason, sales were not. It was later reported that Brian was devastated by the comparative commercial failure of *Pet Sounds* in his own country (US number 10), and mortified a year later when the Beatles' *Sgt Peppers Lonely Hearts Club Band* was released. It was not widely known that Brian had already experienced two nervous breakdowns, retired from performing with the group and had begun to depend on barbiturates. Even less public was the breakdown of his relationship with his father and the festering tension within the band. The brief recruitment of Glen Campbell, followed by Bruce Johnston, filled Brian's place in public. Through all this turmoil the Beach Boys rose to their peak at the end of 1966 with arguably their greatest achievement, 'Good Vibrations'. This glorious collage of musical pattern with its changes of tempo, unusual lyrics and incredible dynamics earned Brian and the band the respect of every musician. The group embarked on a major tour of Europe with a new single, 'Heroes And Villains', another innovative excursion with more intriguing lyrics by Van Dyke Parks. Brian meanwhile attempted a counter attack on the Beatles, with a project to be known as 'Smile'. This became the band's albatross, although it was never officially released. The painstaking hours spent on this project is now one of pop's legendary tales. Parts of the material surfaced on their next three albums, and further tracks appeared on other collections up until 1971.

The conflict between Wilson and the band was surfacing more regularly. Mike Love in particular wanted the other Beach Boys to continue with their immaculate pop music, and argued that Brian was getting too 'far out'. Indeed, Brian's reclusive nature, fast-increasing weight and growing dependence on drugs added fuel to Love's argument. Observers felt that the band could not raise themselves to the musical level visualized in Brian's present state of mind. Many students of the Beach Boys saga feel, retrospectively, that at that point Brian should have completely broken away to concentrate on his symphonic ideas, and made his own records. The band, meanwhile, could have continued along the route that their fans loved. *Smiley Smile* in 1967 and *Wild Honey* the following year were comparative failures in the charts by previous Beach Boys standards. Their music had lost its cohesiveness and their mentor and guiding light had by now retreated to his bed, where he stayed for many years. In Europe the group were still having hits, and even had a surprise UK chart topper in 1968 with 'Do It Again', with Mike Love's nasal vocals taking the lead on a song harping back to better times. Love had now become a devotee of the Maharishi Mahesh Yogi, while Dennis Wilson, who was emerging as a talented songwriter, became involved with Charles Manson, later to become notorious as a murderer. Dennis's naïvety allowed him to be drained of money, parted from his home and ultimately threatened with his life. Manson and Wilson collaborated on a number of songs, notably 'Never Learn Not To Love', which, although a Beach Boys b-side, had the ironic distinction of putting Charles Manson in the charts. To highlight their discontent, three of their next four singles were extraneous compositions, namely 'Bluebirds Over The Mountain', and a competent version of Lead Belly's 'Cottonfields'. The third non-original was the Phil Spector/Jeff Barry/Ellie Greenwich opus 'I Can Hear Music', featuring a passionate lead vocal from Carl, confirming his status as acting leader. He struggled to maintain this role for many years to come.

In April 1969 the Beach Boys left Capitol in a blaze of litigation. No new product surfaced until August the following year, apart from 'Add Some Music To Your Day' in March 1970. They had the ignomy of having an album rejected prior to that. *Sunflower* was an artistic triumph but a commercial disaster, on which Dennis contributed four songs including the sublime 'Forever'. Throughout the following 12 months they set about rebuilding their credibility in the USA, having lost much ground to the new wave bands from San Francisco. They started to tour constantly, even appearing with unlikely compatriots the Grateful Dead. Through determination and hard work they did the seemingly impossible and allied themselves with the hip *cognoscenti*.

The arrival of *Surf's Up* in July 1971 completed their remarkable renaissance. The title track, with surreal lyrics by Van Dyke Parks, was another masterpiece, while on the rest of the album it was Carl's turn to put in strong contributions with the beautiful 'Feel Flows' and 'Long Promised Road'. The record's strong ecological stance was years ahead of its time, and the critics were unanimous in favourably reassessing them. As Dennis co-starred with James Taylor in the cult road movie *Two-Lane Blacktop*, so Brian's life was deteriorating into mental instability. Miraculously the band were able to maintain their career which at times included only one Wilson, Carl, and no longer had the presence of the long-serving Bruce Johnston. The addition of Ricky Fataar, Blondie Chaplin and Daryl Dragon nevertheless gave the depleted band a fuller sound. One further album appeared before the outstanding *Holland* came in 1973. For this project the entire Beach Boys organization, including wives and children, moved to Holland for eight months of recording. Thankfully, even Brian was cajoled into going, because his composition 'Sail On Sailor' was a high point of the record. Murray Wilson died of a heart attack in June 1973, but Brian and Dennis declined to attend the funeral; they were greatly affected by his passing. At the same time the group's fortunes were once again in the descendent as a double live album was badly received. A year later an astonishing thing happened: a compilation, *Endless Summer*, put together by Mike Love, unexpectedly rocketed to the top of the US charts. It spent 71 weeks on the lists, disappeared and returned again the following year to a high position staying for a further 78 weeks. This unparalleled success reinforced Love and Jardine's theory that all anybody wanted of the Beach Boys was surfing and car songs. With the addition of James William Guercio, formerly of Chicago and ex-producer of Blood, Sweat And Tears, the band enjoyed extraordinary concert tour success, and ended 1974 being voted 'Band of the Year' by the influential magazine *Rolling Stone*. *Spirit Of America* (1975), another compilation of earlier tracks, enjoyed enormous success staying on the American charts for almost a year. Meanwhile, Brian's condition had further deteriorated and he was now under the treatment of therapist Eugene Landy. The album *15 Big Ones* in July 1976 gave them a big hit with Chuck Berry's 'Rock And Roll Music'. The publicity centred on a tasteless 'Brian Is Back' campaign, the now obese Wilson being unwillingly pushed into the spotlight. It seemed obvious to all that Brian was not back; here was a sick, confused and nervous man being used as a financial tool.

Subsequent albums, *The Beach Boys Love You* and *M.I.U. Album*, attempted to maintain Brian's high profile as producer, but close observers were well aware that this was a complete sham. The material was of average quality, although the former showed strong glimpses of Wilson's fascination for childlike innocence. In 1977 they signed a recording contract with CBS reputedly worth $8,000,000, on the terms that Brian Wilson contributed at least four new songs and a total of 70 per cent of all the material for each album. The first album under this contract was the patchy *LA (Light Album)*, with Bruce Johnston recalled to bail them out on production duties. The album did manage to produce a sizeable hit with Al Jardine's 'Lady Lynda'. The most controversial track, however, was a remake of 'Here Comes the Night'; this previously innocuous R&B song from *Wild Honey* was turned into an 11-minute extended disco extravaganza. This track alone cost $50,000 to produce. By now Dennis had a serious cocaine habit which hampered the recording of his own solo album *Pacific Ocean Blue*. It was released to excellent reviews, and was an album into which Dennis put his heart, using a host of musicians and singers, with the notable absence of the Beach Boys. Dennis now openly verbally abused the other members of the band except for Brian, whom he defended resolutely. When Carl fell victim to cocaine and alcohol, the fragmentation of the group was at its height.

The next official work was *Keeping The Summer Alive*, a poor album (with an even poorer cover), without the presence of Dennis who had left the group. He was now living with Christine McVie of Fleetwood Mac. During 1980 only Love and Jardine were present from the original group. Carl delivered his first solo album, a beautifully sung, well-produced record that flopped. One track, 'Heaven', later became a regular part of the Beach Boys' repertoire and was dedicated to Dennis during the 80s. In 1982, Brian Wilson was officially dismissed, and was admitted to hospital for detoxification, weighing a massive 320 pounds. In December 1983, Dennis Wilson tragically drowned while diving from his boat. Ironically, his death reportedly snapped Brian out of his stupor, and he gradually re-emerged to participate onstage. A clean and healthy-looking band graced the back of the 1985 Steve Levine-produced, *The Beach Boys*. Following this collection they found themselves without a recording contract, and decided to concentrate purely on being a major concert attraction, travelling the world. While no new albums appeared, they concentrated on singles, including an energetic, well-produced 'Rock And Roll To The Rescue', followed by their version of the Mamas And The Papas' classic 'California Dreaming', with Roger McGuinn featured on 12-string guitar. In 1987, they teamed up with rap act the Fat Boys for a remake of the Surfaris' 'Wipe Out'.

In 1988, a phoenix-like Brian Wilson returned with the solo album for which his fans had waited over 20 years. The much-publicized record showed a slim, healthy-looking man. The critics and fans loved it, but the general public did not respond and the album sold only moderately well. At the same time the Beach Boys released 'Kokomo', which was included in the film *Cocktail*. They found themselves unexpectedly at the top of the US charts, for many weeks. In May 1990, the Beach Boys took Brian Wilson to court in an alleged attempt to wrest his $80 million fortune from him. They maintained that he was insane and unable to look after himself. His medical condition was confirmed (extreme introversion, pathological shyness and manic depression). Wilson defended the case but eventually reluctantly accepted a settlement by which he severed his links with the controversial Landy. Wilson was then officially sacked/resigned and proceeded to get back monies which had been pouring in from his back catalogue. Murray Wilson had sold his son's company Sea Of Tunes to another publisher in 1969. During this latest court case Wilson testified that he was mentally ill and a casualty of drug abuse at the time. Wilson won the case and received substantial back royalties. No sooner had the dust settled when Mike Love issued a writ to Brian Wilson claiming he co-wrote 79 songs with him, including 'California Girls', 'I Get Around' and 'Surfin' USA' (the latter was 'borrowed' from Chuck Berry). In 1993 the band continued to tour, although their show was merely an oldies package. During 1994 mutterings were heard that the pending lawsuit would be settled, as Love and Brian were at least speaking to each other. Late that year it was announced that a substantial settlement had been made to Love, effectively confirming all his claims. In February 1995 a thin, handsome, recently remarried Wilson and a neat sprite-looking Love met at the latter's home. Not only had they mended the rift but they were writing songs together. Early reports indicate both enthusiasm and a desire to make up for many years of wasted time. The non-stop touring carried out by Love, Jardine and Carl Wilson was halted in 1997 when the latter underwent treatment for cancer. Much has been written about the band, and to those wishing to study the band, David Leaf's book is highly recommended. Timothy White's recent book adds information that had previously never surfaced and is a well-written documentary of California life. Their career has been rolling, like the tide their great songs evoked, constantly in and out, reaching incredible highs and extraordinary troughs. Through all these appalling experiences, however, they still reign supreme as the most successful American group in pop history.

●ALBUMS: *Surfin' Safari* (Capitol 1962)★★, *Surfin' USA* (Capitol 1963)★★, *Surfer Girl* (Capitol 1963)★★★, *Little Deuce Coupe* (Capitol 1963)★★★, *Shut Down Vol. 2* (Capitol 1964)★★★★, *All Summer Long* (Capitol 1964)★★★★, *Beach Boys Concert* (Capitol 1964)★★★, *The Beach Boys' Christmas Album* (Capitol 1964)★★★, *The Beach Boys Today!* (Capitol 1965)★★★★, *Summer Days (And Summer Nights!!)* (Capitol 1965)★★★★, *The Beach Boys' Party!* (Capitol 1965)★★, *Pet Sounds* (Capitol 1966)★★★★★, *Smiley Smile* (Capitol 1967)★★★★, *Wild Honey* (Capitol 1967)★★★, *Friends* (Capitol 1968)★★★, *20/20* (Capitol 1969)★★★, *Live In London* (Capitol 1970)★★, *Sunflower* (Brother 1970)★★★★★, *Surf's Up* (Brother 1971)★★★★★, *Carl And The Passions-So Tough* (Brother 1972)★★★, *Holland* (Brother 1973)★★★★, *The Beach Boys In Concert* (Brother 1973)★★, *15 Big Ones* (Brother 1976)★★★, *The Beach Boys Love You* (Brother 1977)★★★, *M.I.U. Album* (Brother 1978)★, *LA (Light Album)* (Caribou 1979)★★★, *Keepin' The Summer Alive* (Caribou 1980)★, *Rarities* (1983)★★★, *The Beach Boys* (Caribou 1985)★★★, *Still Cruisin'* (Capitol 1989)★, *Summer In Paradise* (1993)★, *Stars And Stripes Vol. 1* (River North 1996)★.

●COMPILATIONS: *Endless Summer* (Capitol 1974)★★★★★, *Spirit Of America* (Capitol 1975)★★★★, *20 Golden Greats* (Capitol 1976)★★★, *Ten Years Of Harmony* (Caribou 1981)★★★, *Sunshine Dream* (Capitol 1982)★★★, *The Very Best Of The Beach Boys* (Capitol 1983)★★★★, *Made In The USA* (Capitol 1986)★★★★, *Summer Dreams* (Capitol 1990)★★★, *Good Vibrations: Thirty Years Of...* 5-CD box set (Capitol 1993)★★★★★.

●VIDEOS: *Beach Boys: An American Band* (1988), *Summer Dreams* (1991).

●FURTHER READING: *The Beach Boys: Southern California Pastoral*, Bruce Golden. *The Beach Boys: A Biography In Words & Pictures*, Ken Barnes. *The Beach Boys*, John Tobler. *The Beach Boys And The California Myth*, David Leaf. *The Beach Boys: The Authorized Illustrated Biography*, Byron Preiss. *Surf's Up!: The Beach Boys On Record, 1961-1981*, Brad Elliott. *The Beach Boys*, Dean Anthony. *The Beach Boys: Silver Anniversary*, John Millward. *Heroes And Villains: The True Story Of The Beach Boys*, Steven Gaines. *Look! Listen! Vibrate! SMILE*, Dominic Priore. *Denny Remembered*, Edward Wincentsen. *Wouldn't It Be Nice: My Own Story*, Brian Wilson and Todd Gold. *In Their Own Words*, Nick Wise (compiled). *The Nearest Faraway Place: Brian Wilson, The Beach Boys & The Southern California*, Timothy White. *The Rainbow Files: The Beach Boys on CD*, Rene Hultz and Hans Christian Skotte.

●FILMS: *Girls On The Beach* (1965), *Americation* (1979).

BEACH PARTY

Former Walt Disney 'Mousketeer' Annette Funicello joined clean-cut pop singer Frankie Avalon in this 1963 feature, the first of a succession of 'beach' films from the American International Pictures group. Although inspired by California's surfing scene, *Beach Party* was more closely allied to 50s' formula 'quickies', such as *Disneyland After Dark* and the *Gidet* series, in particular the notion of pitching teenagers against adults. Robert Cummings starred as a 'square' academic adopting farcical disguises in an attempt to observe the sexual antics of beach-orientated youth. Dorothy Provine and Morey Amsterdam (of the rated *Dick Van Dyke* television show) were cast alongside the winsome stars, while Peter Falk, later of *Colombo*, appeared as a member of a motorbike gang. Beach Boys leader Brian Wilson was briefly featured alongside sometime collaborators Gary Usher and Roger Christian, but the chief musical interest was provided by Dick Dale And His Del-Tone, founders of the instrumental 'surfing' sound. Dale's hard-edged guitar style, heard in a succession of stellar recordings, was not especially well served in this film. Indeed his pioneering technique was about to be eclipsed by a host of imitators and an increased interest in vocal harmony groups. Yet the power of his best work remains undiminished; maverick director Quentin Tarantino employed Dale's work in his film *Pulp Fiction*.

BEACON STREET UNION

One of the bands included as part of MGM Records' over-hyped 'Bosstown Sound' advertising campaign of 1968, Beacon Street Union managed to survive for two years and two albums despite a lack of critical support. The band consisted of vocalist John Lincoln Wright, Paul Tartachny (guitar), Robert Rhodes (keyboards), Wayne Ulaky (bass) and Richard Weisberg (percussion). Formed in Boston, Massachusetts, USA, around 1967, the group was signed to MGM along with such bands as Ultimate Spinach and Orpheus - the label's ill-fated intention was to create a Boston music scene to parallel San Francisco's. The group recorded two albums, both of which were hard folk rock albums with jazz and blues leanings and ambitious, often pretentious lyrics. The debut album reached number 75 in the USA and the follow-up number 173 before the band regrouped in 1970 as Eagle.

●ALBUMS: *The Eyes Of The Beacon Street Union* (MGM 1968)★★, *The Clown Died In Marvin Gardens* (1968)★★.

BEAT CLUB

One of the most atmospheric pop showcases of the 60s, this German television magazine was as important in its way as the older UK counterpart *Ready Steady Go!* or the US *Shindig*. Transmitted from Hamburg, it featured Roy Black, the Rattles, the Lords and other domestic acts, and was a crucial inclusion on the European itineraries of bands such as the Spencer Davis Group, the Easybeats, Dave Dee, Dozy, Beaky, Mick And Tich, Aphrodite's Child and Canned Heat, who all became at least as popular in the lucrative German market as they were at home through regular appearances on the show. The final edition was recorded in 1971, but, compounding the growth of nostalgia for 60s pop, editions of *Beat Club* were broadcast on Britain's Channel Four in the early 90s.

BEATLES

The origin of the phenomenon that became the Beatles can be traced to 1957 when Paul McCartney (b. 18 June 1942, Liverpool, England) successfully auditioned at a church fête in Woolton, Liverpool, for the guitarist's position in the Quarrymen, a skiffle group led by John Lennon (b. 9 October 1940, Liverpool, England, d. 8 December 1980, New York, USA). Within a year, two more musicians had been brought in, the 15-year-old guitarist George Harrison (b. 25 February 1943, Liverpool, England) and an art school friend of Lennon's, Stuart Sutcliffe (b. 23 June 1940, Edinburgh, Scotland, d. 10 April 1962). After a brief spell as Johnny And The Moondogs, the band rechristened themselves the Silver Beetles, and, in April 1960, played before impresario Larry Parnes, winning the dubious distinction of a support slot on an arduous tour of Scotland with autumnal idol Johnny Gentle.

By the summer of 1960 the group had a new name, the Beatles, dreamed up by Lennon who said 'a man in a flaming pie appeared and said you shall be Beetles with an a'. A full-time drummer, Pete Best (b. 1941, Liverpool, England) was recruited and they secured a residency at Bruno Koschminder's Indra Club in Hamburg. It was during this period that they honed their repertoire of R&B and rock 'n' roll favourites, and during exhausting six-hour-sets performed virtually every song they could remember. Already, the musical/lyrical partnership of Lennon/McCartney was bearing fruit, anticipating a body of work unparalleled in modern popular music. The image of the group was changing, most noticeably with their fringed haircuts or, as they were later known, the 'mop-tops', the creation of Sutcliffe's German fiancée Astrid Kirchherr. The first German trip ended when the under age Harrison was deported in December 1960 and the others lost their work permits. During this turbulent period, they also parted company with manager Allan Williams, who had arranged many of their early gigs. Following a couple of months recuperation, the group reassembled for regular performances at the Cavern Club in Liverpool and briefly returned to Germany where they performed at the Top Ten club and backed Tony Sheridan on the single 'My Bonnie'. Meanwhile, Sutcliffe decided to leave the group and stay in Germany as a painter. The more accomplished McCartney then took up the bass guitar. This part of their career is well documented in the feature film *Backbeat* (1994).

In November 1961, Brian Epstein, the manager of North End Music Store, a record shop in Liverpool, became interested in the group after he had received dozens of requests from customers for the Tony Sheridan record, 'My Bonnie'. He went to see the Beatles play at the Cavern and soon afterwards became their manager.

Despite Epstein's enthusiasm, several major record companies passed on the Beatles, although the group were granted an audition with Decca on New Year's Day 1962. After some prevarication, the A&R department, headed by Dick Rowe, rejected the group in favour of Brian Poole And The Tremeloes. Other companies were even less enthusiastic than Decca which had at least taken the group seriously enough to finance a recording session. On 10 April, further bad news was forthcoming when the group heard that Stuart Sutcliffe had died in Hamburg of a brain haemorrhage. The following day, the Beatles flew to Germany and opened a seven-week engagement at Hamburg's Star Club. By May, Epstein had at last found a Beatles convert in EMI producer George Martin, who signed the group to the Parlophone label. Three months later, drummer Pete Best was sacked, for although he had looked the part, his drumming was poor. An initial protest was made by his considerable army of fans back in Liverpool. His replacement was Ringo Starr (b. Richard Starkey, 7 July 1940, Liverpool, England), the extrovert and locally popular drummer from Rory Storm And The Hurricanes.

Towards the end of 1962, the Beatles broke through to the UK charts with their debut single, 'Love Me Do', and played the Star Club for the final time. The debut was important as it was far removed from the traditional 'beat combo' sound, and the use of Lennon's harmonica made the song stand out. At this time Epstein signed a deal with the music publisher Dick James that led to the formation of Northern Songs.

On 13 February 1963 the Beatles appeared on UK television's *Thank Your Lucky Stars* to promote their new single, 'Please Please Me', and were seen by six million viewers. It was a pivotal moment in their career at the start of a year in which they would spearhead a working-class assault on music, fashion and the peripheral arts. 'Please Please Me', with its distinctive harmonies and infectious group beat, soon topped the UK charts. It signalled the imminent overthrow of the solo singer in favour of an irresistible wave of Mersey talent. From this point, the Beatles progressed artistically and commercially with each successive record. After seven weeks at the top with 'From Me To You', they released the strident, wailing 'She Loves You', a rocker with the catchphrase 'Yeah, Yeah, Yeah' that was echoed in ever more frequent newspaper headlines. 'She Loves You' hit number 1, went down, then returned to the top seven weeks later as Beatlemania gripped the nation. It was at this point that the Beatles became a household name. 'She Loves You' was replaced by 'I Want To Hold Your Hand', which had UK advance sales of over one million and entered the charts at number 1.

Until 1964 America had proven a barren ground for aspiring British pop artists, with only the occasional record such as the Tornados' 'Telstar' making any impression. The Beatles changed that abruptly and decisively. 'I Want To Hold Your Hand' was helped by the band's television appearance on the top-rated *Ed Sullivan Show* and soon surpassed UK sales. The Beatles had reached a level of popularity that even outshone their pre-eminence in Britain. By April, they held the first five places in the *Billboard* Hot 100, while in Canada they boasted nine records in the Top 10. Although the Beatles' chart statistics were fascinating in themselves, they barely reflected the group's importance. They had established Liverpool as the pop music capital of the world and the beat boom soon spread from the UK across to the USA. In common with Bob Dylan, the Beatles had taught the world that pop music could be intelligent and was worthy of serious consideration beyond the screaming hordes of teendom. Beatles badges, dolls, chewing gum and even cans of Beatle breath, showed the huge rewards that could be earned with the sale of merchandising goods. Perhaps most importantly of all, however, they broke the Tin Pan Alley monopoly of songwriting by steadfastly composing their own material. From the moment they rejected Mitch Murray's 'How Do You Do It?' in favour of their own 'Please Please Me', Lennon and McCartney set in motion revolutionary changes in the music publishing industry. They even had sufficient surplus material to provide hits for fellow artists such as Billy J. Kramer, Cilla Black, the Fourmost and Peter And Gordon. As well as providing the Rolling Stones with their second single 'I Wanna Be Your Man', the Beatles encouraged the Stones to start writing their own songs in order to earn themselves composers' royalties.

By 1965, Lennon and McCartney's writing had matured to a startling degree and their albums were relying less on other material. Previously, they had recorded compositions by Chuck Berry, Buddy Holly, Carl Perkins, Bacharach And David, Leiber And Stoller and Goffin And King, but with each successive release the group were leaving behind their earlier influences and moving towards uncharted pop territory. They carried their audience with them, and even while following traditional pop routes they always invested their work with originality. Their first two films, *A Hard Day's Night* and *Help!*, were not the usual pop celluloid cash-ins but were witty and inventive and achieved critical acclaim as well as box office success. The national affection bestowed upon the lovable mop-tops was best exemplified in 1965, when they were awarded MBEs for services to British industry. The year ended with the release of their first double-sided number 1 single, 'We Can Work It Out'/'Day Tripper', the coupling indicating how difficult it had now become to choose between a- and b-sides.

Both Lennon and McCartney were huge influences on each other and showed themselves equally adept at crafting ballads and rockers, either alone or together. Their symmetry was extraordinary, at once oppositional and complementary. On the ballad side there was 'I'll Follow The Sun' and 'Yesterday', the latter overtly sentimental but pure genius. Lennon displayed a more despairing personal angst on the bleak 'Baby's In Black' and the deceptively uptempo 'Help', arguably the first pop song to use the word 'insecure'. Both writers were huge influences on each other and showed themselves equally adept at crafting ballads and rockers, either alone

or together. Moreover, their handling of cover versions, from Paul's wailing 'Kansas City' to John's screaming 'Twist And Shout', emphasized their dual talent at tackling diverse material.

At Christmas 1965 the Beatles released *Rubber Soul*, an album that was not a collection of would-be hits or favourite cover versions, as the previous releases had been, but a startlingly diverse collection, ranging from the pointed satire of 'Nowhere Man' to the intensely reflective 'In My Life'. As ever with the Beatles, there were some pointers to their future styles, including Harrison's use of sitar on the punningly titled song of Lennon's infidelity 'Norwegian Wood'. That same year, the Byrds, Yardbirds and Rolling Stones incorporated Eastern-influenced sounds into their work, and the music press tentatively mentioned the decidedly unpoplike Ravi Shankar. Significantly, Shankar's champion, George Harrison, was allowed two writing credits on *Rubber Soul*, 'Think For Yourself' and 'If I Needed Someone' (also a hit for the Hollies).

During 1966, the Beatles continued performing their increasingly complex arrangements before scarcely controllable screaming fans, but the novelty of fandom was wearing frustratingly thin. In Tokyo, the group incurred the wrath of militant students who objected to their performance at Budokan. Several death threats followed and the group left Japan in poor spirits, unaware that worse was to follow. A visit to Manila ended in a near riot when the Beatles did not attend a party thrown by President Ferdinand Marcos, and before leaving the country they were set upon by angry patriots. A few weeks later Beatles records were being burned in the redneck southern states of America because of Lennon's flippant remark that: 'We are more popular than Jesus now'. Although his words passed unnoticed in Britain, their reproduction in an American magazine instigated assassination threats and a massed campaign by members of the Ku Klux Klan to stamp out the Beatle menace. By the summer of 1966, the group were exhausted and defeated and played their last official performance at Candlestick Park, San Francisco, USA, on 29 August.

The controversy surrounding their live performances did not detract from the quality of their recorded output. 'Paperback Writer' was another step forward with its gloriously elaborate harmonies and charmingly prosaic theme. It was soon followed by a double-sided chart topper, 'Yellow Submarine'/'Eleanor Rigby', the former a self-created nursery rhyme sung by Ringo, complete with mechanical sounds, and the latter a brilliantly orchestrated narrative of loneliness, untainted by mawkishness. The attendant album *Revolver* was equally varied, with Harrison's caustic 'Taxman', McCartney's plaintive 'For No One' and 'Here, There And Everywhere', and Lennon's drug-influenced 'I'm Only Sleeping', 'She Said She Said' and the mantric and then-scary 'Tomorrow Never Knows'. The latter is seen as the most effective evocation of a LSD experience ever recorded. After 1966, the Beatles retreated into the studio, no longer bound by the restriction of having to perform live. Their image as pin-up pop stars was also undergoing metamorphosis and when they next appeared in photographs, all four had moustaches, and Lennon even boasted glasses, his shortsightedness previously concealed by contact lenses. Their first recording to be released in over six months was 'Penny Lane'/'Strawberry Fields Forever' which broke their long run of consecutive UK number 1 hits, as it was kept off the top by Engelbert Humperdinck's schmaltzy 'Release Me'. Nevertheless, this landmark single brilliantly captured the talents of Lennon and McCartney and is seen as their greatest pairing on disc. Although their songwriting styles were increasingly contrasting, there were still striking similarities, as both songs were about the Liverpool of their childhood. There were also absurdist elements in each song, with Paul recalling 'Penny Lane' presenting a bustling landscape, populated by various occupants including a fire fighter wary of a shower of rain and a nurse selling poppies. Lennon's lyrics to 'Strawberry Fields Forever' dramatize an inner dialogue characterized by stumbling qualifications ('That is, I think, I disagree'). Musically, the songs were similarly intriguing with 'Penny Lane' including a piccolo trumpet and shimmering percussive fade-out, while 'Strawberry Fields Forever' fused two different versions of the same song and used reverse taped cellos to eerie effect.

It was intended that this single would be the jewel in the crown of their next album, but by the summer of 1967 they had sufficient material to release 13 new tracks on *Sgt. Pepper's Lonely Hearts Club Band*. *Sgt. Pepper* turned out to be no mere pop album but a cultural icon embracing the constituent elements of the 60s' youth culture: pop art, garish fashion, drugs, instant mysticism and freedom from parental control. Although the Beatles had previously experimented with collages on *Beatles For Sale* and *Revolver*, they took the idea further on the sleeve of *Sgt. Pepper* which included photos of every influence on their lives that they could remember. The album had a gatefold sleeve, cardboard cut-out figurines, and, for the first time on a pop record, printed lyrics. The music, too, was even more extraordinary and refreshing. Instead of the traditional breaks between songs, one track merged into the next, linked by studio talk, laughter, electronic noises and animal sounds. A continuous chaotic activity of sound ripped forth from the ingenuity of their ideas translator, George Martin. The songs were essays in innovation and diversification, embracing the cartoon psychedelia of 'Lucy In The Sky With Diamonds', the music-hall pastiche of 'When I'm 64', the circus atmosphere of 'Being For The Benefit Of Mr Kite', the eastern philosophical promise of 'Within You, Without You' and even a modern morality tale in 'She's Leaving Home'. Audio tricks and surprises abounded involving steam organs, orchestras, sitars, and even farmyard animals and a pack of foxhounds in full cry at the end of 'Good Morning, Good Morning'. The album closed with the epic 'Day In The Life', the Beatles' most ambitious work to date, featuring what Lennon described as 'a sound building up from nothing to the end of the world'. As a final gimmick, the orchestra was recorded beyond a 20,000 hertz frequency, meaning that the final note was audible only to dogs. Even the phonogram was not allowed to interfere with the proceedings, for a record groove was cut back to repeat slices of backwards recorded tape which played on into infinity.

While *Sgt. Pepper's Lonely Hearts Club Band* topped the album charts, the group appeared on a live television broadcast to the whole world, playing their anthem of the period, 'All You Need Is Love'. The following week it entered many of the world's charts at number 1, echoing the old days of Beatlemania. There was sadness, too, that summer, for on 21 August 1967, Brian Epstein was found dead, the victim of a cumulative overdose of the drug Carbitrol, together with hints of a homosexual scandal cover-up. With spiritual guidance from the Maharishi Mahesh Yogi, the Beatles took Epstein's death calmly and decided to look after their business affairs without a manager. The first fruits of their post-Epstein labour was the film *Magical Mystery Tour*, first screened on national television on Boxing Day 1967. While the phantasmogorical movie got mixed reviews, nobody could complain about the music, initially released in the unique form of a double EP, featuring six well-crafted songs. The EPs reached number 2 in the UK, making chart history in the process. Ironically, the package was robbed of the top spot by the traditional Beatles Christmas single, this time in the form of 'Hello Goodbye'.

In 1968 the Beatles became increasingly involved with the business of running their company, Apple Corps. A mismanaged boutique near Baker Street came and went. The first Apple single, 'Hey Jude', was a warm-hearted ballad that progressed over its seven-minute duration into a rousing singalong finale. Their third film, *Yellow Submarine*, was a cartoon, and the graphics were acclaimed as a landmark in animation. The soundtrack album contained a few desultory tracks issued the following year. With their prolific output, the group crammed the remainder of their most recent material on to a double album, *The Beatles* (now known as 'The White Album'), released in a stark white cover. George Martin's perceptive overview many years later was that it would have made an excellent single album. It had some brilliant moments which displayed the broad sweep of the Beatles' talent, from 'Back In The USSR', the affectionate tribute to Chuck Berry and the Beach Boys, to Lennon's tribute to his late mother, 'Julia', and McCartney's excellent 'Blackbird'. Harrison contributed 'While My Guitar Gently Weeps', which featured Eric Clapton on guitar. Marmalade took 'Ob-La-Di, Ob-La-Da' to number 1 in the UK, while 'Helter Skelter' took on symbolic force in the mind of the murderer Charles Manson. There were also a number of average songs that seemed still to require work, plus some ill-advised doodlings such as 'Revolution No. 9' and 'Goodnight'. *The Beatles* revealed that the four musicians were already working in an isolated neutrality.

The Beatles' inability as business executives was becoming apparent from the parlous state of Apple, to which Allen Klein attempted to restore some order. The new realism that permeated the portals of their headquarters was even evident in their art. Like several other contemporary artists, including Bob Dylan and the Byrds, they chose to end the 60s with a reversion to less complex musical forms. The return-to-roots minimalism was spearheaded by the appropriately titled number 1 single 'Get Back', which featured Billy Preston on organ. Cameras were present at their next recording sessions, as they ran through dozens of songs, many of which they had not played since Hamburg. When the sessions ended there were countless spools of tape which would not be reassembled until the following year. In the meantime, a select few witnessed the band's last 'public' performance on the rooftop of the Apple headquarters in Savile Row, London. Amid the uncertainty of 1969, the Beatles enjoyed their final UK number 1 with 'Ballad Of John And Yoko', on which only Lennon and McCartney performed.

In a sustained attempt to cover the cracks that were becoming increasingly visible in their personal and musical relationships, they reconvened for *Abbey Road*. The album was dominated by a glorious song cycle on side 2, in which such fragmentary compositions as 'Mean Mr. Mustard', 'Polythene Pam', 'She Came In Through The Bathroom Window' and 'Golden Slumbers'/'Carry That Weight' gelled into a convincing whole. The accompanying single coupled Lennon's 'Come Together' with Harrison's 'Something'. The latter song gave Harrison the kudos he deserved, and rightly became the second most covered Beatle song ever, after 'Yesterday'. The album reached only number 4 in the UK, the group's lowest chart position since 'Love Me Do' in 1962. Such considerations were small compared to the fate of their other songs. The group could only watch helplessly as a wary Dick James surreptitiously sold Northern Songs to ATV. The catalogue continued to change hands over the following years and not even the combined financial force of McCartney and Yoko Ono could eventually wrest it from superstar speculator Michael Jackson.

With various solo projects coming up, the Beatles stumbled through 1970, their disunity betrayed to the world in the depressing film *Let It Be*, which shows Harrison and Lennon clearly unhappy about McCartney's attitude towards the band. The subsequent album, finally pieced together by producer Phil Spector, was a controversial and bitty affair, initially housed in a cardboard box containing a lavish paperback book which increased the retail price to a prohibitive level. Musically, the work revealed the Beatles looking back to better days. It included the sparse 'Two Of Us' and the primitive 'The One After 909', a song they used to play as the Quarrymen, and an orchestrated 'Long And Winding Road' which provided their final US number 1, although McCartney pointedly preferred the non-orchestrated version on the film. And there was the aptly titled last official single, 'Let It Be', which entered the UK charts at number 2, only to drop to number 3 the following week. For many it was the final sad anti-climax before the inevitable, yet still unexpected, split. The acrimonious dissolution of the Beatles, like that of no other group before or since, symbolized the end of an era that they had dominated and helped create.

It is inconceivable that any group in the future could shape and influence a generation in the way these four individuals did. Thirty years on, and such is the quality of the songs that none have shown signs of sounding dated either lyrically or musically.

Since the break-up of the band there have been some important releases for fans of the Beatles. In 1988 the two *Past Masters* volumes collected together all the Beatles tracks not available on the CD releases of their original albums. The first volume has 18 tracks from 1962-65; the second 15 from the rest of their career. *Live At The BBC* collected together 56 tracks played live by the Beatles for various shows on the BBC Light Programme in the infancy of their career. Most of the songs are cover versions of 50s R&B standards, including nine by Chuck Berry. The first volume of *Anthology*, released in November 1995, collected 52 previously unreleased outtakes and demo versions recorded between 1958 and 1964, plus eight spoken tracks taken from interviews. The album was accompanied by an excellent six-part television series, made with the help of the three remaining Beatles, that told the complete story of the band, and by the single release of 'Free As A Bird', the first song recorded by the Beatles since their break-up. This consisted of a 1977 Lennon track he had sung into a tape recorder, backed vocally and instrumentally in 1995 by the other three Beatles and produced by Jeff Lynne. It narrowly failed to reach number 1 on both sides of the Atlantic, as did the slightly inferior 'Real Love' in March 1996. The reaction to *Anthology 2* was ecstatic. While it was expected that older journalists would write favourably about *their* generation, it was encouraging to see younger writers having something to say that was fresh. David Quantick of the *New Musical Express* offered one of the best comments in recent years: 'The Beatles only made - they could only make - music that referred to the future. And *that* is the difference between them and every other pop group or singer ever since'. *Anthology 3* could not improve upon the previous collection but there were gems to be found: the acoustic 'While My Guitar Gently Weeps' from Harrison is stunning. 'Because', never an outstanding track when it appeared on *Abbey Road*, is given a stripped a cappella treatment. The result is breathtaking; never have the Beatles sounded so rich and perfect, and the silent pauses in-between have the listener begging for more. The McCartney demo of 'Come And Get It' for Badfinger begs the question, why didn't the fab four release this classic pop song themselves?

In the course of history The Rolling Stones and countless other groups are loved, but the Beatles are universally and unconditionally adored.

●ALBUMS: *Please Please Me* (Parlophone 1963)★★★★, *With The Beatles* (Parlophone 1963)★★★★, *A Hard Day's Night* (Parlophone

1964)★★★, *Beatles For Sale* (Parlophone 1964)★★★★, *The Savage Young Beatles* (USA)(Savage 1964)★, *Ain't She Sweet* (USA)(Atco 1964)★, *The Beatles With Tony Sheridan & Their Guests & Others* (USA)(MGM 1964)★, *Meet The Beatles* (USA)(Capitol 1964)★★★, *The Beatles Second Album* (USA)(Capitol 1964)★★★, *Something New* (USA)(Capitol 1964)★★★, *Beatles '65* (USA)(Capitol 1964)★★★, *The Early Beatles* (USA)(Capitol 1965)★★, *Beatles VI* (USA)(Capitol 1965)★★, *Help!* (Parlophone 1965)★★★★★, *Rubber Soul* (Parlophone 1965)★★★★★, *Yesterday And Today* (Capitol 196)★★★, *Revolver* (Parlophone 1966)★★★★★, *Sgt. Pepper's Lonely Hearts Club Band* (Parlophone 1967)★★★★★, *Magical Mystery Tour* (Capitol 1968)★★★★, *The Beatles* (Apple 1968)★★★★★, *Yellow Submarine* (Apple 1969)★★, *Abbey Road* (Apple 1969)★★★★★, *Let It Be* (Apple 1970)★★★, *Hey Jude* (Capitol 1970)★★★, *The Early Years* (Contour 1971)★★, *The Beatles At The Hollywood Bowl* (Parlophone 1977)★★, *Rarities* (Parlophone 1979)★★★★, *Live At The BBC* (Apple 1994)★★★★, *Anthology 1* (Apple 1995)★★★★, *Anthology 2* (Apple 1996)★★★★, *Anthology 3* (Apple 1996)★★★.

●COMPILATIONS: *A Collection Of Beatles Oldies* (Parlophone 1966)★★★★, *The Beatles 1962-1966* (Apple 1973)★★★★★, *The Beatles 1967-1970* (Apple 1973)★★★★★, Rock & Roll Music (EMI 1976)★★★★, *Love Songs* (EMI 1977)★★★★, *Past Masters Volume 1* (Parlophone 1988)★★★★★, *Past Masters Volume 2* (Parlophone 1988)★★★★★.

●VIDEOS: *Ready Steady Go Special* (1985), *A Hard Days Night* (Vestron 1986), *Compleat Beatles* (MGM 1986), *Magical Mystery Tour* (MPI 1989), *Help* (MPI 1989), *On The Road* (1990), *Alone And Together* (1990), *The First U.S. Visit* (1993), *Beatles Firsts* (Goodtimes 1995), *The Making Of A Hard Day's Night* (VCI 1995), *The Beatles Anthology Vols 1-8* (PMI 1996).

●FURTHER READING: There have been hundreds of books published of varying quality. Our three recommendations are: *The Complete Beatles Chronicle* by Mark Lewisohn, an accurate and definitive career and recording history by their greatest historian. *Shout! The True Story Of The Beatles* by Philip Norman, the most readable and objective biography. *Revolution In The Head* by Ian MacDonald, a beautifully written authoritative study of every song. Others: *The True Story Of The Beatles*, Billy Shepherd. *The Beatles Book*, Norman Parkinson and Maureen Cleave. *A Cellarful Of Noise*, Brian Epstein. *The Beatles: A Hard Day's Night*, John Burke. *Love Me Do: The Beatles' Progress*, Michael Braun. *The Beatles In Help*, Al Hine. *The Beatles: Words Without Music*, Rick Friedman. *The Beatles*, Hunter Davies. *Get Back*, Ethan Russell (photographs). *The Beatles Illustrated Lyrics Vol. 2*, Alan Aldridge (ed.). *Apple To The Core: The Unmaking Of The Beatles*, Peter McCabe and Robert D. Schonfeld. *The Longest Cocktail Party*, Richard DiLello. *As Time Goes By: Living In The Sixties*, Derek Taylor. *Twilight Of The*

Gods: The Beatles In Retrospect, Wilfred Mellers. *The Man Who Gave The Beatles Away*, Allan Williams. *The Beatles: An Illustrated Record*, Roy Carr and Tony Tyler. *All Together Now: The First Complete Beatles Discography 1961-1975*, Harry Castleman and Walter J. Podrazik. *The Beatles: Yesterday, Today, Tomorrow*, Rochelle Larkin. *Beatles In Their Own Words*, Miles. *The Beatles: A Day In The Life: The Day By Day Diary 1960-1970*, Tom Schultheiss. *The Boys From Liverpool: John, Paul, George, Ringo*, Nicholas Schaffner. *The Beatles Illustrated Lyrics*, Alan Aldridge (ed.). *The Beatles Apart*, Bob Woffinden. *Shout! The True Story Of The Beatles*, Philip Norman. *The Beatles: An Illustrated Discography*, Miles. *Thank U Very Much: Mike McCartney's Family Album*, (Peter) Michael McCartney. *All You Needed Was Love: The Beatles After The Beatles*, John Blake. *The Long And Winding Road: A History Of The Beatles On Record*, Neville Stannard. *Abbey Road: The Story Of The World's Most Famous Recording Studios*, Brian Southall. *The Complete Beatles Lyrics*, no author listed. *The Beatles At The Beeb 62-65: The Story Of Their Radio Career*, Kevin Howlett. *With The Beatles: The Historic Photographs*, Dezo Hoffman. *Beatles' England*, David Bacon and Norman Maslov. *Working Class Heroes: The History Of The Beatles' Solo Recordings*, Neville Stannard. *The Beatles: An Illustrated Diary*, H.V. Fulpen. *The Love You Make: An Insider's Story Of The Beatles*, Peter Brown and Steven Gaines. *John Ono Lennon 1967-1980*, Ray Coleman. *John Winston Lennon 1940-1966*, Ray Coleman. *Beatlemania: An Illustrated Filmography*, Bill Harry. *Paperback Writers: An Illustrated Bibliography*, Bill Harry. *The End Of The Beatles*, Harry Castleman and Wally Podrazik. *Beatle! The Pete Best Story*, Pete Best and Patrick Doncaster. *The Beatles Live*, Mark Lewisohn. *It Was Twenty Years Ago*, Derek Taylor. *Yesterday: The Beatles Remembered*, Alistair Taylor. *All Our Loving: A Beatle Fan's Memoir*, Carolyn Lee Mitchell and Michael Munn. *The Beatles: 25 Years In The Life*, Mark Lewisohn. *Brian Epstein: The Man Who Made The Beatles*, Ray Coleman. *The Beatles Album File and Complete Discography*, Jeff Russell. *How They Became The Beatles: A Definitive History Of The Early Years 1960-1964*, Gareth L. Pawlowski. *Complete Beatles Recording Sessions: The Official Story Of The Abbey Road Years*, Mark Lewisohn. *Day By Day*, Mark Lewisohn. *Speak Words Of Wisdom: Reflections On The Beatles*, Spencer Leigh. *In Their Own Words: The Beatles After The Break Up*, David Bennahum. *Complete Beatles Chronicle*, Mark Lewisohn. *Ultimate Beatles Encyclopedia*, Bill Harry. *Tomorrow Never Knows: Thirty Years Of Beatles Music & Memorabilia*, Geoffrey Giuliano. *The Ultimate Recording Guide*, Allen J. Wiener. *Beatles*, John Ewing. *It Was Thirty Years Ago Today*, Terence Spencer. *The Summer Of Love*, George Martin. *A Hard Day's Write*, Steve Turner. *Revolution In The Head: The Beatles Records And The Sixties*, Ian MacDonald. *Backbeat*, Alan Clayson and

Pauline Sutcliffe. *The Essential Guide To The Music Of …*, John Robertson. *The Beatle's London*, Piet Schreuders, Mark Lewisohn And Adam Smith. *A Day In The Life: The Music And Artistry Of The Beatles*, Mark Hertsgaard.

● FILMS: *A Hard Days Night* (1964), *Help* (1965), *Yellow Submarine* (1968), *Magical Mystery Tour* (1968), *Let It Be* (1970).

BEATSTALKERS

Formed in Glasgow, Scotland, in 1962, the Beatstalkers originally comprised Davie Lennox (vocals), Eddie Campbell (guitar), Alan Mair (bass) and 'Tudge' Williamson (drums). Within weeks Ronnie Smith (rhythm guitar) had been added to the line-up. By 1964 the Beatstalkers had become a leading attraction, specialiZing in cover versions of hitherto obscure soul and R&B songs. Such was their popularity, the group was dubbed 'Scotland's Beatles' and in 1965 an open-air concert in Glasgow's George Square was abandoned when fans rioted. The Beatstalkers then secured a recording deal with Decca Records. 'Everybody's Talkin' 'Bout My Baby', 'Left Right Left' and 'A Love Like Yours' followed in succession, but although worthwhile in their own right, these records failed to capture the group's true mettle. The Beatstalkers moved to London in 1967 where they secured a residency at the famed Marquee Club. However, despite switching to CBS Records, the group was still unable to achieve a major breakthrough, in part because they relied on outside material. Their new manager Ken Pitt suggested that the Beatstalkers record songs by his best-known charge, David Bowie. Three of his compositions, 'Silver Tree Top School For Boys', 'Everything Is You' and 'When I'm Five', were released in succession, although only the first title was issued as an a-side. The experiment was neither an artistic nor commercial success, and, as Alan Mair later recalled, 'It was pitiful to watch Davie Lennox rehearse the songs in an English accent.' The Beatstalkers split up in 1969 when their entire equipment was stolen. Late period drummer Jeff Allen found success with East Of Eden, while Mair was later a member of the critically acclaimed Only Ones.

BEAU BRUMMELS

Formed in San Francisco in 1964, the Beau Brummels provided a vital impetus to the city's emergent rock circuit. Vocalist Sal Valentino had previously led his own group, Sal Valentino And The Valentines, which issued 'I Wanna Twist'/'Lisa Marie' in 1962. Ron Elliott (b. 21 October 1943, Healdsburg, California, USA; guitar/vocals), Ron Meagher (b. 2 October 1941, Oakland, California, USA; bass) and John Petersen (b. 8 January 1942, Rudyard, Michigan, USA; drums), formerly of the Sparklers, joined him in a new act taking the name Beau Brummels in deference to their love of British beat music. Playing a staple diet of current hits and material by the Beatles and Searchers, the quartet enjoyed a committed following within the city's Irish community prior to adding Declan Mulligan (b. County Tipperary, Eire;

guitar) to the line-up. Local entrepreneurs Tom Donahue and Bob Mitchell saw their obvious topicality and signed the group to their fledgling Autumn label. 'Laugh Laugh', the Beau Brummels' debut single, broached the US Top 20 in 1964, while its follow-up, 'Just A Little', reached number 8 early the following year. Both songs, which were original compositions, bore an obvious debt to British mentors, but later, more adventurous releases, including 'You Tell Me Why' and 'Don't Talk To Strangers', emphasized an American heritage, presaging the 'West Coast' sound. The group's first two albums offered elements of folk, country and R&B. Producer Sylvester Stewart, later known as Sly Stone, sculpted a clear, resonant sound which outstripped that of many contemporaries. Elliott emerged as a distinctive songwriter, while Valentino's deep, tremulous delivery provided an unmistakable lead. Mulligan's premature departure in March 1965 did little to undermine this progress.

Autumn Records was wound up in 1966 and the group's contract was sold to Warner Brothers Records. A new member, Don Irving, was featured on their next collection, *Beau Brummels 66*, but this sorry affair was a marked disappointment, consisting of throwaway readings of current hits. Its release undermined the quintet's credibility. Irving then left, and, as the band now eschewed live appearances, Petersen opted for another local attraction, the Tikis, who later became Harpers Bizarre. The remaining trio completed the exquisite *Triangle*, one of the era's most cultured and delicate albums, but the loss of Meagher in September 1967 reduced the group to that of Elliott and Valentino. The former undertook several 'outside' projects; producing and/or writing singles for Butch Engle And The Styx, before donating songs and/or arranging skills on albums by Randy Newman, the Everly Brothers and the aforementioned Harpers Bizarre. In 1968 the Beau Brummels' duo completed *Bradley's Barn*, an early excursion into country-rock, before embarking on separate careers. Valentino issued three solo singles before founding Stoneground. Elliott completed the gorgeous *The Candlestickmaker*, formed the disappointing Pan, then undertook occasional session work, including a cameo on Little Feat's *Sailing Shoes*.

The original Beau Brummels regrouped in 1974 but Meagher was an early casualty. He was replaced by Dan Levitt, formerly of Pan and Levitt And McClure. *Beau Brummels* was an engaging collection, but progress halted in 1975 when Petersen opted to assist in a Harpers Bizarre reunion. Peter Tepp provided a temporary replacement, but the project was latterly abandoned. Since then the Beau Brummels have enjoyed several short-lived resurrections, but conflicting interests coupled with Elliott's ill-health have denied them a long-term future. A plethora of archive recordings, many previously unreleased, have nonetheless kept the group's name and music alive.

● ALBUMS: *Introducing The Beau Brummels* (Autumn/Pye International 1965)★★★, *Volume 2* (Autumn 1965)★★★, *Beau Brummels 66* (Warners

1966)★★★, *Triangle* (Warners 1967)★★★, *Bradley's Barn* (Warners 1968)★★, *Volume 44* (Vault 1968)★★, *The Beau Brummels* (1975)★★.
●COMPILATIONS: *The Best Of The Beau Brummels* (1967)★★★, *The Beau Brummels Sing* (Post 1972)★★★, *The Original Hits Of The Beau Brummels* (JAS 1975)★★★, *The Best Of The Beau Brummels* rec. 1964-1968 (1981)★★★, *From The Vaults* (Sundazed 1982)★★★, *Autumn In San Francisco* (1985)★★★, *The Autumn Of Their Years* (Big Beat/Nuggets From The Golden Era 1995)★★★, *San Fran Sessions* (Sundazed 1997)★★.

BEDROCKS

Formed in Leeds, England, in late 1967, this West Indian sextet comprised Trevor Wisdom (b. 1945, Jamaica; organ), Owen Wisdom (b. 1948, Jamaica; bass guitar), Leroy Mills (b. 1949, St Kitts; trumpet), Reg Challenger (b. 1948, St Kitts; drums), William Hixon (b. 1951, Monseratt; lead guitar), Paul Douglas (b. 1947, Jamaica; tenor saxophone). Their big break came in 1968 when they were offered the opportunity to record at EMI with producer Norman Smith (later Hurricane Smith). After borrowing £25 to hire a van for the trip, they completed a single within a day. Two days later, their topical cover version of the Beatles' 'Ob-La-Di, Ob-La-Da' was issued and a fortnight later it was in the UK Top 20. Unfortunately, their ethnic reading was outsold by Marmalade's chart-topping version. For their follow-up, the Bedrocks recorded a version of the rugby song 'The Lovedene Girls', but the single received little airplay and failed to chart. It was to prove their last chance of commercial success.

BEGGARS OPERA

Glasgow, Scotland, rock band Beggars Opera was formed in the late 60s by Marshall Erskine (bass/flute), Ricky Gardiner (guitar/vocals), Martin Griffiths (vocals/percussion), Alan Park (keyboards) and Raymond Wilson (drums). The group's grandiose ambition was to fuse classical and progressive rock elements, an accommodation they achieved well but to moderate critical or commercial interest. Signed to Vertigo Records, they made their debut in 1970 with *Act One*, released concurrently with 'Sarabande'. The single was the most successful of the two releases, charting in several mainland European countries. The album included a preposterous rendition of 'Classical Gas', which was eventually released as a single in its own right four years later. The group then expanded to a quintet with the addition of multi-instrumentalist Gordon Sellar (bass/guitar/vocals) for the follow-up collection, *Waters Of Change*. Abandoning some of the progressive rock elements of earlier recordings, the group pursued a more melodious rock direction on this album, heavily indebted to musical developments on America's west coast. Erskine had left the group by the time they recorded 1972's *Pathfinder*, which included a cover version of Richard Harris's 'MacArthur Park'. Their final effort, 1973's *Get Your Dog Off Me*, was completed as a trio, with Sellar joined by founder-members Gardiner and

Park. Unfortunately, this again proved unsuccessful, and with Vertigo wary of further investment in the group they broke up in 1974. Sellar attempted a reformation in the mid-70s when two further albums were issued in Germany - still the group's most receptive market. Gardiner enjoyed greater success as a member of David Bowie's touring band.
●ALBUMS: *Act One* (Vertigo 1970)★★★, *Waters Of Change* (Vertigo 1971)★★★, *Pathfinder* (Vertigo 1972)★★, *Get Your Dog Off Me* (Vertigo 1973)★★.

BEL-AIRS

Formed in Redondo Beach, California, USA, in 1961, the Bel-Airs were an instrumental surf group best known for their first single, 'Mr. Moto', on Arvee Records. The record never reached the national charts but was a popular local hit in the Los Angeles region and subsequently became a staple of the repertoires of many other surf bands. The group consisted of Paul Johnson (guitar), Richard Delvy (drums), Jim Roberts (piano), Chaz Stewart (saxophone) and Eddie Bertrand (guitar). A later member was drummer Dick Dodd, who went on to play drums and sing lead vocals for the Standells. The Bel-Airs broke up in 1963, having never recorded an album.

BELAFONTE, HARRY

b. Harold George Belafonte, 1 March 1927, New York, USA. In recent years, the former 'King Of Calypso' has become better known for his work with UNICEF and his enterprise with USA For Africa. Prior to that, Belafonte had an extraordinarily varied life. His early career was spent as an actor, until he had time to demonstrate his silky smooth and gently relaxing singing voice. He appeared as Joe in Oscar Hammerstein's *Carmen Jones*; an adaptation of *Carmen* by Bizet, and in 1956 he was snapped up by RCA Victor. Belafonte was then at the forefront of the calypso craze which was a perfect vehicle for his happy-go-lucky folk songs. Early hits included 'Jamaica Farewell', 'Mary's Boy Child' and the classic transatlantic hit 'Banana Boat Song' with its unforgettable refrain: 'Day-oh, dayyy-oh, daylight come and me wanna go home'. *Calypso* became the first ever album to sell a million copies, and spent 31 weeks at the top of the US charts. Belafonte continued throughout the 50s with incredible success. He was able to cross over into many markets appealing to pop, folk and jazz fans, as well as to the 'ethnic population with whom he became closely associated, particularly during the civil rights movement. He appeared in many films including *Island In The Sun*, singing the title song, and *Odds Against Tomorrow*. His success as an album artist was considerable; between 1956 and 1962 he was hardly ever absent from the album chart. *Belafonte At Carnegie Hall* spent over three years in the charts, and similar success befell *Belafonte Returns To Carnegie Hall*, featuring Miriam Makeba, the Chad Mitchell Trio and Odetta with the memorable recording of 'There's A Hole In My Bucket'. Throughout the 60s Belafonte was an ambassador of human rights and a most articulate speaker at rallies and on television.

His appeal as a concert hall attraction was immense; no less than seven of his albums were recorded in concert. Although his appearances in the best-sellers had stopped by the 70s he remained an active performer and recording artist, and continued to appear on film, although in lightweight movies like *Buck And The Preacher* and *Uptown Saturday Night*. In the mid-80s he was a leading light in the USA For Africa appeal and sang on 'We Are The World'. His sterling work continued into the 90s with UNICEF. Belafonte was one of the few black artists who broke down barriers of class and race, and should be counted alongside Dr. Martin Luther King as a major figure in achieving equal rights for blacks in America through his work in popular music.

● ALBUMS: *Mark Twain And Other Folk Favorites* (RCA Victor 1955)★★★, *Belafonte* (RCA Victor 1956)★★★★, *Calypso* (RCA Victor 1956)★★★★, *An Evening With Belafonte* (RCA Victor 1957)★★★★, *Belafonte Sings Of The Caribbean* (RCA Victor 1957)★★★, *Belafonte Sings The Blues* (RCA Victor 1958)★★★, *Love Is A Gentle Thing* (RCA Victor 1959)★★★, *Porgy And Bess* (RCA Victor 1959)★★★★, *Belafonte At Carnegie Hall* (RCA Victor 1959)★★★★, *My Lord What A Mornin'* (RCA Victor 1960)★★★, *Belafonte Returns To Carnegie Hall* (RCA Victor 1960)★★★, *Swing Dat Hammer* (RCA Victor 1960)★★★, *At Home And Abroad* (RCA Victor 1961)★★★, *Jump Up Calypso* (RCA Victor 1961)★★★★, *The Midnight Special* (RCA Victor 1962)★★★, *The Many Moods Of Belafonte* (RCA Victor 1962)★★★, *To Wish You A Merry Christmas* (RCA Victor 1962)★★★, *Streets I Have Walked* (RCA Victor 1963)★★★, *Belafonte At The Greek Theatre* (1964)★★★, *Ballads Blues And Boasters* (1964)★★, *An Evening With Belafonte/Makeba* (1965)★★★, *An Evening With Belafonte/Mouskouri* (1966)★★★, *In My Quiet Room* (1966)★★★, *Calypso In Brass* (1967)★★, *Belafonte On Campus* (1967)★★, *Homeward Bound* (1970)★★, *Turn The World Around* (1977)★★, *Loving You Is Where I Belong* (1981)★★, *Paradise In Gazankulu* (1988)★★, *Belafonte '89* (EMI 1989)★★.

● COMPILATIONS: *Collection - Castle Collector Series* (1987)★★★, *Banana Boat Song* (1988)★★★, *All Time Greatest Hits Vol. 1* (RCA 1989)★★★★, *All Time Greatest Hits Vol. 2* (RCA 1989)★★★, *Day-O And Other Hits* (RCA 1989)★★★, *The Very Best Of* (1992)★★★.

● FURTHER READING: *Belafonte*, A.J. Shaw.

BENNETT, CLIFF

One of the most accomplished British R&B vocalists of his era, Cliff Bennett (b. 4 June 1940, Slough, England) formed the excellent Rebel Rousers in early 1961. Taking their name from a Duane Eddy hit of the period, the group comprised Mick King (lead guitar), Frank Allen (bass), Sid Phillips (piano/saxophone) and Ricky Winters (drums). With a repertoire of rock 'n' roll, blue-eyed soul and R&B, the group were briefly taken under the wing of

madcap producer Joe Meek, with whom they recorded several unsuccessful singles. A succession of R&B covers brought no further success and, early in 1964, bassist Frank Allen departed to replace Tony Jackson in the Searchers. The Rebel Rousers continued their busy touring schedule at home and abroad and were finally rewarded with a Top 10 hit, 'One Way Love', in November 1964. This brassy, upbeat cover version of the Drifters' original augured well for the future, but the follow-up, 'I'll Take You Home', stalled at number 43. Abandoning the Drifters as source material, they covered other R&B artists, without noticeable success. A move to Brian Epstein's NEMs management secured them the invaluable patronage of the Beatles, and Paul McCartney stepped in to produce their sparkling reading of 'Got To Get You Into My Life' from the recently released *Revolver*. Peaking at number 6, the single was their second and last Top 10 hit. Thereafter, Bennett fell victim to changing musical fashions as beat groups were generally dismissed as anachronistic. The Rebel Rousers changed their name to the more prosaic Cliff Bennett And His Band and briefly sought success with contemporary writers such as Mark London and Roy Wood. By mid-1969, Bennett decided to dissolve his group and reinvent himself for the progressive market. The result was Toe Fat, a short-lived ensemble now best remembered for their tasteless album covers rather than their music. In 1972 Bennett tried again with Rebellion, and, three years later, Shanghai, but without success. Weary of traipsing around the country, Cliff eventually worked in the advertising business, but still plays semi-professionally.

● ALBUMS: *Cliff Bennett And The Rebel Rousers* (Parlophone 1965)★★★, *Drivin' You Wild* (MFP 1966)★★★, *Cliff Bennett* (Regal 1966)★★★, *Got To Get You Into Our Lives* (Parlophone 1967)★★★, *Cliff Bennett Branches Out* (Parlophone 1968)★★.

BENNETT, DUSTER

b. Anthony Bennett, c.1940, d. 26 March 1976. Bennett was a dedicated British one-man-band blues performer, in the style of Jesse Fuller and Dr Ross. He played the London R&B club circuit from the mid-60s and was signed by Mike Vernon to Blue Horizon in 1967, releasing 'It's A Man Down There' as his first single. On his first album he was backed by Peter Green and John McVie of Fleetwood Mac. Bennett also played harmonica on sessions for Fleetwood Mac, Champion Jack Dupree, Memphis Slim, Shusha and Martha Velez. He was briefly a member of John Mayall's Bluesbreakers, and in 1974 recorded for Mickie Most's RAK label, releasing a single, 'Comin Home'. He was killed in a road accident on 26 March 1976 in Warwickshire, England, returning home after performing with Memphis Slim.

● ALBUMS: *Smiling Like I'm Happy* (Blue Horizon 1968)★★★, *Bright Lights* (Blue Horizon 1969)★★★, *12 DBs* (1970)★★★, *Fingertips* (1974)★★.

● COMPILATIONS: *Out In The Blue* (Indigo 1994)★★★, *Jumpin' At Shadows* (Indigo 1994)★★, *Blue Inside* (Indigo 1995)★★★.

BENNETT, TONY

b. Anthony Dominick Benedetto, 13 August 1926, Astoria, New York, USA. The son of an Italian father and American mother, Bennett studied music and painting at the High School of Industrial Arts. He later became a talented artist, exhibiting under his real name in New York, Paris and London. Originally possessing a tenor voice which would deepen over the years, Bennett sang during service with the US Army's entertainment unit late in World War II. Upon his discharge he worked in clubs before joining a Pearl Bailey revue in Greenwich Village as singer and master of ceremonies under the name of Joe Bari, where he was spotted by Bob Hope who engaged him to sing in his Paramount show and changed his name to Tony Bennett. In 1950 he successfully auditioned for Columbia Records' producer Mitch Miller, singing 'Boulevard Of Broken Dreams', and a year later topped the US chart with 'Because Of You' and 'Cold, Cold Heart'. Other 50s hits, mostly backed by the Percy Faith Orchestra, included 'Rags To Riches', 'Just In Time', 'Stranger In Paradise' (from Kismet), 'There'll Be No Teardrops Tonight', 'Cinnamon Sinner', 'Can You Find It In Your Heart' and 'In The Middle Of An Island'. In 1958, his album Basie Swings-Bennett Sings was a precursor to later jazz-based work. That same year 'Firefly', by the new songwriting team of Cy Coleman and Carolyn Leigh, was Bennett's last US Top 40 entry until 1962, when he made a major comeback with the 1954 song 'I Left My Heart In San Francisco' (which won a Grammy Award) and a sell-out Carnegie Hall concert, which was recorded and released on a double-album set. During this period he continued his long association with pianist/arranger Ralph Sharon, and frequently featured cornet soloist Bobby Hackett. Often quoted as being unable to find suitable new material, Bennett nevertheless made the 60s singles charts with contemporary songs such as 'I Wanna Be Around', 'The Good Life', 'Who Can I Turn To' and 'If I Ruled The World'. Even so, the future lay with concerts and his prolific album output which included US Top 40 albums such as I Wanna Be Around, The Many Moods Of Tony, The Movie Song Album, and four albums with Canadian composer/conductor Robert Farnon. In the 70s Bennett left Columbia Records and recorded for various labels including his own, and made albums with jazz musicians Ruby Braff and Bill Evans. His return to Columbia in the mid-80s produced The Art Of Excellence, which included a duet with Ray Charles, and Bennett/Berlin, a celebration of America's premier songwriter, on which he was accompanied by the Ralph Sharon Trio. He continued to gain excellent reviews at venues such as the Desert Inn, Las Vegas, and in 1991 celebrated 40 years in the business with a concert at London's Prince Edward Theatre. In 1993 and 1994 he was awarded Grammys for 'Best Traditional Pop Performance' for his albums Perfectly Frank and Steppin' Out. Around the same time, Bennett was 'discovered' by younger audiences following his appearances on the David Letterman Show, benefit shows hosted by 'alternative rock' radio stations, and his Unplugged session on the US cable channel MTV. The latter teamed him with contemporary artists k.d. lang and Elvis Costello. By the time he had gained two more Grammys and a World Music Award in 1995 for his MTV Unplugged, the album had spent 35 weeks at the top of the US Jazz chart. He received a second World Music Award for lifelong contribution to the music industry. Bennett's star continued to shine with Here's To The Ladies, a formidable collection of classic songs with particularly impressive versions of 'God Bless The Child' and 'I Got Rhythm'. He expanded his Billie Holiday catalogue with the excellent Tony Bennett On Holiday: A Tribute To Billie Holiday. The 90s are proving to be his most critically acclaimed decade as his voice ripens with age.

●ALBUMS: Because Of You (Columbia 1952)★★★, Alone At Last With Tony Bennett (Columbia 1955)★★, Treasure Chest Of Songs (1955)★★★, Cloud Seven (Columbia 1955)★★, Tony (Columbia 1957)★★★, The Beat Of My Heart (Columbia 1957)★★★, Long Ago And Far Away (Columbia 1958)★★★, Basie Swings - Bennett Sings (Roulette 1958)★★, Blue Velvet (Columbia 1959)★★★, If I Ruled The World (Columbia 1959)★★★★, with Count Basie Tony Bennett In Person (Columbia 1959)★★★, Hometown, My Town (Columbia 1959)★★★, To My Wonderful One (Columbia 1960)★★, Tony Sings For Two (Columbia 1960)★★★, Alone Together (Columbia 1960)★★★, A String Of Harold Arlen (Columbia 1960)★★★, My Heart Sings (Columbia 1961)★★★, Bennett And Basie Strike Up The Band (Roulette 1962)★★, Mr. Broadway (Columbia 1962)★★★, I Left My Heart In San Francisco (Columbia 1962)★★★★, On The Glory Road (Columbia 1962)★★, Tony Bennett At Carnegie Hall (Columbia 1962)★★★, I Wanna Be Around (Columbia 1963)★★★★, This Is All I Ask (Columbia 1963)★★★, The Many Moods Of Tony (Columbia 1964)★★★, When Lights Are Low (Columbia 1964)★★★, Who Can I Turn To (Columbia 1964)★★★, If I Ruled The World - Songs For The Jet Set (Columbia 1965)★★★, The Movie Song Album (Columbia 1966)★★★, A Time For Love (Columbia 1966)★★★, The Oscar soundtrack (Columbia 1966)★★, Tony Makes It Happen! (Columbia 1967)★★, For Once In My Life (Columbia 1967)★★★, Snowfall/The Tony Bennett Christmas Album (Columbia 1968)★★★, I've Gotta Be Me (Columbia 1969)★★, Tony Sings The Great Hits Of Today! (Columbia 1970)★★, Tony Bennett's 'Something' (Columbia 1970)★★★, Love Story (Columbia 1971)★★★, Get Happy With The London Philharmonic Orchestra (Columbia 1971)★★, Summer Of '42 (Columbia 1972)★★, With Love (Columbia 1972)★★★, The Good Things In Life (MGM/Verve 1972)★★★, Rodgers And Hart Songbook (Columbia 1973)★★, with Bill Evans The Bennett Evans Album (Mobile Fidelity 1975)★★★★, with Bill Evans Together Again (DRG 1977)★★★, Chicago (DCC 1984)★★★, Anything Goes (1985)★★★, The Art Of Excellence (Columbia 1986)★★★, Bennett/Berlin (1987)★★★, Jazz (Columbia 1987)★★★, with Count Basie Some

Pair! (Pair 1989)★★★, *Astoria: Portrait Of The Artist* (Columbia 1990)★★★, *Perfectly Frank* (Columbia 1992)★★, *Steppin' Out* (Columbia 1993)★★★, *MTV Unplugged* (Columbia 1994)★★★★, *Here's To The Ladies* (Columbia 1995)★★★, *Tony Bennett On Holiday: A Tribute To Billie Holiday* (Columbia 1997)★★★.

●COMPILATIONS: *Tony's Greatest Hits* (Columbia 1958)★★★★, *More Tony's Greatest Hits* (Columbia 1960)★★★★, *Tony's Greatest Hits, Volume III* (Columbia 1965)★★★★, *A String Of Tony's Hits* (Columbia 1966)★★★★, *Tony Bennett's Greatest Hits, Volume IV* (Columbia 1969)★★★, *Tony Bennett's All-Time Greatest Hits* (1972)★★★, *The Very Best Of Tony Bennett - 20 Greatest Hits* (1977)★★★, *40 Years, The Artistry Of Tony Bennett* 4-CD box set (Legacy 1991)★★★★.

●VIDEOS: *Tony Bennett In Concert* (1987), *A Special Evening With Tony Bennett* (MIA 1995), *The Art Of The Singer* (SMV 1996).

●FURTHER READING: *What My Heart Has Seen*, Tony Bennett.

BENT FABRIC
b. Bent Fabricus Bjerre, 7 December 1924, Copenhagen, Denmark. A multi-talented Danish musician, known mainly for his piano work. Bent Fabric first formed a jazz band in the 40s when he was still in his teens. They made some of the first ever jazz recordings in Denmark. In 1950, having moved into the pop music of the day, he took over the Danish record company Metronome where he appointed himself A&R manager. Bent Fabric also had his own Saturday night television show, *Around A Piano*. In 1962 he sold a million copies worldwide of the tune 'Alley Cat' which he had written under the pseudonym Frank Bjorn. The subsequent album made the US top 20. He never followed the hit with any success other than the minor hit 'Chicken Feed', the following year, and returned to Denmark and his record company. In recent years he has become one of the most successful music publishers in Europe.

●ALBUMS: *Alley Cat* (1962)★★★.

BENTON, BROOK
b. Benjamin Franklin Peay, 19 September 1931, Camden, South Carolina, USA, d. 9 April 1988. A stylish, mellifluent singer, Benton's most ascendant period was the late 50s/early 60s. Although he began recording in 1953, Benton's first major hit came in 1959 on forging a songwriting partnership with Clyde Otis and Belford Hendricks. 'It's Just A Matter Of Time' reached the US Top 3 and introduced a remarkable string of successes, including 'So Many Ways' (1959), 'The Boll Weevil Song' (1961) and 'Hotel Happiness' (1962). Duets with Dinah Washington, 'Baby (You've Got What It Takes)', a million-seller, and 'A Rockin' Good Way (To Mess Around And Fall In Love)', topped the R&B listings in 1960. Benton's warm, resonant delivery continued to prove popular into the early 60s. A versatile vocalist, his releases encom-

passed standards, blues and spirituals, while his compositions were recorded by Nat 'King' Cole, Clyde McPhatter and Roy Hamilton. Brook remained signed to the Mercury label until 1964 before moving to RCA Records, then Reprise Records. Releases on these labels failed to recapture the artist's previous success, but by the end of the decade Benton rose to the challenge of younger acts with a series of excellent recordings for Atlantic Records' Cotillion subsidiary. His languid, atmospheric version of 'Rainy Night In Georgia' (1970) was an international hit and the most memorable product of an artistically fruitful period. Benton continued to record for a myriad of outlets during the 70s, including Brut (owned by the perfume company), Stax and MGM. Although his later work was less incisive, the artist remained one of music's top live attractions. He died in April 1988, aged 56, succumbing to pneumonia while weakened by spinal meningitis.

●ALBUMS: *Brook Benton At His Best* (Epic 1959)★★, *It's Just A Matter Of Time* (Mercury 1959)★★★, *Brook Benton* (Mercury 1959)★★★, *Endlessly* (1959)★★★, *So Many Ways I Love You* (Mercury 1960)★★★, *Two Of Us - With Dinah Washington* (1960)★★★★, *Songs I Love To Sing* (Mercury 1960)★★★, *The Boll Weevil Song (& Eleven Other Great Hits)* (Mercury 1961)★★★, *Sepia* (1961)★★, *If You Believe* (Mercury 1961)★★★, *Singing The Blues - Lie To Me* (Mercury 1962)★★★, *There Goes That Song Again* (Mercury 1962)★★★, *Best Ballads Of Broadway* (Mercury 1963)★★, *Born To Sing The Blues* (Mercury 1964)★★★, *Laura (What's He Got That I Ain't Got)* (1967)★★, *Do Your Own Thing* (1969)★★, *Brook Benton Today* (1970)★★, *Home Style* (1970)★★★, *The Gospel Truth* (1971)★★, *Something For Everyone* (1973)★★, *Sings A Love Story* (1975)★★, *Mr. Bartender* (1976)★★, *This Is Brook Benton* (1976)★★★, *Makin' Love Is Good For You* (1977)★★, *Ebony* (1978)★★, *Brook Benton Sings The Standards* (1984)★★★.

●COMPILATIONS: *Brook Benton's Golden Hits* (Mercury 1961)★★★, *Golden Hits Volume Two* (Mercury 1963)★★★, *Spotlight On Brook Benton* (1977)★★★, *The Incomparable Brook Benton* (1982)★★★, *Sixteen Golden Classics* (1986)★★★, *The Brook Benton Anthology* (Rhino 1986)★★★★, *His Greatest Hits* (1987)★★★, *40 Greatest Hits* (Mercury 1990)★★★★, *A Rainy Night In Georgia* (1990)★★★, *Greatest Hits* (Curb 1991)★★★.

BERNS, BERT
b. 1929, New York, USA, d. 30 December 1967, New York, USA. This exceptional songwriter and producer was responsible for some of urban, 'uptown' soul's most treasured moments. He began his career as a record salesman, before being drawn into a new role as copywriter and session pianist. Berns then began composing, often under such pseudonyms as 'Bert Russell' and 'Russell Byrd', and in 1960 formed a partnership with Phil Medley, the first of several similar working relationships. Their first major success came with 'Twist And Shout',

originally recorded by the Top Notes but later transformed into an anthem by the Isley Brothers and regularly performed as a show-stopper by the Beatles. Berns's work then appeared on several New York-based outlets, but his next important step came when he replaced the team of Leiber And Stoller as the Drifters' writer/producer. Now firmly in place at the Atlantic label, he was involved with several other artists including Ben E. King and Barbara Lewis, although his finest work was saved for Solomon Burke and such definitive releases as 'Goodbye Baby', 'Everybody Needs Somebody To Love' and 'The Price'. Berns also forged an exceptional partnership with Jerry Ragovoy which included stellar work for Garnet Mimms and Lorraine Ellison, plus 'Piece Of My Heart' which was recorded by Erma Franklin and later on by Janis Joplin. A spell in Britain resulted in sessions with Them and Lulu, Berns returned home to inaugurate the Bang and Shout labels. The former, pop-oriented company boasted a roster including the McCoys, the Strangeloves and former Them lead singer Van Morrison, while Shout was responsible for several excellent soul releases by Roy C, Bobby Harris, Erma Franklin and Freddy Scott. An astute individual, Berns once proffered a photograph of the Beatles to writer Nik Cohn. 'These boys have genius. They may be the ruin of us all.' He was referring to an endangered generation of hustling backroom talent, responsible for gathering songs, musicians and arrangements. He did not survive to see his prophecy fulfilled - Berns died from a heart attack in a New York hotel room on 30 December 1967.

BERNSTEIN, ELMER

b. 4 April 1922, New York, USA. An important and prolific arranger-conductor and composer of over 100 film scores. Bernstein was hailed as a 'musical genius' in the classical field at the age of 12. Despite being a talented actor, dancer and painter, he devoted himself to becoming a concert pianist and toured nationally while still in his teens. His education at New York University was interrupted when he joined the United States Air Force during World War II. Throughout his four years' service he composed and conducted music for propaganda programmes, and produced musical therapy projects for operationally fatigued personnel. After the war he attended the Juilliard School of Music and studied composition with the distinguished composer, Roger Sessions. Bernstein moved to Hollywood and started writing film scores in 1950, and two years later wrote the background music for *Sudden Fear*, a suspense thriller starring Joan Crawford and Jack Palance. Agent and producer Ingo Preminger, impressed by Bernstein's music, recommended him to his brother Otto for the latter's 1955 film project, *The Man With The Golden Arm*. A tense, controversial movie, its theme of drug addiction, accompanied by the Berstein modern jazz score, played by top instrumentalists such as Shelly Manne, Shorty Rogers, Pete Candoli and Milt Bernhart, caused distribution problems in some American states. The film won Oscar nominations for the star, Frank Sinatra, and for Bernstein's powerful, exciting music score. Bernstein made the US Top 20 with his record of the film's 'Main Title', and Billy May entered the UK Top 10 with his version. In 1956, Bernstein wrote the score for Cecil B. De Mille's epic *The Ten Commandments*. Thereafter, he provided the background music for an impressive array of movies with varied styles and subjects, including *Fear Strikes Out* (1957), *Sweet Smell Of Success* (1957), *God's Little Acre* (1958), *Some Came Running* (1958), *The Rat Race* (1960), *The Birdman Of Alcatraz* (1962), *The Great Escape* (1963), *A Walk In The Spring Rain* (1970), *The Shootist* (1976), *National Lampoon's Animal House* (1978), *An American Werewolf In London* (1981), *Ghostbusters* (1984), *¡Three Amigos!* (1986), *Amazing Grace And Chuck* (1987), *Slipstream* (1988), *DA* (1988), *My Left Foot* (1989), *The Grifters* (1990), *The Field* (1990), *Rambling Rose* (1991), *Oscar* (1991), *A Rage In Harlem* (1991), *The Babe* (1992), *The Cemetery Club*, *Mad Dogs And Glory*, *The Good Son*, and *Neil Simon's Lost In Yonkers* (1993). In 1991, Bernstein was the musical director and arranger of Bernard Herrman's original score for the 1962 classic, *Cape Fear*. He has received Academy Award nominations for his work on *The Magnificent Seven* (1960); *Summer And Smoke* (1961), the title song for *Walk On The Wild Side* (1961), with a lyric by Mack David; *To Kill A Mockingbird* (1962), said to be Bernstein's favourite of his own scores; the scores for *Return Of The Seven* (1966), and *Hawaii* (1966) (and a song from *Hawaii*, 'Wishing Doll', lyric by Mack David); the title song from *True Grit* (1969) lyric by Don Black; a song from *Gold* (1974), 'Wherever Love Takes Me', lyric by Don Black; and *Trading Places* (1983). Bernstein won an Oscar for his original music score for the 20s spoof, *Thoroughly Modern Millie* (1967). Coincidentally, Bernstein was the musical arranger and conductor at the Academy Awards ceremony when his award was announced, and had to relinquish the baton before going on stage to receive his Oscar. Bernstein also worked extensively in television: in 1958 he signed for US Revue Productions to provide background music for television dramas. One of his most notable scores was for *Staccato* (1959) (later retitled *Johnny Staccato*), a series about a jazz musician turned private eye, starring John Cassavetes. The shows were extremely well received in the UK, where Bernstein's recording of 'Staccato's Theme' rose to Number 4 in the singles chart in 1959, and re-entered the following year. On a somewhat larger scale instrumentally, an 81-piece symphony orchestra was contracted to record Berstein's score for Martin Scorsese's 1993 film *Age Of Innocence*.
●ALBUMS: *What Is Jazz?* (1958)★★★, *Desire Under The Elms* (1959)★★★, *God's Little Acre* (1959)★★★, *King Go Forth* (1959)★★★, *Some Came Running* (1960)★★★★, *Walk On the Wild Side* (1962)★★★★, *To Kill A Mocking Bird* (1962)★★★, *Movie And TV Themes* (1963)★★, *The Great Escape* (1963)★★★, *The Carpetbaggers* (1964)★★★, *Hallelujah Trail* (1965)★★, *The Sons Of Katie Elder* (1965)★★★, *The Ten Commandments* (1966)★★★, *A Man And His*

Movies (1992)★★★, Elmer Bernstein By Elmer Bernstein (Denon 1993)★★★, Bernard Herrmann Film Scores (Milan 1993)★★★.

BERNSTEIN, LEONARD

b. Louis Bernstein, 25 August 1918, Lawrence, Massachusetts, USA, d. 14 October 1990, New York, USA. Bernstein was a major and charismatic figure in modern classical music and the Broadway musical theatre. He was also a conductor, composer, pianist, author and lecturer. A son of immigrant Russian Jews, Bernstein started to play the piano at the age of 10. In his teens he showed an early interest in the theatre, organizing productions such as The Mikado, and an unconventional adaptation of Carmen, in which he played the title role. Determined to make a career in music, despite his father's insistence that 'music just keeps people awake at night', Bernstein eschewed the family beauty parlour business. He went on to study first with Walter Piston and Edward Burlingaunt Hill at Harvard, then with Fritz Reiner, Isabella Vengerova and Randall Thompson at the Curtis Institute in Philadephia, and finally with Serge Koussevitzky at the Berkshire Music Institute at Tanglewood. Bernstein had entered Harvard regarding himself as a pianist, but became influenced by Dimitri Mitropoulos and Aaron Copland. They inspired him to write his first symphony, Jeremiah. In 1943 he was chosen by Artur Rodzinski to work as his assistant at the New York Philharmonic. On 14 November 1943, Bernstein deputized at the last minute for the ailing Bruno Walter, and conducted the New York Philharmonic in a concert that was broadcast live on network radio. The next day, he appeared on the front pages of the newspapers and became a celebrity overnight. In the same year he wrote the music for Fancy Free, a ballet, choreographed by Jerome Robbins, about three young sailors on 24 hours' shore leave in New York City. It was so successful that they expanded it into a Broadway musical, with libretto and lyrics by Betty Comden and Adolph Green. Retitled On The Town and directed by George Abbott, it opened in 1944, with a youthful, vibrant score which included the memorable anthem 'New York, New York', 'Lonely Town', 'I Get Carried Away' and 'Lucky To Be Me'. The 1949 film version, starring Frank Sinatra and Gene Kelly, and directed by Kelly and Stanley Donen, is often regarded as innovatory in its use of real New York locations, although Bernstein's score was somewhat truncated in the transfer. In 1950 Bernstein wrote both music and lyrics for a musical version of J. M. Barrie's Peter Pan, starring Jean Arthur and Boris Karloff. His next Broadway project, Wonderful Town (1953), adapted from the play My Sister Eileen, by Joseph Fields and Jerome Chodorov, again had lyrics by Comden and Green, and starred Rosalind Russell, returning to Broadway after a distinguished career in Hollywood. Bernstein's spirited, contemporary score for which he won a Tony Award, included 'Conversation Piece', 'Conga', 'Swing', 'What A Waste', 'Ohio', 'A Quiet Girl' and 'A Little Bit Of Love'. The show had a successful revival in

London in 1986, with Maureen Lipman in the starring role. Candide (1956) was one of Bernstein's most controversial works. Lillian Hellman's adaptation of the Voltaire classic, sometimes termed a 'comic operetta', ran for only 73 performances on Broadway. Bernstein's score was much admired, however, and one of the most attractive numbers, 'Glitter And Be Gay', was sung with great effect by Barbara Cook, one year before her Broadway triumph in Meredith Willson's The Music Man. Candide has been revived continually since 1956, at least twice by producer Hal Prince. It was his greatly revised production, which included additional lyrics by Stephen Sondheim and John Latouche (original lyrics by Richard Wilbur), that ran for 740 performances on Broadway in 1974. The Scottish Opera's production, directed by Jonathan Miller in 1988, is said to have met with the composer's approval, and Bernstein conducted a concert version of the score at London's Barbican Theatre in 1989, which proved to be his last appearance in the UK.

Bernstein's greatest triumph in the popular field came with West Side Story in 1957. This brilliant musical adaptation of Shakespeare's Romeo And Juliet was set in the streets of New York, and highlighted the violence of the rival gangs, the Jets and the Sharks. With a book by Arthur Laurents, lyrics by Sondheim in his first Broadway production, and directed by Jerome Robbins, Bernstein created one of the most dynamic and exciting shows in the history of the musical theatre. The songs included 'Jet Song', 'Something's Coming', 'Maria', 'Tonight', 'America', 'Cool', 'I Feel Pretty', 'Somewhere' and 'Gee, Officer Krupke!'. In 1961, the film version gained 10 Academy Awards, including 'Best Picture'. Bernstein's music was not eligible for an award because it had not been written for the screen. In 1984, he conducted the complete score of West Side Story for the first time, in a recording for Deutsche Grammophon, with a cast of opera singers including Kiri Te Kanawa, José Carreras, Tatania Troyanos and Kurt Allman. Bernstein's last Broadway show, 1600 Pennsylvania Avenue (1976) was an anti-climax. A story about American presidents, with book and lyrics by Alan Jay Lerner, it closed after only seven performances. Among Bernstein's many other works was the score for the Marlon Brando film, On The Waterfront (1954), for which he was nominated for an Oscar; a jazz piece, 'Prelude, Fugue and Riffs', premiered on US television by Benny Goodman in 1955; and 'My Twelve Tone Melody' written for Irving Berlin's 100th birthday in 1988. In his celebrated classical career, which ran parallel to his work in the popular field, he was highly accomplished and prolific, composing three symphonies, a full length opera, and several choral works. He was musical director of the New York Philharmonic from 1958-69, conducted most of the world's premier orchestras, and recorded many of the major classical works. In the first week of October 1990, he announced his retirement from conducting because of ill health, and expressed an intention to concentrate on composing. He died one week later on 14 October 1990. In 1993, BBC Radio marked the 75th anniversary of his birth by devoting a complete day to programmes about his varied and distinguished career. A year later, *The Leonard Bernstein Revue: A Helluva Town*, played the Rainbow & Stars in New York, and, on a rather larger scale, in June of that year the New York Philharmonic presented their own celebration entitled *Remembering Lenny*. Further contrasting interpretations of Bernstein's work were heard in 1994 when television coverage of the football World Cup used his 1984 recording of 'America' as its theme, while the new pop band, Thunderballs, 'viciously mugged' the song (with permission from the Bernstein estate) under the title of '1994 America'.

●ALBUMS: *Bernstein Conducts Bernstein* (1984)★★★, *West Side Story* (1985)★★★★★, *Bernstein's America* (1988)★★★, various artists *Leonard Bernstein's New York* (Nonesuch 1996)★★★.

●FURTHER READING: *The Joy Of Music*, Leonard Bernstein. *Leonard Bernstein*, John Briggs. *Leonard Bernstein*, Peter Gadenwitz. *Leonard Bernstein*, Joan Peyser. *Leonard Bernstein*, Humphrey Burton. *Leonard Bernstein - A Life*, Meryle Secrest.

BERRY, CHUCK

b. Charles Edward Anderson Berry, 18 October 1926, St. Louis, Missouri, USA. A seminal figure in the evolution of rock 'n' roll, Chuck Berry's influence as songwriter and guitarist is incalculable. His cogent songs captured adolescent life, yet the artist was 30 years old when he commenced recording. Introduced to music as a child, Berry learned guitar while in his teens, but this period was blighted by a three-year spell in Algoa Reformatory following a conviction for armed robbery. On his release Berry undertook several blue-collar jobs while pursuing part-time spots in St. Louis bar bands. Inspired by Carl Hogan, guitarist in Louis Jordan's Timpani Five, and Charlie Christian, he continued to hone his craft and in 1951 purchased a tape recorder to capture ideas for compositions. The following year Berry joined Johnnie Johnson (piano) and Ebby Hardy (drums) in the houseband at the Cosmopolitan Club. Over the ensuing months the trio became a popular attraction, playing a mixture of R&B, country/hillbilly songs and standards, particularly those of Nat 'King' Cole, on whom Berry modelled his cool vocal style. The guitarist also fronted his own group, the Chuck Berry Combo, at the rival Crank Club, altering his name to spare his father's embarrassment at such worldly pursuits.

In 1955, during a chance visit to Chicago, Berry met bluesman Muddy Waters, who advised the young singer to approach the Chess label. Chuck's demo of 'Ida May', was sufficient to win a recording deal and the composition, retitled 'Maybellene', duly became his debut single. This ebullient performance was a runaway success, topping the R&B chart and reaching number 5 on the US pop listings. Its lustre was partially clouded by a conspiratorial publishing credit which required Berry to share the rights with Russ Fratto and disc jockey Alan Freed, in deference to his repeated airplay. This situation remained unresolved until 1986.

Berry enjoyed further US R&B hits with 'Thirty Days' and 'No Money Down', but it was his third recording session which proved highly productive, producing a stream of classics, 'Roll Over Beethoven', 'Too Much Monkey Business' and 'Brown-Eyed Handsome Man'. The artist's subsequent releases read like a lexicon of pop history - 'School Days' (a second R&B number 1), 'Rock And Roll Music' (all 1957), 'Sweet Little Sixteen', 'Reelin' And Rockin', 'Johnny B. Goode' (1958), 'Back In The USA', 'Let It Rock' (1960), 'Bye Bye Johnny' (1960) are but a handful of the peerless songs written and recorded during this prolific period. In common with contemporary artists, Berry drew from both country and R&B music, but his sharp, often piquant, lyrics, clarified by the singer's clear diction, introduced a new discipline to the genre. Such incomparable performances not only defined rock 'n' roll, they provided a crucial template for successive generations. Both the Beatles and Rolling Stones acknowledged their debt to Berry. The former recorded two of his compositions, taking one, 'Roll Over Beethoven', into the US charts, while the latter drew from his empirical catalogue on many occasions. This included 'Come On', their debut single, 'Little Queenie', 'You Can't Catch Me' and 'Around And Around', as well as non-Berry songs which nonetheless aped his approach. The Stones' readings of 'Route 66', 'Down The Road Apiece' and 'Confessin' The Blues' were indebted to their mentor's versions, while Keith Richards' rhythmic, propulsive guitar figures drew from Berry's style. Elsewhere, the Beach Boys rewrote 'Sweet Little Sixteen' as 'Surfin' USA' to attain their first million-seller while countless other groups scrambled to record his songs which somehow combined immediacy with longevity.

Between 1955 and 1960, Berry seemed unassailable. He enjoyed a run of 17 R&B Top 20 entries, appeared in the films *Go Johnny Go*, *Rock, Rock, Rock* and *Jazz On A Summer's Day*, the last of which documented the artist's performance at the 1958 *Newport Jazz Festival*, where he demonstrated the famed 'duckwalk' to a bemused audience. However, personal impropriety undermined Berry's personal and professional life when, on 28 October 1961, he was convicted under the Mann Act of 'transporting an under-age girl across state lines for immoral purposes'. Berry served 20 months in prison, emerging in October 1963 just as 'Memphis Tennessee', recorded in 1958, was providing him with his first UK Top 10 hit. He wrote several compositions during his incarceration, including 'Nadine', 'No Particular Place To Go', 'You Never Can Tell' and 'Promised Land', each of which reached the UK Top 30. Such chart success soon waned as the R&B bubble burst, and in 1966 Berry sought to regenerate his career by moving from Chess to Mercury Records. However, an ill-advised *Golden Hits* set merely featured re-recordings of old material, while attempts to secure a contemporary image on *Live At The Fillmore Auditorium* (recorded with the Steve Miller Band) and *Concerto In B. Goode* proved equally unsatisfactory. He returned to Chess Records in 1969 and immediately re-established his craft with the powerful 'Tulane'. *Back*

Home and *San Francisco Dues* were cohesive selections and in-concert appearances showed a renewed purpose. Indeed, a UK performance at the 1972 Manchester Arts Festival not only provided half of Berry's *London Sessions* album, but also his biggest-ever hit. 'My Ding-A-Ling', a mildly ribald *double entendre* first recorded by Dave Bartholomew, topped both the US and UK charts, a paradox in the light of his own far superior compositions which achieved lesser commercial plaudits. It was his last major hit, and despite several new recordings, including *Rockit*, a much-touted release on Atco, Berry became increasingly confined to the revival circuit. He gained an uncomfortable reputation as a hard, shrewd businessman and disinterested performer, backed by pick-up bands with which he refused to rehearse. Tales abound within the rock fraternity of Berry's refusal to tell the band which song he was about to launch into. Pauses and changes would come about by the musicians watching Berry closely for an often disguised signal. Berry has insisted for years upon pre-payment of his fee, usually in cash, and he will only perform an encore after a further negotiation for extra payment. Berry's continued legal entanglements resurfaced in 1979 when he was sentenced to a third term of imprisonment following a conviction for income tax evasion. Upon release he embarked on a punishing world tour, but the subsequent decade proved largely unproductive musically and no new recordings were undertaken. In 1986, the artist celebrated his 60th birthday with gala performances in St. Louis and New York. Keith Richards appeared at the former, although relations between the two men were strained, as evinced in the resultant documentary, *Hail! Hail! Rock 'N' Roll*, which provided an overview of Berry's career. Sadly, the 90s began with further controversy and allegations of indecent behaviour at the singer's Berry Park centre. Although these serve to undermine the individual, his stature as an essential figure in the evolution of popular music cannot be underestimated.

●ALBUMS: *After School Session* (Chess 1958)★★★★, *One Dozen Berrys* (Chess 1958)★★★★★, *Chuck Berry Is On Top* (Chess 1959)★★★★, *Rockin' At The Hops* (Chess 1960)★★★★, *New Juke Box Hits* (Chess 1961)★★★, *Chuck Berry Twist* (Chess 1962)★★★, *More Chuck Berry* (Chess 1963)★★★, *Chuck Berry On Stage* (Chess 1963)★★, *The Latest And Greatest* (Chess 1964)★★★, with Bo Diddley *Two Great Guitars* (Chess 1964)★★★, *St. Louis To Liverpool* (Chess 1964)★★★★★, *Chuck Berry In London* (Chess 1965)★★★, *Fresh Berrys* (Chess (1965)★★★, *Golden Hits* new recordings (Mercury 1967)★★, *Chuck Berry In Memphis* (Mercury 1967)★★★, *Live At The Fillmore Auditorium* (Mercury 1967)★★, *From St. Louis To Frisco* (Mercury 1968)★★, *Concerto In B. Goode* (Mercury 1969)★★, *Back Home* (Chess 1970)★★, *San Francisco Dues* (Chess 1971)★★, *The London Chuck Berry Sessions* (Chess 1972)★★, *Bio* (Chess 1973)★★, *Chuck Berry* Chess (1975)★★, *Live In Concert* (Magnum 1978)★★★, *Rockit* (Atco 1979)★★★,

Rock! Rock! Rock 'N' Roll! (1980)★★, *Hail, Hail Rock 'N' Roll* soundtrack (1987)★★, *On The Blues Side* (1993)★★.

●COMPILATIONS: *Chuck Berry's Greatest Hits* (Chess 1964)★★★★★, *Chuck Berry's Golden Decade* (Chess 1967)★★★★★, *Golden Decade, Volume 2* (Chess 1973)★★★★, *Golden Decade, Volume 3* (Chess 1974)★★★★, *Motorvatin'* (1977)★★★ *Spotlight On Chuck Berry* (1980)★★★, *Chess Masters* (1983)★★★, *Reelin' And Rockin' (Live)* (Aura 1984)★★, *Rock 'N' Roll Rarities* (Chess 1986)★★, *More Rock 'N' Roll Rarities* (Chess 1986)★★, *Chicago Golden Years* (1988)★★★, *Decade '55 To '65* (1988)★★★, *Chuck Berry Box Set* (Chess 1989)★★★★, *The Great Twenty-Eight* (Chess 1990)★★★★★, *Chess Box* CD box set (Chess 1990)★★★★, *Oh Yeah!* (Charly 1994)★★★, *Poet Of Rock 'N' Roll* 4-CD set (Charly 1995)★★★★★.

●VIDEOS: *The Legendary Chuck Berry* (1987), *Hail Hail Rock 'N' Roll* (1988), *Live At The Roxy* (1990), *Rock 'N' Roll Music* (1991).

●FURTHER READING: *Chuck Berry: Rock 'N' Roll Music*, Howard A. De Witt. *Chuck Berry: Mr Rock 'N' Roll*, Krista Reese. *Chuck Berry: The Autobiography*, Chuck Berry.

●FILMS: *Go Johnny Go* (1958), *American Hot Wax* (1976).

BERRY, DAVE

b. David Holgate Grundy, 6 February 1941, Woodhouse, Sheffield, Yorkshire, England. With his long-serving backing group, the Cruisers, Berry was signed to Danny Betesh's Manchester-based Kennedy Street Enterprises, and, after signing to Decca Records, found success with a version of Chuck Berry's 'Memphis Tennessee' in 1963. Covers of Arthur Crudup's 'My Baby Left Me' and Burt Bacharach's 'Baby It's You' were also minor hits, but the band's breakthrough came with Geoff Stevens's 'The Crying Game', which reached the UK Top 5 in August 1964. Berry's stage act and image was strong for the period and featured the singer dressed in black, erotically contorting his body and playing with the microphone as although it were a writhing snake. Bobby Goldsboro's chirpy 'Little Things' and Ray Davies's 'This Strange Effect' - the Netherlands' biggest-selling record ever - provided further chart success, which concluded with the much-covered B.J. Thomas opus, 'Mama', in 1966. In the late 70s, Berry was one of the few 60s stars held in any esteem in punk circles, epitomized by the Sex Pistols' revival of 'Don't Gimme No Lip Child', one of Berry's 1964 b-sides. The next decade saw a resumption of his recording career and he continues to tour abroad, appearing regularly on the cabaret/revivalist circuit.

●ALBUMS: *Dave Berry* (Decca 1964)★★★, *The Special Sound Of Dave Berry* (Decca 1966)★★★, *One Dozen Berrys* (Ace Of Clubs 1966)★★★, *Dave Berry '68* (Decca 1968)★★, *Hostage To The Beat* (Butt 1986)★★.

●COMPILATIONS: *Berry's Best* (1988)★★★.

BERRY, MIKE

b. Michael Bourne, 24 September 1942, Northampton, England. Buddy Holly-influenced singer whose Joe Meek-produced recording debut was a Hollyesque cover version of the Shirelles' 'Will You Still Love Me Tomorrow?' on Decca. He narrowly missed reaching the UK Top 20 in 1961 with his heartfelt 'Tribute To Buddy Holly' on HMV Records, a song supposedly given the seal of approval by Buddy at a seance! Berry was backed on this and other early recordings by the Outlaws, a noted group which included Ritchie Blackmore and Chas Hodges. Berry's biggest hit came in 1963 with the first of his two UK Top 10 hits, 'Don't You Think It's Time?', again written by spiritualist/songwriter Geoff Goddard and produced by Meek. Berry's records were picked up in the USA by Holly's old label Coral but did not reach the charts. In the 70s he became a television actor, appearing regularly in television programmes such as the top children's show, *Worzel Gummidge*. In 1980, after a 17-year gap, he returned to the UK Top 10 on Polydor with a MOR revival of 'The Sunshine Of Your Smile', produced by his old colleague Chas Hodges, now of Chas And Dave.
●ALBUMS: *Drifts Away* (1972)★★, *Rocks In My Head* (1976)★★, *I'm A Rocker* (1980)★, *Sunshine Of Your Smile* (1980)★★, *Memories* (1982)★★.

BERRY, RICHARD

b. 11 April 1935, Extension, Louisiana, USA, d. 23 January 1997. Berry was brought to Los Angeles as an infant, where he learned piano, playing along with the records of Joe Liggins And His Honeydrippers. In high school he formed a vocal group and began recording in 1953 under various names (Hollywood Blue Jays; Flairs; Crowns; Dreamers; Pharaohs) as well as doing solo sessions for Modern's Flair subsidiary. His most famous moments on record are his bass vocal contributions to the Robins' 'Riot In Cell Block No. 9' and as 'Henry', Etta James's boyfriend, on her early classic 'Roll With Me Henry (The Wallflower)'. He composed rock 'n' roll's famous standard 'Louie Louie', which he recorded in 1956 on Flip Records, but he had to wait seven years for its success with the Kingsmen's hit. The song spawned over 300 cover versions, including those by the Kinks, the Beach Boys and Paul Revere And The Raiders, none of which approached the Kingsmen's definitive recording. The sensual rhythm and theme of the song led to Berry's being accused of writing pornographic lyrics, but as they were virtually unintelligible, Berry took their secret to the grave with him. During the 60s and 70s, Berry, inspired by Bobby Bland and his wife Dorothy (herself a recording artist), became a soul singer. He recorded for myriad west coast labels (including his debut album for Johnny Otis's Blues Spectrum label) and continued performing into the 90s.
●ALBUMS: *Richard Berry And The Dreamers* (Crown 1963)★★★, with the Soul Searchers *Live At The Century Club* (Pam 60s)★★, with the Soul Searchers *Wild Berry* (Pam 60s)★★, *Great Rhythm & Blues Oldies* (1977)★★★, *Get Out Of The Car* (Ace 1982)★★★★, *Louie, Louie* (1986)★★★.

BEST, PETE

b. Liverpool, England, 1941. A founder member of the Beatles, the luckless drummer was fired from the group in August 1962, prior to their official recording debut. He then joined Lee Curtis And The All-Stars, a group which became the Pete Best All-Stars on its erstwhile leader's departure. The artist enjoyed a temporary notoriety in the wake of the Beatles' success and his group, now known as the Pete Best Four, secured a deal with Decca Records. A perfunctory reading of 'I'm Gonna Knock On Your Door' was the act's sole British release on Decca, but they pursued a career in the USA and Canada under various guises, including the Pete Best Combo and Best Of The Beatles. Singles appeared on a variety of often dubious outlets, the most opportunistic of which was their reading of 'This Boy', a song associated with Ringo Starr. Many of these recordings were collected on a subsequent album, *Best Of The Beatles*. This somewhat tawdry affair ended, against the odds, in 1966 with the excellent 'Carousel Of Love'. The group was then dissolved, but although former members Tony Waddington and Wayne Bickerton achieved success in the 70s with their work for the Rubettes and Flirtations, Best was unable to pursue a full-time career in music, although rumours always persist of a new band being formed. As a result of the Beatles' *Anthology* series, the first CD of which was issued in 1995, Best is set to earn as much as £8 million in royalties, as a number of early tracks feature him on drums: a highly satisfactory redundancy payment 30 years on.
●ALBUMS: *Best Of The Beatles* (1965)★, as the Pete Best Combo *Beyond The Beatles 1963-68* (Cherry Red 1996)★★, *Live At The Adelphi* (Cherry Red 1996)★★.
●FURTHER READING: *Beatle!*, Pete Best and Patrick Doncaster.

BETESH, DANNY

Manchester-based accountant Danny Betesh founded one of most respected agencies in British pop, Kennedy Street Enterprises. He had originally entered show business as a ballroom owner but switched to agency work, booking such local acts as Freddie And The Dreamers and Dave Berry. In 1963, Betesh promoted the first major tour for the Beatles, and the following year launched a Manchester invasion of America, which culminated with Freddie And The Dreamers, Herman's Hermits and Wayne Fontana And The Mindbenders holding the Top 3 positions in the US singles chart. Since that golden era, Kennedy Street has continued to flourish as an agency and management organization. Among the acts they have represented include 10cc, Sad Cafe, Barclay James Harvest, Tony Christie and Godley And Creme. The number of tours they have promoted has been countless and includes celebrated appearances by such stars as Van Morrison, Bruce Springsteen and Morrissey.

BEYOND THE FRINGE

Born in 1960 as a late-night 'fringe entertainment' at the Edinburgh Festival, this four-man satirical revue moved to the tiny Fortune Theatre in London on 10 May 1961. It was written and performed by the cast, consisting of four Oxbridge university graduates: Alan Bennett, Peter Cook, Jonathan Miller and Dudley Moore. Unlike the smart, sophisticated revues popular in the 50s, such as *The Lyric Revue*, *Airs On A Shoestring* and *Look Who's Here!*, *Beyond The Fringe* was, in the words of the distinguished critic Bernard Levin, 'so brilliant, adult, hard-boiled, accurate, merciless, witty, unexpected, alive, exhilarating, cleansing, right, true, and good that my first conscious thought as I stumbled, weak and sick with laughter, up the stairs at the end was one of gratitude.' Moore wrote the music for the 'series of unconnected skits' which included 'The Bollard', 'The Sadder And Wiser Beaver' (based on the press baron Lord Beaverbrook), 'Take A Pew', 'Aftermyth Of War', 'Sitting On A Bench' (a precursor to Cook and Moore's notorious Derek and Clive characters), 'And The Same To You' (shades of David Lean's film, *The Bridge Over The River Kwai*), and 'The End Of The World', (a fashionably anti-nuclear piece). The production was highly acclaimed by public and press alike, and won the London *Evening Standard* award for best musical in 1961. Bennett, Cook, Miller and Moore left early in 1962, but the show continued with a second cast, eventually closing in March 1964 after 1189 performances. The original quartet of performers went to Cape Town, Toronto, Washington and Boston before the Broadway premiere of *Beyond The Fringe* at the John Golden Theatre on 27 October 1962. This edition, which had been revised for US consumption, was widely applauded and the cast received a special Tony Award for 'their brilliance which has shattered all the old concepts of comedy'. Miller stayed with the show for about a year and the other three withdrew soon afterwards. In addition to the New York run of 673 performances, another company toured the USA for seven months. Alan Bennett and Jonathan Miller, the 'serious pair', have devoted much of their time since to the theatre, Bennett as one of the UK's most renowned playwrights, and Miller as a notable director for a variety of productions, including opera. For more than a decade, Peter Cook and Dudley Moore were an immensely popular film and television comedy team, particularly in the series, *Not Only . . . But Also*, before Moore combined a lucrative acting career in Hollywood with occasional flashes of brilliance as an accomplished jazz pianist. Cook continued to be associated with satire through his involvement in the notorious *Private Eye* magazine, as well as being one of Britain's most familiar character actors and chat-show personalities, until his death in 1995. The Original Cast 'live' album of *Beyond The Fringe*, which charted in the UK and the USA, was re-released in 1993 on Broadway Angel.

BIENSTOCK, FREDDY

b. 24 April 1923, Vienna, Austria. The music publishing branch of popular music is often criticized by the very artists the publishers represent. This is not the case for Freddy Bienstock, who has maintained respect and cred-

ibility for over five decades in shark-infested waters. A young Ray Davies, who signed with Bienstock's Carlin Music at the age of 19, stated: 'I went to Carlin because I wanted to get paid for what I was doing. Music publishers when I started were all Denmark Street.'

Bienstock started out as a young man working at the legendary Brill Building in the stockroom at Chappell Music in New York, where his cousins Jean and Julian Aberbach were executives. They eventually left to form their own music company and Freddy joined them a few years later. His first manna from heaven came in 1955 when he was introduced to Colonel Tom Parker. Over the next few years Bienstock was instrumental in presenting new songs to Elvis Presley via the Hill and Range publishing company. This resulted in classics such as 'Blue Suede Shoes' (Carl Perkins) and 'Jailhouse Rock' (Leiber And Stoller). Bienstock moved to London in 1957 to set up Belinda Music to handle the Aberbachs' catalogue. Freddy eventually bought the list and founded Carlin Music in 1966. He originally wanted to name the company after his daughter Caroline but the Pirate Radio ship owner Ronan O'Rahilly had already registered the name, and so Bienstock removed the letters 'o' and 'e' to evade the Companies House legislation. One of his first signings was the Kinks, and it is to Bienstock's credit that he saw the future potential in the songwriting talent of Raymond Douglas Davies. Bienstock also acquired the Motown, Burt Bacharach and Gamble And Huff catalogues, in addition to many classic songs from the beat group era from Cliff Richard, the Shadows and the Animals. Great writers like Phil Spector, Ellie Greenwich, Jeff Barry, Doc Pomus and Mort Shuman also became part of the Carlin list. In 1980 he added over 100,000 American popular songs with the acquisition of the Redwood catalogue. This contained evergreens like 'As Time Goes By', 'Sweet Georgia Brown', 'Button Up Your Overcoat' and the Al Jolson perennial, 'My Mammy'. Bienstock was able to purchase Chappells in 1984 on the condition that he agreed to suspend the Carlin operation. Outside purchasers were also taking an interest in Bienstock's midas touch, and in 1987 his board agreed to sell Chappells to Warner Brothers Records at a hug profit. Bienstock, however, shrewdly retained an outstanding collection with the Carlin catalogue and the company had already established a firm foundation of classic rock 'n' roll, 60s pop, standards of American popular song and 70s progressive rock. Carlin's chief executive David Japp has consolidated this base by building on music from Europe, and contemporary pop and film music. Bienstock is publisher to what is probably the finest independent pop music catalogue in the world and remains a peerless entrepreneur in popular music history. Ray Davies stated in 1977: 'I dealt with a man called Freddy Bienstock. I think he's got a good ear, he's from Vienna.'

BIENSTOCK, JOHNNY

b. 1 March 1927, Vienna, Austria. The younger brother of Freddie Bienstock has also established himself in the music business. Although his elder sibling has become a music business legend, Johnny has been an instigator, creator and an outstanding administrator, as well as a music publisher. He became the first employee of his cousins Julian and Jean Aberbach's company Biltmore Music in 1945, after leaving the US army. In 1958 he was asked to set up Big Top Records, and oversaw four golden years with a string of hits, including those by Sammy Turner, Johnny And The Hurricanes and Del Shannon. After refusing to accept a gift of a new house from one of his cousins (which would have effectively tied him to them for life), he was sacked in 1966. On the same day, he received a call from Jerry Wexler at Atlantic Records who invited him to the company as his executive assistant. Bienstock was with Atlantic through its golden era, and later managed their subsidiary Atco Records. During his time there (1966-72) he worked closely with Aretha Franklin, Tom Dowd, Iron Butterfly, Bobby Darin and Buffalo Springfield. It was Bienstock who suggested that the *Woodstock* album should be a triple record set, much to the astonishment of his colleagues. In addition to publishing some of J.J. Cales's work, Bienstock managed RSO Records from their inception in 1972 and dealt with Cream, Eric Clapton, the Bee Gees and Derek And The Dominos. He rejoined his brother at the Carlin Group offices at the Brill Building in 1983 and administers the E.B. Marks publishing company; he is also involved with the Carlin Music Recorded Library. In 1993 he was responsible for the promotion and eventual release of *Back Out Of Hell,* evidence that even in his sixth decade in the music business, Bienstock still had the midas touch.

BIG BROTHER AND THE HOLDING COMPANY

Formed in September 1965, this pivotal San Franciscan rock group evolved out of 'jam' sessions held in the basement of a communal house. The original line-up featured Sam Andrew (b. 18 December 1941, Taft, California, USA; guitar/vocals), Peter Albin (b. 6 June 1944, San Francisco, California, USA; bass/vocals), Dave Eskerson (guitar) and Chuck Joncs (drums), but within months the latter pair had been replaced, respectively, by James Gurley (b. c.1940, Detroit, Michigan, USA) and David Getz (b. 1938, Brooklyn, New York, USA). The restructured quartet initially eschewed formal compositions, preferring a free-form improvisation centred on Gurley's mesmeric finger-picking style, but a degree of discipline gradually evolved. The addition of Texas singer Janis Joplin in June 1966 emphasized this newfound direction, and her powerful, blues-soaked delivery provided the perfect foil to the unit's instrumental power. The group rapidly became one of the Bay Area's leading attractions, but naïvely struck an immoderate recording deal with the Chicago-based Mainstream label. Although marred by poor production, *Big Brother And The Holding Company* nonetheless contains several excellent performances, notably 'Bye Bye Baby' and 'Down On Me'. The quintet rose to national prominence in 1967 following a sensational appearance at the Monterey Pop Festival. Joplin's charismatic performance engendered a prestigious management deal with Albert Grossman, who in turn secured their release from all contractual obligations. Big Brother then switched outlets to Columbia Records, for which they completed *Cheap Thrills* (1968). This exciting album topped the US charts, but despite the inclusion of in-concert favourites 'Piece Of My Heart' and 'Ball And Chain', the recording was fraught with difficulty. Joplin came under increased pressure to opt for a solo career as critics denigrated the musicians' abilities. The group broke up in November 1968 and while Sam Andrew joined the singer in her next venture, Albin and Getz joined Country Joe And The Fish. The following year the latter duo reclaimed the Big Brother name and with the collapse of an interim line-up, re-established the unit with ex-colleagues Andrew and Gurley. Several newcomers, including Nick Gravenites (vocals), Kathi McDonald (vocals), David Schallock (guitar) and Mike Finnegan (piano) augmented the quartet on an informal basis, but despite moments of inspiration, neither *Be A Brother* (1970) nor *How Hard It Is* (1971) recaptured former glories. The group was disbanded in 1972, but reconvened six years later at the one-off Tribal Stomp reunion. In 1987 singer Michelle Bastian joined Getz, Gurley, Andrew and Albin in a fully reconstituted Big Brother line-up still hoping to assert an independent identity.

●ALBUMS: *Big Brother And The Holding Company* (Mainstream 1967)★★★, *Cheap Thrills* (Columbia 1968)★★★★, *Be A Brother* (Columbia 1970)★★, *How Hard It Is* (Columbia 1971)★, *Big Brother And The Holding Company Live* (Rhino 1985)★★.
●COMPILATIONS: *Cheaper Thrills* (1984)★★, *Joseph's Coat* (1986)★★.
●VIDEOS: *Comin' Home* (BMG 1992), *Live In Studio: San Francisco '67* (Castle Music Pictures 1992).
●FILMS: *American Pop* (1981).

BIG THREE

Formed in Liverpool 1961 as an offshoot from Cass And The Cassanovas, the Big Three comprised Johnny Gustafson (vocals/bass), Johnny Hutchinson (vocals/drums) and Adrian Barber (guitar). During 1962, Barber relocated to Germany and was replaced by Brian Griffiths, who made his debut at the Star Club, Hamburg. A mini-legend in their native Liverpool, the Big Three were revered as one of the loudest, most aggressive and visually appealing acts on the circuit. After signing with the Beatles' manager Brian Epstein, success seemed assured, but their characteristic unruliness proved to be their undoing. They achieved only two minor hits, a cover version of Ritchie Barrett's R&B standard 'Some Other Guy', and Mitch Murray's 'By The Way'. Although a live EP *At The Cavern* gave some indication of their power, their vinyl excursions failed to reveal their true potential. An acrimonious split with Epstein only months into their relationship effectively wrecked their chances. By November 1963, Griffiths and Gustafson found alternative employment with the Seniors; Hutchinson recruited Paddy Chambers and Faron (of the Flamingos) as replacements. Less than a year later, the Big Three disbanded. Gustafson later joined the Merseybeats, formed John And Johnny, then Quatermass, and appeared again in the 70s as the bassist in Roxy Music.

●ALBUMS: *Resurrection* (Polydor 1973)★★, *Cavern Stomp* (1982)★★★, *I Feel Like Steppin' Out* (1986)★★★.

BILK, ACKER

b. Bernard Stanley Bilk, 28 January 1929, Pensford, Somerset, England. A self-taught clarinettist, Bilk made his first public appearance in 1947 while on National Service in Egypt. On his return to the UK, he played as a semi-professional around the Bristol area, before getting his big break with the Ken Colyer band in 1954. Four years later, under the name 'Mr' Acker Bilk, he enjoyed his first UK Top 10 hit with 'Summer Set'. Backed by the Paramount Jazz Band, and promoted by his Bilk Marketing Board, he was at the forefront of the British traditional jazz boom of the early 60s. With their distinctive uniform of bowler hats and striped waistcoats, Bilk and company enjoyed a number of jazzy UK hits in the 60s, including 'White Cliffs Of Dover', 'Buona Sera', 'That's My Home', 'Stars And Stripes Forever', 'Frankie And Johnny', 'Gotta See Baby Tonight' and 'A Taste Of Honey'. However, it was with the Leon Young String Chorale that Bilk achieved his most remarkable hit. 'Stranger On The Shore' was a US number 1 in May 1962, and peaked at number 2 in the UK, staying for a record-breaking 55 weeks in the best-sellers. Although the beat boom all but ended the careers of many traditional jazzmen, Bilk has continued to enjoy a successful career in cabaret and concerts, and returned to the Top 10 in 1976, again with a string backing, with 'Aria'. He continues to tour regularly alongside contemporaries such as Kenny Ball and Chris Barber. The trio had a number 1 album, *The Best Of Ball, Barber And Bilk*, in 1962. Bilk remains a major figure in traditional jazz, and more than 30 years after 'Stranger On The Shore' gained an Ivor Novello Award for 'Most Performed Work', in 1995 it featured in a UK television commercial for Volkswagen cars.

●ALBUMS: *Mr. Acker Requests* (Pye Nixa 1958)★★★, *Mr. Acker Marches On* (1958)★★★, *Mr. Acker Bilk Sings* (1959)★★, *Mr. Acker Bilk Requests (Part One)* (1959)★★★, *Mr. Acker Bilk Requests (Part Two)* (1959)★★★, *The Noble Art Of Mr. Acker Bilk* (1959)★★★, *Seven Ages Of Acker* (1960)★★★, *Mr. Acker Bilk's Omnibus* (Pye 1960)★★★, *Acker* (Columbia EMI 1960)★★★, *A Golden Treasury Of Bilk* (Columbia EMI 1961)★★★★, *Mr. Acker Bilk's Lansdowne Folio* (1961)★★★, *Stranger On The Shore* (Columbia EMI 1961)★★★★, *Above The Stars And Other Romantic Fancies* (1962)★★★, *A Taste Of Honey* (Columbia EMI 1963)★★★, *Great Themes From Great European Movies* (1965)★★, *Acker In Paris* (1966)★★, *Blue Acker* (1968)★★★★, *Some Of My Favourite Things* (PRT 1973)★★★, *That's My Desire* (1974)★★★, *Serenade* (1975)★★★, *The One For Me*

(PRT 1976)★★★, *Invitation* (PRT 1977)★★★, *Meanwhile* (1977)★★★, *Sheer Magic* (Warwick 1977)★★★, *Extremely Live In Studio 1* (1978)★★, *Free* (1978)★★★, *When The Lights Are Low* (1978)★★★, with Max Bygraves *Twogether* (1980)★★, *Unissued Acker* (1980)★★★, *Made In Hungary* (PRT 1980)★★★, *The Moment I'm With You* (1980)★★★, *Mama Told Me So* (PRT 1980)★★★, *The Moment I'm With You* (PRT 1981)★★★, *Relaxin'* (PRT 1981)★★★, *Wereldsuccessen* (Philips 1982)★★★, *I Think The Best Thing About This Record Is The Music* (Bell 1982)★★, *Acker Bilk In Holland* (Timeless 1985)★★, *Nature Boy* (PRT 1985)★★★, *Acker's Choice* (Teldec 1985)★★★, *John, Paul And Acker* (1986)★★, *Love Songs My Way* (Topline 1987)★★, reissued as *Acker Bilk Plays Lennon And McCartney* (GNP 1988)★★, *On Stage* (Start 1988)★★★, with Ken Colyer *It Looks* (Stomp Off 1988)★★★, *That's My Home* (1988)★★★, *The Love Album* (Pickwick 1989)★★★, with Chris Barber, Kenny Ball *Trad Days 1959/60* (1990)★★★★, *Imagine* (Pulse 1991)★★, *Blaze Away* (Timeless 1990)★★★, *The Ultimate!* (1991)★★★, *Heartbeats* (Pickwick 1991)★★★, with Humphrey Lyttelton *At Sundown* (Calligraph 1992)★★★★, with Lyttelton *Three In The Morning* (Calligraph 1995)★★★★, *Oscar Winners* (Carlton 1995)★★.

●COMPILATIONS: *The Best Of Ball, Barber And Bilk* (Pye 1962)★★★★, *Golden Hour Of Acker Bilk* (Knight 1974)★★★★, *Very Best Of Acker Bilk* (1978)★★★★, *Evergreen* (Warwick 1978)★★★, *The Acker Bilk Saga* (Polydor 1979)★★★, *Sheer Magic* (1979)★★★, *The Best Of Acker Bilk, Volume Two* (1979)★★★, *Mellow Music* (1980)★★★, *Spotlight On Acker Bilk* (PRT 1980)★★★, *100 Minutes Of Bilk* (PRT 1982)★★★, *Spotlight On Acker Bilk Vol. 2* (PRT 1982)★★★, *I'm In The Mood For Love* (Philips 1983)★★★, *Finest Moments* (Castle 1986)★★★, *Magic Clarinet Of Acker Bilk* (K-Tel 1986)★★★, *16 Golden Memories* (Spectrum 1988)★★★, *Best Of Acker Bilk His Clarinet And Strings* (PRT 1988)★★★, *Hits Blues And Classics* (Kaz 1988)★★★, *The Collection* (Castle 1989)★★★, *Images* (Knight 1989)★★★, *After Midnight* (Pickwick 1990)★★★, *In A Mellow Mood* (Castle 1992)★★★, *Reflections* (Spectrum 1993)★★★, *Acker Bilk Songbook* (Tring 1993)★★★, *Bridge Over Troubled Water* (Spectrum 1995)★★.

●FURTHER READING: *The Book Of Bilk*, P. Leslie and P. Gwynn-Jones.

●FILMS: *It's Trad, Dad!* (1962), *It's All Over Town* (1964).

BILLINGS, VIC

Vic Billings was an unusual manager in the history of British pop, working for over two decades and yet resisting the temptation to sign a money-spinning group, even at the zenith of the beat boom. From 1954-60, he worked as a theatre house manager before branching out into the pop business. One of his first clients was Michael Cox, who charted with a cover of 'Angela Jones'. Another signing was Paul Raven who recorded a version of 'Tower Of Strength', which lost out to Frankie Vaughan's chart-topping version. Raven subsequently moved to Germany and re-emerged a decade later as Gary Glitter. In 1962, Billings joined the ill-fated management/record company Audio Enterprises, and following its rapid demise inherited the promising Eden Kane. Under Billings' aegis, Kane secured a new contract with Fontana Records, toured regularly and eventually emigrated to Australia. Billings subsequently took on the management of Kane's younger brother, Robin Sarstedt, in 1976. Billings's style of management was based firmly on the precepts of the 50s and contrasted markedly with the hard-sell, flamboyant approach of his contemporaries. Much of the drama and double-dealing that seemed part and parcel of pop group management completely bypassed Billings, who was free to develop his solo artists' long-term careers without interference from potential rivals. His association with Dusty Springfield is still regarded by many as one of the best manager/artist relationships of the 60s: he assumed her management immediately after the breakup of the Springfields and they stayed together until 1968, when she moved to the USA. Some felt that Billings was over-cautious in his handling of her career but it was this very solicitude that sustained the partnership for so long. The consistent chart career of Dusty was some compensation for the puzzling failure of his younger protégée, Kiki Dee, who maintained a career in cabaret but failed to chart during the 60s. Billings eventually moved into a corporate management company, but was later called upon by manager Meg Van Kuyk as adviser to Hazell Dean.

BIRDS

Formed in West Drayton, Middlesex, England, in 1964. Ali McKenzie (vocals), Tony Munroe (guitar/vocals), Ron Wood (guitar/vocals), Kim Gardner (bass/vocals) and Pete McDaniels (drums) were originally known as the Thunderbirds, but truncated their name to avoid confusion with Chris Farlowe's backing group. One of the era's most powerful R&B groups, the Birds' legacy is confined to a mere four singles, but the energy displayed on 'Leaving Here' and 'No Good Without You Baby' (both 1965), show their reputation is deserved. However, the group is better known for a scurrilous publicity stunt, wherein seven writs were served on the American Byrds, demanding they change their name and claiming loss of income. The US group naturally ignored the charges and the UK unit was latterly known as Bird's Birds. They broke up in October 1966 when Gardner joined Creation. Wood was also a member of the latter in-between his two spells with the Jeff Beck Group. Gardner achieved temporary fame in the 70s with Ashton, Gardner And Dyke and Badger, but it was Wood who enjoyed the greater profile, first with the Faces, and latterly, the Rolling Stones.
●ALBUMS: *These Birds Are Dangerous* (1965)★★.

BLACK CAT BONES

The original line-up of this London-based blues band included Paul Kossoff (guitar), Stuart Brooks (bass) and Simon Kirke (drums). Producer Mike Vernon invited the group to back pianist Champion Jack Dupree on his 1968 release, *When You Feel The Feeling*, and attendant live appearances, but momentum faltered when Kossoff and Kirke left to form Free. A restructured Black Cat Bones - Brian Short (vocals), Derek Brooks (guitar), Rod Price (guitar/vocals) and Phil Lenoir (drums) - joined Stuart Brooks for *Barbed Wire Sandwich*, but the revised unit failed to capture the fire of its predecessor.
●ALBUMS: *Barbed Wire Sandwich* (Nova 1970)★★★.

BLACK, BILL

b. William Patton Black, 17 September 1926, Memphis, Tennessee, USA, d. 21 October 1965, Memphis, Tennessee, USA. Black was the bass-playing half of the Scotty And Bill team that backed Elvis Presley on his earliest live performances. After leaving Presley, Black launched the successful Bill Black Combo. Initially playing an acoustic stand-up bass, Black was hired as a session musician by Sun Records, where he met Presley in 1954. He played on the earliest Sun tracks, including 'That's All Right'. Black toured with Presley alongside guitarist Scotty Moore; later, drummer D.J. Fontana was added to the group. Black and Moore left Presley in 1957, owing to what they felt was unfair payment. The Bill Black Combo was formed in 1959, with Black (electric bass guitar), Reggie Young (guitar), Martin Wills (saxophone), Carl McAvoy (piano) and Jerry Arnold (drums). Signed to Hi Records in Memphis, the group favoured an instrumental R&B-based sound tempered with jazz. Their first chart success was 'Smokie Part 2' in late 1959 but it was the follow-up, 'White Silver Sands' that gave the group its biggest US hit, reaching number 9, in 1960 Black retired from touring in 1962, and the group continued performing under the same name without him, with Bob Tucker playing bass. The group also backed other artists, including Gene Simmons on the 1964 number 11 hit 'Haunted House'. Saxophonist Ace Cannon was a member of the group for some time. The group continued playing even after Black died of a brain tumour in October 1965. The Bill Black Combo achieved a total of 19 US chart singles and was still working under the leadership of Tucker in the late 80s.
●ALBUMS: *Smokie* (Hi 1960)★★★, *Saxy Jazz* (Hi 1960)★★★, *Solid And Raunchy* (Hi 1960)★★★★, *That Wonderful Feeling* (Hi 1961)★★★, *Movin'* (Hi 1961)★★★, *Bill Black's Record Hop* (Hi 196)★★★, *Let's Twist Her* (Hi 1962)★★★★, *Untouchable Sound Of Bill Black* (Hi 1963)★★★, *Bill Black Plays The Blues* (Hi 1964)★★★, *Bill Black Plays Tunes By Chuck Berry* (Hi 1964)★★, *Bill Black's Combo Goes Big Band* (Hi 1964)★★, *More Solid And Raunchy* (Hi 1965)★★, *All Timers* (1966)★★, *Black Lace* (1967)★★, *King Of The Road* (1967)★★, *The Beat Goes On* (1968)★★, *Turn On Your Lovelight* (London 1969)★★, *Solid And Raunchy The 3rd* (Hi 1969)★★, *Soulin' The Blues* (London 1969)★★.
●COMPILATIONS: *Greatest Hits* (Hi/London 1963)★★★.

BLACK, CILLA

b. Priscilla White, 27 May 1943, Liverpool, England. While working as a part-time cloakroom attendant at Liverpool's Cavern club, in 1963, Priscilla appeared as guest singer with various groups, and was brought to the attention of Brian Epstein. The Beatles' manager changed her name and during the next few years ably exploited her girl-next-door appeal. Her first single, under the auspices of producer George Martin, was a brassy powerhouse reworking of the Beatles' unreleased 'Love Of The Loved', which reached the UK Top 40 in late 1963. A change of style with Burt Bacharach's 'Anyone Who Had A Heart' saw Black emerge as a ballad singer of immense power and distinction. 'You're My World', a translation of an Italian lyric, was another brilliantly orchestrated, impassioned ballad, which, like its predecessor, dominated the UK number 1 position in 1964. In what was arguably the most competitive year in British pop history, Black was outselling all her Merseyside rivals except the Beatles. For her fourth single, Paul McCartney presented 'It's For You', a fascinating jazz waltz ballad which seemed a certain number 1, but stalled at number 8. By the end of 1964, she was one of the most successful female singers of her era and continued to release cover versions of superb quality, including the Righteous Brothers' 'You've Lost That Lovin' Feelin'' and an excellent reading of Randy Newman's 'I've Been Wrong Before'. A consummate rocker and unchallenged mistress of the neurotic ballad genre, Black was unassailable at her pop peak'. For most of 1965, she ceased recording and worked on her only film, *Work Is A Four Letter Word*, but returned strongly the following year with 'Love's Just A Broken Heart' and 'Alfie'.

The death of Brian Epstein in 1967 and a relative lull in chart success might have blighted the prospects of a lesser performer, but Black was already moving into television work, aided by her manager/husband Bobby Willis. Her highly-rated television series was boosted by the hit title theme 'Step Inside Love', donated by Paul McCartney. Throughout the late 60s, she continued to register Top 10 hits, including the stoical 'Surround Yourself With Sorrow', the oddly paced wish-fulfilling 'Conversations' and the upbeat 'Something Tells Me'. Like many of her contemporaries, Black wound down her recording career in the 70s and concentrated on live work and television commitments. While old rivals such as Lulu, Sandie Shaw and Dusty Springfield were courted by the new rock elite, Black required no such patronage and entered the 90s as one of the highest paid family entertainers in the British music business, with two major UK television shows, *Blind Date* and *Surprise Surprise*. In 1993, she celebrated 30 years in show business with an album, full-length video, book, and television special, all entitled *Through The Years*. Two years later she received a BAFTA award on behalf of *Blind Date*, in recognition of her contribution to this 'significant and popular programme'. Her future as an entertainer is guaranteed: as long as there is television, there will always be a 'Misssa Cilla Blaaaaaack'.

●ALBUMS: *Cilla* (Parlophone 1965)★★★, *Cilla Sings A Rainbow* (Parlophone 1966)★★★, *Sher-oo* (Parlophone 1968)★★★, *Surround Yourself With Cilla* (Parlophone 1969)★★, *Sweet Inspiration* (Parlophone 1970)★★, *Images* (Parlophone 1971)★★, *Day By Day With Cilla* (Parlophone 1973)★★, *In My Life* (EMI 1974)★★★, *It Makes Me Feel Good* (EMI 1976)★★, *Modern Priscilla* (EMI 1978)★★★, *Surprisingly Cilla* (1985)★★, *Love Songs* (1987)★★, *Through The Years* (Columbia 1993)★★★.

●COMPILATIONS: *You're My World* (Starline 1970)★★★, *Especially For You* (K-Tel 1980)★★★, *25th Anniversary Album* (1988)★★★, *Love, Cilla* (1993)★★★.

●VIDEOS: *Throughout The Years* (1993).

●FILMS: *Ferry Cross The Mersey* (1964).

BLACK, DON

b. 21 June 1938, Hackney, London, England. A prolific lyricist for film songs, stage musicals and Tin Pan Alley. One of five children, Black worked part-time as an usher at the London Palladium before getting a job as an office boy and sometime journalist with the *New Musical Express* in the early 50s. Then, after a brief sojourn as a stand-up comic in the dying days of the music-halls, he gravitated towards London's Denmark Street, the centre of UK music publishing, where he worked as a song plugger for firms owned by Dave Toff and Joe 'Mr. Piano' Henderson. He met Matt Monro in 1960, shortly before the singer made his breakthrough with Cyril Ornadel and Norman Newell's 'Portrait Of My Love'. Encouraged by Monro, Black began to develop his talent for lyric writing. Together with another popular vocalist, Al Saxon, Black wrote 'April Fool', which Monro included on his *Love Is The Same Anywhere*. In 1964 Black collaborated with the German composer, Udo Jurgens, and together they turned Jurgens' Eurovision Song Contest entry, 'Warum Nur Warum', into 'Walk Away', which became a UK Top 5 hit for Monro. The singer also charted with 'For Mama', which Black wrote with Charles Aznavour. The song was also popular for Connie Francis and Jerry Vale in the USA. In 1965 Black made his break into films with the lyric of the title song for *Thunderball*, the fourth James Bond movie. The song was popularized by Tom Jones, and it marked the beginning of a fruitful collaboration with composer John Barry. As well as providing Bond with two more themes, 'Diamonds Are Forever' (1971, Shirley Bassey, and for which they received an Ivor Novello Award) and 'The Man With The Golden Gun' (1974, Lulu), the songwriters received a second 'Ivor' and an Academy Award for their title song to *Born Free* in 1966. Black has been nominated on four other occasions: for 'True Grit' (with Elmer Bernstein, 1969), 'Ben' (Walter Scharf, a US number 1 for Michael Jackson in 1972, and a UK hit for Marti Webb in 1985), 'Wherever Love Takes Me', from *Gold* (Bernstein, 1972), and 'Come To Me', from *The Pink Panther Strikes Again* (Henry Mancini, 1976). It has been estimated that Black's lyrics have been heard in well over 100 movies, including *To Sir With*

Love (title song, with Mark London, 1972, a US number 1 for Lulu), *Pretty Polly* (title song, Michel Legrand, 1967), *I'll Never Forget What's 'Is Name* ('One Day Soon', Francis Lai, 1968), *The Italian Job* ('On Days Like These', Quincy Jones, 1969), *Satan's Harvest* ('Two People', Denis King, 1969), *Hoffman* ('If There Ever Is A Next Time', Ron Grainer, 1970), *Mary Queen Of Scots* ('Wish Was Then', John Barry, 1971), *Alice's Adventures In Wonderland* (several songs with Barry, 1972), *The Tamarind Seed* ('Play It Again', Barry, 1974), *The Dove* ('Sail The Summer Winds', Barry, 1974), and *The Wilby Conspiracy* ('All The Wishing In The World', Stanley Myers, 1975). In 1970, Matt Monro invited Don Black to become his manager, and he remained in that role until the singer died in 1985. Black considered Monro to be one of the finest interpreters of his lyrics, particularly with regard to 'If I Never Sing Another Song', which Black wrote with Udo Jurgens in 1977. It was featured on *Matt Monro Sings Don Black* which was released in 1990. The song became a favourite closing number for many artists, including Johnnie Ray and Eddie Fisher. In 1971, Black augmented his already heavy workload by becoming involved with stage musicals. His first score, written with composer Walter Scharf, was for *Maybe That's Your Problem*, which had a limited run (18 performances) at London's Roundhouse Theatre. The subject of the show was premature ejaculation (Black says that his friend, Alan Jay Lerner, suggested that it should be called *Shortcomings*, but the critics regarded it as 'a dismal piece'). However, one of the performers was Elaine Paige, just seven years before her triumph in *Evita*. Paige was also in *Billy*, London's hit musical of 1974. Adapted from the play, *Billy Liar*, which was set in the north of England, Black and John Barry's score captured the 'feel' and the dialect of the original. The songs included 'Some Of Us Belong To The Stars', 'I Missed The Last Rainbow', 'Any Minute Now', and 'It Were All Green Fields When I Were A Lad', which was subsequently recorded by Stanley Holloway. *Billy* ran for over 900 performances and made a star of Michael Crawford in his musical comedy debut. Black's collaborator on the score for his next show, *Bar Mitzvah Boy* (1978), was Jule Styne, the legendary composer of shows such as *Funny Girl* and *Gypsy*, among others. Although *Bar Mitzvah Boy* had a disappointingly short run, it did impress Andrew Lloyd Webber, who engaged Black to write the lyrics for his song cycle, *Tell Me On Sunday*, a television programme and album which featured Marti Webb. Considered too short for theatrical presentation, on the recommendation of Cameron Mackintosh it was combined with Lloyd Webber's *Variations* to form *Song And Dance*, a two part 'theatrical concert', and featured songs such as 'Take That Look Off Your Face', which gave Marti Webb a UK Top 5 hit and gained Black another Ivor Novello Award, 'Nothing Like You've Ever Known', 'Capped Teeth And Caesar Salad', and 'Tell Me On Sunday'. The show ran in the West End for 781 performances before being remodelled and expanded for Broadway, where it starred Bernadette Peters, who

received a Tony Award for her performance. Black teamed with Benny Andersson and Bjorn Ulvaeus, two former members of Abba, for the aptly titled *Abbacadabra*, a Christmas show which played to packed houses in 1983. Earlier that year, he had written the score for *Dear Anyone* with Geoff Stephens, a successful composer of pop hits such as 'Winchester Cathedral' 'You Won't Find Another Fool Like Me' and 'There's A Kind Of Hush'. The show first surfaced as a concept album in 1978, and one of its numbers, 'I'll Put You Together Again', became a Top 20 hit for the group Hot Chocolate. The 1983 stage presentation did not last long, and neither did *Budgie* (1988). Against a background of 'the sleezy subculture of London's Soho', this show starred Adam Faith and Anita Dobson. Black's lyrics combined with Mort Shuman's music for songs such as 'Why Not Me?', 'There Is Love And There Is Love', 'In One Of My Weaker Moments', and 'They're Naked And They Move', but to no avail - Black, as co-producer, presided over a '£1 million flop'. Two years earlier, Anita Dobson had achieved a UK hit with 'Anyone Can Fall In Love', when Black added a lyric to Simon May and Leslie Osborn's theme for BBC Television's *Eastenders*, one of Britain's top television soap operas. He collaborated with the composers again for 'Always There', a vocal version of their theme for *Howard's Way*, which gave Marti Webb a UK hit. In 1989, Black resumed his partnership with Andrew Lloyd Webber for *Aspects Of Love*. Together with *Phantom Of The Opera* lyricist Charles Hart, they fashioned a musical treatment of David Garnett's 1955 novel which turned out to be more intimate than some of Lloyd Webber's other works, but still retained the operatic form. The show starred Michael Ball and Ann Crumb; Ball took the big ballad, 'Love Changes Everything', to number 2 in the UK, and the score also featured the 'subtle, aching melancholy' of 'The First Man You Remember'. *Aspects of Love* was not considered a hit by Lloyd Webber's standards - it ran for three years in the West End, and for one year on Broadway - but the London Cast recording topped the UK album chart. In the 90s Black's activities remain numerous and diverse. In 1992, together with Chris Walker, he provided extra lyrics for the London stage production of *Radio Times*; wrote additional songs for a revival of *Billy* by the National Youth Music Theatre at the Edinburgh Festival; renewed his partnership with Geoff Stephens for a concept album of a 'revuesical' entitled *Off The Wall*, the story of 'six characters determined to end it all by throwing themselves off a ledge on the 34th storey of a London highrise building'; collaborated with Lloyd Webber on the Barcelona Olympics anthem, 'Friends For Life' ('Amigos Para Siempre'), which was recorded by Sarah Brightman and Jose Carreras; and worked with David Dundas on 'Keep Your Dreams Alive', for the animated feature, *Freddie As F.R.O.7*. He spent a good deal of the year co-writing the book and lyrics, with Christopher Hampton, for Lloyd Webber's musical treatment of the Hollywood classic, *Sunset Boulevard*. The show, which opened in London and on Broadway in 1993, brought Black two Tony Awards. He adapted one of the hit songs, 'As If We Never Said Goodbye', for Barbra Streisand to sing in her first concert tour for 27 years. Black has held the positions of chairman and vice-president of the British Academy of Songwriters, Composers and Authors, and has, for the past few years, been the genial chairman of the voting panel for the Vivian Ellis Prize, a national competition to encourage new writers for the musical stage. In 1993, 22 of his own songs were celebrated on *The Don Black Songbook*, and in the following year Black branched out into broadcasting, interviewing Elmer Bernstein, and presenting the six-part *How To Make A Musical* on BBC Radio 2. In 1995 he was presented with the Jimmy Kennedy Award at the 40th anniversary Ivor Novello Awards ceremony. In 1996 he received a Lifetime Achievement Award from BMI, and in the following year provided the lyric for 'You Stayed Away Too Long', a song that made the last four of the British heats of the Eurovision Song Contest, but failed to progress further. Another disappointment in 1997 came when the London production of the flop Broadway musical, *The Goodbye Girl*, for which Black wrote seven new songs with composer Marvin Hamlisch, departed after a brief run.

BLACK, ROY

b. Gerd Hoellerich, 25 January 1943, Augsburg, Germany, d. 10 October 1991. As a teenager, Black fronted a beat group modelled to Merseybeat specifications, often playing Hamburg clubs, but he was uncomfortable with this style. He was signed to Polydor as a solo balladeer after a well-received performance in a televised song festival. Composed by Arland and Hertha, 1965's 'Du Bist Nicht Allein' ('You Are Not Alone') established him as a national star and ensured sell-out tours and high chart placings until the mid-70s. In 1966, 'Ganz In Weiss' ('All In White') was a German number 1 for six weeks, and his second album had advance orders of 50,000. Disinclined to attempt any breakthrough into the English language market, he consolidated his domestic success with 'Deine Schonstes Geschenk' which, in 1970, stayed at the top of the charts even longer than 'Ganz In Weiss'. Identified with and dependent on a particular sound, he lost the knack of consistently picking hits, but wisely invested his royalties and subsequently worked in cabaret.
●ALBUMS: *Roy Black* (1966)★★★, *Roy Black II* (1967)★★★.

BLACKBURN, TONY

b. Kenneth Blackburn, 29 January 1943, Guildford, Surrey, England. Blackburn was Britain's most popular disc jockey of the late 60s and early 70s. He joined the pirate radio station Radio Caroline after replying to an advert in the *New Musical Express*, and Johnny Dankworth's 'Beefeater' became his distinctive theme music. He remained at Caroline for two years before moving on to Radio London, another offshore pop station. After a year he joined the BBC Light Programme hosting the *Midday Spin* record show and was then offered the

breakfast show slot on the new Radio 1 when it was launched in September 1967. After George Martin's specially composed 'Theme One' introduction, Blackburn's voice was the first sound on Radio 1. Blackburn had also diversified into television starting in the mid-60s with *Discs A Go-Go* for Welsh television. He then hosted the *5 O'Clock Club* before getting his own *Time For Blackburn* on Southern Television. Not content with being a broadcaster, Blackburn had already started a secondary career as a recording artist in 1965 when he released 'Don't Get Off That Train' on Fontana. By the end of the decade he had released two more singles, three for MGM, of which 'So Much Love' and 'It's Only Love' were hits. He left Radio 1 in 1984. He also released several more records including 'Cindy', which was written by Chinn And Chapman. His personal life was fraught with difficulty - a marriage and divorce from actress Tessa Wyatt was dragged through the mud by the press, and Blackburn developed a problem with tranquilizers. He joined Radio London during the mid-80s where he became known for his risque humour. He currently broadcasts for Capital Gold in London.
●ALBUMS: *Tony Blackburn Sings* (MGM 1968)★, *Tony Blackburn Meets Matt Monroe* (Fontana 1970)★.

BLACKWELL, ROBERT 'BUMPS'

b. Robert A. Blackwell, 23 May 1918, Seattle, Washington, USA (of mixed French, Negro and Indian descent), d. 9 March 1985. An arranger and studio band leader with Specialty Records, Blackwell had led a band in Seattle. After arriving in California in 1949 he studied classical composition at the University of California, Los Angeles, and within a few years was arranging and producing gospel and R&B singles for the likes of Lloyd Price and Guitar Slim. Previously he had written a series of stage revues - *Blackwell Portraits* - very much in the same vein as the *Ziegfeld Follies*. His Bumps Blackwell Jnr. Orchestra featured, at various times, Ray Charles and Quincy Jones. He also worked with Lou Adler and Herb Alpert before taking over the A&R department at Specialty Records where he first came into contact with Little Richard. His boss, Art Rupe, sent him to New Orleans in 1955 where he recorded 'Tutti Frutti' and established a new base for rock 'n' roll. Blackwell was a key producer and songwriter in the early days of rock 'n' roll, particularly with Little Richard. He was responsible for tracking down Little Richard and buying his recording contract from Peacock in 1955. Blackwell helped to rewrite 'Tutti Frutti' in a cleaned-up version more appropriate to white audiences, which he recorded at Richard's first Specialty session in New Orleans. As well as being involved with the writing of some of Richard's hits, he also produced some of his early work, and became his personal manager. Along with John Marascalco he wrote 'Ready Teddy', 'Rip It Up', and, with Enotris Johnson and Richard Penniman (Little Richard), 'Long Tall Sally'. He also helped launch the secular careers of former gospel singers Sam Cooke and Wynona Carr. After leaving Specialty, he was involved in setting up Keen Records which furthered the careers of Sam Cooke and Johnny 'Guitar' Watson, among others. In 1981 he co-produced the title track of Bob Dylan's *Shot Of Love*, before his death from pneumonia in 1985.

BLAINE, HAL

b. Harold Simon Belsky, 5 February 1929, Holyoke, Massachusetts, USA. Drummer Blaine claims to be the most-recorded musician in history. The Los Angeles-based session musician says he has performed on over 35,000 recordings (*c*.1991), including over 350 that reached the US Top 10. Blaine began playing drums at the age of seven, owning his first drum set at 13. A fan of big band jazz, he joined the high school band when his family moved to California in 1944. After a stint in the army, he became a professional drummer, first with a band called the Novelteers (also known as the Stan Moore Trio) and then with singer Vicki Young, who became the first of his several wives. At the end of the 50s he began working with teen-idol Tommy Sands, then singer Patti Page. At the recommendation of fellow studio drummer Earl Palmer, Blaine began accepting session work in the late 50s, beginning on a Sam Cooke record. His first Top 10 single was Jan And Dean's 'Baby Talk' in 1960. His huge discography includes drumming for nearly all the important sessions produced by Phil Spector, including hits by the Crystals, Ronettes and Righteous Brothers. He played on many of the Beach Boys' greatest hits and on sessions for Elvis Presley, Frank Sinatra, Nancy Sinatra, the Association, Gary Lewis And The Playboys, the Mamas And The Papas, Johnny Rivers, the Byrds, Simon And Garfunkel, the Monkees, Neil Diamond, the Carpenters, John Lennon, Ringo Starr, George Harrison, Herb Alpert, Jan And Dean, the Supremes, the Partridge Family, John Denver, the Fifth Dimension, Captain And Tennille, Barbra Streisand, Grass Roots, Cher and hundreds of other artists. In the late 70s Blaine's schedule slowed down and by the 80s his involvement in the LA studio scene drew to a near halt. In 1990 he wrote a book about his experiences, *Hal Blaine And The Wrecking Crew*.
●ALBUMS: *Deuces, T's, Roadsters & Drums* (RCA Victor 1963)★★, *Drums! Drums! A Go Go* (Dunhill 1966)★★, *Psychedelic Percussion* (Dunhill 1967)★, *Have Fun!!! Play Drums!!!* (Dunhill 1969)★★.

BLAKEY, ART

b. Arthur Blakey, 11 October 1919, Pittsburgh, Pennsylvania, USA, d. 16 October 1990. Although renowned as a drummer, Blakey was a pianist first. His move to the drums has been variously attributed to Erroll Garner's appearance on the scene, the regular session drummer being ill and (Blakey's favourite) a gangster's indisputable directive. Blakey drummed for Mary Lou Williams on her New York debut in 1942, Fletcher Henderson's mighty swing orchestra (1943/4) and the legendary Billy Eckstine band that included Charlie Parker, Dexter Gordon, Dizzy Gillespie, Miles Davis and Thelonious Monk (1944-47). The classic bebop sessions predominantly featured Max Roach or Kenny Clarke on

drums, but Blakey soon became the pre-eminent leader of the hard bop movement. In contrast to the baroque orchestrations of the West Coast Jazz 'cool' school, hard bop combined bebop's instrumental freedoms with a surging gospel backbeat. Ideally suited to the new long-playing record, tunes lengthened into rhythmic epics that featured contrasting solos. Blakey's hi-hat and snare skills became legendary, as did the musicians who passed through the ranks of the Jazz Messengers: the band became an on-the-road 'college' (pianist JoAnne Brackeen was one of his discoveries). His playing combined musicianship with risk, and his drumming encouraged daring and brilliance. He would lean with his elbow on the surface of the drum to change its intonation: such 'press rolls' became a musical trademark. That his power was not from want of subtlety was illustrated by his uncanny sympathy for Thelonious Monk's sense of rhythm: his contribution to Monk's historic 1957 group, which included both Coleman Hawkins and John Coltrane, was devastating, and the London trio recordings he made with Monk in 1971 (*Something In Blue* and *The Man I Love*) are perhaps his most impressive achievements as a player. For a period following his conversion to Islam, Blakey changed his name to Abdullah Ibn Buhaina, which led to his nickname 'Bu'.

Blakey inspired and encouraged the creativity and drive of acoustic jazz through the electric 70s; Miles Davis once remarked 'If Art Blakey's old-fashioned, I'm white'. This comment was substantiated in the 80s when hard bop became popular, a movement led by ex-Jazz Messengers Wynton Marsalis and Terence Blanchard. In England, a televised encounter in 1986 with the young turks of black British jazz, including Courtney Pine and Steve Williamson, emphasized Blakey's influence on generations of jazz fans. Until his death in 1990, Art Blakey continually found new musicians and put them through his special discipline of heat and precision. When he played, Blakey invariably had his mouth open in a grimace of pleasure and concentration: memories of his drumming still makes the jaw drop today. As a drummer Blakey will not be forgotten, but as a catalyst for hundreds of past messengers he will be forever praised.
●ALBUMS: *Blakey* (EmArcy 1954)★★★, *A Night At Birdland Vol. 1* (Blue Note 1954)★★★★★, *A Night At The Birdland Vol. 2* (Blue Note 1954)★★★★★, *A Night At The Cafe Bohemia Vol. 1* (Blue Note 1954)★★★★, *At The Cafe Bohemia Vol. 1* (Blue Note 1956)★★★★★, *At The Cafe Bohemia Vol. 2* (Blue Note 1956)★★★★★, *Hard Bop* (Columbia 1956)★★★, *The Jazz Messengers* (Columbia 1956)★★★, *Drum Suite* (Columbia 1957)★★★, *Cu-Bop* (Jubilee 1957)★★★, *Orgy In Rhythm Vol. 1* (Blue Note 1957)★★★, *Orgy In Rhythm Vol. 2* (Blue Note 1957)★★★, *A Midnight Session With The Jazz Messengers* (Elektra 1957)★★★, *Play Selections From Lerner And Loewe* (Vik 1957)★★, *The Hard Bop Academy* (Affinity 1958)★★★, *Art Blakey's Jazz Messengers With Thelonius Monk* (Atlantic 1958)★★★★, *Ritual* (Pacific Jazz 1958)★★★, *Holiday For Skins Vol. 1* (Blue Note 1958)★★★, *Moanin'* (Blue

Note 1958)★★★★, *At The Jazz Corner Of The World Vol. 1* (Blue Note 1958)★★★★, *At The Jazz Corner Of The World Vol. 2* (Blue Note 1958)★★★★, *Art Blakey's Big Band* (Bethlehem 1958)★★★, *Hard Drive* (Bethlehem 1958)★★★, *Holiday For Skins Vol. 2* (Blue Note 1959)★★★, *A Night In Tunisia* (Blue Note 1960)★★★★, *The Big Beat* (Blue Note 1960),★★★ *Like Someone In Love* (1960)★★★, *Meet You At The Jazz Corner Of The World Vol. 1* (Blue Note 1960)★★★★, *Meet You At The Jazz Corner Of The World Vol. 2* (Blue Note 1960)★★★★, *Paris Concert* (Epic 1960)★★★, *Art Blakey In Paris* (Epic 1961)★★★, *The African Beat* (Blue Note 1961)★★★, *Roots & Herbs* (1961)★★★★, *Jazz Messengers !!!!* (Impulse 1961)★★★, *Mosaic* (Blue Note 1961)★★★★, *Buhaina's Delight* (Blue Note 1962)★★★★, *Three Blind Mice* (United Artists 1962)★★★, *Caravan* (Riverside 1962)★★★, *Ugetsu* (Riverside 1963)★★★, *The Freedom Rider* (Blue Note 1963)★★★, *Indestructible* (Blue Note 1963)★★★, *Like Someone In Love* (Blue Note 1963)★★★★, *A Jazz Message* (Impulse 1963)★★★, *Free For All* (Blue Note 1964)★★★, *Tough!* (Cadet 1965)★★, *'S Make It* (Limelight 1965)★★, *Soul Finger* (Limelight 1965)★★, *Buttercorn Lady* (Limelight 1966)★★, *Kyoto* (Riverside 1966)★★★, *Hold On I'm Coming* (Limelight 1966)★★, *Art Blakey Live* (Mercury 1968)★★★, *Mellow Blues* (Moon 1969)★★★, with Thelonious Monk *Something In Blue* (1971)★★★, *Gypsy Folk Tales* (Roulette 1977)★★, *In This Corner* (Concord 1979)★★★, *Messages* (Vogue 1979)★★★, *Straight Ahead* (Concord 1981)★★★, *Album Of the Year* (Timeless 1981)★★★★, *In My Prime Vol. 1* (Timeless 1981)★★★, *Blues Bag* (Affinity 1981)★★★, *Keystone 3* (Concord 1982)★★★, *In Sweden* (Amigo 1982)★★★, *Oh, By The Way* (Timeless 1982)★★★, *New York Scene* (Concord 1984)★★★, *Blue Night* (Timeless 1985)★★★, *Dr Jeckyl* (Paddle Wheel 1985)★★★, *Blues March* (Vogue 1985)★★★, *Farewell* (Paddle Wheel 1985)★★, *In My Prime Vol 2* (Timeless 1986)★★★, *Live At Ronnie Scott's* (Hendring 1987)★★★, *Not Yet* (Soul Note 1988)★★, *Feeling Good* (Delos 1988)★★, *Hard Champion* (Electric Bird 1988)★★★, *I Get A Kick Out Of Bu* (Soul Note 1989)★★, *Live In Berlin 1959-62* (Jazzup 1989)★★★, *One For All* (A&M 1990)★★, *Live In Europe 1959* (Creole 1992)★★★.

●COMPILATIONS: *The Best Of Art Blakey* (Emarcy 1980)★★★, *Art Collection* (Concord 1986)★★★, *The Best Of Art Blakey And The Jazz Messengers* (Blue Note 1989)★★★★★, *Compact Jazz* (Verve 1992)★★★★, *The History Of Art Blakey & The Jazz Messengers* 3-CD set (Blue Note 1992)★★★★.

●VIDEOS: *Notes From Jazz* (1988), *At Ronnie Scotts* (1988), *Art Blakey & The Jazz Messengers* (1988), *Jazz At The Smithson Vol. 2* (1990), *Concerts And Jam Sessions On Video* (1991), *A Lesson With Art Blakey* (CPP Media Master 1996).

BLAND, BOBBY

b. Robert Calvin Bland, 27 January 1930, Rosemark, Tennessee, USA. Having moved to Memphis with his mother, Bobby 'Blue' Bland started singing with local gospel groups, including, among others, the Miniatures. Eager to expand his interests, he began frequenting the city's infamous Beale Street where he became associated with an *ad hoc* circle of aspiring musicians, named, not unnaturally, the Beale Streeters. Bland's recordings from the early 50s show him striving for individuality, but his progress was halted by a stint in the US Army. When the singer returned to Memphis in 1954 he found several of his former associates, including Johnny Ace, enjoying considerable success, while Bland's recording label, Duke, had been sold to Houston entrepreneur Don Robey. In 1956 Bland began touring with 'Little' Junior Parker. Initially, he doubled as valet and driver, a role he reportedly performed for B.B. King, but simultaneously began asserting his characteristic vocal style. Melodic big-band blues singles, including 'Farther Up The Road' (1957) and 'Little Boy Blue' (1958) reached the US R&B Top 10, but Bland's vocal talent was most clearly heard on a series of superb early 60s releases, including 'Cry Cry Cry', 'I Pity The Fool' and the sparkling 'Turn On Your Lovelight', which was destined to become a much-covered standard. Despite credits to the contrary, many such classic works were written by Joe Scott, the artist's bandleader and arranger.

Bland continued to enjoy a consistent run of R&B chart entries throughout the mid-60s but his recorded work was nonetheless eclipsed by a younger generation of performers. Financial pressures forced the break-up of the group in 1968, and his relationship with Scott, who died in 1979, was irrevocably severed. Nonetheless, depressed and increasingly dependent on alcohol, Bland weathered this unhappy period. In 1971, his record company, Duke, was sold to the larger ABC Records group, resulting in several contemporary blues/soul albums including *His California Album* and *Dreamer*. Subsequent attempts at pushing the artist towards the disco market were unsuccessful, but a 1983 release, *Here We Go Again*, provided a commercial life-line. Two years later Bland was signed by Malaco Records, specialists in traditional southern black music, who offered a sympathetic environment. One of the finest singers in post-war blues, Bobby Bland has failed to win the popular acclaim his influence and talent perhaps deserve.

●ALBUMS: with 'Little' Junior Parker *Blues Consolidated* (1958)★★★, with Parker *Barefoot Rock And You Got Me* (1960)★★★, *Two Steps From The Blues* (Duke 1961)★★★★, *Here's The Man* (Duke 1962)★★★★, *Call On Me* (Duke 1963)★★★, *Ain't Nothin' You Can Do* (Duke 1964)★★★, *The Soul Of The Man* (Duke 1966)★★★, *Touch Of The Blues* (1967)★★, *Spotlighting The Man* (1968)★★, *His California Album* (ABC 1973)★★, *Dreamer* (ABC 1974)★★, with B.B. King *Together For The First Time - Live* (1974)★★★★, with King *Together Again - Live* (MCA 1976)★★★, *Get On Down* (1975)★★, *Reflections*

In Blue (MCA 1977)★★, *Come Fly With Me* (1978)★★, *I Feel Good I Feel Fine* (MCA 1979)★★, *Sweet Vibrations* (1980)★★, *You Got Me Loving You* (1981)★★, *Try Me, I'm Real* (1981)★★, *Here We Go Again* (1982)★★, *Tell Mr. Bland* (1983)★★, *Members Only* (Malaco 1985),★★ *After All* (Malaco 1986)★★, *Blues You Can Use* (Malaco 1987)★★, *First Class Blues* (Malaco 1987)★★★, *Midnight Run* (Malaco 1989)★★★, *Portrait Of The Blues* (Malaco 1991)★★★, *Sad Street* (Malaco 1995)★★★.
●COMPILATIONS: *The Best Of Bobby Bland* (Duke 1967)★★★★, *The Best Of Bobby Bland Vol. 2* (Duke 1968)★★★★, *Introspective Of The Early Years* (MCA 1974)★★★, *Woke Up Screaming* (1981)★★★, *The Best Of Bobby Bland* (1982)★★★, *Foolin' With The Blues* (1983)★★★, *Blues In The Night* (1985)★★★, *The Soulful Side Of Bobby Bland* (1986)★★, *Soul With A Flavour 1959-1984* (1988)★★★, *The '3B' Blues Boy: The Blues Years 1952-59* (Ace 1991)★★★★, *The Voice* (Ace 1992)★★★★, *I Pity The Fool: The Duke Recordings Vol. 1* (1993)★★★.

BLIND FAITH

Formed in 1969, Blind Faith were one of the earliest conglomerations to earn the dubious tag 'supergroup'. The group comprised Eric Clapton (b. 30 March 1945, Ripley, Surrey, England; guitar/vocals), Ginger Baker (b. 19 August 1939, London, England; drums), Steve Winwood (b. 12 May 1948, Birmingham, England; keyboards/vocals) and Rick Grech (b. 1 November 1945, Bordeaux, France, d. 16 March 1990; bass/violin). The band stayed together for one highly publicized, million-selling album and a lucrative major US tour. Their debut was at a free pop concert in front of an estimated 100,000 at London's Hyde Park, in June 1969. The controversial album cover depicted a topless pre-pubescent girl holding a phallic chrome model aeroplane. The content included only one future classic, Clapton's 'Presence Of The Lord'. Baker's 'Do What You Like' was self-indulgent and over-long and their cover of Buddy Holly's 'Well. . . All Right!' was unspectacular. Buried among the tracks was the beautiful Winwood composition 'Can't Find My Way Home', never afforded the attention it deserved. Further live Blind Faith tracks can be heard on the Winwood box set, *The Finer Things*.
●ALBUMS: *Blind Faith* (Polydor 1969)★★★.

BLITZ!

Lionel Bart was back at the top of his form with this follow-up to the smash hit *Oliver!* (1960). For *Blitz!*, which opened at the Adelphi Theatre in London on 8 May 1962, Bart not only wrote the book (with Joan Maitland), music and lyrics, but directed the piece. The show, set in the East End of London during the dark years of World War II, concerns two families: one is Jewish - the other is not. Mrs Blitztein (originally played by Amanda Bayntun) runs a pickled herring stall in Petticoat Lane's Sunday market, next to that of Alfred Locke (Bob Grant). Their dislike of each other is such that messages have to

be passed between them ('Tell Him-Tell Her') by Mrs Blitztein's daughter Carol (Grazina Frame) and Alfred's son Georgie (Graham James). Inevitably, the two young people fall in love, and express their feelings for each other in 'Opposites'. The small children are evacuated to the countryside ('We're Going To The Country'), while Mrs Blitztein pours scorn into 'Who's This Geezer Hitler?' ('He's a nasty little basket with a black moustache/And we don't want him here'). Later, Carol is blinded in a air-raid, Georgie deserts from the Army, and there is a typical East End 'knees-up' wedding before a bomb destroys much of the immediate locality. Mrs Blitztein emerges from the rubble unscathed. Bart's rousing, and sometimes tender score, includes 'Our Hotel', 'I Want To Whisper Something', 'Another Morning', 'Be What You Wanna Be', 'Petticoat Lane (On A Saturday Ain't So Nice)', 'Down The Lane', 'So Tell Me', 'Mums And Dads', and 'Is This Gonna Be A Wedding?'. Grazina Frame sang the haunting 'Far Away', which became a UK chart hit for Shirley Bassey, and the voice of Vera Lynn was heard on the 'radio' with 'The Day After Tomorrow'. The entire production was designed by Sean Kenny, whose huge mechanical sets, a mass of girders and metal platforms, was praised by one critic as 'the most remarkable spectacle to hit the London stage in my time'. The show was a tremendous success and ran for well over two years, with a total of 568 performances. Nearly 30 years later, in September 1990, the National Youth Theatre of Great Britain staged a revival of *Blitz!* at London's Playhouse Theatre, and, in the following year, it was presented again, in the north of England. The Original Cast album, which had featured in the UK charts in 1962, was re-released in 1991 with three additional tracks.

BLONDE ON BLONDE

Blonde On Blonde - Ralph Denver (guitar/vocals), Gareth Johnson (guitar), Richard Hopkins (bass/keyboards) and Les Hicks (drums) - came to prominence on BBC Television's short-lived programme *How Late It Is*. Their debut single, 'All Day All Night' (1968), showed considerable promise, but *Contrasts* was a comparative disappointment, demonstrating little of the group's initial imaginativeness. Blonde On Blonde appeared at the 1969 Isle Of Wight Festival, after which Denver and Hopkins left the line-up. Dave Thomas (guitar/vocals) and Richard John (bass) joined for *Rebirth*, on which the group pursued a musical direction reminiscent of the Moody Blues. They added a mellotron player, known only as Kip, for *Reflections On A Life*, which also featured new bassist Graham Davies in place of John. This somewhat pretentious selection was not a success and Blonde On Blonde broke up soon afterwards.
●ALBUMS: *Contrasts* (Pye 1969)★★, *Rebirth* (Ember 1970)★★, *Reflections On A Life* (Ember 1971)★★.

BLOOD, SWEAT AND TEARS

The jazz/rock excursions made by Blood, Sweat And Tears offered a refreshing change to late 60s guitar dominated rock music. The many impressive line-ups of the band comprised (among others) David Clayton-Thomas (b. David Thomsett, 13 September 1941, Surrey, England; vocals), Al Kooper (b. 5 February 1944, New York, USA; keyboards/vocals), Steve Katz (b. 9 May 1945, New York, USA; guitar), Jerry Weiss, Randy Brecker (b. 27 November 1945, Philadelphia, Pennsylvania, USA; saxophone), Dick Halligan (b. 29 August 1943, New York, USA; trombone/flute/keyboards), Fred Lipsius (b. 19 November 1944, New York, USA; alto saxophone/piano), Bobby Colomby (b. 20 December 1944, New York, USA; drums), Jim Fielder (b. 4 October 1947, Denton, Texas, USA; bass), Lew Soloff (b. 20 February 1944, Brooklyn, New York, USA; trumpet), Chuck Winfield (b. 5 February 1943, Monessen, Pennsylvania, USA; trumpet), Jerry Hyman (b. 19 May 1947, Brooklyn, New York, USA; Trumpet) and Dave Bargeron (b. 6 September 1942, Athol, Massachusetts, USA; trumpet). The band was conceived by Al Kooper, who together with Katz, both from the Blues Project, but Kooper departed soon after the debut *Child Is Father To The Man*, which contained two of his finest songs, 'I Can't Quit Her' and 'My Days Are Numbered'. The record, although cited as a masterpiece by some critics was ultimately flawed by erratic vocals. Kooper, Brecker and Weiss were replaced by Winfield, Soloff and Clayton-Thomas. The latter took over as vocalist to record *Blood Sweat And Tears*, which is now regarded as their finest work, standing up today as a brilliantly scored and fresh-sounding record. Kooper, although working on the arrangements, missed out on the extraordinary success this record achieved. The album topped the US album charts for many weeks during its two-year stay, sold millions of copies, won a Grammy award and spawned three major worldwide hits: 'You've Made Me So Very Happy', 'Spinning Wheel' and 'And When I Die'. The following two albums were both considerable successes, although unoriginal, with their gutsy brass arrangements, occasional biting guitar solos and Clayton-Thomas's growling vocal delivery. Following *BS&T4*, Clayton-Thomas departed for a solo career, resulting in a succession of lead vocalists, including the former member of Edgar Winter's White Trash, Jerry LaCroix (b. 10 October 1943, Alexandria, Lousiana, USA). The band never regained their former glory, even following the return of Clayton-Thomas. *New City* reached the US album charts, but the supper-club circuit ultimately beckoned. The band re-formed briefly in 1988 to play their back catalogue, and deserve a place in rock history as both innovators and brave exponents of psychedelic-tinged jazz/rock.

●ALBUMS: *Child Is Father To The Man* (Columbia 1968)★★★, *Blood, Sweat And Tears* (Columbia 1969)★★★★, *Blood, Sweat And Tears 3* (Columbia 1970)★★★, *BS&T4* (Columbia 1971)★★★, *New Blood* (Columbia 1972)★★, *No Sweat* (Columbia 1973)★★, *Mirror Image* (Columbia 1974)★★, *New City* Columbia (1975)★★, *More Than Ever* (Columbia 1976)★★, *Brand New Day* (1977)★★, *Nuclear Blues* (1980)★★, *Live And Improvised* (Columbia 1991)★★.

●COMPILATIONS: *Greatest Hits* (Columbia 1972)★★★★, *What Goes Up! The Best Of* (Columbia/Legacy 1995)★★★★.

●FURTHER READING: *Blood, Sweat And Tears*, Lorraine Alterman.

BLOOM, BOBBY

d. 28 February 1971. New York-based Bloom began his career during the 60s as one of several backroom entrepreneurs, along with Anders And Poncia, Artie Ripp and Levine/Reisnick, central to the Kama Sutra/Buddah group of labels. He also made several solo recordings, including 'Love Don't Let Me Down' and 'Count On Me', and later formed a partnership with composer/producer Jeff Barry. Together, they contributed material for the Monkees, notably 'Ticket On A Ferry Ride' and 'You're So Good To Me'. Bloom's singing career blossomed with the effervescent 'Montego Bay' which reached the US Top 10 and UK Top 3 in 1970. This adept combination of bubblegum, calypso and rock was maintained on 'Heavy Makes You Happy' and *The Bobby Bloom Album*, which Barry produced. Bloom was killed in an accidental shooting in 1971.

●ALBUMS: *The Bobby Bloom Album* (1970)★★★.

BLOOMFIELD, MIKE

b. 28 July 1944, Chicago, Illinois, USA d. 15 February 1981. For many, both critics and fans, Bloomfield was the finest white blues guitarist America has so far produced. Although signed to Columbia Records in 1964 as the Group (with Charlie Musslewhite and Nick Gravenites), it was his emergence in 1965 as the young, shy guitarist in the Paul Butterfield Blues Band that bought him to public attention. He astonished those viewers who had watched black blues guitarists spend a lifetime trying, but failing to play with as much fluidity and feeling as Bloomfield. That same year he was an important part of musical history, when folk purists accused Bob Dylan of committing artistic suicide at the Newport Folk Festival. Bloomfield was his lead electric guitarist at that event, and again later on Dylan's 60s masterpiece *Highway 61 Revisited.*. On leaving Butterfield in 1967 he immediately formed the seminal Electric Flag, although he left before the first album's subsequent decline in popularity. His 1968 album *Super Session* with Stephen Stills and Al Kooper became his biggest selling record. It led to a short but financially lucrative career with Kooper. The track 'Stop' on the album epitomized Bloomfield's style: clean, crisp, sparse and emotional. The long sustained notes were produced by bending the string with his fingers underneath the other strings so as not to affect the tuning.

It was five years before his next satisfying work appeared, *Triumvirate*, with John Paul Hammond and Dr. John (Mac Rebennack), and following this, Bloomfield became a virtual recluse. Subsequent albums were distributed on small labels and did not gain national distribution. Plagued with a long-standing drug habit he occasionally supplemented his income by scoring music for pornographic movies. He also wrote three film music soundtracks, *The Trip* (1967), *Medium Cool* (1969) and

Steelyard Blues (1973). Additionally, he taught music at Stanford University in San Francisco, wrote advertising jingles and was an adviser to *Guitar Player* magazine. Bloomfield avoided the limelight, possibly because of his insomnia while touring, but mainly because of his perception of what he felt an audience wanted: 'Playing in front of strangers leads to idolatry, and idolatry is dangerous because the audience has a preconception of you, even though you cannot get a conception of them'. In 1975 he was cajoled into forming the 'supergroup' KGB with Rick Grech, Barry Goldberg and Carmine Appice. The album was an unmitigated disaster and Bloomfield resorted to playing mostly acoustic music. He had an extraordinarily prolific year in 1977, when he released five albums, the most notable being the critically acclaimed *If You Love These Blues, Play 'Em As You Please*, released through *Guitar Player* magazine. A second burst of activity occurred shortly before his tragic death, when another three albums' worth of material was recorded. Bloomfield was found dead in his car from a suspected accidental drug overdose, a sad end to a 'star' who constantly avoided stardom in order to maintain his own integrity.
●ALBUMS: *Super Session* (1968)★★★★, *The Live Adventures Of Mike Bloomfield And Al Kooper* (1969)★★★, *Fathers And Sons* (1969)★★, with Barry Goldberg *Two Jews Blues* (1969)★★, *It's Not Killing Me* (1969)★★, with others *Live At Bill Graham's Fillmore West* (1969)★★, with Dr John *Triumvirate* (1973)★★★, *Try It Before You Buy It* (1975)★★, as KGB *KGB* (1976)★, *Bloomfield/Naftalin* (1976)★★, *Mill Valley Session* (1976)★★★, *There's Always Another Record* (1976)★★, *I'm Always With You* (1977)★★, *If You Love These Blues, Play 'Em As You Please* (1977)★★★, *Analine* (1977)★★, *Michael Bloomfield* (1977)★★, *Count Talent And The Originals* (1977)★★, *Mike Bloomfield And Woody Harris* (1979)★★, *Between The Hard Place And The Ground* (1980)★★, *Livin' In The Fast Lane* (1980)★★, *Gosport Duets* (1981)★★, *Red Hot And Blues* (1981)★★, *Cruisin' For A Bruisin'* (1981)★★, *Retrospective* (1984)★★★, *Junco Partners* (1984)★★, *Blues, Gospel And Ragtime Guitar Instrumentals* (Shanachie 1994)★★★.
●COMPILATIONS: *Essential Blues 1964-1969* (Columbia Legacy 1994)★★★.
●FURTHER READING: *The Rise And Fall Of An American Guitar Hero*, Ed Ward.

BLOSSOM TOES

Brian Godding (guitar/vocals/keyboards), Jim Cregan (guitar/vocals), Brian Belshaw (bass/vocals) and Kevin Westlake (drums) were initially known as the Ingoes, but became Blossom Toes in 1967 upon the launch of manager Giorgio Gomelsky's Marmalade label. *We Are Ever So Clean* was an enthralling selection, astutely combining English pop with a quirky sense of humour. The grasp of melody offered on 'Love Is' or 'What's It For' was akin to that of the Idle Race or the Beatles, while the experimental flourish on 'What On Earth' or 'Look At Me

I'm You' captures the prevailing spirit of 1967. *If Only For A Moment* marked the departure of Westlake, who was replaced, in turn, by John 'Poli' Palmer, then Barry Reeves. A noticeably heavier sound was shown to great effect on the revered 'Peace Lovin' Man', but the set was altogether less distinctive. The quartet was dissolved in 1970, but while Belshaw and Godding rejoined Westlake in B.B. Blunder, Cregan formed Stud with Jim Wilson and Charlie McCracken, before joining Family. He later found fame with Cockney Rebel and Rod Stewart.
●ALBUMS: *We Are Ever So Clean* (Marmalade 1967)★★★★, *If Only For A Moment* (Marmalade 1969)★★★.
●COMPILATIONS: *The Blossom Toes Collection* (1989)★★★★.

BLOW UP

This much-feted 1966 film by Italian director Michelangelo Antonioni was an ironic homage to 'swinging London', in which David Hemmings starred as a successful photographer, the character loosely modelled on David Bailey and Terence Donovan. Emotionally detached at the outset, Hemmings later becomes obsessed by a series of seemingly casual shots of a couple on Hampstead Heath. When one of the subjects, played by Vanessa Redgrave, goes to great lengths to retrieve the negatives, he makes several 'blow-ups' of one frame in which he perceives the image of a corpse. He returns to the scene - no body is found - and all shreds of 'evidence' are later removed from his studio. He absent-mindedly wanders into a London club before a encountering a group of mime artists playing tennis. At one point they ask Hemmings to throw back their 'ball', the noise of which becomes audible as he walks away.
Blow Up poses questions about reality to telling effect but musicologists revere the film for a cameo appearance by the Yardbirds. The rare Jeff Beck/Jimmy Page line-up is featured as a guitar-smashing group, a part rejected by the Who. They perform 'Stroll On' to an expressionless audience which becomes frenzied when Beck throws the remains of his instrument to them. Hemmings escapes with this totem, then throws it away, whereupon passers-by examine the object only to decide it worthless. 'Stroll On' is featured on an accompanying soundtrack album which is completed by contributions from jazz musician Herbie Hancock. The soundtrack adds tonal colour to one of the most fascinating films of its, or any other, era.

BLUE CHEER

San Francisco's Blue Cheer, consisting of Dickie Peterson (b. 1948, Grand Forks, North Dakota, USA; vocals/bass), Leigh Stephens (guitar) and Paul Whaley (drums), harboured dreams of a more conventional direction until seeing Jimi Hendrix perform at the celebrated Monterey Pop Festival. Taking their name from a potent brand of LSD, they made an immediate impact with their uncompromising debut album *Vincebus Eruptum*, which featured cacophonous interpretations of Eddie Cochran's 'Summertime Blues' (US number 14) and Mose Allison's

'Parchman(t) Farm'. A second set, *Outsideinside*, was completed in the open air when the trio's high volume levels destroyed the studio monitors. Stephens left the group during the sessions for *New! Improved*, and his place was taken by former Other Half guitarist Randy Holden; they also added Bruce Stephens (bass), and Holden left during the recording sessions. *Blue Cheer* then unveiled a reconstituted line-up of Petersen, Burns Kellogg (keyboards), and Norman Mayell (drums/guitar), who replaced Whaley. Stephens was then replaced by former Kak guitarist, Gary Yoder, for *The Original Human Being*. It featured the atmospheric, raga-influenced 'Babaji (Twilight Raga)', and is widely acclaimed as the group's most cohesive work. The band was dissolved in 1971 but re-formed in 1979 following an emotional reunion between Petersen and Whaley. This line-up made *The Beast Is Back* ... in 1985 and added guitarist Tony Rainer. Blue Cheer continued to pursue the former's bombastic vision, and *Highlights And Lowlives*, coupled the group with Anthrax producer Jack Endino. In the early 90s the band was reappraised, with many of the Seattle grunge rock bands admitting a strong affection for Blue Cheer's ground-breaking work.
●ALBUMS: *Vincebus Eruptum* (Philips 1968)★★★, *Outsideinside* (Philips 1968)★★★, *New! Improved! Blue Cheer* (Philips 1969)★★, *Blue Cheer* (Philips 1970)★★, *The Original Human Being* (Philips 1970)★★, *Oh! Pleasant Hope* (Philips 1971)★, *The Beast Is Back* ... (Important 1985)★, *Blitzkrieg Over Nuremburg* (Thunderbolt 1990)★★, *Dining With Sharks* (Nibelung 1991)★★.
●COMPILATIONS: *The Best Of Blue Cheer* (Phillips 1982)★★★, *Louder Than God* (Rhino 1986)★★★, *Highlights And Lowlives* (Nibelung 1990)★★, *Good Times Are So Hard To Find (The History Of Blue Cheer)* (Mercury 1990)★★★, *Live & Unreleased* (Captain Trip 1996)★★.

BLUE HAWAII

Blue Hawaii was Elvis Presley's third film after leaving the US Army. Released in 1961, its lush production and romantic theme set the tone for the production-line formula which followed. Here, Presley plays a GI who, having returned home to Honolulu, opts for a life as a beachcomber. Despite this mild 'drop-out' theme, the star's assimilation into conventional life culminates with his marriage and his version of the 'Hawaiian Wedding Song'. Glamorous location shots helped enhance the film's appeal, particularly in an austere UK where the soundtrack album remained on the charts for over a year. A double-sided single culled from its content, 'Rock A Hula Baby'/'Can't Help Falling In Love With You', topped the UK singles chart for four weeks.

BLUE NOTE RECORDS

Founded in New York by Alfred Lion, the Blue Note record label became synonymous with the best in bebop and soul jazz. Its origins were, however, somewhat differently orientated. Born in Berlin, Germany, in 1908, Lion visited New York when he was 20 years old, mainly to hear music. Back in Germany he watched the rising tide of fascism with alarm and left the country before things became too dangerous, eventually making his way back to New York in 1938. Prompted by his admiration of boogie-woogie pianists Albert Ammons and Meade 'Lux' Lewis at John Hammond's *Spirituals To Swing* concert at Carnegie Hall he decided to record them at his own expense. He followed this session with others featuring established jazzmen of the day, including Edmond Hall, James P. Johnson and Sidney Bechet. By the early 40s Lion had begun to record many of the most influential figures in the newly emergent strand of jazz known as bebop. Lion's dedication and ear for talent, allied as it was to the perspicacity of his A&R man, tenor saxophonist Ike Quebec, caused him to bring to his Blue Note studios many newcomers who could not find opportunities with the major record companies. In Blue Note's studios, the music was superbly recorded thanks to the skills of sound engineer Rudy Van Gelder. The list of artists recorded during this period reads like a bebop hall of fame; among them were Bud Powell, Thelonious Monk, Tadd Dameron, Wynton Kelly, Horace Silver, Fats Navarro, Howard McGhee, Clifford Brown, Lee Morgan, Freddie Hubbard, Dexter Gordon, Hank Mobley, Jackie McLean, Johnny Griffin, Kenny Barron, Clifford Jordan and Art Blakey. Thanks to such enormous talents, Blue Note's reputation grew, and over the next decade or so, many of the most important figures in contemporary jazz were persuaded to record for Lion and his partner Francis Wolff, whose photographs were often featured on the label's strikingly designed record sleeves. Following Quebec's death in 1963, Lion again appointed a musician as A&R man, this time choosing Duke Pearson. After the unexpected popular success of Lee Morgan's 'The Sidewinder' single in 1964, the label became associated with the 60s soul-jazz movement, including Big John Patten, Jimmy Smith, Grant Green, Kenny Burrell, Stanley Turrentine, Lou Donaldson and Brother Jack McDuff. During this inspired period, the record covers featured the immaculate typography of designer Reid Miles. Lion also released many notable *avant garde* records, including sessions by Ornette Coleman, Andrew Hill, Sam Rivers, Wayne Shorter, Cecil Taylor, Anthony Williams and Larry Young. Ill heath forced Lion to sell Blue Note to Liberty Records with Wolff and Pearson continuing to control the company's musical policy. Eventually, commercial considerations affected the nature of the music with which Blue Note was associated, but an intelligent reissue programme was instigated by producer Michael Cuscuna in the mid-70s and continued through the 80s and into the early 90s. In the 80s Liberty became a part of the EMI group, and, in addition to the reissue programme, the label began to record many new jazz stars, including Bobby McFerrin, John Scofield and Stanley Jordan, while continuing to record the established figures. Alfred Lion died in 1987, his partner Wolff having died in 1971. The label is currently run by Bruce Lundval and Michael Cuscuna.

●COMPILATIONS: *Critics' Choice* (1992)★★★, *The Best Of Blue Note Vol. 2* (1993)★★★.
●FURTHER READING: *The Cover Art Of Blue Note Records*, Graham Marsh, Glyn Callingham and Felix Cromey (eds.).

BLUE, DAVID

b. Stuart David Cohen, 18 February 1941, Providence, Rhode Island, USA, d. 2 December 1982, USA. Having left the US Army, Cohen arrived in Greenwich Village in 1960 hoping to pursue an acting career, but was drawn instead into the nascent folk circle. He joined a generation of younger performers - Eric Anderson, Phil Ochs, Dave Van Ronk and Tom Paxton - who rose to prominence in Bob Dylan's wake. Blue was signed to the influential Elektra label in 1965 and released the *Singer/Songwriter Project* album - a joint collaboration with Richard Farina, Bruce Murdoch and Patrick Sky. Although Blue's first full-scale collection in 1966 bore an obvious debt to the folk rock style of *Highway 61 Revisited*, a rudimentary charm was evident on several selections, notably 'Grand Hotel' and 'I'd Like To Know'. Several acts recorded the singer's compositions, but subsequent recordings with a group, American Patrol, were never issued and it was two years before a second album appeared. *These 23 Days In December* showcased a more mellow performer, best exemplified in the introspective reworking of 'Grand Hotel', before a further release recorded in Nashville, *Me, S. David Cohen*, embraced country styles. Another hiatus ended in 1972 when Blue was signed to David Geffen's emergent Asylum label, and his first album for the company, *Stories*, was the artist's bleakest, most introspective selection. Subsequent releases included the Graham Nash-produced *Nice Baby And The Angel* and *Com'n Back For More*, but although his song, 'Outlaw Man', was covered by the Eagles, Blue was unable to make a significant commercial breakthrough. During this period, he appeared alongside his old Greenwich Village friend, Bob Dylan, in the Rolling Thunder Revue which toured North America. Blue resumed acting later in the decade and made memorable film appearances in Neil Young's *Human Highway* and Wim Wenders' *An American Friend*. His acerbic wit was one of the highlights of Dylan's *Renaldo And Clara* movie, but this underrated artist died in 1982 while jogging in Washington Square Park.
●ALBUMS: with Richard Farina *Singer/Songwriter Project* (1965)★★★, *David Blue* (1966)★★★, *These 23 Days In December* (1968)★★, *Me, S. David Cohen* (1970)★★, *Stories* (Line 1971)★★★, *Nice Baby And The Angel* (1973)★★★, *Com'n Back For More* (Asylum 1975)★★★, *Cupid's Arrow* (1976)★★★.

BLUEJAYS

An R&B vocal group from Los Angeles, California, USA, the Blue Jays perfectly represent the transitional era between 50s R&B and the 60s soul in their renditions of doo-wop-styled songs with a gospel-style lead vocal. Comprising lead singer Leon Peels (b. 1936, Newport, Arkansas, USA), Alex Manigo, Van Earl Richardson, and Leonard Davidson, the group came together in 1961, and the same year were signed by country singer Werly Fairburn to his Milestone label. The Blue Jays' first record, 'Lovers Island' (number 31 in the US pop chart) in 1961 was at the time considered to be one of the last gasps of doo-wop, yet in retrospect, one can hear the first glimmerings of soul in Peels' gospel-edged vocals. Peculiarly, the song only made the local R&B charts. The group followed the hit with some excellent numbers, notably 'Tears Are Falling' (1961) and 'The Right To Love' (1962), but achieved little success; they disbanded in early 1962.
●ALBUMS: *The Blue Jays Meet Little Caesar* (Milestone 1962)★★★.
●COMPILATIONS: *Lovers Island* (Relic 1987)★★★.

BLUES MAGOOS

Formed in the Bronx, New York, USA, in 1964 and initially known as the Bloos Magoos, the founding line-up consisted of Emil 'Peppy' Thielhelm (b. 16 June 1949; vocals/guitar), Dennis LaPore (lead guitar), Ralph Scala (b. 12 December 1947; organ/vocals), Ronnie Gilbert (b. 25 April 1946; bass) and John Finnegan (drums), but by the end of the year LaPore and Finnegan had been replaced by Mike Esposito (b. 1943, Delaware, USA) and Geoff Daking (b. 1947, Delaware, USA). The group quickly became an important part of the emergent Greenwich Village rock scene and in 1966 secured a residency at the fabled Night Owl club. Having recorded singles for Ganim and Verve Forecast, the band was signed to Mercury Records, where they became the subject of intense grooming. However, Vidal Sassoon-styled haircuts and luminous costumes failed to quash an innate rebelliousness, although the group enjoyed one notable hit when '(We Ain't Got) Nothin' Yet' (1966) reached number 5 in the US chart. Its garage-band snarl set the tone for an attendant album, *Psychedelic Lollipop*, which contained several equally virulent selections. The Blues Magoos' dalliance with drugs was barely disguised, and titles such as 'Love Seems Doomed' (LSD) and 'Albert Common Is Dead' (ACID) were created to expound their beliefs. By 1968 tensions arose within the group and they broke up following the release of *Basic Blues Magoos*. The management team re-signed the name to ABC Records, and, as Thielhelm had accumulated a backlog of material, suggested he front a revamped line-up. John Leillo (vibes/percussion), Eric Kaz (keyboards), Roger Eaton (bass) and Richie Dickon (percussion) completed *Never Goin' Back To Georgia*, while the same group, except for Eaton, was augmented by sundry session musicians for the disappointing *Gulf Coast Bound*. The Blues Magoos' name was discontinued when Peppy took a role in the musical *Hair*. As Peppy Castro he has since pursued a varied career as a member of Barnaby Bye, Wiggy Bits and Balance, while Cher and Kiss are among the artists who have recorded his songs.
●ALBUMS: *Psychedelic Lollipop* (Mercury 1966)★★★, *Electric Comic Book* (Mercury 1967)★★★, *Basic Blues Magoos* (Mercury 1968)★★, *Never Goin' Back To*

Georgia (1969)★★, *Gulf Coast Bound* (1970)★★.
●COMPILATIONS: *Kaleidoscopic Compendium: The Best Of The Blues Magoos* (Mercury 1992)★★★.

BLUES PROJECT

The Blues Project was formed in New York City in the mid-60s by guitarist Danny Kalb, and took its name from a compendium of acoustic musicians in which he participated. Tommy Flanders (vocals), Steve Katz (b. 9 May 1945, Brooklyn, New York, USA; guitar), Andy Kulberg b. 1944, Buffalo, New York, USA; bass/flute), Roy Blumenfeld (drums), plus Kalb, were latterly joined by Al Kooper (b. 5 February 1944, Brooklyn, New York, USA; vocals/keyboards), fresh from adding the distinctive organ on Bob Dylan's 'Like A Rolling Stone'. The sextet was quickly established as the city's leading electric blues band, a prowess demonstrated on their debut album *Live At the Cafe Au Go Go*. Flanders then left to pursue a solo career and the resultant five-piece embarked on the definitive *Projections* album. Jazz, pop and soul styles were added to their basic grasp of R&B to create an absorbing, rewarding collection, but inner tensions undermined an obvious potential. By the time *Live At The Town Hall* was issued, Kooper had left the group to form Blood, Sweat And Tears, where he was subsequently joined by Katz. An unhappy Kalb also quit the group, but Kulberg and Blumenfeld added Richard Greene (violin), John Gregory (guitar/vocals) and Don Kretmar (bass/saxophone) for a fourth collection, *Planned Obsolescence*. The line-up owed little to the old group, and in deference to this new direction, changed their name to Seatrain.
In 1971, Kalb reclaimed the erstwhile moniker and recorded two further albums with former members Flanders, Blumenfeld and Kretmar. This particular version of the band was supplanted by a reunion of the *Projections* line-up for a show in Central Park, after which the Blues Project name was abandoned. Despite their fractured history, the group is recognised as one of the leading white R&B bands of the 60s.
●ALBUMS: *Live At The Cafe Au Go-Go* (Verve/Folkways 1966)★★, *Projections* (Verve/Forecast 1967)★★★, *Live At The Town Hall* (Verve/Forecast 1967)★★★, *Planned Obsolescence* (Verve/Forecast 1968)★★, *Flanders Kalb Katz Etc* (Verve Forecast 1969)★★, *Lazarus* (1971)★★, *Blues Project* (Capitol 1972)★★, *Reunion In Central Park* (One Way 1973)★★.
●COMPILATIONS: *Best Of The Blues Project* (Rhino 1989)★★★.

BO STREET RUNNERS

Formed in 1964 in Harrow, Middlesex, England, the Bo Street Runners initially comprised John Dominic (vocals), Gary Thomas (lead guitar), Royston Fry (keyboards), Dave Cameron (bass) and Nigel Hutchinson (drums). Within months of forming they recorded a self-financed EP which was sold at Harrow's Railway Hotel, where the group held a residency. When Cameron's mother sent a copy of the disc to the producers of ATV's *Ready, Steady, Go!*, the Bo Street Runners were added to the list of competitors in the show's talent contest, 'Ready, Steady, Win!'. The group won, securing a prized deal with Decca Records. 'Bo Street Runner' duly became their debut single, but despite the publicity, it failed to chart. Glyn Thomas and Tim Hinkley then replaced Hutchinson and Fry, while Dave Quincy was added on saxophone. Two singles for Columbia Records ensued, 'Tell Me What You're Gonna Do' and 'Baby Never Say Goodbye', the latter of which lost out to the original version by Unit Four Plus Two. Thomas was then replaced by Mick Fleetwood, and with Quincy departing for Chris Farlowe, the reshaped Bo Street Runners released a version of the Beatles' 'Drive My Car' in January 1966. Fleetwood was then replaced in turn by Alan Turner and Barrie Wilson, and when Dominic opted to manage the group, Mike Patto joined as vocalist. The Bo Street Runners disbanded late in 1966, after which Patto recorded a solo single, 'Can't Stop Talkin' 'Bout My Baby'. The b-side, 'Love', represented the final Bo Street Runners' recording. Patto was reunited with Hinkley in the Chicago Line Blues Band, before joining Timebox, who in turn evolved into Patto.

BOB AND EARL

Formed in Los Angeles, California, USA, in 1960, this duo comprised Bobby Day (b. Bobby Byrd, 1 July 1932, Fort Worth, Texas, USA) and Earl Lee Nelson. Day had previously formed the Hollywood Flames, a group best recalled for the rock 'n' roll hit 'Buzz-Buzz-Buzz' (1957), which featured Nelson on lead vocal. Day then secured a solo hit with 'Rockin' Robin' before briefly joining Nelson in the original Bob And Earl. Bob Relf replaced Day when the latter resumed his own career. The Barry White-produced 'Harlem Shuffle', the pairing's best-known song, was originally released in 1963. A minor hit in the US, the single proved more durable in Britain. Although it failed to chart when first released, a reissue reached number 7 in 1969. Bob And Earl had meanwhile continued to record excellent singles, although the prophetically titled 'Baby It's Over' (1966) was their only further hit. Nelson recorded under the name of Jay Dee for Warner Brothers Records in 1973, and also as Jackie Lee, charting in the US with 'The Duck' (1965), 'African Boo-Ga-Loo' (1968) and 'The Chicken' (1970). Relf wrote Love Unlimited's 1974 hit 'Walking In The Rain' and was latterly replaced by Bobby Garrett. The new duo continued to record together, and individually, during the 70s.
●ALBUMS: *Harlem Shuffle* (Tip/Sue 1966)★★★, *Bob And Earl* (Crestview/B&C 1969)★★, *Together* (Joy 1969)★★.

BOB B. SOXX AND THE BLUE JEANS

One of several groups created by producer Phil Spector, this short-lived trio consisted of two members of the Blossoms (Darlene Love and Fanita James), and soul singer Bobby Sheen. The Blue Jeans scored a US Top 10 hit in 1962 with a radical reading of 'Zip-A-Dee-Do-Dah', wherein the euphoric original was slowed to a snail-like pace. Its success spawned an album which mixed restructured standards ('The White Cliffs Of Dover', 'This Land Is Your Land') with original songs, of which 'Why Do Lovers Break Each Other's Heart?' and 'Not Too Young To Get Married' were also issued as singles. The group made a contribution to Phil Spector's legendary *Christmas Album*.

●ALBUMS: *Zip-A-Dee-Doo-Dah* (Philles 1963)★★★.

BOND, GRAHAM

b. 28 October 1937, Romford, Essex, England, d. 8 May 1974, London, England. The young Bond was adopted from the Dr Barnardo's children's home and given musical tuition at school, and has latterly become recognized as one of the main instigators of British R&B, along with Cyril Davies and Alexis Korner. His musical career began with Don Rendell's quintet in 1961 as a jazz saxophonist, followed by a stint with Korner's famous ensemble, Blues Incorporated. By the time he formed his first band in 1963 he had made the Hammond organ his main instrument, although he showcased his talent at gigs by playing both alto saxophone and organ simultaneously. The seminal Graham Bond Organisation became one of the most respected units during 1964, and boasted an impressive line-up of Ginger Baker (drums), Jack Bruce (bass) and Dick Heckstall-Smith (saxophone - replacing John McLaughlin on guitar), playing a hybrid of jazz, blues and rock that was musically and visually stunning. Bond was the prominent musician in Britain to play a Hammond organ through a Leslie speaker cabinet, and the first to use a Mellotron. The original Organisation made two superlative and formative albums, *Sound Of '65* and *There's A Bond Between Us*. Both featured original songs mixed and interpretations of 'Walk On The Wild Side', 'Wade In The Water' and 'Got My Mojo Working'. Bond's own 'Have You Ever Loved A Woman' and 'Walkin' In The Park' demonstrated his songwriting ability, but despite his musicianship he was unable to find a commercially acceptable niche. The jazz fraternity regarded Bond's band as too noisy and rock-based, while the pop audience found his music complicated and too jazzy. Thirty years later the Tommy Chase Band pursued an uncannily similar musical road, now under the banner of jazz. As the British music scene changed, so the Organisation was penalized for its refusal to adapt to more conventional trends in music. Along the way, Bond had lost Baker and Bruce departed to form Cream, although the addition of Jon Hiseman on drums reinforced their musical pedigree. When Hiseman and Heckstall-Smith left to form Colosseum, they showed their debt to Bond by featuring 'Walkin' In The Park' on their debut album. Disenchanted with the musical tide, Bond moved to the USA where he made two albums for the Pulsar label. Both records showed a departure from jazz and R&B, but neither fared well and Bond returned to England in 1969. The music press welcomed his reappearance, but a poorly attended Royal Albert Hall homecoming concert must have bitterly disheartened its subject. His new band, the Graham Bond Initiation, featured his wife Diane Stewart. The unlikely combination of astrological themes, R&B and public apathy doomed this promising unit. Bond started on a slow decline into drugs, depression, mental disorder and dabblings with the occult. Following a reunion with Ginger Baker in his ill-fated Airforce project, and a brief spell with the Jack Bruce Band, Bond formed a musical partnership with Pete Brown; this resulted in one album and, for a short time, had a stabilizing effect on Bond's life. Following a nervous breakdown, drug addiction and two further unsuccessful conglomerations, Bond was killed on 8 May 1974 when he fell under the wheels of a London Underground train at Finsbury Park station. Whether Graham Bond could again have reached the musical heights of his 1964 band is open to endless debate; what has been acknowledged is that he was an innovator, a loveable rogue and a major influence on British R&B.

●ALBUMS: *The Sound Of '65* (Columbia 1965)★★★★, *There's A Bond Between Us* (Columbia 1966)★★★, *Mighty Graham Bond* (Pulsar 1968)★★★, *Love Is The Law* (Pulsar 1968)★★★, - the latter two albums were repackaged as *Bond In America* (Philips 1971)★★★, *Solid Bond* (Warners 1970)★★★, *We Put The Majick On You* (Vertigo 1971)★★★, *Holy Magick* (Vertigo 1971)★★★, *Bond And Brown: Two Heads Are Better Than One* (Chapter One 1972)★★★, *This Is Graham Bond* (Philips 1978)★★★, an edited version of *Bond In America*, *The Beginnings Of Jazz-Rock* (1977)★★★, *The Graham Bond Organisation Live At Klook's Kleek* (Charly 1984)★★★.

●FURTHER READING: *The Smallest Place In The World*, Dick Heckstall-Smith. *Graham Bond; The Mighty Shadow*, Harry Shapiro.

●FILMS: *Gonks Go Beat* (1965).

BONDS, GARY 'U.S.'

b. Gary Anderson, 6 June 1939, Jacksonville, Florida, USA. Having initially sung in various gospel groups, Bonds embraced secular music upon moving to Norfolk, Virginia. A successful spell in the region's R&B clubs resulted in a recording deal with local entrepreneur Frank Guida, whose cavernous production techniques gave Bonds' releases their distinctive sound. The ebullient 'New Orleans' set the pattern for the artist's subsequent recordings and its exciting, 'party' atmosphere reached an apogee on 'Quarter To Three', a US chart-topper and the singer's sole million-seller. Between 1961 and 1962 Bonds scored further similar-sounding hits with 'School Is Out', 'School Is In', 'Dear Lady Twist' and 'Twist Twist Senora', but his career then went into sharp decline. He toured the revival circuit until 1978 when long-time devotee Bruce Springsteen joined the singer onstage during a live engagement. Their friendship resulted in *Dedication*, produced by Springsteen and E Street Band associate Miami Steve Van Zandt. The former contributed three original songs to the set, one of which, 'This Little Girl', reached the US Top 10 in 1981. Their collaboration was maintained with *On The Line*, which included Bonds' version of the Box Tops' 'Soul Deep', but he later asserted his independence with the self-produced *Standing In The Line Of Fire*. Little has been heard of him in the 90s.

● ALBUMS: *Dance 'Til Quarter To Three* (Legrand/Top Rank 1961)★★★, *Twist Up Calypso* (Legrand/Stateside 1962)★★★, *Dedication* (EMI America 1981)★★★, *On The Line* (EMI America (1982)★★, *Gary 'U.S.' Bonds Meets Chubby Checker* (1981)★★, *Standing In The Line Of Fire* (Phoenix 1984)★★.

● COMPILATIONS: *Greatest Hits Of Gary 'U.S.' Bonds* (Legrand/Stateside 1962)★★★★, *Certified Soul* (Rhino 1982)★★, *The School Of Rock 'n' Roll: The Best Of Gary 'U.S' Bonds* (Rhino 1990)★★★★, *Take Me Back To New Orleans* (Ace 1995)★★★, *The Best Of Gary U.S. Bonds* (EMI 1996)★★★★.

● FILMS: *It's Trad, Dad* aka *Ring-A-Ding Rhythm* (1962).

BONO, SONNY

b. Salvatore Bono, 12 February 1935, Detroit, Michigan, USA. Although primarily associated with the 60s folk rock boom, Bono's career began the previous decade as director of A&R at Specialty Records. He co-wrote 'She Said Yeah' for Larry Williams, later covered by the Rolling Stones, and also pursued a recording career with the first of several singles bearing numerous aliases, including Don Christy, Sonny Christy and Ronny Sommers. A fruitful period under the aegis of producer Phil Spector inspired Bono to found the ill-fated Rush label, but he achieved a greater fame when 'Needles And Pins', a collaboration with Jack Nitzsche, was successfully recorded by Jackie DeShannon and the Searchers. In 1963 Bono met, and married, Cherilyn La Pierre, better known as Cher. Her fledgling singing career was subsequently augmented by their work as a duo, firstly as Caesar And Cleo, then Sonny And Cher. In 1965 the couple enjoyed an international smash with 'I Got You Babe', written, arranged and produced by Bono, who resurrected solo ambitions in the wake of its success. Although 'Laugh At Me' reached the Top 10 in the US and UK, 'The Revolution Kind', Sonny's disavowal of the counter-culture, failed to emulate this feat. Bono's lone album, *Inner Views*, was an artistic and commercial disaster and he subsequently abandoned solo recordings. Although Sonny and Cher ended the personal partnership in 1974, they continued to host a popular television show. However, Bono later concentrated on an acting career, with regular appearances on television and in several films, notably *Hairspray* (1988). A registered Republican, he was voted mayor of Palm Springs in 1988, the day after his ex-wife won an Oscar for her role in *Moonstruck*. In 1991, Bono announced his intention to run for the senate at the next election.

● ALBUMS: *Inner Views* (1967)★.

● FURTHER READING: *And The Beat Goes On*, Sonny Bono.

BONZO DOG DOO-DAH BAND

Although this eccentric ensemble was initially viewed as a 20s revival act, they quickly developed into one of the era's most virulent satirists. Formed as the Bonzo Dog Dada Band in 1965 by art students Vivian Stanshall (b. 21 March 1943, Shillingford, Oxfordshire, England, d. March 1995; vocals, trumpet, devices) and Rodney Slater (b. 8 November 1941, Crowland, Lincolnshire, England; saxophone), the group also included Neil Innes (b. 9 December 1944, Danbury, Essex, England; vocals, piano, guitar), Roger Ruskin Spear (b. 29 June 1943, Hammersmith, London, England; props, devices, saxophone) and 'Legs' Larry Smith (b. 18 January 1944, Oxford, England; drums). Various auxiliary members, including Sam Spoons (b. Martin Stafford Ash, 8 February 1942, Bridgewater, Somerset, England), Bob Kerr and Vernon Dudley Bohey-Nowell (b. 29 July 1932, Plymouth, Devon, England), augmented the line-up; the informality was such that no-one knew which members would arrive to perform in the group's early shows. In 1966, two singles, 'My Brother Makes The Noises For The Talkies' and 'Alley Oop', reflected their transition from trad jazz to pop. *Gorilla*, the Bonzo's inventive debut album, still showed traces of their music-hall past, but the irreverent humour displayed on 'Jollity Farm' and the surrealistic 'The Intro And The Outro' confirmed a lasting quality which outstripped that of contemporary 'rivals', the New Vaudeville Band, to whom Kerr, and others, had defected. A residency on the British television children's show, *Do Not Adjust Your Set*, secured the group's unconventional reputation and the songs they performed were later compiled on the *Tadpoles* album. The Bonzo Dog Band was also featured in the Beatles' film *Magical Mystery Tour*, performing the memorable 'Death Cab For Cutie', and in 1968 secured a UK Top 5 hit with 'I'm The Urban Spaceman', which was produced by Paul McCartney under the pseudonym Apollo C. Vermouth. Further albums, *The Doughnut In Granny's Greenhouse* and *Keynsham*, displayed an endearing eclecticism which derided the blues boom ('Can Blue Men Sing The Whites'), suburbia ('My Pink Half Of The Drainpipe') and many points in between, while displaying an increasingly rock-based bent. Newcomers Dennis Cowan (b. 6 May 1947, London, England), Dave Clague and Joel Druckman toughened the group's live sound, but the strain of compressing pre-war English middle class frivolousness (Stanshall), whimsical pop (Innes) and Ruskin Spear's madcap machinery into a united whole ultimately proved too great. Although a reconvened line-up completed *Let's Make Up And Be Friendly* in 1972, this project was only undertaken to fulfil contractual obligations. The group had disbanded two years earlier when its members embarked on their inevitably divergent paths.

● ALBUMS: *Gorilla* (Liberty 1967)★★★, *The Doughnut In Granny's Greenhouse* (Liberty 1968)★★★, *Tadpoles* (Liberty 1969)★★★, *Keynsham* (Liberty 1969)★★★, *Let's Make Up And Be Friendly* (United Artists 1972)★★.

●COMPILATIONS: *The History Of The Bonzos* (United Artists 1974)★★★★, *The Bestiality Of The Bonzo Dog Band* (Liberty 1989)★★★, *Cornology Vols. 1-3* (EMI 1992)★★★.
●FILMS: *Adventures Of The Son Of Exploding Sausage* (1969).

BOOKER T. AND THE MGs

Formed in Memphis, Tennessee, USA, in 1962 as a spin-off from the Mar-Keys, the group comprised Booker T. Jones (b. 12 November 1944, Memphis, Tennessee, USA; organ), Steve Cropper (b. 21 October 1941, Willow Spring, Missouri, USA; guitar), Lewis Steinberg (bass) and Al Jackson Jr. (b. 17 November 1934, Memphis, Tennessee, USA, d. 1 October 1975, Memphis, Tennessee, USA; drums). 'Green Onions', the MGs' renowned first hit, evolved out of a blues riff they had improvised while waiting to record a jingle. Its simple, smoky atmosphere, punctuated by Cropper's cutting guitar, provided the blueprint to a series of excellent records, including 'Jellybread', 'Chinese Checkers', 'Soul Dressing', Mo' Onions and 'Hip Hug-Her'. Pared to the bone, this sparseness accentuated the rhythm, particularly when Steinberg was replaced on bass by Donald 'Duck' Dunn (b. 24 November 1941, Memphis, Tennessee, USA). Their intuitive interplay became the bedrock of classic Stax, the foundation on which the label and studio sound was built. The quartet appeared on all of the company's notable releases, including 'In The Midnight Hour' (Wilson Pickett), 'Hold On I'm Comin'' (Sam And Dave) and 'Walkin' The Dog' (Rufus Thomas), on which Booker T. also played saxophone. Although Jones divided his time between recording and studying at Indiana University, (he subsequently earned a BA in music); the MGs (Memphis Group) continued to chart consistently in their own right. 'Hang 'Em High' (1968) and 'Time Is Tight' (1969) were both US Top 10 singles, while as late as 1971 'Melting Pot' climbed into the same Top 50. The group split that year; Jones moved to California in semi-retirement, recording with his wife, Priscilla, while his three ex-colleagues remained in Memphis. In 1973 Jackson and Dunn put together a reconstituted group. Bobby Manuel and Carson Whitsett filled out the line-up, but the resultant album, *The MGs*, was a disappointment. Jackson meanwhile maintained his peerless reputation, particularly with work for Al Green and Syl Johnson, but tragically in 1975 he was shot dead in his Memphis home after disturbing intruders. Cropper, who had released a solo album in 1969, *With A Little Help From My Friends*, set up his TMI studio/label and temporarily seemed content with a low-key profile. He latterly rejoined Dunn, ex-Bar-Kay drummer Willie Hall and the returning Jones for *Universal Language*. Cropper and Dunn also played musicians' roles in the film *The Blues Brothers*. During the late 70s UK R&B revival, 'Green Onions' was reissued and became a Top 10 hit in 1979. In 1981, *I Want You*, reached the R&B charts although the members still continued with their individual projects. The group did, however, complete some British concert dates in 1990.

●ALBUMS: *Green Onions* (Stax 1962)★★★★, *Mo' Onions* (1963)★★★★, *Soul Dressing* (Stax 1965)★★★★, *My Sweet Potato* (1965)★★★, *And Now!* (Stax 1966)★★★, *In The Christmas Spirit* (Stax 1966)★★, *Hip Hug-Her* (Stax 1967)★★★, with the Mar-Keys *Back To Back* (Stax 1967)★★★, *Doin' Our Thing* (Stax 1968)★★★, *Soul Limbo* (Stax 1968)★★★, *Uptight* (Stax 1969)★★, *Booker T. Set* (Stax 1969)★★★, *McLemore Avenue* (Stax 1970)★★, *Melting Pot* (Stax 1971)★★, as the MG's *The MGs* (Stax 1973)★★, *Memphis Sound* (1975)★★, *Union Extended* (1976)★★, *Universal Language* (Asylum 1977)★. Solo: Booker T. *I Want You* (1981)★★, *That's The Way It Should Be* (Columbia 1994)★★.
●COMPILATIONS: *The Best Of Booker T. And The MGs* (Atlantic 1968)★★★★★, *Greatest Hits* (Stax 1970)★★★★, *The Best Of Booker T And The MG's (Very Best Of)* (Rhino 1993)★★★★★, *Play The Hip Hits* (Stax/Ace 1995)★★★★.

BOONE, PAT

b. Charles Eugene Patrick Boone, 1 June 1934, Jacksonville, Florida, USA. Boone sold more records during the late 50s than any other artist except Elvis Presley. From 1955 to date, only six artists (Presley, the Beatles, James Brown, Elton John, Rolling Stones and Stevie Wonder) are ranked above him in terms of total singles sales and their relative chart positions. Boone had a total of 60 hits in the US singles charts during his career, six of which reached number 1. A bona fide 'teen-idol', Boone was, however, a personality quite unlike Presley. Where Elvis represented the outcast or rebel, Boone was a clean-cut conformist. He was a religious, married family man, who at one point turned down a film role with Marilyn Monroe rather than having to kiss a woman who was not his wife. While Elvis wore long sideburns and greasy hair, Boone was recognised by his 'white buck' shoes and ever-present smile. Boone even attended college during the height of his career. Accordingly, Boone's music, although considered to be rock 'n' roll during his first few years of popularity, was considerably less manic than that being made by Presley and the early black rockers. Boone, in fact, built his career on 'cover' records, tame, cleaned-up versions of R&B songs originally recorded by black artists like Fats Domino, Little Richard, Ivory Joe Hunter, the Flamingos and the El Dorados.
Boone grew up in the Nashville, Tennessee, area, where he began singing in public at the age of 10. He appeared on the national *Ted Mack Amateur Hour* and *Arthur Godfrey's Talent Scouts* television programmes in the early 50s, and had his own radio programme on Nashville's WSIX. In 1953, he married Shirley Foley, daughter of country star Red Foley. The following year, Boone recorded his first of four singles for the small Republic label in Nashville, all of which failed.
That year the Boones moved to Denton, Texas, and began raising a family of four daughters, the third of whom, Debby Boone, had a chart hit in 1977 with the ballad 'You Light Up My Life'. Pat signed to Dot Records and recorded

his first single for the company, 'Two Hearts' (originally by R&B group Otis Williams And The Charms) in February 1955. Admittedly unfamiliar with the genre, Boone quickly adapted the raw music to his own crooning style. His second single, Domino's 'Ain't That A Shame', went to number 1, and was followed by a non-stop procession of hits. Boone stayed with the R&B covers until 1957. Even today it is a controversial question whether Boone's cover records helped open the door to the black originators or shut them out of the white marketplace. By 1957, when Presley had established himself as the reigning white rocker, Boone had given up rock and switched to ballads. Among the biggest sellers were 'Friendly Persuasion', 'Don't Forbid Me', 'Love Letters In The Sand' and 'April Love'. Some of Boone's recordings by this time were taken from films in which he starred. He also frequently appeared on television, toured the country, and was the subject of magazine articles praising his positive image and outlook. Boone even wrote several books giving advice to teenagers.

From 1957-60, Boone hosted his own television show, *The Pat Boone Chevy Showroom*. Although still popular, by the beginning of the 60s, his place at the top had slipped somewhat lower. 'Moody River' in 1961, and 'Speedy Gonzales', a novelty rock number of the following year, were his last major pop hits. By 1966 Boone's contract with Dot ended. He drifted from one label to the next, trying his hand at country music and, primarily, gospel. Although he had started recording Christian music as early as 1957, his concentration on that form was near-total by the late 70s; he recorded over a dozen Christian albums during that decade, several with his wife and children as the Boone Family Singers. He continued to make live appearances into the 90s, and became an outspoken supporter of politically conservative and religious causes. By 1991 he had begun discussing the possibility of singing rock music again. In 1993, Boone joined another 50s legend, Kay Starr, on 'The April Love Tour' of the UK. In 1996, Boone recorded with Ritchie Blackmore and Guns N'Roses' Slash for his heavy metal tribute album. Ridiculous although it may seem, Boone tackled classics such as 'The Wind Cries Mary', 'No More Mr Nice Guy', 'Smoke On The Water' and, of course, 'Stairway To Heaven'.

●ALBUMS: *Pat Boone* (Dot 1956)★★★, *Howdy!* (Dot 1956)★★★, *'Pat'* (Dot 1957)★★★, *Pat Boone Sings Irving Berlin* (Dot 1957)★★, *Hymns We Love* (Dot 1957)★★, *Star Dust* (Dot 1958)★★★, *Yes Indeed!* (Dot 1958)★★★, *White Christmas* (Dot 1959)★★★, *He Leadeth Me* (Dot 1959)★★, *Pat Boone Sings* (Dot 1959)★★★, *Great Millions* (Dot 1959)★★★, with Shirley Boone *Side By Side* (Dot 1959)★★, *Tenderly* (Dot 1959)★★★, *Hymns We Have Loved* (Dot 1960)★★, *Moonglow* (Dot 1960)★★★, *This And That* (Dot 1960)★★★, *Moody River* (Dot 1961)★★, *Great! Great! Great!* (Dot 1961)★★, *My God And I* (Dot 1961)★★, *I'll See You In My Dreams* (Dot 1962)★★★, *Pat Boone Reads From The Holy Bible* (Dot 1962)★, *State Fair* film soundtrack (1962)★★, *Pat Boone Sings*

Guess Who? (Dot 1963)★★, *I Love You Truly* (1963)★★, *The Star Spangled Banner* (1963)★★, *Days Of Wine And Roses* (1963)★★★, *Tie Me Kangaroo Down* (1963)★★, *Sing Along Without* (1963)★★, *Touch Of Your Lips* (1964)★★, *Pat Boone* (1964)★★, *Ain't That A Shame* (1964)★★★, *Lord's Prayer And Other Great Hymns* (1964)★★, *Boss Beat* (1964)★★, *True Love: My Tenth Anniversary With Dot Records* (1964)★★, *Near You* (1965)★★★, *Blest Be Thy Name* (1965)★★, *Golden Era Of Country Hits* (1965)★, *Pat Boone 1965* (1965)★★, *Great Hits Of '65* (1966)★★, *Memories* (1966)★★★, *Pat Boone Sings Winners Of The Readers Digest Poll* (1966)★★, *Wish You Were Here, Buddy* (1966)★★, *Christmas Is A Comin'* (1966)★★★, *How Great Thou Art* (1967)★★, *I Was Kaiser Bill's Batman* (1967)★★, *Look Ahead* (1968)★★, *Departure* (1969)★★★, *The Pat Boone Family In The Holy Land* (1972)★, *The New Songs Of The Jesus People* (1972)★, *I Love You More And More Each Day* (1973)★, *Born Again* (1973)★, *S.A.V.E.D.* (1973)★, *The Family Who Prays* (1973)★, *All In The Boone Family* (1973)★, *The Pat Boone Family* (1974)★, *Songs From The Inner Court* (1974)★, *Something Supernatural* (1975)★, *Texas Woman* (1976)★★, *Country Love* (1977)★★, *The Country Side Of Pat Boone* (1977)★, *Just The Way I Am* (1981)★★, *Songmaker* (1981)★★, *Whispering Hope* (1982)★★, *Pat Boone Sings Golden Hymns* (1984)★★, *Jivin' Pat* (1986)★★, *Let's Get Cooking, America* (1987)★, *Tough Marriage* (1987)★★, *With The First Nashville Jesus Band* (1988)★★, *Pat Boone In A Metal Mood: No More Mr Nice Guy* (Hip O 1997)★★.

●COMPILATIONS: *Pat's Great Hits* (Dot 1957)★★★★, *Pat's Great Hits, Volume 2* (Dot 1960) ★★★, *Pat Boone's Golden Hits* (Dot 1962)★★★★, *Twelve Great Hits* (1964)★★★, *16 Great Performances* (1972)★★★, *Pat Boone Originals* (1976)★★★, *20 Best Loved Gospel Songs* (70s)★★, *Best Of Pat Boone* (1982)★★★, *16 Golden Classics* (1987)★★★, *Greatest Hits* (Curb 1990)★★★, *Golden Greats* (1993)★★★, *More Golden Hits: The Original Dot Recordings* (Varese Sarabande 1995)★★★★.

●FURTHER READING: *A New Song*, Pat Boone. *Together: 25 Years With The Boone Family*, Pat Boone.

BOSSTOWN SOUND

The 'Bosstown sound' was the name of a promotional campaign initiated by MGM Records in 1968 in order to push three psychedelic groups it had signed in Boston, Massachusetts, USA, Orpheus, Ultimate Spinach and the Beacon Street Union. The label's goal was to try to create the appearance of a Boston music scene to rival that taking place in San Francisco at the time. Reaction by music critics to the records - and the hype - was so severely negative that the campaign backfired, killing any chance of success the bands might have had on their own. Record producer Alan Lorber is credited as the architect behind the campaign, having produced the debut albums of Orpheus and Ultimate Spinach. MGM

took out an advertisement in the trade magazine *Billboard* announcing the new 'Bosstown sound' in January 1968, and Boston radio stations as well as other mainstream media jumped on the story. *Newsweek*, for example, devoted an approbatory article to the story. Critics in such influential 'underground' rock magazines as *Crawdaddy* and *Rolling Stone* used words such as 'pretentious' and 'inept' to describe the music, and soon a backlash developed. By that time, several other bands, either by choice or by default, were being lumped in with the 'Bosstown' bands, including a third MGM act, Beacon Street Union, and such groups as Earth Opera, the Apple Pie Motherhood Band, Teddy and the Pandas, Phluph, Bagatelle, Ill Wind, Bo Grumpus, Eden's Children and the Lost. Later, MGM abandoned its campaign, and most of the groups involved disbanded shortly afterwards.
●COMPILATIONS: *Bosstown Sound 1968 - The Music & The Time* (Ace 1996)★★★.

BOWN, ALAN, THE

Trumpeter Alan Bown, formerly of the John Barry Seven, formed this respected group in 1965. Originally known as the Alan Bown Set, the septet - Bown, Jess Roden (vocals), Tony Catchpole (guitar), John Goodsall (saxophone), Geoff Bannister (keyboards), Stan Haldane (bass) and Vic Sweeny (drums) - were stalwarts of London's R&B and soul circuit and appeared on the era's seminal selection, *London Swings Live At The Marquee Club*. By 1967 the unit had abandoned soul music in favour of the emergent 'underground' style and truncated its name to The Alan Bown! *Outward Bown* offered such contemporaneous fare as 'Toyland' and 'Technicolour Dream', but the group subsequently pursued a heavier, more progressive direction on *The Alan Bown!* Brown recruited vocalist Robert Palmer from local support act, Mandrake Paddlesteamer. He replaced Jess Roden, who formed Bronco. The group at that time also included John Anthony on saxophone, who later changed his name to John Helliwell and joined Supertramp. Before he left, Roden had recorded the vocal tracks for a projected album, and it fell to Palmer to dub his voice over these (however, the US version of the group's self-titled debut retained Roden's contributions). Afterwards, Palmer moved on to Dada, then Vinegar Joe, although The Alan Bown continued to play sporadic live dates. In the wake of Palmer's subsequent breakthrough, the group's sole album was reissued twice under different titles by See For Miles Records in 1985 and C5 Records in 1987. Bown continued to lead a fluctuating line-up for two further albums, before dissolving the group. The trumpeter then accepted an A&R appointment with CBS Records.
●ALBUMS: with various artists *London Swings Live At The Marquee Club* (1966)★★, *First Album - Outward Bown* (Music Factory 1967)★★★, *The Alan Bown!* (Deram 1968)★★★, *Listen* (Island 1970)★★★, *Stretchin' Out* (Island 1971)★★.
●COMPILATIONS: *Kick Me Out* (See For Miles 1985)★★★, as Robert Palmer And Alan Brown *The Early Years* (C5 1987)★★★.

BOX TOPS

Formed in 1965, this Memphis-based quintet - Alex Chilton (b. 28 December 1950, Memphis, Tennessee, USA; guitar/harmonica/vocals), Gary Talley (b. 17 August 1947, Memphis, Tennessee, USA; lead guitar), Billy Cunningham (b. 23 January 1950, Memphis, Tennessee, USA; rhythm guitar), John Evans (b. 1949; bass) and Danny Smythe (b. 1949; drums) - sprang to fame two years later when their debut single, 'The Letter', became an international hit. Although nominally a group, their appeal lay in Chilton's raspy delivery and Dan Penn's complementary production, a combination repeated on further successes, 'Neon Rainbow', 'Cry Like A Baby', 'Soul Deep' and the annoyingly infectious 'Choo-Choo Train'. Rick Allen (b. 28 January 1946, Little Rock, Arkansas, USA) replaced Evans in 1968, but the group's gifted singer remained its focal point. The Box Tops adeptly combined southern soul with pop, but any impetus faltered when their backroom mentors were drawn into other projects. The band broke up in 1969, but Chilton subsequently reappeared in the critically acclaimed Big Star.
●ALBUMS: *The Letter/Neon Rainbow* (Bell 1967)★★★, *Cry Like A Baby* (Bell 1968)★★★, *Non Stop* (Bell 1968)★★★, *Dimensions* (1969)★★.
●COMPILATIONS: *Super Hits* (Bell 1969)★★★, *Greatest Hits* (Rhino 1982)★★★, *Ultimate Box Tops* (Warners 1988)★★★.

BOYCE AND HART

Recalled chiefly for their association with the Monkees, this songwriting team also enjoyed a fruitful independent career. Tommy Boyce (b. 29 September 1944, Charlottsville, Virginia, USA, d. 23 November 1994, Nashville, Tennessee, USA) had recorded several singles during the early 60s, charting briefly with 'I'll Remember Carol', while Bobby Hart (b. 1944, Phoenix, Arizona, USA) helped compose hits for Little Anthony And The Imperials and Tommy Sands. The two were originally cast as members of the Monkees, but secured the musical/production rights when this idea was vetoed. Together they wrote several of the group's early classics, including 'Last Train To Clarksville', 'Valleri' and '(I'm Not Your) Steppin' Stone', but they were latterly supplanted during the backroom machinations surrounding the group's progress. Boyce and Hart then embarked on a performing career. They had several US Top 40 hits, the most successful of which was 'I Wonder What She's Doing Tonite' which peaked at number 8 in January 1968. Their interest in the Monkees continued with the release of several previously shelved masters, and in 1975 they joined former members Davy Jones and Mickey Dolenz for a nostalgia tour. This, in turn, engendered a handful of new recordings. The songwriters subsequently pursued a myriad of projects. Bobby Hart recorded a solo album, while Tommy Boyce enjoyed a successful career in London, and produced a series of hits for Showaddywaddy and Darts.
●ALBUMS: *Test Patterns* (A&M 1967)★★, *I Wonder*

What She's Doing Tonite? (A&M 1968)★★, *It's All Happening On The Inside* (A&M 1968)★★, with Mickey Dolenz and Davy Jones *Dolenz, Jones, Boyce And Hart* (1976)★★, *Concert In Japan, 1976* (1981)★★, *The Songs Of Tommy Boyce & Bobby Heart* (Varese Sarabande 1996)★★★.

BREAKAWAYS

Formed in London, England, in 1962, this vocal act comprised Vikki Haseman, Margot Quantrell and Betty Prescott, all former members of the Vernons Girls. The Breakaways made their debut with a poor rendition of the Crystals' 'He's A Rebel', although their arrangement was modelled on Vikki Carr's cover version, rather than Phil Spector's original production. The single was not a success and the Breakaways began working as session singers for fellow Pye Records artists Joe Brown, Julie Grant and Jimmy Justice. A brief split followed, but in 1963 Haseman and Quantrell were reunited with another ex-Vernons Girl, Jean Ryder. Having adopted a 'tougher' visual image - black sweaters, slacks and spike-heeled boots - the Breakaways proceeded to record two superb 'girl group' singles, 'That Boy Of Mine' and 'That's How It Goes', both of which were produced by Tony Hatch. The Breakaways remained an in-demand session act, appearing on discs by Cilla Black ('Anyone Who Had A Heart', 'You're My World'), Dusty Springfield ('Stay Awhile'), the Walker Brothers ('The Sun Ain't Gonna Shine Anymore') and Burt Bacharach ('Trains And Boats And Planes'). In 1965 the Breakaways' fourth single, 'Danny Boy', was released to little effect and it was 1967 before another disc, 'Sacred Love', was issued. Their final single, 'Santo Domingo', appeared in 1968. Nevertheless, the Breakaways remained an integral part of the music scene into the 70s, working with, among others, Cliff Richard and James Last. However, by the middle of the decade the Breakaways' name was dropped. Quantrell left music altogether, Ryder continued in session work while Hasemen - now Vikki Brown following her marriage to Joe Brown - began a solo career with *From The Inside* (1977) which was produced by Shel Talmy. In 1986 she duetted with George Harrison on 'Shanghai Surprise' and her busy studio-based career continued unabated into the 90s; she died of cancer in 1995.

BREL, JACQUES

b. 8 April 1929, Brussels, Belgium, d. 10 October 1978. Brel remains a figurehead of modern songwriting, despite a reluctance to either sing in English or, owing to his bitter opposition to the Vietnam war, perform in North America - or, indeed, anywhere else, after retiring from concert appearances in 1966. Although Flemish, he conversed in French. After studying commercial law, he married and spent several years in the family cardboard merchandising business until, nauseated by bourgeois convention, he began a new career in Paris as a singing composer. Buck-toothed and lanky, his lack of obvious mass appeal was thrust aside by impresario Jacques Canetti, who presented him regularly at Pigalle's Theatre Des

Trois Baudets, where he was accompanied by his own guitar and a small backing band. A sense of dramatic construction resulted in performances that, embracing fierce anger, open romanticism and world-weariness, captivated the audiences; his popularity increased after 'Quand On N'A Que L'Amour', his first record success. Other domestic hits such as 'Le Valse De Mille Temps', 'Les Bourgeois', 'Les Dames Patronesses' and 'Les Flamands' gave vent to social comment via a wryly watchful, literate lyricism. This remained intrinsically Gallic until US recording manager Nat Shapiro enthused about Brel to his CBS superiors, who authorized the issue of 1957's *American Debut*, from which a substantial English-speaking following grew. Brel strongly influenced the output of such diverse wordsmiths as Mort Shuman (an early and lifelong disciple), the Kinks' Ray Davies, Leonard Cohen, David Bowie and - also the foremost interpreter of his work - Scott Walker. Brel was to reach a global market by proxy when his material was translated - and often emasculated, as instanced by the Kingston Trio's 1964 rendition of 'Le Moribund' as 'Seasons In The Sun' (a UK number 1 for Terry Jacks a decade later), and the evolution of 'If You Go Away' into a cabaret 'standard'. He played two sell-out Carnegie Hall shows but was keener on developing himself in movies like *Les Risques Du Metier* and *La Bande A Bonnet* (an account of a French anarchist movement at the turn of the century). After he withdrew to the Polynesian Islands, he returned only fleetingly to Paris for one-take recording sessions: his work remained in the public eye through a three-year Broadway run of the musical *Jacques Brel Is Alive And Well And Living In Paris* (which later became a film), and smaller tributes such as the Sensational Alex Harvey Band's use of 'Next' as the title track of a 1975 album. In 1977, Brel returned to France for treatment for the cancer that killed him the following year - a passing marked by a million-selling compilation album and a posthumous recognition of his popularity.

●COMPILATIONS: *La Chanson Francais* (1979)★★★, *Music For The Millions* (1983)★★★, *Ses Plus Grandes Chansons* (1984)★★★, *Jacques Brel* (1986)★★★, *Le Plat Pays* (1988)★★★, *Greatest Hits* (1993)★★★★.

●FURTHER READING: *Jacques Brel: The Biography*, Alan Clayson.

BRENDA AND THE TABULATIONS

An R&B vocal group from Philadelphia, Pennsylvania, USA, consisting of Brenda Payton, Jerry Jones, Eddie Jackson, and Maurice Coates, characterized by the fetchingly innocent-sounding vocals of Payton on a series of intensely sung ballads. Their biggest hit was their 1967 debut single on the Dionn label, 'Dry My Eyes' (number 8 US R&B chart, number 29 pop chart). Their most successful records were a remake of the Miracles' 'Who's Lovin' You' (number 19 R&B) and 'When You're Gone' (number 27 R&B). Bernard Murphy joined the line-up in 1969, and reorganized in 1970 with Brenda Payton, Pat Mercer, and Deborah Martin, the group achieved their biggest hit the following year with 'Right On The Tip Of

'My Tongue' (number 10 R&B, number 23 pop) on the Top & Bottom label. A stint at Epic produced no big hits, but in 1973 their excellent 'One Girl Too Late' (number 43 R&B) deserved far greater recognition and success. The group's last chart success was in 1977.

● ALBUMS: *Dry Your Eyes* (Dionn 1967)★★, *Brenda And The Tabulations* (Top & Bottom 1970)★★, *I Keep Coming Back For More* (Chocolate City 1977)★★.

BRICUSSE, LESLIE

b. 29 January 1931, London, England. A composer, lyricist, librettist and screenwriter, Bricusse was influenced by the MGM musicals of the 40s, particularly *Words And Music*, the Richard Rodgers and Lorenz Hart biopic. He originally intended to be a journalist, but, while studying at Cambridge University, started to write, direct and appear in the *Footlights Reviews*. In 1953, he wrote the music and lyrics (with Robin Beaumont) for *Lady At the Wheel*, a musical with the Monte Carlo rally as its setting, which included songs such as 'The Early Birdie', 'Pete Y'Know', 'Love Is' and a comedy tango, 'Siesta'. It was staged at the local Arts Theatre, and, five years later, had a limited run in the West End. From 1954-5, Bricusse had appeared on the London stage himself with a theatrical legend, in *An Evening With Beatrice Lillie*. For a while during the 50s, he was under contract as a writer at Pinewood Film Studios, and, in 1954, wrote the screenplay and the songs (with Beaumont) for *Charley Moon*, which starred Max Bygraves. The popular singer/comedian took one of the numbers, 'Out Of Town', into the UK Top 20, and it gained Bricusse his first Ivor Novello Award: he won several others, including one for 'My Kind Of Girl' (words and music by Bricusse), which was a UK Top 5 hit for Matt Monro in 1961. Bricusse also wrote a good deal of special material for Bygraves, including one of his 'catch-phrase' songs, 'A Good Idea - Son!'. Early in 1961, Bricusse went to New York to write for another Beatrice Lillie revue, taking Anthony Newley with him to develop ideas for a show of their own. The result, *Stop The World - I Want To Get Off*, written in around three weeks, opened in London's West End in July of that year, and stayed there until November 1962. It later ran for over 500 performances on Broadway, and was filmed in 1966. Book, music and lyrics were jointly credited to Bricusse and Newley, and the latter starred as the central character, Littlechap, in London and New York. The score included several hit songs, including 'What Kind Of Fool Am I?', 'Once In A Lifetime' and 'Gonna Build A Mountain', as well as other, more specialized numbers, such as 'Lumbered', 'Typically English' and 'Someone Nice Like You'. While Newley went off to appear in the off-beat, parochial movie *The World Of Sammy Lee*, Bricusse collaborated with Cyril Ornadel on the score for the musical *Pickwick* (1963), which starred the 'Goon with the golden voice', Harry Secombe, in the title role. His recording of the show's big ballad, 'If I Ruled The World', was a Top 20 hit in the UK, and, later, after the Broadway production had flopped, it became part of Tony Bennett's repertoire. Reunited in 1964, Bricusse and

Newley's next major stage project, *The Roar Of The Greasepaint - The Smell Of The Crowd* (1965), appeared similar to their previous effort, a moral tale of a downtrodden little man, bucking the system. It toured (Bricusse: 'We managed to empty every provincial theatre in England'), but did not play the West End. Bricusse, and others, felt that comedian, Norman Wisdom, was miscast in the central role, and Newley took over for the Broadway run of 232 performances. Once again, however, the hit songs were there - in this case, 'Who Can I Turn To?' and 'A Wonderful Day Like Today', plus other items such as 'This Dream', 'The Beautiful Land', 'The Joker', 'Where Would You Be Without Me?', 'Nothing Can Stop Me Now' and 'Feeling Good'. The latter number was popularized in the USA by Joe Sherman, and received an impressive, extended treatment from Steve Winwood's UK rock group, Traffic, on their live *Last Exit* (1969). In 1964, Bricusse and Newley turned their attention to the big screen, providing the lyric to John Barry's music for the title song to the James Bond movie *Goldfinger* (1964), sung by Shirley Bassey. Bricusse and Barry later wrote another Bond theme for *You Only Live Twice* (1968), popularized by Nancy Sinatra. In 1967, Bricusse contributed the screenplay and the complete song score to *Doctor Dolittle*, which starred Newley, along with Rex Harrison who sang the Oscar-winning 'Talk To The Animals'. Considered an 'expensive dud', there was no mention of a *Doctor Dolittle II*. Far more to the public's taste was Roald Dahl's *Willy Wonka And The Chocolate Factory* (1971). Bricusse and Newley's score contained 'The Candy Man', a song which gave Sammy Davis Jnr. a US number 1 in the following year. Davis was one of the songwriting team's favourite people - Bricusse estimates that he recorded at least 60 of his songs, including a complete album of *Doctor Dolittle*. Davis also starred in a revival of *Stop The World - I Want To Get Off* during the 1978/9 Broadway season.

After writing several numbers for a 1971 US television adaptation of *Peter Pan*, which starred Danny Kaye and Mia Farrow, Bricusse and Newley returned to the stage with *The Good Old Bad Old Days*. Newley directed and starred in the show, which ran for 10 months in London, and included the jolly title song and several other appealing numbers, such as 'I Do Not Love You', 'It's A Musical World', 'The People Tree' and 'The Good Things In Life'. Since then, their back catalogue has been repackaged in productions such as *The Travelling Music Show* (1978), with Bruce Forsyth, and *Once Upon A Song*, in which Newley occasionally appears when he is not singing for big dollars in Las Vegas. Also in 1978, Bricusse collaborated with composer Armando Trovajoli on *Beyond the Rainbow*, an English language version of the Italian musical *Aggiungi Una Posta Alla Tavola*, which ran for six months in London - a good deal longer than his own *Kings And Clowns*. He also wrote some new songs for a Chichester Festival Theatre production of his film score for *Goodbye, Mr Chips* (1982). By then, he was generally wearing his Hollywood hat, and had received Oscar nominations for his work on *Goodbye, Mr Chips*

(1969, original song score, with John Willams), *Scrooge* (1970, original song score with Ian Fraser and Herbert W. Spencer, and his own song, 'Thank You Very Much'), *That's Life* (1986, 'Life In a Looking Glass', with Henry Mancini), *Home Alone* (1990, 'Somewhere In My Memory', with John Williams), and *Hook* (1991, 'When You're Alone', with John Williams). He won his second Academy Award in 1982, in collaboration with Mancini, for the original song score to *Victor/Victoria*. Bricusse and Newley were inducted into the Songwriters' Hall Of Fame in 1989, a year that otherwise proved something of a disappointment for the partners. For instance, an updated version of *Stop The World*, directed by, and starring Newley, staggered along for five weeks in London, and Bricusse's *Sherlock Holmes*, with Ron Moody and Liz Robertson, opened there as well, to disappointing reviews. *Sherlock Holmes* re-surfaced in 1993, and toured the UK with Robert Powell in the title role. In the same year, Bricusse's stage adaptation of *Scrooge*, with Newley in the title role, was presented for the first time. Also in 1993, Harry Secombe recreated his orginal role in *Pickwick* at Chichester and in the West End. In October 1995, a stage version of *Victor/Victoria*, starring Julie Andrews, opened on Broadway, to be followed in April 1997 by *Jekyll And Hyde*, on which librettist/lyricist Bricusse collaborated with composer Frank Wildhorn.

BRILL BUILDING

The Brill Building, situated in Broadway, New York, was the home of Tin Pan Alley, conveyor-belt produced pop. Housed within the building were tiny cubicles in which some of the leading songwriters of the day provided the soundtrack to a generation of teenage dreams. With talents such as Carole King, Neil Sedaka, Barry Mann, Cynthia Weill, Jeff Barry and Ellie Greenwich, Leiber And Stoller, and Doc Pomus and Mort Shuman, a string of hits in rapid succession seemed almost inevitable. With key bubblegum-pop genius Don Kirshner cracking the whip, a veritable university of young, top-class composers/musicians competed among themselves to produce chart-topping songs. The golden era of New York-based pop lasted from 1960-64 when the emergence of the Beatles and the commercial upsurge of Bob Dylan prompted many artists to compose their own material. Several former Brill Building pupils, including Neil Sedaka and Carole King, re-emerged as major singer-songwriters at the end of the decade.

BROGUES

Formed in San Jose, California, USA, in 1964, the Brogues were one of the region's finest garage bands. Their initial line-up comprised of Eddie Rodrigues (guitar/vocals), Rick Campbell (guitar/vocals), Bill Whittington (bass/vocals) and Greg Elmore (drums), but their reputation was more fully established upon the addition of Gary Grubb (aka Gary Cole; guitar). The group completed two singles, the best known of which was a rivetting reading of 'I Ain't No Miracle Worker', also recorded by the Chocolate Watch Band. The Brogues disbanded in July 1965 when Rodrigues joined the US Army. Whittington then became a founder member of Family Tree, while Elmore and Grubb, now known as Gary Duncan, joined Quicksilver Messenger Service.

BROOK BROTHERS

Geoffrey Brook (b. 12 April 1943) and Ricky Brook (b. 24 October 1940) were a pop duo from Winchester, Hampshire, England, who were often called the British Everly Brothers. The pair made their first appearance in a skiffle group in 1956 and started on the road to fame after winning a talent competition on Southern UK television's programme *Home Grown*. They first recorded in 1960 for Top Rank Records and their first single (which was an Italian hit for them) was a cover version of the Brothers Four's US hit 'Greenfields'. They followed it with a double-sided cover 'Please Help Me I'm Falling'/'When Will I Be Loved'. They then moved to Pye Records with their producer Tony Hatch, and their second release on that label 'Warpaint' entered the UK Top 20, as did 'Ain't Gonna Wash For A Week' a few months later. Again, these were cover versions of US records with the originals coming from Barry Mann and Eddie Hodges, respectively. The duo, backed by the Semi-Tones, toured with acts like Cliff Richard, Bobby Rydell and Jimmy Jones. They had three smaller UK hits in 1962-63, appeared in the film *It's Trad Dad* and recorded on Decca as the Brooks before fading from the scene. The crisp production of their canon of hits placed them above many of their contemporaries during their brief days of glory.
●ALBUMS: *Brook Brothers* (Pye 1961)★★★.
●FILMS: *It's Trad, Dad* aka *Ring-A-Ding Rhythm* (1962).

BROOKLYN BRIDGE

Johnny Maestro (b. John Mastrangelo, 7 May 1939, Brooklyn, New York, USA) had been the lead singer of the Crests in the 50s, and his voice was behind one of the most memorable doo-wop songs ever, '16 Candles', in 1958. He was also the featured vocalist on follow-up hits such as 'The Angels Listened In', 'Step By Step' and 'Trouble In Paradise'. When Maestro left the group to go solo in 1961, his career took a down-turn. In 1968 he formed a new group, Brooklyn Bridge, with singers Les Cauchi, Fred Ferrara, both formerly of the Del-Satins (once the backing group for Dion), and an eight-member backing band, formerly known as the Rhythm Method. The new group fashioned an orchestral, more modernized style of doo-wop, and with the dramatic vocals of Maestro, were signed to Buddah Records. Their first single was a Jimmy Webb song, 'The Worst That Could Happen', which became a number 3 US hit at the beginning of 1969. The group achieved a total of seven chart singles and two albums by the end of 1970. They became a mainstay at revival concerts featuring old rock 'n' roll. Maestro continued to front the band through many personnel changes, and Brooklyn Bridge were still a top concert and club attraction on the east coast in the early 90s.
●ALBUMS: *Brooklyn Bridge* (Buddah 1969)★★★, *The*

Second Brooklyn Bridge (Buddah 1969)★★, with the Isley Brothers and Edwin Hawkins *Live At Yankee Stadium* (T-Neck 1969)★★, *Brooklyn Bridge* (1970)★★★, *Bridge In Blue* (1972)★★.

BROWN, ARTHUR

b. 24 June 1942, Whitby, Yorkshire, England. A distinctive, uncompromising vocalist, Brown formed an R&B group - Blues And Brown - while studying philosophy at Reading University. He made his recording debut in 1965 with two contributions to a student 'Rag Week' flexi-disc, before moving to London where he fronted a succession of bands, known variously as the Southwest Five, the Arthur Brown Union and the Arthur Brown Set. In 1966 the singer moved to Paris where he began honing a theatrical and visual image. He was feted by the city's artisans and contributed two songs to *La Curee*, a Roger Vadim film which starred Jane Fonda.

Arthur returned to London in 1967 and formed the first Crazy World Of Arthur Brown with Vincent Crane (b. 21 May 1943, Reading, Berkshire, England, d. 14 February 1989; organ), Drachen Theaker (drums) and, later, Nick Greenwood (bass). They were quickly adopted by the 'underground' audience, where Brown's facial make-up, dervish dancing and fiery helmet earned them immediate notoriety. Their popularity engendered a recording deal and the following year the group scored a surprise number 1 hit with the compulsive 'Fire'. The attendant album, *The Crazy World Of Arthur Brown*, contained many stage favourites, including 'Spontaneous Apple Creation' and 'Come And Buy', but was marred by poor production. Theaker and Crane left the band during a US tour, and although Crane later returned, Carl Palmer, formerly of Chris Farlowe's Thunderbirds, joined as drummer. However, Brown's most successful group ended in 1969 when the newcomer and Crane formed Atomic Rooster.

Brown moved to Puddletown in Dorset, where a musically fertile commune had been established. Reunited with Theaker, he completed the experimental set latterly issued as *Strangelands*, before embarking on a new direction with Kingdom Come. This intermittently interesting group recorded three albums before disbanding. The singer resumed a solo career in 1974, but despite a memorable cameo as the Priest in Ken Russell's film, *Tommy*, subsequent recordings proved highly disappointing. His voice, which once stood comparison with those of Screaming Jay Hawkins, Little Richard and James Brown, was muted on the tired *Dance* album, and a reconciliation with Crane for *Chisholm In My Bosom* was little better. Brown then went into semi-retirement from the music business and settled in Austin, Texas, where he pursues a career as a carpenter and decorator in partnership with former Mothers Of Invention drummer, Jimmy Carl Black.

●ALBUMS: *The Crazy World Of Arthur Brown* (Track 1968)★★★, *Galactic Zoo Dossier* (1972)★★, *The Journey* (1972)★★, *Dance* (Gull 1974)★★, *Chisholm In My Bosom* (Gull 1978)★, with Vincent Crane *Faster*

Than The Speed Of Light (1980)★★, *Requiem* (1982)★★, *Strangelands* (1988)★★, *Order From Chaos - Live 1993* (Voiceprint 1994)★★★.
●COMPILATIONS: *The Lost Ears* 1968-72 recordings (Gull 1977)★★.

BROWN, JAMES

b. 3 May 1928, Barnwell, South Carolina, USA. Brown claims he was born in 1933 in Macon, Georgia. 'The Hardest Working Man In Show-Business', 'The Godfather Of Soul', 'The Minister Of The New New Super Heavy Funk' – such sobriquets only hint at the protracted James Brown legend. Convicted of theft at 16, he was imprisoned at the Alto Reform School, but secured an early release on the approbation of local singer, Bobby Byrd. Brown later joined his group, the Gospel Starlighters, who evolved into the Flames after embracing R&B. In 1955 they recorded a demo of 'Please Please Please' at WIBB, a Macon, Georgia, radio station. Local airplay was such that talent scout Ralph Bass signed the group to the King/Federal company. A re-recorded version of the song was issued in March 1956. Credited to 'James Brown And The Famous Flames', it eventually climbed to number 5 in the USA R&B list. Further releases fared poorly until 1958, when 'Try Me' rose to number 1 in the same chart. Once again Brown found it difficult to maintain this level of success, but 'I'll Go Crazy' and 'Think' (both 1960) put his progress on a surer footing. From thereon, until 1977, almost every 'official' single charted. However, it was an album, *Live At The Apollo* (1962) which assuredly established the singer. Raw, alive and uninhibited, this shattering collection confirmed Brown as the voice of black America, every track on the album is a breathtaking event. More than 30 years on, with all the advances in recording technology, this album stands as one of the greatest live productions of all time. His singles continued to enthrall: energetic songs such as 'Night Train' and 'Shout And Shimmy', contrasted with such slower sermons as 'I Don't Mind' and 'Bewildered', but it was the orchestrated weepie, 'Prisoner Of Love' (1963), which gave James his first US Top 20 pop single. Such eminence allowed Brown a new manoeuvrability. Dissatisfied with his record label King, he ignored contractual niceties and signed with Smash Records. By the time his former outlet had secured an injunction, 'Out Of Sight' had become another national hit. More importantly, however, the single marked the beginning of a leaner, tighter sound which would ultimately discard accepted western notions of harmony and structure. This innovative mid-60s' period is captured on film in his electrifying performance on the *TAMI Show*.

Throughout the 60s, James proclaimed an artistic freedom with increasingly unconventional songs including 'Papa's Got A Brand New Bag', 'I Got You (I Feel Good)', 'It's A Man's Man's Man's World' (with a beautifully orchestrated string section) and 'Money Won't Change You'. In 1967 Alfred Ellis replaced Nat Jones as Brown's musical director and 'Cold Sweat' introduced further radical refinements to the group's presentation. With

Clyde Stubblefield on drums, 'Say It Loud – I'm Black And I'm Proud' (1968), 'Mother Popcorn' (1969), and 'Get Up (I Feel Like Being A) Sex Machine' (1970) were each stripped down to a nagging, rhythmic riff, over which the singer soared, sometimes screaming, sometimes pleading, but always with an assertive urgency. In 1971 Brown moved to Polydor Records and unveiled a new backing band, the JBs. Led by Fred Wesley, it featured such seasoned players as Maceo Parker and St. Clair Pinckney, as well as a new generation of musicians. Elsewhere, former bassist Bootsy Collins defected with other ex-members to George Clinton's Funkadelic. Such changes, coupled with Sly Stone's challenge, simply reinforced Brown's determination. He continued to enjoy substantial hits; 1974 saw three successive number 1 R&B singles in 'The Payback', 'My Thang' and 'Papa Don't Take No Mess (Part 1)', and Brown also scored two film soundtracks, *Black Caesar* and *Slaughter's Big Rip Off*. However, as the decade progressed, his work became less compulsive, suffering a drop in popularity with the advent of disco. A cameo role in the movie *The Blues Brothers* marked time, and in 1980 Brown left the Polydor label.

Subsequent releases on such smaller labels as TK, Augusta Sound and Backstreet were only marginally successful. However, Brown returned with a vengeance in 1986 with 'Livin' In America', the theme song from the *Rocky IV* film soundtrack. An international hit single, it was followed by two R&B Top 10 entries, 'How Do You Stop' (1987) and 'I'm Real' (1988), the latter of which inspired a compulsive album of the same name. The Brown resurrection was abruptly curtailed that same year when the singer was arrested after a high-speed car chase. Charged with numerous offences, including illegal possession of drugs and firearms, aggravated assault and failure to stop for the police, he was sentenced to six-and-a-half years' imprisonment at the State Park Correctional Centre. He was released in 1991, having reportedly written new material while incarcerated. Brown's considerable influence has increased with the advent of hip-hop. New urban-based styles are indebted to the raw funk espoused by 'The Godfather of Soul', while Stubblefield's rhythmic patterns, particularly those on 1970's 'Funky Drummer', have been heavily sampled, as have Brown's notorious whoops, screams, interjections and vocal improvisations. Artists as disparate as Public Enemy, George Michael, Sinead O'Connor and Candy Flip have featured beats taken from Brown's impressive catalogue. During the 90s he has continued to have further problems with the law and a continuing battle to quit drugs; in 1995 he was forced to cope with a tragic medical accident when his ex-wife Adrienne died during surgery for 'liposuction'. Through all this he is still seen as one of the most dynamic performers of the century and a massive influence on most forms of black music: soul, hip-hop, funk, R&B and disco.

●ALBUMS: *Please Please Please* (King 1959)★★★, *Try Me* (King 1959)★★, *Think* (King 1960)★★★, *The Amazing James Brown* (King 1961)★★★, *James Brown Presents His Band/Night Train* (King 1961)★★★, *Shout And Shimmy* (King 1962)★★★, *James Brown And His Famous Flames Tour The USA* (King 1962)★★, *Excitement Mr Dynamite* (King 1962)★★★, *Live At The Apollo* (King 1963)★★★★★, *Prisoner Of Love* (King 1963)★★★, *Pure Dynamite: Live At The Royal* (King 1964)★★★, *Showtime* (Smash 1964)★★, *The Unbeatable James Brown* (King 1964)★★★, *Grits And Soul* (Smash 1964)★★, *Out Of Sight* (Smash 1964)★★★, *Papa's Got A Brand New Bag* (King 1965)★★★, *I Got You (I Feel Good)* (King 1966)★★★, *James Brown Plays James Brown Today And Yesterday* (Smash 1966)★★, *Mighty Instrumentals* (King 1966)★★, *James Brown Plays New Breed (The Boo-Ga-Loo)* (Smash 1966)★★, *Soul Brother No. 1: It's A Man's Man's Man's World* (King 1966)★★★, *James Brown Sings Christmas Songs* (King 1966)★★, *Handful Of Soul* (Smash 1966)★★, *The James Brown Show* (Smash 1967)★★, *Sings Raw Soul* (King 1967)★★★, *James Brown Plays The Real Thing* (Smash 1967)★★★, *Live At The Garden* (King 1967)★★, *Cold Sweat* (King 1967)★★★, *James Brown Presents His Show Of Tomorrow* (King 1968)★★★, *I Can't Stand Myself (When You Touch Me)* (King 1968)★★, *I Got The Feelin'* (King 1968)★★★, *Live At The Apollo, Volume 2* (King 1968)★★★★, *James Brown Sings Out Of Sight* (King 1968)★★★, *Thinking About Little Willie John And A Few Nice Things* (King 1968)★★★, *A Soulful Christmas* (King 1968)★★, *Say It Loud, I'm Black And I'm Proud* (King 1969)★★★★, *Gettin' Down To It* (King 1969)★★★, *The Popcorn* (King 1969)★★★, *It's A Mother* (King 1969)★★★, *Ain't It Funky* (King 1970)★★★, *Soul On Top* (King 1970)★★★, *It's A New Day - Let A Man Come In* (King 1970)★★★, *Sex Machine* (King 1970)★★★, *Hey America* (King 1970)★★★, *Super Bad* (King 1971)★★, *Sho' Is Funky Down Here* (King 1971)★★, *Hot Pants* (Polydor 1971)★★, *Revolution Of The Mind/Live At The Apollo, Volume 3* (Polydor 1971)★★★, *There It Is* (1972)★★★, *Get On The Good Foot* (Polydor 1972)★★★, *Black Caesar* (Polydor 1973)★★★, *Slaughter's Big Rip-Off* (Polydor 1973)★, *The Payback* (Polydor 1974)★★★, *Hell* (Polydor 1974)★★★, *Reality* (Polydor 1975)★★★, *Sex Machine Today* (Polydor 1975)★★★, *Everybody's Doin' The Hustle And Dead On The Double Bump* (Polydor 1975)★★, *Hot* (Polydor 1976)★★★, *Get Up Offa That Thing* (Polydor 1976)★★, *Bodyheat* (Polydor 1976)★★, *Mutha's Nature* (Polydor 1977)★★★, *Jam 1980's* (Polydor 1978)★★★, *Take A Look At Those Cakes* (Polydor 1979)★★★, *The Original Disco Man* (Polydor 1979)★★★, *People* (Polydor 1980)★★★, *Hot On The One* (Polydor 1980)★★, *Soul Syndrome* (TK 1980)★★★★, *Nonstop!* (Polydor 1981)★★★, *Live In New York* (Audio Fidelity 1981)★★★, *Bring It On* (Churchill 1983)★★★, *Gravity* (Scotti Brothers 1986)★★★, *James Brown And Friends* (1988)★★★, *I'm Real* (Scotti Brothers 1988)★★★, *Love Over-Due* (Scotti Brothers 1991)★★★, *Universal James* (1993)★★, *Funky President* (1993)★★★, *Live At The*

Apollo 1995 (Scotti Brothers 1995)★★★.
●COMPILATIONS: *Soul Classics* (Polydor 1972)★★★, *Soul Classics, Volume 2* (Polydor 1973)★★★, *Solid Gold* (1977)★★★, *The Fabulous James Brown* (HRB 1977)★★★, *Can Your Heart Stand It?* (Solid Smoke 1981)★★★, *The Best Of James Brown* (Polydor 1981)★★★★, *The Federal Years, Part 1* (Solid Smoke 1984)★★★★, *The Federal Years, Part 2* (Solid Smoke 1984)★★★, *Roots Of A Revolution* (1984)★★★, *Ain't That A Groove - The James Brown Story 1966-1969* (Polydor 1984)★★★, *Doing It To Death - The James Brown Story 1970-1973* (Polydor 1984)★★★, *Dead On The Heavy Funk 1974-1976* (Polydor 1985)★★★, *The CD Of JB: Sex Machine And Other Soul Classics* (Polydor 1985)★★★★, *The LP Of JB (Sex Machine And Other Soul Classics)* (Polydor 1986)★★★★, *In The Jungle Groove* (1986)★★★, *Motherlode* (1988)★★★, *Messin' With The Blues* (1991)★★★, *Star Time* 4-CD box set (Polydor 1991)★★★★★, *Chronicles - Soul Pride* (1993)★★★, *JB40: 40th Anniversary Collection* (Polydor 1996)★★★★, *On Stage* (Charly 1997)★★★.
●VIDEOS: *Video Biography* (1988), *Live In London: James Brown* (1988), *James Brown And Friends* (1988), *Live In Berlin* (1989), *Soul Jubilee* (1990), *Live On Stage (With Special Guest B.B. King)* (1990), *Sex Machine (The Very Best Of James Brown)* (1991), *The Lost Years (Live In Santa Cruz)* (1991), *Live In New York* (1991), *James Brown Live* (MIA 1995).
●FURTHER READING: *James Brown: The Godfather Of Soul*, James Brown with Bruce Tucker. *Living In America: The Soul Saga Of James Brown*, Cynthia Rose. *James Brown: A Biography*, Geoff Brown.
●FILMS: *The Blues Brothers* (1980).

BROWN, JOE

b. 13 May 1941, Swarby, Lincolnshire, England. Brown has sustained a career for over 30 years as a cheerful 'cockney' rock 'n' roll singer and guitarist. He was a popular live and television performer in the late 50s, a major UK recording star in the early 60s and is still a well-loved personality in the 90s. In 1956, this cast London-based performer formed the Spacemen skiffle group, which became the backing group on Jack Good's top-rated television series *Boy Meets Girl* in 1959. At this point in his career, Brown was generally regarded as one of the finest guitarists in the UK and his services were frequently in demand. Rechristened Joe Brown And The Bruvvers, the group joined Larry Parnes's successful stable of artists (Parnes allegedly tried to rename him Elmer Twitch!) and signed to Decca Records. He first charted with a unique treatment of 'Darktown Strutters Ball' in 1960 and had a trio of UK Top 10 hits on the Pye Piccadilly label in 1962-63 with 'A Picture Of You', 'It Only Took A Minute' and 'That's What Love Will Do'. Being a happy and cheeky 'character' with a regional accent, it is likely that he could have had success in the USA in the way that Herman's Hermits did (Brown actually recorded 'I'm Henry The VIII, I Am' first). Brown was just two years early, and before the USA was completely receptive to the 'British

invasion'. As it was, his major hits were covered in the USA by acts like Paul Evans, the Kalin Twins and Bobby Goldsboro. He was voted 'Top UK Vocal Personality' in the *New Musical Express* poll in 1962 and 1963. He appeared in the film *What A Crazy World* and in the mid-60s starred in the hit musical *Charlie Girl*. He has recorded sporadically since then on a variety of labels including MCA, Vertigo and Parlophone. During the early 70s Brown put together the country-rock band Home Brew, which featured his wife Vicki, Ray Glynn (guitar), Pete Oakman (bass/violin), Jeff Peters (bass), Dave Hynes (drums) and Kirk Duncan (piano). Vicki was one of Britain's most successful and prolific backing session vocalists until her career was tragically curtailed by illness. She died from cancer in 1991. Brown has occasionally appeared on other artists' recordings; in 1982 he guested on George Harrison's *Gone Troppo*. His daughter Sam Brown has forged her own career as a notable rock singer. Brown's career has suffered insofar that he is always seen as the 'cor blimey mate, what a lovely bloke'. He is a masterful guitarist and singer who commands respect and admiration from a wide spectrum of artists. His 1997 album was a small step in the direction of reaffirming his real talent.
●ALBUMS: *A Picture Of Joe Brown* (Ace Of Clubs 1962)★★★, *Live* (Piccadilly 1963)★★★, *A Picture Of You* (Piccadilly 1965)★★★, *Here Comes Joe!* (Pye 1967)★★, *Joe Brown* (MCA 1968)★★★, *Browns Home Brew* (Bell 1972)★★, *Together* (1974)★★★, *Joe Brown Live* (1977)★★★, *Come On Joe* (1993)★★★, *Fifty Six And Taller Than You Think* (Demon 1997)★★★.
●COMPILATIONS: *Joe Brown Collection* (1974)★★★, *Hits 'N' Pieces* (1988), *The Joe Brown Story* 2-CD (Sequel 1993)★★★.

BROWN, MAXINE

b. Kingstree, South Carolina, USA. Having sung in two New York gospel groups, Maxine made her recording debut on Nomar with 'All In My Mind'. A US hit in 1961, this uptown soul ballad was followed by 'Funny'. A period at ABC-Paramount then passed before Brown signed to Wand Records and proceeded to make a series of excellent singles. She is best recalled for 'Oh No Not My Baby' (1964), a beautifully written David Goffin and Carole King song which was later covered by Manfred Mann, Rod Stewart and Aretha Franklin. Maxine also recorded with Chuck Jackson, their version of 'Something You Got' made the US R&B Top 10, but her position at Wand was undermined by the company's preoccupation with Dionne Warwick. Releases on a new outlet, Commonwealth United, resulted in two R&B chart entries, including the acclaimed 'We'll Cry Together' (1969). Maxine signed with Avco in 1971, but her work there failed to re-establish her former profile.
●ALBUMS: *The Fabulous Sound Of Maxine Brown* (Wand 1962)★★★, *Spotlight On Maxine Brown* (Wand 1964)★★★, *We'll Cry Together* (1969)★★★.
●COMPILATIONS: *Maxine Brown's Greatest Hits* (Wand 1964)★★★, *One In A Million* (1984)★★★, *Like*

Never Before Wand recordings(1985)★★★, *Oh No Not My Baby - The Best Of ...* (1990)★★★, *Not My Baby* (1991)★★★, *Maxine Brown's Greatest Hits* (Tomato 1995)★★★.

BROWN, PETE (UK)

b. 25 December 1940, London, England. During the early 60s Brown was one of the leading 'beat poets'. His recitals at jazz fraternity gatherings and small clubs made him an important figure of the burgeoning 'underground' scene. His work came to national prominence as the lyricist of Jack Bruce's contributions to Cream. No-one before or since has captured more effectively the essence of the drug experience, all the more remarkable since Brown had stopped all drug-taking and drinking by the time he wrote this collection of songs. On *Disraeli Gears*, Brown's outstanding, nonsensical tales contributed to his prodigious success: lines like, 'Its getting near dark, when light close their tired eyes' in 'Sunshine Of Your Love', and the powerful surrealism of 'SWLABR' (She Was Like A Bearded Rainbow), are but two examples of Brown's fertile hallucinogenic imagination. The superlative 'White Room' from *Wheels Of Fire* has stood the test of time, and along with much of the Cream catalogue has enabled Brown to receive continuing financial reward for a series of classic rock songs. Some of his finest lyrics are to be found on Jack Bruce's *Songs For A Tailor* and *How's Tricks*, the former including the evocative 'Theme For An Imaginary Western' and the quirky 'Weird Of Hermiston'. During his most prolific period in the late 60s, he also formed two bands that have now received belated critical acclaim. The Battered Ornaments featured the explorative guitar of Chris Spedding, while Piblokto! recorded two albums that are valuable collector's items. Brown also worked with the pivotal R&B pioneer Graham Bond in a partnership known as Bond And Brown. During the past years Brown has been involved with writing film scripts but has recently returned to the music scene, as well as continuing his long musical partnership with Jack Bruce. His contributions have lost none of their surreal sharpness, as demonstrated on Bruce's *A Question Of Time* in 1989. Brown also continues to work with former Piblokto! colleague Phil Ryan, frequently on musicals and film scores. In the 90s Brown reunited with Bruce for the album *Cities Of The Heart* and was part of Calvin Owens' band for UK gigs. He became a credible record producer, producing, for example Dick Heckstall-Smith's *Where One Is*. Brown is a true original, retaining all the best qualities, humour and aspirations of the 60s underground scene.

●ALBUMS: *A Meal You Can Shake Hands With In The Dark* (Harvest 1969)★★★, *Things May Come And Things May Go But The Art School Dance Goes On Forever* (Harvest 1969)★★★, *Thousands On A Raft* (Harvest 1970)★★★, with Graham Bond *Two Heads Are Better Than One* (1972)★★★, *The 'Not Forgotten' Association* (1973)★★, *Party In The Rain* (1983)★★, *Ardours Of The Lost Rake* (Aura 1991)★★, *Coals To Jerusalem* (Voiceprint)★★★.

●COMPILATIONS: *Before Singing Lessons 1969-1977* (1987)★★★, and Phil Ryan *The Land That Cream Forgot* (Viceroy 1997)★★★.

BRUCE, TOMMY

b. 1939, London, England. This 60s rock 'n' roll vocalist possessed an extraordinary voice that was described as a subtle blending of a corncrake, steam hammer and gravel polisher. Orphaned at the age of 10, he worked for some years as a driver's mate in London's famous Covent Garden fruit market, before his neighbour, the then actor and later successful songwriter, Barry Mason, encouraged him to make the demo record that secured him a contract with Norrie Paramor at Columbia Records in 1960. His first release, the Fats Waller oldie 'Ain't Misbehavin'', was a UK number 2 hit, and his follow-up, another standard, 'Broken Doll', also reached the UK Top 40, but was his last record to do so. The singer, who was either loved or hated, was often accused of emulating the Big Bopper. He hotly disputed this claim, saying he was not particularly familiar with the late singer's work. Together with his group the Bruisers, he appeared on television programmes such as *Wham!!* and on many live shows, often under the auspices of impresario Larry Parnes. This unique cockney performer, who never claimed that he could actually sing, also recorded on Polydor in 1965, RCA in 1966 and CBS in 1969. Bruce is still to be found singing in rock 'n' roll revival and 60s nostalgia shows.

●COMPILATIONS: *Greatest Hits* (1985)★★★.

BRYANT, ANITA

b. 25 March 1940, Barnsdale, Oklahoma, USA. Bryant has had a unique series of career changes: a beauty queen turned hit-maker, turned religious singer and spokesperson against gay liberation. Her first stage appearance was at the age of six and at nine she won her first talent show. She became known as 'Oklahoma's Red Feather Girl', and local television and radio appearances brought her to the attention of Arthur Godfrey, who put her on his television talent show where she won first prize. Her first record was 'Sinful To Flirt' in early 1956. In 1958 she became 'Miss Oklahoma' and at that year's 'Miss America Pageant', where she also sang, she came third. Her first chart entry was her second single on Carlton, a version of 'Till There Was You' (from the musical *The Music Man*), in 1959. She had three US Top 20 singles in 1960-61 with 'Paper Roses', 'In My Little Corner Of The World' (both minor UK hits and both revived later by Marie Osmond) and the vocal version of Bert Kaempfert's number 1 hit 'Wonderland By Night'. She joined Columbia Records in 1962 and later recorded religious material for Myrrh and Word. Still a well-known figure in the USA, she resides in California and is now best known for her outspoken views on the gay community.

●ALBUMS: *Anita Bryant* (Carlton 1959)★★★, *Hear Anita Bryant In Your Home Tonight* (Carlton 1960)★★★, *In My Little Corner Of The World* (Carlton

1961)★★★★, *In A Velvet Mood* (1962)★★★ *Mine Eyes Have Seen The Glory* (1967)★★, *Abide With Me* (70s)★★.

BUCKINGHAMS

Formed in Chicago, Illinois, USA, in 1966, the Buckinghams originally consisted of Dennis Tufano (b. 11 September 1946, Chicago, Illinois, USA; vocals), Carl Giammarese (b. 21 August 1947, Chicago, Illinois, USA; lead guitar), Dennis Miccoli (organ), Nick Fortune (b. 1 May 1946, Chicago, Illinois, USA; bass) and Jon Jon Poulos (b. 31 March 1947, Chicago, Illinois, USA, d. 26 March 1980; drums). Although their first hit, 'Kind Of A Drag' was their only gold disc, the group enjoyed a consistent run of US chart successes throughout 1967, achieved two further Top 10 entries with 'Don't You Care' and 'Mercy Mercy Mercy'. Miccoli was latterly replaced by Marty Grebb (b. 2 September 1946, Chicago, Illinois, USA) before the Buckinghams' staid image was deemed passé by a more discerning audience. Yet despite those slick, commercial singles, their albums showed a desire to experiment. Produced and directed by Jim Guercio, such releases hinted at the brass arrangements this talented individual later brought to protégés Chicago. Unable to reconcile their image and ambitions, the quintet split up in 1970. Poulos later managed several local acts, but died of drug-related causes in 1980. Tufano and Giammarese continued working as a duo, while Grebb later worked with Chicago.

●ALBUMS: *Kind Of A Drag* (USA 1967)★★★, *Time And Changes* (Columbia 1967)★★★, *Portraits* (Columbia 1968)★★★, *In One Ear And Gone Tomorrow* (Columbia 1968)★★, *Made In Chicago* (1969)★★.

●COMPILATIONS: *The Buckinghams' Greatest Hits* (Columbia 1969)★★★.

BUDDAH RECORDS

Neil Bogart, formerly of Cameo-Parkway Records, founded this New York-based label in September 1967. Its early success was derived from several production affiliates, notably that of Super K, which revolved around entrepreneurs Jerry Kasenetz and Jeff Katz. Having sensed a gap in the marketplace caused by the onset of the rock era, the duo assiduously created singles at once both memorable and disposable. Armed with a series of often interchangeable groups, including the 1910 Fruitgum Company, the Ohio Express and the Kasenetz-Katz Singing Orchestral Circus, and songwriters Artie Resnick, Joey Levine and Richie Cordell, the producers concocted a series of mindless, yet eminently danceable releases, including 'Simon Says', 'Yummy Yummy Yummy' and 'Quick Joey Small', each of which were major hits in the US and UK. Dubbed 'bubblegum' by a derisory press, such performances helped Buddah gross over five million dollars during its first year and established the label as one of the most successful, singles-oriented independents. Such prestige, however, was not solely derived from Super K, and the Lemon Pipers, the

Brooklyn Bridge and Anders And Poncia team also provided hits. Buddah also flirted with Californian music, but despite critical approbation, neither Penny Nichols nor Captain Beefheart made a lasting commercial impression. The label later acquired the Kama Sutra catalogue (the Lovin' Spoonful), as well as the distribution rights to Curtis Mayfield's Windy C and Curtom labels, and the Isley Brothers T-Neck company. When the appeal of bubblegum faltered, Buddah found a new lease of life with Melanie, the Edwin Hawkins Singers, Stories and Brewer And Shipley, while the signing of Gladys Knight And The Pips from Motown was a major coup, as this enduring act became one of the label's most popular attractions. Bogart left Buddah in 1974; he subsequently founded Casablanca Records, and his departure signalled the end of the company's most productive period. Despite hits with Barbara Mason, the Five Stairsteps and Michael Henderson, the company was shorn of an impetus and become associated with former, rather than present, glories.

●COMPILATIONS: *Bubblegum Music Is The Naked Truth* (1969)★★★, *Super K's Bubblegum Explosion* (1990)★★★.

BUFFALO SPRINGFIELD

A seminal band in the development of American country-rock and folk-rock, although short-lived, the monumental influence of Buffalo Springfield rivals that of the Byrds. Although the line-up constantly changed, the main members throughout their three turbulent years comprised: Stephen Stills (b. 3 January 1945, Dallas, Texas, USA), Neil Young (b. 12 November 1945, Toronto, Canada), Richie Furay (b. 9 May 1944, Yellow Springs, Ohio, USA), Dewey Martin (b. 30 September 1942, Chesterville, Canada), Bruce Palmer (b. 1947, Liverpool, Canada) and Jim Messina (b. 5 December 1947, Maywood, California, USA). Furay and Stills worked together in the Au Go-Go Singers in the mid-60s, where they met Young, who at that time was a solo singer, having previously worked with Palmer in the Mynah Birds. They eventually congregated in Los Angeles in 1966 and following a series of gigs at the prestigious *Whiskey A Go-Go*, together with verbal endorsements from the Byrds' Chris Hillman and David Crosby, the band were signed by Ahmet Ertegun to his Atco label. Any group containing three main songwriters who could all play lead guitar was heading for trouble, and soon their egos clashed. Their problems were compounded by the continual immigration and drug problems of Palmer. At one point, their manager, Dick Davis masqueraded as bassist on the television. Eventually, Young's former associate Ken Koblin was recruited as a replacement. He, in turn, was replaced by Jim Fielder from the Mothers Of Invention. Their only major hit was in 1967: 'For What Its Worth (Hey Whats That Sound)' remains one of the finest 60s pop songs. This composition exemplified the phenomenon of the 'right song at the right time'. Stills' plaintive yet wry and lethargic plea for tolerance was written after the police used heavy-handed methods to stop an anti-Vietnam student demonstration on Sunset Strip in 1966. The opening lyric 'There's something happening here, what it is ain't exactly clear, there's a man with a gun over there, telling me I've got to beware', innocently sets the scene. The chorus of 'Stop children, what's that sound everybody knows what's going down' became an anthem for west coast students who were unhappy with the Nixon government. Two albums were released; although *Stampede* was recorded, it only appeared as a bootleg. *Last Time Around* was patched together by producer and latter-day bassist Messina, after the band had broken up for the final time. *Buffalo Springfield Again* remains their finest work and is still highly favoured by the cogniscenti. The album demonstrated the developing talents of Stills and Young as major songwriters. Young, with his superb surreal mini-epics 'Expecting To Fly' and 'Broken Arrow' was equalled by Stills's immaculate 'Everydays' and the lengthy 'Bluebird' (Bluebird was Judy Collins). Furay also contributed, among others, the heavily countrified 'A Child's Claim To Fame'. Both the band and the album's essence, however, was encapsulated in one short track, 'Rock And Roll Woman', co-written by an uncredited David Crosby, who briefly appeared with the group as Young's substitute at the 1967 Monterey Pop Festival. The three lead guitars duelled together and the three lead vocals enmeshed brilliantly - all seemingly without ego, to produce for a brief moment what could have been America's greatest rival to the Beatles.

Albums; *Buffalo Springfield* (Atco 1967)★★★★, *Buffalo Springfield Again* (Atco 1967)★★★★★, *Last Time Around* (Atco 1968)★★★.
●COMPILATIONS: *Retrospective* (Atco 1969)★★★★.
●FURTHER READING: *Neil Young: Here We Are In The Years*, Johnny Rogan. *Crosby, Stills And Nash: The Authorized Biography*, Dave Zimmer.

BURDON, ERIC

b. 11 May 1941, Walker, Newcastle-upon-Tyne, Tyne & Wear, England. Burdon originally came to prominence as the lead singer of the Animals in 1963. His gutsy, distinctive voice was heard on their many memorable records in the 60s. Following the demise of the latter-day Eric Burdon And The New Animals, it was announced that he would pursue a career in films. By 1970 no offers from Hollywood were forthcoming so he linked up with the relatively unknown black jazz/rock band Nite Shift, and, together with his friend Lee Oskar, they became Eric Burdon And War. A successful single, 'Spill The Wine', preceded the well-received *Eric Burdon Declares War*. In the song Burdon parodied himself with the lyrics: 'Imagine me, an overfed, long-haired leaping gnome, should be a star of a Hollywood movie.' Both this and the follow-up, *Black Man's Burdon*, combined ambitious arrangements mixing flute with Oskar's harmonica. Eventually the jazz/rock/funk/blues/soul mix ended up merely highlighting Burdon's ultra pro-black stance. While his intentions were honourable, it came over to many as inverted racism. Burdon received a lot of press

in 1970 when he was still regarded as an influential spokesperson of the hippie generation. At the time of Jimi Hendrix's death, he claimed to possess a suicide note, the contents of which he refused to divulge. After parting company, War went on to become hugely successful in the early 70s, while Burdon's career stalled. He teamed up with Jimmy Witherspoon on *Guilty* and attempted a heavier rock approach with *Sun Secrets* and *Stop*. The ponderous Hendrix-influenced guitar style of the last two albums did not suit reworked versions of early Animals' hits, and the albums were not successful. In 1980 Burdon formed Fire Dept in Germany, making one album, *Last Drive*. He finally fulfilled his long-standing big-screen ambitions by appearing in the film *Comeback*, albeit as a fading rock star.

Throughout the 80s Burdon continued to perform with little recorded output, while experiencing drug and alcohol problems. His 1977 and 1983 reunion albums with the original Animals were not well received. Burdon's popularity in Germany continue, while his profile in the UK and USA decreased. His confessional autobiography was published in 1986. Burdon remains one of the finest white blues vocalists of our time, although ultimately typecast as the man who sang 'House Of The Rising Sun'.

●ALBUMS: as Eric Burdon And War *Eric Burdon Declares War* (Polydor 1970)★★★, *Black Man's Burdon* (Liberty 1971)★★★, with the Eric Burdon Band and Jimmy Whitherspoon *Guilty* (United Artists 1971)★★★, *Ring Of Fire* (1974)★★★, *Sun Secrets* (Capitol 1974)★★, *Stop* (Capitol 1975)★★, *Survivor* (Polydor 1978)★★, *Gotta Find My Baby* (1979)★★, *Last Drive* (1980)★★, *Eric Burdon Band Live* (1982)★★, *Comeback* (1982)★★, *I Used To Be An Animal* (1988)★★, *Wicked Man* (1988)★★, *Crawling King Snake* (1992)★★, *Misunderstood* (Aim 1995)★★.
●COMPILATIONS: War featuring Eric Burdon *Love Is All Around* (ABC 1976)★★, *Star Portrait* (80s)★★★, *Sings The Animals Greatest Hits* (Avenue 1994)★★.
●VIDEOS: *Finally* (Warners 1992).
●FURTHER READING: *Wild Animals*, Andy Blackford. *I Used To Be An Animal But I'm All Right Now*, Eric Burdon. *The Last Poet: The Story Of Eric Burdon*, Jeff Kent. *Good Times: The Ultimate Eric Burdon*, Dionisio Castello.

BURKE, SOLOMON

b. 1936, Philadelphia, Pennsylvania, USA. The former 'Wonder Boy Preacher', Burke's first recordings appeared on the New York-based Apollo label. From 1955-59 he attempted various styles until a brisk rocker, 'Be Bop Grandma', attracted the attention of Atlantic Records. An eclectic performer, his reading of a sentimental country song, 'Just Out Of Reach' (1961), was a US Top 30 hit, but the following year the 'King of Soul' began asserting a defined soul direction with 'Cry To Me'. Burke's sonorous voice was then heard on a succession of inspired singles, including 'If You Need Me' (1963), 'Goodbye Baby (Baby Goodbye)' and the declamatory 'Everybody Needs

Somebody To Love' (both 1964). This exceptional period culminated with 'The Price', an impassioned release which marked the end of Burke's relationship with producer Bert Berns. Although further strong records appeared, indeed 'Got To Get You Off My Mind' (1965) became his biggest hit, they lacked the drama of the earlier era. Still based in New York, Solomon was now overshadowed by Otis Redding, Sam And Dave and other acts who recorded at Stax and Fame Records. A belated Memphis session did provide a US Top 50 entry in 'Take Me (Just As I Am)', but Burke left Atlantic for Bell Records in 1968. The ensuing album, *Proud Mary*, was a southern soul classic, while the title track, written by John Fogerty, charted as a single in the US. The 70s saw a move to MGM Records, but his work there was marred by inconsistency. The same was true of his spells at Dunhill and Chess Records although his collaborations with Swamp Dogg on *From The Heart* recalled his old power. This rebirth continued on *Soul Alive*, where recorded in concert, Burke sounds inspired, infusing his 'greatest hits' with a newfound passion. A strong studio collection, *A Change Is Gonna Come*, followed 1987's European tour and displayed Burke's enduring talent. Two albums, *The Best Of Solomon Burke* (1966) and *Cry To Me* (1984), compile his Atlantic singles, while *The Bishop Rides South* (1988) adds four extra tracks to the original *Proud Mary* album.

●ALBUMS: *Solomon Burke* (Apollo 1962)★★★, *If You Need Me* (Atlantic 1963)★★★, *Rock 'N' Soul* (Atlantic 1964)★★★, *I Wish I Knew* (Atlantic 1968)★★★, *King Solomon* (Atlantic 1968)★★★, *Proud Mary* (Bell 1969)★★★, *Electronic Magnetism* (Polydor 1972)★★, *King Heavy* (1972)★★, *We're Almost Home* (1972)★★, *I Have A Dream* (1974)★★, *Music To Make Love By* (1975)★★, *Back To My Roots* (1975)★★, *Sidewalks Fences & Walls* (1979)★★, *Lord I Need A Miracle Right Now* (1981)★★, *Into My Life You Came* (1982)★★, *Take Me, Shake Me* (1983)★★, *This Is His Song* (1984)★★, *Soul Alive* (1985)★★, *A Change Is Gonna Come* (1986)★★★, *Love Trap* (1987)★★★, *Homeland* (1991)★★★, *Soul Of The Blues* (Black Top 1993)★★★, *Live At The House Of Blues* (Black Top 1994)★★, *Definition Of Soul* (Pointblank/Virgin 1997)★★★.

●COMPILATIONS: *Solomon Burke's Greatest Hits* (Atlantic 1962)★★★, *I Almost Lost My Mind* (1964)★★★, *King Of Rock 'N' Soul/From The Heart* (1981)★★★, *Cry To Me* (1984)★★★★, *You Can Run But You Can't Hide* (1987)★★★, *The Bishop Rides South* (1988)★★★, *Hold On I'm Coming* (1991)★★★, *Home In Your Heart* (Rhino 1992)★★★★, *The King Of Soul* (1993)★★★, *Greatest Hits: If You Need Me* (Sequel 1997)★★★.

BURNETTE, JOHNNY

b. 28 March 1934, Memphis, Tennessee, USA, d. 1 August 1964, Clear Lake, California, USA. Having attended the same high school as Elvis Presley, Johnny moved into the rockabilly genre by forming a trio with his brother Dorsey Burnette on string bass and school friend Paul Burlison on guitar. Allegedly rejected by Sun Records supremo Sam Phillips, the group recorded 'Go Mule Go' for Von Records in New York and were subsequently signed to Coral, where they enjoyed a minor hit with 'Tear It Up'. After touring with Carl Perkins and Gene Vincent, the trio underwent a change of personnel in November 1956 with the recruitment of drummer Tony Austin. That same month, the trio were featured in Alan Freed's movie *Rock, Rock, Rock*. During this period, they issued a number of singles, including 'Honey Hush', 'The Train Kept A-Rollin'', 'Lonesome Train', 'Eager Beaver Baby', 'Drinkin' Wine', 'Spo-Dee-O-Dee' and 'If You Want It Enough', but despite the quality of the songs their work was unheralded. By the autumn of 1957, the trio broke up and the Burnette brothers moved on to enjoy considerable success as songwriters. Writing as a team, they provided Ricky Nelson with the hits 'It's Late', 'Believe What You Say' and 'Just A Little Too Much'. After briefly working as a duo, the brothers parted for solo careers. Johnny proved an adept interpreter of teen ballads, whose lyrics conjured up innocent dreams of wish-fulfilment. Both 'Dreamin'' and 'You're Sixteen' were transatlantic Top 10 hits, perfectly suited to Burnette's light but expressive vocal. A series of lesser successes followed with 'Little Boy Sad', 'Big Big World', 'Girls' and 'God, Country And My Baby'. With his recording career in decline, Burnette formed his own label Magic Lamp in 1964. In August that year, he accidentally fell from his boat during a fishing trip in Clear Lake, California and drowned. His son, Rocky Burnette, subsequently achieved recording success at the end of the 70s.

●ALBUMS: as the Johnny Burnette Trio *Rock 'N' Roll Trio* (Coral 1957)★★★★, *Dreamin'* (Liberty 1961)★★★, *You're Sixteen* (Liberty 1961)★★★, *Johnny Burnette* (Liberty 1961)★★★, *Johnny Burnette Sings* (Liberty 1961)★★★, *Burnette's Hits And Other Favourites* (Liberty 1962)★★★, *Roses Are Red* (Liberty 1962)★★★.

●COMPILATIONS: *The Johnny Burnette Story* (Liberty 1964)★★★★, with the Rock 'n' Roll Trio *Tear It Up* (Solid Smoke/Coral 1968)★★★, *Tenth Anniversary Album* (United Artists 1974)★★★, *We're Having A Party* (1988)★★★, *The Best Of Johnny Burnette* (1989)★★★★, *You're Sixteen: The Best Of Johnny Burnette* (Capitol 1992)★★★★.

BURNS, TITO

A former dance-band leader, Burns came to prominence in UK pop with one of the most famous and powerful music business agencies of the 50s and 60s. His major pop client during the rock 'n' roll era was Cliff Richard and within 10 years Burns was handling some of the major pop artists of the day, from Dusty Springfield to the Rolling Stones. The most enduring image of Burns is captured in the film *Don't Look Back* in which he can be seen haggling with Bob Dylan's manager Albert Grossman in what now serves as a fascinating insight into the backrooms of mid-60s pop.

BURNSIDE, R.L.

b. 23 November 1926, Coldwater, Mississippi, USA. Burnside, 'Rule' to his friends, was a keen observer of his neighbour Mississippi Fred McDowell, as well as Son Hibler and Ranie Burnett, and learned from them the modal rhythm-based techniques of the North Mississippi blues. To these he added songs by Muddy Waters, John Lee Hooker and Lightnin' Hopkins heard on the radio. Prior to taking up the guitar, he had moved to Chicago in the late 40s, where he worked in a foundry and witnessed Muddy Waters' music first-hand. In 1950 he returned south and spent the ensuing years doing farm-work by day and playing jukes and house parties at weekends. He was discovered and recorded in 1967 by George Mitchell, and after the release of *Mississippi Delta Blues* was in demand to appear at festivals in North America and Europe. As well as performing solo, Burnside also leads the Sound Machine, a band which features various members of his large family on guitar and bass, and son-in-law Calvin Jackson on drums. *Bad Luck City* features sons Dwayne and Joseph assisting on a wide range of contemporary material, representative of a typical set played at local clubs such as Junior Kimbrough's at Chulahoma. *Too Bad Jim* was recorded there, in part, and consists of songs played in the older, modal tradition with pupil Kenny Brown on second guitar. These latter recordings prove the enduring strength of Mississippi blues as well as Burnside's eminence as a stirring performer of its intricacies. *A Ass Pocket Of Whiskey* was recorded with the rootsy punksters the Jon Spencer Blues Explosion, and Don Van Vliet (Captain Beefheart) and Ry Cooder replicated the Burnside sound for *Strictly Personal* in 1968.

●ALBUMS: *Mississippi Delta Blues Vol. 2* (Arhoolie 1968)★★★, *Hill Country Blues* (Swingmaster 1988)★★★, *Plays And Sings The Mississippi Delta Blues* (Swingmaster)★★★, *Sound Machine Groove* (Blues Today)★★★, *Mississippi Blues* (Arion)★★★, *Bad Lucky City* (Fat Possum 1991)★★★, *Deep Blues* (Atlantic 1992)★★★, *Too Bad Jim* (Fat Possum 1994)★★★, *A Ass Pocket Of Whiskey* (Matador 1996)★★★★, *Mr. Wizard* (Fat Possum 1997)★★★.

BURRELL, KENNY

b. 31 July 1931, Detroit, Michigan, USA. Coming from a family that encouraged music (all his three brothers were musicians), Burrell studied classical guitar for a mere 18 months (1952-53). In 1955 he received a Bachelor of Music degree from Detroit's Wayne University. He played guitar with the Candy Johnson Sextet in 1948, with Count Belcher in 1949 and Tommy Barnett in 1950. In 1951 Dizzy Gillespie visited Detroit and they recorded together. In March 1955 he stood in for Herb Ellis in the Oscar Peterson trio and in 1957 saw work with Benny Goodman. Discovered by the prestigious Blue Note label, he formed an association with organist Jimmy Smith, and recorded with John Coltrane under the name The Cats. Like all jazz guitarists of his generation Burrell was primarily influenced by Charlie Christian, but developed his own particular playing style. His series of 60s albums for Blue Note and Verve contain his classic work. Arguably *Midnight Blue* featuring Stanley Turrentine (with its famous Reid Miles typography and inspiration behind Elvis Costello's *Almost Blue* sleeve) is his best album. The track 'Midnight Blue' has been cited as the influence for Van Morrison's 'Moondance'. The excellent *Guitar Forms* with Gil Evans in 1964 is another important work, the ambitious suite demonstrating wide influences. Along with Grant Green, there is no finer exponent of 'smokey guitar jazz'. In the late 80s his encouragement of young black talent - especially the drummer Kenny Washington - gave his trio an edge that belied his reputation for classy easy listening. In 1994 he was once again touring with the Jimmy Smith Trio.

●ALBUMS: *Introducing Kenny Burrell* (Blue Note 1956)★★★, *Kenny Burrell Vol 2* (Blue Note 1957)★★★, *Kenny Burrell - John Coltrane* (New Jazz 1958)★★★★, *The Cats* (Original Jazz Classics 1957)★★★, *Blue Lights, Vols. 1 and 2* (Blue Note 1959)★★★★, *Night At The Village Vanguard* (Argo 1959)★★★, *On View At The Five Spot Cafe, Vol. 1* (Blue Note 1959)★★★, *Weaver Of Dreams* (Columbia 1961)★★, *Lotsa Bossa Nova* (Kapp 1962)★★, *Bluesy Burrell* (Moodsville 1963)★★★, *All Night Long* (Prestige 1963)★★★, *All Day Long* (Prestige 1963)★★★, *Blue Bash* (Verve 1963)★★★★, *Midnight Blue* (Blue Note 1963)★★★★★, *Blue Moods* (Prestige 1964)★★★★, *Soul Call* (Prestige 1964)★★★, *Crash* (Prestige 1964)★★★, *Man At Work* (Cadet 1965)★★, *Guitar Forms* (Verve 1965)★★★★, *A Generation Ago Today* (Verve 1966)★★★, *The Tender Gender* (Cadet 1966)★★, *Have Yourself A Soulful Little Christmas* (Cadet 1966)★★, *For Charlie Christian And Benny Goodman* (Verve 1967)★★, with John Coltrane *The Kenny Burrell Quintet With John Coltrane* (Prestige 1967)★★★, *Ode To 52nd Street* (Cadet 1967)★★, *Out Of This World* (Prestige 1968)★★★, *Blues, The Common Ground* (Verve 1968)★★★, *Night Song* (Verve 1968)★★★, *Asphalt Canyon Suite* (Verve 1969)★★★, *Ellington Is Forever Vol. 1 & 2* (Fantasy 1975)★★★★, *Handcrafted* (Muse 1978)★★★, *Kenny Burrell In New York* (Muse 1981)★★★, *Listen To The Dawn* (Muse 1983)★★★, *Bluesin' Around* (CBS 1984)★★★, *Al La Carte* (Muse 1986)★★★, *Generations* (Blue Note 1987)★★★, *Groovin' High* (Muse 1987)★★★, *Togethering* (1989)★★, *Recapitulation* (Charly 1989)★★, *Guiding Spirit* (Contemporary 1990)★★★, *Sunnup To Sundown* (Contemporary 1992)★★★, with Jimmy Smith Trio *The Master* (Blue Note 1994)★★★, *Lotus Blossom* (Concord 1995)★★★, *Midnight At The Village Vanguard* (Evidence 1996)★★★, *Live At The Blue Note* (Concord 1997)★★★.

●COMPILATIONS: *The Best Of Kenny Burrell* (Prestige 1967)★★★.

BURTON, GARY

b. 23 January 1943, Anderson, Indiana, USA. After teaching himself to play piano Burton studied music formally before switching to the vibraphone. In 1960 he recorded with Hank Garland, a country guitarist, but then moved into jazz with a two-year stint at Berklee College Of Music, where he began an important musical association with Mike Gibbs. In 1963 he became a member of George Shearing's group, following this with two years with Stan Getz. Later in the 60s, Burton formed his own small band, playing jazz-rock. Throughout the decade and on into the 70s, Burton led a succession of fine bands which included such musicians as Larry Coryell, Steve Swallow, Roy Haynes, Pat Metheny and Eberhard Weber. He was also teamed on record with Stéphane Grappelli, Carla Bley, Keith Jarrett, Chick Corea, Michael Brecker, Peter Erskine and others. From 1971 Burton taught at Berklee, often finding empathetic musicians among his students. In the 80s his musical associates included Tommy Smith. Although he followed many more famous vibraphonists, not least Lionel Hampton and Milt Jackson, Burton was the first player of this instrument to create a new and wholly original musical style. His extensive simultaneous use of four mallets gave him a less percussive sound, allowing him to develop more complex ideas in a manner usually available only to pianists and players of wind instruments. Burton's Six Pack in 1993 was a refreshing excursion featuring six guitar players: B.B. King, John Scofield, Jim Hall, Kurt Rosenwinkel Kevin Eubanks and familiar partner Ralph Towner. His early musical experience of country and rock have all been thoroughly absorbed into a strongly jazz-orientated concept. Burton's interests and enthusiasm, allied as they are to a virtuoso technique, have made him a leading exemplar of contemporary music. However, although others have followed his example, he remains the only vibraphonist of his generation to be measured alongside major interpreters and innovators in jazz.

●ALBUMS: New Vibe Man In Town (RCA Victor 1961)★★★, Who Is Gary Burton (RCA Victor 1963)★★★, with Sonny Rollins and Clark Terry 3 In Jazz (RCA Victor 1963)★★★, Something's Coming (RCA Victor 1964)★★★, The Groovy Sound Of Music (RCA Victor 1965)★★★, The Time Machine (RCA Victor 1966)★★★, Tennessee Firebird (RCA Victor 1966)★★★, Duster (RCA Victor 1967)★★★, Lofty Fake Anagram (RCA Victor 1967)★★★, Country Roads And Other Places (RCA Victor 1968)★★★, with Carla Bley A Genuine Young Funeral (RCA Victor 1968)★★★, Gary Burton In Concert (RCA Victor 1968)★★★★, with Stéphane Grappelli Paris Encounter (1969)★★★, Green Apple (1969)★★, Throb (Atlantic 1969)★★, Gary Burton And Keith Jarrett (Atlantic 1970)★★★★, Alone At Last (Atlantic 1972)★★★, with Chick Corea Crystal Silence (ECM 1972)★★★, The New Quartet (ECM 1973)★★★, with Steve Swallow Hotel Hello (ECM 1974)★★★, Matchbook (ECM 1974)★★★, Dreams So Real (ECM 1975)★★★, with Eberhard Weber Ring (ECM 1974)★★★, with Weber Passengers (ECM 1976)★★★★, with Chick Corea Duet (ECM 1978)★★★★, Easy As Pie (ECM 1980)★★★, Picture This (ECM 1983)★★★,

Somethings Coming (RCA 1984)★★, Real Life Hits (ECM 1984)★★★, with Ralph Towner Slide Show (ECM 1986)★★★, Whiz Kids (ECM 1986)★★, Times Like These (GRP 1988)★★, with Pat Metheny Reunion (ECM 1989)★★★★, Cool Nights (GRP 1990)★★★, with Paul Bley Right Time Right Place (Sonet 1991)★★★, Six Pack (GRP 1993)★★★, with Makoto Ozone Face To Face (GRP 1995)★★★.

●COMPILATIONS: Artists Choice (Bluebird 1988)★★★, Works (ECM 1989)★★★, Collection (GRP 1996)★★.

BURTON, JAMES

b. 21 August 1939, Shreveport, Louisiana, USA. One of the most distinguished of rock and country-rock guitar players, Burton toured and recorded with Ricky Nelson, Elvis Presley and numerous other artists. His first recording was the highly influential 'Suzie Q' sung by Dale Hawkins in 1957. Burton also performed with country singer Bob Luman before moving to Los Angeles where he was hired to work with Nelson, then the latest teen sensation. For six years he toured and recorded with Nelson, perfecting a guitar sound known as 'chicken pickin''. This was achieved by dampening the strings for staccato-sounding single-string riffs and solos. Among the best examples of this style are 'Hello Mary Lou', 'Never Be Anyone Else But You' and the more frantic, rockabilly-flavoured 'Believe What You Say'. During the late 60s and early 70s, Burton was much in demand as a session guitarist, working with Dale Hawkins on a comeback album as well as various artists including Buffalo Springfield, Judy Collins, John Phillips, Joni Mitchell, Michael Nesmith and Longbranch Pennywhistle, a group featuring future Eagles member Glenn Frey. Burton also played dobro on albums by P.F. Sloan and John Stewart. In addition, Burton's powerful rockabilly-influenced guitar work made a major contribution to the harsher country sound developed at this time by Merle Haggard. Burton made two albums of his own during these years, one in collaboration with steel guitarist Ralph Mooney.

During the 70s, Burton's work took him in contrasting directions. With pianist Glen D. Hardin (a former Crickets member), he was a mainstay of Elvis Presley's touring and recording band from 1969-77, but he also played a leading role in the growing trend towards country/rock fusion. Burton's most significant performances in this respect came on the albums of Gram Parsons. After Parsons' death, Burton and Hardin toured with Emmylou Harris and backed her on several solo albums. More recently he has toured with Jerry Lee Lewis. As a session guitarist, Burton played on albums by Jesse Winchester, Ronnie Hawkins, Rodney Crowell, Phil Everly, J.J. Cale and Nicolette Larson. As a result of an accident in 1995, Burton lost the use of his hands and has been receiving treatment to enable him to play the guitar again. He had no medical insurance and faced bankruptcy after financing his own treatment. A fund has been set up to help him and benefit concerts are being held.

●ALBUMS: with Ralph Mooney Corn Pickin' And Slick

Slidin' (1969)★★, *The Guitar Sound Of James Burton* (A&M 1971)★★.

BUTTERFIELD, PAUL

b. 17 December 1942, Chicago, Illinois, USA, d. 3 May 1987. As a catalyst, Butterfield helped shape the development of blues music played by white musicians in the same way that John Mayall and Cyril Davies were doing in the UK. Butterfield had the advantage of performing with Howlin' Wolf, Muddy Waters and his mentor Little Walter. Butterfield sang, composed and led a series of seminal bands throughout the 60s, but it was his earthy Chicago-style harmonica-playing that gained him attention. He was arguably the first white man to play blues with the intensity and emotion of the great black blues harmonica players. Mike Bloomfield, Mark Naftalin, Elvin Bishop, David Sanborn and Nick Gravenites were some of the outstanding musicians that passed through his bands. His now infamous performance at the 1965 Newport Folk Festival gave him the distinction of being the man who supported Bob Dylan's musical heresy by going electric. In 1973 his new venture *Better Days* went on the road to lukewarm response, and during subsequent years he struggled to find success. Ill health plagued him for some time, much of it caused by aggravating stomach hernias caused by his powerful harmonica playing. Butterfield's legacy remains and much of his catalogue is still available. *East-West* remains his best-selling and most acclaimed work, although the rawness of the debut album also has many critical admirers.
●ALBUMS: *Paul Butterfield Blues Band* (Elektra 1966)★★★★, *East-West* (Elektra 1966)★★★★, *The Resurrection Of Pigboy Crabshaw* (Elektra 1968)★★★, *In My Own Dream* (Elektra 1968)★★★, *Keep On Movin'* (Elektra 1969)★★, *Live* (Elektra 1971)★★, *Sometimes I Just Feel Like Smilin'* (Elektra 1971)★★, *Offer You Can't Refuse* (1972)★★, *Better Days* (1973)★★★, as Better Days *It All Comes Back* (Bearsville 1973)★★, as Better Days *Better Days* (Bearsville 1973)★★★, *Put It In Your Ear* (1976)★★, *North South For Bearsville* (1981)★★, *The Legendary Paul Butterfield Rides Again* (1986)★★★, *Strawberry Jam* (Winner 1995)★★, *Lost Elektra Sessions* (Rhino 1995)★★.
●COMPILATIONS: *Golden Butter - Best Of The Paul Butterfield Blues Band* (Elektra 1972)★★★.

BYRDS

Originally formed as a trio, the Jet Set, this seminal group featured Jim (Roger) McGuinn (b. James Joseph McGuinn, 13 July 1942, Chicago, Illinois, USA; vocals/lead guitar), Gene Clark (b. Harold Eugene Clark, 17 November 1941, Tipton, Missouri, USA, d. 24 May 1991; vocals, tambourine, rhythm guitar) and David Crosby (b. David Van Cortlandt, 14 August 1941, Los Angeles, California, USA; vocals, rhythm guitar). Essentially ex-folkies caught up in the Beatles craze of 1964, they were signed to a one-off singles contract with Elektra Records which resulted in the commercially

unsuccessful 'Please Let Me Love You', released under the pseudonym Beefeaters. By late 1964, the trio had expanded to include former bluegrass player turned bassist Chris Hillman (b. 4 December 1942, Los Angeles, California, USA) and drummer Michael Clarke (b. Michael Dick, 3 June 1944, Spokane, Washington State, USA, d. 19 December 1993, Treasure Island, Florida, USA). Under the supervision of manager/producer Jim Dickson, they recorded at Hollywood's World Pacific studios, slowly and painfully perfecting their unique brand of folk rock. In November 1964, they signed to CBS Records as the Byrds, and were placed in the hands of producer Terry Melcher (b. 8 February 1942, New York, USA, d. 1991). Their debut single, 'Mr Tambourine Man', was a glorious creation, fusing the lyrical genius of Bob Dylan with the harmonic and melodious ingenuity of the Beatles (McGuinn later described his vocal on the disc as a cross between that of John Lennon and Bob Dylan). The opening guitar sound is that of a Rickenbacker 12-string, and one that has been linked to the Byrds and McGuinn ever since. By the summer of 1965, the single had topped both the US and UK charts and the Byrds found themselves fêted as teen-idols. They fulfilled this image with their immaculately groomed fringed haircuts and pop trappings, including Crosby's green suede cape and McGuinn's rectangular tinted granny glasses. To coincide with their UK success a tour was hastily arranged on which the group were promoted as 'America's Answer To The Beatles'. This presumptuous and premature labelling backfired and during their exhausting visit they fell victim to over-expectant fans and tetchy critics. To make matters worse, their second single, 'All I Really Want To Do', suffered split sales due to an opportunistic cover version from folk rock rival Cher. The group's management attempted to compensate for this setback by simultaneously promoting the b-side, 'Feel A Whole Lot Better', a stunning slice of cynical romanticism that swiftly became a stage favourite. The Byrds' debut album, *Mr Tambourine Man*, was a surprisingly solid work that featured four Dylan covers, a striking rearrangement of Pete Seeger's 'Bells Of Rhymney' and some exceptionally strong torch songs from Clark, including 'I Knew I'd Want You', 'Here Without You' and 'You Won't Have To Cry'. There was even a strange reworking of the wartime favourite 'We'll Meet Again', which ended the album on a bizarre yet amusing note.

After returning to the USA, the Byrds spent months in the studio before releasing their third single, the biblically inspired 'Turn! Turn! Turn!', which gave them another US number 1. The album of the same name again showed the prolific Gene Clark in the ascendant with the charming 'The World Turns All Around Her' and the densely worded 'Set You Free This Time', their most sophisticated lyric to date and arguably their definitive self-penned folk rock statement. McGuinn's presence was also felt on the driving 'It Won't Be Wrong' and elegiac 'He Was A Friend Of Mine', with lyrics pertaining to the Kennedy assassination. An odd tribute to Stephen Foster closed the album in the form of the sarcastic 'Oh! Susanah'.

By early 1966, the group had parted from producer Melcher and branched out from their stylized folk rock repertoire to embrace raga and jazz. The awesome 'Eight Miles High', with its John Coltrane-inspired lead break and enigmatic lyrics effectively elevated them to the artistic level of the Beatles and the Rolling Stones, but their chart rewards were severely qualified by a radio ban based on spurious allegations that their latest hit was a 'drugs song'. In fact, the lyric had been written following their visit to England and the unusual imagery was based on their sense of culture shock. The b-side of the disc, 'Why', included some raga-like guitar work from McGuinn, and during a press conference of the period the group were pictured studiously playing a sitar, although none of them had mastered the instrument. The setback over the banning of 'Eight Miles High' was worsened by the abrupt departure of leading songwriter Clark, whose fear of flying and distaste for life on the road had proved intolerable burdens. Continuing as a quartet, the Byrds recorded *Fifth Dimension*, a clever amalgam of hard, psychedelic-tinged pop ('I See You' and 'What's Happening?!?!') and rich folk rock orchestration ('Wild Mountain Thyme' and 'John Riley'). Their chart fortunes were already waning by this time and neither the quizzically philosophical '5-D (Fifth Dimension)' nor the catchy 'Mr Spaceman' made much impression on the charts. The Byrds, rather than promoting their latest album with endless tours, became more insular and were the subject of speculation that they were on the point of breaking up.

1967 proved the pivotal year in their career, commencing with the hit single 'So You Want To Be A Rock 'N' Roll Star', an acerbic observation on the manufacturing of pop stars, complete with taped screams from their ill-fated UK tour and a guest appearance from Hugh Masekela on trumpet. Its b-side, 'Everybody's Been Burned', displayed Crosby's songwriting and vocal sensitivity with an exceptionally strong guitar solo from McGuinn and some stupendous jazz-inspired bass work from Hillman. Their fourth album, *Younger Than Yesterday*, proved their best yet, ably capturing the diverse songwriting skills of Crosby, McGuinn and Hillman and ranging in material from the raga-tinged 'Mind Gardens' to the country-influenced 'Time Between', the quirky space rock of 'CTA 102' and even an ironically retrospective Dylan cover, 'My Back Pages'. Their creative ascendancy coincided with intense inter-group rivalry, culminating in the dismissal of the ever-controversial David Crosby, who would later re-emerge as part of the hugely successful Crosby, Stills And Nash. As Crosby told *the* Byrdologist Johnny Rogan: 'They came zooming up my driveway in their Porsches and said that I was impossible to work with and I wasn't very good anyway and they'd do much better without me. It hurt like hell and I just said "it's a shameful waste, goodbye".' The remaining Byrds, meanwhile, recruited former colleague Gene Clark, who lasted a mere three weeks before his aerophobia once more took its toll.

Drummer Michael Clarke was dismissed from the group soon afterwards, leaving McGuinn and Hillman to assemble the stupendous *The Notorious Byrd Brothers*, a classic example of artistic endeavour overcoming adversity. For this album, the Byrds used recording studio facilities to remarkable effect, employing phasing, close microphone technique and various sonic experiments to achieve the sound they desired. Producer Gary Usher who worked on this and their previous album contributed significantly towards their ascension as one of rock's most adventurous and innovative bands. Once again, however, it was the songs rather than the studio gimmickry that most impressed. Successful readings of Gerry Goffin and Carole King's 'Goin' Back' and 'Wasn't Born To Follow' were placed alongside Byrds originals such as 'Change Is Now', 'Dolphin's Smile', 'Tribal Gathering' and 'Draft Morning'.

In early 1968, Hillman's cousin Kevin Kelley took over on drums and the talented Gram Parsons added musical weight as singer/composer/guitarist. Under Parsons' guidance, the group plunged headlong into country, recording the much-acclaimed *Sweetheart Of The Rodeo*. A perfectly timed reaction to the psychedelic excesses of 1967, the album predated Dylan's *Nashville Skyline* by a year and is generally accepted as the harbinger of country rock. Although Parsons directed the work and included one of his best compositions, 'Hickory Wind', his lead vocals on such country standards as 'You Don't Miss Your Water' and 'You're Still On My Mind' were replaced by those of McGuinn due to contractual complications. It was not until 1990 that the public heard the rough original vocals, which were incorporated into a retrospective boxed set package. McGuinn re-established the Bob Dylan links on *Sweetheart Of The Rodeo* by featuring two songs from the then unreleased *Basement Tapes*, 'You Ain't Going Nowhere' and 'Nothing Was Delivered'. The critical plaudits heaped upon the Byrds were not translated into sales, however, and further conflict ensued when Gram Parsons dramatically resigned on the eve of their ill-advised tour of South Africa in the summer of 1968.

From 1965-68, the Byrds produced some of the greatest and most memorable work ever recorded in the history of popular music. Their remarkable ability to ride trends and incorporate stylistically diverse material ranging from folk and country to raga, jazz and space rock demonstrated a profound vision and a wondrous spirit of adventure and innovation that few of their contemporaries could dream of, let alone match. Their work from this period still sounds fresh and contemporary, which is a testament to their pioneering worth. Their achievement is all the more remarkable given the loss of several key personnel over the years. Rather than destroying the Byrds, their frequent and often inflammatory internal acrimony served as a creative catalyst, prompting a combative and proprietorial sense that resulted in some of the era's most spectacular recordings. Among their contemporaries only the Beatles could boast a body of work of such consistency, and the Byrds were probably unmatched in terms of musical diversity and eclecticism. Late 1968 saw the group at their lowest ebb with Hillman quitting after a dispute with their new manager Larry Spector. The embittered bassist soon reunited with the errant Parsons in the Flying Burrito Brothers. McGuinn, meanwhile, assumed total control of the Byrds and assembled an entirely new line-up featuring Clarence White (vocals, guitar), John York (vocals, bass) and Gene Parsons (vocals, drums). This new phase began promisingly enough with the single 'Bad Night At The Whiskey', backed by the McGuinn/Gram Parsons song 'Drug Store Truck Driving Man'. York lasted long enough to contribute to two albums, *Dr Byrds & Mr Hyde* and *Ballad Of Easy Rider*, before being replaced by journeyman Skip Battin. This unlikely but stable line-up lasted from 1969-72 and re-established the Byrds' reputation with the hit single 'Chestnut Mare' and the bestselling album *(Untitled)*. The latter album, a two-disc set, demonstrated just what an excellent live attraction they had become. McGuinn was given freedom to expand three minute songs into sets that began to resemble the Grateful Dead. Battin stretched out with bass solos, and White grew in stature as an exemplary lead guitarist. Regular concert appearances brought the Byrds a strong groundswell support, but the quality of their early 70s output lacked consistency. McGuinn often took a back seat and his familiar nasal whine was replaced with inferior vocals from the other members. After three successive albums with their first producer Melcher, they again severed their connections with him owing to his decision to include orchestration on *Byrdmaniax*. The Byrds hurriedly attempted to record a compensatory work, *Farther Along*, but it only served to emphasize their disunity. On this final album some of their worst efforts appeared; even the dreadful 'B.B. Class Road' was beaten by a song that tops the poll as the worst Byrds song ever committed to record, the unbelievably bad 'America's Great National Pastime'. This nadir was briefly improved by two songs, 'Tiffany Queen' and White's poignant vocal on 'Buglar'. McGuinn eventually elected to dissolve the group after agreeing to participate in a recorded reunion of the original Byrds for Asylum Records. Released in 1973, *Byrds* received mixed reviews, prompting the group to revert to their various solo/offshoot ventures. On this perplexing release they attempted Neil Young's 'Cowgirl In The Sand' and Joni Mitchell's 'For Free'. That same year tragedy struck when ex-Byrd Clarence White was killed by a drunken driver. Less than three months later, Gram Parsons died from a drug overdose.

The Byrds' legacy has continued in a host of new groups who either borrowed their Rickenbacker sound or traded off their folk/country roots (Tom Petty in particular). The individual members later featured in a host of offshoot groups such as Dillard And Clark, various permutations of the Flying Burrito Brothers, Manassas, Souther Hillman Furay and, of course, Crosby, Stills, Nash And Young. Ironically, the ex-Byrds (with the exception of Crosby) failed to exploit their superstar potential, even after reuniting as McGuinn, Clark And Hillman. By the

80s, the individual members were either recording for small labels or touring without a record contract. Crosby, meanwhile, had plummeted into a narcotic netherworld of free-base cocaine addiction and after several seizures and arrests was confined to prison. He emerged reformed, corpulent and enthusiastic, and amid a flurry of activity set about resurrecting the Byrds moniker with McGuinn and Hillman. Crosby, for once humble, acknowledged in interviews that 'McGuinn was, is and will always be the very heart of the Byrds', and added that no reunion was possible without his participation. An acrimonious lawsuit with Michael Clarke ended with the drummer assuming the right to the group name. Although a proposed five-way reunion of the Byrds for a live album and world tour was mooted, the old conflicts frustrated its immediate fruition. However, McGuinn, Crosby and Hillman completed four songs in Nashville during August 1990 which were subsequently included on a boxed set featuring 90 songs. The nearest that the group reached to a full reunion was when they were each inducted into the rock 'n' roll Hall of Fame in January 1991. The chance of playing together again finally elapsed with the deaths of Gene Clark later that year and Michael Clarke in 1993. By the mid-90s the Byrds were acknowledged as one of the most influential groups of the rock era, and like the Beatles, little of their catalogue sounds dated. This was confirmed in 1996/7 when the first eight albums were expertly remastered and reissued with bonus tracks that had previously only been heard by the Byrds' serious followers. Albums such as *Notorious Byrd Brothers* and *Younger Than Yesterday* are certified classics, and much of their earlier catalogue is indispensable. McGuinn continues to tour small venues with his Rickenbacker and Martin 12-string acoustic, happy to reprise 'Mr Tambourine Man' and his devastating solo on 'Eight Miles High'. Crosby has a new kidney and a new baby and the rounder he gets, the sweeter his voice becomes. Hillman is producing some excellent bluegrass with Larry Rice and Herb Pedersen. It is sad that Gene Clark, the group's best songwriter, is only now receiving universal acclaim. His great song, 'Feel A Whole Lot Better', is recognized as a classic of the 60s; ironic that it only appeared as a b-side in 1965.

●ALBUMS: *Mr Tambourine Man* (Columbia 1965)★★★★, *Turn! Turn! Turn!* (Columbia 1965)★★★★, *Fifth Dimension* (Columbia 1966)★★★★, *Younger Than Yesterday* (Columbia 1967)★★★★★, *The Notorious Byrd Brothers* (Columbia 1968)★★★★★, *Sweetheart Of The Rodeo* (Columbia 1968)★★★★, *Dr Byrds & Mr Hyde* (Columbia 1969)★★★, *Ballad Of Easy Rider* (Columbia 1969)★★★, *The Byrds (Untitled)* (Columbia 1970)★★★★, *Byrdmaniax* (Columbia 1971)★★, *Farther Along* (Columbia 1972)★, *Byrds* (Asylum 1973)★★★.

Three archive albums are also available: *Preflyte* (Together 1969)★★, *Never Before* (Murray Hill 1989)★★★, *In The Beginning* (Rhino 1989)★★★.

●COMPILATIONS: *Greatest Hits* (Columbia 1967)★★★★, *Greatest Hits, Vol. II* (Columbia 1971)★★★, *History Of The Byrds* (CBS 1973)★★★★, *The Byrds Play Dylan* (CBS

1979)★★★,*The Original Singles* (CBS 1980)★★★★, *The Original Singles, Vol. II* (CBS 1982)★★★, *The Byrds Collection* (Castle 1989)★★★, *The Byrds* 4-CD box set (CBS Legacy 1990)★★★★, *20 Essential Tracks* (1993)★★★★, *The Very Best Of The Byrds* (Columbia 1997)★★★★.
●FURTHER READING: *Timeless Flight: The Definitive Biography Of The Byrds*, Johnny Rogan. *The Byrds*, Bud Scoppa. *Timeless Flight Revisited*, Johnny Rogan.

BYRNES, EDD

b. Edward Breitenberger, 30 July 1933, New York City, New York, USA. Byrnes gained fame as the character Gerald Lloyd Kookson III in the US television series *77 Sunset Strip* during the late 50s and early 60s. Sporting a large pompadour hairstyle, the character, known as 'Kookie', could often be seen combing his hair. Byrnes, who became popular among teenage girls, took the nickname in his off-screen career. In 1959 he recorded a novelty single, 'Kookie, Kookie, Lend Me Your Comb', on Warner Brothers Records, a duet with actress-singer Connie Stevens, which reached number 4 in the US. Only one follow-up single, 'Like I Love You', with Joanie Sommers charted; two further singles did poorly and Byrnes returned to acting without repeating his early success.
●ALBUMS: *Kookie* (Warners 1959)★.
●FILMS: *Beach Ball* (1964), *Grease* (1978).

BYSTANDERS

Formed in Merthyr Tydfil, Mid-Glamorgan, Wales, in 1962, the Bystanders initially comprised Lynn Mittell (vocals), Mickey Jones (guitar), Clive John (organ), Ray Williams (bass) and Jeff Jones (drums), but Mittell was later replaced by Vic Oakley. The group became a fixture on the small, but thriving, Welsh club circuit and their debut release, 'That's The End' (1965), was issued on a Swansea-based independent label. This promising single engendered a deal with Pye/Piccadilly. An excellent, and versatile, harmony group, the Bystanders' career was plagued by misfortune. Although their attractive reading of '98.6' was a minor hit in February 1967, it was outstripped by Keith's original version, while the following year the quintet's haunting ballad, 'When Jesamine Goes', flopped. The song was then recorded by the Casuals, and, as 'Jesamine', it reached number 2 in the UK and enjoyed massive success in Europe. However, the Bystanders were growing increasingly tired of their pop image, and experimented with more imaginative original material on their b-sides. Oakley left the group in 1968, unsettled by this new direction, and was replaced by Deke Leonard, from fellow Welsh band the Dream. The reconstituted quintet then embraced progressive rock under a new name, Man.
●COMPILATIONS: *Birth Of Man* (1990)★★★.

C., ROY

b. Roy Charles Hammond, 1943, New York City, New York, USA. A member of the Genies, with whom he recorded for several labels, Roy C's most enduring moment came with 'Shotgun Wedding' (1965). A US R&B Top 20 hit, it proved even more popular in the UK, reaching number 6 the following year, and made the Top 10 again in 1972. The singer later recorded, without luck, for Black Hawk and Shout, but 'Got To Get Enough (Of Your Sweet Love Stuff)' was a soul hit in 1971. Released on C's own Alaga label, he subsequently secured further success on Mercury Records. He also wrote 'Honey I Still Love You', a 1972 bestseller for the Mark IV.
●ALBUMS: *Sex And Soul* (1973)★★★, *More Sex And Soul* (1977)★★.

CABARET

Before arriving on Broadway as a musical comedy, *Cabaret* had enjoyed success in other forms. In 1935 Christopher Isherwood had published *Berlin Stories*, which told of the decadence of contemporary German society. The story was adapted for the stage by John Van Druten in 1951 under the title *I Am A Camera*, starring Julie Harris who also starred in the 1955 screen version. Van Druten's stage play was adapted as a musical by Joe Masteroff with music by John Kander and lyrics by Fred Ebb. *Cabaret* opened at the Broadhurst Theatre in New York on 20 November 1966 and was a great popular and critical success. It starred Jill Haworth as Sally Bowles, an amoral American nightclub singer living, working and loving, the latter somewhat indiscriminately, in Berlin. Joel Grey, as the egregious master of ceremonies at the Kit Kat Club where Sally works, gave the show's outstanding performance. Also in the cast was Lotte Lenya. The songs included 'Wilkommen', 'Tomorrow Belongs To Me', 'If You Could See Her Through My Eyes', 'Meeskite', 'Perfectly Marvelous', 'Don't Tell Mama', 'The Money Song', 'Married', 'What Would You Do?', and 'Cabaret'. Effectively evoking the contrasting social phenomena of cultural decay and the nascent National Socialist (Nazi) Party, the show combined high drama, realistic if unconventional morality, and strong characters with good songs. It ran for 1,165 performances, and won Tony Awards for best musical, supporting actor (Grey), supporting actress (Peg Murray), score, director (Harold Prince), choreographer (Ronald Field), scenic design (Boris Aronson) and costumes (Patricia Zipprodt). The 1968 London production bravely, and, as it turned out, successfully, starred classical actress Judi Dench as Sally

Bowles. *Cabaret* was revived on Broadway in 1987 when Joel Grey recreated his original role, and in the West End in 1986 with ballet dancer Wayne Sleep as the Emcee. In 1993 and 1994, the Donmar Warehouse on the London Fringe presented the show in the manner of a play with music, which prompted *Variety* to comment: 'In taking *Cabaret* away from Broadway, an essential verve that can only be defined as Broadway has been taken from *Cabaret*'. The 1972 film version starred Liza Minnelli as Sally with Grey reprising his role. Although making certain alterations to the plot, notably changing it from a loser's tale into a success story, the film version was highly successful and benefited from the performances of Grey and Minnelli, the latter having since become inseparable from the title song.

CADETS

The Cadets were one of the more colourful Irish showbands of the early to mid-60s. The original line-up comprised Eileen Reid (vocals), Patrick Murphy (harmonica), Jas Fagan (trombone), Paddy Burns (vocals/trumpet), Gerry Hayes (piano), Brendan O'Connell (lead guitar), Jimmy Day (tenor saxophone/guitar) and Willie Devey (drums). The band played the usual showband fare of C&W and cover hits, but gained considerable attention for their fancy naval-inspired uniforms and exotic lead vocalist. Eileen Reid, with her enormous beehive hair-do, was an instant hit with audiences, and before long the Cadets were attracting record company interest. After a false start with 'Hello Trouble' on Decca, they switched to Pye Records and were soon number 1 in Eire with their version of Jim Reeves' 'Fallen Star'. During this period, they also toured America and appeared on the UK television show *Thank Your Lucky Stars*. They were even given their own show on Radio Eireann, *Carnival Time With The Cadets*. In late 1964, they charted with their most famous song, 'I Gave My Wedding Dress Away'. For this melancholic C&W ballad Reid regularly appeared onstage dressed in a wedding dress, which caused a minor sensation at the time. The Cadets continued to tour the showband circuit and notched up an impressive run of hits including 'Right Or Wrong', 'If I Had My Life To Live Over', 'More Than Yesterday', 'At The Close Of A Long Day' and 'Land Of Gingerbread'. The group split in 1970, just before the showband scene went into a sharp decline.
●ALBUMS: *The Cadets* (1966)★★★.

CAIOLA, AL

b. Alexander Emil Caiola, 7 September 1920, Jersey City, New Jersey, USA. A highly respected studio guitarist, Caiola played with many renowned musical directors such as Percy Faith, Hugo Winterhalter and Andre Kostelanetz. After serving as musical arranger and conductor for United Artists Records, Caiola released several singles on RCA during the 50s, including 'Delicado', a Brazilian song written by Walter Azevedo, which became a hit for Percy Faith, Stan Kenton, Ralph Flanagan and Dinah Shore. Caiola also released *Serenade In Blue* and

Deep In A Dream, recorded by his Quintet. In 1961 he entered the US Top 40 charts with the movie theme *The Magnificent Seven* and *Bonanza*, the title music from the popular western television series; he had his own television show for a short time in the USA.
●ALBUMS: *Deep In A Dream* (Savoy/London 1956)★★, *Serenade In Blue* (Savoy/London 1957)★★★, with Don Arnone *Al Caiola And Don Arnone* (Chancellor 1960)★★★, *Soft Guitars* (60s)★★★, *Guitar Of Plenty* (60s)★★★, *Cleopatra And All That Jazz* (United Artists 1962)★★★, *Italian Guitars* (60s)★★, *Tough Guitar* (United Artists 1964)★★, *Music To Read James Bond By* (1965)★★★, *Sounds For Spies And Private Eyes* (United Artists 1965)★★★.

CALDER, TONY

b. 27 June 1943, Surbiton, Surrey, England. Born to Scottish parents, Calder became one of the more aspiring and hustling agents on the mid-60s UK pop scene. Following a stint at Decca Records by day and Mecca dancehalls by night, he worked as a publicist with Mark Wynter and the Beatles. He formed a successful business partnership with the young svengali Andrew Loog Oldham, an involvement went from the business management of the Rolling Stones to the creation of the PR company Image, which represented among others, the Beach Boys and Freddie And The Dreamers. Together they founded Immediate Records, one of the first independent labels. Immediate became one of the most innovative and fondly remembered (but ill-fated) record companies of the 60s. Calder also managed Marianne Faithfull and produced two of her hits, 'Come And Stay With Me' and 'This Little Bird'. Calder was always the backroom boy of British pop, perpetually on the horizon, but not well known outside the business. During the 70s, he discovered and secured the Bay City Rollers their recording contract with Bell Records and represented Eddie Grant during his most successful period. It was Calder that was responsible for Grant's 'I Don't Wanna Dance' being issued, a song that would have remained a demo but for his ear for a good pop song. He remained in various areas of the pop world, giving Jive Bunny three UK number 1 hits in a row, and enjoyed success with his publishing company, Marylebone Music, which he sold to London Festival Productions in 1991. When the re-launch of Immediate was announced in 1993 both Calder and Oldham enjoyed considerable media attention, indicating that, contrary to their press in the past, their brand of outspoken honesty is still very much welcomed. No launch took place, but the inimitable pair attracted further media attention in 1995 having written a book on Abba.

CAMELOT

Alan Jay Lerner and Frederick Loewe brought the stage musical *Camelot* to New York on 1 December 1960, despite the fact that their previous show, *My Fair Lady*, was still running. Inevitably compared and contrasted with that blockbuster, *Camelot* was generally considered to be an inferior show. Pre-opening events had also militated against success. Director Moss Hart suffered a heart attack, Loewe was hospitalized with bleeding ulcers, and technical problems beset out-of-town previews. Although there were good advance sales for Broadway, the critics greeted it with a lukewarm response . Nevertheless, *Camelot* established a good following with the public and ran for almost 900 performances. The show starred Julie Andrews as Queen Guenevere, Richard Burton as King Arthur, and Robert Goulet as Lancelot. Based upon T.H. White's *The Once And Future King*, a new version of the Arthurian legends, the score contained several good songs, including 'How To Handle A Woman', 'Follow Me', 'I Wonder What The King Is Doing Tonight', 'The Lusty Month Of May', 'C'est Moi', 'If Ever I Would Leave You' and the title number. During the show's run, several cast changes were made, but of the originals Goulet was most striking, building a successful career upon this, his Broadway debut. The 1964 London production starred Laurence Harvey, later replaced by Paul Daneman, as the King. In 1993 the show was revived on Broadway following a long US tour. In this production Robert Goulet took the role of King Arthur, and received what were probably some of the worst reviews of his career so far. A moderately successful version of *Camelot* was filmed in 1967 with Richard Harris, Vanessa Redgrave and David Hemmings.

CAMPBELL, IAN, FOLK GROUP

This highly respected British folk group were formed in Birmingham, West Midlands, in 1956 and were originally called the Clarion Skiffle Group. With his parents, Campbell had moved from his home town of Aberdeen, Scotland, to Birmingham in 1946. The original line-up was Ian Campbell (b. 10 June 1933, Aberdeen, Scotland; guitar/vocals), his sister Lorna Campbell (b. 1939, Aberdeen, Scotland; vocals), Dave Phillips (guitar) and Gordon McCulloch (banjo). In 1958, they became the Ian Campbell Folk Group. McCulloch departed in 1959 and was replaced by John Dunkerley (b. 1942; banjo/guitar/accordion) who remained until 1976. In 1960, Dave Swarbrick (b. 5 April 1941, London, England; fiddle/mandola) joined, remaining until 1966. Issued in 1962, it is notable that *Ceilidh At The Crown* was the first ever live folk club recording to be released. In 1963, the group were signed to Transatlantic Records and Brian Clark (guitar/vocals) joined the line-up as a replacement for Phillips. Clark also became a long term member, staying until 1978.

By now Ian had taken a place at university as a mature student, but the group still had bookings to honour. Various session players were recruited for live performances, including Aiden Ford (b. 1960; banjo/mandola) and Colin Tommis (b. 1960; guitar), who stayed for 18 months, touring Scandinavia. In 1984, Neil Cox (guitar) was added, and the group were booked by former bass player Mansell Davies to play dates in Canada. Cox then left, and the group of Ian, Lorna, Neil and Aiden played occasionally for special dates. An album recorded in Denmark in 1977 has never been released because there

was no group to promote it. The sessions included Luke Kelly of the Dubliners, Dave Swarbrick and Martin Carthy. Many of Ian Campbell's songs are often thought of as traditional, but those such as 'The Sun Is Burning' have been covered by countless others, including Simon And Garfunkel.

During the early 60s, the group appeared on television programmes such as the *Hootenanny Show*, *Barn Dance* and *Hullabaloo*. In addition, they regularly played to full houses in concert at venues such as the Royal Albert Hall, and the Royal Festival Hall in London. In 1964, they were invited to perform at the Newport Folk Festival in the USA, and in 1965, they became the first non-US group to record a Bob Dylan song; their version of 'The Times They Are A-Changin'' reached the UK Top 50 in March 1965. The group added bass player Mansell Davies in 1966, but he emigrated to Canada three years later, and he later became an organizer of Canadian festivals such as Calgary. After Swarbrick's departure in 1966, the group worked with George Watts (flute), who appeared on only two albums: *New Impressions* and *The Ian Campbell Folk Group* which was recorded in Czechoslovakia. Unfortunately, due to the prevailing political climate of the time, the record was never released outside the country, and the group did not receive royalties. Watts left in 1968, but a year earlier the group took on bassist Dave Pegg, who remained with them for three years before joining Fairport Convention. In 1969, Andy Smith (banjo/mandolin/guitar/fiddle) joined, leaving in 1971. That same year, Mike Hadley (bass) joined the ever-changing line-up, leaving in 1974. *Adam's Rib* was a suite of 12 songs written by Ian for his sister Lorna; the songs dealt with the different crisis points in a woman's life. John Dunkerley left the group, owing to ill health, in 1976, and died the following year from Hodgkinson's disease, aged just 34. The group disbanded in 1978.

●ALBUMS: *Ceilidh At The Crown* (1962)★★★, *Songs Of Protest* (1962)★★★, *This Is The Ian Campbell Folk Group* (Transatlantic 1963)★★★, *The Ian Campbell Folk Four* (1964)★★★, *Across The Hills* (Transatlantic 1964)★★★, *Coaldust Ballads* (1965)★★★, *The Ian Campbell Folk Group* (1965)★★★, *The Singing Campbells* (1965)★★★, *Contemporary Campbells* (1966)★★, *New Impressions Of The Ian Campbell Folk Group* (1967)★★★, *Circle Game* (1968)★★★, *The Cock Doth Crow* (1968)★★★, Ian Campbell, John Dunkerley *Tam O'Shanter* (1968)★★★, *Ian Campbell-With The Ian Campbell Folk Group And Dave Swarbrick* (1969)★★★, *The Ian Campbell Folk Group and Dave Swarbrick* (1969)★★★, *The Sun Is Burning* (1970)★★★, *Something To Sing About* (1972)★★★, *The Ian Campbell Folk Group Live* (1974)★★, *Adam's Rib* (1976)★★★.

●COMPILATIONS: *The Ian Campbell Folk Group Sampler Vol.1* (1969)★★★★, *The Ian Campbell Folk Group Sampler Vol.2* (1969)★★★, *And Another Thing* (Celtic Music 1994)★★★.

CANNED HEAT

This popular, but ill-fated blues/rock group was formed in 1965 by two Los Angeles-based blues aficionados: Alan Wilson (b. 4 July 1943, Boston, Massachusetts, USA; vocals/harmonica/guitar) and Bob 'The Bear' Hite (b. 26 February 1943, Torrance, California, USA; vocals). Wilson, nicknamed 'Blind Owl' in deference to his thick-lensed spectacles, was already renowned for his distinctive harmonica work and had accompanied Son House on the veteran bluesman's post 'rediscovery' album, *Father Of Folk Blues*. Wilson's obsession with the blues enabled him to build up a massive archive blues collection by his early twenties. The duo was joined by Frank Cook (drums) and Henry Vestine (b. 25 December 1944, Washington, DC, USA; guitar), a former member of the Mothers Of Invention. They took the name Canned Heat from a 1928 recording by Tommy Johnson and employed several bassists prior to the arrival of Larry Taylor, an experienced session musician who had worked with Jerry Lee Lewis and the Monkees.

Canned Heat's debut album was promising rather than inspired, offering diligent readings of such 12-bar standards as 'Rollin' And Tumblin'', 'Dust My Broom' and 'Bullfrog Blues'. However, the arrival of new drummer Alfredo Fito (b. Adolfo De La Parra, 8 February 1946, Mexico City, Mexico) coincided with a newfound confidence displayed almost immediately on *Boogie With Canned Heat*. This impressive selection introduced the extended 'Fried Hookey Boogie', a piece destined to become an in-concert favourite, and the hypnotic remake of Jim Oden's 'On The Road Again', which gave the group a UK Top 10 and US Top 20 hit single in 1968. Wilson's distinctive frail high voice, sitar-like guitar introduction and accompanying harmonica have made this version a classic. A double set, *Livin' The Blues*, includes an enthralling version of Charley Patton's 'Pony Blues' and a 19-minute *tour de force* 'Parthenogenesis', which captures the quintet at their most experimental. However, it was Wilson's adaptation of a Henry Thomas song, 'Bulldoze Blues', which proved most popular. The singer retained the tune of the original, rewrote the lyric and emerged with 'Goin' Up The Country', whose simple message caught the prevalent back-to-nature attitude of the late 60s. This evocative performance charted in the US and UK Top 20, and was one of the highlights of the successful *Woodstock* movie.

In 1969 and 1970 Canned Heat recorded four more albums, including a spirited collaboration with blues boogie mentor John Lee Hooker, and a fascinating documentary of their 1970 European tour. *Hallelujah* boasted one of artist George Hunter's finest album covers. It also featured 'Get Off My Back', which in its day was used by hi-fi buffs to check their systems were in phase, as the cross-channel switching in the mix was outrageously overdone. *Future Blues* marked the arrival of guitarist Harvey Mandel, replacing Vestine, who could no longer tolerate working with Taylor. The reshaped band enjoyed two further UK hits with a cover of Wilbert Harrison's 'Let's Work Together', which reached number 2, and the

cajun-inspired 'Sugar Bee', but were shattered by the suicide of Wilson, whose body was found in Hite's backyard on 3 September 1970. His death sparked a major reconstruction within the group: Taylor and Mandel left to join John Mayall, the former's departure prompting Vestine's return, while Antonio De La Barreda became Canned Heat's new bassist. The new quartet completed *Historical Figures And Ancient Heads*, before Hite's brother Richard replaced Barreda for the band's 1973 release, *The New Age*. The changes continued throughout the decade, undermining the band's strength of purpose. Bob Hite, the sole remaining original member, attempted to keep the group afloat, but was unable to secure a permanent recording deal. Spirits lifted with the release of *Human Condition*, but the years of struggle had taken their toll. On 5 April 1981, following a gig at the Palomino Club, the gargantuan vocalist collapsed and died of a heart attack. Despite the loss of many key members, the Canned Heat name has survived. Inheritors Larry Taylor and Fito De La Parra completed 1989's *Re-heated* album with two new guitarists, James Thornbury and Junior Watson. They now pursue the lucrative nostalgia circuit with various former members coming and going. Vestine is allowed to perform when he sticks to soft alcohol and herbal substances; Taylor now has a heart condition, and the band is led by De La Parra.

●ALBUMS: *Canned Heat* (Liberty 1967)★★★, *Boogie With Canned Heat* (Liberty 1968)★★★, *Livin' The Blues* (Liberty 1968)★★★, *Hallelujah* (Liberty 1969)★★★★, *Vintage - Canned Heat* early recordings (Pye International 1969)★★, *Future Blues* (Liberty 1970)★★★, *Live At The Topanga Canyon* (Wand 1970)★★, with John Lee Hooker *Hooker 'N' Heat* (Liberty 1971)★★★, *Canned Heat Concert (Recorded Live In Europe)* (Liberty 1971)★★, with Memphis Slim *Memphis Heat* (Barclay 1971)★★, with Clarence 'Gatemouth' Brown *Gates Of Heat* (Barclay 70s)★★★, *Historical Figures And Ancient Heads* (United Artists 1972)★★★, *The New Age* (United Artists 1973)★★, *Rollin' And Tumblin'* (1973)★★, *One More River To Cross* (Atlantic 1974)★★, *Human Condition* (Takoma 1978)★★, *Boogie Assault - Live In Australia* (1981)★★, *Captured Live* (1981)★★, with Hooker *Hooker 'N' Heat - Live* (1981)★★★, *Kings Of The Boogie* (1982)★★, *Dog House Blues* (1983)★★, *Re-Heated* (Dali 1989)★★, *Internal Combustion* (River Road 1995)★★.

●COMPILATIONS: *Canned Heat Cook Book (The Best Of Canned Heat)* (1969)★★★, *The Very Best Of Canned Heat* (1973)★★★, *Greatest Hits* (1988)★★★, *The Best Of Hooker 'N' Heat* (1989)★★★, *Let's Work Together - The Best Of Canned Heat* (1989)★★★, *The Big Heat* (1992)★★★, *Uncanned - The Best Of Canned Heat* (Liberty 1994)★★★★.

CANNIBAL AND THE HEADHUNTERS

Formed in 1965 in Los Angeles, California, USA, Cannibal and the Headhunters were a Mexican-American group whose only chart hit, 'Land Of 1000 Dances', is considered a 'garage pop' and soul classic, despite its only having reached number 30 nationally. The trio consisted of Frankie 'Cannibal' Garcia (b. *c*.1950, Los Angeles, d. 21 January 1996), Robert 'Rabbit' Jaramillo and Joe 'Yo Yo' Jaramillo, all residents of the Hispanic East L.A. area. Garcia had earned the nickname 'Cannibal' as a child after biting another boy in a fight. In his early teens he sang with the Royal Jesters and the Rhythm Playboys, with whom he stayed until 1963. The Jaramillo brothers were in the Romanos when they met Garcia, and the trio formed a vocal group, using Headhunters as a complement to the name Cannibal. Their one chart hit was written by Fats Domino with lyrics by Chris Kenner, who had a minor hit with it in 1963. The Headhunters first heard it sung by Rufus Thomas in concert, and they began performing the song themselves, substituting the nonsense phrase 'Na na na na na, na na na na' in place of some of the lyrics. Discovered by entrepreneur Eddie Davis, they recorded their new version, which was issued on the small Rampart Records label. Despite several other singles on Rampart, and follow-ups on Date and Capitol, as well as two albums and tour dates with the Beatles, Beach Boys and Rolling Stones, the group never had another hit. They reunited in 1983, led by Eddie Serrano and have been playing concerts sporadically into the early 90s. 'Land Of 1000 Dances' has also been a US chart hit for Thee Midniters, Wilson Pickett (number 6 in 1966), Electric Indian and the J. Geils Band. Up until his death Garcia worked as a hospital research nurse.

●ALBUMS: *Land Of 1000 Dances* (Rampart/CBS1966)★★.

CANNON, FREDDY

b. Freddy Picariello, 4 December 1940, Lynn, Massachusetts, USA. A frantic and enthusiastic vocalist, known as the 'last rock 'n' roll star', Cannon was the link between wild rock 'n' roll and the softer Philadelphia-based sounds that succeeded it. The son of a dance-band leader, he fronted Freddy Karmon And The Hurricanes and played guitar on sessions for the G-Clefs. He was spotted by Boston disc jockey Jack McDermott, who gave a song that Freddy and his mother had written, entitled 'Rock 'N' Roll Baby', to top writing and production team Bob Crewe and Frank Slay: they improved the song, retitled it 'Tallahassee Lassie', and renamed him Freddy Cannon. The record was released in 1959 on Swan, a label part-owned by Dick Clark, who often featured Cannon on his US *Bandstand* television programme and road shows. The single was the first of 21 US hits that 'Boom Boom' (as the ex truck driver was known) had over the next seven years. He had five US and four UK Top 20 singles, the biggest being his revival of 'Way Down Yonder In New Orleans' in 1959 and 'Palisades Park', written by television personality Chuck Barris, in 1962. His only successful album was *The Explosive! Freddy Cannon* in 1960, which made history as the first rock album to top the UK charts. During his long career, Cannon also recorded with Warner Brothers, Buddah,

Claridge (where he revived his two biggest hits), We Make Rock 'N' Roll Records, Royal American, MCA, Metromedia and Sire. He returned briefly to the charts in 1981 in the company of Dion's old group, the Belmonts, with a title that epitomized his work: 'Let's Put The Fun Back Into Rock 'N' Roll'.

●ALBUMS: *The Explosive! Freddy Cannon* (Swan/Top Rank 1960)★★★★, *Happy Shades Of Blue* (Swan 1960)★★★, *Freddy Cannon's Solid Gold Hits* (Swan 1961)★★★, *Twistin' All Night Long* (Swan 1961)★★★, *Freddy Cannon At Palisades Park* (Swan 1962)★★★, *Freddy Cannon Steps Out* (Swan 1963)★★, *Freddy Cannon* (Warners 1964)★★, *Action!* (Warners 1966)★★.

●COMPILATIONS: *Freddy Cannon's Greatest Hits* (Warners 1966)★★★, *Big Blast From Boston! The Best Of ...* (Rhino 1995)★★★.

CAPITOL (EIRE)

One of the biggest Irish showbands of the 60s, the Capitol was formed in 1960 with a line-up comprising Butch Moore (vocals), Jimmy Hogan (lead guitar), Des Kelly (vocals/bass), Johnny Kelly (drums), Eddie Monahan (piano), Paul Sweeney (trumpet) Patrick Loughman (trombone) and Eddie Ryan (saxophone). When hey became professional the following year, Loughman and Ryan were replaced by Don Long and Paddy Cole, respectively. Based in Dublin, the Capitol became the first showband to appear on Irish television. After signing to Pye Records, they recruited the songwriting services of the then unknown Phil Coulter, whose 'Foolin' Time' took them into the Irish Top 10. In common with Coulter, they fell into the hands of manager/agent Phil Solomon, whose powerful influence brought them a prestigious appearance on the stage of the London Palladium. By November 1964, the band were number 1 in Eire with 'Down Came The Rain', an achievement they repeated with the Coulter-arranged 'Born To Be With You'. In 1965 Eire was admitted to the Eurovision Song Contest for the first time, and the Capitol were the chosen representatives. Moore's stirring 'Walking The Streets In The Rain' came sixth in the final, and also provided the Capitol with their third successive Irish number 1 hit. At their peak, the Capitol were second only to the Royal Showband in popularity. With their distinctive uniform of white trousers, white shoes and blue jackets, they looked particularly slick. During 1965-66, their success continued, with 'Born To Be With You', 'Our Love Will Go On', 'So Many Ways' and 'Christmas', but, their impact was severely weakened after Moore was bought out and launched a career as a cabaret artist. He subsequently sang with the Kings, then married singer Maeve Mulvany and emigrated to the USA. A revamped Capitol replaced Moore with Noel McNeill, and later, John Drummond. With Des Kelly as vocalist, the band made a strong return with 'The Streets Of Baltimore', but by the late 60s, their star was in the descendant and the original group split up. Cole subsequently joined the showband supergroup Big 8, while Kelly became a successful manager with the Irish folk group, Sweeney's Men.

● ALBUMS: *Presenting The Capitol Showband* (Pye 1963)★★.

● FURTHER READING: *Send 'Em Home Sweatin'*, Vincent Power.

CAPITOLS

An R&B trio from Detroit, Michigan, USA, originally known as the Three Caps, the Capitols were best known for their 1966 hit 'Cool Jerk'. Originally formed around 1962 as a quintet, the two principal members were Donald Storball (guitar/vocals) and Samuel George (drums/lead vocals). Discovered by record producer Ollie McLaughlin and signed to his Karen label, their first single was 'Dog And Cat', which failed to have any impact. Four years later, after splitting from the other members, Storball and George added pianist/vocalist Richard McDougall to the line-up and they recorded the soulful dance number 'Cool Jerk', which became their only hit, reaching the US Top 10. The group was unable to produce a successful follow-up and disbanded in 1969. Storball enrolled in the Detroit police force, while George was fatally stabbed in March 1982.

● ALBUMS: *Dance The Cool Jerk* (Atco 1966)★★, *We Got A Thing That's In The Groove* (Atco 1966)★★.

● COMPILATIONS: *Their Greatest Recordings* (Solid Smoke 1984)★★, *Golden Classics* (Collectables 1991)★★.

CAPRIS

Formed in Queens, New York, USA, in 1958, this vocal quintet consisted of Nick Santamaria (lead vocals), Mike Mincelli (first tenor), Vinny Nacardo (second tenor), Frank Reins (baritone) and John Apostol (bass). They were best known for the doo-wop ballad 'There's A Moon Out Tonight', a US number 3 single in early 1961, a song recorded by the Capris in 1958 and released on the small Planet Records label. It was not a hit and the group disbanded. Late in 1960, the owners of Lost Nite Records, one of the first labels to specialize in reissuing earlier rock and roll recordings, purchased the master of the recording and re-released it. It was then leased to the larger, more established Old Town Records, and due to the revived interest in group harmony singing, the record nearly to the top of the chart. The group re-formed and recorded further singles for Old Town and the Mr. Peeke label, but although three reached the charts, they never again had another hit. The group has stayed together since the early 60s, however, and in 1982 recorded an album for Ambient Sound Records which included an update of their hit.

● ALBUMS: *There's A Moon Out Again* (Ambient Sound 1982)★★, re-released as *Morse Code Of Love* (Collectables 1992).

CAPTAIN BEEFHEART

b. Don Van Vliet, 15 January 1941, Glendale, California, USA. As a child he achieved some fame as a talented sculptor, but for more than three decades the enigmatic and charismatic 'Captain', together with his various Magic Bands, has been one of rock music's more interesting subjects. During his teens he met Frank Zappa, who shared the same interest in R&B, and while an attempt to form a band together failed, Zappa (and members of the Mothers Of Invention) reappeared frequently during Beefheart's career. The first Magic Band was formed in 1964, although it was not until 1966 that they secured a record contract. The unit comprised, in addition to Beefheart, Alex St. Clair Snouffer (guitar), Doug Moon (guitar), Paul Blakely (drums) and Jerry Handley (bass). The ensuing singles, including 'Diddy Wah Diddy', were a commercial disaster and he was dropped by A&M Records. Beefheart reappeared with the pioneering *Safe As Milk* in April 1967, and was immediately adopted by the underground scene as a mentor. The album was helped by Ry Cooder's unmistakable guitar and it was a critical success throughout the 'summer of love'. Beefheart found that Europe was more receptive to his wonderfully alliterated lyrics, full of nonsensical juxtaposition that defied the listener to decode them. The follow-up, *Strictly Personal*, has fallen from grace as a critics' favourite, but at the time it was considered one of the most innovative albums of the 60s. It is now regarded as more of a blues-based album, with a heavily phased and nearly unlistenable recording. Titles such as 'Beatle Bones And Smokin' Stones' and 'Ah Feel Like Ahcid' were astonishing hallucinogenic voyages. It was with the remarkable *Trout Mask Replica* that Beefheart reached his peak. The double album, crudely recorded by Frank Zappa, contained a wealth of bizarre pieces, including 'Old Fart At Play', 'Veterans Day Poppy', 'Hair Pie Bake One' and 'Neon Meat Dream Of A Octofish'. Beefheart used his incredible octave range to great effect as he narrated and sang a wealth of lyrical 'malarkey'. The definitive Magic Band were present on this record, consisting of the Mascara Snake (unidentified, reputedly Beefheart's cousin), Antennae Jimmy Semens (Jeff Cotton), Drumbo (John French), Zoot Horn Rollo (Bill Harkelroad) and Rockette Morton (Mark Boston). It was reliably reported that the band recorded and played most of the tracks in one studio, while Beefheart added his lyrics in another (out of earshot). The structure and sound of many of the pieces was reminiscent of Ornette Coleman. At one stage on the record, Beefheart is heard laconically stating: 'Shit, how did the harmony get in there?' The listener requires a high tolerance level, and while Beefheart and Zappa may have intended to perpetrate one of the greatest musical jokes of our time, the album is cherished as one of the classic albums from the psychedelic era of the 60s. A similar theme was adopted for *Lick My Decals Off, Baby* and *Spotlight Kid*, although the latter had a more structured musical format. This album contained the delightfully perceptive 'Blabber And Smoke', written by Jan Van Vliet commenting on her husband. Beefheart sings her lyrics: 'Why don't you stop acting like a silly dope? / All you ever do is blabber and smoke'. Beefheart also received considerable attention by contributing the vocals to 'Willie The Pimp' on Zappa's *Hot Rats* in 1969. Following the release of the overtly commercial (by

Beefheart standards) *Clear Spot* and a heavy touring schedule, the Magic Band split from Beefheart to form Mallard. Beefheart signed to the UK Virgin Records label, releasing two albums, including the critically acclaimed *Unconditionally Guaranteed*. In 1975 Beefheart and Zappa released *Bongo Fury*, a superb live set recorded in Austin, Texas. However, the release of the album resulted in protracted litigation with Virgin, which won an injunction over Warner Brothers Records on the sale of the album in the UK. Beefheart began to spend more time with his other interest, painting. His colourful oils were in the style of Francis Bacon, and it eventually became his main interest. Beefheart has toured and recorded only occasionally and seemed destined to be an important cult figure until the release of *Ice Cream For Crow* in 1982. This excellent return to form saw him writing and performing with renewed fervour. It reached number 90 in the UK charts but was completely ignored in his homeland. Since that time there have been no new recordings and Don Van Vliet, as he is now known, is a respected artist, exhibiting regularly; his paintings are now fetching considerable prices. In 1993 it was alleged that Beefheart was suffering from multiple sclerosis.

●ALBUMS: *Safe As Milk* (Buddah 1967)★★★★, *Strictly Personal* (Blue Thumb/Liberty 1968)★★★★, *Trout Mask Replica* (1969)★★★★★, *Lick My Decals Off, Baby* (1970)★★★★, *The Spotlight Kid* (1972)★★★, *Clear Spot* (1972)★★★, *Mirror Man* (1973)★★★, *Unconditionally Guaranteed* (1974)★★, *Bluejeans And Moonbeams* (1974)★★, with Frank Zappa *Bongo Fury* (1975)★★★, *Shiny Beast (Bat Chain Puller)* (1978)★★★, *Doc At The Radar Station* (1980)★★★, *Ice Cream For Crow* (1982)★★★, *I May Be Hungry But I Sure Ain't Weird* alternate takes and new tracks (1992)★★★.

●COMPILATIONS: *The Best Beefheart* (1993)★★★, *Zig Zag Wanderer: The Best Of The Buddah Years* (Wooden Hill 1997)★★★.

●FURTHER READING: *The Lives And Times Of Captain Beefheart*, no editor listed. *Captain Beefheart: The Man And His Music*, Colin David Webb.

CARAVELLES

Former office workers Lois Wilkinson (b. 3 April 1944, Sleaford, Lincolnshire, England) and Andrea Simpson (b. 1946) achieved international success with their distinctive version of 'You Don't Have To Be A Baby To Cry'. This light, breathy single reached the UK Top 10 in August 1963 where it formed an antidote to the more powerful, emergent British beat. Despite touring the USA, where the single was a number 3 hit, the duo was unable to maintain a consistent profile in spite of recording several excellent, if novelty-bound releases. Wilkinson began a solo career as Lois Lane, while Simpson maintained the Caravelles' name with a series of replacements and was actively performing throughout the 80s.

●ALBUMS: *You Don't Have To Be A Baby To Cry* US release (Smash 1963)★★, *The Caravelles* UK release (Decca 1963)★★.

CARR, JAMES

b. 13 June 1942, Coahoma, Mississippi, USA. One of soul music's greatest and most underrated voices, Carr sang gospel in the Sunset Travellers and the Harmony Echoes and was discovered by Memphis gospel-group mentor Roosevelt Jamison. This budding manager and songwriter brought Carr to the Goldwax label. It took four singles to define the singer's style, but the deep, magnificent 'You've Got My Mind Messed Up' burned with an intensity few contemporaries could match. A US Top 10 R&B hit in 1966, 'Love Attack' and 'Pouring Water On A Drowning Man' also followed that year. In 1967 Carr released 'Dark End Of The Street', southern soul's definitive guilt-laced 'cheating' song, which inspired several cover versions. His later work included 'Let It Happen' and 'A Man Needs A Woman', but his fragile personality was increasingly disturbed by drug abuse. 'To Love Somebody' (1969) was Carr's final hit. Goldwax Records collapsed the following year and Carr moved to Atlantic Records for 'Hold On' (1971), which was recorded at Malaco Studios in Jackson, Mississippi. His problems worsened until 1977 when a now-impoverished Carr was reunited with Jamison. One single, the rather average 'Let Me Be Right', appeared on the River City label and the singer temporarily disappeared from the scene. Carr resurfaced in 1979 on a tour of Japan, the first concert of which was a disaster when he 'froze' on stage, having taken too much medication before his performance. In 1991 he had an album of new material entitled *Take Me To The Limit* released by Goldwax Records in the USA (Ace Records in the UK), with Quinton Claunch and Roosevelt Jamison back among the production credits. The following year, Carr appeared at the Sweet Soul Music annual festival in northern Italy, and three of his songs were included on a 'live' album of the festival on the Italian '103' label. By 1993, Claunch had left Goldwax and set up his own Soultrax Records, for which Carr recorded his *Soul Survivor* album (again also on UK Ace), the title track of which had a single release in the US. Meanwhile, having lost Carr to Claunch, Goldwax's new President, E.W. Clark, exhumed some prime late 60s Carr material for inclusion on *Volume 1* of the projected (and perhaps optimistically titled) *Complete James Carr* (a US only release).

●ALBUMS: *You Got My Mind Messed Up* (Goldwax 1966)★★★★, *A Man Needs A Woman* (1968)★★★, *Freedom Train* (1968)★★★, *Take Me To The Limit* (Ace 1991)★★★, *Soul Survivor* (1993)★★★.

●COMPILATIONS: *At The Dark End Of The Street* (1987)★★★, *A Man Needs A Woman* (late 80s)★★★, *The Complete James Carr, Volume 1* (Goldwax 1993)★★★★, with the Jubilee Hummingbirds *Guilty Of Serving God* (Ace 1996)★★.

CARR, PEARL, AND TEDDY JOHNSON

Both were popular solo vocalists prior to their marrage in 1955. Carr (b. Pearl Lavina Carr, 2 November 1923, Exmouth, Devon, England) worked with several popular bands and was lead singer with the Keynotes, the resident vocal group on BBC Radio's *Take It From Here*. She also appeared on radio as a comedienne and singer on *Breakfast* (and *Bedtime*) *With Braden*, and had her own series, *In The Blue Of The Evening*. Johnson (b. Edward Victor Johnson, 4 September 1920, Surbiton, Surrey, England) led his own five-piece amateur band at the age of 14 and sang and played drums professionally at the age of 17. He recorded extensively for Columbia in the early 50s, worked as a disc jockey for Radio Luxembourg, and regularly appeared on television on programmes such as *Crackerjack* and *Music Shop*. The couple's professional liaison proved to be extremely successful, especially during the late 50s when they became known as Britain's Mr and Mrs Music. They toured the UK variety circuit, and in 1959 made the UK Top 20 chart with the catchy 'Sing Little Birdie', a song that they had taken to second place in the *Eurovision Song Contest*. They had another hit in 1961 with the Italian 'Aneme e Core (How Wonderful To Know)'. More recently they have been involved in biographical stage presentations such as *The Bing Crosby Story* and *London To Hollywood Songbook*, which they devised and appeared in. In 1987 they were contemplating retirement when they accepted an offer to appear as two ageing Vaudeville stars in Stephen Sondheim's *Follies*, their first West End musical. In the late 80s and early 90s Johnson continued to write and present programmes for the BBC World Service and Radio 2.

CARR, VIKKI

b. Florencia Bisenta De Casillas Martinez Cardona, 19 July 1941, El Paso, Texas, USA. The eldest of seven children, Carr made her public debut at the age of four singing 'Silent Night' in Latin at a Christmas concert, before moving to LA where she took leading roles in school musicals and studied music. After graduating she auditioned for a job at the Chi Chi Club in Palm Springs where she worked as singer with the 'Irish Mexican' Pepe Callahan Orchestra. With them she travelled to Las Vegas, Hawaii and Reno, where she teamed up with the Chuck Leonard Quartette, before pursuing a solo career. After doing some club work she recorded some demos which enticed Liberty Records to sign her. As part of a host of television variety appearances, she was regularly featured as vocalist on the *Ray Anthony Show* in 1962, and enjoyed a much publicized friendship with Elvis Presley. Her biggest hit was 'It Must Be Him (Seul Sur Son Etoile)' in 1967, which sold in excess of a million copies. Follow-up hits in the UK included 'There I Go' and 'With Pen In Hand'. She became a popular MOR concert performer and performed live in the White House for Presidents Nixon in 1970 and Ford in 1974. A Royal Command Performance became the equivalent seal of approval in the UK. As the 70s progressed she became more involved in charity work, setting up a scholarship fund for Chicano children. Her popularity in the 90s was very much in the Latin market, singing in her native language.

●ALBUMS: *Color Her Great* (1963)★★★, *Discovery!* (Liberty 1964)★★★, *Way Of Today* (1967)★★★, *It Must Be Him* (Liberty 1967)★★★, *Vikki!* (Liberty 1968)★★★, *For Once In My Life* (Liberty 1969)★★★, *Nashville By Carr* (1970)★★, *Vikki Carr's Love Story* (1971)★★★, *Superstar* (1971)★★★, *The First Time Ever (I Saw Your Face)* (1972)★★★, *Song Sung Blue* (CBS 1972)★★★, *En Espanol* (1972)★★★, *Ms. America* (1973)★★, *Live At The Greek Theatre* (1973)★★, *One Hell Of A Woman* (1974)★★★, *Y El Amor* (1980)★★★, *Emociones* (Polygram 1996)★★★.

●COMPILATIONS: *The Vikki Carr Collection* (United Artists 1973)★★★, *The Liberty Years - The Best Of Vikki Carr* (1989)★★★.

CARROLL, RONNIE

b. Ronald Cleghorn, 18 August 1934, Belfast, Northern Ireland. A singer with an extremely high baritone voice, who became known as 'The Minstrel'. Carroll has been a baker, plumber, greengrocer, milkman, car mechanic and auctioneer's assistant. He began his career in shows promoted by Ruby Murray's father, then joined Eddie Lee's *Hollywood Doubles Show*, blacking up to provide Nat 'King' Cole impressions. Cole attended his performance in Liverpool and asked, 'What are you trying to do, cripple me?' Carroll toured the UK Variety circuit with the show, adding Billy Eckstine material to his repertoire. After BBC producer Albert Stevenson gave him his television debut, he met singer and actress Millicent Martin on a show and they were married in 1959. Carroll was signed to Philips by A&R manager Johnny Franz who had seen him at the London Metropolitan, Edgware Road. In the late 50s he had UK hits with 'Walk Hand In Hand' (1956) and 'The Wisdom Of A Fool' (1957), and in the early 60s with 'Footsteps' (1960), 'Roses Are Red' (1962 - a number 3 hit), 'If Only Tomorrow' (1962) and two songs with which he won the British heats of the *Eurovision Song Contest*, 'Ring-A-Ding Girl' (1962) and 'Say Wonderful Things' (1963 - Top 10). He was still working in the 80s, but the recession in the UK northern club business forced him to seek work in holiday camps and in Singapore and Kuala Lumpur hotels. In 1989, Carroll was discharged from bankruptcy with reported debts of many thousands of pounds. In 1997 Carroll stood as a parliamentary candidate at the general election.

●ALBUMS: with Bill McGuffie *From Ten Till One* (Philips 1956)★★★, *Lucky Thirteen* (Philips 1959)★★★, *Sometimes I'm Happy, Sometimes I'm Blue* (Philips 1963)★★★, with Millicent Martin *Mr & Mrs Is The Name* (Philips 1964)★★, *Carroll Calling* (1965)★★★, *Wonderful Things And Other Favourites* (Wing 1967)★★★, with Anna Pollack *Phil The Fluter* (Fontana 1969)★★, with Aimi McDonald *Promises Promises* (Fontana 1970)★★.

●COMPILATIONS: *Roses Are Red: The Ronnie Carroll Story* (Diamond 1996)★★★.

CARTER AND LEWIS

John Carter (John Shakespeare) and Ken Lewis (Kenneth Hawker) were born in 1942 in Small Heath, Birmingham,

England. They initially found fame leading Carter-Lewis And The Southerners, a group which briefly included guitarist Jimmy Page and recorded several singles including So Much In Love (1961), Here's Hoping' (1962) and 'Sweet And Tender Romance' and 'Your Mama's Out Of Town' (both 1963). The duo's ability to create unabashed pop had been confirmed with 'Will I What?', a UK number 1 hit for Mike Sarne, and having disbanded their group, Carter/Lewis compositions were adopted by scores of acts, including the Marauders, Brenda Lee, P.J. Proby and the McKinleys, the last of whom they also produced. In 1964 the songwriters resurrected the idea of a group, forming the Ivy League with Perry Ford. This harmony trio enjoyed several hits, but lost momentum when first Carter, then Lewis, left the line-up in 1966. The pair resumed a back room role with the Flowerpot Men, before scoring further success as composers and/or producers with, among others, White Plains and First Class. Carter and Lewis also persued joint and individual projects writing for commercials and jingles.
● ALBUMS: *Carter-Lewis Story* (Sequel 1993)★★★.

CASCADES

Formed in the late 50s in San Diego, California, USA, the Cascades were best known for their 1963 number 3 US hit 'Rhythm Of The Rain'. The group consisted of John Gummoe (vocals/guitar), Eddy Snyder (piano), Dave Stevens (bass), Dave Wilson (saxophone) and Dave Zabo (drums). They were discovered at a club called the Peppermint Stick in 1962 and signed to Valiant Records. Their first single, 'Second Chance', failed but 'Rhythm Of The Rain' became a soft-rock classic that still receives radio airplay in the 90s. One other chart single for Valiant and one for RCA Records charted but the group was unable to repeat its main success. Two more albums recorded in the late 60s did not revive the group's fortunes. They disbanded in 1969, with only one original member remaining at that time.
● ALBUMS: *Rhythm Of The Rain* (Valiant 1963)★★★, *What Goes On* (Cascade 1968)★★, *Maybe The Rain Will Fall* (UNI 1969)★★.
● FILMS: *Catalina Caper* (1967).

CASH, ALVIN

b. Alvin Welch, 15 February 1939, St. Louis, Missouri, USA. Cash's first group, the Crawlers, was named after a dance troupe completed by the singer's three younger brothers, Robert, Arthur and George. Although credited, this line-up did not perform on Alvin's early singles, where their place on the label's credits were taken by the Registers, a back-up group Cash had encountered on tour and who were initially called the Nightlighters. Together they released a series of records generally based on popular dance routines, including 'Twine Time' (1965 - a US Top 20 pop hit) and 'The Barracuda' (both 1965) and 'Philly Freeze' (1966). Cash continued this theme into the 70s, but later expanded on his rather limited repertoire by recording several tributes to the boxer, Muhammad Ali.
● ALBUMS: *Twine Time* (Mar-V-Lus 1965)★★, *The*

Philly Freeze (President 1966)★★, *Alvin Cash Does The Greatest Hits Of Muhammad Ali* (1980)★.

CASH, JOHNNY

b. 26 February 1932, Kingsland, Arkansas, USA. Cash has traced his ancestry to seventeenth-century Scotland and has admitted that he fabricated the much-publicized story that he was a quarter Cherokee. Cash's father, Ray, worked on sawmills and the railway; in 1936, the family was one of 600 chosen by the Federal Government to reclaim land by the Mississippi River, known as the Dyess Colony Scheme. Much of it was swampland and, in 1937, they were evacuated when the river overflowed. Cash recalled the circumstances in his 1959 country hit, 'Five Foot High And Risin''. Other songs inspired by his youth are 'Pickin' Time', 'Christmas As I Knew It' and 'Cisco Clifton's Filling Station'. Carl Perkins wrote 'Daddy Sang Bass' about Cash's family and the 'little brother' is Jack Cash, who was killed when he fell across an electric saw. Cash was posted to Germany as a radio-operator in the US Army. Many think the scar on his cheek is a knife wound but it is the result of a cyst being removed by a drunken doctor, while his hearing was permanently damaged by a German girl playfully sticking a pencil down his left ear. After his discharge, he settled in San Antonio with his bride, Vivian Liberto. One of their four children, Rosanne Cash, also became a country singer. Cash auditioned as a gospel singer with Sam Phillips of Sun Records in Memphis, who told him to return with something more commercial. Cash developed his 'boom chicka boom' sound with two friends: Luther Perkins (lead guitar) and Marshall Grant (bass). Their first record, 'Hey Porter'/'Cry, Cry, Cry', credited to Johnny Cash And The Tennessee Two, was released in June 1955, but Cash was irritated that Phillips had called him 'Johnny' as it sounded too young. 'Cry, Cry, Cry' made number 14 on the US country charts and was followed by 'Folsom Prison Blues', which Cash wrote after seeing a film called *Inside The Walls Of Folsom Prison*. They played shows with Carl Perkins (no relation to Luther Perkins). Perkins' drummer, W.S. Holland, joined Cash in 1958 to make it the Tennessee Three. Cash encouraged Perkins to complete the writing of 'Blue Suede Shoes', while he finished 'I Walk The Line' at Perkin's insistence. 'I got the idea from a Dale Carnegie course. It taught you to keep your eyes open for something good. I made a love song out of it. It was meant to be a slow, mournful ballad but Sam had us pick up the tempo until I didn't like it at all.' 'I Walk The Line' made number 17 on the US pop charts and was the title song for a 1970 film starring Gregory Peck. Among his other excellent Sun records are 'Home Of The Blues', which was the name of a Memphis record shop, 'Big River', 'Luther Played The Boogie', 'Give My Love To Rose' and 'There You Go', which topped the US country charts for five weeks. Producer Jack Clement added piano and vocal chorus. They achieved further pop hits with the high school tale, 'Ballad Of A Teenage Queen' (number 14), 'Guess Things Happen That Way' (number 11) and 'The Ways Of A Woman In Love' (number 24).

While at Sun Records, Cash wrote 'You're My Baby' and 'Rock 'N' Roll Ruby' which were recorded by Roy Orbison and Warren Smith, respectively. Despite having his photograph taken with Elvis Presley, Jerry Lee Lewis and Carl Perkins, he did not take part in the 'million dollar session' but went shopping instead.

At a disc jockey's convention in Nashville in November 1957, Sun launched their first ever album release, *Johnny Cash With His Hot And Blue Guitar*, but Phillips was reluctant to record further LPs with Cash. This, and an unwillingness to increase his royalties, led to Cash joining Columbia Records in 1958. His cautionary tale about a gunfighter not listening to his mother, 'Don't Take Your Guns To Town', sold half a million copies and prompted a response from Charlie Rich, 'The Ballad Of Billy Joe', which was also recorded by Jerry Lee Lewis. Its b-side, 'I Still Miss Someone', is one of Cash's best compositions, and has been revived by Flatt And Scruggs, Crystal Gayle and Emmylou Harris. Cash started to take drugs to help get himself through his schedule of 300 shows a year; however, his artistic integrity suffered and he regards *The Sound Of Johnny Cash* as his worst album. Nevertheless, he started on an inspiring series of concept albums about the working man (*Blood, Sweat And Tears*), cowboys (*Ballads Of The True West*) and the American Indian (*Bitter Tears*). The concepts are fascinating, the songs excellent, but the albums are bogged down with narration and self-righteousness, making Cash sound like a history teacher. His sympathy for a maligned American Indian, 'The Ballad Of Ira Hayes', led to threats from the Ku Klux Klan. Cash says, 'I didn't really care what condition I was in and it showed up on my recordings, but *Bitter Tears* was so important to me that I managed to get enough sleep to do it right.' For all his worthy causes, the drugged-up country star was a troublemaker himself, although, despite press reports, he only ever spent three days in prison. His biggest misdemeanor was starting a forest fire for which he was fined $85,000. He wrecked hotel rooms and toyed with guns. He and his drinking buddy, country singer Carl Smith, rampaged through Smith's house and ruined his wife's Cadillac. Smith's marriage to June Carter of the Carter Family was nearing its end but few could have predicted Carter's next marriage. In 1963, Mexican brass was added to the ominous 'Ring Of Fire', written by Carter and Merle Kilgore, which again was a pop hit. Without Cash's support, Bob Dylan would have been dropped by Columbia, and Cash had his first British hit in 1965 with Dylan's 'It Ain't Me Babe'. Their off beat duet, 'Girl From The North Country', was included on Dylan's *Nashville Skyline*, and the rest of their sessions have been widely bootlegged. Dylan also gave Cash an unreleased song, 'Wanted Man'. Cash said, 'I don't dance, tell jokes or wear my pants too tight, but I do know about a thousand songs.' With this in mind, he has turned his road show into a history of country music. In the 60s it featured Carl Perkins (who also played guitar for Cash after Luther Perkins' death in a fire), the Statler Brothers and the Carter Family. The highlight of Cash's act was 'Orange Blossom Special' played with two har-

monicas. One night Cash proposed to June Carter on stage; she accepted and they were married in March 1968. Their successful duets include 'Jackson' and 'If I Were A Carpenter'.

In 1968 Columbia finally agreed to record one of Cash's prison concerts and the invigorating album, *Johnny Cash At Folsom Prison* is one of the most atmospheric of all live albums. It remains, arguably, Cash's best album and a contender for the best country record of all time. Cash explains, 'Prisoners are the greatest audience that an entertainer can perform for. We bring them a ray of sunshine and they're not ashamed to show their appreciation.' He included 'Graystone Chapel' written by an inmate, Glen Sherley, which he had been given by the Prison Chaplain. Sherley subsequently recorded an album with Cash's support, but he died in 1978. The Folsom Prison concert was followed by one at San Quentin, which was filmed for a television documentary. Shortly before that concert, Shel Silverstein gave Cash a poem, 'A Boy Named Sue'. Carl Perkins put chords to it and, without any rehearsals, the humorous song was recorded, giving Cash his only Top 10 on the US pop charts and a number 4 success in the UK. Cash's popularity led to him hosting his own television series from 1969-71 but, despite notable guests such as Bob Dylan, the show was hampered by feeble jokes and middle-of-the-road arrangements. Far better was the documentary, *Johnny Cash - The Man, His World, His Music*. Cash's catch phrase 'Hello, I'm Johnny Cash' became so well-known that both Elvis Presley and the Kinks' Ray Davies sometimes opened with that remark. Cash championed Kris Kristofferson, wrote the liner notes for his first album, *Kristofferson*, and recorded several of his songs. 'To Beat The Devil' celebrated Cash overcoming drugs after many years, while 'The Loving Gift' was about the birth of Cash's son, John Carter Cash, who has since joined his stage show. Cash has often found strength and comfort in religion and he has recorded many spiritual albums. One of his most stirring performances is 'Were You There (When They Crucified My Lord)?' with the Carter Family. He made a documentary film and double album *The Gospel Road* with Kristofferson, Larry Gatlin and the Statler Brothers, but, as he remarked, 'My record company would rather I'd be in prison than in church.' He justified himself commercially when 'A Thing Called Love', written by Jerry Reed, made with the Evangel Temple Choir, became one of his biggest-selling UK records, reaching number 4 in 1972.

Cash is an imposing figure with his huge muscular frame, black hair, craggy face and deep bass voice. Unlike other country singers, he shuns lavish colours and in his song 'Man In Black' he explains that he wears black because of the injustice in the world. In truth, he started wearing black when he first appeared on the *Grand Ole Opry* because he felt that rhinestone suits detracted from the music. With little trouble, Cash could have been a major Hollywood star, particularly in westerns, and he acquitted himself well when the occasion arose. He made his debut in *Five Minutes To Live* in 1960 and his best role is opposite Kirk Douglas in the 1972 film *A Gunfight*, which was financed by Apache money, although religious principles prevented a scene with a naked actress. He was featured alongside Kris Kristofferson and Willie Nelson in a light-hearted remake of *Stagecoach* and starred in a television movie adaptation of his pool-hall song *The Baron*. Cash also gave a moving portrayal of a coalminer overcoming illiteracy in another television movie, *The Pride Of Jesse Hallam*. He recorded the theme for the US television series *The Rebel - Johnny Yuma* and, among the previously unissued tracks released by Bear Family Records, is his submission for a James Bond theme, 'Thunderball'. By opening his own recording studios, House Of Cash, in 1972, he became even more prolific. His family joined him on the quirky *The Junkie And The Juicehead Minus Me* and his son-in-law J.W. Routh wrote several songs and performed with him on *The Rambler*. He has always followed writers and the inclusion of Nick Lowe, former husband of Carlene Carter, and Rodney Crowell, husband of Rosanne Cash, into his family increased his awareness. His recordings include the Rolling Stones' 'No Expectations', John Prine's 'Unwed Fathers', Guy Clark's 'The Last Gunfighter Ballad' and a touching portrayal of Bruce Springsteen's 'Highway Patrolman'. He showed his humour with 'Gone Girl', 'One Piece At A Time' and 'Chicken In Black'. He said, 'I record a song because I love it and let it become a part of me.' Cash moved to Mercury Records in 1986 and scored immediately with the whimsical 'The Night Hank Williams Came To Town'. He made an all-star album, *Water From The Wells Of Home* with Emmylou Harris, the Everly Brothers, Paul McCartney and many others. His 60s composition 'Tennessee Flat-Top Box' became a US country number 1 for daughter Rosanne in 1988. In the same year, various UK modern folk artists recorded an album of his songs *'Til Things Are Brighter*, with proceeds going to an AIDS charity. Cash particularly enjoyed Sally Timms' waltz-time treatment of 'Cry, Cry, Cry'. On the crest of a revival, Cash has been hampered by pneumonia, heart surgery and a recurrence of drug problems. He has now returned to the stage, either touring with the Carter Family or as part of the Highwaymen with Kristofferson, Waylon Jennings and Nelson. He is still passionate about his beliefs. 'A lot of people think of country singers as right-wing, redneck bigots,' he says, 'but I don't think I'm like that.' Few would dare argue with the imposing figure of the man in black. Cash has made over 70 albums of original material, plus countless guest appearances. His music reflects his love of America (a recent compilation was called *Patriot*), his compassion, his love of life, and, what is often lacking in country music, a sense of humour. His limited range is staggeringly good on particular songs, especially narrative ones. Like Bo Diddley's 'shave and a haircut' rhythm, he has developed his music around his 'boom chicka boom', and instilled enough variety to stave off boredom. In a genre now dominated by new country, Cash has found it difficult to obtain record deals of late, but this worked to his advantage with the low-key *American Recordings*, produced by Rick Rubin in 1994. Featuring just his craggy voice and simple guitar, it reaffirmed his talent for storytelling. Among the many excellent songs included Nick Lowe's 'The Beast In Me' (Lowe was a former son-in-law), Tom Waits' 'Down There By The Train' and Loudon Wainwright's 'The Man Who Couldn't Cry'. An appearance at the Glastonbury Festival in 1994 also introduced him to a new audience, this time indie and new wave rockers. In the USA during 1994 Cash became a media star and was featured on the cover on many magazines (not just music ones). It was an astonishing rebirth of interest. *Unchained* continued his renaissance with effortless covers of Don Gibson's 'Sea Of Heartbreak' and the Dean Martin classic 'Memories Are Made Of This'. His continuing popularity assured, Cash states he heeded the advice he was given during his one and only singing lesson, 'Never change your voice.' His gigantic contribution to country music's history is inestimable and, as he says, 'They can get all the synthesizers they want, but nothing will ever take the place of the human heart.'

●ALBUMS: *Johnny Cash With His Hot And Blue Guitar* (Sun 1957)★★★, *Johnny Cash Sings The Songs That Made Him Famous* (Sun 1958)★★★, *The Fabulous Johnny Cash* (Columbia 1958)★★★, *Hymns By Johnny Cash* (Columbia 1959)★, *Songs Of Our Soil* (Columbia 1959)★★, *Now There Was A Song* (Columbia 1960)★★, *Johnny Cash Sings Hank Williams And Other Favorite Tunes* (Sun 1960)★★★, *Ride This Train* (Columbia 1960)★★★★, *Now Here's Johnny Cash* (Sun 1961)★★★, *The Lure Of The Grand Canyon* (Columbia 1961)★★, *Hymns From The Heart* (Columbia 1962)★, *The Sound Of Johnny Cash* (Columbia 1962)★★, *All Aboard The Blue Train* (Sun 1963)★★★, *Blood, Sweat And Tears* (Columbia 1963)★★★, *The Christmas Spirit* (Columbia 1963)★★, with the Carter Family *Keep On The Sunny Side* (1964)★★★, *I Walk The Line* (Columbia 1964)★★★, *Bitter Tears (Ballads Of The American Indian)* (Columbia 1964)★★★, *Orange Blossom Special* (Columbia 1965)★★★★, *Ballads Of The True West* (Columbia 1965)★★★, *Mean As Hell* (Columbia 1965)★★, *The Sons Of Katie Elder* film soundtrack (Columbia 1965)★★, *Ballads Of The True West, Volume 2* (Columbia 1966)★★★, *Everybody Loves A Nut* (Columbia 1966)★, *Happiness Is You* (Columbia 1966)★★, with June Carter *Carryin' On* (1967)★★, *Old Golden Throat* (Columbia 1968)★★, *From Sea To Shining Sea* (Columbia 1968)★★, *Johnny Cash At Folsom Prison* (Columbia 1968)★★★★, *More Of Old Golden Throat* (Columbia 1969)★★, *The Holy Land* (Columbia 1969)★, *Johnny Cash At San Quentin* (Columbia 1969)★★★★, *Hello I'm Johnny Cash* (Columbia 1970)★★★, *The Johnny Cash Show* (1970)★★★, *The Rough Cut King Of Country* (Sun 1970)★★★, *I Walk The Line* (1970)★★★, *Man In Black* (1971)★★★, *A Thing Called Love* (1972)★★, *Christmas And The Cash Family* (Columbia 1972)★★, *America (A 200-Year Salute In Story And Song)*

(1972)★★, *The Gospel Road* (1973)★★, *Any Old Wind That Blows* (Columbia 1973)★★, with June Carter *Johnny Cash And His Woman* (Columbia 1973)★★, *Inside A Swedish Prison* (1974)★★, *The Junkie And The Juicehead Minus Me* (Columbia 1974)★★, *Ragged Old Flag* (Columbia 1974)★★, *John R. Cash* (Columbia 1975)★★★, *Look At Them Beans* (Columbia 1975)★★, *The Johnny Cash Children's Album* (1975)★★, *Destination Victoria Station* (1976)★★, *Strawberry Cake* (Columbia 1976)★★★, *One Piece At A Time* (Columbia 1976)★★★★, *The Last Gunfighter Ballad* (Columbia 1977)★★★, *The Rambler* (Columbia 1977)★★★, *Gone Girl* (Columbia 1978)★★★, *The Unissued Johnny Cash* (1978)★★, *I Would Like To See You Again* (Columbia 1978)★★★, *Silver* (Columbia 1979)★★★, *A Believer Sings The Truth* (Columbia 1979)★★, *Johnny And June* (1980)★★, *Rockabilly Blues* (Columbia 1980)★★★★, *Tall Man* (1980)★★★, *The Baron* (Columbia 1981)★★★, with Jerry Lee Lewis, Carl Perkins *The Survivors* (Columbia 1982)★★★, *The Adventures Of Johnny Cash* (Columbia 1982)★★, *Johnny 99* (Columbia 1983)★★, *Rainbow* (Columbia 1985)★★★, with Kris Kristofferson, Waylon Jennings, Willie Nelson *Highwayman* (1985)★★★★, with Jerry Lee Lewis, Roy Orbison, Carl Perkins *Homecoming* (1986)★★★, with Waylon Jennings *Heroes* (Columbia 1986)★★★, *Believe In Him* (Word 1986)★★, *Johnny Cash Is Back In Town* (Mercury 1987)★★★, *Classic Cash* (Mercury 1988)★★★, *Water From The Wells Of Home* (Mercury 1988)★★★★, *Boom Chicka Boom* (Mercury 1989)★★★, with Kristofferson, Jennings and Nelson *Highwayman 2* (1990)★★★, *The Mystery Of Life* (Mercury 1991)★★★, *Get Rhythm* (Sun 1991)★★★, *American Recordings* (American 1994)★★★★, *Unchained* (American 1996)★★★.

●COMPILATIONS: *Johnny Cash's Greatest* (Sun 1959)★★★, *Ring Of Fire (The Best Of Johnny Cash)* (1963)★★★, *The Original Sun Sound Of Johnny Cash* (Sun 1965)★★★, *Johnny Cash's Greatest Hits, Volume 1* (1967)★★★, *Get Rhythm* (1969)★★★, *Story Songs Of The Trains And Rivers* (1969)★★★, *Showtime* (1969)★★★, *The Singing Story Teller* (1970)★★★, *The Best Of The Sun Years 1959-1962* 5-CD box set (1992)★★★★, *The Man In Black: The Definitive Collection* (Columbia 1994)★★★★, *Get Rhythm: The Best Of The Sun Years* (Pickwick 1995)★★★, *Ring Of Fire* (Spectrum 1995)★★★, *The Man In Black 1963-1969 Plus* 6-CD box set (Bear Family 1996)★★★★, *All American Country* (Spectrum 1997)★★★.

●VIDEOS: *Live In London: Johnny Cash* (1987), *In San Quentin* (1987), *Riding The Rails* (1990), *Johnny Cash Live!* (1993), *The Tennessee Top Cat Live 1955-1965* (Jubilee 1995), *The Man, His World, The Music* (1995).

●FURTHER READING: *Johnny Cash Discography And Recording History 1954-1969*, John L. Smith. *A Boy Named Cash*, Albert Govoni. *The Johnny Cash Story*, George Carpozi. *Johnny Cash: Winners Get Scars Too*, Christopher S. Wren. *The New Johnny Cash*, Charles Paul Conn. *Man In Black*, Johnny Cash. *The Johnny Cash Discography 1954-1984*, John L. Smith. *The Johnny Cash Record Catalogue*, John L. Smith (ed.).

CASINOS

Formed in 1958 in Cincinnati, Ohio, USA, the Casinos originally consisted of Gene and Glen Hughes, Pete Bolton, Joe Patterson and Ray White. After gaining popularity locally, they signed with the small Terry Records and covered the Carla Thomas R&B ballad 'Gee Whiz', with no success. They then switched to the local Fraternity Records and recorded a series of singles which also failed commercially. The group, still sporting a clean-cut look and a 50s-orientated doo-wop sound, grew to nine members by the mid-60s, including Bob Armstrong, Tom Mathews, Bill Hawkins and Mickey Denton. Finally, in 1967, the group reached the US Top 10 with a cover of John D. Loudermilk's ballad, 'Then You Can Tell Me Goodbye'. The Casinos continued to record into the 70s and a version of the group was still performing in Cincinnati by the early 90s, but there have been no further hits.

●ALBUMS: *Then You Can Tell Me Goodbye* (Fraternity 1967)★★★.

CASTAWAYS

Formed in Richfield, Minnesota, USA, in 1962 with the express purpose of playing at a fraternity party, the Castaways made one appearance on the US charts in 1965 with 'Liar, Liar', a 'garage-rock' gem marked by overbearing organ and heavily echoed vocals. Roy Hensley (guitar), Denny Craswell (drums) and Dick Roby (bass) originated the group, with Bob Folschow (guitar) and Jim Donna (keyboards) completing the line-up. Their only hit was also their first single, recorded for the local Soma label which was intended to gain the band a better footing from which to sell itself to local club owners. The group recorded several other singles but none charted. Denny Craswell left the band to join Crow in 1970, while the remaining four members still performed together in the late 80s and hope to eventually record an album. Meanwhile, 'Liar, Liar' remains popular, having received a boost in 1987 via placement in the film *Good Morning Vietnam*.

●FILMS: *It's A Bikini World* (1967).

CASTELLS

Based in Santa Rosa, California, USA, this vocal quartet was originally formed as a trio in 1958. By mid-1959 they had become a quartet with the line-up of teenagers Tom Hicks, Chuck Girard, Bob Ussery and Joe Kelly. They were taken to the successful independent label, Era Records by west coast disc jockey Dan Dillon. Their first release, 'Little Sad Eyes', was a local hit and in 1961 their second single 'Sacred', a sweet and innocent semi-religious song, written by Adam Ross and Bill Laundau, gave them their only Top 20 record. This classy, doo-wop-orientated pop vocal quartet also reached the US Top 40 with 'So This Is Love' in 1962. Kelly and Girard were later members of the Hondells. They later recorded unsuccessfully for United Artists, Warner Brothers, Decca, Solomon and Laurie.

●ALBUMS: *So This Is Love* (Era 1962)★★★.
●COMPILATIONS: *Sweet Sounds Of The Castelles* (Collectables 1987)★★★.

CASUALS

Three times winners on *Opportunity Knocks*, British television's hugely popular talent show of the late 60s, the Casuals subsequently left the UK for Italy, where they became a leading attraction. Alan Taylor (b. Halifax, Yorkshire, England; guitar/bass), Johnny Tebb (b. 1 October 1945, Lincoln, England; organ), Howard Newcombe (b. Lincoln, England; guitar/trumpet) and Robert O'Brien (b. Bridge Of Allan, Central Scotland; drums) were based in Milan for several years before returning to Britain in 1968, when their single, 'Jesamine', entered the charts. The song was originally recorded by the Bystanders, but the Casuals' inherently commercial reading coincided with a prevailing trend for emotional ballads. The single ultimately reached number 2 but later releases were less successful and 'Toy' (1968), which peaked at number 30, was their only other hit. The Casuals continued to record superior pop: Move leader Roy Wood wrote and produced the polished 'Caroline' (1969), but as the decade closed, so their style of music grew increasingly anachronistic.

●ALBUMS: *Hour World* (Decca 1969)★★★.

CATTINI, CLEM

b. 28 August 1939, London, England. As pop exponents tend to accelerate and slow down *en bloc* to inconsistencies of tempo in concert, it is not uncommon for drumming on record to be ghosted by someone more technically adept than a given act's regular player. From the 60s onwards, chief among those Britons earning Musicians Union-regulated tea breaks in this fashion was Clem Cattini, one of the first dyed-in-the-wool rock 'n' rollers to be thus employed and heard on countless UK chart hits. His professional life began in 1959 in the Beat Boys, led by saxophonist Ray McVay, who accompanied Johnny Gentle, Dickie Pride and similar vocalists managed by the celebrated Larry Parnes. Nevertheless, prospects with Johnny Kidd And The Pirates proved more attractive, particularly when a contract with HMV enabled Cattini to drum on all the group's early recordings - including the classic 'Shakin' All Over'. By 1961, however, Cattini left Kidd for an Italian tour with Colin Hicks (Tommy Steele's younger brother) and the Cabin Boys, for which he retained his Pirate stage costume. On returning, he joined the Tornados house band at producer Joe Meek's north London studio, remaining with them throughout their period of greatest celebrity as a respected session unit, and chart entrants in their own right with 'Telstar', 'Globetrotter' *et al*. With flop singles reducing engagement fees, Cattini quit the Tornados - with whom his name would always be synonymous - in March 1965 for a more lucrative post with Division Two who backed the

Ivy League, then at the peak of their fame. He was also much in demand for hundreds of record dates by artists from every trackway of pop. His 60s work included Dusty Springfield, the Kinks, P.J. Proby, Herman's Hermits, Marianne Faithfull, Tom Jones, Love Affair, Joe Cocker and Marmalade. The sharp-eyed would also spot stout Clem on television and in prestigious auditoriums 'rattling the traps' behind artists such as Cliff Richard, Roy Orbison, the Everly Brothers and Engelbert Humperdinck.

During the next decade, he was cajoled into oddball album projects under the direction of Slapp Happy, Bob Downes, Beggar's Opera, as well as Hungry Wolf, Edward's Hand, Rumplestiltskin and other obscure 'progressive' acts. As usual, his 'bread-and-butter' was in mainstream pop - notably the Bay City Rollers and Kenny, but he also continued to serve old friends like Phil Everly, Chris Spedding, Hank Marvin and, from the Meek era, Mike Berry. By the mid 80s, Cattini was seen more often in theatrical productions such as *The Rocky Horror Show*'s West End run in 1989. Two years later, he was mainstay of a new Tornados with a repertoire that spanned every familiar avenue of his distinguished career.

●ALBUMS: as Rumplestiltskin *Rumplestiltskin* (Bell 1970)★★.

CAVERN, THE

Unquestionably, the Cavern - the Beatles' stomping ground - is the best-known club in the UK, and yet it was not intended as a rock venue. In the mid-50s, a doctor's son, Alan Sytner, ran jazz evenings in Liverpool at the Temple restaurant, but the place lacked atmosphere and he wanted a club totally devoted to jazz. Sytner visited Mathew Street, a narrow alley with seven-storey warehouses on either side. The basement of No. 10 was typical - it had been used for storing food and drink, but in 1956, it was empty. It was comprised of three subway tunnels, each 100 foot long and 10 feet wide, with the archways strengthened so that it could double as an air-raid shelter during the war. Sytner had been impressed with Le Caveau Français in Paris and this, the Cavern, was to be Liverpool's answer. He took the £400 proceeds of a coming-of-age insurance policy and invested it in the club. One subway was for collecting admission money and cloakroom facilities, one for performing and listening with a small wooden stage and wooden chairs, and one for dancing - a dance for beatniks requiring minimal space, the Cavern Stomp, evolved. There were no decorations, no stage curtains, no coloured lights and this did not change with the years. The Cavern opened its dimly lit doorway on 16 January 1957, admitting 600 of the 2,000 queuing youngsters. The attraction was the Merseysippi Jazz Band, who were still going strong in 1996, but the celebrity intended for the opening, the jazz-drumming Earl Of Wharncliffe, never materialized as he had been ordered to return to his studies. Apart from the itinerant Earl, patrons and performers alike went down the stone steps to the cellar. There was no ventilation, everybody smoked and condensation dripped from the walls. There was only one exit and if health and safety legislation had been as strict as today, the Cavern would never have opened.

Local musicians playing the Cavern included the Ralph Watmough Jazz Band and the Gin Mill Skiffle Group (later the Spinners) while visiting performers included Acker Bilk, John Dankworth, Clinton Ford and Ronnie Scott. Lonnie Donegan opened a skiffle club there and Hank Walters performed country, but rock 'n' roll was not allowed. The Cavern's membership soared to 25,000 and riverboat shuffles on the Royal Iris were organised. At the first Liverpool Jazz Festival in 1960, Rory Storm And The Hurricanes (with drummer Ringo Starr) defied instructions by rampaging through 'Whole Lotta Shakin' Goin' On'. The audience showed their disapproval by throwing, old pennies at them and the new Cavern owner, Ray McFall, docked their fee. (They made it up by collecting the pennies!) This had been a storm warning as McFall noticed that clubs in the Liverpool suburbs, often known as Jive Hives, were presenting rock 'n' roll and a city centre venue was needed. He also sensed that jazz was losing its popularity. He asked the Swinging Blue Jeans (then the Bluegenes and a skiffle/trad jazz group) to host guest nights. As a result, the Beatles made their debut at the Cavern on 21 March 1961. They had already been to Germany and had developed their own brand of raucous, pounding rock 'n' roll. Within months, beat music had taken over and jazz at the Cavern became a rarity.

The beat groups became fans of each other and often performed similar material - 'What'd I Say', 'You Better Move On' and 'Roll Over Beethoven' - although they did not copy each other's arrangements, evidenced if one listens to the Beatles', the Big Three's and the Searchers' versions of 'Some Other Guy' back-to-back. Over 350 groups could be heard on Merseyside and typically, a group might play the Orrell Park Ballroom early in the evening, move to St. Luke's Hall in Crosby and finish at a Cavern all-nighter. The scene was so unique and close-knit that it fostered its own newspaper, *Mersey Beat*, owned and edited by Bill Harry. The groups wrote their names on painted bricks on the wall behind the stage, while key staff at the Cavern included the genial doorman Paddy Delaney (who has written but not published his memoirs), cloakroom attendant Priscilla White (renamed by accident in *Mersey Beat* as Cilla Black) and, most of all, the disc jockey Bob Wooler. Wooler was far more than a DJ: he organized the bookings, usually employing three or four bands a session, acted as a talent scout, offered advice on recording and management contracts, and advised performers on their repertoires. Gerry And The Pacemakers recorded 'I'll Be There' because Wooler closed evening sessions with Bobby Darin's original record, while both the Beatles and the Swinging Blue Jeans were impressed by Wooler's constant playing of Chan Romero's 'Hippy Hippy Shake'. The Cavern served only Coca-Cola and sandwiches and had no alcohol licence, although many performers drank beforehand at The Grapes public house opposite, or the nearby White

Star and Why Not. People came for the music - often in their lunchtimes - and, for example, the bill for 26 July 1961 consisted of the Beatles, Gerry And The Pacemakers, the Searchers and the Fourmost. Admission was five shillings (25p) and the bill cost Ray McFall £50 in performing fees. At a push, he could cram 1,100 punters into the club.

A few hundred yards away in Whitechapel was NEMS, an electrical store owned by the Epstein family. Brian Epstein, who managed the record department, had been intrigued by the interest in the Beatles and he went to the Cavern on 9 November 1961 with his assistant Alistair Taylor to see them for himself; within a couple of days Epstein was their manager. This led to the sacking of drummer Pete Best, which in turn led to George Harrison being given a black eye by a Cavern member. The act was symbolic as well as physical as many Cavern-dwellers feared that they would lose the Beatles from Liverpool when they signed to Parlophone Records. When Bob Wooler ammounced the news that 'Please Please Me' would be number 1 that week, the Cavern fell silent. They had lost their favourite band forever.

Many American musicians played the Cavern (Ben E. King, Stevie Wonder, Solomon Burke, Sonny Boy Williamson) and Petula Clark presented a live show for French television from there. Decca Records recorded a live album *At The Cavern* featuring the Dennisons, Lee Curtis and Beryl Marsden (who were local) and Dave Berry, Heinz and the Fortunes (who were not), but the most atmospheric recording is the sweat-drenched EP, *The Big Three At The Cavern*. On both records, you hear the carefully crafted introductions of disc jockey Wooler, who, revealingly (and astonishingly for a 1964 record), calls the Big Three 'the boys with the Benzedrine beat'. The Big Three was the only group to immortalise the Cavern in song - the repetitive but compelling 'Cavern Stomp'. The Cavern was also the premier venue for Manchester groups such as the Hollies (who were greatly influenced by what they saw in the Beatles), Freddie And The Dreamers and Herman's Hermits. When the Newcastle group the Animals were carrying their equipment downstairs to the Cavern, Alan Price was approached by two Scouse girls. 'What do you do then?' they asked. 'We play rhythm and blues,' said Alan Price proudly, 'have you heard of it?' 'Heard it?' said one of the girls, 'We invented it.'

As expected, the Beatles soon grew too big to play the Cavern, but almost as a joke, they returned to play their 292nd (and last) appearance on 3 August 1963 for a fee of £20. 'They were the same old Beatles,' recalls Paddy Delaney, 'John Lennon would say, "Okay, tatty-head, we'll do this number for you."' By then, several of the major groups had left Liverpool and a second wave was taking hold with the Roadrunners, the Escorts and the Merseybeats, who single-handedly played an eight-hour marathon at the Cavern. One band, the Hideaways, played the Cavern over 400 times, but their only national success was with the Radio Luxembourg campaign for 'tick-a-tick Timex'. In 1965 the Cavern started its own record label with country singer Phil Brady's 'An American Sailor At The Cavern', but its dream of records made in Liverpool and performed by local talent never materialized. The club was making money but its downfall lay in its lack of hygiene. Instead of proper sewage facilities, waste products had been collecting in a vast vat and its contents were starting to seep through onto the hapless railwaymen working in Liverpool's underground railway. It cost thousands of pounds to correct. At the final all-night session in February 1966, the fans barricaded the door to keep the bailiffs out. The siege made the national news and the publicity helped an appeal for funds. In June 1966 a new-look Cavern, under new management, was opened by the Prime Minister and MP for Huyton, Harold Wilson. Showing a knowledge of beat group economics, he recommended that the groups should appear at the Cavern each year for the same fee as they were getting at present!

The Cavern continued for some years but its magic had disappeared and it lost its direction. One evening Adrian Henri of the Liverpool Scene organized a 'happening' called Bomb at the Cavern, adding a false ceiling which collapsed and covered the participants with mock fallout. The club experienced further problems when British Rail wanted to expand its underground network. A ventilation shaft was needed and the ideal site was that of the Cavern. A repossession order was issued to the then owner, Roy Adams, and in March 1973 the bulldozers moved in, burying the Cavern in rubble - in retrospect (even at the time), this was an act of corporate vandalism. Once the rail network was complete, the site became a carpark. The New Cavern, specializing in heavy metal, opened in a cellar across the street, but it was another club on Mathew Street that heralded the new punk music, Eric's. In the late 70s, a Beatles statue by Liverpool sculptor Arthur Dooley was erected on its front wall. When John Lennon was assassinated, fans covered the site with flowers and messages. On that day, a Liverpool architect David Backhouse had a vision to develop a Cavern quarter, and the new Cavern club is now part of a shopping precinct, Cavern Walks. It is a surprisingly good recreation and at the signing of the new wall, Merseybeat musicians met with each other for the first time in 20 years - this led to new friendships and the successful Merseycats charity. The Cavern is now the centre of an organization including the Cavern and the Abbey Road pubs, also in Mathew Street, and the club is put to particular good use during the annual Merseybeatle and Mathew Street Festivals. Another recreation of the Cavern occurs at the Beatles Story at the Albert Dock, and the Cavern has fared better than the site of NEMS, which houses an Ann Summers sex store. Many of the original Cavern bricks were used in building the new Cavern, but 5,000 of them were sold at £5 each for charity and now regularly make over £100 each at Beatle auctions.

Go into the Cavern Quarter today and one finds many Merseybeat figures in the thriving pubs and clubs. Like the Ghosts of Merseybeat Past, Bob Wooler and the Beatles' first manager, Allan Williams, hold court in The Grapes, while one can chat to Uncle Charlie Lennon at the John Lennon club. There are lighthearted attempts to con the gullible tourists - one story that made the national papers concerned a sailor in the 60s, who was about to attack Ringo Starr in The Grapes with a piece of lead piping, but was stopped by a visiting student, Bill Clinton. In fact, Starr and Clinton were never in Mathew Street at the same time. As Bob Wooler advises, 'Make sure the stories you hear are from the horse's mouth and not the other end.'

● ALBUMS: *At The Cavern* (Decca 1964)★★★, *Liverpool Today - At The Cavern* (Ember 1965)★★, various Liverpool artists *Cavern Days* (1992)★★. Very few acts were recorded at the Cavern but part of a 1965 performance by Gene Vincent is included on *Rebel Heart, Vol. 3* (Magnum Force 1996)★★★.

● FURTHER READING: *Let's Go Down The Cavern*, Spencer Leigh and Pete Frame. *The Best Of Cellars - The Story Of The World Famous Cavern Club*, Phil Thompson.

CHAD AND JEREMY

Chad Stewart (b. 10 December 1943, England; vocals/guitar/banjo/keyboards/sitar) and Jeremy Clyde (b. 22 March 1944, England; vocals/guitar) became acquainted as students at London's Central School of Speech and Drama. Inspired by a common interest in music, the pair began performing together with Stewart providing the musical accompaniment to Clyde's lyrics. Their early releases offered a brand of folk-influenced pop similar to that of Peter And Gordon, but the duo was unable to make commercial inroads in the UK. However, their quintessential Englishness inspired four US Top 30 hits, including 'Yesterday's Gone' and 'A Summer Song' the latter of which reached number 7. A concept album, *Of Cabbages And Kings*, produced by Gary Usher, signalled a switch to progressive styles, but this ambitious and sadly neglected work was not a commercial success and the pair broke up in 1969. Clyde, who made frequent appearances on the popular television show, *Rowan And Martin's Laugh-In*, later pursued an acting career, while Stewart began writing musicals.

● ALBUMS: *Yesterday's Gone* (1964)★★★, *Chad And Jeremy Sing For You* (Ember 1965)★★★, *Before And After* (Columbia 1965)★★★, *I Don't Want To Lose You Baby* (Columbia 1965)★★★, *Second Album* (Ember 1966)★★★, *More Chad And Jeremy* (1966)★★★, *Distant Shores* (Columbia 1966)★★★, *Of Cabbages And Kings* (Columbia 1967)★★, *Yesterday's Gone* (World Artists 1967)★★★, *The Ark* (1968)★★, *Three In An Attic* soundtrack (1969)★★.

● COMPILATIONS: *The Best Of Chad And Jeremy* (1966)★★★, *5 Plus 10 Equals 15 Fabulous Hits* (1965)★★★, *Chad And Jeremy* (1968)★★★, *Painted Dayglo Smile* (Legacy 1992)★★★, *The Essential Chad And Jeremy* (1993)★★★, *Yesterday's Gone* (Drive Archive 1994)★★★, *The Best Of Chad And Jeremy* (One Way 1996)★★★.

CHAMBERLAIN, RICHARD

b. George Richard Chamberlain, 31 March 1935, Los Angeles, California, USA. The well-known television and film star had a brief spell as a successful recording artist in the early 60s. In 1960, after serving in Korea and attending the LA Conservatory of Music, he had his first television role in *Gunsmoke* and appeared in the film *The Secret Of The Purple Reef*. In 1961 he landed the lead role in the television series *Dr. Kildare*, which made the photogenic fresh-faced actor a top pin-up on both sides of the Atlantic. In 1962, his first single, a vocal version of the television series' theme song, 'Three Stars Will Shine Tonight', became the first of four UK and three US Top 40 singles for the pleasant-voiced MOR/pop singer. His debut album 'Richard Chamberlain Sings', on which he was accompanied by David Rose's 40-piece orchestra, also shot into the transatlantic Top 10s. Chamberlain, who at the height of his career as Dr. Kildare was reputedly receiving 2,500 letters a day, quickly faded from the pop scene but has gone on to star in many more television programmes and films. In 1993 he starred on Broadway as Henry Higgins in a drastically revised revival of the classic musical *My Fair Lady*.

●ALBUMS: *Richard Chamberlain Sings* (MGM 1963)★★, *Joy In The Morning* (MGM 1964)★, *Theme Fom Dr Kildare* (Metro 1966)★★.

CHAMBERS BROTHERS

Born and raised in Lee County, Mississippi, USA, the four brothers, George (b. 26 September 1931; bass), Willie (b. 3 March 1938; guitar), Lester (b. 13 April 1940; harmonica) and Joe (b. 22 August 1942; guitar), moved to Los Angeles during the early 50s. The group's gospel-based origins were evident in their first recordings, which included an unpolished reading of Curtis Mayfield's 'People Get Ready'. In 1965 they were joined by drummer Brian Keenan and an appearance at that year's Newport Folk Festival reinforced the group's 'R&B combo' approach, the basis for their later direction. The title track to a 1968 album, *Time Has Come Today*, with its exciting, extended instrumental break, introduced the Brothers to the white, counter-culture audience. They cultivated a hippie image and part of a subsequent album, *Love Peace And Happiness*, was recorded live at the Fillmore East, then one of rock's prestigious venues. The group continued to maintain their popularity into the 70s, but in embracing such a transient fashion they were unable to secure a committed following when tastes changed. In the 90s their music found a new generation, given the wink by their elders. The band continue to perform the hits together with blues standards, and it appears that the Chambers' children have boosted the line-up. 'Time Has Come Today' is still an encore worth waiting for.

●ALBUMS: *Barbara Dane And The Chamber Brothers* (Folkways 1964)★★, *People Get Ready* (Vault 1966)★★★, *The Chamber Brothers Now* (Vault 1967)★★★, *The Time Has Come* (Columbia 1967)★★★, *The Chamber Brothers Shout* (Vault 1968)★★★, *A New Time - A New Day* (Columbia 1968)★★, *Groovin' Time* (Riverside 1968)★★, *Feelin' The Blues* (Vault 1969)★★★, with various artists *Love, Peace And Happiness* (Columbia 1969)★★, *A New Generation* (Columbia 1971)★★, *Oh My God* (Columbia 1972)★★, *Unbonded* (Avco 1974)★★, *Right Move* (Avco 1975)★★, *Live In Concert On Mars* (Roxbury 1976)★★★.

●COMPILATIONS: *The Chamber Brothers Greatest Hits* (Columbia 1970)★★★, *Best Of ...* (Fantasy 1973)★★★.

CHANDLER, CHAS

b. Bryan James Chandler, 18 December 1938, Heaton, Tyne And Wear, England, d. 17 July 1996. Chandler's career can be placed in two distinct sections. In the 60s he was the giant figure wielding a bass guitar with the pioneering R&B group the Animals. Following the break-up of the original Animals in 1967, the businesslike Chandler had the foresight to spot the potential of a black guitarist, whom he had watched playing in a New York club. He brought this young man, now renamed Jimi Hendrix, over to London. After recruiting two further musicians, Noel Redding and Mitch Mitchell, the shrewd Chandler succeeded in making the Jimi Hendrix Experience one of the most talked-about groups since the Beatles. The summer of 1967 was a perfect time to launch psychedelic rock music to the awaiting 'underground' scene. Chandler proved that his midas-like touch was no fluke, and after selling out his managerial interest in Hendrix to former Animals manager Mike Jeffries, he nurtured Slade. With wily foresight Chandler led them through extraordinary success in the early 70s with no less than six UK chart-toppers. He built up a mini-empire of companies, including music publishing, agency, management, production and recording studio under the Barn Group banner. In 1977 the original Animals re-formed and recorded their comeback album in his barn in Surrey. Six years later they re-formed once again, prompting Chandler to sell up his business interests and become a musician again. While the obligatory world tour made money, it also opened old wounds and the group collapsed for a third time.

●FURTHER READING: *Wild Animals*, Andy Blackford.

CHANDLER, GENE

b. Eugene Dixon, 6 July 1937, Chicago, Illinois, USA. Recalled for the gauche, but irresistible 1962 US number 1, 'Duke Of Earl', Chandler's million-selling single in fact featured the Dukays, a doo-wop quintet he fronted (Eugene Dixon, Shirley Jones, James Lowe, Earl Edwards and Ben Broyles). His record company preferred to promote a solo artist and thus one of soul's most enduring careers was launched. Temporarily bedevilled by his 'dandy' image, the singer was rescued by a series of excellent Curtis Mayfield-penned songs. 'Rainbow' and 'Man's Temptation'. These were hits in 1963, but the relationship blossomed with 'Just Be True' (1964) and the sublime 'Nothing Can Stop Me' (1965), both US Top 20 singles. Chandler later recorded under the aegis of producer Carl

Davis including '(The) Girl Don't Care', 'There Goes The Lover' and 'From The Teacher To The Preacher', a duet with Barbara Acklin. Switching to Mercury Records in 1970, 'Groovy Situation' became another major hit, while an inspired teaming with Jerry Butler was an artistic triumph. Chandler's career was revitalized during the disco boom when 'Get Down' was an international hit. Further releases, 'When You're Number 1' and 'Does She Have A Friend', consolidated such success, while recordings for Salsoul, with Jaime Lynn and Fastfire continued his career into the 80s.

●ALBUMS: *The Duke Of Earl* (Vee Jay 1962)★★★★, *Just Be True* (1964)★★★, *Live On Stage In '65* (Constellation 1965)★★ , reissued as *Live At The Regal*), *The Girl Don't Care* (1967)★★★, *The Duke Of Soul* (Checker 1967)★★★, *There Was A Time* (1968)★★, *The Two Sides Of Gene Chandler* (1969)★★, *The Gene Chandler Situation* (Mercury 1970)★★★, with Jerry Butler *Gene And Jerry - One & One* (Mercury 1971)★★★, *Get Down* (Chi-Sound 1978)★★★, *When You're Number One* (20th Century 1979), *80* (20th Century 1980)★★★, *Live At The Regal* (1986)★★.

●COMPILATIONS: *Greatest Hits By Gene Chandler* (Constellation 1964)★★★, *Just Be True* (1980)★★★, *Stroll On With The Duke* (Solid Smoke 1984)★★★, *60s Soul Brother* (1986)★★★, *Get Down* (1992)★★★, *Nothing Can Stop Me: Gene Chandler's Greatest Hits* (Varese Saranbande 1994)★★★.

●FILMS: *Don't Knock The Twist* (1962).

CHANNEL, BRUCE

b. 28 November 1940, Jacksonville, Texas, USA. Born into a musical family, Channel was actively performing while still in high school. He secured a six-month residency on the prestigious *Louisiana Hayride* show, which in turn resulted in a recording deal with Smash Records. In 1962 the singer scored a US chart-topper with the infectious 'Hey Baby' which also achieved gold record status on climbing to number 2 in the UK. Much of the song's appeal, however, was derived from its distinctive harmonica passage, which was played by Delbert McClinton. His plaintive style influenced that of several subsequent releases, including the Beatles' 'Love Me Do', although John Lennon later denied his influence. Channel's career floundered over the ensuing years and his releases were confined to low-key labels including Le Cam and Mel-O-Dy. He was signed to Mala in 1968, but although this made no difference to his fortune in America, the singer enjoyed another UK Top 10 hit with the exuberant 'Keep On'. Longtime fans were perplexed by a figure vowing to return with a blues group featuring McClinton and guitarist Bobby Turner, but Channel's newfound success proved short-lived, and the frantic 'Mr. Bus Driver' failed to chart. He has nonetheless continued to perform and in 1988 made a surprise guest appearance while on a visit to the UK, as a disc jockey on BBC Radio 2. He appeared with the Memphis Horns on their album *The Memphis Horns* in 1995.

●ALBUMS: *Hey! Baby (And 11 Other Songs About Your Baby)* (Smash 1962)★★★, *Goin' Back To Louisiana* (1964)★★, *Keep On* (Bell 1968)★★★.

CHANTAYS

This US-based group was comprised of the Californian Santa Ana High School students Bob Spickard (lead guitar), Brian Carman (guitar/saxophone), Bob Marshall (piano), Warren Waters (bass) and Bob Welsh (drums). They formed the Chantays in 1962, and secured immortality with 'Pipeline' the following year. Initially released as the b-side to a vocal track, this atmospheric surfing instrumental brought a new level of sophistication to an often one-dimensional genre and deservedly became a hit in the USA and Britain. It was a standard the quintet were unable to repeat and although Steve Kahn replaced Welsh, the group broke up following a handful of unsuccessful releases. However, a re-formed line-up emerged during the 80s in the wake of a surfing resurgence.

●ALBUMS: *Pipeline* (Downey 1963)★★★, *Two Sides Of The Chantays* (Dot 1964)★★★.

●COMPILATIONS: *The Story Of Rock 'N' Roll* (1976)★★★.

CHANTELS

Regarded as the first true 'girl group', this New York vocal quintet - Arlene Smith (b. 5 October 1941, New York, USA), Sonia Goring, Rene Minus, Lois Harris and Jackie Landry were all members of a high school choir when they auditioned for producer Richie Barrett in 1957. The group made its recording debut with 'He's Gone', and this plaintive offering set the tone for the Chantels' subsequent work. Their impassioned style culminated with 'Maybe', wherein Smith's heart-wrenching plea carried an inordinate passion. Barely 16 years old on its release, the singer's emotional delivery belies her youth. The single reputedly sold in excess of one million copies, but pirated pressings were prevalent in many American states, undermining the group's potential. Subsequent releases failed to match its quality and the Chantels grew disenchanted with their management and label. Harris had already dropped out of the line-up and Smith embarked on a solo career under the tutelage of Phil Spector, while Barrett continued to produce the remaining trio with different singers in place of the former vocalist. The Chantels enjoyed two US Top 30 hits with 'Look In My Eyes' and 'Well I Told You', but they lacked the distinctiveness of the earlier releases.

●ALBUMS: *The Chantels* aka *We're The Chantels* (End 1958)★★★, *The Chantels On Tour* (Carlton 1961)★★, *There's Our Song Again* (Carlton 1962)★★★, *The Chantels Sing Their Favorites* (Forum 1964)★★★.

●COMPILATIONS: *Arlene Smith And The Chantels* (1987)★★★, *The Best Of The Chantels* (Rhino 1990)★★★.

CHARLATANS (USA)

The first of San Francisco's 'underground' rock groups, the Charlatans were formed in 1964 by George Hunter (autoharp/tambourine), Mike Wilhelm (guitar/vocals) and Richard Olsen (bass/clarinet/vocals). They were then augmented by pianist Michael Ferguson, whom Hunter had met in line at an unemployment office, and Sam Linde (drums). The incompatible Linde was replaced by Dan Hicks, by which time the group had adopted their striking visual image, reminiscent of turn-of-the-century western outlaws. Their waistcoats, stiff-necked collars, high boots and long hair so impressed the owner of the Red Dog Saloon, a bar in Virginia City, Nevada, that he booked them as his resident houseband. It was here that the group honed their melange of blues, folk, R&B and good-time music, while Ferguson's artwork for their debut performance is recognized as America's first psychedelic poster.

The Charlatans returned to San Francisco late in 1965 but their eminent position did not result in a coherent recording career. Demos for the local Autumn label were rejected, and although the quintet completed an album for Kama Sutra Records, the results were shelved. 'The Shadow Knows', a single issued against the group's preference, was the sole release by this pioneering line-up. Hicks, Ferguson and Hunter then left, disillusioned at this seeming impasse. Olsen and Wilhelm persevered and in 1969 completed the Charlatans' self-titled album with Darrell De Vore (piano) and Terry Wilson (drums). Although the group's erstwhile fire was muted, glimpses of their legacy appeared in 'Alabama Bound' and 'Fulsom Prison Blues'. The Charlatans then dissolved, but its individual members remained active. Hicks formed the impressive Dan Hicks And His Hot Licks, and while Wilhelm fronted Loose Gravel, Ferguson joined Lynne Hughes, barmaid at the Red Dog Saloon, in Tongue And Groove. Olsen became a producer at Pacific High Studios and Hunter, the group's visionary, founded the Globe Propaganda design company. Hunter's artwork graced numerous magnificent covers including *Happy Trails* (Quicksilver Messenger Service), *Hallelujah* (Canned Heat) and *Its A Beautiful Day* (Its A Beautiful Day). Although the Charlatans were denied the acclaim accorded to those in their wake, the élan of San Francisco's renaissance is indebted to their influence.

●ALBUMS: *The Charlatans* (Philips 1969)★★★, *The Autumn Demos* (1982)★★ .

●COMPILATIONS: *The Charlatans* (Ace 1996)★★★, *The Amazing Charlatans* (Ace/Big Beat 1996)★★★.

CHARLES, RAY

b. Ray Charles Robinson, 23 September 1930, Albany, Georgia, USA. Few epithets sit less comfortably than that of genius; Ray Charles has borne this title for over thirty years. As a singer, composer, arranger and pianist, his prolific work deserves no other praise. Born in extreme poverty, Charles was slowly blinded by glaucoma until, by the age of seven, he had lost his sight completely. Earlier he had to cope with the tragic death of his brother, who he had seen drown in a water tub. He learned to read and write music in braille and was proficient on several instruments by the time he left school. His mother

Aretha died when Charles was 15, and he continued to have a shared upbringing with Mary Jane (the first wife of Charles' absent father). Charles drifted around the Florida circuit, picking up work where he could, before moving across the country to Seattle. Here he continued his itinerant career, playing piano at several nightclubs in a style reminiscent of Nat 'King' Cole.

Ray began recording in 1949 and this early, imitative approach was captured on several sessions. Three years later Atlantic Records acquired his contract, but initially the singer continued his 'cool' direction, revealing only an occasional hint of the passions later unleashed. 'It Should've Been Me', 'Mess Around' and 'Losing Hand' best represent this early R&B era, but Charles' individual style emerged as a result of his work with Guitar Slim. This impassioned, almost crude, blues performer sang with a gospel-based fervour that greatly influenced Charles' thinking. He arranged Slim's million-selling single, 'Things That I Used To Do', of which the riffing horns and unrestrained voice set the tone for Charles' own subsequent direction. This effect was fully realized in 'I Got A Woman' (1954), a song soaked in the fervour of the Baptist Church, but rendered salacious by the singer's abandoned, unrefined delivery. Its extraordinary success, commercially and artistically, inspired similarly compulsive recordings including 'This Little Girl Of Mine' (1955), 'Talkin' 'Bout You' (1957) and the lush and evocative 'Don't Let The Sun Catch You Crying' (1959), a style culminating in the thrilling call and response of 'What'd I Say' (1959). This acknowledged classic is one of the all-time great encore numbers performed by countless singers and bands in stadiums, clubs and bars all over the world. However, Charles was equally adept at slow ballads, as his heartbreaking interpretations of 'Drown In My Own Tears' and 'I Believe To My Soul' (both 1959) clearly show. Proficient in numerous styles, Charles' recordings embraced blues, jazz, standards and even country, as his muscular reading of 'I'm Movin' On' attested.

In November 1959 Charles left the Atlantic label for ABC Records, where he secured both musical and financial freedom. Commentators often cite this as the point at which the singer lost his fire, but early releases for this new outlet simply continued his groundbreaking style. 'Georgia On My Mind' (1960) and 'Hit The Road Jack' (1961) were, respectively, poignant and ebullient, and established the artist as an international name. This stature was enhanced further in 1962 with the release of the massive-selling album, *Modern Sounds In Country And Western*, a landmark collection that produced the million-selling single 'I Can't Stop Loving You'. Its success defined the pattern for Charles' later career; the edges were blunted, the vibrancy was stilled as Charles' repertoire grew increasingly inoffensive. There were still moments of inspiration, 'Let's Go Get Stoned' and 'I Don't Need No Doctor' brought a glimpse of a passion now too often muted, while *Crying Time*, Charles' first album since kicking his heroin habit, compared favourably with any Atlantic release. This respite was, however, temporary and as the 60s progressed so the singer's work became less compulsive and increasingly MOR. Like most artists, he attempted cover versions of Beatles songs and had substantial hits with versions of 'Yesterday' and 'Eleanor Rigby'. Two 70s releases, *A Message From The People* and *Renaissance*, did include contemporary material in Stevie Wonder's 'Living In The City' and Randy Newman's 'Sail Away', but subsequent releases reneged on this promise. Charles' 80s work included more country-flavoured collections and a cameo appearance in the film *The Blues Brothers*, but the period is better marked by the singer's powerful appearance on the USA For Africa release, 'We Are The World' (1985). It brought to mind a talent too often dormant, a performer whose marriage of gospel and R&B laid the foundations for soul music. His influence is inestimable, his talent widely acknowledged and imitated by formidable white artists such as Steve Winwood, Joe Cocker, Van Morrison and Eric Burdon. Charles has been honoured with countless awards during his career including the Lifetime Achievement Award. He has performed rock, jazz, blues and country with spectacular ease but it is 'father of soul music' that remains his greatest title; it was fitting that, in 1992, an acclaimed documentary, *Ray Charles: The Genius Of Soul*, was broadcast by PBS television. *My World* was a sparkling return to form, and is one of his finest albums in many years, particularly noteworthy for his version of Leon Russell's 'A Song For You', a song that sounds like it has always been a Charles song, such is the power of this man's outstanding voice. *Strong Love Affair* continued in the same vein with a balance of ballads matching the up-tempo tracks; however, it was clear that low register, slow songs such as 'Say No More', 'Angelina' and 'Out Of My Life' is where Charles should be concentrating.

●ALBUMS: *Hallelujah, I Love Her So* aka *Ray Charles* (Atlantic 1957)★★★, *The Great Ray Charles* (Atlantic 1957)★★★★, with Milt Jackson *Soul Brothers* (Atlantic 1958)★★★, *Ray Charles At Newport* (Atlantic 1958)★★★, *Yes Indeed* (Atlantic 1959)★★★, *Ray Charles* (Hollywood 1959)★★★★, *The Fabulous Ray Charles* (Hollywood 1959)★★★, *What'd I Say* (Atlantic 1959)★★★, *The Genius Of Ray Charles* (Atlantic 1959)★★★★★, *Ray Charles In Person* (1960)★★★, *Genius Hits The Road* (ABC 1960)★★★, *The Genius After Hours* (1961)★★★★, *The Genius Sings The Blues* (Atlantic 1961)★★★★, with Milt Jackson *Soul Meeting* (Atlantic 1961)★★★, *Do The Twist With Ray Charles* (Atlantic 1961)★★★, *Dedicated To You* (ABC 1961)★★★, *Genius + Soul = Jazz* (1961)★★★★★, with Betty Carter *Ray Charles And Betty Carter* (1961)★★★★, *Modern Sounds In Country And Western* (ABC 1962)★★★★★, *Modern Sounds In Country And Western Volume 2* (ABC 1962)★★★★, *Ingredients In A Recipe For Soul* (DCC 1963)★★★★, *Sweet And Sour Tears* (1964)★★★, *Have A Smile With Me* (ABC 1964)★★★, *Live In Concert* (ABC 1965)★★★, *Country And Western Meets Rhythm And Blues* aka *Together Again* (ABC 1965)★★★, *Crying Time* (ABC

1966)★★★, *Ray's Moods* (ABC 1966)★★★, *Ray Charles Invites You To Listen* (ABC 1967)★★★, *A Portrait Of Ray* (ABC 1968)★★, *I'm All Yours, Baby!* (1969)★★, *Doing His Thing* (ABC 1969)★★★, *My Kind Of Jazz* (Tangerine 1970)★★★, *Love Country Style* (ABC 1970)★★, *Volcanic Action Of My Soul* (ABC 1971)★★, *A Message From The People* (Tangerine 1972)★★, *Through The Eyes Of Love* (ABC 1972), *Jazz Number II* (Tangerine 1972)★★★, *Jazz Number II* (1973)★★★, *Come Live With Me* (Crossover 1974)★★, *Renaissance* (Crossover 1975)★★, *My Kind Of Jazz III* (Crossover 1975)★★, *Live In Japan* (1975)★★★, with Cleo Laine *Porgy And Bess* (1976)★★★, *True To Life* (Atlantic 1977)★★, *Love And Peace* (Atlantic 1978)★★, *Ain't It So* (Atlantic 1979)★★, *Brother Ray Is At It Again* (Atlantic 1980)★★, *Wish You Were Here Tonight* (Columbia 1983)★★, *Do I Ever Cross Your Mind* (Columbia 1984)★★, *Friendship* (Columbia 1985)★★, *The Spirit Of Christmas* (Columbia 1985)★★, *From The Pages Of My Mind* (Columbia 1986)★★, *Just Between Us* (1988)★★, *Seven Spanish Angels And Other Hits* (Columbia 1989)★★, *Would You Believe* (Warners 1990)★★, *My World* (Warners 1993)★★★★, *Strong Love Affair* (Qwest 1996)★★, *Berlin, 1962* (Pablo 1996)★★★.

●COMPILATIONS: *The Ray Charles Story* (1962)★★★, *A Man And His Soul* (1967)★★★, *The Best Of Ray Charles 1956-58* (Atlantic 1970)★★★★, *25th Anniversary In Show Business Salute To Ray Charles* (ABC 1971)★★★★, *The Right Time* (1987)★★★, *A Life In Music 1956-59* (Atlantic 1982)★★★★, *Greatest Hits Vol. 1 1960-67* (Rhino 1988)★★★★, *Anthology* (Rhino 1989)★★★★, *The Collection* ABC recordings (1990)★★★, *Blues Is My Middle Name* rec. 1949-52 (Double Play 1991)★★★, *The Birth Of Soul 1952-59* (Atlantic 1991)★★★★★, *The Complete Atlantic Rhythm And Blues Recordings* 4-CD box set (1992)★★★★★, *The Living Legend* (1993)★★★, *The Best Of … The Atlantic Years* (Rhino/Atlantic 1994)★★★, *Classics* (Rhino 1995)★★★.

●FURTHER READING: *Ray Charles*, Sharon Bell Mathis. *Brother Ray, Ray Charles' Own Story*, Ray Charles and David Ritz.

●FILMS: *Blues For Lovers* aka *Ballad In Blue* (1964), *The Blues Brothers* (1980).

CHARLIE GIRL

One of the biggest blockbusters in the history of the London musical theatre (pre-Andrew Lloyd Webber), *Charlie Girl* opened at the Adelphi Theatre on 15 December 1965. Initial reviews were of the 'it takes geniuses of inspired mediocrity to produce rubbish such as this' variety, but the public loved it from the start. As with that other enormously popular musical, Me And My Girl, whose long and glorious run was inconveniently interrupted (temporarily) by World War II, *Charlie Girl* utilises the age-old formula of mixing the English upper and lower classes, and allowing the latter to come off best. Hugh and Margaret Williams' book (with some humorous help from Ray Cooney) tells the sad tale of Lady Hadwell (Anna Neagle), who was on the stage as one of Cochran's Young Ladies before she married the late earl. It is not enough that she is beset by death duties, leaky roofs, and nosey tourists, but she also has a daughter Charlotte (Christine Holmes), who prefers to be known as Charlie and rides motorcycles. With this kind of laidback attitude, Charlie is obviously destined to marry Lady Hadwell's Cockney *aide de camp*, Joe Studholme (60s pop star Joe Brown), who wants to be loved for himself alone, and not for his life-enhancing win on the football pools, the news of which has been brought to him by Nicholas Wainright (Derek Nimmo). Charlie's brief (innococent) affair with wealthy Jack Connor (Stuart Damon), the son of Kay Connor (Hy Hazell), Lady Hadwell's buddy from the Cochran days, is only a minor hitch before fireworks in the sky blaze out the message, 'Isn't It Flippin' Well Marvellous!' Adelphi audiences certainly thought so, and *Charlie Girl* ran there for nearly five and a half years, a total of 2202 performances, and won an Ivor Novello Award for best musical. The show's score, by David Heneker (*Half A Sixpence*) and John Taylor, showcased Brown's charming, cheeky style in numbers such as 'My Favourite Occupation', 'Charlie Girl', 'I 'ates Money' (with Nimmo), 'Fish 'N' Chips', and 'You Never Know What You Can Do Until You Try' (with Neagle). Christine Holmes, had the delightful 'Bells Will Ring', 'I Love Him, I Love Him' and 'Like Love', while Hy Hazell excelled in 'Party Of A Lifetime', 'Let's Do A Deal' (with Neagle), and 'What Would I Get From Being Married?' Neagle brought the house down regularly at the end of the first act with 'I Was Young'. During the run, this much-loved actress was created a Dame of the British Empire, and the cast borrowed the band parts from *South Pacific*, which was at the Prince of Wales Theatre, and sang 'There Is Nothing Like A Dame' to her at the close of the evening's performance. She stayed with the show throughout, except for holidays, but Joe Brown was replaced by Gerry Marsden, without his Pacemakers (the role was 'tweaked' to explain his Liverpudlian accent). When the show closed in 1971 Neagle and Nimmo joined the successful Australian and New Zealand productions which included John Farnham, a British singer who was popular down-under. In 1986 a revised version of *Charlie Girl* was mounted at London's Victoria Palace, starring Paul Nicholas, Dora Bryan, Mark Wynter, Nicholas Parsons, and the dancing star of many MGM musical films, Cyd Charisse, but times had changed, and the production lasted for only six months.

CHECKER, CHUBBY

b. Ernest Evans, 3 October 1941, Philadelphia, Pennsylvania, USA. Checker's musical career began in 1959 while working at a local chicken market. His employer introduced the teenager to songwriter Kal Mann, who penned the singer's debut single, 'The Class'. He was given his new name by the wife of the legendary disc jockey Dick Clark as a derivation of Fats Domino. Chubby Checker became one of several artists to enjoy the patronage of Clark's influential *American Bandstand* television show and the successful Cameo-Parkway label. He achieved national fame in 1960 with 'The Twist', a compulsive dance-based performance which outgrew its novelty value to become an institution. The song, initially recorded in 1958 by Hank Ballard And The Midnighters, was stripped of its earthy, R&B connotation as Checker emphasized its carefree quality. 'The Twist' topped the US chart on two separate occasions (1960 and 1961), and twice entered the UK charts, securing its highest position, number 14, in 1962. 'Pony Time' (1961), a rewrite of Clarence 'Pine Top' Smith's 'Boogie Woogie', became Checker's second gold disc and second US number 1, before 'Let's Twist Again' established him as a truly international attraction. A Top 10 hit on both sides of the Atlantic, it became the benchmark of the twist craze, one of the memorable trends of the immediate pre-Beatles era. It inspired competitive releases by the Isley Brothers ('Twist And Shout'), Joey Dee ('Peppermint Twist') and Sam Cooke ('Twisting The Night Away') while Checker mined its appeal on a surprisingly soulful 'Slow Twistin' (with Dee Dee Sharp) and 'Teach Me To Twist' (with Bobby Rydell). Eager for more dance-orientated success, he recorded a slew of opportunistic singles including 'The Fly' (1961) and 'Limbo Rock' (1962), both of which sold in excess of one million copies. However, the bubble quickly burst, and dance-inspired records devoted to the Jet, the Swim and the Freddie were much less successful. Even so, Checker had in a comparatively short time a remarkable run of 32 USA chart hits up to 1966. Checker was latterly confined to the revival circuit, reappearing in 1975 when 'Let's Twist Again' re-entered the UK Top 5. The Fat Boys' single, 'The Twist (Yo Twist)', with Chubby guesting on vocals, climbed to number 2 in the UK in 1988.

● ALBUMS: *Chubby Checker* (Parkway 1960)★★★, *Twist With Chubby Checker* (Parkway 1960)★★★, *For Twisters Only* (Parkway 1960)★★★, *It's Pony Time* (Parkway 1961)★★★, *Let's Twist Again* (Parkway 1961)★★★★, *Bobby Rydell/Chubby Checker* (Parkway 1961)★★★, *Twistin' Round The World* (Parkway 1962)★★, *For Teen Twisters Only* (Parkway 1962)★★★, *Don't Knock The Twist* soundtrack (Parkway 1962)★★, *All The Hits (For Your Dancin' Party)* (Parkway 1962)★★★, with Dee Dee Sharp *Down To Earth* (1962)★★★, *Limbo Party* (Parkway 1962)★★★, *Let's Limbo Some More* (Parkway 1963)★★, *Beach Party* (Parkway 1963)★★, *Chubby Checker In Person* (Parkway 1963)★★, *Chubby's Folk Album* (Parkway 1964)★, *Chubby Checker With Sy Oliver* (Parkway 1964)★★, *Discotheque* (Parkway 1965)★★, *The Other Side Of Chubby Checker* (1971)★★, *Chequered* (London 1971)★★, *The Change Has Come* (1982)★★.

● COMPILATIONS: *Your Twist Party* (1961)★★★, *Chubby Checker's Biggest Hits* (1962)★★★★, *Chubby Checker's Eighteen Golden Hits* (Parkway 1966)★★★★, *Chubby Checker's Greatest Hits* (ABKCO 1972)★★★★.

●FILMS: *It's Trad, Dad* aka *Ring-A-Ding Rhythm* (1962), *Don't Knock The Twist* (1962).

CHENIER, CLIFTON

b. 25 June 1925, Opelousas, Louisiana, USA, d. 12 December 1987. This singer, guitarist, harmonica and accordion player is regarded by many as the 'king of zydeco music'. Chenier was given lessons on the accordion by his father, and started performing at dances. He also had the advantage of being able to sing in French patois, English and Creole. In 1945, Chenier was working as a cane cutter in New Iberia. In 1946, he followed his older brother, Cleveland, to Lake Charles. He absorbed a wealth of tunes from musicians such as Zozo Reynolds, Izeb Laza, and Sidney Babineaux, who, despite their talent, had not recorded. The following year, Chenier travelled to Port Arthur, along with his wife Margaret, where he worked for the Gulf and Texaco oil refineries until 1954. Still playing music at weekends, Chenier was discovered by J.R. Fulbright, who recorded Clifton at radio station KAOK, and issued records of these and subsequent sessions. In 1955, 'Ay Tee Tee' became his best-selling record, and he became established as an R&B guitarist. By 1956, having toured with R&B bands, he had turned to music full-time. In 1958, Chenier moved to Houston, Texas, and from this base played all over the South. Although ostensibly a cajun musician, he had also absorbed zydeco, and R&B styles influenced by Lowell Fulson. Chenier's first ventures into recording saw his name mistakenly spelled 'Cliston'. During the 60s Chenier played one concert in San Francisco, backed by Blue Cheer. Chenier recorded for a number of notable labels, including Argo and Arhoolie, in a bid to reach a wider audience. 'Squeeze Box Boogie' became a hit in Jamaica in the 50s. The style of music he played was not widely heard before the 60s. In later life, in addition to suffering from diabetes, he had part of his right foot removed due to a kidney infection in 1979. Although this prevented him from touring as frequently, his influence was already established. *Sings The Blues* was compiled from material previously released on the Prophecy and Home Cooking labels. His son C.J. Chenier carries on the tradition into a third generation of the family.

●ALBUMS: *Louisiana Blues And Zydeco* (Arhoolie 1965)★★★★, *Black Snake Blues* (Arhoolie 1966)★★★★, with Lightnin' Hopkins, Mance Lipscomb *Blues Festival* (1966)★★★, *Bon Ton Roulet* (1967)★★★, *Sings The Blues* (Arhoolie 1969)★★★★, *King Of The Bayous* (1970)★★★, *Bayou Blues* (Specialty/Sonet 1970)★★★★, *Live At St. Marks* (Arhoolie 1971)★★★, *Live At A French Creole Dance* (1972)★★★, *Out West* (Arhoolie 1974)★★★, *Bad Luck And Trouble* (1975)★★★, *Bogalusa Boogie* (Arhoolie 1975)★★★★, *Red Hot Louisiana Band* (Arhoolie 1978)★★★★, *In New Orleans* (GNP Crescendo 1979)★★★, *Frenchin' The Boogie* (1979)★★★, *King Of Zydeco* (Home Cooking 1980)★★★, *Boogie 'N' Zydeco* (1980)★★★, *Live At The 1982 San Francisco Blues Festival* (Arhoolie 1982)★★★, *I'm Here* (Alligator 1982)★★★★, with Rob Bernard *Boogie In Black And White* (mid-80s)★★★, *Live At St. Mark's* (late 80s)★★★, *The King Of Zydeco, Live At Montreux* (late 80s)★★★, *Playboy* (1992)★★★.

●COMPILATIONS: *Clifton Chenier's Very Best* (Harvest 1970)★★★★, *Classic Clifton* (Arhoolie 1980)★★★★, *Sixty Minutes With The King Of Zydeco* (Arhoolie 1987)★★★★.

●VIDEOS: *King Of Zydeco* (1988), *Hot Pepper* (1988).

CHEROKEES

Sons of Worcester, England, John Kirby (vocals), David Dower (rhythm guitar), Terry Stokes (lead guitar), Mike Sweeney (bass) and drummer Jim Green's moment of glory came in autumn 1964 when their revival of Lonnie Donegan's trudging b-side 'Seven Daffodils' spent five weeks in the UK Top 40, almost outpacing a version by the better-known Mojos. This feat was mostly attributable to generous pirate radio plugging and the production skills of Mickie Most, fresh from a chart-topper with the Animals, an act also signed to EMI Columbia. The Cherokees' future looked rosy but their follow-up, 'Wondrous Face', flopped. Further impetus was lost by procrastination about their next release - 1966's 'Land 0f 1,000 Dances'. This Chris Kenner opus proved to be an error of judgement as it battled in vain against more simultaneous covers than had 'Seven Daffodils'. By 1967, the Cherokees were back on the Worcester orbit of engagements - a classic local group.

CHESS RECORDS

Polish-born brothers Leonard and Philip Chess were already proprietors of several Chicago nightclubs when they bought into the Aristocrat label in 1947. Its early repertoire consisted of jazz and jump-blues combos, but these acts were eclipsed by the arrival of Muddy Waters. This seminal R&B performer made his debut with 'I Can't Be Satisfied', the first of many superb releases which helped establish the fledgling company. Having then secured the services of Sunnyland Slim and Robert Nighthawk, the brothers confidently bought out a third partner, Evelyn Aron, renaming their enterprise Chess in 1950. Initial releases consisted of material from former Aristocrat artists, but the new venture quickly expanded its roster with local signings Jimmy Rogers and Eddie Boyd, as well as others drawn from the southern states, including Howlin' Wolf. Their recordings established Chess as a leading outlet for urban blues, a position emphasized by the founding of the Checker subsidiary and attendant releases by Little Walter, Sonny Boy Williamson (Rice Miller) and Elmore James. Other outlets, including Argo and Specialist were also established, and during the mid-50s the Chess empire successfully embraced rock 'n' roll with Chuck Berry and Bo Diddley. White acts, including Bobby Charles and Dale Hawkins also provided hits, while the label's peerless reputation was sufficient to attract a new generation of virtuoso blues performers, led by Otis Rush and Buddy Guy. The R&B boom of the 60s, spearheaded by the Rolling Stones and later emphasized by John Mayall and Fleetwood Mac, brought renewed interest in the company's catalogue, but the rise of soul in turn deemed it anachronistic. Although recordings at the Fame studio by Etta James, Irma Thomas and Laura Lee matched the artistic achievements of Motown and Atlantic, ill-advised attempts at aiming Waters and Wolf at the contemporary market with *Electric Mud* and *The New Howlin' Wolf Album*, marked the nadir of their respective careers. The death of Leonard Chess on 16 October 1969 signalled the end of an era and Chess was then purchased by the GRT corporation. Phil left the company to run the WVON radio station, while Leonard's son, Marshall, became managing director of Rolling Stones Records. Producer Ralph Bass remained in Chicago, cataloguing master tapes and supervising a studio reduced to recording backing tracks, but he too vacated the now moribund empire. Chess was later acquired by the All Platinum/Sugarhill companies, then MCA who, in tandem with European licensees Charly, have undertaken a major reissue programme.

●COMPILATIONS: *Chess: The Rhythm And The Blues* (1988)★★★★, *The Chess Story: Chess Records 1954-1969* (1989)★★★★, *First Time I Met The Blues* (1989)★★★, *Second Time I Met The Blues* (1989)★★★, *Chess Blues* 4-CD box set (1993)★★★★, 4-CD box set *Chess Rhythm & Roll* (MCA 1995)★★★★.

●FURTHER READING: *The Chess Labels*, Michel Ruppli. *Chess Blues Discography*, L. Fancourt.

CHESSMEN

One of the more adventurous Irish showbands of the mid-60s, the Chessmen featured singer Alan Dee who was also a strong songwriter. It was almost unprecedented for a showband to compose their own material, but Dee penned several hit songs such as 'Fighting' and 'What In The World Has Come Over You'. His greatest success, however, came with an evocative ballad of emigration, 'Michael Murphy's Boy'. With its haunting chorus ('My name is Patrick Joseph, I'm Michael Murphy's Boy') the song was played frequently on Radio Eireann and reached number 4 in the Irish charts in the summer of 1966. The Chessmen enjoyed the privilege of being managed by Noel Pearson, a talented impresario who wrote and was on the board of the Abbey Theatre and producer of such acclaimed Irish films as *My Left Foot* and *The Field*. Although the Chessmen were a promising act, they felt restricted by the showband routine and fragmented in the late 60s following the departure of Dee.

CHEYNES

Formed in London, England, in July 1963, the Cheynes' founding line-up consisted of Roger Peacock (vocals), Eddie Lynch (lead guitar), Peter Bardens (organ/vocals), Peter Hollis (bass) and Mick Fleetwood (drums). Within weeks Lynch was replaced by Phil Sawyer. The Cheynes were one of the most popular and exciting R&B acts of their era, but the group was unable to emulate the success of the Yardbirds or Manfred Mann. They made their

recording debut in 1963 with a version of the Isley Brothers' 'Respectable'. It was succeeded in 1964 by the gospel-tinged 'Goin' To The River' and in 1965 by the equally confident 'Down And Out'. They disbanded in April 1965. Peacock joined the Mark Leeman Five, Fleetwood joined the Bo Street Runners, Sawyer joined (Les) Fleur De Lys and Bardens joined Them.

CHICKEN SHACK

Chicken Shack was the product of eccentric guitarist Stan Webb, veteran of several R&B groups including the Blue 4, Sound Five and the Sounds Of Blue. The latter, active between 1964 and 1965, included Webb, Christine Perfect (b. 12 July 1943, Birmingham, England; piano/vocals) and Andy Sylvester (bass), as well as future Traffic saxophonist Chris Wood. Webb and Sylvester formed the core of the original Chicken Shack, who enjoyed a long residency at Hamburg's famed Star Club before returning to England in 1967. Perfect then rejoined the line-up which was augmented by several drummers until the arrival of Londoner Dave Bidwell. Producer Mike Vernon then signed the quartet to his Blue Horizon label. *Forty Blue Fingers Freshly Packed And Ready To Serve* was a fine balance between original songs and material by John Lee Hooker and Freddie King, to whom Webb was stylistically indebted. *OK Ken?* emphasized the guitarist's own compositions, as well as his irreverence, as he introduces each track by impersonating well-known personalities, including UK disc jockey John Peel, ex-Prime Minister Harold Wilson and UK comedian Kenneth Williams. The quartet also enjoyed two minor hit singles with 'I'd Rather Go Blind' and 'Tears In The Wind', the former of which featured a particularly moving vocal from Perfect, who then left for a solo career (later as Christine McVie). Her replacement was Paul Raymond from Plastic Penny. Ensuing releases, *100 Ton Chicken* and *Accept*, lacked the appeal of their predecessors and their heavier perspective caused a rift with Vernon, who dropped the band from his blues label. Friction within the line-up resulted in the departure of Raymond and Bidwell for Savoy Brown, a group Sylvester later joined.

Webb reassembled Chicken Shack with John Glassock (bass, ex-Jethro Tull) and Paul Hancox (drums) and embarked on a period of frenetic live work. They completed the disappointing *Imagination Lady* before Bob Daisley replaced Glassock, but the trio broke up, exhausted, in May 1973 having completed *Unlucky Boy*. The guitarist established a completely new line-up for *Goodbye Chicken Shack*, before dissolving the band in order to join the ubiquitous Savoy Brown for a USA tour and the *Boogie Brothers* album. Webb then formed Broken Glass and the Stan Webb Band, but he has also resurrected Chicken Shack on several occasions, notably between 1977 and 1979 and 1980 and 1982, in order to take advantage of a continued popularity on the European continent which, if not translated into record sales, assures this instinctive virtuoso a lasting career. In the 90s, Stan Webb was once again delighting small club audiences with his latest version of Chicken Shack.

●ALBUMS: *Forty Blue Fingers Freshly Packed And Ready To Serve* (Blue Horizon 1968)★★★★, *OK Ken?* (Blue Horizon 1969)★★★, *100 Ton Chicken* (1969)★★★, *Accept! Chicken Shack* (1970)★★★, *Imagination Lady* (Deram 1972)★★★, *Unlucky Boy* (Deram 1973)★★, *Goodbye Chicken Shack* (Deram 1974)★★, *The Creeper* (1978)★★, *The Way We Are* (1979)★★, *Chicken Shack* (1979)★★, *Roadie's Concerto* (1981)★★, *Changes* (1992)★★★, *Webb's Blues* (Indigo 1994)★★★, *Plucking Good* (Inak 1994)★★★, *Stan 'The Man' Live* (Indigo 1995)★★★.
●COMPILATIONS: *Stan The Man* (1977)★★★, *The Golden Era Of Pop Music* (1977)★★★, *In The Can* (1980)★★★, *Collection: Chicken Shack* (1988)★★★.

CHIFFONS

Formed in the Bronx, New York, USA, where all the members were born, erstwhile backing singers Judy Craig (b. 1946), Barbara Lee (b. 16 May 1947), Patricia Bennett (b. 7 April 1947) and Sylvia Peterson (b. 30 September 1946), are best recalled for 'He's So Fine', a superb girl-group release and an international hit in 1963. The song later acquired a dubious infamy when its melody appeared on George Harrison's million-selling single, 'My Sweet Lord'. Taken to court by the original publishers, the ex-Beatle was found guilty of plagiarism and obliged to pay substantial damages. This battle made little difference to the Chiffons, who despite enjoying hits with 'One Fine Day' (1963) and 'Sweet Talkin' Guy' (1966), were all too soon reduced to a world of cabaret and 'oldies' nights. They did, however, record their own version of 'My Sweet Lord'.
●ALBUMS: *He's So Fine* (Laurie 1963)★★, *One Fine Day* (Laurie 1963)★★, *Sweet Talkin' Guy* (Laurie 1966)★★.
●COMPILATIONS: *Everything You Ever Wanted To Hear ... But Couldn't Get* (1984)★★★, *Doo-Lang Doo-Lang Doo-Lang* (1985)★★★, *Flips, Flops And Rarities* (1986)★★, *Greatest Recordings* (1990)★★★.

CHILTON, JOHN

b. 16 July 1932, London, England. A sound trumpeter and skilful arranger, Chilton led his own band in the mid-50s before joining the Bruce Turner Jump Band in 1958. He remained with Turner for five years, playing and writing arrangements. In the early 60s he was with Alex Welsh and Mike Daniels before forming another band of his own. At the end of the 60s he became co-leader with Wally Fawkes of a band they named the Feetwarmers, taking over as leader in 1974. Almost at once, Chilton became musical director for George Melly and ever since has toured, recorded and broadcast with the singer. as far as the wider public is concerned, Chilton's place in British jazz may rest on his relationship with Melly, but for the *cogniscenti* it is his role as a writer and tireless researcher into jazz history that makes him a figure of considerable importance. Among his many publications are *Who's Who Of Jazz: Storyville To Swing Street*, a work which ably demonstrates the awe-inspiring meticu-

lousness of his research; *Louis: The Louis Armstrong Story*, a biography written in collaboration with Max Jones; *Jazz*, a history written for the 'Teach Yourself' series of publications; *Billie's Blues*, a partial biography of Billie Holiday, plus historical accounts of the Jenkins Orphanage bands, McKinney's Cotton Pickers, the Bob Crosby Bobcats, and definitive biographies of Sidney Bechet and Coleman Hawkins. In the early 90s Chilton was still on the road with Melly and writing about his branch of jazz, on which he is an acknowledged expert.

CHIMES (USA)

Formed in Brooklyn, New York, in 1959, this vocal quintet consisted of Lenny Cocco (lead), Joe Croce (baritone), Pat DePrisco (first tenor), Rich Mercado (second tenor) and Pat McGuire (bass). Signed to the small Tag label, the group reached the US Top 20 in 1961 with 'Once In Awhile'. A cover of 'I'm In The Mood For Love' managed a US Top 40 placing the following year but the Chimes had no subsequent hits, disbanding in 1965. They re-formed in 1970 and performed at oldies shows until 1973. Cocco assembled a new Chimes group in 1981, which was still performing in the New York area in the early 90s. 'Once In Awhile' has actually grown in stature, and routinely features among the 10 all-time favourite hits by listeners of New York's 'oldies' radio station. A re-recording was made in the 80s that did not have the patina of the original.
●ALBUMS: *Once In Awhile* (Ambient Sound 1987)★★.
●COMPILATIONS: *Best Of Chimes And Classics* (Rare Bird 1974)★★★.

CHIPMUNKS

A fictional group, the Chipmunks were three cartoon characters, Alvin, Theodore and Simon, who were created by Ross Bagdasarian (b. 27 January 1919, Fresno, California, USA), a multi-faceted performer, who had earlier had an international hit as David Seville with 'Witch Doctor' in early 1958. On that hit, Bagdasarian had manipulated a tape recorder so that normally sung vocals played back at a faster speed. Using the same technique, he experimented with the sound of three voices harmonizing at that faster speed and it reminded him of the chattering of chipmunks. Bagdasarian had recorded 'Witch Doctor' for Liberty Records (the three Chipmunks were named after Liberty executives), which released 'The Chipmunk Song' for the Christmas 1958 season. It reached number 1 in the US and was quickly followed by 'Alvin's Harmonica' which climbed to number 3. In all, the Chipmunks placed 15 songs on the US charts between 1958 and 1962, spawning a hit television programme. They continued well into the 60s, recording an album of Beatles songs. Bagdasarian died in January 1972 but the Chipmunks were revived in 1980 by his son, Ross Bagdasarian Jnr., and his partner Janice Karmen, this time recording albums of punk, country and current rock!
●ALBUMS: *Let's All Sing With The Chipmunks* (Liberty 1959)★, *Sing Again With The Chipmunks*

(Liberty 1960)★, *Christmas With The Chipmunks* (Liberty 1962)★, *Christmas With The Chipmunks - Volume Two* (Liberty 1963)★, *The Chipmunks Sing The Beatles Hits* (Liberty 1964)★, *The Chipmunks Sing With Children* (Liberty 1965)★, *Chipmunk Punk* (Liberty 1980)★, *Urban Chipmunk* (Liberty 1981)★, *A Chipmunk Christmas* (Liberty 1981)★, *Chipmunk Rock* (Liberty 1982)★, *Merry Christmas Fun With The Merry Chipmunks* (Liberty 1984)★.
●COMPILATIONS: *Twenty All-Time Greatest Hits* (Liberty 1982)★★★.

CHISHOLM, GEORGE

b. 29 March 1915, Glasgow, Scotland. In his early 20s Chisholm arrived in London, where he played trombone in the popular dance bands led by Teddy Joyce and Bert Ambrose. Inspired originally by recordings of Jack Teagarden, Chisholm naturally gravitated towards the contemporary jazz scene and was thus on hand for informal sessions and even the occasional recording date with visiting American stars such as Benny Carter, Coleman Hawkins and Fats Waller. During World War II he played with the Royal Air Force's dance band, the Squadronaires, with whom he remained in the post-war years. Later he became a regular studio and session musician, playing with several of the BBC's house bands. In the late 50s and on through the 60s Chisholm's exuberant sense of humour led to a succession of television appearances, both as musician and comic, and if his eccentric dress, black tights and George Robey-style bowler hat caused jazz fans some displeasure, the music he played was always excellent. During this period he made many records with leading British and American jazz artists including Sandy Brown and Wild Bill Davison. In the 80s, despite having had heart surgery, Chisholm played on, often working with Keith Smith's Hefty Jazz or his own band, the Gentlemen of Jazz. He continued to delight audiences with his fluid technique and his ability to blend an urgent attack with a smooth style of playing and endless touches of irreverent humour. He was awarded an OBE in 1984. In 1990 he was still on the road, touring with visiting Americans, such as Spike Robinson. Soon afterwards, however, his state of health forced him to retire from active playing but did nothing to damage his high spirits and sense of humour.
●ALBUMS: *George Chisholm And His Band* (1956)★★★, *Stars Play Jazz* (1961)★★★, *George Chisholm* (1967)★★★, with Sandy Brown *Hair At Its Hairiest* (1968)★★★, *Along The Chisholm Trail* (1971)★★★, *In A Mellow Mood* (1973)★★★, *Trombone Showcase* (1976)★★★, *The Swingin' Mr C* (Zodiac 1986)★★★, *That's A-Plenty!* (Zodiac 1987)★★★, with John Petters *Swinging Down Memory Lane* (CMJ 1989)★★★.
●COMPILATIONS: with Benny Carter *Swingin' At Maida Vale* (1937)★★★, *Fats Waller In London* (1938)★★★ with the Squadronaires *There's Something In The Air* (1941-50)★★★.

CHOCOLATE WATCH BAND

The original line-up of this tempestuous US pop group - Ned Torney (guitar), Mark Loomis (guitar/vocals), Jo Kleming (organ), Richard Young (bass), Danny Phay (lead vocals) and Pete Curry (drums) - was assembled in San Jose, California, USA, in 1964. Gary Andrijasevich replaced Curry within weeks of the quintet's inception. The following year Torney, Kleming and Phay defected to another local outfit, the Topsiders, later known as the Other Side, while the latter's guitarist, Sean Tolby (bass), joined Loomis and Andrijasevich. The revitalised quintet was completed by Dave Aguilar (vocals) and Bill Flores (bass).
Producer Ed Cobb, already renowned for his work with the Standells, signed the group in 1966. He matched the Watch Band's instinctive love of British R&B with a tough, metallic sound, and the best of their work - 'Don't Need No Lovin'', 'No Way Out' and 'Are You Gonna Be There (At The Love In)' - is among the finest to emerge from America's garage-band genre. However, the group's potential was undermined by personal and professional problems. Several Chocolate Watch Band masters featured studio musicians, while a substitute vocalist, Don Bennett, was also employed on certain sessions. A disillusioned Aguilar quit the line-up prior to the release of *The Inner Mystique*. Phay resumed his place on *One Step Beyond*, but this album proved disappointing, despite a cameo appearance by Moby Grape guitarist Jerry Miller. The Chocolate Watch Band split up in March 1970.
●ALBUMS: *No Way Out* (Tower 1967)★★★, *The Inner Mystique* (Tower 1968)★★★, *One Step Beyond* (Tower 1969)★★.
●COMPILATIONS: *The Best Of The Chocolate Watch Band* (Rhino 1983)★★★, *44* (1987)★★★.

CHRISTIAN, NEIL

b. Christopher Tidmarsh, 14 February 1943, Hoxton, East London, England. With backing group the Crusaders, Christian was one of the pioneering acts of Britain's pre-Beatles era. His first line-up included guitarist Jimmy Page, who was later featured as a session musician on the singer's 1964 release, 'Honey Hush'. Albert Lee, Mick Abrahams and Alex Dmochowski (later of Aynsley Dunbar Retaliation) also graced the Crusaders at various times in its career, while Ritchie Blackmore (guitar), Elmer Twitch (piano), Bibi Blange (bass) and Tornado Evans (drums) supported Christian when he toured to promote 'That's Nice'. This perky single reached the UK Top 20 in 1966, but when the similarly styled 'Oops' failed to chart, the singer moved to Germany where he had attracted a fanatical following. Christian subsequently returned to Britain and continued to record sporadically, but, unable to secure a consistent success, he later retired from active performing.

CHRISTIE, LOU

b. Lugee Alfredo Giovanni Sacco, 19 February 1943, Glen Willard, Pennsylvania, USA. A former student of classical music, Christie moved to New York in 1963 where he sang backing vocals on a variety of sessions. Before beginning his string of hits, Christie recorded unsuccessfully with such groups as the Classics and Lugee and the Lions. Although his high falsetto was reminiscent of an earlier era, and similar to that used successfully by Frankie Valli and Del Shannon, 'The Gypsy Cried', the artist's debut solo single, achieved sales in excess of one million in 1963. The following year 'Two Faces Have I' proved equally successful but, unable to avoid the US military draft, Christie's career was interrupted. He achieved a third golden disc with 'Lightnin' Strikes' (1966), arguably his finest record, which pitted the singer's vocal histrionics against a solid, Tamla/Motown-styled backbeat. The single also charted in the UK, where its follow-up, 'Rhapsody In The Rain' (1966), was another Top 20 entry, despite a ban in deference to its 'suggestive lyric'. In 1969, this time signed to Buddah Records, Christie had his final Top 10 hit with 'I'm Gonna Make You Mine', his style virtually unchanged from the earlier hits. Numerous singles followed on small labels into the 80s, but Christie was unable to regain any commercial ground. An almost anachronistic performer, he has spent most of the past two decades playing on the US rock 'n' roll revival circuit.

●ALBUMS: *Lou Christie* (Roulette 1963)★★, *Lightnin' Strikes* (MGM 1966)★★★, *Lou Christie Strikes Back* (Co&Ce 1966)★★★, *Lou Christie Strikes Again* (Colpix 1966)★★★, *Lou Christie Painter Of Hits* (MGM 1966)★★, *I'm Gonna Make You Mine* (Buddah 1969)★★★, *Paint America Love* (Buddah 1971)★★, *Lou Christie - Zip-A-Dee-Doo-Dah* (CTI 1974)★★.

●COMPILATIONS: *This Is Lou Christie* (1969)★★★, *Beyond The Blue Horizon: More Of The Best Of ...* (Varese Sarabande 1995)★★★.

CIRCUS

Circus was originally known as the Stormsville Shakers, a London-based R&B group led by Philip Goodhand-Tait, which supported Larry Williams on his 1965 UK tour. The band recorded several singles in its own right for the Parlophone label, the last two of which - 'Sink Or Swim' and 'Do You Dream' - featured their newly acquired Circus appellation. The sextet: Goodhand-Tait (vocals/keyboards), Mel Collins (saxophone), Clive Burrows (saxophone, ex-Zoot Money), Ian Jelfs (guitar), Kirk Riddell (bass) and Alan Bunn (guitar) was then signed to Transatlantic, for whom they completed *Circus* in 1969, which featured a lengthy improvised version of the Beatles' 'Norwegian Wood'. This progressive set was the group's sole album, as Goodhand-Tait then left to pursue a singer/songwriter career in the mode of Elton John. Mel Collins meanwhile recorded with King Crimson and Alexis Korner.

●ALBUMS: *Circus* (Transatlantic 1969)★★★.

CLANCY BROTHERS AND TOMMY MAKEM

Although born in Carrick on Suir, Eire, Tom (b. 1923, d. 7 November 1990, Cork, Eire), Paddy (b. 1923) and Liam Clancy (b. 1936) were among the founders of the New York folk revival during the 50s. From a musical family, Tom and Paddy emigrated to the USA to become actors. Paddy was soon assisting the Folkways and Elektra labels in recording Irish material and in 1956 he set up his own small label, Tradition. This released material by Josh White and Odetta. By now, the younger brother Liam had also moved to America, and was collecting songs in the Appalachian mountains. He encouraged whistle player Tommy Makem (b. 1932, Keady, Co. Armagh, Northern Ireland) to move to New York. In the late 50s, the quartet began to perform in clubs and at hootenannies, eventually recording collections of Irish material in 1959. Among them were many, including 'Jug Of Punch' and 'The Leaving Of Liverpool', that became widely sung in folk clubs on both sides of the Atlantic. The Clancys attracted a large following with their boisterous approach and gained national prominence through an appearance on Ed Sullivan's television show. The group recorded frequently for Columbia throughout the 60s. Their sister, Peg Clancy Power made a solo album of Irish songs in the late 60s. Makem left to follow a solo career in 1969, later recording with producer Donal Lunny for Polydor in Ireland. The Clancys continued to make occasional appearances, notably their annual St. Patrick's Day concerts in New York. Louis Killen, a traditional singer from north-east England joined for a 1973 record of *Greatest Hits* on Vanguard. There were other albums for Warner Brothers in the 70s and the original group re-formed for a 1984 concert and album. Although Tom Clancy died in November 1990, the remaining brothers continued to perform together occasionally in the early 90s.

●ALBUMS: *The Rising Of The Moon* (Tradition 1959)★★★, *Come Fill Your Glass With Us* (Tradition 1959)★★★, *The Clancy Brothers And Tommy Makem* (Tradition 1961)★★★★, *A Spontaneous Performance Recording* (Columbia 1961)★★★★, *The Boys Won't Leave The Girls Alone* (Columbia 1962)★★★, *In Person At Carnegie Hall* (Columbia 1964)★★★★, *Isn't It Grand Boys* (Columbia 1966)★★★, *The Irish Uprising* (1966)★★★, *Freedom's Son's* (Columbia 1967)★★★, *Home Boys Home* (1968)★★★, *Sing Of The Sea* (Columbia 1968)★★★, *Bold Fenian Men* (1969)★★★, *Seriously Speaking* (1975)★★★, *Every Day* (1976)★★★, *Reunion* (1984)★★★, *In Concert* (1992)★★★. Solo: Tommy Makem *In The Dark Green Woods* (1974)★★, *Ever The Winds* (1975)★★, *Tommy Makem And Liam Clancy* (1976)★★.

●COMPILATIONS: *Greatest Hits* (1973)★★★,

CLANTON, JIMMY

b. 2 September 1940, Baton Rouge, Louisiana, USA. Pop vocalist Clanton celebrated his 18th birthday with his co-written debut hit, the R&B ballad 'Just A Dream', at number 4 in the US Hot 100. His smooth singing style appealed to the teen market and his subsequent releases were aimed in that direction. These included 'My Own True Love', which used the melody of 'Tara's Theme' from *Gone With The Wind*. The title track of the film

Go, Jimmy, Go, in which he starred, gave him another US Top 5 smash and the ballad 'Another Sleepless Night' reached the UK Top 50 in July 1960. His most famous record, 'Venus In Blue Jeans', co-written by Neil Sedaka, gave him his last US Top 10 hit, in late 1962. The song became a bigger hit in the UK, when Mark Wynter took his version into the Top 5.

●ALBUMS: *Just A Dream* (Ace 1959)★★★, *Jimmy's Happy* (Ace 1960)★★★, *Jimmy's Blue* (Ace 1960)★★★, *My Best To You* (Ace 1961)★★★, *Teenage Millionaire* (Ace 1961)★★★, *Venus In Bluejeans* (Ace 1962)★★★.
●COMPILATIONS: *The Best Of Jimmy Clanton* (Philips 1964)★★★.
●FILMS: *Go Johnny Go* (1958).

CLARENDONIANS

While Jamaican music is packed with child prodigies, to find three in one group is unusual even by reggae standards. The Clarendonians, originally Fitzroy 'Ernest' Wilson and Peter Austin, formed during 1965 in their home parish of Clarendon in rural Jamaica, and after several talent competition victories came to the attention of producer Coxsone Dodd, owner of the Studio One label, while they were in their early teens. Dodd liked their feisty approach and soon put the pair in the studio, where they helped define the 'rude boy' era of ska alongside Dodd's other youthful protégés, Bob Marley And The Wailers. If anything, the Clarendonians were more successful than Marley's group at the time, scoring heavily with brash, loud singles like 'You Can't Be Happy', 'You Can't Keep A Good Man Down', 'Sho Be Do Be', 'Rudie Gone A Jail', 'Be Bop Boy', and their anthem, 'Rudie Bam Bam'. As young as their audience and the music they worked with, the Clarendonians were briefly the perfect ska vocal group. Somewhere along the line Dodd added another member, Freddie McGregor, who at the age of seven had to stand on a box to reach the microphone, and Dodd permutated the members as Freddie And Fitzie, Freddie And Peter, or simply recorded them solo. Ernest Wilson was the first member to really strike out as a solo act with a cover of Billy Vera's 'Storybook Children' and Tim Hardin's 'If I Were A Carpenter', as well as recording under the unlikely moniker of King Shark. He is still something of a star in Jamaica today, if only sporadically successful. McGregor was not so immediately successful, but after a series of excellent records with Studio One lasting right into the early 70s, he finally hit with 'Bobby Babylon'. Peter Austin's attempt at a solo career sadly faltered.

●COMPILATIONS: *The Best Of The Clarendonians* (Studio One 1968)★★★.

CLARK, CHRIS

Christine Clark joined Motown Records as a receptionist in 1964 and followed a familiar career structure within the company by graduating from office work to a recording contract. Her strident, bluesy vocals led her to be nicknamed 'The White Negress' by British fans, but this style excluded her from Motown's musical mainstream. After scoring an R&B hit with 'Love Gone Bad' in 1966 on the VIP subsidiary label, she graduated to Tamla in 1967, where she found some success with 'From Head To Toe'. In 1969 she became the Vice-President of Motown's film division, co-writing the screenplay for *Lady Sings The Blues* in 1971. In 1981 she was appointed Vice-President of Motown Productions, with jurisdiction over the company's creative affairs. Clark left the organisation in 1989 and re-recorded 'From Head To Toe' with producer Ian Levine for Motor City Records in 1991.

●ALBUMS: *Soul Sounds* (Tamla 1967)★★★, *CC Rides Again* (Weed 1969)★★★.

CLARK, DAVE, FIVE

One of the most popular British beat groups of the mid-60s, the Dave Clark Five's career stretched back as far as 1958. Originally a backing group for north London singer Stan Saxon, the Five comprised Dave Clark (b. 15 December 1942, London, England; drums/vocals), backed by various musicians, whose ranks included bassist Chris Wells and lead guitarist Mick Ryan. After splitting from Saxon, the Five established their own identity and nominated their date and place of formation as the South Grove Youth Club, Tottenham, London in January 1962. The evolving and finally settled line-up featured Mike Smith (b. 6 December 1943, London, England; organ/vocals), Rick Huxley (b. 5 August 1942, Dartford, Kent, England; bass guitar), Lenny Davidson (b. 30 May 1944, Enfield, Middlesex, England; lead guitar) and Denis Payton (b. 8 August 1943, London, England; saxophone). Smith's throaty vocals and Clark's incessant thumping beat were the group's most familiar trademarks. After losing out to Brian Poole And The Tremeloes with the much covered Contours classic 'Do You Love Me', the group elected to record their own material. The Clark/Smith composition 'Glad All Over' proved one of the most distinctive and recognizable beat songs of its era and reached number 1 in the UK during January 1964. Its timing could not have been more opportune as the record fortuitously removed the Beatles' 'I Want To Hold Your Hand', after its six-week reign at the top. The national press, ever fixated with Beatles stories, pronounced in large headlines: 'Has The Five Jive Crushed The Beatles' Beat?' The Five took advantage of the publicity by swiftly issuing the less memorable, but even more boot-thumping, 'Bits And Pieces', which climbed to number 2. Over the next couple of years, the group's chart career in the UK was erratic at best, although they enjoyed a sizeable Top 10 hit in 1965 with 'Catch Us If You Can' (*Having A Wild Weekend* in the USA) from the film of the same name in which they starred.

Even as their beat group charm in Britain faded, surprisingly new opportunities awaited them in the USA. A series of appearances on the *Ed Sullivan Show* saw them at the forefront of the mid-60s beat invasion and they racked up a string of million sellers. A remarkable 17 *Billboard* Top 40 hits included 'Can't You See That She's Mine', 'Because', 'I Like It Like That' and their sole US number 1 'Over And Over'. Back in the UK, they enjoyed a belated and highly successful shift of style with the Barry Mason/Les Reed ballad, 'Everybody Knows'. Slipping into the rock 'n' roll revivalist trend of the early 70s, they charted with the medleys 'Good Old Rock 'N' Roll' and 'More Good Old Rock 'N' Roll', before bowing out in 1971. In reappraising their work, their flow of singles between 1964 and 1966 was of an incredibly high standard, and such was their output that most of the b-sides were quite excellent. In terms of production Clark employed a kitchen sink approach; throw in everything. The remarkable 'Anyway You Want It' is one of the most exciting records of the decade, although many are unaware of its existence. This blockbuster has reverb, echo and treble recorded at number 11 volume, with an ear-shattering result that does not distort.

The simultaneous strength and weakness of the group lay in their no-risk policy and refusal to surrender the hit-making formula for a more ambitious approach. Far from serious rivals to the Beatles, as their initial press implied, they were actually a limited but solid outfit. Smith was the most talented with a huge rasping voice and great songwriting ability. Their astute leader, Clark, had a canny sense of the moment and astute business know-how, which enabled them to enjoy lucrative pickings in the US market long after their beat contemporaries had faded. He subsequently became a successful entrepreneur and multi-millionaire, both in the video market, where he purchased the rights to the pop show *Ready Steady Go!*, and onstage where his musical *Time* (starring Cliff Richard) enjoyed box office success. Clark retains the rights to all the band's material, and by sitting on the catalogue has sucessfully held out for the most lucrative offer to reissue the hits in the age of CD. This was achieved in fine style with the definitive History double CD. Old fans will relish the excellent running order and new fans will be astonished to discover how fresh these 60s pop songs sound in the 90s. A highly underrated group.

● ALBUMS: *A Session With The Dave Clark Five* (Columbia 1964)★★★★, *Glad All Over* (Epic 1964)★★★, *The Dave Clark Five Return* (Epic 1964)★★★, *American Tour Volume 1* (Epic 1964)★★★, *Coast To Coast* (Epic 1965)★★★, *Weekend In London* (Epic 1965)★★★, *Catch Us If You Can* soundtrack *Having A Wild Weekend* in the USA (Columbia 1965)★★★★, *I Like It Like That* (Epic 1965)★★★, *Try Too Hard* (Epic 1966)★★★, *Satisfied With You* (Epic 1966)★★★, *You Got What It Takes* (Epic 1967)★★★, *Everybody Knows* (Epic 1968)★★★, *If Somebody Loves You* (Columbia 1970)★★★, *Glad All Over Again* (Epic 1975)★★★.

● COMPILATIONS: *The Dave Clark Five's Greatest Hits* (Columbia 1967)★★★★, *5x5 - Go!* (Epic 1969)★★★★, *The Best Of The Dave Clark Five* (Regal Starline 1970)★★★★, *25 Thumping Great Hits* (Polydor 1977)★★★★, *The History Of The Dave Clark Five* (Hollywood 1993)★★★★★.

● VIDEOS: *Glad All Over Again* (PMI 1993).

● FILMS: *Get Yourself A College Girl* (1964), *Catch Us If You Can* (USA: *Having A Wild Weekend*) (1965).

CLARK, DEE

b. Delecta Clark, 7 November 1938, Blytheville, Arkansas, USA, d. 7 December 1990. Clark had a wonderfully impassioned tenor voice and enjoyed a spate of rock 'n' roll hits in the late 50s and a lesser body of soul work in the 60s. Clark's entertainment career began in 1952 as a member of the Hambone Kids, who, with band leader Red Saunders, recorded a novelty number in which Clark's group patted a rhythm known as the Hambone. Clark later joined a vocal group, the Goldentones, who won first prize in a talent show at Chicago's Roberts Show Lounge. Noted disc jockey Herb 'Kool Gent' Kent then took the group to Vee Jay Records, where they recorded as the Kool Gents. Clark's distinctive stylings soon engendered a solo contract and in 1958 he had a US hit with 'Nobody But You' (R&B number 3 and pop Top 30). 'Just Keep It Up' (R&B number 9 and pop Top 20) and 'Hey Little Girl' (R&B number 2 and pop Top 20) proved equally popular the following year. The artist's major success came in 1962 with 'Raindrops' (R&B number 3 and pop number 2). This plaintive offering, co-written by Clark and Phil Upchurch, eventually sold in excess of one million copies. Sadly, Clark was unable to repeat this feat, but continued on Chicago-based Constellation with a spate of moderate R&B hits, namely 'Crossfire Time' (1963), 'Heartbreak' (1964), and 'TCB' (1965). His career faded after Constellation went out of business in 1966. In the UK he had a sizable hit in 1975 with 'Ride A Wild Horse'; in the US the record failed to chart. Clark died of a heart attack in 1990.

● ALBUMS: *Dee Clark* (Abner 1959)★★★, *How About That* (Abner 1960)★★★, *You're Looking Good* (Vee Jay 1960)★★★, *Hold On, It's Dee Clark* (Vee Jay 1961)★★★, *Hey Little Girl* (1982)★★★.

● COMPILATIONS: *The Best Of Dee Clark* (Vee Jay 1964)★★★★, *Keep It Up* (1980)★★★, *The Delectable Sound Of Dee Clark* (1986)★★★★, *Raindrops* (1987)★★★★.

CLARK, DICK

b. Richard Wagstaff Clark, 30 November 1929, Mount Vernon, New York, USA. Clark became a showbusiness giant via the US television dance programme *American Bandstand*, the longest-running variety show in television history. As its host for over 30 years, Clark brought rock 'n' roll music and dancing into millions of American homes. He has been nicknamed 'America's Oldest Living Teenager'. Clark's career began in 1947, upon his graduation from high school. After working at minor jobs at his uncle's radio station, WRUN (Utica, New York), Clark debuted on the air at WAER, the radio station at Syracuse University, which he attended. Further radio jobs followed, until Clark took his first television job, as a newscaster, in 1951. He returned to radio upon moving to Philadelphia's WFIL, but by 1956 WFIL's television outlet needed a replacement host for its *Bandstand* show. Clark was offered the position and started his new job on 9 July 1956.

Bandstand's format was simple: play current hit records and invite local teenagers to come in and dance to them. The programme was a surprise success and a year later the ABC network decided to broadcast it nationally, changing the name to *American Bandstand* on 5 August 1957. Clark continued to host, bringing in guest artists - particularly top rock 'n' roll artists of the day - and the programme became a national phenomenon. Record promoters coveted airplay on *Bandstand*, as its power to 'break' records was unparalleled, and managers clamoured to land their artists on the programme to 'lip-sync' their latest hits. Many artists, particularly such Philadelphia-based singers as Fabian, Bobby Rydell, Chubby Checker and Frankie Avalon, largely owed their success to *Bandstand* exposure. Bobby Darin, Paul Anka and Connie Francis were also regulars.

By this time Clark's own power within the music industry had grown, and when in 1959-60 the US government cracked down on so-called 'payola', the practice of disc jockeys accepting money or gifts in exchange for airplay, Clark was called to Washington to testify. He claimed innocence and was cleared with his reputation intact, although he divested himself of some $8 million in music business-related investments. Clark had formed a production company early in his career, and in the mid-60s began producing other music television programmes, such as *Where The Action Is* and *Happening*. He also produced television game shows and films (including *Psych-Out* and *Because They're Young*). Clark's later creations include the *American Music Awards*, the *Country Music Awards* and television films about the Beatles and Elvis Presley - ironically, the only two major pop artists never to appear on *American Bandstand*. He also arranged tours called the Caravan of Stars, which took top musical stars on one-night-stand concerts throughout the USA in the early 60s.

In 1964 *Bandstand* moved to Los Angeles from Philadelphia, and eventually it was scaled down from a daily to a weekly show. It continued until the late 80s, featuring contemporary artists such as Madonna, Prince and Cyndi Lauper. Clark remained an enormously powerful and influential figure in the entertainment industry into the 90s.

● FILMS: *Because They're Young* (1960).
● FURTHER READING: *Rock, Roll & Remember*, Dick Clark and Richard Robinson.

CLARK, PETULA

b. 15 November 1932, Epsom, Surrey, England. Her Welsh mother, a soprano, taught Petula to sing, which enabled her to commence a stage career at the age of seven and a broadcasting career two years later. Her youthful image and crystal-clear enunciation were ideal for radio and by 1943, she had her own programme with the accent on wartime, morale-building songs. She made her first film, *Medal For The General*, in 1944 and then signed for the J. Arthur Rank Organization appearing in over 20 feature films, including the *Huggett* series, alongside other young hopefuls such as Anthony Newley and Alec Guinness. By 1949 she was recording, and throughout the 50s had several hits including 'The Little Shoemaker', 'Suddenly There's A Valley' 'With All My Heart' and 'Alone'. Around this period, Clark's success in France led to many concert appearances in Paris and recordings, in French, for the Vogue label. Eventually, in 1959, at the age of 27 and unhappy with the British audiences' reluctance to see her as anything but a sweet adolescent, she moved to France, where she married Vogue's PR representative, Claude Wolff. At the Olympia Theatre, Paris, in 1960, she introduced her new sound, retaining the ultra-clear vocals, but adding to them electronic effects and a hefty beat. Almost immediately her career took off. She had a massive hit with 'Ya-Ya Twist', for which she received the Grand Prix du Disque, and by 1962 was France's favourite female vocalist, ahead even of the legendary Edith Piaf. Meanwhile, in Britain, Clark's versions of 'Romeo', 'My Friend The Sea' and 'Sailor', were chasing Elvis Presley up the charts. Her international breakthrough began in 1964 when the British songwriter/arranger Tony Hatch presented Clark with 'Downtown'. It became a big hit in western Europe, and a year later climbed to the top of the US charts, clinching her popularity in a country where she was previously unknown. The record sold over three million copies worldwide and gained a Grammy Award in the USA as the best rock 'n' roll single. Clark's subsequent recordings of other Hatch songs, frequently written with his lyricist wife, Jackie Trent, including 'Don't Sleep In The Subway', 'The Other Man's Grass', 'I Couldn't Live Without Your Love', 'My Love' and 'I Know A Place', all made the US Top 10. Her recording of 'This Is My Song', written by Charles Chaplin for the Marlon Brando/Sophia Loren epic, *A Countess From Hong Kong* (1967), reached number 1 in the UK charts. Tours of the USA and television guest shots followed. As well as hosting her own BBC television series, she was given her own US NBC television special *Petula*, in 1968. This was marred by the programme sponsor's request that a sequence in which she touched the arm of black guest Harry Belafonte, should be removed in deference to the southern States. The show was eventually transmitted complete. That same year Clark revived her film career when she appeared as Sharon, the 'Glocca Morra' girl in E.Y. 'Yip' Harburg and Burton Lane's *Finian's Rainbow*, co-starring with Fred Astaire and Tommy Steele. While the film was generally regarded as too old-fashioned for 60s audiences, Clark's performance, with just a touch of the blarney, was well received, as was her partnership with Peter O'Toole in MGM's 1969 remake of *Goodbye, Mr. Chips*, marking her 30 years in show business. She was, by now, not only a major recording star, but an international personality, able to play all over the world, in cabaret and concerts. Between 1981 and 1982 she played the part of Maria in the London revival of Richard Rodgers/Oscar Hammerstein II's *The Sound Of Music*. It ran for 14 months, and was a great personal success. In 1989 PYS

Records issued a 'radically remixed' version of her 60s hit, 'Downtown', with the original vocal accompanied by 'acid house' backing. It went to number 10 in the UK chart. To date she has sold over 30 million records worldwide and has been awarded more gold discs than any other British female singer. From early in her career she has written songs, sometimes under the pseudonym of Al Grant; so it was particularly pleasing for Clark to write the music, and appear in a West End musical, *Someone Like You*. The show opened in March 1990 to mixed reviews, and had only a brief run. Two years later Clark made her first concert tour of the UK for 10 years, and in 1993 took over one of the starring roles in Willy Russell's musical *Blood Brothers* on Broadway.

●ALBUMS: *Petula Clark Sings* (Pye Nixa 1956)★★★, *A Date With Pet* (Pye Nixa 1956)★★★, *You Are My Lucky Star* (Pye Nixa 1957)★★★, *Pet Clark* (1959)★★★, *Petula Clark In Hollywood* (Pye Nixa 1959)★★★, *In Other Words* (Pye 1962)★★★, *Petula* (Pye 1962)★★★, *Les James Dean* (Pye-Vogue 1962)★★★, *Downtown* (Pye 1964)★★★★, *I Know A Place* (1965)★★★, *The World's Greatest International Hits!* (1965)★★★, *The New Petula Clark Album* (Pye 1965)★★★, *Uptown With Petula Clark* (1965)★★★, *In Love* (1965)★★★, *Petula '65* (1965)★★★★, *My Love* (1966),★★★★ *Petula '66* (1966)★★★, *Hello Paris, Vol. I* (Pye-Vogue 1966)★★★, *Hello Paris, Vol. II* (Pye-Vogue 1966)★★★, *Petula Clark Sings For Everybody* (1966)★★★, *I Couldn't Live Without Your Love* (1966),★★★★, *Colour My World/Who Am I?* (1967)★★★, *These Are My Songs* (Pye 1967)★★★, *The Other Man's Grass Is Always Greener* (Pye 1968)★★★★, *Petula* (Pye 1968)★★★, *Portrait Of Petula* (Pye 1969)★★★, *Just Pet* (Pye 1969)★★★, *Memphis* (Pye 1970)★★, *The Song Of My Life* (Pye 1971)★★★, *Wonderland Of Sound* (1971)★★, *Today* (Pye 1971)★★★, *Petula '71* (Pye 1971)★★★, *Warm And Tender* (1971)★★★, *Live At The Royal Albert Hall* (Pye 1972)★★★, *Now* (Polydor 1972)★★★, *Live In London* (1974)★★★, *Come On Home* (1974)★★★, *C'est Le Befrain De Ma Vie* (1975)★★★, *La Chanson De Marie-Madeleine* (1975)★★★, *I'm The Woman You Need* (1975)★★★, *Just Petula* (Polydor 1975)★★★, *Noel* (Pet Projects 1975)★★, *Beautiful Sounds* (Pet Projects 1976)★★, *Destiny* (CBS 1978)★★★, *An Hour In Concert With Petula Clark* (1983)★★★.

●COMPILATIONS: *Petula's Greatest Hits, Volume 1* (1968)★★★★, *Petula Clark's Hit Parade* (Pye 1969)★★★★, *Petula Clark's 20 All Time Greatest* (1977)★★★★, *Spotlight On Petula Clark* (1980)★★★, *100 Minutes Of Petula Clark* (1982)★★★, *Early Years* (1986)★★★, *The Hit Singles Collection* (1987)★★★★, *My Greatest* (1989)★★★, *Downtown* (1989)★★★, *Treasures Vol. 1* (1992)★★★, *Jumble Sale: Rarities And Obscurities 1959-64* 2-CD set (1992)★★★★, *The EP Collection Volume 2* (See For Miles 1993)★★★★, *The Nixa Years Volume One* 2-CD set (1994)★★★★, *The Polygon Years Volume One: 1950-1952* (RPM 1994)★★★, *The Polygon Years Volume Two: 1952-1955* (RPM 1994)★★★, *I Love To Sing* 3-CD set (Sequel 1995)★★★★, *The Nixa Years Volume Two* 2-CD set (1995)★★★★, *Downtown* (Spectrum 1995)★★★, *The Pye Years Volume Two* (RPM 1996)★★★, *These Are My Songs* (Start 1996)★★★, *The Pye Years Volume Three* (RPM 1997)★★★★.

●VIDEOS: *Petula Clark Spectacular* (Laserlight 1996).
●FURTHER READING: *This Is My Song: Biography Of Petula Clark*, Andrea Kon.

CLASSICS IV

Formed in Jacksonville, Florida, USA, the Classics IV were 'discovered' by entrepreneur Bill Lowery upon their move to Atlanta in 1967. This strongly commercial quintet comprised Dennis Yost (vocals), James Cobb (lead guitar), Wally Eaton (rhythm guitar), Joe Wilson (bass) and Kim Venable (drums). Seasoned session musicians, they had already worked on records by Lowrey protégés Tommy Roe, Billy Joe Royal and the Tams. Between 1968 and 1969, they enjoyed three soft-rock US hits with 'Spooky' (which sold in excess of one million copies), 'Stormy' and 'Traces', all expertly arranged by producer Buddie Buie. For a time, lead singer Dennis Yost was billed independently of the group, as Gary Puckett and Diana Ross had been in the Union Gap and the Supremes during the same period. Despite expanding the line-up to that of an octet with Dean Daughtry, the eventual loss of major songwriter Cobb proved insurmountable. Yost failed to emerge as a star in spite of the new billing and, somewhat adrift in the early 70s, Classics IV enjoyed only one more minor hit, 'What Am I Crying For' (1972). James Cobb and Daughtry later formed the Atlanta Rhythm Section.

●ALBUMS: *Spooky* (Liberty 1968)★★★, *Mamas And Papas/Soul Train* (1969)★★, *Traces* (1969)★★.
●COMPILATIONS: *Dennis Yost And The Classics IV Golden Greats Volume 1* (1969)★★★, *The Very Best Of The Classic IV* (EMI 1975)★★★, *Greatest Hits* (CEMA 1992)★★★.

CLAYTON SQUARES

Named after Clayton Square in their home town of Liverpool, England, the Clayton Squares were a driving R&B band formed too late to cash in on the Mersey boom. The founding line-up comprised Mike Evans (tenor saxophone/leader), Denny Alexander (vocals/rhythm guitar), Pete Dunn (lead guitar/organ), Les Smith (alto saxophone), Geoff Jones (bass), and Bobby Scott (drums). They recorded two excellent singles for Decca Records, 'Come And Get It' and 'There She Is', but despite consistent touring and numerous international television appearances, the group was unable to achieve commercial success. The Clayton Squares disbanded in 1966 after which Evans joined late-period guitarist Andy Roberts in the Liverpool Scene.

CLEAR LIGHT

Despite releasing only one album, peaking at number 126 on the *Billboard* chart, Los Angeles-based septet

Clear Light sent out ripples across the entertainment business. Their music, heavy rock featuring an innovative early use of double drummers, was intriguing with flashes of potential greatness but, after a cameo appearance in James Coburn's 1967 political satire flick, *The President's Analyst*, they imploded in 1968. After two solo albums, Cliff de Young (vocals) pursued an acting career which continues to this day with regular television credits. Ralph Shuckett (keyboards) joined the Peanut Butter Conspiracy before making a name for himself in television soundtracks. Douglas Lubahn (bass) went into session work, notably for the Doors before joining Dreams and even turning up with Billy Squier in the 80s. Dallas Taylor (drums) became the regular drummer for Crosby, Stills, Nash And Young, and after a brief excursion into the obscure Ohio Knox, worked with Steven Stills Band and Manassas. Danny Kortchmar (lead guitar) and Michael Ney (second drummer) both joined up with Carole King in her early band the City, and Kortchmar remained her regular guitarist for many years and was a mainstay friend, guitarist in James Taylor's career. Only Bob Seal (guitar) seems to have returned to oblivion.

●ALBUMS: *Clear Light* (Elektra 1967)★★★. Subsequent albums under the name Clearlight belong to a Scandinavian band unconnected to the original.

CLIFFORD, BUZZ

b. Reese Francis Clifford III, 8 October 1942, Berwyn, Illinois, USA. Buzz Clifford is best known for his one US Top 10 single, 'Baby Sittin' Boogie', in 1961. Clifford learned to play guitar as a child and, enamoured of television westerns, created his own cowboy songs. After winning a talent contest in New Jersey as a teenager, he was signed to Columbia Records. His first single, 'Hello Mr. Moonlight', did not chart but 'Baby Sittin' Boogie', a novelty rock 'n' roll number, charted on the pop, country and R&B charts. Clifford went on to record further singles for Columbia and became a producer for ABC-Paramount in the late 60s. He attempted a comeback first as a folk rock singer for RCA Records and later as a long-haired country rock artist in 1969. He released a final album on Dot Records that year, which did not reach the charts.

●ALBUMS: *Baby Sittin' With Buzz* (Columbia 1961)★★★, *See Your Way Clear* (Dot 1969)★★.

CLINE, PATSY

b. Virginia Patterson Hensley, 8 September 1932, Gore, near Winchester, Virginia, USA, d. 5 March 1963, Camden, Tennessee, USA. Her father, Sam Hensley, already had two children from a previous marriage, when he married Hilda, Patsy's mother - a woman many years his junior. Hilda was only 16 when Patsy was born and they grew up like sisters. At the age of four Patsy, influenced by a film of Shirley Temple and, without tuition, learned tap dancing and showed an interest in music that was encouraged by the piano-playing of her step-sister whenever she was taken to her house. In spite of financial hardships, her parents gave her a piano for her seventh birthday, which she soon learned to play by ear.

Hilda could never understand her daughter's affinity with country music, since neither she nor Sam was interested in the genre. At the age of 10, Patsy was eagerly listening to broadcasts from the *Grand Ole Opry* and informing everyone that one day she would be an *Opry* star.

In the early 40s, the Hensleys relocated to Winchester, where Patsy became interested in the country show on WINC presented by Joltin' Jim McCoy. Apart from playing records, he also fronted his own band in live spots on the show. At 14 Patsy contacted McCoy and told him she wanted to sing on his show. He was impressed by her voice and Virginia Hensley quickly became a regular singer with his Melody Playboys. She also became associated with pianist William 'Jumbo' Rinker with whom she sang at local venues, and she left school to work in Gaunt's Drug Store to help the family finances. In 1948, Wally Fowler, a noted *Opry* artist whose gospel show was broadcast live on WSM, appeared at the Palace Theatre in Winchester. Patsy brazenly manoeuvred herself backstage on the night and confronted Fowler. She told him that she was a singer and, taken aback by her approach, he sarcastically suggested that maybe she was Winchester's answer to Kitty Wells, but nevertheless let her sing for him. Realizing this might be her big chance, she sang unaccompanied and impressed Fowler so much that he included her on that night's show. Afterwards, he took Patsy home to seek Hilda's permission for her to audition for WSM in Nashville. A few weeks later, Hilda received his call to take Patsy to see Jim Denny, the manager of the *Opry*. With accompaniment from the legendary pianist, Moon Mullican, she successfully auditioned. Denny was impressed and asked her to remain in Nashville so that he could arrange an *Opry* appearance. Without money, although too embarrassed to admit it, and accompanied by the two younger children, Hilda pleaded they must return to Winchester that day. Before they left, Roy Acuff, who had heard Patsy's singing from an adjoining studio, asked her to sing on his *Noon Time Neighbours* broadcast that day.

Her hopes that she would hear from Denny were never realized and Patsy returned to the drug store and singing locally. In 1952, she met Bill Peer, a man destined to have great influence on her life. A disc jockey and musician, who had run bands for some years, Peer was then touring the Tri-State Moose Lodge circuit with his band, the Melody Boys and Girls. He hired Patsy as lead vocalist and on 27 September 1952, she made her first appearance with him at the Brunswick Moose Club in Maryland. Peer did not think the name Virginia was suitable and wrongly assuming that her second name was Patricia, he billed her as Patsy Hensley. Peer quickly realised her potential and began to push Patsy's career to the neglect of his own family. On 27 February 1953, Patsy married Gerald Cline, whom she had met at a show only a few weeks earlier. On the night of her marriage, Patsy appeared on stage for the first time as Patsy Cline.

Although Patsy Cline's name was known over a considerable area, Peer knew that she needed national exposure. He realized that she could not achieve this with his band

and sought a recording contract for her. A demo tape attracted attention and on 30 September 1954, she signed a two year contract with Four-Star, a Pasadena-based independent company, once owned by Gene Autry, whose president was now William A. McCall, a man not highly regarded by many in the music business. The contract said that all Patsy Cline's recordings would remain Four-Star property. In effect, she could only record songs that McCall published and, being a non-writer herself, she was faced with any material he chose. Cline made her first four recordings on 1 June 1955, in Bradley's 'Quonset' hut studios in Nashville, under the production of pianist, guitarist and arranger Owen Bradley. 'A Church, A Courtroom And Then Goodbye', penned by Eddie Miller and W.S. Stevenson, was the selected song but it failed to make the country charts. (W.S. Stevenson was a pseudonym used by McCall, seemingly for his own songs, but it is known that, on occasions, he applied the name to songs that were written by other writers, such as Donn Hecht, who were under contract to his label.) Cline made further recordings on 5 January and 22 April 1956, including the toe-tapping 'I Love You Honey' and the rockabilly 'Stop, Look And Listen'. The anticipated country chart entries did not occur and she became despondent. Her private life took a new turn in April 1956, when she met Charlie Dick, the man destined to be her second husband, when her marriage to Cline ended in 1957.

In an effort to find a country hit, McCall commissioned songwriter Hecht to produce one. Hecht suggested 'Walking After Midnight' a blues type number that he had initially written for Kay Starr, but she had turned it down. Cline did not like the song either, claiming it was 'nothing but a little old pop song'. Under pressure from Decca (who leased her records from Four-Star), she recorded it, on 8 November 1956, in a session that also included 'A Poor Man's Roses (Or A Rich Man's Gold)' and 'The Heart You Break May Be Your Own'. On 28 January 1957, although preferring 'A Poor Man's Roses', she sang 'Walking After Midnight' on the Arthur Godfrey *Talent Scouts* show. On 11 February, Decca released the two songs in a picture sleeve on 78 rpm and it immediately entered both country and pop charts. Cline first sang 'Walking After Midnight' on the *Opry* on 16 February. The song finally peaked as a number 2 country and number 12 pop hit, while 'A Poor Man's Roses' also made number 14 on the country chart. It was later estimated that the record sold around three-quarters of a million copies.

In July 1959, she recorded two fine gospel numbers 'Life's Railroad To Heaven' and 'Just A Closer Walk With Thee' but although Decca released various records the follow-up chart hit did not materialize. In truth, Decca had only 11 songs, recorded between February 1958 and November 1960, from which to choose. It was possible Cline chose to record the minimum number necessary under the terms of her Four-Star contract in the hope McCall would drop her, thus enabling her to pick up a promised Decca contract. The first song she recorded under her new association with Decca, on 16 November 1960, was 'I Fall To Pieces' by Hank Cochran and Harlan Howard. It quickly became a country number 1 and also peaked at number 12 on the pop charts.

In August 1961 she completed a four day recording session which included 'True Love', 'The Wayward Wind', 'San Antonio Rose' and her now legendary version of 'Crazy'. Willie Nelson, who had written the song, had demoed it almost as a narration, which Cline did not like. With Owen Bradley's persuasion she produced her stunning version in one take. The recording was a number 2 country and a number 9 pop hit. In 1962, 'She's Got You' was an even bigger country hit, spending five weeks at number 1, while peaking at number 14 in the pop charts. It also became her first entry in the Top 50 UK pop charts. Meanwhile her marriage to Charlie Dick was becoming more stormy. She had long ago discarded her cowgirl outfits for more conventional dress and she seemed indifferent to her weight problem. Her wild life style included affairs, particularly an enduring affair with Faron Young. Her last recording session took place on 7 February 1963, when she recorded 'He Called Me Baby', 'You Took Him Off My Hands' and 'I'll Sail My Ship Alone'. The latter, ironically, was a song written by Moon Mullican, the pianist who had played for her *Opry* audition in 1948.

Patsy appeared in Birmingham, Alabama with Tex Ritter and Jerry Lee Lewis on 2 March 1963, following which she agreed with other artists to appear in a charity show in Kansas City the next day, a show staged for the widow of Jack Call, a noted disc jockey on KCMK, known as Cactus Jack, who had died in a car crash. The weather was bad on 4 March but early on the afternoon of 5 March, in spite of further adverse weather forecasts, Patsy, together with country singers Cowboy Copas and Hawkshaw Hawkins, set off on the five-hundred-mile flight to Nashville, in a small aircraft piloted by Randy Hughes, the son-in-law of Copas and Patsy's lover and manager. Hughes first landed at Little Rock to avoid rain and sleet and then at Dyersburg to refuel, where he was warned of bad weather in the area. They encountered further bad weather and, although the exact reason for the crash is unknown, the life of Patsy Cline came to an end some fifty minutes later, when the aircraft came down in woodland about a mile off Highway 70, near Camden, Tennessee. At the time of her death, Patsy's recording of 'Leaving On Your Mind' was in both country and pop charts and before the year was over, both 'Sweet Dreams' and 'Faded Love' became Top 10 country and minor pop hits.

It has been suggested that Patsy Cline was not an outstanding performer of up-tempo material, but it is an undisputed fact that she could extract every possible piece of emotion out of a country weepie. Her versions of 'Walking After Midnight', 'I Fall To Pieces', 'Crazy', 'She's Got You' and 'Sweet Dreams' represent five of the greatest recordings ever made in country music. Those in any doubt of her standing should consult the *Billboard* back-catalogue country chart; her *Greatest Hits* has been number 1 for over four years!

●ALBUMS: *Patsy Cline* (Decca 1957)★★★★, *Showcase* (Decca 1961)★★★★, *Sentimentally Yours* (Decca 1962)★★★★, *Tribute To Patsy Cline* (1963)★★★★, *Legend* (1964)★★★, *Portait Of Patsy Cline* (Decca 1964)★★★★, *How A Heartache Begins* (1965)★★★, *Reflections* (1965)★★★, *Gotta Lot Of Rhythm* (1965)★★★, *The Last Sessions* (MCA 1980)★★★★, *Sweet Dreams* film soundtrack (1985)★★★, *Live At The Opry* (MCA 1988)★★★, *Live - Volume Two* (1989)★★★.
●COMPILATIONS: *The Patsy Cline Story* (Decca 1963)★★★★, *Golden Hits* (1966)★★★, *Patsy Cline's Greatest Hits* (Decca 1967)★★★, *Greatest Hits* (MCA 1973)★★★★★, *Golden Greats* (MCA 1979)★★★★★, *20 Classic Tracks* (Starburst 1987)★★★, *12 Greatest Hits* (MCA 1988)★★★, *Dreaming* (Platinum Music 1988,)★★★, *20 Golden Hits* (Deluxe 1989)★★★, *The Patsy Cline Collection* 4-CD box set (MCA 1991)★★★★★, *The Definitive* (1992)★★★, *Discovery* (Prism Leisure 1994)★★★, *Premier Collection* (Pickwick 1994)★★★, *The Patsy Cline Story* (MCA 1994)★★★★, *Thinking Of You* (Summit 1995)★★★, *Today, Tomorrow And Forever* 2-CD (Parade 1995)★★★.
●VIDEOS: *The Real Thing* (1989), *The Real Patsy Cline* (Prism Leisure 1991), *Remembering Patsy* (1993).
●FURTHER READING: *Patsy Cline: Sweet Dreams* Ellis Nassour. *Honky Tonk Angel: The Intimate Story Of Patsy Cline* Ellis Nassour. *Patsy: The Life And Times Of Patsy Cline* Margaret Jones.

CLOUDS

As part of the expanding UK progressive music boom in 1969, the musically competent Clouds sadly failed to capture record buyers' imagination. Billy Ritchie (keyboards), Harry Hughes (drums) and Ian Ellis (bass), made the trek to London to find fame and fortune. They had previously been members of various Scottish bands but left their homeland in November 1966 and were signed to Robert Stigwood's NEMS Group as One Two Three. They supported Jimi Hendrix at his famous Saville Theatre gig but were dropped soon afterwards by the tough Stigwood. The Chrysalis agency signed and rechristened them Clouds. They made two interesting albums before they disintegrated, unable to find a niche among an overcrowded progressive music scene.
●ALBUMS: *Scrapbook* (Island 1969)★★★, *Watercolour Days* (Island 1971)★★★.

COLLECTORS

Formed in Vancouver, Canada, in 1961 and originally known as the C-Fun Classics, the original line-up - Howie Vickers (vocals), Brian Russell (guitar), Claire Lawrence (saxophone), Glenn Miller (bass) and Gary Taylor (drums) - recorded locally with some success before unveiling a new name, the Collectors, with the single 'Looking At A Baby' in 1967. By this point Russell and Taylor had been replaced by Bill Henderson and Ross Turney. The Collectors were then drawn towards US west

coast venues where they established a positive reputation for their complex arrangements, soaring harmonies and extended improvisations. Their debut album, *The Collectors* aka *New Vibrations From Canada* admirably displayed such diverse talents. The group's second album, *Grass And Wild Strawberries*, was a loosely framed concept album. Although their imaginative use of time signatures and woodwind garnered critical plaudits, this was not transferred into sales, and the Collectors' career ebbed with two non-album singles. The departure of Vickers prompted an internal rethink and the remaining quartet abandoned the name and emerged as Chilliwack in 1971.
●ALBUMS: *The Collectors* aka *New Vibrations From Canada* (Warners 1968)★★★, *Grass And Wild Strawberries* (Warners 1969)★★★.
●COMPILATIONS: *Seventeenth Summer* (1986)★★★.

COLLINS, GLENDA

b. 1945, London, England. Glenda Collins sang on numerous radio shows and in cabaret at the age of 12. In 1960 she was signed by Decca Records who issued her first three singles, 'Take A Chance', 'The Age For Love' and 'Find Another Fool'. In 1962 Collins was introduced to enigmatic producer Joe Meek, who oversaw the rest of her output. 'I Lost My Heart At The Fairground' contains all of Meek's trademarks - sound effects, echo, pulsating beat and strong melody. On this recording Collins was backed by the Tornadoes, whereas the equally powerful follow-up, 'If You've Got To Pick A Baby', featured the Outlaws, with guitarist Ritchie Blackmore adding already distinctive accompaniment. Six more singles followed, the best of which was Collins' final release, 'It's Hard To Believe It', issued in 1966. Her recording career ended when Meek committed suicide in February 1967. Collins persevered on the cabaret circuit until the end of the 60s before opting to retire from music. Although denied commercial success, Collins' records remain among the finest Meek produced.
●COMPILATIONS: *Been Invited To A Party: The Singles 1963-1966* (Connoisseur Collection 1990)★★★.

COLLINS, JUDY

b. 1 May 1939, Seattle, Washington, USA. One of the leading female singers to emerge from America's folk revival in the early 60s, Judy Collins was originally trained as a classical pianist. Having discovered traditional music while a teenager, she began singing in the clubs of Central City and Denver, before embarking on a full-time career with engagements at Chicago's Gate Of Horn and New York's famed Gerde's. Signed to Elektra Records in 1961, Collins' early releases emphasized her traditional repertoire. However, by the release of *Judy Collins #3*, her clear, virginal soprano was tackling more contemporary material. This pivotal selection, which included Bob Dylan's 'Farewell', was arranged by future Byrds' guitarist Jim (Roger) McGuinn. *Judy Collins' Fifth Album* was the artist's last purely folk collection. Compositions by Dylan, Richard Farina, Eric Andersen and Gordon Lightfoot had gained the ascendancy, but Collins henceforth combined such talent with songs culled from theatre's bohemian fringes. *In My Life* embraced Jacques Brel, Bertolt Brecht, Kurt Weill and the then-unknown Leonard Cohen; on *Wildflower* she introduced Joni Mitchell and in the process enjoyed a popular hit with 'Both Sides Now'. These releases were also marked by Joshua Rifkin's studied string arrangements, which also became a feature of the singer's work. Collins' 1968 release, *Who Knows Where The Time Goes* is arguably her finest work. A peerless backing group, including Stephen Stills and Van Dyke Parks, added sympathetic support to her interpretations, while her relationship with the former resulted in his renowned composition, 'Suite: Judy Blue Eyes'. The singer's next release, *Whales And Nightingales*, was equally impressive, and included the million-selling single, 'Amazing Grace'. However, its sculpted arrangements were reminiscent of earlier work and although Collins' own compositions were meritorious, she was never a prolific writer. Her reliance on outside material grew increasingly problematic as the era of classic songwriters drew to a close and the artist looked to outside interests. She remained committed to the political causes born out of the 60s protest movement and fashioned a new career by co-producing *Antonia: Portrait Of A Woman*, a film documentary about her former teacher which was nominated for an Academy Award. Collins did secure another international hit in 1975 with a version of Stephen Sondheim's 'Send In The Clowns'. Although subsequent recordings lack her former perception, and indeed have grown increasingly infrequent, she remains an immensely talented interpreter. In recent years Collins has shown a gift for writing novels.

●ALBUMS: *A Maid Of Constant Sorrow* (Elektra 1961)★★★, *The Golden Apples Of The Sun* (Elektra 1962)★★★, *Judy Collins #3* (Elektra 1964)★★★, *The Judy Collins Concert* (Elektra 1964)★★, *Judy Collins' Fifth Album* (Elektra 1965)★★★, *In My Life* (1966)★★★★, *Wildflowers* (Elektra 1967)★★★★, *Who Knows Where The Time Goes* (Elcktra 1968)★★★★, *Whales And Nightingales* (Elektra 1970)★★★, *Living* (Elektra 1971)★★★, *True Stories And Other Dreams* (Elektra 1973)★★★, *Judith* (Elektra 1975)★★★, *Bread And Roses* (Elektra 1976)★★★, *Hard Times For Lovers* (Elektra 1979)★★, *Running For My Life* (Elektra 1980)★★★, *Time Of Our Lives* (Elektra 1982)★★, *Home Again* (1984)★★, *Trust Your Heart* (Gold Castle 1987)★★, *Sanity And Grace* (Gold Castle 1987)★★, *Fires Of Eden* (CBS 1990)★★, *Judy Sings Dylan ... Just Like A Woman* (Geffen 1994)★★, *Come Rejoice: A Judy Collins Christmas* (Mesa 1994)★★★, *Shameless* (Mesa 1995)★★★.

●COMPILATIONS: *Recollections* (Elektra 1969)★★★★, *Colours Of The Day: The Best Of Judy Collins* (Elektra 1972)★★★★, *So Early In The Spring, The First 15 Years* (Elektra 1977)★★★★, *Most Beautiful Songs Of Judy Collins* (Elektra 1979)★★★★, *Amazing Grace* (1985)★★★, *Live At Newport* (Vanguard 1994)★★★,

●FURTHER READING: *Trust Your Heart: An Autobiography*, Judy Collins. *The Judy Collins Songbook*, Judy Collins and Herbert Haufrecht. *Judy Collins*, Vivian Claire. *Shameless*, Judy Collins.

COLOSSEUM

The commercial acceptance of jazz rock in the UK was mainly due to Colosseum. The band was formed in 1968 from the nucleus of the musicians who accompanied John Mayall on his influential album *Bare Wires*. Colosseum comprised Jon Hiseman (b. 21 June 1944, London, England; drums), Dick Heckstall-Smith (b. 26 September 1934, Ludlow, Shropshire, England; saxophone), Dave Greenslade (b. 18 January 1943, Woking, Surrey, England; keyboards), Tony Reeves (b. 18 April 1943, London, England; bass), James Litherland (b. 6 September 1949, Manchester, England; guitar/vocals). Ex-Graham Bond Organisation members Heckstall-Smith and Hiseman took their former boss's pivotal work and made a success of it. From the opening track of their strong debut, *Those Who Are About To Die Salute You* (1969), with Bond's 'Walkin' In The Park', the band embarked on a brief excursion that would showcase each member as a strong musical talent. Heckstall-Smith, already a seasoned jazz professional, combined with 19-year-old Litherland to integrate furious wah-wah guitar with bursting saxophone. Greenslade's booming Hammond organ intertwined with Reeves' melodically inventive bass patterns. This sparkling cocktail was held together by the masterful pyrotechnics of Hiseman, whose solos, featuring his dual bass drum pedal technique, were incredible. *Valentyne Suite* the same year maintained the momentum, notably with the outstanding Heckstall-Smith composition 'The Grass Is Greener'. As with many great things, the end came quite soon, although the departing member Litherland was replaced with a worthy successor in Dave 'Clem' Clempson (b. 5 September 1949, England). In order to accommodate Clempson's wish to concentrate on guitar they further enlisted Greenslade's former boss in the Thunderbirds, Chris Farlowe. His strong vocals gave a harder edge to their work. Following the departure of Reeves and the recruitment of Mark Clarke, their work took on a more rock-orientated approach. The end came in October 1971 with their last studio album, *Daughter Of Time*, quickly followed by *Colosseum Live*. Hiseman and Clarke formed Tempest, but after two mediocre albums he resurrected the name in the shape of Colosseum II in 1975. The new version was much heavier in sound and featured ex-Thin Lizzy guitarist Gary Moore, future Whitesnake bassist Neil Murray and future Rainbow keyboard player Don Airey. Vocalist Mike Starrs completed the line-up and they progressed through the mid-70s with three albums, before Colosseum II finally collapsed through Hiseman's exhaustion, and his wish to return to his jazz roots. He eventually joined his wife Barbara Thompson playing jazz with her band Paraphernalia. Colosseum will be remembered for their initial pioneering work in making jazz rock accessible to a wider market. In 1997 most of the original band reconvened with Farlowe as vocalist. Although Hiseman had often mooted the idea of a reunion, he stated in 1997 that the time 'seemed right'.

● ALBUMS: *Those Who Are About To Die Salute You* (Fontana 1969)★★★★, *Valentyne Suite* (Vertigo 1969)★★★★, *The Daughter Of Time* (Vertigo 1970)★★, *Live* (1971)★★★, *Strange New Flesh* (1976)★★, *Electric Savage* (1977)★★, *Wardance* (1977)★★.

● COMPILATIONS: *The Grass Is Greener* (1969)★★★, *Collector's Colosseum* (1971)★★★, *Pop Chronik* (1974)★★★, *Epitaph* (1986), *The Golden Decade Of Colosseum* (1990)★★★.

COLTRANE, JOHN

b. John William Coltrane, 23 September 1926, Hamlet, North Carolina, USA, d. 17 July 1967. Coltrane grew up in the house of his maternal grandfather, Rev. William Blair (who gave him his middle name), a preacher and community spokesman. While he was taking clarinet lessons at school, his school band leader suggested his mother buy him an alto saxophone. In 1939 his grandfather and then his father died. After finishing high school he joined his mother in Philadelphia. He spent a short period at the Ornstein School of Music and the Granoff Studios, where he won scholarships for both performance and composition, but his real education began when he started gigging. Two years' military service was spent in a navy band (1945-46), after which he toured in the King Kolax and Eddie 'Cleanhead' Vinson bands, playing goodtime, rhythmic big band music. It was while playing in the Dizzy Gillespie Big Band (1949-51) that he switched to tenor saxophone. Coltrane's musical roots were in acoustic black music that combined swing and instrumental prowess in solos, the forerunner of R&B.

He toured with Earl Bostic (1952), Johnny Hodges (1953-54) and Jimmy Smith (1955). However, it was his induction into Miles Davis's band of 1955 - rightly termed the Classic Quintet - that he was noticed. Next to Davis's filigree sensitivity, Coltrane sounds awkward and crude, and Davis received criticism for his choice of saxophonist. The only precedent for such modernist interrogation of tenor harmony was John Gilmore's playing with Sun Ra. Critics found Coltrane's tone raw and shocking after years in which the cool school of Lester Young and Stan Getz had held sway. It was generally acknowledged, however, that his ideas were first rate. Along with Sonny Rollins, he became New York's most in-demand hard bop tenor player: 1957 saw him appearing on 21 important recordings, and enjoying a brief but fruitful association with Thelonious Monk. That same year he returned to Philadelphia and kicked his longtime heroin habit and started to develop his own music (Coltrane's notes to the later *A Love Supreme* refer to a 'spiritual awakening'). He also found half of his 'classic' quartet: at the Red Rooster (a nightclub that he visited with trumpeter Calvin Massey, an old friend from the 40s), he discovered pianist McCoy Tyner and bassist Jimmy Garrison.

After recording numerous albums for the Prestige label, Coltrane signed to Atlantic Records and, on 15 August 1959, he recorded *Giant Steps*. Although it did not use the talents of his new friends from Philadelphia, it featured a dizzying torrent of tenor solos that harked back to the pressure-cooker creativity of bebop, while incorporating the muscular gospel attack of hard bop. Pianist Tommy Flanagan (later celebrated for his sensitive backings for singers like Ella Fitzgerald and Tony Bennett) and drummer Art Taylor provided the best performances of their lives. Although this record is rightly hailed as a masterpiece, it encapsulated a problem: where could hard bop go to from here? Coltrane knew the answer: after a second spell with Davis (1958-60), he formed his best-known quartet with Tyner, Garrison and the amazing polyrhythmic drummer Elvin Jones. Jazz has been recovering ever since.

The social situation of the 60s meant that Coltrane's innovations were simultaneously applauded as *avant garde* statements of black revolution and efficiently recorded and marketed. The Impulse! label, to which he switched from Atlantic in 1961, has a staggering catalogue that includes most of Coltrane's landmark records plus several experimental sessions from the mid-60s that still remain unreleased (although they missed *My Favourite Things*, recorded in 1960 for Atlantic, in which Coltrane established the soprano saxophone as an important instrument). Between 1961 and his death in 1967, Coltrane made music that has become the foundation of modern jazz. For commercial reasons Impulse! Records had a habit of delaying the release of his music: fans emerged from the live performances in shock at the pace of his evolution. A record of *Ballads* and an encounter with Duke Ellington in 1962 seemed designed to deflect criticisms of coarseness, although Coltrane later attributed their relatively temperate ambience to persistent problems with his mouthpiece. *A Love Supreme* was more hypnotic and lulling on record than in live performance, but nevertheless a classic. After that the records became wilder and wilder. The unstinting commitment to new horizons led to ruptures within the group. Elvin Jones left after Coltrane incorporated a second drummer (Rashied Ali). McCoy Tyner was replaced by Alice McLeod (who married Coltrane in 1966). Coltrane was especially interested in new saxophone players and *Ascension* (1965) made space for Archie Shepp, Pharoah Sanders, Marion Brown and John Tchicai. Eric Dolphy, although he represented a different tradition of playing from Coltrane (a modernist projection of Charlie Parker), had also been a frequent guest player with the quartet in the early 60s, touring Europe with them in 1961. *Interstellar Space* (1967), a duet record, pitched Coltrane's tenor against Ali's drums, and provides a fascinating hint of new directions. Coltrane's death in 1967 robbed *avant garde* jazz of its father figure. The commercial ubiquity of fusion in the 70s obscured his music and the 80s jazz revival concentrated on his hard bop period. Only Reggie Workman's Ensemble and Ali's Phalanx carried the huge ambition of Coltrane's later music into the 90s. As soloists, though, few tenor players have remained untouched by his example. It is interesting that the saxophonists Coltrane encouraged did not sound like him: since his death, his 'sound' has become a mainstream commodity, from the Berklee College Of Music style of Michael Brecker to the 'European' variant of Jan Garbarek. New stars like Andy Sheppard have established new audiences for jazz without finding new ways of playing. Coltrane's music - like that of Jimi Hendrix - ran parallel with a tide of mass political action and consciousness. Perhaps those conditions are required for the creation of such innovative and intense music. Nevertheless, Coltrane's music reached a wide audience, and was particularly popular with the younger generation of listeners who were also big fans of rock music. *A Love Supreme* sold sufficient copies to win a gold disc, while the Byrds used the theme of Coltrane's tune 'India' as the basis of their hit single 'Eight Miles High'. Perhaps by alerting the rock audience to the presence of jazz, Coltrane can be said to have - inadvertently - prepared the way for fusion.

●ALBUMS: with Hank Mobley *Two Tenors* (1956)★★★, with various artists *Tenor Conclave* (1957)★★★, *Thelonious Monk With John Coltrane* (1957)★★★, *Dakar* (Original Jazz Classics 1957)★★★, *John Coltrane - Paul Quinichette Quintet* (1957)★★★, *Cattin' With Coltrane And Quinichette* (Original Jazz Classics 1957)★★★, *Wheelin' And Dealing* (Original Jazz Classics 1957)★★★, *The First Trane* (1957)★★★, *Miles Davis And John Coltrane Play Richard Rodgers* (1958)★★★, *Lush Life* (Original Jazz Classics 1958)★★★, *Traneing In* (Original Jazz Classics 1958)★★★, *Tenor Conclave* (Original Jazz Classics 1958)★★★, *Blue Train* (Blue Note 1958)★★★, *Trane's Reign* (1958)★★★, *Soultrane* (Original Jazz Classics 1958)★★★★, *Kenny Burrell - John Coltrane* (1958)★★★, *Settin The Pace* (Original Jazz Classics 1958)★★★, *Coltrane Plays For Lovers* (1959)★★★, *The Believer* (1959)★★★, *The Last Trane* (Original Jazz Classics 1959)★★★, *Black Pearls* (Original Jazz Classics 1959)★★★, *Stardust* (1959)★★★, *The Standard Coltrane* (Prestige 1959)★★★, *Bahia* (Original Jazz Classics 1959)★★★, John Coltrane And The Jazz Giants (Prestige 1959)★★★, *Coltrane Time* (1959)★★★, with Milt Jackson *Bags And Trane* (1959)★★★, *Giant Steps* (Atlantic 1960)★★★★★, *Coltrane Jazz* (Atlantic 1961)★★★★, with Don Cherry *The Avant-Garde* (Atlantic 1961)★★★, *My Favourite Things* (Atlantic 1961)★★★★, *Coltrane Plays The Blues* (Atlantic 1961)★★★★, *Coltrane's Sound* (Atlantic 1961)★★★★, *Africa/Brass* (MCA 1961)★★★★, *Live At The Village Vanguard* (MCA 1961)★★★, *Olé Coltrane* (Atlantic 1962)★★★, *John Coltrane Quartet* (1962)★★★, *Coltrane* (MCA 1962)★★★★, *Ballads* (Impulse 1963)★★★★, *Duke Ellington And John Coltrane* (1963)★★★, *... And Johnny Hartman* (Impulse 1963)★★★, *Impressions* (MCA 1963)★★★★, *Live At Birdland* (Charly 1964)★★★, *Crescent* (Impulse 1964)★★★, *A Love Supreme* (MCA

1965)★★★★★, *The John Coltrane Quartet Plays* (Impulse 1965)★★★, *Kule Se Mama* (1965)★★★, *Ascension* (1965)★★★★, *Transition* (Impulse 1965)★★★★, *Selflessness* rec. 1963, 1965 (1966)★★★, *Meditations* (Impulse 1966)★★★★, with Archie Shepp *New Thing At Newport* (Impulse 1966)★★★, *Om* (Impulse 1966)★★★, *Live At The Village Vanguard Again!* (Impulse 1966)★★★, *Expression* (Impulse 1967)★★★, *Sun Ship* rec. 1965 (1971)★★★, *Dear Old Stockholm* (Impulse 1965)★★★, *Live In Seattle* rec. 1965 (Impulse 1971)★★★, *Africa Brass, Volume Two* rec. 1961 (1974)★★★★, *Interstellar Space* rec. 1967 (Impulse 1974)★★★, *First Meditations - For Quartet* rec. 1965 (Impulse 1977)★★★, *The Other Village Vanguard Tapes* rec. 1961 (1977)★★★, *Afro-Blue Impressions* rec. 1962 (Pablo 1977)★★★, *The Paris Concert* rec. 1962 (1979)★★★, *The European Tour* rec. 1962 (1980)★★★, *Bye Bye Blackbird* rec. 1962 (1981)★★★, *Live At Birdland - Featuring Eric Dolphy* rec. 1962 (1982)★★★, *Stellar Regions* rec. 1967 (Impulse 1995).

●COMPILATIONS: *The Art Of John Coltrane - The Atlantic Years* (1973)★★★★, *The Mastery Of John Coltrane, Vols. 1-4* (1978)★★★★, *The Gentle Side Of John Coltrane* (Impulse 1992)★★★★, *The Major Works Of John Coltrane* (Impulse 1992)★★★★, *The Impulse! Years* (Impulse 1993)★★★★, *The Heavyweight Champion* 7-CD box set (Rhino/Atlantic 1995)★★★★★.

●VIDEOS: *The World According To John Coltrane* (1993).

●FURTHER READING: *Trane 'N ' Me*, Andrew Nathaniel White. *About John Coltrane*, Tim Gelatt (ed.). *John Coltrane, Discography*, Brian Davis. *The Artistry Of John Coltrane*, John Coltrane. *The Style Of John Coltrane*, William Shadrack Cole. *Chasin' The Trane*, J. C. Thomas. *Coltrane*, Cuthbert Ormond Simpkins. *John Coltrane*, Brian Priestley. *John Coltrane*, Bill Cole. *Ascension: John Coltrane And His Quest*, Eric Nisenson.

CONCORDS

Formed in 1959 in the Brighton Beach enclave of Brooklyn, New York, USA, the Concords' membership originally teamed Mike Lewis (lead and tenor), Dickie Goldman (lead and tenor), Murray Moshe (baritone), Charles 'Chippy' Presti (second tenor) and Steve Seider (bass). Signed by RCA Records, the Concords made their debut with a vocal group standard, 'Again'. Songwriter Stu Wiener then took them to his father's Gramercy Records label, where they released two singles, 'Cross My Heart' and 'My Dreams'. After losing Goldman and deciding to continue as a quartet, they chose to re-release 'Again' on Rust Records in 1962, before finding a more permanent home at Herald Records. Their most successful single, 'Marlene', followed, which became a major regional hit in the north west, and led to them performing in Detroit with the Supremes. However, it was not enough to dampen disquiet in the ranks and the Concords broke up

in 1963. Lewis briefly formed the Planets but returned to a reshuffled Concords in 1964, wherein he and Seider were joined by Teddy Graybill (ex-Stardrifts), Sal Tepedino (ex-Travelers) and Bobby Ganz. A new contract with Epic Records led to the release of 'Should I Cry', although Lewis and Wiener enjoyed more success with their production of Roddie Joy's 'Come Back Baby'. A remake of the Quintones' 'Down The Aisle Of Love' was the final Concords' single in 1966, with only Lewis remaining in the music industry thereafter (principally as a writer and producer).
●ALBUMS: *The Concords* (Crystal Ball 1991)★★.

CONLEY, ARTHUR

b. 4 January 1946, Atlanta, Georgia, USA. Recalled as something of a one-hit-wonder, this Otis Redding protégé remains underrated. Conley first recorded for the NRC label as Arthur And The Corvets. After signing to his mentor's, Otis Redding's, Jotis label, further singles were leased to Volt and Stax Records before 'Sweet Soul Music' (1967) hit both the US R&B and pop charts. A thin reworking of Sam Cooke's 'Yeah Man' saw the song's original lyrics amended to pay homage to several contemporary soul singers. Although 'Funky Street' was a US Top 20 hit, Redding's tragic death forestalled Conley's progress. Minor successes followed throughout 1968 and 1969 before the singer switched to the Capricorn label in 1971. His debut album, *Sweet Soul Music*, is a strong collection, highlighted by each of his first five singles and two Redding originals. Later Conley had a set of recordings for Swamp Dogg released, and then, having relocated to Europe, a live album recorded in Amsterdam in 1980 under his pseudonym of Lee Roberts finally emerged some eight years later.
●ALBUMS: *Sweet Soul Music* (Atco 1967)★★★★, *Shake, Rattle And Roll* (Atlantic 1967)★★★, *Soul Directions* (Atlantic 1968)★★★, *More Sweet Soul* (Atco 1969)★★★, *One More Sweet Soul Music* (1988)★★, as Lee Roberts And The Sweater *Soulin'* (1988)★★★.
●COMPILATIONS: *Arthur Conley* (1988)★★★.
●FURTHER READING: *Sweet Soul Music*, Peter Guralnick.

CONNIFF, RAY

b. 6 November 1916, Attelboro, Massachusetts, USA. Taught to play the trombone by his father, Conniff studied arranging with the aid of a mail-order course while still at college. In 1934, after graduation, he worked with small bands in Boston before joining Bunny Berigan as trombonist/arranger in 1936. After a spell with Bob Crosby's Bobcats, Conniff spent four years with Artie Shaw and featured on several successful records including 'Concerto For Clarinet', 'Dancing In The Dark' and 'St James Infirmary'. During this period he was also studying at the New York Juilliard School of Music in New York. After army service in World War II Conniff spent some time as an arranger with Harry James, then freelanced while searching for a successful formula for producing hit records. He joined Columbia Records in

1954 and worked with several of their artists, including Johnnie Ray, Rosemary Clooney, Guy Mitchell and Marty Robbins. In 1954 he provided the arrangement for Don Cherry's million-seller, 'Band Of Gold', and in 1956 was given the chance, by Columbia producer Mitch Miller, to make an album featuring his 'new sound'. The successful result, *'S Wonderful*, was a set of familiar songs with an orchestra, and a cleverly blended mixed chorus of wordless voices, sometimes used as extra instruments within the songs' arrangements. *'S Wonderful* was followed, naturally, by *'S Marvellous* and *'S Awful Nice*, all in the same vein. *It's The Talk Of The Town*, in 1960, featured a larger chorus, and for the first time they sang words. From 1957-68 Conniff had 28 albums in the US Top 40, including *Say It With Music (A Touch Of Latin)*, *Memories Are Made Of This*, and in 1966, the million-seller, *Somewhere My Love*. The album's title track, 'Lara's Theme' from the film *Doctor Zhivago* (1965), also made the US Top 10 singles chart. In 1969 he topped the UK album charts with *His Orchestra, His Chorus, His Singers, His Sound*, and in 1974 became the first American popular musician to record in Russia, where he made *Ray Conniff In Moscow*, using a local chorus. More recent albums have included three Spanish sets, *Amor, Amor*, *Exclusivamente Latino* and *Fantastico*, and *The Nashville Collection* with country guest stars including Barbara Mandrell, George Jones and Charly McClain who featured on songs as diverse as 'Oh, Lonesome Me' and 'Smoke Gets In Your Eyes'.
●ALBUMS: with Don Cherry *Swingin' For Two* (1956)★★★, *'S Wonderful!* (1957)★★★★, *'S Marvelous* (1957)★★★★, *'S Awful Nice* (1958)★★★★, *Concert In Rhythm* (1958)★★★, *Broadway In Rhythm* (1959)★★★, *Hollywood In Rhythm* (1959)★★★, with Billy Butterfield *Conniff Meets Butterfield* (1959)★★★, *Christmas With Conniff* (1959)★★★, *It's The Talk Of The Town* (1960)★★★, *Concert In Rhythm - Volume II* (1960)★★★, *Young At Heart* (1960)★★★, *Hi-fi Companion Album* (1960)★★★★, *Say It With Music (A Touch Of Latin)* (1960)★★★, *Memories Are Made Of This* (1961)★★★, *Somebody Loves Me* (1961)★★★, *So Much In Love* (1962)★★★, *'S Continental* (1962)★★★★, *Rhapsody In Rhythm* (1962)★★★★, *We Wish You A Merry Christmas* (1962)★★★, *The Happy Beat* (1963)★★★, with Butterfield *Just Kiddin' Around* (1963)★★★, *You Make Me Feel So Young* (1964)★★★★, *Speak To Me About Love* (1964)★★★, *Invisible Tears* (1964)★★★, *Friendly Persuasion* (1965)★★★, *Music From Mary Poppins, The Sound Of Music, My Fair Lady & Other Great Movie Themes* (1965)★★, *Love Affair* (1965)★★★, *Happiness Is* (1966)★★★, *Somewhere My Love* (1966)★★★, *Ray Conniff's World Of Hits* (1967)★★★, *En Espanol!* (1967)★★★, *This Is My Song* (1967)★★★, *Hawaiian Album* (1967)★★, *It Must Be Him* (1968)★★★, *Honey* (1968)★★★, *Turn Around Look At Me* (1968)★★★, *I Love How You Love Me* (1969)★★★, *Jean* (1969)★★★, *Bridge Over Troubled Water* (1970)★★, *Concert In Stereo/Live At The Sahara/Tahoe* (1970)★★★, *We've*

Only Just Begun (1970)★★★, *Love Story* (1971)★★★, *Great Contemporary Instrumental Hits* (1971)★★★, *I'd Like To Teach The World To Sing* (1972)★★, *Love Theme From The 'Godfather'* (1972)★★★, *Alone Again (Naturally)* (1972)★★★, *I Can See Clearly Now* (1973)★★★, *You Are The Sunshine Of My Life* (1973)★★★, *Harmony* (1973)★★★, *Evergreens* (1973)★★★, *Love Will Keep Us Together* (1975)★★★, *Plays The Carpenters* (1975)★★★, *Laughter In The Rain* (1975)★★★, *Send In The Clowns* (1976)★★★, *I Write The Songs* (1976)★★★, *Smoke Gets In Your Eyes* (1977)★★★, *If You Leave Me Now* (1977)★★★, *Sentimental Journey* (1978)★★★, *I Will Survive* (1979)★★★, *The Perfect Ten Classics* (1981)★★★, *The Nashville Connection* (1982)★★★, *Amor, Amor* (1984)★★★, *Exclusivamente Latino* (1984)★★★, *Fantastico* (1984)★★★, *Smoke Gets In Your Eyes* (1984)★★★, *Always In My Heart* (1988).
●COMPILATIONS: *'S Wonderful's 'S Marvellous* (1962)★★★★, *Ray Conniff's Greatest Hits* (1969)★★★★, *His Orchestra, His Chorus, His Singers, His Sound* (1969)★★★★, *Happy Beat Of Ray Conniff* (1975)★★★, *The Ray Conniff Songbook* (1984)★★★★, *16 Most Requested Songs* (1993)★★★.

CONRAD, JESS

b. 1935, Brixton, London, England. Christened Jesse James, Conrad began his career as a repertory actor and film extra before being cast as a pop singer in a television play, *Rock-A-Bye Barney*. Initially, his singing voice was overdubbed by that of Gary Mills, but before long life imitated art and Conrad was transformed into a pop adonis. Championed by television producer Jack Good, he appeared in *Oh Boy!*, *Wham!* and *Boy Meets Girl*, which led to a recording contract with Decca Records and some minor early 60s hits with 'Cherry Pie', 'Mystery Girl' and 'Pretty Jenny'. When his recording career waned, he continued acting in low budget movies and pantomime, and in the 70s appeared in the musicals *Joseph And The Amazing Technicolor Dreamcoat* and *Godspell* as well as taking a cameo part in the Sex Pistols' celluloid excursion, *The Great Rock 'N' Roll Swindle*. One of Conrad's early singles, 'This Pullover', was belatedly named the worst single ever made in a novelty compilation of pop atrocities. Conrad continued to work throughout the 80s, and, in 1993, shed his 'squeaky-clean' image when he appeared as Prince Charming, with comedians Charlie Drake and Jim Davidson, in Davidson's 'blue' pantomime, *Sinderella*.
●ALBUMS: *Jess For You* (Decca 1961)★.

CONTOURS

The Contours formed as an R&B vocal group in Detroit in 1959, featuring lead vocalist Billy Gordon, Billy Hoggs, Joe Billingslea and Sylvester Potts. Hubert Johnson joined the line-up in 1960, and it was his cousin Jackie Wilson who secured the group an audition and then a contract with Motown Records in 1961. Initial singles proved unsuccessful, but in 1962 the dance-orientated number 'Do You Love Me' became one of the label's biggest hits to date, topping the R&B charts and reaching number 3 in the US pop listing. The same frantic blend of R&B and the twist dance craze powered the follow-up, 'Shake Sherry', in 1963. Both songs heavily influenced the British beat group scene, with 'Do You Love Me' being covered by Brian Poole And The Tremeloes, Faron's Flamingos and the Dave Clark Five. Unfortunately the Contours were unable to capitalize on their early success, and their exciting, slightly chaotic sound lost favour at Motown, usurped by the choreographed routines and tight harmonies of acts like the Temptations and the Four Tops. As the Contours' line-up went through a rapid series of changes, they scored occasional R&B successes with 'Can You Jerk Like Me', Smokey Robinson's witty 'First I Look At The Purse', and the dance number 'Just A Little Misunderstanding'. Although 'It's So Hard Being A Loser' (1967) was the Contour's last official single, posthumous releases, particularly in Britain, kept their name alive. Former lead vocalist, Dennis Edwards, later enjoyed consistent success with the Temptations, and as a soloist. Versions of the Contours appeared on the revival circuit from 1972 onwards, and while Johnson committed suicide on 11 July 1981, a trio consisting of Billingslea, Potts and Jerry Green were still performing into the 80s. In 1988, 'Do You Love Me' returned to the US Top 20 on the strength of its inclusion in the film, *Dirty Dancing*. The current line-up of Billingslea, Potts, Arthur Hinson, Charles Davis and Darrel Nunlee issued *Running In Circles* on Ian Levine's Motor City label in 1990. The former lead vocalist Joe Stubbs also recorded *Round And Round* for the same label.
●ALBUMS: *Do You Love Me* (Gordy 1962)★★★.
●COMPILATIONS: *Baby Hit And Run* (1974)★★★, *Running In Circles* (1990)★★★, *The Very Best* (Essential Gold 1996)★★★.

CONWAY, RUSS

b. Trevor Stanford, 2 September 1925, Bristol, Avon, England. Conway not only played the piano as a young boy, but won a scholarship to join the choir at the Bristol Cathedral School. He was conscripted into the Royal Navy in 1942 and, during a varied career, was awarded the DSM for service during campaigns in the Mediterranean and Aegean sea and lost part of a finger while using a bread slicer. In 1955, following spells in the post-war Merchant Navy, Conway played piano in nightclubs, worked as rehearsal pianist for choreographer Irving Davies and audition pianist for Columbia (UK) record producer Norman Newell. He later served as accompanist for star singers such as Dennis Lotis, Gracie Fields and Joan Regan. Signed to Columbia, his first hit, 'Party Pops', in 1957, was an instrumental medley of standard songs. It was the first of 20 UK chart entries featuring his catchy piano-playing through to 1963, including two number 1 singles, 'Side Saddle' and 'Roulette', and Top 10 entries 'China Tea' and 'Snowcoach', all of which were his own compositions. He headlined several times at the London Palladium, had his own television show and regularly guested on others, including the Billy Cotton Band Show on BBC television where his cross-talk and vocal duets with the host revealed a genuine flair for comedy and an acceptable light baritone voice. During the 60s his career was marred by ill health, a nervous breakdown while on stage and a mild stroke which prevented him from working during 1968-1971. Since then, still an anachronism, his combination of lively tunes, light classical themes and shy smile have consistently proved a big draw abroad and in the UK, where he promotes his own nostalgia package shows and charity concerts. After fighting stomach cancer for five years, in June 1994 Conway was told by doctors that he was in good health. Two years earlier he had been awarded the Lord Mayor of Bristol's Medal for his contributions to popular music and the cancer fund he set up after learning that he had the disease. Early in 1995, Conway's career was under threat once more after he trapped a thumb in the door of his Rolls Royce car.

●ALBUMS: *Pack Up Your Troubles* (1958)★★★, *Songs To Sing In Your Bath* (1958)★★★, *Family Favourites* (1959)★★★, *Time To Celebrate* (1959)★★★, *My Concerto For You* (1960)★★★, *Party Time* (1960)★★★, *At The Theatre* (1961)★★★, *At The Cinema* (1961)★★★, *Happy Days* (1961)★★★, *Concerto For Dreamers* (1962)★★★, *Russ Conway's Trad Party* (1962)★★★, *Something For Mum* (1963)★★★, *Enjoy Yourself* (1964)★★★, *Concerto For Lovers* (1964)★★★, *Once More It's Party Time* (1965)★★★, *Pop-A-Conway* (1966)★★★, *Concerto For Memories* (1966)★★★, *Russ Hour* (1966)★★★, *New Side Of Russ Conway* (1971)★★★, *Songs From Stage And Screen* (1974)★★★, *The One And Only* (1979)★★★, *Always You And Me* (1981)★★★, *A Long Time Ago* (1986)★★★.

●COMPILATIONS: *The Very Best Of Russ Conway* (1976)★★★★, *24 Piano Greats* (1977)★★★, *Russ Conway Playing Great Piano Hits* (1980)★★★, *The Two Sides Of Russ Conway* (1986)★★★, *Greatest Hits* (1986)★★★★, *The Magic Of Russ Conway* (1988)★★★, *The EMI Years: The Best Of Russ Conway* (1989)★★★★.

●FILMS: *It's All Happening* (1963).

COOKE, SAM

b. Sam Cook, 22 January 1931, Clarksdale, Mississippi, USA, d. 11 December 1964, Los Angeles, California, USA. Cooke first performed publicly with his brother and two sisters in their Baptist quartet, the Soul Children. As a teenager he joined the Highway QCs, before replacing Rebert 'R.H.' Harris in the Soul Stirrers. Between 1951 and 1956 Cooke sang lead with this innovative gospel group. His distinctive florid vocal style was soon obvious on 'Touch The Hem Of His Garment' and 'Nearer To Thee'. The Soul Stirrers recorded for the Specialty label, where the singer's popularity encouraged producer 'Bumps' Blackwell to provide Sam with pop material. 'Loveable'/'Forever' was issued as a single, disguised

under the pseudonym 'Dale Cook' to avoid offending the gospel audience. Initially content, the label's owner, Art Rupe, then objected to the sweetening choir on a follow-up recording, 'You Send Me', and offered Cooke a release from his contract in return for outstanding royalties. The song was then passed to the Keen label, where it sold in excess of two million copies. Further hits, including 'Only Sixteen' and 'Wonderful World', followed. The was latter used extensively in a television jeans commercial and in 1986 the reissue reached number 2 in the UK charts. Sam left the label for RCA Records where 'Chain Gang' (1960), 'Cupid' (1961) and 'Twistin' The Night Away' (1962), displayed a pop craft later offset by such grittier offerings as 'Bring It On Home To Me' and 'Little Red Rooster'. Cooke also founded the Sar and Derby labels on which the Simms Twins' 'Soothe Me' and the Valentinos' 'It's All Over Now' were issued. Cooke's own career remained in the ascendant with '(Ain't That) Good News' and 'Good Times' but the purity of such music made his tawdry fate all the more perplexing. On 11 December 1964, following an altercation with a girl he had picked up, the singer was fatally shot by the manageress of a Los Angeles motel. The ebullient 'Shake' became a posthumous hit, but its serene coupling, 'A Change Is Gonna Come', was a more melancholic epitaph. Arguably his finest composition, its title suggested a metaphor for the concurrent Civil Rights movement. Cooke's legacy continued through his various disciples - Johnnie Taylor, who had replaced Cooke in the Soul Stirrers, bore an obvious debt, as did Bobby Womack of the Valentinos. Sam's songs were interpreted by acts as diverse as Rod Stewart, the Animals and Cat Stevens, while the Rolling Stones' version of 'Little Red Rooster' echoed Cooke's reading rather than that of Howlin' Wolf. Otis Redding, Aretha Franklin, Smokey Robinson - the list of those acknowledging Cooke's skill is a testimony in itself. A seminal influence on soul music and R&B, his effortless and smooth delivery has rarely been surpassed. *Sam Cooke: A Man And His Music* provides an excellent overview of the singer's career.

●ALBUMS: *Sam Cooke* i (Keen 1958)★★★, *Sam Cooke Encore* (Keen 1959)★★★, *Tribute To The Lady* (Keen 1959)★★★, *Hit Kit* (Keen 1960)★★★, *I Thank God* (Keen 1960)★★★, *Wonderful World Of Sam Cooke* (Keen 1960)★★★, *Cooke's Tour* (RCA 1960)★★★, *Hits Of The 50s* (RCA 1960)★★★, *Swing Low* (1961)★★★, *My Kind Of Blues* (RCA 1961)★★★★, *Twisting The Night Away* (RCA 1962)★★★★, *Mr. Soul* (RCA 1963)★★★★, *Night Beat* (RCA 1963)★★★, *Live At Harlem Square Club Harlem* (RCA 1963)★★★, *Ain't That Good News* (RCA 1964)★★★, *Sam Cooke At The Copa* (RCA 1964)★★★★, *Shake* (RCA 1965)★★★, *Try A Little Love* (RCA 1965)★★★, *Sam Cooke Sings Billie Holiday* (RCA 1976)★★★,

●COMPILATIONS: *The Best Of Sam Cooke, Volume 1* (RCA 1962)★★★★, *The Best Of Sam Cooke, Volume 2* (RCA 1965)★★★★, *The Late And Great* (1969)★★★, *The Gospel Sound Of Sam Cooke With The Soul Stirrers* (Spcialty 1969)★★★★, *The Two Sides Of Sam Cooke* (Specialty 1971)★★★, *This Is Sam Cooke*

(1971)★★★, *The Golden Age Of Sam Cooke* (1976)★★★, *The Man And His Music* (RCA 1986)★★★★★, *Forever* (Specialty 1986)★★★, *Sam Cooke* ii (1987)★★★, *You Send Me* (1987)★★★, *20 Greatest Hits* (1987)★★★★, *Sam Cooke* iii (1988)★★★, *Wonderful World* (1988)★★★★, *The World Of Sam Cooke* (1989)★★★★, *Sam Cooke* iv (1989)★★★, *Legend* (1990)★★★, *The Magic Of Sam Cooke* (1991)★★★, *Sam Cooke With The Soul Stirrers* (Specialty 1991)★★★★, *Sam Cooke's Sar Records Story* (1994)★★★.

●FURTHER READING: *Sam Cooke: The Man Who Invented Soul: A Biography In Words & Pictures*, Joe McEwen. *You Send Me: The Life And Times*, S.R. Crain, Clifton White and G. David Tenenbaum.

COOKIES

This US vocal group trio was formed in the early 50s by Doretta (Dorothy) Jones (b. South Carolina, USA). Early members included Pat Lyles, Ethel 'Dolly' McCrae and Margorie Hendrickse. They were signed by Atlantic Records in 1956 where they recorded four singles, of which 'In Paradise' reached the R&B Top 10. However, the group was better known for session work, and can be heard on successful releases by Joe Turner ('Lipstick, Powder And Paint') and Chuck Willis ('It's Too Late'). The Cookies also backed Ray Charles on several occasions and Hendrickse, now known as Margie Hendrix, left to form Charles' own singing ensemble, the Raelettes. Her erstwhile colleagues continued their career as contract singers with newcomer Margaret Ross. Work with Neil Sedaka resulted in their meeting songwriter Carole King, who in turn brought the trio to the Dimension label. Here they scored two US Top 20 hits with the effervescent 'Chains' (later covered by the Beatles) and 'Don't Say Nothin' Bad (About My Baby)', while their voices also appeared on various releases by Little Eva, herself an auxiliary member of the group. The Cookies later moved to Warner Brothers following Dimension's collapse. Altogether the trio recorded seven singles, all of which are excellent examples of the girl-group genre. Jones and McCrae also recorded in their own right, the latter under the name Earl-Jean.

●COMPILATIONS: *The Complete Cookies* (Sequel 1994)★★★.

CORDELL, DENNY

b. Dennis Cordell-Laverack, 1942, Brazil, d. 18 February 1995, Dublin, Eire. Cordell's earliest musical involvement was as a manager for jazz trumpeter Chet Baker. Cordell discovered Bessie Banks' original version of 'Go Now' while an employee of Saltaeb, a company marketing Beatles-related merchandise. He gave the song to the Moody Blues, then contracted to the parent NEMS organization, and in turn created one of 1964's memorable releases. Cordell produced the group's output until 1966, but despite an undoubted artistic merit, none emulated that early success. He also supervised recordings by other acts, including the Mark Leeman Five, but did not regain his commercial touch until 1966 when he scored UK Top 10 hits with Georgie Fame ('Getaway') and the Move ('Night Of Fear'). He then founded the *Straight Ahead* and *New Breed* production companies before achieving monumental success with the newly formed Procol Harum and 'A Whiter Shade Of Pale'. Along with entrepreneur Tony Secunda, he helped revive the defunct record label Regal Zonophone. Cordell later worked with Joe Cocker, shaping the singer's major hit, 'With A Little Help From My Friends'. It was through this association that the producer met Leon Russell, and together they continued to fashion Cocker's career before establishing their own label, Shelter, in 1970. Based in Russell's hometown of Tulsa, Oklahoma, the new outlet was responsible for launching J.J. Cale and Tom Petty, as well as revitalizing the career of bluesman Freddie King. The label sadly encountered major distribution problems during the late 70s. Cordell and Chris Blackwell started Mango Records in 1972 and had an immediate hit with the now legendary Jamaican film *The Harder They Come*. In the 80s Cordell retired from music and bred racehorses on his farm in Ireland, but was tempted back to Island Records; he brought with him his golden touch by producing Melissa Etheridge and introducing the Cranberries. His death came after a short battle with lymphoma: he will be remembered as one of the main 'progressive' producers of the 60s, still retaining his musical vision in the 90s.

CORDET, LOUISE

b. Louise Boisot, 1946, Buckinghamshire, England. The daughter of cabaret and television actress Helene Cordet - and god-daughter of HRH Prince Phillip - Louise assumed her mother's stage-surname upon signing with Decca Records in 1962. Her first single for the label, 'I'm Just A Baby', was written by Jerry Lordan and recorded under the aegis of former Shadows drummer Tony Meehan; her perky delivery was rewarded with a UK number 13 hit. Later releases included her original rendition of 'Don't Let The Sun Catch You Crying', specifically written for Cordet by Gerry Marsden and later recorded, more successfully, by his group, Gerry And The Pacemakers. Despite appearances in the lightweight pop films *Just For Fun* and *Just For You*, Cordet was unable to sustain her performing career and by 1965 was described as a 'former singer' when the *New Musical Express* announced her intention to help publicize Marianne Faithfull.

CORNELL, LYNN

b. Liverpool, England. Cornell had been a prominent member of the Vernons Girls when she married drummer Andy White and subsequently recorded solo for Decca when the original troupe was nearing its 1961 disbandment. She is remembered chiefly for the much-covered, Greek-flavoured film title theme to 1960's *Never On Sunday* (her only UK Top 30 entry) and an ebullient 'African Waltz', which paled in the shdow of the bigger-selling Johnny Dankworth instrumental. Its b-side, an arrangement of the Jon Hendricks jazz standard 'Moanin'', illustrated that, beyond mere pop, Cordell could unfurl a suppleness of vocal gesture that was denied to luckier but less stylistically adventurous contemporaries. In more light-hearted vein was Jack Good's eccentric production of her 1962 duplication of the Blue-Belles' US hit, 'I Sold My Heart To The Junkman', but despite airplay on the BBC Light Programme, this, too, could not supersede even the chart honours gained by 'Never On Sunday'.

CORSAIRS

An R&B vocal quartet from LaGrange, North Carolina, USA. A family group consisting of three brothers - lead Jay 'Bird' Uzzell (b. 13 July 1942), James Uzzell (1 December 1940), and Moses Uzzell (b. 13 September 1939) - and a cousin, George Wooten (b. 16 January 1940). Their songs have a nice mid-tempo pop feel, yet have an edge provided by Jay Uzzell's wailing lead, burbling bass and strong chorusing. The Corsairs made their opportunity by moving from their native North Carolina to New Jersey in 1961 to be nearer to the New York recording business. They were discovered in a Jersey club by independent producer Abner Spector, who released their records on his Tuff Record label. In 1962 they reached the charts twice, with 'Smokey Places' (number 10 R&B, number 12 pop) and 'I'll Take You Home' (number 26 R&B, number 68 pop). One unrecognized classic in their repertoire is 'Stormy' (their 1963 remake of a 1956 hit by Illinois group the Prophets). The Corsairs ideally evoke that fuzzy, in-between era when the shuffle beats and the doo-wop harmonies of the 50s were fast fading and had yet to be superseded by gospelized soul stylings. By 1965 Abner's well had run dry and the Corsairs' recording career was finished.

CORTEZ, DAVE 'BABY'

b. David Cortez Clowney, 13 August 1938, Detroit, Michigan, USA. Cortez played piano in church as a boy and progressed from there to Hammond organ, performing on the chittlin' circuit through the Midwest and California in the late 50s. From 1955-57 he performed with vocal group the Pearls and in 1956-57 also worked with the Valentines. In 1956 he made his first recording (under the name of Dave Clooney) for the Ember label. He recorded for RCA Victor in September 1959 and had a hit with Clock Records ('Happy Organ') in the same year. In 1962 he hit again with 'Rinky Dink', a crude 'Louie Louie'-type instrumental that sounds like a definition of 60s teen rock naïvety. He recorded an album for Chess Records in 1963 called, predictably, *Rinky Dink* and then signed with Roulette Records, who issued 'Shindig', 'Tweetie Pie' and 'In Orbit'. In February 1966 *The Fabulous Dave 'Baby' Cortez* appeared on Metro. In 1972 All Platinum released *Soul Vibration* with Frank Prescod (bass) and Bunky Smith (drums). Producer Joe Richardson gave the bass a funk depth comparable to reggae dub experiments. The hilarious dialogue of 'Tongue Kissing', plus liner notes by the organist's mum,

make the album a gem. Signed to the T-Neck label - a Buddha subsidiary - he worked with the Isley Brothers to produce *The Isley Brothers Go All The Way*.
●ALBUMS: *Dave 'Baby' Cortez And His Happy Organ* (RCA Victor 1959)★★★★, *Dave 'Baby' Cortez* (Clock 1960)★★★, *Rinky Dink* (Chess 1962)★★★, *Organ Shindig* (Roulette 1965)★★★, *Tweety Pie* (Roulette 1966)★★★, *In Orbit With Dave 'Baby' Cortez* (Roulette 1966)★★★, *The Fabulous Dave 'Baby' Cortez* (1966)★★★, *Soul Vibration* (1972)★★★.
●COMPILATIONS: *Happy Organs, Wild Guitars And Piano Shuffles* (Ace 1993)★★★★.

CORVETTES

This Los Angeles, USA, country rock band was founded in 1968 by Chris Darrow (guitar/vocals) and Jeff Hanna (guitar/vocals), both ex-members of the Nitty Gritty Dirt Band. John London (bass) and John Ware (drums) completed the line-up featured on the act's two singles, 'Back Home Girl'/'Beware Of Time' and 'Level With Your Senses'/'Lion In Your Heart', but this promising quartet was unable to find commercial success. In January 1969 they became the backing group for Linda Ronstadt, touring with the singer as she promoted *Home Grown*. Bernie Leadon replaced Hanna in May when the latter rejoined the Dirt Band, but by September the Corvettes had disbanded. Darrow then pursued a solo career, Leadon switched to the Flying Burrito Brothers, while Ware and London became founder members of Mike Nesmith's First National Band.

COTTON, MIKE

b. 12 August 1939, London, England. Trumpeter Cotton had led the Mike Cotton Jazzband during the 'Trad' craze of the early 60s, but incurred the wrath of purists by increasingly adopting beat-styled material. In 1963 the group, now known as the Mike Cotton Sound, enjoyed a Top 30 entry with 'Swing That Hammer', and the following year completed their lone, highly regarded album. The group included Dave Rowberry (keyboards), later of the Animals, and future Argent and Kinks bassist Jim Rodford (b. 7 July 1941, St. Albans, Hertfordshire, England), while Johnny Crocker (trombone) Derek Tearle (bass) and Jim Garforth (drums) were among the other musicians featured in its changeable line-up. Vocalist Lucas was added in 1967 as the group switched from jazz-based R&B to soul, but by the end of the decade Cotton had jettisoned its now-anachronistic name, replacing it with Satisfaction. This new aggregation broke up on completing its sole album, following which the trumpeter retained the brass section for session work, notably with the Kinks, whom they supported both live and in the studio throughout the early 70s.
●ALBUMS: *The Mike Cotton Sound* (Columbia 1964)★★★.

COUGARS

Formed in 1961 in Bristol, England, the Cougars consisted of Keith 'Rod' Owen (guitar/arranger), Dave Tanner (rhythm guitar), Adrian Morgan (bass) and Dave Hack (drums). An instrumental group in the mould of the Shadows, the quartet was signed to EMI by A&R manager Norrie Paramor following a talent contest. Their debut single, 'Saturday Night At The Duck Pond', a frenetic reworking of Tchaikovsky's 'Swan Lake', incurred a BBC ban on the grounds that it 'defaced a classical melody', but nonetheless reached the number 33 spot in 1963. The same composer was the inspiration for several ensuing releases, including 'Red Square' and 'Caviare And Chips', but the group was unable to repeat its initial success.

COUNT FIVE

Formed in 1964 in San Jose, California, USA. The Count Five were a classic one-hit-wonder whose Yardbirds-inspired psychedelic-punk hit 'Psychotic Reaction', reached the US Top 5 in 1966. The band's line-up consisted of Ken Ellner (b. 1948, Brooklyn, New York, USA; vocals/harmonica), Sean Byrne (b. 1947, Dublin, Eire; guitar/vocals), John Michalski (b. 1949, Cleveland, Ohio, USA; lead guitar), Roy Chaney (b. 1948, Indianapolis, Indiana, USA; bass) and Craig Atkinson (b. 1947, Springfield, Missouri, USA; drums). They first drew attention by wearing Dracula-style capes to their gigs. After recording one album, also titled *Psychotic Reaction*, they continued to release singles into 1968 before disbanding. Byrne returned to Eire and featured on one album in 1973 as a member of Public Foot The Roman and in 1978 he turned up yet again for the group Legover on their album *Wait Till Nightime*.
●ALBUMS: *Psychotic Reaction* (Double Shot 1966)★★★.

COUNTRY JOE AND THE FISH

Formed in Berkeley, California, USA, in 1965, this imaginative quintet began life as the Instant Action Jug Band. Former folk singer Country Joe McDonald (b. 1 January 1942, El Monte, California, USA) established the group with guitarist Barry Melton (b. 1947, Brooklyn, New York, USA), the only musicians to remain in the line-up throughout its turbulent history. Part of a politically active family, McDonald immersed himself in the activism centred on Berkeley, and his group's earliest recording, 'I Feel Like I'm Fixin' To Die Rag' (1965), was a virulent attack on the Vietnam war. The following year an expanded line-up, McDonald, Melton, David Cohen (guitar/keyboards), Paul Armstrong (bass) and John Francis Gunning (drums) embraced electricity with a privately pressed EP. By 1967 Armstrong and Gunning had been replaced, respectively, by Bruce Barthol and Gary 'Chicken' Hirsh. This reshaped quintet was responsible for *Electric Music For The Mind And Body*, one of the 60s' 'west coast' era's most striking releases. Although politics were still prevalent on 'Superbird', this excellent collection also included shimmering instrumentals ('Section 43'), drug songs ('Bass Strings') and unflinching romanticism ('Porpoise Mouth'). It was followed by *I Feel Like I'm Fixin' To Die*, which not only featured a new version of that early composition, but also contained a poignant tribute to singer Janis Joplin. The controversial and outspoken McDonald instigated the famous 'fish cheer' which, more often than not, resulted in thousands of deliriously stoned fans spelling out not F.I.S.H. but F.U.C.K. with carefree abandon. Beset by internal problems, the group's disappointing third album, *Together*, marked the end of this innovative line-up. *Here We Are Again* was completed by various musicians, including Peter Albin and Dave Getz from Big Brother And The Holding Company, and although piecemeal, included the haunting country-tinged 'Here I Go Again' (later a hit for the 60s model, Twiggy). Mark Kapner (keyboards), Doug Metzner (bass) and Greg Dewey (drums - formerly of Mad River), joined McDonald and Melton in the summer of 1969. The new line-up was responsible for the group's final album, *C.J. Fish*, on which glimpses of the former fire were present. The 'classic' line-up, which appeared on the group's first three albums, was briefly reunited between 1976 and 1977 but the resultant release, *Reunion*, was a disappointment. McDonald aside, Barry Melton has enjoyed the highest profile, recording several albums under his own name and performing with the San Francisco 'supergroup', the Dinosaurs.
●ALBUMS: *Electric Music For The Mind And Body* (Vanguard 1967)★★★, *I Feel Like I'm Fixin' To Die* (Vanguard 1967)★★★, *Together* (Vanguard 1968)★★, *Here We Are Again* (Vanguard 1969)★★, *C.J. Fish* (Vanguard 1970)★★, *Reunion* (Fantasy 1977)★, *Live Fillmore West 1969* (Ace 1996)★★.
●COMPILATIONS: *Greatest Hits* (Vanguard 1969)★★★, *The Life And Times Of Country Joe And The Fish From Haight-Ashbury To Woodstock* (Vanguard 1971)★★★, *Collectors' Items - The First Three EPs* (1980)★★★, *The Collected Country Joe And The Fish* (Vanguard 1987)★★★.
●FILMS: *Gas! Or It Became Necessary ...* (1970).

COUNTRYMEN

Formed in Hull, Yorkshire, England, in the early 60s, singing guitarists Alan Beach, David Kelsey and David Waite sported uniform waistcoats and embroidered shirts while performing commercial folk - 'I Know Where I'm Going' reached the lower reaches of the UK Top 50 in spring 1962. They were also noted as the first UK act to cover a Paul Simon opus when 'Carlos Dominguez' was issued in Britain a month prior to the version by the composer (as 'Jerry Landis') in May 1964. They had the advantage, too, of a virtual residency on UK television's *Five O'Clock Club*, before being lost to the archives of oblivion when this ITV children's series ended.
●ALBUMS: *The Countrymen* (Piccadilly 1963)★★.

COVAY, DON

b. March 1938, Orangeburg, South Carolina, USA. Covay resettled in Washington during the early 50s and initially sang in the Cherry Keys, his family's gospel quartet. He crossed over to secular music with the Rainbows, a formative group which also included Marvin Gaye and Billy Stewart. Covay's solo career began in 1957 as part of the

Little Richard revue. The most tangible result of this liaison was a single, 'Bip Bop Bip', on which Covay was billed as 'Pretty Boy'. Released on Atlantic, it was produced by Richard and featured the weight of his backing band, the Upsetters. Over the next few years Covay drifted from label to label. His original version of 'Pony Time' (credited to the Goodtimers) lost out to Chubby Checker's cover version, but a further dance-oriented offering, 'Popeye Waddle', was a hit in 1962. Covay meanwhile honed his songwriting skill and formed partnerships with several associates including Horace Ott and Ronnie Miller. Such work provided Solomon Burke with 'I'm Hanging Up My Heart For You' while Gladys Knight And The Pips reached the US Top 20 with 'Letter Full Of Tears'. Covay's singing career continued to falter until 1964 when he signed with New York's Rosemart label. Still accompanied by the Goodtimers (Ace Hall, Harry Tiffen and George Clane), his debut single there, the vibrant 'Mercy Mercy', established his effortless, bluesy style. Atlantic subsequently bought his contract but while several R&B hits followed, it was a year before Covay returned to the pop chart. 'See-Saw', co-written with Steve Cropper and recorded at Stax Records, paved the way for other exceptional singles, including 'Sookie Sookie' and 'Iron Out The Rough Spots' (both 1966). Covay's late 60s output proved less fertile, while the ill-founded Soul Clan (with Solomon Burke, Wilson Pickett, Joe Tex and Ben E. King) ended after one single. Covay's songs still remained successful, Aretha Franklin won a Grammy for her performance of his composition, 'Chain Of Fools'. Covay switched to Janus in 1971; from there he moved to Mercury Records where he combined recording with A&R duties. *Superdude 1* (1973), a critics' favourite, reunited the singer with Horace Ott. Further releases appeared on the Philadelphia International (1976), U-Von (1977) and Newman (1980) labels, but while Randy Crawford and Bonnie Raitt resurrected his songs, Covay's own career continued to slide downhill. In 1993 the Rhythm & Blues Foundation honoured the singer/songwriter with one of its prestigious Pioneer Awards. Covay, unfortunately, was by then suffering the after-effects of a stroke. A tribute album, *Back To The Streets: Celebrating The Music Of Don Covay*, recorded by many first-rate artists including Chuck Jackson, Ben E. King, Bobby Womack, Robert Cray and Todd Rundgren, was released by Shanachie in 1994. The same year the Razor & Tie label released a fine 23 track retrospective of his best work, compiled and annotated by soulman and producer Billy Vera.
● ALBUMS: *Mercy* (Atlantic 1964)★★★, *See Saw* (Atlantic 1966)★★★★, with the Lemon Jefferson Blues Band *House Of Blue Lights* (Atlantic 1969)★★★, *Different Strokes* (1970)★★, *Superdude 1* (1973)★★, *Hot Blood* (1975)★★, *Travellin' In Heavy Traffic* (1976)★★.
● COMPILATIONS: *Sweet Thang* (1987)★★★, *Checkin' In With Don Covay* (1989)★★★, *Mercy Mercy - The Definitive Don Covay* (Razor & Tie 1994)★★★★.

COWSILLS

Billed as 'America's First Family Of Music', the Cowsills were all born in Newport, Rhode Island, USA. The group featured Bill (b. 9 January 1948; guitar/vocals), Bob (b. 26 August 1949; guitar/vocals), Paul (b. 11 November 1952; keyboards/vocals), Barry (b. 14 September 1954; bass/vocals), John (b. 2 March 1956; drums) and Susan (b. 20 May 1960; vocals). Occasionally augmented by their mother Barbara (b. 1928; vocals), they came to the attention of writer/producer Artie Kornfeld who co-wrote and produced their debut single 'The Rain, The Park And Other Things' which reached number 2 in the US charts in December 1967. Featuring lyrics by Bill, their happy, bouncy harmonies were evident on the subsequent singles 'We Can Fly', 'In Need Of A Friend' and the 1968 Top 10 hit 'Indian Lake'. Their energetic interpretation of the title song from the rock musical *Hair* reached number 2 in May 1969 and proved to be their swansong. Shortly afterwards Bill left to pursue a career in composing. Before they split up in 1972, they became the inspiration for the NBC US television series *The Partridge Family*, starring David Cassidy, in 1970. In January 1985 Barbara died of emphysema, aged 56, in Tempe, Arizona, USA.
● ALBUMS: *The Cowsills* (1967)★★★, *We Can Fly* (1968)★★★, *Captain Sad And His Ship Of Fools* (1968)★★, *The Cowsills In Concert* (1969)★★, *On My Side* (London 1971)★★.
● COMPILATIONS: *The Best Of The Cowsills* (1968)★★★.

COX, MICHAEL

b. Michael James Cox, Liverpool, England. After his sisters wrote to producer Jack Good demanding an audition, Cox found himself transformed into a television singing star. Fellow pop singer Marty Wilde kindly presented him with a demo of John D. Loudermilk's 'Angela Jones', which brought Cox a UK Top 10 hit in 1960. Only one minor success followed, 'Along Came Caroline', but the singer enjoyed considerable success in Scandinavia where he toured with the Outlaws, featuring Ritchie Blackmore. Several continental jaunts kept Cox in regular work during the mid-60s and beyond. Following a bizarre experience with a ouija board, he decided to abandon his surname and call himself simply Michael James. Today he still plays the cabaret circuit and has also acted in several minor film productions.

COXSONE, LLOYD

An influential figure in the growth of the UK reggae scene, Lloyd Coxsone (b. Lloyd Blackwood) left his home in Morant Bay, Jamaica, and arrived in the UK in 1962, settling in south west London and setting up his first sound system, Lloyd The Matador. This venture floundered due to inexperience and Lloyd joined the UK-based Duke Reid sound, but he eventually left in 1969, taking some of that operation's personnel with him, to form his own sound system, adopting the name of the biggest sound in Jamaica at the time, and also, pointedly, the main rival to Jamaica's Duke Reid, Sir Coxsone. Coxsone sound soon gained a strong following that eventually led to his residency at the famous London nightclub the Roaring Twenties in Carnaby Street. Throughout the 70s Sir Coxsone Sound's success lay with maintaining the sound to rigorous standards, playing the most exclusive dub plates direct from Jamaica, and keeping abreast of trends within the music. Rather than specializing in one particular style, Coxsone Sound offered music for all tastes.

Coxsone, like other sound men, also expanded into the record business, licensing music from Jamaica at first, then trying his hand at his own productions using local UK artists. In 1975 he enjoyed huge success, and kick-started the UK lovers rock phenomenon in the process, with his production of 'Caught You In A Lie' - originally a US soul hit by Robert Parker - featuring the vocal talents of 14-year-old south London schoolgirl Louisa Marks. That same year he issued one of the best dub albums of the era, *King Of The Dub Rock*, which featured dubwise versions of his own productions and those of Gussie Clarke, mixed in part at King Tubby's. Other notable records appeared on his Tribesman and Lloyd Coxsone Outernational imprints and elsewhere during the late 70s and early 80s, including Faybiene Miranda's Jack Ruby-produced 'Prophecy', 'Love And Only Love' and 'Voice Of The Poor' by Fred Locks. Others included 'Stormy Night' and 'Homeward Bound' by the Creation Steppers, a version of the Commodores' 'Easy' by Jimmy Lindsay (many of which are available on *12 The Hard Way*) and many more. During the mid-80s Coxsone handed control of his sound over to the younger elements in his team, notably Blacker Dread, and a new breed of DJs. Blacker released his own productions by the likes of Fred Locks, Frankie Paul, Mikey General, Sugar Minott, Michael Palmer, Don Carlos, Earl Sixteen and Coxsone DJ, Jah Screechy. Recently, as interest in the roots music of the 70s has increased, Coxsone has emerged from his semi-retirement to once again stand at the controls of his sound.

●ALBUMS: *King Of The Dub Rock* (Safari 1975)★★★★, *King Of The Dub Rock Part 2* (1982)★★★, *12 The Hard Way* (Tribesman 1989)★★★.

CRAMER, FLOYD

b. 27 October 1933, Shreveport, Louisiana, USA. The style and sound of Cramer's piano-playing is arguably one of the biggest influences on post 50s country music. His delicate rock 'n' roll sound is achieved by accentuating the discord in rolling from the main note to a sharp or flat, known as 'slip note'. This is perfectly highlighted in his first major hit 'Last Date' in 1960. Cramer was already a vastly experienced Nashville session player, playing on countless records during the 50s. He can be heard on many Jim Reeves and Elvis Presley records, often with his long-time friend Chet Atkins. During the early 60s he regularly made the US charts. Two notable hits were the superb 'On The Rebound', which still sounds fresh and lively more than 30 years later, and his sombre reading of Bob Wills' 'San Antonio Rose'. After dozens of albums Cramer was still making commercially successful record-

ings into the 80s, having a further hit in 1980 with the theme from the television soap-opera *Dallas*. With Atkins, Cramer remains Nashville's most prolific musician.

●ALBUMS: *That Honky Tonk Piano* (MGM 1957)★★★, *Hello Blues* (1960)★★★, *Last Date* (RCA 1960)★★★★, *On The Rebound* (1961)★★★★, *America's Biggest Selling Pianist* (1961)★★★, *Floyd Cramer Get Organized* (1962)★★, *I Remember Hank Williams* (1962)★★★, *Swing Along With Floyd Cramer* (1963)★★★, *Comin' On* (1963)★★★, *Country Piano - City Strings* (1964)★★★, *Goes Honky Tonkin'* (1964)★★★, *Cramer At The Console* (1964)★★★, *Hits From The Country Hall Of Fame* (1965)★★★, *The Magic Touch Of Floyd Cramer* (1965)★★★, *Class Of '65* (1965)★★★, *The Distinctive Piano Styling Of Floyd Cramer* (1966)★★★, *The Big Ones* (1966)★★★, *Class Of '66* (1966)★★★, *Here's What's Happening* (1967)★★★, *Floyd Cramer Plays The Monkees* (1967)★★★, *Class Of '67* (1967)★★★, *Floyd Cramer Plays Country Classics* (1968)★★★, *Class Of '68* (1968)★★★, *Floyd Cramer Plays MacArthur Park* (1968)★★, *Class Of '69* (1969)★★★, *More Country Classics* (1969)★★★, *Floyd Cramer Country* (1976)★★★, *Looking For Mr. Goodbar* (1968)★★★, *The Big Ones - Volume 2* (1970)★★★, *Floyd Cramer With The Music City Pops* (1970)★★★, *Class Of '70* (1970)★★, *Sounds Of Sunday* (1971)★★, *Class Of '71* (1971)★★★, *Floyd Cramer Detours* (1972)★★★, *Class Of '72* (1972)★★★, *Super Country Hits Featuring Crystal Chandelier And Battle Of New Orleans* (1973)★★, *Class Of '73* (1973)★★, *The Young And The Restless* (1974)★★, *In Concert* (1974)★★, *Class Of '74 And '75* (1975)★★, *Floyd Cramer And The Keyboard Kick Band* (1977)★★★, *Superhits* (1979)★★, *Dallas* (1980)★★, *Great Country Hits* (1981)★★, *The Best Of The West* (1981)★★, *Originals* (1991)★★, *Classics* (1992)★★★.

●COMPILATIONS: *The Best Of Floyd Cramer* (RCA 1964)★★★★, *The Best Of Floyd Cramer - Volume 2* (1968)★★★, *This Is Floyd Cramer* (1970)★★★★, *The Big Hits* (1973)★★★, *Best Of The Class Of* (1973)★★★, *Spotlight On Floyd Cramer* (1974)★★★, *Piano Masterpieces 1900-1975* (1975)★★★, *All My Best* (1980)★★★, *Treasury Of Favourites* (1984)★★★, *Country Classics* (1984)★★★★, *Our Class Reunion* (1987)★★★, *The Best Of Floyd Cramer* (1988)★★★★, *Easy Listening Favorites* (1991)★★★, *King Of Country Piano* (Pickwick 1995)★★★, *The Essential Floyd Cramer* (RCA 1996)★★★★.

CRAZY ELEPHANT

A studio group created by Jerry Kasenetz and Jeff Katz (see Kasenetz-Katz Singing Orchestral Circus), the mastermind producers behind such bubblegum confections as the Ohio Express and the 1910 Fruitgum Company, Crazy Elephant were signed to Bell Records in 1969. With Robert Spencer, a former member of the Cadillacs ('Speedoo' and 'Gloria') singing lead, the 'group' landed a

transatlantic Top 20 hit with the soul-inflected bub-blegum-pop 'Gimme Gimme Good Lovin''. The song was penned by Joey Levine and Ritchie Cordell, who had written Tommy James And The Shondells' international hit, 'Mony Mony'. The promoted line-up of the group comprised Hal King (lead vocals), Larry Laufer (vocals/organ), Ronnie Bretone (bass), Bob Avery (drums) and 'Jethro' (pretty much anything he could lay his hands on). Their follow-up 'Sunshine Red Wine' featured King's gutsy vocal and the classic formula of organ, rasping saxophones, handclaps and throbbing beat. Although Crazy Elephant released a number of subsequent singles (including one on which the newly formed 10cc participated), they never had another hit.
●ALBUMS: *Crazy Elephant* (Major Minor 1969)★★.

CREAM

Arguably the most famous trio in rock music, Cream comprised Jack Bruce (b. John Symon Asher Bruce, 4 May 1943, Glasgow, Lanarkshire, Scotland; bass/vocals), Eric Clapton (b. Eric Patrick Clapp, 30 March 1945, Ripley, Surrey, England; guitar) and Ginger Baker (b. Peter Baker, 19 August 1939, Lewisham, London, England; drums). In their two-and-a-half years together, Cream made such an impression on fans, critics and musicians as to make them one of the most influential bands since the Beatles. They formed in the height of swinging London during the 60s and were soon thrust into a non-stop turbulent arena, hungry for new and interesting music after the Merseybeat boom had quelled. Cream were announced in the music press as a pop group, Clapton from John Mayall's Bluesbreakers, Bruce from Manfred Mann and Baker from the Graham Bond Organisation. Their debut single 'Wrapping Paper' was a comparatively weird pop song, and made the lower reaches of the charts on the strength of its insistent appeal. Their follow-up single, 'I Feel Free' unleashed such energy that it could only be matched by Jimi Hendrix. The debut *Fresh Cream* confirmed the promise: this band were not what they seemed. With a mixture of blues standards and exciting originals, the album became a record that every credible music fan should own. It reached number 6 in the UK charts. That same crucial year, *Disraeli Gears*, with its distinctive day-glo cover, went even higher, and firmly established Cream in the USA where they spent most of their touring life. This superb album showed a marked progression from their first, in particular the songwriting of Jack Bruce and his lyricist, former beat poet, Pete Brown. Landmark songs such as 'Sunshine Of Your Love', 'Strange Brew' and 'SWLABR' (She Was Like A Bearded Rainbow) were performed with precision.

Already rumours of a split prevailed as news filtered back from America of fights and arguments between Baker and Bruce. Meanwhile, their live performances did not reflect the music thus far committed to vinyl. The long improvisational pieces, based around fairly simple blues structures were awesome. Each member had a least one party piece during concerts, Bruce with his frantic har-

monica solo on 'Traintime', Baker with his trademark drum solo on 'Toad' and Clapton with his strident vocal and fantastic guitar solo on 'Crossroads'. One disc of the superb two-record set *Wheels Of Fire* captured Cream live, at their inventive and exploratory best. Just a month after its release, while it sat on top of the US charts, they announced they would disband at the end of the year following two final concerts. The famous Royal Albert Hall farewell concerts were captured on film; the posthumous *Goodbye* repeated the success of its predecessors, as did some later scrapings from the bottom of the barrel. The three members came together in 1993 for an emotional one-off performance at the Rock 'n' Roll Hall Of Fame awards in New York. Cream came and went almost in the blink of an eye, but left an indelible mark on rock music.
●ALBUMS: *Fresh Cream* (Polydor 1966)★★★★, *Disraeli Gears* (Polydor 1967)★★★★★, *Wheels Of Fire* (Polydor 1968)★★★★, *Goodbye* (Polydor 1969)★★★, *Live Cream* (Polydor 1970)★★★, *Live Cream, Volume 2* (Polydor 1972)★★★.
●COMPILATIONS: *The Best Of Cream* (Polydor 1969)★★★★, *Heavy Cream* (Polydor 1973)★★★, *Strange Brew - The Very Best Of Cream* (Polydor 1986)★★★★.
●VIDEOS: *Farewell Concert* (1986), *Stange Brew* (1992), *Fresh Live Cream* (1994).
●FURTHER READING: *Cream In Gear (Limited Edition)*, Gered Mankowitz and Robert Whitaker (Photographers). *Strange Brew*, Chris Welch.

CREATION

Revered as one of Britain's most inventive mod/pop-art acts, the Creation evolved out of the Enfield, Middlesex, England, beat group, the Mark Four. Kenny Pickett (b. 1942, Middlesex, England, d. 10 January 1997; vocals), Eddie Phillips (lead guitar), Mick Thompson (rhythm guitar), John Dalton (bass) and Jack Jones (drums) completed four singles under this appellation before Dalton left to join the Kinks and Thompson abandoned music altogether. The remaining trio added Bob Garner, formerly of the Merseybeats, and Tony Sheridan, and changed their name in 1966 upon securing a deal with producer Shel Talmy. The Creation's early singles, 'Making Time' and 'Painter Man', offered the same propulsive power as the Who, while Phillips' distinctive bowed guitar sound was later popularized by Jimmy Page. Although both releases were only minor hits in Britain, they proved highly successful on the Continent, but the group's undoubted promise was undermined by personality clashes between Pickett and Garner. The singer left the group in June 1967 and although several strong records followed, they lacked the impact of earlier recordings. The group broke up in February 1968, but re-formed the following month around Pickett, Jones, Kim Gardner (bass) and ex-Birds member, Ron Wood (guitar). This realignment proved temporary and, impromptu reunions apart, the Creation broke up in June 1968. However, after 25 years, the band re-formed and made a live album, *Lay The Ghost*, in 1993. An all-new album

was issued on Alan McGee's Creation label in 1996.
●ALBUMS: *We Are Paintermen* (Hi-Ton 1967)★★★, *Lay The Ghost* (1993)★★, *The Creation* (Creation 1996)★★, *Power Surge* (Creation 1996)★★.
●COMPILATIONS: *The Best Of Creation* (Pop Schallplatten 1968)★★★, *The Creation 66-67* (Charisma 1973)★★★, *How Does It Feel To Feel* (Edsel 1982)★★★, *Recreation* (1984)★★.

CREEDENCE CLEARWATER REVIVAL

Although generally bracketed with the post-psychedelic wave of San Franciscan groups, Creedence Clearwater Revival boasted one of the region's longest pedigrees. John Fogerty (b. 28 May 1945, Berkeley, California, USA; lead guitar/vocals), Tom Fogerty (b. 9 November 1941, Berkeley, California, USA, d. 6 September 1990, Scottsdale, Arizona, USA; rhythm guitar/vocals), Stu Cook (b. 25 April 1945, Oakland, California, USA; bass) and Doug Clifford (b. 24 April 1945, Palo Alto, California, USA; drums) began performing together in 1959 while attending high school. Initially known as the Blue Velvets, then Tommy Fogerty And The Blue Velvets, the quartet became a popular attraction in the Bay Area suburb of El Cerritto and as such completed a single, 'Bonita', for a local independent outlet. In 1964 they auditioned for the more prestigious Fantasy label, who signed them on the understanding that they change their name to the more topical Golliwogs to monopolize on the concurrent 'British Invasion'. Between 1965 and 1967, the rechristened group recorded seven singles, ranging from the Beatles-influenced 'Don't Tell Me No More Lies' to the compulsive 'Fight Fire' and 'Walk Upon The Water', two superb garage band classics. The quartet turned fully professional in December 1967 and in doing so became known as Creedence Clearwater Revival.

Their debut album reflected a musical crossroads. Revamped Golliwogs tracks and new John Fogerty originals slotted alongside several rock 'n' roll standards, including 'Suzie Q' and 'I Put A Spell On You', the former reaching number 11 in the US charts. *Bayou Country*, issued within a matter of months, was a more substantial affair, establishing Fogerty as a perceptive composer, and the group as America's consummate purveyors of late 60s pop. 'Proud Mary' reached the Top 10 in both the US and UK and in the process become the quartet's first gold disc. More importantly, it introduced the mixture of Southern creole styles, R&B and rockabilly through which the best of the group's work was filtered. *Green River* consolidated the group's new-found status and contained two highly successful singles, 'Green River' and 'Bad Moon Rising', the latter of which topped the UK charts. The set confirmed Fogerty's increasingly fertile lyricism which ranged from personal melancholia ('Lodi') to a plea for mutual understanding ('Wrote A Song For Everyone'). This social perspective flourished on the 'Fortunate Son', an acerbic attack on a privileged class sending others out to war, one of several highlights captured on *Willie And The Poor Boys*. By this point the group was indisputably America's leading attraction, marrying commercial success with critical approbation. 'Down On The Corner', a euphoric tribute to popular music, became their fifth US Top 10 single and confirmed a transformation from gutsy bar band to international luminaries.

CCR reached a peak with *Cosmo's Factory*. It included three gold singles, 'Travellin' Band', 'Up Around The Bend' and 'Looking Out My Back Door', as well as an elongated reading of the Tamla/Motown classic 'I Heard It Through The Grapevine'. The album defined the consummate Creedence Clearwater Revival sound: tight, economical and reliant on an implicit mutual understanding, and deservedly became 1970's best-selling set. However, relationships between the Fogerty brothers grew increasingly strained, reflected in the standard of the disappointing *Pendulum*. Although it featured their eighth gold single in 'Have You Ever Seen The Rain', the set lacked the overall intensity of its immediate predecessors, a sparkle only occasionally rekindled in 'Pagan Baby' and 'Molina'. Tom Fogerty left for a solo career in February 1971, but although the remaining members continued to work as a trio, the band had lost much of its impetus. Major tours of the USA, Europe, Australia and Japan did ensue, but a seventh collection, *Mardi Gras*, revealed an artistic impasse. Cook and Clifford were granted democratic rights, but their uninspiring compositions only proved how much the group owed to John Fogerty's vision: Creedence Clearwater Revival was officially disbanded in July 1972. It was a dispiriting close to one of the era's most compulsive and successful groups, a combination rarely found. While the rhythm section followed low-key pursuits both independently and together, their erstwhile leader began an erratic path dogged by legal and contractual disputes, but that was marked by a deserved re-emergence in 1985.

●ALBUMS: *Creedence Clearwater Revival* (Fantasy 1968)★★★, *Bayou Country* (Fantasy 1969)★★★★, *Green River* (Fantasy 1969)★★★★, *Willie And The Poor Boys* (Fantasy 1969)★★★★, *Cosmo's Factory* (Fantasy 1970)★★★★, *Pendulum* (Fantasy 1970)★★★, *Mardi Gras* (Fantasy 1972)★★, *Live In Europe* (Fantasy 1973)★★, *Live At The Royal Albert Hall* aka *The Concert* (Fantasy 1980)★★.
●COMPILATIONS: *Creedence Gold* (Fantasy 1972)★★★★, *More Creedence Gold* (Fantasy 1973)★★★★, *Chronicle: The 20 Greatest Hits* (Fantasy 1976)★★★★, *Greatest Hits* (Fantasy 1979)★★★, *Creedence Country* (Fantasy 1981)★★★, *Creedence Clearwater Revival Hits Album* (Fantasy 1982)★★★★, *The Creedence Collection* (Impression 1985)★★★, *Chronicle II* (Fantasy 1986)★★★★, *Best of Volume 1* (Fantasy 1988)★★★★, *Best of Volume 2* (Fantasy 1988)★★★★, as the Golliwogs *The Golliwogs* (1975)★★.
●FURTHER READING: *Inside Creedence*, John Hallowell.

CRICKETS

The Crickets have continued occasionally to record and tour as a group ever since Buddy Holly's death in 1959. In addition to Holly, the original long-serving members were drummer Jerry Allison (b. 31 August 1939, Hillsboro, Texas, USA), bassist Joe B. Mauldin and guitarist Nicky Sullivan. When Holly was signed to Decca Records in 1957, it was decided that these Nashville-produced tracks produced by Norman Petty should be released under two names, as Holly solo items (on Coral) and as the Crickets (on Brunswick). It was 'That'll Be The Day', credited to the Crickets which was the first number 1 hit. Other Crickets successes with Holly on lead vocals included 'Oh Boy', 'Maybe Baby' and 'Think It Over'. However, by the end of 1958, Holly had moved to New York to concentrate on his solo career and the Crickets did not accompany him on his final tour. Petty and Allison had already begun recording independently of Holly, issuing 'Love's Made A Fool Of You' with Earl Sinks on lead vocals. On the later singles 'Peggy Sue Got Married' and 'More Than I Can Say' Sinks was replaced by Sonny Curtis (b. 9 May 1937, Meadow, Texas, USA; guitar/vocals), who was an early Texas associate of Holly and Allison. Written by Curtis and Allison, 'More Than I Can Say' was a hit for Bobby Vee, and in 1961 the Crickets moved to Vee's label, Liberty Records and recorded an album of Holly numbers with the singer the following year. Glen D. Hardin (b. 18 April 1939, Wellington, Texas, USA; piano) joined at this point. The group also released a series of singles between 1962 and 1965. These made little impact in the USA but 'Please Don't Ever Change' (a Carole King/Gerry Goffin number) and 'My Little Girl' were Top 20 hits in the UK, where the group continued to tour.

There followed a five-year hiatus in the group's career as Curtis and Allison worked as songwriters and session musicians. They were persuaded to re-form the Crickets in 1970, to record a rock revival album for the Barnaby label. This led to a contract with Mercury and two albums containing mostly original country rock style songs, such as Allison's powerfully nostalgic 'My Rockin' Days'. The producer was Bob Montgomery who had been Holly's earliest songwriting partner. The group now included singer/writer Steve Krikorian and two English musicians: guitarist Albert Lee and ex-Family and Blind Faith bassist Ric Grech.

The most recent phase of the Crickets' career was stimulated by the purchase from Paul McCartney's publishing company of Petty's share of the Holly/Allison song catalogue. During the 80s, Allison led the band for revival tours and he returned to recording in 1987 with original bassist Mauldin and newcomer Gordon Payne on guitar and vocals. They released *Three-Piece* on Allison's own Rollercoaster label, which became *T-Shirt* on CBS with the addition of the title track, the winner of a UK songwriting competition organized by McCartney's company MPL.

●ALBUMS: *In Style With The Crickets* (Coral 1960)★★★★, *Bobby Vee Meets The Crickets* (Liberty 1962)★★★, *Something Old, Something New, Something Borrowed, Something Else* (Liberty 1963)★★★, *California Sun* (Liberty 1964)★★★, *Rockin' 50s Rock 'N' Roll* (1970)★★★, *Bubblegum, Bop, Ballads And Boogies* (1973)★★, *A Long Way From Lubbock* (1975)★★, *Three-Piece* (1988)★★, *T-Shirt* (1989)★★, *Too Much Monday Morning* (Carlton 1997)★★.

●COMPILATIONS: *The Singles Collection 1957-1961* (Pickwick 1994)★★★.

●VIDEOS: *My Love Is Bigger Than A Cadillac* (Hendring 1990).

●FILMS: *Girls On The Beach* (1965).

CRITTERS

This US group was founded in 1964 by guitarists Jim Ryan and Don Ciconne. Kenny Gorka (bass), Chris Darway (organ) and Jack Decker (drums) then completed the line-up. Initially based in Plainfield, New Jersey, USA. 'Children And Flowers', a Jackie DeShannon song, was their first release on a major label, but it was a follow-up single, 'Younger Girl', that gave the Critters their major hit. This harmonious reading of the John Sebastian (Lovin' Spoonful) song established the quintet as a leading folk rock ensemble while later releases, 'Mr. Dieingly Sad', 'Bad Misunderstanding' and 'Don't Let The Rain Fall Down On Me', embellished this facet with classic New York-styled productions. Ciconne, who also enjoyed a brief, but fruitful partnership with songwriters Anders And Poncia, left the line-up on his induction into the army. Jeff Pelosi (drums) and Bob Spinella (keyboards), joined the group in late 1967, but despite several further releases, the Critters were unable to recapture the magic of that original quintet. Ryan became a session musician following the band's final collapse, while Ciconne returned to the limelight in 1974 on replacing Clay Jordan in the Four Seasons.

●ALBUMS: *Younger Girl* (Kapp 1966)★★★, *Touch 'N' Go* (1967)★★, *Project 3 aka The Critters* (1968)★★.

●COMPILATIONS: *New York Bound* (1968)★★★, *Anthology: The Complete Kapp Recordings: 1965-1967* (Taragon 1995)★★★.

CROME CYRCUS

Lee Graham (vocals/bass/flute); John Garborit (lead guitar), Ted Sheffler (keyboards), Dick Powell (harmonica) and Rod Pilloud (drums) made up this enigmatic 'progressive' San Francisco group. Their lone album, *The Love Cycle*, featured an ambitious, extended title-track in which the musicians attempted to compress much of the city's experimental musical styles. Although not wholly convincing, Crome Cyrcus were applauded for their ambition and in 1969 won a Bay Area songwriting award. However, the group dissolved soon afterwards.

●ALBUMS: *The Love Cycle* (Command 1968)★★.

CROPPER, STEVE

b. 21 October 1942, Willow Spring, Missouri, USA. This economical but effective guitarist was a founder member of the Mar-Keys, a high school band whose instrumental single, 'Last Night', provided a cornerstone for the emerging Stax label in 1961. Cropper worked with several groups constructed around the company's house musicians, the most successful of which was Booker T. And The MGs. The latter group not only had several hits under its own identity, but over the next few years was the muscle behind almost every performance released via the Stax studio. However, Cropper's prowess was not only confined to playing. His songwriting and arranging skills were prevalent on many of these performances, including 'Knock On Wood' (Eddie Floyd), 'Sookie Sookie' (Don Covay), 'In The Midnight Hour' (Wilson Pickett) and 'Mr. Pitiful' and '(Sittin' On) The Dock Of The Bay' (Otis Redding). The MGs continued to record until the end of the decade, but they broke up when organist Booker T. Jones moved to California. Cropper preferred to maintain a low-key profile and although he recorded a pleasant solo album, *With A Little Help From My Friends*, he chose to concentrate on running his Memphis-based studio, TMI, rather than embrace the public acclaim he richly deserved. TMI subsequently folded and Cropper resettled in Los Angeles, returning to session work and production. He featured largely on the Rod Stewart 1975 UK number 1, *Atlantic Crossing*. The surviving MGs were reunited following the death of drummer Al Jackson, and the group has since pursued this erratic existence.

The guitarist was also a member of the Blues Brothers, a band formed by comedians John Belushi and Dan Ackroyd which led to the successful film of the same name. The group recorded three albums, following which Cropper released his second solo collection, *Playing My Thang*. Cropper has continued a low-key approach to his art during the 80s although he has made several live appearances in the UK in the early 90s, particularly in the wake of a revived interest in the Blues Brothers. His distinctive sparse, clipped, high treble sound with his Fender Telecaster has been heard on literally hundreds of singles and albums. His reluctance to hog the limelight cannot disguise the fact that he is one of the major figures in soul music, remarkable in that he is an 'all-American white boy'.

●ALBUMS: with Albert King, 'Pops' Staples *Jammed Together* (1969)★★★, *With A Little Help From My Friends* (1971)★★, *Playing My Thang* (1980)★★.
●FILMS: *The Blues Brothers* (1980).

CROSBY, STILLS AND NASH

David Crosby (b. 14 August 1941, Los Angeles, California, USA), Stephen Stills (b. 3 January 1945, Dallas, Texas, USA) and Graham Nash (b. 2 February 1942, Blackpool, Lancashire, England) joined forces in 1969 after parting with their previous groups, the Byrds, Buffalo Springfield and the Hollies, respectively. Inevitably, they attracted considerable media attention as a 'supergroup' but unlike similar aggregations of their era, they were a genuine team who respected each other's work and recognized the importance of their contribution to American popular music. Their self-titled debut album was a superlative achievement containing several of the finest songs that they would ever write: 'Long Time Gone', 'Suite: Judy Blue Eyes', (with possibly the most joyous climax ever recorded), 'Lady Of The Island' and the powerfully thought-provoking 'Wooden Ships'. Strong lyrics, solid acoustic musicianship and staggeringly faultless three-part harmonies was the mixture that they concocted and it was enough to influence a new generation of American performers for the next decade. The need to perform live convinced them to extend their ranks and with the induction of Neil Young they reached an even bigger international audience as Crosby, Stills, Nash And Young. Internal bickering and policy differences split the group at its peak and although Crosby And Nash proved a successful offshoot, the power of the original trio was never forgotten and only occasionally matched by its descendants. It was not until 1977 that the CS&N permutation reunited for *CSN*, a strong comeback album with such highlights as 'Shadow Captain', 'Dark Star' and 'Cathedral'. The trio toured the USA and seemed more united than at any time since its inception, but subsequent recording sessions proved unsatisfactory and the individuals once more drifted apart. A further five years passed, during which Crosby's drug abuse gradually alienated him from his colleagues. In a previously untried combination, Stills and Nash set about recording an album, but were eventually persuaded by Atlantic Records' founder Ahmet Ertegun to bring back Crosby to the fold. He returned late in the sessions and although his contribution was not major, he did proffer one of the strongest tracks, 'Delta'. The resulting album, *Daylight Again*, was disproportionately balanced as a result of Crosby's late arrival, but the songs were nevertheless good. The title track from Stills was one of his best, borrowed from the memorable live set of his 1973 group, Manassas. Nash's offerings included the US Top 10 hit 'Wasted On The Way' and provided the commercial clout to sustain CS&N as one of the major concert attractions of the day. Following a tour of Europe, the trio again splintered and with Crosby incapacitated by cocaine addiction it seemed that their zigzag story had finally ended. Fortunately, imprisonment reached Crosby before the Grim Reaper and upon his release he reunited CSN&Y for an album and took CS&N on the road. *Live It Up*, their first recording as a trio in 10 years, boasted a tasteless sleeve while the material lacked the edge of their best work. Now the doyens of the 70s rock circuit, their concerts still show flashes of the old brilliance while overly relying on former classics that occasionally come dangerously close to nostalgia at the expense of their finest quality: innovation. A CD box set was put together by Nash in 1991. This collection included unreleased tracks and alternative versions and led to a critical reappraisal that year. Recent live concerts (1994) indicate that the trio are singing with more passion and confidence than ever, although their recent studio recordings have suffered from a lack of strong songs. This was highlighted on *After The Storm*, a disappointing collection, against which the public reacted.

●ALBUMS: *Crosby, Stills And Nash* (Atlantic 1969)★★★★, *CSN* (Atlantic 1977)★★★★, *Daylight Again* (Atlantic 1982)★★★, *Allies* (Atlantic 1983)★★★, *Live It Up* (Atlantic 1990)★★, *Crosby, Stills And Nash* 4-CD box set (Atlantic 1991)★★★★★, *After The Storm* (Atlantic 1994)★★.

●COMPILATIONS: *Replay* (Atlantic 1980)★★★★.

●VIDEOS: *Daylight Again* (CIC 1983), *Acoustic* (Warner Music Vision 1991), *Crosby, Stills And Nash: Long Time Comin'* (Wienerworld 1994).

●FURTHER READING: *Crosby, Stills & Nash: The Authorized Biography*, Dave Zimmer. *Prisoner Of Woodstock*, Dallas Taylor. *The Visual Documentary*, Johnny Rogan.

CRYAN' SHAMES

Two 60s groups claimed the above name , although a misspelling differentiated the British and American bands. Formed in Chicago in 1965, the Cryan Shames - Tom 'Toad' Doody (b. 1945; vocals), Jim (Hook) Pilster (b. 1947; tambourine), Jim Fairs (b. 1948; lead guitar), Gerry Stone (b. 1945; rhythm guitar), Dave Purple (b. 1945; bass) and Dennis Conroy (b. 1948; drums) - made their debut with a version of 'Sugar And Spice', previously a hit for the Searchers. Although the single only rose to number 49 in the US charts, interest in the group proved sufficient to warrant an album. *Sugar And Spice* was a hurried affair, indebted to the Byrds and British beat, but the Cryan' Shames asserted a greater individuality on a second selection, *A Scratch In The Sky*. Here they showed an understanding of harmony pop akin to that of the Association, while the group's final album, *Synthesis*, blended such talent with some truly lavish instrumentation. The sextet was later hampered by personnel changes. Purple and Stone were replaced by Isaac Guillory (b. 27 February 1947, US Naval Base, Guantanamo Bay, Cuba) and Lenny Kerley, but such alterations had little effect on the group's ultimate progress. By 1970 they had broken up; Guillory embarked on a solo career, Fairs began session work, Kerley and Conroy formed Possum River, and the brief career of the Cryan' Shames was ended.

●ALBUMS: *Sugar And Spice* (Columbia 1966)★★, *A Scratch In The Sky* (Columbia 1967)★★★, *Synthesis* (1969)★★★.

●COMPILATIONS: *Sugar And Spice* (1988)★★★.

CRYSTALS

This highly influential 60s US female vocal group were the product of Phil Spector, for his pioneering Philles record label. They, along with the Ronettes, were one of the definitive 'wall of sound' groups of the 60s. They came together after meeting in the legendary Brill Building where the group were preparing demos for the Aberbach's famous publishing company Hill and Range. The line-up comprised Dee Dee Kennibrew (b. Dolores Henry, 1945, Brooklyn, New York, USA), La La Brooks (b. 1946, Brooklyn, New York, USA), Pat Wright (b. 1945, Brooklyn, New York, USA), Mary Thomas (b. 1946, Brooklyn, New York, USA) and Barbara Alston who was their manager's niece. Spector was impressed and produced the debut 'There's No Other (Like My Baby)' in 1961. At this time Spector was developing his unique sound by mixing numerous layers of vocals and instruments on to one mono track. The blurred result was demonstrated on 'Uptown' but it was taken to its glorious extreme on Gene Pitney's song 'He's A Rebel'. The latter featured the lead vocals of Darlene Wright (Love), and, as Spector owned the name, he could use whoever he wanted as the Crystals. It became a number 1 single in the USA (UK number 19). La la Brooks returned to the lead vocal on two further hits which have since become timeless classics, 'Da Doo Ron Ron (When He Walked Me Home)' and 'Then He Kissed Me', both major hits in 1963. The Beach Boys attempted a Spector-like production with their own version, 'Then I Kissed Her', in 1967. The Crystals were soon overtaken when their mentor devoted more time to the Ronettes, and consequently their career faltered. New members passed through, including Frances Collins, and the band were prematurely banished to the nostalgia circuit.

●ALBUMS: *Twist Uptown* (Philles 1962)★★, *He's A Rebel* (Philles 1963)★★★.

●COMPILATIONS: *The Crystals Sing Their Greatest Hits* (Philles 1963)★★★, *Uptown* (1988)★★★, *The Best Of* (ABKCO 1992)★★★.

CUBY AND THE BLIZZARDS

The Netherlands' premier blues band, Cuby And The Blizzards originated in the town of Grolloo and was founded when Harry 'Cuby' Muskee (vocals/harmonica) joined forces with Eelco Gelling (lead guitar). The group, also known as C + B, was later completed by Hans Kinds (guitar), Willy Middel (bass) and Dick Beekman (drums). Their debut single, 'Stumble And Fall' (1965), bore a debt to the Pretty Things, but successive releases, including 'Your Body Is Not Your Soul' and 'Back Home A Man', revealed a startling individuality. Gelling's incisive style, which drew praise from John Mayall, was already evident on *Desolation*, while the group also completed the excellent *Praise The Blues* with veteran US pianist Eddie Boyd. Their kudos was further enhanced by accompanying Van Morrison during a tour of The Netherlands undertaken following the singer's departure from Them. Although Muskee and Gelling remained at the helm, changes in personnel undermined the group's progress. Pianist Herman Brood was one of many musicians passing through the Blizzards' ranks as they fused their blues-based style to progressive rock. However, by 1976 the duo had tired of their creation and while Muskee formed the Harry Muskee Band, Gelling opted to join Golden Earring. The long career of Cuby And The Blizzards was then maintained by Herman Deinum (bass), Hans Lafaille (drums) - both of whom had joined in 1969 - Rudy van Dijk (vocals), Paul Smeenk (guitar) and Jeff Reynolds (trumpet). This line-up remained active into the 80s.

●ALBUMS: *Desolation* (1966)★★★, with Eddie Boyd

Praise The Blues (1967)★★★★, *Groeten Uit Grolloo* (1967)★★★, *Trippin' Thru' A Midnight Blues* (1968)★★★, *Live!* (1968)★★, *On The Road (Boek En Plaat)* (1968)★★★, *Cuby's Blues* (1969)★★★, *Appleknockers Flophouse* (1969)★★★, *Too Blind To See* (1970)★★★, *King Of The World* (1970)★★★, *Simple Man* (1971)★★, *Sometimes* (1972)★★, *Ballads* (1973)★★, *Afscheidsconsert* (1974)★★, *Kid Blue* (1976)★★, *The Forgotten Tapes* (1979)★★, *Cuby And The Blizzards, Featuring Herman Brood - Live* (1979)★★.

●COMPILATIONS: *The Best Of Cuby And The Blizzards* (1974)★★★, *Old Times Good Times* (1977)★★★.

CUFF LINKS

The brainchild of Pat Rizzo (formerly of Joey Dee And The Starliters), the Cuff Links were a studio group featuring Ron Dante, lead singer of the Archies. Rizzo had recruited songwriters Paul Vance and Lee Pockriss who had previously composed hits for Perry Como ('Catch A Falling Star') and Brian Hyland ('Itsy Bitsy Teenie Weenie Yellow Polkadot Bikini'). The songwriting duo came up with the catchy, bubblegum singalong 'Tracy', which became an international hit. Dante was the sole multi-voiced singer on the original recording but once the song charted, a group was specially created comprising Pat Rizzo (vocals), Rick Dimino (keyboards), Bob Gill (trumpet/flugelhorn/flute), Dave Loxender (guitar), Andrew 'Junior' Deno (bass), Joe Cord (vocals) and Davy Valentine (drums). The group recorded further singles and two albums before disbanding in the early 70s.

●ALBUMS: *Tracy* (MCA 1969)★★★, *The Cuff Links* (1970)★★.

CUPID'S INSPIRATION

Based in Stamford, Lincolnshire, England, and initially known as the Ends, this pop attraction secured a recording deal with NEMS on the strength of vocalist T. (Terry) Rice-Milton (b. 5 June 1946). The line-up was completed by Wyndham George (b. 20 February 1947; guitar), Laughton James (b. 21 December 1946; bass) and Roger Gray (b. 29 April 1949) and featured on 'Yesterday Has Gone' (1968), a song originally recorded by Little Anthony And The Imperials. Cupid's cover version rose to number 4 in the UK chart, during which time pianist Garfield Tonkin (b. 28 September 1946) was added to the group. However, despite enjoying a subsequent minor hit with 'My World', the quintet was unable to repeat the success of their powerful and catchy debut single. The line-up was disbanded at the end of the year, but within weeks Rice-Milton and Gray re-emerged alongside newcomers Bernie Lee (guitar) and Gordon Haskell (bass). A new-found, more 'progressive' style, failed to reverse declining fortunes and the group disintegrated. Its vocalist began a short-lived solo career in 1970 with a revival of Cilla Black's 'You're My World', while Haskell, formerly of Fleur De Lys, later found fame with King Crimson.

●ALBUMS: *Yesterday Has Gone* (Nems 1968)★★.

CYMBAL, JOHNNY

b. 3 February 1945, Ochiltree, Clyde, Scotland. Cymbal's family moved to Canada while he was a child. He became infatuated with music in his teens and in 1960 the singer, then living in Cleveland, Ohio, USA, secured a recording deal with MGM Records. His early releases included 'The Water Is Red', a macabre 'death disc' in which Cymbal's girlfriend was eaten by a shark. In 1963 the artist switched outlets to Kapp Records for whom he recorded 'Mr. Bass Man', a humorous paean to the vocalist carrying the bottom line in a harmony group, in this case one Ronnie Bright. The single, evocative of a passing singing style, reached number 16 in the US and number 24 in the UK, and has since become one of the most memorable novelty songs of the pre-Beatles era. However, despite a succession of subsequent releases, Cymbal was unable to secure another hit and instead forged a new career in songwriting. He penned 'Mary In The Morning', a US hit for Al Martino in 1967 and later produced several records for David Cassidy and Gene Pitney. Domiciled in Nashville since 1980, Cymbal now concentrates on country material.

●ALBUMS: *Mr. Bass Man* (Kapp 1963)★★.

CYRKLE

Founder members of this harmony pop act, Don Dannemann (b. Albany, New York, USA; guitar/vocals) and Tom Dawes (b. Brooklyn, New York, USA; guitar/vocals) met while studying at Lafayette College. Together they formed a 'frat' band, the Rhondells, with Earl Pickens (keyboards) and Marty Fried (drums) which honed a set drawn from songs by the Beach Boys and Four Seasons. They were 'discovered' playing at New Jersey's Alibi Lounge by New York attorney Nat Weiss, who introduced the group to Beatles manager Brian Epstein. He signed the Rhondells to his NEMS roster; John Lennon reported by suggested their new name, the Cyrkle. The incipient act then broke up temporarily, leaving Dawes free to tour with Simon And Garfunkel. Paul Simon offered the bassist 'Red Rubber Ball', a song he co-wrote with Bruce Woodley of the Seekers' which gave the reconvened Cyrkle a number 2 US hit in 1966. The group supported the Beatles on the latter's final tour but having passed on another Simon composition, '59 Street Bridge Song (Feeling Groovy)', later a hit for Harpers Bizarre, the Cyrkle enjoyed their final Top 20 entry with 'Turn Down Day', which featured Dawes' memorable sitar line. Pickens was replaced by Mike Losecamp for *Neon*, but the death of Epstein in 1967 virtually ended the Cyrkle's career. They broke up in January 1968 when Dawes and Losecamp quit the line-up. The former later found success penning advertising jingles, a career Dannemann also followed.

●ALBUMS: *Red Rubber Ball* (Columbia 1966)★★, *Neon* (Columbia 1967)★★.

●COMPILATIONS: *Red Rubber Ball (A Collection)* (Columbia Legacy 1991)★★.

D'ABO, MICHAEL

b. 1 March 1944, Betchworth, Surrey, England. Vocalist D'Abo was a founder member of beat group A Band Of Angels, formed at Harrow School. A highly competent songwriter, he penned the last of the group's four singles, 'Invitation', before replacing Paul Jones in Manfred Mann in 1966. D'Abo proved a worthy successor, and was featured on many of their best-known releases, including 'Semi Detached Suburban Mr. Jones' (1966), 'Ha Ha Said The Clown' (1967) and 'Mighty Quinn' (1968). D'Abo also won plaudits for his much-covered composition, 'Handbags And Gladrags', while 'Build Me Up Buttercup', a collaboration with Tony Macauley, was a million-selling hit for the Foundations. D'Abo left Manfred Mann in 1969 when they embraced a 'progressive rock' style, and subsequently unveiled his affection for crafted pop. Broken Rainbows featured a stellar cast, including Graham Nash and Mike Bloomfield, but the singer was unable to achieve commercial success. In 1976 he joined Mike Smith, ex-Dave Clark Five, in a performing/songwriting partnership, Smith And D'Abo. Once again widespread acclaim proved elusive, and the artist has since pursued a less public, yet still productive, career. D'Abo composed several advertising jingles, including television's long-running 'finger of fudge' for Cadbury's chocolate.
●ALBUMS: *Gulliver's Travels* (Instant 1968)★★, *D'Abo* (MCA 1970)★★, *Down At Rachel's Place* (A&M 1972)★★, *Broken Rainbows* (A&M 1974)★★, with Mike Smith *Smith & D'Abo* (1976)★★★, *Indestructible* (1987)★★, *Tomorrow's Troubadour* (1988)★★.

DAILY FLASH

Formed in Seattle, Washington, USA, in 1965, the Daily Flash was the confluence of former bluegrass veteran Don MacAllister (bass), ex-folk singer Steve Lalor (guitar), jazz drummer Jon Keliehor and lead guitarist Doug Hastings. The unit boasted a repertoire drawn from all these sources and was quickly established as the city's leading 'alternative' attraction. Their debut single, 'Jack Of Diamonds'/Bob Dylan's 'Queen Jane Approximately', was released in 1965 and preceded a successful series of concerts in San Francisco and Los Angeles the following year. Despite an acclaimed second single, 'The French Girl'/'Green Rocky Road', and a bizarre appearance in television's The Girl From UNCLE, the group did not achieve commercial success and the line-up then fragmented. Keliehor left in May 1967, while Hastings briefly replaced Neil Young in Buffalo Springfield before becoming a founder member of Rhinoceros. Craig

Tarwater (guitar) and Tony Dey (drums) subsequently joined Daily Flash, but the group broke up the following year. MacAllister became immersed in the blues circuit prior to his premature death in 1969, while Keliehor and Lalor pursued several projects both together and individually. The most notable of those was *1 Flash Daily*, a collection of previously issued and archive selections, which featured a lengthy live rendition of Herbie Hancock's 'Canteloupe Island'.
●ALBUMS: *1 Flash Daily* (Psycho 1984)★★.

DAKOTAS

Originally formed in Manchester, England, the Dakotas - Mike Maxfield (b. 23 February 1944, Manchester, England; guitar), Robin McDonald (b. 18 July 1943, Nairn, Scotland; guitar), Ray Jones (b. 22 October 1939, Oldham, Lancashire, England; bass) and Tony Mansfield (b. Anthony Bookbinder, 28 May 1943, Salford, Lancashire, England; drums) - achieved fame as the backing group to Liverpudlian singer Billy J. Kramer. His success inspired the quartet's own recording career which enjoyed a promising beginning when their debut single, 'The Cruel Sea', reached the UK Top 20 in July 1963. This surf-influenced instrumental was succeeded by 'Magic Carpet', but this release failed to achieve a similar profile. When Jones left the line-up in July 1964, McDonald switched to bass in order to accommodate former Pirates guitarist Mick Green. The Dakotas continued to support Kramer, and over the next four years they recorded three further singles in their own right. The group was reduced to a trio in 1965 when Maxfield left to concentrate on songwriting. Another ex-Pirate, drummer Frank Farley, replaced Mansfield in 1966. He, Green and MacDonald later joined singer Cliff Bennett following the Dakotas' demise in 1968.

DALE AND GRACE

Dale Houston (b. 1944, Baton Rouge, Louisiana, USA), and Grace Broussard (b. 1944, Prairieville, Louisiana, USA). Both singers had sung solo and Grace had also sang with her brother Van (later of soul duo Van And Titus) before they teamed up at a recording session for the local Montel label in 1963. Their first recording, a revival of Don And Dewey's ballad 'I'm Leaving It Up To You', found success in the south and soon went to number 1 in the US charts and narrowly missed the UK Top 40. The duo also put their follow-up 'Stop And Think It Over' into the US Top 10 and had a minor hit with 'The Loneliest Night'. Their debut album also made the US Top 100. This distinctive R&B-orientated pop duo later had unsuccessful releases on Guyden and Hanna-Barbera. Their biggest hit song became a transatlantic Top 10 record in 1974 for Donny and Marie Osmond.
●ALBUMS: *I'm Leaving It Up To You* (Montel 1964)★★.

DALE, DICK

b. Richard Monsour, 4 May 1937, Boston, Massachusetts, USA. (Note: Dale himself has been quoted in interviews as saying he was born in Beirut, Lebanon, and that his family emigrated to Quincy, Massachusetts, when he was a child. Now, however Dale denies that story and claims to have been born in Boston.) Dale is usually credited as the inventor of the instrumental surf music style and the major influence on surf guitar. With his group the Del-Tones, Dale's early 60s records sparked the surf music craze on the US west coast. His guitar-playing influenced hundreds of other musicians. Dale started out as a pianist at the age of nine, and also played trumpet and harmonica. His first musical interest was country music and his idol was Hank Williams. Dale switched to the ukulele and then finally guitar. Dale's family moved to El Segundo, California in 1954 and he took a job at an aircraft company after graduating from high school. Having learned country guitar, he entered talent contests, still performing under his real name. The name Dick Dale was suggested to him by a Texas disc jockey named T. Texas Tiny. Dale gained popularity as a local country singer and also appeared in concerts with rhythm and blues artists. He also gained a small role in a Marilyn Monroe film, *Let's Make Love*. Dale's first record was 'Ooh-Whee-Marie' on the Del-Tone label, which his father owned. He eventually recorded nine singles for that label between 1959 and 1962, and also recorded for the Cupid label. One of those Del-Tone singles, 'Let's Go Trippin'', released in 1961, is generally considered to be the first instrumental surf record. According to Dale, he and his cousin were riding motorcycles to the beach on the Balboa Peninsula in southern California, where Dale befriended the local surfers. There he also began playing with a band at a club called the Rinky Dink. Another guitar player showed him how to make certain adjustments to the pickup settings on his Stratocaster guitar to create different sounds, and that sound, aided by other sonic developments and featuring Dale's staccato attack, became his trademark. Although he was still playing country music, he moved closer to the beach and began surfing during the day and playing music at night, adding rock 'n' roll to his repertoire. By then Dale had formed his own band, the Del-Tones, including piano, guitars, bass, drums and saxophone, and shifted his home base to the Rendezvous Ballroom down the beach from the Rinky Dink. The group, like most others, performed vocal compositions, until one patron asked Dale if the band could play an instrumental song. Inspired by his surfing hobby, Dale composed a tune that he felt captured the feeling of riding the waves and the power of the ocean. Once the group began adding more instrumental songs in this style to its repertoire, the crowd grew in size until the Rendezvous was packed to capacity. At one point city officials tried to run Dale out of town, believing that his music was having a negative effect on the local youth. Playing left-handed without reversing the strings, Dale started to fine-tune the surf guitar style. He met with Leo Fender, the inventor of the Fender guitar and amplifier line, and worked with him on designing equipment that would be more suited to that style of music (Dale helped to develop the popular Showman amp). Along with other

innovations, such as the first outboard reverb unit, which helped define the surf sound, the JBL speaker and the Rhodes piano, Dale was able virtually to reinvent this new style of rock 'n' roll as he went along. 'Let's Go Trippin'' was the first instrumental recording by Dale, and one of only two singles to make the US national charts (at number 60, based entirely on local sales in California), with 'Shake 'N' Stomp' and 'Misirlou' also popular early Dale singles on Del-Tone. Dale released his first album, Surfer's Choice, also on Del-Tone, in 1962. Recorded live, it was one of the first albums to feature a surfer (Dale) on the cover. (At the same time, vocal surf music, as pioneered by the Beach Boys, began to take off, but the two styles have little in common musically. Moreover Dale's first recording preceded theirs by two months.) The instrumental surf music craze was initially largely confined to the Orange County area, but its popularity there became so overwhelming that Los Angeles radio stations began playing the music of Dale and the other new surf groups. In 1963, after *Surfer's Choice* made the national album charts (number 59), Capitol Records signed Dale to a seven-album contract (only five were released). One of Dale's singles for Capitol, 'The Scavenger', made the US charts, as did the *Checkered Flag* album that year, but Dale never charted again, remaining almost entirely a local phenomenon while becoming a major influence on other musicians. Dale appeared on the *Ed Sullivan Show* on US television and received national press coverage, but his reluctance to travel, combined with the brief popularity of surf music, hindered his career advancement. He appeared in the 1964 film *Muscle Beach Party* but that same year, with the arrival of the British groups, Capitol had shifted its priorities and Dale was dropped from the label less than two years after signing to it. He continued to record sporadically throughout the rest of the 60s and 70s for numerous labels but a cancer scare, which he overcame, effectively sidelined his career. His music was rediscovered in the 80s, and he recorded a scorching duet with Stevie Ray Vaughan of the old Chantays surf instrumental 'Pipeline' in 1987 for the film *Back To The Beach*. In 1989, Rhino Records released a compilation of Dale's best recordings, and in the early 90s Dale signed with the US label Hightone Records. His 1993 album *Tribal Thunder* and the 1994 follow-up, *Unknown Territory*, as well as numerous live gigs across the USA, have showed that Dale's influence remains strong and that his powers as a musician, although limited, are undiminished. In 1994 his recording of 'Misirlou' was prominently featured in the Quentin Tarantino film *Pulp Fiction*, bringing Dale new recognition to a much younger audience. This resulted in a new phase of his career, being able to trade on the word 'legendary' wherever he went and launched a revitalized recording career.

●ALBUMS: *Surfer's Choice* (Deltone 1962)★★★, *King Of The Surf Guitar* (Capitol 1963)★★★, *Checkered Flag* (Capitol 1963)★★★, *Mr. Eliminator* (Capitol 1964)★★★, *Summer Surf* (Capitol 1964)★★★, *Rock Out - Live At Ciro's* (Capitol 1965)★★, *The Tiger's*

Loose (1983)★★, *Tribal Thunder* (Hightone 1993)★★, *Unknown Territory* (Hightone 1994)★★★, *Calling Up Spirits* (Beggars Banquet 1996)★★★.
●COMPILATIONS: *Dick Dale's Greatest Hits* (1975)★★★, *King Of The Surf Guitar* (Rhino 1986)★★★, *The Best Of Dick Dale* (1989)★★★.

DANTALIAN'S CHARIOT

Formed in London, England, in 1967, Dantalian's Chariot comprised four ex-members of Zoot Money's Big Roll Band; Zoot Money (vocals/keyboards), Andy Somers (guitar), Pat Donaldson (bass) and Colin Allen (drums). The new act eschewed the R&B style of its predecessor in favour of the prevailing 'flower power' trend. Indeed, Dantalian's Chariot boasted one of the most innovative light shows of the era. The group issued one single during its short life span. 'The Madman Running Through The Fields' is a quintessential slice of English psychedelia, replete with sound effects, backward-running tapes and escapist lyrics. Other tracks, recorded at the same time, remained unissued, although some were resurrected for Money's 'solo' release *Transition* (1968). He and Somers subsequently joined Eric Burdon And The New Animals. Donaldson was later a member of Fotheringay, while Allen played with John Mayall and Stone The Crows. Money has remained a popular attraction both as a singer and actor, while Somers, as Andy Summers, found fame in the Police.
●ALBUMS: *Chariot Rising* (Wooden Hill 1997)★★★.

DARIN, BOBBY

b. Walden Robert Cassotto, 14 May 1936, New York, USA, d. 20 December 1973. Darin's entry to the music business occurred during the mid-50s following a period playing in New York coffeehouses. His friendship with co-writer/entrepreneur Don Kirshner resulted in his first single, 'My First Love'. A meeting with Connie Francis' manager George Scheck led to a prestigious television appearance on the Tommy Dorsey television show and a contract with Decca. An unsuccessful attempt at a hit with a cover version of Lonnie Donegan's 'Rock Island Line' was followed by a move towards pop novelty with 'Splish Splash'. Darin's quirky vocal ensured that his song was a worldwide hit, although he was outsold in Britain by a rival version from comedian Charlie Drake. During this period, Darin also recorded in a group called the Ding Dongs, which prompted a dispute between Atco and Brunswick Records, culminating in the creation of a new group, the Rinky Dinks, who were credited as the backing artists on his next single, 'Early In The Morning'. Neither that, nor its successor, 'Mighty Mighty', proved commercially viable, but the intervening Darin solo release, 'Queen Of The Hop', sold a million. The period charm of 'Plain Jane' presaged one of Darin's finest moments - the exceptional 'Dream Lover'. An enticing vocal performance allied to strong production took the song to number 1 in the UK and number 2 in the USA.
Already assured of considerable status as a pop artist, Darin dramatically changed direction with his next

recording and emerged as a finger-clicking master of the supperclub circuit. 'Mack The Knife', composed by Bertolt Brecht and Kurt Weill for the celebrated musical *The Threepenny Opera*, proved a million-seller and effectively raised Darin to new status as a 'serious singer' - he even compared himself favourably with Frank Sinatra, in what was a classic example of pop hubris. Darin's hit treatments of 'La Mer (Beyond The Sea)', 'Clementine', 'Won't You Come Home Bill Bailey?' and 'You Must Have Been A Beautiful Baby' revealed his ability to tackle variety material and transform it to his own ends.
In 1960, Darin adeptly moved into film and was highly praised for his roles in *Come September* (whose star Sandra Dee he later married), *State Fair*, *Too Late Blues*, *If A Man Answers*, *Pressure Point*, *Hell Is For Heroes* and *Captain Newman MD*. He returned to form as a pop performer with the lyrically witty 'Multiplication' and the equally clever 'Things'. In the meantime, he had recorded an album of Ray Charles' songs, including the standard 'What'd I Say'. During the beat boom era Darin briefly reverted to show tunes such as 'Baby Face' and 'Hello Dolly', but a further change of style beckoned with the folk rock boom of 1965. Suddenly, Darin was a protest singer, summing up the woes of a generation with the surly 'We Didn't Ask To Be Brought Here'. Successful readings of Tim Hardin songs, including 'If I Were A Carpenter' and 'The Lady Came From Baltimore', and John Sebastian's 'Lovin' You' and 'Darling Be Home Soon' demonstrated his potential as a cover artist of seemingly limitless range. A more contemporary poetic and political direction was evident on the album *Born Walden Robert Cassotto*, and its serious follow-up *Commitment*. As the 60s ended Darin was more actively involved in related business interests, although he still appeared regularly on television. One of the great vocal chameleons of pop music, Darin suffered from a weak heart and after several operations, time finally caught up with the singer at Hollywood's Cedars of Lebanon Hospital in December 1973.
●ALBUMS: *Bobby Darin* (Atco 1958)★★★★, *That's All* (Atco 1959)★★★, *This Is Darin* (Atco 1960)★★★, *Darin At The Copa* (Atco 1960)★★★, *For Teenagers Only* (Atco 1960)★★★, *It's You Or No-One* (Atco 1960)★★★, *The 25th December* (Atco 1960)★★★, soundtrack *Pepe* (Colpix 1960)★★, with Johnny Mercer *Two Of A Kind* (Atco 1961)★★★, *Love Swings* (Atco 1961)★★★, *Twist With Bobby Darin* (Atco 1962)★★★, *Darin Sings Ray Charles* (Atco 1962)★★★, *Oh Look At Me Now* (Capitol 1962)★★★, *It's You Or No One* (Atco 1962)★★★, *Earthy* (Capitol 1963)★★★, *You're The Reason I'm Living* (Capitol 1963)★★★, *Eighteen Yellow Roses* (Capitol 1963)★★★, *Golden Folk Hits* (Capitol 1963)★★★, *Winners* (Atco 1964)★★★, *From Hello Dolly To Goodbye Charlie* (Capitol 1964)★★, *Venice Blue* (Capitol 1965)★★, *In A Broadway Bag* (Atlantic) (1966)★★, *The Shadow Of Your Smile* (Atlantic 1966)★★, *If I Were A Carpenter* (Atlantic 1966)★★★★, *Inside Out* (Atlantic 1967)★★★, *Bobby*

Darin Sings Doctor Doolittle (Atlantic 1967)★, *Bobby Darin Something Special* (1967)★★★, *Born Walden Robert Cassotto* (Direction 1968)★★★, *Commitment* (Direction 1969)★★★.
●COMPILATIONS: *The Bobby Darin Story* (Atco 1961)★★★★, *Things And Other Things* (Atco 1962)★★★, *The Best Of Bobby Darin* (Capitol 1966)★★★, *The Versatile Bobby Darin* (1985)★★★, *The Legend Of Bobby Darin* (1985)★★★, *His Greatest Hits* (1985)★★★, *Bobby Darin: Collectors Series* (Capitol 1989)★★★, *Splish Splash: The Best Of Bobby Darin Vol . 1* (Atco 1991)★★★, *Mack The Knife: The Best Of Bobby Darin Vol. 2* (Atco 1991)★★★, *Spotlight On Bobby Darin* (Capitol 1995)★★★, *As Long As I'm Singing: The Bobby Darin Collection* 4-CD box set (Rhino 1995)★★★★.
●FURTHER READING: *Borrowed Time: The 37 Years Of Bobby Darin*, Al Diorio. *Dream Lovers*, Dodd Darin.
●FILMS: *Pepe* (1960), *Come September* (1961), *If A Man Answers* (1962), *Hell Is For Heroes* (1962), *Too Late Blues* (1962), *Pressure Point* (1962), *Captain Newman M.D.* (1963), *That Funny Feeling* (1965), *Gunfight In Abilene* (1967), *Stranger In The House/Cop-Out* (1968), *The Happy Ending* (1969), *Happy Mother's Day-Love George/Run Stranger Run* (1973).

DARREN, JAMES

b. James Ercolani, 3 October 1936, Philadelphia, Pennsylvania, USA. The photogenic actor/singer was signed to Columbia Pictures in the mid-50s, his first film being *Rumble On The Docks* in 1956. He first sang in the film *Gidget* in 1959 and the title song made the US chart. He also starred in *Because They're Young* in 1960 and the epic *The Guns Of Navarone* in 1961. In 1962 he debuted in the US Top 20 with his lucky 13th single 'Goodbye Cruel World' and followed it with two more US Top 20 and UK Top 40 hits 'Her Royal Majesty', a Carole King song, and 'Conscience', written by Barry Mann. Darren later recorded with little success on Warner Brothers in 1965, Kirshner in 1969, Buddah in 1970, MGM in 1973, Private Stock in 1975 (where he returned briefly to the US Top 100 in 1977) and RCA in 1978. This distinctively voiced pop/MOR singer is perhaps now best remembered for playing the role of Tony Newman in the popular and often re-run 60s television series *The Time Tunnel*, although the memorable fairground atmosphere of 'Goodbye Cruel World' was probably his finest moment on record.
●ALBUMS: *James Darren Vol. 1* (Colpix 1960)★★, *Gidget Goes Hawaiian* (Colpix 1961)★★, *James Darren Sings For All Sizes* (Colpix 1962)★★★, *Love Among The Young* (Colpix 1962)★★, *Bye Bye Birdie* (Colpix 1963)★★, with Shelly Fabares, Paul Peterson *Teenage Triangle* (1963)★★, *The Lively Set* soundtrack (Decca 1964)★, with Fabares, Peterson *More Teenage Triangle* (Colpix 1964), *All* (1967)★.
●COMPILATIONS: *The Best Of ...* (Sequel 1994)★★★.
●FILMS: *Because They're Young* (1960).

DASSIN, JOE

b. 5 November 1938, New York, USA, of Hungarian descent. Dassin changed secondary schools 11 times in three years owing to the peripatetic career of his father, renowned film director Jules Dassin, whom he assisted during the Crete shoot of *Celui Qui Doit Mourir* in the interim before a ethnology course at the University of Michigan. This led eventually to a doctorate in philosophy and a reputation in local folk clubs as a singing guitarist with a penchant for the songs of Georges Brassens. His formal education over, he was re-employed by his father in minor roles, such as a gypsy in the 1964 film *Topkapi* and an anarchist in *Lady L* (starring Sophia Loren). He was initially contracted to record 'Bip Bip', 'Katy Cruel' and other lightweight singles produced by Jacques Plait and distributed throughout France and her colonies, but it was only when Dassin made surprising headway in North America that he was able to stoke up greater interest at home. In January 1967, he hosted the first MIDEM festival in Cannes, which provided an opportunity to plug 'Les Dalton', his vocal interpretation of a Plait instrumental, which sold well that spring. However, Dassin's days as a pop idol were numbered - although a more lucrative destiny awaited him as a media personality.

DAVE DEE, DOZY, BEAKY, MICK AND TICH

Formed in 1961 as Dave Dee And The Boston, this zany quintet found a settled hit line-up as Dave Dee (b. David Harman, 17 December 1943, Salisbury, Wiltshire, England; vocals), Dozy (b. Trevor Davies, 27 November 1944, Enford, Wiltshire, England; bass), Beaky (b. John Dymond, 10 July 1944, Salisbury, Wiltshire, England; guitar), Mick (b. Michael Wilson, 4 March 1944, Amesbury, Wiltshire, England; lead guitar) and Tich (Ian Amey, 15 May 1944, Salisbury, Wiltshire, England). The group established their power as live performers during residencies at various Hamburg clubs in 1962. Their act featured rock 'n' roll spiced with comedy routines and an element of risqué patter from their engaging frontman. While supporting the Honeycombs on a 1964 UK tour, they came to the attention of managers Howard And Blaikley (Ken Howard and Alan Blaikley) and were subsequently signed to Fontana Records by Jack Baverstock and assigned to producer Steve Rowland. After two unsuccessful singles, 'No Time' and 'All I Want', they hit the UK chart with the upbeat 'You Make It Move'. Thereafter, they had an incredible run of a dozen strong chart hits, all executed with a camp flair and costume-loving theatricalism that proved irresistible. With songs provided by Howard & Blaikley, they presented a veritable travelogue of pop, filled with melodramatic scenarios. 'Bend It' was their 'Greek' phase, and allowed Dave Dee to wiggle his little finger while uttering the curiously suggestive lyric; 'Zabadak' was an exotic arrangement sung in a unknown language; 'The Legend Of Xanadu' was a ripping yarn, which allowed Dee to brandish a bullwhip in live performance; 'Last Night In

Soho' was a leather-boy motorbike saga portraying lost innocence in London's most notorious square mile. The sheer diversity of the hits maintained the group's appeal but they lost ground at the end of the 60s and Dave Dee left for an unsuccessful solo career before venturing into A&R. The others continued as a quartet, but after one minor hit, 'Mr President', and an album, *Fresh Ear*, they broke up. A couple of brief nostalgic reunions later occurred, but not enough to encourage a serious relaunch. *Zabadak*, a fascinating fanzine, is published in France for those fans who wish to monitor their every move.

●ALBUMS: *Dave Dee, Dozy, Beaky, Mick And Tich* (Fontana 1966)★★★, *If Music Be The Food Of Love* (Fontana 1967)★★★, *If No One Sang* (Fontana 1968)★★★, *The Legend Of Dave Dee, Dozy, Beaky, Mick And Tich* (1969)★★, *Together* (1969)★★.
●COMPILATIONS: *The Best Of Dave Dee, Dozy, Beaky, Mick And Tich* (Spectrum 1996)★★★, *The Complete Collection* (Mercury 1997)★★★.

DAVID AND JONATHAN

Songwriting duo Roger Greenaway ('David') and Roger Cook ('Jonathan') began their partnership in 1965 after the demise of the former's beat group, the Kestrels, and enjoyed instant success when an early collaboration, 'You've Got Your Troubles', was a number 2 hit for the Fortunes. The pair began a performing/recording career at the end of the year, but paradoxically scored their first chart entry with a version of the Beatles' 'Michelle'. Although the Overlanders enjoyed a concurrent UK chart topper with the same song, David And Jonathan reached a respectable number 11, before securing a Top 10 slot with their self-penned follow-up, 'Lovers Of The World Unite'. Although the duo continued to record under their adopted appellation, they found much greater commercial success with a series of crafted compositions including 'Gasoline Alley Bred' (the Hollies), 'Home Lovin' Man' (Andy Williams), 'I'd Like To Teach The World To Sing' (the New Seekers) and 'Something Tells Me (Somethin's Gonna Happen Tonight)' (Cilla Black). Such work was often undertaken with other songwriters, including Tony Macauley and Albert Hammond, but were copyrighted to the duo's Cookaway publishing company. Their commercial touch was maintained into the 70s with Blue Mink, a group comprising of session musicians fronted by Cook and Madeline Bell, and they remain one of the most efficacious pop songwriting teams the UK ever produced.

●ALBUMS: *David And Jonathan* (Columbia 1966)★★★.
●COMPILATIONS: *Lovers Of The World Unite* aka *The Very Best Of David And Jonathan* (1984)★★★.

DAVIES, CYRIL

b. 1932, Buckinghamshire, England, d. 7 January 1964. Along with Alexis Korner and Graham Bond, the uncompromising Davies was a seminal influence in the development of British R&B during the beat boom of the early 60s. His superb wailing and distorted harmonica shook the walls of many clubs up and down Britain. Initially he played with Alexis Korner's Blues Incorporated and then formed his own band, the All-Stars, featuring Long John Baldry, renowned session pianist Nicky Hopkins and drummer Mickey Waller. Their Chicago-based blues was raw, loud and exciting. Like Bond he died at a tragically young age, after losing his battle with leukaemia.

●ALBUMS: *The Legendary Cyril Davies* (Folklore 1970)★★★.

DAVIS, BILLIE

b. Carol Hedges, 1945, Woking, Surrey, England. Discovered by entrepreneur Robert Stigwood, this blue-eyed soul singer first came to chart prominence in 1962, duetting with Mike Sarne on the novelty hit, 'Will I What?' The following year, she emerged in her own right with an upbeat rendition of the Exciters' 'Tell Him'. Although well poised to take advantage of the beat boom, Davis' strong voice proved insufficient to take the follow-up, 'He's The One', into the Top 30. Her romantic entanglement with former Shadows' guitarist Jet Harris gained considerable publicity, especially when both were involved in a car crash. With singles, however, further success proved elusive, although 'I Want You To Be My Baby' scraped into the lower chart regions in 1968. Thereafter, Davis concentrated on the European market, particularly Spain, where she retained a healthy following.

●ALBUMS: *Billie Davis* (Decca 1970)★★.

DAVIS, MILES

b. 25 May 1926, Alton, Illinois, USA, d. 28 September 1991. Davis was born into a comparatively wealthy middle-class family and both his mother and sister were capable musicians. He was given a trumpet for his thirteenth birthday by his dentist father, who could not have conceived that his gift would set his son on the road to becoming one of the giant figures in the development of jazz. Notwithstanding his outstanding talent as master of the trumpet, Davis' versatility encompassed flügelhorn and keyboards together with a considerable gift as a composer. This extraordinary list of talents earned Davis an unassailable reputation as the greatest leader/catalyst in the history of jazz. Such accolades were not used lightly, and he can justifiably be termed a 'musical genius'. Davis quickly progressed from his high school band into Eddie Randall's band in 1941, after his family had moved to St. Louis. He studied at the Juilliard School of Music in New York in 1945 before joining Charlie 'Bird' Parker, with whom he had previously played in the Billy Eckstine band.

By 1948 Davis had played or recorded with many jazz giants, most notably Coleman Hawkins, Dizzy Gillespie, Benny Carter, John Lewis, Illinois Jacquet and Gerry Mulligan. That year was to be a landmark for jazz and Davis, in collaboration with Gil Evans, made a series of 78s which were eventually released in 1957 as the highly influential album *The Birth Of The Cool*. Davis had now refined his innovative style of playing, which was based upon understatement rather than the hurried action of the great bebop players.

During the early 50s Davis became dependant on heroin and his career was put on hold for a lengthy period. This spell of inactivity lasted until as late as 1954. The following year his seminal quintet included variously Red Garland, John Coltrane, Charles Mingus, Paul Chambers, Philly Joe Jones, Bill Evans and Sonny Rollins. Among their output was the acclaimed series of collections *Cookin'*, *Relaxin'*, *Workin'* and *Steamin'*. During this time Miles was consistently voted the number 1 artist in all the major jazz polls. Now no longer dependent on drugs, he set about collaborating with Gil Evans once again. The orchestral albums made with Evans between 1957 and 1959 have all become classics: *Miles Ahead*, *Porgy And Bess* and the sparsely beautiful *Sketches Of Spain* (influenced by composer Joaquin Rodrigo). Evans was able to blend lush and full orchestration with Davis' trumpet - allowing it the space and clarity it richly deserved. Davis went on further, assembling a sextet featuring a spectacular line-up including Coltrane, Chambers, Bill Evans, Jimmy Cobb and Cannonball Adderley. Two further landmark albums during this fertile period were the aptly titled *Milestones*, followed by *Kind Of Blue*. The latter album is cited by many critics as the finest in jazz history. More than 30 years later his albums are still available. They form an essential part of any jazz record collection, with *Kind Of Blue* at the top of the list. 'So What', the opening track, has been covered by dozens of artists, the most recent offerings from guitarist Ronnie Jordan, Larry Carlton, saxophonist Candy Dulfer and reggae star Smiley Culture, who added his own lyrics and performed it in the film *Absolute Beginners*. Ian Carr, Davis' leading biographer, perceptively stated of *Kind Of Blue* in 1982: 'The more it is listened to, the more it reveals new delights and fresh depths'.

In 1959, following the bizarre arrest and beating he received from the New York Police, Davis took out a lawsuit, which he subsequently and wisely dropped. Davis entered the 60s comfortably, still the leading innovator in jazz, and shrugged off attempts from John Coltrane to dethrone him in the jazz polls. Davis chose to keep to his sparse style, allowing his musicians air and range. In 1964 while the world experienced Beatlemania, Davis created another musical landmark when he assembled arguably his finest line-up. The combination of Herbie Hancock, Wayne Shorter, Ron Carter and Tony Williams delivered the monumental *E.S.P.* in 1965. He continued with this acoustic line-up through another three recordings, including *Miles Smiles* and ending with *Nefertiti*. By the time of *Filles De Kilimanjaro* Miles had gradually electrified his various groups and took bold steps towards rock music, integrating multiple electric keyboards and utilizing a wah-wah pedal connected to his electrified trumpet. Additionally, his own fascination with the possibilities of electric guitar, as demonstrated by Jimi Hendrix, took an increasing position in his bands. Young

American west coast rock musicians had begun to produce a form of music based upon improvisation (mostly through the use of hallucinogenics). This clearly interested Davis who saw the potential of blending traditional rock rhythms with jazz, although he was often contemptuous of some white rock musicians at this time. The decade closed with his band being accepted by rock fans. Davis appeared at major festivals with deliriously stoned audiences appreciating his line-up, which now featured the brilliant electric guitarist John McLaughlin, of whom Miles stated in deference to black musicians: 'Show me a black who can play like him, and I'd have him instead'. Other outstanding musicians Davis employed included Keith Jarrett, Airto, Chick Corea, Dave Holland, Joe Zawinul, Billy Cobham and Jack DeJohnette. Two major albums from this period were *In A Silent Way* and *Bitches Brew*, which unconsciously invented jazz rock and what was later to be called fusion. These records were marketed as rock albums, and consequently appeared in the regular charts. By the early 70s Davis had alienated himself from the mainstream jazz purists by continuing to flirt with rock music. In 1975, after a succession of personal upheavals including a car crash, further drug problems, a shooting incident, more police harassment and eventual arrest, Davis, not surprisingly, retired. During this time he became seriously ill, and it was generally felt that he would never play again.

As unpredictable as ever, Davis returned six years later healthy and fit with the comeback album, *The Man With The Horn*. He assembled a new band and received favourable reviews for live performances. Among the personnel were guitarist John Scofield and saxophonist Bill Evans. On the predominantly funk-based *You're Under Arrest*, he tackled pure pop songs, and although unambitious by jazz standards, tracks like Cyndi Lauper's 'Time After Time' and Michael Jackson's 'Human Nature' were given Davis' brilliant master touch. The aggressive disco album *Tutu* followed with his trumpet played through a synthesizer. A recent soundtrack recording for the Dennis Hopper film, *The Hot Spot*, found Davis playing the blues alongside Taj Mahal, John Lee Hooker, Tim Drummond and Roy Rogers.

During his final years Davis settled into a comfortable pattern of touring the world and recording, able to dictate the pace of his life with the knowledge that ecstatic audiences were waiting for him everywhere. Following further bouts of ill health during which times he took to painting, Miles was admitted to hospital in California and died in September 1991. The worldwide obituaries were neither sycophantic nor morose: great things had already been said about Davis for many years. Django Bates stated that his own favourite Davis recordings were those between 1926 and mid-1991. Ian Carr added, in his impressive obituary, with regard to Davis' music: 'unflagging intelligence, great courage, integrity, honesty and a sustained spirit of enquiry always in the pursuit of art - never mere experimentation for its own sake'. Miles Davis' influence on rock music is considerable; his influence on jazz is inestimable.

●ALBUMS: *Young Man With A Horn* (Blue Note 1952)★★★, *The New Sounds Of Miles Davis* (Prestige 1952)★★★, *Miles Davis Vol. 2* (Blue Note 1953)★★★★, *Bopping The Blues* rec. 1946 (Black Lion)★★★, *Cool Boppin'* rec. 1948-49 (Fresh Sounds)★★★, *Miles Davis With Horns* (Original Jazz Classics 1953)★★★, *Collector's Items* rec. 1953, 1956 (Original Jazz Classics)★★★, *Blue Period* (Prestige 1953)★★★, *Miles Davis Plays Al Cohn Compositions* (Prestige 1953)★★★, *Miles Davis Quintet* (Prestige 1953)★★★, *Miles Davis Quintet Featuring Sonny Rollins* (Prestige 1953)★★★, *Miles Davis Vol. 3* (Blue Note 1954)★★★, *Miles Davis Sextet* (Prestige 1954)★★★, *Jeru* (Capitol 1954)★★★★★, *Miles Davis Vols. 1 & 2* (Blue Note 1954)★★★★, *Walkin'* (Prestige 1955)★★★★, *Miles Davis All Stars Vol. 1* (Prestige 1955)★★★★, *Miles Davis All Stars Volume 2* (Prestige 1955)★★★★, *Blue Moods* (Debut 1955)★★★, *Musings Of Miles* (Prestige 1955)★★★, *Miles Davis And The Modern Jazz Giants* (Original Jazz Classics 50s)★★★, with Sonny Rollins *Dig Miles Davis/Sonny Rollins* (Prestige 1956), *Workin'* (Prestige 1956)★★★★, *Collectors Item* (Prestige 1956)★★★, *Steamin'* (Prestige 1956)★★★★, *Cookin'* (Prestige 1956)★★★★, *Relaxin'* (Prestige 1956)★★★★, *Miles - The New Miles Davis Quintet* (Prestige 1956)★★★, *Blue Haze* (Prestige 1956)★★★, *The Birth Of The Cool* rec. 1949-50 (Capitol 1956)★★★★★, *Miles* (Original Jazz Classics 1956)★★★, *Miles Davis And Horns* (Prestige 1956)★★★, *Quintet/Sextet* (Original Jazz Classics 1956)★★★, *Cookin' With The Miles Davis Quintet* (Prestige 1957)★★★★, *Bags Groove* (Prestige 1957)★★★★, *Round About Midnight* (Columbia 1957)★★★★, *Miles Ahead* (Columbia 1957)★★★★★, *'58 Miles* (Columbia 1958)★★★★, *Miles Davis And The Modern Jazz Giants* (Prestige 1958)★★★, with John Coltrane *Miles And Coltrane* (Columbia 1958)★★★★, *Milestones* (Columbia 1958)★★★★★, *Porgy And Bess* (Columbia 1958)★★★★, *Workin' With The Miles Davis Quintet* (Prestige 1959)★★★★, *Kind Of Blue* (Columbia 1959)★★★★★, *Sketches Of Spain* (Columbia 1960)★★★★, *On Green Dolphin Street* rec. 1960 (Jazz Door)★★★, *Live In Zurich* (Jazz Unlimited 1960)★★★, *Live In Stockholm 1960* (Royal Jazz 1960)★★★, *Miles Davis In Person (Friday And Saturday Nights At The Blackhawk)* (Columbia 1961)★★★★, *Someday My Prince Will Come* (Columbia 1961)★★★★, *Steamin' With The Miles Davis Quintet* (Prestige 1961)★★★★, *The Beginning* (Prestige 1962)★★★, *At Carnegie Hall* (Columbia 1962)★★★, *Seven Steps To Heaven* (Columbia 1963)★★★, *Diggin'* (Prestige 1963)★★★, *Quiet Nights* (Columbia 1963)★★★, *Miles In Antibes* (Columbia 1964)★★★, (Prestige 1964)★★★, with Thelonious Monk *Miles And Monk At Newport* (Columbia 1964)★★★, *Miles Davis In Europe* (1964)★★★, *My Funny Valentine* (1964)★★★★, *'Four' And More* (1964)★★★, *ESP* (Columbia 1965)★★★★, *Miles Davis Plays For Lovers* (Prestige 1965)★★★, *Jazz Classics* (Prestige 1965)★★★, *Miles Smiles* (Columbia 1966)★★★, *Sorcerer* (Columbia 1967)★★★, *Nefertiti* (Columbia 1967)★★★, *Miles In The Sky* (Columbia 1968)★★★, *Filles De Kilimanjaro* (Columbia 1968)★★★★, *In A Silent Way* (Columbia 1969)★★★★★, *Double Image* (Moon 1969)★★★, *Paraphernalia* (JMY)★★★, *Bitches Brew* (Columbia 1970)★★★★★, *At The Fillmore* (Columbia 1970)★★★, *A Tribute To Jack Johnson* (Columbia 1971)★★★★, *What I Say?* Vols. 1 & 2 (JMY 1971)★★★, *Live-Evil* (Columbia 1972)★★★, *On The Corner* (Columbia 1972)★★★, *Tallest Trees* (1973)★★★, *In Concert* (1973)★★★, *Black Beauty* (1974)★★★, *Big Fun* (Columbia 1974)★★★, *Get Up With It* (1974)★★★, *Jazz At The Plaza Vol. 1* (1974)★★★, *Agharta* (1976)★★★★, *Pangaea* (Columbia 1976)★★★, *Live At The Plugged Nickel* (Columbia 1976)★★★★, *Water Babies* (1977)★★★, *Circle In The Round* rec. 1955-70 (Columbia 1979)★★★, *Directions* (1981)★★★, *Man With The Horn* (1981)★★★, *A Night In Tunisia* (1981)★★★, *We Want Miles* (1982)★★★, *Star People* (1983)★★★, *Blue Christmas* (1983)★★★, *Heard 'Round the World* (1983)★★★, *Blue Haze* (1984/6)★★★, *At Last* (1985)★★★, *Decoy* (Columbia 1984)★★★, *Your Under Arrest* (Columbia 1985)★★★★, *Tutu* (Warners 1986)★★★★, *Music From Siesta '88* (Warners 1988)★★★, *Amandla* (Warners 1989)★★★, *Aura* (Columbia 1989)★★★★, *Mellow Miles* rec. 1961-63 (Columbia 1989)★★★, *Ballads* rec. 1961-63 (Columbia 1989)★★★★, *The Hot Spot* (1990)★★★, *Dingo* (Warners 1991)★★★, *Doo-Bop* (1993)★★★, *Live In Europe 1988* (1993)★★★, with Quincy Jones *Miles And Quincy Jones Live At Montreux* rec. 1991 (Warners 1993)★★★, *The Complete Live At The Plugged Nickel 1965* 8-CD box set (Columbia 1995)★★★★, *Highlights From The Plugged Nickel* (Columbia 1995)★★★★, *Live Around The World* (Warners 1996), *Dig* rec. 1951 (Original Jazz Classics)★★★.

●COMPILATIONS: *The CBS Years 1955-1985* (1989)★★★★, *The Collection* (1990)★★★★, *Gold Collection* (1993)★★★★, *Ballads And Blues* (Blue Note 1996)★★★★, *This Is Jazz No. 8 - Miles Davis Acoustic* (Legacy 1996)★★★, with Gil Evans *Miles Davis And Gil Evans: The Complete Columbia Studio Recordings* 6-CD box set (Columbia/Legacy 1996)★★★★★.

●VIDEOS: *Miles Davis And Jazz Hoofer* (1988), *Miles In Paris* (1990), *Miles Davis And Quincy Jones: Live At Montreux* (1993).

●FURTHER READING: *Miles Davis Transcribed Solos*, Miles Davis. *Miles: The Autobiography*, Miles Davis. *Milestones: 1. Miles Davis, 1945-60*, J. Chambers. *Milestones: 2. Miles Davis Since 1960*, J. Chambers. *Miles Davis*, Barry McRae. *Miles Davis: A Critical Biography*, Ian Carr. *Miles Davis For Beginners*, Daryl Long. *The Man In The Green Shirt: Miles Davis*, Richard Williams.

DAVIS, SAMMY, JNR.

b. 8 December 1925, Harlem, New York, USA, d. 16 May 1990, Los Angeles, California, USA. A dynamic and versatile all-round entertainer - a trouper in the old-fashioned tradition. The only son of two dancers in a black vaudeville troupe, called Will Mastin's Holiday In Dixieland, Davis made his professional debut with the group at the age of three, as 'Silent Sam, The Dancing Midget'. While still young he was coached by the legendary tap-dancer, Bill 'Bojangles' Robinson. Davis left the group in 1943 to serve in the US Army, where he encountered severe racial prejudice for the first, but not the last, time. After the war he rejoined his father and adopted uncle in the Will Mastin Trio. By 1950 the Trio were headlining at venues such as the Capitol in New York and Ciro's in Hollywood with stars including Jack Benny and Bob Hope, but it was Davis who was receiving the standing ovations for his singing, dancing, drumming, comedy and apparently inexhaustible energy. In 1954 he signed for Decca Records, and released two albums, *Starring Sammy Davis Jr* (number 1 in the US chart), featuring his impressions of stars such as Dean Martin, Jerry Lewis, Johnnie Ray and Jimmy Durante, and *Just For Lovers*. He also made the US singles chart with 'Hey There' from *The Pajama Game*, and in the same year he lost his left eye in a road accident. When he returned to performing in January 1955 wearing an eyepatch he was greeted even more enthusiastically than before. During that year he continued to break the US Top 20 with 'Something's Gotta Give', 'Love Me Or Leave Me' and 'That Old Black Magic'. In 1956 he made his Broadway debut in the musical *Mr Wonderful*, music and lyrics by Jerry Bock, Larry Holofcener and George Weiss. Also in the show were the rest of the Will Mastin Trio, Sammy's uncle and Davis Snr. The show ran for nearly 400 performances and produced two hits, 'Too Close For Comfort', and the title song, which was very successful for Peggy Lee. Although generally regarded as the first popular American black performer to become acceptable to both black and white audiences, Davis attracted heavy criticism in 1956 over his conversion to Judaism, and later for his marriage to Swedish actress Mai Britt. He described himself as a 'one-eyed Jewish nigger'. Apart from a few brief appearances when he was very young, Davis started his film career in 1958 with *Anna Lucasta*, and was critically acclaimed in the following year for his performance as Sporting Life in *Porgy And Bess*. By this time Davis was a leading member of Frank Sinatra's 'inner circle', called variously, the 'Clan', or the 'Rat Pack'. He appeared with Sinatra in three movies, *Ocean's Eleven* (1960), *Sergeants 3* (1962), and *Robin And The Seven Hoods* (1964), but made, perhaps, a greater impact when he co-starred with another member of the 'Clan', Shirley MacLaine, in the Cy Coleman and Dorothy Fields film musical, *Sweet Charity*. The 60s were good times for Davis, who was enormously popular on records and television, but especially 'live', at Las Vegas and in concert. In 1962 he made the US chart with the Anthony Newley/Leslie Bricusse number 'What Kind Of Fool Am I?', and thereafter featured several of their songs in his act. He sang Bricusse's nominated song, 'Talk To The Animals', at the 1967 Academy Awards ceremony, and collected the Oscar on behalf of the songwriter when it won. In 1972, he had a million-selling hit record with another Newley/Bricusse song, 'The Candy Man', from the film *Willy Wonka And The Chocolate Factory*. He appeared again on Broadway in 1964 in *Golden Boy*, Charles Strouse and Lee Adams' musical adaptation of Clifford Odet's 1937 drama of a young man torn between the boxing ring and his violin. Also in the cast was Billy Daniels. The show ran for 569 performances in New York, and went to London in 1968. During the 70s Davis worked less, suffering, it is said, as a result of previous alcohol and drug abuse. He entertained US troops in the Lebanon in 1983, and five years later undertook an arduous comeback tour of the USA and Canada with Sinatra and Dean Martin. In 1989 he travelled further, touring Europe with the show, *The Ultimate Event*, along with Liza Minnelli and Sinatra. While he was giving everything to career favourites such as 'Birth Of The Blues', 'Mr Bojangles' and 'Old Black Magic' he was already ill, although did not let it show. After his death in 1990 it was revealed that his estate was almost worthless. In 1992, an all-star tribute, led by Liza Minnelli, was mounted at the Royal Albert Hall in London, the city that had always welcomed him. Proceeds from the concert went to the Royal Marsden Cancer Appeal.

●ALBUMS: *Starring Sammy Davis Jr* (Decca 1955)★★★, *Just For Lovers* (Decca 1955)★★★, *Mr. Wonderful* soundtrack (Decca 1956)★★, *Here's Looking At You* (Decca 1956)★★★, with Carmen McRae *Boy Meets Girl* (late 50s)★★★, *Sammy Swings* (Decca 1957)★★★★, *It's All Over But The Swingin'* (Decca 1957)★★★★, *Mood To Be Wooed* (Decca 1958)★★★, *I Got A Right To Swing* (Decca 1958)★★★★, *All The Way And Then Some* (Decca 1958)★★★★, *Sammy Davis Jr. At Town Hall* (Decca 1959)★★★★, *Porgy And Bess* (Decca 1959)★★★, *Sammy Awards* (Decca 1960)★★★, *What Kind Of Fool Am I And Other Show-Stoppers* (1962)★★★★, *Sammy Davis Jr. At The Cocoanut Grove* (1963)★★★★, *Johnny Cool* soundtrack (United Artists 1963)★★★, *As Long As She Needs Me* (1963)★★★, *Sammy Davis Jr. Salutes The Stars Of The London Palladium* (1964)★★★, *The Shelter Of Your Arms* (1964)★★★, *Golden Boy* soundtrack (Capitol 1964★★, with Count Basie *Our Shining Hour* (1965)★★★, *Sammy's Back On Broadway* (1965)★★★, *A Man Called Adam* soundtrack (Reprise 1966)★★, *I've Gotta Be Me* (1969)★★★, *Sammy Davis Jr. Now* (1972)★★★, *Portrait Of Sammy Davis Jr.* (1972)★★★, *It's A Musical World* (1976)★★★, *The Song And Dance Man* (1977)★★★★, *Sammy Davis Jr. In Person 1977* (1983)★★★, *Closest Of Friends* (1984).
●COMPILATIONS: *The Best Of Sammy Davis Jr.* (1982)★★★, *Collection* (1989)★★★, *The Great Sammy Davis Jr.* (1989)★★★, *Sammy Davis Jr Capitol Collectors Series* (1990)★★★.
●VIDEOS: *Mr Bojangles* (1992).

●FILMS:*The Benny Goodman Story* (1956), *Anna Lucasta* (1958), *Porgy And Bess* (1959), *Pepe* (1960), *Ocean's Eleven* (1960), *Convicts Four* (1962), *Sergeants Three* (1962), *Johnny Cool* (1963), *The Threepenny Opera* (1963), *Robin And The Seven Hoods* (1964), *Nightmare In The Sun* (1964), *A Man Called Adam* (1966), *Salt And Pepper* (1968), *Man Without Mercy* (1969), *Sweet Charity* (1969), *One More Time* (1970), *Diamonds Are Forever* (1972), *Save The Children* concert film (1973), *Stop The World - I Want To Get Off* (1978), *The Cannonball Run II* (1984), *Moon Over Parador* (1988), *Tap* (1989).

DAVIS, SPENCER, GROUP

Formed in Birmingham, England, in 1962 as the Rhythm And Blues Quartet, the group featured Spencer Davis (b. 17 July 1941, Swansea, South Wales; guitar/vocals), Steve Winwood (b. 12 May 1948, Birmingham, England; guitar/organ/vocals), Muff Winwood (b. Mervyn Winwood, 15 June 1943, Birmingham, England; bass) and Pete York (b. 15 August 1942, Middlesborough, Cleveland, England; drums). School teacher Davis, the elder Winwood brother and drummer York were already experienced performers with backgrounds in modern and traditional jazz, blues, and skiffle. The group was gradually dwarfed by the younger Winwood's immense natural musical talent. While they were much in demand on the fast-growing club scene as performers, their bluesy/pop records failed to sell, until they made a breakthrough in 1965 with 'Keep On Running', which reached number 1 in the UK. This was followed in quick succession by another chart-topper, 'Somebody Help Me', and three more notable hits 'When I Come Home', 'Gimme Some Lovin'', and 'I'm A Man'. In keeping with 60s pop tradition they also appeared in a low budget British film, *The Ghost Goes Gear*. Throughout their career they were managed by Chris Blackwell, founder of Island Records. Amid press reports and months of speculation, Steve Winwood finally left to form Traffic in 1967. A soundtrack album *Here We Go Round The Mulberry Bush*, released that year, ironically had both Traffic and the Spencer Davis Group sharing the billing. Muff Winwood also left, joining Island as head of A&R. Davis soldiered on with the addition of Phil Sawyer, who was later replaced by guitarist Ray Fenwick from After Tea and Eddie Hardin (keyboards). The latter had an uncannily similar voice to Steve Winwood. They were unable to maintain their previous success but had two further minor hits, 'Mr Second Class' and the richly psychedelia-phased 'Time Seller'. After a number of line-up changes including Dee Murray and Nigel Olsson, Hardin And York departed to form their own band, and enjoyed some success mainly on the continent during the progressive boom of 1969-70. Davis eventually went to live in America where he became involved in the business side of music, working in A&R for various major record companies. The Davis/York/Hardin/Fenwick team re-formed briefly in 1973 with the addition of Charlie McCracken on bass, formerly with Taste, and made a further two albums. The infectious single 'Catch Me On The Rebop' almost become a belated hit. Today, York can still be found playing in various jazz style bands; his acknowledged talent as a drummer being regularly in demand. Spencer Davis is still making the occasional album from his base on the west coast of America. Muff Winwood is presently head of Artist Development at CBS Records and among his signings have been Shakin' Stevens, Bros, Paul Young and Terence Trent D'Arby. Steve Winwood, after progressing through Blind Faith and Air Force, is currently a highly successful solo artist. In 1997 Davis was touting a new version of the group, which included the original drummer York together with ex-Keef Hartley Band vocalist/guitarist Miller Anderson.

●ALBUMS: *The First Album* (Fontana 1965)★★★, *The Second Album* (Fontana 1966)★★★, *Autumn '66* (Fontana 1966)★★★, *Here We Go Round The Mulberry Bush* (United Artists 1967)★★★, *Gimme Some Lovin'* (United Artists 1967)★★★, *I'm A Man* (United Artists 1967)★★★, *With Their New Face On* (United Artists 1967)★★, *Heavies* (United Artists 1969)★★, *Funky* (Columbia 1969)★★, *Gluggo* (Vertigo 1973)★★★, *Living In The Back Street* (Vertigo 1974)★★, *Catch You On The Rebop: Live In Europe* (RPM 1995)★★★.

●COMPILATIONS: *The Best Of The Spencer Davis Group* (Island 1968)★★★★, *The Best Of Spencer Davis Group* (EMI America 1987)★★★, *Keep On Running* (Royal Collection 1991)★★★, *Taking Out Time 1967-69* (RPM 1994)★★, *Spotlight On Spencer Davis* (Javelin 1994)★★, *Live Together* 1988 recordings (In Akustik 1995)★, *24 Hours Live In Germany* 1988 recordings (In Akustik 1995)★, *Eight Gigs A Week: The Steve Winwood Years* (Island/Chronicles 1996)★★★★.

●FURTHER READING: *Keep On Running: The Steve Winwood Story*, Chris Welch. *Back In The High Life: A Biography Of Steve Winwood*, Alan Clayson.

DEARIE, BLOSSOM

b. 28 April 1928, East Durham, New York, USA. A singer, pianist and songwriter, with a 'wispy, little-girlish' voice, Dearie is regarded as one of the great supperclub singers. Her father was of Scottish and Irish descent; her mother emigrated from Oslo, Norway. Dearie is said to have been given her unusual first name after a neighbour brought peach blossoms to her house on the day she was born. She began taking piano lessons when she was five, and studied classical music until she was in her teens, when she played in her high school dance band and began to listen to jazz. Early influences included Art Tatum, Count Basie, Duke Ellington and Martha Tilton, who sang with the Benny Goodman Band. Dearie graduated from high school in the mid-40s and moved to New York City to pursue a music career. She joined the Blue Flames, a vocal group within the Woody Herman Big Band, and then sang with the Blue Reys, a similar formation in the Alvino Rey Band. In 1952, while working at the Chantilly Club in Greenwich Village, Dearie met Nicole Barclay who, with her husband, owned Barclay Records. At her

suggestion she went to Paris and formed a vocal group, the Blue Stars. The group consisted of four male singers/instrumentalists, and four female singers; Dearie contributed many of the arrangements. They had a hit in France and the USA with one of their first recordings, a French version of 'Lullaby Of Birdland'. While in Paris, Dearie met impresario and record producer Norman Granz, who signed her Verve Records, for whom she eventually made six solo albums, including the highly regarded *My Gentleman Friend*. Unable to take the Blue Stars to the USA because of passport problems (they later evolved into the Swingle Singers), she returned to New York and resumed her solo career, singing to her own piano accompaniment at New York nightclubs such as the Versailles, the Blue Angel and the Village Vanguard. She also appeared on US television with Jack Paar, Merv Griffin and Johnny Carson. In 1966 she made the first of what were to become annual appearances at Ronnie Scott's Club in London, receiving excellent reviews as 'a singer's singer', whose most important asset was her power to bring a personal interpretation to a song, while showing the utmost respect for a composer's intentions'. In the 60s she also made some albums for Capitol Records, including *May I Come In?*, a set of standards arranged and conducted by Jack Marshall. In the early 70s, disillusioned by the major record companies' lack of interest in her kind of music, she started her own company, Daffodil Records in 1974. Her first album for the label, *Blossom Dearie Sings*, was followed by a two-record set entitled *My New Celebrity Is You*, which contained eight of her own compositions. The album's title song was especially written for her by Johnny Mercer, and is said to be the last piece he wrote before his death in 1976. During the 70s Dearie performed at Carnegie Hall with former Count Basie blues singer Joe Williams and jazz vocalist Anita O'Day in a show called *The Jazz Singers*. In 1981 she appeared with Dave Frishberg for three weeks at Michael's Pub in Manhattan. Frishberg, besides being a songwriter, also sang and played the piano, and Dearie frequently performed his songs, such as 'Peel Me A Grape', 'I'm Hip' and 'My Attorney Bernie'. Her own compositions include 'I Like You, You're Nice', 'I'm Shadowing You' and 'Hey John'. From 1983, she performed regularly for six months a year at the Ballroom, a nightclub in Manhattan, and in 1985 was the first recipient of the Mabel Mercer Foundation Award, which is presented annually to an outstanding supper-club performer. Appreciated mostly in New York and London, where she appeared several times in the late 80s/early 90s at the Pizza On The Park, Dearie, with her intimate style and unique voice remains one of the few survivors of a specialized art.
●ALBUMS: *Blossom Dearie* (Verve 1957)★★★, *Give Him The Ooh-La-La* (Verve 1958)★★★, *Once Upon A Summertime* (Verve 1958)★★★★, *Blossom Dearie Sings Comden And Green* (Verve 1959)★★★, *My Gentleman Friend* (Verve 1959)★★★★, *Broadway Song Hits* (Verve 1960)★★★, *Blossom Dearie* (Verve 1961)★★★★, *May I Come In?* (1966)★★★, *My New*

Celebrity Is You (1979)★★★, *Blossom Dearie Sings 1973* (1979)★★★, *Blossom Dearie Sings 1975* (Daf 1979)★★★, *Winchester In Apple Blossom Time* (Daf 1979)★★★, *Needlepoint Magic* (Daf 1988)★★★, *Featuring Bobby Jasper* (1988)★★★, *Songs Of Chelsea* (1988)★★★, *Et Tu Bruce* (1989)★★★.
●COMPILATIONS: *The Special Magic Of Blossom Dearie* (1975)★★★.

DEE, JOEY, AND THE STARLITERS

The US group that helped revitalize the Twist were Joey Dee (b. Joseph DiNicola, 11 June 1940, Passaic, New Jersey, USA; vocals), Carlton Latimer (keyboards), Willie Davis (drums), Larry Vernieri (backing vocals) and David Brigati (backing vocals). Formed in 1958, this lively and entertaining group took up residency at New York's famed Peppermint Lounge club in 1960, the year of their first recordings on Bonus and Scepter. In late 1961, a year after Chubby Checker's 'The Twist' topped the US chart, the wealthy socialites who frequented the club belatedly discovered the dance. Dee incorporated it into his act and even wrote a special club song, 'Peppermint Twist'. The memorable, uplifting single shot to the top of the charts and *Doin' The Twist At The Peppermint Lounge* reached number 2. In 1962 the group, which now included a 10-piece dance team, starred in the low-budget films *Hey Let's Twist* and *Vive Le Twist* with the soundtrack album and title track of the former both reaching the US Top 20. They followed this with a breakneck version of the Isley Brothers' 'Shout', which reached number 6. Dee appeared in the film *Two Tickets To Paris* and his solo version of Johnny Nash's 'What Kind Of Love is This?', taken from it, became his fourth and final Top 20 entry in 1962. In all, this distinctive group, which never graced the UK Top 20, notched up nine US chart singles and three albums between 1961 and 1963. Dee opened his own club The Starliter in New York in 1964. That year he formed a new band which included Gene Cornish, Felix Cavaliere and Eddie Brigati, who became the very successful (Young) Rascals and a couple of years later he hired guitarist Jimi Hendrix for the group. Dee recorded on Jubilee in 1966 and Janus in 1973 and is now the spokesman of an association representing American 'oldies' acts.
●ALBUMS: *Doin' The Twist At The Peppermint Lounge* (Roulette 1961)★★★, soundtrack *Hey, Let's Twist* (Roulette 1962)★★, *Back At The Peppermint Lounge-Twistin* (Roulette 1961)★★★, *All The World Is Twistin'* (Roulette 1961)★★, *Two Tickets To Paris* soundtrack (Roulette 1962)★★, *The Peppermint Twisters* (Scepter 1962)★★★, *Joey Dee* (Roulette 1963)★★★, *Dance, Dance, Dance* (Roulette 1963)★★, *Hitsville* (Jubilee 1966)★★.
●FILMS: *Hey Let's Twist* (1961).

DEENE, CAROL

b. 1944, Thurnscoe, Yorkshire, England. The daughter of a singing miner, the clean-cut pop singer moved to

London at the age of 16, and, after appearing on the Joan Regan television show in 1961, was snapped up by HMV. Deene had four UK Top 50 entries in a 12 month period, all with cover versions, but none made the Top 20. The songs were 'Sad Movies' and the irritating 'Norman' (which were both John D. Loudermilk songs that had been US hits for Sue Thompson), 'Johnny Get Angry' (a US hit for Joanie Sommers) and 'Some People', which was originally performed by UK act Valerie Mountain & The Eagles in the film of the same name. In 1962 she had her own series as a disc jockey on Radio Luxembourg and was seen in the Acker Bilk film *Band Of Thieves*. She later had unsuccessful releases on Columbia in 1966, CBS in 1968, Conquest in 1969, Pye in 1970; and reappeared in the late 70s on the Koala and Rim labels.
● ALBUMS: *A Love Affair* (World Records 1970)★★.
● FILMS: *It's All Happening* (1963).

DEEP FEELING

After disbanding his Hellions in 1966, drummer Jim Capaldi re-entered the fray on congas and vocals with guitarist David Meredith (from Evesham's Wavelengths) and John Palmer (flute/vibraphone). With a set that included erudite soul covers, Deep Feeling's ear-catching sound netted an impressive tally of London club dates plus sporadic singles such as the self-penned 'If You're Mine' and the US-only 'Pretty Colours'. Both featured on a French EP. Throughout this period, ex-Hellion guitarists Dave Mason and Luther Grosvenor served the outfit intermittently before Palmer was absorbed into Family, and Capaldi and Mason into Traffic. There next evolved a more fixed line-up of John Swail (vocals), Derek Elson (keyboards), Martin Jenner (guitar) and Dave Green (bass/flute). Their funereal arrangement of the Contours' 'Do You Love Me' reached the UK Top 40 in spring 1970, marking the group's commercial climax.
● ALBUMS: *Deep Feeling* (DJM 1971)★★.

DEL-SATINS

R&B artists the Del-Satins had few peers as practitioners of white doo-wop in the 60s. They were formed in 1958 in Manhattan, New York, USA, by Stan Ziska (lead), Fred Ferrara (baritone), his brother Tom Ferrara (bass), Leslie Cauchi (first tenor) and Bobby Fiela (second tenor). The Del-Satins was chosen as their name in open tribute to their principal influences, the Dells and Five Satins. Under the new name they secured a recording contract with End Records. Their debut single, 'I'll Pray For You', was released in 1961. New management was sought with Passions manager Jim Gribble, who found them a more permanent contract at Laurie Records. Their label star Dion was currently grappling with diminishing chart returns after an impressive start, and wanted to replace his existing backing band, the Belmonts, with a 'rockier' troupe. The Del-Satins were instantly sent to work on Dion's new song, 'Runaround Sue', a two week number 1 in the *Billboard* charts. They stepped out on their own for 'Counting Teardrops' for Winn Records, before reuniting with Dion for 'The Wanderer', which stalled just

one place short of the number 1 spot in the US charts. The follow-up, 'Lovers Who Wander', peaked at number 3, emphasizing the power of the Dion/Del-Satins coalition. While the combination was charting once more with the kazoo-led 'Little Dianne', the Del-Satins released 'Teardrops Follow Me', their first own-name outing to garner serious sales, after which they found regular work on television (Alan Freed) and radio (Freed and Murray The K). Back with Dion for the number 5 'Love Came To Me', the Del-Satins' own 'Does My Love Stand A Chance' did not fare well. In 1962 they moved to Columbia Records as part of Dion's new deal, which began with a version of the Drifters' 'Ruby Baby', another substantial hit at number 2. Still frustrated by their lack of recognition, in 1963 the Del-Satins auditioned for Phil Spector but declined his subsequent invitation to record with him. Meanwhile, in appreciation for their past efforts on his behalf, Dion wrote a song for the Del-Satins for single release, 'Feeling No Pain', but without his name to accompany it there was no chart return. Two more hits with their mentor followed, 'Donna The Prima Donna' and 'Drip Drop', before new manager Jay Fontana found the group a home at Mala Records. This relationship lasted for only one single, 'Two Broken Hearts', before three more efforts at B.T. Puppy Records. These included a rendering of the Drifters 'Sweets For My Sweet', but afterwards Ziska left (for the Magnificent Men) and was temporarily replaced by Carl Parker. In 1966 the Vietnam War robbed the group of Cauchi and Tommy Ferrara, but the Del-Satins continued to play live with the addition of Richard Green, Mike Gregorio and Johnny Maestro. When Cauchi returned he and the Del-Satins became Brooklyn Bridge. In 1991 the original Del-Satins reformed for nostalgia shows.
● ALBUMS: *Out To Lunch* (BT Puppy 1972)★★.

DEMENSIONS

A New York-based vocal group formed in 1960, the Demensions had one Top 20 hit, a doo-wop version of the *Wizard Of Oz* classic 'Over The Rainbow', that same year. Consisting of Lenny Dell (b. 1944, Bronx, New York, USA), Howie Margolin (b. 1943, Bronx, New York, USA), Marisa Martelli (b. 1944, Bronx, New York, USA) and Peter Del Giudice (b. 1938, Bronx, New York, USA), they were signed to the small Mohawk Records. Following a then-current trend of remaking older pop tunes rock 'n' roll style, the Demensions, with an arrangement by Seymour Barab, worked up their version of the one-time Judy Garland hit in a ballad style. They recorded other standards in that style, but only one other song, a cover of Billy Eckstine's 'My Foolish Heart', charted, reaching number 95 on Coral Records in 1963.
● ALBUMS: *My Foolish Heart* (Coral 1963)★★.
● COMPILATIONS: *Seven Days A Week* (Crystal Ball 1982)★★, *Over The Rainbow* (Relic 1992)★★.

DENNISONS

One of the youngest Liverpool beat groups, the Dennisons - Eddie Parry (vocals), Steve McLaren (guitar),

Clive Hornsby (drums), Alan Willis and Ray Scragge - made their debut at the Cavern Club in May 1962. The following year the quintet came third in the prestigious *Mersey Beat* poll, trailing behind only the Beatles and Gerry And The Pacemakers, and released their first single, the lightweight 'Come On Be My Girl'. Willis was later replaced by Terry Carson as the Dennisons continued their recording career with enthusiastic versions of 'Walking The Dog' and 'Lucy (You Sure Did It This Time)', the latter produced by Shel Talmy. The group was sadly unable to convert regional popularity into national prominence and split up in 1965.

DENNY, MARTIN

b. 10 April 1911, New York, USA. A pianist, composer, arranger, and conductor, Denny trained as a classical pianist and toured with various bands before moving to Hawaii in 1954. The story goes that while playing in the Shell Bar of the alfresco Hawaiian Village night club in Honolulu, he began to incorporate the sounds of the frogs, birds, and various other nocturnal creatures into his music. He also used unusual (some say, weird) instruments to create a kind of Latin/Hawaiian 'exotic fruit cocktail'. The recipe was a tremendous success, and the Exotic Sounds Of Martin Denny had a US number one album in 1959 with *Exotica*. One of the tracks, 'Quiet Village', a 1951 Les Baxter composition, also made the Top 5. The group, which initially consisted of Denny (piano), John Kramer (bass), August Colon (bongos), and Arthur Lyman (vibes), later featured Julius Wechter (vibes and marimba), who went on to form the Baja Marimba Band. There followed a series of phenomenally successful albums as Denny's music permeated into the most unexpected areas. In the late 70s, Genesis P-Orridge of Throbbing Gristle was an enthusiastic fan. After touring throughout America in his heyday, Denny eventually opted for semi-retirement in Honolulu. He emerged in 1995 to take part in *Without Walls: The Air-Conditioned Eden*, a UK Channel 4 television documentary which reflected post-war America's obsession with the 'tiki' culture. His catalogue was revived following the rediscovery of people like Esquivel and 'space age bachelor pad music' in the mid-90s.
●ALBUMS: *Exotica* (Liberty 1957)★★★★, *Exotica Vol. II* (Liberty 1957)★★★★, *Primitiva* (Liberty 1958)★★★, *Forbidden Island* (Liberty 1958)★★★, *Exotica Volume III* (Liberty 1959)★★★, *Hypnotique* (Liberty 1959)★★★, *Afro-Desia* (Liberty 1959)★★★, *Quiet Village* (Liberty 1959)★★★, *Exotic Sounds From The Silver Screen* (Liberty 1960)★★★, *Exotic Sounds Visits Broadway* (Liberty 1960)★★★, *Enchanted Sea* (Liberty 1960)★★★, *Romantica* (Liberty 1961)★★★, *Exotic Percussion* (Liberty 1961)★★★, *In Person* (Liberty 1962)★★★, *A Taste Of Honey* (Liberty 1962)★★★, *Exotica Suite* (Liberty 1962)★★★, *Versatile* (Liberty 1963)★★★, *Latin Village* (Liberty 1964)★★★, *Golden Hawaiian Hits* (Liberty 1965)★★★, *Golden Greats* (Liberty 1966)★★★, *Hawaii Tattoo* (Liberty 1966)★★★, *Paradise Moods* (Sunset 1966)★★★★, *Hawaiian A Go-Go* (Liberty 1966)★★★, *Hawaii* (Liberty 1967)★★★, *Exotica Classica* (Liberty 1967)★★★, *Sayonara* (Sunset 1967)★★★, *Exotica Today* (Liberty 1969)★★★, *Exotic Moog* (Liberty 1969).
●COMPILATIONS: *Best Of* (Liberty 1962)★★★, *The Best Of Martin Denny* (Rhino 1995)★★★★, *The Exotic Sounds Of ...* (Capitol 1997)★★★.

DENVER, KARL

b. Angus McKenzie, 16 December 1934, Glasgow, Scotland. Denver, a former merchant seaman, was aged 23 before he began a career in show business. During his travels the singer developed a love of contrasting folk forms and his repertoire consisted of traditional material from the Middle East, Africa and China. Denver's flexible voice spanned several octaves and his unusual inflections brought much contemporary comment. The artist enjoyed four UK Top 10 hits during 1961/62, including 'Marcheta' and 'Wimoweh', the latter reaching number 4. Denver continued to enjoy minor chart success over the next two years, but he progressively turned to cabaret work. The singer has been based in Manchester for many years, which in part explains 'Lazyitis (One Armed Boxer)', his 1989 collaboration with the city's neo-psychedelic favourites, the Happy Mondays.
●ALBUMS: *Wimoweh* (Decca 1961)★★★, *Karl Denver* (Ace Of Clubs 1962)★★★, *Karl Denver At The Yew Tree* (Decca 1962)★★, *With Love* (Decca 1964)★★★, *Karl Denver* (1970)★★.

DERAM RECORDS

The Decca label established its Deram subsidiary in 1966 with a view to exploiting experimental British pop. The new outlet, named after a brand of cartridge, made its debut with Beverley (Martyn)'s 'Happy New Year', but achieved commercial success with singles by the Move ('Night Of Fear', 'I Can Hear The Grass Grow') and Cat Stevens ('I Love My Dog', 'Matthew And Son', 'I'm Gonna Get Me A Gun'). Such hits were accompanied by several excellent 'one-off' recordings intended to fulfil the label's original premise. These included singles by Timebox, the Eyes Of Blue and Denny Laine, but the international approbation greeting Procol Harum's 'A Whiter Shade Of Pale' (1967) helped change Deram's direction. Producer Denny Cordell used the status it garnered to take his acts elsewhere, thus robbing the label of several prime assets. Session group the Flowerpot Men did score with the opportunistic 'Let's Go To San Francisco' and although Amen Corner enjoyed hits with 'Gin House Blues' (1967), 'Bend Me Shape Me' and 'High In The Sky' (both 1968), they too moved to another outlet. Deram was also responsible for MOR recordings led by Les Reed and Roberto Mann, while a collaboration between the London Festival Orchestra and a moribund Moody Blues relaunched the latter's career, in particular through the recurrent favourite 'Nights In White Satin'. However, by the end of the 60s the outlet had lost its remaining identity and during the ensuing decade re-promoted its David Bowie catalogue in the light of the artist's new-found success, rather than breaking new acts. Deram's release schedule lessened as the 70s unfolded, although post-punk signings the Modettes and Splodgenessabounds scored several hits. While never acclaimed in the manner of Vertigo, Elektra and Harvest, the label was nonetheless responsible for several excellent releases.

●COMPILATIONS: *Staircase To Nowhere* (1986)★★★, *Deram Dayze* (1987)★★★.

DeSanto, Sugar Pie

b. Umpeylia Marsema Balinton, 16 October 1935, Brooklyn, New York, USA. Raised in San Francisco, DeSanto was discovered at a talent show by Johnny Otis, who later dubbed her 'Little Miss Sugar Pie'. She recorded for Federal and Aladdin before 'I Want To Know' (1960) on Veltone reached the R&B charts. Signed to Checker in 1961, her first releases made little impact and for two years she toured as part of the James Brown Revue. 'Slip In Mules' (1964), an amusing 'answer' to Tommy Tucker's 'Hi-Heeled Sneakers', regained her chart position. It was followed by the sassy 'Soulful Dress', while an inspired pairing with Etta James produced 'Do I Make Myself Clear' (1965) and 'In The Basement' (1966). Although her recording career at Checker was drawing to a close, DeSanto's songs were recorded by such acts as Billy Stewart, Little Milton and Fontella Bass. DeSanto returned to San Francisco during the 70s where she continues to perform and record today.

●ALBUMS: *Sugar Pie* (Checker 1961)★★★, *Hello San Francisco* (1984)★★.

●COMPILATIONS: *Loving Touch* (1987)★★★ *Down In The Basement - The Chess Years* (1988)★★★, with Fontella Bass *Sisters Of Soul* (1990)★★★.

DeShannon, Jackie

b. 21 August 1944, Hazel, Kentucky, USA. This highly talented singer and songwriter was introduced to gospel, country and blues styles while still a child. She was actively performing by the age of 15 and, having travelled to Los Angeles, commenced a recording career in 1960 with a series of releases on minor labels. DeShannon's collaborations with Sharon Sheeley resulted in several superior pop songs including 'Dum Dum' and 'Heart In Hand' for Brenda Lee and 'Trouble' for the Kalin Twins. DeShannon then forged equally fruitful partnerships with Jack Nitzsche and Randy Newman, the former of which spawned 'When You Walk In The Room', a 1964 smash for the Searchers. Resultant interest in the UK inspired several television appearances and DeShannon's London sojourn was also marked by several songwriting collaborations with Jimmy Page. Despite a succession of excellent singles, Jackie's own recording career failed to achieve similar heights, although her work continued to be covered by Helen Shapiro, Marianne Faithfull, the Byrds and the Critters. DeShannon enjoyed a US Top 10 single with the Burt Bacharach/Hal David-penned 'What The World Needs Now Is Love' (1965), but her biggest hit came four years later when 'Put A Little Love In Your Heart' reached number 4 in the same chart. Although she

continued to write and record superior pop, as evinced on *Jackie* and *Your Baby Is A Lady*, DeShannon was unable to sustain the same profile during the 70s and 80s. Her songs continued to provide hits for others, notably 'Bette Davis Eyes' (Kim Carnes in 1981), 'Breakaway' (Tracey Ullman in 1983) and 'Put A Little Love In Your Heart' (Annie Lennox and Al Green in 1988). Jackie DeShannon's position as one of the 60s' leading pop composers remains undiminished.

●ALBUMS: *Jackie DeShannon* (Liberty 1963)★★, *Breakin' It Up On The Beatles Tour* (Liberty 1964)★★, *Don't Turn Your Back On Me* (1964)★★★, *Surf Party* soundtrack (1964)★★, *This Is Jackie DeShannon* (Imperial 1965)★★★, *You Won't Forget Me* (Imperial 1965)★★, *In The Wind* (Imperial 1965)★★, *C'Mon Let's Live A Little* soundtrack (1966)★★, *Are You Ready For This?* (1966)★★★, *New Image* (1967)★★, *For You* (1967)★★, *Me About You* (1968)★★, *What The World Needs Now Is Love* (1968)★★★, *Laurel Canyon* (1969)★★, *Put A Little Love In Your Heart* (1969)★★, *To Be Free* (1969)★★, *Songs* (1971)★★★, *Jackie* (Atlantic 1972)★★, *Your Baby Is A Lady* (1974)★★★, *New Arrangement* (1975)★★, *You're The Only Dancer* (1977)★★, *Quick Touches* (1978)★★.

●COMPILATIONS: *You Won't Forget Me* (1965)★★★, *Lonely Girl* (1970)★★, *What The World Needs Now Is ... The Definitive Collection* (EMI 1997)★★★, *The Best Of Jackie DeShannon* (Rhino 1991)★★★★.

Desmond, Paul

b. Paul Breitenfeld, 25 November 1924, San Francisco, California, USA, d. 30 May 1977. Alto saxophonist Desmond is best known as a member of the Dave Brubeck quartet, in which he played from 1951-67 and to whose popular success he greatly contributed by writing the hit 'Take Five'. However, aficionados and critics alike agree that much of his best work was done away from Brubeck's often stiff improvisations and tricky time signatures, in particular on two albums with Gerry Mulligan (*Blues In Time*, *Two Of A Mind*) and five with Jim Hall (*East Of The Sun*, *Bossa Antigua*, *Glad To Be Unhappy*, *Take Ten*, *Easy Living*), which Mosaic Records later reissued in one of their splendidly packaged box sets. Influenced by Lee Konitz, but very much his own man, Desmond's pure tone and fluid, inventive solos - into which he often wove witty quotes from other songs - marked him out as one of modern jazz's most original and distinctive voices. A noted humorist too, he once declared his aim was to make his saxophone 'sound like a dry martini' and also claimed to have won prizes as 'the world's slowest alto player'. In fact, Desmond's pellucid tone and relaxed, floating style required an architect's sense of structure and the lightning reflexes of a master improviser. In the late 60s/early 70s he sometimes sounded out of place on the CTI label, amid fusion, strings, Simon And Garfunkel songs and the other accoutrements of Creed Taylor's production; but a 1971 date with the Modern Jazz Quartet, and two albums from a 1975 concert with his own quartet, catch him back at his best. In 1975 he also recorded a set of duets with Brubeck and rejoined the pianist's quartet for a reunion tour. In 1976 his doctor diagnosed lung cancer - 'I only went with swollen feet,' Desmond wryly remarked - and he died the following May. Desmond is remembered as one of the most literate, amusing and reflective of jazzmen.

●ALBUMS: *The Paul Desmond Quintet* (Fantasy 1954)★★★, *The Paul Desmond Quartet* (Fantasy 1956)★★★, with Gerry Mulligan *Blues In Time* (1957)★★★, *First Place Again!* (Warners 1959)★★★, *Desmond Blue* (RCA Victor 1961)★★★★, with Mulligan *Two Of A Mind* (RCA Victor 1962)★★★★, *Take Ten* (RCA Victor 1962)★★★, *Bossa Antigua* (RCA Victor 1965)★★★, *Glad To Be Unhappy* (RCA Victor 1965)★★★, *Easy Living* (RCA Victor 1966)★★★, *Polka Dots And Moonbeams* (Bluebird 1966)★★★, *Summertime* (A&M 1969)★★★, *From The Hot Afternoon* (A&M 1969)★★★, *Crystal Illusions* (1969)★★★, *Bridge Over Troubled Water* (A&M 1970)★★, *Skylark* (CBS 1974)★★★, *Pure Desmond* (CTI 1975)★★★, with Dave Brubeck *1975: The Duets* (1975)★★★, *The Paul Desmond Quartet Live* (1976)★★★★, *Like Someone In Love* (Telarc 1976)★★★★, *Paul Desmond* rec. 1975 (1978)★★★, with the MJQ *The Only Recorded Performance* rec. 1971 (1984)★★★.

●COMPILATIONS: *Greatest Hits* (RCA 1986)★★★, *The Complete Recordings Of The Paul Desmond Quartet With Jim Hall* rec. 1959-65, 6-LP box set (1987)★★★★, *Late Lament* rec. 1961-62 (1987)★★★.

DETERGENTS

Formed in the New York City area, the Detergents were a trio consisting of Ron Dante, Danny Jordan and Tommy Wynn. Dante had been a songwriter and demo singer at New York's Brill Building, where his compositions had been placed with such artists as Johnny Mathis, Bobby Vee and Gene Pitney. In 1964, Dante joined up with Jordan and Wynn and recorded a parody of the Shangri-Las', 'Leader Of The Pack'. Entitled 'Leader Of The Laundromat' composed by Paul Vance and Lee Pockriss, who wrote hits such as 'Itsy Bitsy Teeny Weeny Yellow Polka Dot Bikini' and 'Catch A Falling Star'. The song was released on the Roulette label and eventually climbed to number 19 in the US singles chart. By the time the follow-up single, was released, Jordan and Wynn were replaced by Phil Patrick and Tony Favio. The single, 'Double-O-Seven', made the lower regions of the US charts in 1965 and the group released one album. Dante went on to become the vocalist behind the hits by the Archies in the late 60s and produced some of the earliest recordings by Barry Manilow for Bell Records. Jordan later produced the 1972 novelty hit 'Popcorn' by Hot Butter.

●ALBUMS: *The Many Faces Of The Detergents* (Roulette 1965)★★.

DEVIANTS

Originally known as the Social Deviants, this pioneering British underground group merged R&B, pseudo-politics and an amateurism inspired by New York radicals, the Fugs. The 'Social' prefix was dropped in 1967 with the departure of Clive Muldoon and Pete Munroe, while the remaining core, Mick Farren (vocals), Sid Bishop (guitar), Cord Rees (bass) and Russell Hunter (drums) began work on the Deviants' debut album, *Ptooff*. This characteristically rabblehouse collection was initially issued on the group's own label and distributed through the network purveying the era's alternative publications, *International Times* and *Oz*. Rees was replaced by Duncan Sanderson for *Disposable*, memorable for Farren's call-to-arms composition, 'Let's Loot The Supermarket'. Canadian guitarist Paul Rudolph joined the group on Bishop's departure and the reconstituted quartet completed *Deviants* prior to embarking for America. Farren was fired during the tour and on their return his former colleagues dropped their erstwhile name and became the Pink Fairies upon the addition of former Pretty Things drummer Twink. Farren, who pursued a multi-faceted career as a novelist, rock journalist and sometime musician, later re-established the Deviants' appellation for an EP, *Screwed Up* (1977) and an informal live performance captured on the *Human Garbage* album.

●ALBUMS: *Ptooff* (Underground Impressarios 1967)★★, *Disposable* (Stable 1968)★★, *Deviants* (Transatlantic 1969)★★, *Human Garbage* (Psycho 1984)★★, *Eating Jello With A Heated Fork* (Alive 1996)★★.

DEVOTIONS

Formed in 1960 in Astoria, New York, USA, the Devotions were a doo-wop group best known for their 1964 novelty recording 'Rip Van Winkle'. The group included Ray Sanchez, who sang bass-lead, Bob Weisbrod, Bob Hovorka and brothers Frank and Joe Pardo. With their manager, the group auditioned in 1960 for a small record label, Delta, whose owner, Bernie Zimming, was not impressed with their sound. The group wrote 'Rip Van Winkle' that day and Zimming liked it. However, it did not sell, but two years later, when the larger Roulette Records acquired Delta, it was released again. It still did not reach the charts, and the group disbanded. In 1964, however, Roulette included the song as part of a *Golden Goodies* album series and it attracted more attention. Roulette issued the single for a third time and this time it made the US Top 40. A new Devotions group was assembled including three original members, but when further singles flopped, they disbanded in 1965.

DICK AND DEE DEE

This American boy/girl vocal duo was formed in 1961 by Dick St John Gostine (b. 1944, Santa Monica, California, USA) and Dee Dee Sperling (b. 1945, Santa Monica, California, USA) while they were at a local high school. The Gostine-written 'The Mountain's High' was originally released on the small local label Lama, but was picked up by Liberty and became a US hit. Gostine had already made some solo recordings for the label. The fact that they were still at college while this happened precluded touring, however. Visually, the duo dressed as high school kids for an end of term 'prom', and remained highly popular in the US for several years. They switched to Warner Brothers in 1962, and had several more hits before fading out of fashion in the mid-60s. Afterwards they retired from pop music.

●ALBUMS: *Tell Me/The Mountain's High* (Liberty 1962)★★★, *Young And In Love* (Warners 1963)★★★, *Turn Around* (Warners 1964)★★★, *Thou Shalt Not Steal* (Warners 1965)★★★, *Songs We've Sung On Shindig* (Warners 1966)★★.

●COMPILATIONS: *The Best Of ...* (Varese Sarabande 1996)★★★.

DIDDLEY, BO

b. Elias Bates (later known as Elias McDaniel), 28 December 1928, McComb, Mississippi, USA. After beginning his career as a boxer, where he received the sobriquet 'Bo Diddley', the singer worked the blues clubs of Chicago with a repertoire influenced by Louis Jordan, John Lee Hooker and Muddy Waters. In late 1954, he teamed up with Billy Boy Arnold and recorded demos of 'I'm A Man' and 'Bo Diddley'. Re-recorded at Chess Studios with a backing ensemble comprising Otis Spann (piano), Lester Davenport (harmonica), Frank Kirkland (drums) and Jerome Green (maracas), the a-side 'Bo Diddley' became an R&B hit in 1955. Before long, Diddley's distorted, amplified, custom-made guitar, with its rectangular shape and pumping rhythm style became a familiar, much-imitated trademark, as did his self-referential songs with such titles as 'Bo Diddley's A Gunslinger', 'Diddley Daddy' and 'Bo's A Lumberjack'. His jive-talking routine with 'Say Man' (a US Top 20 hit in 1959) and 'Pretty Thing' and 'Hey Good Lookin'', which reached the lower regions of the UK charts in 1963. By then, Diddley was regarded as something of an R&B legend and found a new lease of life courtesy of the UK beat boom. The Pretty Things named themselves after one of his songs while his work was covered by such artists as the Rolling Stones, Animals, Manfred Mann, Kinks, Yardbirds, Downliner's Sect and the Zephyrs. Diddley subsequently jammed on albums by Chuck Berry and Muddy Waters and appeared infrequently at rock festivals. His classic version of 'Who Do You Love' became a staple cover for a new generation of USA acts ranging from Quicksilver Messenger Service to the Doors, Tom Rush and Bob Seger, while the UK's Juicy Lucy took the song into the UK Top 20.

Like many of his generation, Diddley attempted to update his image and in the mid-70s released *The Black Gladiator* in the uncomfortable guise of an ageing funkster. *Where It All Begins*, produced by Johnny Otis (whose hit 'Willie And The Hand Jive' owed much to Diddley's style), was probably the most interesting of his post 60s albums. In 1979, Diddley toured with the Clash and in 1984 took a cameo roll in the film *Trading Places*. A familiar face on the revival circuit, Diddley is rightly regarded as a seminal figure in the history of rock 'n' roll. His continued appeal to younger performers was empha-

sized by Craig McLachlan's hit recording of 'Mona' in 1990. Bo's sound and 'chunk-a-chunka-cha' rhythm continues to remain an enormous influence on pop and rock, both consciously and unconsciously. It was announced in 1995, after many years of relative recording inactivity, that Diddley had signed for Mike Vernon's Code Blue record label; the result was *A Man Amongst Men*. Even with the assistance of Richie Sambora, Jimmie Vaughan, Ronnie Wood, Keith Richards, Billy Boy Arnold, Johnny 'Guitar' Watson and the Shirelles the anticipation was greater than the result.

●ALBUMS: *Bo Diddley* (Checker 1957)★★★, *Go Bo Diddley* (Checker 1958)★★★, *Have Guitar Will Travel* (Checker 1959)★★★, *Bo Diddley In The Spotlight* (Checker 1960)★★★, *Bo Diddley Is A Gunslinger* (Checker 1961)★★★, *Bo Diddley Is A Lover* (Checker 1961)★★★, *Bo Diddley* (Checker 1962)★★★, *Bo Diddley Is A Twister* (Checker 1962)★★★, *Hey Bo Diddley* (1963)★★★, *Bo Diddley And Company* (Checker 1963)★★★, *Bo Diddley Rides Again* (1963)★★★, *Bo Diddley's Beach Party* (Checker 1963)★★★, *Bo Diddley Goes Surfing* (USA *Surfin' With Bo Diddley*) (Checker 1963)★★★, *Hey Good Looking* (Checker 1964)★★★, with Chuck Berry *Two Great Guitars* (Checker 1964)★★★, *500% More Man* (Checker 1965)★★★, *Let Me Pass* (1965)★★★, *The Originator* (Checker 1966)★★★, *Superblues* (Checker 1968)★★★, Boss Man (Checker 1967)★★★, *The Super Super Blues Band* (Checker 1968)★★★, *Big Bad Bo* (Chess 1974)★★★, *Another Dimension* (Chess 1971)★★★, *The Bo Diddley London Sessions* (Chess 1973)★★, *Got My Own Bag Of Tricks* (Chess 1974)★★★, *The Black Gladiator* (Checker 1969)★★, *Where It All Begins* (Chess 1972)★★, *The 20th Anniversary Of Rock 'N' Roll* (1976)★★, *I'm A Man* (1977)★★, *Signifying Blues* (1993)★★★, *Bo's Blues* (1993)★★, *A Man Amongst Men* (Code Blue 1996)★★.

●COMPILATIONS: *Chess Master* (Chess 1988)★★★, *EP Collection* (1991)★★★★, *Bo Diddley: The Chess Years* 12-CD box set (Charly 1993)★★★★★, *Bo Diddley Is A Lover ... Plus* (See For Miles 1994)★★★, *Let Me Pass ... Plus* (See For Miles 1994)★★★.

●FURTHER READING: *Where Are You Now Bo Diddley?*, Edward Kiersh. *The Complete Bo Diddley Sessions*, George White (ed.).

DILLARD AND CLARK

Refugees from the Dillards and the Byrds, respectively, Doug Dillard (b. 6 March 1937) and Gene Clark (b. Harold Eugene Clark, 17 November 1941, Tipton, Missouri, USA, d. 24 May 1991) joined forces in 1968 to form one of the first country rock groups. Backed by the Expedition featuring Bernie Leadon (banjo/guitar), Don Beck (dobro/mandolin) and David Jackson (string bass), they recorded two albums for A&M Records, which confirmed their standing among the best of the early country rock exponents. *The Fantastic Expedition Of Dillard And Clark* featured several strong compositions by Clark and Leadon including 'The Radio Song', 'Out On The Side',

'Something's Wrong' and 'Train Leaves Here This Mornin''. Leadon later took the latter to his next group, the Eagles, who included the song on their debut album. By the time of their second album, Dillard and Clark displayed a stronger country influence with the induction of Flying Burrito Brothers drummer Jon Corneal, champion fiddle player Byron Berline and additional vocalist Donna Washburn. *Through The Morning, Through The Night* combined country standards with Clark originals and featured some sumptuous duets between Clark and Washburn which pre-empted the work of Gram Parsons and Emmylou Harris. Although the Expedition experiment showed considerable promise, the group scattered in various directions at the end of the 60s, with Clark reverting to a solo career.

●ALBUMS: *The Fantastic Expedition Of Dillard And Clark* (A&M 1968)★★★, *Through The Morning, Through The Night* (A&M 1969)★★★.

DINO, DESI AND BILLY

The trio comprised the son of actor/singer Dean Martin, Dino (b. Dean Paul Anthony Martin Jnr, 12 November 1951, Los Angeles, California, USA, d. 21 March 1987), the son of actors Desi Arnaz and Lucille Ball, Desi (b. Desiderio Alberto Arnaz IV, 19 January 1953, Los Angeles, California, USA) and Billy (b. William Ernest Joseph Hinsche, 29 June 1951, Manilla, The Philippines), a friend from school. The trio met while playing Little League baseball in Beverly Hills in 1965 and decided to form a pop group. With their connections, they were easily signed to Frank Sinatra's Reprise label. Their first single, the easy listening 'I'm A Fool', was their biggest hit, reaching number 17 in the summer of 1965, and they placed five other singles and two albums on the charts before breaking up in 1970. Although Martin and Arnaz joined a blues band in the 70s, Hinsche kept the highest musical profile, as a session musician and briefly a member of the Beach Boys' stage back-up band. Martin was killed in 1987 when his Air National Guard jet crashed.

●ALBUMS: *I'm A Fool* (Reprise 1965)★★★, *Our Times Are Coming* (Reprise 1966)★★, *Memories Are Made Of This* (Reprise 1966)★★, *Souvenir* (Reprise 1966)★★★, *Follow Me* (1969)★★.

●COMPILATIONS: *The Rebel Kind* (Sundazed 1996)★★★.

DION AND THE BELMONTS

b. Dion DiMucci, 18 July 1939, Bronx, New York, USA. During his peak, from 1958-63, Dion was the quintessential Italian-American New York City rocker and was, perhaps, the first major white rock singer who was not from a southern city. The career of one of America's legendary artists has spanned five decades, during which time he has made numerous musical style changes. Between 1958 and 1960 Dion And The Belmonts were one of the leading doo-wop groups. The Belmonts comprised Angelo D'Aleo (b. 3 February 1940, Bronx, New York, USA), Carlo Mastrangelo (b. 5 October 1938, Bronx, New York, USA),

and Freddie Milano (b. 22 August 1939, Bronx, New York, USA). The slick besuited Italian look rivalled the black harmony groups that dominated the era. They had nine hits in two years, including two of the all-time great examples of white doo-wop, 'I Wonder Why' and 'No One Knows'. Their classic reading of the Doc Pomus and Mort Shuman song 'Teenager in Love' with the memorable line of teenage despair 'each night I ask, the stars up above, (bom, bom, bom, bom), why must I be a teenager in love?' It poignantly articulated growing pains in an era when conservative values were being challenged by a new moral climate.

In 1960 they attempted a version of 'When You Wish Upon A Star' from Walt Disney's *Pinocchio* and followed with a worthy cover of Cole Porter's 'In The Still Of The Night'. Dion left for a solo career in 1960 and had immediate success in the USA with 'Lonely Teenager'. The following year he had two consecutive hits that made him one of America's biggest artists. Both 'Runaround Sue' and 'The Wanderer' are rock classics; the former, warning everybody to keep away from Sue, while the latter warns Flo, Jane and Mary to steer clear of the wanderer. The similarity of the theme can be forgiven as they are both wonderfully uplifting songs, great dance records and two of the finest of the era. Dion sustained an incredible output of hits; in 1963 with seven major singles he was in the US charts for the entire year. In 1964 Dion disappeared from the scene to fight a serious addiction to heroin, a drug to which he had fallen victim in 1960. Although he and the Belmonts reunited briefly in 1967, little was heard of him until December 1968. He returned during a turbulent year in American history; the escalation of the Vietnam War had received strong opposition, particularly from the music world, and the assassinations of Robert Kennedy and Martin Luther King were fresh in people's minds. The emotional Dick Holler song, 'Abraham, Martin And John' was a perfectly timed stroke of genius. This lilting folksy ballad barely left a dry eye as it climbed to number 4 in the US charts.

The following year a heroin-free Dion delighted festival and concert audiences with a striking solo act, accompanied on acoustic guitar. That same year the excellent *Dion* was released, including sensitive covers of songs by Bob Dylan, Joni Mitchell, Leonard Cohen, and a brave attempt at Jimi Hendrix's 'Purple Haze'. Dion's critical ranking was high but his commercial standing dwindled, and two acoustic-based albums were commercial disasters. Wily entrepreneurs encouraged another reunion with the Belmonts in 1973, and in 1975 Phil Spector produced 'Born To Be With You'. An album of the same name (on Spector's own label) failed, and one underrated album, *The Return Of The Wanderer*, appeared in 1978 on Lifesong Records. For the next few years Dion became a devout born-again Christian and recorded sporadically, releasing Christian albums including *Inside Job* and *Kingdom Of The Street*. He returned to rock 'n' roll in 1988 playing with Bruce Springsteen and released the Dave Edmunds-produced *To Frankie*; he toured the UK as recently as 1990. Dion is one of the few survivors from a school of American vocalists who had genuine talent, and should be forever applauded for a series of great uplifting songs that still sound remarkably fresh. He was elected to the Rock and Roll Hall of Fame in 1989.

●ALBUMS: Dion And The Belmonts: *Presenting Dion And The Belmonts* (Laurie 1959)★★★, *Wish Upon A Star* (Laurie 1960)★★, *Together* (Laurie 1963)★★★, *Together Again* (ABC 1967)★★★, *Live 1972* (Reprise 1973).

●COMPILATIONS: *20 Golden Greats* (1980)★★★★. Dion: *Alone With Dion* (Laurie 1961)★★★, *Runaround Sue* (Laurie 1961)★★★, *Lovers Who Wander* (Laurie 1962)★★★, *Dion Sings His Greatest Hits* (Laurie 1962)★★★, *Love Came To Me* (Laurie 1963)★★★, *Ruby Baby* (Columbia 1963)★★★, *Dion Sings The 15 Million Sellers* (Laurie 1963)★★★★, *Donna The Prima Donna* (Columbia 1963)★★★★, *Dion Sings To Sandy* (Laurie 1963)★★★, *Dion* (1968)★★★, *Sit Down Old Friend* (1969)★★★, *Wonder Where I'm Bound* (1969)★★★, *You're Not Alone* (1971)★★★, *Sanctuary* (1971)★★★, *Suite For Late Summer* (1972)★★★, *Born To Be With You* (1975)★★★, *Sweetheart* (1976)★★★, *The Return Of The Wanderer* (1978)★★★, *Inside Job* (1980)★★★, *Kingdom Of The Street* (1985)★★★, *Velvet And Steel* (1986)★★★, *Yo Frankie!* (1989)★★★, *Bronx Blues: The Columbia Recordings (1962-1965)* (1991)★★★★, *The Road I'm On: A Retrospective* (Columbia Legacy 1997)★★★.

●FURTHER READING: *The Wanderer*, Dion DiMucci with Davin Seay.

DIXIE CUPS

Formed in New Orleans, Louisiana, USA, in 1963, the Dixie Cups were a female trio best known for the original recording of the hit 'Chapel Of Love' in the early 60s. The group consisted of sisters Barbara Ann Hawkins (b. 23 October 1943) and Rosa Lee Hawkins (b. 24 September 1944) and their cousin Joan Marie Johnson (b. January 1945, New Orleans, Louisiana, USA). Having sung together in church and at school, the girls formed a group called the Meltones for a high school talent contest in 1963. There they were discovered by Joe Jones, a New Orleans singer who had secured a hit himself with 'You Talk Too Much' in 1960. He became their manager and signed the trio with producers/songwriters Jerry Leiber and Mike Stoller, who were then starting their own record label, Red Bird, with industry veteran George Goldner.

The Dixie Cups recorded Jeff Barry and Ellie Greenwich's 'Chapel Of Love' despite the fact that both the Ronettes and the Crystals had failed to have hits with the song, which was described by co-producer Mike Leiber as 'a record I hated with a passion'. Released as the debut Red Bird single, the trio's first single reached number 1 in the USA during the summer of 1964. (The trio later claimed that they received only a few hundred dollars for their part in the recording.) Following that hit, the Dixie Cups toured the USA and released a number of follow-up singles for Red Bird, four of which charted. 'People Say', the second, made number 12 and the last, 'Iko Iko', a tradi-

tional New Orleans chant, reached number 20. The song was subsequently used in soundtracks for a number of films, in common with 'Chapel Of Love'.

After Red Bird closed down in 1966, the Dixie Cups signed with ABC-Paramount Records. No hits resulted from the association, and the trio have not recorded since, although they continue to perform (the two sisters are the only originals still in the act).

●ALBUMS: *Chapel Of Love* (Red Bird 1964)★★★, *Iko Iko* reissue of first album (Red Bird 1965)★★★, *Ridin' High* (ABC/Paramount 1965)★★.

DOCTOR WEST'S MEDICINE SHOW AND JUG BAND

Founded in Los Angeles, California, USA, Doctor West's Medicine Show And Jug Band were led by former Boston-based folk singer, Norman Greenbaum. Bonnie Wallach (guitar/vocals), Jack Carrington (guitar/vocals/percussion) and Evan Engber (percussion) completed the original line-up. The group played a mixture of jug and good-time music similar to Sopwith Camel. They enjoyed a minor US hit in 1967 with the novelty song, 'The Eggplant That Ate Chicago' and attracted attention for the title of its follow-up, 'Gondoliers, Overseers, Playboys And Bums'. They broke up at the end of that year after which Greenbaum formed several low-key acts before teaming with producer Erik Jacobsen and scoring international success with 'Spirit In The Sky'.

●ALBUMS: *The Eggplant That Ate Chicago* (Go Go 1967)★★.

DODD, KEN

b. 8 November 1927, Liverpool, England. Primarily one of Britain's all-time great stand-up comedians, Dodd has also had a successful recording career singing romantic ballads in a warm mezzo-tenor voice. His only comedy record - as the Diddy Men in 1965 - was a flop. He grew up in Liverpool and sang in a church choir before developing a comedy act as Professor Yaffle Chuckabutty, Operatic Tenor and Sausage Knotter, in which he sang comic versions of well-known songs. Dodd worked in sales before becoming a professional comic in 1954, playing theatres and summer shows at Blackpool's Central Pier, where he topped the bill in 1958. This led to appearances at the London Palladium and a television series in the 60s. Like other comedians of his generation, Dodd was a competent singer and frequently closed his shows with a romantic ballad.

In 1960 he signed to Decca and recorded 'Love Is Like A Violin', a 20s ballad which became a Top 10 hit. This was followed by 'Once In Every Lifetime' (1961) and 'Pianissimo' (1962). He next switched to EMI's Columbia label, where Geoff Love was the musical director for the minor hits 'Still' (1963) and the exuberant 'Happiness' (1964). But the biggest hit of his career was the contrasting 'Tears' (1965), a weepie of a ballad produced by Norman Newell. After five weeks at number 1 in the UK, it was displaced by the Rolling Stones' 'Get Off Of My Cloud'. A hit for Rudy Vallee in 1931, 'Tears' sold nearly

two million copies for Dodd and led to six more Top 20 singles in the next few years. Among these were translations of three Italian Ken Dodd hits ('The River, 'Broken Hearted' and 'When Love Comes Round Again') and 'Promises', based on Beethoven's *Pathetique Sonata*. During the 80s, Dodd had modest success with 'Hold My Hand' (1981). In 1990 he hit the headlines following a controversial High Court action brought by the Inland Revenue, which he won. Four years later, he began a six-part BBC Radio 2 series, *Ken Dodd's Comedy Club*, explaining: 'I'm an intellectual entertainer; at one time there was only me and Noël Coward doing this sort of stuff.'
●ALBUMS: *Tears Of Happiness* (1965)★★★, *Hits For Now And Always* (1966)★★★, *For Someone Special* (1967)★★★, *Now And Forever* (1983)★★★.

DOLPHY, ERIC

b. 20 June 1928, Los Angeles, California, USA, d. 29 June 1964. A fluent performer on several reed instruments, Dolphy began to play clarinet while still at school. On the west coast of America in the second half of the 40s he worked with Roy Porter's band, before spending a couple of years in the US army. After his discharge, he played with several leading musicians, including Gerald Wilson, before becoming a member of the popular Chico Hamilton quintet. The stint with Hamilton brought Dolphy to the attention of a wide audience and many other young musicians. In New York in 1959 Dolphy joined Charles Mingus, all the time freelancing at clubs and on recording dates with such influential musicians as George Russell and John Coltrane. In the early 60s, Dolphy began a hugely prolific and arduous period of touring and recording throughout the USA and Europe. He played in bands led by Ornette Coleman (on the seminal *Free Jazz* sessions), John Lewis, Ron Carter, Mal Waldron, Oliver Nelson, Max Roach, Gil Evans, Andrew Hill, Booker Little, Abbey Lincoln, Mingus and Coltrane, with whose quartet he toured Europe in 1961. He also recorded a series of albums as leader, perhaps most notably the *At The Five Spot* sessions, with the brilliant young trumpeter Booker Little (later reissued as *The Great Concert Of Eric Dolphy*), and his Blue Note debut *Out To Lunch*. The latter, with its dislocated rhythms and unusual instrumental textures (Bobby Hutcherson's vibes sharing front line duties with Freddie Hubbard's trumpet and Dolphy's reeds) is a landmark of modern music, and was voted best post-war jazz LP in a 1984 poll of *Wire* magazine critics. Shortly after recording *Out To Lunch* Dolphy left the USA to live in Europe because, as he told writer A.B. Spellman, 'if you try to do anything different in this country, people put you down for it'. He was working in Germany when he suffered a complete circulatory collapse caused by too much sugar in the bloodstream (he was diabetic), and died suddenly on 29 June 1964.

A major influence on jazz, and especially on alto saxophone players, Dolphy was a remarkably gifted musician. During his short career he established himself as a sig-nificant force, playing alto, flute and bass clarinet, an instrument before and since unusual in jazz. He was comfortable in the varied idioms of the bands in which he played, from the relatively orthodox Hamilton to the forward-thinking Coltrane and the third-stream innovations of Gunther Schuller. He was, however, very much his own man, creating strikingly original solo lines, frequently dashed off at breakneck tempos and encompassing wide intervallic leaps. Although he is rightly associated with the concept of free jazz, Dolphy brought to this area of music his own carefully reasoned attitude, and he is perhaps better thought of as someone who stretched bebop to its very limits. Thirty years after his death, the importance of Dolphy's contribution to jazz is still being explored by musicians.
●ALBUMS: with Chico Hamilton *Goings East* (1958)★★★, with Ornette Coleman *Free Jazz* (1960)★★★, *Charles Mingus Presents Charles Mingus* (1960)★★★, with Gunther Schuller *Jazz Abstractions* (1960)★★★, *Out There* (Original Jazz Classics 1960)★★★★, *Outward Bound* (New Jazz 1960)★★★★, *Candid Dolphy* (Candid 1960-61)★★★, *Great Concert Of Eric Dolphy* (1961)★★★, *Eric Dolphy At The Five Spot* (New Jazz 1961)★★★★, *Stockholm Sessions* (1961)★★★, with John Coltrane *Live At The Village Vanguard* (1961)★★★, with Coltrane *European Impressions* (1961)★★★, *Far Cry* (Prestige 1962)★★★★, with Mingus *Town Hall Concert* (1962)★★★, *The Great Concert Of Charles Mingus* (1962)★★★, *Eric Dolphy Quartet* (Tempo 1962)★★★, *In Europe; Vols.1-3* (Prestige 1962)★★★, *Music Matador* (1963)★★★, *Conversations* (FM 1963)★★★, *Unrealized Tapes* (1964)★★★, *Naima* (West Wind 1964)★★★, *Memorial Album* (Vee Jay 1964)★★★★, *Last Date* (Emarcy 1964)★★★, *Eric Dolphy At The Five Spot Vol. 2* (Prestige 1964)★★★★, *Out To Lunch* (Blue Note 1964)★★★★★, *Eric Dolphy In Europe Vol. 2* (Prestige 1965)★★★, *Eric Dolphy In Europe Vol. 3* (Prestige 1965)★★★, *Here And There* (Prestige 1965)★★★★, *Eric Dolphy And Cannonball Adderley* (Archive Of Folk And Jazz 1969)★★★, *Iron Man* (Douglas 1969)★★★, *Other Aspects* rec. 1960-1962 (Blue Note 1982)★★★, *The Complete Prestige Recordings* 9-CD box set (Prestige 1995)★★★★.
●FURTHER READING: *Like A Human Voice - The Eric Dolphy Discography*, Uwe Reichardt. *Eric Dolphy: A Musical Biography And Discography*, Vladimir Simosko and Barry Tepperman. *The Importance Of Being Eric Dolphy*, Raymond Horricks.

DON'T KNOCK THE TWIST

Mindful of Don't Knock The Rock, a follow-up to Rock Around The Clock, *Don't Knock The Twist* succeeded Twist Around The Clock. Few could accuse its producers of possessing imagination. This 1962 feature revolved around a television executive, who hurriedly stages a twisting marathon to pre-empt a similar plan by a rival station. Chubby Checker contributed the title song and 'Slow Twistin', the latter with the help of Dee Dee Sharp.

Inspired by another dance craze, Ms. Sharp offered the memorable 'Mashed Potato Time', while the Dovels sang 'Do The New Continental' and 'Bristol Stomp'. Soul singer Gene Chandler provided the undoubted highlight when, replete with top hat, cape and monocle, he performed the classic 'Duke Of Earl'. Yet despite these interesting cameos, *Don't Knock The Twist* is not one of pop cinema's better features.

DON'T LOOK BACK

Arguably the finest documentary in rock, *Don't Look Back* is a *cinéma verité* film of Bob Dylan's 1965 tour of England. Director D.A. Pennebaker shot the proceedings in black and white with a 16mm, hand-held camera. Indeed, the opening scene, in which 'Subterranean Homesick Blues' plays while the singer holds up placards with words from its lyric, has become a much-copied pop legend. The subsequent pace is almost relentless and, having gained access both onstage and off, Pennebaker exposes Dylan in various moods. The concert footage itself is superb, in particular because this would be Dylan's final all-acoustic tour.

He performs excellent versions of 'Gates Of Eden' and 'It's Alright Ma (I'm Only Bleeding)', but these are over-shadowed by other events captured on film. Dylan's verbal demolition of the *Time* magazine reporter is revelatory, as is his anger when some glasses are thrown from a window at a party. Yet a sense of mischief abounds when, in the company of US companion Bobby Neuworth, a running joke about Donovan only ends when Dylan finally meets his supposed 'rival'. Joan Baez, Marianne Faithfull, Alan Price, John Mayall, Derroll Adams and sundry Pretty Things are also caught on camera, but Dylan is always the focus of attention. *Don't Look Back* was released in 1967, but screenings were generally restricted to independent cinemas. It was withdrawn on Dylan's instructions for a period during the 70s, but was reactivated again in the 80s and finally released on video.

DONAHUE, TOM

b. 21 May 1928, South Bend, Indiana, USA, d. 28 April 1975. Affectionately known as 'Big Daddy' in deference to his massive girth, Donahue played a pivotal role in the evolution of San Franciscan music. He arrived in the city in 1961, having already established himself as a leading disc jockey with Philadelphia's top station WBIG. At KYA he befriended colleague Bob Mitchell, and together they began promoting concerts at the Cow Palace auditorium. The Beatles and the Rolling Stones were two of the acts presented there. Donahue and Mitchell founded Autumn Records in 1964. They scored a national hit with Bobby Freeman's 'C'mon And Swim', before embracing nascent American rock with the Beau Brummels. Fellow disc jockey Sylvester Stewart, aka Sly Stone, produced many of the label's acts. The entrepreneurs also established a North Beach club, Mothers, which showcased some of the early acts synonymous with the San Franciscan sound, including the Great Society. However, they singularly

failed to sign other important acts, including the Charlatans, the Grateful Dead and Dino Valenti, despite recording demos with them. This hesitancy was one of the factors contributing to Autumn's demise. Mitchell died in 1966, but Donahue retained his influential position. He managed several artists, including Ron Nagle, Sal Valentino and the aforementioned Valenti, and revolutionized radio at station KSAN-FM by adopting a bold 'album' format. He masterminded an ambitious touring revue, the *Medicine Ball Caravan*, which later spawned a film, and Donahue remained a fixture within the city until his premature death from a heart attack in 1975.

DONALDSON, LOU

b. 1 November 1926, Badin, North Carolina, USA. Donaldson started on clarinet but, while playing in a band in the US Navy alongside Willie Smith and Clark Terry, he switched to alto saxophone. In the early 50s he was in New York, playing with Thelonious Monk, Horace Silver, Blue Mitchell, Art Blakey and other leading jazzmen. In 1954 he and Clifford Brown joined Blakey's Jazz Messengers. During the 60s and 70s he toured extensively, usually as leader of a small band, playing concerts and festivals in the USA and Europe. He recorded prolifically for Blue Note, producing a number of excellent soul-jazz albums, including *Alligator Boogaloo*. During this period, Donaldson made some stylistic changes, experimenting with an R&B-inflected style and playing jazz-funk; but by the 80s he was back in a hard bop groove, where his striking technique and inventiveness assured him of a welcome place on the international circuit.

●ALBUMS: *New Faces, New Sounds* i (1952)★★★, *New Faces, New Sounds* ii (1953)★★★, *Lou Donaldson Quintet-Quartet* (Blue Note 1953)★★★, *Lou Donaldson With Clifford Brown* (1953)★★★, with Art Blakey *A Night At Birdland* (1954)★★★, *Lou Donaldson Sextet, Vol. 2* (Blue Note 1955)★★★, *Wailing With Lou* (Blue Note 1955)★★★, *Lou Donaldson Quartet Quintet Sextet* (Blue Note 1957)★★★, *Swing And Soul* (Blue Note 1957)★★★, *Lou Takes Off* (Blue Note 1958)★★★, *Blues Walk* (Blue Note 1958)★★★, *LD+3* (Blue Note 1959)★★★, *The Time Is Right* (Blue Note 1959)★★★, *Sunny Side Up* (Blue Note 1960)★★★★, *Light Foot* (Blue Note 1960)★★★, *Here 'Tis* (Blue Note 1961)★★★★, *The Natural Soul* (Blue Note 1962)★★★★, *Gravy Train* (Blue Note 1962)★★★, *Good Gracious* (Blue Note 1963)★★★, *Signifyin'* (Argo 1963)★★★, *Possum Head* (Argo 1964)★★★, *Cole Slaw* (Argo 1964)★★★, *Musty Rusty* (Cadet 1964)★★★, *Rough House Blues* (Cadet 1965)★★★, *At His Best* (1966)★★★, *Lush Life* (Blue Note 1967)★★★★, *Alligator Boogaloo* (Blue Note 1967)★★★★, *Mr Shing-a-ling* (Blue Note 1967)★★★, *Blowin' In The Wind* (Cadet 1967)★★★, *Fried Buzzard-Lou Donaldson Live* (Cadet 1968)★★★, *Hot Dog* (Blue Note 1969)★★★, *Pretty Things* (Blue Note 1970)★★★, *Sophisticated Lou* (1972)★★★, *Back Street* (Muse 1972)★★★, *A Different Scene* (1976)★★★, *Sweet Poppa Lou* (1981)★★★, *Forgotten Man*

(Timeless 1981)★★★, *Life In Bologna* (Timeless 1984)★★★, *Play The Right Thing* (Milestone 1990)★★★, *Birdseed* (Milestone 1992)★★★, *Caracas* (Milestone 1992)★★★.

DONOVAN

b. Donovan Leitch, 10 May 1946, Glasgow, Scotland. Uncomfortably labelled 'Britain's answer to Bob Dylan' the young troubadour did not fit in well with the folk establishment. Instead, it was the pioneering UK television show *Ready Steady Go* that adopted Donovan, and from then on success was assured. His first single, 'Catch The Wind', launched a career that lasted through the 60s with numerous hits, developing as fashions changed. The expressive 'Colours' and 'Turquoise' continued his hit folk image, although hints of other influences began to creep into his music. Donovan's finest work, however, was as ambassador of 'flower power' with memorable singles like 'Sunshine Superman' and 'Mellow Yellow'. His subtle drug references endeared him to the hippie movement, although some critics felt his stance was just a bit fey and insipid. He enjoyed several hits with light material such as the calypso influenced 'There Is A Mountain' and 'Jennifer Juniper' (written for Jenny Boyd during a much publicized sojourn with the guru, Maharishi Mahesh Yogi). Donovan's drug/fairy tale imagery reached its apotheosis on the Lewis Carroll-influenced 'Hurdy Gurdy Man'. As the 60s closed, however, he fell from commercial grace. Undeterred, Donovan found greater success in the USA; indeed, many of his later records were first issued in America and some gained no UK release. His collaboration with Jeff Beck on 'Goo Goo Barabajagal (Love Is Hot)' showed a more gutsy approach, while a number of the tracks on the boxed set *A Gift From A Flower To A Garden* displayed a jazzier feel. He had previously flirted with jazz on his b-sides, notably the excellent 'Sunny Goodge Street' and 'Preachin' Love'. *Cosmic Wheels* in 1973 was an artistic success; it sold well and contained his witty 'Intergalactic Laxative'. In anticipation of continued success, *Essence To Essence* was a bitter disappointment, and thereafter Donovan ceased to be a major concert attraction.

In 1990 after many inactive years the Happy Mondays bought him back into favour by praising his work and invited him to tour with them in 1991. Their irreverent tribute 'Donovan' underlined this new-found favouritism. Shortly before this, he was back on television as part of a humorous remake of 'Jennifer Juniper' with UK comedians Trevor and Simon. A new album was released and a flood of reissues arrived; for the moment at least the cognoscenti decreed that Donovan was 'okay' again. He undertook a major UK tour in 1992. *Troubadour*, an excellent CD box set was issued in 1992 covering the vital material from his career. The highest profile he has received in the recent past is by becoming Black Grape's Shaun Ryder's father-in-law. *Sutras* was released to a considerable amount of press coverage but achieved little in terms of sales. On this, his first album in many years, he revisited the territory that was whimsical and 'cosmic'.

Instead of catchy folk songs (early period) and acid soaked rockers (late period), he opted for cloying (though sincere) material.

●ALBUMS: *What's Bin Did And What's Bin Hid* (Pye 1965)★★★★, *Catch The Wind* (1965 Pye/Hickory)★★★, *Fairytale* (Pye/Hickory1965)★★★★, *Sunshine Superman* (Epic 1966)★★★★, *Mellow Yellow* (Epic 1967)★★★★, *Wear Your Love Like Heaven* (Epic 1967)★★★, *For Little Ones* (Epic 1967)★★★, *A Gift From A Flower To A Garden* (Epic 1967)★★★, *Donovan In Concert* (Epic 1968)★★★, *Hurdy Gurdy Man* (Epic 1968)★★★★, *Barabajagal* (Epic 1969)★★★★, *Open Road* (Dawn 1970)★★, *HMS Donovan* (Dawn 1971)★★★, *Brother Sun, Sister Moon* soundtrack (TKR 1972)★★, *Colours* (Hallmark 1972)★★★, *The Pied Piper* soundtrack (1973)★★, *Cosmic Wheels* (Epic 1973)★★★, *Live In Japan* (Sony 1973)★★★, *Essence To Essence* (Epic 1973)★★★, *7-Tease* (Epic 1974)★★★, *Slow Down World* (Epic 1976)★★, *Donovan* (Arista 1977)★★, *Neutronica* (RCA 1981)★★, *Love Is Only Feeling* (RCA 1981)★★, *Lady Of The Stars* (Allegiance 1984)★★, *The Classics Live 1991* (Great Northern Arts 1993)★★★, *Sutras* (American Recordings 1996)★★★.

●COMPILATIONS: *Universal Soldier* (Pye 1967)★★★★, *Like It Is* (Hickory 1968)★★★, *The World Of Donvan* (Pye 1969)★★★★, *Hear Me Now* (Janus 1970)★★★, *The Golden Hour Of Donovan* (Pye 1971)★★★★, *Early Treasures* (Bell 1973)★★★, *The Donovan File* (Pye 1977)★★★, *Spotlight On Donovan* (Pye 1981)★★★★, *Greatest Hits And More* (EMI 1989)★★★, *The EP Collection* (See For Miles 1990)★★★★, *Donovan Rising* (Permanent 1990)★★★, *The Trip: A Collection Of Donovan Originals From The Psychedelic Era* (EMI 1991)★★★★★, *25 Years In Concert* (1991)★★★, *Troubadour: The Definitive Collection 1964-1976* box set (Legacy 1992)★★★★★, *The Hits* (Disky 1993)★★★, *Till I See You Again* (Success 1994)★★★, *Josie* (Castle 1994)★★★, *Universal Soldier* (Spectrum 1995)★★★★, *Sunshine Troubadour* (Hallmark 1996)★★★, *Catch The Wind: The Best Of Donovan* (Pulse 1996)★★★.

DOONICAN, VAL

b. Michael Valentine Doonican, 3 February 1928, Waterford, Eire. Doonican learned to play the mandolin and guitar as a boy, and later toured northern and southern Ireland in various bands before travelling to England in 1951 to join an Irish vocal quartet, the Four Ramblers. He wrote the group's vocal arrangements as well as singing and playing guitar in their BBC radio series *Riders Of The Range*. In the late 50s, on the advice of Anthony Newley, he went solo, and appeared on television in *Beauty Box*, and on radio in *Dreamy Afternoon*, later retitled, *A Date With Val*. In 1963 he was recommended to impresario Val Parnell by comedian Dickie Henderson, and gained a spot on ITV's top-rated television show *Sunday Night At The London Palladium*. He made an immediate impact with his friendly, easy-going style and in 1964 commenced an annual series for BBC television, which ran until the 80s. He soon became one of the most popular entertainers in the UK, and was voted Television Personality Of The Year three times. The closing sequence of his TV show, in which he sang a song while seated in a rocking chair, was especially effective. The idea was later used as a self-deprecating album title, *Val Doonican Rocks, But Gently*. Later, in the age of video tape, he still preferred his shows to be transmitted 'live'. His first record hit, 'Walk Tall', in 1964, was followed by a string of chart entries through to the early 70s, including 'The Special Years', 'Elusive Butterfly', 'What Would I Be', 'Memories Are Made Of This', 'If The Whole World Stopped Loving', 'If I Knew Then What I Know Now' and 'Morning'. Equally popular, but not chart entries, were a number of novelty songs such as 'O'Rafferty's Motor Car', 'Delaney's Donkey' and 'Paddy McGinty's Goat', written by the prolific English team of Bob Weston and Bert Lee. By the early 90s Doonican was semi-retired - performing 'laps of honour', as he put it. In 1993 he released a video, 'a tribute to his favourite artists', entitled *Thank You For The Music*.

●ALBUMS: *Lucky 13 Shades Of Val Doonican* (1964)★★★, *Gentle Shades Of Val Doonican* (1966)★★★, *Val Doonican Rocks, But Gently* (1967)★★★, *Val* (1968)★★★, *Sounds Gentle* (1969)★★★, *The Magic Of Val Doonican* (1970)★★★, *This Is Val Doonican* (1971)★★★, *Morning Has Broken* (1973)★★★, *Song Sung Blue* (1974)★★★, *I Love Country Music* (1975)★★★, *Life Can Be Beautiful* (1976)★★★, *Some Of My Best Friends Are Songs* (1977)★★★, *Quiet Moments* (1981)★★★, *Val Sings Bing* (1982)★★★, *The Val Doonican Music Show* (1984)★★★, *By Request* (1987)★★★, *Mr Music Man* (1988)★★★, *Portrait Of My Love* (1989)★★★, *Songs From My Sketch Book* (1990)★★★.

●COMPILATIONS: *The World Of Val Doonican* (1969)★★★★, *The World Of Val Doonican, Volume Two* (1969)★★★★, *The World Of Val Doonican, Volume Three* (1970)★★★★, *The World Of Val Doonican, Volume Four* (1971)★★★★, *The World Of Val Doonican, Volume Five* (1972)★★★, *Rocking Chair Favourites* (1973)★★★★, *Spotlight On Val Doonican* (1974)★★★, *Focus On Val Doonican* (1976)★★★, *Memories Are Made Of This* (1981)★★★, *Forty Shades Of Green* (1983)★★★, *The Very Best Of Val Doonican* (1984)★★★★, *Twenty Personal Favourites For You* (1986)★★★, *It's Good To See You* (1988)★★★.

●FURTHER READING: *The Special Years: An Autobiography*, Val Doonican.

DOORS

'If the doors of perception were cleansed, everything would appear to man as it is, infinite.' This quote from poet William Blake, via Aldous Huxley, was an inspiration to Jim Morrison (b. James Douglas Morrison, 8 December 1943, Melbourne, Florida, USA, d. 3 July 1971, Paris, France), a student of theatre arts at the University of California and an aspiring musician. His dream of a rock band entitled 'the Doors' was fulfilled in 1965, when he sang a rudimentary composition, 'Moonlight Drive', to fellow scholar Ray Manzarek (b. 12 February 1935, Chicago, Illinois, USA; keyboards). Impressed, he invited Morrison to join his campus R&B band, Rick And The Ravens, which also included the organist's two brothers. Ray then recruited drummer John Densmore (b. 1 December 1945, Los Angeles, California, USA), and the reshaped group recorded six Morrison songs at the famed World Pacific studios. The session featured several compositions that the group subsequently re-recorded, including 'Summer's Almost Gone' and 'End Of The Night'. Manzarek's brothers disliked the new material and later dropped out of the group. They were replaced by Robbie Krieger (b. 8 January 1946, Los Angeles, California, USA), an inventive guitarist, whom Densmore met at a meditation centre. Morrison was now established as the vocalist and the quartet began rehearsing in earnest.

The Doors' first residency was at the London Fog on Sunset Strip, but they later found favour at the prestigious Whisky-A-Go-Go. They were, however, fired from the latter establishment, following a performance of 'The End', Morrison's chilling, oedipal composition. Improvised and partly spoken over a raga/rock framework, it proved too controversial for timid club owners, but the group's standing within the music fraternity grew. Local rivals Love, already signed to Elektra Records, recommended the Doors to the label's managing director, Jac Holtzman who, despite initial caution, signed the group in 1966.

The Doors, released the following year, unveiled a group of many contrasting influences. Manzarek's thin sounding organ (he also performed the part of bassist with the aid of a separate bass keyboard) recalled the garage-band style omnipresent several months earlier, but Krieger's liquid guitar playing and Densmore's imaginative drumming were already clearly evident. Morrison's striking, dramatic voice added power to the exceptional compositions, which included the pulsating 'Break On Through' and an 11-minute version of 'The End'. Cover versions of material, including Willie Dixon's 'Back Door Man' and Bertolt Brecht/Kurt Weill's 'Alabama Song (Whisky Bar)', exemplified the group's disparate influences.

The best-known track, however, was 'Light My Fire', which, when trimmed down from its original seven minutes, became a number 1 single in the USA. Its fiery imagery combined eroticism with death, and the song has since become a standard. Its success created new problems and the Doors, perceived by some as underground heroes, were tarred as teenybop fodder by others. This dichotomy weighed heavily on Morrison who wished to be accepted as a serious artist. A second album, *Strange Days*, showcased 'When The Music's Over', another extended piece destined to become a *tour de force* within the group's canon. The quartet enjoyed further chart success when 'People Are Strange' broached the US Top 20, but it was 1968 before they secured another number 1 single with the infectious 'Hello I Love You'. The song was also the group's first major UK hit, although some of this lustre was lost following legal action by Ray Davies of the Kinks, who claimed infringement of his own composition, 'All Day And All Of The Night'.

The action coincided with the Doors' first European tour. A major television documentary, *The Doors Are Open*, was devoted to the visit and centred on their powerful performance at London's Chalk Farm Roundhouse. The group showcased several tracks from their third collection, *Waiting For The Sun*, including the declamatory 'Five To One', and a fierce protest song, 'The Unknown Soldier', for which they also completed an uncompromising promotional film. However, the follow-up album, *The Soft Parade*, on which a horn section masked several unremarkable songs, was a major disappointment, although the tongue-in-cheek 'Touch Me' became another US Top 3 single and 'Wishful Sinful' was a Top 50 hit.

Continued commercial success exacted further pressure on Morrison, whose frustration with his role as a pop idol grew more pronounced. His anti-authoritarian persona combined with a brazen sexuality and notorious alcohol and narcotics consumption to create a character bedevilled by doubt and cynicism. His confrontations with middle America reached an apogee in July 1969 when, following a concert at Miami's Dinner Key auditorium, the singer was indicted for indecent exposure, public intoxication and profane, lewd and lascivious conduct. Although Morrison was later acquitted of all but the minor charges, the incident clouded the group's career when live dates for the next few months were cancelled. Paradoxically, this furore re-awoke the Doors' creativity. *Morrison Hotel*, a tough R&B-based collection, matched the best of their early releases and featured seminal performances in 'Roadhouse Blues' and 'You Make Me Real'. *Absolutely Live*, an in-concert set edited from a variety of sources, gave the impression of a single performance and exhibited the group's power and authority. However, Morrison, whose poetry had been published in two volumes, *The Lords* and *The New Creatures*, now drew greater pleasure from this more personal art form. Having completed sessions for a new album, the last owed to Elektra, the singer escaped to Paris where he hoped to follow a literary career and abandon music altogether. Tragically, years of hedonistic excess had taken its toll and on 3 July 1971, Jim Morrison was found dead in his bathtub, his passing recorded officially as a heart attack.

LA Woman, his final recording with the Doors, is one of their finest achievements. Recorded in the group's workshop, its simple intimacy resulted in some superb performances, including 'Riders On The Storm', whose haunting imagery and stealthy accompaniment created a timeless classic. The survivors continued to work as the Doors, but while *Other Voices* showed some promise, *Full Circle* was severely flawed and the group soon dissolved. Densmore and Krieger formed the Butts Band, with whom they recorded two albums before splitting to pursue different paths. Manzarek undertook several projects as either artist, producer or manager, but the spectre of the Doors refused to die. Interest in the group flourished throughout the decade and in 1978 the remaining trio supplied newly recorded music to a series of poetry recitations, which Morrison had taped during the *LA Woman* sessions. The resultant album, *An American Prayer*, was a major success and prompted such archive excursions as *Alive She Cried*, a compendium of several concert performances and *The Doors Live At Hollywood Bowl*. The evocative use of 'The End' in Francis Ford Coppola's Vietnam war film, *Apocalypse Now* (1979), also generated renewed interest in the group's legacy, and indeed, it is on those first recordings that the Doors' considerable reputation, and influence, rest. Since then the Doors' catalogue has never been out of print, and future generations of rock fans will almost certainly use them as a major role model. In 1991, director Oliver Stone's film biography *The Doors*, starring Val Kilmer confirmed Morrison as one of the 60s' great cultural icons.

● ALBUMS: *The Doors* (Elektra 1967)★★★★★, *Strange Days* (Elektra 1967)★★★★, *Waiting For The Sun* (Elektra 1968)★★★, *The Soft Parade* (Elektra 1969)★★, *Morrison Hotel* (Elektra 1970)★★★★, *Absolutely Live* (Elektra 1970)★, *LA Woman* (Elektra 1971)★★★★, *Other Voices* (Elektra 1971)★★, *Full Circle* (Elektra 1972)★, *An American Prayer* (Elektra 1978)★★, *Alive She Cried* (Elektra 1983)★★, *The Doors Live At The Hollywood Bowl* (Elektra 1987)★★, *In Concert* (Elektra 1991)★★.

● COMPILATIONS: *13* (Elektra 1971)★★★★, *Weird Scenes Inside The Goldmine* (Elektra 1972)★★★, *The Best Of The Doors* (Elektra 1974)★★★★, *Greatest Hits* (Elektra 1980)★★★★, *The Doors* soundtrack (1991)★★★, *Greatest Hits* enhanced CD (East West 1996)★★★.

● VIDEOS: *Live At The Hollywood Bowl* (1987), *Tribute To Jim Morrison* (1988), *The Doors In Europe* (Castle Hendring 1990), *The Doors Are Open* (Castle Hendring 1990), *The Doors* (1991), *Dance On Fire* (1991), *Doors: A Tribute To Jim Morrison* (1991).

● FURTHER READING: *Jim Morrison And The Doors: An Unauthorized Book*, Mike Jahn. *An American Prayer*, Jim Morrison. *The Lords & The New Creatures*, Jim Morrison. *Jim Morrison Au Dela Des Doors*, Herve Muller. *No One Here Gets Out Alive*, Jerry Hopkins and Danny Sugerman. *Burn Down The Night*, Craig Kee Strete. *Jim Morrison: The Story Of The Doors In Words And Pictures*, Jim Morrison. *Jim Morrison: An Hour For Magic*, Frank Lisciandro. *The Doors: The Illustrated History*, Danny Sugerman. *The Doors*, John Tobler and Andrew Doe. *Jim Morrison: Dark Star*, Dylan Jones. *Images Of Jim Morrison*, Edward Wincentsen. *The End: The Death Of Jim Morrison*, Bob Seymore. *The American Night Volume 2*, Jim Morrison. *The American Night: The Writings Of Jim Morrison*, Jim Morrison. *Morrison: A Feast of*

Friends, Frank Lisciandro. *Light My Fire*, John Densmore. *Riders On The Storm: My Life With Jim Morrison And The Doors*, John Densmore. *The Doors Complete Illustrated Lyrics*, Danny Sugerman (ed.). *Break On Through: The Life and Death Of Jim Morrison*, James Riordan and Jerry Prochnicky. *The Doors: Lyrics, 1965-71*, no author. *The Lizard King: The Essential Jim Morrison*, Jerry Hopkins. *The Doors: Dance On Fire*, Ross Clarke. *The Complete Guide To The Music Of ...*, Peter K. Hogan. *The Doors: Moonlight Drive*, Chuck Crisafulli.
●FILMS: *American Pop* (1981).

DORSEY, LEE

b. Irving Lee Dorsey, 24 December 1926, New Orleans, Louisiana, USA, d. 1 December 1986. An ex-boxer (nicknamed 'Kid Chocolate') turned singer, Dorsey first recorded for Joe Banashak's Instant label. One song, 'Lottie Mo', became a regional hit and led to a contract with Fury. The infectious 'Ya Ya' (1961) was a number 1 US R&B and pop Top 10 single. A year later a version by Petula Clark, retitled 'Ya Ya Twist', made the US Top 10 and reached the UK Top 20. Dorsey's next release 'Do-Re-Mi' (regularly performed by Georgie Fame and Dusty Springfield) was also a hit, although this time reaching no higher than 27 in the *Billboard* pop chart, and subsequent releases on Fury Records were less successful. His career stalled temporarily when Fury collapsed but Lee re-emerged in 1965 with the classic 'Ride Your Pony' on the Amy label. Written by Allen Toussaint and produced by Marshall Sehorn, this combination created a series of impeccable singles that blended crisp arrangements with the singer's easy delivery. In 1966 he reached the peak of his success by scoring four Top 40 hits in the UK, including two Top 10 singles with 'Working In The Coalmine', with its wonderful bass riff, and 'Holy Cow', with Dorsey's voiced mixed so far back he sounds tearful. Both songs reached the US R&B and pop charts. The sweetly doom-laden 'Get Out Of My Life Woman' was another excellent song that deserved a better commercial fate. 'Everything I Do Gohn Be Funky (From Now On)' became Dorsey's last substantial hit in 1969, although the title track to his concept 'concept' album, 'Yes We Can', did reach the US R&B Top 50. Dorsey continued to record for Polydor and ABC and remained a popular figure, so much so that he guested on the 1976 debut album by Southside Johnny And The Asbury Dukes and supported the Clash on their 1980 tour of north America. Sadly, he died of emphysema in December 1986 and deserves to be remembered for six outstanding examples of melodic soul.
●ALBUMS: *Ya Ya* (Fury 1962)★★★, *Ride Your Pony* (Amy/Stateside 1966)★★★, *The New Lee Dorsey* (Amy/Stateside 1966)★★★★, *Yes We Can* (Polydor 1970)★★, *Night People* (1978)★★.
●COMPILATIONS: *The Best Of Lee Dorsey* (Sue 1965)★★, *Gohn Be Funky* (1985)★★★, *All Ways Funky* (1982)★★★, *Holy Cow! The Best Of Lee Dorsey* (1985)★★★★, *Am I That Easy To Forget?*

(1987)★★★, *Can You Hear Me* (1987)★★★, *Ya Ya* (Relic 1992)★★★, *Working In A Coalmine* (1993)★★★, *Freedom For The Funk* (Charly 1994)★★★.

DOUGLAS, CRAIG

b. Terence Perkins, 12 August 1941, Newport, Isle Of Wight, England. After moving to London in the mid-50s, Douglas came under the wing of agent Bunny Lewis, appeared on the television show *6.5 Special*, and won a record contract with Decca before moving to Dick Rowe's label, Top Rank. Covering American hits was the classic route to chart success, and in 1959 Douglas scored with Dion's 'A Teenager In Love' and reached number 1 with Sam Cooke's 'Only Sixteen'. He co-starred with Helen Shapiro in the film *It's Trad Dad* (1961). Several more hits followed but after four consecutive number 9s with 'A Hundred Pounds Of Clay', 'Time', 'When My Little Girl Is Smiling' and 'Our Favourite Melodies', Craig felt the sting of the approaching beat boom. He then travelled the world, returning for a career in cabaret in the UK, where he still resides. In 1992 he joined other 60s survivors, including Helen Shapiro, on the Walkin' Back To Happiness Tour. Douglas possesses a good singing voice that should have moved into the classic pop song. His recycled past hits now sound trite and tired, although the voice is still intact.
●ALBUMS: *Craig Douglas* (Top Rank 1960)★★★, *Bandwagon Ball* (Top Rank 1961)★★★, *Our Favourite Melodies* (Columbia 1962)★★★, *Oh Lonesome Me* (Jackson 1981)★★.
●COMPILATIONS: *The Best Of The EMI Years* (EMI 1993)★★★.
●FILMS: *It's Trad, Dad* aka *Ring-A-Ding Rhythm* (1962).

DOVELLS

Originally called the Brooktones, this Philadelphia-based R&B vocal group comprised Len Barry (b. Leonard Borisoff), Jerry Summers (b. Jerry Gross), Mike Dennis (b. Michael Freda) and Danny Brooks (b. Jim Meeley). Signed to the Parkway Records label, the group had a US number 2 hit in 1961 with 'Bristol Stomp', succeeded the following year by the Top 40 hits, 'Do The Continental', 'Bristol Twistin' Annie' and 'Hully Gully Baby', all of which became dance favourites of the era. Len Barry was responsible for introducing their contemporaneous friends, the Orlons, to Cameo Records and after the departure of Brooks, in 1962, the Dovells achieved another major US hit with a cover of the Phil Upchurch Combo hit, 'You Can't Sit Down'. Barry departed from the group later that year and they continued as a trio. The Dovells recorded for MGM Records in the late 60s under the name of the Magistrates, but met with little success.
●ALBUMS: *The Bristol Stomp* (Parkway 1961)★★★, *All The Hits Of The Teen Groups* (Parkway 1962)★★★, *Don't Knock The Twist* soundtrack (Parkway 1962)★★, *For Your Hully Gully Party* (Parkway 1963)★★, *You Can't Sit Down* (Parkway 1963)★★★, with Len Barry

Len Barry Sings With The Dovells (Cameo 1964)★★★, *Discotheque* (1965)★★.
●COMPILATIONS: *Golden Hits Of The Orlons And The Dovells* (1963)★★★, *The Dovells' Biggest Hits* (1965)★★★.
●FILMS: *Don't Knock The Twist* (1962).

DOWD, TOM

b. *c*.1930. This much-respected engineer began his career in 1947 at New York's Ampex Studio. Here he became acquainted with Ahmet Ertegun, co-founder of Atlantic Records, who invited Dowd, then still a teenager, to join the label. His early sessions included releases by Joe Turner, Ray Charles and Ruth Brown, to whom he brought a clarity hitherto unheard in R&B recordings. Always striving for new techniques, Dowd engineered the first stereo album, by the Wilbur De Paris Dixieland Band, which required customized equipment, including two needles, to play it. His collaborations with producers Leiber And Stoller brought commercial success to the Coasters and Drifters, while in the 60s Dowd engineered Atlantic's sessions at the Stax Records and Fame studios. His first work with Otis Redding, *Otis Blue*, is generally regarded as the singer's finest album and was responsible for taking the artist into the pop market. Dowd also enjoyed commercially fruitful recordings with the (Young) Rascals, Dusty Springfield and Aretha Franklin and later helped create the label's custom-built studio, Criteria, in Miami. Dowd later became a fully-fledged producer, and during the 70s left the Atlantic staff to pursue freelance work, notably with Eric Clapton *Layla* (1971), *461 Ocean Boulevard* (1974), *E.C. Was Here* and *There's One In Every Crowd* (both 1975) and on the Allman Brothers' *At Fillmore East* (1971) and Rod Stewart's *Atlantic Crossing* (1975) and *A Night On The Town* (1976).

DOWNLINERS SECT

Formed in 1962, this enduring UK act was initially known as the Downliners, but the original line-up fell apart following a brief tour of US air bases. Founder members Don Craine (vocals/rhythm guitar) and Johnny Sutton (drums) then reshaped the group around Keith Grant (bass) and Terry Gibson (lead guitar) and, having added the 'Sect' suffix, the quartet secured a residency at London's Studio 51 club. A privately pressed EP, *A Nite In Great Newport Street*, captured their brash interpretation of Chicago R&B, and was a contributory factor to a subsequent recording deal with EMI. A version of Jimmy Reed's 'Baby What's Wrong' became the group's first single in June 1964, by which time Ray Sone (harmonica) had been added to the line-up. The Sect's brazen musical approach, redolent of the contemporaneous Pretty Things, was showcased on their debut album, but not only did its irreverence anger purists, Craine's ever-present deerstalker hat and autoharp also did little to attract a younger, more fashion-conscious audience. The group, however, seemed unmoved by such considerations and in 1965 further confused any prospective audience with

The Country Sect, an album of folk and country material, and *The Sect Sing Sick Songs* EP, which included the ghoulish 'I Want My Baby Back', and 'Leader Of The Sect', a riposte to the Shangri-Las' death-disc, 'Leader Of The Pack'. Sone left the group prior to recording *The Rock Sect's In*, which neatly combined almost all of the group's diverse styles. It is now notable for the inclusion of 'Why Don't You Smile Now', which was part-composed by Lou Reed and John Cale prior to their founding the Velvet Underground. The Sect, however, were still struggling to find commercial success and the line-up disintegrated when two pop-oriented singles, 'Glendora' and the Graham Gouldman-penned 'Cost Of Living', failed to chart. Gibson and Sutton were replaced, respectively, by Bob Taylor and Kevin Flanagan, while pianist Matthew Fisher, later of Procol Harum, was also briefly a member. Craine abandoned his creation following the release of 'I Can't Get Away From You', after which Grant and the prodigal Sutton took the group to Sweden, where they recorded a handful of tracks before disbanding altogether. Craine and Grant revived Sect in 1976 in the wake of the pub rock/R&B phenomenon, and the resultant *Showbiz* invoked the gutsy styles of Dr. Feelgood or Count Bishops. The duo continued to lead the group throughout the 80s, and they are also an integral part of the British Invasion All-Stars with former members of the Yardbirds, Creation and Nashville Teens. However, it is their 60s recordings which afford the Sect their cult-based appeal.
●ALBUMS: *The Sect* (Columbia 1964)★★★, *The Country Sect* (Columbia 1965)★★, *The Rock Sect's In* (Columbia 1966)★★, *Showbiz* (1979)★★★.
●COMPILATIONS: *Be A Sect Maniac* (80s)★★★, *Savage Return* (1991)★★, *The Definitive Downliners Sect - Singles A's & B's* (See For Miles 1994)★★★.

DOZIER, LAMONT

b. 16 June 1941, Detroit, USA. Schooled in the blossoming vocal group scene of the late 50s, Lamont Dozier sang alongside several Motown notables in the Romeos and the Voice Masters during 1957-58. He befriended local songwriter and producer Berry Gordy around this time, and was one of Gordy's first signings when he launched the Motown label at the end of the decade. Dozier issued his debut single, 'Let's Talk It Over', under the pseudonym 'Lamont Anthony' in 1960, and issued two further singles in the early 60s. In 1963, he recorded a one-off release with Motown songwriter Eddie Holland and was soon persuaded into a writing and production team with Eddie and his brother Brian Holland. The Holland/Dozier/Holland credit graced the majority of Motown's hit records for the next five years, as the trio struck up particularly successful working relationships with the Supremes and the Four Tops. Dozier contributed both lyrics and music to the partnership's creations, proving the initial impetus for hits like 'Stop! In The Name Of Love' by the Supremes, 'Bernadette' by the Four Tops, and 'Jimmy Mack' by Martha And The Vandellas. As a pianist, arranger and producer, Dozier was also prominent in the studio, supporting the central role of

Brian Holland in the recording process.

Holland/Dozier/Holland left Motown in 1967, unhappy at the financial and artistic restrictions imposed by Gordy. The following year, they set up their own rival companies, Invictus and Hot Wax Records, who produced hits for artists like Freda Payne and the Chairmen Of The Board. Dozier resumed his own recording career in 1972, registering a US hit with 'Why Can't We Be Lovers', and receiving critical acclaim for a series of duets with Brian Holland. The Holland/Dozier/Holland partnership was fragmenting, however, and in 1973 Dozier severed his ties with Invictus and signed to ABC. *Out Here On My Own* and *Black Bach* demonstrated the creative liberation Dozier felt outside the constraints of the HDH team, and he scored major USA hits in 1974 with 'Trying To Hold Onto My Woman', the anti-Nixon diatribe 'Fish Ain't Bitin'', and 'Let Me Start Tonite'. Dozier switched labels to Warner Brothers in 1976, issuing the highly regarded *Peddlin' Music On The Side* the following year. That album included the classic 'Goin' Back To My Roots', an avowal of black pride which became a big hit in the hands of Odyssey in the early 80s. Dozier also continued his production work, overseeing Aretha Franklin's *Sweet Passion* in 1977, plus recordings by Zingara and Al Wilson. In the late 70s and early 80s, Dozier's brand of soul music lost ground to the burgeoning disco scene. After several overlooked albums on Warners and M&M, he re-emerged in 1983 on his own Megaphone label, cutting the muscular *Bigger Than Life*, and paying tribute to his own heritage with a remarkable 18-minute hits medley, 'The Motor City Scene'. Since then, he has remained out of the public eye, working sporadically on production projects with the Holland brothers.

●ALBUMS: *Out Here On My Own* (ABC 1973)★★, *Black Bach* (ABC 1974)★★, *Love And Beauty* (1975)★★, *Right There* (1976)★★, *Peddlin' Music On The Side* (1977)★★★, *Bittersweet* (1979)★★, *Working On You* (1981)★★, *Lamont* (1982)★★★, *Bigger Than Life* (1983)★★.

DR. STRANGELY STRANGE

This Irish folk group - Ivan Pawle (vocals/bass), Tim Booth (vocals/guitar) and Tim Goulding (vocals/keyboards) - made its recording debut in 1969. Although *Kip Of The Serenes* betrayed an obvious debt to the Incredible String Band (both groups were produced by Joe Boyd), the album nonetheless offered a whimsical charm. The trio then embraced a rock-based style on *Heavy Petting*, despite the assistance of traditional musicians Andy Irvine and Johnny Moynahan. Guitarist Gary Moore guested on four of the tracks, including the catchy yet subtly humorous 'I Gave My Love An Apple', but this electric album lacked the purpose of its predecessor. Dr. Strangely Strange disbanded in 1971 following their appearance on Mike Heron's all-star solo album, *Smiling Men With Reputations*.

●ALBUMS: *Kip Of The Serenes* (1969)★★, *Heavy Petting* (1970)★★★.

DRAKE, CHARLIE

b. Charles Sprigall, 19 June 1925, London, England. The enormously popular actor/comedian Charlie Drake is always instantly recognizable with his shock of red hair, diminutive 5 feet 1 inch frame and distinctive cockney voice. In 1958, he hit the UK charts, outselling Bobby Darin with a cover version of 'Splish Splash'. Further hits followed over the next three years, including 'Volare', 'Mr. Custer' and 'My Boomerang Won't Come Back'. The latter was co-written by Drake, in collaboration with Max Diamond. The duo also provided Drake's theme song and irritating catchphrase 'Hullo, My Darlings!' With strong managerial backing from Colonel Bill Alexander and the producing talents of George Martin, Drake was in good hands and his comedy workouts translated well on to disc. Although he continued recording, acting commitments increasingly took precedence, although he did make a brief chart reappearance in 1972 with 'Puckwudgie'. His most recent appearances have been in fellow comedian Jim Davidson's 'blue' pantomime, *Sinderella*.

●ALBUMS: *Hello My Darlings* (MFP 1967)★★★.

DREAMLOVERS

Formed as the Romances in Philadelphia, Pennsylvania, USA, in 1956, the Dreamlovers notched up two claims to fame: their own US Top 10 doo-wop ballad, 1961's 'When We Get Married', and their role as Chubby Checker's back-up group on his top-selling dance hit 'The Twist'. The quintet initially consisted of lead vocalist William Johnson, tenor Tommy Ricks, tenor Cleveland Hammock Jnr., baritone Conrad Dunn and bass James Ray Dunn. After Johnson was killed in a street fight, Morris Gardner was brought in as his replacement, and a new name, the Dreamlovers, was taken. In 1960 they recorded their first tracks for the Len and V-Tone labels, which failed to sell, but that same year Cameo-Parkway Records hired the group to provide vocals behind Chubby Checker on his future hit, as well as subsequent Cameo label tracks by Checker, Dee Dee Sharp, and the Dovells. The Dreamlovers made their mark in the pop history books with 'When We Get Married', written by Don Hogan, a part-time member of the group. One single for End Records also charted and in 1973, after making a single under the name A Brother's Guiding Light, the group disbanded. Some of the members formed a new Dreamlovers in 1980 and were still performing in the early 90s.

●ALBUMS: *The Bird And Other Golden Dancing Grooves* (Columbia 1963)★★★.

●COMPILATIONS: *Best Of ...* (Collectables 1990)★★★, *Best Of ... Vol. 2* (Collectables 1990)★★, *The Best Of ...* (Sequel 1994)★★★, *The Heritage Masters Plus ...* (Sequel 1997)★★★.

DRIFTERS

Formed in 1953 in New York, USA, at the behest of Atlantic Records, this influential R&B vocal group was initially envisaged as a vehicle for ex-Dominoes singer,

Clyde McPhatter. Gerhart Thrasher, Andrew Thrasher and Bill Pinkney completed the new quartet which, as Clyde McPhatter and the Drifters, scored a number 1 R&B hit with their debut single, 'Money Honey'. Follow-up releases, including 'Such A Night', 'Lucille' and 'Honey Love' (a second chart-topper), also proved highly successful, while the juxtaposition of McPhatter's soaring tenor against the frenzied support of the other members provided a link between gospel and rock 'n' roll styles. The leader's interplay with bassist Pinkey breathed new life into 'White Christmas', the group's sixth R&B hit, but McPhatter's induction into the armed forces in 1954 was a blow the Drifters struggled to withstand. The vocalist opted for a solo career upon leaving the services, and although his former group did enjoy success with 'Adorable' (number 1 R&B 1955), 'Steamboat' (1955), 'Ruby Baby' (1956) and 'Fools Fall In Love' (1957), such recordings featured a variety of lead singers, including David Baughn and Johnny Moore. A greater emphasis on pop material ensued, but tension between the group and manager, George Treadwell, resulted in an irrevocable split. Having fired the extant line-up in 1958, Treadwell, who owned the copyright to the Drifters' name, invited another act, the Five Crowns, to adopt the appellation. Ben E. King (tenor), Charlie Thomas (tenor), Doc Green Jnr. (baritone) and Elsbearry Hobbes (b. c.1936, d. 31 May 1996, New York, USA; bass), plus guitarist Reggie Kimber, duly became 'the Drifters', and declared their newfound role with 'There Goes My Baby'. Written and produced by Leiber And Stoller, this pioneering release contained a Latin rhythm and string section, the first time such embellishments had appeared on an R&B recording. The single not only topped the R&B chart, it also reached number 2 on the US pop listings, and anticipated the 'symphonic' style later developed by Phil Spector.

Further excellent releases followed, notably 'Dance With Me' (1959), 'This Magic Moment' (1960) and 'Save The Last Dance For Me', the last of which topped the US pop chart and reached number 2 in the UK. However, King left for a solo career following 'I Count The Tears' (1960), and was replaced by Rudy Lewis, who fronted the group until his premature death in 1964. The Drifters continued to enjoy hits during this period and songs such as 'Sweets For My Sweet', 'When My Little Girl Is Smiling', 'Up On The Roof' and 'On Broadway' were not only entertaining in their own right, but also provided inspiration, and material, for many emergent British acts, notably the Searchers, who took the first-named song to the top of the UK chart. Johnny Moore, who had returned to the line-up in 1963, took over the lead vocal slot from Lewis. 'Under The Boardwalk', recorded the day after the latter's passing, was the Drifters' last US Top 10 pop hit, although the group remained a popular attraction. Bert Berns had taken over production from Leiber and Stoller, and in doing so brought a soul-based urgency to their work, as evinced by 'One Way Love' and 'Saturday Night At The Movies' (1964). When he left Atlantic to found the Bang label, the Drifters found themselves increasingly over-shadowed by newer, more contemporary artists and,

bedevilled by lesser material and frequent changes in personnel, the group began to slip from prominence. However, their career was revitalized in 1972 when two re-released singles, 'At The Club' and 'Come On Over To My Place', reached the UK Top 10. A new recording deal with Bell was then secured and British songwriters/producers Tony Macauley, Roger Cook and Roger Greenaway fashioned a series of singles redolent of the Drifters' 'classic' era. Purists poured scorn on their efforts, but, between 1973 and 1975, the group, still led by Moore, enjoyed six UK Top 10 hits, including 'Come On Over To My Place', 'Kissin' In The Back Row Of The Movies', 'Down On The Beach Tonight' and 'There Goes My First Love'. This success ultimately waned as the decade progressed, and in 1982 Moore left the line-up. He was replaced, paradoxically, by Ben E. King, who in turn brought the Drifters back to Atlantic. However, despite completing some new recordings, the group found it impossible to escape its heritage, as evinced by the numerous 'hits' repackages and corresponding live appearances on the cabaret and nostalgia circuits.

●ALBUMS: *Save The Last Dance For Me* (Atlantic 1961)★★★★, *The Good Life With The Drifters* (Atlantic 1964)★★★★, *The Drifters* (Clarion 1964)★★, *I'll Take You Where The Music's Playing* (Atlantic 1965)★★★, *Souvenirs, Love Games* (1975)★★★, *There Goes My First Love* (1975)★★★, *Every Night's A Saturday Night* (1976)★★★, *Greatest Hits Live* (1984)★★.

●COMPILATIONS: *The Drifters Greatest Hits, Our Biggest Hits* (1964)★★★, *The Drifters' Golden Hits, Rockin' And Driftin', Good Gravy* (1964)★★★, *The Drifters' Story, 24 Original Hits, Diamond Series: The Drifters* (1988)★★★, *Kissin' In The Back Row: The 70s Classics* (1993) *Let The Boogie Woogie Roll - Greatest Hits (1953-58)* (Atlantic 1993)★★★, *All Time Greatest Hits And More (1958-65)* (Atlantic 1993)★★★★, *Up On The Roof, On Broadway & Under The Boardwalk* (Rhino/Pickwick 1995)★★★, *Rockin' And Driftin': The Drifters Box* 3-CD box set (Rhino 1996)★★★★, *Anthology One: Clyde & The Drifters* (Sequel 1996)★★★★, *Anthology Two: Rockin' & Driftin'* (Sequel 1996)★★★, *Anthology Three: Save The Last Dance For Me* (Sequel 1996)★★★★, *Anthology Four: Up On The Roof* (Sequel 1996)★★★★, *Anthology Five: Under The Boardwalk* (Sequel 1997)★★★★, *Anthology Six: The Good Life With The Drifters* (Sequel 1997)★★★, *Anthology Seven: I'll Take You Where The Music's Playing* (Sequel 1997)★★★★.

●FURTHER READING: *The Drifters: The Rise And Fall Of The Black Vocal Group*, Bill Millar. *Save The Last Dance For Me: The Musical Legacy 1953-92*, Tony Allan and Faye Treadwell.

DRISCOLL, JULIE

b. 8 June 1947, London, England. Driscoll was employed by producer/manager Giorgio Gomelsky as administrator of the Yardbirds' fan club when the former suggested a singing career. Her singles included a version of the Lovin' Spoonful's 'Didn't Want To Have To Do It' (1965) and an early Randy Newman composition 'If You Should Ever Leave Me' (1967), but this period is better recalled for Driscoll's membership of Steam Packet, an R&B-styled revue which also featured Long John Baldry, Rod Stewart and the Brian Auger Trinity. Driscoll remained with the last-named act when the larger group folded, and in 1968 had a number 5 hit with Bob Dylan's 'This Wheel's On Fire'. Her striking appearance engendered much publicity, and a cool, almost disinterested vocal style formed the ideal counterpoint to Auger's jazz-based ambitions. 'Jools' left the group following the release of *Streetnoise* in order to pursue a more radical direction. She contributed to B.B. Blunder's *Workers Playtime*, and released the excellent *Julie Driscoll*, which featured support from members of the Soft Machine, Nucleus and Blossom Toes as well as pianist Keith Tippett, whom the singer later married. She has since appeared on many of her husband's *avant garde* jazz creations, notably Centipede's *Septober Energy* (1971) and the expansive *Frames* (1978), as well appearing and recording with Brian Eley and the experimental vocal quartet Voice.

●ALBUMS: with Brian Auger *Open* (1967)★★★, with Auger *Streetnoise* (1968)★★★, *Julie Driscoll* (Polydor 1971)★★.

●COMPILATIONS: *Jools/Brian* (1968)★★★, both shared with Brian Auger *London 1964-1967* (1977)★★★, *The Best Of Julie Driscoll* (1982)★★★, both with the Brian Auger Trinity *The Road To Vauxhall 1967-1969* (1989)★★★.

DUBLINERS

The band comprised Barney MacKenna (b. 16 December 1939, Donnycarney, Dublin, Eire), Luke Kelly (b. 16 November 1940), Ciaran Bourke (b. 18 February 1936, Dublin, Eire) and former teacher Ronnie Drew (b. 18 September 1935, Dun Laoghaire, Co. Dublin, Eire). They formed in 1962, in the back of O'Donoghue's bar in Merron Row, Dublin, Eire, and were originally named the Ronnie Drew Group. The members were known faces in the city's post-skiffle folk haunts before pooling their assorted singing and fretboard skills in 1962. In 1964 Kelly left the group and went to England where he continued to play on the folk scene. Two other members joined shortly after Kelly had left: Bob Lynch (b. Dublin, Eire) and ex-draughtsman John Shehan (b. 19 May 1939, Dublin, Eire). *Dubliners In Concert* was the result of a live recording on 4 December 1964 in the concert hall at Cecil Sharp House in London. The band played various theatre bars, made several albums for Transatlantic and gained a strong following on the Irish folk circuit. After an introduction by Dominic Behan, they were signed by manager Phil Solomon and placed on his label, Major Minor. In 1965, the group took the desicion to turn professional, and Kelly wanted to return. He replaced Lynch who had wished to stay semi-professional. Throughout their collective career, each member pursued outside projects - among them Kelly's stints as an actor and

MacKenna's 'The Great Comic Genius', a solo single issued after the Irishmen transferred from Transatlantic to the Major Minor label in 1966. During this time they received incessant plugging on the Radio Caroline pirate radio station. Bigoted folk purists were unable to regard them with the same respect as the similarly motivated Clancy Brothers And Tommy Makem after the Dubliners were seen on *Top Of The Pops* promoting 1967's censored 'Seven Drunken Nights' and, next, 'Black Velvet Band'. 'Never Wed An Old Man' was only a minor hit, but high placings for *A Drop Of The Hard Stuff* and three of its successors in the album list were a firm foundation for the outfit's standing as a thoroughly diverting international concert attraction. A brain haemorrhage forced Bourke's retirement in 1974, and Drew's return to the ranks - after a brief replacement by Jim McCann (b. 26 October 1944, Dublin, Eire) - was delayed by injuries sustained in a road accident. Nevertheless, Drew's trademark vocal, 'like coke being crushed under a door', was heard on the group's 25th anniversary single, 'The Irish Rover', a merger with the Pogues that signalled another sojourn in the Top 10.

●ALBUMS: *Dubliners In Concert* (1965)★★★, *Finnegan Wakes* (Transatlantic 1966)★★★★, *A Drop Of The Hard Stuff* (1967)★★★★, *More Of The Hard Stuff* (1967)★★★, *The Dubliners* (Major Minor 1968)★★★★, *Drinkin' And Courtin'* (1968)★★★, *At It Again* (Major Minor 1968)★★★, *A Drop Of The Dubliners* (1969)★★★★, *Live At The Albert Hall* (1969)★★★, *At Home With The Dubliners* (Columbia 1969)★★★, *Revolution* (Columbia 1970)★★★, *Hometown!* (1972)★★★, *Double Dubliners* (1973)★★★, *Plain And Simple* (Polydor 1973)★★★, *The Dubliners Live* (1974)★★★, *Dubliners Now* (1975)★★★, *A Parcel Of Rogues* (1976)★★★, *The Dubliners - Fifteen Years On* (1977)★★★, *Prodigal Sons* (1983)★★★, *The Dubliners 25 Years Celebration* (1987)★★★, *The Dubliners Ireland* (1992)★★★, *Thirty Years A-Greying* (1992)★★★, *The Original Dubliners* (1993)★★★, *Milestones* (Transatlantic 1995)★★★.

●COMPILATIONS: *Best Of The Dubliners* (1967)★★★, *Very Best Of The Dubliners* (1975)★★★★, *20 Greatest Hits: Dubliners* (1989)★★★★, *20 Original Greatest Hits* (1988)★★★, *20 Original Greatest Hits Vol. 2* (1989)★★★, *The Best Of ...* (Wooden Hill 1996)★★★.

●FURTHER READING: *The Dubliners Scrapbook*, Mary Hardy.

DUKE, PATTY

b. Anna Marie Patricia Duke, 14 December 1946, Elmhurst, New York, USA. A child actress, Duke first came to the fore in the 1959 Broadway play *The Miracle Worker*, in which she played Helen Keller. In 1962 she reprised the role on film, for which she became the youngest person ever to win an Academy Award. The following year she starred in her own US television situation comedy in which she played two roles as 'identical cousins'. The programme became a great success (still seen in re-runs today) and lasted until 1966. In 1965 Duke signed a record deal with United Artists; her first single, 'Don't Just Stand There', was a teen-oriented ballad, reminiscent of Lesley Gore. It hit number 8 on the US charts and her follow-up, 'Say Something Funny', reached number 22 that same year. Duke subsequently recorded several other singles and albums, but never repeated her initial success. Today she is still involved in television and film acting.

●ALBUMS: *Billie* soundtrack (United Artists 1965)★★, *Don't Just Stand There* (United Artists 1965)★★★, *Songs From The Valley Of The Dolls* (United Artists 1968)★★.

DUMMER, JOHN, BLUES BAND

This UK band came into being in 1965, evolving from the Muskrats and the Grebbells, and lasted until the early 70s, surviving numerous personnel changes. The line-up included prominent British blues artists such as pianist Bob Hall, guitarist Dave Kelly and his sister Jo Ann Kelly, Mike Cooper, and Tony McPhee. The band backed touring American artists John Lee Hooker and Howlin' Wolf, and recorded albums for Mercury and Vertigo between 1969 and 1973. Drummer John Dummer went on to work with English pop vocal group Darts in the mid-70s. In recent years all Dummer's albums have become much sought after items in the collectors' market and currently carry very high prices.

●ALBUMS: *Cabal* (Mercury 1969)★★★, *John Dummer's Blues Band* (Mercury 1969)★★★★, *Famous Music Band* (Philips 1970)★★, *This Is John Dummer* (Philips 1972)★★★, *Volume II, Try Me One More Time* (Philips 1973)★★, *Blue* (Vertigo 1973)★★, *Oobleedooblee Jubilee* (Vertigo 1973)★★.

DUNBAR, AYNSLEY, RETALIATION

This unit was formed in 1967 by ex-John Mayall drummer Aynsley Dunbar. Having recorded an informal version of Buddy Guy's 'Stone Crazy' with an embryonic line-up of Rod Stewart (vocals), Peter Green (guitar) and Jack Bruce (bass), Dunbar created a permanent Retaliation around ex-Johnny Kidd And The Pirates and Shotgun Express guitarist, Jon Morshead, Keith Tillman (bass) and ex-Alexis Korner vocalist, Victor Brox. This line-up completed a solitary single, 'Warning'/'Cobwebs', for the Blue Horizon label before Tillman was replaced by Alex Dmochowski (ex-Neil Christian's Crusaders). *The Aynsley Dunbar Retaliation* showcased this superior blues group's self-assurance, with one side devoted to concise performances and the other to freer, instrumentally based workouts. Although it lacked the overall strength of its predecessor, *Dr. Dunbar's Prescription* was another worthwhile album which offered strong original songs and several judicious cover versions. However, the group is best recalled for *Retaliation* aka *To Mum From Aynsley And The Boys*, which was produced by John Mayall. Former Grease Band keyboard player Tommy Eyre was added for this powerful, moody collection on which the unit created some of its finest record-

ings, including 'Don't Take The Power Away' and 'Journey's End'. In November 1969 Dunbar and Eyre left the group to form Aynsley Dunbar's Blue Whale. A fourth set, *Remains To Be Heard*, was culled from remaining masters and newer recordings by the extant trio with singer Annette Brox, but the Retaliation broke up soon after its completion.

●ALBUMS: *The Aynsley Dunbar Retaliation* (Liberty 1968)★★★, *Dr. Dunbar's Prescription* (Liberty 1968)★★★, *Retaliation* aka *To Mum From Aynsley And The Boys* (Liberty 1969)★★★, *Remains To Be Heard* (Liberty 1970)★★.

DUNHILL RECORDS

The Dunhill label was inaugurated in Los Angeles, USA, in 1965 by Lou Adler, Jay Lasker and Bobby Roberts. Of the three partners, it was Adler who proved the driving force. An experienced songwriter, record producer and manager, he was the guiding light behind Jan And Dean and Johnny Rivers, and already operated the successful Trousdale publishing house. Its premier compositional team, P.F. Sloan and Steve Barri, were responsible for many of Dunhill's early releases, notably 'Eve Of Destruction', a million-selling protest disc for Barry McGuire. In turn this singer introduced the fledgling Mamas And The Papas to Adler. Their sumptuous harmonies were captured in a series of memorable singles, notably 'California Dreamin'' and 'Monday Monday', and such releases established Dunhill at the vanguard of the folk rock movement. Another melodically-inclined act, the Grass Roots, emerged from a Sloan/Barri experiment to enjoy consistent chart success with their distinctive brand of mainstream pop. Steppenwolf and Three Dog Night were among Dunhill's bestselling acts of the late 60s, but by this point the label's character had completely altered. The Mamas and The Papas had split up, the Sloan/Barri partnership was sundered and Adler had sold his share in the company to ABC/Paramount. In 1967 he founded Ode, striking an international hit with Scott McKenzie's 'San Francisco (Be Sure To Wear Flowers In Your Hair)'. The Dunhill name was retained until 1974, when its roster switched to the parent company.

DUPREE, SIMON, AND THE BIG SOUND

Formed in Portsmouth, England, by the Shulman brothers, Derek (b. 11 February 1947, Glasgow, Scotland; lead vocals), Ray (b. 3 December 1949, Portsmouth, Hampshire, England; lead guitar) and Phil (b. 27 August 1937, Glasgow, Scotland; saxophone/trumpet). The siblings had led several local groups, including the Howlin' Wolves and Roadrunners, before a newly acquired manager suggested the above appellation in 1966. Eric Hine (keyboards), Pete O'Flaherty (bass) and Tony Ransley (drums) completed the line-up which then became a regular attraction in London's soul and R&B clubs. 'I See The Light', 'Reservations' and 'Daytime Nightime' (penned by Manfred Mann drummer Mike Hugg) were all radio hits and a *de rigueur* compendium of dance-floor favourites

Without Reservations, preceded the sextet's switch to flower-power with 'Kites'. The group disliked the song's overt trappings - gongs, finger cymbals and Jackie Chan's Chinese narration - but it became their biggest hit, rising to number 9 in 1967. Subsequent singles failed to emulate this success, but the band achieved a measure of notoriety the following year when their psychoactive single, 'We Are The Moles', credited pseudonymously to the Moles, was assumed to be the Beatles in disguise. The unit was disbanded in 1969 when Derek Shulman, tired of being 'Simon Dupree', suffered a nervous breakdown. Upon recovery he joined his brothers in Gentle Giant.

●ALBUMS: *Without Reservations* (Parlophone 1967)★★.

●COMPILATIONS: *Amen* (1982)★★, *Kites* (1987)★★.

DYLAN, BOB

b. Robert Allen Zimmerman, 24 May 1941, Duluth, Minnesota, USA. Bob Dylan is unquestionably one of the most influential figures in the history of popular music. He is the writer of scores of classic songs and is generally regarded as the man who brought literacy to rock lyrics. The son of the middle-class proprietor of an electrical and furniture store, as a teenager, living in Hibbing, Minnesota, he was always intrigued by the romanticism of the outsider. He loved James Dean movies, liked riding motorcycles and wearing biker gear, and listened to R&B music on radio stations transmitting from the south. A keen fan of folk singer Odetta and country legend Hank Williams, he was also captivated by early rock 'n' roll. When he began playing music himself, with schoolfriends in bands such as the Golden Chords and Elston Gunn And The Rock Boppers, it was as a clumsy but enthusiastic piano player, and it was at this time that he declared his ambition in a high school yearbook 'to join Little Richard'. In 1959, he began visiting Minneapolis at weekends and on his graduation from high school, enrolled at the University of Minnesota there, although he spent most of his time hanging around with local musicians in the beatnik coffeehouses of the Dinkytown area. It was in Minneapolis that he first discovered blues music, and he began to incorporate occasional blues tunes among the primarily traditional material that made up his repertoire as an apprentice folk singer. Dylan, who by this time had changed his name, played occasionally at local clubs but was, by most accounts, a confident but, at best, unremarkable performer. In the summer of 1960, however, Dylan spent some time in Denver, and developed as an artist in several extraordinary and important ways. First, he adopted a persona based upon the Woody Guthrie romantic hobo figure of the film *Bound For Glory*. Dylan had learned about Guthrie in Minnesota and had quickly devoured and memorized as many Guthrie songs as he could. In Denver, he assumed a new voice, began speaking with an Okie twang, and adopted a new 'hard travellin'' appearance. Second, in Denver Dylan had met Jesse Fuller, a blues performer who played guitar and harmonica simultaneously by using a harp rack. Dylan was intrigued and soon afterwards

began to teach himself to do the same. By the time he returned to Minneapolis, he had developed remarkably as a performer. By now sure that he intended to be a professional musician, he returned briefly to Hibbing, then set out, via Madison and Chicago, for New York, where he arrived on 24 January 1961.

For a completely unknown and still very raw performer, Dylan's impact on the folk scene of Greenwich Village was immediate and enormous. He captivated anyone who saw him with his energy, his charisma and his rough-edged authenticity. He spun stories about his background and family history, weaving a tangled web of tall tales and myths about who he was and where he was from. He played in the coffeehouses of the Village, including Cafe Wha?, The Commons, The Gaslight and, most importantly, Gerde's Folk City, where he made his first professional appearance, supporting John Lee Hooker, in April 1961. He was also paid for playing harmonica on records by Harry Belafonte and Carolyn Hester, as a result of which he came the attention of producer John Hammond, who signed him to Columbia Records in Autumn 1961. At the same time, a gig at Gerde's was reviewed favourably in the *New York Times* by Robert Shelton, who declared that Bob Dylan was clearly destined for fortune and fame.

His first album, called simply *Bob Dylan*, was released in March 1961. It presented a collection of folk and blues standards, often about death and sorrows and the trials of life, songs that had been included in Dylan's repertoire over the past year or so, performed with gusto and an impressive degree of sensitivity for a 20-year-old. But it was the inclusion of two of his own compositions, most notably the affectionate tribute, 'Song To Woody', that pointed the way forward. Over the next few months, Dylan wrote dozens of songs, many of them 'topical' songs. Encouraged by his girlfriend, Suze Rotolo, Dylan became interested in, and was subsequently adopted by, the Civil Rights movement. His song 'Blowin' In The Wind', written in April 1962, was to be the most famous of his protest songs and was included on his second album, *The Freewheelin' Bob Dylan*, released in May 1963. In the meantime, Dylan had written and recorded several other noteworthy early political songs, including 'Masters Of War' and 'A Hard Rain's-A-Gonna Fall', and, during a nine-month separation from Suze, one of his greatest early love songs, 'Don't Think Twice, It's All Right'. At the end of 1962, he recorded a single, a rock 'n' roll song called 'Mixed Up Confusion', with backing musicians. The record was quickly deleted, apparently because Dylan's manager, Albert Grossman, saw that the way forward for his charge was not as a rocker, but as an earnest acoustic folky. Similarly, tracks that had been recorded for Dylan's second album with backing musicians were scrapped, although the liner notes which commented on them and identified the players remained carelessly unrevised. The *Freewheelin'* record was so long in coming that four original song choices were substituted at the last moment by other, more newly composed songs. One of the tracks omitted was 'Talking John

Birch Society Blues', which Dylan had been controversially banned from singing on the *Ed Sullivan Show* in May 1963. The attendant publicity did no harm whatsoever to Dylan's stature as a radical new 'anti-establishment' voice. At the same time, Grossman's shrewd decision to have a somewhat saccharine version of 'Blowin' In The Wind' recorded by Peter, Paul And Mary also paid off, the record becoming a huge hit in the USA, and bringing Dylan's name to national, and indeed international, attention for the first time.

At the end of 1962, Dylan flew to London to appear in the longlost BBC television play, *The Madhouse On Castle Street*. The experience did little to further his career as an actor, but while he was in London, he learned many English folk songs, particularly from musician Martin Carthy, whose tunes he subsequently 'adapted'. Thus, 'Scarborough Fair' was reworked as 'Girl From The North Country', 'Lord Franklin' as 'Bob Dylan's 'Dream', and 'Nottamun Town' as 'Masters Of War'. The songs continued to pour out and singers began to queue up to record them. It was at this time that Joan Baez first began to play a prominent part in Dylan's life. Already a successful folk singer, Baez covered Dylan songs at a rapid rate, and proclaimed his genius at every opportunity. Soon she was introducing him to her audience and the two became lovers, the King and Queen of folk music. Dylan's songwriting became more astute and wordy as the months passed. Biblical and other literary imagery began to be pressed into service in songs like 'When The Ship Comes In' and the anthemic 'Times They Are A-Changin'', this last written a day or two after Dylan had sung 'Only A Pawn In Their Game' in front of 400,000 people at the March On Washington, 28 August 1963. Indeed, the very next day, Dylan read in the local newspaper of the murder of black waitress Hattie Carroll, which inspired the best, and arguably the last, of his protest songs, 'The Lonesome Death Of Hattie Carroll', included on his third album, *The Times They Are A-Changin'*, released in January 1964.

Dylan's songwriting perspectives underwent a huge change in 1964. Now finally separated from Suze Rotolo, disenchanted with much of the petty politics of the Village, and becoming increasingly frustrated with the 'spokesman of a generation' tag that had been hung around his neck, the everrestless Dylan sloughed off the expectations of the old folky crowd, and, influenced by his reading the poetry of John Keats and French symbolist Arthur Rimbaud, began to expand his own poetic consciousness. He then wrote the songs that made up his fourth record, *Another Side Of Bob Dylan* - including the disavowal of his past, 'My Back Pages', and the Illuminations-inspired 'Chimes Of Freedom' – while yet newer songs such as 'Mr Tambourine Man' (which he recorded for but did not include on *Another Side*), 'Gates Of Eden' and 'It's Alright Ma, I'm Only Bleeding', which he began to include in concert performances over the next few weeks, dazzled with their lyrical complexity and literary sophistication. Here, then, was Dylan the poet, and here the arguments about the relative merits of high

art and popular art began. The years 1964-66 were, unarguably, Dylan's greatest as a writer and as a performer; they were also his most influential years and many artists today still cite the three albums which followed, *Bringing It All Back Home* and *Highway 61 Revisited* from 1965 and 1966's double album *Blonde On Blonde* as being seminal in their own musical development.

Another Side Of Bob Dylan was to be Dylan's last solo acoustic album for almost 30 years. Intrigued by what the Beatles were doing – he had visited London again to play one concert at the Royal Festival Hall in May 1964 – and particularly excited by the Animals' 'folk-rock' cover version of 'House Of The Rising Sun', a track Dylan himself had included on his debut album, he and producer Tom Wilson fleshed out some of the *Bringing It All Back Home* songs with rock 'n' roll backings – the proto-rap 'Subterranean Homesick Blues' and 'Maggie's Farm', for instance. However, the song that was perhaps Dylan's most important mid-60s composition, 'Like A Rolling Stone', was written immediately after the final series of acoustic concerts played in the UK in April and May 1965, and commemorated in D.A. Pennebaker's famous documentary film, *Don't Look Back*. Dylan said that he began to write 'Like A Rolling Stone' having decided to 'quit' singing and playing. The lyrics to the song emerged from six pages of stream-of-consciousness 'vomit'; the sound of the single emerged from the immortal combination of Chicago blues guitarist Michael Bloomfield, bass man Harvey Brooks and fledgling organ-player Al Kooper. 'Like A Rolling Stone' was producer Tom Wilson's last, and greatest, Dylan track. At six minutes, it destroyed the formula of the sub-three-minute single forever. It was a huge hit and was played, alongside the Byrds' equally momentous version of 'Mr Tambourine Man', all over the radio in the summer of 1965. Consequently, it should have come as no surprise to those who went to see Dylan at the Newport Folk Festival on July 25 that he was now a fully fledged folk rocker; but, apparently, it did.

Backed by the Paul Butterfield Blues Band, Dylan's supposedly 'new sound' – although admittedly it was his first concert with supporting musicians – was met with a storm of bewilderment and hostility. Stories vary as to how much Dylan was booed that night, and why, but Dylan seemed to find the experience both exhilarating and liberating. If, after the UK tour, he had felt ready to quit, now he was ready to start again, to tour the world with a band and to take his music, and himself, to the farthest reaches of experience, just like Rimbaud. Dylan's discovery of the Hawks, a Canadian group who had been playing roadhouses and funky bars until introductions were made via John Hammond Jnr. and Albert Grossman's secretary Mary Martin, was one of those pieces of alchemical magic that happen hermetically. The Hawks, later to become the Band, comprised Robbie Robertson, Richard Manuel, Garth Hudson, Rick Danko and Levon Helm. Dylan's songs and the Hawks' sound were made for each other. After a couple of stormy warmup gigs, they took to the road in the autumn of 1965 and travelled through the USA, then, via Hawaii, to Australia, on to Scandinavia and finally to Britain, with a hop over to Paris for a birthday show, in May 1966. Dylan was deranged and dynamic, the group wild and mercurial. Their set, the second half of a show that opened with Dylan playing acoustically to a reverentially silent house, was provocative and perplexing for many. It was certainly the loudest thing anyone had ever heard, and, almost inevitably, the electric set was greeted with mayhem and dismay. Drummer Levon Helm was so disheartened by the ferocity of the booing that he quit before the turn of the year – drummers Sandy Konikoff and Mickey Jones completed the tour. Offstage, Dylan was spinning out of control, not sleeping, not eating, and apparently heading rapidly for rock 'n' roll oblivion. Pennebaker again filmed the tour, this time in Dylan's employ. The 'official' record of the tour was the rarely seen *Eat The Document*, a film originally commissioned by ABC TV. The unofficial version compiled by Pennebaker himself was *You Know Something Is Happening*. 'What was happening,' says Pennebaker, 'was drugs . . .'

Dylan was physically exhausted when he got back to America in June 1966, but had to complete the film and finish *Tarantula*, the book that was overdue for Macmillan. He owed Columbia two more albums before his contract expired, and was booked to play a series of concerts right up to the end of the year in increasingly bigger venues, including Shea Stadium. Then, on 29 July 1966, Dylan was injured in a motorcycle accident near his home in Bearsville, near Woodstock, upper New York State.

Was there really a motorcycle accident? Dylan still claims there was. He hurt his neck and had treatment. More importantly, the accident allowed him to shrug off the responsibilities that had been lined up on his behalf by manager Grossman. By now, the relationship between Dylan and Grossman was less than cordial and litigation between the two of them was ongoing until Grossman's death almost 20 years later. Dylan was nursed through his convalescence by his wife, Sara – they had been married privately in November 1965 – and visited only rarely. Rumours spread that Dylan would never perform again. Journalists began to prowl around the estate, looking for some answers but finding no-one to ask.

After several months of doing little but feeding cats, bringing up young children, and cutting off his hair, Dylan was joined in the Bearsville area by the Hawks, who rented a house called Big Pink in West Saugerties. Every day they met and played music. It was the final therapy that Dylan needed. A huge amount of material was recorded in the basement of Big Pink – old folk songs, old pop songs, old country songs – and, eventually, from these sessions came a clutch of new compositions, which came to be known generically as the *Basement Tapes*. Some of the songs were surreally comic – 'Please Mrs Henry', 'Quinn The Eskimo', 'Million Dollar Bash'; others were soul-searchingly introspective musings on fame, guilt, responsibility and redemption – 'Tears Of Rage',

'Too Much Of Nothing', 'I Shall Be Released'. Distributed by Dylan's music publisher on what became a widely bootlegged tape, many of these songs were covered by, and became hits for, other artists and groups. Dylan's own recordings of some of the songs were not issued until 1975.

In January 1968, Dylan appeared with the Hawks, at this time renamed the Crackers, at the Woody Guthrie Memorial Concert at Carnegie Hall in New York. The following month *John Wesley Harding* was released, a stark, heavily moralistic collection of deceptively simple songs such as 'All Along The Watchtower', 'The Ballad Of Frankie Lee & Judas Priest', 'Dear Landlord' and 'Drifter's Escape', many of which can be heard as allegorical reflections on the events of the previous couple of years. The record's final song, however, 'I'll Be Your Baby Tonight', was unambivalently simple and presaged the warmer love songs of the frustratingly brief *Nashville Skyline*, released in April 1969. After the chilly monochrome of *John Wesley Harding*, here was Dylan in full colour, smiling, apparently at ease at last, and singing in a deep, rich voice, which, oddly, some of his oldest acquaintances maintained was how 'Bobby' used to sound back in Minnesota when he was first learning how to sing. 'Lay Lady Lay', 'Tonight I'll Be Staying Here With You', a duet with Johnny Cash on 'Girl From The North Country' – it was all easy on the ear, lyrically unsophisticated and, for some, far too twee. Nevertheless, *Nashville Skyline* was an extraordinarily influential record. It brought a new hipness to the hopelessly out-of-fashion Nashville (where, incidentally and incongruously, *Blonde On Blonde* had also been recorded) and it heralded a new genre of music – country rock – and a new movement that coincided with, or perhaps helped to spawn, the Woodstock Festival of the same summer. A return to simplicity and a love that was in truth only a distant relation of that psychedelically celebrated by the hippies in San Francisco a couple of years earlier, to whom Dylan paid no heed whatsoever. There are, therefore, no photographs of Bob Dylan in kaftan, beads and flowers or paisley bell-bottoms.

Dylan chose to avoid the Woodstock Festival (though the Band – the newly rechristened Crackers, who by now had two of their own albums, *Music From Big Pink* and *The Band*, to their credit – did play there), but he did play at the Isle Of Wight Festival on 31 August 1969. In a baggy Hank Williams-style white suit, it was a completely different Bob Dylan from the fright-haired, rabbit-suited marionette who had howled and screamed in the teeth of audience hostility at the Albert Hall more than three years earlier. This newly humble Dylan cooed and crooned an ever-so-polite, if ever-so-unexciting, set of songs and in doing so left the audience just as bewildered as those who had booed back in 1966.

But that bewilderment was as nothing compared with the puzzlement which greeted the release, in June 1970, of *Self Portrait*. This new record most closely resembled the Dylan album which preceded it – the bootleg collection *Great White Wonder*. Both were double albums; both offered mish-mash mix-ups of undistinguished live tracks, alternate takes, odd cover versions, botched beginnings and endings. Some even heard *Self Portrait*'s opening track, 'All The Tired Horses', as a caustic comment on the bootleggers' exploitation of ages-old material – was Dylan complaining 'How'm I supposed to get any ridin' done?' or 'writin' done?' There was little new material on *Self Portrait*, but there was 'Blue Moon'. The critics howled. Old fans were (yes, once again) dismayed. Rolling Stone was vicious: 'What is this shit?', the review by Greil Marcus began.

'We've Got Dylan Back Again,' wrote Ralph Gleason in the same magazine just four months later, heralding the hastily released *New Morning* as a 'return to form'. There was Al Kooper; there was the Dylan drawl; there were some slightly surreal lyrics; there was a bunch of new songs; but these were restless times for Dylan. He had left Woodstock and returned to New York, to the heart of Greenwich Village, having bought a townhouse on MacDougal Street. It was, he later realized, an error, especially when A.J. Weberman, the world's first Dylanologist, turned up on his doorstep to rifle through his garbage in search of clues to unlocking the secret code of his poetry and (unintentionally) scaring his kids. Weberman saw it as his duty to shake Dylan out of his mid-life lethargy and reanimate him into embracing political and moral causes, and remarkably, met with some success. On 1 August 1971, Dylan appeared at the Concert For Bangladesh benefit, his only live performance between 1970 and 1974, and in November of the same year released 'George Jackson', a stridently powerful protest song, as a single. Little else happened for some time. Dylan cropped up so frequently as a guest on other people's albums that it ceased to be seen as a coup. He began to explore his Jewishness and was famously pictured at the Wailing Wall in Jerusalem. In 1973 he played, with some aplomb, the enigmatic Alias in Sam Peckinpah's brilliant *Pat Garrett & Billy The Kid*, for which film he also supplied the soundtrack music, including the hit single 'Knocking On Heaven's Door'.

Also in 1973, in a move which confounded industry-watchers, Dylan left CBS Records, having been persuaded by David Geffen of the advantages of signing to his Asylum Records label. The disadvantage, some might say, was the cruelly spurned Columbia's misguided desire to exact a kind of revenge. They put out *Dylan*, an album of outtakes and warm-ups, presumably intending to either embarrass Dylan beyond endurance or to steal some of the thunder from his first Asylum album, *Planet Waves*, newly recorded with the Band. In terms of the records' merits, there was no contest, although a few of the *Dylan* tracks were actually quite interesting, and the only embarrassment suffered was by Columbia, who were widely condemned for their petty-minded peevishness.

A US tour followed. Tickets were sold by post and attracted six million applications. Everybody who went to the shows agreed that Dylan and the Band were fantastic. The recorded evidence, *Before The Flood*, also released by Asylum, certainly oozes energy, but lacks subtlety: Dylan seems to be trying too hard, pushing everything too fast. It is good, but not that good.

What is *that* good, unarguably and incontestably, is *Blood On The Tracks*. Originally recorded (for CBS, no hard feelings, etc.) in late 1974, Dylan substituted some of the songs with versions reworked in Minnesota over the Christmas period. They were his finest compositions since the *Blonde On Blonde* material. 'Tangled Up In Blue', 'Idiot Wind', 'If You See Her Say Hello', 'Shelter From The Storm', 'Simple Twist Of Fate', 'You're A Big Girl Now' . . . one masterpiece followed another. It was not so much a divorce album as a separation album (Dylan's divorce from Sara wasn't completed until 1977), but it was certainly a diary of despair. 'Pain sure brings out the best in people, doesn't it?' Dylan sang in 1966's 'She's Your Lover Now'; *Blood On The Tracks* gave the lie to all those who had argued that Dylan was a spent force.

If Dylan the writer was reborn with *Blood On The Tracks*, Dylan the performer re-emerged on the Rolling Thunder Revue. A travelling medicine show, moving from small town to small town, playing just about unannounced, the line-up extensive and variable, but basically consisting of Dylan, Joan Baez, Roger McGuinn, Rambling Jack Elliott, Allen Ginsberg, Mick Ronson, Bobby Neuwirth and Ronee Blakley, the Revue was conceived in the Village in the summer of 1975 and hit the road in New England, in Plymouth, Massachusetts, on 31 October. It was a long wished-for dream, and Dylan, face painted white, hat festooned with flowers, was inspired, delirious, imbued with a new vitality and singing like a demon. Some of those great performances are preserved in the four-hour movie Renaldo And Clara, the self-examination through charade and music that Dylan edited through 1977 and defended staunchly and passionately on its release to the almost inevitable uncomprehending or downright hostile barrage of criticism which greeted it. The Revue reconvened for a 1976 tour of the south, musical glimpses of its excitement being issued on the live album *Hard Rain*. A focal point of the Revue had been the case of wrongly imprisoned boxer Hurricane Carter, to whose cause Dylan had been recruited after having read his book, *The Sixteenth Round*. Dylan's song 'Hurricane' was included just about every night in the 1975 Revue, and also on the follow-up album to *Blood On the Tracks*, *Desire*, which also offered several songs co-written with Jacques Levy. *Desire* was an understandably popular record; 'Isis', 'Black Diamond Bay', 'Romance In Durango' represented some of Dylan's strongest narrative ballads.

This was further borne out by the songs on *Street-Legal*, the 1978 album that was released in the middle of a year-long stint with the biggest touring band with which Dylan ever played. Some critics dubbed it the alimony tour, but considerably more funds could have been generated if Dylan had gone out with a four-piece. Many of the old songs were imaginatively reworked in dramatic new arrangements. *At Budokan*, released in 1979, documents the tour at its outset; the Earl's Court and Blackbushe concerts caught it memorably mid-stream; while an exhausting trip around the USA in the latter part of the year seemed to bring equal amounts of acclaim and disapproval. 'Dylan's gone Vegas,' some reviewers moaned. True, he wore trousers with lightening flashes while behind him flutes and bongos competed for attention with synthesizers and keyboards, but some of the performances were quite wonderful and the new songs, 'Senor (Tales Of Yankee Power)', 'Changing Of The Guard', 'Where Are You Tonight? (Journey Through Dark Heat)', 'True Love Tends To Forget', sounded terrific. Who would have thought that . . .

In 1979, Dylan became a born-again Christian, released an album of fervently evangelical songs, *Slow Train Coming*, recorded in Muscle Shoals, Alabama, with Jerry Wexler and Barry Beckett, and featuring Mark Knopler and Pick Withers from Dire Straits, and in November and December played a series of powerful concerts featuring nothing but his new Christian material. Cries of disbelief? Howls of protest? Well, naturally; but the record was crisp and contemporary-sounding, the songs strong, the performances admirable (Dylan was to win a Grammy for best rock vocal performance on 'Gotta Serve Somebody'), and the concerts, which continued in 1980, among the most powerful and spine-tingling as any in his entire career. The second Christian album, *Saved*, was less impressive, however, and the fervour of the earlier months was more muted by the end of the year. Gradually, old songs began to be reworked into the live set and by the time of 1981's *Shot Of Love*, it was no longer clear whether or not – or to what extent – Dylan's faith remained firm. The sarcastic 'Property Of Jesus' and the thumping 'Dead Man, Dead Man' suggested that not much had changed, but the retrospective 'In The Summertime' and the prevaricating 'Every Grain Of Sand' hinted otherwise.

After three turbulent years, it was hardly surprising that Dylan dropped from sight for most of 1982, but the following year he was back in the studio, again with Mark Knopfler, having, it was subsequently established, written a prolific amount of new material. The album that resulted, *Infidels*, released in October 1983, received a mixed reception. Some songs were strong – 'I&I' 'Jokerman' among them – others relatively unimpressive. Dylan entered the video age by making promos for 'Sweetheart Like You' and 'Jokerman', but did not seem too excited about it. Rumours persisted about his having abandoned Christianity and re-embraced the Jewish faith. His name began to be linked with the ultra-orthodox Lubavitcher sect: the inner sleeve of *Infidels* pictured him touching the soil of a hill above Jerusalem, while 'Neighbourhood Bully' was a fairly transparent defence of Israel's policies towards its neighbours. Dylan, as ever, refused to confirm or deny his state of spiritual health.

In 1984, he appeared live on the David Letterman television show, giving one of his most extraordinary and thrilling performances, backed by a ragged and raw Los Angeles trio, the Cruzados. However, when, a few weeks later, he played his first concert tour for three years, visiting Europe on a package with Santana put together by impresario Bill Graham, Dylan's band was disappointingly longer in the tooth (with Mick Taylor on guitar and Ian McLagan on organ). An unimpressive souvenir album, *Real Live*, released in December, was most notable for its inclusion of a substantially rewritten version of 'Tangled Up In Blue'.

1985 opened with Dylan contributing to the 'We Are The World' USA For Africa single, and in summer, after the release of *Empire Burlesque*, a patchy record somewhat over-produced by remix specialist Arthur Baker but boasting the beautiful acoustic closer 'Dark Eyes', he was the top-of-the-bill act at Live Aid. Initially, Dylan had been supposed to play with a band, but then was asked to perform solo, to aid the logistics of the grande finale. In the event, he recruited Rolling Stones Ron Wood and Keith Richards to help him out. The results were disastrous. Hopelessly under-rehearsed and hampered both by the lack of monitors and the racket of the stage being set up behind the curtain in front of which they were performing, the trio were a shambles. Dylan, it was muttered later, must have been the only artist to appear in front of a billion television viewers worldwide and end up with fewer fans than he had when he started. Matters were redeemed a little, however, at the Farm Aid concert in September, an event set up as a result of Dylan's somewhat gauche onstage 'charity begins at home' appeal at Live Aid. Backed by Tom Petty And The Heartbreakers, it was immediately apparent that Dylan had found his most sympathetic and adaptable backing band since the Hawks. The year ended positively, too, with the release of the five album (3-CD) retrospective, *Biograph*.

The collaboration with Tom Petty having gone so well, it was decided that the partnership should continue, and a tour was announced to begin in New Zealand, Australia and Japan with more shows to follow in the USA. It was the summer's hottest ticket and the Petty/Dylan partnership thrived for a further year with a European tour, the first shows of which saw Dylan appearing in Israel for the very first time. Unfortunately, the opening show in Tel Aviv was not well received either by the audience or by the press, whose reviews were vitriolic. The second show in Jerusalem was altogether more enjoyable, until the explosion of the PA system brought the concert to an abrupt end.

Between the two tours, Dylan appeared in his second feature film, the Richard Marquand-directed *Hearts Of Fire*, made in England and Canada and co-starring Rupert Everett and Fiona Flanagan. Dylan played Billy Parker, a washed-up one-time mega-star who in all but one respect (the washed-up bit) bore an uncanny resemblance to Dylan himself. Despite Dylan's best efforts – and he was arguably the best thing in the movie – the film was a clunker. Hoots of derision marred the premiere in October 1987 and its theatrical release was limited to one week in the UK. The poor movie was preceded by a poor album, *Knocked Out Loaded*, which only had the epic song 'Brownsville Girl', co-written with playwright Sam Shepard, to recommend it.

Increasingly, it appeared that Dylan's best attentions were being devoted to his concerts. The shows with Tom Petty had been triumphant. Dylan also shared the bill with the Grateful Dead at several stadium venues, and learned from the experience. He envied their ability to keep on playing shows year in, year out, commanding a following wherever and whenever they played. He liked their two drummers and also admired the way they varied their set each night, playing different songs as and when they felt like it. These peculiarly Deadian aspects of live performance were soon incorporated into Dylan's own concert philosophy.

Down In The Groove, an album of mostly cover versions of old songs, was released in the same month, June 1988, as Dylan played the first shows of what was to become known as the Never-Ending Tour. Backed by a three-piece band led by G.E. Smith, Dylan had stripped down his sound and his songs and was, once again, seeminglyre-energised. His appetite for work had never been greater, and this same year he found himself in the unlikely company of George Harrison, Jeff Lynne, Tom Petty and Roy Orbison as one of the Traveling Wilburys, a jokey band assembled on a whim in the Spring. Their album, *Volume One*, on which Dylan's voice was as prominent as anyone's, was, unexpectedly, a huge commercial success.

His Wilbury star in the ascendancy, Dylan's next album emerged as his best of the 80s. *Oh Mercy*, recorded informally in New Orleans and idiosyncratically produced by Daniel Lanois, sounded fresh and good, and the songs were as strong a bunch as Dylan had come up with in a long time. However, for reasons best known only to himself, it transpired from bootleg tapes that Dylan had been excluding many excellent songs from the albums he had been releasing in the 80s, most notably the masterpiece 'Blind Willie McTell', which was recorded for, but not included on, *Infidels*. Indeed, despite the evident quality of the songs on *Oh Mercy* – 'Shooting Star' and 'Most Of The Time' were, for once, both songs of experience, evidence of a maturity that many fans had long been wishing for in Dylan's songwriting – it turned out that Dylan was still holding back. The crashing, turbulent 'Series Of Dreams' and the powerful 'Dignity' were products of the Lanois sessions, but were not used on *Oh Mercy*. Instead, both later appeared on compilation albums.

Not without its merits (the title track and 'God Knows' are still live staples, while 'Born In Time' is a particularly emotional love song), the nursery-rhyme-style *Under The Red Sky*, released in September 1990, was for most a relative, probably inevitable, disappointment, as was the Roy-Orbison-bereft Wilburys follow-up, *Volume Three*. However, the touring continued, with Dylan's performances becoming increasingly erratic – sometimes splendid, often shambolic. It was one thing being spontaneous and improvisatory, but it was quite another being slapdash and incompetent. Dylan could be either, and

was sometimes both. His audiences began to dwindle, his reputation started to suffer. The three-volume collection of outtakes and rarities, *The Bootleg Series, Volumes 1-3 (Rare And Unreleased) 1961-1991*, redeemed him somewhat, as did the 30th Anniversary Celebration concert in Madison Square Garden in 1992, in which some of rock music's greats and not-so-greats paid tribute to Dylan's past achievements as a songwriter.

There was, however, precious little present songwriting to celebrate. Both *Good As I Been To You* (1992) and *World Gone Wrong* (1993), although admirable, were collections of old folk and blues material, performed, for the first time since 1964, solo and acoustically. *Greatest Hits Volume 3* (1994) threw together a clump of old non-hits and *Unplugged* (1995) saw Dylan revisiting a set of predominantly 60s songs in desultory fashion. Even the most ambitious CD-ROM so far, *Highway 61 Interactive*, while seemingly pointing to a Dylan-full future, wallowed nostalgically in, and was marketed on the strength of, past glories. Although Dylan's live performances became more coherent and controlled, his choice of material grew less imaginative through 1994, while many shows in 1995, which saw continued improvement in form, consisted almost entirely of songs written some 30 years earlier. In 1997 it was rumoured that Dylan was knocking on heaven's door. Although he had suffered a serious inflammation of the heart muscles he was discharged from hospital after a short time, eliciting this priceless quote to the press: 'I really thought I'd be seeing Elvis soon'. Time, perhaps, for doubters to begin to consign Dylan to the pages of history. However, as time has often proved, you can never write off Bob Dylan. He is a devil for hopping out of the hearse on the way to the cemetery.

●ALBUMS: *Bob Dylan* (Columbia 1962)★★★, *The Freewheelin' Bob Dylan* (Columbia 1963)★★★★, *The Times They Are A-Changin'* (Columbia 1964)★★★★, *Another Side Of Bob Dylan* (Columbia 1964)★★★★, *Bringing It All Back Home* (Columbia 1965)★★★★★, *Highway 61 Revisited* (Columbia 1965)★★★★★, *Blonde On Blonde* (Columbia 1966)★★★★★, *John Wesley Harding* (Columbia 1968)★★★★, *Nashville Skyline* (Columbia 1969)★★★, *Self Portrait* (Columbia 1970)★★, *New Morning* (Columbia 1970)★★★, *Dylan* (Columbia 1973)★, *Planet Waves* (Island 1974)★★★★, *Before The Flood* (Asylum 1974)★★★, *Blood On The Tracks* (Columbia 1975)★★★★★, *The Basement Tapes* (Columbia 1975)★★★, *Desire* (Columbia 1976)★★★★, *Hard Rain* (Columbia 1976)★★, *Street-Legal* (Columbia 1978)★★★, *Slow Train Coming* (Columbia 1979)★★★, *At Budokan* (Columbia 1979)★★★, *Saved* (Columbia 1980)★, *Shot Of Love* (Columbia 1981)★★★, *Infidels* (Columbia 1983)★★★, *Real Live* (Columbia 1984)★★, *Empire Burlesque* (Columbia 1985)★★, *Knocked Out Loaded* (Columbia 1986)★★, *Down In The Groove* (Columbia 1988)★★★, *Dylan And The Dead* (Columbia 1989)★, *Oh Mercy* (Columbia 1989)★★★★, *Under The Red Sky* (Columbia 1990)★★★, *Good As I Been To You* (Columbia 1992)★★, *World Gone Wrong* (Columbia 1993)★★, *The 30th Anniversary Concert*

Celebration (Columbia 1993)★★★, *MTV Unplugged* (Columbia 1995)★★★.
●COMPILATIONS: *Bob Dylan's Greatest Hits* (Columbia 1971)★★★★★, *More Bob Dylan Greatest Hits* (Columbia 1972)★★★★, *Biograph* (CBS 1985)★★★★, *The Bootleg Series, Vols 1-3, Rare And Unreleased 1961-1991* (CBS/Legacy 1991)★★★★★, *Greatest Hits Volume 3* (Columbia 1994)★★★.
●VIDEOS: *Hard To Handle* (1987), *Don't Look Back* (1988), *30th Anniversary Concert Celebration* (1993), *MTV Unplugged* (1995).
●FURTHER READING: *Bob Dylan In His Own Write*, Bob Dylan. *Eleven Outlined Epitaphs & Off The Top Of My Head*, Bob Dylan. *Folk-Rock: The Bob Dylan Story*, Sy and Barbra Ribakove. *Don't Look Back*, D.A. Pennebaker. *Bob Dylan: An Intimate Biography*, Anthony Scaduto. *Positively Main Street: An Unorthodox View Of Bob Dylan*, Toby Thompson. *Bob Dylan: A Retrospective*, Craig McGregor. *Song And Dance Man: The Art Of Bob Dylan*, Michael Gray. *Bob Dylan: Writings And Drawings*, Bob Dylan. *Knocking On Dylan's Door*, Rolling Stone editors. *Rolling Thunder Logbook*, Sam Shepard. *On The Road With Bob Dylan: Rolling With The Thunder*, Larry Sloman. *Bob Dylan: The Illustrated Record*, Alan Rinzler. *Bob Dylan In His Own Words*, Miles. *Bob Dylan: An Illustrated Discography*, Stuart Hoggard and Jim Shields. *Bob Dylan: An Illustrated History*, Michael Gross. *Bob Dylan: His Unreleased Recordings*, Paul Cable. *Dylan: What Happened?*, Paul Williams. *Conclusions On The Wall: New Essays On Bob Dylan*, Liz Thomson. *Twenty Years Of Recording: The Bob Dylan Reference Book*, Michael Krogsgaard. *Voice Without Restraint: A Study Of Bob Dylan's Lyrics And Their Background*, John Herdman. *Bob Dylan: From A Hard Rain To A Slow Train*, Tim Dowley and Barry Dunnage. *No Direction Home: The Life And Music Of Bob Dylan*, Robert Shelton. *Bringing It All Back Home*, Robbie Wolliver. *All Across The Telegraph: A Bob Dylan Handbook*, Michael Gray and John Bauldie (eds.). *Raging Glory*, Dennis R. Liff. *Bob Dylan: Stolen Moments*, Clinton Heylin. *Jokerman: Reading The Lyrics Of Bob Dylan*, Aidan Day. *Dylan: A Biography*, Bob Spitz. *Performing Artist: The Music Of Bob Dylan Vol. 1, 1960-1973*, Paul Williams. *Dylan Companion*, Elizabeth M. Thomson and David Gutman. *Lyrics: 1962-1985*, Bob Dylan. *Bob Dylan: Performing Artist*, Paul Williams. *Oh No! Not Another Bob Dylan Book*, Patrick Humphries and John Bauldie. *Absolutely Dylan*, Patrick Humphries and John Bauldie.*Dylan: Behind The Shades*, Clinton Heylin. *Bob Dylan: A Portrait Of the Artist's Early Years*, Daniel Kramer. *Wanted Man: In Search Of Bob Dylan*, John Bauldie (ed.). *Bob Dylan: In His Own Words*, Chris Williams. *Tangled Up In Tapes*, Glen Dundas. *Hard Rain: A Dylan Commentary*, Tim Riley. *Complete Guide To The Music Of Bob Dylan*, Patrick Humphries. *Bob Dylan Drawn Blank (Folio of drawings)*, Bob Dylan. *Watching The River Flow (1966-1995)*, Paul Williams.

EARL, ROBERT

b. 17 November 1926, England. This popular ballad singer enjoyed several UK hits in the late 50s. After becoming a semi-professional with the dance bands of Sydney Lipton and Nat Temple, he turned full-time professional in 1950, and appeared frequently on radio and television programmes such as the *Jack Jackson Show* and *Off The Record*. In 1958, he narrowly beat Perry Como to the UK chart with his version of 'I May Never Pass This Way Again'. Later that year, however, his 'More Than Ever (Come Prima)' was kept out of the Top 10 by Malcolm Vaughan. Earl's last hit was 'Wonderful Secret Of Love' in 1959. During the 60s, he retained a small but faithful audience. Subsequently, Earl's occasional releases, such as *Robert Earl Showcase* and *Shalom*, often featured Jewish favourites, including 'Yaas', 'My Son, My Son' and 'Mom-e-le'. Favourably reviewed in a London cabaret appearance in 1991, the 'veteran song stylist' maintained the Hebrew connection by including 'If I Was A Rich Man' from *Fiddler On The Roof*, among a selection of other nostalgic items. Earl's son, also named Robert, is listed among the UK's Top 100 richest people. In his early 40s, he heads the Hard Rock Cafe chain, and co-owns Planet Hollywood, 'New York's newest eating experience', and its London subsidiary, along with Bruce Willis, Sylvester Stallone and Arnold Schwarzenegger.
●ALBUMS: *Robert Earl Showcase* (Philips 1960)★★★.

EARLS

Although 'Remember Then' was their only hit, the Earls were one of the most accomplished white doo-wop groups of the early 60s. The lead singer Larry Chance (b. Larry Figueiredo, 19 October 1940, Philadelphia, Pennsylvania, USA) formed the group in New York's Bronx area in the late 50s. The other members were first tenor Robert Del Din (b. 1942), second tenor Eddie Harder (b. 1942), baritone Larry Palumbo (b. 1941) and bass John Wray (b. 1939). For their first single, the group revived the Harptones' 1954 R&B hit 'Life Is But A Dream'. This was released by the local Rome label in 1961. The following year, the group moved to another New York label, Old Town, and made 'Remember Then' which reached the Top 30. The Earls continued to release singles on Old Town until 1965, but the only record to make an impact was a maudlin version of 'I Believe', dedicated to Palumbo, who had died in a parachute accident. With various personnel changes, including the addition of Hank DiScuillo on guitar, Chance continued to lead the group on occasional records for Mr G and ABC. With their

big hit on numerous oldies compilations during the 70s, the Earls appeared on rock revival shows. 'Remember Then' was a UK Top 20 hit in 1979 for revivalist band Showaddywaddy.
●ALBUMS: *Remember Me Baby* (Old Town 1963)★★★.
●COMPILATIONS: *Remember Rome - The Early Years* (Crystal Ball 1982)★★, *Remember Then: The Best Of ...* (Ace 1992)★★, *Remember Me Baby: The Golden Classic Edition* (Collecatbles 1992)★★.

EARTH OPERA

Formed in Boston, New England, USA, in 1967, Earth Opera revolved around Peter Rowan (vocals/guitar) and David Grisman (b. 1945, Hackensack, New Jersey, USA; mandocello/mandolin). Both were veterans of the blue-grass and old-time circuit; Rowan with Bill Monroe And The Bluegrass Boys and the Mother State Bay Entertainers, and Grisman as leader of the New York Ramblers and member of the Even Dozen Jug Band. The two musicians worked as a duo, performing Rowan's original songs, before adding John Nagy (bass) and Bill Stevenson (keyboards/vibes). *Earth Opera* was produced by fellow folk music associate Peter Siegel, who shared an unerring empathy with the material. Rowan's lyrical, highly visual compositions were enhanced by his unusual, expressive tenor, particularly on the graphic 'Death By Fire' and 'The Child Bride'. Elsewhere the material reflected the questioning rootlessness prevalent in the immediate post-1967 era.

Drummer Paul Dillon was then added to the line-up, but Bill Stevenson left the group prior to recording a second album. Although worthy, *The Great American Eagle Tragedy* featured a roughshod horn section which altered the tone of several songs, with only one track, 'Mad Lydia's Waltz', retaining the delicacy of the previous set. The collection was marked by its uncompromising title track, a lengthy impassioned attack on the Vietnam War. A compulsive example of the genre, replete with images of terror and madness, this accomplished piece over-shadowed much of the remaining content, although Rowan's talent was equally obvious on 'Home To You' and 'Sanctuary From The Law'. The former contained the memorably quirky lyric, 'It's tired and I'm getting late'. Earth Opera broke up soon after the set was issued. Rowan later joined Sea Train, before enjoying a successful solo career, while Grisman became a leading figure in traditional music circles.
●ALBUMS: *Earth Opera* (Elektra 1968)★★, *The Great American Eagle Tragedy* (Elektra 1969)★★★.

EAST OF EDEN

Formed in 1968, this versatile UK group originally consisted of Dave Arbus (violin), Ron Gaines (alto saxophone), Geoff Nicholson (lead guitar), Andy Sneddon (bass) and Geoff Britton (drums). Their debut, *Mercator Projected*, offered an imaginative brew of progressive rock, jazz and neo-eastern predilections, but this robust, *avant garde* direction contrasted with the novelty tag placed on the group in the wake of their surprise hit

single, 'Jig A Jig'. This lightweight, fiddle-based instrumental reached number 7 in the UK in April 1971, and in the process confused prospective audiences. East Of Eden was plagued by personnel problems and by 1972 had shed every original member. Joe O'Donnell (violin), Garth Watt-Roy (guitar, ex-Greatest Show On Earth), Martin Fisher (bass) and Jeff Allen (drums, ex-Beatstalkers) then maintained the group's name before their demise later in the decade. Meanwhile, Arbus gained further acclaim for his contributions to the Who's *Who's Next* album while Geoff Britton later joined Wings.
●ALBUMS: *Mercator Projected* (Deram 1969)★★, *Snafu* (Deram 1970)★★★, *East Of Eden* (Harvest 1971)★★★, *New Leaf* (Harvest 1971)★★, *Another Eden* (1975)★★, *Here We Go Again* (1976)★★ *It's The Climate* (1976)★★, *Silver Park* (1978)★★.
●COMPILATIONS: *The World Of East Of Eden* (Deram 1971)★★★, *Masters Of Rock* (1975)★★★, *Things* (1976)★★★.

EASY RIDER

Released in 1969, *Easy Rider* is one of the lynchpin films of the 60s, encapsulating the mood of its time upon release. Co-stars Peter Fonda and Dennis Hopper, who also directed, play two bikers who, having finalized a drugs deal, ride to New Orleans to celebrate the Mardi Gras. En route they encounter friendship and animosity in equal doses but as the film progresses the 'American Dream' - and indeed the idealism of the central characters - gradually sours. 'We blew it,' states Fonda in the scene preceding the still numbing finale, referring both to his immediate circle and society in general. Fonda and Hopper apart, *Easy Rider* features a superb performance from Jack Nicholson playing drunken lawyer George Hansen, and the normally reclusive Phil Spector has a small role as the Connection. *Easy Rider* is also a technical triumph. The usually profligate Hopper is remarkably disciplined, although he would later claim 'his' film was cut to ribbons. Laszlo Kovak's photography is breathtaking and Terry Southern's script is suitably economic. *Easy Rider* also boasted a superb soundtrack and two songs in particular, Steppenwolf's 'Born To Be Wild' and the Byrds' 'I Wasn't Born To Follow', are forever linked to the imagery they accompany. Material by the Band, Bob Dylan, Jimi Hendrix, Roger McGuinn, the Holy Modal Rounders, Fraternity Of Man and Electric Prunes is also well selected, creating a new standard for the cinematic use of rock music. Indeed the whole style and content of *Easy Rider* became much copied, but few films came close to cmulating it.

EASYBEATS

Formed in Sydney, Australia, in 1964, this beat group comprised Harry Vanda (b. Harold Wandon, 22 March 1947, The Hague, Holland; guitar), Dick Diamonde (b. 28 December 1947, Hilversum, Holland; bass), Steve Wright (b. 20 December 1948, Leeds, Yorkshire, England; vocals), George Young (b. 6 November 1947, Glasgow, Scotland; guitar) and Gordon 'Snowy' Fleet (b. 16 August 1946,

Bootle, Lancashire, England; drums). Originally known as the Starfighters, they changed their name after the arrival of Fleet, who modelled their new style on that of the Liverpool beat groups of the period. After a series of hits in their homeland, including six number 1 singles, the group relocated to England in the summer of 1966 and were offered the opportunity to work with top pop producer Shel Talmy. The combination resulted in one of the all-time great beat group singles of the 60s: 'Friday On My Mind'. Strident guitars, clever counter harmonies and a super-strong beat were the ingredients that provided the disc with its power. Following a solid push on pirate radio, it peaked at number 6 in the UK. Unfortunately, the group found it difficult to follow up their hit and their prospects were not helped after splitting with Talmy during the recording of their first UK-released album. When they finally returned to the UK charts in 1968, it was with the ballad 'Hello How Are You', the mood of which contrasted sharply with that of their first hit. Lack of morale and gradual line-up changes subtly transformed the group into a vehicle for key members Vanda and Young, who were already writing material for other artists. In 1969, after an Australian tour, the Easybeats split up. Ironically, they enjoyed a US hit some months later with 'St Louis'. In the wake of their demise, Vanda/Young went into production, released records under a variety of pseudonyms and were largely responsible for the Australian success of such artists as John Paul Jones and William Shakespeare. George Young and his two brothers, Angus and Malcolm, were part of the original line-up of AC/DC, while Vanda/Young found success in their own right during the early 80s as Flash In The Pan.

●ALBUMS: *Easy* (1965)★★, *It's 2 Easy* (1966)★★, *Volume 3* (1966)★★★, *Good Friday* (United Artists 1967)★★★, *Vigil* (United Artists 1968)★★, *Friends* (Polydor 1969)★★, *The Shame Just Drained* (1977)★★, *Live Studio And Stage* (Raven 1995)★★.
●COMPILATIONS: *The Best Of The Easybeats, Plus Pretty Girl* (1967)★★★, *Rock Legend* (1980)★★★, *Absolute Anthology* (1980)★★★, *Best Of The Easybeats* (1986)★★★, *The Best Of ...* (Repertoire 1995)★★★, *Aussie Beat That Shook The World* (Repertoire 1996)★★★.

ECHOES

The Echoes were a white doo-wop group from Brooklyn, New York, USA, that logged one Top 20 hit, 'Baby Blue', in 1961. The group consisted of Harry Boyle (b. 1943, Brooklyn, New York, USA), Thomas Duffy (b. 1944, Brooklyn, New York, USA), and Tom Morrissey (b. 1943, Brooklyn, New York, USA). Originally called the Laurels, the group was given 'Baby Blue', written by teachers Sam Guilino and Val Lagueux, by a member of another group who had decided not to record it. The Laurels changed their name to the Echoes and financed their own demo recording of the song, and Jack Gold, owner of Paris Records, decided to release it on another label he was starting, SRG Records. The record was picked up by

another label, Seg-Way, and it went up to number 12. The Echoes were unable to follow up their one hit, despite several fine subsequent recordings, and the group split up. When a revival scene for white doo-wop emerged in the New York area in the 80s, an album of the Echoes best material was released.
●COMPILATIONS: *The Echoes Greatest Hits* (Crystal Ball 1984)★★.

ECLECTION

Formed in London, England, in 1967, Eclection took their name from the contrasting backgrounds of its original line-up. Although Mike Rosen (guitar), Kerilee Male (vocals), Georg Hultgren (bass) and Gerry Conway (drums) were not well-known figures, guitarist Trevor Lucas had established himself on the folk circuit following his arrival from Australia. The quintet used his undoubted talent to forge an imaginative folk rock style which used influences from both British and American sources. Male left the group in October 1968, following the release of Eclection's debut album. Her replacement was Dorris Henderson, a black American singer who had previously recorded two folk-influenced collections with guitarist John Renbourn. A further change occurred when John 'Poli' Palmer succeeded Rosen, but the group was sadly unable to fulfil its obvious potential. In October 1969 Palmer left to join Family, and Eclection simply folded. Lucas and Conway soon resurfaced in Fotheringay, while Hultgren later changed his surname to Kajanus and found fame with the pop group Sailor. In the 70s Henderson attempted to revive Eclection with different musicians, but she was largely unsuccessful.
●ALBUMS: *Eclection* (Elektra 1968)★★★.

EDDY, DUANE

b. 26 April 1938, Corning, New York, USA. The legendary simple 'twangy' guitar sound of Duane Eddy has made him one of rock 'n' roll's most famous instrumental artists. The sound was created after hearing Bill Justis's famous 'Raunchy' (the song that George Harrison first learned to play). Together with producer Lee Hazelwood, Eddy co-wrote a deluge of hits mixed with versions of standards, using the bass strings of his Grestch guitar recorded through an echo chamber. The debut 'Movin' 'N' Groovin'' made the lower end of the US chart, and for the next six years Eddy repeated this formula with greater success. His backing group, the Rebel Rousers was a tight, experienced band with a prominent saxophone sound played by Jim Horn and Steve Douglas, completed by pianist Larry Knechtel. Among their greatest hits were 'Rebel-Rouser', 'Shazam', 'Peter Gunn', 'Ballad Of Paladin' and 'Theme From Dixie'. The latter was a variation on the Civil War standard written in 1860. One of Eddy's most memorable hits was the superlative theme music for the film *Because They're Young*, brilliantly combining his bass notes with evocative strings. The song has been used by UK disc jockey Johnny Walker as his theme music for over 25 years and this classic still sounds fresh. Eddy's '(Dance With The) Guitar Man' was another major hit, which was unusual for the fact that the song had lyrics, sung by a female group. Eddy's albums played heavily on the use of 'twang' in the title, but that was exactly what the fans wanted.

The hits dried up in 1964 at the dawn of the Beatles' invasion, and for many years his sound was out of fashion. An attempt in the contemporary market was lambasted with *Duane Goes Dylan*. Apart from producing Phil Everly's excellent *Star Spangled Springer* in 1973, Eddy travelled the revival circuit, always finding a small but loyal audience in the UK. Tony Macauley wrote 'Play Me Like You Play Your Guitar' for him in 1975, and after more than a decade he was back in the UK Top 10. He slipped back into relative obscurity but returned to the charts in 1986 when he was flattered to be asked to play with the electro-synthesizer band Art Of Noise, all the more complimentary was that it was his song, 'Peter Gunn'. The following year Jeff Lynne produced his first album for many years, being joined by Paul McCartney, George Harrison and Ry Cooder, all paying tribute to the man who should have legal copyright on the word 'twang'.

●ALBUMS: *Have Twangy Guitar Will Travel* (1958)★★★, *Especially For You* (1958)★★★, *The 'Twang's The 'Thang'* (1959)★★★★, *Songs Of Our Heritage* (1960)★★★, *$1,000,000 Worth Of Twang* (1960)★★★★, *Girls! Girls! Girls!* (1961)★★★, *$1,000,000 Worth Of Twang Volume 2* (1962)★★★, *Twistin' And Twangin'* (RCA Victor 1962)★★★★, *Twisting With Duane Eddy* (1962)★★★, *Twangy Guitar-Silky Strings* (RCA Victor 1962)★★★★, *Dance With The Guitar Man* (RCA Victor 1963)★★★★, *In Person* (1963)★★★, *Surfin' With Duane Eddy* (1963)★★★, *Twang A Country Song* (RCA Victor 1963)★★, *Twanging Up A Storm!* (RCA Victor 1963)★★★, *Lonely Guitar* (RCA Victor 1964)★★★, *Water Skiing* (RCA Victor 1964)★★, *Twangsville* (RCA Victor 1965)★★, *Twangin' The Golden Hits* (RCA Victor 1965)★★★, *Duane Goes Bob Dylan* (RCA Victor 1965)★★, *Duane A Go Go* (RCA Victor 1965)★★, *Biggest Twang Of Them All* (RCA Victor 1966)★★, *Roaring Twangies* (RCA Victor 1967)★★, *Twangy Guitar* (1970)★★★, *Duane Eddy* (1987)★★★,

●COMPILATIONS: *The Best Of Duane Eddy* (RCA Victor 1966)★★★★, *The Vintage Years* (Sire 1975)★★★, *Legends Of Rock* (1975)★★★, *Twenty Terrific Twangies* (1981)★★★, *Greatest Hits* (1991)★★★★, *Twang Thang: The Duane Eddy Anthology* (1993)★★★★, *That Classic Twang* 2-CD (Bear Family 1994)★★★★, *Twangin' From Phoenix To L.A. - The Jamie Years* (Bear Family 1995)★★★★.

●FILMS: *Because They're Young* (1960).

EDISON LIGHTHOUSE

This UK conglomeration was essentially a vehicle for session singer Tony Burrows, who also sang with White Plains, the Brotherhood Of Man and the Pipkins. The backing musicians were originally part of a group called Greenfield Hammer before they became a studio 're-creation' and hit group. The Tony Macauley/Barry Mason composition 'Love Grows (Where My Rosemary Goes)' provided the breakthrough and zoomed to number 1 in the UK and also hit the US Top 5. While this was occurring, Burrows had already moved on to other projects, leaving his backing musicians to continue under the name Edison. Macauley, meanwhile, still owned the name Edison Lighthouse and conjured up another group with that title for recording and touring purposes. The manufactured spin-off group failed to exploit their chart-topping name, although they did manage to scrape into the lower rungs of the Top 50 with a weak follow-up, 'It's Up To You, Petula'.

EDSELS

This R&B vocal ensemble from Campbell, Ohio, USA, led by George Jones Jnr. (lead vocal), also included Marshall Sewell, James Reynolds, and brothers Harry and Larry Greene. They were named after the popular make of car. In 1959 they auditioned for a local music publisher who helped them secure a recording contract. Their debut single was the fast doo-wop outing 'Rama Lama Ding Dong' (written by Jones), originally released under the incorrect title of 'Lama Rama Ding Dong'. It was a local hit but flopped nationally. Two years later when Marcels had a big hit with the similar sounding doo-wop version of 'Blue Moon', a disc jockey was reminded of 'Rama Lama Ding Dong' and started playing it. Demand grew and it was re-released under its correct title and became a hit in the USA. By this time the Edsels had moved on and could not capitalize on their success. Although the original failed in the UK the song was a hit in 1978 when it was covered by Rocky Sharpe And The Replays.

●COMPILATIONS: *Rama Lama Ding Dong* (Relic 1993)★★.

EDWARDS, JACKIE

b. Wilfred Edwards, 1938, Jamaica, d. 15 August 1992. The honeyed tones of Jackie Edwards have graced hundreds of ska, R&B, soul, rocksteady, reggae and ballad recordings since he composed and sang 'Your Eyes Are Dreaming', a sentimental ballad, and the gentle Latin-beat 'Tell Me Darling', for future Island Records owner Chris Blackwell in 1959. Probably the most accomplished romantic singer and songwriter that Jamaica has ever produced, he has always had enough soul in his voice to escape the descent into schmaltz. In 1962, when Blackwell set up Island Records in London, Edwards made the trip to Britain with him. At Island in the early years, his duties included not only singing and songwriting but also delivering boxes of ska records by bus to the capital's suburban shops. His persistence paid off when, in 1966, the Spencer Davis Group scored two consecutive UK number 1 pop hits with his now classic compositions, 'Keep On Running' and 'Somebody Help Me'. In more recent years he has continued to issue records whose standards of production have been variable but on which his crooning has substantiated his sobriquet of 'the original cool ruler'.

●ALBUMS: *The Most Of ...* (Island 1963)★★★, *Stand*

Up For Jesus (Island 1964)★★★, *Come On Home* (Island 1966)★★★, *By Demand* (Island 1967)★★★, *Premature Golden Sands* (Island 1967)★★★, *I Do Love You* (Trojan 1973)★★★, *Sincerely* (Trojan 1978)★★, *King Of The Ghetto* (Black Music 1983)★★, *Original Cool Ruler* (Vista Sounds 1983)★★. With Millie Small: *Pledging My Love* (1967)★★★, *The Best Of Jackie & Millie* (1968)★★★.

●COMPILATIONS: *The Best Of* (Island 1966)★★★.

EIRE APPARENT

Originally known as the People, this Irish quartet - Mike Cox (lead guitar), Ernie Graham (vocals/guitar), Chris Stewart (bass) and Dave Lutton (drums) - came to prominence in 1967 when they were signed by the Mike Jeffery/Chas Chandler management team, which they shared with Jimi Hendrix and the Soft Machine. Hendrix produced and guested on the group's sole album, *Sunrise*. A crafted blend of pop and neo-psychedelia, this underrated collection featured several excellent performances, including the vibrant 'Yes I Need Someone'. In 1968 Eire Apparent supported Hendrix on a gruelling US tour, and they split up after its completion. Ernie Graham later joined Help Yourself, before recording a solo album on which he was backed by Brinsley Schwarz. Although he did not record with them, Henry McCullough was another former member of Eire Apparent. This respected guitarist subsequently featured in the Grease Band and Wings.

●ALBUMS: *Sunrise* (Buddah 1969)★★★.

ELBERT, DONNIE

b. 25 May 1936, New Orleans, Louisiana, USA, d. 31 January 1989. Elbert's prolific career began in the 50s as a member of the Vibraharps. His first solo hit, 'What Can I Do?', was released in 1957, but the singer's career was interrupted by a spell in the US Army. Discharged in 1961, recordings for Parkway Records and Checker then followed, before Elbert founded his own labels, Gateway/Upstate in 1964. His reputation was secured by 'Run Little Girl' and 'A Little Piece Of Leather', compulsive performances highlighting Donnie's irrepressible falsetto. The latter single became a standard in UK soul clubs when it was released on the Sue label and on the strength of this popularity Elbert came to the UK where he married and settled. The singer pursued his career with several releases, including an album of Otis Redding cover versions, *Tribute To A King*. Elbert returned to the USA in 1970 although his pounding version of the Supremes' 'Where Did Our Love Go?' (1972), was recorded in London. A hit on both sides of the Atlantic, it was followed in 1972 by 'I Can't Help Myself', another reworking of a Tamla/Motown classic. Elbert's last UK chart entry came with a new, but inferior, version of 'A Little Bit Of Leather' (1972), although he continued to appear in the US R&B listings up until 1977. Elbert later moved to Canada where he became an A&R director with Polygram Records.

●ALBUMS: *The Sensational Donnie Elbert Sings* (King 1959)★★★, *Tribute To A King* (1968)★★, *Where Did Our Love Go* (1971)★★, *Have I Sinned* (1971)★★, *Stop In The Name of Love* (1972)★★, *A Little Bit Of Leather* (1972)★★, *Roots Of Donnie Elbert* (1973)★★★, *Dancin' The Night Away* (1977)★★.

ELECTRIC FLAG

The brief career of the much vaunted Electric Flag was begun in 1967 by the late Mike Bloomfield, following his departure from the influential Paul Butterfield Blues Band. The original group comprised Bloomfield (b. 28 July 1944, Chicago, Illinois, USA, d. 15 February 1981; guitar), Buddy Miles (drums/vocals), Nick Gravenites (b. Chicago, Illinois, USA; vocals), Barry Goldberg (keyboards), Harvey Brooks (bass), Peter Strazza (tenor saxophone), Marcus Doubleday (trumpet) and Herbie Rich (baritone saxophone). All members were well-seasoned professionals coming from a variety of musical backgrounds. Their debut at the 1967 Monterey Pop Festival was a noble start. Their excellent *A Long Time Comin'* was released in 1968 with additional members Stemziel (Stemsy) Hunter and Mike Fonfara and was a significant hit in the USA. The tight brassy-tinged blues numbers were laced with Bloomfield's sparse but bitingly crisp Fender Stratocaster guitar. Tracks such as 'Killing Floor' were perfect examples of vintage Flag. The band was unable to follow this release, and immediately began to dissolve, with founder Bloomfield being the first to go. Miles attempted to hold the band together but the second album was a pale shadow of their debut, with only 'See To Your Neighbour' showing signs of a unified performance. Miles then left to form the Buddy Miles Express, while Gravenites became a songwriting legend in San Francisco. Brooks, following years of session work that included the Bloomfield/Kooper/Stills *Super Session*, reappeared as a member of Sky. An abortive Flag reunion produced the lacklustre and inappropriately titled *The Band Kept Playing*.

●ALBUMS: *The Trip* film soundtrack (Sidewalk 1967)★★, *A Long Time Comin'* (Columbia 1968)★★★★, *The Electric Flag* (Columbia 1969)★★, *The Band Kept Playing* (1974)★.

ELECTRIC PRUNES

Formed in Los Angeles in 1965, the Electric Prunes originally consisted of Jim Lowe (b. San Luis Obispo, California, USA; vocals/guitar/autoharp), Ken Williams (b. Long Beach, California, USA; lead guitar), James 'Weasel' Spagnola (b. Cleveland, Ohio, USA; guitar), Mark Tulin (b. Philadelphia, Pennsylvania, USA; bass) and Michael Weakley aka Quint (drums), although the latter was quickly replaced by Preston Ritter (b. Stockton, California, USA). The quintet made its debut with the low-key 'Ain't It Hard', before achieving two US Top 20 hits with 'I Had Too Much To Dream (Last Night)' and 'Get Me To The World On Time'. These exciting singles blended the drive of garage/punk rock, the rhythmic pulse of the Rolling Stones and the experimentalism of the emerging psychedelic movement. Such performances were enhanced by Dave Hassinger's accomplished production. The Prunes' debut album was hampered by indifferent material, but the excellent follow-up, *Underground*, featured three of the group's finest achievements, 'Hideaway', 'The Great Banana Hoax' and 'Long Day's Flight'. However the Prunes were sadly unable to sustain their hit profile and grew increasingly unhappy with the artistic restrictions placed on them by management and producer. Ritter was replaced by the prodigal Quint before the remaining original members dropped out during sessions for *Mass In F Minor*. This acclaimed combination of Gregorian styles and acid rock was composed and arranged by David Axelrod, who fulfilled the same role on a follow-up set, *Release Of An Oath*. An entirely new line-up - Ron Morgan (guitar), Mark Kincaid (b. Topeka, Kansas, USA; guitar), Brett Wade (b. Vancouver, British Columbia, Canada; bass) and Richard Whetstone (b. Hutchinson, Kansas, USA; drums) - completed the lacklustre *Just Good Old Rock 'N' Roll*, which bore no trace of the founding line-up's sense of adventure. The Electric Prunes' name was then abandoned.

●ALBUMS: *The Electric Prunes (I Had Too Much To Dream Last Night)* (Reprise 1967)★★★, *Underground* (Reprise 1967)★★★, *Mass In F Minor* (Reprise 1967)★★, *Release Of An Oath* (Reprise 1968)★★, *Just Good Old Rock 'N' Roll* (Reprise 1969)★.
●COMPILATIONS: *Long Day's Flight* (1986)★★★.

ELEKTRA RECORDS

Founded in New York, USA, in 1950 by student and traditional music enthusiast Jac Holtzman, this much respected label initially showcased recordings drawn from America's rich heritage. Early releases included Jean Ritchie's *Songs Of Her Kentucky Mountain Family* and Ed McCurdy's *Songs Of The Old West*, but the catalogue also boasted collections encompassing material from international sources. Elektra also made several notable jazz and blues recordings but, as the 50s progressed, became renowned for its interest in contemporary folk. It thus attracted many of the performers from the Greenwich Village and New England enclaves, notably Judy Collins, Tom Paxton, Koerner, Ray And Glover, Fred Neil and Phil Ochs, before embracing electric styles in 1966 with the Paul Butterfield Blues Band and Love. Elektra then became established on America's west coast and its transformation from folk to rock was confirmed the following year with the Doors. Subsequent signings included the MC5, Rhinoceros, the Stooges and Earth Opera, while the label achieved concurrent commercial success with Bread. Elektra also became an important outlet for many singer-songwriters, and its catalogue included superior releases by David Ackles, Tom Rush, Tim Buckley, Harry Chapin, Incredible String Band and Carly Simon. In 1971 Elektra was absorbed into the WEA conglomerate and incongruous releases by the New Seekers and Queen robbed the company of its individuality. Two years later, and with the departure of Holtzman, the label was amalgamated with Asylum and

for much of the decade remained the junior partner. Television's *Marquee Moon* rekindled memories of the outlet's classic era, while during the 80s Elektra was responsible for releases by 10,000 Maniacs, the Screaming Blue Messiahs and the Pixies (the latter US only). The label was unwilling, or unable, to shake off its early heritage which was commemorated in a series of boxed sets under the umbrella title *The Jac Holtzman Years*. Elektra's 40th anniversary was celebrated with *Rubiayat*, in which representatives from the current roster performed songs drawn from the 'classic' era.

●ALBUMS: *What's Shakin'* (1966)★★★, *Select Elektra* (1967)★★★, *Begin Here* (1969)★★★, *O Love Is Teasing: Anglo-American Mountain Balladry* (1983)★★★, *Bleecker & MacDougal: The Folk Scene Of The 60s* (1983)★★★, *Crossroads: White Blues In The 60s* (1985)★★★, *Elektrock: The Sixties* (c.1985)★★★.

ELGINS

US-born Johnny Dawson, Cleo Miller and Robert Fleming, later replaced by Norbert McClean, sang together in three Detroit vocal groups in the late 50s, the Sensations, the Five Emeralds and the Downbeats. Under the last of these names, they recorded two singles for Motown in 1959 and 1962. Also in 1962, Saundra Mallett (later Saundra Mallett Edwards) issued 'Camel Walk' for Tamla, backed by the Vandellas. Motown suggested that she join forces with the Downbeats, and the new group was named the Elgins after the title originally used by the Temptations when they first joined Motown. In the fiercely competitive climate of Motown Records in the mid-60s, the Elgins were forced to wait three years before they could issue a single, but 'Darling Baby' - written and produced by Holland/Dozier/Holland - reached the US R&B Top 10 early in 1966. 'Heaven Must Have Sent You', which also exhibited the traditional Motown sound of the period, matched that success, but after one further hit in 1967, the group broke up. In 1971, the group enjoyed two unexpected UK Top 20 hits when Motown reissued 'Heaven Must Have Sent You' and the former b-side 'Put Yourself In My Place'. The Elgins re-formed to tour Britain, with Yvonne Allen (a former session vocalist) taking the place of Saundra Mallett; but plans for the revitalized group to renew their recording career foundered. In 1989 Yvonne Allen, Johnny Dawson, Norman Mclean and Jimmy Charles recorded a new arrangement of 'Heaven Must Have Sent You' for producer Ian Levine. They continued working for his Motor City label in the 90s, releasing *Take The Train* and *Sensational*. The original lead vocalist on all their Motown material, Saundra Edwards, was also recording for the same label.

●ALBUMS: *Darling Baby* (VIP 1966)★★★, *Take The Train* (1990)★★, *Sensational* (1991)★★.

ELLIOT, 'MAMA' CASS

b. Ellen Naiomi Cohen, 19 September 1941, Baltimore, Maryland, USA, d. 29 July 1974, London, England. Elliot's professional singing career began in the early 60s as a member of the Big Three, a pivotal folk group that included her first husband, James Hendricks, and Tim Rose. When Rose embarked on a solo career, the remaining duo founded the Mugwumps with Denny Doherty and Zalman Yanovsky. Elliot later joined the former in the Mamas And The Papas, one of the most enduring folk rock attractions of the 60s. Her assured, soaring voice proved ideal for songwriter John Phillips' optimistic compositions, but internal disputes robbed the group of its momentum. In 1968 Cass began an independent career with *Dream A Little Dream*, the title track from which reached the US and UK Top 20s. 'It's Getting Better' from *Bubblegum, Lemonade And ... Something For Mama* fared better still, climbing to number 8 in the UK despite competition from Paul Jones' cover version. Elliot's third set, *Make Your Own Kind Of Music*, preceded a temporary Mamas And The Papas reunion, after which she forged an equally short-lived partnership with ex-Traffic singer/guitarist Dave Mason. Tiring of her erstwhile image, Cass began courting a wider MOR audience, but later recordings lacked the naïve charm of their predecessors. Elliot nonetheless remained a popular figure and her death in July 1974, reportedly from choking on a sandwich, robbed pop of one of its most endearing characters.

●ALBUMS: *Dream A Little Dream* (1968)★★, *Bubblegum, Lemonade And ... Something For Mama* (1969)★★, *Make Your Own Kind Of Music* (1969)★★, *Cass Elliot* (1971)★★, *Dave Mason And Mama Cass* (1971)★★, *The Road Is No Place For A Lady* (1972)★★, *Don't Call Me Mama Anymore* (1973)★★.
●COMPILATIONS: *Mama's Big Ones* (1971)★★.

ELLIOTT, BERN, AND THE FENMEN

Formed in Erith, Kent, England, in 1961, Bern Elliott And The Fenmen spent many of their early years playing in German clubs. Signed to Decca in 1963, they had a UK Top 20 hit with their debut single, 'Money', arguably the finest cover version of this recurrent beat group favourite. A rendition of 'New Orleans' provided another chart entry, but the singer and backing group broke up following the release of 'Good Times'. While the Fenmen: Alan Judge (guitar), Wally Allen (guitar), Eric Willmer (bass) and Jon Povey (drums) - continued to record in an engaging, close-harmony style, Elliott formed a new group, the Klan, around Dave Cameron (organ), Tim Hamilton (guitar), John Silby-Pearce (bass) and Pete Adams (drums). Despite several excellent singles, including 'Voodoo Woman' (1965), the vocalist was unable to regain their initial success. Former colleagues Allen and Povey later found fame in the Pretty Things.
●ALBUMS: *The Beat Years* (1988)★★.

ELLIOTT, RAMBLIN' JACK

b. Elliott Charles Adnopoz, 1 August 1931, Brooklyn, New York, USA. The son of an eminent doctor, Elliott forsook his middle-class upbringing as a teenager to join a travelling rodeo. Embarrassed by his family name, he dubbed

himself Buck Elliott, before adopting the less-mannered first name, Jack. In 1949 he met and befriended Woody Guthrie who in turn became his mentor and prime influence. Elliott travelled and sang with Guthrie whenever possible, before emerging as a talent in his own right. He spent a portion of the 50s in Europe, introducing America's folk heritage to a new and eager audience. By the early 60s he had resettled in New York where he became an inspirational figure to a new generation of performers, including Bob Dylan. *Jack Elliott Sings The Songs Of Woody Guthrie* was the artist's first American album. This self-explanatory set was succeeded by *Ramblin' Jack Elliott*, in which he shook off the imitator tag by embracing a diverse selection of material, including songs drawn from the American tradition, the Scottish music-hall and Ray Charles. Further releases included *Jack Elliott*, which featured Dylan playing harmonica under the pseudonym Tedham Porterhouse, and *Young Brigham* in 1968, which offered songs by Tim Hardin and the Rolling Stones as well as an adventurous use of dobros, autoharps, fiddles and tablas. The singer also guested on albums by Tom Rush, Phil Ochs and Johnny Cash. In 1975 Elliott was joined by Dylan during an appearance at the New York, Greenwich Village club, The Other End, and he then became a natural choice for Dylan's nostalgic carnival tour, the Rolling Thunder Revue. Elliot later continued his erratic, but intriguing, path and an excellent 1984 release, *Kerouac's Last Dream*, showed his power undiminished.

●ALBUMS: *Jack Elliott Sings The Songs Of Woody Guthrie* (1960)★★★, *Ramblin' Jack Elliott* (1961)★★★, *Jack Elliott* (1964)★★★, *Ramblin' Cowboy* (mid-60s)★★★, *Young Brigham* (1968)★★★, *Jack Elliott Sings Guthrie And Rogers* (1976)★★★, *Kerouac's Last Dream* (1984)★★★, *South Coast* (Red House 1995)★★★, *Me And Bobby McGee* (Rounder 1996).
●COMPILATIONS: *Talking Dust Bowl - The Best Of Ramblin' Jack Elliott* (1989)★★★, *Hard Travelin'* (1990)★★★, *Ramblin' Jack - The Legendary Topic Masters* (Topic 1996)★★★.

ELLIS, SHIRLEY

b. New York, New York, USA. Before striking out on a solo career in 1963, Ellis served an apprenticeship singing with an unsuccessful vocal group, the Metronones. Her strong voice was used for good effect on dance-floor ravers 'The Nitty Gritty' (number 4 R&B and number 8 pop in 1963) and '(That's) What The Nitty Gritty Is' (number 14 R&B 1964), and her future looked bright. Ellis, however, soon found herself in novelty song territory with catchy ditties written by her manager Lincoln Chase, namely 'The Name Game' (number 4 R&B and number 3 pop in 1965) and 'The Clapping Song (Clap Pat Clap Slap)' (number 16 R&B and number 8 pop in 1965). The latter was the only UK success for Ellis, amazingly hitting twice, in 1965, when it reached number 6, and on an EP in 1978. The Belle Stars successfully revived 'The Clapping Song' in 1982.

●ALBUMS: *In Action* (Congress 1964)★★, *The Name*

Game (Congress 1965)★★★, *Sugar, Let's Shing A Ling* (Columbia 1967)★★.
●COMPILATIONS: *The Very Best Of ...* (Taragon 1995)★★★.

ELLISON, ANDY

b. England. Ellison has had a varied musical career. He began as a solo singer but later worked with John's Children, Jet and eventually late 70s quirky pop/punk band the Radio Stars. In all he released three solo singles for three different labels in the late 60s - 'It's Been A Long Time' (Track), 'Fool From Upper Eden' (CBS) and 'You Can't Do That' (S.N.B.). None breached the charts or sold in substantial quantities, although each has become a collector's item due to Ellison's subsequent musical activities. In the 90s Allison was involved in a re-formation of the ever-popular John's Children.

ELLISON, LORRAINE

b. 1943, Philadelphia, Pennsylvania, USA, d. 17 August 1985. Although only associated with a few minor hits in the history of R&B, Ellison's intense, dramatic, and highly gospelized vocal delivery helped define deep soul as a particular style. Ellison recorded with two gospel groups, the Ellison Singers and the Golden Chords, but left the latter in 1964 to pursue a solo career in R&B music. 'I Dig You Baby' (number 22 R&B) in 1965 was her first chart entry, but it was the powerful 'Stay With Me' (number 11 R&B, number 64 pop) in 1966 that established her reputation. Written and produced by Jerry Ragovoy, the song with Ellison's awe-inspiring vocal pleas ultimately proved to be a spectacular one-off performance. Nothing in her subsequent recordings emulated its naked emotion, and even the excellent 'Heart Be Still' (number 43 R&B, number 89 pop), from 1967, was something of an anti-climax. Ellison never charted again, not even with the original version of 'Try Just A Little Bit Harder' (1968), which rock singer Janis Joplin later remade with great success. Ellison's compositions on which she often collaborated with her manager, Sam Bell (of Garnet Mimms And The Enchanters fame), were recorded by Howard Tate and Garnet Mimms.
●ALBUMS: *Heart And Soul* (Warners 1966)★★, *Stay With Me* (Warners 1970)★★★, *Lorraine Ellison* (Warners 1974)★★.
●COMPILATIONS: *The Best Of Philadelphia's Queen* (1976)★★★, *Stay With Me* (1985)★★★.

END

Comprising Hugh Attwool (drums), Dave Brown (bass/vocals), Nick Graham (keyboards/vocals), Colin Griffin (steel guitar/vocals) and Terry Taylor (guitar), most of the initial enthusiasm surrounding this London, England, quintet was due to the fact that they were managed by Bill Wyman. The group's sound was a superior blend of late 60s psychedelic elements with forthright hard rock properties, and much was expected of their 1969 Decca Records debut album *Introspection*. However, despite the presence of Wyman's fellow Rolling Stone Charlie Watts (playing tabla on the excellent 'Shades Of Orange', which was recorded during breaks from the sessions that resulted in the Stones' *Their Satanic Majesties Request* album) and Nicky Hopkins, it proved commercially unsuccessful. Previously they had released two singles, 'I Can't Get Any Joy' and an earlier version of 'Shades Of Orange', but after the failure of their debut album the group transmuted into Tucky Buzzard. That group, still under the stewardship of Wyman as producer, released three further albums in the 70s but again success eluded them.
●ALBUMS: *Introspection* (Decca 1969)★★, *In The Beginning ... The End* (Tenth Planet 1996)★★.

EPISODE SIX

This respected beat group evolved in 1964 when two amateur groups amalgamated. Roger Glover (bass), Harvey Shields (drums) and Tony Lander (guitar) were former members of the Madisons; Sheila Carter-Dimmock (organ), her brother Graham (rhythm guitar) and Andy Ross (vocals) were from the Lightnings. Ross, who quickly tired of touring, left in May 1965, and was replaced by Ian Gillan. The sextet had already secured a recording deal with Pye; 'Put Yourself In My Place', written by the Hollies' team, Clarke/Hicks/Nash, duly became their debut single the following January. Episode Six specialized in releasing cover versions, bringing strong harmony work to the Beatles' 'Here, There And Everywhere', the Tokens' 'I Hear Trumpets Blow' and Tim Rose's 'Morning Dew'. Lack of direction doubtlessly doomed their commercial prospects, but despite this, two solo singles, by Sheila Carter-Dimmock and Graham Carter, were also issued. The latter's release, credited to 'Neo Maya', was a cover version of 'I Won't Hurt You', originally recorded by the West Coast Pop Art Experimental Band.
Shields was replaced by former Pirates drummer John Kerrison in 1967. The following year the sextet switched to MGM, dropping the 'Six' suffix for one single, 'Little One'. Mick Underwood (ex-Outlaws) then joined in place of a disenchanted Kerrison, after which the group joined the Chapter One label for two more singles. Their final release, 'Mozart Versus The Rest', was a brazen pop/classical workout. Plans for an album, *The Story So Far* were mooted, but in July 1969 Ian Gillan was invited to join Deep Purple. Within weeks he was joined by Roger Glover, although Underwood kept Episode Six alive with the addition of Johnny Gustafson (bass, ex-Big Three) and Peter Robinson (keyboards). In 1970 the three broke away to found progressive act Quatermass, effectively ending the career of Episode Six.
●COMPILATIONS: *Put Yourself In My Place* (1987)★★★, *The Roots Of Deep Purple: The Complete Episode Six* (1992)★★★.

EPSTEIN, BRIAN

b. Brian Samuel Epstein, 1934, Liverpool, England, d. 27 August 1967. One of the most famous pop managers in music business history, Epstein began his working life as a provincial shopkeeper, overseeing the North End Road Music Stores (NEMS) in central Liverpool. His life took a new direction on Saturday 28 October 1961 when a customer requested a record entitled 'My Bonnie' by a group called the Beatles. When Epstein subsequently attended one of their gigs at the Cavern club in Mathew Street he was drawn into the alien netherworld of leather-clad beat groups and, against the advice of his friends, became a pop manager. His early efforts at promoting the Beatles proved haphazard, but using his influence with record companies he secured a number of interviews with important A&R representatives. A slew of rejections followed, but Decca Records at least offered the Beatles an audition before finally turning them down. Epstein took his revenge by crediting the unfortunate Dick Rowe with the immortal words: 'Groups of guitarists are on the way out'.

Epstein's tardiness in securing a record deal did not diminish his abilities in other areas. He transformed the Beatles into a more professional outfit, banned them from swearing or eating on stage and even encouraged the establishment of a rehearsed repertoire. Perhaps his most lasting contribution at this point was persuading them to replace their menacing, black leather garb with smart, grey lounge suits, with eye-catching matching collars. By the spring of 1962, Epstein at last won a record deal thanks to the intuitive intervention of producer George Martin. A near crisis followed shortly afterwards when Epstein had to oversee the dismissal of drummer Pete Best, who was replaced by Ringo Starr. During October 1962, a management contract was belatedly finalized with the Beatles by which Epstein received 25 per cent of their earnings, a figure he maintained for all future signings. Weeks later, he struck a deal with music publisher Dick James, which culminated in the formation of Northern Songs, a company dealing exclusively with compositions by John Lennon and Paul McCartney. In an extremely clever and unusual deal for the period, the powers agreed on a 50/50 split: half to Dick James and his partner Charles Emmanuel Silver; 20 per cent each to Lennon and McCartney, and 10 per cent to Epstein.

Long before the Beatles became the most successful entertainers in British music history, Epstein had signed his second group Gerry And The Pacemakers. Scouring the Cavern for further talent he soon added Tommy Quickly, the Fourmost, Billy J. Kramer And The Dakotas, the Big Three and Cilla Black. The spree of NEMS signings during 1963 was the most spectacular managerial coup since Larry Parnes' celebrated discoveries during the late 50s. More importantly, the artists dominated the UK charts throughout the year, logging an incredible nine number 1 hits spanning 32 weeks at the top. By early 1964, Beatlemania had crossed from Britain to America and NEMS had transformed from a small family business into a multi-million pound organization. The strength of the company ensured that the Beatles had few administrative problems during the Epstein era. Scrupulously fair, he even allowed his charges a 10 per cent interest in

NEMS. One area where Epstein was deemed fallible was in the merchandising agreements that he concluded on behalf of the Beatles. Ironically, it was the result of delegating the matter to the inexperienced solicitor David Jacobs that the group found themselves receiving a mere 10 per cent of the sums received by the company set up to merchandise goods in their name. By the mid-60s, licences had been granted for every product that the American merchandising mentality could conceive. This meant not only badges, dolls and toys, but even cans of Beatle breath. The lost revenue that Brian had allowed to slip through his fingers was gruesomely revealed in the pages of the *Wall Street Journal*. According to their figures, Americans spent approximately $50 million on Beatles goods up to the end of 1964, while the world market was estimated at roughly £40 million. Although Epstein attempted to rectify the poor merchandising deal through litigation and even contributed massive legal expenses from his own pocket, the stigma of the unfortunate deal remained. Few pointed out that it was less Epstein's error than that of the inexperienced Jacobs, who had agreed to the arrangement without consulting his client.

The merchandising dispute has all too often eclipsed Epstein's achievements in other areas. It deserves to be remembered that the Liverpudlian effectively ushered in the era of stadium rock with the Beatles' Hollywood Bowl concert, an event which changed rock economics for ever. Even while the Beatles were conquering the New World, Epstein was expanding his empire. Although he signed a couple of unsuccessful artists, most of the NEMS stable enjoyed tremendous success. The career of Cilla Black was a tribute to Epstein's creative management. He helped her adapt to the rigours of showbusiness success with a feminine solicitude typical of a would-be dress designer. More importantly, however, he immediately recognized her lasting charm as the gauche, unpretentious girl-next-door, an image that another manager might have suppressed. Epstein's expert exploitation of her appeal paved the way for her eventual acceptance and remarkable success as a television host.

When the Beatles ceased touring after the summer of 1966, Epstein's role in their day-to-day lives was minimal. For a time, he attempted to find satisfaction in other areas, purchasing the Savile Theatre in London's Shaftesbury Avenue and alternating serious drama with Sunday pop shows. Ever-puzzling, Epstein even sponsored an Anglo-Spanish bullfighter named Henry Higgins and astonished his colleagues by attempting to persuade the perpetually nervous Billy J. Kramer to pursue an acting career. NEMS, meanwhile, ceased to inspire the entrepreneur and he inexplicably offered a 51 per cent controlling interest to the Australian adventurer Robert Stigwood. By 1967, Epstein was losing control. Drug dependence and homosexual guilt brought him to the verge of a nervous breakdown and attempted suicide. He suffered at the hands of the press for advocating the use of the drug LSD. On August Bank Holiday 1967 the Beatles were in north Wales attending a course in transcendental meditation with their new mentor the Maharishi Mahesh Yogi. Brian, meanwhile, was lying dead at his London home. The inquest subsequently established that he had died from a cumulative overdose of the sleep-inducing drug Carbitrol. Although suicide was suspected and some fanciful conspiracy theories have suggested the remote possibility of foul play, the coroner concluded with a prosaic verdict of accidental death from 'incautious self-overdoses'.

In spite of his foibles, Epstein is rightly regarded as a great manager, possibly the greatest in British pop history. Judged in the context of his era, his achievements were remarkable. Although it is often claimed that he did not exploit the Beatles' earning power to its maximum degree, he most certainly valued their reputation above all else. During his tenure as manager, he insulated them from corporate avarice and negotiated contracts that prevented EMI from marketing cheap reissues or unauthorized compilations. In this sense, he was the complete antithesis of Elvis Presley's manager, Colonel Tom Parker, who allowed his artist to atrophy through a decade of bad movies. As the custodian of the Beatles' international reputation, Epstein's handling of their career was exemplary. For Epstein, honour meant more than profit and he brought an integrity to pop management that few of his successors have matched.

●FURTHER READING: *A Cellarfull Of Noise*, Brian Epstein. *Brian Epstein: The Man Who Made The Beatles*, Ray Coleman.

EQUALS

Twins Derv and Lincoln Gordon (b. 29 June 1948, Jamaica; vocals and rhythm guitar, respectively), Eddie Grant (b. 5 March 1948, Guyana; lead guitar), Patrick Lloyd (b. 17 March 1948, Holloway, London, England; rhythm guitar) and John Hall (b. 25 October 1947, Holloway, London, England; drums) began playing together in 1965 on a council estate in Hornsey Rise, north London. Their best-remembered single, 'Baby Come Back', was recorded the following year as a b-side, but the quintet's early releases made little impression. Over the ensuing months the group became highly regarded on the Continent, where they toured extensively. 'Baby Come Back' became a major hit in Germany during 1967 and later topped the charts in Holland and Belgium. This propulsive, infectious song was then reissued in Britain where it eventually rose to number 1. Although the Equals enjoyed other hits, only 'Viva Bobby Joe' (1969) and 'Black Skinned Blue-Eyed Boys' (1970) reached the Top 10 as their reliance on a tested formula wore thin. Chief songwriter Grant left for a solo career in 1971, after which the group underwent several changes in personnel before finding security on the cabaret circuit. However, their career was resurrected in 1978 when Grant, by then a self-sufficient artist and entrepreneur, signed them to his Ice label for *Mystic Synster*.

●ALBUMS: *Unequalled Equals* (President 1967)★★★, *Equals Explosion* aka *Equal Sensational Equals* (President 1968)★★★, *Equals Supreme* (President 1968)★★★, *Baby Come Back* (1968)★★★, *Equals Strike Back* (President 1969)★★, *Equals At The Top* (President 1970)★★, *Equals Rock Around The Clock* (1974)★★, *Doin' The 45s* (1975)★★★, *Born Ya* (Mercury 1976)★★, *Mystic Synster* (1978)★★.

●COMPILATIONS: *The Best Of The Equals* (President 1969)★★★, *Greatest Hits* (1974)★★★, *The Very Best Of* (1993)★★★.

ESCORTS (UK)

Terry Sylvester (vocals/guitar), John Kinrade (lead guitar) and Mike Gregory (b. 1947; vocals/bass) formed the Escorts at Liverpool's Rose Lane school in 1962. They were originally augmented by drummer John Foster, aka Johnny Sticks, a cousin of Ringo Starr, replaced by Pete Clark (b. 1947) in 1963. The quartet made their debut in April 1964 with a powerful interpretation of 'Dizzie Miss Lizzie', before scoring a minor hit two months later with 'The One To Cry'. Their next release, 'I Don't Want To Go On Without You', was also recorded by the Moody Blues, who secured the chart entry. This undermined the Escorts' confidence, and subsequent releases, although carefully crafted, proved unsuccessful. The group's line-up was also unstable. Sylvester left for the Swinging Blue Jeans, from where he later replaced Graham Nash in the Hollies and by mid-1966, Kinrade and Gregory were the sole original members. Paddy Chambers (guitar, ex-Big Three; Paddy, Klaus And Gibson) and Paul Comerford (drums, ex-Cryin' Shames) completed the group featured on 'From Head To Toe', the Escorts' final single. This accomplished performance featured Paul McCartney on tambourine, but the quartet split up within weeks of its release.

●ALBUMS: *3 Down 4 To Go* (1973)★★.

●COMPILATIONS: *From The Blue Angel* (1982)★★.

ESQUIRES

Formed in Milwaukee, USA, in 1957 with a line-up featuring Gilbert Moorer, Alvis Moorer and Betty Moorer. Originally conceived as a doo-wop group, the Esquires were briefly augmented by Harvey Scales before Sam Pace joined in 1961. In 1965 Betty Moorer was replaced by Shawn Taylor. The group then moved to Chicago where they signed to the Bunky label. An original song, 'Get On Up', was recorded with the help of Millard Edwards, who sang its distinctive bass line. Edwards became a permanent member when this infectious single was an R&B hit in 1967. Shawn Taylor left before a similar-sounding follow-up, 'And Get Away', was issued, but rejoined in 1971. That same year, 'Girls In The City', featuring Taylor as lead, was a Top 20 US R&B hit. The opportunistic 'Get Up '76' was the Esquires most recent hit; by the early 80s only Gilbert and Alvis Moorer remained from the group's heyday.

●ALBUMS: *Get On Up And Get Away* (1967)★★, with the Marvelows *Chi-Town Showdown* (1982)★★★.

ESQUIVEL!

b. Juan Garcia Esquivel, 1918, Mexico. Although he was a

huge inspiration for the revival of 'lounge' or 'easy listening' music in the 90s, Esquivel in fact began recording his heavily orchestrated pop muzak four decades earlier. Although none of his recordings from this period charted, he was widely recognized as an influence on Californian music of the time with his swinging pop arrangements. Indeed, in the 70s Steely Dan acknowledged Esquivel as the reason they introduced marimba, vibes and percussion into the recording of *Pretzel Logic*. Esquivel's intention was to realize the possibilities allowed by the development of stereo technology, and his records were thus infused with all manner of diverting intrusions such as whistling and pinball percussion, which adorned big band Latin pop. He had been brought to America in 1957 by the RCA Records executive Herman Diaz Jnr. and became a prolific bandleader, overseeing singers including Yvonne DeBourbon and Randy Van Horne. As 'The Sights And Sounds Of Esquivel' they toured widely in the USA, appearing in New York, Hollywood and Las Vegas. A visual as well as aural perfectionist, one anecdote from these times concerns Esquivel's development of a special 'walk' so as not to crease his shoes. The women in his band were severely disciplined. Forced to step on scales before each performance, they would be summarily fined $5 for each pound of weight gained. By the artist's own reckoning, his music has been used in over 200 television shows, including *Baywatch*. In the 90s Esquivel was widely celebrated as 'the father of Lounge Music' with the release of compilation albums on Bar/None Records which became staples of US college radio. Contemporary groups including Combustible Edison, Stereolab and Black Velvet Flag appropriated his style, while Chicago's Vinyl Dance nightclub dedicated itself to his music. Despite being bed-ridden after a fall, he relished this new wave of attention. 'Perhaps I was too far ahead of my time,' he told *Rolling Stone* in 1995.

●ALBUMS: *To Love Again* (RCA Victor 1957)★★★, *Four Corners Of The World* (RCA Victor 1958)★★★, *Other Worlds, Other Sounds* (RCA Victor 1958)★★★★, *Exploring New Sounds In Hi-Fi* (RCA Victor 1959)★★★, *Exploring New Sounds In Stereo* (RCA Victor 1959)★★★, *Strings Aflame* (RCA Victor 1959)★★★, *Infinity In Sound* (RCA Victor 1960) *Infinity In Sound Vol. 2* (RCA Victor 1961)★★★, *Latin-Esque* (RCA Victor 1962)★★★, *More Of Other Worlds Other Sounds* (Reprise 1962)★★★, *Other Sounds, Other Worlds, Exploring New Sounds In Stereo* (RCA 1963)★★★.

●COMPILATIONS: *Esquivel!* (Bar/None 1994)★★★★, *Space Age Bachelor Pad Music* (Bar/None 1994)★★★★, *Music From A Sparkling Planet* (Bar/None 1995)★★★★, *Merry Xmas* (Bar/None 1996)★★.

ESSEX

A rock 'n' roll vocal group formed in the early 60s by members of the US Marine Corps at Camp LeJeune, North Carolina, USA. Members were lead Anita Humes, Walter Vickers, Rodney Taylor, Rudolph Johnson, and Billie Hill. The group exploded on the scene in 1963 with three singles, 'Easier Said Than Done' (number 1 R&B and pop), 'A Walkin' Miracle' (number 11 R&B, number 12 pop), and 'She's Got Everything' (number 56 pop). The vocal sound of the group, unlike many African-American groups of the day, featured meagre vocal harmony and concentrated on the warm engaging voice of Humes, and the group never sang R&B. After the initial hits, their company, Roulette, focused on Humes, and on their final album put only her picture on the cover, calling the artist Anita Humes With The Essex. The Essex's later soul-styled recordings, although thoroughly appealing, never found a market. In 1966 the group recorded a final single for Bang Records before disbanding.

●ALBUMS: *Easier Said Than Done* (Roulette 1963)★★, *A Walkin' Miracle* (Roulette 1963)★★, *Young And Lively* (Roulette 1964)★★.

●COMPILATIONS: *The Best Of The Essex* (Sequel 1994)★★.

EVANS, BILL (PIANIST)

b. 16 August 1929, Plainfield, New Jersey, USA, d. 15 September 1980. One of the most important and influential of modern jazz pianists, Evans studied at Southeastern Louisiana University, while summer jobs with Mundell Lowe and Red Mitchell introduced him to the jazz scene. He was in the army from 1951-54; played with Jerry Wald in 1954-55; studied at the Mannes School of Music, New York 1955-56; then began a full-time jazz career with clarinettist Tony Scott. Through Lowe he was introduced to Riverside Records and made his recording debut as leader (of a trio) in 1956. Evans then recorded with Charles Mingus and George Russell. In 1958 he joined Miles Davis, playing a central role on the album *Kind Of Blue*, which was so influential in the development of modal jazz. Evans left Davis after less than a year to form his own trio, and favoured that format thereafter. His recordings with Scott La Faro and Paul Motian (1959-61) represent the summit of the genre (*Portrait In Jazz*, *Explorations*, live sessions at the Village Vanguard). The tragic loss of La Faro in a car accident deprived Evans of his most sympathetic partner, and the later recordings do not quite approach the level of those on Riverside; Eddie Gomez was the most compatible of later bassists. Evans recorded solo, most interestingly on the double-tracked *Conversations With Myself*; in duo with Jim Hall, Bob Brookmeyer and Tony Bennett; and in larger groups with such players as Lee Konitz, Zoot Sims and Freddie Hubbard. Towards the end of his life Evans was establishing a new trio with Marc Johnson and Joe LaBarbera, and playing with new-found freedom. Although he eventually kicked his heroin habit, he experienced continuing drug problems and these contributed to his early death from a stomach ulcer and other complications.

Evans' background is significant; he matured away from the bebop scene in New York. Although his earlier playing was indebted to bopper Bud Powell and more strikingly to hardbop pianist Horace Silver, as well as to Lennie Tristano, he gradually developed a more lyrical, 'impressionistic' approach, with an understated strength far removed from the aggression of bebop. His ideas were influential in the development of modal jazz and hence of the John Coltrane school, whose major pianistic voice was McCoy Tyner; however, he did not pursue that direction himself, finding it insufficiently lyrical and melodic for his needs. The softer, understated, less obviously dissonant idiom of the great trio with La Faro and Motian embodies the rival pianistic tradition to that of the eventually overbearing Tyner. Contemporary jazz piano tends towards a synthesis of the Evans and Tyner styles, but the Evans legacy is with hindsight the richer one. Technically, Evans led the way in the development of a genuinely pianistic modern jazz style. Most important was his much-imitated but completely distinctive approach to harmony, in particular to the way the notes of the chord are arranged or 'voiced'. Red Garland, who preceded Evans in the Miles Davis group, had moved away from Bud Powell's functional 'shell voicings', but it was Evans (and to a lesser extent Wynton Kelly) who first fully defined the new style of 'rootless voicings'. These retain only the essential tones of the chord (dispensing with the root itself, often played by the bassist), and form the grammatical basis of contemporary jazz piano. Evans employed a wider variety of tone-colour than is usual in jazz piano, with subtle use of the sustaining pedal and varying emphasis of notes in the chord voicing. He improvises thematically, 'rationally'; as he said, 'the science of building a line, if you can call it a science, is enough to occupy somebody for 12 lifetimes'. His influence on pianists is as considerable as that of Coltrane on saxophonists , most notably on several artists known to a wider public than he was, such as Herbie Hancock, Keith Jarrett and Chick Corea, but also on Hampton Hawes, Paul Bley and more recently Michel Petrucciani. Legions of imitators have tended to conceal from listeners the complete originality of his style as it developed in the late 50s and early 60s, and Evans's music still continues to yield up secrets.

A trio setting was Evans's ideal format, and his solo piano style is (with the exception of the double-tracked *Conversations With Myself*) less compelling. The trio with La Faro and Motian is surely one of the great combinations in jazz history. The 'collective improvisation' of this group involved rhythmic innovation, with the bass in particular escaping its standard timekeeping role. Evans commented that 'at that time nobody else was opening trio music in quite that way, letting the music move from an internalized beat, instead of laying it down all the time explicitly'. However, the apparent lassitude of Evans' mature style has led to much misunderstanding and criticism. Archie Shepp commented (incorrectly) that 'Debussy and Satie have already done those things'; Cecil Taylor found Evans 'so uninteresting, so predictable and so lacking in vitality'. As James Collier wrote, 'If Milton can write 'Il Pensero', surely Bill Evans can produce a 'Turn Out The Stars'. But Milton also wrote 'L'Allegro', and Evans is not often seen dancing in the chequer'd shade'. Melancholy is Evans' natural mood, and rhythm his

greatest weakness; he does not swing powerfully, and is not interested enough in the 'groove'. Cannonball Adderley commented that when the pianist joined Davis, 'Miles changed his style from very hard to a softer approach. Bill was brilliant in other areas, but he couldn't make the real hard things come off . . . '. When Evans plays in a determined uptempo (as on *Montreux 1968*) the result can sound merely forced and frantic, and unlike Wynton Kelly or Tommy Flanagan, he is not a first-choice accompanist. Nonetheless, he swings effectively when pushed by a drummer such as Philly Joe Jones on *Everybody Digs Bill Evans* (listen to 'Minority'), and there are many powerful swinging musicians whose music has a fraction of the interest of Evans'. In common with an unusual handful of great jazz musicians, Bill Evans was not a master of the blues. He rapidly learned to avoid straight-ahead blues settings, although his grasp of minor blues (e.g. John Carisi's wonderful 'Israel') was assured, partly because melodic minor harmony is the basis of the modern jazz sound that he helped to develop. Evans increasingly played his own compositions, which are unfailingly fine and inventive, often involving irregular phrase lengths and shifting metres, and many, incidentally, named after female friends ('Waltz For Debby', 'One for Helen', 'Show-Type Tune', 'Peri's Scope', 'Laurie', 'Turn Out The Stars', 'Blue In Green'). His originality was equally apparent in his transformations of standard songs ('Beautiful Love', 'Polka Dots And Moonbeams', 'Someday My Prince Will Come', 'My Romance', 'My Foolish Heart'). His recorded legacy is extensive.

●ALBUMS: *New Jazz Conceptions* (Riverside 1956)★★★, *Everybody Digs Bill Evans* (Riverside 1958)★★★★, *Portrait In Jazz* (Riverside 1959)★★★★, *Explorations* (Riverside 1961)★★★★, *Sunday At The Village Vanguard* (Riverside 1961)★★★★★, *Waltz For Debby* (Riverside 1961)★★★★★, *More From The Vanguard* (1961)★★★★, *Empathy* (Verve 1962)★★★, *Moonbeams* (Riverside 1962)★★★, *How My Heart Sings* (Riverside 1962)★★★★, with Freddie Hubbard *Interplay* (Riverside 1962)★★★, *Conversations With Myself* (Verve 1963)★★★★, with Jim Hall *Undercurrent* (Blue Note 1963)★★★★, *Trio '64* (Verve 1964)★★★★, *The Bill Evans Trio Live* (1964)★★★, *At Shelly's Manne Hole* (Riverside 1964)★★★, *Trio '65* (Verve 1965)★★★, *Bill Evans Trio With The Symphony Orchestra* (Verve 1965)★★★, *Bill Evans At Town Hall* (Verve 1966)★★★, with Hall *Intermodulation* (Verve 1966)★★★, *A Simple Matter Of Conviction* (Verve 1966)★★★, *Further Conversations With Myself* (Verve 1967)★★★★, *Polka Dots And Moonbeams* (Riverside 1967)★★★, *California Here I Come* (1967)★★★★, *Alone* (Verve 1968)★★★, *Bill Evans At The Montreux Jazz Festival* (Verve 1968)★★★, *Jazzhouse* (1969)★★★, *What's New* (Verve 1969), *Montreux ii* (1970)★★★, *You're Gonna Hear From Me* (Milestone 1970)★★★, *The Bill Evans Album* (Columbia 1971)★★★, with George Russell *Living Time* (1972)★★★, *Live In Tokyo* (Fantasy 1972)★★★★, *Yesterday I Heard The Rain* (Bandstand

1973)★★★, *Since We Met* (Original Jazz Classics 1974)★★★, *Re: Person I Knew* (Original Jazz Classics 1974)★★★, *Intuition* (1974)★★★, *Blue Is Green* (Milestone 1974)★★★, *Jazzhouse* (Milestone 1974)★★★, *Montreux iii* (Original Jazz Classics 1975)★★★, *The Tony Bennett/Bill Evans Album* (Original Jazz Classics 1975)★★★★, with Tony Bennett *Together Again* (1976)★★★, *Alone (Again)* (Original Jazz Classics 1976)★★★, *Eloquence* (1976)★★★, with Harold Land *Quintessence* (Original Jazz Classics 1976)★★★, with Lee Konitz, Warne Marsh *Crosscurrents* (Original Jazz Classics 1977)★★★, *From The 70's* (1977)★★★, *You Must Believe In Spring* (1977)★★★, *New Conversations* (1978)★★★, with Toots Thielemans *Affinity* (1978)★★★, *I Will Say Goodbye* (Original Jazz Classics 1979)★★★, *We Will Meet Again* (1979)★★★, *The Complete Fantasy Recordings* (Fantasy 1980)★★★★, *The Paris Concert: Edition One* rec. 1979 (1983)★★★, *The Paris Concert: Edition Two* rec. 1979 (1984)★★★, *The Complete Riverside Recordings* (Fantasy 1985)★★★★, *Consecration i and ii* rec. 1980 (Timeless 1990)★★★, *The Brilliant* rec. 1980 (Timeless 1990)★★★, *Letter To Evan* (Dreyfus 1993)★★★, *Turn Out The Stars* rec. 1980 (Dreyfus 1996)★★★, *The Secret Sessions* 8-CD box set (Fantasy 1996)★★★★.
●VIDEOS: *In Oslo* (K-Jazz 1994), *The Bill Evans Trio* (Rhapsody 1995).

EVANS, MAUREEN
b. 1940, Cardiff, Wales. Evans began her singing career on the Embassy label, which made budget-priced recordings of contemporary hits for the UK's Woolworths chainstore. She later enjoyed chart success in her own right, beginning in 1960 with 'The Big Hurt', and peaking two years later with 'Like I Do'. This perky offering, more teen-orientated than Evans' normal fare, reached the UK Top 3, but later releases failed to emulate its success. Her rather dated style was quickly surpassed by younger-minded artists, although 'Never Let Him Go', one of the singer's final releases, was an excellent interpretation of a David Gates song.
●ALBUMS: *Like I Do* (Oriole 1963)★★.

EVERETT, BETTY
b. 23 November 1939, Greenwood, Mississippi, USA. Having moved to Chicago in the late 50s, Everett recorded unsuccessfully for several local labels, including Cobra and One-derful. Her hits came on signing to Vee Jay Records where 'You're No Good' (1963) and 'The Shoop Shoop Song (It's In His Kiss)' (1964) established her pop/soul style. A duet with Jerry Butler, 'Let It Be Me' (1964), consolidated this position, but her finest moment came with 'Getting Mighty Crowded', a punchy Van McCoy song. Her career faltered on Vee Jay's collapse, and an ensuing interlude at ABC Records was unproductive. However, in 1969, 'There'll Come A Time' reached number 2 in the R&B charts, a momentum which continued into the early 70s with further releases

on UNI and Fantasy Records. Everett's last chart entry was in 1978 with 'True Love (You Took My Heart)'. Cher took her version of 'The Shoop Shoop Song' to the top of the charts in 1991.
●ALBUMS: *You're No Good* (Vee Jay 1964)★★★, *It's In His Kiss* (Vee Jay/Fontana1964)★★★, with Jerry Butler *Delicious Together* (1964)★★★, *There'll Come A Time* (Uni 1969)★★, *Love Rhymes* (1974)★★, *Black Girl* (1974)★★, *Happy Endings* (1975)★★.
●COMPILATIONS: *The Very Best Of Betty Everett* (Vee Jay 1965)★★★, *Betty Everett* (1974)★★★, *Hot To Handle* (1982)★★★, with Lillian Offitt *1957-1961* (1986)★★, *The Shoop Shoop Song* (1993)★★★, *Love Rhymes/Happy Endings* (1993)★★★.

EVERLY BROTHERS
Don (b. 1 February 1937, Brownie, Kentucky, USA) and Phil (b. 19 January 1939, Chicago, Illinois, USA), the world's most famous rock 'n' roll duo had already experienced a full career before their first record 'Bye Bye Love' was released. As sons of popular country artists Ike and Margaret, they were pushed into the limelight from an early age. They regularly appeared on their parents' radio shows throughout the 40s and accompanied them on many tours. In the mid-50s, as rockabilly was evolving into rock 'n' roll, the boys moved to Nashville, the mecca for such music. Don had a minor hit when Kitty Wells recorded his composition 'Thou Shalt Not Steal' in 1954. In 1957 they were given a Felice and Boudleaux Bryant song that was finding difficulty being placed. They took 'Bye Bye Love' and made it their own; it narrowly missed the US number 1 position and scored in the UK at number 6. The brothers then embarked on a career that made them second only to Elvis Presley in the rock 'n' roll popularity stakes. Their blend of country and folk did much to sanitize and make respectable a phenomenon to which many parents showed hostility. America, then still a racially segregated country, was not ready for its white teenagers to listen to black-based rock music. The brothers' clean looks and even cleaner harmonies did much to change people's attitudes. They quickly followed this initial success with more irresistible Bryant songs, 'Wake Up Little Susie', 'All I Have To Do Is Dream', 'Bird Dog', 'Problems', 'So Sad' and the beautiful 'Devoted To You'. The brothers were supremely confident live performers both with their trademark Gibson Dove and later, black J50 guitars. By the end of the 50s they were the world's number 1 vocal group.
Amazingly, their career gained further momentum when, after signing with the newly formed Warner Brothers Records for $1 million, they delivered a song that was catalogued WB1. This historical debut was the superlative 'Cathy's Clown', written by Don. No Everly record had sounded like this before; the echo-laden production and the treble-loaded harmonies stayed at number 1 in the US for 5 weeks. In the UK it stayed on top for over two months, selling several million and making it one of the most successful records of all time. The brothers continued to release immaculate records,

many of them reached the US Top 10, although in England their success was even greater, with two further number 1 hits during 1961. Again the echo and treble dominated in two more classics, 'Walk Right Back' and a fast-paced reworking of the former Bing Crosby hit 'Temptation'. At the end of 1961 they were drafted into the US Marines, albeit for only six months, and resumed by making a European tour. Don became dependent on drugs, the pressures from constant touring and recording began to show; during one historic night at London's East Ham Granada, England, a nervous Phil performed solo. The standard 'food poisoning/exhaustion' excuse was used. What was not known by the doting fans, was that Don had attempted a suicidal drug overdose twice in 48 hours. Phil completed the tour solo. Don's addiction continued for another three years, although they were able to work during part of this time.

The advent of the beat boom pushed the brothers out of the spotlight and while they continued to make hit records, none came near their previous achievements. The decline was briefly halted in 1965 with two excellent major UK hits, 'The Price Of Love' and 'Love Is Strange'. The former, a striking chart topper, sounded like their early Warner sound, while the latter harked back even earlier, with a naïve but infectious call and answer, talking segment. In 1966 they released *Two Yanks In England*, a superb album which contained eight songs by Nash/Clarke/Hicks of the Hollies; surprisingly the album failed to chart. The duo were recognized only for their superb singles, and many of their albums were less well-received. The stunning *Stories We Could Tell*, with an array of guest players, threatened to extend their market into the rock mainstream, but it was not to be. After a few years of declining fortunes and arrival at the supper-club circuit, the brothers acrimoniously parted. Following a show at Knotts Berry Farm, California, in 1973 during which a drunken Don had insulted Phil, the latter walked off, smashed one of his beloved Gibsons and vowed, 'I will never get on a stage with that man again'. The only time they met over the next 10 years was at their father's funeral. Both embarked on solo careers with varying degrees of accomplishment. Their country-flavoured albums found more favour with the Nashville audience of their roots. Don and his band, the Dead Cowboys, regularly played in Nashville, while Phil released the critically acclaimed *Star Spangled Springer*. Inexplicably the album was a relatively poor seller, as was his follow-up *Mystic Line*. Phil made a cameo appearance in the film *Every Which Way But Loose*, performing with actress Sondra Locke. While Don maintained a steady career, playing with ex-Heads, Hands And Feet maestro Albert Lee, Phil concentrated on writing songs. 'She Means Nothing To Me' was a striking duet with Cliff Richard which put the Everly name back in the UK Top 10. Rumours began to circulate of a reunion, which was further fueled by a UK television advertisement for an Everly Brothers' compilation. In June 1983 they hugged and made up and their emotional reunion was made to an ecstatic wet-eyed audience at London's Royal Albert

Hall. The following year *EB84* was released and gave them another major hit with Paul McCartney's 'Wings Of A Nightingale'. In 1986 they were inducted into the Rock 'n' Roll Hall Of Fame and the following year Phil gave Don a pound of gold and a handmade guitar for his 50th birthday. The Everly Brothers' influence over a generation of pop and rock artists is inestimable; they set the standard for close harmony singing which has rarely been bettered. They now perform regularly together, with no pressure from record companies. Don lives quietly in Nashville and tours with his brother a few months every year. To date their ceasefire has held.

●ALBUMS: *The Everly Brothers* (Cadence 1958)★★★, *Songs Our Daddy Taught Us* (Cadence 1958)★★★, *It's Everly Time* (Warners 1960)★★★, *The Fabulous Style Of The Everly Brothers* (Cadence 1960)★★★★, *A Date With The Everly Brothers* (Warners 1960)★★★★, *Both Sides Of An Evening* (Warners 1961)★★★, *Folk Songs Of the Everly Brothers* (Cadence 1962)★★★, *Instant Party* (Warners 1962)★★★, *Christmas With The Everly Brothers And The Boys Town Choir* (Warners 1962)★★★, *The Everly Brothers Sing Great Country Hits* (Warners 1963)★★★, *Gone Gone Gone* (Warners 1965)★★★★, *Rock 'N' Soul* (Warners 1965)★★★, *Beat 'N' Soul* (Warners 1965)★★★, *In Our Image* (Warners 1966)★★★, *Two Yanks In England* (Warners 1966)★★★, *The Hit Sound Of The Everly Brothers* (Warners 1967)★★★, *The Everly Brothers Sing* (Warners 1967)★★★, *Roots* (Warners 1968)★★★, *The Everly Brothers Show* (Warners 1970)★★★, *Chained To A Memory* (1970)★★, *End Of An Era* (Barnaby/CBS 1971)★★★, *Stories We Could Tell* (RCA 1972)★★, *Pass The Chicken And Listen* (RCA 1973)★★, *The Exciting Everly Brothers* (1975)★★★, *Living Legends* (1977)★★★, *The New Album* (Warners 1977)★★★, *The Everly Brothers Reunion Concert* (Impression 1984)★★★★, *Nice Guys* (Magnum Force 1984)★★, *EB84* (1984)★★★, *Some Hearts* (1985)★★★, *Home Again* (1985)★★★, *Born Yesterday* (1986). Solo: Don Everly *Don Everly* (A&M 1970)★★, *Sunset Towers* (A&M 1974)★★, *Brother Juke Box* (Hickory 1976)★★. Phil Everly *Star Spangled Springer* (1973)★★, *Phil's Diner (There's Nothing Too Good For My Baby)* (Pye 1974)★★, *Mystic Line* (1975)★★, *Living Alone* (Elektra 1979)★★, *Phil Everly* (Capitol 1983)★★.

●COMPILATIONS: *The Golden Hits Of The Everly Brothers* (1962)★★★★, *15 Everly Hits* (1963)★★★, *The Very Best Of The Everly Brothers* (1964)★★★★, *The Very Best Of The Everly Brothers* (1964)★★★★, *The Everly Brothers Original Greatest Hits* (1970)★★★★, *The Most Beautiful Songs Of The Everly Brothers* (1973)★★★, *Don's And Phil's Fabulous Fifties Treasury* (1974)★★★, *Walk Right Back With The Everlys* (1976)★★★★, *The Sensational Everly Brothers* (Reader Digest 1979)★★★, *Hidden Gems* (1990)★★★, *Perfect Harmony* (1990)★★★, *Their 24 Greatest Hits* (1993)★★★★, *Heartaches And Harmonies* 4-CD box set (Rhino 1995)★★★★★, *Walk Right Back: On Warner Bros.*

1960 To 1969 2-CD (Warners 1996)★★★★.
●FURTHER READING: *Everly Brothers: An Illustrated Discography*, John Hosum. *The Everly Brothers: Walk Right Back*, Roger White. *Ike's Boys*, Phyllis Karpp. *The Everly Brothers: Ladies Love Outlaws*, Consuelo Dodge. *For-Everly Yours*, Peter Aarts and Martin Alberts.

EXCITERS
Formed in the Jamaica district of Queens, New York City, this aptly named group, which included Herb Rooney (b. 1941, New York City, New York, USA), Brenda Reid (b. 1945), Carol Johnson (b. 1945) and Lillian Walker (b. 1945), first came to prominence with the vibrant 'Tell Him', a US Top 5 hit in 1962 (also a hit in the UK for Billie Davis in 1963). Produced by Leiber And Stoller and written by Bert Berns (under his pseudonym Bert Russell), the single's energy established the pattern for subsequent releases. 'Do Wah Diddy' (later a hit by Manfred Mann) and 'He's Got The Power' took elements from both uptown soul and the girl-group genre, but later singles failed to fully exploit this powerful combination. The group had lesser hits with 'I Want You To Be My Boy' (1965), a revival of 'A Little Bit Of Soap' (1966) and 'You Don't Know What You're Missing (Till It's Gone)' (1969), but failed to recapture the verve of those first releases. The group re-entered the UK charts in 1975 with 'Reaching For The Best'. Ronnie Pace and Skip McPhee later replaced Johnson and Walker, while Rooney and Reid (his wife) had a minor 1978 hit as Brenda And Herb, releasing one album in 1979, *In Heat Again*.
●ALBUMS: *Tell Him* (United Artists 1963)★★★, *The Exciters* (Roulette 1965)★★★, *Caviar And Chitlins* (1969)★★, *Black Beauty* (1971)★★, *Heaven Is Where You Are* (1976)★★, *The Exciters* (1977)★★.
●COMPILATIONS: *The Hit Power Of The Exciters* (1986)★★★, *Tell Him* (EMI 1991)★★★.
●FILMS: *Bikini Beach* (1964).

EYES OF BLUE
Founded in Neath, Wales, by Ritchie Francis (guitar), Gary Pickford Hopkins (vocals), Phil Ryan (keyboards), Ray Williams (bass) and Wyndham Rees (drums), Eyes Of Blue started out as a soul revival band before gradually attuning their musical sensibilities to the emergent US west coast rock scene. They initially recorded two singles for Deram Records, 'Heart Trouble' and 'Supermarket Full Of Cans', in 1966 and 1967, but for their debut album moved to Mercury Records. The group covered two Graham Bond songs on the album and he also wrote the sleevenotes. *The Crossroads Of Time* was a satisfying mix of diverse musical influences, ranging from psyche-delic and ethnic instrumentation to jazz and classical styles. However, their own songwriting suffered in comparison to Bond's songs and their cover version of the Beatles' 'Yesterday'. For their second album, 1969's rein-carnation-themed *In Fields Of Ardath*, they replaced their original rhythm section with R. Bennett (bass) and John Weathers (drums). The album featured their collaboration with Quincy Jones, 'Merry Go Round', which was included on the soundtrack to Jones' *Toy Grabbers* film score, and the group itself was later seen on film in *Connecting Rooms*. Other tracks revealed a debt to the UK progressive rock movement, although another Bond cover, 'Spanish Blues', was present as continuity. It was the group's final release, although they did also record an album as backing band to US singer-songwriter Buzzy Linhart (*Buzzy*). After the group's demise the members scattered. Ryan joined Man, Weathers worked with Pete Brown and Gentle Giant, while Francis recorded a solo album.
●ALBUMS: *The Crossroads Of Time* (Mercury 1968)★★★, *In Fields Of Ardath* (Mercury 1969)★★.

FABARES, SHELLEY

b. Michelle Fabares, 19 January 1944, Santa Monica, California, USA. Fabares, whose music career was highlighted by the 1962 number 1 song 'Johnny Angel', was the niece of actress Nanette Fabray. Turning to acting herself, Fabares landed roles in such 50s films as *Never Say Goodbye, Rock, Pretty Baby* and *Summer Love* before being offered the part of Mary Stone in the US television situation comedy *The Donna Reed Show* in 1958. As the show's popularity rose, both she and series co-star Paul Petersen signed recording contracts with Colpix Records. Fabares was given the ballad 'Johnny Angel', written by Lee Pockriss and Lyn Duddy, and after its debut on the television show, the single quickly rose to number 1. Three follow-up singles did not fare nearly as well, nor did the two albums she recorded for Colpix. In 1964 Fabares married record producer Lou Adler, who arranged a record deal for Fabares with Vee Jay Records. There were no hits and Fabares then became the first artist signed to his new Dunhill Records label. Again there were no hits and Fabares returned to acting, working with Herman's Hermits in their film *Hold On* and with Elvis Presley in *Girl Happy, Spinout* and *Clambake*. She divorced Adler in the late 60s and continued to work in film and television. In the late 80s and early 90s she was a member of the cast of *Coach*, a popular television situation comedy.

● ALBUMS: *Shelley!* (Colpix 1962)★★, *The Things We Did Last Summer* (Colpix 1962)★★, *A Time To Sing* (MGM 1968)★★.
● COMPILATIONS: *The Best Of ...* (Sequel 1994)★★.
● FILMS: *Hold On* (1965).

FABIAN

b. Fabiano Forte Bonaparte, 6 February 1943, Philadelphia, USA. Fabian, almost despite himself, was among the more endurable products of the late 50s when the North American charts were infested with a turnover of vapid boys-next-door - all hair spray, doe eyes and coy half-smiles - groomed for fleeting stardom. Fabian was 'discovered' by two local talent scouts, Peter De Angelis and Bob Marucci, in Frankie Avalon's Teen And Twenty youth club in 1957. Enthralled by the youth's good looks, the pair shortened his name and contracted him to their Chancellor Records where a huge budget was allocated to project him as a tamed Elvis Presley. Accompanied by the Four Dates, Fabian's first two singles - 'I'm In Love' and 'Lilly Lou' - were only regional hits, but a string of television performances on Dick Clark's nationally-

broadcast *American Bandstand* plus a coast-to-coast tour had the desired effect on female teenagers, and Fabian found himself suddenly in *Billboard*'s Top 40 with 'I'm A Man,' composed by the top New York songwriting team Doc Pomus/Mort Shuman, who also delivered more lucrative hits in 'Turn Me Loose' and 'Hound Dog Man', the main theme from Fabian's silver screen debut of the same name.

More substantial movie roles came Fabian's way after his recording career peaked with 1959's million-selling 'Tiger' and *Hold That Tiger*. As well as the predictable teen-pics with their vacuous storylines and mimed musical sequences, he coped surprisingly well as John Wayne's sidekick in 1960's *North To Alaska* and with Bing Crosby and Tuesday Weld in *High Time*. Fabian's decline was as rapid as his launch after Congress pinpointed him as an instance of one of the exploited puppets in the payola scandal. Questioned at the time, Fabian made matters worse by outlining the considerable electronic doctoring necessary to improve his voice on record. His first serious miss came in 1960 with 'About This Thing Called Love' and an irredeemable downward spiral mitigated by 1962's 'Kissin' And Twistin'' and other small hits. Nevertheless, he could be seen in films such as the 1962 war epic *The Longest Day*, but more commensurate with his talent were productions such as *Fireball 500* (a 1966 hot-rod epic with his old friend Frankie Avalon) and 1965's *Ride The Wild Surf*. Fabian's limited vocal range should not be held against him: he became a puppet and he danced; out of it he traded a doomed musical career for a credible movie career.

● ALBUMS: *Hold That Tiger* (Chancellor 1959)★★, *The Fabulous Fabian* (Chancellor 1960)★★, *Fabian Facade* (Chancellor 1961)★★, *The Good Old Summertime* (Chancellor 1961)★★, *Rockin' Hot* (Chancellor 1961)★★, *16 Fabulous Hits* (Chancellor 1962)★★, *All The Hits* (1993)★★.
● COMPILATIONS: *The Best Of ...* (Varese Sarabande 1996)★★.
● FILMS: *Hound Dog Man* (1959), *Dr Goldfoot And The Girl Bomb* (1966), *American Pop* (1981).

FAHEY, JOHN

b. 28 February 1939. Fahey grew up in Takoma Park, Maryland, USA, and learned to play country-style guitar in the footsteps of Hank Williams and Eddie Arnold at the age of 13, inspired by the recordings of Blind Willie Johnson, and other blues greats. He toured during his teens with Henry Vestine (later of Canned Heat), in addition to gaining a BA in Philosophy and Religion. Fahey's style is based on an original folk blues theme, encompassing blues, jazz, country and gospel music, and at times incorporating classical pieces, although he still retains an almost traditional edge in his arrangements. His 12-string work often features open tunings. He has now become a major influence on other American acoustic guitarists. Having set up his own Takoma Records label with a $300 loan, he released *The Transfiguration Of Blind Joe Death*. This perplexing album subsequently became a cult record during the late 60s. It was a record with which to be seen, rather than actually play. He later signed with Vanguard Records in 1967, and released virtually one album a year until quitting the company. Later still, after a brief sojourn with Reprise Records, he was dropped due to insufficient sales. Fahey was also quick to spot other talent and was the first to record Leo Kottke. His work was heard in the film *Zabriskie Point*, but generally, his influence is greater than his own success. Having overcome drug problems, Fahey retains a cult following. His recorded output is prolific and he continues to perform, although only occasionally. He wrote a thesis on Charley Patton which has been published. In 1997 the experimental *City Of Refuge* received a good reception, appealing to the alternative rock audience having dedicated a song 'Hope Slumbers Eternal' to Mazzy Star's vocalist Hope Sandoval.

●ALBUMS: *Blind Joe Death* (Takoma 1959)★★★, *Death Chants Breakdowns And Miltary Waltzes* (Takoma 1963)★★★★, *Dance Of Death And Other Plantation Favorites* (Takoma 1964)★★★, *John Fahey* i (1966)★★★, *The Great San Bernadino Birthday Party And Other Excursions* (1966)★★★, *Guitar* (1967)★★★, *Days Have Gone By* (1967)★★★, *Requia* (1967)★★★, *John Fahey* ii (1968)★★★, *The Voice Of The Turtle* (1968)★★★, *The Yellow Princess* (takoma 1968)★★★★, *The New Possibility: Christmas Album* (Takoma 1968)★★★, *The Transfiguration Of Blind Joe Death* (Takoma/Transatlantic 1968)★★★★, *Of Rivers And Religion* (1972)★★★, *After The Ball* (1973)★★★, *Fare Forward Voyagers* (1973)★★★, *John Fahey, Leo Koettke, Peter Lang* (Takoma 1974)★★★★, *Fahey, Kelly, Mann, Miller, Seidler* (Blue Goose 1974)★★★, *Old Fashioned Love* (Takoma 1975)★★★, *Yes! Jesus Loves Me* (1980)★★★, *John Fahey Visits Washington, D.C.* (1980)★★★, *Live In Tasmania* (Takoma 1981)★★★, *Let Go* (Varrick 1984)★★★, *Railroad* (Takoma 1984)★★★, *Rain Forests, Oceans And Other Themes* (Varrick 1985)★★★, *I Remember Blind Joe Death* (Varrick 1987)★★★, *Popular Songs Of Christmas And New Years* (Rounder 1988)★★★, *Christmas Guitar, Vol. 1* (Varrick 1988)★★★, *God, Time And Casualty* (Shanachie 1990)★★★, *Old Fashioned Love* (Shanachie 1990★★★, *Fast Forward Voyagers* (Shanachie 1992)★★★★, *Old Girlfriends And Other Horrible Memories* (1992), *City Of Refuge* (Tim Kerr 1997).

●COMPILATIONS: *The Best Of John Fahey 1959-1977* (Takoma 1977)★★★★, *The Essential John Fahey* (1979)★★★★.

FAITH, ADAM

b. Terence Nelhams, 23 June 1940, Acton, London, England. During the British 'coffee bar' pop music phenomenon of the late 50s two artists reigned supreme: Cliff Richard and Adam Faith. While the former has shown astonishing staying power the young Faith had a remarkable run of hit records during the comparatively short time before he retired from singing. In seven years he made the UK chart 24 times, opening his career with two chart toppers. Both, 'What Do You Want' and 'Poor Me' lasted only two minutes; both featured the infectious pizzicato strings of John Barry's orchestra, both were written by Les Vandyke (alias Johnny Worth) and both featured the hiccuping delivery with the word, 'baby' pronounced 'bybeee'. This became Adam's early 'gimmick'. Faith's continued success rivalled that of Cliff's, when in a short period of time he appeared in three films: *Beat Girl*, *Never Let Go* and *What A Whopper*, and made a surprisingly confident appearance, being interviewed by John Freeman in a serious BBC television programme, *Face To Face*. Adults were shocked to find that during this conversation, this lucid teenager admitted to pre-marital sex and owned up to listening to Sibelius. The following year, still enjoying chart hits, he appeared in the film *Mix Me A Person*. His career continued until the dawn of the Beatles, then Faith was assigned the Roulettes (featuring a young Russ Ballard). Songwriter Chris Andrews proceeded to feed Adam with a brief second wave of infectious beat-group hits most notably 'The First Time'. In the mid-60s he gave up singing and went into repertory theatre and in 1971 became an acting star in the UK television series *Budgie*. Additionally Faith has produced records for Roger Daltrey and Lonnie Donegan and managed Leo Sayer. His two supporting actor roles in *Stardust* and *McVicar* bought him critical success in addition to appearing in *Yesterday's Hero*. For a number of years he has been a wealthy financial consultant, although in the 90s he returned to the stage with *Budgie* and *Alfie*, and to UK television as lead actor in *Love Hurts*. Faith still works on the perimeter of the musical world, and released an album in 1993. While he will readily admit that his vocal range was limited, his contribution to popular music was significant insofar as he was the first British teenager to confront a hostile world of respectable parents and adults, and demonstrate that pop singers were not all mindless 'layabouts and boneheads'.

●ALBUMS: *Adam* (Parlophone 1960)★★★, *Beat Girl* soundtrack (Columbia 1960)★★★, *Adam Faith* (Parlophone 1962)★★★, *From Adam With Love* (Parlophone 1962)★★★, *For You - Adam* (Parlophone 1963)★★★, with the Roulettes *On The Move* (Parlophone 1964)★★★, with the Roulettes *Faith Alive* (Parlophone 1965)★★, *I Survive* (1974)★★, *Midnight Postcards* (1993)★★.

●COMPILATIONS: *20 Golden Greats* (1981)★★★, *Not Just A Memory* (1983)★★★★, *The Best Of Adam Faith* (MFP 1989)★★★★, *The Adam Faith Singles Collection: His Greatest Hits* (1990)★★★, *The Best Of The EMI Years* (EMI 1994)★★★★.

●FURTHER READING: *Adam, His Fabulous Year*, Adam Faith. *Poor Me*, Adam Faith. *Acts Of Faith*, Adam Faith.

●FILMS: *Beat Girl* (1960), *Never Let Go* (1960), *What A Whopper* (1961), *Mix Me A Person* (1962), *Stardust* (1974), *McVicar* (1980).

FAITHFULL, MARIANNE

b. 29 December 1946, Hampstead, London, England. Ex-convent schoolgirl Faithfull began her singing career upon meeting producer Andrew Loog Oldham at a London party. She was thus introduced into the Rolling Stones' circle and a plaintive Jagger/Richard song, 'As Tears Go By', became her debut single in 1964. This folksy offering reached number 9, the first of four UK Top 10 hits which also included 'Come And Stay With Me' (penned by Jackie DeShannon) and the pounding 'Summer Nights'. Her albums reflected an impressive balance between folk and rock, featuring material by Donovan, Bert Jansch and Tim Hardin, but her doomed relationship with Mick Jagger undermined ambitions as a performer. Faithfull also pursed her thespian aspirations appearing on stage in Chekhov's *Three Sisters* and on celluloid in the title role of *Girl On A Motorcycle*, but withdrew from the public eye following a failed suicide attempt upon her break with Jagger. Drug problems bedeviled her recovery, but Marianne re-emerged in 1976 with *Dreamin' My Dreams*, a mild country set on which she was backed by the Grease Band. A further period of seclusion followed but the singer rekindled her career three years later with the impressive *Broken English*. The once-virginal voice was now replaced by a husky drawl, particularly effective on the atmospheric title track and her version of Shel Silverstein's 'The Ballad Of Lucy Jordan', a minor UK hit. Faithfull's later releases followed a similar pattern, but nowhere was the trauma of her personal life more evident than on *Blazing Away*, a live album on which the singer reclaimed songs from her past. Recorded live in Brooklyn's St. Ann's Cathedral, her weary intonation, although artistically effective, contravened the optimism of those early recordings. Her autobiography was a revealing and fascinating insight into a true survivor of the 60s and all that followed. *A Secret Life* was a return to the brooding atmosphere of *Broken English*, but, although her voice was still captivating, the songs were generally uninspiring. *20th Century Blues* was a an ill-chosen live album from a Paris gig featuring songs by Kurt Weill, Noel Coward and in Marlene Deitrich pose, 'Falling In Love Again'.

●ALBUMS: *Come My Way* (Decca 1965)★★, *Marianne Faithfull* (Decca 1965)★★★, *Go Away From My World* (1965)★★★, *Faithfull Forever* (1966), *North Country Maid* (Decca 1966)★★, *Loveinamist* (Decca 1967)★★, *Dreamin' My Dreams* (Nems 1976)★, *Faithless* (Immediate 1977)★★, *Broken English* (Island 1979)★★★★, *Dangerous Acquaintances* (Island 1981)★★★, *A Child's Adventure* (Island 1983)★★★, *Strange Weather* (Island 1987)★★★, *Blazing Away* (Island 1990)★★★, *A Secret Life* (Island 1995)★★, *20th Century Blues* (RCA 1996)★★.

●COMPILATIONS: *The World Of Marianne Faithfull* (Decca 1969)★★★, *Marianne Faithfull's Greatest Hits* (Abkco 1969)★★★, *As Tears Go By* (1981)★★★, *Summer Nights* (1984)★★★, *The Very Best Of Marianne Faithfull* (1987)★★★, *Rich Kid Blues* (1988)★★★, *Faithfull: A Collection Of Her Best Recordings* (Island 1994)★★★.

●FURTHER READING: *Marianne Faithfull: As Tears Go By*, Mark Hodkinson. *Faithfull*, Marianne Faithfull and David Dalton.

FAME, GEORGIE

b. Clive Powell, 26 June 1943, Leigh, Lancashire, England. Entrepreneur Larry Parnes gave the name to this talented organist during the early 60s following a recommendation from songwriter Lionel Bart. Parnes already had a Power, a Wilde, an Eager and a Fury. All he now needed was Fame. It took a number of years before Fame and his band the Blue Flames had commercial success, although he was a major force in the popularizing of early R&B, bluebeat and ska at London's famous Flamingo club. The seminal *Rhythm And Blues At The Flamingo* was released in 1964. Chart success came later that year with a UK number 1, 'Yeh Yeh'. Fame's jazzy nasal delivery, reminiscent of Mose Alison, made this record one of the decade's classic songs. He continued with another eleven hits, including two further UK chart toppers, 'Get Away' and 'The Ballad Of Bonnie And Clyde', the latter of which was his only US Top 10 single in 1968. The former maintained his jazz feel, which continued on such striking mood pieces as 'Sunny' and 'Sitting In The Park'. Thereafter, he veered towards straight pop. His recent change of record labels had attempted to re-market him and at one stage teamed him with the Harry South Big Band. While his albums showed a more progressive style his singles became lightweight, the nadir being when he teamed up with Alan Price to produce some catchy pop songs. Fame has also played straight jazz at Ronnie Scott's club, performed a tribute to Hoagy Carmichael with singer Annie Ross, and has sung over Esso advertisements. In recent times Fame has been content touring with Van Morrison as keyboard player, given a brief cameo to perform the occasional hit. During the renaissance of the Hammond B3 organ (an instrument that Fame had originally pioneered in the London clubs) during the jazz boom of the early 90s it was announced that Georgie had recorded a new album *Cool Cat Blues*; its subsequent release to favourable reviews and regular concert appearances indicated a new phase. The album was recorded to the highest standards and featured smooth contributions from Steve Gadd, Robben Ford, Richard Tee, Jon Hendricks and Boz Scaggs. A reggae reworking of 'Yeh Yeh' and a graceful version of Carmichael's 'Georgia' are but two outstanding tracks. Van Morrison duets with Fame on the former's classic 'Moondance'. He followed this with *The Blues And Me*, an album of a similar high standard. Tragedy struck Fame in 1994 when his wife committed suicide. Since then he has continued to work and record with Morrison as well as gigging with his latter-day version of the Blue Flames, which features his son.

●ALBUMS: *Rhythm And Blues At The Flamingo* (Columbia 1963)★★★★, *Fame At Last* (Columbia 1964)★★★★, *Sweet Things* (Columbia 1966)★★★, *Sound Venture* (Columbia 1966)★★★, *Two Faces Of*

Fame (CBS 1967)★★★, *The Ballad Of Bonnie And Clyde* (Epic 1968)★★★, *The Third Face Of Fame* (CBS 1968)★★★, *Seventh Son* (CBS 1969)★★, *Georgie Does His Things With Strings* (CBS 1970)★★, *Going Home* (CBS 1971)★★, with Alan Price *Fame And Price, Price And Fame Together* (CBS 1971)★★, *All Me Own Work* (Reprise 1972)★★★, *Georgie Fame* (Island 1974)★★, *That's What Friends Are For* (1979)★★★, *Georgie Fame Right Now* (1979)★★★, *Closing The Gap* (1980)★★, with Annie Ross *Hoagland* (1981)★★★, *In Goodman's Land* (1983)★★★, *My Favourite Songs* (1984)★★, *No Worries* (1988)★★, *Cool Cat Blues* (Go Jazz 1991)★★★★, *The Blues And Me* (1994)★★★, *Three Line Whip* (1994)★★★, with Van Morrison *How Long Has This Been Going On* (Verve 1995)★★★, with Morrison, Ben Sidran, Mose Allison *Tell Me Something: The Songs Of Mose Allison* (Verve 1996)★★★.
●COMPILATIONS: *Hall Of Fame* (Columbia 1967)★★★★, *Georgie Fame* (Starline 1969)★★★★, *Fame Again* (Starline 1972)★★★, *20 Beat Classics* (Polydor 1982)★★★★, *The First Thirty Years* (1990)★★★.

FAMILY DOGG

Formed in the UK in 1969, the original line-up comprised Steve Rowland, Albert Hammond, Mike Hazelwood, Doreen De Veuve and Zooey. Rowland already had a chequered history as a film-maker, actor and continental recording artist before forming the Double R production company with Ronnie Oppenheimer. With the backing of Fontana A&R head Jack Baverstock, Rowland produced a string of hits for Dave Dee, Dozy, Beaky, Mick And Tich and the Herd, while his company also recorded such artists as P.J. Proby, the Magic Lanterns and Amory Kane. After assembling a talented back-up crew, Rowland launched Family Dogg and soon scaled the charts with 'Way Of Life', written by Roger Cook and Roger Greenaway. Specializing in high harmony and classy covers, the Dogg followed up unsuccessfully with Paul Simon's 'Save The Life Of My Child' and recorded an album of hit standards with backing by several members of the newly formed Led Zeppelin. Although the Dogg had considerable commercial potential they were clearly a studio group with a tendency to lose members at short notice. In July 1969, De Veuve was replaced by the glamorous ex-*Charlie Girl* star Christine Holmes, and several months later Ireen Scheer took over Zooey's role. With Hammond and Hazelwood busy writing the 13-piece suite *Oliver In The Overworld* for Freddie And The Dreamers, Rowland was forced to explain that his group was a concept that only came together occasionally before dissipating into individual projects. The UK music press, unconvinced by such rhetoric, made sarcastic news item remarks such as 'No change in Family Dogg line-up this week'. Nobody was too surprised when the Dogg ceased operations early in the new decade.
●ALBUMS: *Way Of Life* (Bell 1969)★★, *The View From Rowland's Head* (Polydor 1972)★.

FAMILY TREE

Bob Segarini (guitar/vocals), Mike Olsen (keyboards), Bill Whittington (bass) and Newman Davis (drums) formed Family Tree in 1965. This San Franciscan rock group was bedevilled by internal unrest, and by the time their debut album was released, Segarini was the only remaining original member. *Miss Butters* unveiled the anglophile persuasion that marked his subsequent music, but was deemed out of step with the prevailing musical trend. Mike Dure (guitar), Jim De Cocq (keyboards), Bill 'Kootch' Troachim (bass) and Vann Slatter (drums) completed the band's final line-up, which broke apart in 1970. Segarini and De Cocq formed Roxy, while founder member Olsen found fame as virtuoso Lee Michaels.
●ALBUMS: *Miss Butters* (1968)★★.

FAMOUS JUG BAND

This UK quartet featured Jill Johnson (vocals/guitar), Pete Berryman (guitar/vocals) Clive Palmer (guitar/vocals) and Henry Bartlett (vocals/jug). Initial attention focused on Palmer, a former member of the Incredible String Band, and some of that group's quirkiness prevailed on *Sunshine Possibilities*, the Jug Band's debut album. His premature departure from this fledgling venture robbed them of a pivotal member. Although a second album was completed, it lacked the depth of its predecessor and the Famous Jug Band broke up soon afterwards. Palmer subsequently formed COB while Berryman later recorded with folk guitarist John James.
●ALBUMS: *Sunshine Possibilities* (Liberty 1969)★★★, *Chameleon* (Liberty 1970)★★.

FANTASTIC BAGGYS

The Fantastic Baggys was a recording outlet for songwriting team P.F. Sloan (herein known as 'Flip') and Steve Barri. The duo supplied surfing act Jan And Dean with several compositions, notably 'Summer Means Fun' and 'From All Over The World', and added backing harmonies on several sessions, factors which in turn inspired this concurrent career. Bob Myman (drums) and Jerry Cargman completed the nominal Baggys line-up, but the venture was, in essence, studio-based. The Sloan/Barri team wrote arranged and produced every track on *Tell 'Em I'm Surfin'*, but the duo quickly tired of their creation and ceased using the name following the release of the Gary Paxton-penned 'It Was I' (1965). However, the Fantastic Baggys had proved highly popular in South Africa and a second album, *Ride The Wild Surf*, was compiled the following year. Although five tracks, drawn from singles and out-takes, did feature Sloan and Barri, more than half the set featured anonymous musicians imitating the original group. By the release of *Surfer's Paradise*, the ruse had run its course. Here any connection was even more tenuous and the sole Sloan/Barri performance, 'Only When You're Lonely', was mistakenly drawn from another studio project, the Grass Roots. When the album proved commercially moribund, the Baggy's appellation was mercifully abandoned.
●ALBUMS: *Tell 'Em I'm Surfin'* (Imperial 1964)★★★,

Ride The Wild Surf soundtrack (1964)★★, *Surfer's Paradise* (1967)★.
●COMPILATIONS: *Surfin' Craze* (1983)★★★.

FARDON, DON

b. Don Maughn, *c.*1943, Coventry, West Midlands, England. As the vocalist with the Sorrows, Maughn was featured on this cult group's most durable release, the pulsating 'Take A Heart'. A number 21 hit in September 1965, its hypnotic, throbbing beat was maintained on subsequent releases, several of which the singer co-composed. Here, however, he preferred to use an alternative surname, Fardon, which was then retained for the artist's solo career. His version of John D. Loudermilk's '(The Lament Of The Cherokee) Indian Reservation' gave him his first and only US hit single in 1968, reaching the Top 20. He broke into the UK charts in 1970 with 'Belfast Boy', a homage to the talented, but troubled footballer, George Best. This success paved the way for the re-issue of 'Indian Reservation' which, when resurrected, climbed to a respectable number 3 and became one of that year's most distinctive chart entries. Yet despite several further releases, some of which were remakes of former Sorrows material, Fardon was unable to secure consistent success.
●ALBUMS: *I've Paid My Dues* (Young Blood 1970)★★, *Released* (Young Blood 1970)★★.
●COMPILATIONS: *Indian Reservation: The Best Of* (See For Miles 1996)★★.

FARINA, MIMI

b. Mimi Margharita Baez, 30 April 1945, Stanford, California, USA. The younger sister of folk singer Joan Baez, Mimi was pursuing a solo career when she met and married Richard Farina. The couple began performing together in 1964 and completed two exceptional albums, *Celebrations For A Grey Day* and *Reflections In A Crystal Wind*, before Richard was killed in a motorcycle accident on 30 April 1966. Two years later Mimi helped to compile the commemorative *Memories*, as well as *Long Time Coming And A Long Time Gone*, a collection of her husband's lyrics, poetry and short stories. She later joined the Committee, a satirical theatre group, working as an improvisational actor before returning to singing. Having forged a short-lived partnership with Tom Jans, which resulted in one low-key album, she resumed her solo career. Farina later founded Bread And Roses, an organization which brought live music into convalescent homes, psychiatric wards and drug rehabilitation centres.
●ALBUMS: with Richard Farina *Celebrations For A Grey Day* (Vanguard 1965)★★★, *Reflections In A Crystal Wind* (Vanguard 1966)★★, *Memories* (Vanguard 1968)★★, with Tom Jans *Mimi Farina And Tom Jans* (1971)★★.
●COMPILATIONS: *The Best Of Mimi And Richard Farina* (Vanguard 1970)★★★.

FARINA, RICHARD

b. 1937, Brooklyn, New York, USA, d. 30 April 1966. A songwriter, novelist and political activist, Farina was drawn into folk music following his marriage to singer Carolyn Hester. Their ill-starred relationship ended in 1961 when, following a European tour, Richard decided to remain 'in exile' to work on his first novel *Been Down So Long It Looks Like Up To Me*. It was during this time that Farina's first recordings were made. *Dick Farina & Eric Von Schmidt*, the product of a two-day session in the cellar of London's Dobell's Jazz Shop, also featured an impromptu appearance by Bob Dylan, masquerading under his celebrated pseudonym, Blind Boy Grunt. Farina returned to America in 1963 where he married Mimi Baez, the sister of folk singer Joan Baez. The couple began performing together and were latterly signed to Vanguard Records. Their two superb albums were released in 1965, the first of which, *Celebrations For A Grey Day*, included Richard's classic song, 'Pack Up Your Sorrows'. *Been Down So Long* was published in 1966, but its author was killed in a motorbike crash during a celebratory party. Farina's death robbed a generation of an excellent writer and gifted musician.
●ALBUMS: *Dick Farina & Eric Von Schmidt* (1964)★★★, with Mimi Farina *Celebrations For A Grey Day* (1965)★★★, *Reflections In A Crystal Wind* (1965)★★.
●COMPILATIONS: *Memories* (Vanguard 1968)★★.

FARINAS

Formed at Leicester Art College, Leicestershire, England, in 1962, the Farinas originally comprised Jim King (saxophone), Harry Overnall (drums), Charlie Whitney (guitar/vocals) and Tim Kirchin (bass). Their primary influence was the Chess Records catalogue of the 50s, and blues rock 'n' rollers such as Chuck Berry in particular. The group recorded its solitary single, 'You'd Better Stop' backed by a cover version of Chris Kenner's 'I Like It Like That', for Fontana Records in 1964. A year later Ric Grech replaced Kirchin, while Roger Chapman came in to take over lead vocals in 1966. Shortly thereafter they abandoned the name Farinas and became first the Roaring Sixties then Family at the suggestion of Kim Fowley.

FARLOWE, CHRIS

b. John Henry Deighton, 13 October 1940, Islington, London, England. Farlowe's long career began during the 50s skiffle boom when the John Henry Skiffle Group won the all-England championship. He then formed the original Thunderbirds, which remained semi-professional until 1962 when they embarked on a month's engagement in Frankfurt, Germany. Farlowe then met Rik Gunnell, owner of London's Ram Jam and Flamingo clubs, and the singer quickly became a stalwart of the city's R&B circuit. He made his recording debut that year with the pop-oriented 'Air Travel', but failed to secure commercial success until 1966 when his version of the Rolling Stones' song, 'Out Of Time', produced by Mick Jagger, soared to the top of the UK charts. Several minor hits, including 'Ride On Baby' (1966) and 'Handbags And Gladrags' (1967), followed, as well as a brace of pop/soul albums, but Farlowe's intonation proved too craggy for popular consumption. He and the Thunderbirds - which between 1964 and 1967 featured Albert Lee (guitar), Dave Greenslade (organ), Bugs Waddell (bass), Ian Hague (drums) and Jerry Temple (congas) - remained one of the country's most impressive R&B acts, although session musicians were increasingly employed for recording purposes. By 1968 the group had been reduced to that of Farlowe, Lee, Pete Solley (keyboards) and Carl Palmer (drums), but two years later the singer founded an all-new group, the Hill. The venture's sole album, *From Here To Mama Rosa*, was not a commercial success and Chris joined ex-colleague Greenslade in Colosseum. This powerful jazz-rock group disbanded in 1971, and having briefly switched allegiances to Atomic Rooster, Farlowe retired from rock to pursue an interest in military and Nazi memorabilia. He re-emerged in 1975 with *The Chris Farlowe Band, Live*, but has conspicuously failed to find a satisfactory niche for his powerful, gritty voice. Cameo appearances during the 80s on sessions for Jimmy Page engendered the widely acclaimed *Out Of The Blue* and *Born Again* which together served notice that the singer's feeling for the blues remained intact. Although he gigs infrequently he can still be seen performing in the mid-90s as a support act, and he can still cause goosebumps with his sensational version of 'Stormy Monday Blues'. He rejoined his colleagues in Colosseum in 1996 for a reunion tour and album. Farlowe is blessed with a magnificent voice; with it he should have been a giant.

●ALBUMS: *Chris Farlowe And The Thunderbirds* aka *Stormy Monday* (Columbia 1966)★★★, *Fourteen Things To Think About* (Immediate 1966)★★★, *The Art Of Chris Farlowe* (Immediate 1966)★★★, *The Fabulous Chris Farlowe* (EMI Regal 1967)★★★, *Paint It Farlowe* (1968)★★★, *The Last Goodbye* (Immediate 1969)★★, as Chris Farlowe And The Hill *From Here To Mama Rosa* (Polydor 1970)★★, *The Chris Farlowe Band, Live* (Polydor 1976)★★★, *Out Of The Blue* (1985)★★, *Born Again* (1988)★★★, *Waiting In The Wings* (1992)★★★, *Lonesome Road* (Indigo 1995)★★★, with Zoot Money *Alexis Korner Memorial Concert Volume 2* (Indigo 1995)★★★.

●COMPILATIONS: *The Best Of Chris Farlowe Vol. 1* (Immediate 1968)★★★, *Out Of Time* (1975)★★★, *Out Of Time - Paint It Black* (1977)★★★, *Hot Property (The Rare Tracks)* (1983)★★, *Mr. Soulful* (1986)★★★, *Buzz With The Fuzz* (1987)★★★, *I'm The Greatest* (See For Miles 1994)★★★.

FARON'S FLAMINGOS

Formed in Liverpool, England, in 1961, Faron's Flamingos were one of the pivotal acts of the Merseybeat era who completely missed the ferry (sic) with no commercial success whatsoever. Founding members Nicky Crouch (guitar/vocals), Billy Jones (guitar/vocals), Eric London (bass) and Trevor Morias (drums) had worked together since 1959 as the Ravens, before adding vocalist Faron (b. Bill Roughley). Cavern Club DJ Bob Wooler suggested the name Faron's Flamingos. In 1962 London and Jones left the group which continued as a four-piece with ex-Undertakers bassist Mushy Cooper. Following a tour of France, Paddy Chambers (guitar/vocals) was added to the line-up and when Cooper left for Lee Curtis in 1963, Faron took over on bass. This version of Faron's Flamingos recorded four tracks for *This Is Merseybeat*, before securing a deal with Oriole Records. Sadly, their rousing version of 'Do You Love Me' was eclipsed by Brian Poole And The Tremeloes' inferior reading and an equally ebullient 'Shake Sherry' made little impression. The disillusioned group broke up in November 1963. Faron and Chambers joined the Big Three, while Morias later found success in the Peddlers.

FARREN, MICK

Born in Cheltenham but raised in Worthing and educated in London, Farren first entered music as a member of the group the Mafia around 1962. He then passed through a couple of R&B bands before forming a Fugs-type outfit which evolved into the Social Deviants in 1967. After his time with the Deviants (from which he was kicked out and stranded in America) and a brief spell in the first line-up of the Pink Fairies, Farren released his debut solo album, *Mona The Carnivorous Circus* in 1970. That same year Farren also worked on the original production of Twink's first solo album *Think Pink*. Farren then retired from performing music and turned to writing. At first he wrote science fiction but later produced a number of books such as *The Feelies*, *Watch Out Kids*, and *The Tale Of Willy's Rats*. He also started the underground comic *Nasty Tales*, edited *IT*, contributed to the *New Musical Express*, organized the Phun City Festival and still found time to collect toy robots. He re-entered the musicworld around 1976/7 when he began writing songs with Lemmy from Motorhead. He also recorded some tracks, including a reworking of the Deviants' anthem 'Let's Loot The Supermarket', which was released as an EP on Stiff Records. In 1977 he recorded a version of 'To Know Him Is To Love Him' for the Phil Spector tribute album *Bionic Gold*, before he eventually recorded his second solo album in 1978. *Vampires Stole My Lunch Money* featured contributions from Wilko Johnson, Andy Colquhoun, Sonja Kristina, Chrissie Hynde, Larry Wallis and others. To promote the album Farren assembled the Good Guys with Colquhoun and Wallis on guitars, Will Stallybrass on harmonica, Gary Tibbs on bass, and Alan Powell on drums. Colquhoun and Powell were both from Tanz Der Youth while Tibbs had just left the Vibrators. Farren later married Betsy Volck of Ze Records and moved to New York where he released a single on Ork. He continues to write.

●ALBUMS: *Mona The Carnivorous Circus* (Transatlantic 1970)★★, *Vampires Stole My Lunch Money* (Logo 1978)★★, *Partial Recall* (1992).

●FURTHER READING: *The Quest Of The DNA Cowboys*, *Synaptic Manhunt*, *The Neural Atrocity*, *The Textx Of Festival*.

FELIX, JULIE

b. 14 June 1938, Santa Barbara, California, USA. Felix arrived in the UK during the early 60s at a time when several US folk singers, including Paul Simon and Jackson C. Frank, had also relocated to London. Her early recordings revealed a commercial, rather than innovative talent, a fact emphasized by weekly appearances on UK television's *The Frost Report* (1967/68). She followed the liberal tradition of Tom Paxton or Pete Seeger, rather than that of the radical left, although she was an early champion of the folk-styled singer/songwriter movement, notably Leonard Cohen, and was proclaimed as 'Britain's Leading Lady of Folk'. Her humanitarian beliefs had, however, been put to practical use by the singer's tour of the African states of Kenya and Uganda, working for the Christian Aid and Freedom From Hunger charities. Felix enjoyed two successful British television series in her own right, *Once More With Felix* (1969/70) and *The Julie Felix Show* (1971), and enjoyed a UK Top 20 hit in 1970 with a version of 'El Condor Pasa', produced by pop svengali Mickie Most. The singer's 'wholesome' image was tarred by a conviction for possession of marijuana, but she continued a prolific recording career, albeit to less publicity, into the 80s, as well as performing for Women's Rights, Green and environmental benefits, and founding Britain's first 'New Age Folk Club'.

●ALBUMS: *Julie Felix* (Decca 1964)★★★, *2nd Album* (Decca 1965)★★★, *3rd Album* (Decca 1966)★★★, *Julie Felix Sings Dylan And Guthrie* (Decca 1966)★★★, *Changes* (Fontana 1966)★★★, *Julie Felix In Concert* (Fontana 1967)★★★, *Flowers* (Fontana 1968)★★, *This World Goes Round And Round* (Fontana 1969)★★★, *Going To The Zoo* (1970)★★★, *Clotho's Web* (1971)★★, *Lightning* (1974)★★★, *London Palladium* (1974)★★★, *Hota Chocolata* (1977)★★, *Blowing In The Wind* (1982)★★★, *Bright Shadows* (1989)★★★.

●COMPILATIONS: *The World Of Julie Felix* (Decca 1969)★★★, *The World Of Julie Felix Volume 2* (Decca 1970)★★★, *This Is Julie Felix* (1970)★★★, *The Most Collection* (1972)★★★, *This Is Julie Felix Volume 2* (1974)★★★, *Amazing Grace* (1987)★★★, *El Condor Pasa* (Start 1995)★★★.

FENDER, LEO

Along with Les Paul and Adolph Rickenbacker, Leo Fender (b. 10 August 1909, Anaheim, California, USA, d. 21 March 1991) was one of the key names in the development of the electric guitar in the middle of the twentieth century. He first came to the attention of the musical instrument manufacturing industry when he was working with 'Doc' Kauffman producing guitar amplifiers in the mid-40s. He had developed a new smaller pick-up and designed a solid body guitar based on the Hawaiian steel, with which to demonstrate it. Although the pick-up itself was quite revolutionary, local musicians were more intrigued with the guitar, and so Fender decided to concentrate his efforts in that direction. In 1946 he left Kauffman and formed the Fender Electrical Instrument Company. The idea of a solid body guitar had been in the forefront of manufacturer's minds since the advent of electrical amplification which meant that hollow sound boxes were no longer essential. It was Fender, along with Californian neighbours Les Paul and Paul Bigsby, who spearheaded the forthcoming wave of electric guitars. In 1948 Fender launched the Broadcaster (later called the Telecaster) which remained virtually unchanged for the next 30 or so years; there were a few variations such as the Esquire (1954), the Thinkline (1969), the Deluxe (1972) and the Custom (1972). Famous rock 'n' roll guitarist James Burton favours a Telecaster, as does Bruce Welch of the Shadows, Steve Cropper, Roy Buchanan and Bruce Springsteen. Fender's next major instrument was the Stratocaster, developed in 1953 with his chief engineer Leo Tavares, and put into production the following year. Like the Telecaster, the Stratocaster was virtually untouched in design over the next few decades and became a favourite of Buddy Holly, Hank B. Marvin, Eric Clapton, Rory Gallagher, Mark Knopfler and the master - Jimi Hendrix, to name just a few of thousands. In 1990 a Stratocaster once owned by Hendrix was sold at auction for almost £200,000. The design, shape, feel and colour of the Stratocaster became an art form, and arguably, the accepted icon for the electric guitar. In 1955 Fender contracted a virus that would dog him for the next decade. In the mid-60s, convinced that he had little time to live, Leo decided to order his affairs. The Fender Electrical Instrument Company was sold to CBS in January 1965 for $13 million, shortly after which Fender made a complete recovery. CBS employed him as a consultant and he continued to help to design and develop new guitars. Later he formed the CLF Research Company before returning to consultancy for Music Man guitars, started by former Fender employees Thomas Walker and Forrest White. In the 80s he formed G&L (George and Leo) Guitars with long time associate George Fullerton. They continued to make popular instruments, although names like the F100-1 series were less appealing than their forebears. Leo Fender died in the spring of 1991 aged 82. As well as the guitars mentioned, the Fender name is also attached to the Musicmaster (1956), the Jazzmaster (1958), the Jaguar (1961), and the Starcaster (1975). He also moved into electric basses in 1951 with the Precision and then the Jazz Bass (1960), Bass VI (1962) and the Telecaster Bass (1968).

●FURTHER READING: *The Fender Book: A Complete History Of Fender Electric Guitars*, Tony Bacon and Paul Day. *Fender Custom Shop Guitar Gallery*, Richard Smith.

FENDERMEN

Formed in 1959 in Milwaukee, Wisconsin, USA, the Fendermen were a trio best known for the 1960 US chart Top 5 rock 'n' roll adaptation of the Jimmie Rodgers country standard 'Muleskinner Blues'. The group consisted of guitarists Jim Sundquist and Phil Humphrey (both b. 26 November 1937, Sundquist in Niagara, Wisconsin, USA, and Humphrey in Stoughton, Wisconsin, USA) and drummer John Howard, of LaCrosse,

Wisconsin, USA. The two guitarists, who preferred the Fender brand of electric guitar, hence the name of the group, recorded 'Muleskinner Blues' initially for the small Cuca label. It was picked up by the somewhat larger Minnesota-based Soma label and became a hit in May 1960. (Howard was added at that time, for live appearances.) The group recorded one album for Soma, now a valued rarity in the USA, and continued together until 1966, with no other chart successes.

●ALBUMS: *Mule Skinner Blues* (Soma 1960)★★.

FENTON, SHANE

b. Bernard Jewry, 1942, London, England. Fenton achieved his first notable success after securing a spot on *Saturday Club*, BBC Radio's influential show. Backed by the Fentones and sporting a distinctive silver lamé suit, the singer quickly became a part of Britain's pre-beat enclave, beside other home-grown talent including Cliff Richard, Marty Wilde, Duffy Power and Billy Fury. Fenton had a UK Top 30 hit in 1961 with the mythologizing 'I'm A Moody Guy', but despite several similarly structured releases, only 'Cindy's Birthday' (1962) broached the UK Top 20. Deemed passé on the rise of the Beatles, Fenton eked out a living from the rock 'n' roll/cabaret circuit until revitalizing his career in the 70s under a new guise, Alvin Stardust.

●ALBUMS: *Good Rockin' Tonight* (Contour 1974)★★.
●FILMS: *It's All Happening* (1963).

FENTONES

Jerry Wilcox (b. 1940; lead guitar), Mickey Eyre (b. 1942; rhythm guitar), William Walter Edward 'Bonney' Oliver (bass) and Tony Hinchcliffe (b. 1940; drums) provided the backing to singer Shane Fenton. They became a popular attraction in their own right, recording several instrumental singles, including 'The Mexican' and 'The Breeze And I', both of which reached the UK Top 50 in 1962. Briefly touted as possible rivals to the Shadows, such aspirations proved over-ambitious and in keeping with many pre-beat contemporaries, the Fentones were later eclipsed by the Beatles and the new generation following in their wake

●FILMS: *It's All Happening* (1963).

FEVER TREE

Although a Texas group, Fever Tree made its mark with a tribute to the Summer of Love's host city with their 1968 anthem 'San Francisco Girls (Return Of The Native)'. Comprising Rob Landes (keyboards), Dennis Keller (vocals), E.E. Wolfe (bass), John Tuttle (drums) and Michael Knust (guitar), the psychedelic group formed in Houston, Texas, in the mid-60s as Bostwick Vine. The name change came in 1967 and the group subsequently signed with Chicago-based Mainstream Records. Two unsuccessful singles were recorded, and the group then signed to Uni Records, and recorded their self-titled debut album in 1968. 'San Francisco Girls (Return Of The Native)' was penned by Vivian Holtzman, one of the group's producers. Although only a minor chart hit, it received much airplay on the new USA FM rock stations and on John Peel's *Top Gear* radio programme in the UK. The group recorded four albums, three of which charted in the USA, before splitting up in 1970. Interest in the group was renewed in the mid-80s psychedelic revival, and compilation albums were issued in both the USA and UK.

●ALBUMS: *The Fever Tree* (Uni 1968)★★★, *Another Time, Another Place* (Uni 1968)★★, *Creation* (Uni 1969)★★, *Angels Die Hard* soundtrack (Uni 1970)★, *For Sale* (Ampex 1970)★★.
●COMPILATIONS: *Best Of Fever Tree* (1985)★★★, *San Francisco Girls* (1986)★★★.

FIDDLER ON THE ROOF

With music by Jerry Bock, lyrics by Sheldon Harnick and book by Joseph Stein, *Fiddler On The Roof* opened at the Imperial Theatre in New York on 22 September 1964. The story was based on tales by Sholom Aleichem which recounted episodes in the life of Tevye, a milkman living in a Jewish village in Czarist Russia. Set in the early years of the twentieth century, a time when Jewish orthodoxy, especially in matters of religion, language and custom, was under threat, *Fiddler On The Roof* was itself unorthodox. For one thing, religion was not traditional musical-comedy fare. Tevye's problems in coming to terms with change, his response to the wish of one of his daughters to marry outside the faith, and the ever-threatening presence of anti-Semitism gave *Fiddler On The Roof* a depth and intensity more in keeping with straight drama than with song and dance. The show also had an unhappy ending, with Tevye and his wife and two of his daughters leaving for America, hoping, but uncertain, that a married daughter will be able to follow with her husband, and unable through religious belief to bid farewell to another daughter who has married a gentile. Bock's music drew upon traditional folk forms, and the libretto and lyrics used language replete with cultural references that gave audiences a strong sense of social awareness, while simultaneously providing entertainment of the highest order. The show starred Zero Mostel as Tevye with Maria Karnilova as his wife, Golde, with other roles taken by Beatrice Arthur, as Yente the matchmaker, Joanna Merlin, Julia Migenes and Tanya Everett as the three older daughters, and Austin Pendleton, Bert Convy and Michael Grainger. Among the songs were 'Matchmaker, Matchmaker', 'To Life', 'Sunrise, Sunset', 'Now I Have Everything', 'Do You Love Me?', 'Miracle Of Miracles', 'Tradition', and, unusually for any Broadway musical show, a song written especially with a particular performer in mind, 'If I Were A Rich Man', which was sung by Mostel. Indeed, although *Fiddler On The Roof* had many strengths, Mostel was the tower that ensured the show's massive success. Nevertheless, the show continued to do good business after Mostel left at the end of the first year. His successors included Luther Adler, Herschel Bernardi and Jan Peerce. *Fiddler On The Roof*'s first Broadway run lasted for 3,242 performances and it was revived in 1976 with Mostel reprising the role of Tevye. The show won many awards including the New York Drama Critics' Circle Award as best musical, and Tony Awards for best musical, score, book, actor (Mostel), featured actress (Karnilova), choreographer (Jerome Robbins) and costumes (Patricia Zipprodt). The enormously popular 'If I Were A Rich Man' also became a surprise UK Top 10 hit in a version by Topol, who played the role of Tevye in the London production, which ran for over 2,000 performances, and the 1971 film version. He also starred in the 1990 Broadway revival, and the show's 30th anniversary world tour which called in at the London Palladium in June 1994.

FIFTH DIMENSION

Originally known as the Versatiles and later as the Vocals, Marilyn McCoo (b. 30 September 1944, Jersey City, New Jersey, USA), Florence LaRue (b. 4 February 1944, Philadelphia, Pennsylvania, USA), Billy Davis Jnr. (b. 26 June 1940, St. Louis, Missouri, USA), Lamont McLemore (b. 17 September 1940, St. Louis, Missouri, USA) and Ron Townsend (b. 29 January 1941, St. Louis, Missouri, USA), were a soul-influenced harmony group, based in Los Angeles. They sprang to fame in 1967 as an outlet for the then unknown talents of songwriter Jimmy Webb. Ebullient singles on the pop charts, including, 'Go Where You Wanna', 'Up Up And Away' and 'Carpet Man', established their fresh voices which wrapped themselves around producer Bones Howe's dizzy arrangements. Having completed two albums containing a number of Webb originals, the group then took to another composer, Laura Nyro, whose beautiful soul-styled songs, 'Stoned Soul Picnic', 'Sweet Blindness' (both 1968), 'Wedding Bell Blues' (1969) and 'Save The Country' (1970) continued the Fifth Dimension's success and introduced the group to the R&B charts. These popular recordings were punctuated by 'Aquarius/Let The Sunshine In', a medley of songs from the rock musical *Hair* that topped the US chart in 1969 and reached number 11 in Britain that same year. In 1971 the group reached number 2 in the US with the haunting 'One Less Bell To Answer'. From then on, however, the MOR elements within their style began to take precedence and the quintet's releases grew increasingly bland. In 1976 Marilyn McCoo and Billy Davis Jnr. (who were now married) left for a successful career both as a duo and as solo artists. They had a US number 1 hit together in 1976 with 'You Don't Have To Be A Star' which was followed up in 1977 by their last Top 20 hit, 'Your Love'. Marilyn went on to host the US television show *Solid Gold* for much of the early 80s.

●ALBUMS: *Up Up And Away* (Soul City 1967)★★★, *Magic Garden* (Soul City 1967)★★★, *Stoned Soul Picnic* (Soul City 1968)★★★, *Age Of Aquarius* (Soul City 1969)★★★, *Fantastic* (1970)★★, *Portrait* (Bell 1970)★★, *Love's Lines, Angles And Rhymes* (Bell 1971)★★★, *Live!* (Bell 1971)★★, *Individually And Collectively* (1972)★★, *Living Together, Growing Together* (1973)★★, *Earthbound* (1975)★★.

●COMPILATIONS: *Greatest Hits* (Soul City 1970)★★★, *The July 5th Album* (Soul City 1970)★★★, *Reflections* (1971), *Greatest Hits On Earth* (Arista 1972)★★★, *Anthology* (Rhino 1986)★★★, *Greatest Hits* (1988)★★★.

FIFTH ESTATE

The Fifth Estate is recalled for a novelty hit, 'Ding Dong! The Witch Is Dead' (from *The Wizard Of Oz*), which reached number 11 in the US charts during the summer of 1967. The group had been formed three years earlier and, inspired by the 'British Invasion', they began a career which took them through a variety of short-lived record deals until they secured their one-off success. The quintet - Wayne 'Wads' Wadham (vocals/keyboards), Rick Engler (vocals/guitar/kazoo/violin/clarinet/bass), D. Bill Shute (guitar/mandolin), Dick 'Duck' Ferrar (vocals/guitar/bass) and Furvus Evans (drums) - broke up when Shute was drafted. He later returned to music and has forged a successful career as a folk musician. His partner, Lisa Null, formed Green Linnet records with Patrick Sky and this outlet was responsible for several of Shute's subsequent recordings.

●ALBUMS: *Ding Dong The Witch Is Dead* (Jubilee 1967)★★.

FIREBALLS

Formed in the autumn of 1957 in Raton, New Mexico, USA, the Fireballs comprised George Tomsco (b. 24 April 1940, Raton, USA; guitar), Chuck Tharp (b. 3 February 1941; vocals), Danny Trammell (b. 14 July 1940; rhythm guitar), Stan Lark (b. 27 July 1940; bass) and Eric Budd (b. 23 October 1938; drums). The group placed 11 singles in the US charts between 1959-69, including the Top 10 hits 'Sugar Shack' (as Jimmy Gilmer And The Fireballs) and 'Bottle Of Wine', under their own name. Tomsco and Tharp formed the foundation of the group after meeting in high school. After the others came in, they rehearsed and won a talent contest in January 1958. After a shaky start that found members leaving for college and then returning, they recorded at Norman Petty's studio in Clovis, New Mexico, in August 1958. After several failed singles, they recorded the instrumental 'Torquay' in early 1959, which scraped into the Top 40. After two other minor chart singles on Top Rank and one on Warwick (as well as several non-charting singles on other labels and a Warwick album), Tharp left the group and was replaced by Jimmy Gilmer (b. 15 September 1940, LaGrange, Illinois, USA). During 1961 the group was used to overdub music behind unfinished tapes recorded by Buddy Holly before his death in 1959.

During 1962 the Fireballs were signed to Dot Records, where they recorded *Torquay*, after which Budd entered the army and was replaced by Doug Roberts. In early 1963, now billed as Jimmy Gilmer And The Fireballs, they recorded 'Sugar Shack', using an unusual keyboard called a Solovox to give the record a distinctive sound. The result was one of the best-selling hits of 1963 - 'Sugar Shack' stayed at number 1 for five weeks late in the year. An album of the same title also charted. Although several other singles and albums were released, the group was unable to capitalize on that success; the follow-up, 'Daisy Petal Pickin'', made number 15. Such efforts as *Folk Beat*, a 1965 album crediting only Gilmer, were unsuccessful. By the following year, Dot was sold and in 1967 the Fireballs signed to Atco Records. Before Christmas that year they recorded a Tom Paxton song, 'Bottle Of Wine', which reached number 9 in early 1968. There were three other minor chart singles by the end of 1969, including the politically charged 'Come On, React!', but the Fireballs' time had clearly expired, and they disbanded.

● ALBUMS: *The Fireballs* (Top Rank 1960)★★★, *Vaquero* (Top Rank 1960)★★★, *Here Are The Fireballs* (Warwick 1961)★★★, *Torquay* (Dot 1963)★★★, *Sugar Shack* (Dot 1963)★★★, *The Sugar Shackers* (1963)★★★, *Sensational* (1963)★★★, *Buddy's Buddy* (Dot 1964)★★, *Lucky 'Leven* (Dot 1965)★★, *Folk Beat* (Dot 1965)★★, *Campusology* (Dot 1966)★★, *Firewater* (Dot 1968)★★, *Bottle Of Wine* (Atco 1968)★★, *Come On, React!* (Atco 1969)★★.

● COMPILATIONS: *Blue Fire & Rarities* (Ace 1993)★★★.

FLOWERPOT MEN

This UK group was formed in 1967 by the Carter And Lewis songwriting team to exploit the concurrent flower-power boom. The ensuing single, 'Let's Go To San Francisco', became a Top 5 hit and a quartet of session vocalists - Tony Burrows, Robin Shaw, Pete Nelson and Neil Landon - then assumed the name. Despite this undoubtedly mercenary instigation, the group completed several well-sculpted releases, notably 'A Walk In The Sky'. An instrumental section, comprising Ged Peck (guitar), Jon Lord (organ), Nick Simper (bass) and Carlo Little (drums), accompanied the singers on tour, but this line-up was dissolved when Lord and Simper founded Deep Purple. Burrows later reverted to session work, and while Landon resurfaced in Fat Mattress, Shaw and Nelson retained their relationship with Carter And Lewis in White Plains.

● ALBUMS: *Let's Go To San Francisco* (1988)★★★.

FLOYD, EDDIE

b. 25 June 1935, Montgomery, Alabama, USA. A founder-member of the Detroit-based Falcons, Floyd was present on both their major hits, 'You're So Fine' (1959) and 'I Found A Love' (1962). He then recorded solo for Lupine in Detroit and Safice in Washington, DC, before moving to Memphis in 1965 to join the Stax organization. He first made his mark there as a composer, penning Wilson Pickett's '634-5789' among others. During Floyd's recording tenure at Stax, he enjoyed the use of the session bands Booker T. And The MGs and the Mar-Keys. He opened his account with 'Things Get Better' (1965), followed by the anthem-like 'Knock On Wood' (1966), one of soul's enduring moments. Probably the only time lightning and frightening can be coupled without sounding trite: 'just like thunder and lightning, the way you love me is frightening think I'd better knock on wood'. Although subsequent releases failed to match its success,

a series of powerful singles, including 'Love Is A Doggone Good Thing' (1967) and 'Big Bird' (1968), confirmed Floyd's stature both as performer and songwriter. Although his compositions were recorded by several acts, his next US Top 20 pop hit came with Sam Cooke's 'Bring It On Home To Me' in 1968. Floyd stayed with Stax until its bankruptcy in 1975, whereupon he moved to Malaco Records. His spell there was thwarted by commercial indifference and he left the label for Mercury in 1977, but met with no better results. In 1988, Floyd linked up with William Bell's Wilbe venture and issued his *Flashback* album. Briefly relocated to London, he recorded under the aegis of Mod resurrectionists Secret Affair, before surfacing in New York with the album *Try Me* (1985). In 1990 Floyd appeared live with a re-formed Booker T. And The MGs.

● ALBUMS: *Knock On Wood* (Stax 1967)★★★, *I've Never Found A Girl* (Stax 1968)★★★, *You've Got To Have Eddie* (Stax 1969)★★★, *California Girl* (Stax 1970)★★, *Down To Earth* (Stax 1971)★★, *Baby Lay Your Head Down* (Stax 1973)★★, *Soul Street* (1974)★★, *Experience* (1977)★★, *Try Me* (1985)★★, *Flashback* (1988)★★.

● COMPILATIONS: *Rare Stamps* (Stax 1968)★★★, *Chronicle* (1979)★★★, *The Best Of Eddie Floyd* (1988)★★★, *I've Never Found A Girl* (1992)★★★, *Rare Stamps/I've Never Found A Girl* (1993)★★★.

FOLKS BROTHERS

To be labelled a one-hit-wonder is generally something of an insult, but to be a one-record wonder is an accolade. The Jamaican artists who have made one perfect recording and then vanished, leaving a reputation forever untarnished by later lapses, could be counted on the fingers of one hand. The Folks Brothers are among that number: in 1961 or early 1962 they recorded 'Oh Carolina', a unique and perfect single, and never appeared again. The record has Count Ossie's Rastafarian drummers thundering out complex African cross-rhythms, Owen Gray contrastingly American-styled on piano, and the Brothers, a soulful lead singer and two lighter-voiced male accompanists, delivering the song. In 1993 an updated version of 'Oh Carolina' breached the number 1 position in the UK charts for Shaggy.

FONTANA, WAYNE

b. Glyn Ellis, 28 October 1945, Manchester, England. After changing his name in honour of Elvis Presley's drummer D.J. Fontana, Wayne was signed to the appropriately named Fontana Records by A&R head Jack Baverstock. Wayne's backing group, the Mindbenders from the horror film of the same name, were as accomplished as their leader and provided a gritty accompaniment. Their first minor hit was with the unremarkable 'Hello Josephine' in 1963. Specializing in mild R&B covers, the group finally broke through with their fifth release, the Major Lance cover 'Um, Um, Um, Um, Um', which reached number 5 in the UK. The 1965 follow-up, 'The Game Of Love', hit number 2 and spearheaded a

Kennedy Street Enterprises Manchester invasion of the US which lifted the group to number 1. Thereafter, the group struggled, with 'Just A Little Bit Too Late' and the below par 'She Needs Love' being their only further hits. In October 1965, Wayne decided to pursue a solo career, first recording the Bert Berns and Jerry Ragovoy ballad 'It Was Easier To Hurt Her' before finding success with Jackie Edwards' catchy 'Come On Home'. Erratic progress followed, with only the Graham Gouldman composition 'Pamela Pamela' breaking a run of misses. After giving up music during the early 70s, Fontana joined the revivalist circuit, although his progress was frequently dogged by personal problems.
●ALBUMS: *Wayne Fontana And The Mindbenders* (Fontana 1965)★★★,*The Game Of Love* (Fontana 1965)★★★, *Eric, Rick Wayne And Bob* (Fontana 1966)★★★, *Wayne One* (Fontana 1966)★★, *Wayne Fontana* (MGM 1967)★★.

FORD, DEAN, AND THE GAYLORDS

Formed in 1960 in Glasgow, Scotland, Dean Ford And The Gaylords were a musically accomplished act before the dawning of the Beat age. William 'Junior' Campbell (lead guitar), Pat Fairley (rhythm guitar), Bill Irving (bass) and Raymond Duffy (drums) had been fronted by various vocalists prior to the arrival of Thomas MacAlise in 1963, who assumed the Dean Ford name. The group was signed to Columbia Records by Norrie Paramor following an audition in Glasgow's Locarno Ballroom. Dean Ford And The Gaylords first single, released in 1964, was a breezy version of Chubby Checker's 'Twenty Miles'. It was succeeded by the less distinguished 'Mr. Heartbreak's Here Instead', which in turn was followed by a powerhouse reading of Shirley Ellis's 'The Name Game'. In 1965 Graham Knight replaced Bill Irving as the group made plans to relocate in London, England. Upon their arrival in 1966 they dropped the Dean Ford prefix and, as the Gaylords, released their strongest single to date, 'He's A Good Face (But He's Down And Out).' Despite its mod connotations, the song was written by US team Al Kooper and Irwin Levine. Although not a chart hit, the single was often played on pirate radio and helped solidify the Gaylords' career. Somewhat bravely they then decided to change their name completely, rechristening themselves the Marmalade.

FORD, EMILE, AND THE CHECKMATES

b. 16 October 1937, Castries, St. Lucia, West Indies. Having arrived in Britain to study at technical college, Ford later began singing professionally in London's dancehalls and coffee bars. In 1958 he formed the Checkmates with step-brothers George and Dave Sweetman (bass and saxophone, respectively), Ken Street (guitar), Les Hart (saxophone), Peter Carter (guitar), Alan Hawkshaw (piano) and John Cuffley (drums) and the following year secured a recording deal as first prize in a Soho talent contest. The group's debut single, 'What Do

You Want To Make Those Eyes At Me For?', topped the charts that year and this Caribbean-influenced rendition of a popular standard remains their best-known release. The octet enjoyed further success with the similarly styled 'Slow Boat To China', 'Them There Eyes' (credited solely to Ford) and 'Counting Teardrops'. A concurrent album featured material drawn from Elvis Presley, Lloyd Price and Les Paul and Mary Ford, but Ford's novelty aspect quickly faltered. Having parted from the Checkmates, who later accompanied P.J. Proby, the singer spent many years performing in British clubs before emigrating to Los Angeles, California.
●ALBUMS: *New Tracks With Emile* (Pye 1960)★★★, *Emile* (Piccadilly 1961)★★★, *Emile Ford* (1972)★★★.
●COMPILATIONS: *Under The Midnight Sun* (Pye Golden Guinea 1965)★★★, *The Best Of Emile Ford And The Checkmates* (1991)★★★, *Greatest Hits* (1993)★★★, *The Very Best Of ...* (Sound Waves 1994)★★★.

FORTUNE, LANCE

b. Chris Morris, 1940, Birkenhead, Cheshire, England. Until he received a guitar at Christmas 1956, this grammar school student had studied classical piano. Morris sacrificed a scholarship at a Welsh university to work as an odd-job man at the famous London coffee bar, the 2 I's, and it was there that he was heard singing by top manager and impresario Larry Parnes in 1959. Although he did not manage him, Parnes rechristened him Lance Fortune (a name he had previously given to Clive Powell, a singer and pianist, whom he later renamed Georgie Fame). Fortune recorded his first single 'Be Mine', an Adam Faith-styled pop song, backed by John Barry's musicians, which was released by Pye and eventually climbed to number 4 in the UK. During the time it took to reach the charts in Britain, Fortune toured with his idol, Gene Vincent. He also managed to put the follow-up 'This Love I Have For You' into the Top 30 but it was his last taste of success - long-term fame was not on the cards for Mr. Fortune.

FORTUNES

Originally formed in March 1963 as a trio, this UK beat group comprised Glen Dale (b. 24 April 1943, Deal, Kent, England; guitar); Rod Allen (b. Rodney Bainbridge, 31 March 1944, Leicester, England; bass) and Barry Pritchard (b. 3 April 1944, Birmingham, England; guitar). The group had come together at Clifton Hall, the pop academy in the Midlands masterminded by their manager Reg Calvert. After perfecting their harmonic blend, the group recruited David Carr (b. 4 August 1943, Leyton, Essex, England; keyboards) and Andy Brown (b. 7 July 1946, Birmingham, England; drums) and toured consistently in the Midlands. Their debut single, 'Summertime Summertime' passed without notice, but the follow-up 'Caroline' was taken up as the theme song for the pirate radio station of the same name. By 1965 the group had broken into the UK and US Top 10 with 'You've Got Your Troubles' and modestly stated their ambition of recording pop ballads and harmonious standards. 'Here It Comes Again' and 'This Golden Ring' displayed their easy listening appeal and suggested the possibility of a long-term showbusiness career. Unfortunately, the group was hampered by the departure of vocalist Glen Dale who went on to pursue an unsuccessful solo career. To make matters worse, their manager was shot dead in a dispute over the ownership of the UK pirate station Radio City. The group continued and after switching record labels scored an unexpectedly belated US hit with 'Here Comes That Rainy Day Feeling Again' in 1971. Back in the UK, they also enjoyed their first hits in over five years with 'Freedom Come Freedom Go' and 'Storm In A Teacup' and have since sustained their career, albeit with changing personnel, on the cabaret circuit.

Albums; *The Fortunes* i (Decca 1965)★★★, *The Fortunes* ii (Capitol 1972)★★.

●COMPILATIONS: *Remembering* (1976)★★★, *Best Of The Fortunes* (1983)★★★, *Music For The Millions* (1984)★★★, *Greatest Hits* (1985)★★★, *Here It Comes Again* (Deram 1996)★★★.

FOUNDATIONS

Formed in January 1967, the Foundations were discovered by London record dealer Barry Class as they rehearsed in the Butterfly, a club situated in a basement below his office. He introduced the group to songwriters Tony Macauley and John MacLeod whose composition, 'Baby, Now That I've Found You', became the group's debut release. An engaging slice of commercial pop, soul, the single soared to the top of the UK charts and by February 1968 had reached number 9 in the USA, with global sales eventually exceeding three million.

The group's multiracial line-up included Clem Curtis (b. 28 November 1940, Trinidad, West Indies; vocals), Alan Warner (b. 21 April 1947, London, England; guitar), Tony Gomez (b. 13 December 1948, Colombo, Sri Lanka; organ), Pat Burke (b. 9 October 1937, Jamaica, West Indies; tenor saxophone, flute), Mike Elliot (b. 6 August 1929, Jamaica, West Indies; tenor saxophone), Eric Allan Dale (b. 4 March 1936, Dominica, West Indies; trombone), Peter Macbeth (b. 2 February 1943, London, England; bass) and Tim Harris (b. 14 January 1948, London, England; drums). Dale was a former member of the Terry Lightfoot and Alex Welsh jazz bands, while Elliot had backed Colin Hicks, brother of British rock 'n' roll singer Tommy Steele. This mixture of youth and experience drew much contemporary comment. The Foundations scored a second multi-million seller in 1968 with 'Build Me Up, Buttercup'. Written by Macauley in partnership with Manfred Mann's Michael D'Abo, this compulsive song reached number 2 in Britain before topping the US chart for two weeks. The group enjoyed further success with several similarly styled releases, including 'Back On My Feet Again' and 'Any Old Time' (both 1968), but their momentum faltered when Curtis embarked on an ill-starred solo career. He was replaced by Colin Young (b. 12 September 1944, Barbados, West Indies), but the departure of Elliot signalled an internal

dissatisfaction. 'In The Bad Bad Old Days' (1969) returned the group to the UK Top 10, but that year's minor hit, 'Born To Live And Born To Die', was their last chart entry. The septet split up in 1970 when the rhythm section broke away to form the progressive group Pluto. A completely new line-up later resurrected the Foundations' name with little success.

●ALBUMS: *From The Foundations* (Pye 1967)★★, *Rocking The Foundations* (Pye 1968)★★, *Digging The Foundations* (Pye 1969)★★.

●COMPILATIONS: *Back To The Beat* (1983)★★, *The Best Of The Foundations* (1987)★★★.

●FILMS: *The Cool Ones* (1967).

FOUR PENNIES

This Lancastrian-born Blackburn beat group was comprised of Lionel Morton (14 August 1942, Blackburn, Lancashire, England; vocals/rhythm guitar), Fritz Fryer (b. David Roderick Carnie Fryer, 6 December 1944, Oldham, England; lead guitar), Mike Wilsh (b. 21 July 1945, Stoke-on-Trent, England; bass) and Alan Buck (b. 7 April 1943, Brierfield, Lancashire, England; drums). They scored a notable UK number 1 hit in 1964 with 'Juliet' - a Morton-penned ballad that was originally the b-side of the less immediate 'Tell Me Girl', which had a stark simplicity that enhanced its plaintive qualities. The quartet enjoyed three further Top 20 entries with 'I Found Out The Hard Way', 'Black Girl' (both 1964) and 'Until It's Time For You To Go' (1965), but were unable to sustain a long career. Fryer, having briefly fronted a new act, Fritz, Mike and Mo, later became a successful record producer, while Morton, who married actress Julia Foster, made frequent appearances in children's television programmes.

●ALBUMS: *Two Sides Of The Four Pennies* (Philips 1964)★★★, *Mixed Bag* (Philips 1966)★★★.

●COMPILATIONS: *Juliet* (Wing 1967)★★★.

FOUR SEASONS

This highly acclaimed USA vocal group first came together in 1956 with a line-up comprising vocalists Frankie Valli (b. Francis Castelluccio, 3 May 1937, Newark, New Jersey, USA), brothers Nick and Tommy DeVito (b. 19 June 1936, Bellville, New Jersey, USA) and Hank Majewski. Initially known as the Variatones, then the Four Lovers, they enjoyed a minor US hit with 'You're The Apple Of My Eye', composed by Otis Blackwell. After being dropped by RCA Records, they recorded a single for Epic, following which Valli departed in 1958. As a soloist he released 'I Go Ape', composed by singer Bob Crewe. Meanwhile, the Four Lovers released several records under pseudonymous names, during which Nick DeVito and Majewski departed to be replaced by Nick Massi (b. 19 September 1935, Newark, New Jersey, USA) and Bob Gaudio (b. 17 December 1942, Bronx, New York, USA), a former member of the Royal Teens. After combining with Crewe and Gaudio, the group evolved into the Four Seasons, recording the single 'Spanish Lace' for the End label, before signing with Vee Jay Records. There, they released 'Sherry', which reached number 1 in the USA in

September 1962. A brilliant example of falsetto, harmony pop, the track established the group as one of America's most popular. Two months later, they were back at the top with the powerful 'Big Girls Don't Cry' and achieved the same feat the following March with the equally powerful 'Walk Like A Man'. All these hits were underpinned by lustrous, soaring harmonies and thick up-front production, which gave the Seasons a sound that was totally unique in pop at that time. Their international fame continued throughout 1964 when they met fierce competition from the Beatles. A sign of their standing was evinced by Vee Jay's release of a battle of the bands album featuring the Seasons and the Beatles. Significantly, when the Fab Four held four of the Top 5 positions in the *Billboard* chart during early 1964, the Four Seasons represented the solitary competition with 'Dawn (Go Away)' at number 3. The sublime 'Rag Doll' brought them back to the top in the summer of 1964.

In 1965, Nick Massi left the group and was replaced by Joe Long. It was during this period that they playfully released a version of Bob Dylan's 'Don't Think Twice It's All Right' under the pseudonym Wonder Who. Valli, meanwhile, was continuing to enjoy solo hits. By the end of the 60s, the group reflected the changing times by attempting to establish themselves as a more serious act with *Genuine Imitation Life Gazette*. The album was poorly received, however, and following its release Gaudio replaced Crewe as producer. When Tommy DeVito left in 1970, the lucrative Four Seasons back catalogue and rights to the group name rested with Valli and Gaudio. A brief tie-up with Berry Gordy's Motown label saw the release of *Chameleon*, which despite favourable reviews sold poorly. Meanwhile, Valli was receiving unexpected success in the UK thanks to a northern soul dancefloor revival of 'You're Ready Now', which reached number 11 in 1971. Throughout the early 70s, membership of the Four Seasons was erratic, and Gaudio retired from performing in 1974 to concentrate on producing. Despite impending deafness, Valli was back at number 1 in 1975 with 'My Eyes Adored You'. With an old track from *Chameleon*, 'The Night', adding to the glory and the latest group line-up charting with 'Who Loves You', it was evident that the Four Seasons were as popular as ever. Immense success followed as the group became part of the disco boom sweeping America. The nostalgic 'December 1963 (Oh What A Night)' was a formidable transatlantic number 1 in 1976, but the following year, Valli left the group to concentrate on his solo career. While he again hit number 1 in the USA with the Barry Gibb film theme, *Grease*, the Four Seasons continued with drummer Gerry Polci taking on lead vocals. Valli returned to the group for a double album recorded live at Madison Square Garden. A team-up with the Beach Boys on the single 'East Meets West' in 1984 was followed by a studio album, *Streetfighter*, which featured Valli. Still going strong, the Four Seasons have become an institution whose illustrious history spans several musical eras, from the barber shop harmonies of the 50s to the disco beat of the 70s and beyond. It is however the timeless hit

singles of the 60s to which the group are indelibly linked.
●ALBUMS: *Sherry And 11 Others* (Vee Jay 1962)★★★, *Ain't That A Shame And 11 Others* (Vee Jay 1963)★★★, *The 4 Seasons Greetings* (Vee Jay 1963)★★★, *Big Girls Don't Cry* (Vee Jay 1963)★★★, *Folk-Nanny* (Vee Jay 1963)★★★, *Born To Wander* (Philips 1964)★★★, *Dawn And 11 Other Great Songs* (Philips 1964)★★★, *Stay And Other Great Hits* (Vee Jay 1964)★★★, *Rag Doll* (Philips 1964)★★★, *We Love Girls* (Vee Jay 1965)★★★, *The Four Seasons Entertain You* (Philips 1965)★★★, *Recorded Live On Stage* (Vee Jay 1965)★★, *The Four Seasons Sing Big Hits By Bacharach, David And Dylan* (Philips 1965)★★, *Working My Way Back To You* (Philips 1966)★★★, *Lookin' Back* (Philips 1966)★★★, *Christ mas Album* (Philips 1967)★★★, *Genuine Imitation Life Gazette* (Philips 1969)★★★, *Edizione D'Oro* (Philips 1969)★★★, *Chameleon* (1972)★★, *Streetfighter* (1975)★★, *Inside You* (1976)★★, *Who Loves You* (Warners 1976)★★★, *Helicon* (1977)★★★, *Reunited Live* (Sweet Thunder 1981)★★.
●COMPILATIONS: *Golden Hits Of The Four Seasons* (Vee Jay 1963)★★★★, *More Golden Hits By The Four Seasons* (Vee Jay 1964)★★★★, *Gold Vault Of Hits* (Philips 1965)★★★★, *Second Vault Of Golden Hits* (Philips 1967)★★★★, *Seasoned Hits* (Fontana 1968)★★★★, *The Big Ones* (Philips 1971)★★★★, *The Four Seasons Story* (Private Stock 1976)★★★★★, *Greatest Hits* (K-Tel 1976)★★★, *The Collection* (Telstar 1988)★★★★, *Anthology* (Rhino 1988)★★★★★, *Rarities Vol 1* (Rhino 1990)★★★, *Rarities Vol. 2* (Rhino 1990)★★★, *The Very Best Of Frankie Valli And The Four Seasons* (Polygram 1992)★★★★.
●FILMS: *Beach Ball* (1964).

FOUR TOPS

Levi Stubbs (b. *c*.1938, Detroit, Michigan, USA), Renaldo 'Obie' Benson (b. 1937, Detroit, Michigan, USA), Lawrence Peyton (b. *c*.1938, Detroit, Michigan, USA, d. 1997) and Abdul 'Duke' Fakir (b. *c*.1938, Detroit, Michigan, USA), first sang together at a party in Detroit in 1954. Calling themselves the Four Aims, they began performing at supper clubs in the city, with a repertoire of jazz songs and standards. In 1956, they changed their name to the Four Tops to avoid confusion with the popular singing group the Ames Brothers, and recorded a one-off single for the R&B label Chess. Further unsuccessful recordings appeared on Red Top, Columbia and Riverside between 1958 and 1962, before the Four Tops were signed to the Motown jazz subsidiary, Workshop, in 1963. Motown boss Berry Gordy elected not to release their initial album, *Breaking Through*, in 1964, and suggested that they record with the label's Holland/Dozier/Holland writing and production team. The initial release from this liaison was 'Baby I Need Your Loving', which showcased the group's strong harmonies and the gruff, soulful lead vocals of Levi Stubbs; it reached the US Top 20. The following year, another Holland, Dozier, Holland song, 'I Can't Help Myself', topped the charts, and established the Four Tops as one of Motown's most successful groups.

Holland/Dozier/Holland continued to write and produce for the Four Tops until 1967. The pinnacle of this collaboration was 'Reach Out I'll Be There', a transatlantic hit in 1966. This represented the peak of the traditional Motown style, bringing an almost symphonic arrangement to an R&B love song; producer Phil Spector described the record as 'black (Bob) Dylan'. Other major hits like 'It's The Same Old Song' and 'Bernadette' were not as ambitious, although they are still regarded as Motown classics today. In 1967, the Four Tops began to widen their appeal with soul-tinged versions of pop hits, such as the Left Banke's 'Walk Away Renee' and Tim Hardin's 'If I Were A Carpenter'. The departure of Holland, Dozier, Holland from Motown later that year brought a temporary halt to the group's progress, and it was only in 1970, under the aegis of producer/writers like Frank Wilson and Smokey Robinson, that the Four Tops regained their hit status with a revival of the Tommy Edwards hit, 'It's All In The Game', and the socially aware ballad, 'Still Waters'. That same year, they teamed up with the Supremes for the first of three albums of collaborations.

Another revival, Richard Harris's hit 'MacArthur Park', brought them success in 1971, while Renaldo Benson also co-wrote Marvin Gaye's hit single 'What's Going On'. But after working with the Moody Blues on 'A Simple Game', in 1972, the Four Tops elected to leave Motown when the corporation relocated its head office from Detroit to California. They signed a deal with Dunhill, and immediately restored their chart success with records that marked a return to their mid-60s style, notably the theme song to the 'blaxploitation' movie *Shaft In Africa*, 'Are You Man Enough'. Subsequent releases were less dynamic, and for the remainder of the 70s the Four Tops enjoyed only sporadic chart success, although they continued touring and performing their Motown hits. After two years of inactivity at the end of the decade, they joined Casablanca Records, and immediately secured a number 1 soul hit with 'When She Was My Girl', which revived their familiar style. Subsequent releases in a similar vein also charted in Britain and America.

In 1983, the group performed a storming medley 'duel' of their 60s hits with the Temptations during the Motown 25th Anniversary television special. They re-signed to the label for the aptly titled *Back Where I Belong*, one side of which was produced by Holland, Dozier, Holland. But disappointing sales and disputes about the group's musical direction led them to leave Motown once again for Arista, where they found immediate success in 1988 with the singles 'Indestructible' and 'Loco In Acapulco', the latter taken from the soundtrack to the film *Buster*. The Four Tops have retained a constant line-up since their inception, and the group's immaculate choreography and harmonies have ensured them ongoing success as a live act from the mid-60s to the present day - notably in the UK and Europe, where they have always been held in higher regard than in their homeland.

●ALBUMS: *Four Tops* (Motown 1964)★★★, *Four Tops No. 2* (Motown 1964)★★★★, *On Top* (Motown 1966)★★★★, *Live!* (Motown 1966)★★★, *On Broadway* (Motown 1967)★★★, *Reach Out* (Motown 1967)★★★★, *Yesterday's Dreams* (Motown 1968)★★★, *Now* (Motown 1969)★★★, *Soul Spin* (Motown 1969)★★★, *Still Waters Run Deep* (Motown 1970)★★★, *Changing Times* (Motown 1970)★★★, with the Supremes *The Magnificent Seven* (1970)★★★, with the Supremes *The Return Of The Magnificent Seven* (1971)★★★, with the Supremes *Dynamite* (1971)★★★, *Nature Planned It* (1972)★★★, *Keeper Of The Castle* (Command/Probe 1972)★★★, *Shaft In Africa* soundtrack (Probe 1973)★★, *Main Street People* (Command/Probe 1973)★★, *Meeting Of The Minds* (Probe 1974)★★, *Live And In Concert* (ABC 1974)★★, *Night Lights Harmony* (ABC 1975)★★, *Catfish* (1976)★★, *The Show Must Go On* (1977)★★, *At The Top* (1978)★★, *Tonight* (1981)★★, *One More Mountain* (1982)★★, *Back Where I Belong* (1983)★★, *Magic* (1985)★★, *Hot Nights* (1986)★★, *Indestructible* (1988)★★.
●COMPILATIONS: *Four Tops Greatest Hits* (Motown 1968)★★★★★, *Four Tops Greatest Hits Vol. 2* (Motown 1971)★★★★, *Four Tops Anthology* (Motown 1974)★★★★★.

FOUR-EVERS

The Four-Evers formed in Brooklyn, New York, USA, in the early 60s and consisted of Joe Di Benedetto (lead), John Cipriani (first tenor), Steve Tudanger (second tenor) and Nick Zagami (baritone). Their debut came in 1962 with 'I'll Be Seeing You', which saw them signed to Columbia Records at an average collective age of just 15. Although this received a strong local reception, it was not until the song was covered by the Duprees the following year that it became a chart hit. By 1963 the Four Evers had moved to Smash Records, a subsidiary operation run by Mercury Records, for whom they recorded 'It's Love' in September. However, a better reaction was afforded to its follow-up, 'Please Be Mine' (aka 'Be My Girl'), written by Bob Gaudio, which reached number 75 in the *Billboard* national charts. Joining Leslie Gore and Bobby Rydell on tours of the US and Canada, the Four-Evers also backed Eddie Rambeau and Vinnie Monte on record. However, when their last single for Smash, '(Doo Bee Dum) Say I Love You', flopped, and their remaining outings for three successive labels fared poorly, they dissolved in 1968. Tudanger and Di Benedetto formed a new group, Playhouse, to back recordings made with producer Jeff Barry. In this guise they performed uncredited behind a number of hits including those ascribed to the Archies, Andy Kim and Robin McNamara. By the time they broke up in 1970, Playhouse had also recorded two singles on their own account, for Barry's Steel Records. Afterwards Di Benedetto joined New York's Joe Casey Orchestra.

FOURMOST

Originally known as the Blue Jays, then the Four Jays, then the Four Mosts; Brian O'Hara (b. 12 March 1942, Liverpool, England; lead guitar/vocals), Mike Millward (b. 9 May 1942, Bromborough, Cheshire, England, d. 1966; rhythm guitar/vocals), Billy Hatton (b. 9 June 1941, Liverpool, England; bass) and Dave Lovelady (b. 16 October 1942, Liverpool, England; drums) achieved momentary fame under the management wing of Brian Epstein. Two commercial John Lennon and Paul McCartney songs, 'Hello Little Girl' and 'I'm In Love', served as their initial a-sides, but the unflinchingly chirpy 'A Little Lovin'' became the quartet's biggest hit on reaching number 6 in April 1964. An archetypal merseybeat group, the Fourmost's later releases veered from Tamla, Motown ('Baby I Need Your Lovin'') to George Formby ('Aunt Maggie's Remedy') and their unswerving 'show business' professionalism was deemed anachronistic in the wake of the R&B boom. The death in 1966 of leukaemia victim Millward undermined the group's confidence, and despite McCartney's continued patronage - he produced their 1969 rendition of 'Rosetta' - the Fourmost were later consigned to cabaret and variety engagements.

●ALBUMS: *First And Fourmost* (Parlophone 1965)★★★.
●COMPILATIONS: *The Most Of The Fourmost* (1982)★★★.
●FILMS: *Ferry Cross The Mersey* (1964).

FOWLEY, KIM

b. 27 July 1942, Los Angeles, California, USA. A prodigious talent, Fowley's role as a producer, songwriter, recording artist and catalyst proved important to 60s and 70s pop. He recorded with drummer Sandy Nelson during the late 50s and later worked with several short-lived hit groups including the Paradons ('Diamonds And Pearls') and the Innocents ('Honest I Do'). Durable success came from his collaborations with schoolfriends Gary S. Paxton and Skip Battin, who performed as Skip And Flip. Fowley produced 'Cherry Pie' (1960), their US Top 20 entry and, with Paxton, created the Hollywood Argyles whose novelty smash, 'Alley Oop' (1960) topped the US charts. The pair were also responsible for shaping Paul Revere And The Raiders' debut hit, 'Like Long Hair' and in 1962 they assembled the Rivingtons, whose gloriously nonsensical single, 'Papa-Oom-Mow-Mow', was a minor success. That same year Fowley produced 'Nut Rocker' for B. Bumble And The Stingers, which was a hit on both sides of the Atlantic and a UK number 1. In 1964 Fowley undertook promotional work for singer P.J. Proby and the following year began embracing the Los Angeles counter-culture through his association with scene guru Vito and Frank Zappa's nascent Mothers Of Invention.

Fowley came to Britain on several occasions. The Rockin' Berries recorded 'Poor Man's Son' at his suggestion, he composed 'Portobello Road' with Cat Stevens, and produced sessions for Deep Feeling (which included Dave Mason and Jim Capaldi, later of Traffic), the Farinas

(which evolved into Family), the Belfast Gypsies and the Soft Machine. Fowley also recorded in his own right, completing a cover version of the Napoleon XIV hit, 'They're Coming To Take Me Away, Ha-Haaa!', and 'The Trip', a hypnotic paean to underground predilections. He became closely associated with flower-power, recording *Love Is Alive And Well* in 1967. This debut album was the first of a prolific output which, although of undoubted interest and merit, failed to match the artist's intuitive grasp of current trends for other acts. He produced material for the Seeds, A.B. Skhy, Warren Zevon and Gene Vincent, while maintaining his links with Europe through Finnish progressive act Wigwam.

Skip Battin joined the Byrds in 1970 and several collaborations with Fowley became a part of the group's late period repertoire, although long-time fans baulked at such ill-fitting material as 'Citizen Kane' and 'America's Great National Pastime'. Battin's first solo album, *Skip*, consisted of songs written with Fowley, while their partnership continued when the bassist joined the New Riders Of The Purple Sage. Fowley's role as a pop svengali continued unabated and he was responsible for piecing together the Runaways, an all-girl group whose average age was 16. They quickly outgrew the initial hype and abandoned their mentor, who in turn formed a new vehicle, Venus And The Razorblades. The advent of punk provided scope for further exploitation, but as the 80s progressed Fowley's once-sure touch seemed to desert him. He remains a cult name and as such can still release the occasional record. *Let the Madness In* was idiosyncratic and unfunny.

●ALBUMS: *Love Is Alive And Well* (Tower 1967)★★, *Born To Be Wild* (Imperial 1968)★★, *Outrageous* (Imperial 1968)★★, *Good Clean Fun* (Imperial 1968)★★, *The Day The Earth Stood Still* (1970)★★, *I'm Bad* (1972)★★, *International Heroes* (1973)★★, *Visions Of The Future* (1974)★★, *Animal God Of The Street* (1975)★★, *Living In The Streets* (1978)★★, *Sunset Boulevard* (1978)★★, *Legendary Dog Duke Sessions* (1979)★★, *Snake Document Masquerade* (1979)★★, *Hollywood Confidential* (1980)★★, *Hotel Insomnia* (1993)★★, *White Negroes In Deutschland* (1993)★★, *Let The Madness In* (Receiver 1995)★, *Mondo Hollywood* (Rev-Ola 1995)★★.

FOXX, INEZ AND CHARLIE

Inez Foxx (b. 9 September 1942, Greensboro, North Carolina, USA) and Charlie Foxx (b. 23 October 1939, Greensboro, North Carolina, USA) formed this brother and sister duo. Inez was a former member of the Gospel Tide Chorus, and her first solo single, 'A Feeling', was issued on Brunswick Records, credited to 'Inez Johnston'. Charlie was meanwhile a budding songwriter and his reworking of a nursery rhyme, 'Mockingbird', became their first single together. Released on the Sue label subsidiary Symbol, it was a US Top 10 hit in 1963, although it was not until 1969 that the song charted in the UK Top 40. Their immediate releases followed the same contrived pattern but later recordings for Musicor, Dynamo, in particular 'I Stand Accused', were more adventurous. However, their final hit together, '(1-2-3-4-5-6-7) Count The Days' (1967), was modelled closely on that early style.

Solo again, Inez continued to record for Dynamo before signing with Stax, Volt, in 1972. Although apparently uncomfortable with their recording methods, the results, including the *Inez Foxx In Memphis* album, were excellent.

●ALBUMS: *Mockingbird* (Sumbol 1963)★★★★, *Inez And Charlie Foxx* (Sue 1965)★★★★, *Come By Here* (Dynamo 1965)★★★. Solo: Inez Foxx *In Memphis* (1972).

●COMPILATIONS: *Inez And Charlie Foxx's Greatest Hits* (Dynamo 1967)★★★, *Mockingbird: The Best Of Charlie And Inez Foxx* (EMI America 1986)★★★, *At Memphis And More* (1990)★★★.

FRANCIS, CONNIE

b. Concetta Rosa Maria Franconero, 12 December 1938, Newark, New Jersey, USA. A popular singer of tearful ballads and jaunty up-tempo numbers, Francis was one of the most successful female artists of the 50s and 60s. She began playing the accordion at the age of four, and was singing and playing professionally when she was 11. After winning an *Arthur Godfrey Talent Show*, she changed her name, at Godfrey's suggestion. Signed for MGM Records in 1955, her first record was a German import, 'Freddy', which was also recorded by Eartha Kitt and Stan Kenton. 'Majesty Of Love', her 10th release, a duet with Marvin Rainwater, was her first US chart entry. In 1957 she was persuaded by her father, against her will, to record one of his favourites, the 1923 song 'Who's Sorry Now', by Harry Ruby, Bert Kalmar and Ted Snyder. It went to number 4 in the US charts and number 1 in the UK, and was the first of a string of hits through to 1962. These included reworkings of more oldies, such as 'My Happiness', 'Among My Souvenirs' and 'Together'. Among her more jaunty, upbeat songs were 'Stupid Cupid' (another UK number 1 coupled with 'Carolina Moon') and 'Where The Boys Are' by the new songwriting team of Neil Sedaka and Howard Greenfield. Her other US Top 10 entries included 'Lipstick On Your Collar', 'Frankie', 'Mama', 'Everybody's Somebody's Fool' (her first US number 1), 'My Mind Has A Heart Of Its Own' (another US number 1), 'Many Tears Ago', 'Breakin' In A Brand New Broken Heart', 'When The Boy In Your Arms (Is The Boy In Your Heart)', 'Don't Break The Heart That Loves You' (US number 1), 'Second Hand Love' and 'Vacation'. Francis made her film debut in 1960 with *Where The Boys Are*, and followed it with similar 'frothy' comedy musicals such as *Follow The Boys* (1963), *Looking For Love* (1964) and *When The Boys Meet The Girls* (1965). Outdated by the 60s beat boom, she worked in nightclubs in the late 60s, and did much charity work for UNICEF and similar organizations, besides entertaining US troops in Vietnam. She also extended her repertoire, and kept her options open by recording albums in several languages, including French, Spanish and Japanese, and one

entitled, *Connie Francis Sings Great Jewish Favorites*. Late 70s issues included more country music selections, including *Great Country Hits* with Hank Williams Jnr.

In 1974 she was the victim of a rape in her motel room after performing at the Westbury Theatre, outside New York. She later sued the motel for negligence, and was reputedly awarded damages of over three million dollars. For several years afterwards she did not perform in public, and underwent psychiatric treatment for long periods. She returned to the Westbury in 1981, to an enthusiastic reception, and resumed performing in the USA and abroad, including appearances at the London Palladium in 1989, and in Las Vegas in the same year, where she received a standing ovation after a mature performance ranging from her opening number, 'Let Me Try Again', to the climactic, 'If I Never Sing Another Song'. While at the Palladium, her speech became slurred and she was suspected of being drunk. In 1991 she had trouble speaking on a US television show, and, a year later, collapsed at a show in New Jersey. She was diagnosed as suffering from 'a complex illness', and of 'having been toxic for 18 years'. After drastically reducing her daily lithium intake, in 1993 she signed a new recording contract with Sony, buoyed up by the fact that her 1959 hit, 'Lipstick On Your Collar', was climbing high in the UK charts, triggered by its use as the title of a Dennis Potter television drama.

●ALBUMS: *Who's Sorry Now?* (MGM 1958)★★★★, *The Exciting Connie Francis* (MGM 1959)★★★★, *My Thanks To You* (MGM 1959)★★★★, *Christmas In My Heart* (MGM 1959)★★★, *Italian Favorites* (MGM 1960)★★★, *More Italian Favorites* (MGM 1960)★★★, *Rock 'N' Roll Million Sellers* (MGM 1960)★★★, *Country And Western Golden Hits* (MGM 1960)★★, *Spanish And Latin American Favorites* (MGM 1960)★★★, *Connie Francis At The Copa* (MGM 1961)★★, *Connie Francis Sings Great Jewish Favorites* (MGM 1961)★★, *Songs To A Swingin' Band* (MGM 1961)★★, *Never On Sunday And Other Title Songs From Motion Pictures* (MGM 1961)★★★, *Folk Song Favorites* (MGM 1961)★★★, *Do The Twist* (MGM 1962)★★★, *Second Hand Love And Other Hits* (MGM 1962)★★★, *Country Music Connie Style* (MGM 1962)★★★, *Modern Italian Hits* (MGM 1963)★★★, *Follow The Boys* soundtrack (MGM 1963)★★★, *German Favorites* (MGM 1963)★★, *Award Winning Motion Picture Hits* (MGM 1963)★★, *Great American Waltzes* (MGM 1963)★★★, *In The Summer Of His Years* (MGM 1964)★★★, *Looking For Love* soundtrack (MGM 1964)★★, with Hank Williams Jnr. *Great Country Favorites* (MGM 1964)★★, *A New Kind Of Connie* (MGM 1964)★★★, *Connie Francis Sings For Mama* (MGM 1965)★★★, *When The Boys Meet The Girls* soundtrack (MGM 1965)★★★, *Movie Greats Of The Sixties* (MGM 1966)★★★, *Live At The Sahara In Las Vegas* (MGM 1966)★★, *Love Italian Style* (MGM 1967)★★★, *Happiness* (MGM 1967)★★, *My Heart Cries For You* (MGM 1967)★★, *Hawaii Connie* (MGM 1968)★★, *Connie And Clyde* (MGM 1968)★★, *Connie*

Sings Bacharach And David (MGM 1968)★★★, *The Wedding Cake* (MGM 1969)★★★, *Connie Francis Sings Great Country Hits, Volume Two* (MGM 1973)★★, *Sings The Big Band Hits* (MGM 1977)★★, *I'm Me Again - Silver Anniversary Album* (MGM 1981)★★★, *Connie Francis And Peter Kraus, Volumes 1 & 2* (MGM 1984)★★★, *Country Store* (MGM 1988)★★.

●COMPILATIONS: *Connie's Greatest Hits* (MGM 1960)★★★★, *More Greatest Hits* (MGM 1961)★★★★, *Mala Femmena And Connie's Big Hits From Italy* (MGM 1963)★★★, *The Very Best Of Connie Francis* (MGM 1963)★★★★, *The All Time International Hits* (MGM 1965)★★★★, *20 All Time Greats* (1977)★★★★, *Connie Francis In Deutschland* 8-album box set (1988)★★★★, *The Very Best Of Connie Francis, Volume Two* (1988)★★★, *The Singles Collection* (1993)★★★, *White Sox, Pink Lipstick ... And Stupid Cupid* 5-CD box set (1993)★★★★, *Souvenirs* 4-CD box set (Polydor/Chronicles 1996)★★★★.

●FURTHER READING: *Who's Sorry Now?*, Connie Francis.

●FILMS: *Jamboree* aka *Disc Jockey Jamboree* (1957), *Follow The Boys* (1962).

FRANCOIS, CLAUDE

b. 4 February 1942, Suez, Egypt, d. 11 March 1978. He inherited musical skills from his parents who, with worsening political antagonism in the East, returned him to France where, on leaving school, he drummed in a Monte Carlo jazz combo before ambition drove him to Paris where, demonstrating the Twist, Mashed Potato and similar dance crazes in the Caramel Club, he was noticed by record company talent scouts. Steve Lawrence's 'Girls Girls Girls' was, in 1961, the first of many swift translations of US hits for home consumers by Francois. His strategy was best exemplified by a version of 'If I Had A Hammer', in the shops a mere week after Trini Lopez's 1963 original. More idiosyncratic smashes included 'Marche Tout Troit' and an up-tempo revival of Noël Coward's 'Poor Little Rich Girl'. Adored as 'Clo-Clo' by teenagers, Francois next addressed himself to their parents with a greater proportion of largely self-composed ballads such as 'J'Y Pense Et Puis J'Oublie', 'J'Attendrai' and 'Qu'Est-Ce Que Tu Deviens'. Although 1976's 'Tears 0n The Telephone' inched into Britain's Top 40, his deepest penetration into markets beyond French regions had been by proxy with the reflective 'Comme D'Habitude' - written with Jacques Revaux and Gilles Thibaut - which, with English lyrics by Paul Anka, was covered (as 'My Way') by artists as diverse as Frank Sinatra and the Sex Pistols. While this syndication enabled Francois to purchase a mansion near Fontainbleau, his private life was marred by divorce and maladies that included chronic insomnia. His death (by electrocution) on 11 March 1978 was mourned in microcosm as passionately as that of Elvis Presley - another of the many who recorded 'My Way'.

●ALBUMS: *Album Souvenir* (1988)★★★.

FRANK, JACKSON C.

b. Jackson Carey Frank, 1943, Buffalo, New York, USA. Singer/songwriter Frank made a strong impression in the mid-60s with songs such as 'Blues Run The Game'. This was contained on his 1965 debut, recorded in London with production from Paul Simon and guitar from Al Stewart. Like Simon and Shawn Phillips, he was one of several American folk performers who temporarily resided in Britain during this period. Jackson's life thus far had already been a troubled one. At the age of 11 he had been badly burned in a fire at his school in Cheektowago, Buffalo, his life only saved when classmates patted snow on his burning back (18 other children died). The reason for his journey to England was the belated arrival of his compensation cheque, which he intended to invest in a brand new Jaguar car. He wrote 'Blues Run The Game', his very first song despite experience in several rock 'n' roll bands, while aboard the Queen Elizabeth cruise ship *en route*. However, after the success of his debut album he became something of a recluse, although he was continually celebrated by other artists of the period. John Renbourn included a cover of 'Blues Run The Game' on his *So Clear* album, while Sandy Denny wrote a song about him as well as interpreting his compositions both as a solo artist and member of Fairport Convention. Roy Harper, too, celebrated him in song ('My Friend'). When he returned to England in 1968 he joined Fairport on tour, but was unable to pick up the impetus of his career. As Stewart recalled: 'he started doing songs that were completely impenetrable, they were basically about psychological angst played at full volume with lots of thrashing.' Disillusioned, Frank returned to America to edit a local paper, but his marriage to an English fashion model broke up, and his baby son died of cystic fibrosis. Frank suffered a nervous breakdown and entered hospital. In 1984 he travelled to New York in order to set up a meeting with old friend Paul Simon, but fell to begging in the streets, his mind blurred by medicinal drug use. Interned in institution after institution, he was diagnosed as a paranoid schizophrenic, which Frank justly refutes, putting these 'lost years' down to the trauma caused by the death of his child. It was only in the 90s, and through the efforts of record collector Jim Abbott, that the artist was traced. Abbott found him new accommodation in Woodstock, but not before Frank had been the victim of a point blank shooting which left him blind in his left eye. Dishevelled and overweight (due to a parathyroid malfunction resulting from his original injuries in the fire), he at last began to write songs again. One of the most tragic lives in the history of popular music may yet have a shot of salvation.

●ALBUMS: *Jackson C. Frank* reissued in 1978 by B&C as *Jackson Frank Again* (Columbia 1965)★★★.

●COMPILATIONS: *Blues Run The Game* (1987)★★★.

FRANKLIN, ARETHA

b. 25 March 1942, Memphis, Tennessee, USA. Aretha's music is steeped in the traditions of the church. Her father, C.L. Franklin was a Baptist preacher who, once he had moved his family to Detroit, became famous throughout black America for his fiery sermons and magnetic public appearances. He knew the major gospel stars, Mahalia Jackson and Clara Ward, who in turn gave his daughter valuable tutelage. At 12, Aretha was promoted from the choir to become a featured soloist. Two years later she began recording for JVB and Checker. Between 1956 and 1960, her output consisted solely of devotional material but the secular success of Sam Cooke encouraged a change of emphasis. Franklin auditioned for John Hammond, who signed her to Columbia. Sadly, the company was indecisive on how best to showcase her remarkable talent. They tried blues, cocktail jazz, standards, pop songs and contemporary soul hits, each of which wasted the singer's natural improvisational instincts. There were some occasional bright spots - 'Running Out Of Fools' (1964) and 'Cry Like A Baby' (1966) - but in both cases content succeeded over style. After a dozen albums a disillusioned Franklin joined Atlantic Records in 1966 where the magnificent 'I Never Loved A Man (The Way I Loved You)', recorded in January 1967 in New York declared her liberation. The album was scheduled to be made in Muscle Shoals but Franklin's husband Ted White had an argument with the owner of Fame Studios, Rick Hall. At short notice Wexler flew the musicians to New York. The single soared into the US Top 10 and, coupled with the expressive 'Do Right Woman – Do Right Man', only the backing track of which was recorded in Alabama, it announced the arrival of a major artist. The releases which followed – 'Respect', 'Baby I Love You', '(You Make Me Feel Like) A Natural Woman', 'Chain Of Fools' and '(Sweet Sweet Baby) Since You've Been Gone' – many of which featured the Fame rhythm section 'borrowed' by Jerry Wexler for sessions in New York, confirmed her authority and claim to being the 'Queen Of Soul'. The conditions and atmosphere created by Wexler and the outstanding musicians gave Franklin such confidence that her voice gained amazing power and control.

Despite Franklin's professional success, her personal life grew confused. Her relationship with husband and manager White disintegrated and while excellent singles such as 'Think' still appeared, others betrayed a discernible lethargy. She followed 'Think' with the sublime cover of Hal David and Burt Bacharach's 'I Say A Little Prayer' giving power and authority to simple yet delightful lyrics: 'the moment I wake up, before I put on my make-up, I say a little prayer for you'. Written by Burt Bacharach and Hal David, but crafted for Franklin, it remains one of the greatest working-class lyrics of all time. The subject catches a bus to work and has a coffee break: the song deals with simple values and has stood the test of time. Following a slight dip in her fortunes during the late 60s, she had regained her powers in 1970 as 'Call Me', 'Spirit In The Dark' and 'Don't Play That Song' ably testified. An album, *Aretha Alive At The Fillmore West* (1971), meanwhile, restated her in-concert power. The following year another live appearance resulted in *Amazing*

Grace, a double gospel set recorded with James Cleveland and the Southern California Community Choir. Its passion encapsulated her career to date. Franklin continued to record strong material throughout the early 70s and enjoyed three R&B chart-toppers, 'Angel', 'Until You Come Back To Me (That's What I'm Gonna Do)' and 'I'm In Love'. Sadly, the rest of the decade was marred by recordings which were at best predictable, at worst dull. It was never the fault of Franklin's voice, merely that the material was often poor and indifferent. Her cameo role in the film *The Blues Brothers*, however, rekindled her flagging career. Franklin moved to Arista Records in 1980 and she immediately regained a commercial momentum with 'United Together' and two confident albums, *Aretha* and *Love All The Hurt Away*. 'Jump To It' and 'Get It Right', both written and produced by Luther Vandross, and *Who's Zoomin' Who?* (1985), continued her rejuvenation. From the album, produced by Narada Michael Walden, Franklin had hit singles with 'Freeway Of Love', 'Another Night', and the superb title track. In the late, mid-80s, she made the charts again, in company with Annie Lennox ('Sisters Are Doin' It For Themselves') and George Michael ('I Knew You Were Waiting (For Me)'), which went to number 1 in the US and UK in 1987. Franklin's *Through The Storm* (1989) contained more powerful duets, this time with Elton John on the title track, James Brown ('Gimme Some Lovin'', remixed by Prince for 12-inch), and Whitney Houston ('It Isn't, It Wasn't, It Ain't Never Gonna Be'). The album also included a remake of her 1968 US Top 10 title, 'I Think'. In 1991, her *What You See Is What You Sweat* was criticized for its cornucopia of different styles: a couple of tracks by Burt Bacharach and Carole Bayer Sager; a collaboration with Luther Vandross; a fairly thin title ballad; and the highlight, 'Everyday People', a mainstream disco number, written by Sly Stone and brilliantly produced by Narada Michael Walden. Franklin may now lack the instinct of her classic Atlantic recordings, but as her 'return to gospel' *One Lord One Faith One Baptism* (1987) proved, she is still a commanding singer. Franklin possesses an astonishing voice that has often been wasted on a poor choice of material. She is rightfully heralded as the Queen of Soul, even although that reputation was gained in the 60s. There are certain musical notes that can be played on a saxophone that are chilling, similarly there are sounds above the 12th fret on a guitar which are orgasmic. Aretha Franklin is better than any instrument, she can hit notes that do not exist in instrumental terms. The 4-CD box set *Queen Of Soul* highlighting the best of her Atlantic recordings confirmed her position as one of the greatest voices in recording history.

● ALBUMS: *Aretha* (Columbia 1961)★★, *The Electrifying Aretha Franklin* (Columbia 1962)★★, *The Tender Swinging Aretha Franklin* (Columbia 1962)★★, *Laughing On The Outside* (Columbia 1963)★★, *Unforgettable* (Columbia 1964)★★, *Songs Of Faith* (Columbia 1964)★★, *Running Out Of Fools* (Columbia 1964)★★, *Yeah!!!* (Columbia 1965)★★, *Queen Of Soul* (1965)★★★, *Once In A Lifetime* (1965)★★★, *Soul*

Sister (Columbia 1966)★★★, *Take It Like You Give It* (Columbia 1967)★★★, *Take A Look* (Columbia 1967)★★★, *I Never Loved A Man The Way That I Love You* (Atlantic 1967)★★★★★, *Aretha Arrives* (Atlantic 1967)★★★★, *Aretha: Lady Soul* (Atlantic 1968)★★★★★, *Aretha Now* (Atlantic 1968)★★★★★, *Aretha In Paris* (1968)★★★, *Soul '69* (Atlantic 1969)★★★★, *Today I Sing The Blues* (Columbia 1969)★★★★, *Soft And Beautiful* (Columbia 1969)★★★, *I Say A Little Prayer* (1969)★★★, *Aretha Franklin Live* (1969)★★★, *This Girl's In Love With You* (Atlantic 1970)★★★, *Spirit In The Dark* (Atlantic 1970)★★★, *Two Sides Of Love* (1970)★★★, *Aretha Live At The Fillmore West* (Atlantic1971)★★★, *Young, Gifted And Black* (Atlantic 1971)★★★, *Amazing Grace* (Atlantic 1972)★★★, *Hey Now Hey (The Other Side Of The Sky)* (Atlantic 1973)★★, *Let Me Into Your Life* (Atlantic 1974)★★★, *With Everything I Feel In Me* (Atlantic 1974)★★★, *You* (Atlantic 1975)★★, *Sparkle* (Atlantic 1976)★★, *Sweet Passion* (Atlantic 1977)★★, *Satisfaction* (1977)★★★, *Almighty Fire* (1978)★★, *La Diva* (1979)★★, *Aretha* (1980)★★, *Love All The Hurt Away* (1981)★★, *Jump To It* (1982)★★, *Get It Right* (1983)★★, *Who's Zoomin' Who?* (Arista 1985)★★★, *Aretha* (Arista 1986)★★★, *One Lord, One Faith, One Baptism* (1987)★★, *Through The Storm* (Arista 1989)★★, *What You See Is What You Sweat* (1991)★★, *Love All The Hurt Away* (1993)★★.

●COMPILATIONS: *Aretha Franklin's Greatest Hits Columbia recordings 1961-66* (1967)★★★, *Aretha's Gold* (1969)★★★★, *Aretha's Greatest Hits* (1971)★★★★, *In The Beginning* (1972)★★★, *The First 12 Sides* (1973)★★★, *Ten Years Of Gold* (1976)★★★★, *Legendary Queen Of Soul* (1983)★★★★, *Aretha Sings The Blues* (1985)★★★, *The Collection* (1986)★★★★, *Never Grow Old* (1987)★★★, *20 Greatest Hits* (1987)★★★★, *Aretha Franklin's Greatest Hits 1960-1965* (1987)★★★★, *Queen Of Soul: The Atlantic Recordings* 4-CD box set (Rhino, Atlantic 1992)★★★★★, *Aretha's Jazz* (1993)★★★, *Greatest Hits 1980 1994* (Arista 1994)★★★, *Love Songs* (Rhino/Atlantic 1997)★★★.

●VIDEOS: *Live At Park West* (PVE 1995).
●FURTHER READING: *Aretha Franklin*, Mark Bego.
●FILMS: *The Blues Brothers* (1980).

FRATERNITY OF MAN

This US group was formed in Los Angeles, California, USA in 1967 when Elliot Ingber (guitar, ex-Mothers Of Invention) joined forces with three members of struggling aspirants the Factory: Warren Klein (guitar/sitar), Martin Kibbee (bass) and Richard Hayward (drums). Lawrence 'Stash' Wagner (lead vocals/guitar) completed the line-up featured on *Fraternity Of Man*, a musically disparate selection ranging from melodic flower-power ('Wispy Paisley Skies') to rhetorical politics ('Just Doin' Our Job'). The album also featured a version of Frank Zappa's 'Oh No I Don't Believe It', but is best recalled for the 'dopers' anthem 'Don't Bogart Me', later immortalized

in the film Easy Rider. The blues-influenced *Get It On* lacked the charm of its predecessor, but featured contributions from pianist Bill Payne and former Factory guitarist Lowell George, both of whom resurfaced, with Hayward, in Little Feat. Ingber was also involved with the last-named act during its embryonic stages, but left to join Captain Beefheart, where he was rechristened Winged Eel Fingerling. In later years he emerged as a member of the Mothers' offshoot, Grandmothers.
●ALBUMS: *Fraternity Of Man* (ABC 1968)★★★, *Get It On* (Dot 1969)★★.

FRED, JOHN, AND HIS PLAYBOY BAND

b. John Fred Gourrier, 8 May 1941, Baton Rouge, Louisiana, USA. John Fred was a 6 foot 5 inch, blue-eyed soul singer who originally worked with Fats Domino's backing group in the late 50s. During the early 60s various versions of the Playboy Band recorded for small independent record labels but it was not until the end of 1967 that success finally came with the international hit, 'Judy In Disguise (With Glasses)'. An amusing satire on the Beatles' 'Lucy In The Sky With Diamonds', the single beat off a rival version by Amboy Dukes. Although the Playboy Band were generally perceived as a novelty group, they were tight and well organized and Fred's blue-eyed soul vocals were evident on their album *Agnes English*, which included a rasping version of 'She Shot A Hole In My Soul'. By the end of the 60s the group split and Fred went on to become a producer.
●ALBUMS: *John Fred And His Playboys* (Paula 1966)★★★, *34:40 Of John Fred And His Playboys* (Paula 1967)★★, *Agnes English* (Paula 1967)★★.

FREDDIE AND THE DREAMERS

This Lancastrian, Manchester-born and raised group, comprising Freddie Garrity (b. 14 November 1940; vocals), Roy Crewsdon (b. 29 May 1941; guitar), Derek Quinn (b. 24 May 1942; guitar), Pete Birrell (b. 9 May 1941; bass) and Bernie Dwyer (b. 11 September 1940; drums), was briefly renowned for its mixture of beat music and comedy. Garrity formed the group in 1959 and it remained semi-professional until passing a BBC audition in 1963. Although their debut, 'If You Gotta Make A Fool Of Somebody', was an R&B favourite (James Ray and Maxine Brown), subsequent releases were tailored to the quintet's effervescent insouciant image. 'I'm Telling You Now' and 'You Were Made For Me' also reached the UK Top 3, establishing the group at the height of the beat boom. Although Garrity displayed his songwriting skill with strong ballads such as 'Send A Letter To Me', his work was not used for a-side recordings. Further hits followed in 1964 with 'Over You', 'I Love You Baby', 'Just For You', and the Christmas season favourite 'I Understand'. The group's appeal declined in the UK but early in 1965, they made a startling breakthrough in America where 'I'm Telling You Now' topped the charts. American audiences were entranced by Garrity's zany stage antics (which resulted in frequent twisted ankles) and eagerly demanded the name of his unusual dance routine. 'It's called the Freddie', he innocently replied. A US Top 20 hit rapidly followed with 'Do The Freddie'. Although the group appeared in a couple of films, *Just For You* And *Cuckoo Patrol*, their main audience was in pantomime and cabaret. They broke up at the end of the decade, but Garrity and Birtles remained together in the children's show *Little Big Time*. During the mid-70s the group was revived by Freddie Garrity, with new personnel, for revival concerts at home and abroad. In 1988, Garrity began a parallel career of performing in cabaret and an acting career.

●ALBUMS: *Freddie And The Dreamers* (Columbia 1963)★★★, *You Were Made For Me* (Columbia 1964)★★★, *Freddie And The Dreamers* (Mercury 1965)★★★, *Sing-Along Party* (Columbia 1965)★★, *Do The Freddie* (Mercury 1965)★★, *Seaside Swingers* aka *Everyday's A Holiday* film soundtrack (Mercury 1965)★★, *Frantic Freddie* (Mercury 1965)★★, *Freddie And The Dreamers In Disneyland* (Columbia 1966)★, *Fun Lovin' Freddie* (Mercury 1966)★★, *King Freddie And His Dreaming Knights* (Columbia 1967)★★, *Oliver In The Underworld* (1970)★★.

●COMPILATIONS: *The Best Of Freddie And The Dreamers* (1982)★★★, *The Hits Of Freddie And The Dreamers* (1988)★★★, *The Best Of Freddie And The Dreamers - The Definitive Collection* (EMI 1992)★★★.

●FILMS: *Every Day's A Holiday* aka *Seaside Swingers* (1965).

FRUMIOUS BANDERSNATCH

This highly promising quintet was based in Berkeley, California, USA in the late 60s. They completed an album for Fantasy Records that was never issued and consequently, their sole recorded legacy lies in a privately pressed EP. The group - Jimmy Warner (solo guitar/vocals), David Denny (b. 5 February 1948, Berkeley, California, USA; lead guitar/vocals), Bob Winkelman (rhythm guitar/vocals), Ross Vallory (b. 2 February 1949, San Francisco, California, USA; bass/vocals) and Jackson King (drums/vocals) - were highly accomplished musicians and the opening track, 'Hearts To Cry', offered some exciting, *de rigueur*, acid-rock. Denny was later replaced by George Tickner, but the band subsequently folded in the face of corporate disinterest. Winkelman, Warner, King and Vallory all appeared at various times as members of the Steve Miller Band. Vallory then found greater success with Tickner as members of Journey.

●COMPILATIONS: *A Young Man's Song* (Big Beat 1996)★★.

FUGS

Formed in 1965, the Fugs combined the bohemian poetry of New York's Lower East Side with an engaging musical naïvety and the shock tactic of outrage. Writers Ed Sanders, Tuli Kupferberg and Ken Weaver made their recording debut on the Broadside label, which viewed the group's work as 'ballads of contemporary protest'. The set included poetry by William Blake alongside such irreverent offerings as 'I Couldn't Get High' and 'Slum Goddess', while the original trio was supported by several musicians, including Peter Stampfel and Steve Weber from fellow cultural dissidents the Holy Modal Rounders. The Fugs' album was subsequently issued by ESP, a notorious outlet for the *avant garde*. A projected second collection was withheld when the company deemed it 'too obscene', and a feverish rock album, entitled *The Fugs*, was issued instead. This excellent collection featured Kupferberg's satirical 'Kill For Peace' and the almost lyrical 'Morning Morning'. The disputed second album was then released as *Virgin Fugs*. In 1967 the group switched outlets to Reprise. Although *Tenderness Junction* featured a more proficient backing group, including Danny Kootch (b. Dan Kortchmar; guitar) and Charles Larkey (bass), the subject matter - hippie-politics and sex - remained as before. *It Crawled Into My Hand, Honest*, released the following year, was another idiomatic record, but subsequent releases undermined the balance between literary and carnal pursuits, erring in favour of the latter. They disbanded to avoid the dangers of self-parody, although Ed Sanders continued his musical pursuits with two country-influenced selections and wrote an acclaimed book, The Family, about the hippie-cult leader Charles Manson. *Fugs 4 Rounder Score*, in 1975, contained unreleased Holy Modal Rounders material. Sanders and Kupferberg resumed work as the Fugs during the 80s. Contemporary releases invoke a world-consciousness portrayed in the group's earlier political work, and they retain the same idealistic optimism. During the 90s Sanders and Kupferberg retrieved the rights to their ESP recordings. The material was then licensed to Ace Records on the recommendation of the Grateful Dead. Subsequent repackages have been augmented by archive photographs and previously unissued recordings. Sanders and Kupferberg attempted to hold a rival Woodstock anniversary festival in 1994. The results were issued on a double CD in 1995, the satire and humour is now sadly dated.

●ALBUMS: *The Village Fugs* aka *The Fugs First Album* (ESP 1965)★★★★, *The Fugs* (ESP 1966)★★★★, *Virgin Fugs* (ESP 1966)★★★★, *Fugs 4 Rounders Score* (ESP 1967)★★★, *Tenderness Junction* (Reprise 1967)★★★, *It Crawled Into My Hand, Honest* (Reprise 1968)★★★, *The Belle Of Avenue A* (Reprise 1969)★★, *Refuse To Be Burnt Out* (1985)★★, *No More Slavery* (1986)★★★, *Star Peace* (1987)★★, *The Fugs Live In The 60s* (Fugs 1994)★★★, *The Real Woodstock Festival* (Fugs 1995)★★.

●COMPILATIONS: *Golden Filth* (Reprise 1969)★★★★.

FULLER, BOBBY

b. 22 October 1943, Baytown, Texas, USA, d. 18 July 1966. An inventive and compulsive musician, Bobby Fuller made his recording debut in 1961. 'You're In Love' was the first of several outings for local independent labels, but the artist's development was more apparent on the many demos completed in his home-based studio. Fuller later moved to Los Angeles where his group, the Bobby Fuller Four - Randy Fuller (bass), Jim Reese (rhythm guitar) and DeWayne Quirico (drums) - became a leading attraction, infusing Buddy Holly-styled rockabilly with the emergent British beat. Their early releases were regional hits; nevertheless, in January 1966 the group reached the US Top 10 with an ebullient reading of the Crickets' 'I Fought The Law'. This pop classic, later covered by the Clash, was followed up by a Top 30 hit, 'Love's Made A Fool Of You'. The singer's stature now seemed assured, but on 18 July that same year any hope for a bright future was cut short when Fuller's badly beaten body was discovered in a parked car in Los Angeles. His death was attributed to asphyxia through the forced inhalation of gasoline, but further investigations as to the perpetrators of this deed remain unresolved.

●ALBUMS: *KRLA King Of The Wheels* (Mustang 1965)★★★, *I Fought The Law* aka *Memorial Album* (Mustang 1966)★★★★, *Live Again* (Eva 1984)★★.

●COMPILATIONS: *The Best Of The Bobby Fuller Four* (Rhino 1981)★★★★, *The Bobby Fuller Tapes, Volume 1* (1983)★★★, *Bobby Fuller Tapes Vol. 2* (Voxx 1984)★★, *The Bobby Fuller Instrumental Album* (Rockhouse 1985)★★.

FURY, BILLY

b. Ronald Wycherley, 17 April 1940, Dingle, Liverpool, England, d. 28 January 1983. An impromptu audition in a Birkenhead dressing room resulted in Wycherley joining Larry Parnes' management stable. The entrepreneur provided the suitably enigmatic stage name, and added the aspirant to the bill of a current package tour. Fury enjoyed a UK Top 20 hit with his debut single, 'Maybe Tomorrow', in 1959 and the following year completed *The Sound Of Fury*, which consisted entirely of the artist's own songs. Arguably Britain's finest example of the rockabilly genre, it owed much of its authenticity to sterling support from guitarist Joe Brown, while the Four Jays provided backing vocals. However, Fury found his greatest success with a series of dramatic ballads which, in suggesting a vulnerability, enhanced the singer's undoubted sex appeal. His stylish good looks complimented a vocal prowess blossoming in 1961 with a cover version of Tony Orlando's 'Halfway To Paradise'. This superior single, arranged and scored by Ivor Raymonde, established a pattern that provided Fury with 16 further UK Top 30 hits, including 'Jealousy' (1961), 'Last Night Was Made For Love' (1962), 'Like I've Never Been Gone' (1963), 'It's Only Make Believe' (1964), and 'In Thoughts Of You' (1965). Fury also completed two exploitative pop movies, *Play It Cool* (1962) and *I've Gotta Horse* (1964) and remained one of Britain's leading in-concert attractions throughout the early 60s. Supported initially by the Tornados, then the Gamblers, the singer showed a wider repertoire live than his label would allow on record. Bedevilled by ill health and overtaken by changing musical fashions, Fury's final hit came in 1965 with 'Give Me Your Word'. The following year he left Decca for Parlophone, debuting with a Peter And

Gordon song, 'Hurtin' Is Lovin'. Subsequent recordings included David Bowie's 'Silly Boy Blue', the Bee Gees' 'One Minute Woman' (both 1968) and Carole King's 'Why Are You Leaving' (1970), but the singer was unable to regain his erstwhile success. In 1971 he underwent open-heart surgery, but recovered to record 'Will The Real Man Stand Up' on his own Fury label, and played the part of 'Stormy Tempest' in the film *That'll Be The Day* (1973). A second major operation in 1976 forced Billy to retire again, but he re-emerged at the end of the decade with *Memories*, new recordings of his best-known songs, and several live and television appearances. In 1981 Fury struck a new deal with Polydor, but his health was rapidly deteriorating and on 28 January 1983 he succumbed to a fatal heart attack. Unlike many of his pre-Beatles contemporaries, the artist's reputation has grown over the years, and Billy Fury is now rightly regarded as one of the finest rock 'n' roll singers Britain ever produced.

●ALBUMS: *Sound Of Fury* (Decca 1960)★★★★, *Billy Fury* (Ace Of Clubs 1960)★★★, *Halfway To Paradise* (Ace Of Clubs 1961)★★★, *Billy* (Decca 1963)★★★, *We Want Billy* (Decca 1963)★★, *I've Got A Horse* (1965)★★★, *The One And Only* (1983)★★★.

●COMPILATIONS: *The Best Of Billy Fury* (1967)★★★★, *The World Of Billy Fury* (Decca 1972)★★★★, *The Billy Fury Story* (1977)★★★, *The World Of Billy Fury, Volume 2* (1980)★★★, *Hit Parade* (1982)★★★, *The Missing Years 1967-1980* (1983)★★★, *The Billy Fury Hit Parade* (1983)★★★, *Loving You* (1984)★★★, *The Other Side Of Billy Fury* (1984)★★★, *Stick 'N' Stones* (1985)★★★, *The EP Collection* (1985)★★★★, *Jealousy* (1986)★★★, *The Collection* (1987)★★★, *The Best Of Billy Fury* (1988)★★★, *The Sound Of Fury + 10* (1988)★★★, *Am I Blue?* (1993)★★★, *The Other Side Of Fury* (See For Miles 1994)★★★★.

●FILMS: *I've Gotta Horse* (1965).

GANTRY, ELMER'S, VELVET OPERA

As 'Elmer Gantry's Velvet Opera', Gantry (vocals), Colin Foster (guitar), Richard Hudson (b. Richard William Stafford Hudson, 9 May 1948, London, England; drums) and John Ford (b. 1 July 1948, Fulham, London, England; bass), were fixtures on Britain's 'underground' circuit. Their reputation was enhanced by regular appearances on BBC Radio 1's *Top Gear*, presented by John Peel. In 1967, the group recorded its debut album which contained self-composed material - notably the up-tempo 'Flames' which re-appeared on CBS as a highlight of *The Rock Machine Turns You On*, the first mid-price sampler album. Truncating to just 'Velvet Opera', the outfit disbanded in the early 70s after two more flop singles (including the excellent 'Anna Dance Square'); Ford and Hudson were absorbed into the Strawbs. By 1974, Gantry was fronting a band which, until checked by litigation, accepted illicit bookings as 'Fleetwood Mac' while the genuine article were off the road. A year later, Gantry emerged once more as singer on Stretch's solitary UK chart entry, 'Why Did You Do It'.

●ALBUMS: *Elmer Gantry's Velvet Opera* (CBS 1967)★★★, as Velvet Opera *Ride A Hustler's Dream* (CBS 1969)★★★.

●COMPILATIONS: *The Very Best Of Elmer Gantry* (See For Miles 1996)★★★.

GAYE, MARVIN

b. Marvin Pentz Gay Jnr., 2 April 1939, Washington, DC, USA, d. 1 April 1984. Gaye was named after his father, a minister in the Apostolic Church. The spiritual influence of his early years played a formative role in his musical career, particularly from the 70s onwards, when his songwriting shifted back and forth between secular and religious topics. He abandoned a place in his father's church choir to team up with Don Covay and Billy Stewart in the R&B vocal group the Rainbows. In 1957, he joined the Marquees, who recorded for Chess under the guidance of Bo Diddley. The following year the group were taken under the wing of producer and singer Harvey Fuqua, who used them to re-form his doo-wop outfit, the Moonglows. When Fuqua moved to Detroit in 1960, Gay went with him: Fuqua soon joined forces with Berry Gordy at Motown, and Gaye became a session drummer and vocalist for the label.

In 1961, he married Gordy's sister, Anna, and was offered a solo recording contract. Renamed Marvin Gaye, he began his career as a jazz balladeer, but in 1962 he was persuaded to record R&B, and notched up his first hit single with the confident 'Stubborn Kind Of Fellow', a Top 10 R&B hit. This record set the style for the next three years, as Gaye enjoyed hits with a series of joyous, dance-flavoured songs which cast him as a smooth, macho Don Juan figure. He also continued to work behind the scenes at Motown, co-writing Martha And The Vandellas' hit 'Dancing In The Street', and playing drums on several early recordings by Little Stevie Wonder. In 1965, Gaye dropped the call-and-response vocal arrangements of his earlier hits and began to record in a more sophisticated style. 'How Sweet It Is (To Be Loved By You)' epitomized his new direction, and it was followed by two successive R&B number 1 hits, 'I'll Be Doggone' and 'Ain't That Peculiar'. His status as Motown's best-selling male vocalist left him free to pursue more esoteric avenues on his albums, which in 1965 included a tribute to the late Nat 'King' Cole and a collection of Broadway standards.

To capitalize on his image as a ladies' man, Motown teamed Gaye with their leading female vocalist, Mary Wells, for some romantic duets. When Wells left Motown in 1964, Gaye recorded with Kim Weston until 1967, when she was succeeded by Tammi Terrell. The Gaye/Terrell partnership represented the apogee of the soul duet, as their voices blended sensuously on a string of hits written specifically for the duo by Ashford And Simpson. Terrell developed a brain tumour in 1968, and collapsed onstage in Gaye's arms. Records continued to be issued under the duo's name, although Simpson allegedly took Terrell's place on some recordings. Through the mid-60s, Gaye allowed his duet recordings to take precedence over his solo work, but in 1968 he issued the epochal 'I Heard It Through The Grapevine' (written by Whitfield/Strong), a song originally released on Motown by Gladys Knight And The Pips, although Gaye's version had actually been recorded first. With its tense, ominous rhythm arrangement, and Gaye's typically fluent and emotional vocal, the record represented a landmark in Motown's history - not least because it became the label's biggest-selling record to date. Gaye followed up with another number 1 R&B hit, 'Too Busy Thinking 'Bout My Baby', but his career was derailed by the insidious illness and eventual death of Terrell in March 1970. Devastated by the loss of his close friend and partner, Gaye spent most of 1970 in seclusion. The following year, he emerged with a set of recordings that Motown at first refused to release, but that eventually became his most successful solo album.

On 'What's Going On', a number 1 hit in 1971, and its two chart-topping follow-ups, 'Mercy Mercy Me (The Ecology)' and 'Inner City Blues', Gaye combined his spiritual beliefs with his increasing concern about poverty, discrimination and political corruption in American society. To match his shift in subject matter, Gaye evolved a new musical style, which influenced a generation of black performers. Built on a heavily percussive base, Gaye's arrangements mingled jazz and classical influences into his soul roots, creating a fluid instrumental backdrop for his sensual, almost despairing vocals. The three singles were all contained on *What's Going On*, a conceptual masterpiece on which every track contributed to the spiritual yearning suggested by its title. After making a sly comment on the 1972 US presidential election campaign with the single 'You're The Man', Gaye composed the soundtrack to the 'blaxploitation' thriller, *Trouble Man*. His primarily instrumental score highlighted his interest in jazz, while the title song provided him with another hit single.

Gaye's next project saw him shifting his attention from the spiritual to the sexual with *Let's Get It On*, which included a quote from T.S. Eliot on the sleeve and devoted itself to the art of talking a woman into bed. Its explicit sexuality marked a sea-change in Gaye's career; as he began to use cocaine more and more regularly, he became obsessed with his personal life, and rarely let the outside world figure in his work. Paradoxically, he continued to let Motown market him in a traditional fashion by agreeing to collaborate with Diana Ross on a sensuous album of duets in 1973 - although the two singers allegedly did not actually meet during the recording of the project. The break-up of his marriage to Anna Gordy in 1975 delayed work on his next album. *I Want You* was merely a pleasant reworking of the *Let's Get It On* set, albeit cast in slightly more contemporary mode. The title track was another number 1 hit on the soul charts, however, as was his 1977 disco extravaganza, 'Got To Give It Up'. Drug problems and tax demands interrupted his career, and in 1978 he fled the US mainland to Hawaii in a vain attempt to salvage his second marriage. Gaye devoted the next year to the *Here My Dear* double album, a bitter commentary on his relationship with his first wife. Its title was ironic: he had been ordered to give all royalties from the project to Anna as part of their divorce settlement.

With this catharsis behind him, Gaye began work on an album to be called *Lover Man*, but he cancelled its release after the lukewarm sales of its initial single, the sharply self-mocking 'Ego Tripping Out', which he had presented as a duet between the warring sides of his nature. In 1980 under increasing pressure from the Internal Revenue Service, Gaye moved to Europe where he began work on an ambitious concept album, *In My Lifetime*. When it emerged in 1981, Gaye accused Motown of remixing and editing the album without his consent, of removing a vital question-mark from the title, and of parodying his original cover artwork. The relationship between artist and record company had been shattered, and Gaye left Motown for Columbia in 1982. Persistent reports of his erratic personal conduct and reliance on cocaine fuelled pessimism about his future career, but instead he re-emerged in 1982 with a startling single, 'Sexual Healing', which combined his passionate soul vocals with a contemporary electro-disco backing. The subsequent album, *Midnight Love*, offered no equal surprises, but the success of the single seemed to herald a new era in Gaye's music. He returned to the USA, where he took up residence at his parents' home. The intensity of his cocaine addiction made it impossible for him to work on another album, and he fell into a prolonged bout of depression. He repeatedly announced his wish to commit suicide in the early weeks of 1984, and his abrupt shifts of mood brought him into heated conflict with his father, rekindling animosity that had festered since Gaye's adolescence. On 1 April 1984, another violent disagreement provoked Marvin Gay Snr. to shoot his son dead, a tawdry end to the life of one of soul music's premier performers.

Motown and Columbia collaborated to produce two albums based on Gaye's unfinished recordings. *Dream Of A Lifetime* mixed spiritual ballads from the early 70s with sexually explicit funk songs from a decade later; while *Romantically Yours* offered a travesty of Gaye's original intentions in 1979 to record an album of big band ballads. Although Gaye's weighty canon is often reduced to a quartet of 'I Heard It Through The Grapevine', 'Sexual Healing', *What's Going On* and *Let's Get It On*, his entire recorded output signifies the development of black music from raw rhythm and blues, through sophisticated soul to the political awareness of the early 70s, and the increased concentration on personal and sexual politics thereafter. Gaye's remarkable vocal range and fluency remains a touchstone for all subsequent soul vocalists, and his 'lover man' stance has been frequently copied as well as parodied.

●ALBUMS: *The Soulful Moods Of Marvin Gaye* (Tamla Motown 1961)★★★, *That Stubborn Kind Of Fella* (Tamla Motown 1963)★★★★, *Recorded Live: On Stage* (Tamla Motown 1964)★★★, *When I'm Alone I Cry* (Tamla Motown 1964)★★★, with Mary Wells *Together* (Tamla Motown 1964)★★★, *Hello Broadway This Is Marvin* (Tamla Motown 1965)★★★, *How Sweet It Is To Be Loved By You* (Tamla Motown 1965)★★★, *A Tribute To The Great Nat King Cole* (Tamla Motown 1965)★★★, *Moods Of Marvin Gaye* (Tamla Motown 1966)★★★, with Kim Weston *Take Two* (Tamla Motown 1966)★★★, with Tammi Terrell *United* (Tamla Motown 1967)★★★, *In The Groove* (Tamla Motown 1968)★★★, with Terrell *You're All I Need* (Tamla Motown 1968)★★★, *Marvin Gaye And His Girls* (Tamla Motown 1969)★★★, *MPG* (Tamla Motown 1969)★★★, *That's The Way Love Is* (Tamla Motown 1970)★★★, *What's Going On* (Tamla Motown 1971)★★★★★, *Trouble Man* soundtrack (Tamla Motown 1972)★★, *Let's Get It On* (Tamla Motown 1973)★★★★★, with Diana Ross *Diana And Marvin* (Tamla Motown 1973)★★★, *Live* (Tamla Motown 1974)★★, *I Want You* (Tamla Motown 1976)★★★, *Live At The London Palladium* (Motown 1977)★★★, *Here My Dear* (Motown 1978)★★★, *In Our Lifetime* (Motown 1981)★★★, *Midnight Love* (CBS 1982)★★★, *Dream Of A Lifetime* (CBS 1985)★★★, *Romantically Yours* (CBS 1985)★★★, *The Last Concert Tour* (Giant 1991)★★, *For The Very Last Time* (1994)★★.

●COMPILATIONS: *Marvin Gaye's Greatest Hits* (Tamla 1964)★★★★, *Marvin Gaye's Greatest Hits Vol. 2* (Tamla 1967)★★★★, *18 Greatest Hits* (Motown 1988)★★★★, *Love Songs* (Telstar 1990)★★★★, *The*

Marvin Gaye Collection 4-CD box set (Motown 1990)★★★★★, *Night Life* (1993)★★★, *The Master: 1961-1984* (Motown 1995)★★★, *Early Classics* (Spectrum 1996).

●FURTHER READING: *Divided Soul: The Life Of Marvin Gaye*, David Ritz. *I Heard It Throught The Grapevine: Marvin Gaye, The Biography*, Sharon Davis.

GENTLE, JOHNNY

b. John Askew, 1941, Liverpool, England. Askew was a merchant seaman who sang as a semi-professional before he was spotted and rechristened by the celebrated 50s svengali, Larry Parnes. Beginning with 1959's 'Boys And Girls Were Meant For Each Other' on Philips, this square-jawed hunk's singles all missed the UK chart but he was often seen on British television pop series such as *Oh Boy* and *Drumbeat* and was, therefore, guaranteed a period of well-paid one-nighters. His backing groups for these included fellow Merseysiders the Beatles and Cass And The Cassanovas with entertainments that embraced mutually familiar rock 'n' roll standards and the simpler sides of Gentle's singles, such as the self-penned 'Wendy'. Without a recording contract in 1963, Gentle replaced Gordon Mills in the Viscounts before retiring from show-business by the mid-60s.

GENTRY, BOBBIE

b. Roberta Lee Streeter, 27 July 1944, Chicasaw County, Mississippi, USA. Gentry, of Portuguese descent, was raised on a poverty-stricken farm in Greenwood, Mississippi and was interested in music from an early age. She wrote her first song at the age of seven ('My Dog Sergeant Is A Good Dog') and learned piano - black keys only! - guitar, banjo and vibes. By her teens, she was regularly performing and she took her stage name from the film, *Ruby Gentry*. After studying both philosophy and music, she was signed to Capitol Records and recorded 'Mississippi Delta' for an a-side. To her own guitar accompaniment, Gentry recorded for the b-side one of her own songs, 'Ode To Billie Joe', in 30 minutes. Violins and cellos were added, the song was reduced from its original seven minutes, and, because of disk jockey's reactions, it became the a-side. Despite competition from Lee Hazlewood, Gentry's version topped the US charts for four weeks and reached number 13 in the UK. Capitol's truncated version added to the song's mystery: what did Billie Joe and his girlfriend throw off the Tallahatchie Bridge and why did Billie Joe commit suicide? The song's main thrust, however, was the callousness of the girl's family over the event, and it can be twinned with Jeannie C. Riley's subsequent story of 'Harper Valley PTA'. Gentry became a regular headliner in Las Vegas and she married Bill Harrah, the manager of the Desert Inn Hotel. (Gentry's second marriage, in 1978, was to singer-songwriter Jim Stafford.) Gentry made an easy listening album with Glen Campbell, which included successful revivals of the Everly Brothers hits, 'Let It Be Me' (US Top 40) and 'All I Have To Do Is Dream' (US Top 30/UK

number 3). Gentry, with good looks similar to Priscilla Presley, was given her own UK television series, *The Bobbie Gentry Show*, which helped her to top the charts in 1969 with the Burt Bacharach and Hal David song from *Promises, Promises*, 'I'll Never Fall In Love Again'. The 1976 film, *Ode To Billy Joe* (sic), starred Robby Benson and Glynnis O'Connor, and had Billy Joe throw his girlfriend's ragdoll over the bridge and commit suicide because of a homosexual affair. Gentry herself retired from performing to look after her business interests.

●ALBUMS: *Ode To Billie Joe* (Capitol 1967)★★★, *Delta Sweetie* (Columbia 1968)★★★, with Glen Campbell *Bobbie Gentry And Glen Campbell* (Capitol 1968)★★★, *Local Gentry* (1968)★★, *Touch 'Em With Love* (Capitol 1969)★★★, *I'll Never Fall In Love Again* (1970)★★★, *Fancy* (Capitol 1970)★★, *Patchwork* (1971)★★, *Sittin' Pretty/Tobacco Road* (1971)★★.

●COMPILATIONS: *Bobby Gentry's Greatest* (Capitol 1969)★★★, *The Best Of* (Music For Pleasure 1994)★★★.

GERRY AND THE PACEMAKERS

Gerry Marsden (b. Gerard Marsden, 24 September 1942; guitar/vocals), Freddie Marsden (b. 23 October 1940; drums) and John 'Les' Chadwick (b. 11 May 1943; bass) formed the original Pacemakers in 1959. Two years later they were joined by Les Maguire (b. 27 December 1941, Wallasey, Cheshire; piano) and having completed highly successful spells in German beat clubs, became the second group signed to Brian Epstein's management stable. The effervescent 'How Do You Do It', rejected as unsuitable by the Beatles, gave the more pliant Pacemakers a number 1 hit. Further chart-toppers 'I Like It' and 'You'll Never Walk Alone' (both 1963) followed in quick succession, earning the group the distinction of becoming the first act to have their first three releases reach number 1. The latter song, taken from the musical *Carousel*, was later adopted as the anthem of Liverpool Football Club. Although the group's lone album revealed a penchant for R&B, their singles often emphasized Gerry Marsden's cheeky persona. The exceptions included two excellent in-house compositions 'Don't Let The Sun Catch You Crying' (1964) and 'Ferry Cross The Mersey' (1965), the theme song to the Pacemakers' starring film. A follow-up release, 'I'll Be There', was the quartet's final Top 20 entry and in 1967 Gerry embarked on a solo career. He remained a popular figure in television and on the cabaret circuit, but regained the national spotlight in 1985 following the Bradford City Football Club fire tragedy, when a charity recording, credited to the Crowd and featuring an all-star cast, took a new version of 'You'll Never Walk Alone' to the top of the UK chart for the second time. Another re-recording of an earlier hit for charity, 'Ferry Cross The Mersey', this time for the victims of the Hillsborough crowd disaster, involving supporters of Liverpool FC in 1989, reached number 1.

●ALBUMS: *How Do You Like It* (Columbia 1963)★★★★, *Second Album* (1964)★★★, *I'll Be There!* (1965)★★★, *Ferry Cross The Mersey* sound-

track (1965)★★★, *Girl On A Swing* (1965)★★★, *20 Year Anniversary Album* (1983)★★.
●COMPILATIONS: *Don't Let The Sun Catch You Crying* (1964)★★★, *Gerry And The Pacemakers' Greatest Hits* (1965)★★★★, *The Best Of Gerry And The Pacemakers* (1977)★★★★, *The Very Best Of Gerry And The Pacemakers* (1984)★★★★, *Hit Singles Album* (1986)★★★★, *The EP Collection* (1987)★★★★, *The Singles Plus* (1987)★★★★, *The Very Best Of ... 20 Superb Tracks* (1993)★★★★.
●VIDEOS: *In Concert* (Legend 1990).
●FURTHER READING: *I'll Never Walk Alone*, Gerry Marsden with Ray Coleman.

GIBSON, BOB

b. 16 November 1931, New York City, New York, USA. Although commercial success proved illusive, Gibson was one of folk music's most influential figures. His songs were recorded by the Kingston Trio and Peter, Paul And Mary and he was responsible for launching and/or furthering the careers of Bob Camp, Judy Collins and Joan Baez. Having recorded his debut single, 'I'm Never To Marry', in 1956, Gibson embarked on a series of excellent albums including *Offbeat Folksongs* and *Carnegie Concert*. Indifferent to marketplace pressure, his novelty collection, *Ski Songs*, was issued at the height of the hootenanny boom while *Yes I See*, arguably the nadir of his recording career, appeared as Bob Dylan began to attract peer group acclaim. These disappointing releases were followed by a duet with Bob (Hamilton) Camp, *At The Gate Of Horn*, paradoxically one of American folk's definitive works. Gibson was absent from music for much of the 60s, but he re-emerged early in the 70s with a melodic album which featured Roger McGuinn, Spanky McFarland and Cyrus Faryar. This respected artist has since pursued a more public path. During the 80s he toured with Tom Paxton and was a frequent performer at international folk festivals.
●ALBUMS: *Folksongs Of Ohio* (Stateside 1956)★★★, *Offbeat Folksongs* (Riverside 1956)★★★, *I Come For To Sing* (Riverside 1957)★★★★, *Carnegie Concert* (Riverside 1957)★★★★, *There's A Meeting Here Tonight* (Riverside 1959)★★★, *Ski Songs* (Elektra 1959)★★★, *Yes I See* (Elektra 1961)★★★, with Bob 'Hamilton' Camp *At The Gate Of Horn* (1961)★★, *Hootenanny At Carnegie* (Riverside 1963)★★★★, *Where I'm Bound* (Elektra 1963),★★★ *Bob Gibson* (70s)★★★, *Funky In The Country* (1974)★★, with Camp *Homemade Music* (1978)★★★.

GILBERTO, ASTRUD

b. 1940, Bahia, Brazil. Gilberto's career began by accident in March 1963 during a recording session featuring her husband, guitarist Joao Gilberto, and saxophonist Stan Getz. A projected track, 'The Girl From Ipanema', required a singer conversant with English and although strictly a non-professional, Astrud was coaxed into performing the soft, *sang-froid* vocal. Her contribution was considered relatively unimportant - early pressings of the resultant *Stan Getz/Joao Gilberto* did not credit the singer - even when the track was issued as a single the following year. 'The Girl From Ipanema' eventually reached the US Top 5 and UK Top 20, garnering sales in excess of one million and forever binding the artist to the subject of the song. Astrud later toured with Getz; their collaboration was chronicled on *Getz A-Go-Go*, but she later pursued an independent career, bringing her distinctive, if limited, style to a variety of material, including standards, Brazilian samba/bossa nova and contemporary songs from Tim Hardin, Jimmy Webb and the Doors. Gilberto was the subject of renewed attention when 'Ipanema' re-entered the UK charts in 1984 as a result of the UK bossa nova/jazz revival perpetrated by artists such as Everything But The Girl, the Style Council, Weekend and Sade.
●ALBUMS: *The Astrud Gilberto Album* (Verve 1965)★★★★, *The Shadow Of Your Smile* (Verve 1965)★★★, *Look To The Rainbow* (Verve 1965)★★★, *A Certain Smile, A Certain Sadness* (Verve 1966)★★★, *Beach Samba* (Verve 1967)★★★, *Windy* (Verve 1968)★★, *I Haven't Got Anything Better To Do* (Verve 1969)★★★, with James Last *Plus* (1986)★★, *September 17 1969* (Verve 1969)★★, *So & So* (1988)★★.
●COMPILATIONS: *Once Upon A Summertime* (1971)★★★, *That Girl From Ipanema* (1977)★★★★, *The Best Of Astrud Gilberto* (1982)★★★★, *The Essential Astrud Gilberto* (1984)★★★★ *Compact Jazz* (1987)★★★★.

GIRLS ON THE BEACH, THE

Taking its cue from a succession of 'quickie' films emanating from the American International Pictures company, *The Girls On The Beach* tied a flimsy plot to a series of pop act cameos. In this 1965 feature, girl students wishing to raise funds decide to organize a concert which they mistakenly believe will feature the Beatles. Fortunately other performers step into the breech, including the Crickets, who offer a version of 'La Bamba', and Leslie Gore. The latter sings three numbers, 'Leave Me Alone', 'It's Got To Be You' and 'I Don't Wanna Be A Loser', the last of which was a minor US hit the previous year. Topping the bill are the Beach Boys with 'Little Honda', 'The Lonely Sea' and the title song itself. Prolific surf and drag music producer/composer Gary Usher was responsible for the bulk of the soundtrack score, but the appeal of the 'beach' genre was waning by the time this film was released. The Byrds' 'Mr. Tambourine Man', also issued in 1965, signalled the rise of an altogether different Californian sub-culture.

GLASS MENAGERIE

After moving from their native Lancashire to seek commercial success in London, England, this psych-pop quartet released a series of singles for Pye Records and Polydor Records without ever completing an album. Comprising Bill Atkinson (drums), John Medley (bass), Alan Kendall (guitar) and Lou Stonebridge (vocals/harmonica), the group made their debut in 1968 with the typically floral 'She's A Rainbow'. Two further singles followed for Pye in the same year, 'You Don't Have To Be So Nice' and 'Frederick Jordan', but neither reached the charts. Transferring to Polydor in 1969, 'Have You Forgotten Who You Are' and 'Do My Thing Myself' failed to rectify their commercial misfortune. By now the group had adopted a heavier, progressive rock styled sound, which might have been better sampled on a full album release. However, despite the existence of an album acetate, Polydor declined to release it officially and the group broke up. Kendall subsequently joined Toe Fat, while Stonebridge worked with Paladin and McGuinness Flint.

GODS

Formed in 1965 in Hatfield, England, the first incarnation of the Gods consisted of Mick Taylor (guitar), Ken Hensley (keyboards/vocals), John Glassock (bass/vocals) and Brian Glassock (drums). They remained active until 1967, but broke up when Taylor joined John Mayall's Bluesbreakers. Within months Hensley had reconstituted the band around Joe Konas (guitar/vocals), Paul Newton (bass) and Lee Kerslake (drums). Greg Lake then replaced Newton, but the newcomer left to help found King Crimson in 1968. John Glassock returned to the fold as the Gods secured a recording deal with Columbia Records. *Genesis* was an ambitious concept album, brimming with late 60s naïve pretension, but it was not a commercial success. The Gods did create a minor stir with their reading of the Beatles' 'Hey Bulldog', but they disbanded in February 1969. *To Samuel A Son* was issued posthumously when various ex-members had achieved a higher profile elsewhere. Hensley, Kerslake and both Glassock brothers were all members of Toe Fat, before Hensley, Kerslake and Paul Newton found fame at various different points in Uriah Heep.
●ALBUMS: *Genesis* (Columbia 1968)★★★, *To Samuel A Son* (Columbia 1970)★★, *Gods* (Harvest 1976)★★.
●COMPILATIONS: *The Gods: Featuring Ken Hensley* (Harvest Heritage 1976)★★★.

GOFFIN, GERRY

b. 11 February 1939, New York City, New York, USA. Goffin was a chemistry major at New York's Queens College when he met fellow student Carole King. Both harboured songwriting ambitions and pooled resources when the former's lyrical gifts gelled with the latter's musical talent. The now-married couple were introduced to publisher Don Kirshner in 1960 following the release of 'Oh! Neil', King's answer disc to Neil Sedaka's 'Oh! Carol'. They joined the staff of the magnate's Aldon company where their early compositions included 'Will You Still Love Me Tomorrow?' (the Shirelles), 'Take Good Care Of My Baby' (Bobby Vee), 'Go Away Little Girl' (Steve Lawrence) and 'Up On The Roof' (the Drifters). Goffin also enjoyed success with Jack Keller and Barry Mann, but the compositions he produced with his wife ultimately proved the most memorable. Together they wrote 'The Loco-Motion' (Little Eva), 'One Fine Day' (the Chiffons), 'I'm Into Something Good' (Earl-Jean/Herman's Hermits), 'Just Once In My Life' (the Righteous Brothers) and 'Oh No Not My Baby' (Maxine Brown/Manfred Mann), and as the 60s developed so Goffin's lyrics developed from the mundane to the meaningful. 'Don't Bring Me Down', a 1966 hit for the Animals, established a personal perspective, while the images evoked in Aretha Franklin's 'A Natural Woman' - 'when my soul was in the lost and found, you came along to claim it' - verged on the poetic. His ability to assume a feminine perspective emphasized a now incontrovertible skill, consolidated in the introspection of 'Goin' Back' (Dusty Springfield/the Byrds) and the anti-suburbia protest of 'Pleasant Valley Sunday' (the Monkees). However, pressure both professional and personal undermined the couple's relationship and their marriage ended in 1967. Whereas King forged a second successful career during the 70s singer/songwriter boom, Goffin enjoyed a less public profile. Bereft of a melodious partner and out of place in an era where musicians both composed and performed, he remained in the public eye due to the enduring popularity of his early compositions. Blood, Sweat And Tears recorded 'Hi De Hi', Grand Funk Railroad covered 'The Loco-Motion', while his ex-wife later paid tribute to their partnership with *Pearls*, a selection of their 60s collaborations. During the 70s Goffin worked as a producer for several artists, including Diana Ross. He did record a solo album, *It Ain't Exactly Entertainment*, in 1973, but it failed to emulate the popularity of his former partner. Goffin's contribution to popular music is considerable and many of former hits are now classics. Always literate and melodic, his work remains timeless. He had a second attempt at fame as a recording artist in 1996.
●ALBUMS: *It Ain't Exactly Entertainment* (1973). A compilation of various artists interpretations of Goffin And King compositions is also available: *The Goffin And King Songbook* (1989)★★★, *Back Room Blood* (Adelphi 1996)★★.

GOINS, HERBIE

Goins, like Geno Washington, was a former US servicemen who remained in the UK when his military service ended. In 1963 he joined Alexis Korner's Blues Incorporated and is featured vocalist on several of this seminal band's releases, including *Red Hot From Alex* and *At The Cavern*. In 1965 he left to lead Herbie Goins And The Night Timers, which became a highly popular attraction in London's clubs. The group was signed to Parlophone Records for whom they recorded several excellent dance-orientated soul singles, including 'The Music Played On' (1965), 'Number One In Your Heart' and 'Incredible Miss Brown' (both 1966). In 1967 the Night Timers recorded their only album. *Number One In Your Heart* is an exciting set, with swinging versions of such club standards as 'Pucker Up Buttercup', 'Knock On Wood' and 'Look At Granny Run', but it was deemed anachronistic when compared to concurrent, psychedelic trends. The group broke up in 1968.

●ALBUMS: *Number One In Your Heart* (Parlophone 1967)★★★.

GOLDBERG, BARRY

b. 1941, Chicago, Illinois, USA. Goldberg was one of several white aspirants frequenting Chicago's blues clubs during the early 60s. He befriended guitarist Michael Bloomfield prior to forming the Goldberg-Miller Blues Band with itinerant Texan Steve Miller. Goldberg assumed the group's leadership on his partner's departure, and the resultant album is a fine example of pop-influenced R&B. An accomplished keyboard player, Goldberg was part of the back-up band supporting Bob Dylan on his controversial appearance at 1965's Newport Folk Festival. Sessions supporting Mitch Ryder preceded a brief spell with Chicago Loop before Goldberg joined the Electric Flag. The artist resumed his own career in 1968 with the Barry Goldberg Reunion. Several erratic albums followed including *Two Jews Blues*, which featured contributions from Bloomfield and Duane Allman and a collaboration with Neil Merryweather and Charlie Musselwhite, *Ivar Avenue Reunion*. Goldberg also continued his session work and produced albums for Musselwhite and the Rockets, but has been unable to translate his status as a sideman into a coherent solo path.

●ALBUMS: *Blowing My Mind* (Epic 1966)★★, *The Barry Goldberg Reunion* (Buddah 1968)★★★, with Mike Bloomfield *Two Jews Blues* (1969)★★, *Barry Goldberg And Friends* (1969)★★, *Chicago Anthology* (1969)★★★, *Streetman* (1970)★★★, with Neil Merryweather, Charlie Musselwhite *Ivar Avenue Reunion* (1970)★★★, *Barry Goldberg* (1974)★★, *Barry Goldberg And Friends Recorded Live* (1970)★★★.

GOLDIE AND THE GINGERBREADS

Formed in Brooklyn, New York, USA, in 1963, Goldie And The Gingerbreads made their debut at the city's famed Peppermint Lounge. They were discovered by British group the Animals who, impressed by the quartet's musical abilities, suggested they move to the UK. Goldie Zelkowitz (b. 1943, Brooklyn, New York, USA; vocals), Carol McDonald (b. 1944, Wilmington, Delaware, USA; guitar), Margo Crocitto (b. 1943, Brooklyn, New York, USA; organ) and Ginger Panebianco (b. 1945, Long Island, New York, USA; drums) arrived in London in November 1964 and their debut single was issued the following year in the wake of successful appearances at the Crazy Elephant and Flamingo clubs. Animals keyboard player Alan Price produced the excellent 'Can't You Hear My Heart Beat?', a UK Top 30 entry, but two further singles failed to achieve similar success. The group toured with the Rolling Stones and Kinks, but despite their undoubted dexterity - Crocitto made several session appearances - they were unfairly perceived as a novelty. The quartet split up in October 1965 when Goldie embarked on a solo career, but the remaining trio maintained contact and the group continued to record upon returning to New York,

releasing 'Song To The Moon'/'Walking In Different Circles' in 1967. They later re-emerged during the 70s as part of Isis, an all-woman group.

GOMELSKY, GIORGIO

b. 1934, Georgia, formerly USSR. Exiled to Switzerland and educated in Italy, Gomelsky later settled in Britain where he became a leading figure of London's jazz scene during the 50s. He organized the first Richmond Jazz Festival and was later responsible for bringing bluesman Sonny Boy 'Rice Miller' Williamson to Europe. Giorgio's first club was the Piccadilly, but in 1963 he established the famed Crawdaddy Club in Richmond's Station Hotel, which quickly became one of the country's leading venues for rhythm and blues. The Rolling Stones enjoyed a successful residency there prior to recording and Gomelsky initially acted as the group's manager before being supplanted by Andrew Loog Oldham. However, the impresario fared better with their successors, the Yardbirds, whom he guided and produced between 1964 and 1966. Gomelsky subsequently managed the T-Bones and the Steampacket before founding the Marmalade label in 1967. He enjoyed a modicum of success with Blossom Toes, before securing international hits with protégés Julie Driscoll and Brian Auger And The Trinity. The company, however, proved short-lived and Giorgio subsequently left England for Paris where he established an alternative music circuit for radical groups Magma, whom he also managed, and Gong. Gomelsky also enjoyed a fruitful relationship with BYG Records, who issued several albums culled from tapes he had recorded during the 60s. Having founded a new label, Utopia, in 1975, he then moved to New York, where he continues to supervise releases drawn from his considerable archive.

GONKS GO BEAT

Inspired by the plot from the AIP film, *Pajama Party*, this 1965 feature offered a wafer-thin premise whereby a space-travelling alien versed in the wonder of pop attempts to placate rivalry between Beatland and Balladisle. This is achieved through an unlikely combination of acts, most of which were culled from the Decca Records roster. Although the bulk of the acts were undistinguished - precocious child stars Elaine and Derek were set beside second-string beat groups the Long And The Short and Trolls - the film did include otherwise unavailable recordings by chart acts the Nashville Teens and Lulu And The Luvvers. The latter featured future Stone The Crows and Robin Trower member Jimmy Dewar on bass. However, the highlight of *Gonks Go Beat* was unquestionably an appearance by the Graham Bond Organization, one of the finest - and most influential - 60s groups. Vocalist/keyboard player Bond was herein joined by Jack Bruce and Ginger Baker, both later of Cream, and future Colosseum saxophonist, Dick Heckstall-Smith. Their contribution, 'Harmonica', was shot in a studio bedecked in tropical style, but the ill-fitting setting did not undermine the quartet's charismatic power. It did nothing to salvage the film's commercial prospects and an attendant soundtrack album enjoyed negligible success. Another in a line of British 'quickie' pop films, *Gonks Go Beat* does at least boast one highly memorable sequence.

GOOD RATS

This US group was formed while the members were at college in 1964 by Peppi and Mickey Marchello, both from Long Island, New York, USA. Their debut was a mixture of rock 'n' roll and progressive rock. A succession of poor selling albums coupled with regular changes of record labels hampered their commercial prospects. They broke up for three years during 1969-72. By the time of their fourth and best album - *From Rats To Riches* - (which was later issued on Radar in the UK), the line-up was the gruff-voiced Peppi, Mickey (guitar), John 'the Cat' Gatto (guitar), Lenny Kotke (bass) and Joe Franco (drums). This album was recorded on Long Island in late 1977 with Flo And Eddie (Mark Volman and Howard Kaylan) producing. Although their place in the market was never clear they were essentially a good old-fashioned, basic US rock 'n' roll band.
●ALBUMS: *The Good Rats* (Kapp 1968)★★★, *Tasty* (1974)★★, *Ratcity In Blue* (1976)★★, *From Rats To Riches* (1978)★★★, *Rats The Way You Like It Live* (Passport 1978)★★, *Birth Comes To Us All* (1978)★★, *Live At Last* (1980)★★, *Great American Music* (1981)★★.

GOOD, JACK

b. 1931, London, England, This founder of British pop television was president of Oxford University Drama Society and then a stand-up comic before enrolling on a BBC training course. His final test film was centred on Freddie Mills. The late boxer was also an interlocutor on 1957's *6.5 Special*, a magazine series for 'teenagers produced by Good and Josephine Douglas. While he became evangelical about rock 'n' roll, Good's staid superiors obliged him to balance the pop with comedy sketches, string quartets and features on sport and hobbies. He was fired for flaunting Corporation dictates by presenting a stage version of the show. Snapped up by ITV, he broke ground with *Oh Boy!* which introduced Cliff Richard, Marty Wilde and other homegrown rockers to the nation. So swiftly did its atmospheric parade of idols - mostly male - pass before the cameras that the screaming studio audience, urged on by Good, scarcely had pause to draw breath. While overseeing the less exciting *Boy Meets Girls* and *Wham!*, Good branched out into publishing and record production, such as Billy Fury's *Sound Of Fury*.
In 1962 Good was in North America where he worked intermittently as an actor - notably on Broadway in C.P. Snow's *The Affair* and, in 1967, as a hotelier in *Clambake*, an Elvis Presley vehicle. His self-financed pilot programme, *Young America Swings The World*, fell on stony ground but, after Brian Epstein commissioned him for *Around The Beatles*, he superintended the nationally broadcast pop showcase *Shindig* which, as

well as making 'discoveries' such as the Righteous Brothers and Sonny And Cher, represented a media breakthrough for diverse black artists from Howlin' Wolf to the Chambers Brothers - and held its own in a ratings war against *The Beverley Hillbillies* on a main rival channel. Leaving *Shindig* to fend for itself, his most interesting career tangent of the later 60s was *Catch My Soul*, 1968's rock adaptation in a Los Angeles theatre of Shakespeare's *Othello* with Jerry Lee Lewis as Iago. For a season in London, P.J. Proby assumed the Lewis role with Good himself as the Moor. Back in the USA, he ticked over with one-shot television specials concerning, among others, Andy Williams, the Monkees and 1970's Emmy award-winning classical/pop hybrid of Ray Charles, Jethro Tull, the Nice and the LA Philharmonic. On an extended visit to England from his Santa Fe home, Good put on *Elvis*, a biographical musical starring, initially, Proby and Shakin' Stevens before daring an updated reconstruction of *Oh Boy!* (later transferred to television) at the same London West End theatre. By the 80s, income from the inspired Good's less frequent television and stage ventures underwrote another vocational episode - as a painter. In the early 90s it was reported that Good was training to become a monk, but, while he was contemplating it, he travelled to London to oversee the West End launch of his own autobiographical musical, *Good Rockin' Tonite*, which had them dancing in the aisles - just like the old days.

GORDY, BERRY

b. Berry Gordy Jnr., 28 November 1929, Detroit, Michigan, USA. Gordy took his first tentative steps into the music business in 1955, when he opened a jazz record store in Detroit. When it folded, he returned to the automobile assembly lines until he met the manager of young R&B singer Jackie Wilson. Gordy wrote Wilson's first major hit, the novelty and now classic 'Reet Petite', and joined the singer's entourage, composing four further chart successes over the next two years. In 1958, Gordy set himself up as an independent producer, working with young unknowns such as the Miracles, Marv Johnson and Eddie Holland. That year he formed the Jobete Music company to handle songs by himself and his associates. At the suggestion of the Miracles' vocalist Smokey Robinson, Gordy went a stage further in 1959 by launching his own record company, Tamla Records. This was merely the first of a succession of labels gathered under his Motown Records umbrella, which rapidly became one of America's most important independent concerns.
Gordy masterminded Motown from the outside, choosing the artist-roster, writing and producing many of the early releases, and chairing weekly meetings that determined every aspect of the company's artistic direction. Having co-produced and co-written Motown's first major hit, the Miracles' 'Shop Around' in 1960, Gordy was also responsible for hits such as 'Do You Love Me' and 'Shake Sherry' by the Contours, 'Fingertips (Part 2)' by Stevie Wonder, 'Try It Baby' by Marvin Gaye and 'Shotgun' by Junior

Walker And The All Stars. As Motown's influence and reputation grew, Gordy groomed a school of producers and writers to create the style that he dubbed 'The Sound of Young America'. Gradually his own artistic input lessened, although he continued to collaborate on Supremes hits such as 'Love Child' and 'No Matter What Sign You Are' until the end of the decade. His time was primarily devoted to increasing Motown's market share, and to dealing with a series of bitter clashes between artists and company which threatened to halt the label's progress by the early 70s. Anxious to secure new power bases, Gordy shifted Motown's main offices from Detroit to California, and inaugurated a new films division with the highly acclaimed *Lady Sings The Blues*. This movie starred former Supreme Diana Ross, with whom Gordy had long been rumoured to be enjoying a romantic liaison. Their relationship was part of the company backbone, and her eventual decision to leave Motown in the early 80s was read as an indicator of the label's declining fortunes.

Having lost many of its major creative talents, Motown subsisted through the 70s and early 80s on the backs of several unique individuals, notably Stevie Wonder and Lionel Richie. Gordy was no longer finding significant new talent, however; ironically, one of his company's most successful newcomers of the 80s was his own son, Rockwell. Gordy's personal career has long since been synonymous with the fortunes of his company, and he surprised the industry when he sold Motown Records to MCA in 1988 - just weeks after he had been inducted into the Rock 'n' Roll Hall Of Fame in recognition of his pioneering talents as a major songwriter, impresario and executive.

●FURTHER READING: *Movin' Up*, Berry Gordy. *To Be Loved*, Berry Gordy.

GORE, LESLEY

b. 2 May 1946, New York City, USA, and raised in Tenafly, New Jersey. Having secured a recording contract with Mercury on the basis of a privately financed demonstration disc, Gore enjoyed a sensational debut when 'It's My Party' topped the US chart, reached number 9 in the UK and grossed sales in excess of one million. This tale of adolescent trauma has retained its timeless appeal - the singer's birthday celebrations are irrevocably marred on losing boyfriend Johnny to Judy - and it remains one of the era's most memorable releases. The vengeful follow-up, 'Judy's Turn To Cry', earned another gold disc, but successive releases, including 'You Don't Own Me', a powerful call for independence, and 'Maybe I Know', confirmed that the singer was not simply a novelty act. Gore made several appearances in teen-oriented films and television shows, including *Batman*, but her career was marred by periods of inactivity. She re-emerged in 1972 with *Something Else Now*, released on Motown's Mowest subsidiary and three years later was briefly reunited with producer/songwriter Quincy Jones, who had produced her early Mercury recordings, which resulted in the exceptional 'Immortality'. Despite the frailty exhibited on her debut single, Lesley Gore is now

viewed by commentators as an early champion of women's rights.

●ALBUMS: *I'll Cry If I Want To* (Mercury 1963)★★★★, *Lesley Gore Sings Of Mixed-Up Hearts* (Mercury 1963)★★★★, *Boys, Boys, Boys* (Mercury 1964)★★★, *Girl Talk* (Mercury 1964)★★★, *My Town, My Guy And Me* (Mercury 1965)★★★, *Lesley Gore Sings All About Love* (Mercury 1966)★★★, *California Nights* (Mercury 1967)★★, *Someplace Else Now* (Mowest 1972)★★.

●COMPILATIONS: *The Golden Hits Of Lesley Gore* (Mercury 1965)★★★★, *The Golden Hits Of Lesley Gore, Volume 2* (Mercury 1968)★★★, *Start The Party Again* (Raven 1993)★★★.

●FILMS: *Girls On The Beach* (1965).

GRADUATE, THE

One of the biggest grossing films of 1968 - and one which has proved enduringly popular - *The Graduate* launched Dustin Hoffman's acting career. He plays the part of the graduate, Benjamin Braddock, unsure about his future. He is seduced by his father's business partner's wife, Mrs. Robinson, memorably played by Anne Bancroft, before falling in love, and eloping with Bancroft's screen daughter (Katherine Ross). A mild comment on US middle-class values, *The Graduate*'s strengths are derived from Hoffman's portrayal of Braddock, suitably lost and decisive when the need arose. The film's charm was enhanced by a soundtrack featuring Simon And Garfunkel. Although the duo had enjoyed chart success with 'Homeward Bound' and 'Sound Of Silence', they were not a household name prior to this film. The latter song enhanced one of the film's most poignant scenes, a feature shared with 'Scarborough Fair' and 'April Come She Will'. The album reached number 3 in the UK charts, while the duo's recording of 'Mrs. Robinson' broached the UK Top 5. Indeed, such was the attendant popularity, an EP comprising the aforementioned four songs peaked at number 9 in the singles chart early the following year. Simon And Garfunkel were no longer viewed as an alternative, if coy, act; their next album *Bridge Over Troubled Waters* effortlessly topped the UK chart and remained on the list for 303 weeks.

GRAHAM, BILL

b. Wolfgang Wolodia Grajonca, 8 January 1931, Berlin, Germany, d. 25 October 1991. Born into a Russian-Jewish family, Graham arrived in New York during 1941, a refugee from Nazi persecution. After earning a degree in business administration, he moved to the west coast. By 1965 he was managing the San Francisco Mime Troupe, organizing the requisite benefit gigs to keep the revue afloat. Such work brought him into contact with the nascent rock fraternity and Graham began promoting concerts at the city's Fillmore Auditorium. The venue became the leading showcase for the 'San Francisco Sound', exemplified by Jefferson Airplane, Quicksilver Messenger Service, the Grateful Dead and Big Brother And The Holding Company. Graham, in turn, became a leading impresario, and by 1968 had bought the larger Carousel Ballroom, renaming it the Fillmore West. Within weeks he had opened a corresponding Fillmore East in a vacant cinema on New York's Second Avenue.

As a hard-headed entrepreneur, he often came into conflict with the free-loading hippie idealism inherent in running a music venue. Yet Graham often confounded his critics by contributing to local organizations in the form of benefits. In addition, the presentation of concerts at his venues paved the way for future promoters by way of introducing light shows, showing films between acts, free apples and taking a personal interest in the musicians giving a professional performance. He was also instrumental in efforts to integrate black artists on billings, so introducing many musicians to a predominantly white audience. These artists included B.B. King, Leon Thomas, Raahsan Roland Kirk, Miles Davis, Muddy Waters and Ravi Shankar.

By the end of 1971, Graham had closed down both halls and was determined to retire from a business for which he was losing respect. The final performances at the Fillmore West were captured on the film and accompanying album box-set, *Fillmore - The Last Days* (1972). The sabbatical was brief and during the next decade he was involved in national tours by Bob Dylan and Crosby, Stills, Nash And Young, as well as major one-off events. Such work culminated on 13 July 1985 when Graham organized the American segment of the Live Aid concert for famine relief. A controversial and outspoken character, he also pursued a successful career in management, guiding, at different times, the paths of Jefferson Airplane, Santana, Van Morrison and Dylan.

Graham's tragic death in a helicopter crash occurred while returning from a Huey Lewis And The News concert he had promoted in South County, California. It robbed the rock music business of one its most legendary characters and greatest promoters. His funeral service was attended by members of the Grateful Dead, Santana and Quicksilver Messenger Service who offered musical tributes.

●FURTHER READING: *Bill Graham Presents*, Bill Graham and Robert Greenfield.

GRAHAM, DAVEY

b. 22 November 1940, Leicester, England, of Scottish and Guyanese parents. An influential guitarist in British folk circles, Graham's itinerant travels throughout Europe and North Africa resulted in a cosmopolitan and unorthodox repertoire. By the early 60s he was a fixture of the London fraternity and his 1961 recording with Alexis Korner, *3/4 A.D.*, showcased his exceptional talent. The EP included the much-feted 'Angie', an evocative instrumental that Paul Simon and Bert Jansch later covered using Graham's innovative DADGAD guitar tuning. *Folk, Blues & Beyond* showcased Graham's eclectic talent, with material drawn from Charles Mingus, Lead Belly, Bob Dylan and Blind Willie Johnson. The expressive instrumental, 'Maajun (A Taste Of Tangier)', emphasized the modal element of Graham's playing and although

never more than adequate as a singer, his inspired guitar work was a revelation. *Folk Roots New Routes* was an unlikely collaboration with traditional vocalist Shirley Collins, and while the latter's purity was sometimes at odds with Graham's earthier approach, the album is rightly lauded as a milestone in British folk music. Graham maintained his idiosyncratic style throughout the 60s, experimenting with western and eastern musical styles, but although the respect of his peers was assured, commercial success proved elusive. Drug problems and ill health undermined the artist's progress, but he later re-emerged with two excellent albums for the specialist Kicking Mule outlet. During his latter years, he has resided in west Scotland where he has taught guitar, while continuing to perform on the folk club circuit, often performing on double bills with Bert Jansch, and demonstrating his credentials as one of Britain's finest folk-blues guitarists, although his profile deserves to be much higher.

●ALBUMS: *Guitar Player* (Pye Golden Guinea 1963)★★★, *Folk, Blues & Beyond* (Decca 1964)★★★★, with Shirley Collins *Folk Roots New Routes* (Decca 1965)★★★, *Midnight Man* (Decca 1966)★★★, *Large As Life And Twice As Natural* (Decca 1968)★★★, *Hat* (Decca 1969)★★★, *Holly Kaleidoscope* (Decca 1970)★★★, *Godington Boundary* (President 1970)★★, *All That Moody* (Eron 1976)★★★, *Complete Guitarist* (Kicking Mule 1978)★★★, *Dance For Two People* (Kicking Mule 1979)★★★, *Playing In Traffic* (1993)★★★.

●COMPILATIONS: *Folk Blues And All Points In Between* (See For Miles 1990)★★★★, *The Guitar Player ... Plus* (See For Miles 1992)★★★★.

GRANT, JULIE

A product of early 60s vintage UK pop, Grant found some success with a string of singles for Pye Records. Her half-beehive hairstyle and angular eye make-up was seen regularly on package tours and UK television. Her manager was Eric Easton, who briefly managed the Rolling Stones, with whom she shared the bill on their first major package tour. Her 1962 cover of the Drifters' 'Up On The Roof' made the UK hit parade but was overtaken by Kenny Lynch's version. Nevertheless, she bounced back with 'Count On Me', reaching number 24 - her highest (and penultimate) chart placing. However, after 1964's 'Come To Me', a tempestuous ballad that was frequently played on the BBC Light Programme, and, consequently wended its way to the edge of the Top 30, Grant's fortunes on record declined irrecoverably.

GRAPEFRUIT

Formed in Britain during 1967, Grapefruit was originally comprised of three former members of harmony group Tony Rivers And The Castaways - John Perry (b. 16 July 1949, London, England; lead guitar/vocals), Pete Sweetenham (b. 24 April 1949, London, England; rhythm guitar/vocals), Geoff Sweetenham (b. 8 March 1948, London, England; drums) and songwriter George

Alexander (b. 28 December 1946; Glasgow, Scotland; bass/vocals). The quartet, named by John Lennon, was the first act signed to the Beatles' Apple publishing company, whose faith was confirmed when Grapefruit's debut single, 'Dear Delilah', became a UK Top 30 hit. Alexander's penchant for high-quality British pop was matched by Terry Melcher's sympathetic production, but despite several equally excellent follow-up releases, the group's only other chart entry was 'C'mon Marianne', originally recorded by the Four Seasons. By 1969 Mick Fowler (keyboards) had been added to the line-up while Geoff Sweetenham was later replaced by Bobby Ware. *Deep Water* revealed an unsatisfactory soul/rock perspective and Alexander subsequently dissolved the band. He joined former Easybeats members George Young and Harry Vanda (Young and Alexander were brothers) for a variety of projects issued under different names. The Grapefruit appellation was briefly revived in 1971 for 'Universal Party', a melodic pop song redolent of the act's initial releases, although it failed to make a similar impact on the singles chart.

●ALBUMS: *Around Grapefruit* (Dunhill 1968)★★★, *Deep Water* (RCA Victor 1969)★★.

GRASS ROOTS

Although several Californian groups claimed this sobriquet, including the embryonic Love, it was appropriated by songwriters P.F. Sloan and Steve Barri, who employed the name pseudonymously on several folk rock performances. When 'Where Were You When I Needed You?' reached the US Top 30 in 1966, the need for a permanent line-up arose and the duo enticed Warren Entner (b. 7 July 1944, Boston, Massachusetts, USA; vocals/guitar), Creed Bratton (b. 8 February 1943, Sacramento, California, USA; guitar), Rob Grill (b. 30 November 1944, Los Angeles, California, USA; vocals/bass) and Rick Coonce (b. Erik Michael Coonce, 1 August 1947, Los Angeles, California, USA; drums) to adopt the Grass Roots name. The new group enjoyed immediate success with 'Let's Live For Today', a remake of an Italian hit. This distanced the quartet from their mentors, but although Sloan's input decreased dramatically, Barri retained his role as producer. The Grass Roots then became one of America's leading commercial attractions with a series of confident performances, including 'Midnight Confessions' (1968), 'Bella Linda' (1968), 'I'd Wait A Million Years' (1969) and 'Sooner Or Later' (1971). In the 80s the group remained a popular attraction, although the verve of their early work had, by then, evaporated.

●ALBUMS. *Where Were You When I Needed You?* (Dunhill 1966)★★★, *Let's Live For Today* (Dunhill 1967)★★★, *Feelings* (Dunhill 1968)★★★, *Lovin' Things* (Dunhill 1969)★★★, *Leaving It All Behind* (Dunhill 1969)★★★, *Move Along* (Dunhill 1972)★★, *A Lotta' Mileage* (1973)★★.

●COMPILATIONS: *Golden Grass (Their Greatest Hits)* (Stateside 1968)★★★, *More Golden Grass* (1970)★★, *Their Sixteen Greatest Hits* (Dunhill 1974)★★★, *Anthology 1965-1975* (Rhino 1991)★★★.

GRATEFUL DEAD

The enigmatic and mercurial (cliché, but absolutely true) Grateful Dead evolved from Mother McCree's Uptown Jug Champions to become the Warlocks in 1965. The legendary name was chosen from a randomly opened copy of the *Oxford English Dictionary*, the juxtaposition of words evidently appealing to members of the band, who were at the time somewhat chemically stimulated. The original line-up comprised Jerry Garcia (b. Jerome John Garcia, 1 August 1942, San Francisco, California, USA, d. 9 August 1995, Forest Knolls, California, USA; lead guitar), Bob Weir (b. Robert Hall, 16 October 1947, San Francisco, California, USA; rhythm guitar), Phil Lesh (b. Philip Chapman, 15 March 1940, Berkeley, California, USA; bass), Ron 'Pigpen' McKernan (b. 8 September 1945, San Bruno, California, USA. d. 8 March 1973; keyboards) and Bill Kreutzmann (b. 7 April 1946, Palo Alto, California, USA; drums). The Grateful Dead have been synonymous with the San Francisco/Acid Rock scene since its inception in 1965 when they took part in Ken Kesey's Acid Tests. Stanley Owsley manufactured the then legal LSD and plied the band with copious amounts. This hallucinogenic opus was duly recorded onto tape over a six-month period, and documented in Tom Wolfe's book *The Electric Kool-Aid Acid Test*. Wolfe stated that 'They were not to be psychedelic dabblers, painting pretty pictures, but true explorers.'

Their music, which started out as straightforward rock, blues and R&B, germinated into a hybrid of styles, but has the distinction of being long, wandering and improvisational. By the time their first album was released in 1967 they were already a huge cult band. *Grateful Dead* sounds raw in the light of 90s record production, but it was a brave, early attempt to capture a live concert sound on a studio album. The follow-up *Anthem Of The Sun* was much more satisfying. On this 'live' record, 17 different concerts and four different live studios were used. The non-stop suite of ambitious segments with tantalizing titles such as 'The Faster We Go The Rounder We Get' and 'Quadlibet For Tenderfeet' was an artistic success. Their innovative and colourful album covers were among the finest examples of San Franciscan art, utilizing the talents of Kelley Mouse Studios (Alton Kelley and Stanley Mouse). The third album contained structured songs and was not as inaccessible as the palindrome title *Aoxomoxoa* suggested. Hints of a mellowing Grateful Dead surfaced on 'China Cat Sunflower' and the sublime 'Mountains Of The Moon', complete with medieval-sounding harpsichord. In concert, the band were playing longer and longer sets, sometimes lasting six hours with only as many songs.

Their legion of fans, now known as 'Deadheads' relished the possibility of a marathon concert. It was never ascertained who imbibed more psychedelic chemicals, the audience or the band. Nevertheless, the sounds produced sometimes took them to breathtaking heights of musical achievement. The interplay between Garcia's shrill, flowing solos and Lesh's meandering bass lines complemented the adventurous chords of Weir's rhythm guitar.

The band had now added a second drummer, Micky Hart, and a second keyboard player, Tom Constanten, to accompany the unstable McKernan. It was this line-up that produced the seminal *Live Dead* in 1970. Their peak of improvisation is best demonstrated on the track 'Dark Star'. During its 23 minutes of recorded life, the music simmers, builds and explodes four times, each with a crescendo of superb playing from Garcia and his colleagues. On the two following records *Workingman's Dead* and *American Beauty*, a strong Crosby, Stills And Nash harmony influence prevailed. The short, country-feel songs brought Garcia's pedal steel guitar to the fore (he had recently guested on Crosby, Stills, Nash And Young's *Déja Vu*). Paradoxically, the 'Dead' reverted to releasing live sets by issuing a second double album closely followed by the triple, *Europe '72*. After years of ill health through alcohol abuse, McKernan died in 1973. He was replaced by Keith Godcheaux from Dave Mason's band, who, together with his wife Donna on vocals, compensated for the tragic loss. *Wake Of The Flood* in 1973 showed a jazz influence and proved to be their most commercially successful album to date. With this and subsequent studio albums the band produced a more mellow sound. It was not until *Terrapin Station* in 1977 that their gradual move towards lethargy was averted. Producer Keith Olsen expertly introduced a fuller, more orchestrated sound.

As a touring band the Grateful Dead continued to prosper, but their studio albums began to lose direction. For their funky *Shakedown Street* they enlisted Lowell George. Although they had been with the band for some years, Keith and Donna Godcheaux had never truly fitted in. Donna had trouble with her vocal pitch, resulting in some excruciating performances, while Keith began to use hard drugs. They were asked to leave at the end of 1979 and on 21 July 1980, Keith was killed in a car crash. *Go To Heaven* (1980) with new keyboard player Brent Mydland betrayed a hint of disco-pop. The album sleeve showed the band posing in white suits which prompted 'Deadheads' to demand: 'Have they gone soft?' Ironically, it was this disappointing record that spawned their first, albeit minor, success in the US singles chart with 'Alabama Getaway'. All of the band had experimented with drugs for many years and, unlike many of their contemporaries, had survived. Garcia, however, succumbed to heroin addiction in 1982. This retrospectively explained his somnolent playing and gradual decline as a guitarist, together with his often weak and shaky vocals. By the mid-80s, the band had become amorphous but still commanded a massive following. Garcia eventually collapsed and came close to death when he went into a diabetic coma in 1986.

The joy and relief of his survival showed in their first studio album in seven years, *In The Dark*. It was a stunning return to form, resulting in a worldwide hit single 'Touch Of Grey', with Garcia singing his long-time co-songwriter Robert Hunter's simplistic yet honest lyric: 'Oh well a touch of grey, kinda suits you anyway, that's all I've got to say, it's alright'. The band joined in for a joyous repeated chorus of 'I will survive' followed by 'We will survive'. They were even persuaded to make a video and the resulting exposure on MTV introduced them to a whole new generation of fans. The laconic Garcia humorously stated that he was 'appalled' to find they had a smash hit on their hands. While *Built To Last* (1989) was a dull affair, they continued to play to vast audiences. They have since received the accolade of being the largest grossing band in musical history. In August 1990 Mydland died from a lethal combination of cocaine and morphine. Remarkably, this was the third keyboard player to die in the band. Mydland's temporary replacement was Bruce Hornsby until Vince Welnick was recruited full-time. In 1990, the band's live album catalogue was increased with the release of the erratic *Without A Net*.

The transcendental Grateful Dead have endured, throughout the many difficult stages in their long career. Their progress was again halted when Garcia became seriously ill with a lung infection. After a long spell in hospital Garcia returned, this time promising to listen to doctors' advice. They continued to tour throughout 1993 and 1994, after which they began to record a new studio album. However, on 9 August 1995, Garcia suffered a fatal heart attack while staying in a drug treatment centre in California. The reaction from the world press was surprisingly significant: Garcia would have had a wry grin at having finally achieved respectibility all over the world. The press was largely in agreement, concurring that a major talent in the world of music had passed on (either that or all the news editors on daily newspapers are all 40-something ex-hippies). In the USA the reaction was comparable to the death of Kennedy, Luther King, Elvis Presley and John Lennon. Over 10,000 postings were made on the Internet, an all night vigil took place in San Francisco and the president of the USA gave him high praise and called him a genius. The mayor of San Francisco called for flags to be flown at half mast and, appropriately, flew a tie dyed flag from city hall. Bob Dylan said that there was no way to measure his greatness or magnitude. Garcia's high standing in the USA is undisputed, but it is hoped that he will be remembered elsewhere in the world not just as the man who played the opening pedal steel guitar solo on Crosby, Stills And Nash's 'Teach Your Children'. Garcia was a giant who remained hip, humorous, humble and credible right up to his untimely death. At a press conference in December 1995 the band announced that they would bury the band name along with Garcia. With no financial worries, all of the members except for Kreutzmann have a number of forthcoming solo projects that will see them well into the twenty-first century, which is precisely where many of their fans believed they always belonged.

●ALBUMS: The *Grateful Dead* (Warners 1967)★★★, *Anthem Of The Sun* (Warners 1968)★★★★, *Aoxomoxoa* (Warners 1969)★★★★, *Live/Dead* (Warners 1970)★★★★, *Workingman's Dead* (Warners 1970)★★★★★, *Vintage Dead* (Sunflower 1970)★, *American Beauty* (Warners 1970)★★★★★, *Historic*

Dead (Sunflower 1971)★, *Grateful Dead* (Warners 1971)★★★, *Europe '72* (Warners 1972)★★★, *History Of The Grateful Dead, Volume 1 - (Bear's Choice)* (Warners 1973)★★★, *Wake Of The Flood* (Grateful Dead 1973)★★, *From The Mars Hotel* (Grateful Dead 1974)★★★, *For Dead Heads* (United Artists)★★★, *Blues For Allah* (Grateful Dead 1975)★★, *Steal Your Face* (Grateful Dead 1976)★★, *Terrapin Station* (Arista 1977)★★★, *Shakedown Street* (Arrista 1978)★★, *Go To Heaven* (Arista 1980)★, *Reckoning* (Arista 1981)★★★, *Dead Set* (Arista 1981)★★, *In The Dark* (Arista 1987)★★★★, *Built To Last* (Arista 1989)★★, with Bob Dylan *Dylan And The Dead* (Columbia 1990)★, *Without A Net* (Arista 1990)★★, *One From The Vault* (Grateful Dead 1991)★★★, *Infrared Roses* (Grateful Dead 1991)★★, *Two From The Vault* (Grateful Dead 1992)★★★, *Dick's Picks Volume 1* (Grateful Dead 1993)★★★, *Hundred Year Hall* (Arista 1995)★★★, *Dick's Picks Volume 2* (Grateful Dead 1995)★★★, *Dick's Pick's Volume 3* (Grateful Dead 1996)★★★, *Dozin' At The Knick* (Arista 1996)★★★.

●COMPILATIONS: *The Best Of: Skeletons From The Closet* (Warners 1974)★★★★, *What A Long Strange Trip It's Been: The Best Of The Grateful Dead* (Warners 1977)★★★★, *The Arista Years* (Arista 1996)★★★.

●VIDEOS: *Grateful Dead In Concert* (RCA Video 1984), *So Far* (Virgin Vision 1988), *The Grateful Dead Movie* (Palace Premiere 1990), *Infrared Sightings* (Trigon 1995), *Dead Ahead* (Monterey 1995), *Backstage Pass: Acess All Areas* (Pearson 1995), *Ticket To New Year's* (Monterey Home Video 1996), *Tie Died: Rock 'n' Roll's Most Dedicated Fans* (BMG Video 1996).

●FURTHER READING: *The Grateful Dead*, Hank Harrison. *Grateful Dead: The Official Book Of The Deadheads*, Paul Grushkin, Jonas Grushkin and Cynthia Bassett. *History Of The Grateful Dead*, William Ruhlmann. *Built To Last: Twenty-Five Years Of The Grateful Dead*, Jamie Jensen. *Drumming At The Edge Of Magic*, Mickey Hart. *Grateful Dead Family Album*, Jerilyn Lee Brandelius. *Sunshine Daydreams: Grateful Dead Journal*, Herb Greene. *One More Saturday Night: Reflections With The Grateful Dead*, Sandy Troy. *Drumming At the Edge Of Magic*, Mickey Hart and Jay Stevens. *Planet Drum*, Mickey Hart and Fredric Lieberman. *Book Of The Dead: Celebrating 25 Years With The Grateful Dead*, Herb Greene. *Conversations With The Grateful Dead*, David Gans. *Story Of The Grateful Dead*, Adrian Hall. *Dead Base IX: Complete Guide To Grateful Dead Song Lists*, Nixon and Scot Dolgushkin. *Living With The Dead*, Rock Scully with David Dalton.

GREAT AWAKENING

This little-known band made a brief impression in 1969 with an outstanding instrumental version of 'Amazing Grace', long before Judy Collins popularized the song. The mantra-like fuzz guitar added a spiritual quality that was missing from later versions. So little was known of the group that they were often referred to as Amazing Grace, and the song as 'The Great Awakening'! For years it was thought that the man responsible was guitarist David Cohen from Country Joe And The Fish; others suggested it was by members of the Band. Later it was discovered that it was a different David Cohen, helped out by Joe Osborn (bass) and Jimmy Gordon (drums). The latter Cohen has worked as session guitarist for Bobby Darin, Tim Hardin and Frank Sinatra.

GREAT SOCIETY

The Great Society was formed in August 1965 by Grace Slick (b. Grace Barnett Wing, 30 October 1939, Evanston, Illinois, USA; vocals, piano, recorder, guitar), her husband Jerry (drums) and his brother Darby Slick (lead guitar). David Minor (rhythm guitar) and Bard DuPont (bass) completed the original line-up, although the latter was replaced by Peter Vandergelder, who also doubled on saxophone. One of the first San Franciscan rock groups, the quintet was active for 13 months, during which they issued one single, 'Someone To Love' (later known as 'Somebody To Love') on Tom Donahue's Autumn Records/Northbeach label. This intriguing Darby Slick composition achieved fame when it was adopted by Jefferson Airplane, the group Grace joined in October 1966. The Great Society broke up on her departure, but two live collections, released solely in the wake of the singer's subsequent fame, show a group of rare imagination. The first album features 'White Rabbit', another composition Grace introduced to her new-found companions, which is preceded by a lengthy instrumental passage performed in a raga style that typified the Great Society's approach to many of their songs. Indeed, on the dissolution of the group, Darby Slick, Vandergelder and Minor went to study music in India, while Jerry was briefly a member of Final Solution before returning to film work.

●ALBUMS: *Conspicuous Only In Its Absence* (Columbia 1968)★★★, *How It Was* (Columbia 1968)★★.

●COMPILATIONS: *Live At The Matrix* (1989)★★, *Born To Be Burned* (Sundazed 1996)★★★.

●FURTHER READING: *The Jefferson Airplane And The San Francisco Sound*, Ralph J. Gleeson. *Grace Slick - The Biography*, Barbara Rowe. *Don't You Want Somebody To Love*, Darby Slick.

GREEN, GRANT

b. 6 June 1931, St Louis, Missouri, USA, d. 31 January 1979. Heavily influenced by Charlie Christian, guitarist Green first played professionally with Jimmy Forrest. Although noted particularly for his work in organ-guitar-drum trios in the 50s, throughout his career Green was associated with post-bop musicians and in the 60s he recorded for the Blue Note label with Stanley Turrentine, Hank Mobley, McCoy Tyner, Herbie Hancock and others. The flowing, single-line solos characteristic of Christian's early experiments in bebop were evident in much of Green's work. At home in several areas of jazz, he had a particularly strong affinity with the blues, while one album, *Feelin' The Spirit,* features gospel music. Nevertheless, he was essentially modern in his approach to music. Drug addiction severely limited his career in the 70s and he died in 1979.

●ALBUMS: *Grant's First Stand* (Blue Note 1961)★★★, *Reaching Out* (Black Lion 1961)★★★, *Green Street* (Blue Note 1961)★★★, *Sunday Mornin'* (Blue Note 1961)★★★, *Grantstand* (Blue Note 1961)★★★★, *Gooden's Corner* (1961)★★★, *Nigeria* (1962)★★★, *Remembering* (c.1962)★★★, *The Latin Bit* (Blue Note 1962)★★★, *Goin' West* (Blue Note 1962)★★★, *Feelin' The Spirit* (Blue Note 1962)★★★, *Born To Be Blue* (Blue Note 1962)★★★, *Am I Blue* (Blue Note 1963)★★★, *Idle Moments* (Blue Note 1963)★★★★, *Matador* (Blue Note 1964)★★★★, *Solid* (1964)★★★, *Talkin' About!* (1964)★★★★, *Street Of Dreams* (Blue Note 1964)★★★, *I Want To Hold Your Hand* (Blue Note 1964)★★★, *His Majesty King Funk* (Verve 1965)★★★, *Iron City* (1967)★★★, *All The Gin Is Gone* (Delmark 1967)★★★, *Black Forrest* (Delmark 1967)★★★, *Carryin' On* (Blue Note 1969)★★★, *Grant Green Alive!* (Blue Note 1970)★★★, *Visions* (1971)★★★, *Shades Of Green* (1971)★★★, *The Final Comedown* soundtrack (1972)★★, *Live At The Lighthouse* (1972)★★★, *The Main Attraction* (1976)★★★, *Easy/Last Session* (1978)★★, *Iron City* (Black Lion 1981)★★, *Last Session* (Atlantis 1987)★★.

●COMPILATIONS: *Best Of* (Blue Note 1993)★★★.

GREENWICH, ELLIE

b. 23 October 1940, Brooklyn, New York, USA. Greenwich's singing career began in 1958 with 'Cha-Cha-Charming', released under the name Ellie Gaye. Two years later she met budding songwriter Jeff Barry and, following a release as Ellie Gee And The Jets, the couple formed the Raindrops in 1963. The group enjoyed a US Top 20 hit with 'The Kind Of Boy You Can't Forget', but increased demand on the now-married duo's compositional skills led to the band's demise. Having abandoned respective partnerships with Toni Powers and Art Resnick, Greenwich and Barry enjoyed a sustained period of success with a series of notable compositions, including 'Do Wah Diddy' (the Exciters/Manfred Mann), 'I Wanna Love Him So Bad' (the Jelly Beans) and 'Hanky Panky' (Tommy James And The Shondells). Collaborations with Phil Spector generated hits for the Crystals ('Da Doo Ron Ron' and 'Then He Kissed Me'), the Ronettes ('Be My Baby' and 'Baby, I Love You') and Ike And Tina Turner ('River Deep - Mountain High') while work with George 'Shadow' Morton reaped commercial success for the Shangri-Las, notably 'Leader Of The Pack'. Ellie also rekindled her solo career with 'You Don't Know', but her divorce from Barry in 1965 put an intolerable strain on their working relationship. Together they produced Neil Diamond's early recordings, but in 1967 she severed their partnership and made an exclusive songwriting deal with Unart Music. *Ellie Greenwich Composes, Produces, Sings* combined original songs with current favourites, but was a commercial failure,

while her subsequent Pineywood Productions company was similarly ill-starred in the wake of changing musical tastes. 'I couldn't understand what (acid rock) was all about', she later stated, and instead switched to writing jingles. She re-emerged during the singer/songwriter boom with *Let It Be Written, Let It Be Sung*, but this excellent album failed to rekindle her career when stage fright blighted an attendant tour. Ellie remained in seclusion for most of the ensuing decade but re-emerged in the 80s as a performer in the acclaimed biographical revue *Leader Of The Pack*. A new generation of acts, including Nona Hendryx, Cyndi Lauper and Ellen Foley, have recorded her songs, insuring Greenwich's position as one of pop's finest composers.

●ALBUMS: *Ellie Greenwich Composes, Produces And Sings* (United Artists 1968)★★, *Let It Be Written, Let It Be Sung* (1973)★★.

GROSSMAN, ALBERT

b. 1926, Chicago, Illinois, USA, d. 25 January 1986. Nicknamed 'the floating Buddha', this stout impressario's Windy City club, Gate Of Horn, was a showcase for Big Bill Broonzy, Odetta and other entertainers who reached a wider audience via his annual Newport Festivals - the most important date on the US folk/blues devotee's calendar in the early 60s. As manager, his most famous charges were Peter, Paul And Mary until, on the advice of CBS producer John Hammond, Bob Dylan signed up with him for seven years in 1962. Grossman's faith in the youth as a composer as well as a performer was justified with all manner of remunerative covers of his songs, from Peter, Paul And Mary's million-selling 'Blowing In The Wind' to Manfred Mann's cache of UK smashes, which were initiated through Grossman's scraping acquaintance with their manager during Dylan's British tour of 1964. Grossman's bellicose stance in negotiation was instanced in *Don't Look Back*, the film documentary of the visit. Although the Band and the late Janis Joplin later also came under his wing, his name became as synonymous with Dylan's as Colonel Tom Parker's was with Elvis Presley. Nevertheless, their contract was not renewed and the song 'Dear Landlord', on *John Wesley Harding* was widely interpreted as an acerbic response by the artist. Grossman subsequently devoted more attention to Paul Butterfield, Todd Rundgren, Jesse Winchester and other artists on his Bearsville record label - named after the town of which he became something of a patriarch.

GTOs

An acronym for Girls Together Outrageously, this all-female group was lauded in 1969 as part of Frank Zappa's Straight label roster. Initially known as the Laurel Canyon Ballet Company, they were, alongside the notorious Plaster Casters, the best-known members of the 60s groupie sub-culture. After meeting the overtly polite Tiny Tim, each member abandoned her respective surname and became Miss Lucy, Miss Pamela, Miss Christine, Miss Sparky, Miss Mercy, Miss Sandra and Miss Cynderella.

The septet decamped to Zappa's home when Miss Christine became governess to his daughter Moon, and they occasionally performed live with his group, the Mothers Of Invention. Zappa produced the bulk of the GTOs, audio-verite *Permanent Damage*, while future Little Feat guitarist Lowell George took charge of two tracks - his distinctive slide style is apparent on 'I Have A Paintbrush In My Hand To Colour A Triangle'. Members of the Mothers and the Jeff Beck Group also made several contributions, but the album's release was almost cancelled when Misses Mercy, Cynderella and Sparky were arrested on drugs charges. The GTOs split into two camps, and the final recordings were made solely by Pamela and Sparky. Each member then went her separate way, but their collective flirtation with the rock élite continued. Miss Christine was pictured emerging from a tomb on the cover of Zappa's *Hot Rats* and on the inner sleeve of Todd Rundgren's *Runt*. She was also the subject of the Flying Burrito Brothers' song 'Christine's Tune', but this title was later amended to 'She's The Devil In Disguise' following her death in 1972. Miss Mercy and Miss Pamela joined the chorus on the same group's 'Hippie Boy' and Miss Cynderella was briefly married to John Cale. Pamela later sang on tour with the Pink Fairies, married former Silverhead vocalist Michael Des Barres and in 1989 penned a kiss-and-tell autobiography, *I'm With The Band*.
●ALBUMS: *Permanent Damage* (Straight 1969)★★.

GUARALDI, VINCE

b. 17 July 1928, San Francisco, California, USA, d. 6 February 1976. Jazz pianist and latter day easy listening jazz composer Guaraldi played with Cal Tjaader in the early 50s before moving through Bill Harris' combo, and worked with Sonny Criss and George Auld. He also served as part of Woody Herman's touring band in the late 50s. It was in the 60s, however, that Guaraldi made a name for himself as a composer of light romantic jazz-influenced songs. His most famous and deservedly long-lasting classic is 'Cast Your Fate To The Wind', which was a hit for his trio in 1962 and subsequently won him a Grammy award. A surprise cover version appeared high in the UK charts at the end of 1964 by a studio-only group Sounds Orchestral. In recent years the song has been covered many times, one of the better interpretations was by David Benoit from his 1989 album *Waiting For Spring*. Less credible although also widely known is his soundtrack theme music for the Charlie Brown *Peanuts* cartoon television series. He also recorded with Conte Candoli and Frank Rosolino in the 60s. His music received an unexpected boost in the mid-90s when some of his work was reappraised during the 'space age bachelor pad music' cult boom.
●ALBUMS: *Modern Music From San Francisco* (Fantasy 1956)★★★, *Vince Guaraldi Trio* (Fantasy 1956)★★★, *A Flower Is A Lovesome Thing* (Fantasy 1958)★★★, *Cast Your Fate To The Wind; Jazz Impressions Of Black Orpheus* (Fantasy 1962)★★★, *Vince Guaraldi In Person* (Fantasy 1963)★★★, with

Frank Rosolino *Vince Guaraldi/Frank Rosolino Quintet* (Premier 1963)★★★, with Conte Candoli *Vince Guaraldi/Conte Candoli Quartet* (Premier 1963)★★★, *Vince Guaraldi, Bola Sete And Friends* (Fantasy 1963)★★★, *Tour De Force* (Fantasy 1963)★★★, *Jazz Impressions Of Charlie Brown* (Fantasy 1964)★★★, *Jazz Impressions* (Fantasy 1964)★★★, *A Boy Named Charlie Brown* (Fantasy 1964)★★★, *The Latin Side Of Vince Guaraldi* (Fantasy 1964)★★★, *Vince Guaraldi At Grace Cathedral* (Fantasy 1965)★★★, *From All Sides* (Fantasy 1965)★★★, *Live At The El Matador* (Fantasy 1966)★★★, *Oh Good Grief!* (Warners 1968)★★★.

GUN (60s)

This late 60s high-powered UK trio had an interesting ancestry, as two of their number were the offspring of the Kinks' irreverent and exuberant road manager Sam Curtis. Paul Curtis (b. Paul Gurvitz, 6 July 1947) and Adrian Curtis (b. Adrian Gurvitz, 26 June 1949) joined drummer Louie Farrell (b. Brian Farrell, 12 December 1947) at a time when the boundaries between pop and progressive music were still a matter of hot debate. Gun were featured on John Peel's influential BBC Radio show, *Top Gear*, and enjoyed a strong chart hit with the driving, riff-laden 'Race With The Devil' in 1968, which was uncannily similar to Moby Grape's 'Can't Be So Bad'. Uncertain of their appeal in the pop market, they came unstuck with their follow-up, the frantic 'Drives You Mad', and when 'Hobo' also flopped, it was clear that their chart days were over. Their record label attempted to market them as counter-culture heroes with advertisements proclaiming 'the revolutionaries are on CBS', but the group failed to establish themselves as album artists. After dissolving the group in the early 70s, Adrian Gurvitz teamed up with Ginger Baker to form the Baker Gurvitz Army, and later achieved a hit single, 'Classic', as a soloist in 1982.
●ALBUMS: *Gun* (CBS 1969)★★, *Gunsight* (CBS 1969)★★.

GYPSY (60s)

This Leicester-based group made its debut in 1968 under the name Legay. Having completed only one single, John Knapp (vocals/guitar/keyboards), Robin Pizer (guitar/vocals), Rod Read (guitar/vocals), David McCarthy (bass/vocals) and Moth Smith (drums) took a new name, Gypsy, and were one of the attractions featured at the 1969 Isle Of Wight festival. Their debut album showed great promise and showcased an engaging, tight-harmony style reminiscent of Moby Grape. Ray Martinez then replaced Rod Read, but the group's second album lacked the purpose of its predecessor and Gypsy broke up soon after its release.
●ALBUMS: *Gypsy* (United Artists 1971)★★★, *Brenda And The Rattlesnake* (United Artists 1972)★★.

H.P. LOVECRAFT

This imaginative group were formed in Chicago, Illinois, USA, by George Edwards (guitar/vocals) and David Michaels (keyboards-woodwind/vocals). They made their debut in 1967 with a folk rock reading of 'Anyway That You Want Me', a Chip Taylor composition successfully revived by the Troggs. The duo was initially backed by a local outfit, the Rovin' Kind, until Tony Cavallari (lead guitar), Jerry McGeorge (bass, ex-Shadows Of Knight) and Michael Tegza (drums) completed the new venture's line-up. Their debut album, *H.P. Lovecraft*, fused haunting, folk-based material with graphic contemporary compositions. It featured stirring renditions of 'Wayfaring Stranger' and 'Let's Get Together', but the highlight was 'The White Ship', a mesmerizing adaptation of a short story penned by the author from whom the quintet took its name. McGeorge was replaced by Jeffrey Boylan for *H.P. Lovecraft II*. This enthralling set included 'At The Mountains Of Madness', in which the group's distinctive harmonies cultivated an eerie, chilling atmosphere. Commercial indifference sadly doomed their progress and the quintet disintegrated, although Tezga re-emerged in 1971 with three new musicians, Jim Dolinger (guitar), Michael Been (bass) and Marty Grebb (keyboards). Now dubbed simply Lovecraft, the group completed *Valley Of The Moon*, a set that bore little resemblance to those of its pioneering predecessor. In 1975 the drummer employed a completely new line-up for *We Love You Whoever You Are*, before finally laying the name to rest.
●ALBUMS: *H.P. Lovecraft* (Philips 1967)★★★, *H.P. Lovecraft II* (Philips 1968)★★★, as Lovecraft *Valley Of The Moon* (1971)★★, as Lovecraft *We Love You Whoever You Are* (1975)★★, as H.P. Lovecraft *Live - May 11, 1968* (Sundazed 1992)★★.

HAIR

After an off-Broadway opening, the stage musical *Hair* came to Broadway at the Biltmore Theatre on 29 April 1968. To use an anachronism, *Hair* was what might today be described as 'alternative entertainment'. Among many things that differentiated the show from other contemporary productions was its forceful stand on matters like sex, politics, drugs, the draft and religion. It was the first musical of the hippie peace and love generation; many of the performers wore wigs as they had yet to grow their own hair. Strong language and nudity ensured a measure of shock value and doubtless helped fill seats with the prurient. Despite, or perhaps because of, its irreverence and decidedly contemporary attitude, *Hair* was received favourably by critics. The music was by Galt MacDermot with book and lyrics by Gerome Ragni and James Rado. Cast with mostly unknown young actors, *Hair* offered a joyous theatrical experience unlike that to which most Broadway regulars were accustomed. Among the cast were Lynn Kellogg, Melba Moore, Sally Eaton, Diane Keaton and Lamont Washington. The songs included 'I Believe In Love', 'Hair', 'Hare Krishna', 'Walking In Space' and 'Good Morning, Starshine'; other titles broke newer ground for establishment-Broadway: 'Prisoners In Niggertown', 'Hashish' and 'Sodomy'. Several artists had hits with songs from the show, notably the Fifth Dimension who topped the US chart with a medley that included 'Aquarius' and 'Let The Sunshine In'. The successfull 1968 London production had Paul Nicholas, Oliver Tobias and Marsha Hunt among the cast (Alex Harvey was in the pit orchestra). A 1993 revival at London's Old Vic ('this show is about as topical as *The Pirates Of Penzance*') folded after two months. In the USA, a 1994 '25th anniversary' tour was directed by James Rado, incorporated three new musical numbers. A film version of *Hair* appeared in 1979.

HALLYDAY, JOHNNY

b. Jean-Philippe Smet, 15 June 1943, Paris, France. After his Belgian father's desertion, Smet was adopted by his aunt Helene Mar, wife of North American song-and-dance man Lee Hallyday, from whom the child later derived his stage surname. His aptitude for the performing arts earned him a role in his uncle's act, and he developed a passable mastery of the guitar after giving up violin lessons. By the late 50s, he had become an incorrigible *ye-ye* - a Parisian species of rock 'n' roller that trod warily amid official disapproval. His stamping ground was Le Golf Drouot club with its jukebox of US discs. Singing in public was second nature to him, and he sounded so much like the genuine American article during his 1960 radio debut that, via the brother who managed him, Vogue contracted Hallyday for an immediate single, 'T'Ai Mer Follement'. However, it was a million-selling bilingual cover of Chubby Checker's 'Let's Twist Again' on Philips in 1961, a film part (in *Les Parisiennes*) that same year, and, crucially, the intensity of his recitals that convinced most that this svelte, blond youth was to France what Elvis Presley was to the USA. The title of 1962's *Johnny Hallyday Sings America's Rockin' Hits* was a reliable indicator of future direction. The preponderance of English language material in his concert sets was commensurate with recorded interpretations of songs such as 'The House Of The Rising Sun', 'Black Is Black', 'In The Midnight Hour', 'Hey Joe' and in the 70s and 80s 'Delta Lady' and - in a remarkable 1985 duet with Emmylou Harris - 'If I Were A Carpenter'. An appearance in 1964 on *Ready Steady Go* had been well received but he was unable to duplicate even Richard Anthony's modest triumphs in the UK chart. If neither made much headway in the USA, Johnny eclipsed his rival in Africa and South America, where a 25,000 attendance at a Hallyday show in Argentina was not atypical. Several degrees from blatant bandwagon-jumping, Hallyday continued to thrive on a certain hip sensibility, manifested in his block-bookings of fashionable studios in Britain and the USA, and employment of top session musicians like Bobby Keyes, Jim Price and Gary Wright - all prominent on 1975's *Flagrant Delit* which, like most of his albums, contained a few Hallyday originals. Details of his stormy marriage to Sylvie Vartan and a more recent hip operation attracted headlines as he entered middle age. Yet Hallyday maintained a jocular bonhomie in interview, and on stage he remained as melodramatic as ever, evolving less as France's Presley, more its 'answer' to Cliff Richard, as he is still one of the few European stars in direct artistic debt to US pop to be regarded with anything approaching strong interest beyond his country's borders. Dozens of albums have been released, but mainly in France. An extraordinary box set containing 42 CDs was issued for his 50th birthday.

●ALBUMS: *Johnny Hallyday Sings America's Rockin' Hits* (Philips 1961)★★★, *Flagrant Delit* (1975)★★★, *Drole De Metier* (1986)★★★, *Trift De Rattles* (1986)★★★, *Les Grands Success De Johnny Hallyday* (1988)★★★, *La Peur* (1988)★★★, *La Nuit Johnny* 42-CD box set (1993)★★★.

HAPPENINGS

This was a vocal harmony group from Paterson, New Jersey, USA that specialized in reviving classic songs; it comprised Bob Miranda (lead), Ralph DeVito (baritone), David Libert (bass) and Thomas Giuliano (tenor). They met while in military service at Fort Dix, New Jersey, and after leaving formed the Four Graduates. In addition to their roles as session singers, the quartet recorded a couple of singles for Crystal Ball Records and Rust, the latter being produced in 1963 by members of the successful group the Tokens. When the Tokens formed their own B.T. Puppy label in 1965 they signed the group, now called the Happenings, and their second release, a revival of the Tempos' 1959 hit, 'See You In September', reached number 3 in the US charts. Despite the fact that their distinctively dated yet somehow contemporary style seemed out of place with other 60s groups, they strung together an enviable nine US chart entries between 1966 and 1969. The biggest of these were their revivals of Steve Lawrence's 'Go Away Little Girl', George Gershwin's 'I Got Rhythm' and Al Jolson's 'My Mammy', which were all hits in the US Top 20. They later recorded for Jubilee, Big Tree and Midland International, and in the 80s Miranda and Giuliano were fronting a new line-up of the group on oldies shows.

●ALBUMS: *The Happenings* (BT Puppy 1966)★★★, *Psycle* (BT Puppy 1967)★★★, *Piece Of Mind* (Jubilee 1969)★★.

●COMPILATIONS: *Happenings Golden Hits* (BT Puppy 1968)★★★, *The Happening's Greatest Hits* (Jubilee 1969)★★★, *The Best Of ...* (Sequel 1995)★★★.

HAPSHASH AND THE COLOURED COAT

Hapshash And The Coloured Coat was the name adopted by graphic artists Michael English and Nigel Weymouth. They met in London, England, in 1966, collaborating on the Love Festival poster that showed the joint influence of Man Ray and US pop artist Tom Wesselman. Their work defined the romanticism of the English Underground movement and included posters promoting the Soft Machine, Tomorrow, Jimi Hendrix and Arthur Brown, as well as concerts held at the UFO Club and Brian Epstein's Saville Theatre, both located in London. Having become acquainted with producer/svengali Guy Stevens, English and Weymouth recorded their debut album. *Hapshash And The Coloured Coat* featured lengthy, semi-improvised pieces fused to hard, repetitive riffs and chanted vocals. The accompaniment was supplied by Stevens' protégés Art. Housed in a *de rigeur* psychedelic sleeve and pressed on red vinyl, the album became a lynchpin release of the English 'underground' movement. However, with Stevens now in absentia and English preferring art to music, it was largely left to Weymouth to record *Western Flyer*. Groundhogs' guitarist Tony McPhee and future Wombles producer/songwriter Mike Batt assisted on a set encompassing pop, progressive and cajun styles, all delivered in a suitably quirky manner. English and Weymouth sundered their partnership soon afterwards.

●ALBUMS: *Hapshash And The Coloured Coat Featuring The Human Host And The Heavy Metal Kids* (Minit 1967)★★, *Western Flyer* (Liberty 1969)★.

HARD DAY'S NIGHT, A

When it was released in 1964, the first Beatles feature broke many pop film taboos. Director Richard Lester, famed for his work with the madcap Goons, brought elements of that tradition to this innovative venture. Shot in black and white with the merest whiff of kitchen-sink realism, it captured the quartet's natural humour and left their Liverpudian accents intact. Superb support from Wilfred Brambell, as McCartney's 'grandfather', and Victor Spinetti as the harassed television producer, complement the Beatles' performances superbly. If the plot was slight, the imagery and camera work were captivating, buoyed by a slew of superior John Lennon/Paul McCartney compositions. The sequence featuring 'I Should Have Known Better', set in a train, is particularly memorable, but the entire film is a fast-moving kaleidoscope of sound and picture. 'If I Fell', 'Tell Me Why' and 'Can't Buy Me Love' encapsulate Beatlemania at its height, while the six songs completing the *A Hard Day's Night* album, not featured in the film, show its sound and scope maturing. A landmark in British cinema and pop.

HARD MEAT

Taking its cue from Traffic, this trio were among many outfits who, in the late 60s, 'got it together in the country' - in their case, the wilds of Cornwall. To make ends meet, guitarist Michael Dolan, his bass-plucking brother Steve -

with whom he shared both vocals and a Birmingham upbringing - and drummer Mick Carless took on a summer residency as the Ebony Combo at Bude's Headland Pavilion before assuming their genital moniker in 1969. By then, they had cultivated a faintly sinister 'stoned hippie' image, and their repertoire hinged on originals of 'progressive' rock plus reinventions of works by Bob Dylan ('Most Likely You Go Your Way') and Richie Havens. After amassing an extensive work schedule they were signed to Warner Brothers Records for whom they recorded two unremarkable albums and a single - an arrangement of the Beatles' 'Rain' - before disbanding in 1971. Two years later, Steve Dolan was among the cast on Pete Sinfield's *Under The Sky*.

●ALBUMS: *Hard Meat* (Warners 1970)★★, *Through A Window* (Warners 1970)★★.

HARDIN, TIM

b. 23 December 1941, Eugene, Oregon, USA, d. 29 December 1980. Hardin arrived in New York following a tour of duty with the US Marines. He initially studied acting, but dropped out of classes to develop his singing and songwriting talent. By 1964 he was appearing regularly in New York's Greenwich Village cafés, where he forged a unique blend of poetic folk/blues. Hardin's first recordings were made in 1964 although the results of this traditional-based session were shelved for several years and were only issued, as *This Is Tim Hardin*, in the wake of the singer's commercial success. His debut album, *Tim Hardin 1*, was a deeply poignant affair, wherein Tim's frail, weary intonation added intrigue to several magnificent compositions, including 'Don't Make Promises', 'Misty Roses' (sensitively covered by Colin Blunstone) and 'Hang On To A Dream' (which became a regular part of the Nice's live performances) as well as the much-covered 'Reason To Believe'. *Tim Hardin 2*, featured his original version of 'If I Were A Carpenter', an international hit in the hands of Bobby Darin and the Four Tops, which confirmed Hardin's position as a writer of note. However, the artist was deeply disappointed with these releases and reportedly broke down upon hearing the finished master to his first selection. Hardin's career then faltered on private and professional difficulties. As early as 1970 he was experiencing alcohol and drug problems. A conceptual work, *Suite For Susan Moore And Damion* reclaimed something of his former fire but his gifts seemed to desert him following its release. Hardin's high standing as a songwriter has resulted in his work being interpreted by many artists over the past four decades, including Wilson Phillips and Rod Stewart ('Reason to Believe') and Scott Walker ('Lady Came From Baltimore'). As Hardin's own songs grew less incisive, he began interpreting the work of other songwriters. Beset by heroin addiction, his remaining work is a ghost of that early excellence. Tim Hardin died, almost forgotten and totally underrated, in December 1980, of a heroin overdose. Over the past few years Hardin's work has received a wider and more favourable reception.

●ALBUMS: *Tim Hardin 1* (Verve Forecast 1966)★★★, *Tim Hardin 2* (Verve Forecast 1967)★★★, *This Is Tim Hardin* (Atco 1967)★★, *Tim Hardin 3 Live In Concert* (Verve Forecast 1968)★★★, *Tim Hardin 4* (Verve Forecast 1969)★★★, *Suite For Susan Moore And Damion/We Are - One, One, All In One* (Columbia 1969)★★★, *Golden Archive Series* (MGM 1970)★★★, *Bird On A Wire* (Columbia 1971)★★, *Painted Head* (Columbia 1972)★★★, *Archetypes* (MGM 1973)★★★, *Nine* (GM/Antilles 1974)★★★, *The Shock Of Grace* (Columbia 1981)★★★, *The Homecoming Concert* (Line 1981)★★★.

●COMPILATIONS: *Best Of Tim Hardin* (Verve Forecast 1969)★★★★, *Memorial Album* (Polydor 1981)★★★, *Reason To Believe (The Best Of)* (Polydor 1987)★★★★, *Hang On To A Dream - The Verve Recordings* (Polydor 1994)★★★★, *Simple Songs Of Freedom: The Tim Hardin Collection* (Columbia 1996)★★★★.

HARDY, FRANÇOISE

b. 17 January 1944, Paris, France. After graduating from the Le Bruyère College, Hardy pursued a musical career as a singer/songwriter. Signed to the prestigious French record label Vogue, she had an international million-selling hit in 1962 with the self-composed 'Tous Les Garçons Et Les Filles'. Three years later, she enjoyed her only major UK hit with the softly sung 'All Over The World'. A major star in her home country, she extended her appeal as a result of various modelling assignments and appearances in several films by Roger Vadim. Her international recording career gradually declined towards the end of the 60s due to stage fright. In the mid-90s she reappeared together with Malcolm McLaren on a duet 'The Revenge Of The Flowers'.

●ALBUMS: *Golden Hour Presents The Best Of Françoise Hardy* (1974)★★★, *Greatest Hits* (1984)★★★, *The Françoise Hardy Hit Parade* (1984)★★★, *In Vogue* (1988)★★★, *All Over the World* (1989)★★★, *Le Danger* (Virgin 1996)★★★.

HARMONY GRASS

Formed in Essex, England, in 1968, this close harmony pop group developed from Tony Rivers And The Castaways, a superior beat attraction heavily influenced by the Beach Boys. Longtime associate Ray Brown (bass) joined Rivers (lead vocals) in a venture completed by third former Castaway, Kenny Rowe (second bass), and newcomers Tony Ferguson (lead guitar), Tom Marshall (rhythm guitar/piano) and Bill Castle (drums). Signed to RCA Records, the sextet enjoyed a UK Top 30 hit in 1969 with their debut single, 'Move In A Little Closer', which was produced by Chris Andrews, previously successful with Sandie Shaw and Adam Faith. However, despite recording several equally high-class singles, including a cover version of Paul Simon's 'Cecilia', Harmony Grass was unable to consolidate this early commercial promise. Rivers later pursued a career as a successful session singer, while the rump of his erstwhile group evolved into Capability Brown and J.J. Foote.

●ALBUMS: *This Is Us* (1969)★★.

HARPERS BIZARRE

Evolving from Santa Cruz band the Tikis, the orginal Harpers Bizarre emerged in late 1966 with a line-up comprising lead vocalist/guitarist Ted Templeman (b. Theodore Templeman, 24 October 1944), vocalist/guitarist Dick Scoppettone (b. 5 July 1945), vocalist/bassist Dick Young (9 January 1945), vocalist/guitarist Eddie James and former Beau Brummels drummer/vocalist John Peterson. A sprightly cover of Simon And Garfunkel's '59th Street Bridge Song (Feelin' Groovy)' brought them a US Top 20 hit and became a perennial radio favourite. Their first album, boasting the arranging skills of Leon Russell and the composing talents of Randy Newman, backed by Harpers' exceptional vocal talent, proved an enticing debut. After covering Van Dyke Parks' 'Come To The Sunshine', they worked with the man himself on the hit follow-up, a revival of Cole Porter's 'Anything Goes'. An album of the same name combined similar standards with material by Parks and Newman. After two more albums, the group split in 1969 with Templeman becoming a name staff producer for Warner Brothers Records. Three members of the original line-up reunited briefly six years later for the album *As Time Goes By*.
●ALBUMS: *Feelin' Groovy* (Warners 1967)★★★, *Anything Goes* (Warners 1967)★★, *The Secret Life Of Harpers Bizarre* (Warners 1968)★★, *Harpers Bizarre 4* (1969)★★, *As Time Goes By* (1976)★.

HARRIS, JET, AND TONY MEEHAN

Terence 'Jet' Harris (b. 6 July 1939, Kingsbury, Middlesex, England; guitar) and Daniel Joseph Anthony Meehan (b. 22 March 1943, Hampstead, London, England; drums) began their partnership in 1959 as members of the Shadows. Meehan left the group in October 1961 to take up an A&R position at Decca, and the following year Harris began a solo career with 'Besame Mucho'. 'The Man With The Golden Arm' gave the guitarist a UK Top 20 hit prior to reuniting with Meehan in 1963. The duo's debut single, 'Diamonds', was a startling instrumental composition which topped the UK charts, while two ensuing releases, 'Scarlett O'Hara' and 'Applejack', also reached the Top 5. Each performance matched Harris' low-tuned Fender Jaguar guitar with Meehan's punchy drum interjections, and although a bright future was predicted, a serious car crash undermined Harris' confidence and the pair split up. Existing contracts were fulfilled by the Tony Meehan Combo, although Harris did resume recording with 'Big Bad Bass'. His subsequent career was blighted by personal and professional problems, and successive attempts at rekindling former glories fell flat. Meehan, meanwhile, enjoyed an increasingly backroom role as a producer and arranger.
●COMPILATIONS: *Remembering: Jet Harris And Tony Meehan* (Decca 1976)★★★, *The Jet Harris And Tony Meehan Story Volumes 1 & 2* (1976)★★★, *Diamonds* (1983)★★★.

HARRISON, NOEL

b. 1934. Harrison's career was furnished with both the best and worst start by the long shadow of Rex Harrison, his famous father. Before capitulating to full-time acting too, Noel - an urbane and accomplished singing guitarist - was well known on the British folk club circuit before achieving his only hit in 1969. Assisted by its inclusion in *The Thomas Crown Affair* film soundtrack, 'Windmills Of Your Mind' peaked at number 8 in the UK charts, but only 'A Young Girl' elicited further interest. Having tested the thespian water with minor appearances in television's *Man From UNCLE* series, he took over from Tommy Steele in a touring production of *Half A Sixpence*. After several similar starring roles, his talents were directed exclusively towards the theatre.
●ALBUMS: *At The Blue Angel* (Philips 1960)★★, *The Great Electric Experiment Is Over* (Reprise 1969)★★.
●COMPILATIONS: *The World Of Noel Harrison* (Decca 1970)★★★.

HARTLEY, KEEF, BAND

b. 8 March 1944, Preston, Lancashire, England. Together with Colosseum, the Keef Hartley Band of the late 60s, forged jazz and rock music sympathetically to appeal to the UK progressive music scene. Drummer Hartley had already had vast experience in live performances as Ringo Starr's replacement in Rory Storm And The Hurricanes. When Merseybeat died, Hartley was enlisted by the London-based R&B band the Artwoods, whose line-up included future Deep Purple leader Jon Lord. Hartley was present on their only album *Art Gallery* (now a much sought-after collector's item). He joined John Mayall's Bluesbreakers and was present during one of Mayall's vintage periods. Both *Crusade* and *Diary Of A Band* highlighted Hartley's economical drumming and faultless timing. The brass-laden instrumental track on John Mayall's *Bare Wires* is titled 'Hartley Quits'. The good natured banter between Hartley and his ex-boss continued onto Hartley's strong debut *Half Breed*. The opening track 'Hearts And Flowers' has the voice of Mayall on the telephone officially sacking Hartley, albeit tongue-in-cheek, while the closing track 'Sacked' has Hartley dismissing Mayall! The music intervening features some of the best ever late 60s jazz-influenced blues, and the album remains an undiscovered classic. The band for the first album comprised Miller Anderson (b. 12 April 1945, Johnston, Renfrewshire, Scotland; guitar and vocals), Gary Thain (b. 15 May 1948, Wellington, New Zealand, d. 19 March 1976; bass), Peter Dines (organ) and Spit James (guitar). Later members to join Hartley's fluid line-up included Mick Weaver (aka Wynder K. Frog) organ, Henry Lowther (b. 11 July 1941, Leicester, England; trumpet/violin), Jimmy Jewell (saxophone), Johnny Almond (flute), Jon Hiseman (who guested on percussion and congas) and Harry Beckett. Hartley, often dressed as an American Indian, sometimes soberly, sometimes in full head-dress and war-paint, was a popular attraction on the small club scene. His was one of the few British bands to play the Woodstock Festival, where his critics compared him favourably with Blood Sweat And Tears. *The Battle Of NW6* in 1969 further enhanced his club reputation, although chart success still eluded him. By the time of the third album both Lowther and Jewell had departed, although Hartley always maintained that his band was like a jazz band, in that musicians could come and go and be free to play with other aggregations.

Dave Caswell and Lyle Jenkins came in and made *The Time Is Near*. This album demonstrated Miller Anderson's fine songwriting ability, and long-time producer Neil Slaven's excellent production. They were justly rewarded when the album briefly nudged its way into the UK and US charts. Subsequent albums lost the fire that Hartley kindled on the first three, although the formation of his Little Big Band and the subsequent live album had some fine moments. The recording at London's Marquee club saw the largest ever band assembled on the tiny stage; almost the entire British jazz/rock fraternity seemed to be present, including Chris Mercer, Lynn Dobson, Ray Warleigh, Barbara Thompson, and Derek Wadsworth. By the time *Seventy Second Brave* was released, Anderson had departed having signed a contract as a solo artist. He was clearly the jewel in Hartley's crown (or headgear) and the cohesion that Anderson gave the band as the main songwriter, lead vocalist and lead guitar was instantly lost. Future recordings also lacked Slaven's even production. Hartley and Anderson came together again in 1974 for one album as Dog Soldier but Hartley has been largely inactive in music for many years apart from the occasional tour with John Mayall and sessions with Michael Chapman. In the mid-90s he had a carpentry business in Preston, Lancashire, and although it is alleged that he no longer owns a drumkit attempts were being made in the mid-90s to re-form the original band.

●ALBUMS: *Halfbreed* (Deram 1969)★★★, *Battle Of NW6* (Deram 1970)★★★, *The Time Is Near* (Deram 1970)★★★★, *Overdog* (Deram 1971)★★, *Little Big Band* (Deram 1971)★★★, *Seventy Second Brave* (Deram1972)★, *Lancashire Hustler* (Deram 1973)★, as Dog Soldier *Dog Soldier* (1975)★★ .

●COMPILATIONS: *The Best Of Keef Hartley* (Decca 1972)★★★.

HARVEY, ALEX

b. 5 February 1935, Gorbals, Glasgow, Scotland, d. 4 February 1982. Having left school at the age of 15, Harvey undertook a multitude of occupations before opting for music. Inspired by Jimmie Rodgers, Woody Guthrie and Cisco Houston, he became acquainted with several musicians who rehearsed regularly at the city's Bill Patterson Studios. In 1955 Harvey joined saxophonist Bill Patrick in a group that combined rock 'n' roll and traditional jazz. Known jointly as the Clyde River Jazz Band or the Kansas City Skiffle Band, depending on the booking, the unit later evolved into the Kansas City Counts, and joined the Ricky Barnes All-Stars as pioneers of the Scottish rock 'n' roll circuit. By the end of the

decade, and with their singer the obvious focal point, the group had became known as Alex Harvey's (Big) Soul Band, the appellation derived from a new form of small group jazz championed by Horace Silver. The band's repertoire consisted of Ray Charles, the Isley Brothers and urban R&B versions, while their innovative use of conga drums and other percussive instruments emphasized the swinging nature of their sound. Harvey moved to Hamburg where he recorded *Alex Harvey And His Soul Band* in October 1963. Curiously, this excellent set did not feature the singer's regular group, but musicians drawn from Kingsize Taylor And The Dominoes. The following year Alex returned to the UK. His group made its London debut on 6 February 1964 and for several months remained a highly popular attraction in the capital. However, another opportunity to capture them on record was lost when *The Blues* consisted of largely solo material with support derived solely from Harvey's younger brother, Leslie. This disparate set included suitably idiosyncratic readings of 'Danger Zone', 'Waltzing Matilda' and 'The Big Rock Candy Mountain'. Despite initial intentions to the contrary, Harvey dissolved the Soul Band in 1965 with a view to pursuing a folk-based direction. However subsequent releases, including 'Agent 00 Soul' and 'Work Song', continued the artist's love of R&B. Having briefly fronted the houseband at Glasgow's Dennistoun Palais, Alex returned to London in 1967 to form the psychedelic Giant Moth. The remnants of this short-lived group - Mox (flute), Jim Condron (guitar/bass) and George Butler (drums) - supported the singer on two invigorating singles, 'Someday Song' and 'Maybe Someday'. Stung by their commercial failure, Harvey took a job in the pit band for the musical *Hair*, which in turn inspired *Hair Rave Up Live From The Shaftesbury Theatre*. The singer re-established his own career in 1969 with the uncompromising *Roman Wall Blues*. This powerful set included the original version of 'Midnight Moses', a composition that the singer brought to his next substantial group, the Sensational Alex Harvey Band. Galvanized by the tragic death of his brother Leslie while on stage with Stone The Crows, Harvey formed SAHB with Tear Gas, a struggling Glasgow hard rock band. Together they became one of the most popular live attractions of the early 70s. He abandoned the group in October 1977 to resume a less frenetic solo career, but *The Mafia Stole My Guitar* failed to recapture former glories. Harvey succumbed to a fatal heart attack on 4 February 1982 in Belgium at the end of a four-week tour of Europe. He was an enigmatic and endearing character who still has stories told about his exploits long after his death.

●ALBUMS: *Alex Harvey And His Soul Band* (Polydor 1964)★★★, *The Blues* (Polydor 1964)★★★, *Hair Rave Up Live From The Shaftesbury Theatre* (1969)★★, *Roman Wall Blues* (Fontana 1969)★★, *Alex Harvey Narrates The Loch Ness Monster* (K-Tel 1977)★★, *The Mafia Stole My Guitar* (RCA 1979)★★, *The Soldier On The Wall* (Power Supply 1983)★★★.

●COMPILATIONS: *The Alex Harvey Collection* (1986)★★★.

HATHAWAY, DONNY

b. 1 October 1945, Chicago, Illinois, USA, d. 13 January 1979. Originally schooled in the gospel tradition, this versatile artist majored in musical theory before performing in a cocktail jazz trio. Hathaway was then employed as a producer with Curtis Mayfield's Curtom label, while a duet with June Conquest, 'I Thank You Baby', became his first hit in 1969. The following year he was signed by Atlantic Records for whom he recorded several imaginative singles, including 'The Ghetto (1970) and 'Love Love Love' (1973). His crafted compositions were recorded by such acts as Aretha Franklin and Jerry Butler, but Hathaway is best remembered for his cool duets with Roberta Flack. Their complementary voices were honed to perfection on 'Where Is The Love' (1972) and 'The Closer I Get To You' (1978), both of which reached the US Top 5. Why this gifted musician should have taken his own life remains unexplained, but on 13 January 1979, Hathaway threw himself from the 15th floor of New York's Essex House hotel. The following year, the singer scored a posthumous hit in the UK with another Roberta Flack duet, 'Back Together Again', which reached number 3.

●ALBUMS: *Everything Is Everything* (Atlantic 1970)★★★, *Donny Hathaway* (Atlantic 1971)★★★, *Live* (Atlantic 1972)★★, *Come Back Charleston Blue* soundtrack (1972)★, *Roberta Flack And Donny Hathaway* (1972)★★★, *Extension Of A Man* (Atlantic 1973)★★, *Roberta Flack Featuring Donny Hathaway* (1980)★★★, *In Performance* (1980)★★★.
●COMPILATIONS: *Best Of Donny Hathaway* (1978)★★★.

HAVENS, RICHIE

b. Richard Pierce Havens, 21 January 1941, Bedford-Stuyvesant, Brooklyn, New York, USA. Havens' professional singing career began at the age of 14 as a member of the McCrea Gospel Singers. By 1962 he was a popular figure on the Greenwich Village folk circuit with regular appearances at the Cafe Wha?, Gerdes, and The Fat Black Pussycat. Havens quickly developed a distinctive playing style, tuning his guitar to the open E chord which in turn inspired an insistent percussive technique and a stunningly deft right hand technique. A black singer in a predominantly white idiom, Havens' early work combined folk material with New York-pop inspired compositions. His soft, yet gritty, voice adapted well to seemingly contrary material and two early releases, *Mixed Bag* and *Something Else Again*, revealed a blossoming talent. However, the artist established his reputation interpreting songs by other acts, including the Beatles and Bob Dylan, which he personalized through his individual technique. Havens opened the celebrated Woodstock Festival and his memorable appearance was a highlight of the film. A contemporaneous release, *Richard P. Havens 1983*, was arguably his artistic apogee, offering several empathic cover versions and some of the singer's finest compositions. He later established an independent label, Stormy Forest, and enjoyed a US Top 20 hit with 'Here Comes The Sun'. A respected painter, writer and sculptor, Havens currently pursues a lucrative career doing voice-overs for US television advertisements.

●ALBUMS: *Mixed Bag* (Verve/Forecast 1967)★★★★, *Richie Havens Record* (Douglas 1968)★★, *Electric Havens* (Douglas 1968)★★, *Something Else Again* (Forecast 1968)★★★, *Richard P. Havens 1983* (Forecast 1969)★★★★, *Stonehenge* (Stormy Forest 1970)★★, *Alarm Clock* (Stormy Forest 1971)★★★, *The Great Blind Degree* (Stormy Forest 1971)★★, *Richie Havens On Stage* (Stormy Forest 1972)★★★, *Portfolio* (Stormy Forest 1973)★★★, *Mixed Bag II* (Stormy Forest 1974)★★, *The End Of The Beginning* (A&M 1976)★★, *Mirage* (A&M 1977)★★, *Connections* (Elektra 1980)★★, *Common Ground* (Connexion 1984)★★, *Simple Things* (RBI 1987)★, *Richie Havens Sings The Beatles And Dylan* (Rykodisc 1987)★★, *Live At The Cellar Door* (Five Star 1990)★★★, *Now* (Solar/Epic 1991)★★★, *Cuts To The Chase* (Rhino/Forward 1994)★★★.
●COMPILATIONS: *A State Of Mind* (1971)★★★, *Resumé* (Rhino 1993)★★★★.
●FILMS: *Catch My Soul* (1974), *Hearts of Fire* (1989).

HAWKINS, EDWIN, SINGERS

As directors of music at their Berkeley church, the Ephresian Church of God in Christ, Edwin Hawkins (b. August 1943, Oakland, California, USA) and Betty Watson began in 1967 to absorb the leading soloists from other San Franciso-based choirs to inaugurate the North California State Youth Choir. In 1969, the 50-strong ensemble recorded an album to boost their funds, and when San Francisco DJ Tom Donahue began playing one of its tracks, 'Oh Happy Day', the assemblage found itself with both a record contract with the Buddah label and a surprise international hit. Although renamed the Edwin Hawkins Singers, the featured voice belonged to Dorothy Combs Morrison (b. 1945, Longview, Texas) and much of the single's attraction comes from her powerful delivery. The singer subsequently embarked on a solo career which failed to maintain its initial promise while Hawkins, deprived of such an important member, struggled in the wake of this 'novelty' hit, although they enjoyed a period of great demand for session singing. One such session put them back into the US charts in 1970 while guesting on Melanie's Top 10 hit 'Lay Down (Candle In The Wind)'. It was their last chart appearence to date and eventually the group's fortunes faded. The Singers, now somewhat reduced in numbers, continue to tour and occasionally record.

●ALBUMS: *Oh Happy Day* (Fixit 1969)★★★, *Lets Us Go Into The House Of The Lord* (1969)★★★, *Peace Is Blowing In The Wind* (1969)★★★, *Live At The Yankee Stadium* (1969)★★, *I'd Like To Teach The World To Sing* (1972)★★★, *New World* (1973)★★★, *Live - Amsterdam* (1974)★★★, *Live At The Bitter End, N.Y.* (1974)★★★, *Wonderful* (1977)★★★, *Love Alive II* (1979)★★★, *Imagine Heaven* (Fixit 1982)★★★, *Live With The Oakland Symphony Orchestra* (1982)★★★,

Give Us Peace (1982)★★★, *Face To Face* (Fixit 1991)★★★. Solo: Edwin Hawkins *Children (Get Together)* (1971)★★★, *Love Alive* (1977)★★★.
●COMPILATIONS: *The Best Of The Edwin Hawkins Singers* (1985)★★★.

HAWKINS, RONNIE

b. 10 January 1935, Huntsville, Arkansas, USA. Hawkins, who is rock 'n' roll's funniest storyteller says: 'I've been around so long, I remember when the Dead Sea was only sick'. Hawkins' father played at square dances and his cousin, Dale Hawkins, staked his own claim to rock 'n' roll history with 'Susie Q'. Hawkins, who did some stunt diving for Esther Williams' swimming revue, earned both a science and physical education degree at the University of Arkansas, but his heart was in the 'chitlin' starvation circuit' in Memphis. Because the pay was poor, musicians went from one club to another using the 'Arkansas credit card' - a siphon, a rubber hose and a five gallon can. Hawkins befriended Elvis Presley: 'In 1954 Elvis couldn't even spell Memphis: by 1957 he owned it'. After Hawkins' army service, he followed Conway Twitty's recommendation by working Canadian clubs. While there, he made his first recordings as the Ron Hawkins Quartet, the tracks being included on *Rrrracket Time*. In 1959 Hawkins made number 45 on the US charts with 'Forty Days', an amended version of Chuck Berry's 'Thirty Days'. He explains, 'Chuck Berry had simply put new lyrics to 'When The Saints Go Marching In'. My record company told me to add ten days. They knew Chess wouldn't sue as they wouldn't want to admit it was 'The Saints''. Hawkins' version of Young Jessie's 'Mary Lou' then made number 26 in the US charts. With his handstands and leapfrogging, he became known as Mr. Dynamo and pioneered a dance called the Camel Walk. In 1960 Hawkins became the first rock 'n' roller to involve himself in politics with a plea for a murderer on Death Row, 'The Ballad Of Caryl Chessman', but to no avail. The same year Hawkins with his drummer, Levon Helm, travelled to the UK for the ITV show *Boy Meets Girls*. He was so impressed by guitarist Joe Brown that he offered him a job, but, on returning home, the Hawks gradually took shape - Levon Helm, Robbie Robertson, Garth Hudson, Richard Manuel and Rick Danko. Their wild 1963 single of two Bo Diddley songs, 'Bo Diddley' and 'Who Do You Love', was psychedelia before its time. 'Bo Diddley' was a Canadian hit, and by marrying a former Miss Toronto, Hawkins made the country his home. He supported local talent and refused, for example, to perform in clubs that did not give equal time to Canadian artists. Meanwhile, the Hawks recorded for Atlantic Records as Levon and the Hawks and were then recruited by Bob Dylan, becoming the Band. The various incarnations of the Hawks have included many fine musicians, notably the pianist Stan Szelest. Hawkins had Canadian Top 10 hits with 'Home From The Forest' and 'Bluebirds Over The Mountain', while his experience in buying a Rolls-Royce was recounted in Gordon Lightfoot's 'Talkin' Silver Cloud Blues'. In 1970 Hawkins befriended John Lennon and

Yoko Ono, and the promotional single on which Lennon praises Hawkins' 'Down In The Alley' is a collectors' item. Kris Kristofferson wrote humorous liner notes for Hawkins' album, *Rock And Roll Resurrection* and it was through Kristofferson that Hawkins had a role in the disastrous film, *Heaven's Gate*. Hawkins is better known for extrovert performance in the Band's film, *The Last Waltz*. The burly singer has also appeared in Bob Dylan's Rolling Thunder Revue and he has some amusing lines as 'Bob Dylan' in the film, *Renaldo And Clara*. Hawkins' segment with 'happy hooker' Xaviera Hollander includes the line; 'Abraham Lincoln said all men are created equal, but then he never saw Bo Diddley in the shower'. In 1985 Hawkins joined Joni Mitchell, Anne Murray, Neil Young and several others for the Canadian Band Aid record, 'Tears Are Not Enough' by Northern Lights. Hawkins has a regular Canadian television series, *Honky Tonk*, and owns a 200 acre farm and has several businesses. It gives the lie to his colourful quote: '90 per cent of what I made went on women, whiskey, drugs and cars. I guess I just wasted the other 10 per cent'.
●ALBUMS: *Ronnie Hawkins* (Roulette 1959)★★, *Mr. Dynamo* (Roulette/Columbia 1960)★★, *The Folk Ballads Of Ronnie Hawkins* (Roulette 1960)★★, *Ronnie Hawkins Sings The Songs Of Hank Williams* (Roulette 1960)★★, *Ronnie Hawkins* (1969)★★, *Ronnie Hawkins* (Cotillion 1970)★★, *Arkansas Rock Pile* (Roulette 1970)★★, *The Hawk* i (1971)★★, *Rock And Roll Resurrection* (Monument 1972)★★, *The Giant Of Rock And Roll* (1974)★★, *The Hawk* ii (1979)★★, *Rrrracket Time* (1979)★★, *A Legend In His Spare Time* (1981)★★, *The Hawk And Rock* (1982)★★, *Making It Again* (1984)★★, *Hello Again ... Mary Lou* (1991)★★.
●COMPILATIONS: *The Best Of Ronnie Hawkins & His Band* (Roulette 1970)★★★, *The Best Of Ronnie Hawkins And The Hawks* (Rhino 1990)★★★.
●VIDEOS: *The Hawk In Concert* (1988), *This Country's Rockin' - Reunion Concert* (1993).

HAYES, TUBBY

b. Edward Brian Hayes, 30 January 1935, London, England, d. 8 June 1973. Born into a musical family, Hayes studied violin as a child but took up the tenor saxophone before reaching his teens. He matured rapidly and at the age of 15 became a professional musician. In the early 50s he played with several leading jazzmen, including Kenny Baker, Vic Lewis and Jack Parnell. In the mid-50s he formed his own bop-orientated group and later in the decade was co-leader with Ronnie Scott of the Jazz Couriers. In the early 60s he continued to lead small groups for clubs, concerts, record dates and tours of the UK and USA. By this time Hayes had become adept on other instruments, including the vibraphone, flute and most of the saxophone family. He occasionally formed a big band for concerts and television dates and was active as arranger and composer. Towards the end of the 60s Hayes' health was poor and he underwent a heart operation. He returned to playing, but early in the 70s a second heart operation was deemed necessary and he died on the operating table. A virtuoso performer on tenor saxophone, Hayes was a fluent improviser, and through his energy, enthusiasm and encouragement he created a new respect for British musicians, especially in the USA. Hayes was world-class almost from the outset of his career, and his death in 1973, while he was still very much in his prime, was a grievous loss.

●ALBUMS: *After Lights Out* (Jasmine 1956)★★★★, *Little Giant Of Jazz* (Imperial 1957)★★★★, *Tubby Hayes With The Jazz Couriers* (1958)★★★★, *Message From Britain* (1959)★★★★, *Tubby's Groove* (Jasmine 1959)★★★★, *Tubbs In NY* (1961)★★★★, *Palladium Jazz Date* (1961)★★★★, *Introducing Tubbs* (Epic 1961)★★★★, *Tubby The Tenor* (Epic 1961)★★★★, *Almost Forgotten* (1961)★★★★, *Tubby Hayes And The All Stars: Return Visit* (1962)★★★★, *Down In The Village* (Fontana 1962)★★★★, *Tubby's Back In Town* (Smash 1962)★★★★, *A Tribute: Tubbs* (Spotlite 1963)★★★★, *Tubb's Tours* (Mole 1963)★★★★, *100% Proof* (1966)★★★★, *Mexican Green* (1967)★★★★, *The Tubby Hayes Orchestra* (1969)★★★★, *Where Am I Going To Live* (Harlequin 1986)★★★★, *New York Sessions* (CBS 1989)★★★★, *For Members Only* rec. 1967 (Miles Music 1990)★★★★, *Live 1969* (Harlequin 1991)★★★, *200% Proof* (Mastermix 1992)★★★★, *Jazz Tete A Tete* (Progressive 1994)★★★.

HEAD, ROY

b. 1 September 1941, Three Rivers, Texas, USA. This respected performer first formed his group, the Traits, in 1958, after moving to San Marcos. The line-up included Jerry Gibson (drums) who later played with Sly And The Family Stone. Head recorded for several local labels, often under the supervision of famed Texas producer Huey P. Meaux, but it was not until 1965 that he had a national hit when 'Treat Her Right' reached number 2 on both the US pop and R&B charts. This irresistible song, with its pumping horns and punchy rhythm, established the singer alongside the Righteous Brothers as that year's prime blue-eyed soul exponent. Head's later releases appeared on a variety of outlets, including Dunhill and Elektra Records, and embraced traces of rockabilly ('Apple Of My Eye') and psychedelia ('You're (Almost) Tuff'). However, by the 70s he had honed his style and was working as a country singer, and in 1975 he earned a notable US C&W Top 20 hit with 'The Most Wanted Woman In Town'.

●ALBUMS: *Roy Head And The Traits* (TNT 1965)★★★, *Treat Me Right* (Scepter 1965)★★★, *A Head Of His Time* (1968)★★, *Same People* (Stateside 1970)★★, *Dismal Prisoner* (1972)★★, *Head First* (1976),★★ *Tonight's The Night* (1977)★★, *Boogie Down* (1977)★★, *Rock 'N' Roll My Soul* (1977)★★, *In Our Room* (1979)★★, *The Many Sides Of Roy Head* (1980)★★.

●COMPILATIONS: *His All-Time Favourites* (1974)★★★, *Treat Her Right* (1988)★★★.

HEARTS AND FLOWERS

Formed in 1964 at the Troubador Club in Los Angeles, California, when Rick Cunha (guitar/vocals) and Dave Dawson (autoharp/vocals), then working as a duo, met Larry Murray (guitar/vocals, ex-Scotsville Squirrel Barkers). Together they formed an acoustic country/folk act which quickly became an integral part of the west coast circuit. *Now Is The Time For Hearts And Flowers* revealed a group of breathtaking confidence, whose three-part harmonies and gift for melody brought new perspectives to a range of material drawn from Donovan, Carole King, Tim Hardin and Kaleidoscope. Terry Paul and Dan Woody were then added to the line-up, but Hearts And Flowers were a trio again for *Of Horses, Kids And Forgotten Women*. Although Rick Cunha had been replaced by another former Barker, Bernie Leadon, the blend of styles remained the same with Murray emerging as the group's chief songwriter. Commercial success did not ensue, and the band broke up soon after the album's release. Leadon and associate bassist David Jackon reappeared in Dillard And Clark and while Dawson dropped out of music altogether, both Murray and Cunha recorded as solo artists.

●ALBUMS: *Now Is The Time For Hearts And Flowers* (Capitol 1967)★★★, *Of Horses, Kids And Forgotten Women* (Capitol 1968)★★.

HEAVY JELLY

The complexities surrounding this intriguing UK progressive group belie its brief lifespan. The name 'Heavy Jelly' first appeared in a fictitious review, run late in 1968 in the London listings magazine, *Time Out*. Interest was such that two labels, Island and Head, released singles bearing the name. Island's Heavy Jelly was the rock group Skip Bifferty in disguise, although their lone single, 'I Keep Singing That Same Old Song', achieved a higher profile when it was placed on a popular budget-priced sampler, *Nice Enough To Eat*. The Head release, in the spring of 1969, 'Time Out (The Long Wait)', featured John Moreshead (guitar), Alex Dmochowski (bass) - both from the Aynsley Dunbar Retaliation - drummer Carlo Little and an individual dubbed Rocky. When this single proved popular, the label's managing director, John Curd, registered the Heavy Jelly, name and Moreshead and Dmochowski instigated a full-time line-up. Initial album sessions featured Chris Wood and Jim Capaldi from Traffic, but they were latter replaced by ex-Animals drummer Barry Jenkins and vocalist Jackie Lomax. Further upheavals followed, the projected album was shelved and the final blow came when Lomax accepted a solo recording deal.

●ALBUMS: *Take Me Down To The Water* (1984)★★★.

HEBB, BOBBY

b. 26 July 1941, Nashville, Tennessee, USA. An accomplished musician and songwriter, Hebb appeared on the *Grand Ole Opry* at 12 and studied guitar with Chet Atkins. He later moved to New York, ostensibly to play with Mickey And Sylvia. When that duo split, a new combination emerged: Bobby And Sylvia. This short-lived partnership was followed by several solo Hebb releases that culminated in 'Sunny' (1966). Written in memory of his brother Hal, who died the day after the assassination of John F. Kennedy, this simple, melancholic song reached number 2 in the US and number 12 in the UK. It was recorded by many artists, including Cher and Georgie Fame, whose version reached number 13 in the UK in 1966. Despite his tag as 'the song a day man', Hebb chose the country standard, 'A Satisfied Mind', as the follow-up. It fared less well commercially, although the singer later secured a reputation in UK northern soul circles with 'Love Me' and 'Love Love Love', which reached the Top 40 in the UK in 1972. Hebb returned to the fringes of the soul chart with 'Sunny 76', a reworking of his best-known moment.

●ALBUMS: *Sunny* (Philips 1966)★★.

HEDGEHOPPERS ANONYMOUS

Formed in November 1963 and originally known as the Trendsetters, this short-lived quintet consisted of ex-members of the Royal Air Force. Mick Tinsley (b. 16 December 1940), Ray Honeyball (b. 6 June 1941), Leslie Dash (b. 3 April 1943), Alan Laud (b. 13 March 1946) and John Stewart (b. 18 March 1941) were managed by Jonathan King, who wrote and produced their UK Top 5 hit 'It's Good News Week' in 1965. A somewhat contrived cash-in on the then-current 'protest' trend, the single was undeniably catchy, but the group was unable to repeat its success. Although a follow-up, 'Don't Push Me', was given considerable airplay, it failed to chart and the quintet disbanded soon afterwards.

HEINZ

b. Heinz Burt, 24 July 1942, Germany. Bassist Burt was a founder member of the Tornados, a studio group assembled by UK producer Joe Meek. The quintet enjoyed international fame with 'Telstar', but the photogenic dyed-blond Heinz was then groomed for a solo career. Although his debut disc, 'Dreams Do Come True', failed to chart despite magnanimous publicity, the singer later enjoyed a UK Top 5 hit with the 'tribute' to the late Eddie Cochran, 'Just Like Eddie' (1963). An immoderate vocalist, Heinz was bolstered by a crack studio group, the Outlaws, and was accompanied live by the Wild Boys, who included guitarist Ritchie Blackmore. However further minor hits, 'Country Boy' (1963), 'You Were There' (1964) and 'Diggin' My Potatoes' (1965), revealed his limitations and an acrimonious split with Meek ended his chart career. Burt has nonetheless remained popular through rock 'n' roll revival shows and cabaret.

●ALBUMS: *Tribute To Eddie* (Decca 1964)★★.
●COMPILATIONS: *Remembering ... Heinz* (1977)★★, *Dreams Do Come True: The 45s Collection* (Castle 1994)★★.

HELLO, DOLLY! (STAGE MUSICAL)

Opening at the St. James Theatre in New York on 16 January 1964, the stage musical *Hello, Dolly!* swiftly became one of the most talked-about shows in the history of the American musical theatre. Michael Stewart's book was adapted from the Thornton Wilder play *The Matchmaker*, which itself was based on other sources. *Hello, Dolly!* recounts the tale of Dolly Gallagher Levi, a self-appointed matchmaker who seeks to inveigle into marriage a wealthy New York merchant, Horace Vandergelder. Sub-plots follow the love life of Vandergelder's clerk, Cornelius Hackl, and Mrs Molloy, the lady Vandergelder thinks Dolly is trying to match with him. With a fine score by Jerry Herman, choreography and direction by Gower Champion, and excellent central performances, the show survived near-disaster in out-of-town previews, and by the time it reached New York was set to become a massive box-office hit. For its New York opening the show starred Carol Channing as Dolly, and she was succeeded during its 2,844-performance run by Betty Grable, Ginger Rogers, Martha Raye, and Ethel Merman, among others, while various touring companies starred Channing, Grable, Raye, Dorothy Lamour, Mary Martin and Eve Arden. In the original cast, David Burns played Vandergelder, Eileen Brennan was Mrs Molloy, with Charles Nelson Reilly as Cornelius. The splendid score included 'Dancing', 'Put On Your Sunday Clothes', 'Before The Parade Passes By' (with Charles Strouse and Lee Adams), 'Elegance', 'It Takes A Woman', 'Ribbons Down My Back', 'It Only Take A Moment', and 'So Long, Dearie'. Numerous recordings were made of the rousing title number, with Louis Armstrong's version topping the US chart, and winning Grammy Awards as Best Song and Best Male Vocal. *Hello, Dolly!* won Tony Awards for best musical, book, score, actress (Channing), director-choreographer, producer (David Merrick), musical director (Shepard Coleman), scenic design (Oliver Smith), and costumes (Freddy Wittop). The 1969 film version, which composer Jerry Herman apparently regards as definitive, starred Barbra Streisand, Walter Matthau, Marianne McAndrew and Michael Crawford. Mary Martin took the lead in the 1965 London stage presentation, and an all-black production with Pearl Bailey and Billy Daniels played on Broadway in 1975. Three years later, another Broadway revival starred Carol Channing, giving audiences a second chance to see the outstanding interpreter of one of the great roles of the modern musical theatre in America. London audiences were also granted the same opportunity when Channing reprised her role in the West End in 1979. In 1995, *Hello, Dolly!*, with Channing on board once more, was on the road in the USA, bound for Broadway.

HELP! (FILM)

The Beatles' second feature film was, like *A Hard Day's Night*, directed by Richard Lester. His eccentricity was still evident, but the simple plot and location scenes resulted in a finished work closer in style to classic 60s teen movies than its predecessor. This is not to deny *Help!*'s many good qualities, particularly the Beatles' unpretentious performances, superb comedic support by Victor Spinetti and Roy Kinnear and the dazzling array of original songs providing the soundtrack. 'Ticket To Ride', which accompanies antics on an Alpine ski-slope, and 'You've Got To Hide Your Love Away', set in a communal living room, are particularly memorable. The corresponding album is completed by several more superb John Lennon/Paul McCartney compositions, notably 'Yesterday', plus a handful of cover versions, including a rousing take of Larry Williams' 'Dizzy Miss Lizzy'. *Help!*'s breathtaking scope complements the film from which it takes its cue.

HENDERSON, DORRIS

Although best known for her spell with the innovative Eclection, this American-born singer and autoharpist became a well-known attraction in Britain's folk clubs in the 60s. She moved to England from her native Los Angeles, California, USA, in 1965, on the advice of her US Air Force brother who was temporarily stationed there, and recommended the work opportunities. She brought little more than her savings, autoharp and Alan Lomax songbooks with her. Previously she had performed in the celebrated Greenwich Village folk melting pot, at one point as backing singer to beat poet Lord Buckley. After finding her feet at the Troubador Club in London she cultivated a profitable partnership with guitarist John Renbourn and completed two excellent albums, the second of which saw her switch from traditional Appalachian to contemporary styles. Henderson replaced Kerilee Male in Eclection in October 1968. However, the single, 'Please Mark 2', was the new singer's only creative involvement with this respected group , and she resumed her solo carer after the group's demise. Henderson did attempt to resurrect the Eclection name during the 70s, but this proved an ill-fated exercise. She continues to perform in the UK from her base in Twickenham, often with her husband, guitar player Mac McGann, while her daughter has also gone on to a singing career in Los Angeles.

●ALBUMS: with John Renbourn *There You Go* (Columbia 1965)★★★, *Watch The Stars* (Fontana 1967)★★★.

HENDRIX, JIMI

b. Johnny Allen Hendrix, 27 November 1942, Seattle, Washington, USA, d. 18 September 1970. (His father subsequently changed his son's name to James Marshall Hendrix). More superlatives have been bestowed upon Hendrix than any other rock guitarist. Unquestionably one of music's most influential figures, he brought an unparalleled vision to the art of playing electric guitar Self-taught (and with the burden of being left-handed with a right-handed guitar) he spent hours absorbing the recorded legacy of southern-blues practitioners, from Robert Johnson to B.B. King. The aspiring musician joined several local R&B bands while still at school, before enlisting as a paratrooper in the 101st Airborne Division. It was during this period that Hendrix met Billy Cox, a bass player upon whom he called at several stages in his career. Together they formed the King Kasuals, an

in-service attraction later resurrected when both men returned to civilian life. Hendrix was discharged in July 1962 after breaking his right ankle. He began working with various touring revues backing, among others, the Impressions, Sam Cooke and the Valentinos. He enjoyed lengthier spells with the Isley Brothers, Little Richard and King Curtis, recording with each of these acts, but was unable to adapt to the discipline their performances required. The experience and stagecraft gained during this formative period proved essential to the artist's subsequent development. By 1965 Hendrix was living in New York. In October he joined struggling soul singer Curtis Knight, signing a punitive contract with the latter's manager, Ed Chaplin. This ill-advised decision returned to haunt the guitarist. In June the following year, Hendrix, now calling himself Jimmy James, formed a group initially dubbed the Rainflowers, then Jimmy James And The Blue Flames. The quartet, which also featured future Spirit member Randy California, was appearing at the Cafe Wha? in Greenwich Village when Chas Chandler was advised to see them. The Animals' bassist immediately recognized the guitarist's extraordinary talent and persuaded him to come to London in search of a more receptive audience. Hendrix arrived in England in September 1966. Chandler became his co-manager in partnership with Mike Jeffries (aka Jeffreys), and immediately began auditions for a suitable backing group. Noel Redding (b. 25 December 1945, Folkestone, Kent, England) was selected on bass, having recently failed to join the New Animals, while John 'Mitch' Mitchell (b. 9 July 1947, Ealing, Middlesex, England), a veteran of the Riot Squad and Georgie Fame's Blue Flames, became the trio's drummer. The new group, dubbed the Jimi Hendrix Experience, made its debut the following month at Evereux in France. On returning to England they began a string of club engagements that attracted pop's aristocracy, including Pete Townshend and Eric Clapton. In December the trio released their first single, the understated, resonant 'Hey Joe'. Its UK Top 10 placing encouraged a truly dynamic follow-up in 'Purple Haze'. The latter was memorable for Hendrix's guitar pyrotechnics and a lyric that incorporated the artist's classic line: "Scuse me while I kiss the sky'. On tour his trademark Fender Stratocaster and Marshall Amplifier were punished night after night, as the group enhanced its reputation with exceptional live appearances. Here Hendrix drew on black culture and his own heritage to produce a startling visual and aural bombardment. Framed by a halo of long, wiry hair, his slight figure was clad in a bright, rainbow mocking costume. Although never a demonstrative vocalist, his delivery was curiously effective. Hendrix's playing technique, meanwhile, although still drawing its roots from the blues, encompassed an emotional range far greater than any contemporary guitarist. Rapier-like runs vied with measured solos, matching energy with ingenuity, while a wealth of technical possibilities - distortion, feedback and even sheer volume - brought texture to his overall approach. This assault was enhanced by a flamboyant stage persona in which Hendrix used the guitar as a physical appendage. He played his instrument behind his back, between his legs or, in simulated sexual ecstasy, on the floor. Such practices brought criticism from radical quarters, who claimed the artist had become an 'Uncle Tom', employing tricks to carry favour with a white audience - accusations that denied a similar showmanship from generations of black performers, from Charley Patton to 'T-Bone' Walker. Redding's clean, uncluttered bass lines provided the backbone to Hendrix's improvisations, while Mitchell's drumming, as instinctive as his leader's guitar work, was a perfect foil.

Their concessions to the pop world now receding, the Experience completed an astonishing debut album which ranged from the apocalyptic vision of 'I Don't Live Today', to the blues of 'Red House' and the funk of 'Fire' and 'Foxy Lady'. Hendrix returned to America in June 1967 to appear, sensationally, at the Monterey Pop Festival. During one number (Dylan's 'Like A Rolling Stone') he paused to inform the crowd that he was re-tuning his guitar, later in the same song admitting he had forgotten the words. Such unparalleled confidence only served to endear him to the crowd. His performance was a musical and visual feast, topped off by a sequence which saw him playing the guitar with his teeth, and then burning the instrument with lighter fuel. He was now fêted in his homeland, and following an ill-advised tour supporting the Monkees, the Experience enjoyed reverential audiences in the country's nascent concert circuit. *Axis: Bold As Love* revealed a new lyrical capability, notably in the title-track and the jazz-influenced 'Up From The Skies'. 'Little Wing', a delicate love song bathed in unhurried guitar splashes, offered a gentle perspective, closer to that of the artist's shy, offstage demeanour. Released in December 1967, the collection completed a triumphant year, artistically and commercially, but within months the fragile peace began to collapse. In January 1968 the Experience embarked on a gruelling American tour encompassing 54 concerts in 47 days. Hendrix was now tiring of the wild man image that had brought initial attention, but he was perceived as diffident by spectators anticipating gimmickry. An impulsive artist, he was unable to disguise below-par performances, while his relationship with Redding grew increasingly fraught as the bassist rebelled against the set patterns he was expected to play. *Electric Ladyland*, the last official Experience album, was released in October. This extravagant double set was initially deemed 'self-indulgent', but is now recognized as a major work. It revealed the guitarist's desire to expand the increasingly limiting trio format, and contributions from members of Traffic (Chris Wood and Steve Winwood) and Jefferson Airplane (Jack Casady) embellished several selections. The collection featured a succession of virtuoso performances - 'Gypsy Eyes', 'Crosstown Traffic' - while the astonishing 'Voodoo Chile (Slight Return)', a posthumous number 1 single, showed how Hendrix had brought rhythm, purpose and mastery to the recently invented wah-wah pedal. *Electric Ladyland* included two UK hits, 'The Burning Of The

Midnight Lamp' and 'All Along The Watchtower'. The latter, an urgent restatement of the Bob Dylan song, was particularly impressive, and received the ultimate accolade when the composer adopted Hendrix's interpretation when performing it live on his 1974 tour. Despite such creativity, the guitarist's private and professional life was becoming problematic. He was arrested in Toronto for possessing heroin, but although the charges were later dismissed, the proceedings clouded much of 1969. Chas Chandler had meanwhile withdrawn from the managerial partnership and although Redding sought solace with a concurrent group, Fat Mattress, his differences with Hendrix were now irreconcilable. The Experience played its final concert on June 29 1969; Jimi subsequently formed Gypsies Sons And Rainbows with Mitchell, Billy Cox (bass), Larry Lee (rhythm guitar), Juma Sultan and Jerry Velez (both percussion). This short-lived unit closed the Woodstock Festival, during which Hendrix performed his famed rendition of the 'Star Spangled Banner'. Perceived by some critics as a political statement, it came as the guitarist was being increasingly subjected to pressures from different causes. In October he formed an all-black group, Band Of Gypsies, with Cox and drummer Buddy Miles, intending to accentuate the African-American dimension in his music. The trio made its debut on 31 December 1969, but its potential was marred by Miles' comparatively flat, pedestrian drumming and unimaginative compositions. Part of the set was issued as *Band Of Gypsies*, but despite the inclusion of the exceptional 'Machine Gun', this inconsistent album was only released to appease former manager Chaplin, who acquired the rights in part-settlement of a miserly early contract. The Band Of Gypsies broke up after a mere three concerts and initially Hendrix confined his efforts to completing his Electric Ladyland recording studio. He then started work on another double set, the unreleased *First Rays Of The New Rising Sun*, and later resumed performing with Cox and Mitchell. His final concerts were largely frustrating, as the aims of the artist and the expectations of his audience grew increasingly separate. His final UK appearance, at the Isle Of Wight festival, encapsulated this dilemma, yet still drew an enthralling performance.

The guitarist returned to London following a short European tour. On 18 September 1970, his girlfriend, Monika Danneman, became alarmed when she was unable to rouse him from sleep. An ambulance was called, but Hendrix was pronounced dead on arrival at a nearby hospital. The inquest recorded an open verdict, with death caused by suffocation due to inhalation of vomit. Eric Burdon claimed at the time to possess a suicide note, but this has never been confirmed. Two posthumous releases, *Cry Of Love* and *Rainbow Bridge*, mixed portions of the artist's final recordings with masters from earlier sources. These were fitting tributes, but many others were tawdry cash-ins, recorded in dubious circumstances, mispackaged and mistitled. This imbalance has been redressed of late with the release of fitting archive recordings, but the Hendrix legacy also rests in his prevailing influence on fellow musicians. Many guitarists have imitated his technique; few have mastered it, while none at all have matched him as an inspirational player. In November 1993 a tribute album, *Stone Free*, was released, containing a formidable list of performers including the Pretenders, Eric Clapton, Cure, Jeff Beck, Pat Metheny and Nigel Kennedy, a small testament to the huge influence Hendrix has wielded and will continue to wield as the most inventive rock guitarist of all time. The litigation regarding ownership of his recordings that had been running for many years was resolved in January 1997. The Hendrix family finally won back the rights from Alan Douglas. This was made possible by the financial weight of Microsoft co-founder Paul Allen, who in addition to helping with legal expenses has financed the Jimi Hendrix Museum, which will be located in Seattle. A major reissuing programme was underway for 1997 including outtakes from the recording of *Electric Ladyland*. The reissued catalogue on Experience/MCA records is now the definitive and final word. The quality is as good as twenty five year-old tapes will allow.

●ALBUMS: *Are You Experienced?* (Track 1967)★★★★★, *Axis: Bold As Love* (Track 1967)★★★★★, *Electric Ladyland* (Track 1968)★★★★, *Band Of Gypsies* (Track 1970)★★★, *Cry Of Love* (Polydor 1971)★★★, *Experience* (Ember 1971)★, *Isle Of Wight* (Polydor 1971)★★, *Rainbow Bridge* (Reprise 1971)★★, *Hendrix In The West* (Polydor 1971)★★★, *More Experience* (Ember 1972)★, *War Heroes* (Polydor 1972)★★, *Loose Ends* (Polydor 1974)★★, *Crash Landing* (Polydor 1975)★★, *Midnight Lightnin'* (Polydor 1975)★★, *Nine To The Universe* (Polydor 1980)★★, *The Jimi Hendrix Concerts* (CBS 1982)★★★, *Jimi Plays Monterey* (Polydor 1986)★★★, *Live At Winterland* (Polydor 1987)★★★, *Radio One* (Castle 1988)★★★★, *Live And Unreleased* (Castle 1989)★★★, *First Rays Of The New Rising Sun* (Experience/MCA 1997)★★★.

●COMPILATIONS: *Smash Hits* (Track 1968)★★★★, *The Essential Jimi Hendrix* (Polydor 1978)★★★★, *The Essential Jimi Hendrix Volume Two* (Polydor 1979)★★★, *The Singles Album* (Polydor 1983)★★★★, *Kiss The Sky* (Polydor 1984)★★★, *Cornerstones* (Polydor 1990)★★★, *Blues* (Polydor 1994)★★★, *Exp Over Sweden* (Univibes 1993)★★, *Jimi In Denmark* (Univibes 1995)★★.

●VIDEOS: *Jimi Hendrix Plays Berkeley* (1986), *Jimi Plays Monterey* (1986), *Rainbow Bridge* (Castle Hendring 1988), *Jimi Hendrix* (1988), *Live At The Isle Of Wight 1970* (Rhino Home Video 1990), *Experience* (1991), *Jimi Hendrix Live At Monterey* (1994), *Jimi At Woodstock* (BMG 1995), *Jimi At The Atlanta Pop Festival* (BMG 1995), *Jimi Hendrix Experience* (BMG 1995), *Jimi Hendrix Plays The Great Pop Festivals* (BMG 1995).

●FURTHER READING: *Jimi: An Intimate Biography Of Jimi Hendrix*, Curtis Knight. *Jimi Hendrix*, Alain Dister. *Jimi Hendrix: Voodoo Child Of The Aquarian Age*, David Henderson. *Scuze Me While I Kiss The Sky:*

The Life Of Jimi Hendrix, David Henderson. *Hendrix: A Biography*, Chris Welch. *Hendrix: An Illustrated Biography*, Victor Sampson. *The Jimi Hendrix Story*, Jerry Hopkins. *Crosstown Traffic: Jimi Hendrix And Post-War Pop*, Charles Shaar Murray. *Jimi Hendrix: Electric Gypsy*, Harry Shapiro and Caesar Glebbeek. *Are You Experienced?*, Noel Redding and Carole Appleby. *Hendrix Experience*, Mitch Mitchell and John Platt. *And The Man With The Guitar*, Jon Price and Gary Geldeart. *The Jimi Hendrix Experience In 1967 (Limited Edition)*, Gerad Mankowitz and Robert Whitaker (Photographers). *Jimi Hendrix: A Visual Documentary, His Life, Loves And Music*, Tony Brown. *The Hendrix Experience*, Mitch Mitchell with John Platt. *Jimi Hendrix: Starchild*, Curtis Knight. *Hendrix: Setting The Record Straight*, John McDermott with Eddie Kramer. *The Illustrated Jimi Hendrix*, Geoffrey Guiliano. *Cherokee Mist - The Lost Writings Of Jimi Hendrix*, Bill Nitopi (compiler). *Voodoo Child: The Illustrated Legend Of Jimi Hendrix*, Martin L. Green and Bill Sienkiewicz. *The Ultimate Experience*, Adrian Boot and Chris Salewicz. *The Lost Writings Of Jimi Hendrix*, Jimi Hendrix. *The Complete Studio Recording Sessions 1963-1970*, John McDermott. *Complete Guide To The Music Of*, John Robertson. *The Inner World Of Jimi Hendrix*, Monika Dannemann. *Jimi Hendrix Experience*, Jerry Hopkins. *Jimi Hendrix: Voices From Home*, Mary Willix. *The Man, The Music, The Memorabilia*, Caesar Glebbeek and Douglas Noble.

HENRY, CLARENCE 'FROGMAN'

b. 19 March 1937, Algiers, Louisiana, USA. Henry began performing during the 50s with a New Orleans-based R&B group led by Bobby Mitchell. The singer later began work with bandleader Paul Gayten who accompanied him on his 1957 smash 'Ain't Got No Home'. However it was not until 1961 that 'But I Do' provided a follow-up to this novelty song, earning Henry a US number 4 and UK number 3 hit. Co-written by Bobby Charles, the song featured several seasoned New Orleans musicians, including the young Allen Toussaint, and relaunched Henry's career. The same year a further international success, 'You Always Hurt The One You Love' - previously a hit for the Mills Brothers in 1944 - echoed the same effortless style. The following single fared better in the UK, with 'Lonely Street'/'Why Can't You' just missing out the Top 40, but it was the artist's last substantial hit. He continued to record for a variety of companies, and a 1969 collection, *Is Alive And Well*, was acclaimed as a fine example of the 'Crescent City' style. Since then Henry has remained a popular live attraction in his adopted city.

●ALBUMS: *You Always Hurt The One You Love* (Pye 1961)★★★, *Is Alive And Well And Living In New Orleans* (1969)★★, *New Recordings* (1979)★★, *Little Green Frog* (1987)★★.

●COMPILATIONS: *Legendary Clarence 'Frogman' Henry* (1983)★★★.

HERBAL MIXTURE

Formed in London, England in 1966, Herbal Mixture consisted of Tony McPhee (guitar/vocals), Pete Cruickshank (bass) - both ex-members of John Lee's Groundhogs - and Mike Meeham (drums). The new act's name was inspired by McPhee's interest in alternative medicine. Herbal Mixture secured a deal with Columbia Records, for whom they recorded two inventive singles. 'A Love That's Died' married pop and psychedelia through McPhee's fuzz guitar playing, while the atmospheric 'Machines' opens with startling effects, before progressing through contrasting moods heightened by further compelling guitar work. Herbal Mixture split up in 1967 having failed to achieve commercial success either on record or as a live attraction. In 1968 McPhee and Cruickshank were reunited in the Groundhogs. *Please Leave My Mind* compiles singles, demo versions and two previously unreleased tracks.
●COMPILATIONS: *Please Leave My Mind* (Distortions 1993)★★.

HERD

This UK group originally formed in 1965 as a quintet featuring Terry Clark (vocals), Andy Bown (bass), Gary Taylor (guitar) and Tony Chapman (drums). After several line-up shuffles, Bown took over on lead vocals and organ, occasionally relieved by the new guitarist Peter Frampton. In 1967, however, songwriting managers Ken Howard and Alan Blaikley were taken on in place of Billy Gaff and immediately promoted the reluctant Frampton to centre stage. A near miss with the psychedelic 'I Can Fly' was followed by a portentous adaptation of *Orpheus In The Underworld* (retitled 'From The Underworld'), which became a UK Top 10 hit. Having translated Virgil into pop, Howard And Blaikley next tackled Milton with 'Paradise Lost'. Despite their strange mix of literate pop and jazz rhythms, the Herd were marketed for teenzine consumption and Frampton was voted the 'Face of '68' by *Rave* magazine. Not surprisingly, a more straightforward hit followed with 'I Don't Want Our Loving To Die'. Ambivalent feelings about their pop star status convinced them to dump Howard and Blaikley in favour of the mercurial Andrew Loog Oldham, but their next single, the Frampton-composed 'Sunshine Cottage', missed by a mile. A brief tie-up with yet another manager, Harvey Lisberg, came to nothing and by this time Frampton had left to form Humble Pie. For a brief period, the remaining members struggled on, but to no avail. Bown later teamed up with Andy Fairweather-Low and appeared on the road with Status Quo, while Taylor and Steele guested on various sessions.
●ALBUMS: *Paradise Lost* (1968)★★★, *Lookin' Thru You* (Fontana 1968)★★★, *Nostalgia* (Bumble 1973)★★★.

HERMAN'S HERMITS

Originally known as the Heartbeats, Herman's Hermits were discovered in 1963 by manager Harvey Lisberg and his partner Charlie Silverman. After restructuring the group, the line-up emerged as Peter Noone (b. 5 November 1947, Manchester, England; vocals), Karl Green (b. 31 July 1947, Salford, Manchester, England; bass), Keith Hopwood (b. 26 October 1946, Manchester, England; rhythm guitar), Lek Leckenby (b. Derek Leckenby, 14 May 1946, Leeds, England, d. 4 June 1994, Manchester, England; lead guitar) and Barry Whitwam (b. 21 July 1946, Manchester, England; drums - formerly a member of Leckenby's first group, the Wailers). A link with producer Mickie Most and an infectious cover of Earl Jean's US hit, 'I'm Into Something Good' gave the quintet a UK number 1 in 1964. By early 1965, the group had settled into covering 50s songs such as the Rays' 'Silhouettes' and Sam Cooke's 'Wonderful World', when an extraordinary invasion of America saw them challenge the Beatles as a chart act with over 10 million record sales in under 12 months. A stream of non-stop hits over the next two years, including the vaudevillian 'Mrs Brown You've Got A Lovely Daughter' and 'I'm Henry VIII, I Am', effectively transformed them into teen idols. Director Sam Katzman even cast them in a couple of movies, *When The Boys Meet The Girls* (co-starring Connie Francis) and *Hold On!* Although their music-hall-inspired US chart-toppers were not issued as singles in the UK, they enjoyed a run of hits penned by the leading commercial songwriters of the day. 'A Must To Avoid' and 'No Milk Today' were inventive as well as catchy, although by 1968/9 their repertoire had become more formulaic. The hits continued until as late as 1970 when Noone finally decided to pursue a solo career. Thereafter, Herman's Hermits drifted into cabaret. Although a reunion concert did take place at Madison Square Garden in New York in 1973, stage replacements for Noone were later sought, including Peter Cowap, Karl Green, Garth Elliott and Rod Gerrard. Noone eventually settled in California, where he presented his own music show on television, and rekindled an acting career which had begun many years earlier on the top UK soap opera, *Coronation Street*. Leckenby died in 1994 following a long fight with cancer.
●ALBUMS: *Herman's Hermits* (Columbia 1965)★★★, *Introducing Herman's Hermits* (Columbia 1965)★★★, *Herman's Hermits On Tour* (Columbia 1965)★★★, *Hold On!* soundtrack (Columbia 1966)★★, *Both Sides Of Herman's Hermits* (Columbia 1966)★★★, *There's A Kind Of Hush* (Columbia 1967)★★★, *Mrs Brown You've Got A Lovely Daughter* (Columbia 1968)★★★, *Blaze* (Columbia 1967)★★★.
●COMPILATIONS: *The Best Of* (Columbia 1969)★★★, *The Most Of* (MFP 1971)★★★, *The Most Of Vol. 2* (MFP 1972)★★★, *Twenty Greatest Hits* (K-Tel 1977)★★★, *The Very Best Of* (MFP 1984)★★★, *The Collection* (Castle 1990)★★★, *The EP Collection* (See For Miles 1990)★★★★, *Best Of The EMI Years Vol. 1* (EMI 1991)★★★★, *Best Of The EMI Years Vol. 2* (EMI 1992)★★★.
●FILMS: *Hold On* (1965).

HILL, BENNY

b. Alfred Hawthorne Hill, 25 January 1925, England, d. 18 April 1992. Hill entered showbusiness at an early age and played the variety circuit, specializing in comedy and impressions. He was already a well-known comedian in Britain when he was signed to Pye as a recording artist in the early 60s. His whimsical tunes, 'Gather In The Mushrooms', 'Transistor Radio' and 'Harvest Of Love' were all minor hits during this period. Hill went on to star in one of the decade's most successful comedy television series, *The Benny Hill Show*. Amazingly, the series later became hugely popular in the USA and many other countries, despite its peculiarly English 'saucy seaside postcard' humour. Hill usually had musical guests on the show and a segment was reserved for his own stories in song, which were usually filled with mild innuendo and grinning puns. One such song was 'Ernie (The Fastest Milkman In The West)' which captured the public's imagination and became the UK's Christmas number 1 in 1971. His saucy narrative ballads are available on album. His death in April 1992 resulted in considerable media coverage, praising his talent and probing his considerable fortune.
●COMPILATIONS: *Benny Hill: The Best Of* (1992)★★★.

HINNEN, PETER

b. 19 September 1941, Zurich, Switzerland. Hinnen displayed musical talent at an early age. He studied bass and piano at music school and at 14, he had also appeared in three films. He learned guitar and became interested in traditional Swiss folk music (Volksmusik) and especially in yodelling. His first record release, 'Columbus Boogie', was on a Polydor 78 in 1955. By 1959, he was working as a singer, yodeller and instrumentalist with a folk band but also visited the USA, where he appeared on New York's *Radio City Music Hall*. He made two further visits to America in 1961 (when he appeared on a show with Judy Garland) and 1962. He enjoyed country music success in German-speaking countries with 'Auf Meiner Ranch Bin Ich Konig' ('El Rancho Grande') and 'Siebentausend Rinder' ('Seven Thousand Cattle') and clearly demonstrated his yodelling skills with his own composition 'Mein Pferd Tonky' ('My Horse Tonky'), which he based on the melody of Elton Britt's 'Chime Bells'. These numbers later appeared on a 16-track country album. During the mid-60s, he had 15 Top 10 hits. He toured extensively and appeared on television in Europe and even Japan. He recorded a live album of Swiss folk music at Zurich's famous Kindli venue, which gained a UK release through the World Record Club and clearly demonstrated his outstanding yodelling ability. In 1967, tiring of the hectic life style, he decided to take things easier. Resisting offers to play in Las Vegas and the London Palladium, he became a band leader. In 1990, he was persuaded to record an album of yodelling songs. He re-recorded some of his old hits, including 'Siebentausend Rinder', with more modern backing and the resultant success of the recordings saw him coaxed back into the entertainment business. In 1991, he undertook a 54-concert tour that saw him play to large audiences at venues in Germany, Austria and Switzerland. On 9 February 1992, in Zurich, he gained a place in the *Guinness Book Of Records* as the World's most rapid yodeller, when he yodelled 22 tones (15 falsetto) in one second. (This may sound totally impossible but the event was seemingly officially witnessed by Norris McWhirter.) The success of the tour saw him return to the public appearance circuits and, at the time of writing, he continues to record. The material is mainly country but naturally the yodel is never far away.
●ALBUMS: *Souvenirs Of Switzerland (Live At Kindli)* (Ariola 1964)★★★, *Star Album* (Ariola 1964)★★★, *Jodel Echo* (Ariola 1968)★★★, *Auf Meiner Ranch Bin Ich Konig* (Baccarola 1969)★★★, *Yodel Feeling* (Schnoutz 1974)★★★, *16 Seiner Erfolgreichsten Hits* cassette (SR International mid-70s)★★★, *20 Jahre Peter Hinnen* (Ariola 1984)★★★, *Der Generation Jodler* (Baur 1990)★★★, *Country Music* (Gruezi 1991)★★★, *Volksmusik & Country Music* (Koch 1991)★★★, *Treu Wie Gold* (UHU 1994)★★★.

HOLLAND/DOZIER/HOLLAND

Brothers Eddie Holland (b. 30 October 1939, Detroit, Michigan, USA) and Brian Holland (b. 15 February 1941, Detroit, Michigan, USA), and Lamont Dozier (b. 16 June 1941, Detroit, Michigan, USA) formed one of the most successful composing and production teams in popular music history. Throughout the mid-60s, they almost single-handedly fashioned the classic Motown sound, creating a series of hit singles which revolutionized the development of black music. All three men were prominent in the Detroit R&B scene from the mid-50s, Brian Holland as lead singer with the Satintones, his brother Eddie with the Fideltones, and Dozier with the Romeos. By the early 60s, they had all become part of Berry Gordy's Motown concern, working both as performers and as writer/arrangers. After masterminding the Marvelettes' 1961 smash 'Please Mr Postman', Brian Holland formed a production team with his brother Eddie, and Freddy Gorman. In 1963, Gorman was replaced by Dozier, and the trio made their production debut with a disregarded record by the Marvelettes, 'Locking Up My Heart'.

Over the next five years, the triumvirate wrote and produced scores of records by almost all the major Motown artists, among them a dozen US number 1 hits. Although Smokey Robinson can claim to have been the label's first true auteur, Holland/Dozier/Holland created the records that transformed Motown from an enthusiastic Detroit soul label into an international force. Their earliest successes came with Marvin Gaye, for whom they wrote 'Can I Get A Witness?', 'Little Darling', 'How Sweet It Is (To Be Loved By You)' and 'You're A Wonderful One', and Martha And The Vandellas, who had hits with the trio's 'Heatwave', 'Quicksand', 'Nowhere To Run' and 'Jimmy Mack'. Impressive although these achievements were, they paled alongside the team's run of success with the Supremes. Ordered by Berry Gordy to construct suitable vehicles for the wispy, feminine vocal talents of Diana Ross, they produced 'Where Did Our Love Go?', a simplistic but irresistible slice of lightweight pop-soul. The record reached number 1 in the USA, as did its successors, 'Baby Love', 'Come See About Me', 'Stop! In The Name Of Love' and 'Back In My Arms Again' - America's most convincing response to the otherwise overwhelming success of British beat groups in 1964 and 1965.

These Supremes hits charted the partnership's growing command of the sweet soul idiom, combining unforgettable hooklines with a vibrant rhythm section that established a peerless dance groove. The same process was apparent - albeit with more sophistication - on the concurrent series of hits that Holland/Dozier/Holland produced and wrote for the Four Tops. 'Baby I Need Your Loving' and 'I Can't Help Myself' illustrated their stylish way with uptempo material; '(It's The) Same Old Song' was a self-mocking riposte to critics of their sound; while 'Reach Out I'll Be There', a worldwide number 1 in 1966, pioneered what came to be known as 'symphonic soul', with a towering arrangement and a melodic flourish that was the peak of their work at Motown. Besides the Supremes and the Four Tops, Holland/Dozier/Holland found success with the Miracles ('Mickey's Monkey' and 'I'm The One You Need'), Kim Weston ('Take Me In Your Arms'), and the Isley Brothers ('This Old Heart Of Mine', 'Put Yourself In My Place' and 'I Guess I'll Always Love'). Their long-standing commitments continued to bring them recognition in 1966 and 1967, however, as the Supremes reached the top of the US charts with 'You Can't Hurry Love', 'You Keep Me Hanging On', 'Love Is Here And Now You're Gone', and the mock-psychedelic 'The Happening', and the Four Tops extended their run of success with 'Bernadette' and 'Standing In The Shadows Of Love'.

In 1967, when Holland/Dozier/Holland effectively commanded the US pop charts, they split from Berry Gordy and Motown, having been denied more control over their work and more reward for their labours. Legal disputes officially kept them out of the studio for several years, robbing them of what might have been their most lucrative period as writers and producers. They were free, however, to launch their own rival to Motown, in the shape of the Invictus and Hot Wax labels. Neither concern flourished until 1970, and even then the names of the company's founders were absent from the credits of their records - although there were rumours that the trio were moonlighting under the names of their employees. On the evidence of Invictus hits by artists like the Chairmen Of The Board and Freda Payne, the case was convincing, as their records successfully mined the familiar vein of the trio's Motown hits, at a time when their former label was unable to recapture that magic without them. Business difficulties and personal conflicts gradually wore the partnership down in the early 70s, and in 1973 Lamont Dozier left the Holland brothers to forge a solo career. Invictus and Hot Wax were dissolved a couple of years later, and since then there have been only occasional reunions by the trio, none of which have succeeded in rekindling their former artistic fires. The Holland/Dozier/Holland partnership will be remembered for its five halcyon years of success in the 60s, not the two decades or more of disappointment and unfulfilled potential that followed.

HOLLIES

Formed in Manchester in 1962 by childhood friends Allan Clarke (b. 15 April 1942, Salford, Lancashire, England; vocals), and Graham Nash (b. 2 February 1942, Blackpool, Lancashire, England; vocals/guitar). They had already been singing together locally for a number of years as a semi-professional duo under a number of names such as the Guytones, the Two Teens and Ricky And Dane. They enlarged the group by adding Eric Haydock (b. 3 February 1943, Burnley, Lancashire, England; bass) and Don Rathbone (drums), to became the Fourtones and then the Deltas. Following the recruitment of local guitar hero Tony Hicks from the Dolphins (b. 16 December 1943, Nelson, Lancashire, England) they became the Hollies. Almost immediately they were signed to the same label as the Beatles, the prestigious Parlophone. Their first two singles were covers of the Coasters' '(Ain't That) Just Like Me' and 'Searchin''. Both made the UK charts and the group set about recording their first album. At the same time Rathbone left to become their road manager and was replaced by Bobby Elliott (b. 8 December 1942) from Shane Fenton (Alvin Stardust) And The Fentones. The group's excellent live performances throughout Britain had already seasoned them for what was to become one of the longest beat group success stories in popular music. Their first two albums contained the bulk of their live act and both albums became long-time residents in the UK charts. Meanwhile, the band was enjoying a train of singles hits that continued from 1963-74, and their popularity almost rivalled that of the Beatles and Rolling Stones. Infectious, well-produced hits such as Doris Troy's 'Just One Look', 'Here I Go Again' and the sublime 'Yes I Will' all contained their trademark soaring harmonies. The voices of Clarke, Hicks and Nash combined to make one of the most distinctive sounds to be heard in popular music.

As their career progressed the aforementioned trio developed into a strong songwriting team, and wrote most of their own b-sides (under the pseudonym 'L. Ransford'). On their superb third collection, *Hollies* in 1965, their talents blossomed with 'Too Many People', an early song about over-population. Their first UK number 1 came in 1965 with 'I'm Alive' and was followed within weeks by Graham Gouldman's uplifting yet simple take 'Look Through Any Window'. By Christmas 1965 the group experienced their first lapse when their recording of George Harrison's 'If I Needed Someone' just scraped the UK Top 20 and brought with it some bad press. Both the Hollies and John Lennon took swipes at each other, venting frustration at the comparative failure of a Beatles song. Early in 1966, the group enjoyed their second number 1, 'I Can't Let Go', which topped the *New*

Musical Express chart jointly with the Walker Brothers' 'The Sun Ain't Gonna Shine Anymore'. 'I Can't Let Go', co-written by Chip Taylor, had already appeared on the previous year's *Hollies* and was one of their finest recordings, combining soaring harmonies with some exceptionally strong, driving guitar work.

The enigmatic and troublesome Eric Haydock was sacked in April 1966 and was replaced by Hick's former colleague in the Dolphins, Bernie Calvert (b. 16 September 1942, Brierfield, Lancashire, England). The Hollies success continued unabated with Graham Gouldman's 'Bus Stop', the exotic 'Stop! Stop! Stop!' and the poppier 'On A Carousel', all UK Top 5 hits, and (at last) became major hits in the US charts. The Hollies were quick to join the 'flower power' bandwagon, as a more progressive feel had already pervaded their recent album, *For Certain Because*, but with *Evolution*, their beads and kaftans were everywhere. That same year (1967) the release of the excellent *Butterfly* showed signs of discontent. Inexplicably, the album failed to make the charts in either the UK or the US. It marked two distinct types of songs from the previously united team of Nash/Clarke/Hicks. On one hand there was a Clarke-influenced song, 'Charley And Fred', and on the other an obvious Nash composition like 'Butterfly'. Nash took a more ambitious route. His style was perfectly highlighted with the exemplary 'King Midas In Reverse', an imaginative song complete with brass and strings. It was, by Hollies standards, a surprising failure (UK number 18). The following year during the proposals to make *Hollies Sing Dylan*, Nash announced his departure for Crosby, Stills And Nash. His replacement was Terry Sylvester of the Escorts. Clarke was devastated by the departure of his friend of more than 20 years and after seven further hits, including 'He Ain't Heavy He's My Brother', Clarke decided to leave for a solo career. The band soldiered on with the strange induction of Mickael Rickfors from Sweden. In the USA the million-selling 'Long Cool Woman (In A Black Dress)' narrowly missed the top spot, ironic also because Allan Clarke was the vocalist on this older number taken from *Distant Light*.

Clarke returned after an abortive solo career which included two average albums, *My Real Name Is 'Arold* and *Headroom*. The return was celebrated with the worldwide hit, 'The Air That I Breathe', composed by Albert Hammond. Over the next five years the Hollies pursued the supper-club and cabaret circuit as their chart appearances began to dwindle. Although their albums were well produced they were largely unexciting and sold poorly. In 1981 Sylvester and Calvert left the group. Sensing major problems ahead, EMI suggested they put together a Stars On 45-type segued single. The ensuing 'Holliedaze' was a hit, and Graham Nash was flown over for the television promotion. This reunion prompted the album *What Goes Around*, which included a minor hit with the Supremes' 'Stop In The Name Of Love'. The album was justifiably slammed by the critics, and only made the US charts because of Nash's name.

Following this, the Hollies went back to the oldies path,

until in 1988 a television beer commercial used 'He Ain't Heavy', and once again they were at the top of the charts for the first time in over a dozen years. In 1993 they were given an Ivor Novello award in honour of their contribution to British music. The mid-90s lineup in addition to Clarke, Elliott and the amazingly youthful Hicks featured Alan Coates (guitar), Ray Stiles (bass) and Ian Parker (keyboards). The Hollies' catalogue of hits, like those of the Beach Boys, Beatles and Kinks will continue to be reissued for future generations. Their longevity is assured as their expertly crafted, harmonic songs represent some of the greatest music of all mid-60s pop.

●ALBUMS: *Stay With The Hollies* (Parlophone 1964)★★★★, *In The Hollies' Style* (Parlophone 1964)★★★★, *Here I Go Again* (Imperial 1964)★★★, *Hear! Hear!* (Imperial 1965)★★★, *The Hollies* (Parlophone 1965)★★★★, *Would You Believe* (Parlophone 1966)★★★★, *For Certain Because* (Parlophone 1966)★★★★, *The Hollies - Beat Group* (Imperial 1966)★★★, *Bus Stop* (Imperial 1966)★★★, *Stop! Stop! Stop!* (Imperial 1966)★★★, *Evolution* (Parlophone 1967)★★★, *Butterfly* (Parlophone 1967)★★★, *The Hollies Sing Dylan* (Parlophone 1969)★★, *Hollies Sing Hollies* (Parlophone 1969)★★, *He Ain't Heavy He's My Brother* (Epic 1969)★★, *Reflection* reissue of *The Hollies* (Regal Starline 1969)★★★★, *Moving Finger* (Epic 1970)★★, *Confessions Of The Mind* (Parlophone 1970)★★, *Distant Light* (Parlophone 1971)★★, *The Hollies* reissue of *Evolution* (MFP 1972)★★★, *Romany* (Polydor 1972)★★, *Out On The Road* (Hansa 1973)★★, *The Hollies* (Polydor 1974)★★, *Another Night* (Polydor 1975)★★, *Write On* (Polydor 1976)★★, *Russian Roulette* (Polydor 1976)★★, *Hollies Live Hits* (Polydor 1977)★★, *A Crazy Steal* (Polydor 1978)★★, *The Other Side Of The Hollies* (Parlophone 1978)★★★, *Five Three One-Double Seven O Four* (Polydor 1979)★★, *Long Cool Woman In A Black Dress* (MFP 1979)★★★, *Buddy Holly* (Polydor 1980)★★, *What Goes Around* (WEA 1983)★★, *Rarities* (EMI 1988)★★★★.

●COMPILATIONS: *The Hollies' Greatest* (Parlophone 1968)★★★★, *The Hollies Greatest Hits Vol. 2* Parlophone (1972)★★★, *The History Of The Hollies* (1975)★★★★, *The Best Of The Hollies EPs* (1978)★★★★, *20 Golden Greats* (1978)★★★★, *The EP Collection* (See For Miles 1987)★★★★, *Not The Hits Again* (See For Miles 1987)★★★★, *All The Hits And More* (EMI 1988)★★★★, *The Air That I Breath: Greatest Hits* (1993)★★★, *Singles A's And B's 1970-1979* (1993)★★★★, *Treasured Hits And Hidden Treasures* 3-CD box set (EMI 1993)★★★, *Four Hollies Originals* 4-CD set (EMI 1995)★★★★, *Four More Hollies Originals* (EMI 1996)★★★, *The Best Of ...* (EMI 1997)★★★★.

●FILMS: *It's All Over Town* (1964).

HOLLOWAY, BRENDA

b. 21 June 1946, Atascadero, California, USA. Brenda Holloway began her recording career with three small

Los Angeles labels, Donna, Catch and Minasa, in the early 60s, recording under the aegis of producer Hal Davis. In 1964, Holloway made an uninvited performance at a disc jockeys' convention in California, where she was spotted by a Motown Records talent scout. She signed to the label later that year, becoming its first west coast artist. Her initial Tamla single, 'Every Little Bit Hurts', established her bluesy soul style, and was quickly covered by the Spencer Davis Group in Britain. She enjoyed further success in 1964 with 'I'll Always Love You', and the following year with 'When I'm Gone' and 'Operator'. Her consistent record sales led to her winning a place on the Beatles' 1965 US tour, but subsequent Tamla singles proved less successful.

Holloway began to devote increasing time to her songwriting, forming a regular writing partnership with her sister Patrice, and Motown staff producer Frank Wilson. This combination produced her 1968 single 'You've Made Me So Very Happy', a song which proved more successful via the million-selling cover version by the white jazz-rock group, Blood, Sweat And Tears. In 1968, Holloway's contract with Motown was terminated. The label issued a press release stating that the singer wished to sing for God, although Holloway blamed business differences for the split. She released a gospel album in 1983 and worked with Ian Levine from 1987. She teamed with Jimmy Ruffin in 1989 for a duet 'On The Rebound'.
●ALBUMS: *Every Little Bit Hurts* (Tamla 1964)★★★, *The Artistry Of Brenda Holloway* (Motown 1968)★★★, *All It Takes* (1991)★★★.
●COMPILATIONS: *Greatest Hits And Rare Classics* (1991)★★★.

HOLLYWOOD ARGYLES

The Hollywood Argyles was a group assembled after a record, 'Alley Oop', had already been released under that name. The song was written by Dallas Frazier and recorded by vocalist Gary S. Paxton and producer Bobby Rey while Paxton was a member of the Arizona-based duo Skip And Flip. Because that duo was contracted to Brent Records, and 'Alley Oop' was issued on Lute Records, the name Hollywood Argyles was created for the occasion, named after the intersection where the recording studio was located, Hollywood Boulevard and Argyle Street. When the Coasters-like novelty single made its way to number 1 in the US charts in May 1960, a group was created, including Paxton, Rey, Ted Marsh, Gary Webb, Deary Weaver and Ted Winters. Further singles by the Hollywood Argyles, on such labels as Paxley (co-owned by Paxton and producer Kim Fowley), Chattahoochie, Felsted and Kammy failed to reach the charts. Paxton later started the Garpax label, which released the number 1 'Monster Mash' by Bobby 'Boris' Pickett. More recently, as a born-again Christian, Paxton was rumoured to be romantically linked with fallen US evangelist Tammy Faye Bakker.
●ALBUMS: *The Hollywood Argyles* (Lute 1960)★★★.

HOLMES, RICHARD 'GROOVE'

b. 2 May 1931, Camden, New Jersey, USA, d. 29 June 1991, St. Louis, Missouri, USA. A self-taught organist, early in his career Holmes worked along the east coast. A 1961 recording session with Les McCann and Ben Webster resulted in widespread interest in his work. He toured and recorded throughout the 60s, achieving widespread acceptance among mainstream and post-bop jazz audiences. Customarily working in a small group format, Holmes developed a solid working relationship with Gene Ammons, and their playing exemplified the soul-heavy, organ-tenor pairings that proliferated in the early and mid-60s. Displaying his wide-ranging interests, Holmes also played with big bands including that led by Gerald Wilson, with whom he made a fine album, and recorded with singer Dakota Staton. His powerful playing style, with its thrusting swing and booming bass notes lent itself to soul music but his playing had much more than this to offer. Later in his career Holmes's appeal to crossover audiences sometimes led to the unjustified indifference of many jazz fans. Holmes understood the power of a simple riff and like Jimmy Smith and Jimmy McGriff, 'he had soul'.
●ALBUMS: *Richard Groove Holmes* (Pacific Jazz 1961)★★★, with Gene Ammons *Groovin' With Jug* (1961)★★★★, *Something Special* (Pacific Jazz 1962)★★★, *The Groove Holmes Trio* (1962)★★★, *The Groove Holmes Quintet* (1962)★★★, *After Hours* (Pacific Jazz 1962)★★★, *Groove Holmes With Onzy Matthews And His Orchestra* (1964)★★★, Book Of The Blues (Warners 1964)★★★, *Soul Message* (Prestige 1965)★★★, *Tell It Like It Is* (Pacific Jazz 1966)★★★, *Living Soul* (Prestige 1966)★★★, *Misty* (Prestige 1966)★★★, *Spicy* (Prestige 1966)★★★, *Super Cool* (Prestige 1967)★★★, *Soul Message* (Prestige 1967)★★★, *Get Up And Get It* (Prestige 1967)★★★, *The Groover* (Prestige 1968)★★★, *That Healin' Feelin'* (Pretige 1968)★★★, *Welcome Home* (1968)★★★, *Blues Groove* (Prestige 1968)★★★, *Workin' On A Groovy Thing* (1969)★★★, with Gerald Wilson *You Better Believe It!* (60s)★★★, *Dakota Staton* (60s)★★★, *X-77* (c.1970)★★★, *Night Glider* (c.1973)★★, *Comin' On Home* (c.1974)★★, *Six Million Dollar Man* (1975)★★, *I'm In The Mood For Love* (c.1975)★★★, *Slippin' Out* (Muse 1977)★★★, *Star Wars-Close Encounters* (1977)★★, *Good Vibrations* (Muse 1977)★★★, *Nobody Does It Better* (Manhattan 1980)★★, *Broadway* (Muse 1980)★★, *Swedish Lullaby* (1984)★★★, *Hot Tat* (Muse 1989)★, *Blues All Day Long* (Muse 1992)★★★.
●COMPILATIONS: *The Best Of Richard Groove Holmes* (Prestige 1969)★★★.

HOLY MODAL ROUNDERS

Peter Stampfel (b. 1938, Wauwautosa, Wisconsin, USA) and Steve Weber (b. 1942, Philadelphia, Pennsylvania, USA). This on-off partnership was first established in New York's Greenwich Village. The two musicians shared a passion for old-time music and unconventional behaviour, and together they created some of the era's most distinctive records. The duo completed their debut album, *The Holy Modal Rounders* in 1963. It contained several of their finest moments, including the influential 'Blues In The Bottle', which the Lovin' Spoonful, among others, later recorded. The Rounders' second collection, although less satisfying, continued the same cross-section of 20s/30s-styled country and blues. Having accompanied the Fugs on their early releases, Stampfel and Weber broke up; the former began writing for 'alternative' publications. The musicians were reunited in 1967 to complete the experimental, but flawed, *Indian War Whoop*. This often incoherent collection also featured drummer Sam Shepard, an off-Broadway playwright from a parallel Stampfel venture, the Moray Eels. The amalgamation of the two groups led to another album, *The Moray Eels Eat The Holy Modal Rounders*, which was a marked improvement on its predecessor. It featured the sweeping 'Bird Song', later immortalized in the film *Easy Rider*. Shepard left the Rounders in 1970, from where he became a successful writer and actor. Three albums of varying quality were then completed until the group, which suffered a plethora of comings and goings, ground to a halt in 1977. Weber and Stampfel were reunited five years later. *Goin' Nowhere Fast* was an excellent set, evocative of the duo's first recordings together, but their revitalized relationship proved temporary. The latter later worked with an all-new group, Pete Stampfel And The Bottlecaps.

● ALBUMS: *The Holy Modal Rounders* (Folklore 1964)★★★, *The Holy Modal Rounders 2* (Prestige 1965)★★, *Indian War Whoop* (ESP 1967)★★, *The Moray Eels Eat The Holy Modal Rounders* (Elektra 1968)★★, *Good Taste Is Timeless* (Metromedia 1971)★★, *Alleged In Their Own Time* (1975)★★, *Last Round* (1978)★★, *Goin' Nowhere Fast* (1982)★★★★ .

HOLZMAN, JAC

b. 15 September 1931, New York City, New York, USA. Holzman, a trained engineer, founded Elektra Records in 1950 and remained its guiding light over the next 23 years. His label was renowned for traditional music, and early releases featured such artists as Theodore Bikel, Ed McCurdy and Cynthia Gooding. Elektra's foremost reputation was secured during the folk revival of the early 60s. Holzman provided a natural home for a new generation of committed performers, and Judy Collins, Tom Paxton, Fred Neil and Phil Ochs recorded their most lasting work for the label. The company began signing electric acts with the acquisition of the Butterfield Blues Band. Having failed to secure the Lovin' Spoonful and the embryonic Byrds, Holzman's long-term commitment to rock was established with Love. He produced their debut album, a release that paved the way for early seminal work by the Doors and Tim Buckley. Elektra's songwriter tradition was maintained through the work of David Ackles, Steve Noonan and Carly Simon, while Bread's sweet pop achieved international commercial success. Holzman's direct involvement in Elektra's direction lessened as the 60s progressed, although he continued his role of pro-

duction supervisor. However, in 1970 the label was acquired by the Kinney Corporation, who grouped it as WEA with the emergent Asylum Records roster three years later. By then Elektra had forsaken the quest for excellence that marked its epochal era, and Holzman, now senior vice president at Warner Communications, abandoned music for computer technology. In 1991, Holzman purchased the west coast-based Discovery/Trend conglomerate, specialists in jazz reissues, and continues to be very active in the music business.

HONDELLS

The Hondells were a non-existent group when they released their Top 10 single 'Little Honda' in 1964. The mastermind behind the record was producer Gary Usher, a friend and songwriting partner of Beach Boys leader Brian Wilson. Usher had created a series of surf music records using a revolving team of musicians and singers and assigning different group names to the finished products. The Hondells were one such creation. Usher and his hired hands for the day recorded a version of the Brian Wilson song extolling the virtues of Honda motorcycles, which was released on Mercury Records and reached number 9 in the US. With the record a success, the company asked Usher to assemble a touring group of Hondells. He hired Ritchie Burns, one of the background singers on the record, to lead the group. Burns still had not left his job at a bank when the album cover photos were taken, and he had friends of his (who were not involved with the record) pose for its cover. The Hondells continued to make records, and appeared on popular television programmes and in a number of 'beach party' films, including *Beach Blanket Bingo*. Only two further singles charted, 'My Buddy Seat' in 1964-65, and a cover of the Lovin' Spoonful's 'Younger Girl' in 1966. Following this release the group assembled to masquerade as the Hondells began to sing and play on the records, recording a version of Bob Lind's 'Cheryl's Going Home'. Subsequent singles on Columbia Records and Amos did not chart and only the first of the Hondells' albums made the charts. The group and the Hondells name were retired in 1970.

● ALBUMS: *Go Little Honda* (Mercury 1964)★★★, *The Hondells* (Mercury 1965)★★★.

● FILMS: *Beach Ball* (1964), *Beach Blanket Bingo* (1965).

HONEYBUS

Originally managed by one-time Them drummer Terry Noon, Honeybus was a vehicle for minor hit songwriters Pete Dello and Ray Cane. Following the recruitment of Colin Hare (vocals/guitar) and Peter Kircher (drums), the group was signed to the hip Decca subsidiary Deram Records. Their second single, 'Do I Still Figure In Your Life', with its plaintive lyric and striking string arrangement, received extensive airplay but narrowly failed to reach the Top 50. The similarly paced 'I Can't Let Maggie Go' fared better, entering the charts in March 1968 and

peaking at number 8. Rather than exploiting the group's success, however, Dello dramatically left Honeybus only months later. Deprived of their main songwriter and gifted arranger, the group failed to escape the one-hit-wonder trap, but almost broke through with 'Girl Of Independent Means'. After advice from their management they folded in 1969. The post-demise release, *Story* (1970), testifies to their fledgling talent. Their single moment of chart glory was later resurrected as the long-running theme for a UK television bread commercial.
●ALBUMS: *Story* (Deram 1970)★★★.

HONEYCOMBS

Formed in north London in November 1963, the group was originally known as the Sherabons and comprised: Denis D'ell (b. Denis Dalziel, 10 October 1943, London, England; vocals), Anne 'Honey' Lantree (b. 28 August 1943, Hayes, Middlesex, England; drums), John Lantree (b. 20 August 1940, Newbury, Berkshire, England; bass), Alan Ward (b. 12 December 1945, Nottingham, England; lead guitar) and Martin Murray (rhythm guitar), later replaced by Peter Pye (b. 12 July 1946, London, England). Producer Joe Meek had selected one of their songs as a possible single and the group's chances were enhanced following a management agreement with Ken Howard and Alan Blaikley. Although several record companies passed on the quintet's debut, 'Have I The Right', Pye Records' managing director Louis Benjamin agreed to release the disc. First, however, there was the obligatory name change, with Benjamin selecting Honeycombs after a track by Jimmie Rodgers. The fact that the focus of attention in the group was the red-haired drummer 'Honey' made the rechristening even more appropriate. When 'Have I The Right' hit number 1 in the UK in the summer of 1964, the group's pop star future seemed assured. However, a dramatic flop with the follow-up 'Is It Because' caused concern, and although Howard and Blaikley came to the rescue with 'That's The Way', the group faltered amid line-up changes and poor morale, before moving inexorably towards cabaret and the revivalist circuit.
●ALBUMS: *The Honeycombs* (Pye 1964)★★★, *All Systems Go* (Pye 1965)★★★, *Here Are The Honeycombs* (Vee Jay 1964)★★★.
●COMPILATIONS: *Meek And Honey* (PRT 1983)★★★, *It's The Honeycombs/All Systems Go* (Sequel 1990)★★★, *The Best Of The Honeycombs* (1993)★★★.

HOPKIN, MARY

b. 3 May 1950, Pontardawe, Glamorganshire, Wales. Hopkin's career began while she was still a schoolgirl. Briefly a member of a local folk rock band, she completed several Welsh-language releases before securing a slot on the televised talent show, *Opportunity Knocks*. Fashion model Twiggy was so impressed by Hopkin's performance she recommended the singer to Paul McCartney as a prospective signing for the newly formed Apple label. 'Those Were The Days', a traditional song popular-ized by Gene Raskin of the Limelighters, was selected as the artist's national debut and this haunting, melancholic recording, produced by McCartney, topped both the UK and US charts in 1968. Her follow-up single, 'Goodbye' reached number 2 the following year, but despite its excellent versions of Donovan's 'Happiness Runs' and 'Lord Of The Reedy River', the concurrent *Post Card* showed a singer constrained by often inappropriate material. Nevertheless, the Mickie Most-produced 'Temma Harbour' was another Top 10 hit, while 'Knock Knock Who's There?', Britain's entry to the 1970 Eurovision Song Contest, peaked at number 2.
'Think About Your Children', penned by Most protégés Hot Chocolate, was Hopkin's last Top 20 entry, as the singer became increasingly unhappy over the style of her releases. However, a second album *Earth Song/Ocean Song*, was more representative of Hopkin's talent, and sympathetic contributions from Ralph McTell and Danny Thompson enhanced its enchanting atmosphere. Paradoxically, the set was issued as her contract with Apple expired and, having married producer Tony Visconti, Mary retired temporarily from recording.
She resumed her career in 1972 with 'Mary Had A Baby' and enjoyed a minor hit four years later with 'If You Love Me'. The singer also added backing vocals on several sessions, notably David Bowie's *Sound And Vision*, before joining Mike Hurst (ex-Springfields) and Mike D'Albuquerque (ex-Electric Light Orchestra) in Sundance. Having left this short-lived aggregation, Hopkin resurfaced in 1983 as a member of Oasis (not the UK indie band). Peter Skellern and Julian Lloyd Webber were also members of this act which enjoyed a Top 30 album, but was brought to a premature end when Hopkin was struck by illness. Mary's subsequent work includes an appearance on George Martin's production of *Under Milk Wood*, but she remains indelibly linked to her million-selling debut hit.
●ALBUMS: *Post Card* (Apple 1969)★★, *Earth Song/Ocean Song* (Apple 1971)★★, *Those Were The Days* (Apple 1972)★★, *The King Of Elfland's Daughter* (Chrysalis 1977)★★, with Oasis *Oasis* (WEA 1984)★★, with George Martin *Under Milk Wood* (EMI 1988)★★★.
●COMPILATIONS: *The Welsh World Of Mary Hopkin* (Decca 1979)★★, *Those Were The Days: The Best Of Mary Hopkin* (EMI 1995)★★.

HOUR GLASS

Formed in Decatur, Alabama, USA, in 1967 from the ashes of the Allman Joys, the group was fronted by Gregg Allman (vocals/organ) and his brother Duane Allman (guitar). Paul Hornsby (keyboards), Mabron McKinney (bass) and Johnny Sandlin completed the original line-up, 'discovered' playing juke-box favourites by the Nitty Gritty Dirt Band and their manager, Bill McEwan. The Hour Glass then moved to California, where they became a popular live attraction. Although their debut album consisted largely of pop/soul cover versions, it did include 'Cast Off All My Fears', an early Jackson Browne composition. However, the set was essentially a vehicle for Gregg's voice, and with session musicians replacing the group proper, the results bore no relation to the quintet's own ambitions. Jesse Willard Carr replaced McKinney for *Power Of Love*, in which several 'southern' soul songs vied with group originals. Once again the album failed to capture their full potential and in a final act of defiance, the Hour Glass booked themselves into the fabled Fame studios (see Muscle Shoals), where they completed a searing B.B. King medley. When their label rejected the master as unsuitable, the quintet decided to go their separate ways. Gregg and Duane later formed the Allman Brothers Band, an act later produced by Johnny Sandlin. Hornsby became manager of the group's Capricorn Sound studios while Carr enjoyed a lucrative session career.

●ALBUMS: *Hour Glass* (Liberty 1967)★★, *The Power Of Love* (Liberty 1968)★★.
●COMPILATIONS: *Hour Glass 1967-1969* (1973)★★, *The Soul Of Time* (1985)★★.

HOUSTON, THELMA

Thelma Houston left her hometown of Leland, Mississippi, USA in the late 60s to tour with the gospel group, the Art Reynolds Singers. Her impassioned vocal style and innate mastery of phrasing brought her to the attention of the prodigal writer/arranger Jimmy Webb in 1969. He composed and produced *Sunshower*, a remarkable song cycle which also included an adaptation of the Rolling Stones' 'Jumpin' Jack Flash'. The album transcended musical barriers, mixing the fluency of jazz with the passion of soul, and offering Houston the chance to bite into a sophisticated, witty set of lyrics. *Sunshower* won great critical acclaim, and helped her secure a contract with Motown Records. Initially, the company made inadequate use of her talents, failing to provide material that would stretch her vocal capacities to the full. The stasis was broken in 1976 when Houston reworked 'Don't Leave Me This Way', previously a hit for Harold Melvin And The Bluenotes. Her disco interpretation brought a refreshing touch of class to the genre, and achieved impressive sales on both sides of the Atlantic. Ever enthusiastic to repeat a winning formula, Motown made several attempts to reproduce the verve of the hit single. Houston issued a series of interesting, if slightly predictable, albums in the late 70s, and also collaborated on two efforts with Jerry Butler, in an attempt to echo Motown's great duets of the 60s. The results were consistent sellers among the black audience, without ever threatening to rival Houston's earlier pop success. A switch to RCA in 1981 failed to alter her fortunes. Houston enjoyed wider exposure in the late 70s with film roles in *Death Scream*, *Norman ... Is That You?* and *The Seventh Dwarf*, and for a while it seemed as if acting would become her main source of employment. She retired from recording during the mid-80s, re-emerging in 1987 on MCA with a critically-acclaimed but commercially disappointing album. Houston's inconsistent chart record over the last two decades belies the impressive calibre of her vocal talents.

●ALBUMS: *Sunshower* (Stateside 1969)★★, *Thelma Houston* (Mowest 1973)★★, *Anyway You Like It* (1977)★★, with Jerry Butler *Thelma And Jerry* (1977)★★★, *The Devil In Me* (1978)★★, with Butler *Two To One* (1978)★★★, *Ready To Roll* (1978)★★, *Ride To The Rainbow* (1979)★★, *Breakwater Cat* (1980)★★, *Never Gonna Be Another One* (1981)★★, *I've Got The Music In Me* (1981)★★, *Qualifying Heats* (1987)★★.

HOWARD, JOHNNY

b. 5 February 1931, Croydon, Surrey, England. Howard learned to play the saxophone at school and, after playing semi-professionally for several years, became a full-time professional musician in 1959. Two years later he followed Lou Preager as the resident leader at London's prestigious Lyceum Ballroom and, during the next few years, fronted bands at most of London's major dance venues. During the 60s he led his own band on popular UK radio shows such *Easy Beat* and *Saturday Club* and, through the years, has become a familiar name in BBC Radio's music programmes. He also formed and led the Capital Radio Big Band, and features in concerts, sometimes accompanying visiting star vocalists and musicians from the USA.

●ALBUMS: *The Velvet Touch Of Johnny Howard* (Deram 1967)★★★, *Domee Craze* (1975)★★★, *Johnny Howard Plays Cole Porter* (1980)★★★, *Irving Berlin Hit Parade* (1980)★★★.
●COMPILATIONS: *The World Of Johnny Howard* (Decca 1970)★★★.

HULLABALLOOS

Formed in 1963 in Hull, England, and originally known as Ricky And The Crusaders, the Hullaballoos comprised Rick Knight, Andrew Woonton, Geoffrey Mortimer and Harold Dunn. The quartet made its recording debut the following year with a version of Buddy Holly's 'I'm Gonna Love You Too', but although their singles made no commercial impression in Britain, the group became popular in the USA. Adopted by producers Hugo And Luigi, they enjoyed an association with the successful *Hullaballoo* USA television show, but by the end of 1965 the lustre of their now anachronistic brand of beat had faded. Guitarist Mick Wayne, later of Juniors Eyes and the Pink Fairies, joined the group towards the end of its career, but was not featured on any recordings.

●ALBUMS: *The Hullaballoo Show* (Columbia 1965)★, *The Hullaballoos On Hullaballoo* (1965)★.

HUMAN BEINZ

This Ohio-based quartet - Richard Belley (lead guitar), Ting Markulin (rhythm guitar), Mel Pachuta (bass) and Mike Tatman (drums) - made their recording debut on the local Gateway label. Their early releases featured spirited versions of Bob Dylan's 'Times They Are A-Changin'' and Them's 'Gloria' while other covers revealed an affection for the Who and Yardbirds. Signed to Capitol

Records in 1967, the Beinz enjoyed a US Top 10 hit that year with an interpretation of 'Nobody But Me', originally recorded by the Isley Brothers. The quartet embraced a more original direction with the competent *Evolutions*, but disbanded when this brand of superior pop/rock proved unsuccessful.

●ALBUMS: *Nobody But Me* (Capitol 1967)★★, *Evolutions* (Capitol 1968)★★.

●COMPILATIONS: *The Human Beinz With The Mammals* (1968)★★.

HUMBLEBUMS

This Scottish folk-singing duo originally consisted of Tam Harvey (guitar/mandolin) and Billy Connolly (b. 1942, Anderston, Glasgow, Scotland; guitar/banjo). Their debut, *First Collection of Merrie Melodies*, showcased a quirky sense of humour, but it was not until Harvey was replaced by Gerry Rafferty (b. 16 April 1946, Paisley, Scotland), that the group forged an individuality. Rafferty, a former member of the beat group, Fifth Column, introduced a gift for melody and the first release with Connolly, *The New Humblebums*, featured several excellent compositions, including 'Please Sing A Song For Us' and 'Her Father Didn't Like Me Anyway'. A further collection, *Open Up The Door*, confirmed Rafferty's skills but the contrast between his Paul McCartney-influenced compositions ('My Singing Bird') and his partner's lighter, more whimsical offerings was too great to hold under one banner. Connolly returned to the folk circuit, where his between-songs banter quickly became the focal point of his act and introduced a newfound role as a successful comedian. Meanwhile his erstwhile partner began his solo career in 1971 with *Can I Have My Money Back*, before forming a new group, Stealers Wheel.

●ALBUMS: *First Collection Of Merrie Melodies* (1968)★★★, *The New Humblebums* (1969)★★★, *Open Up The Door* (1970)★★★.

●COMPILATIONS: *The Humblebums* (1981)★★★, *Early Collection* (1987)★★★, *The New Humblebums/Open Up The Door* (Transatlantic 1997)★★★.

HUMPERDINCK, ENGELBERT

b. Arnold George Dorsey, 2 May 1936, Madras, India. Originally known as Gerry Dorsey, this singer had attempted to achieve mainstream success in the UK during the 50s. He was a featured artist on the television series *Oh Boy*, toured with Marty Wilde and recorded a failed single, 'I'll Never Fall In Love Again'. It was during this period that he first met Gordon Mills, a singer in the Viscounts, who later moved into songwriting and management. By 1963, Dorsey's career had hit rock bottom. The beat boom hampered his singing career and to make matters worse, he fell seriously ill with tuberculosis. Mills, meanwhile, was beginning to win international success for Tom Jones and in 1967 decided to help his old friend Gerry Dorsey. Soon after, the singer was rechristened Engelbert Humperdinck, a name inspired by the composer of Hansel And Gretel, and relaunched as a bal-

ladeer. His first single for Decca Records, 'Dommage Dommage', failed to chart, but received considerable airplay. There was no mistake with the follow-up, 'Release Me', which sold a million copies in the UK alone, dominated the number 1 spot for five weeks and, most remarkably, prevented the Beatles from reaching the top with the magnificent 'Penny Lane'/'Strawberry Fields Forever'. Humperdinck's follow-up, 'There Goes My Everything', climbed to number 2 in the UK and by the end of the summer he was back at the top for a further five weeks with 'The Last Waltz'. The latter once again sold in excess of a million copies in the UK alone. In a year dominated by psychedelia and experimentation in rock, Humperdinck was the biggest-selling artist in England. His strong vocal and romantic image ensured regular bookings and brought a further series of UK Top 10 hits including 'Am I That Easy To Forget', 'A Man Without Love', 'Les Bicyclettes De Belsize', 'The Way It Used To Be' and 'Winter World Of Love'. Although he faded as a hit-making artist after the early 70s, his career blossomed in America where he was a regular on the lucrative Las Vegas circuit. Like his stablemate Tom Jones he went through a long period without recording, which ended in 1987 with the release of a comeback album, *Remember I Love You*, which featured a duet with Gloria Gaynor. In 1990, it was estimated that he had earned 58 Gold records, 18 Platinum albums, and several Grammy Awards He was still selling plenty of albums, and filling venues such as London's Royal Albert Hall, well into the 90s.

●ALBUMS: *Release Me* (Decca 1967)★★★, *The Last Waltz* (Decca 1967)★★★, *A Man Without Love* (1968)★★★, *Engelbert* (1969)★★★, *Engelbert Humperdinck* (1969)★★★, *We Made It Happen* (1970)★★, *Another Time, Another Place* (1971)★★, *Live At The Riviera* (1972)★★★, *Getting Sentimental* (1975)★★, *Remember I Love You* (1987)★★★, *Hello Out There* (1992)★★★, with Tom Jones *Back To Back* (1993)★★★.

●COMPILATIONS: *Engelbert Humperdinck - His Greatest Hits* (1974)★★★, *The Engelbert Humperdinck Collection* (1987)★★★, *The Best Of ... Live* (Repertoire 1995)★★★.

●FURTHER READING: *Engelbert Humperdinck: The Authorized Biography*, Don Short.

HYLAND, BRIAN

b. 12 November 1943, Woodhaven, Queens, New York, USA. A demonstration disc, recorded with the artist's high school group the Delphis, alerted Kapp Records to Hyland's vocal talent. In 1960 he enjoyed a US chart-topper with 'Itsy Bitsy Teenie Weenie Yellow Polkadot Bikini', one of the era's best-known 'novelty' recordings which subsequently sold over one million copies. Having switched outlets to the larger ABC Paramount, the singer enjoyed further success with 'Let Me Belong To You (1961 - a US Top 20 hit) 'Ginny Come Lately' (1962 - a UK Top 10 hit), before securing a second gold award for 'Sealed With a Kiss'. Its theme of temporary parting was empathetic to the plight of many lovestruck teenagers and the song returned to the UK Top 10 in 1975 before being revived in 1990 by Jason Donovan. Hyland continued to enjoy US chart entries, notably with 'The Joker Went Wild' and 'Run, Run, Look And See' (both 1966), but reasserted his career in 1970 with a sympathetic version of the Impressions' 'Gypsy Woman'. This third million-seller was produced by long-time friend Del Shannon, who co-wrote several tracks on the attendant album, but this rekindled success proved shortlived and the artist later ceased recording.

●ALBUMS: *The Bashful Blonde* (Kapp 1960)★★, *Let Me Belong To You* (ABC 1961)★★, *Sealed With A Kiss* (ABC 1962)★★★, *Country Meets Folk* (ABC 1964)★, *Here's To Our Love* (Philips 1964)★★, *Rockin' Folk* (Philips 1965)★★, *The Joker Went Wild* (Philips 1966)★★★, *Tragedy* (1969)★★, *Stay And Love Me All Summer* (1969)★★, *Brian Hyland* (1970)★★.

●COMPILATIONS: *Golden Decade 1960-1970* (1988)★★★, *Ginny O Ginny* (1988)★★★.

IAN AND THE ZODIACS

This pop group, formed in Crosby, Liverpool, England, in 1960, played a significant role in the development of the Hamburg beat scene, and initially comprised Ian Edwards (vocals/guitar), Peter Wallace (guitar), Charlie Flynn (bass; aka Charlie Wade and Wellington Wade), John Bethel (keyboards) and Cliff Roberts (drums). Oriole Records released two singles, before they switched to Fontana Records in 1964. After recording an album for the label's budget series, housed on the Wing subsidiary, they arrived in Hamburg, Germany, in May. By this time the group was a quartet, having left behind Bethel and having found a new drummer, Geoff Bamford. They quickly became regulars at Hamburg's famed Star Club, mixing beat pop with soul, hallmarked by the group's out-standing harmonies. Although their progress was minor compared to that of the Beatles, they remained pillars of the venue and scene, and by the mid-60s specialized in covering the Fab Four's material to appreciative late-coming audiences. By this time there had been a series of line-up shuffles - new drummer Fred Smith (ex-Big Six) arrived in 1966, while later in the year Wallace was replaced on guitar by Arthur Ashton. Tony Coates became their fourth drummer in 1967, at which time the group recorded two albums of Beatles cover versions under the guise of the Koppycats. However, they dis-banded in late 1967, remaining quiet for two decades before playing a reunion gig in Hamburg in 1988.

●ALBUMS: *Gear Again* (Wing 1964)★★, *Star-Club Show 7* (1965)★★, *Just Listen To ...* (1965)★★, *Locomotive* (1966)★★, *The Beatles Best Done By The Koppycats* (1966)★, *More Beatles Best Done By The Koppycats* (1967)★.

ICE

UK psychedelic pop quintet Ice were formed in the mid-60s while John Carter (bass), Glyn James (vocals), Lynton Naiff (organ), Grant Serpell (drums) and Steve Turner (guitar) were attending Sussex University in Brighton. Their debut single, 'Anniversary (Of Love)', was released in 1967 after the group signed a recording con-tract with Decca Records. The single revealed a band clearly in the thralls of a Procol Harum fixation, with its layered keyboards and nostalgic lyrics. A second single followed a year later, but 'Whisper Her Name (Maria Laine)' also failed to impress commercially. As a result Ice returned to their studies/professional employment and have not recorded since, although both singles have been compiled on numerous psychedelic compilations.

IDLE RACE

Dave Pritchard (guitar), Greg Masters (bass) and Roger Spencer (drums) spent several years in the Nightriders, backing Birmingham singer Mike Sheridan. Their frontman left for a solo career in 1966, but with the addition of guitarist/composer Jeff Lynne (b. 30 December 1947, Birmingham, West Midlands, England), the restructured group embarked on an enthralling, independent direction. The quartet took the name the Idle Race in the wake of an unsuccessful debut single released under their former appellation. By 1967 Lynne had become the group's focal point, contributing the bulk of their original material and shaping its sound and direction. *The Birthday Party* showcased his gift for melody and quirky sense of humour, facets prevalent in two of its undoubted highlights, 'Follow Me Follow' and 'The Skeleton And The Roundabout'. The guitarist's grasp on the group was strengthened with their second album, *Idle Race*, which he produced. This evocative selection featured some of Lynne's finest compositions, many of which bore a debt to the Beatles, but without seeming plagiaristic. Any potential, however, was bedevilled by public indifference. Repeated overtures to join the Move ultimately proved too strong for Lynne to ignore. Highly commercial pop songs like 'Come With Me' and 'At The End Of The Road' surprisingly failed to become hits.

Lynne's departure in January 1970 to form the Electric Light Orchestra precipitated several changes. Pritchard, Masters and Spencer drafted Mike Hopkins and Roy Collum into the line-up, the latter of whom was then replaced by Dave Walker. This reshaped quintet was responsible for *Time Is*, a progressive rock collection at odds with the erstwhile group's simple pop. Walker then left for Savoy Brown and his place was taken by Birmingham veteran Steve Gibbons. Founder members Pritchard and Spencer abandoned their creation, Bob Lamb and Bob Wilson from Tea And Symphony joined, before a third member of that august ensemble, Dave Carroll, replaced Mike Hopkins. When Greg Masters left the Idle Race in 1971, the group became known as the Steve Gibbons Band.

● ALBUMS: *The Birthday Party* (Liberty 1968)★★★, *Idle Race* (Liberty 1969)★★★, *Time Is* (Regal Zonophone 1971)★★.

● COMPILATIONS: *On With The Show* (Sunset 1973)★★★, *Imposters Of Life's Magazine* (1976)★★★, *Light At The End Of The Road* (1985)★★★, *Back To The Story* (Premier 1996)★★★.

IFIELD, FRANK

b. 30 November 1937, Coventry, Warwickshire, England. The most successful recording artist in the UK during the early 60s, Ifield is now also one of the most underrated. At the age of nine, his family emigrated to Australia, and Ifield entered show business during his teens. He first came to prominence in Australia during 1957 with 'Whiplash', a song about the 1851 Australian goldrush which was later used as the theme for a long-running television series. After returning to England in the late 50s, Ifield was signed to the EMI subsidiary Columbia Records and soon found success working with producer Norrie Paramor. After scoring minor hits with 'Lucky Devil' and 'Gotta Get A Date', he broke through spectacularly with the chart-topping 'I Remember You'. The song had a wonderfully elegiac feel, complemented by Ifield's relaxed vocal and a pleasing harmonica break. The track dominated the UK chart listings staying at number 1 for a staggering seven weeks and was the first record ever to sell a million copies in England alone. The song also charted in America, a rare feat for a British-based singer in the early 60s. Late in 1962, Ifield was back at the top of the UK charts for a further five weeks with 'Lovesick Blues', which betrayed his love of C&W and emphasized his extraordinary ability as a yodeller. His engaging falsetto became something of a trademark, which differentiated him from other UK vocalists of the period. A revival of Gogi Grant's 'The Wayward Wind' put Ifield into the record books. No artist in British pop history had previously logged three consecutive number 1 records, but during February 1963 Ifield achieved that honour. Ironically, he shared the number 1 spot jointly with the Beatles' 'Please Please Me', and it was their abrupt rise that year which tolled the death knell for Ifield as a regular chart contender. After stalling at number 4 with 'Nobody's Darlin' But Mine' Ifield experienced his fourth UK chart-topper with the breezy 'Confessin''. His version of the perennial 'Mule Train' added little to the Frankie Laine version and Ifield's last Top 10 hit in the UK was almost an apology for his previous release; the beautifully arranged 'Don't Blame Me'. Thereafter, the material chosen for him seemed weaker and his chart career atrophied. He became the most celebrated victim of the beat boom that was sweeping the UK and never regained the seemingly unassailable position that he enjoyed in the early 60s. He continued his career, playing regularly in pantomime and in stage productions like *Up Jumped A Swagman*, before reverting to cabaret work. During the 80s Ifield concentrated singing his beloved country music, performing regularly in Australia and the USA. In the 90s following lengthy bouts of ill health, Ifield was residing in Australia, and in 1996 following further illness (an abcess on the lung) his singing was permanently impaired. He now works as a television presenter.

● ALBUMS: *I'll Remember You* (1963)★★★, *Portrait In Song* (Columbia 1965)★★★, *Blue Skies* (Columbia 1964), *Up Jumped A Swagman* soundtrack (Columbia 1965)★★, *Someone To Give My Love To* (Spark 1973)★★, *Barbary Coast* (Fir 1978)★★, *Sweet Vibrations* (Fir 1980)★★, *If Love Must Go* (Fir 1982)★★, *At The Sandcastle* (Fir 1983)★★.

● COMPILATIONS: *Greatest Hits* (1964)★★★, *Best Of The EMI Years* (1991)★★★★, *The EP Collection* (1991)★★★★.

● FILMS: *Up Jumped A Swagman* (1965).

ILLINOIS SPEED PRESS

The Chicago-based Illinois Speed Press was originally known as the Gentrys. The quintet - Kal David (vocals/guitar), Paul Cotton (vocals/guitar), Mike Anthony (organ), Frank Bartoli (bass) and Fred Pappalardo (drums) - was later known as the Rovin' Kind and as such recorded several singles including covers of the Who's 'My Generation' and John Sebastian's 'Didn't Want To Have To Do It'. The group assumed the name Illinois Speed Press in February 1968. Rob Lewine replaced Bartoli prior to recording their first album. This debut showed a promising grasp of melody, but within a year, David and Cotton were the only remaining members. They completed *Duet* together before the latter guitarist accepted an offer to join Poco. His erstwhile colleague was later a founder member of the Fabulous Rhinestones.

●ALBUMS: *The Illinois Speed Press* (Columbia 1969)★★, *Duet* (Columbia 1970)★★★.

IMMEDIATE RECORDS

Rolling Stones manager Andrew Loog Oldham and publicist Tony Calder joined forces to found Immediate in 1965. The label enjoyed success when its first release, 'Hang On Sloopy' by the McCoys, reached number 5 in the UK charts. The single was licensed from USA outlet Bang, and other master purchases included recordings by the Strangeloves and Turtles. Early UK signings included the Poets, the Mockingbirds and comedian Jimmy Tarbuck, who recorded an exclusive Mick Jagger/Keith Richard composition, '(We're) Wasting Time'. Gothic chanteuse Nico made her debut, 'I'm Not Saying', for Immediate. It featured stellar guitarist Jimmy Page, who enjoyed an association with the company during its early stages. Oldham's *laissez-faire* attitude helped attract several acts seeking greater freedom of expression, notably the Small Faces. The quartet enjoyed chart success on the label with 'Here Comes The Nice', 'Itchycoo Park', 'Tin Soldier' and 'Lazy Sunday'. Chris Farlowe emerged from the R&B circuit under the tutelage of Mick Jagger, reaching the number 1 spot with 'Out Of Time'. Amen Corner reached the same position in 1969 with '(If Paradise Is) Half As Nice', but by this point Immediate was in considerable financial trouble. Fleetwood Mac remained on its books for a solitary single, the poignant 'Man Of The World', before departing for Reprise, and although enjoying success in the 'underground' market with the Nice, Immediate was unable to survive the crisis. In a last attempt to salvage the company, Oldham and Calder switched supergroup Humble Pie from the Instant subsidiary to the parent label, but it was too late. Immediate was wound up in 1970. It has nevertheless retained a fascination and its back catalogue has been reactivated many times over the years. In 1994 the founding partners announced plans to relaunch the company with new signings.

IMPRESSIONS

Formed in Chicago in 1957 and originally known as the Roosters, this group comprised Jerry Butler (b. 8 December 1939, Sunflower, Mississippi, USA), Curtis Mayfield (b. 3 June 1942, Chicago, Illinois, USA), Sam Gooden (b. 2 September 1939, Chattanooga, Tennessee, USA), and brothers Richard Brooks and Arthur Brooks (both born Chattanooga, Tennessee, USA). Mayfield and Butler first met in the choir of the Travelling Soul Spiritualists Church, from where they formed the Modern Jubilaires and Northern Jubilee Singers. The two teenagers then drifted apart, and while Curtis was involved in another group, the Alphatones, Butler joined Gooden and the Brooks brothers in the Roosters. Mayfield was subsequently installed as their guitarist. Dubbed the Impressions by their manager, the group's first single for Abner/Falcon, 'For Your Precious Love', was a gorgeous ballad and substantial hit, reaching number 11 in the US pop chart in 1958. The label credit, which read 'Jerry Butler And The Impressions', caused internal friction and the two sides split after one more release. While Butler's solo career gradually prospered, that of his erstwhile colleagues floundered. He and Mayfield were later reconciled on Butler's 1960 single, 'He Will Break Your Heart', the success of which, and other Curtis-penned songs, rekindled the Impressions' career. Signed to ABC-Paramount in 1961, they had a hit with the haunting 'Gypsy Woman'. Subsequent releases were less well received until 'It's All Right' (1963) soared to number 1 in the R&B chart and to number 4 in pop chart. The group was now a trio of Mayfield, Gooden and Fred Cash, and their rhythmic harmonies were set against Johnny Pate's stylish arrangements. Magnificent records - including 'I'm So Proud', 'Keep On Pushing', 'You Must Believe Me' (all 1964) and 'People Get Ready' (1965) – showed how Mayfield was growing as an incisive composer, creating lyrical songs which were alternately poignant and dynamic. During this period the Impressions scored what was to be their last US pop Top 10 hit, 'Amen', which was featured in the film *Lilies Of The Field*. Mayfield then set up two short-lived record companies, Windy C, in 1966 and Mayfield, in 1967. However, it was the singer's third venture, Curtom, which proved most durable. In the meantime, the Impressions had emerged from a period when Motown had provided their prime influence. 'You Been Cheatin'' (1965) and 'You Always Hurt Me' (1967), however good in themselves, lacked the subtlety of their predecessors, but were part of a transition in Mayfield's musical perceptions. Statements, previously implicit, were granted a much more open forum. 'This Is My Country' (1968), 'Mighty Mighty Spade And Whitey' (1969) and 'Check Out Your Mind' (1970) were tougher, politically-based performances, while his final album with the group, the quintessential *Young Mod's Forgotten Story*, set the framework for his solo work. Mayfield's replacement, Leroy Hutson, left in 1973. Reggie Torian and Ralph Johnson were subsequently added, and the new line-up topped the R&B chart in 1974 with 'Finally Got Myself Together (I'm A Changed Man)'. 'First Impressions' (1975) became their only British hit, but the following year Johnson left. Although Mayfield, Butler, Cash and Gooden have, on occasions, re-formed, the latter pair have also kept active their version of the Impressions.

●ALBUMS: *The Impressions* (ABC 1963)★★★, *The Never Ending Impressions* (ABC 1964)★★★, *Keep On Pushing* (ABC 1964)★★★, *People Get Ready* (ABC 1965)★★★, *One By One* (ABC 1965)★★★, *Riding High* (ABC 1966)★★★, *The Fabulous Impressions* (ABC 1967)★★★, *We're A Winner* (1968)★★, *This Is My Country* (1968)★★, *The Versatile Impressions* (1969)★★, *The Young Mod's Forgotten Story* (1969)★★, *Check Out Your Mind* (1970)★★, *Times Have Changed* (1972)★★, *Preacher Man* (1973)★★, *Finally Got Myself Together* (1974)★★, *Three The Hard Way* (1974)★★, *First Impressions* (1975)★★★, *It's About Time* (1976)★★, *Loving Power* (1976)★★, *Come To My Party* (1979)★★, *Fan The Fire* (1981)★★.
●COMPILATIONS: *The Impressions Greatest Hits* (1965)★★★★, *The Best Of The Impressions* (1968)★★★★, *Your Precious Love* (1981)★★★★, as Curtis Mayfield And The Impressions *The Anthology 1961 - 1977* (1992)★★★★, *All The Best* (Pickwick 1994)★★★★.

INCREDIBLE STRING BAND

This UK folk group was formed in 1965 in Glasgow, Scotland, at 'Clive's Incredible Folk Club' by Mike Heron (b. 12 December 1942, Glasgow, Scotland), Robin Williamson (b. 24 November 1943, Edinburgh, Scotland) and Clive Palmer (b. London, England). In 1966 the trio completed *The Incredible String Band*, a collection marked by an exceptional blend of traditional and original material, but they broke up upon its completion. Heron and Williamson regrouped the following year to record the exceptional *5000 Spirits Or The Layers Of The Onion*. On this the duo emerged as a unique and versatile talent, employing a variety of exotic instruments to enhance their global folk palate. Its several highlights included Mike's 'Painting Box' and two of Robin's most evocative compositions, 'Way Back In The 1960s' and 'First Girl I Loved'. The latter was later recorded by Judy Collins. A *de rigueur* psychedelic cover encapsulated the era and the pair were adopted by the emergent underground. Two further releases, *The Hangman's Beautiful Daughter* and *Wee Tam And The Big Huge*, consolidated their position and saw Williamson, in particular, contribute several lengthy, memorable compositions. *Changing Horses*, as its title implies, reflected a growing restlessness with the acoustic format and the promotion of two previously auxiliary members, Licorice McKechnie (vocals/keyboards/guitar/ percussion) and Rose Simpson (vocals/bass/violin/percussion), indicated a move to a much fuller sound. The album polarized aficionados with many lamenting the loss of an erstwhile charm and idealism. *I Looked Up* continued the transformation to a rock-based perspective although *U*, the soundtrack to an ambitious ballet-cum-pantomime, reflected something of their earlier charm. *Liquid Acrobat As Regards The Air* in 1971, was stylistically diverse and elegiac in tone. Dancer-turned-musician Malcolm Le Maistre was introduced to the group's circle and, with the departure of both Rose and Licorice, a

woodwinds/keyboard player, Gerald Dott, joined the String Band for *No Ruinous Feud*. By this point the group owed little to the style of the previous decade although Williamson's solo, *Myrrh*, invoked the atmosphere of *Wee Tam* rather than the apologetic rock of *No Ruinous Feud*. The two founding members were becoming estranged both musically and socially and in 1974 they announced the formal end of their partnership.
●ALBUMS: *The Incredible String Band* (Elektra 1966)★★★, *5000 Spirits Or The Layers Of The Onion* (Elektra 1967)★★★★, *The Hangman's Beautiful Daughter* (Elektra 1968)★★★★, *Wee Tam And The Big Huge* (Elektra 1968)★★★, *Changing Horses* (Elektra 1969), *I Looked Up* (Elektra 1970)★★, *U* (Elektra 1970)★★, *Be Glad For The Song Has No Ending* (Island 1971)★★, *Liquid Acrobat As Regards The Air* (Island 1971)★★, *Earthspan* (Island 1972)★★, *No Ruinous Feud* (Island 1973)★★, *Hard Rope And Silken Twine* (Island 1974)★★, *On Air* (1991)★★★, *In Concert* (Windsong 1992)★★★, *The Chelsea Sessions* (Pig's Whisker Music 1997).
●COMPILATIONS: *Relics Of The Incredible String Band* (1971)★★★, *Seasons They Change* (Island 1976)★★★.
●VIDEOS: *Be Glad For The Song Has No Ending* (1994).

INCREDIBLES

A vocal group from Los Angeles, California, USA. Original members were lead Cal Waymon (b. 1942, Houston, Texas, USA), Carl Gilbert (b. 1943, Toledo, Ohio, USA) and Jean Smith (b. 1945, Arkansas, USA), all graduates of Los Angeles' Jefferson High School. Waymon, the writer and producer of the group, had a background as a folk singer, and had for a time lived in New York were he played guitar and sang topical songs in Greenwich Village coffeehouses. On his return to Los Angeles in 1966, he formed the Incredibles, and within months had a moderate national R&B success with 'I'll Make It Easy (If You'll Come On Home)' (number 39 R&B). The group then added a fourth member, Alda Denise Erwin (b. St. Louis, Missouri, USA), and the following year achieved another moderate hit with a remake of the old standard, 'Heart And Soul' (number 45 R&B). The Incredibles - featuring Waymon, Erwin, and new member Don Rae Simpson, from Montreal, Canada - were still recording and touring in 1969, when their only album was released, but their career was all behind them. The Incredibles boasted a smooth relaxed sound that had staying power; their songs are eminently listenable decades later.
●ALBUMS: *Heart & Soul* (Audio Arts 1969)★★.

INTERNATIONAL SUBMARINE BAND

This country rock group were formed in New England, USA, in 1965 by Gram Parsons (vocals/keyboards/guitar), Ian Dunlop (bass/vocals), John Nuese (guitar, ex-Trolls) and Tom Snow (piano) who was later replaced by a drummer, Mickey Gauvin. It was Gauvin and Dunlop who came up the group's new name; a reference to the 'International Silverstream Submarine Band' from the 'Our Gang' film series of the 1930s. They moved to New York where they backed former child actor Brandon De Wilde on a series of demos for RCA Records and also made two singles. The first, an instrumental version of the title song to the film *The Russians Are Coming, The Russians Are Coming*, was backed by a version of Buck Owens' 'Truck Driving Man' and was issued on Ascot Records in 1966. Later that year the quartet switched to Columbia for 'Sum Up Broke'/'One Day Week', the a-side of which was an impressive synthesis of folk rock and pop. When these singles were unsuccessful, the group followed De Wilde to Los Angeles where they supported several acts, including Love and Iron Butterfly, but their blend of R&B, C&W and rock 'n' roll was at odds with prevailing psychedelic trends. Footage of the ISB appeared in the film *The Trip*. Lee Hazlewood showed interest in the C&W element of their music but internal disputes broke apart the founding line-up. In 1967 Dunlop and Gauvin left to form the original Flying Burrito Brothers while Parsons and Nuese were joined in the International Submarine Band by Bob Buchanan (bass) and Jon Corneal (drums). *Safe At Home* was released on Hazlewood's LHI label. It featured material by Johnny Cash and Merle Haggard, alongside four Parsons originals, notably 'Luxury Liner' and 'Blue Eyes'. Both of these songs were completed prior to Buchanan's arrival and feature Chris Ethridge on bass. The album, however, was not a success and the band dissolved. Parsons briefly joined the Byrds, then formed a revamped Flying Burrito Brothers, initially including both Corneal and Ethridge. Gauvin formed Vegelava with two ex-members of the Blues Magoos before retiring from music. Dunlop returned to his native Cornwall where he formed the Muscletones while Nuese fronted a version of the International Submarine Band during the early 70s. At the same time Parsons was enjoying an influential solo career.

●ALBUMS: *Safe At Home* (LHI 1967)★★★.

IRON BUTTERFLY

During the progressive music revolution in the late 60s one of the most surprising successes was that of Iron Butterfly. The band was formed by Doug Ingle (b. 9 September 1946, Omaha, Nebraska, USA; organ/vocals) who added Ron Bushy (b. 23 September 1941, Washington DC, USA; drums), Eric Brann (b. 10 August 1950, Boston, Massachusetts, USA; guitar), Lee Dorman (b. 19 September 1945, St. Louis, Missouri, USA; bass/vocals) and, briefly, Danny Weiss. Together they were arguably the first to amalgamate the terms 'heavy' and 'rock', following the release of their debut in 1968. Their second effort, *In-A-Gadda-Da-Vida* (In The Garden Of Eden), became a multi-million seller and was for a number of years the biggest selling item in Atlantic Records' catalogue. The album also became the record industy's first 'Platinum' disc. The 17-minute title-track contained everything a progressive rock fan could want - neo-clas-

sical organ with Far East undertones, a solid beat, screeching guitar parts, barbed-wire feedback and an overlong drum solo. Magnificently overwrought at the time, the intervening years have been less kind to its standing. The follow-up, *Ball*, was a lesser success, despite containing a better collection of songs, notably the invigorating 'It Must Be Love' and more subtle 'Soul Experience'. Brann departed after a poor live album and was replaced by two guitarists: Larry 'Rhino' Rheinhart (b. 7 July 1948, Florida, USA) and Mike Pinera (b. 29 September 1948, Florida, USA; ex-Cactus, Alice Cooper). No further success ensued. *Metamorphosis* was a confused collection recorded when the band was disintegrating. They re-formed in the mid-70s with two disappointing albums but Iron Butterfly ultimately suffered from an identity crisis. Another re-formation, this time in 1992, was masterminded by Mike Pinera. A new version of 'In-A-Gadda-da-Vida' was recorded and Pinera recruited Dorman and Bushy for extensive touring in the USA. By 1993 their legendary second album had sold an astonishing 25 million copies and in 1995 the band re-formed once more for a further anniversary tour.

●ALBUMS: *Heavy* (Atco 1968)★★, *In-A-Gadda-da-Vida* (Atco 1968)★★★★, *Ball* (Atco 1969)★★★, *Iron Butterfly Live* (Atco 1970)★, *Metamorphosis* (Atco 1970)★★, *Scorching Beauty* (MCA 1975)★★, *Sun And Steel* (MCA 1976)★★★.

●COMPILATIONS: *Evolution* (Atco 1971)★★★, *Star Collection* (1973)★★★, *Light And Heavy: The Best Of* (1993)★★★.

IRWIN, BIG DEE

b. Difosco Ervin, 4 August 1939, New York City, New York, USA, d. 27 August 1995, Las Vegas, Nevada, USA. The corpulent R&B singer first made his mark as lead for the doo-wop group the Pastels, who hit with two sumptuous ballads, 'Been So Long' (1957) and 'So Far Away' (1958). As a solo artist, he is recalled for a series of tongue-in-cheek singles, the most successful of which was a version of the Bing Crosby hit 'Swingin' On A Star' in 1963, an irreverent performance on which he was joined by a perky Little Eva. Irwin's other releases included 'Everybody's Got A Dance But Me', on which he begrudged the dance-based releases of other artists, and 'Happy Being Fat', where Eva, once again, provided the spiky interjections. Irwin later enjoyed intermittent success as a songwriter, including 'What Kind Of Boy', recorded on the Hollies' debut album. He died in 1995 of heart failure.

IVEYS

Originally comprising Tom Evans (bass), Mike Gibbins (drums), Ron Griffiths (guitar) and Pete Ham (guitar/vocals), the Iveys formed in Swansea, South Wales, in the late 60s. An initial demo tape was sent to Apple Records and so impressed Paul McCartney that he immediately invited them to sign with the label. They made their debut in 1968 with 'Maybe Tomorrow'/'And Her Daddy's A Millionaire'. Although it did not chart in the UK, it did reach number 67 in the US charts. A projected album of the same title was never issued in the UK, but was pressed in Europe and Japan. Frustrated by the lack of coverage for the band, Griffiths left to be replaced by guitarist Joey Molland. A second single, 'Dear Angie'/'No Escaping Your Love', was also released in Europe but not the UK, in 1969. They then set about recording a McCartney composition, 'Come And Get It', but by the time this was released they had changed their name to Badfinger. *Maybe Tomorrow* was belatedly released in the UK in 1992 on CD along with previously unissued tracks. Several of the songs it contained were later reprised by Badfinger on their *Magic Christian Music* album.

●ALBUMS: *Maybe Tomorrow* (Apple 1968)★★★.

IVY LEAGUE

Formed in 1964, the Ivy League was an outlet for songwriters John Carter (b. John Shakespeare, 20 October 1942, Birmingham, England) and Ken Lewis (b. James Hawker, 3 December 1942, Birmingham, England). The duo's talent had been established through compositions for several acts, including Mike Sarne's UK novelty hit, 'Will I What', and their own beat group, Carter-Lewis And The Southerners, which featured guitarist Jimmy Page. Perry Ford (b. Bryan Pugh, 1940, Lincoln, England), a former member of Bert Weedon's backing band, completed the Ivy League line-up which had three UK hits in 1965 with 'Funny How Love Can Be' (number 8), 'That's Why I'm Crying' (number 22) and 'Tossing And Turning' (number 3). Their close harmony, falsetto style was modelled on that of the Four Freshmen and Four Seasons and while obviously competent, grew increasingly out-of-step as contemporary pop progressed. The trio reached a creative peak with the atmospheric 'My World Fell Down', but John Carter was now tiring of his creation. Tony Burrows replaced him in 1966 and although Ken Lewis left the group several months later, Perry Ford remained at its helm until the end of the decade, fronting an ever-changing line-up. By then, however, the Ivy League had been surpassed by newer Carter/Lewis projects including the Flowerpot Men and White Plains.

●ALBUMS: *This Is The Ivy League* (1965)★★★.

●COMPILATIONS: *Sounds Of The Ivy League* (Marble Arch 1967)★★★, *Tomorrow Is Another Day* (Marble Arch 1969)★★★, *The Best Of The Ivy League* (1988)★★★.

JACKSON, CHUCK

b. 22 July 1937, Latta, South Carolina, USA. Jackson travelled the traditional 50s route into soul music via a spell in the gospel group, the Raspberry Singers. In 1957, he joined the hit doo-wop group, the Dell-Vikings, taking a prominent role on their US Top 10 success 'Whispering Bells'. His strong baritone vocals enabled him to launch a solo career with Beltone Records in 1960, before signing to the more prestigious Wand label the following year. Jackson's early 60s singles for Wand epitomized the New York uptown soul style, with sophisticated arrangements - often crafted by Burt Bacharach - supporting his sturdy vocals with female vocalists and orchestras. He enjoyed enormous success in the R&B market for several years with a run of hits which have become soul classics, like 'I Don't Want To Cry', 'I Wake Up Crying', 'Any Day Now' and 'Tell Him I'm Not Home', although only the majestic 'Any Day Now', co-written by Bacharach, crossed into the USA Top 30. In 1965 he was teamed with Maxine Brown on a revival of Chris Kenner's R&B favourite, 'Something You Got', the first of three hit duets over the next two years. Their partnership was severed in 1967 when Jackson joined Motown, a decision he later described as 'one of the worst mistakes I ever made in my life'. Although he notched up a minor hit with Freddie Scott's 'Are You Lonely For Me Baby?' in 1969, the majority of his Motown recordings found him pitched against unsympathetic backdrops in a vain attempt to force him into the label's formula. Jackson left Motown in 1971 for ABC, where again he could muster just one small hit, 'I Only Get This Feeling' in 1973. Another switch of labels, to All-Platinum in 1975, produced the chart entry 'I'm Wanting You, I'm Needing You' in his traditional style. In 1980, he joined EMI America, where his most prominent role was as guest vocalist on two hit albums by Gary 'U.S.' Bonds. In the late 80s Jackson was one of many ex-Motown artists signed to Ian Levine's Motor City label, with whom he released two singles.

●ALBUMS: *I Don't Want To Cry* (Wand 1961)★★★, *Any Day Now* (Wand 1962)★★★★, *Encore* (Wand 1963)★★★, *Chuck Jackson On Tour* (Wand 1964)★★★, *Mr Everything* (Wand 1965)★★★, with Maxine Brown *Saying Something* (1965)★★★, *A Tribute To Rhythm And Blues* (Wand 1966)★★★, *A Tribute To Rhythm And Blues Vol. 2* (Wand 1966)★★★, with Brown *Hold On We're Coming* (1966)★★★, *Dedicated To The King* (Wand 1966)★★★, *The Early Show* (1967)★★★, *Chuck Jackson Arrives* (Motown 1968)★★★, *Goin' Back To Chuck Jackson* (Motown 1969)★★★,

Teardrops Keep Falling On My Heart (Motown 1970)★★★, *Through All Times* (ABC 1974)★★★, *Needing You, Wanting You* (1975)★★★, *The Great Chuck Jackson* (1977)★★★, *I Wanna Give You Some Love* (EMI America 1980)★★★, with Cissy Houston *I'll Take Care Of You* (1992)★★★.

●COMPILATIONS: *Chuck Jackson's Greatest Hits* (Wand 1967), *Mr. Emotion* (1985)★★★, *A Powerful Soul* (1987)★★★, *Good Things Any Day Now* (1991)★★★, *I Don't Want To Cry/Any Day Now* (Ace 1993)★★★, *Encore/Mr. Everything* (1994)★★★, *The Great Recordings* (Tomato 1995)★★★.

JAMES, ETTA

b. Jamesetta Hawkins, 25 January 1938, Los Angeles, California, USA. James, introduction to performing followed an impromptu audition for Johnny Otis backstage at San Francisco's Fillmore Auditorium. 'Roll With Me Henry', her 'answer' to the Hank Ballard hit, 'Work With Me Annie', was re-titled 'The Wallflower' in an effort to disguise its risque lyric and became an R&B number 1. 'Good Rockin' Daddy' provided another hit, but the singer's later releases failed to chart. Having secured a deal with the Chess group of labels, James, also known as Miss Peaches, unleashed a series of powerful songs including 'All I Could Do Was Cry' (1960), 'At Last' (1961), 'Trust In Me' (1961), 'Don't Cry Baby' (1961), 'Something's Got A Hold On Me' (1962), 'Stop The Wedding' (1962) and 'Pushover' (1963). She also recorded several duets with Harvey Fuqua. Heroin addiction sadly blighted both her personal and professional life, but in 1967 Chess took her to the Fame studios. The resultant *Tell Mama*, was a triumph, and pitted James' abrasive voice with the exemplary Muscle Shoals houseband. Its highlights included the proclamatory title track, a pounding version of Otis Redding's 'Security' (both of which reached the R&B Top 20) and the despairing 'I'd Rather Go Blind', which was later a UK Top 20 hit for Chicken Shack. The 1973 album *Etta James* earned her a US Grammy nomination, despite her continued drug problems, which she did not overcome until the mid-80s. A 1977 album, *Etta Is Betta Than Evah*, completed her Chess contract, and she moved to Warner Brothers. A renewed public profile followed her appearance at the opening ceremony of the Los Angeles Olympics in 1984. *Deep In The Night*, was a critics' favourite. A live album, *Late Show*, released in 1986, featured Shuggie Otis and Eddie 'Cleanhead' Vinson, and was followed by *Seven Year Itch*, her first album for Island Records in 1989. This, and the subsequent release, *Stickin' To My Guns*, found her back on form, aided and abetted once more by the Muscle Shoals team. Her ability to take and shape a song demonstrates the depth of her great ability to 'feel' the essence of the lyric and melody. All her cover versions from 'Need Your Love So Bad' to 'The Night Time Is The Right Time' are given her indelible stamp. Following the use in a television advertisement of her version of Muddy Waters' 'I Just Want To Make Love To You' she must have been surprised to find herself near the top of the UK charts in 1996. She is both emotional and 'foxy', yet still remains painfully underexposed; perhaps this hit will open the door to her extraordinary voice.

●ALBUMS: *Miss Etta James* (Crown 1961)★★★★, *At Last!* (Argo 1961)★★★★, *Second Time Around* (Argo 1961)★★★★, *Twist With Etta James* (Crown 1962)★★★★, *Etta James* (Argo 1962)★★★★, *Etta James Sings For Lovers* (Argo 1962)★★★★, *Etta James Top Ten* (Argo 1963)★★★, *Etta James Rocks The House* (Argo 1964)★★★, *The Queen Of Soul* (Argo 1965)★★★★, *Call My Name* (Cadet 1967)★★★, *Tell Mama* (Cadet 1968)★★★★★, *Etta James Sings Funk* (Cadet 1970)★★★, *Losers Weepers* (Cadet 1971)★★★, *Etta James* (Chess 1973)★★★, *Come A Little Closer* (Chess 1974)★★★, *Etta Is Betta Than Evah!* (Chess 1977)★★★, *Deep In The Night* (Warners 1978)★★★, *Changes* (MCA 1980)★★★, *Good Rockin' Mama* (1981)★★★, *Red, Hot And Live* (1982)★★★, *The Heart And Soul Of* (1982)★★★, *Tuff Lover* (1983)★★★, with Eddie 'Cleanhead' Vinson *Blues In The Night: The Early Show* (Fantasy 1986)★★★, *Blues In The Night: Late Show* (Fantasy 1986)★★★, *Etta James On Chess* (Vogue 1988)★★★, *Seven Year Itch* (Island 1989)★★★, *Stickin' To My Guns* (Island 1990)★★★★, *Something's Gotta Hold On Me (Etta James Vol. 2)* (Roots 1992)★★★, *The Right Time* (Elektra 1992)★★★, *Mystery Lady: Songs Of Billie Holiday* (Private Music 1994)★★★, *Love's Been Rough On Me* (Private 1997)★★★.

●COMPILATIONS: *The Best Of ...* (Crown 1962)★★★★, *Etta James Top Ten* (1963)★★★, *The Soul Of Etta James* (Ember 1968)★★★★, *Golden Decade* (Chess 1972)★★★★, *Peaches* (Chess 1973)★★★★, *Good Rockin' Mama* (Ace 1981)★★★★, *Chess Masters* (Chess 1981)★★★, *Tuff Lover* (Ace 1983)★★★★, *Juicy Peaches* (Chess 1985, 1988)★★★, *R&B Queen* (Crown 1986)★★★, *Her Greatest Sides, Volume One* (Charly 1987)★★★★, *R&B Dynamite* (Ace 1987)★★★★, *Rocks The House* (Charly 1987)★★★, *Tell Mama* (1988)★★★★, *Chicago Golden Years* (1988)★★★, *On Chess* (1988)★★★, *Come A Little Closer* (Charly 1988)★★★, *Chicago Golden Years* (Vogue 1988)★★★, *Juicy Peaches* (Charly 1989)★★★★, *Etta James Volume 1* and *2* (1990)★★★★, *Legendary Hits* (Jazz Archives 1992)★★★, *Back In The Blues* (Zillion 1992)★★★, *The Soulful Miss Peaches* (Charly 1993)★★★★, *Something's Got A Hold* (Charly 1994)★★★, *I'd Rather Go Blind - The World Of Etta James* (Trace 1993)★★★, *The Gospel Soul Of Etta James* (Disky 1993)★★★, *Blues In The Night, The Early Show* (Fantasy 1994)★★★, *Blues In The Night, The Late Show* (Fanatsy 1994)★★★, *Miss Peaches Sings The Soul* (That's Soul 1994)★★★, *Live From San Franscisco '81* (Private Music 1994)★★★, *The Genuine Article: The Best Of* (MCA/Chess 1996)★★★★.

●FURTHER READING: *Rage To Survive*, Etta James with David Ritz.

JAMES, NICKY

Based in Birmingham, Midlands, England, Nicky James had previously led local band the Lawmen, and been a member of Denny Laine's Diplomats, before embarking on a solo career. Signing to Columbia Records, he then added a suffix to his name to produce the Nicky James Movement. That group made its debut in 1965 with a version of 'Stagger Lee'. When the single did not sell he moved from Columbia to Philips Records and reverted to solo billing. As such he made his debut in 1967 with 'So Glad We Made It'. Four further singles, 'Would You Believe', 'Nobody But Me', 'Time' and 'Reaching For The Sun', ensued, but it was not until 1971 that he made his self-titled album debut. By now he had perfected a vocal technique which melded the blues with prevalent beat pop tendencies, although he found it difficult to make a commercial breakthrough. In 1972 he switched to Threshold Records, a label established by the Moody Blues, who were clearly a major influence on him. Two more albums followed alongside four further singles, which increasingly moved towards blues rock. The last of these, 'Maggie', was released in 1976, by which time he had also appeared on solo albums by Moody Blues members Graeme Edge and Ray Thomas. With the advent of punk, however, James's career declined and 'Maggie' proved to be his final recording.

●ALBUMS: *Nicky James* (Philips 1971)★★★, *Every Home Should Have One* (Threshold 1973)★★, *Thunderthroat* (Threshold 1976)★★.

JAMES, TOMMY, AND THE SHONDELLS

Tommy James formed his first group Tommy And The Tornadoes at the age of 13, by which time he had already recorded his debut single, 'Long Pony Tale'. The Shondells comprised James, Larry Coverdale (guitar), Craig Villeneuve (keyboards), Larry Wright (bass) and Jim Payne (drums) and were assembled to fulfil weekend engagements, but they secured a deal with the local Snap label in 1962. Their first release, 'Hanky Panky', was a regional success, but a chance discovery four years later by Pittsburg disc jockey Bob Mack led to its becoming a national smash, selling in excess of 1one million copies. Now signed to the Roulette label, James assembled a new Shondells which, following defections, settled around a nucleus of Eddie Gray (guitar), Ronnie Rossman (keyboards), Mike Vale (b. 17 July 1949; bass) and Pete Lucia (drums). The addition of producer/songwriting team Ritchie Cordell and Bo Gentry resulted in a string of classic, neo-bubblegum hits, including 'I Think We're Alone Now', 'Mirage' (both gold discs from 1967) and 'Out Of The Blue' (1968). The group's effortless grasp of hooklines and melody culminated with the pulsating 'Mony Mony' (1968), a UK number 1 which invoked the style of the classic garage band era. James then assumed complete artistic control of his work, writing, arranging and producing the psychedelic-influenced 'Crimson And Clover'. This haunting, atmospheric piece, described by the singer as 'our second renaissance', topped the US chart and garnered sales of over five million copies. This desire to experiment continued with two further gold-selling singles, 'Sweet Cherry Wine' and 'Crystal Blue Persuasion' (both 1969), and the album *Cellophane Symphony*. In 1970 the group and singer parted on amicable terms. The latter continued under the name Hog Heaven, while an exhausted James retired to a farm before launching a solo career. 'Draggin' The Line' (1971) provided a US Top 5 hit although subsequent releases from the early 70s failed to broach the Top 30. In 1980 the singer had another million-seller with 'Three Times In Love', since when he has continued to record, albeit with less success. Tommy James And The Shondells' power was encapsulated in their danceability and bracing fusion of soulful voices, garage group riffs, effervescent pop and occasional bubblegum appeal. This pop pourri legacy was picked up by younger artists over a decade on when Joan Jett charted with 'Crimson And Clover' and both Billy Joel and Tiffany took Shondells' covers back to number 1 in the US charts.

●ALBUMS: *Hanky Panky* (Roulette 1966)★★★, *It's Only Love* (Roulette 1967)★★★, *I Think We're Alone Now* (Roulette 1967)★★★, *Gettin' Together* (Roulette 1968)★★, *Mony Mony* (Roulette 1968)★★★, *Crimson & Clover* (Roulette 1968)★★★, *Cellophane Symphony* (1969)★★, *Travelin'* (1970)★★. The Shondells solo: *Hog Heaven* (1971)★★.

●COMPILATIONS: *Something Special! The Best Of Tommy James And The Shondells* (Roulette 1968)★★★, *The Best Of Tommy James And The Shondells* (1969)★★★, *Anthology* (Rhino 1990)★★★★, *Tommy James: The Solo Recordings 1970-1981* (1991)★★★, *The Best Of ...* (Rhino 1994)★★★★.

JAN AND DEAN

Jan Berry (b. 3 April 1941, Los Angeles, California, USA) and Dean Torrance (b. 10 March 1940, Los Angeles, California, USA). Students at Emerson Junior High School, Berry and Torrance began singing together on an informal basis. They formed an embryonic group, the Barons, with Bruce Johnston and Sandy Nelson, but its members gradually drifted away, leaving Berry, Torrance and singer Arnie Ginsburg to plot a different course. The trio recorded 'Jennie Lee' in 1958. A homage to the subject of Ginsburg's affections, a local striptease artist, the single became a surprise hit, reaching number 8 in the US chart. Although featured on the song, Torrance was drafted prior to its success, and the pressing was credited to Jan And Arnie. Subsequent releases failed to achieve success and the pair split up. Berry and Torrance were reunited the following year. They completed several demos in Berry's makeshift studio and, having secured the production and management services of local entrepreneur Lou Adler, the reshaped duo enjoyed a Top 10 entry with 'Baby Talk'. Jan And Dean scored several minor hits over the ensuing four years until a 1963 release, 'Linda', heralded a departure in their style. Here the duo completed all the backing voices, while the lead was sung in falsetto. The sound was redolent of the Beach

Boys and the two performers' immediate future became entwined.

Brian Wilson co-wrote 'Surf City', Jan And Dean's first number 1 hit; this glorious summer hit evokes fun, sunshine and 'two girls for every boy'. The Beach Boys' leader also made telling contributions to several other notable classics, including 'Drag City', 'Dead Man's Curve' and 'Ride The Wild Surf', although Berry's contribution as writer, and later producer, should not be underestimated. However, despite the promise of a television series, and a role in the film *Easy Come - Easy Go*, relations between he and Torrance became increasingly strained. Dean added fuel to the fire by singing lead on 'Barbara Ann', an international hit pulled from the informal *Beach Boys Party*. The exploitative 'Batman' single, released in January 1966, was the last session the pair recorded together. Within weeks Jan Berry had crashed his sports car receiving appalling injuries. He incurred severe brain damage, but although recovery was slow, the singer did complete a few singles during the early 70s. Torrance kept the Jan And Dean name alive, but failed to recapture the duo's success and subsequently found his true vocation with his highly respected design company, Kittyhawk Graphics. However, the pair were reunited in 1978 when they undertook the support slot for that year's Beach Boys tour.

●ALBUMS: *Jan And Dean* (Dore 1960)★★, *Jan And Dean Take Linda Surfin'* (Liberty 1963)★★★, *Surf City (And Other Swinging Cities)* (Liberty 1963)★★★, *Drag City* (Liberty 1964)★★★, *Dead Man's Curve/New Girl In School* (Liberty 1964)★★★, *Ride The Wild Surf* (Liberty 1964)★★★, *The Little Old Lady From Pasadena* (Liberty 1964)★★★, *Command Performance - Live In Person* (Liberty 1965)★, *Folk 'N' Roll* (Liberty 1966)★★, *Filet Of Soul - A 'Live' One* (Liberty 1966)★, *Jan And Dean Meet Batman* (Liberty 1966)★★, *Popsicle* (1966)★★, *Save For A Rainy Day* (1967)★★.

●COMPILATIONS: *Jan And Dean's Golden Hits* (Liberty 1962)★★★, *Golden Hits Volume 2* (1965)★★★, *The Jan And Dean Anthology Album* (1971)★★★, *Gotta Take That One Last Ride* (1973)★★★, *Ride The Wild Surf (Hits From Surf City, USA)* (1976)★★★★, *Teen Suite 1958-1962* (1995)★★★★.

●FURTHER READING: *Jan And Dean*, Allan Clark.

JAN DUKES DE GREY

Originally formed in Yorkshire, England, as a duo of Michael Bairstow (flute, clarinet, saxophone, trumpet, percussion, keyboards) and Derek Noy (vocals, guitar, keyboards, bass, percussion), Jan Dukes De Grey were among the least conventional folk musicians of their time. Their debut album, *Sorcerers*, was composed entirely of Noy originals, the 18 tracks varying wildly in tone and quality, but occasional compositions, with their unusual arrangements and Noy's highly mannered singing, did succeed. By the advent of a second album, the group had expanded with the inclusion of drummer Denis Conlan. For *Mice And Rats In The Loft* the trio

had transferred to the better-distributed Transatlantic Records. Instead of the numerous short songs on their debut, this set comprised just three tracks, one of them a side long. The dissonant tones of its forerunner were given free reign over these expanded tracks, although again the quality of musicianship sometimes failed to match the imagination and invention displayed by Noy's songcraft.

●ALBUMS: *Sorcerers* (Decca Nova 1969)★★, *Mice And Rats In The Loft* (Transatlantic 1971)★★.

JANKOWSKI, HORST

b. 30 January 1936, Berlin, Germany. Jankowski's family was driven from the city and his father killed during World War 11. He returned to Berlin to study at its Conservatory of Music while moonlighting as a multi-instrumental session player. From 1952-64, he was part of Caterina Valente's touring band, an experience that began the gradual recognition of him as one of Germany's most polished mainstream jazz pianists. In 1960, he merged his 18-voice amateur choir with an orchestra to mine a similar easy-listening seam to that of Lawrence Welk and Ray Conniff. Issued as a single in 1965, the self-composed title track of *Eine Schwarzwaldfahrt* - translated as 'A Walk In The Black Forest' - was a huge global smash. He was also accorded the dubious attribute of 'genius' recorded and a tie-in album that sold a million in the USA. A precursor of sorts to James Last, he was, nonetheless, unable to recreate that 'Schwarzwaldfahrt' miracle by protracting a prolific recording career. Before his death, Jankowski reverted to the style in which he felt most comfortable through prestigious employment as an arranger for artists including Benny Goodman, Oscar Peterson, Ella Fitzgerald and Miles Davis. His extraordinary success in Germany resulted in being voted the top Jazz pianist for 11 consecutive years (1955-65).

●ALBUMS: *The Genius Of Jankowski!* (1965)★★★, *Horst Jankowski And His Orchestra* (1979)★★★, *Piano Interlude* (1979)★★★.

JANSCH, BERT

b. 3 November 1943, Glasgow, Scotland. This highly gifted acoustic guitarist and influential performer learned his craft in Edinburgh's folk circle before being absorbed into London's burgeoning folk circuit, where he established a formidable reputation as an inventive guitar player. His debut, *Bert Jansch*, is a landmark in British folk music and includes 'Do You Hear Me Now', a Jansch original later covered by Donovan, the harrowing 'Needle Of Death', and an impressive version of Davey Graham's 'Angie'. The artist befriended John Renbourn who played supplementary guitar on Bert's second selection, *It Don't Bother Me*. The two musicians then recorded the exemplary *Bert And John*, which was released alongside *Jack Orion*, Jansch's third solo album. This adventurous collection featured a nine-minute title track and a haunting version of 'Nottamun Town', the blueprint for a subsequent reading by Fairport Convention. Bert continued to make exceptional records, but his own career was overshadowed by his participation in the Pentangle alongside Renbourn, Jacqui McShee (vocals), Danny Thompson (bass) and Terry Cox (drums). Between 1968 and 1973 this accomplished, if occasionally sterile, quintet was one of folk music's leading attractions, although the individual members continued to pursue their own direction during this time. The Danny Thompson-produced *Moonshine* marked the beginning of his creative renaissance with delightful sleevenotes from the artist: 'I hope that whoever listens to this record gets as much enjoyment as I did from helping me to make it'. *LA Turnaround*, released following the Pentangle's dissolution, was a promising collection and featured assistance from several American musicians including former member of the Monkees, Michael Nesmith. Although Jansch rightly remains a respected figure, his later work lacks the invention of those early releases. It came to light that much of this lethargy was due to alcoholism, and by his own admission, it took six years to get himself into a stable condition. In the late 80s he took time out from solo folk club dates to join Jacqui McShee in a regenerated Pentangle line-up with whom he continues to tour. In the mid-90s he was performing regularly once again with confidence and fresh application. This remarkable reversal after a number of years of indifference was welcomed by his loyal core of fans. *When The Circus Comes To Town* was an album that easily matched his early pivotal work. Not only does Jansch sing and play well but he brilliantly evokes the atmosphere and spirit of the decade in which he first came to prominence. *Live At The 12 Bar* is an excellent example of his sound in the mid-90s, following a successful residency at London's 12 Bar Club.

●ALBUMS: *Bert Jansch* (Transatlantic 1965)★★★★, *It Don't Bother Me* (Transatlantic 1965)★★★★, *Jack Orion* (Transatlantic 1966)★★★★, with John Renbourn *Bert And John* (1966)★★★★, *Nicola* (Transatlantic 1967)★★★, *Birthday Blues* (Transatlantic 1968)★★★, *Lucky Thirteen* (1969)★★★, with Renbourn *Stepping Stones* (Vanguard 1969)★★★, *Rosemary Lane* (Transatlantic 1971)★★★, *Moonshine* (Reprise 1973)★★★, *LA Turnaround* (Charisma 1974)★★, *Santa Barbara Honeymoon* (Charisma 1975)★★, *A Rare Conundrum* (Charisma 1978)★★, *Avocet* (1979)★★, *Thirteen Down* (Sonet 1980)★★, *Heartbreak* (1982)★★, *From The Outside* (Konexion 1985)★★, *Leather Launderette* (1988)★★, *The Ornament Tree* (Run River 1990)★★, *When The Circus Comes To Town* (Cooking Vinyl 1995)★★★★, *Live At The 12 Bar* (Jansch 1996)★★★

●COMPILATIONS: *The Bert Jansch Sampler* (Transatlantic 1969)★★★★, *Box Of Love* (Transatlantic 1972)★★★, *The Essential Collection Vol. 1* (1987)★★★★, *The Essential Collection Vol. 2* (1987)★★★, *The Gardener: Essential Bert Jansch 1965-71* (1992)★★★★, *The Collection* (Castle 1995)★★★★.

JAY AND THE AMERICANS

This New York-based act was formed in 1961 when former Mystics vocalist John 'Jay' Traynor (b. 2 November 1938) joined ex-Harbor Lites duo Kenny Rosenberg, aka Kenny Vance, and Sandy Yaguda, aka Sandy Deane. Howie Kane (b. Howard Kerschenbaum) completed the line-up, which in turn secured a recording deal through the aegis of the songwriting and production team, Leiber And Stoller. Jay And The Americans scored a US Top 5 hit with their second single, the dramatic 'She Cried', but a series of misses exacerbated tension within the group and in 1962 Traynor left for a low-key solo career. Bereft of a lead vocalist, the remaining trio recruited David 'Jay' Black (b. 2 November 1941) from the Empires. Dubbed 'Jay' to infer continuity, Black introduced fifth member Marty Saunders (guitar) to the line-up, and the following year established his new role with the powerful 'Only In America'. Initially intended for the Drifters, the song's optimism was thought hypocritical for a black act and the Americans' vocal was superimposed over the original backing track. In 1964 Artie Ripp assumed the production reins for the quintet's 'Come A Little Bit Closer', a US Top 3 entry. The following year the group was assigned to Gerry Granahan who in turn secured a greater degree of consistency. 'Cara Mia', 'Some Enchanted Evening' and 'Sunday And Me' (the last-named penned by Neil Diamond) all reached the US Top 20, and although 'Livin' Above Your Head' was less successful, this enthralling performance is now recognized as one of the group's finest recordings. The quintet's brand of professional pop proved less popular as the 60s progressed, although revivals of 'This Magic Moment' (1968) and 'Walkin' In The Rain' (1969) were US Top 20 hits. The latter featured Donald Fagen and Walter Becker, later of Steely Dan. By the turn of the decade the group's impetus was waning and with Vance embarking on solo recordings, Sanders writing and Deane producing, Jay Black was granted the rights to the group's name. Further recordings did ensue, and although chart entries have long since ended, he continues to perform on the nostalgia circuit.

●ALBUMS: *She Cried* (United Artists 1962)★★★, *Jay And The Americans At The Cafe Wha?* (United Artists 1963)★★, *Come A Little Bit Closer* (United Artists 1964)★★★, *Blockbusters* (United Artists 1965)★★, *Sunday And Me* (United Artists 1966)★★★, *Livin' Above Your Head* (United Artists 1966)★★★, *Wild, Wild Winter* soundtrack (1966)★★, *Try Some Of This* (United Artists 1967)★★, *Sands Of Time* (1969)★★, *Wax Museum* (1970)★★.

●COMPILATIONS: *Jay And The Americans' Greatest Hits* (United Artists 1965)★★★, *Very Best Of* (1979)★★★, *Jay And The Americans' Greatest Hits Volume Two* (United Artists 1966)★★★, *Come A Little Bit Closer* (1990)★★★.

JAY AND THE TECHNIQUES

Formed in Allentown, Pennsylvania, USA, in the mid-60s, Jay And The Techniques were an inter-racial pop group

best known for the Top 10 debut single 'Apples, Peaches, Pumpkin Pie' in 1967. The group consisted of vocalist Jay Proctor and six other members: Karl Landis, Ronald Goosly, John Walsh, George Lloyd, Charles Crowl and Dante Dancho. The group built a following in the northeast and was discovered by producer Jerry Ross, who arranged to have them signed to Smash Records, a subsidiary of Mercury Records. 'Apples, Peaches, Pumpkin Pie', was their biggest hit, reaching number 6 in the US in 1967. 'Keep The Ball Rolling' was, like the first, based on a children's game, and it climbed to number 14. The formula held up for one further game-orientated single, 'Strawberry Shortcake', which scraped into the Top 40 in 1968. A final chart success, 'Baby Make Your Own Sweet Music', ended their run on the pop charts in 1968, but a revived Jay And The Techniques placed 'Number Onederful' on the R&B charts in 1976, on Event Records. This was the group's swan song.
●ALBUMS: *Apples, Peaches, Pumpkin Pie* (Smash 1967)★★, *Love, Lost & Found* (Smash 1968)★★.
●COMPILATIONS: *Apples, Peaches, Pumpkin Pie* (Collectables 1995)★★, *The Best Of Jay And The Techniques* (Mercury 1995)★★.

JAY, PETER, AND THE JAYWALKERS
Originally based in East Anglia, England, the Jaywalkers - Peter Miller (lead guitar), Tony Webster (rhythm guitar), Mac McIntyre (tenor saxophone/flute), Lloyd Baker (piano/baritone saxophone), Geoff Moss (acoustic bass), Johnny Larke (electric bass), and Peter Jay (drums), predated the British beat boom. They scored a minor hit in 1962 with 'Can Can 62', but despite an unquestioned competence, their rather stilted act became increasingly anachronistic. The group attempted a more contemporary image with several R&B-based releases, and in 1966 a restructured line-up emerged under the name Peter Jay And The New Jaywalkers. Now reduced to a quintet, the unit featured vocalist Terry Reid, but despite an impressive appearance on the Rolling Stones' UK tour, they disbanded by the end of that year.

JAYHAWKS (R&B)
The R&B novelty song 'Stranded In The Jungle' was a hit in 1956 for two USA groups. The Cadets' version remains the best-known (although the New York Dolls' 70s cover is also highly regarded by some) but the Jayhawks actually beat them to the US charts by one week. The doo-wop quartet consisted of lead Jimmy Johnson, baritone Dave Govan, tenor Carl Fisher and bass Carver Bunkum. They formed while in high school in Los Angeles, USA, in the early 50s. 'Stranded In The Jungle' was co-written by Johnson and friend Ernest Smith. It reached number 18 while the Cadets' cover landed three positions higher. Subsequent records by the group failed and by 1960, with a few personnel changes, they had metamorphosed into the Vibrations, who scored with the dance hit 'The Watusi' (1961) and 'My Girl Sloopy' (1964), the latter adapted by the McCoys as 'Hang On Sloopy'. The

Vibrations also moonlighted in 1961 as the Marathons, another one-hit-wonder with the novelty tune 'Peanut Butter'.

JAYNETTS
Songwriter Zelma 'Zell' Sanders formed this New York-based act around her daughter, Johnnie Louise Richardson, previously half of hit duo Johnnie And Joe. Ethel Davis, Mary Sue Wells, Yvonne Bushnell and Ada Ray completed the line-up featured on 'Sally, Go Round The Roses', the quintet's debut single and sole US chart entry. This haunting performance reached number 2 in 1963, and has since become an early classic of the 'girl group' genre, but the Jaynetts' progress was undermined when Richardson left following its release. Ensuing singles, including 'Keep An Eye On Her' and 'Johnny Don't Cry', were not successful, and the group ceased recording in 1965. Johnnie Louise died on 25 October 1988.
●ALBUMS: *Sally, Go 'Round The Roses* (Tuff 1963)★★.

JEFFERSON AIRPLANE
Along with the Grateful Dead, Jefferson Airplane are regarded as the most successful San Francisco band of the late 60s. The group were formed in 1965 by Marty Balin (b. Martyn Jerel Buchwald, 30 January 1942, Cincinnati, Ohio, USA; vocals/guitar). The other members in the original line-up were Paul Kantner (b. 17 March 1941, San Francisco, California, USA; guitar/vocals) and Jorma Kaukonen (b. 23 December 1940, Washington DC, USA; guitar/vocals). Bob Harvey and Jerry Peloquin gave way to Alexander 'Skip' Spence and Signe Anderson (b. Signe Toly Anderson, 15 September 1941, Seattle, Washington, USA). Their replacements; Spencer Dryden (b. 7 April 1938, New York, USA; drums) and Jack Casady (b. 13 April 1944, Washington, DC, USA), made up a seminal band that blended folk and rock into what became known as west coast rock. Kantner, already a familiar face on the local folk circuit and Balin, formerly of the Town Criers and co-owner of the Matrix club, soon became highly popular locally, playing gigs and benefits organized by promoter Bill Graham. Eventually they became regulars at the Fillmore Auditorium and the Carousel Ballroom, both a short distance from their communal home in the Haight Ashbury district. Anderson departed shortly after the release of their moderately successful debut *Takes Off* and was replaced by Grace Slick (b. Grace Barnett Wing, 30 October 1939, Evanston, Illinois, USA; vocals). Slick was already well known with her former band, the Great Society, and donated two of their songs, 'White Rabbit' and 'Somebody To Love' to the Airplane. Both titles were on their second influential collection, *Surrealistic Pillow*, and both became US Top 10 hits. They have now achieved classic status as definitive songs from that era. 'White Rabbit's' lyrics combined the harmless tale of *Alice In Wonderland* with an LSD trip. Their reputation was enhanced by a strong performance at the legendary Monterey Pop Festival in 1967. This national success continued with the erratic *After Bathing At Baxters* and the brilliant *Crown Of Creation*. The latter

showed the various writers in the band maturing and developing their own styles. Balin's 'If You Feel', Kaukonen's 'Ice Cream Phoenix' and Slick's tragi-comic 'Lather' gave the record great variety. This album also contained 'Triad', a song their friend David Crosby had been unable to include a Byrds album. They maintained a busy schedule and released a well-recorded live album, *Bless Its Pointed Little Head* in 1969. The same year they appeared at another milestone in musical history: the Woodstock Festival. Later that year they were present at the infamous Altamont Festival, where a group of Hells Angels killed a young spectator and attacked Balin.

Slick and Kantner had now become lovers and their hippie ideals and political views were a major influence on *Volunteers*. While it was an excellent album, it marked the decline of Balin's role in the band. Additionally, Dryden departed and the offshoot Hot Tuna began to take up more of Casady and Kaukonen's time. Wizened fiddler Papa John Creach (b. 28 May 1917, Beaver Falls, Pennsylvania, USA, d. 22 February 1994; violin) joined the band full-time in 1970, although he still continued to play with Hot Tuna. Kantner released a concept album, *Blows Against The Empire*, bearing the name Paul Kantner And The Jefferson Starship. The 'Starship' consisted of various Airplane members, plus Jerry Garcia, David Crosby, Graham Nash, *et al*. This majestic album was nominated for the science fiction Hugo Award. Slick meanwhile gave birth to a daughter, China, who later in the year graced the cover of Slick And Kantner's *Sunfighter*.

Following a greatest hits selection, *Worst Of* and the departure of Balin, the band released the cleverly packaged *Bark*. Complete with brown paper bag, the album offered some odd moments, notably Slick's 'Never Argue With A German', sung in spoof German, and Covington's 50s-sounding accapella, 'Thunk'. It also marked the first release on their own Grunt label. The disappointing *Long John Silver* was followed by a gutsy live outing, *30 Seconds Over Winterland*. This was the last album to bear their name, although an interesting compilation consisting of single releases and studio out-takes later appeared as *Early Flight*. Hot Tuna became Casady and Kaukonen's main interest and Slick and Kantner released further 'solo' albums. The name change evolved without any fuss, and one of the most inventive bands in history prepared for a relaunch as the Jefferson Starship. Kantner, Balin and Casady regrouped briefly as the KBC Band in 1986. The Airplane title was resurrected in 1989 when Slick, Kaukonen, Casady, Balin and Kantner re-formed and released *Jefferson Airplane* to an indifferent audience. By the early 90s Hot Tuna had re-formed, Kantner was rebuilding his Jefferson Starship and Slick had apparently retired from the music business.

●ALBUMS: *Jefferson Airplane Takes Off* (RCA 1966)★★, *Surrealistic Pillow* (RCA 1967)★★★★, *After Bathing At Baxter's* (RCA 1967)★★★, *Crown Of Creation* (RCA 1968)★★★★, *Bless Its Pointed Little Head* (RCA 1969)★★★, *Volunteers* (RCA 1969)★★★, *Bark* (Grunt 1971)★★★, *Long John Silver* (Grunt 1972)★★★, *30 Seconds Over Winterland* (Grunt 1973)★★★, *Early Flight* (Grunt 1974)★★★, *Jefferson Airplane* (Epic 1989)★.

●COMPILATIONS: *Worst Of Jefferson Airplane* (RCA 1970)★★★, featuring Jefferson Airplane and Starship *Flight Log (1966-1976)* (Grunt 1977)★★★★, *2400 Fulton Street* (RCA 1987)★★★★, *Journey ... Best Of* (Camden 1996)★★★.

●FURTHER READING: *The Jefferson Airplane And The San Francisco Sound*, Ralph J. Gleason. *Grace Slick - The Biography*, Barbara Rowe.

JOBIM, ANTONIO CARLOS

b. Antonio Carlos Brasileiro de Almeida Jobim, 25 January 1927, Rio de Janiero, Brazil, d. 8 December 1994. Jobim can rightfully claim to have started the bossa nova movement when, as director of Odeon Records, he gave his friend João Gilberto his own composition 'Chega De Saudade'. The influence of the resulting record soon spread to the USA, where Stan Getz and Charlie Byrd made his compositions hugely popular. Although Jobim did record, and performed at Carnegie Hall with Getz, Byrd, and Dizzy Gillespie in 1962, it is as a composer that Jobim's influence remains huge, with tunes including 'Desafinado', 'How Insensitive', 'The Girl From Ipanema', 'One Note Samba' and 'Wave' still jazz standards. Enigmatic and cruelly underrated, his praises have been sung for many years by Frank Sinatra, and in recent times the mantle has fallen to Lee Ritenour.

●ALBUMS: *Black Orpheus* soundtrack (1958)★★★, *The Composer Of Desafinado Plays* (Verve 1963)★★★, *Wave* (1967)★★★, *Stone Flower* (1992)★★★, *Compact Jazz* (Verve 1993)★★★★, *A Certain Mr Jobim* (1993)★★★, *Verve Jazz Masters Vol. 13* (Verve 1995)★★★, *The Man From Ipanema* (Verve 1996)★★★★, tribute album *A Twist Of Jobim* (I.E. 1997)★★.

JODY GRIND

UK-based Jody Grind was formed in 1968 by the late pianist/organist Tim Hinkley. Their name was culled from a Horace Silver album title. A veteran of the Bo Street Runners and the Chicago Line Blues Band, he was initially joined by two colleagues, Iav Zagni (guitar) and Barry Wilson (drums). The trio completed an album, *One Step On*, prior to Wilson's departure. He was replaced by Martin Harryman, who in turn made way for Pete Gavin. Guitarist Bernie Holland (who is now an excellent jazz guitarist), meanwhile, took over from Zagni and the restructured line-up recorded *Far Canal* with the help of bassist Louis Cennamo. Jody Grind broke up in March 1970. Hinkley later became part of the *ad hoc* bands Dick And The Firemen and Hinkley's Heroes, while Gavin joined Heads, Hands And Feet. Hinkley produced an album for Chris Farlowe in 1992.

●ALBUMS: *One Step On* (Transatlantic 1969), *Far Canal* (Transatlantic 1970).

JOHN'S CHILDREN

Formed in Leatherhead, Surrey, England, in 1964, John's Children's earliest antecedent was known as the Clockwork Onions. Louie Grooner (vocals), Andy Ellison (harmonica), Geoff McClelland (guitar), Chris Dawsett (bass) and Chris Townson (drums) made up this short-lived ensemble. The following year they emerged under a new name, the Silence, wherein Ellison (now vocalist), McClelland and Townson were joined by bassist John Hewlett. The group became John's Children in 1966 after meeting manager/producer Simon Napier-Bell. They made their debut in October with 'The Love I Thought I'd Found', an experimental composition made memorable by a start-stop, staccato tempo. This unusual release was known by its original title, 'Smashed Blocked', in the USA and Europe. A debut album, entitled *Orgasm*, was then readied for release. The set consisted of rudimentary material overdubbed by fake applause, but was withheld until 1970 in deference to its questionable quality and then controversial title. The group's second single, 'Just What You Want, Just What You Get', was a minor UK hit, but marked the departure of McClelland. His replacement was Napier-Bell protégé and budding singer-songwriter, Marc Bolan, whose spell in John's Children, although brief, proved contentious. His first offering, 'Desdemona', incurred a BBC ban over the line 'lift up your skirt and fly', and when a second composition, 'A Midsummer Night's Scene', had been recorded unsatisfactorily, Bolan left to form Tyrannosaurus Rex. His former colleagues then released the felicitous flower-power anthem, 'Come And Play With Me In The Garden', before exhuming another Bolan song, 'Go Go Girl', from an earlier session. A final John's Children line-up - Ellison, Hewlett, Townson (now guitar) and Chris Colville (drums) completed several outstanding engagements before disbanding. Ellison embarked on a brief solo career, later re-emerging with Townson in 1974 as Jet and from there on to Radio Stars. John Hewlett became a successful manager with Sparks, while also handling Jook, a less celebrated ensemble which also featured Chris Townson.

●ALBUMS: *Orgasm* (1971)★★★.
●COMPILATIONS: *Instant Action* (Hawkeye 1985)★★★, *A Midsummer Night's Scene* (Bam Caruso 1987)★★★, *Legendary Orgasm Album* (Cherry Red 1994)★★★, *Smashed Blocked!* (New Millenium 1997)★★★.
●FURTHER READING: *John's Children*, Dave Thompson.

JOHNNY AND THE HURRICANES

Formed by tenor saxophonist Johnny Paris (b. 1940, Walbridge, Ohio, USA), this instrumental group went through a series of line-up changes from 1957-63. With bassist Lionel 'Butch' Mattice and drummer Tony Kaye, the group recorded the single 'Crossfire' under the name the Orbits in 1959. Under the name Johnny And The Hurricanes, they released the rivetting 'Red River Rock', which featured the trademark sound of rasping saxo-phone, combined with the swirling organ of Paul Tesluk. After enlisting new drummers Don Staczek and Little Bo Savitch along the way, the group continued the hit run in the USA and UK with such instrumentals as 'Reveille Rock', 'Beatnik Fly', 'Down Yonder', 'Rocking Goose' and 'Ja-Da'. In 1963, an entirely new group of Johnny Paris-led Hurricanes toured the UK comprising Eddie Wagenfeald (organ), Billy Marsh (guitar), Bobby Cantrall (bass) and Jay Drake (drums). By this time, however, their instrumental sound was becoming anachronistic and they were soon consumed by the beat boom, which swept the UK and USA. Various line-ups of Hurricanes continued for live performances and cabaret.

●ALBUMS: *Johnny And The Hurricanes* (Warwick 1959)★★★, *Stormsville* (1960)★★★, *Big Sound Of Johnny And The Hurricanes* (Big Top 1960)★★★, *Live At The Star Club* (Attila 1965)★★.

JOHNSON, JOHNNY, AND THE BANDWAGON

Formed in 1967 and originally known simply as the Bandwagon, this popular soul group consisted of four former solo singers who decided to pool their resources. John Johnson (b. 1945, Florida, USA), Terry Lewis (b. 1946, Baltimore, Ohio, USA), Arthur Fullilove (b. 1947, New York City, USA) and Billy Bradley (b. 1945, Rochester, New York, USA) scored a hit with their debut UK release when 'Breaking Down The Walls Of Heartache' reached number 4 in October 1968. This pulsating dance song was the quartet's biggest hit, but two years later they enjoyed further success with 'Sweet Inspiration' and 'Blame It On The Pony Express', both of which reached the UK Top 10. The group was latterly based in Britain where, unlike in America, they had been well received. Johnson assumed leadership as original members dropped out until the billing eventually read 'Johnny Johnson And His Bandwagon'. However the singer's frenetic vocal style proved inflexible and as the band's recordings grew increasingly predictable so their commercial success waned.

●ALBUMS: *Johnny Johnson And The Bandwagon* (Direction 1968)★★, *Soul Survivor* (Bell 1970)★★.

JOHNSON, MARV

b. Marvin Earl Johnson, 15 October 1938, Detroit, Michigan, USA, d. 16 May 1993, Columbia, South Carolina, USA. The gospel training which Johnson received as a teenager in the Junior Serenaders was a major influence on his early R&B releases. In 1958, he formed a partnership with the young Berry Gordy, who was then working as a songwriter and producer for Jackie Wilson. Gordy produced Johnson's earliest releases on Kudo, and launched his Tamla label with Johnson's single 'Come To Me', which became a hit when it was licensed to United Artists. Johnson remained with the label until 1965, scoring a run of chart entries in the early 60s with 'You Got What It Takes', 'I Love The Way You Move', and 'Move Two Mountains' - all produced by Gordy. Johnson's tracks showcased his delicate tenor vocals against a female gospel chorus, and he maintained this style when he signed to Gordy's Motown stable in 1965. His initial release on the Gordy Records label, the soul favourite 'I Miss You Baby', was a US hit, although it proved to be a false dawn. His subsequent US releases failed, and Johnson eventually abandoned his recording career in 1968. Ironically, the UK Tamla-Motown label chose this moment to revive Johnson's 1966 recording, 'I'll Pick A Rose For My Rose', which became an unexpected Top 20 hit amidst a dramatic revival in the label's popularity in Britain. Johnson quickly travelled to the UK to capitalize on this success, before retiring to become a sales executive at Motown. After almost two decades working behind the scenes in the music business, he returned to performing in 1987, touring with the 'Sounds Of Motown' package and re-recording his old hits for the Nightmare label. He was teamed with Carolyn Gill (of the Velvelettes) by record producer Ian Levine to release 'Ain't Nothing Like The Real Thing' in 1987. He released *Come To Me* on Levine's Motor City label.

●ALBUMS: *Marvellous Marv Johnson* (United Artists 1960)★★★, *More Marv Johnson* (United Artists 1961)★★, *I Believe* (United Artists 1966)★★, *I'll Pick A Rose For My Rose* (Motown 1969)★★, *Come To Me* (1990)★★.

●COMPILATIONS: *The Best Of Marv Johnson - You Got What It Takes* (1992)★★★, *The Very Best* (Essential Gold 1996)★★★.

JONES, JIMMY (R&B)

b. 2 June 1937, Birmingham, Alabama, USA. Jones, who had spent a long apprenticeship singing in the R&B doo-wop groups, became a rock 'n' roll star in the early 60s singing 'Handy Man' and other hits with a dramatic and piercingly high falsetto. He began his career as a tap dancer, and in 1955 joined a vocal group, the Sparks Of Rhythm. In 1956 Jones formed his own group, the Savoys, which were renamed the Pretenders in 1956. With all these groups, tracks were recorded in the prevailing doo-wop manner but with no discernable success beyond a few local radio plays in the New York/New Jersey area. Success finally came when Jones began a solo career, signing with MGM's Cub subsidiary in 1959 and hitting with his debut, 'Handy Man' (number 3 R&B/number 2 pop chart in 1960). Retaining the same falsetto style, he followed up with 'Good Timin'' (number 8 R&B/number 3 pop chart in 1960), but the decline in sales was considerable for his two other US chart entries, 'That's When I Cried' (number 83 pop chart in 1960) and 'I Told You So' (number 85 pop chart in 1961). In the UK, Jones's chart success was exceptional compared to most of his US contemporaries. In 1960 'Handy Man' reached number 3, 'Good Timin'' number 1, 'I Just Go For You' number 35, 'Ready For Love' number 46 and 'I Told You So' number 33. 'Handy Man' was revived on the charts twice, by Del Shannon in 1964 and by James Taylor in 1977.

●ALBUMS: *Good Timin'* (MGM 1960)★★★.

JONES, TOM

b. Thomas Jones Woodward, 7 June 1940, Pontypridd, Mid-Glamorgan, Wales. One of the most famous pop singers of the past three decades, Jones began his musical career in 1963 as vocalist in the group Tommy Scott And The Senators. The following year, he recorded some tracks for Joe Meek, which were initially rejected by record companies. He was then discovered by Decca A&R producer/scout Peter Sullivan and, following the recommendation of Dick Rowe, was placed in the hands of the imperious entrepreneur Phil Solomon. That relationship ended sourly, after which Scott returned to Wales. One evening, at the Top Hat Club in Merthyr Tydfil, former Viscounts vocalist Gordon Mills saw Scott's performance and was impressed. He soon signed the artist and changed his name to Tom Jones. His first single, 'Chills And Fever', failed to chart but, early in 1965, Jones' second release 'It's Not Unusual', composed by Mills and Les Reed, reached number 1 in the UK. The exuberant arrangement, reinforced by Jones's gutsy vocal and a sexy image, complete with hair ribbon, brought him instant media attention. Jones enjoyed lesser hits that year with the ballads 'Once Upon A Time' and 'With These Hands'. Meanwhile, Mills astutely insured that his star was given first choice for film theme songs, and the Burt Bacharach/Hal David composition 'What's New Pussycat?' was a major US/UK hit. By 1966, however, Jones's chart fortunes were in decline and even the title track of a James Bond movie, *Thunderball*, fell outside the UK Top 30. Before long, the former chart topper was back playing working men's clubs and his period of stardom seemed spent. Mills took drastic action by regrooming his protégé for an older market. Out went the sexy clothes in favour of a more mature, tuxedoed image. By Christmas 1966, Jones was effectively relaunched owing to the enormous success of 'Green Green Grass Of Home', which sold over a million copies in the UK alone and topped the charts for seven weeks. Jones retained the country flavour with a revival of Bobby Bare's 'Detriot City' and 'Funny Familiar Forgotten Feelings'. In the summer of 1966, he enjoyed one of his biggest UK hits with the intense 'I'll Never Fall In Love Again', which climbed to number 2. The hit run continued with the restrained 'I'm Coming Home', and the dramatic, swaggering 'Delilah', which added a sense of Victorian melodrama with its macabre line: 'I felt the knife in my hand, and she laughed no more'. In the summer of 1968, Jones again topped the *New Musical Express* charts with 'Help Yourself'.

As the 60s reached their close, Mills took his star to America where he hosted the highly successful television show, *This Is Tom Jones*. Unlike similar series, Jones' show attracted some of the best and most critically acclaimed acts of the era. An unusual feature of the show saw Jones duetting with his guests. Some of the more startling vocal workouts occurred when Jones teamed-up with David Crosby during a Crosby, Stills And Nash segment, and on another occasion with Blood, Sweat And Tears' David Clayton-Thomas. Although Jones logged a handful of hits in the UK during the early 70s, he was now an American-based performer, whose future lay in the lucrative Las Vegas circuit. Jones became enormously wealthy during his supper-club sojourn and had no reason to continue his recording career, which petered out during the 70s. It was not until after the death of Mills, when his son Mark Woodward took over his management, that the star elected to return to recording. His recording of 'The Boy From Nowhere' (from the musical *Matador*) was perceived as a personal anthem and reached number 2 in the UK. It was followed by a re-release of 'It's Not Unusual' which also reached the Top 20. In 1988, a most peculiar collaboration occurred between Jones and the Art Of Noise on an appealing kitsch version of Prince's 'Kiss'. The song reached the UK Top 5 and Jones performed the number at the London Palladium. Soon after, he appeared with a number of other Welsh entertainers on a recording of Dylan Thomas's play for voices *Under Milk Wood*, produced by George Martin. Jones's continued credibility was emphasized once more when he was invited to record some songs written by the mercurial Van Morrison. After more than a decade on the Las Vegas circuit, Jones could hardly have hoped for a more rapturous welcome in the UK, both from old artists and the new élite. He entered the digital age with a hard dance album produced by various hands including Trevor Horn, Richard Perry, Jeff Lynne and Youth. Jones clearly demonstrated that his voice felt comfortable with songs written by Lynne, the Wolfgang Press and Diane Warren.

●ALBUMS: *Along Came Jones* (Decca 1965)★★★, *A-Tom-Ic Jones* (Decca 1966)★★★★, *From The Heart* (Decca 1966)★★★, *Green, Green, Grass Of Home* (Decca 1967)★★★★, *Live At The Talk Of The Town* (Decca 1967)★★★, *Delilah* (Decca 1968)★★★, *Help Yourself* (Decca 1968)★★★★, *Tom Jones Live In Las Vegas* (Decca 1969)★★★, *This Is Tom Jones* (Decca 1969)★★★, *Tom* (1970)★★★, *I, Who Have Nothing* (1970)★★★, *Tom Jones Sings She's A Lady* (1971)★★★, *Tom Jones Live At Caeser's Palace, Las Vegas* (1971)★★★, *Close Up* (1972)★★★, *The Body And Soul Of Tom Jones* (1973)★★★, *Somethin' 'Bout You Baby I Like* (1974)★★★, *Memories Don't Leave Like People* (1975)★★★, *Say You'll Stay Until Tomorrow* (1977)★★★, *Rescue Me* (1980)★★★, *Darlin'* (1981)★★★, *Matador - The Musical Life Of El Cordorbes* (1987)★★★, *At This Moment* (1989)★★★, *After Dark* (1989)★★★, with Engelbert Humperdinck *Back To Back* (1993)★★★, *Velvet Steel Gold* (1993)★★★, *The Lead And How To Swing It* (ZTT 1994)★★★★.

●COMPILATIONS: *13 Smash Hits* (Decca 1967)★★★★, *Tom Jones: Greatest Hits* (1973)★★★★, *Tom Jones: 20 Greatest Hits* (1975)★★★★, *The World Of Tom Jones* (1975)★★★★, *Tom Jones Sings 24 Great Standards* (1976)★★★, *What A Night* (1978)★★★, *I'm Coming Home* (1978)★★★, *Super Disc Of Tom Jones* (1979)★★★, *Tom Jones Sings The Hits* (1979)★★★, *Do You Take This Man* (1979)★★★, *The Very Best Of*

Tom Jones (1980)★★★, *Rescue Me* (1980)★★★, *The Golden Hits* (1980)★★★, *16 Love Songs* (1983)★★★, *The Tom Jones Album* (1983)★★★, *The Country Side Of Tom Jones* (1985)★★★, *The Soul Of Tom Jones* (1986)★★★, *Love Songs* (1986)★★★, *The Great Love Songs* (1987)★★★, *Tom Jones - The Greatest Hits* (1987)★★★, *It's Not Unusual - His Greatest Hits* (1987)★★★★, *The Complete Tom Jones* (1993)★★★, *The Ultimate Hit Collection: 1965-1988* (Repertoire 1995)★★★, *Collection* (Spectrum 1996)★★★, *In Nashville* (Spectrum 1996)★★★.

●FURTHER READING: *Tom Jones: Biography Of A Great Star*, Tom Jones. *Tom Jones*, Stafford Hildred and David Griffen.

JOPLIN, JANIS

b. 19 January 1943, Port Arthur, Texas, USA, d. 4 October 1970. Having made her performing debut in December 1961, this expressive singer subsequently enjoyed a tenure at Houston's Purple Onion club. Drawing inspiration from Bessie Smith and Odetta, Joplin developed a brash, uncompromising vocal style quite unlike accustomed folk madonnas Joan Baez and Judy Collins. The following year she joined the Waller Creek Boys, an Austin-based act which also featured Powell St. John, later of Mother Earth. In 1963 Janis moved to San Francisco where she became a regular attraction at the North Beach Coffee Gallery. This initial spell was blighted by her addiction to amphetamines and in 1965 Joplin returned to Texas in an effort to dry out. She resumed her university studies, but on recovery turned again to singing. The following year Janis was invited back to the Bay Area to front Big Brother And The Holding Company. This exceptional improvisational blues act was the ideal foil to her full-throated technique and although marred by poor production, their debut album fully captures an early optimism.

Joplin's reputation blossomed following the Monterey Pop Festival, of which she was one of the star attractions. The attendant publicity exacerbated growing tensions within the line-up as critics openly declared that the group was holding the singer's potential in check. *Cheap Thrills*, a joyous celebration of true psychedelic soul, contained two Joplin 'standards', 'Piece Of My Heart' and 'Ball And Chain', but the sessions were fraught with difficulties and Joplin left the group in November 1968. Electric Flag members Mike Bloomfield, Harvey Brooks and Nick Gravenites helped assemble a new act, initially known as Janis And The Joplinaires, but later as the Kozmic Blues Band. Former Big Brother Sam Andrew (guitar/vocals), plus Terry Clements (saxophone), Marcus Doubleday (trumpet), Bill King (organ), Brad Campbell (bass) and Roy Markowitz (drums) made up the band's initial line-up which was then bedeviled by defections. A disastrous debut concert at the Stax/Volt convention in December 1968 was a portent of future problems, but although *I Got Dem Ol' Kozmic Blues Again Mama* was coolly received, the set nonetheless contained several excellent Joplin vocals, notably 'Try',

'Maybe' and 'Little Girl Blue'. However, live shows grew increasingly erratic as her addiction to drugs and alcohol deepened. When a restructured Kozmic Blues Band, also referred to as the Main Squeeze, proved equally uncomfortable, the singer dissolved the band altogether, and undertook medical advice. A slimmed-down group, the Full Tilt Boogie Band, was unveiled in May 1970. Brad Campbell and latecomer John Till (guitar) were retained from the previous group, while the induction of Richard Bell (piano), Ken Pearson (organ) and Clark Pierson (drums) created a tighter, more intimate sound. In July they toured Canada with the Grateful Dead, before commencing work on a 'debut' album. The sessions were all but complete when, on 4 October 1970, Joplin died of a heroin overdose at her Hollywood hotel.

The posthumous *Pearl* was thus charged with poignancy, yet it remains her most consistent work. Her love of 'uptown soul' is confirmed by the inclusion of three Jerry Ragovoy compositions 'My Baby', 'Cry Baby' and the suddenly anthemic 'Get It While You Can' - while 'Trust Me' and 'A Woman Left Lonely' show an empathy with its southern counterpart. The highlight, however, is Kris Kristofferson's 'Me And Bobby McGee', which allowed Janis to be both vulnerable and assertive. The song deservedly topped the US chart when issued as a single and despite numerous interpretations, this remains the definitive version. Although a star at the time of her passing, Janis Joplin has not been accorded the retrospective acclaim afforded other deceased contemporaries. Her impassioned approach was her attraction - Joplin knew few boundaries, artistic or personal - and her brief catalogue is marked by bare-nerved honesty.

●ALBUMS: *I Got Dem Ol' Kozmic Blues Again Mama!* (Columbia 1969)★★★, *Pearl* (Columbia 1971)★★★, *Janis Joplin In Concert* (Columbia 1972)★★★.

●COMPILATIONS: *Greatest Hits* (Columbia 1973)★★★★, *Janis* film soundtrack including live and rare recordings (1975)★★★, *Anthology* (1980)★★★, *Farewell Song* (1981)★★★, *Janis* 3-CD box-set (Legacy 1995)★★★★, *18 Essential Songs* (Columbia 1995)★★★.

●FURTHER READING: *Janis Joplin: Her Life And Times*, Deborah Landau. *Going Down With Janis*, Peggy Caserta as told to Dan Knapp. *Janis Joplin: Buried Alive*, Myra Friedman. *Janis Joplin: Piece Of My Heart*, David Dalton. *Love, Janis*, Laura Joplin. *Pearl: The Obsessions And Passions Of Janis Joplin*, Ellis Amburn.

●FILMS: *American Pop* (1981).

JOURNEYMEN

This US folk trio comprising Scott McKenzie (guitar/vocals), Dick Weissman (b. Richard Weissman; banjo/guitar/vocals), and John Phillips (b. John Edmund Andrew Phillips, 30 August 1935, Parris Island, South Carolina, USA; guitar/vocals). The group were formed, like many others at the time, as a result of the folk revival of the late 50s and 60s, and featured strong harmonies and a commercial sound that made folk such a saleable commodity at the time. The Journeymen made their debut in 1961 at Gerde's Folk City, New York, and shortly afterwards signed to Capitol Records, releasing *The Journeymen* later the same year. The group's popularity, and commerciality, waned after a relatively short life span, and the members went their separate ways. John attempted to revive the trio's fortunes with the New Journeymen, which featured his wife Michelle Phillips and Marshall Brickman. Phillips went on to form the Mamas And The Papas, while McKenzie found fame as the singer of the hit song 'San Francisco'. Weissman continued in the music business, recording *The Things That Trouble My Mind* and *Dick Weissman Sings And Plays Songs Of Protest*.

●ALBUMS: *The Journeymen* (Capitol 1961)★★★, *Coming Attraction-Live* (Capitol 1962)★★★, *New Directions* (Capitol 1963)★★★.

JUKE BOX JURY

Perhaps the least progressive of all pop television programmes of the 60s, BBC Television's *Juke Box Jury* followed a rigid presentational format where four panellists (typically a disc jockey, a celebrity and two musical or theatrical artists) passed verdicts on current releases. Chaired by presenter David Jacobs, they would be encouraged to predict whether the records played would enter the UK Top 20 ('hit') or not ('miss'). Part of the show's problem lay in this formula - its main substance was the panellists' judgement of an item's musical and artistic worth, yet they were forced to vote on entirely different criteria (whether it would be successful as a chart record). Each record was played for only 30 seconds or so before opinions were declared, and even then chairman Jacobs soothed the discourse - extreme negative reactions, for instance, were frowned upon. Richard Mabey caricatured the show's vapidity in his book, *The Pop Process*: 'The comedian made a joke about the title, the disc jockey explained how he had lunch with the recording manager, and the starlet said how lovely it would be "after the party's over, and you're left alone with someone special".' It was not an ideal programme, then, to document the rise of pop music in the 60s, although it did serve the purpose of informing the public about new releases and forming a body of critical opinion - however spurious - about them. The format was revived in the 70s to limited success, with some of its conventions relaxed. Guests even included John Lydon of PiL, a panellist guaranteed to mock and sneer his way through any recording that was not his own. In the 90s it was revived for a third time, and presented by Jools Holland, but again found limited audience approval. Regardless of the presence of *Juke Boy Jury*, the space for a critical programme on popular music in the UK remains open.

JUSTICE, JIMMY

b. 1940, Carlshalton, Surrey, England. Justice signed to Pye in 1960, owing partly to fellow stable-mate singer, Emile Ford, who had spotted Jimmy singing in a coffee-bar. When Justice's first two releases failed in the UK, he

relocated to Sweden where his cover of the Jarmels' 'Little Lonely One' charted. In 1962 with the help of producer Tony Hatch, he strung together three UK Top 20 hits: the remarkably fresh cover of the Drifters US hit 'When My Little Girl Is Smiling', 'Ain't That Funny' - an original song penned by Johnny Worth - and 'Spanish Harlem'. Jimmy spent 1962 commuting between England and Sweden (where he had many previous bookings to honour) but managed, together with his group the Exchequers, to join a Larry Parnes UK tour headed by Billy Fury and Joe Brown. This white singer who possessed a mature, soulful voice, was sometimes called 'Britain's Ben E. King', and caused some controversy when he covered King's 'Spanish Harlem' with an uncannily similar vocal style. Justice also recorded for Decca in 1969, RCA in 1968 and B&C in 1972.
●ALBUMS: *Two Sides Of Jimmy Justice* (Pye 1962)★★★, *Smash Hits* (Pye 1962)★★★, *Justice For All* (Kapp 1964)★★★.

JUSTIS, BILL

b. 14 October 1927, Birmingham, Alabama, USA, d. 15 July 1982. Justis was a saxophonist, arranger and producer who created 'Raunchy', one of the classic rock 'n' roll instrumentals (and, coincidentally, the first song that George Harrison learned to play). He grew up in Memphis playing jazz and dance band music before joining Sam Phillips' Sun label in 1957 as musical director. Phillips liked a tune called 'Backwoods', composed by Justis and guitarist Sid Manker, but renamed it 'Raunchy'. It was issued as a single and Justis' own honking saxophone solo made it a million-seller. Cover versions by Billy Vaughn and Ernie Freeman also sold well, while there were later recordings by the Shadows and Duane Eddy. Later singles such as 'College Man' and 'Flea Circus' (written by Steve Cropper) were unsuccessful and Justis concentrated on his arrangements for Sun artists. His most important A&R work was with Charlie Rich, whom he discovered singing ballads. Urging him to listen to Jerry Lee Lewis, Justis produced Rich's biggest rock era hit, 'Lonely Weekends', in 1960 and also co-wrote the answer record 'After The Hop' for Bill Pinky And The Turks. Leaving Sun, Justis recorded rockabilly artist Ray Smith for Sam's brother Judd Phillips and briefly ran his own label (Play Me) before working again with Rich at RCA. By 1963 he was with Monument, another significant southern record company, where he produced hits by vocal group the Dixiebelles. Kenny Rogers was among those for whom he later wrote arrangements. Justis occasionally also made his own instrumental albums. He died in July 1982.
●ALBUMS: *Cloud Nine* (Philips 1958)★★★, *Enchanted Sea* (1972)★★.

K-DOE, ERNIE

b. Ernest Kador Jnr., 22 February 1936, New Orleans, Louisiana, USA. Previously a singer with touring gospel groups, K-Doe's earliest non-secular recordings were made in the mid-50s as a member of the Blue Diamonds. His first solo record, 'Do Baby Do', was released on Specialty in 1956. The singer's biggest hit came with the Allen Toussaint song, 'Mother-In-Law' (1961) which reached number 1 in the US pop charts. This pointed 'novelty' song was followed by 'Te-Ta-Te-Ta-Ta', and a strong double-sided release, 'I Have Cried My Last Tear'/'A Certain Girl'. The latter track proved popular in Britain where it was covered by the Yardbirds and the Paramounts. Further K-Doe singles included 'Popeye Joe' and 'I'm The Boss', but it was not until 1967 that he returned to the R&B chart with two singles for the Duke label, 'Later For Tomorrow' and 'Until The Real Thing Comes Along'. He remains a popular, energetic performer and occasional recording artist in New Orleans.
●ALBUMS: *Mother-In-Law* (Minit 1961)★★★★.
●COMPILATIONS: *Burn, K-Doe, Burn!* (1989)★★★★.

KAEMPFERT, BERT

b. Berthold Kaempfert, 16 October 1923, Hamburg, Germany, d. 21 June 1980, Majorca, Spain. A conductor, arranger, composer, multi-instrumentalist and record producer. Kaempfert played the piano as a child, and later studied at the Hamburg Conservatory of Music. By the time he joined Hans Bussch and his Orchestra during World War II, he was capable of playing a variety of instruments, including the piano, piano-accordion and all the reeds. After the war he formed his own band, and became a big draw in West Germany before joining Polydor Records as a producer, arranger and musical director. In the latter role he had some success with the Yugoslavian Ivor Robic's version of 'Morgen', which made the US Top 20 in 1959, and Freddie Quinn's 'Die Gitarre Und Das Meer'. A year later he made his own global breakthrough when he topped the US charts with his studio orchestra's recording of 'Wonderland By Night'. It was the precursor to a series of similar recordings in which a solo trumpet (usually Fred Moch) and muted brass were set against a cushion of lush strings and wordless choral effects, all emphasized by the insistent rhythm of a two-beat bass guitar. This treatment was effectively applied by Kaempfert to several of his own compositions, which were also successful for other artists, such as 'Spanish Eyes (Moon Over Naples)' (Al Martino), 'Danke Schoen' (Wayne Newton), 'L-O-V-E' (Nat

'King' Cole), 'A Swinging Safari' (Billy Vaughn), and 'Wooden Heart', which Elvis Presley sang in his film, *G.I. Blues*, and Joe Dowell took to the US number 1 spot in 1961. Two other Kaempfert numbers, 'The World We Knew' (Over And Over)' and 'Strangers In The Night' benefited from the Frank Sinatra treatment. The latter song, part of Kaempfert's score for the James Garner/Melina Mercouri comedy/thriller, *A Man Could Get Killed*, topped the US and UK charts in 1966. Lyrics for his most successful songs were written by Charles Singleton, Eddie Snyder, Carl Sigman, Kurt Schwabach, Milt Gabler, Fred Wise, Ben Weisman and Kay Twomey. Kaempfert himself had easy listening worldwide hits in his own inimitable style with revivals of 'golden oldies' such as 'Tenderly', Red Roses For A Blue Lady', 'Three O'Clock In The Morning' and 'Bye Bye Blues'. In 1961, *Wonderland By Night* spent five weeks at number 1 in the US, and Kaempfert continued to chart in the US and UK throughout the 60s, but his records failed to achieve Top 40 status in the 70s, although he still sold a great many, and continued to tour. Apart from his skill as an arranger and orchestra leader, Bert Kaempfert has another claim to fame in the history of popular music - he was the first person to record the Beatles. While they were playing a club in Hamburg in 1961, Kaempfert hired them to back Tony Sheridan, a singer who had a large following in Germany. After supplying the additional vocals on 'My Bonnie Lies Over The Ocean' and 'When The Saints Go Marching In', Kaempfert allowed Lennon & Co. to record 'Ain't She Sweet' and 'Cry For A Shadow'. 'My Bonnie', as it was then called, made the US Top 30 in 1964, and 'Ain't She Sweet' became a minor hit in the UK. By the end of the decade the Beatles had broken up, and Kaempfert's best days were behind him, too. In 1980, after completing a successful series of concerts in the UK, culminating in an appearance at the Royal Albert Hall, he was taken ill and died while on holiday in Majorca. The 'New Bert Kaempfert Orchestra' was advertising its availability in UK trade papers in the early 90s.

●ALBUMS: *Wonderland* (1960)★★★, *Wonderland By Night* (1960)★★★, *That Happy Feeling* (1962)★★★, *With A Sound In My Heart* (1962)★★★, *That Latin Feeling* (1963)★★★, *Lights Out, Sweet Dreams* (1963)★★★, *Living It Up* (1963)★★★, *Afrikaan Beat* (1964)★★★, *Blue Midnight* (1965)★★★, *3 O'Clock In The Morning* (1965)★★★, *The Magic Music Of Far Away Places* (1965)★★★, *Strangers In The Night* (1966)★★★, *Bye Bye Blues* (1966)★★★, *A Swinging Safari* (1966)★★★, *Relaxing Sound Of Bert Kaempfert* (1966)★★★, *Bert Kaempfert - Best Seller* (1967)★★★, *Hold Me* (1967)★★★, *The World We Knew* (1967)★★★, *Kaempfert Special* (1967)★★★, *Orange Coloured Sky* (1971)★★★, *A Drop Of Christmas Spirit* (1974)★★★, *Everybody Loves Somebody* (1976)★★★, *Swing* (1978)★★★, *Tropical Sunrise* (1978)★★★, *Sounds Sensational* (1980)★★★, *Springtime* (1981)★★★, *Moods* (1982)★★★, *Now And Forever* (1983)★★★, *Famous Swing Classics* (1984)★★★, *Live In London* (1985)★★★.

KALEIDOSCOPE (UK)

Psychedelic pop band Kaleidoscope were formed in west London, England, in 1964 as the Side Kicks. Comprising Eddie Pumer (guitar), Peter Daltrey (vocals/keyboards), Dan Bridgeman (percussion) and Steve Clarke (bass), they initially worked as an R&B cover band. After changing names to the Key, they switched tempo and style and became Kaleidoscope, and were signed to Fontana Records following the intervention of music publisher Dick Leahy, who became their producer. Their debut single, September 1967's 'Flight From Ashiya', adopted the in-vogue hippy ethos and terminology. Although it failed to chart the subsequent album, *Tangerine Dream*, became a cult success, a position it sustains to this day among fans of 60s psychedelic rock (with a rarity value in excess of £100). Despite a strong underground following, this proved insufficient to launch subsequent singles 'A Dream For Julie' or 'Jenny Artichoke', nor second album *Faintly Blowing*, into the charts. Two further singles, 'Do It Again For Jeffrey' and 'Balloon' in 1969 were issued, but a projected third album was 'lost' when Fontana dropped the band. It was eventually issued in 1991 on the group's own self-titled label. By 1970 the group had transmuted into progressive rock band Fairfield Parlour, whose most vociferous fan was the late UK disc jockey Kenny Everett.

●ALBUMS: *Tangerine Dream* (Fontana 1967)★★★, *Faintly Blowing* (Fontana 1969)★★, *White-Faced Lady* (Kaleidoscope 1991)★★.

●COMPILATIONS: *Dive Into Yesterday* (Fontana 1997)★★.

KALEIDOSCOPE (USA)

Formed in 1966, this innovative group owed its origins to California's jugband and bluegrass milieu. Guitarists David Lindley and Chris Darrow were both former members of the Dry City Scat Band, while Solomon Feldthouse (vocals/oud/caz) had performed in the region's folk clubs. John Vidican (drums) and Charles Chester Crill - aka Connie Crill, Max Buda, Fenrus Epp or Templeton Parceley (violin/organ/harmonica/vocals) - completed the line-up which, having flirted with the name Bagdhad Blues Band, then settled on Kaleidoscope. *Side Trips* revealed a group of enthralling imagination, offering a music drawn from the individual members' disparate interests. Blues, jazz, folk and ethnic styles abounded as the quintet forged a fascinating collection, but although the album was comprised of short songs, Kaleidoscope's reputation as a superior live attraction was based on lengthy improvised pieces. The group tried to address this contrast with *A Beacon From Mars*, which contrasted six concise performances with two extended compositions, the neo-Eastern 'Taxim' and the feedback-laden title track. The album marked the end of this particular line-up as Darrow then opted to join the Nitty Gritty Dirt Band. Vidican also left the group, and thus newcomers Stuart Brotman (bass) and Paul Lagos (drums) were featured on *Incredible Kaleidoscope*, which in turn offered a tougher, less acid-folk perspective. There were, nonetheless, several highlights, including the expanded 'Seven Ate Sweet' and propulsive 'Lie To Me', but the album was not a commercial success, despite the publicity generated by the group's sensational appearance at the 1968 Newport Folk Festival. Further changes in the line-up ensued with the departure of Brotman, who was fired during sessions for a prospective fourth album. His replacement, Ron Johnson, introduced a funk-influenced element to the unit's sound, while a second newcomer, Jeff Kaplan, surprisingly took most of the lead vocals. Kaleidoscope's muse sadly failed to accommodate these changes, and *Bernice* was a marked disappointment. The late-period group did complete two excellent songs for the film soundtrack of *Zabriskie Point*, but the departures of Feldthouse and Crill in 1970 signalled their demise. Despite the addition of Richard Aplan to the line-up, Kaleidoscope dissolved later in the year in the wake of Kaplan's death from a drugs overdose. David Lindley subsequently embarked on a career as a session musician and solo artist, a path Chris Darrow also followed, albeit with less commercial success. The latter subsequently joined Feldthouse, Brotman, Lagos and Crill in the re-formed unit completing *When Scopes Collide* which, although lacking the innovation of old, was nonetheless entertaining. The same line-up reconvened to complete the equally meritorious *Greetings From Kartoonistan ... (We Ain't Dead Yet)*. Such sets simply enhanced the Kaleidoscope legend, which was considerably buoyed by a series of excellent compilations. They remain one of the era's most innovative acts.

●ALBUMS: *Side Trips* (Epic 1967)★★★, *A Beacon From Mars* (Epic 1968)★★★, *Incredible Kaleidoscope* (Epic 1969)★★★, *Bernice* (Epic 1970)★★, *When Scopes Collide* (Island 1976)★★★★★, *Greetings From Kartoonistna ... (We Ain't Dead Yet)* (Curb 1991)★★★.
●COMPILATIONS: *Bacon From Mars* (1983)★★★, *Rampe Rampe* (Edsel 1984)★★★, *Egyptian Candy* (Legacy 1990)★★★, *Blues From Bhagdad - The Very Best Of* (1993)★★★.

KALIN TWINS

A classic example of the one-hit-wonder syndrome, the Kalin Twins have a more interesting history than many who fall into that bracket. Herbie and Harold 'Hal' Kalin, who are twins, were born on 16 February 1934 in Port Jervis, New York State, USA (many references give their birth date as 1939 but this was a Decca Records diversion, in an attempt to make them appear younger than they in fact were). Their first public performances came at just five years of age at a local Christmas party, and the bug stayed with them. They graduated from Port Jervis High School in June 1952, but plans to break into the music industry were delayed when Hal was drafted into the Air Force as a radio operator. They kept in touch during this period, recording and writing songs on a tape recorder and sending them back and forth. After Hal's discharge in 1956 they set about resurrecting their double act. During these early struggles a demo single was pressed, combining the compositions 'Beggar Of Love' and 'The Spider And The Fly'. The result was an audition for Decca, and their first single proper, 'Jumpin' Jack'/'Walkin' To School'. While searching through piles of writers' demo tapes to find a suitable follow-up the twins discovered a song entitled 'When', written by Paul Evans and Jack Reardon. It became their second single. However, the record company chose to plug its flip side, 'Three O'Clock Thrill', instead. It was not until disc jockeys belatedly began to play 'When' that the single took off. It reached number 5 in the *Billboard* charts but topped the UK charts for no less than five weeks (selling over two million copies worldwide). Coast to coast touring of the US ensued before a two week engagement at the Prince Of Wales Theatre in England (later dates introduced Cliff Richard as support artist on his first national tour). The subsequent 'Forget Me Not' and 'Oh My Goodness!' both made reasonable showings in the *Billboard* charts, but neither entered the UK equivalent. Two more minor US hits followed, 'Cool' and 'Sweet Sugarlips', but their remaining Decca sides failed to sell. With the arrival of the Beatles there seemed little place in the market for the Kalin Twins' innocent harmonies, although a further single, 'Sometimes It Comes, Sometimes It Goes' for Amy Records, did appear in 1966. Disillusioned with their diminishing rewards, the brothers mutually agreed to return to their day jobs, with each pursuing college degrees. They did not perform again until 1977 when a friend booked them to appear weekly at his new night spot, the River Boat Club. This led to further one-off engagements, in which they were sometimes joined by younger sibling Jack to appear as the Kalin Brothers. A brace of singles appeared for small labels: 'Silver Seagull' and 'American Eagle' both used the same backing track. A 16-track compilation was released by Bear Family Records in 1983. They disappeared again until old support hand Cliff Richard invited them to play at his 30th Anniversary shows in 1989.

●ALBUMS: *The Kalin Twins* (Decca 1958)★★★, *When* (Vocalion 1966)★★★.
●COMPILATIONS: *When* (Bear Family 1983)★★★.

KAMA SUTRA RECORDS

This innovative record label was launched in New York in 1965 as an extension of Kama Sutra Productions, a publishing/production company headed by Artie Ripp and the Koppelman/Rubin team. The latter pair managed the Lovin' Spoonful who gave Kama Sutra a Top 10 hit with their first release, 'Do You Believe In Magic'. The group became the label's greatest asset, achieving international success with 'Daydream', 'Summer In The City' and 'Nashville Cats'. Although initially issued under the Pye International imprint, Kama Sutra established a UK division with the second of these singles. The Spoonful's melodic blend of folk, blues and pop; dubbed 'good-time music', was heard in several of the company's subsequent releases, notably 'Hello Hello' by Sopwith Camel and 'There's Got To Be A Word' by the Innocence. The latter act revolved around the songwriting/production team of Pete Anders and Vinnie Poncia. They also recorded for

Kama Sutra as the Tradewinds and were heavily involved in releases by the Goodtimes, Vincent Edwards and Bobby Bloom.

Kama Sutra productions enjoyed success with the lyrical Critters, who recorded for Kapp. However, despite embracing the west coast-sound with *Safe As Milk* by Captain Beefheart And The Magic Band, the label's star began to wane as the decade progressed. The demise of the Lovin' Spoonful, coupled with the decampment of Anders, Poncia and Bloom, undermined Kama Sutra considerably. In 1970 it sundered its US deal with MGM Records to become a subsidiary of Neil Bogert's Buddah Records. In 1972 the Canadian group Ocean reached number 2 in the US charts with 'Put Your Hand In The Hand', and followed with three further hits in 1973. Although enjoying success with Stories, Brewer And Shipley, Sha Na Na and Charlie Daniels, Kama Sutra was no longer the creative force it had been as an independent concern.

●COMPILATIONS: *Mynd Excursions* (Sequel 1992)★★★.

KANE, EDEN

b. Richard Sarstedt, 29 March 1942, Delhi, India. When his family returned to England from India during the mid-50s, Kane formed a skiffle group with his brothers. In 1960, he won a talent contest and came under the wing of managers Michael Barclay and Philip Waddilove. They changed his name to Eden Kane, inspired by the movie *Citizen Kane* and the biblical name Cain. Promoted by the chocolate firm, Cadbury's, Kane's first single was 'Hot Chocolate Crazy'. For the follow-up, Kane recorded the catchy, colloquial 'Well I Ask You', which took him to number 1 in the UK during the summer of 1961. Over the next year, three more Top 10 hits followed: 'Get Lost', 'Forget Me Not' and 'I Don't Know Why'. Kane's career suffered a serious setback early in 1963 when Barclay and Waddilove's company Audio Enterprises went into liquidation. The star's management was passed on to Vic Billings, who persuaded Fontana's influential A&R manager Jack Baverstock to sign him. In early 1964, Kane returned to the UK Top 10 with 'Boys Cry', which also proved a major hit in Australia. In the autumn of that year, Kane made the momentous decision to emigrate to Australia, later relocating to the USA. Although his chart days were over, his younger brothers Peter Sarstedt and Robin Sarstedt both enjoyed hits in their own right. The brothers combined their talents in 1973 for the album, *Worlds Apart Together*. Thereafter, Kane continued to play regularly on the revivalist circuit.

●ALBUMS: *Eden Kane* (Ace Of Clubs 1962)★★, *It's Eden* (Fontana 1964, reissued as *Smoke Gets In Your Eyes* in 1965)★★, with the Sarstedt brothers *Worlds Apart Together* (1973)★★.

KASENETZ-KATZ SINGING ORCHESTRAL CIRCUS

The brainchild of bubblegum pop producers, Jerry Kasenetz and Jeff Katz, the Singing Orchestral Circus was a sprawling aggregation of eight groups on one record: the Ohio Express, the 1910 Fruitgum Company, Music Explosion, Lt. Garcia's Magic Music Box, Teri Nelson Group, Musical Marching Zoo, JCW Rat Finks and the St. Louis Invisible Marching Band. Together, they were responsible for one of bubblegum's more memorable moments with the international hit, 'Quick Joey Small' in 1968. With an attendant array of acrobats, clowns, fire-eaters and scantily-clad girls, the circus played a concert at Carnegie Hall with a repertoire which included such hits as 'Yesterday', 'We Can Work It Out', 'Hey Joe' and 'You've Lost That Lovin' Feelin''. The prestige of this event did not prevent them from taking their place as one-hit-wonders.

KASSNER, EDDIE

b. 1920, Vienna, Austria, d. 19 November 1996, London, England. An 'old school' music publisher, Kassner fled from his native Austria as a child to seek refuge from Nazi expansion. He served in the British Army during World War II, before founding the Edward Kassner Music Co. in the 50s. The catalogue of songs he established provided material for Frank Sinatra, Perry Como, Dinah Shore, Nat 'King' Cole and Vera Lynn, among others. In 1951 he opened a branch in New York's Brill Building, from where his catalogue-acquisition efforts expanded. The group's financial stability was assured by a single song in the mid-50s, 'Rock Around The Clock', acquired for an advance of $250. Other major earners included 'Bobby's Girl' (Susan Maughan), 'The White Rose Of Athens' (Nana Mouskouri) and 'I Feel So Bad' (Elvis Presley). However, by the mid-60s, Kessner had become well aware of the trend towards groups and artists writing their own compositions. As a consequence he established President Records in 1966, releasing hits by the Equals, Symbols and KC And The Sunshine Band. He also signed the Kinks to a management deal and began a highly successful 12-year association with Rick Wakeman.

KAYE, CAROL

b. Carol Everett, 1935, Washington, USA. Bass guitarist Kaye was one of the few women musicians, as opposed to vocalists, prospering in the enclosed Los Angeles session fraternity. During the 60s she joined, among others, Glen Campbell, Tommy Tedesco, Billy Strange (guitars) and Larry Knechtal (piano) as a member of a group affectionately known as Hal Blaine's Wrecking Crew. Kaye contributed to innumerable recordings, the most notable of which were with Phil Spector protégés the Crystals, the Ronettes and Darlene Love. Her bass work also appeared on many west coast Tamla/Motown sessions and, by contrast, *Freak Out*, the first album by the Mothers Of Invention. Her affinity with soul/blues-influenced artists was exemplified in appearances on Joe Cocker's *With A Little Help From My Friends* (1969) and Robert Palmer's *Some People Can Do What They Like* (1976). Classical-styled sessions for David Axelrod contrasted singer-song-writer work with Dory Previn and exemplified the versatility of this talented and prolific musician. Those milestone singles that Kaye claims to have played on (some dispute that James Jamerson was on the final mix) are: 'River Deep Mountain High' (Ike And Tina Turner), 'Theme From Shaft' (Isaac Hayes), 'Get Ready' (Temptations), 'Reach Out I'll Be There' (Four Tops), 'I Was Made To Love Her' (Stevie Wonder), 'Everybody's Talkin'' (Nilsson), 'Homeward Bound' (Simon And Garfunkel), 'Good Vibrations' (Beach Boys), 'It's My Party' (Lesley Gore), 'Light My Fire' (Doors), 'You Can't Hurry Love' (Supremes) and 'Young Girl' by (Gary Puckett).

KEITH

b. James Barry Keefer, 7 May 1949, Philadelphia, Pennsylvania, USA. Keith was best known for his Top 10 folk rock single '98.6' in January 1967. Keefer started with a band called the Admirations in the early 60s, recording one single for Columbia Records, 'Caravan Of Lonely Men'. He was then discovered by journalist Kal Rudman, who took Keefer to Mercury Records executive Jerry Ross. Signed to that label, and renamed Keith, he recorded his first solo single, 'Ain't Gonna Lie', which narrowly made the US Top 40. '98.6' followed and was his biggest hit, although Keith charted twice in 1967 with lesser hits, 'Tell Me To My Face' and 'Daylight Savin' Time'. He recorded a few more singles for Mercury and two albums, only the first of which made the charts. After spending time in the armed forces, he returned to a changed musical direction, recording a single, 'In And Out Of Love', for Frank Zappa's Discreet label, and singing briefly with Zappa's band (he did not record with them). Keefer recorded one last album, for RCA Records, with no luck, and then left the music business until 1986, when an attempted comeback under his real name proved unsuccessful.
●ALBUMS: *98.6/Ain't Gonna Lie* (Mercury 1967)★★, *Out Of Crank* (1968), *The Adventures Of Keith* (1969).

KELLER, JERRY

b. 20 June 1938, Fort Smith, Arkansas, USA. After moving to Tulsa in 1944 Keller formed the Lads Of Note Quartet in the 50s before joining the Tulsa Boy Singers. He won a talent contest organized by bandleader Horace Heidt which earned him the vocalist job with Jack Dalton's Orchestra. He then spent nine months as a disc jockey in Tulsa before moving to New York in 1956. He recorded a series of demos for record companies before fellow performer Pat Boone introduced him to Marty Mills who became his manager. Keller recorded the self-penned 'Here Comes Summer' for the Kapp record label, and it became a US summer hit in 1959. Ironically it only entered the UK charts in late August as the warmer months lapsed into autumn, but it still went to number 1. Follow-ups such as 'If I Had A Girl', and 'Now Now Now' failed to repeat the success. In 1960, he toured the UK replacing Eddie Cochran in a package tour engagement after Cochran had died in a car crash. Despite the lack of subsequent hits as a singer, his songs charted handsomely for artists such as Andy Williams and the Cyrkle. In 1977, he appeared in the film *You Light Up My Life*

and the following year in *If I Ever See You Again*.
●ALBUMS: *Here Comes Jerry Keller* (Kapp 1960).

KELLY, WYNTON

b. 2 December 1931, Jamaica, West Indies, d. 12 April 1971. Raised in New York, Kelly first played piano professionally with various R&B bands, where his musical associates included Eddie 'Lockjaw' Davis. In the early 50s, he played with Dizzy Gillespie, Dinah Washington and Lester Young. In 1954, after military service, he rejoined both Gillespie and Washington for brief stints and later played with many important contemporary musicians, notably Charles Mingus and Miles Davis, with whom he worked from 1959-63. Kelly also led his own trio, using the bass (Paul Chambers) and drums (Jimmy Cobb) from Davis' band, and also recorded successfully with a variety of artists such as Wes Montgomery, Freddie Hubbard and George Coleman. A subtle and inventive player, Kelly's style was individual even if his work denotes his awareness both of his contemporaries and the piano masters of an earlier generation. Throughout his records there is a constant sense of freshness and an expanding maturity of talent, which made his death, in April 1971, following an epileptic fit, all the more tragic.
●ALBUMS: *New Faces, New Sounds* (1951)★★★, *Piano Interpretations By Wynton Kelly* (Blue Note 1951)★★★, *The Big Band Sound Of Dizzy Gillespie* (1957)★★★, *Wynton Kelly Piano* (Riverside 1957)★★★, *Wynton Kelly i* (1958)★★★, *Autumn Leaves* (1959)★★★, *Kelly Blue* (Riverside 1959)★★★★★, *Kelly Great!* (Vee Jay 1959)★★★, *Kelly At Midnight* (Vee Jay 1960)★★★, *Wynton Kelly ii* (Vee Jay 1961)★★★, with Miles Davis *Some Day My Prince Will Come* (Columbia 1961)★★★★, *Miles Davis At Carnegie Hall* (1961)★★★★, *The Wynton Kelly Trio With Claus Ogermann And His Orchestra i* (1963)★★★, *The Wynton Kelly Trio With Claus Ogermann And His Orchestra ii* (1964)★★★, *Comin' In The Back Door* (Verve 1964)★★★, *It's All Right* (Verve 1964)★★★, *Undiluted* (Verve 1965)★★★, with Wes Montgomery *Smokin' At The Half Note* (Verve 1965)★★★, *Blues On Purpose* (Xanadu 1965)★★★, *Wynton Kelly And Wes Montgomery* (1965)★★★, *Full View* (1967)★★★, *Wynton Kelly And George Coleman In Concert* (1968)★★★, *In Concert* (Affinity 1981)★★★, *Live In Baltimore* (Affinity 1984)★★★, *Wrinkles* (Affinity 1986)★★★, *Last Trio Session* (Delmark 1988)★★★, *Takin' Charge* (Le Jazz 1993)★★★.

KENNER, CHRIS

b. 25 December 1929, Kenner, Louisiana, USA, d. 25 January 1977. This New Orleans-based artist had a US Top 20 R&B hit in 1957 on the Imperial label with his own composition, 'Sick And Tired', a song later revived by Fats Domino. Kenner was one of the first signings to the Instant label on which he recorded his three best-known songs. In 1961, a song co-written with Fats Domino, 'I Like It Like That, Part 1', reached number 2 in the US pop charts. Kenner later received a Grammy nomination for the song. This was followed by 'Something You Got' and 'Land Of A 1,000 Dances' (1963). The latter, based on a gospel song, 'Children Go Where I Send You', later became a hit for Cannibal And The Headhunters (1965) and Wilson Pickett (1966 - US Top 10/UK Top 30). Although Kenner was beset throughout much of his career by alcohol problems, a prison sentence in 1968 for statutory rape of a minor, and to a lesser degree, a reputation as a poor live performer, he recorded some of the best R&B to emanate from the Crescent City. He died of a heart attack in January 1977.

●ALBUMS: *Land Of 1,000 Dances* (Atlantic 1966)★★★.
●COMPILATIONS: *I Like It Like That* (1987)★★★.
●FILMS: *Be My Guest* (1965).

KIDD, JOHNNY, AND THE PIRATES

Kidd (b. Frederick Heath, 23 December 1939, Willesden, London, England, d. 7 October 1966), is now rightly revered as an influential figure in the birth of British rock. Although his backing group fluctuated, this enigmatic figure presided over several seminal pre-Beatles releases. Formed in January 1959, the original line-up consisted of two former members of the Five Nutters skiffle group, Kidd (lead vocals) and Alan Caddy (b. 2 February 1940, London, England; lead guitar), joined by Tony Docherty (rhythm guitar), Johnny Gordon (bass) and Ken McKay (drums), plus backing singers Mike West and Tom Brown. Their compulsive debut single, 'Please Don't Touch' barely scraped into the UK Top 20, but it remains one of the few authentic home-grown rock 'n' roll performances to emerge from the 50s. Its immediate successors were less original and although they featured session men, most of Kidd's group were then dropped in favour of experienced hands.

By 1960, Kidd and Caddy were fronting a new rhythm section consisting of Brian Gregg (bass) and Clem Cattini (drums). Their first single, 'Shakin' All Over', was another remarkable achievement, marked by its radical stop/start tempo, Kidd's feverish delivery and an incisive lead guitar solo from session man Joe Moretti. The song deservedly topped the charts, but its inspiration to other musicians was equally vital. Defections resulted in the formation of a third line-up - Kidd, Johnny Spence (bass), Frank Farley (drums) and Johnny Patto (guitar) - although the last was replaced by Mick Green. Onstage, the group continued to wear full pirate regalia while the singer sported a distinctive eye-patch, but they were under increasing competition from the emergent Liverpool sound. Two 1963 hits, 'I'll Never Get Over You' and 'Hungry For Love', although memorable, owed a substantial debt to Merseybeat at the expense of the unit's own identity. The following year, Green left to join the Dakotas, precipitating a succession of replacements, and although he continued to record, a depressed leader talked openly of retirement. However, the singer re-emerged in 1966, fronting the New Pirates, but Kidd's

renewed optimism ended in tragedy when, on 7 October, he was killed in a car crash. This pivotal figure is remembered both as an innovator and for the many musicians who passed through his ranks. John Weider (the Animals and Family), Nick Simper (Deep Purple) and Jon Morshead (Aynsley Dunbar Retaliation) are a few of those who donned the requisite costume, while the best-known line-up, Green, Spence and Farley, successfully re-established the Pirates' name during the late 70s.

●COMPILATIONS: *Shakin' All Over* (Regal Starline 1971)★★★, *Johnny Kidd - Rocker* (EMI France 1978)★★★, *The Best Of Johnny Kidd And The Pirates* (EMI 1987)★★★, *Rarities* (See For Miles 1987)★★★, *The Classic And The Rare* (See For Miles 1990)★★★, *The Complete Johnny Kidd* (EMI 1992)★★★★.
●FURTHER READING: *Shaking All Over*, Keith Hunt.

KILEY, RICHARD

b. 31 March 1922, Chicago, Illinois, USA. An actor and singer, with an imposing bearing and inimitable voice, Kiley studied at Loyala University and spent more than three years in the US Navy, before moving to New York in 1947. Although he appeared out of town with Nancy Walker in the musical *A Month Of Sundays*, during the late 40s and early 50s Kiley worked mostly in dramatic parts off-Broadway and in first-class televisions productions such as *Patterns* (*Kraft Television Theatre*) and *P.O.W.* (*United States Steel Hour*). His career in the musical theatre really began in 1953 when he created the role of Caliph in *Kismet*, in which he introduced, with others, several memorable numbers, including 'Stranger In Paradise' and 'And This Is My Beloved'. Following a gap of six years, Kiley returned to Broadway in the murder mystery musical *Redhead* (1959), for which he and his co-star Gwen Verdon won Tony Awards. *No Strings* followed in 1962, and with Diahann Carroll he sang the lovely 'The Sweetest Sounds'. After taking over from Craig Stevens in Meredith Willson's *Here's Love*, Kiley played pitchman Sam the Shpieler in *I Had A Ball* (1964) - and then came the role of a lifetime. Kiley won a second Tony Award for his memorable portrayal of Don Quixote in *Man Of La Mancha* (1965), and introduced Mitch Leigh and Joe Darion's 'The Impossible Dream', a song with which he is always identified. He reprised the part on several occasions, including the 1969 London revival, two further New York productions, and on tour. Since his triumph in *Man Of La Mancha*, Kiley's appearances in musical productions have been limited. He played Julius Caesar in *Her First Roman* (1968), an adaptation of Bernard Shaw's *Caesar And Cleopatra*; took part in the one-night tribute, *A Celebration Of Richard Rodgers* (1972); played an aviator in Alan Jay Lerner and Frederick Loewe's poorly received fantasy movie, *The Little Prince* (1974); appeared in a brief revival of *Knickerbocker Holiday* (1977) at Town Hall, New York; and starred out of town in a musical version of *A Christmas Carol* (1981), with music and lyrics by Michel Legrand and Sheldon Harnick. However, he has continued to appear in dramatic roles in the theatre and on television, and won an Emmy in 1984 for his performance in *The Thorn Birds*.

●ALBUMS: *The Rodgers And Hammerstein Songbook* (RCA Camden 1960)★★★, and Original Cast and spoken word recordings.

●FILMS: *The Mob* (1951), *Eight Iron Men* (1952), *The Sniper* (1952), *Pickup On South Street* (1953), *The Blackboard Jungle* (1955), *The Phenix City Story* (1955), *Spanish Affair* (1958), *Pendulum* (1969), *AKA Cassius Clay* (1970), *The Little Prince* (1974), *Looking For Mr. Goodbar* (1977), *Endless Love* (1981), *Howard The Duck* voice only (1986).

KING CURTIS

b. Curtis Ousley, 7 February 1934, Fort Worth, Texas, USA, d. 13 August 1971. A respected saxophonist and session musician, Curtis appeared on countless releases, including those as disparate as Buddy Holly and Andy Williams. He is, however, best recalled for his work on the Atlantic label. A former member of Lionel Hampton's band, Curtis moved to New York and quickly became an integral part of its studio system. He also scored a number 1 US R&B single, 'Soul Twist', billed as King Curtis And The Noble Knights. The same group switched to Capitol Records, but the leader took a solo credit on later hits 'The Monkey' (1963) and 'Soul Serenade' (1964). Curtis continued his session work with the Coasters, the Shirelles and Herbie Mann, while releases on Atco, backed by the Kingpins, progressively established his own career. Several were simply funky instrumental versions of current hits, but his strongest release was 'Memphis Soul Stew' (1967). The saxophonist had meanwhile put together a superb studio group: Richard Tee, Cornell Dupree, Jerry Jemmott and Bernard 'Pretty' Purdie, all of whom contributed to several of Aretha Franklin's finest records. Curtis guested on John Lennon's *Imagine* and was capable of attracting the best session musicians to put in appearances for his own albums, including guitarist Duane Allman on *Instant Groove* and organist Billy Preston on *Live At Fillmore West*. Curtis did venture to the Fame and American studios, but he preferred to work in New York. 'In the south you have to restrain yourself to make sure you come back alive', Ousley said to writer Charlie Gillett. Six months later, in August 1971, he was stabbed to death outside his West 86th Street apartment.

●ALBUMS: *Have Tenor Sax, Will Blow* (Atco 1959)★★★, *The New Scene Of King Curtis* (New Jazz 1960)★★★, *Azure* (Everest 1961)★★★, *Trouble In Mind* (Tru-Sound 1961)★★★, *Doin' The Dixie Twist* (Tru-Sound 1962)★★★, *It's Party Time* (Tru-Sound 1962)★★★★, *Soul Meeting* (Prestige 1962)★★★, *Arthur Murray's Music For Dancing: The Twist* (RCA Victor 1962)★★, *Soul Twist* (Enjoy 1962)★★★, *Country Soul* (Capitol 1963)★★, *The Great King Curtis* (Clarion 1964)★★, *Soul Serenade* (Capitol 1964)★★★, *King Curtis Plays The Hits Made Famous By Sam Cooke* (Capitol 1965)★★★, *That Lovin' Feelin'* (Atco 1966)★★★, *Live At Small's Paradise* (Atco 1966)★★★,

Plays The The Great Memphis Hits (Atco 1967)★★★, *King Size Soul* (Atco 1967)★★, *Sax In Motion* (1968)★★, *Sweet Soul* (Atco 1968)★★★, *Instant Groove* (1969)★★, *Eternally Soul* (1970)★★★, *Get Ready* (1970)★★★, *Blues At Montreux* (1970)★★★, *Live At Fillmore West* (1971)★★, *Mr. Soul* (1972)★★★, *Everybody's Talkin'* (1972)★★, *Jazz Groove* (1974)★★★.

●COMPILATIONS: *Best Of King Curtis* (Capitol 1968)★★★★, *20 Golden Pieces* (1982)★★★, *Didn't He Play!* (1988)★★★, *It's Partytime With King Curtis* (1989)★★★, *Instant Groove* (1990)★★★★, *The Capitol Years 1962-65* (1993)★★★★, *Instant Soul - The Legendary King Curtis* (1994)★★★★.

KING, BEN E.

b. Benjamin Earl Nelson, 28 September 1938, Henderson, North Carolina, USA. King began his career while still a high school student singing in a doo-wop group, the Four B's. He later joined the Five Crowns who, in 1959, assumed the name the Drifters. King was the featured lead vocalist and occasional composer on several of their recordings including 'There Goes My Baby' and 'Save The Last Dance For Me' (written by Doc Pomus and Mort Shuman). After leaving the group in 1960, he recorded the classic single, 'Spanish Harlem' (1961), which maintained the Latin quality of the Drifters' work and deservedly reached the US Top 10. The follow-up, 'Stand By Me' (1961), was even more successful and was followed by further hits including 'Amor' (1961) and 'Don't Play That Song (You Lied)' (1962). Throughout this period, King's work was aimed increasingly at the pop audience. 'I (Who Have Nothing)' and 'I Could Have Danced All Night' (both 1963) suggested showbusiness rather than innovation, although Bert Berns' 'It's All Over' (1964) was a superb song. 'Seven Letters' and 'The Record (Baby I Love You)' (both 1965) prepared the way for the rhetorical 'What Is Soul?' (1967) which effectively placed King alongside such soul contemporaries as Otis Redding, Wilson Pickett and Joe Tex. Unfortunately, King's commercial standing declined towards the end of the 60s when he left the Atlantic/Atco group of labels. Unable to reclaim his former standing elsewhere, King later re-signed with his former company and secured a US Top 5 hit in 1975 with 'Supernatural Thing Part 1'. In 1977, a collaboration with the Average White Band resulted in two R&B chart entries and an excellent album, *Benny And Us*. However, King's later recordings, including *Music Trance* (1980) and *Street Tough* (1981), proved less successful. In 1986, 'Stand By Me' was included in a film of the same name and once more became an international hit, reaching the US Top 10 and number 1 in the UK, thereby briefly revitalizing the singer's autumnal career.

●ALBUMS: *Spanish Harlem* (Atco 1961)★★★, *Ben E. King Sings For Soulful Lovers* (Atco 1962)★★★, *Don't Play That Song* (Atco 1962)★★★, *Young Boy Blues* (Clarion 1964), *Seven Letters* (Atco 1965)★★★, *What Is Soul* (1967)★★★, *Rough Edges* (1970)★★★, *Beginning*

Of It All (1971)★★★, *Supernatural* (1975)★★★, *I Had A Love* (1976)★★, with the Average White Band *Benny And Us* (1977)★★, *Let Me Live In Your Life* (1978)★★, *Music Trance* (1980)★★, *Street Tough* (1981)★★, *Save The Last Dance For Me* (1988)★★★.
●COMPILATIONS: *Greatest Hits* (1964)★★★, *Here Comes The Night* (1984)★★★, *Stand By Me (The Ultimate Collection)* (1987)★★★★, *Anthology One: Spanish Harlem* (RSA 1996)★★★, *Anthology Two: For Soulful Lovers* (RSA 1996)★★★, *Don't Play That Song* (RSA 1996)★★★, *Anthology Four: Seven Letters* (RSA 1997)★★★, *Anthology Five: What Is Soul?* (RSA 1997)★★★, *Anthology Six: Supernatural* (RSA 1997)★★★, *Anthology Seven: Benny And Us* (RSA 1997)★★.

KING, SOLOMON

This US singer came to prominence in 1968 with the powerful hit ballad 'She Wears My Ring'. It was based on a classical piece of music called *Golandrina (The Swallow)*. King was signed by manager/entrepreneur Gordon Mills but failed to emulate the phenomenal success of his stablemates, Tom Jones and Engelbert Humperdinck. He continued to record well into the 70s, and his version of 'Say A Little Prayer' (1970) is a prized rarity among soul fans.
●ALBUMS: *She Wears My Ring* (Columbia 1968)★★★, *You'll Never Walk Alone* (Columbia 1971)★★.

KINGSMEN

Jack Ely (vocals/guitar), Mike Mitchell (guitar) Bob Nordby (bass) and Lynn Easton (drums) began working as the Kingsmen in 1958. Based in Portland, Oregon, USA, they became a staple part of the region's thriving circuit prior to the arrival of Don Gallucci (keyboards) in 1962. The group's debut single, 'Louie Louie', was released the following year. The song was composed and originally recorded by Richard Berry in 1956, and its primitive, churning rhythm was later adopted by several northwest state bands, including the Wailers and Paul Revere And The Raiders. However, it was the Kingsmen who popularized this endearing composition when it rose to number 2 in the US chart. Its classic C-F-G chord progression, as simple as it was effective, was absorbed by countless 'garage bands', and 'Louie Louie' has subsequently become one of rock's best-known and most influential creations. Indeed, a whole album's worth of recordings of the song by various artists, including the Kingsmen and Richard Berry, was issued by Rhino Records entitled, *The Best Of Louie Louie*. Relations between the individual Kingsmen were sundered on the single's success. Easton informed Ely that he now wished to sing lead, and furthered his argument by declaring himself the sole proprietor of the group's name, having judiciously registered the moniker at their inception. Ely and Norby walked out, although the former won a victory of sorts when a judgement declared that every pressing of the Kingsmen's greatest hit must include the words 'lead vocals by Jack Ely'. His former cohorts added Norm

Sundholm (bass) and Gary Abbot (drums), but despite a succession of dance-related releases including 'The Climb', 'Little Latin Lupe Lu' and 'The Jolly Green Giant', the group was unable to maintain a long-term livelihood. Gallucci formed Don And The Goodtimes, Kerry Magnus and Dick Petersen replaced Sundholm and Abbot, but the crucial alteration came in 1967 when Easton left the group. Numerous half-hearted reincarnations aside, his departure brought the Kingsmen to an end.
●ALBUMS: *The Kingsmen In Person* (Wand 1963)★★, *The Kingsmen, Volume 2 (More Great Sounds)* (Wand 1964)★★, *The Kingsmen, Volume 3* (Wand 1965)★★, *The Kingsmen On Campus* (Wand 1965)★★, *How To Stuff A Wild Bikini* film soundtrack (1965)★, *Up Up And Away* (Wand 1966)★★.
●COMPILATIONS: *15 Great Hits* (Wand 1966)★★, *The Kingsmen's Greatest Hits* (1967)★★, *Louie Louie/Greatest Hits* (1986)★★.
●FILMS: *How To Stuff A Wild Bikini* (1965).

KINKS

It is ironic that one of Britain's most enduring and respected groups spawned from the beat boom of the early 60s has for the best part of two decades received success, adulation and financial reward in the USA. Today this most 'English' institution can still fill a vast stadium in any part of the USA, while in Britain, a few thousand devotees watch their heroes perform in a comparatively small club or hall. The Kinks is the continuing obsession of one of Britain's premier songwriting talents, Raymond Douglas Davies (b. 21 June 1944, Muswell Hill, London, England; vocals/guitar/piano). Originally known as the Ravens, the Kinks formed at the end of 1963 with a line-up comprising: Dave Davies (b. 3 February 1947, Muswell Hill, London; guitar/vocals) and Peter Quaife (b. 31 December 1943, Tavistock, Devon, England; bass), and were finally joined by Mick Avory (b. 15 February 1944, London; drums). Their first single 'Long Tall Sally' failed to sell, although they did receive a lot of publicity through the efforts of their shrewd managers Robert Wace, Grenville Collins and Larry Page. Their third single, 'You Really Got Me', rocketed to the UK number 1 spot, boosted by an astonishing performance on the UK television show *Ready Steady Go*. This and its successor, 'All Day And All Of The Night', provided a blueprint for hard rock guitar playing, with the simple but powerful riffs supplied by the younger Davies. Over the next two years Ray Davies emerged as a songwriter of startling originality and his band were rarely out of the best-sellers list. Early in 1965, the group returned to number 1 with the languid 'Tired Of Waiting For You'. They enjoyed a further string of hits that year, including 'Everybody's Gonna Be Happy', 'Set Me Free', 'See My Friend' and 'Till The End Of The Day'. Despite the humanity of his lyrics, Davies was occasionally a problematical character, renowned for his eccentric behaviour. The Kinks were equally tempestuous and frequently violent. Earlier in 1965, events had reached a head when the normally placid drummer, Avory, attacked Dave Davies on stage with the hi-hat of his drum kit, having been goaded beyond endurance. Remarkably, the group survived such contretemps and soldiered on. A disastrous US tour saw them banned from that country, amid further disputes. Throughout all the drama, Davies the songwriter remained supreme. He combined his own introspection with humour and pathos. The ordinary and the obvious were spelled out in his lyrics, but, contrastingly, never in a manner that was either. 'Dedicated Follower Of Fashion' brilliantly satirized Carnaby Street narcissism while 'Sunny Afternoon' (another UK number 1) dealt with capitalism and class. 'Dead End Street' at the end of 1966 highlighted the plight of the working-class poor: 'Out of work and got no money, a Sunday joint of bread and honey', while later in that same song Davies comments: 'What are we living for, two-roomed apartment on the second floor, no money coming in, the rent collector knocks and tries to get in'. All these were embraced with Davies' resigned laconic music-hall style. Their albums, prior to *Face To Face* had contained a staple diet of R&B standards and comparatively harmless Davies originals. With *Face To Face* and *Something Else*, however, he set about redefining the English character, with sparkling wit and steely nerve. One of Davies' greatest songs was the final track on the latter: 'Waterloo Sunset' was a simple but emotional *tour de force* with the melancholic singer observing two lovers (many have suggested actor Terence Stamp and actress Julie Christie, but Davies denies this) meeting and crossing over Hungerford Bridge in London. It narrowly missed the top of the charts, as did the follow-up 'Autumn Almanac', with its gentle chorus summing up the English working-class of the 50s and 60s: 'I like my football on a Saturday, roast beef on Sunday is all right, I go to Blackpool for my holiday, sit in the autumn sunlight'.

Throughout this fertile period, Ray Davies, along with John Lennon, Paul McCartney and Pete Townshend, was among Britain's finest writers. But by 1968 the Kinks had fallen from public grace in the UK, despite remaining well respected by the critics. Two superb concept albums, *The Kinks Are The Village Green Preservation Society* and *Arthur Or The Decline And Fall Of The British Empire*, failed to sell. This inexplicable quirk was all the harder to take as they contained some of Davies' finest songs. Writing honestly about everyday events seemingly no longer appealed to Davies' public. The former was likened to Dylan Thomas's *Under Milk Wood*, while *Arthur* had to compete with Pete Townshend's *Tommy*. Both were writing rock operas without each other's knowledge, but as Johnny Rogan stats in his biography of the Kinks: 'Davies' celebration of the mundane was far removed from the studious iconoclasm of *Tommy* and its successors'. The last hit single during this 'first' age of the Kinks was the glorious 'Days'. This lilting and timeless ballad is another of Davies' many classics and was a major hit for Kirsty MacColl in 1989.

Pete Quaife permanently departed in 1969 and was replaced by John Dalton. The Kinks returned to the UK best-sellers lists in July 1970 with 'Lola', an irresistible fable of transvestism, which marked the beginning of their breakthrough in the USA by reaching the US Top 10. The resulting *Lola Vs Powerman And The Moneygoround Part One* was also a success there. On this record Davies attacked the music industry and in one track, 'The Moneygoround', openly slated his former managers and publishers, while alluding to the lengthy high court action in which he had been embroiled. The group now embarked on a series of mammoth US tours and rarely performed in Britain, although their business operation centre and recording studio, Konk, was based close to the Davies' childhood home in north London. Having signed a new contract with RCA in 1971 the band had now enlarged to incorporate a brass section, amalgamating with the Mike Cotton Sound. Following the interesting country-influenced *Muswell Hillbillies*, however, they suffered a barren period. Ray experienced drug and marital problems and their ragged half-hearted live performances revealed a man bereft of his driving, creative enthusiasm. Throughout the early 70s a series of average, over-ambitious concept albums appeared as Davies' main outlet. *Preservation Act I*, *Preservation Act II*, *Soap Opera* and *Schoolboys In Disgrace* were all thematic, and *Soap Opera* was adapted for British television as *Starmaker*. At the end of 1976 Dalton departed, as their unhappy and comparatively unsuccessful years with RCA ended. A new contract with Arista Records engendered a remarkable change in fortunes. Both *Sleepwalker* (1977) and *Misfits* (1978) were excellent and successful albums; Ray had rediscovered the knack of writing short, punchy rock songs with quality lyrics. The musicianship of the band improved, in particular, Dave Davies, who after years in his elder brother's shadow, came into his own with a more fluid style.

Although still spending most of their time playing to vast audiences in the USA, the Kinks were adopted by the British new wave, and were cited by many punk bands as a major influence. Both the Jam ('David Watts') and the Pretenders ('Stop Your Sobbing') provided reminders of Davies' 60s songwriting skill. The British music press, then normally harsh on 60s dinosaurs, constantly praised the Kinks and helped to regenerate a market for them in Europe. Their following albums continued the pattern started with *Sleepwalker*, hard-rock numbers with sharp lyrics. Although continuing to be a huge attraction in the USA they have so far never reappeared in the UK album charts, although they are regular victims of ruthless 'Greatest Hits' packages. As Ray Davies' stormy three-year relationship with Chrissie Hynde of the Pretenders drew to its close, so the Kinks appeared unexpectedly back in the UK singles chart with the charming 'Come Dancing'. The accompanying video and high publicity profile prompted the reissue of their entire and considerable back catalogue. Towards the end of the 80s the band toured sporadically amid rumours of a final break-up. In 1990 the Kinks were inducted into the Rock 'n' Roll Hall of Fame, at the time only the fourth UK group to take the honour behind the Beatles, Rolling Stones and the Who. During the ceremony both Pete Quaife and Mick Avory were present. Later that year they received the Ivor Novello award for 'outstanding services to British music'. After the comparative failure of *UK Jive* the band left London Records, and after being without a recording contract for some time, signed with Sony in 1991. Their debut for that label was *Phobia*, a good album which suffered from lack of promotion (the public still perceiving the Kinks as a 60s band). A prime example was in 'Scattered', as good a song as Davies has ever written, that when released was totally ignored apart from a few pro-Kinks radio broadcasters. Following the commercial failure of *Phobia* the band were released from their contract and put out *To The Bone*, an interesting album on their own Konk label, which satisfied long-standing fans. This unplugged session was recorded in front of a small audience at their own headquarters in Crouch End, north London, and contained semi-acoustic versions of some of Davies' classic songs. Both brothers had autobiographies published in the 90s; Ray came first with the cleverly constructed *X-Ray* and Dave responded with *Kink*, a pedestrian, although revealing book in 1996. Whether or not they can maintain their reputation as a going concern beyond the mid-90s, Ray Davies has made his mark under the Kinks' banner as one of the most perceptive and prolific popular songwriters of our time. His catalogue of songs observing ordinary life is one of the finest available. Much of the Britpop movement from the mid-90s acknowledged a considerable debt to Davies as one of the key influences. Bands such as Supergrass, Oasis, Cast and especially Damon Alban of Blur are some of the Kinks' most admiring students.

●ALBUMS: *Kinks* (Pye 1964)★★★, *You Really Got Me* (Reprise 1964), *Kinda Kinks* (Pye 1965)★★★, *Kinks Size* (Reprise 1965)★★★, *Kinkdom* (Reprise 1965)★★★, *The Kink Kontroversy* (Pye 1966)★★★, *Face To Face* (Pye 1966)★★★★, *Live At The Kelvin Hall* (Pye 1967)★, *Something Else* (Pye 1967)★★★★★, *The Kinks Are The Village Green Preservation Society* (Pye 1968)★★★★, *Arthur Or The Decline And Fall Of The British Empire* (Pye 1969)★★★★, *Lola Versus Powerman And The Moneygoround, Part One* (Pye 1970)★★★, *Percy* film soundtrack (Pye 1971)★★, *Muswell Hillbillies* (RCA 1971)★★★★, *Everbody's In Showbiz, Everybody's A Star* (RCA 1972)★★★, *Kink Kronikles* (Reprise 1972)★★★★, *The Great Lost Kinks Album* (Reprise 1973)★★★★, *Preservation Act 1* (RCA 1973)★★, *Preservation Act 2* double album (RCA 1974)★★, *Soap Opera* (RCA 1975)★★, *Schoolboys In Disgrace* (RCA 1975)★★★, *Sleepwalker* (Arista 1977)★★★, *Misfits* (Arista 1978)★★★★, *Low Budget* (Arista 1979)★★★, *One For The Road* (Arista 1980)★★★, *Give The People What They Want* (Arista 1982)★★★, *State Of Confusion* (Arista 1983)★★★, *Word Of Mouth* (Arista 1984)★★, *Think Visual* (London 1986)★★, *The Road* (London 1988)★★, *UK Jive* (London 1989)★★, *Phobia* (Columbia 1993)★★★, *To The Bone* (Konk 1994)★★★, *To The Bone (USA)* (Guardian 1996)★★★★.

●COMPILATIONS: *Well Respected Kinks* (Marble Arch 1986)★★★★, *Sunny Afternoon* (Marble Arch 1964)★★★★, *The Kinks* (Pye 1970)★★★★, *A Golden Hour Of The Kinks* (Golden Hour 1973)★★★, *All The Good Times* 4-LP box set (Pye 1973)★★★★, *The Kinks File* (Pye 1977)★★★★, *Second Time Around* (RCA 1980)★★★, *Greatest Hits* (PRT 1983)★★★, *29th Anniversary Box Set* 3-LP set (PRT 1983)★★★★, *The Ultimate Collection* (Castle 1989)★★★★, *The EP Collection* (See For Miles 1990)★★★★, *Fab Forty: The Singles Collection, 1964-70* (Descal 1991)★★★★, *Tired Of Waiting For You* (Rhino 1995)★★★★.

●FURTHER READING: *The Kinks: The Sound And The Fury*, Johnny Rogan. *The Kinks: The Official Biography*, Jon Savage. *You Really Got Me: The Kinks Part One*, Doug Hinman. *X-Ray*, Ray Davies. *Kink: An Autobiography*, Dave Davies. *The Kinks: Well Respected Men*, Neville Marten and Jeffrey Hudson..

KIPPINGTON LODGE

Best remembered as the vehicle for the earliest Nick Lowe (b. 25 March 1949, Woodbridge, Suffolk, England) recordings, Kippington Lodge stemmed from Lowe's first band, Sounds 4 + 1, which he formed with school pal, Brinsley Schwarz. On leaving school, Lowe, already used to a nomadic existence as his father was in the Royal Air Force, decided to go and see some more of the world leaving, Schwarz to return to his native Tunbridge Wells in Kent. Here Schwarz formed Three's A Crowd who were signed to EMI in 1967. Changing their name to Kippington Lodge they released their debut 'Shy Boy' in October. This effective pop song was accompanied by the equally good 'Lady On A Bicycle'. At this point, Lowe returned to England and joined his friends in time for the second single 'Rumours' which was produced by Mark Wirtz. Lowe's arrival fixed the line-up as Schwarz (guitar/vocals), Lowe (bass/vocals), Barry Landerman (organ) and Pete Whale (drums). Landerman soon departed - later resurfacing in Vanity Fare - and was replaced by Bob Andrews (b. 20 June 1949). To supplement their lack of income from record sales, Kippington Lodge became Billie Davies' backing group and released three further singles during 1968-69. These releases were produced by EMI stalwarts such as Mike Collier, Roger Easterby and Des Champ. The last single, a version of the Beatles' 'In My Life', came out in April 1969 and, after doing as poorly as previous efforts, left the group at a loose end. In September they replaced Pete Whale with the American drummer Billy Rankin and the name Kippington Lodge was dropped in favour of that of lead guitarist Brinsley Schwarz.

KIRBY, KATHY

b. 20 October 1940, Ilford, Essex, England. Her *bel canto* eloquence when in a convent school choir had her earmarked for a career in opera until 1956, when an unscheduled performance with Ambrose And His Orchestra at a local dancehall precipitated three years as the outfit's featured singer - with Ambrose as her mentor until his death in 1971. After stints with the big bands of

Denny Boyle and Nat Allen, she headlined seasons in Madrid and London nightspots, and won recording contracts on Pye and then Decca - but it was only when her strawberry blonde, moist-lipped appeal was transferred to UK television in 1963, as a regular on the *Stars And Garters* variety show, that her records started selling. Her biggest UK smashes were with consecutive revivals of Doris Day's 'Secret Love' and Teresa Brewer's 'Let Me Go Lover', but these were adjuncts to her earnings for personal appearances and two BBC series (*Kathy Kirby Sings*). After a spot on 1965's Royal Command Performance - the apogee of British showbusiness - signs of danger were not yet perceptible. However, with that year's Eurovision Song Contest entry ('I Belong') her Top 40 farewell, and her aspirations to be a film actress frustrated, Ambrose's managerial arrogance and old-fashioned values upset BBC (and ITV) executives, thus consigning his cocooned client to a cabaret ghost-kingdom. Confused by post-Ambrose administrative chaos, Kirby's prima donna tantrums and failure to honour contracts made her a booker's risk. The 70s were further underscored by a disastrous marriage, bankruptcy, failed comebacks and, in 1979, a spell in a mental hospital following her arrest for an unpaid hotel bill (of which she was innocent). Just as unwelcome was publicity concerning her cohabitation with another woman. When the latter was jailed, the affair ended, and Kirby returned to the stage as an intermission act in a Kent bingo hall. Since then, she has played one-nighters, nostalgia revues and has sold the story of her tragic downfall to a Sunday newspaper. In more recent years Kirby has become a recluse, and speculation as to her whereabouts is constantly being expressed in the UK media. In 1994, 'an exciting new play' entitled *Whatever Happened To Kathy Kirby?*, was presented in the London provinces, while a year later, an unauthorized biography was published.
●ALBUMS: *16 Hits From Stars And Garters* (1964)★★, *Make Someone Happy* (Decca 1967)★★★, *My Thanks To You* (Columbia 1968)★★.
●COMPILATIONS: *The Best Of Kathy Kirby* (Ace of Clubs 1968)★★★, *The World Of Kathy Kirby* (Decca 1970)★★★, *Let Me Sing And I'm Happy* (1983)★★★, *Secret Love* (1989)★★★.
●FURTHER READING: *Kathy Kirby: Is That All There Is?*, James Harman.

KLEIN, ALLEN

b. 1932, Newark, New Jersey, USA. A name synonymous with 'notorious', Allen Klein has a reputation as one of the most litigious, and thus feared, entrepreneurs in the music business. He spent his formative years at a Hebrew orphanage, then studied accountancy, paying for his own tuition along the way. During the early 60s, he took over the affairs of singer Buddy Knox and claimed to discover irregularities in the royalties he was due from his record company. The technique was habitual. Again and again, Klein would accost record companies, insist on audits, and produce writs at a moment's notice. His client roster soon extended to include Steve Lawrence, Eydie Gorme,

Bobby Darin, Bobby Vinton and Sam Cooke. Always an over-reacher, Klein's grand ambition was to win the management of the Beatles. During the mid-60s, he infiltrated the British music scene with the notable acquisition of Donovan. His greatest coup, however, was effectively ousting first Eric Easton, then the charismatic Andrew Loog Oldham, as managers of the Rolling Stones. Klein and Oldham had originally formed a partnership in 1965, cemented by the American's success in securing a million-dollar advance from Sir Edward Lewis at Decca Records. Klein's history with the Rolling Stones and Andrew Loog Oldham ended in protracted litigation during the late 60s. In the meantime, Klein had bought the Cameo-Parkway Record label, an acquisition that prompted an investigation from the Securities and Exchange Commission. As his reputation grew, he reiterated his dream of managing the Beatles and, following the death of Brian Epstein in 1967, that ambition at last seemed feasible. In early 1969, Klein had a meeting with John Lennon and Yoko Ono and won them over. Both George Harrison and Ringo Starr also accepted Klein, but Paul McCartney preferred to place his future in the hands of his father-in-law, Lee Eastman. Just as he had done with the Rolling Stones, Klein renegotiated the Beatles contract to spectacular effect and also reorganized their business empire Apple, firing many personnel along the way. Although he boasted that he would win Epstein's company NEMS, he was thwarted when the company was sold to the Triumph Investment Trust. Music publisher Dick James had similar reservations about the American and, wary of provoking a legal battle, he sold the lucrative Beatles catalogue Northern Songs to Lew Grade's ATV network. Klein's hopes of reuniting the Beatles onstage also proved chimerical. Indeed, he seemed to represent a wedge between McCartney and the others and in 1971 the High Court ordered the dissolution of the Beatles' partnership. Klein's career in the echelons of pop was more prosaic during the late 70s, and in 1979 he suffered the indignity of a prison sentence after the US Internal Revenue Service indicted him on charges of tax evasion. By the 80s, Klein had switched his attention from rock music to feature films and the Broadway stage with varying degrees of success.

KNICKERBOCKERS

The Knickerbockers was formed in 1964 by Buddy Randell (saxophone), a former member of the Royal Teens and Jimmy Walker (drums/vocals). The line-up was completed by the Charles brothers, John (bass) and Beau (lead guitar). Originally known as the Castle Kings, the group took its name from an avenue in their hometown of Bergenfield, New Jersey, USA. Signed to the Challenge label, owned by singing cowboy Gene Autry, the quartet initially forged its reputation recording cover versions, but in 1965 they scored a US Top 20 hit with 'Lies', a ferocious rocker which many listeners assumed was the Beatles in disguise. However, the Knickerbockers were more than mere copyists and later releases, which featured the instrumental muscle of experienced studio hands, established an energetic style which crossed folk rock and the Four Seasons. The group broke up in 1968, unable to rekindle that first flame of success. Randell and Walker both attempted solo careers and for a short time the latter replaced Bill Medley in the Righteous Brothers.

●ALBUMS: *Sing And Sync-Along With Lloyd: Lloyd Thaxton Presents The Knickerbockers* (Challenge 1965)★★, *Jerk And Twine Time* (Challenge 1966)★★★, *Lies* (Challenge 1966)★★★.

●COMPILATIONS: *The Fabulous Knickerbockers* (1988)★★★, *A Rave-Up With The Knickerbockers* (Big Beat 1993)★★★, *Hits, Rarities, Unissued Cuts And More ...* (Sundazed 1997)★★★.

KNIGHT, CURTIS

b. 1945, Fort Scott, Kansas, USA. Having completed his national service, Knight settled in California where he hoped to pursue a career in music. He appeared in a low-budget film, *Pop Girl*, before relocating to New York during the early 60s. Knight then recorded for several minor labels, but these releases have been eclipsed by the singer's collaborations with Jimi Hendrix who joined Curtis's group, the Squires, in 1965. Hendrix's tenure there was brief, but the contract he signed with Knight's manager, Ed Chaplin, had unfortunate repercussions, particularly as the guitarist ill-advisedly undertook another recording session in 1967. His spells with Knight yielded 61 songs, 26 studio and 35 live, which have since been the subject of numerous exploitative compilations. Although some of this material is, in isolation, worthwhile, such practices have undermined its value. As Curtis Knight continued to pursue his career throughout the 60s using whatever musicians were available, he increasingly relied on his Hendrix association, and in 1974 published *Jimi*, 'an intimate biography'. By this point Knight was based in London where he led a new group, Curtis Knight - Zeus. This band comprised Eddie Clarke (guitar; later in Motörhead), Nicky Hogarth (keyboards), John Weir (bass) and Chris Perry (drums). They completed two albums, but only one was issued in the UK. The singer undertook a European tour and an unremarkable album before returning to the USA.

●ALBUMS: *Down The Village* (early 70s)★★, *Second Coming* (1974)★★, *Live In Europe* (1989)★★. Selected recordings with Jimi Hendrix *Get That Feeling* (1968)★, *Strange Things* (1968)★★, *Flashing/Jimi Hendrix Plays Curtis Knight Sings* (1968)★★, *The Great Jimi Hendrix In New York* (1968)★★, *In The Beginning* (1973)★, *Looking Back With Jimi Hendrix* (1975)★, *My Best Friend* (1981)★, *Second Time Around* (1981)★★, *Hush Now* (1981)★ *Last Night* (1981)★, *Mr. Pitiful* (1981)★★, *Welcome Home* (1981)★.

●FURTHER READING: *Jimi*, Curtis Knight.

KNIGHT, PETER

b. 23 June 1917, Exmouth, Devon, England, d. 30 July 1985. An arranger, composer and musical director, Knight played the piano by ear as a young child, and studied piano, harmony and counterpoint privately before making his first broadcast on BBC Radio's *Children's Hour* in 1924. After working in semi-professional bands at venues such as London's Gig club, he won the individual piano award with Al Morter's Rhythm Kings in the 1937 *Melody Maker* All London Dance Band Championship. Three years later he played with the Ambrose Orchestra at the Mayfair Hotel before joining the Royal Air Force for service in World War II. On his discharge, he worked with Sydney Lipton at the Grosvenor House in London for four years before forming a vocal group, the Peter Knight Singers, which became popular on stage and radio. His wife Babs was a founder member and remained with the group for over 30 years. Besides operating the Singers, Knight also worked for Geraldo for a year before becoming a musical director for London West End shows such as *Cockles And Champagne* and *The Jazz Train*, a revue which gave American actress Bertice Reading her first London success. In the late 50s, Knight became musical director for Granada Television, and worked on popular programmes such as *Spot The Tune* and *Chelsea At Nine*. When he resumed freelance work, he arranged and conducted records by artists such as Harry Secombe, Petula Clark, Sammy Davis Jnr. and the Moody Blues (*Days Of Future Passed*). Knight was musical director for a 1964 touring version of Leslie Bricusse and Anthony Newley's show, *The Roar Of The Greasepaint - The Smell Of The Crowd*, and for several series of the extremely popular *Morecambe And Wise Show* on television. In the late 70s, Knight spent some time in Hollywood, and conducted the Los Angeles Philharmonic Orchestra in concerts by the Carpenters. In 1979, he scored and conducted the music for Roman Polanski's Oscar-nominated film *Tess*. His other film credits include the scores for *Sunstruck* (1972) and *Curse Of The Crimson Altar* (1968). Shortly after his death in 1985, Yorkshire television inaugurated the annual Peter Knight Award which 'celebrates and rewards the craft of musical arranging'. Knight rarely put a foot wrong throughout his career and is remembered still with the utmost respect and affection.

●ALBUMS: with the Peter Knight Singers *Vocal Gems From My Fair Lady* (1959)★★★, with his orchestra *A Knight Of Merrie England* (1960)★★★, with two pianos and orchestra *The Best Of Ivor Novello And Noël Coward* (1961)★★★, with the Peter Knight Singers *Voices In The Night* (Deram 1967)★★★, *Sgt Pepper* (Mercury 1967)★★, with the Moody Blues *Days Of Future Passed* (Deram 1967)★★★★, with Bob Johnson *The King Of Elfland's Daughter* (1977)★★★.

KNIGHT, ROBERT

b. 24 April 1945, Franklin, Tennessee, USA. Knight made his professional vocal debut with the Paramounts, a harmony quintet consisting of schoolfriends. Signed to Dot Records, they recorded 'Free Me' in 1961, a US R&B hit, outselling the cover version by Johnny Preston. After this initial success their subsequent releases flopped and resulted in the group breaking up. Unfortunately, they also broke their contract with Dot and were prevented

from recording for four-and-a-half years. Knight continued his studies in chemistry at the Tennessee State University where he formed vocal trio the Fairlanes. In 1967, Knight was spotted performing with the Fairlanes in Nashville, and was offered a contract as a solo artist by the Rising Sons label. His first recording, 'Everlasting Love', written by label owners Buzz Cason and Mac Gayden, was an immediate success and earned him a US Top 20 hit. This enduring song was an even bigger success in Britain the following year where a cover version by Love Affair reached number 1, and in doing so, kept the singer from progressing further than a Top 40 position. Knight scored two further pop hits at home, 'Blessed Are The Lonely' and 'Isn't It Lonely Together'. In 1973, he overshadowed his previous chart entry in the UK when 'Love On A Mountain Top' reached the Top 10. However, the reissued 'Everlasting Love' went some way to making amends the following year, this time achieving Top 20 status. He continues, perhaps wisely, to advance his career in chemical research, while occasionally performing and recording.
●ALBUMS: *Everlasting Love* (Monument 1967)★★★, *Love On A Mountain Top* (Monument 1968)★★★.

KOOBAS

Formed in Liverpool, England, in 1962 and initially known as the Kubas, this superior beat group was comprised of two ex-members of the Midnighters - guitarists Stu Leatherwood and Roy Morris - alongside Keith Ellis (bass) and Tony O'Riley (drums), formerly of the Thunderbeats. The Koobas enjoyed a role in *Ferry Across The Mersey* and in 1965 supported the Beatles on a national tour. The group secured a deal with Pye Records and their debut, 'Take Me For A Little While' (1965), showed considerable promise. Following 'You'd Better Make Up Your Mind' (1966) the Koobas switched to Columbia Records for the exceptional 'Sweet Music'. A misguided version of Gracie Fields' 'Sally' (1967) undermined the group's growing reputation, as did the equally insubstantial 'Gypsy Fred'. However, they closed their singles career with a superb rendition of Cat Stevens' 'The First Cut Is The Deepest', before completing *The Koobas*. The content of this excellent album ranges from a rendition of Erma Franklin's 'Piece Of My Heart' to the musically complex 'Barricades', one of the finest songs of its era. The group had actually disbanded prior to its release, after which Ellis joined Van Der Graaf Generator.
●ALBUMS: *The Koobas* (Columbia 1969)★★★.

KORNER, ALEXIS

b. 19 April 1928, Paris, France, d. 1 January 1984. An inspirational figure in British music circles, Korner was already versed in black music when he met Cyril Davies at the London Skiffle Club. Both musicians were frustrated by the limitations of the genre and transformed the venue into the London Blues And Barrelhouse Club where they not only performed together but also showcased visiting US bluesmen. When jazz trombonist Chris Barber introduced an R&B segment into his live reper-

toire, he employed Korner (guitar) and Davies (harmonica) to back singer Ottilie Patterson. Inspired, the pair formed Blues Incorporated in 1961 and the following year established the Ealing Rhythm And Blues Club in a basement beneath a local cinema. The group's early personnel included Charlie Watts (drums), Art Wood (vocals) and Keith Scott (piano), but later featured Long John Baldry, Jack Bruce, Graham Bond and Ginger Baker in its ever-changing line-up. Mick Jagger and Paul Jones were also briefly associated with Korner, whose continued advice and encouragement proved crucial to a generation of aspiring musicians. However, disagreements over direction led to Davies' defection following the release of *R&B From The Marquee*, leaving Korner free to pursue a jazz-based path. While former colleagues later found success with the Rolling Stones, Manfred Mann and Cream, Korner's excellent group went largely unnoticed by the general public, although he did enjoy a residency on a children's television show backed by his rhythm section of Danny Thompson (bass) and Terry Cox (drums). The name 'Blues Incorporated' was dropped when Korner embarked on a solo career, punctuated by the formation of several temporary groups, including Free At Last (1967), New Church (1969) and Snape (1972). While the supporting cast on such ventures remained fluid, including for a short time singer Robert Plant, the last two units featured Peter Thorup who also collaborated with Korner on CCS, a pop-based big band that scored notable hits with 'Whole Lotta Love' (1970), 'Walkin'' and 'Tap Turns On The Water' (both 1971). Korner also derived success from his BBC Radio 1 show that extended a highly individual choice of material. He also broadcast on a long-running programme for the BBC World Service. Korner continued to perform live, often accompanied by former Back Door virtuoso bassist Colin Hodgkinson, and remained a highly respected figure in the music fraternity. He joined Charlie Watts, Ian Stewart, Jack Bruce and Dick Heckstall-Smith in the informal Rocket 88, and Korner's 50th birthday party, which featured appearances by Eric Clapton, Chris Farlowe and Zoot Money, was both filmed and recorded. In 1981, Korner began an ambitious 13-part television documentary on the history of rock, but his premature death from cancer in January 1984 left this and many other projects unfulfilled. However, Korner's stature as a vital catalyst in British R&B was already assured.
●ALBUMS: by Alexis Korner's Blues Incorporated *R&B From The Marquee* (Ace Of Clubs 1962)★★★★, *Red Hot From Alex* aka *Alexis Korner's All Star Blues Incorporated* (Transatlantic 1964)★★★★, *At The Cavern* (Oriole 1964)★★★, *Alexis Korner's Blues Incorporated* (Ace Of Clubs 1964)★★★, *Sky High* (Spot 1965)★★, *Blues Incorporated (Wednesday Night Prayer Meeting)* (1967); by Alexis Korner *I Wonder Who* (Fontana 1967)★★★, *A New Generation Of Blues* aka *What's That Sound I Hear* (Liberty 1968)★★★, *Both Sides Of Alexis Korner* (1969)★★★, *Alexis* (Rak 1971)★★★, *Mr. Blues* (1974)★★★, *Alexis Korner* (1974)★★★, *Get Off My Cloud* (CBS 1975)★★★, *Just*

Easy (1978)★★★, *Me* (1979)★★★, *The Party Album* (1980)★★★, *Juvenile Delinquent* (1984)★★, *Live In Paris: Alexis Korner* (1988)★★★; by New Church *The New Church* (1970); by Snape *Accidentally Born In New Orleans* (Transatlantic 1973)★★★, *Snape Live On Tour* (1974)★★★.

●COMPILATIONS: *Bootleg Him* (Rak 1972)★★★, *Profile* (1981)★★★, *Alexis 1957* (1984)★★★, *Testament* (1985)★★★, *Alexis Korner 1961-1972* (1986)★★★, *Hammer And Nails* (1987)★★★, *The Alexis Korner Collection* (1988)★★★, *And ....* (Castle Communications 1994)★★★, *On The Move* (Castle Communications 1996)★★★.

●FURTHER READING: *Alexis Korner: The Biography*, Harry Shapiro.

KRAMER, BILLY J., AND THE DAKOTAS

b. William Howard Ashton, 19 August 1943, Bootle, Merseyside, England. Kramer originally fronted Merseybeat combo the Coasters, but was teamed with the Manchester-based Dakotas - Mike Maxfield (b. 23 February 1944; lead guitar), Robin McDonald (b. 18 July 1943; rhythm guitar), Ray Jones (bass) and Tony Mansfield (b. 28 May 1943; drums) - upon signing to Brian Epstein's management agency. Having topped the UK charts with the Beatles' 'Do You Want To Know A Secret' (1963), Kramer's UK chart success was maintained with a run of exclusive John Lennon/Paul McCartney songs, including the chart-topping 'Bad To Me', 'I'll Keep You Satisfied' (number 4) and 'From A Window' (number 10). 'Little Children' (1964), penned by US writers Mort Shuman and John McFarland, gave the group a third number 1 and their first taste of success in the USA, reaching number 7. This was quickly followed by the reissued 'Bad To Me' which also reached the Top 10. Their chart reign ended the following year with the Burt Bacharach-composed 'Trains And Boats And Planes' peaking at number 12 in the UK. Although subsequent efforts, most notably the lyrical 'Neon City', proved effective, Kramer's career was firmly in the descendent. He embarked on a solo career in January 1967, but having failed to find a new audience, sought solace on the cabaret and nostalgia circuit.

●ALBUMS: *Listen - To Billy J. Kramer* (Parlophone 1963)★★★, *Little Children* (Imperial 1964)★★★, *I'll Keep You Satisfied* (Imperial 1964)★★★, *Trains And Boats And Planes* (Imperial 1965)★★, *Kramer Versus Kramer* (1986)★★.

●COMPILATIONS: *The Best Of Billy J. Kramer* (1984)★★★, *The EMI Years* (1991)★★★, *The EP Collection* (See For Miles 1995)★★★.

KWESKIN, JIM, JUG BAND

b. 18 July 1940, Stamford, Connecticut, USA. Kweskin began to forge a ragtime/jugband style in the New England folk haunts during the early 60s. His early groups were largely informal and it was not until 1963, when he secured a recording deal, that this singer and guitarist began piecing together a more stable line-up. Geoff Muldaur (guitar/washboard/kazoo/vocals), Bob Siggins, Bruno Wolf and Fritz Richmond (jug/washtub bass) joined Kweskin on his enthusiastic, infectious debut. Siggins dropped out of the group prior to a second album, *Jug Band Music*. Bill Keith (banjo/pedal steel guitar) and Maria D'Amato (vocals/kazoo/tambourine) were now enlisted, while Kweskin's extended family also included several other individuals, the most notorious of whom was Mel Lyman, who added harmonica on *Relax Your Mind*, the leader's 'solo' album. D'Amato married Geoff Muldaur and later became better known for her solo career as Maria Muldaur. *See Reverse Side For Title*, arguably the Jug Band's finest album, featured versions of 'Blues In The Bottle' and 'Fishing Blues', both of which were recorded by the Lovin' Spoonful. 'Chevrolet', a magnificent duet between Muldaur and D'Amato, was another highlight and the entire selection balanced humour with a newfound purpose. Fiddler Richard Greene worked with the line-up for what was the group's final album, *Garden Of Joy*. He subsequently joined Keith on several projects, including the excellent bluegrass quintet, Muleskinner, while Geoff and Maria commenced work as a duo. Kweskin's own progress was rather overshadowed by his immersion in Lyman's dark, quasi-religious, Charles Manson-like commune, but he emerged as a solo performer in the early 70s and has since continued to forge an idiosyncratic, traditional musical-based path.

●ALBUMS: *Jim Kweskin And The Jug Band* i (Vanguard 1965)★★★, *Jug Band Music* (Vanguard 1965)★★★★, *Relax Your Mind* (Vanguard 1966)★★★, *Jim Kewskin And The Jug Band* ii (1966)★★★★, *See Reverse Side For Title* (Vanguard 1967)★★★, *Jump For Joy* (Vanguard 1967)★★★, *Garden Of Joy* (Reprise 1967)★★★, *Whatever Happened To Those Good Old Days* (Vanguard 1968)★★★, *American Aviator* (1969)★★★, *Jim Kweskin's America* (1971)★★★, *Jim Kweskin* (1978)★★★, *Jim Kweskin Lives Again* (1978)★★★, *Side By Side* (1980)★★★, *Swing On A Star* (1980)★★★.

●COMPILATIONS: *Best Of Jim Kweskin And The Jug Band* (Vanguard 1968)★★★★, *Greatest Hits* (1990)★★★★, *Strange Things Happening* (Rounder 1994)★★★.

LAINE, DENNY

b. Brian Hines, 29 October 1944, Jersey, Channel Islands. An integral part of the Birmingham beat scene, this vocalist/guitarist formed his own group, Denny Laine And The Diplomats, in 1962. Two years later, he became a founder-member of the Moody Blues, and was the featured singer on the group's international hit, 'Go Now'. Later recordings were less successful and, in November 1966, Laine abandoned the group to embark on an ill-starred solo career. Although his debut release, 'Say You Don't Mind', failed to chart, the single garnered considerable critical plaudits. Colin Blunstone's sympathetic cover version later became a UK Top 20 hit in 1972. Laine's experimental ensemble, the Electric String Band, collapsed prematurely, and he spent much of the late 60s drifting between several short-lived groups, including Balls and Ginger Baker's Airforce. He also completed a solo album, but this remained unissued for several years. Between 1971 and 1980, Laine was an integral member of Wings, co-writing the multi-million selling 'Mull Of Kintyre'. His departure followed adverse publicity in the wake of leader Paul McCartney's arrest on drugs charges. An intermittently talented individual, Denny Laine has since pursued a solo path, which has failed to match its original promise.
● ALBUMS: *Aah Laine* (Wizard 1973)★★, with Paul McCartney *Holly Days* (EMI 1976)★★, *Japanese Tears* (Scratch 1980)★★, *In Flight* (Breakaway 1984)★★, *Weep For Love* (1985)★★, *Hometown Girls* (1985)★★, *Wings On My Feet* (1987)★★, *Master Suite* (1988), *Lonely Road* (1988)★★, *Blue Nights* (President 1993)★★★, *The Rock Survivor* (WCP 1994)★★★.

LAMBERT, KIT

Initially a budding film-maker, Lambert became involved with music when he and partner Chris Stamp sought a group to star in a short feature film. They discovered the Who - then known as the High Numbers - in September 1964, but having abandoned their initial intention, assumed management duties within a week. A mutual acquaintance brought Lambert together with producer Shel Talmy and although a recording deal ensued, the former quickly grew disillusioned with its terms. He broke the deal in 1966 by producing the Who's fourth single, 'Substitute', but although an out-of-court settlement awarded Talmy substantial damages, the group was free to record elsewhere. The following year Lambert and Stamp created Track Records, the roster of which included not only the Who, but Jimi Hendrix, Arthur Brown, Thunderclap Newman and John's Children. Lambert played an important role in the conception of the Who's pop-opera *Tommy* - he was the son of noted composer/arranger Constant Lambert - and his suggestions and inspiration were later acknowledged by its creator, Pete Townshend. The resultant album, however, was the last to bear Lambert's production credit and during the ensuing decade, relations between the group and management gradually deteriorated. Two years of legal wrangling were finally settled in 1975. The Who adopted a new manager, Bill Curbishley, and label, Polydor, while the subsequent collapse of Track effectively ended Lambert's active tenure in the music business. Whereas Stamp resumed his interest in film work, his former partner embarked on a life of excess which ended tragically on 7 April 1981 when he died of a brain haemorrhage following a fall at his mother's home.

LANCE, MAJOR

b. 4 April 1939, Winterville, Mississippi, USA, d. 3 September 1994, Decatur, Georgia, USA. A former amateur boxer and a dancer on the Jim Lounsbury record-hop television show, Lance also sang with the Five Gospel Harmonaires and for a brief period with Otis Leavill and Barbara Tyson in the Floats. His 1959 Mercury release, 'I Got A Girl', was written and produced by Curtis Mayfield, a high school contemporary, but Lance's career was not truly launched until he signed with OKeh Records three years later. 'Delilah' opened his account there, while a further Mayfield song, the stylish 'The Monkey Time' in 1963, gave the singer a US Top 10 hit. The partnership between singer and songwriter continued through 1963-64 with a string of US pop chart hits: 'Hey Little Girl', 'Um Um Um Um Um Um', 'The Matador' and 'Rhythm'. Although Lance's range was more limited than that of his associate, the texture and phrasing mirrored that of Mayfield's work with his own group, the Impressions. 'Ain't That A Shame' in 1965, marked a pause in their relationship as its commercial success waned. Although further vibrant singles followed, notably 'Investigate' and 'Ain't No Soul (In These Rock 'N' Roll Shoes)', Lance left OKeh for Dakar Records in 1968 where 'Follow The Leader' was a minor R&B hit. Two 1970 releases on Curtom, 'Stay Away From Me' and 'Must Be Love Coming Down', marked a reunion with Mayfield. From there lance moved to Volt, Playboy and Osiris, the last of which he co-owned with Al Jackson, a former member of Booker T. And The MGs. These spells were punctuated by a two-year stay in Britain (1972-74), during which Lance recorded for Contempo and Warner Brothers. Convicted of selling cocaine in 1978, the singer emerged from prison to find his OKeh recordings in demand as part of America's 'beach music' craze, where aficionados in Virginia and the Carolinas maintain a love of vintage soul. A heart attack in September 1994 proved fatal for Lance, who died at the age of 55.
● ALBUMS: *Monkey Time* (OKeh 1963)★★★, *Major Lance's Greatest Hits - Recorded 'Live' At The Torch* (OKeh 1973)★★, *Now Arriving* (Motown 1978)★★, *The*

Major's Back (1983)★★, *Live At Hinkley* (1986)★★.
●COMPILATIONS: *Um Um Um Um Um - The Best Of Major Lance* (OKeh 1964)★★★, *Major's Greatest Hits* (1965)★★★, *The Best Of ...* (Epic 1976)★★★, *The Major's Back* (1983), *Monkey Time* rec. 60s (Edsel 1983)★★★, *Swing'est Hits Of ...* (1984)★★★, *Best Of ...* (1994)★★★.

LANG, DON

b. Gordon Langhorn, 19 January 1925, Halifax, Yorkshire, England, d. 3 August 1992, London, England. Lang started as a dance band trombonist working with the bands of Peter Rose, Teddy Foster and Vic Lewis. It was with Lewis that he made his first recordings. He began singing with Ken Mackintosh's Band and is credited under his real name on some of their records and also one recording with the Cyril Stapleton Orchestra. Lang went solo in the mid-50s and after a couple of singles on Decca he made the UK Top 20 with a 'vocalese' (scat jazz) version of 'Cloudburst' in 1956/56 on HMV Records. Together with his Frantic Five (which included the late saxophonist Red Price) he was one of the first UK acts to get involved with rock 'n' roll and skiffle, although his jazz roots were always audible. The group appeared regularly on UK television's seminal *6.5 Special* and sang the theme song over the credits. After many unsuccessful singles he charted with a cover of Chuck Berry's 'School Day' and reached the Top 10 with a version of David Seville's 'Witch Doctor' (with the curious lyric, 'ooh ee ooh aha bing bang walla walla bing bang'). When the hits dried up for this elder statesman of UK pop, he formed a new band and played the dancehall and club circuit for many years. At times he sang alongside such notable acts as the Mike Sammes and Cliff Adams Singers and played on records like the Beatles' 'white album' (*The Beatles*). Alongside 50s acts like Wee Willie Harris and Tommy Bruce, he could still be seen on the UK rock 'n' roll circuit. For a time he returned to his first love - jazz, but for the last few years of his life he was in virtual retirement, emerging for the occasional rock 'n' roll revival show or recording session. He died of cancer in the Royal Marsden Hospital in August 1992. His son Brad has played bass for ABC and Toyah.
●ALBUMS: *Skiffle Special* (HMV 1957)★★★, *Introducing The Hand Jive* (HMV 1958)★★★, *Twenty Top 20 Twists* (HMV 1962)★★.
●COMPILATIONS: *Rock Rock Rock* (1983)★★★, with the Twisters *20 Rock 'n' Roll Twists* (1988)★★★.

LAST, JAMES

b. Hans Last, 17 April 1929, Bremen, Germany. This phenomenally successful bandleader and arranger brought up to date the tradition of big band arrangements for current pop hits. By the end of the 80s, Last had released over 50 albums and had sold 50 million copies worldwide. Trained as a bass player, in 1946 he joined Hans-Gunther Oesterreich's Radio Bremen Dance Orchestra. Two years later he was leading the Becker-Last Ensemble. When that folded in 1955 Last worked as an arranger for radio stations and for Polydor Records. There he worked with Caterina Valente, Freddy Quinn and bandleader Helmut Zacharias, and in 1965 released *Non-Stop Dancing*. Blending together well-known tunes with a jaunty dance beat, this was the first of 20 volumes that helped make Last a star across Europe by the mid-80s. Hansi, as he was known to his fans, varied the formula in several other ways. He took material from different musical genres (classics, country, Beatles, Latin), from various countries (Ireland, Russia, Switzerland, Scotland) and he added guest artists. Among these were bossa nova singer Astrud Gilberto (*Plus* 1987) and pianist Richard Clayderman (*Together At Last* 1991). One 'added attraction' to his party sets is the technique Last employs of 'non-stop' atmosphere by incorporating claps, cheers and laughter between each segueing track. Relying on albums and tours for his success, Last had only one hit single in the USA and the UK, 'The Seduction', the theme from the 1980 film, *American Gigolo*.
●ALBUMS: *Non Stop Dancing Vol. 1* (1965)★★★, *This Is James Last* (1967)★★★, *Hammond A-Go Go* (1967)★★★, *Dancing '68 Vol. 1* (1968)★★★, *James Last Goes Pop* (1968)★★★, *Classics Up To Date Vols. 1-6* (1970-84)★★★, *Beach Party 2* (1971)★★★, *Voodoo Party* (1972)★★★, *Ole* (1973)★★★, *Country & Square Dance Party* (1974)★★★, *Ten Years Non Stop Party Album* (1975)★★★, *Make The Party Last* (1975)★★★, *Christmas James Last* (1976)★★★, *In London* (1978)★★★, *East To West* (1978)★★★, *Last The Whole Night Long* (1979)★★★, *Christmas Classics* (1979)★★★, *Caribbean Nights* (1980)★★★, *Seduction* (1980)★★★, *Classics For Dreaming* (1980)★★★, *Hansimania* (1981)★★★, *Roses From The South - The Music Of Johann Strauss* (1981)★★★, *Bluebird* (1982)★★★, *Biscaya* (1982)★★★, *Tango* (1983)★★★, *Christmas Dancing* (1983)★★★, *Greatest Songs Of The Beatles* (1983)★★★, *Games That Lovers Play* (1984)★★★, *Rose Of Tralee And Other Irish Favourites* (1984)★★★, *All Aboard With Cap'n James* (1984)★★★, *In Russia* (1984)★★★, *At St. Patrick's Cathedral, Dublin* (1984)★★★, *Im Allgau (In The Alps)* (1984)★★★, *In Scotland* (1985)★★★, *In Holland* (1987)★★★, *Everything Comes To An End, Only A Sausage Has Two* (1987)★★★, *Plus* (1987)★★★, *The Berlin Concert* (1987)★★★, *Dance, Dance, Dance* (1987)★★★, *Flute Fiesta* (1988)★★★, *Plays Bach* (1988)★★★, *Happy Heart* (1989)★★★, *Classics By Moonlight* (1990)★★★, *Together At Last* (1991)★★★.
●COMPILATIONS: *The Best From 150 Gold* (1980)★★★, *By Request* (1988)★★★.
●FURTHER READING: *James Last Story*, James Last. *James Last*, Bob Willcox, *James Last*, Howard Elson.

LAWRENCE, STEVE

b. Stephen Leibowitz, 8 July 1935, Brooklyn, New York, USA. The son of a cantor in a Brooklyn synagogue, Lawrence was in the Glee club at Thomas Jefferson High School, where he began studying piano, saxophone, composition and arranging. He made his recording debut for

King Records at the age of 16. The record, 'Mine And Mine Alone', based on 'Softly Awakes My Heart' from *Samson & Delilah*, revealed an amazingly mature voice and style. Influenced by Frank Sinatra, but never merely a copyist, he was an individual singer of great range and warmth. He got his first break on Steve Allen's *Tonight* television show, where he met, sang with and later married Eydie Gorme. He recorded for Coral Records and had his first hit in 1957 with 'The Banana Boat Song'. It was the infectious 'Party Doll' which gave him a Top 5 hit in 1957 and he followed that same year with four further, although lesser successes, namely 'Pum-Pa-Lum', 'Can't Wait For Summer', 'Fabulous' and 'Fraulein'. During his US Army service (1958-60) he sang with military bands on recruiting drives and bond rallies. Back home he and Eydie embarked on a double act, their most memorable hit was 'I Want To Stay Here' in 1963. As Steve And Eydie they made albums for CBS, ABC and United Artists, including *Steve & Eydie At The Movies*, *On Broadway*, *We Got Us*, *The Golden Hits* and *Our Love Is Here To Stay*, the latter a double album of great George Gershwin songs, which was the soundtrack of a well-received television special. Lawrence, on his own, continued to have regular hits with 'Portrait Of My Love' and 'Go Away Little Girl' in 1961/2, and enjoyed critical success with albums such as *Academy Award Losers* and *Portrait Of My Love*. As an actor he starred on Broadway in *What Makes Sammy Run?*, took the lead in *Pal Joey* in summer stock, and has acted in a crime series on US television.

●ALBUMS: *About That Girl* (Coral 1956)★★★, *Songs By Steve Lawrence* (Coral 1957)★★★, *Here's Steve Lawrence* (Coral 1958)★★★, *All About Love* (Coral 1959)★★★, *Steve Lawrence* (King 1959)★★★, *Swing Softly With Me* (ABC 1959)★★★★, with Eydie Gorme *We Got Us* (ABC 1960)★★★★, with Eydie Gorme *Steve And Eydie Sing The Golden Hits* (ABC 1960)★★★, *The Steve Lawrence Sound* (United Artists/HMV 1960)★★★★, *Steve Lawrence Goes Latin* (United Artists 1960)★★, *Portrait Of My Love* (United Artists 1961)★★★, *Winners* (1963)★★★, with Eydie Gorme *Two On The Aisle* (ABC 1963)★★★, *Come Waltz With Me* (CBS 1963)★★★, *People Will Say We're In Love* (United Artists 1963)★★★, *Steve Lawrence Conquers Broadway* (United Artists 1963)★★★, with Eydie Gorme *Our Best To You* (ABC 1964)★★★, *Academy Award Losers* (1964)★★★, *Songs Everybody Knows* (Coral 1964)★★★, *What Makes Sammy Run* soundtrack (Columbia 1964)★★, *The Steve Lawrence Show* (1965)★★★, *Together On Broadway* (1967)★★★, *What It Was, Was Love* (1969)★★★, *Real True Lovin'* (1969)★★★, *We Got Us* (1984)★★★, *We're All Alone* (1985)★★★, *I Still Believe In Love* (1985)★★★.

●COMPILATIONS: *Best Of Steve Lawrence* (ABC 1960)★★★, *The Very Best Of Steve Lawrence* (United Artists 1962)★★★, *Best Of Steve And Eydie* (1977)★★★, *The Best Of ...* (Taragon 1995)★★★.

LEAVES

Formed in Northridge, California, USA, in 1964, this folk rock group began its career as the Rockwells, a college-based 'frat' band. Founder-members Robert Lee Reiner (guitar) and Jim Pons (bass) were joined by Bill Rinehart (guitar) and Jimmy Kern (drums) in an attraction offering a diet of surf tunes and R&B-styled oldies. By the end of the year vocalist John Beck had been added to the line-up, while Kern was replaced by Tom Ray early in 1965. Having branched into the Los Angeles club circuit, the Rockwells were among the finalists auditioning to replace the Byrds at the fabled Ciro's on Sunset Strip. They duly won the residency whereupon the group took a more contemporary name, the Leaves. Having secured a recording contract with Mira Records via a production deal with singer Pat Boone's Penhouse production company, the Leaves made their recording debut with 'Too Many People' in September 1965. For a follow-up the quintet opted to record 'Hey Joe', a song popularized by the aforementioned Byrds, Love and Music Machine and a subsequent hit for Jimi Hendrix. Their initial recording was not a success, prompting the departure of Rinehart in February 1966. He later surfaced in the Gene Clark Group and, later, Merry Go Round. Bobby Arlin, veteran of the Catalinas with Leon Russell and Bruce Johnson, took his place. A second version of 'Hey Joe' was released, then withdrawn, before the group proclaimed themselves happy with a third interpretation, which featured fuzz guitar and a vibrant instrumental break. It reached the US Top 40 in May that year, much to the chagrin of those initially playing the song. However, ensuing releases were not well received, placing a strain on the group. Reiner left the line-up, but although the remaining quartet were signed to Capitol Records, further ructions ensued. Pons joined the Turtles during sessions for *All The Good That's Happening*, Ray was fired by the producer, and Beck quit in disgust leaving Arlin to tidy the proceedings. The last-named pair did reunite in 1967 to record a handful of songs, but plans to work as the New Leaves, with the aid of Buddy Sklar (bass) and Craig Boyd (drums), were abandoned when Beck quit. The remaining trio took a new name, Hook. Of the remaining ex-members only Pons retained a high profile as a member of Flo And Eddie and the Mothers Of Invention.

●ALBUMS: *Hey Hoe* (Mira 1966)★★, *All The Good That's Happening* (Capitol 1967)★★.

●COMPILATIONS: *The Leaves 1966* (Panda 1985)★★.

●FILMS: *The Cool Ones* (1967).

LEE, BRENDA

b. Brenda Mae Tarpley, 11 December 1944, Lithonia, Georgia, USA. Even in early adolescence, she had an adult husk of a voice that could slip from anguished intimacy through sleepy insinuation to raucous lust even during 'Let's Jump The Broomstick', 'Speak To Me Pretty' and other jaunty classics that kept her in the hit parade from the mid-50s to 1965. Through local radio and, by 1956, wider exposure on Red Foley's Ozark Jubilee broadcasts, 'Little Brenda Lee' was ensured enough airplay for her first single, a revival of Hank Williams' 'Jambalaya', to crack the US country chart before her *Billboard* Hot 100 debut with 1957's 'One Step At A Time'. The novelty of her extreme youth facilitated bigger triumphs for 'Little Miss Dynamite' with the million-selling 'Rockin' Around The Christmas Tree' and later bouncy rockers before the next decade brought a greater proportion of heartbreak ballads such as 'I'm Sorry' and 'Too Many Rivers' - plus an acting role in the children's fantasy movie, *The Two Little Bears*. 1963 was another successful year - especially in the UK with the title song of *All Alone Am I*, 'Losing You' (a French translation), 'I Wonder' and 'As Usual' each entering the Top 20. While 1964 finished well with 'Is It True' and 'Christmas Will Be Just Another Lonely Day', only minor hits followed. Although she may have weathered prevailing fads, family commitments caused Lee to cut back on touring and record only intermittently after 1966's appositely titled *Bye Bye Blues*.

Lee resurfaced in 1971 with a huge country hit in Kris Kristofferson's 'Nobody Wins' and later recordings that established her as a star of what was then one of the squarest seams of pop. When country gained a younger audience in the mid-80s, respect for its older practitioners found her guesting with Loretta Lynn and Kitty Wells on k.d. lang's *Shadowland*. - produced in 1988 by Owen Bradley (who had also supervised many early Lee records). In Europe, Brenda Lee remained mostly a memory - albeit a pleasing one as shown by Coast To Coast's hit revival of 'Let's Jump The Broomstick', a high UK placing for 1980's *Little Miss Dynamite* greatest hits collection and Mel Smith And Kim Wilde's 'Rockin' Around The Christmas Tree'. Lee is fortunate in having a large rock 'n' roll catalogue destined for immortality in addition to her now-high standing in the country music world. In 1993, billed as 'the biggest-selling female star in pop history', Brenda Lee toured the UK and played the London Palladium, headlining a nostalgia package that included Chris Montez, Len Barry and Johnny Tillotson. From her opening 'I'm So Excited', through to the closing 'Rockin' All Over The World', she fulfilled all expectations, and won standing ovations from packed houses. In keeping with many of their packages, the Bear Family box set is a superb retrospective.

●ALBUMS: *Grandma, What Great Songs You Sang* (Decca 1959)★★, *Brenda Lee* (Decca 1960)★★★★, *This Is ... Brenda* (Decca 1960)★★★★, *Miss Dynamite* (Brunswick 1960)★★★★, *Emotions* (Decca 1961)★★★, *All The Way* (Decca 1961)★★★, *Sincerely Brenda Lee* (Decca 1962)★★★★, *Brenda, That's All* (Decca 1962)★★★★, with Tennessee Ernie Ford *The Show For Christmas Seals* (1962)★★★, *All Alone Am I* (Decca 1963)★★★, *Let Me Sing* (Decca 1963)★★★, *By Request* (Decca 1964)★★★, *Merry Christmas From Brenda Lee* (Decca 1964)★★★, *Top Teen Hits* (Decca 1965)★★★, *The Versatile Brenda Lee* (1965)★★★, *Too Many Rivers* (Decca 1965)★★★, *Bye Bye Blues* (Decca 1966)★★★, *Coming On Strong* (Decca 1966)★★★, *Call Me Brenda* (MCA 1967)★★★, *Good Life* (MCA

1967)★★★, with Pete Fountain *For The First Time* (MCA 1968)★★★, *Johnny One Time* (MCA 1969)★★★, *Memphis Portrait* (Decca 1970)★★★, *Let It Be Me* (Vocalion 1970)★★★, *A Whole Lotta* (MCA 1972)★★★, *Brenda* (MCA 1973)★★★, *New Sunrise* (MCA 1974)★★★, *Brenda Lee Now* (MCA 1975)★★★, *The LA Sessions* (MCA 1977)★★★, *Even Better* (MCA 1980)★★★, *Take Me Back* (MCA 1981)★★★, *Only When I Laugh* (MCA 1982)★★★, *Greatest Country Hits* (MCA 1982)★★★, with Dolly Parton, Kris Kristofferson, Willie Nelson *The Winning Hand* (Monument 1983)★★★, *Feels So Right* (MCA 1985)★★★, *Brenda Lee* (Warners 1991)★★★, *A Brenda Lee Christmas* (Warners 1991)★★★, *Greatest Hits Live* (MCA 1992)★★★, *Coming On Strong* (Muskateer 1995)★★★.

●COMPILATIONS: *10 Golden Years* (1966)★★★, *The Brenda Lee Story* (MCA 1974)★★★★, *Little Miss Dynamite* (MCA 1976)★★★★, *25th Anniversary* (1984)★★★★, *The Early Years* (MCA 1984)★★★, *The Golden Decade* (1985)★★★★, *The Best Of Brenda Lee* (1986)★★★★, *Love Songs* (1986)★★★, *Brenda's Best* (1989)★★★★, *Very Best Of Brenda Lee Vol. 1* (1990)★★★★, *Very Best Of Brenda Lee Vol. 2* (1990) *Anthology Vol. 1* (MCA 1991)★★★★, *Anthology Vol. 2* (MCA 1991)★★★, *Little Miss Dynamite* 4-CD box set (Bear Family 1996)★★★★, *The EP Collection* (See For Miles 1996)★★ ★★.

LEE, JACKIE (EIRE)

b. 29 May 1936, Dublin, Eire. A great lover of pseudonyms, Lee began her career touring Ireland under the billing 'Child Star'. In 1956, she made her recording debut with 'The Outskirts Of Paris' and by the end of the decade had joined the Squadronaires showband. After several years on the road, she married musician Len Beadle in 1963 and together they formed Jackie And The Raindrops. Two years later, she went solo again for the tear-jerker, 'I Cry Alone'. In 1967, she was relaunched as Emma Rede but failed with 'Just Like A Man'. By now, she had recorded for Columbia, Decca, Polydor and CBS, but it was with Philips that she finally found chart success courtesy of 'White Horses', the theme from a UK children's television series. The single was recorded under the name Jacky and its success coincided with a serious assault on the US market via film soundtrack recordings. Most notable among these was Lee's contribution to the 1968 film *Barberella*, in which she sang over the credits. Dismissed as a 60s one-hit-wonder, she defied the odds by signing to her umpteenth label, Pye, reverting to her real name and winning through with yet another children's song, 'Rupert', in 1971.

LEEMAN, MARK, FIVE

A popular attraction in London's clubs, the Mark Leeman Five made their debut in January 1965 with the Manfred Mann-produced 'Portland Town'. Mark Leeman (vocals/guitar), Alan Roskams (lead guitar), Terry Goldberg (keyboards), David Hyde (bass) and Brian

'Blinky' Davidson (drums) showed an impressive, almost 'progressive' grasp of R&B, a feature confirmed on their next release 'Blow My Blues Away'. Leeman was killed in a car crash in June 1965 and his place was taken by former Cheynes frontman Roger Peacock. Thomas Parker then replaced Goldberg, but despite two further excellent singles, the quintet was unable to achieve chart success. Peacock left for a solo career in July 1966 and although the remaining musicians were augmented by Pete Hodges (vocals) and Pat 'Rave' Sandy (saxophone), the group subsequently split up. Drummer Davidson later found fame in the Nice.

●COMPILATIONS: *The Mark Leeman Five Memorial Album* (1991)★★.

LEFT BANKE

Formed in 1966, the Left Banke was the brainchild of pianist/composer Michael Brown (b. Michael Lookofsky, 25 April 1949, New York City, New York, USA). The son of a noted arranger and producer, Brown's early work appeared on releases by Reparata And The Delrons and Christopher And The Chaps, prior to the founding of the Left Banke. Steve Martin (vocals), Jeff Winfield (guitar), Tom Finn (bass) and George Cameron (drums) completed the original Left Banke line-up, which scored a US Top 5 hit with 'Walk Away Renee'. This gorgeous song adeptly combined elements drawn from the Beatles and baroque, and became a major hit the following year when covered by the Four Tops. The Left Banke enjoyed further success with 'Pretty Ballerina', but underwent the first of several changes when Rick Brand replaced Winfield during sessions for an attendant album. Internal ructions led to Brown completing a third release, 'Ivy Ivy', with the aid of session musicians, but the band was reunited for 'Desiree', their final chart entry. Michael then abandoned his creation - he later formed Stories - and when Brand also departed, Finn, Cameron and Martin completed *The Left Banke Too* as a trio. Although bereft of their principal songwriter, the group still captured the spirit of earlier recordings, but broke up in 1969 in the wake of a final single, 'Myrah', which was issued in an unfinished state. However, a New York independent, Camerica, coaxed the final line-up back into the studio in 1978. Although initially shelved, the set, which successfully echoed the group's glory days, was belatedly issued eight years later as *Voices Calling* (UK title)/*Strangers On A Train* (US).

●ALBUMS: *Walk Away Renee/Pretty Ballerina* (Smash 1967)★★★, *The Left Banke, Too* (Smash 1968)★★, *Voices Calling* aka *Strangers On A Train* (1906)★★★.

●COMPILATIONS: *And Suddenly It's … The Left Banke* (1984)★★★, *The History Of The Left Banke* (1985)★★★, *Walk Away Renee* (1986)★★★.

LEMON PIPERS

This New York-based quintet - Ivan Browne (vocals/rhythm guitar), Bill Bartlett (lead guitar), R.G. (Reg) Nave (organ), Steve Walmsley (bass) and Bill Albuagh (drums) - made its debut in 1967 with 'Turn Around And Take A Look'. Its rudimentary style was then replaced by the measured approach of aspiring songwriting/production team, Paul Leka and Shelly Pinz. Together they created a distinctive Lemon Pipers sound, a sparkling mélange of sweeping strings and percussive vibraslaps exemplified on the group's million-selling hit, 'Green Tambourine'. The attendant album contained several songs - 'Rice Is Nice', 'Shoeshine Boy' - which were recorded in a similar style, but the set also contained the startling 'Through With You', an extended *tour de force* for Bartlett's rampaging guitarwork and a surprise for those anticipating easy-on-the-ear fare. Subsequent recordings failed to match their early success, and although a second album, *Jungle Marmalade*, offered several inventive moments, the Lemon Pipers were tarred as a bubblegum attraction on the strength of that first hit. The group broke up in 1969, although Bartlett later found success as a member of Ram Jam.

●ALBUMS: *Green Tambourine* (Buddah 1967)★★★, *Jungle Marmalade* (1968)★★.

●COMPILATIONS: *The Lemon Pipers* (1990)★★★.

LESTER, KETTY

b. Revoyda Frierson, 16 August 1934, Hope, Arkansas, USA. Ketty Lester began her singing career on completing a music course at San Francisco State College. A residency at the city's Purple Onion club was followed by a successful tour of Europe before she joined bandleader Cab Calloway's revue. Later domiciled in New York, Lester's popular nightclub act engendered a recording deal of which 'Love Letters' was the first fruit. The singer's cool-styled interpretation of this highly popular standard, originally recorded by Dick Haymes, reached the Top 5 in both the US and UK in 1962, eventually selling in excess of one million copies. The song has been covered many times, with notable successes for Elvis Presley and Alison Moyet. Its attractiveness was enhanced by a memorable piano figure but Lester was sadly unable to repeat the single's accomplished balance between song, interpretation and arrangement. She later abandoned singing in favour of a career as a film and television actress with appearances in *Marcus Welby MD*, *Little House On The Prairie*, *The Terminal Man* and *The Prisoner Of Second Avenue*, to name but a few. She was later coaxed back into the studio, but only on her stipulation that it would be to perform sacred music only.

●ALBUMS: *Love Letters* (Era 1962)★★, *Soul Of Me* (RCA Victor 1964)★★, *Where Is Love* (RCA Victor 1965)★★, *When A Woman Loves A Man* (1967)★★, *I Saw Him* (1985)★★.

LETTERMEN

This very successful US close-harmony pop trio comprised Bob Engemann (b. 19 February 1936, Highland Park, Michigan, USA), Tony Butala (b. 20 November 1940, Sharon, Pennsylvania, USA), Jim Pike (b. 6 November 1938, St. Louis, Missouri, USA). Pike, a letterman at Utah's Brigham Young University, released an unsuccessful single on Warner Brothers Records in 1959. In

1960, he and fellow student and ex-Mormon missionary Engemann formed a trio with supper-club singer Butala, who had recorded previously on Topic and Lute. After two unsuccessful singles, they joined Capitol Records and struck gold immediately with 'The Way You Look Tonight'. The smooth ballad singers put an impressive 24 albums in the US chart in the 60s, with 10 of them reaching the Top 40. The popular live act also had another 19 chart singles including the Top 10 hits 'When I Fall In Love' in 1961 and the medley 'Goin' Out Of My Head/Can't Take My Eyes Off You' in 1967. In 1968, Jim's brother Gary replaced Engemann and six years later their brother Donny replaced Jim. In the 70s they were a top-earning club act and were much in demand for television commercial work. The group recorded on their own Alfa Omega label in 1979 and signed with Applause in 1982. In all, the distinctive harmonic vocal group, who have never charted in the UK, have earned nine gold albums and sold over $25 million worth of records.

●ALBUMS: *A Song For Young Love* (1962)★★★, *Once Upon A Time* (1962)★★★, *Jim, Tony And Bob* (1962)★★★, *College Standards* (1963)★★★, *The Lettermen In Concert* (1963)★★★, *A Lettermen Kind Of Love* (Capitol 1964)★★★, *The Lettermen Look At Love* (1964)★★★, *She Cried* (1964)★★★, *Portrait Of My Love* (1965)★★★, *The Hit Sounds Of The Lettermen* (1965)★★★, *You'll Never Walk Alone* (1965)★★★, *More Hit Sounds Of The Lettermen!* (1966)★★★, *A New Song For Young Love* (1966)★★★, *For Christmas This Year* (1966)★★★, *Warm* (1967)★★★, *Spring!* (1967)★★★, *The Lettermen!!! ... And Live!* (1967)★★★, *Goin' Out Of My Head* (1968)★★★, *Special Request* (1968)★★★, *Put Your Head On My Shoulder* (1968)★★★, *I Have Dreamed* (1969)★★★, *Hurt So Bad* (1969)★★★, *Traces/Memories* (1970)★★★, *Reflections* (1970)★★★, *Everything's Good About You* (1971)★★★, *Feelings* (1971)★★★, *Love Book* (1971)★★★, *Lettermen 1* (1972)★★★, *Alive Again ... Naturally* (1973)★★★, *Evergreen* (1985).

●COMPILATIONS: *The Best Of The Lettermen* (1966)★★★, *The Best Of The Lettermen, Vol. 2* (1969)★★★, *All Time Greatest Hits* (1974)★★★.

LEWIS, GARY, AND THE PLAYBOYS

One of the most commercially successful US pop groups of the mid-60s, the original Playboys comprised Gary Lewis (b. Gary Levital, 31 July 1946, New York, USA; vocals/drums), Alan Ramsey (b. 27 July 1943, New Jersey, USA; guitar), John West (b. 31 July 1939, Unrichville, Ohio, USA; guitar), David Costell (b. 15 March 1944, Pittsburgh, Pennsylvania, USA; bass) and David Walker (b. 12 May 1943, Montgomery, Alabama, USA; keyboards). Group leader Gary Lewis was the son of comedian Jerry Lewis and had been playing drums since the age of 14. After appearing at selected Hollywood parties, the ensemble was offered a residency at the Disneyland Park and soon after was signed by Liberty Records and producer Leon Russell. Their debut single, 'This Diamond Ring' (co-written by Al Kooper and originally intended for former idol, Bobby Vee), topped the American charts in February 1965 and spearheaded a remarkable run of Top 10 hits that included 'Count Me In', 'Save Your Heart For Me', 'Everybody Loves A Clown', 'She's Just My Style', 'She's Gonna Miss Her' and 'Green Grass'. The latter, although written by UK composers Cook And Greenaway (alias David And Jonathan), predictably failed to make any impact in the UK market where the group remained virtually unknown. Undoubtedly the best-selling US group of the mid-60s without a UK hit to their name, they nevertheless enjoyed healthy record sales all over the world, appeared regularly on television, and even participated in a couple of low-budget movies, *A Swingin' Summer* and *Out Of Sight*. Their relative decline in 1967 probably had less to do with changing musical fashions than the induction of Gary Lewis to the US Armed Forces. By the time of his discharge in 1968, a set of Playboys were ready to return him to the charts with a remake of Brian Hyland's 'Sealed With A Kiss'. A revival of the Cascades' 'Rhythm Of The Rain' pointed to the fact that the group were running short of ideas while also indicating their future on the revivalist circuit. After disbanding the group at the end of the 60s, Lewis was unsuccessfully relaunched as a singer/songwriter but later assembled a new version of the Playboys for cabaret and festival dates.

●ALBUMS: *This Diamond Ring* (Liberty 1965)★★★, *Everybody Loves A Clown* (1965)★★★, *Out Of Sight* soundtrack (1966)★★★, *She's Just My Style* (1966)★★★★, *Gary Lewis Hits Again!* (1966)★★★, *You Don't Have To Paint Me A Picture* (Liberty 1967)★★, *New Directions* (1967)★★, *Gary Lewis Now!* (1968)★★, *Close Cover Before Playing* (1968)★★, *Rhythm Of The Rain* (1969)★★, *I'm On The Road Now* (1969)★★.

●COMPILATIONS: *Golden Greats* (1966)★★★, *More Golden Greats* (1968)★★, *Twenty Golden Greats* (1979)★★★, *Greatest Hits: Gary Lewis And The Playboys* (1986)★★★.

LEWIS, RAMSEY

b. 27 May 1935, Chicago, Illinois, USA. Lewis started playing piano at the age of six. He graduated from school in 1948, after winning both the American Legion Award as an outstanding scholar and a special award for piano services at the Edward Jenner Elementary School. He began his career as an accompanist at the Zion Hill Baptist Church, an experience of gospel that never left him. He later studied music at Chicago Music College with the idea of becoming a concert pianist, but left at the age of 18 to get married. He found a job working in a record shop and joined the Clefs, a seven-piece dance band. In 1956, he formed a jazz trio with the Clefs' rhythm section (whom he had known since high school); bassist Eldee Young and drummer Isaac 'Red' Holt. Lewis made his debut recordings with the Argo record label, which later became Chess. He also had record dates with prestigious names such as Sonny Stitt, Clark Terry and Max Roach. In 1959, he played at Birdland in New York City and at the Randall's Island Festival. In 1964, 'Something You Got' was a minor hit, but it was 'The In Crowd', an instrumental cover of Dobie Gray's hit, that made him famous, reaching number 5 in the US charts and selling over a million copies by the end of 1965. Lewis insisted on a live sound, complete with handclaps and exclamations, an infectious translation of a black church feel into pop. His follow-up, 'Hang On Sloopy' reached number 11 and sold another million. These hits set the agenda for his career. Earnings for club dates increased tenfold. His classic 'Wade In The Water' was a major hit in 1966, and became a long-standing encore number for Graham Bond. The rhythm section left and resurfaced as a funk outfit in the mid-70s variously known as Redd Holt Unlimited and Young-Holt Unlimited. Lewis had an astute ear for hip, commercial sounds: his replacement drummer Maurice White left in 1971 to found the platinum mega-sellers Earth, Wind And Fire. Lewis never recaptured this commercial peak; he attempted to woo his audience by using synthesizers and disco rhythms, and continued securing *Billboard* Top 100 hits well into the 70s. His album success was quite an achievement with over 30 of his albums making the *Billboard* Top 200 listings. *The In Crowd* stayed on the list for almost a year, narrowly missing the top spot. *Mother Nature's Son* was a tribute to the Beatles, while the *Newly Recorded Hits* in 1973 was a dreadful mistake: the originals were far superior. By the 80s he was producing middle-of-the-road instrumental albums and accompanying singers, most notably Nancy Wilson. Nevertheless, it is his 60s hits - simple, infectious and funky - that will long endure.

●ALBUMS: *Down To Earth* (EmArcy 1958)★★★, *Gentleman Of Swing* (Argo 1958)★★★, *Gentlemen Of Jazz* (Argo 1958)★★★, *An Hour With The Ramsey Lewis Trio* (Argo 1959)★★★, *Stretching Out* (Argo 1960)★★★, *The Ramsey Lewis Trio In Chicago* (Argo 1961)★★★, *More Music From The Soil* (Argo 1961)★★★, *Sound Of Christmas* (Argo 1961)★★★, *The Sound Of Spring* (Argo 1962)★★★, *Country Meets The Blues* (Argo 1962)★★★, *Bossa Nova* (Argo 1962)★★★, *Pot Luck* (Argo 1962)★★★, *Barefoot Sunday Blues* (Argo 1963)★★★, *At The Bohemian Caverns* (Argo 1964)★★★, *Bach To The Blues* (Argo 1964)★★★, *More Sounds Of Christmas* (Argo 1964)★★★, *You Better Believe It* (Argo 1965)★★★★, *The In Crowd* (Argo 1965)★★★★, *Hang On Ramsey!* (Cadet 1965)★★★★, *Swingin'* (Cadet 1966)★★★★, *Wade In The Water* (Cadet 1966)★★★★, *Goin' Latin* (Cadet 1967)★★, *The Movie Album* (Cadet 1967)★★, *Dancing In The Street* (Cadet 1967)★★★, *Up Pops Ramsey Lewis* (Cadet 1968)★★★, *Maiden Voyage* (Cadet 1968)★★★, *Mother Nature's Son* (Cadet 1969)★★, *Another Voyage* (Cadet 1969)★★, *Ramsey Lewis: The Piano Player* (1970)★★★, *Them Changes* (1970)★★★, *Back To The Roots* (1971)★★★, *Upendo Ni Pamoja* (1972)★★★, *Funky Serenity* (1973)★★★,

Sun Goddess (Columbia 1974)★★★, *Don't It Feel Good* (Columbia 1975)★★★, *Salongo* (Columbia 1976)★★★, *Love Notes* (1977)★★★, *Tequila Mockingbird* (Columbia 1977)★★★, *Legacy* (Columbia 1978)★★★, *Routes* (1980)★★★, *Three Piece Suite* (Columbia 1981)★★★, *Live At The Savoy* (Columbia 1982)★★★, *Les Fleurs* (1983)★★, *Chance Encounter* (Columbia 1983)★★, with Nancy Wilson *The Two Of Us* (1984)★★★, *Renunion* (1984)★★★, *Fantasy* (1986)★★, *Keys To The City* (1987)★★, *Classic Encounter* (1989)★★, *Ivory Pyramid* (GRP 1992)★★, with King Curtis *Instrumental Soul Hits* (1993)★★, *Between The Keys* (GRP 1996)★★.

●COMPILATIONS: *Choice: The Best Of Ramsey Lewis Trio* (Cadet 1965)★★★, *The Best Of Ramsey Lewis* (1970)★★★, *Newly Recorded All-Time Non-Stop Golden Hits* (1973)★★★, *The Greatest Hits Of Ramsey Lewis* (1990)★★★, *20 Greatest Hits* (1992)★★★, *Collection* (More Music 1995)★★★.

●FILMS: *Gonks Go Beat* (1965).

LEYTON, JOHN

b. 17 February 1939, Frinton-on-Sea, Essex, England. Originally a small-time actor in the television series *Biggles*, Leyton's good looks won him a recording contract with Top Rank Records. Backed by the strong management of Robert Stigwood and talented producer Joe Meek, he recorded 'Tell Laura I Love Her', but lost out to the chart-topping Ricky Valence. A second flop with 'Girl On The Floor Above' was followed by the timely intervention of songwriter Geoff Goddard with the haunting 'Johnny Remember Me'. Stigwood ensured that the song was incorporated into Leyton's latest television role as pop singer Johnny St. Cyr in *Harpers, West One*. The nationwide exposure focused attention on the record and its otherworldly ambience and elaborate production were enough to bring Leyton a UK number 1. The Goddard-composed follow-up 'Wild Wind' reached number 2, and there were further minor hits with 'Son This Is She', 'Lone Rider' and 'Lonely City'. Avoiding the ravages of the beat boom, Leyton continued his acting career in such films as *The Great Escape* (1963), *Von Ryan's Express* (1965) and *Krakatoa* (1968). After a 10-year recording hiatus, he made a return in 1974 with an album written entirely by Kenny Young. Thereafter, Leyton concentrated on television work and related business interests.

●ALBUMS: *The Two Sides Of John Leyton* (HMV 1961)★★★, *Always Yours* (HMV 1963)★★, *John Leyton* (York 1974)★★.

●COMPILATIONS: *Rarities* (1984)★★, *The Best Of John Leyton* (1988)★★★, *The EP Collection ... Plus* (See For Miles 1994)★★★.

●FILMS: *It's Trad, Dad* aka *Ring-A-Ding Rhythm* (1962), *Every Day's A Holiday* aka *Seaside Swingers* (1965).

LIMELITERS

The Limeliters were one of the popular forces behind the 50s folk revival in America. The group comprised Lou

Gottleib (b. 10 October 1923, Los Angeles, California, USA, d. 11 July 1996, Sebastopol, California, USA; bass), Alex Hassilev (b. 11 July 1932, Paris, France; guitar/banjo/vocals) and Glenn Yarbrough (b. 12 January 1930, Milwaukee, Wisconsin, USA; guitar/vocals). They formed in Los Angeles in 1959 and took their name from a club, run by Hassilev and Yarbrough, called The Limelite in Aspen, Colorado, USA. Gottleib was a Doctor of Musicology, having studied under the Austrian composer Arnold Schoenberg. The group had a minor hit with 'A Dollar Down' in April 1961 on RCA Records, but their albums sold better than singles. Many of their albums were live recordings, including the popular *Tonight: In Person*, which reached number 5 in the US charts in 1961. The follow-up, *The Limeliters*, narrowly reached the Top 40 the same year. A third release, *The Slightly Fabulous Limeliters* made the US Top 10, also in 1961. A series of albums followed, with *Sing Out!* making the US Top 20 in 1962. Gradually their popularity waned, and when Yarbrough left in November 1963 to pursue a solo career, the group replaced him with Ernie Sheldon. In 1965, Yarbrough, also with RCA, reached the Top 40 in the US album charts with 'Baby The Rain Must Fall'. The title track, taken from a film of the same title, made the Top 20 the same year.

●ALBUMS: *The Limeliters* (RCA Victor 1960)★★★★, *Tonight: In Person* (RCA Victor 1961)★★★, *The Slightly Fabulous Limeliters* (RCA Victor 1961)★★★, *Sing Out!* (RCA Victor 1962)★★★★, *Through Children's Eyes* (RCA Victor 1962)★★, *Folk Matinee* (RCA Victor 1962)★★★, *Our Men In San Francisco* (RCA Victor 1963)★★★, *Makin' A Joyful Noise* (RCA Victor 1963)★★★, *Fourteen 14K Folk Songs* (RCA Victor 1963)★★★, *More Of Everything!* (RCA Victor 1964)★★★, *London Concert* (RCA Victor 1965)★★★, *The Limeliters Look At Love In Depth* (RCA Victor 1965)★★★, *The Original 'Those Were The Days'* (RCA Victor 1968)★★, *Time To Gather Seeds* (RCA Victor 1970)★★★, *Their First Historic Album* (RCA Victor 1986)★★★★, *Alive In Concert* (RCA Victor 1988)★★★.

●COMPILATIONS: *The Best Of The Limeliters* (RCA Victor 1964)★★★.

LIND, BOB

b. 25 November 1944, Baltimore, Maryland, USA. Lind is best known for writing and recording the Top 5 folk rock song 'Elusive Butterfly' in 1966. He moved around frequently with his family, and while settled in Denver, Colorado, he began singing folk music in clubs. He moved to the west coast and was signed to World Pacific Records, a division of the larger Liberty Records. Produced by Jack Nitzsche, Lind played guitar on his recordings for the label, while piano was handled by Leon Russell. His first single, 'Cheryl's Goin' Home', failed to catch on but was later covered by Cher and the Blues Project. 'Elusive Butterfly' was its b-side and became an international Top 10 hit. Lind was widely touted as 'the new Bob Dylan' and the latest spokesperson for youth during 1966. Despite his pop star looks and sensitive lyrics, however, his subsequent singles failed to reach the charts. *Don't Be Concerned* contained a number of sentimental, but attractive songs. His compositions continued to find interpreters, among them the Turtles, Noel Harrison, Nancy Sinatra and Bobby Sherman. Lind continued to record into the early 70s, switching to Capitol Records without a revival of his commercial fortunes. He was still performing in folk and country music circles in the early 80s.

●ALBUMS: *Don't Be Concerned* (World Pacific 1966)★★, *The Elusive Bob Lind* (Verve/Forecast 1966)★★, *Photographs Of Feeling* (World Pacific 1966)★★, *Since There Were Circles* (1971)★★.

LITTLE ANTHONY AND THE IMPERIALS

Formed in Brooklyn, New York, USA, in 1957 and originally called the Chesters, the group comprised 'Little' Anthony Gourdine (b. 8 January 1940, Brooklyn, New York, USA), Ernest Wright Jnr. (b. 24 August 1941, Brooklyn, New York, USA), Clarence Collins (b. 17 March 1941, Brooklyn, New York, USA), Tracy Lord and Glouster Rogers (b. 1940). A vital link between doo-wop and sweet soul, the Imperials were the prototype for the Delfonics and Stylistics. Gourdine first recorded in 1956 as a member of the Duponts. From there he helped form the Chesters, who became the Imperials on signing to the End label. The 'Little Anthony' prefix was subsequently added at the suggestion of the influential disc jockey Alan Freed. The group's first hit, the haunting 'Tears On My Pillow' (1958), encapsulated the essence of street-corner harmony. Further success came with 'So Much' (1959) and 'Shimmy Shimmy Ko-Ko-Bop' (1960), before Gourdine was persuaded to embark on an ill-fated solo career. In 1964, he formed a 'new' Imperials around Wright, Collins and Sammy Strain (b. 9 December 1940). Their first hit, 'I'm On The Outside (Looking In)' showcased Gourdine's dazzling falsetto, a style continued on 'Goin' Out Of My Head' and 'Hurt So Bad' (both of which reached the US pop Top 10). Complementing these graceful releases were such uptempo offerings as 'Better Use Your Head' and 'Gonna Fix You Good' (both 1966). The line-up later drifted apart and in 1974 Sammy Strain replaced William Powell in the O'Jays. Three years later, Collins formed his own 'Imperials', touring Britain on the strength of two hit singles, a reissued 'Better Use Your Head', and a new recording, 'Who's Gonna Love Me'. In the 80s Gourdine released *Daylight* on the religious outlet, Songbird.

●ALBUMS: *We Are Little Anthony And The Imperials* (End 1959)★★★, *Shades Of The 40's* (End 1961)★★★, *I'm On The Outside Looking In* (DCP 1964)★★★, *Goin' Out Of My Head* (DCP 1965)★★★, *Paying Our Dues* (1967)★★★, *Reflections* (1967)★★, *Movie Grabbers* (1968)★★, *Out Of Sight, Out Of Mind* (United Artists 1969)★★, *On A New Street* (1974)★★. Solo: Anthony Gourdine *Daylight* (1980)★★.

●COMPILATIONS: *Little Anthony And The Imperials Greatest Hits* (Roulette 1965)★★★, *The Best Of Little*

Anthony And The Imperials (DCP 1966)★★★, *The Best Of Little Anthony And The Imperials* (1989)★★★.

LITTLE EVA

b. Eva Narcissus Boyd, 29 June 1943, Bellhaven, North Carolina, USA. Discovered by songwriters Carole King and Gerry Goffin, Little Eva burst to fame in 1962 with the international hit, 'The Loco-Motion', a driving, dance-based song. Its ebullient, adolescent approach was muted on a follow-up single, 'Keep Your Hands Off My Baby', but although further releases from the following year, 'Let's Turkey Trot' and 'Old Smokey Locomotion', revived its novelty appeal, they lacked its basic excitement. Eva continued to record until 1965, but her only other substantial hit came with 'Swinging On A Star', a duet with Big Dee Irwin on which she was, unfortunately, uncredited. She made a UK chart comeback in 1972 with 'The Loco-Motion' reissue peaking at number 11, and the song's lasting appeal was reaffirmed in 1988 when Kylie Minogue emulated Eva's original UK chart position.

●ALBUMS: *L-L-L-L-Loco-Motion* (Dimension 1962)★★★.

●COMPILATIONS: *Lil' Loco'Motion* (1982)★★★, *The Best Of Little Eva* (1988)★★★, *Back On Track* (1989)★★★.

LITTLE MILTON

b. James Milton Campbell Jnr., 7 September 1934, Inverness, Mississippi, USA. Having played guitar from the age of 12, Little Milton (he legally dropped the James when he discovered that he had a brother of the same name on his father's side) made his first public appearances as a teenager in the blues bars and cafes on Greenville's celebrated Nelson Street. He first appeared on record accompanying pianist Willie Love in the early 50s, then under his own name appearing on three singles issued on Sam Phillips' Sun label under the guidance of Ike Turner. Although their working relationship continued throughout the decade, it was on signing to Chicago's Chess/Checker outlet that Milton's career flourished. An R&B-styled vocalist in the mould of Bobby Bland and 'T-Bone' Walker, his work incorporated sufficient soul themes to maintain a success denied to less flexible contemporaries. Propelled by an imaginative production, Milton had a substantial hit in 1965 with the optimistic 'We're Gonna Make It', and followed with more expressive performances, including 'Who's Cheating Who?' (1965) plus the wry 'Grits Ain't Groceries' (1968). Campbell remained with Chess until 1971, whereupon he switched to Stax. 'That's What Love Will Do' returned the singer to the R&B chart after a two-year absence, but despite his appearance in the pivotal *Wattstax* film, Little Milton was unable to maintain a consistent recording career. A series of ill-fitting funk releases from the late 70s reinforced the perception that the artist was at his peak with blues-edged material, something proved by his excellent contemporary work for Malaco Records. In the 90s he was with Delmark Records and experienced some-

thing of a resurgence during the most recent blues boom.

●ALBUMS: *We're Gonna Make It* (Checker 1965)★★★, *Little Milton Sings Big Blues* (Checker 1966)★★★, *Grits Ain't Groceries* (1969)★★★, *If Walls Could Talk* (1970)★★★, *Blues 'N' Soul* (1974)★★★, *Waiting For Little Milton* (1973)★★★, *Montreux Festival* (1974)★★★, *Friend Of Mine* (1976)★★★, *Me For You, You For Me* (1976)★★★, *In Perspective* (1981)★★★, *I Need Your Love So Bad* (1982)★★★, *Age Ain't Nothing But A Number* (1983)★★★, *Playin' For Keeps* (1984)★★★, *Annie Mae's Cafe* (1987)★★★, *Movin' To The Country* (1987)★★★, *I Will Survive* (1988)★★★, *Too Much Pain* (1990)★★★, *Reality* (1992)★★★, *I'm A Gambler* (Malaco 1994)★★★, *Live At Westville Prison* (Delmark 1995)★★★, *Cheatin' Habit* (Malaco 1996)★★★.

●COMPILATIONS: *Little Milton's Greatest Hits* (1972)★★★★, *Little Milton* (1976)★★★, *Sam's Blues* (1976)★★★, *Walkin' The Back Streets* (1981)★★★, *Raise A Little Sand* (1982)★★★, *His Greatest Hits* (1987)★★★, *Chicago Golden Years* (1988)★★★, *Hittin' The Boogie* sun recordings (1988)★★★, *The Sun Masters* (1990)★★★, *Welcome To The Club: The Essential Chess Recordings* (MCA 1994)★★★★, *Little Milton's Greatest Hits* (Malaco 1995)★★★★, *The Complete Stax Singles* (Ace 1995)★★★★.

LIVERPOOL SCENE

The name 'Liverpool Scene' was derived from a poetry anthology which featured Roger McGough, Adrian Henri and Brian Patten. The writers subsequently appeared on UK television's *Look Of The Week*, where their readings were accompanied by guitarist Andy Roberts. McGough and Henri then recorded *The Incredible New Liverpool Scene*, which included definitive performances of their best-known work, including 'Let Me Die A Young Man's Death' (McGough) and 'Tonight At Noon' (Henri). While McGough pursued a career within Scaffold, Henri and Roberts added Mike Hart (guitar/vocals), Mike Evans (saxophone/vocals), Percy Jones (bass) and Brian Dodson (drums) to create an explicitly rock-based ensemble. UK disc jockey John Peel was an early patron and the group quickly found itself an integral part of music's underground circuit, culminating in their impressive appearance at the 1969 Isle Of Wight Festival. *The Amazing Adventures Of ...* captured the sextet at their most potent, but successive albums, although worthwhile, failed to match the crucial balance between musical and lyrical content and the group broke up in 1970. Hart embarked on a solo career, but while Roberts initially found fame in Plainsong, he was later reunited with both Henri and McGough in Grimms.

●ALBUMS: *The Incredible New Liverpool Scene* (CBS 1967)★★, *The Amazing Adventures Of ...* (RCA 1968)★★★★, *Bread On The Night* (RCA 1969)★★★, *Saint Adrian Co. Broadway And 3rd* (RCA 1970)★★★, *Heirloom* (RCA 1970)★★.

●COMPILATIONS: *Recollections* (1972)★★★.

LOCOMOTIVE

Formed in Birmingham, England, Locomotive initially achieved fame as a ska/bluebeat band and by the fact that one of their early members, Chris Wood had departed in 1967 to join the fledgling Traffic. Having made their debut with 'Broken Heart' on the dance-oriented Direction label, they switched to Parlophone for 'Rudi's In Love'. This enchanting rock-steady ballad reached the UK Top 30 in 1968, but by the following year the group had completely changed its musical direction. Norman Haines (guitar/vocals) took control of the band on 'Mr. Armageddon', a haunting progressive rock piece drawing an air of mystery from its pulsating, yet distant, horn section. Mick Taylor (trumpet), Bill Madge (saxophone), Mick Hincks (bass) and Bob Lamb (drums) completed the line-up featured on *We Are Everything You See* which, despite contemporary commercial indifference, has become one of the era's most fêted releases. Locomotive split up soon after its release and while its erstwhile leader founded the Norman Haines Band. Lamb, Hincks and associate member Keith Millar formed the Dog That Bit People. The drummer then went on to join the Steve Gibbons Band.

●ALBUMS: *We Are Everything You See* (Parlophone 1969)★★★★.

LOMAX, JACKIE

b. 10 May 1944, Wallasey, Merseyside, England. A former vocalist with the 60s beat group the Undertakers, Lomax began a new career in America when this respected Liverpool unit disbanded. Spells with two short-lived bands, the Mersey Lads and the Lost Souls, preceded a return to England where the singer worked with his own group, the Lomax Alliance, and as a solo act. Two strong, but unsuccessful, singles followed before he was signed to the fledgling Apple label but his opening release, 'Sour Milk Sea', written for him by George Harrison, was unfortunately overshadowed by hits for stablemates the Beatles and Mary Hopkin. Lomax's debut, *Is This What You Want*, featured contributions from a host of star names including Harrison, Paul McCartney, Ringo Starr and Eric Clapton. The artist's stylish compositions and superb voice were equal to such esteemed company. Sadly, Apple's internal problems doomed his undoubted potential and following an interlude as part of the elusive Heavy Jelly, Lomax returned to America where he completed two more excellent albums, *Home Is In My Head* and *Three*. In 1973, the singer joined the British-based Badger, a group formed by ex-Yes organist, Tony Kaye. Lomax helped transform them from a progressive rock band into a more soulful aggregation, exemplified on *White Lady*, which was produced by Allen Toussaint and consisted solely of Lomax's songs. Badger then split into two factions, with Lomax and bassist Kim Gardner instigating an offshoot unit named after the album. Jackie subsequently resumed his solo career, but the releases that followed were disappointing and the bad luck which had often dogged this worthwhile performer further undermined his career. Lomax did resurface in 1990 as

one of several acts contributing to the 'tribute' album *True Voices*, wherein he sang a version of Tim Buckley's 'Devil Eyes'.

●ALBUMS: *Is This What You Want* (Apple 1969)★★★, *Home Is In My Head* (1971)★★★, *Three* (1972)★★, with Badger *White Lady* (1974)★★, *Livin' For Lovin'* (1976)★★★, *Did You Ever* (1977)★★.

LOPEZ, TRINI

b. Trinidad Lopez III, 15 May 1937, Dallas, Texas, USA. Trini Lopez took folk songs and rocked them up into Latin rhythms, recording 14 chart albums and 13 chart singles between 1963 and 1968. Propelled by a strong R&B-influenced backbeat (usually provided by bassist Dave Shriver and drummer Gene Riggio) and his own incessantly rhythmic guitar, Lopez was at his best when playing live. A number of his nightclub performances were recorded and released as albums. Lopez listened to R&B music while growing up, and formed his first band in Wichita Falls, Texas, at the age of 15. At the recommendation of Buddy Holly, Lopez went to the producer Norman Petty in Clovis, New Mexico, but Lopez did not record with him as Petty wanted to record only instrumental music. In 1958, however, Petty did secure Lopez and his group the Big Beats a contract with Columbia Records, which released the single 'Clark's Expedition'/'Big Boy', ironically, an instrumental. Lopez made his first solo recording, his own composition 'The Right To Rock', for the Dallas-based Volk Records, and then signed with King Records in 1959, recording more than a dozen singles for that label, none of which charted. In late 1962, after the King contract expired, Lopez followed up on an offer by producer Snuff Garrett to join the post-Holly Crickets as vocalist. After a couple of weeks of auditions in Los Angeles that idea did not bear fruit and Lopez formed his own group.

He landed a steady engagement at the nightclub PJ's, where his audience soon grew. He was heard there by Frank Sinatra, who had started his own label, Reprise Records, and who subsequently signed Lopez. He was placed with arranger/producer Don Costa, who wisely chose to record Lopez in concert at the club. His first album, *Trini Lopez At PJ's*, rose to number 2 in the summer of 1963 and stayed in the US charts for nearly two years. The first single from the album, an uptempo party-like version of Pete Seeger's 'If I Had A Hammer', reached number 3 (number 4 in the UK), out-performing Peter, Paul And Mary's more sedate rendering a year earlier. Lopez's subsequent recordings for Reprise displayed a musical eclecticism - he recorded a folk album, an R&B album, two Latin albums, country, in foreign languages (Spanish and German) and even Broadway show tunes, all in his infectiously simple singalong style. Only one other Top 20 single resulted, 'Lemon Tree' in 1965, and he appeared in a number of films, including *The Dirty Dozen* and *Marriage On The Rocks*, but by the end of the 60s Lopez had largely disappeared from public view. He recorded sporadically in the 70s, including *Viva* and a number of singles for Capitol Records in 1971-72, and

Transformed By Time for Roulette Records in 1978, and although he continued to sing in Las Vegas during the 80s little has been heard from Lopez since his heyday. There are numerous budget-label album releases of his music available, and several anthologies on European labels.

●ALBUMS: *Teenage Love Songs* (King 1963)★★, *Trini Lopez At PJ's* (1963)★★★★, *More Of Trini Lopez* (King 1964)★★, *More Trini Lopez At PJ's* (1963)★★★, *On The Move* (1964)★★★, *The Latin Album* (1964)★★★, *Live At Basin St. East* (1964)★★★, *The Folk Album* (1965)★★, *The Love Album* (1965)★★★, *The Rhythm & Blues Album* (1965)★★, *The Sing-Along World Of Trini Lopez* (1965)★★★, *Trini* (1966)★★★, *24 Songs By The Great Trini Lopez* (King 1966)★★, *The Second Latin Album* (1966)★★★, *Trini Lopez In London* (1967)★★★, *Now!* (1967)★★★, *It's A Great Life* (1968)★★★, *Trini Country* (1968)★, *Viva* (1972)★★, *Transformed By Time* (Roulette 1978)★★.

●COMPILATIONS: *Greatest Hits!* (1966)★★★, *La Bamba - 28 Greatest Hits* (1988)★★★.

LORDAN, JERRY

b. Jeremiah Patrick Lordan, 30 April 1934, London, England, d. 24 July 1995. After leaving the Royal Air Force in 1955, Lordan sought work as a comedian before forming a short-lived duo, Lee And Jerry Elvin. During this unsatisfying time he was busy writing songs, and one of his demos, 'A Home, A Car And A Wedding Ring', with Emile Ford guesting on piano, became a minor US hit for Mike Preston. When Anthony Newley took Lordan's 'I've Waited So Long' to number 3 in the UK, the composer was signed as a soloist by Parlophone. Five low-ranking Top 50 hits in the first six months of 1960 confirmed Lordan's promise but it was as a songwriter for other people that he shone. His biggest solo hit was 'Who Could Be Bluer?' The shimmering 'Apache' gave the Shadows a momentous UK number 1, while Jorgen Ingmann almost achieved the same position in the USA. Thereafter, Lordan was lauded as the great composer of many instrumentals, enjoying chart toppers with the Shadows' 'Wonderful Land', and Jet Harris And Tony Meehan's 'Diamonds'. He still wrote lyrics for artists including Cleo Laine, Petula Clark, Matt Monro, Shane Fenton (I'm A Moody Guy' and 'Walk Away') and one-hit-wonder Louise Cordet ('I'm Just A Baby'). At the end of the 60s, two more Lordan hits were high in the charts, courtesy of Cilla Black ('Conversations') and Cliff Richard ('Good Times'). After an all too brief recording comeback in 1970 with 'Old Man And The Sea', which was rumoured to have sold only two hundred copies, Lordan's musical career ended and he ceased writing altogether. Following a spell as an alcoholic he suffered serious mental problems. During the 70s his financial problems prompted him to sell the copyrights to most of his major songs. In the 80s his personal life improved and he started to write songs once again as a hobby. The Shadows recognized his massive contribution to their career and Bruce Welch participated during the memorial service.

●ALBUMS: *All My Own Work* (Parlophone 1960)★★.

LOS BRAVOS

Originally known as Los Sonor, Mike Kogel (b. 25 April 1945, Beuliu, Germany; vocals), Antonio Martinez (b. 3 October 1945, Madrid, Spain; guitar), Manolo 'Manuel' Fernandez (b. 29 September 1943, Seville, Spain; organ), Miguel Vicens Danus (b. 21 June 1944, Palma de Mallona, Spain; bass) and Pablo 'Gomez' Samllehi (b. 5 November 1943, Barcelona, Spain; drums) were voted Spain's top beat group following two Top 10 hits in their own country. They achieved international recognition in 1966 when 'Black Is Black', a song composed by two Englishmen, Tony Hayes and Steve Wadey, rose to number 2 in the UK charts in the wake of heavy promotion on pirate radio. The song's compulsive hookline proved equally popular in the USA where it reached number 4, but the quintet was sadly unable to repeat this success. Despite a series of superior pop performances, including an effervescent reading of an Easybeats composition, 'Bring A Little Lovin'', 'I Don't Care' (1966) was the group's last UK Top 20 entry.

●ALBUMS: *Black Is Black* (Press 1966)★★, *Los Bravos* aka *Bring A Little Lovin'* (Parrott 1968)★★.

LOTHAR AND THE HAND PEOPLE

Although this splendidly named quintet became fixtures of New York's underground circuit, they were formed in Denver, Colorado, USA, in 1965. College drop-out John Arthur Emelin (vocals/theremin) was initially joined by Richard Lewis (rhythm guitar), Russell 'Rusty' Ford (bass) and Tom Lyle (drums), before William C. Wright (lead guitar) completed the line-up. Lewis and Wright were later replaced by Kim King (guitar) and Paul Conly (keyboards). Much attention to the group was given due to Emelin's use of the theremin, an instrument capable of eerie electronic 'cries' similar to those used in horror movies and previously heard on the Beach Boys' 'Good Vibrations'. Lothar headed east at the behest of the Lovin' Spoonful whom they supported on a provincial tour. The new arrivals quickly secured a recording deal, but the apathy that greeted their first three singles delayed a debut album. *Presenting Lothar And The Hand People* was not issued until late 1968, although its simple, folksy atmosphere recalled a more innocent era. The album was produced by Robert Margouleff who went on to form the experimental Tonto's Expanding Headband. A second collection, *Space Hymn*, followed within a matter of months and showed a group embracing synthesized technology. The set maintained a love of melody, but despite positive reviews, the album was not a commercial success and Lothar And The Hand People broke up in 1971.

●ALBUMS: *Presenting Lothar And The Hand People* (Capitol 1968)★★, *Space Hymn* (Capitol 1969)★★.

●COMPILATIONS: *This Is It ... Machines* (1986)★★.

LOUDERMILK, JOHN D.

b. 31 March 1934, Durham, North Carolina, USA. Loudermilk's first musical experience was banging a drum for the Salvation Army; he played various instruments as a child and appeared regularly on the radio from the age of 11. In 1956, George Hamilton IV recorded his song 'A Rose And A Baby Ruth', which went from the local to the national charts, reaching number 6. A few months later Eddie Cochran made his debut in the US Top 20 with 'Sittin' In The Balcony', another Loudermilk song that he had recorded himself under the pseudonym, Johnny D.

When Loudermilk moved to Nashville, a stream of hits followed, the UK chart successes being 'Waterloo' (Stonewall Jackson, 1959), 'Angela Jones' (Michael Cox, 1960), 'Tobacco Road' (Nashville Teens, 1964), 'Google Eye' (which was a catfish, Nashville Teens, 1964), 'This Little Bird' (Marianne Faithfull, 1965, and subsequently parodied by the Barron Knights), 'Then You Can Tell Me Goodbye' (Casinos, 1967, and a US country number 1 for Eddy Arnold), 'It's My Time' (the Everly Brothers, 1968), 'Indian Reservation (The Lament Of The Cherokee Reservation Indian)' (Don Fardon, 1970 and a US number 1 for the Raiders, 1971) and 'Sunglasses' (a revival of a Skeeter Davis record by Tracey Ullman, 1984). His controversial 'death' song, 'Ebony Eyes', was the b-side of the Everly Brothers' 1961 number 1, 'Walk Right Back'. Other successful b-sides include 'Weep No More My Baby' (Brenda Lee's 'Sweet Nuthins'), 'Stayin' In' (Bobby Vee's 'More Than I Can Say'); 'Heaven Fell Last Night' (the Browns' 'The Three Bells') and 'In A Matter Of Moments' (Louise Cordet's 'I'm Just A Baby'). Near misses include 'All Of This For Sally' (Mark Dinning), 'The Guitar Player (Him And Her)' for Jimmy Justice and 'To Hell With Love' for Adam Faith. He arranged an old song, 'Abilene', for George Hamilton IV, which made the US charts in 1963 and became a country standard. His other country music successes include 'Talk Back Trembling Lips' (Ernest Ashworth and Johnny Tillotson), 'Bad News' (Johnny Cash and Boxcar Willie), 'Break My Mind' (George Hamilton IV, Gram Parsons and the Hillsiders), 'You're Ruinin' My Life' (Hank Williams Jnr.) and 'Half-Breed' (Marvin Rainwater). He wrote clever novelty songs for Bob Luman ('The Great Snowman' and 'The File') and for Sue Thompson ('Sad Movies (Make Me Cry)', 'Norman', 'James (Hold The Ladder Steady)' and 'Paper Tiger', all US Top 30 hits).

Loudermilk had his own hit with 'The Language Of Love', which made number 13 in the UK in 1962. He made several albums of his own material and they have been collected on two Bear Family compilations, *Blue Train* and *It's My Time*, which contain two previously unreleased tracks in 'The Little Wind Up Doll' and 'Giving You All My Love'. He has often worked in the UK and performs his songs in a similar manner to Burl Ives. He produced Pete Sayers' best album, *Bogalusa Gumbo*, in 1979, but an album that he recorded at the same sessions has not been released.

●ALBUMS: *The Language Of Love* (RCA Victor 1962)★★★, *Twelve Sides Of Loudermilk* (RCA Victor 1962)★★★, *John D. Loudermilk Sings A Bizarre Collection Of Unusual Songs* (RCA Victor 1965)★★★, *Suburban Attitudes In Country Verse* (1967)★★, *Country Love Songs* (1968)★★, *The Open Mind Of John D. Loudermilk* (1969)★★, *Elloree* (70s)★★, *Just Passing Through* (1977)★★.

●COMPILATIONS: *The Best Of John D. Loudermilk* (RCA 1970)★★★, *Encores* (RCA 1975)★★★, *Blue Train* (Bear Family 1989)★★★, *It's My Time* (Bear Family 1989)★★★, *Sittin' In The Balcony* (Bear Family 1995)★★★.

LOUSSIER, JACQUES

b. 26 October 1934, Angers, France. A classically taught pianist, he found a career in commercial popular music more lucrative. Then, in 1959, he hit upon the idea of performing the classical piano works of Johann Sebastian Bach in a quasi-jazz style. Together with Pierre Michelot and Christian Garros, the trio had enormous international success with the wider public. Their records were popular and they toured extensively. The concept, the low-key detached style, and possibly the huge commercial success, failed to endear the group to the hardcore jazz audience. The trio played on into the mid-70s.

●ALBUMS: *Play Bach* i (Decca 1960)★★★★, *Play Bach* ii (Decca 1961)★★★★, *Play Bach* iii (Decca 1962)★★★, *Play Bach* iv (London 1963)★★★, *The World Of Jacques Loussier - Live* (Decca 70s)★★★★, *Bach To The Future* (State Of The Art 70s)★★★, *The Jacques Loussier Trio In Concert At The Royal Festival Hall* (Philips 70s)★★★.

LOVE

For many, the doyens of Los Angeles progressive rock in the 60s, brilliantly erratic and producers of one of the finest rock albums ever made: *Forever Changes*. Love were formed in 1965 as the Grass Roots by Bryan Maclean (b. 1947, Los Angeles, California, USA; guitar/vocals), Arthur Lee (b. 1945, Memphis, Tennessee, USA; guitar/vocals), John Echols (b. 1945, Memphis, Tennessee, USA; lead guitar). Don Conka (drums) and Johnny Fleckenstein were soon replaced by Alban 'Snoopy' Pfisterer (b. 1947, Switzerland) and ex-Surfaris Ken Forssi (b. 1943, Cleveland, Ohio, USA). They become the first rock band to be signed by the expanding Elektra Records, just beating the Doors by a whisker. Their debut single was Burt Bacharach and Hal David's 'My Little Red Book', in a different form from the way the writers imagined it. Love were an instant sensation on the LA club scene, outrageous, loud, innovative and stoned. The furiously energetic '7 And 7 Is' was released in the summer of 1966 and became their second hit. Although 'The Castle' on *Da Capo* pointed to a new direction, it was *Forever Changes* that put them in the history books. That album, 25 years later, is still found on most critics' recommended lists and no comprehensive record collection should be without it. It is a superlative record, unassumingly brilliant, gentle, biting and full of surprises. It proved to be Arthur Lee's finest work and marked the end of the partnership with Bryan Maclean. A new Love featuring Lee, Frank Fayad (bass), Jay Donnellan (guitar) and the drumming pyrotechnics of George Suranovitch, proved to be the most stable line-up and lasted for two

albums. Both records contained rare glimpses of *Forever Changes*, but ultimately they were bitter disappointments. *False Start* featured a few memorable moments, one being a guitar solo from Jimi Hendrix. *Reel To Real* is a truly wretched affair. The long-held opinion that Lee had become a casualty of too many chemicals was strengthened throughout the 70s, 80s and 90s with various stories chronicling his erratic and eccentric behaviour. In 1996 the latest rumours to surface were that Lee and former member Johnny Echols were working together again. Later that year it was confirmed that he now suffers from Parkinson's disease, followed by the astonishing news that he was awaiting a 12-year prison sentence for threatening behaviour with a firearm. Many attempts to resurrect his career have faltered, although any news of Lee is always greeted with enthusiasm. Like Brian Wilson, Syd Barrett, and Skip Spence he is another wayward genius who took one trip too many.
● ALBUMS: *Love* (Elektra 1966)★★★, *Da Capo* (Elektra 1967)★★★★, *Forever Changes* (Elektra 1967)★★★★★, *Four Sail* (Elektra 1969)★★★, *Out Here* (Blue Thumb 1969)★★, *False Start* (Blue Thumb 1970)★★, *Reel To Real* (RSO 1974)★★, *Love Live* (Rhino 1982)★★, *Love* (1982)★★, as Arthur Lee And Love *Arthur Lee And Love* (New Rose 1992)★★.
● COMPILATIONS: *Love Revisited* (Elektra 1970)★★★, *Love Masters* (Elektra 1973)★★★, *Out There* (Big Beat 1988)★★★, *Comes In Colours* (Big Beat 1993)★★★★, *Love Story* (Rhino 1995)★★★★.

LOVE AFFAIR

Originally formed in 1966, this London-based quintet comprised Steve Ellis (vocals), Morgan Fisher (keyboards), Rex Brayley (guitar), Mick Jackson (bass) and Maurice Bacon (drums). Although Ellis was barely 16 years old, the group performed frequently in clubs on a semi-professional basis. Fisher was briefly replaced by Lynton Guest and the following year Ellis, backed by session musicians, recorded a sparkling cover of Robert Knight's 'Everlasting Love' for CBS Records. By January 1968, the single unexpectedly hit number 1 in the UK and Love Affair became instant pop stars with Ellis' cherubic looks gracing teen magazines throughout the nation. With Bacon's father Sid overseeing the management, the group resisted the solicitations of more powerful entrepreneurs, yet failed to exploit their potential. Four more hits followed, 'Rainbow Valley', 'A Day Without Love', 'One Road' and 'Bringing On Back The Good Times', but by the end of the 60s, the lead singer left to form his own group, Ellis. Fisher reappeared in Mott The Hoople, Bacon became a music publisher and the group name was successively plundered for cabaret/revivalist bookings.
● ALBUMS: *The Everlasting Love Affair* (CBS 1968)★★★, *New Day* (CBS 1970)★★.
● COMPILATIONS: *Greatest Hits* (1985)★★★, *Everlasting Hits* (1993)★★★, *Everlasting Love* (Columbia 1996)★★★.

LOVE SCULPTURE

Having recorded as the Human Beans, Dave Edmunds (b. 15 April 1944, Cardiff, South Glamorgan, Wales; guitar) and John Williams (bass) formed Love Sculpture in 1967 with Bob 'Congos' Jones (drums). This Cardiff-based trio enjoyed modest airplay with their debut single, 'River To Another Day', before a rousing interpretation of Aram Khachaturian's 'Sabre Dance', initially aired as a radio session by BBC disc jockey John Peel, became a surprising hit single. Its success bestowed a novelty tag on a group already hampered by a lack of musical direction and although their debut album offered worthy blues interpretations, the psychedelic tinges on a second set were somewhat anachronistic. This impasse led to a split in the original line-up and Mickey Gee (bass) and Terry Williams (drums, later of Man and Dire Straits) joined the guitarist for a final flourish. Edmunds then disbanded the group and embarked on a solo career.
● ALBUMS: *Blues Helping* (Parlophone 1968)★★★, *Forms And Feelings* (Parlophone 1969)★★.
● COMPILATIONS: *The Classic Tracks 1968/72* (1974)★★★, *The Dave Edmunds And Love Sculpture Singles As And Bs* (1990)★★★.

LOVIN' SPOONFUL

Few American pop groups have gathered as much universal affection over the years as the brilliant and underrated Lovin' Spoonful. Their back catalogue of hits is constantly repackaged and reissued as their stature increases. They were formed in 1965 by John Sebastian (b. 17 March 1944, New York, USA; vocal/guitar/harmonica/autoharp) and Zalman Yanovsky (b. 19 December 1944, Toronto, Canada; guitar/vocals) following their time together in the Mugwumps (as eulogized in the Mamas And The Papas hit 'Creeque Alley'). The band were completed by Steve Boone (b. 23 September 1943, Camp Lejeune, North Carolina, USA; bass) and Joe Butler (b. 19 January 1943, Long Island, New York, USA; drums/vocals). Their unique blend of jug-band, folk, blues and rock 'n' roll synthesized into what was termed as 'electric good-time music', kept them apart from every other American pop group at that time. In two years they notched up 10 US Top 20 hits, all composed by John Sebastian. From the opening strum of Sebastian's autoharp on 'Do You Believe In Magic?' the party began; from the evocative 'You Didn't Have To Be So Nice', to the languid singalong 'Daydream'; from the punchy and lyrically outstanding 'Summer In The City': 'Hot town summer in the city, back of my neck getting dirt and gritty', to the gentle romanticism of 'Rain On The Roof': 'You and me and the rain on the roof, caught up in a summer shower, drying while it soaks the flowers, maybe we'll be caught for hours', their four regular albums were crammed full of other gems in addition to the hits. Additionally Sebastian wrote the music for two films, Woody Allen's *What's Up Tiger Lily* and Francis Ford Coppola's *You're A Big Boy Now*, the latter featuring the beautiful 'Darling Be Home Soon'. Sadly the non-stop party came to an end in 1968 following the departure of Yanovsky and the arrival, albeit briefly, of Jerry Yester. The quality of Sebastian's lyrics and melodies makes him one of the finest American songwriters. In 1991, Steve Boone, Joe Butler and the Yester brothers announced the re-formation of the band for a tour - however, without Yanovsky and Sebastian, the 'magic' cannot be present.

●ALBUMS: *Do You Believe In Magic* (Kama Sutra 1965)★★★★, *Daydream* (Kama Sutra 1966)★★★★, with others *What's Shakin'* (Elektra 1966)★★★★, *What's Up Tiger Lily* soundtrack (Kama Sutra 1966)★★, *Hums Of The Lovin' Spoonful* (Kama Sutra 1966)★★★★, *You're A Big Boy Now* soundtrack (Kama Sutra 1967)★★, *Everything Playing* (Kama Sutra 1968)★★★, *Revelation: Revolution* (Kama Sutra 1968)★.

●COMPILATIONS: *The EP Collection* (1988)★★★★, *Collection: Lovin' Spoonful, 20 Hits* (1988)★★★★, *The Very Best Of The Lovin' Spoonful* (1988)★★★★, *Go To The Movies* (1991)★★, *Summer In The City* (Spectrum 1995)★★★.

LULU

b. Marie MacDonald McLaughlin Lawrie, 3 November 1948, Lennox Castle, Glasgow, Scotland. Lulu was originally a beat group vocalist with her own backing group the Luvvers, who comprised Ross Nelson (guitar), Jim Dewar (rhythm guitar), Alec Bell (keyboards), Jimmy Smith (saxophone), Tony Tierney (bass) and David Miller (drums). The 15-year-old singer first came to prominence with a rasping version of the Isley Brothers' 'Shout' in 1964. Under the tutelage of manager Marian Massey she survived a stormy couple of years during which only two of her eight singles charted. Abandoning the Luvvers along the way, she switched record labels from Decca to EMI/Columbia Records and found a new hitmaker in the form of Mickie Most. A cover of Neil Diamond's 'The Boat That I Row' saw an upsurge in her career during 1967, which was punctuated by an acting part in the movie *To Sir With Love*. The theme tune from the film gave her a million-selling US number 1, and in the UK it reached number 6, despite being relegated to b-side of the inferior 'Let's Pretend'. Further UK hits followed, notably 'Me, The Peaceful Heart', 'Boy' and 'I'm A Tiger'. Having established herself as an entertainer of wide appeal, Lulu was granted her own television series and later represented Britain in the Eurovision Song Contest. The painfully trite 'Boom-Bang-A-Bang' tied for first place and provided her highest UK chart placing at number 2. Her brief marriage to Maurice Gibb of the Bee Gees was followed by another switch of labels and musical styles when she worked with famed producer Jerry Wexler on two albums. A lean period of flop singles ended when David Bowie intervened to produce and arrange her hit version of 'The Man Who Sold The World'. During the 70s, she concentrated increasingly on stage work and developed her career as an all-round entertainer, a spin-off of which was becoming the long-standing model/endorser for the Freeman's mail-order catalogue. Appearances in *Guys And Dolls, Song And Dance* and the television programme, *The Secret Diary Of Adrian Mole* distracted her from the studio but a disco re-recording of 'Shout', in 1986, repeated the Top 10 success of 22 years before. In 1993, Lulu released *Independence*, an album of 'modern disco-pop with a flavour of classic soul and R&B'. Co-produced by Bobby Womack and Londonbeat, the title track registered strongly in the UK and US charts, and was followed by another single, 'I'm Back For More', on which Lulu duetted with Womack. She was, by then, creating some of her own material, and one of her songs, 'I Don't Wanna Fight Any More', written with her brother, Billy Laurie, was recorded by Tina Turner.

●ALBUMS: *Something To Shout About* (Decca 1965)★★★★, *Love Loves To Love Lulu* (Columbia 1967)★★★, *Lulu's Album* (Columbia 1969)★★★, *New Routes* (Atco 1970)★★, *Melody Fair* (Atco 1971)★★, *Don't Take Love For Granted* (Rocket 1979)★★★, *Lulu* (Alfa 1981)★★★, *Take Me To Your Heart Again* (Alfa 1982)★★★, *Shape Up And Dance With Lulu* (Life Style 1984)★, *The Man Who Sold The World* (Start 1989)★★★, *Independence* (Dome 1993)★★★.

●COMPILATIONS: *The World Of Lulu* (Decca 1969)★★★★, *The World Of Lulu Vol. 2* (Decca 1970)★★★, *The Most Of Lulu* (MFP 1971)★★★★, *The Most Of Lulu Vol. 2* (MFP 1972)★★★, *The Very Best Of Lulu* (Warwick 1980)★★★★, *Shout* (MFP 1983)★★★, *I'm A Tiger* (MFP 1989)★★★, *From Crayons To Perfume: The Best Of ...* (Rhino 1995)★★★, *Supersneakers* (Sundazed 1997)★★★.

●FILMS: *Gonks Go Beat* (1965).

LYNCH, KENNY

b. 18 March 1939, Stepney, London, England. Britain's best-known black all-round entertainer has been a television personality for three decades. The youngest of 13 children, he first appeared on stage at the age of 12 with his sister, singer Maxine Daniels. At 16 he joined Ed Nichol's Band and before going into the services in 1957 worked in a string of bands including Bob Miller's. He joined HMV Records and hit the UK Top 40 in 1960 with his debut single, a cover of 'Mountain Of Love'. He appeared in several films and hit his recording peak in 1963 with two successive Top 10 entries - a cover of 'Up On The Roof' and 'You Can Never Stop Me Loving You' (which made the US Top 20 when covered by Johnny Tillotson). Over the next 20 years he was one of the UK's busiest and most popular entertainers and was also awarded an OBE. He co-wrote the Small Faces' number 1, 'Sha La La La Lee', and has recorded spasmodically since then on Columbia, Atlantic Records, Polydor, Laser, Towerbell and Spartan. In 1983, he had a surprise chart return with a Brit-funk track 'Half The Day's Gone And We Haven't Earned A Penny' on Satril.

●ALBUMS: *Up On The Roof* (HMV 1963)★★★, *We Like Kenny* (MFP 1966)★★★★, *Half The Day's Gone And We Haven't Earned A Penny* (1983)★★.

●COMPILATIONS: *The Very Best Of Kenny Lynch* (1987)★★★.

LYNN, BARBARA

b. Barbara Lynn Ozen, 16 January 1942, Beaumont, Texas, USA. Barbara was signed up by producer Huey P. Meaux after hearing a demo tape and watching her perform in a Texas club. Her early records were recorded at Cosimo's New Orleans studio and leased to the Jamie label. Composed by Lynn, 'You'll Lose A Good Thing' (1962) was an R&B chart topper and pop Top 10 in the USA, and was followed by 'You're Gonna Need Me' and 'Oh! Baby (We Got A Good Thing Goin')'. The last of these was revived by the Rolling Stones on *Out Of Our Heads*. Barbara issued several singles on Meaux's own label, Tribe, among which was her version of 'You Left The Water Running' (1966). Subsequent releases for Atlantic Records included 'This Is The Thanks I Get' (1968), '(Until Then) I'll Suffer' (1972), both of which reached the R&B chart for this accomplished singer, songwriter and guitarist, who continued to tour, including visits to Japan, and also recorded albums for Ichiban and Rounder/Bullseye.

●ALBUMS: *You'll Lose A Good Thing* (Jamie 1962)★★★★, *Here Is Barbara Lynn* (Atlantic 1968)★★★, *You Don't Have To Go* (Ichiban 1988)★★★, *So Good* (Bullseye Blues 1994)★★.

●COMPILATIONS: *The Barbara Lynn Story* (1965)★★★, with Bettye Swan *Elegant Soul* (1982)★★, *We Got A Good Thing Goin'* (1984)★★, *Barbara Lynn* (Good Thing 1989)★★★, *You'll Lose A Good Thing* (Sound Of The Fifties 1992)★★★, *Barbara Lynn Live In Japan* (1993)★★★, *The Atlantic Years* (Ichiban/Soul Classics 1994)★★★.

MAD RIVER

Laurence Hammond (vocals/harmonica), David Robinson (lead guitar), Greg Druian (rhythm guitar), Tom Manning (bass) and Greg Dewey (drums) formed the Mad River Blues Band in 1965. Initially based in Yellow Springs, Ohio, USA, the group subsequently moved to California, by which time Druian had been replaced by Rick Bockner. The quintet, now dubbed simply Mad River, initially struggled to assert themselves, but a privately pressed EP helped secure a series of gigs at prestigious San Franciscan venues. Mad River's debut album was released in 1968. Although mastered too fast owing to a technical error, it remains an enthralling slice of vintage acid rock, where traces of Country Joe And The Fish and Quicksilver Messenger Service blend with Hammond's reedy, quivering voice. A second album, *Paradise Bar And Grill*, was an altogether different affair. A handful of the tracks echoed the style of that first selection, while others were indebted to C&W, a genre towards which the singer was increasingly drawn. Two haunting acoustic instrumentals and a cameo appearance by the late writer Richard Brautigan completed one of the late 60s most engaging collections. Mad River broke up soon after its release. Dewey later joined Country Joe And The Fish, and has subsequently played with numerous Bay Area groups. Hammond pursued his love of country music with his Whiplash Band and recorded an engaging album, *Coyote's Dream*, in 1976. The remainder of the group retired from active performance.

●ALBUMS: *Mad River* (Capitol 1968)★★★, *Paradise Bar And Grill* (Capitol 1969)★★★.

MAGIC LANTERNS

Formed in the UK and based in the Manchester area, this soft rock band were formed from the Sabres who were in existence around 1962. At one point the Sabres also included Kevin Godley and Lol Creme, later of 10cc and Godley And Creme. After the temporary title of the Hammers, they became the Magic Lanterns. Their founding members were Jimmy Bilsbury (vocals), Peter Shoesmith (guitar), Ian Moncur (bass) and Allan Wilson (drums). While working in a local nightclub they were approached by compere Roy Hastings who liked Bilsbury's songs and introduced them to his publisher, Mike Collier. Collier arranged for the band to record a new version of Artie Wayne's US release 'Excuse Me Baby', on the strength of which CBS signed them and released 'Excuse Me Baby' as a single in June 1966. It was a minor hit and was followed by such misses as 'Knight

In Rusty Armour', 'Rumplestiltskin', and 'Auntie Griselda', by which time they were sounding increasingly psychedelic. In 1969, Collier switched their management to American Ronnie Oppenheimer who got Steve Rowland (Family Dogg) and Albert Hammond involved. They co-wrote 'Shame Shame' which became the band's first US hit. Moncur left in 1969 and some time later Shoesmith and Wilson followed suit. The band struggled on for a few more months, but broke up while in Hamburg. The final line-up was Bilsbury, Alistair Beveridge (guitar), Paul Garner (guitar), Mike Osbourne (bass) and Paul Ward (drums). Bilsbury joined the Les Humphries Singers who were popular on the continent and had several singles released in the UK in the 70s. Boney M's Liz Mitchell was a founding member, along with Humphreys.
●ALBUMS: *Lit Up With The Magic Lanterns* (1968)★★★, *One Night Stand* (Polydor 1971)★★.

MAMAS AND THE PAPAS

Formed in Los Angeles in 1965, this enthralling harmony group embodied the city's astute blend of folk and pop. John Phillips (b. 30 August 1935, Parris Island, South Carolina, USA) had been a founder-member of the popular Journeymen, before establishing this new attraction with his wife Michelle Phillips (b. Holly Michelle Gilliam, 6 April 1944, Long Beach, California, USA), and former Mugwumps' members Denny Doherty (b. 29 November 1941, Halifax, Nova Scotia, Canada) and Cass Elliot (b. Ellen Naimoi Cohen, 19 September 1943, Alexandria, Virginia, USA, d. 29 July 1974, London, England). Although drawing inspiration from the flourishing milieu of New York's Greenwich Village, the quartet quickly moved to California, where they met producer Lou Adler through the interjection of mutual acquaintance Barry McGuire. The then unnamed Mamas And Papas contributed backing vocals to the latter's second album, which in turn inspired the group's own career. Their debut single, 'California Dreamin'', was originally recorded by McGuire, whose voice was simply erased and replaced by that of Doherty. Penned by Phillips and Gilliam, the song provided a vivid contrast between the cold New York winter and the warmth and security of life on the west coast and effectively established the group as arguably the finest vocal ensemble form their era working in the pop field. The group's bohemian image was reinforced by their compositional skill and distinctive individual personalities. Visually, they seemed eccentrically contrasting: John, a towering 6 foot 4 inches, thin as a rake, and cast in the role of group intellectual; Denny the 'good-looking Canadian' and master of the sarcastic one-liner; Cass, overweight, uproarious and charming; and Michelle, quiet, beautiful and 'angelic when she wants to be'. With 'California Dreamin'' they infiltrated the US Top 5 and the song became a standard, covered by many artists, most notably Jose Feliciano. The richly-harmonic follow-up, 'Monday Monday' reached number 1 in the US and also established the group in the UK. Further timeless hit singles followed, including the soaring 'I Saw Her Again' and a brilliant revival of the Shirelles 'Dedicated To The One I Love'. Michelle's sensual, semi-spoken introduction, backed by a solitary acoustic guitar remains one of the most classic and memorable openings to any pop recording.

The group's albums achieved gold status and while the first was sprinkled with cover versions, the second documented Phillips' development as a songwriter. He was involved in no less than 10 compositions, two of which ('No Salt On Her Tail' and 'Strange Young Girls') were particularly outstanding. Marital problems between John and Michelle eroded the stability of the group and she was fired in 1966 and briefly replaced by lookalike Jill Gibson. The group reconvened for *Deliver*, another strong album, which was followed by the autobiographical 'Creeque Alley', which humorously documented their rise to fame. During the summer of 1967 Phillips organized the Monterey Pop Festival and helped launch the career of former Journeyman Scott McKenzie by writing the chart-topping hippie anthem 'San Francisco'. In the winter of 1967, the group arrived in the UK for concerts at London's Royal Albert Hall. After docking at Southampton, Cass was arrested by police, charged with stealing blankets and keys from the Royal Garden Hotel in Kensington on an earlier visit. The charges were dropped but the concerts were subsequently cancelled, amid rumours of a break-up. The group managed to complete one last album, *The Papas And Mamas*, a superb work that highlighted Phillips' brilliance as a songwriter. 'Safe In My Garden', 'For The Love Of Ivy' and the sublime 'Twelve Thirty' were all minor classics, while 'Rooms' and 'Mansions' incisively documented the spiritual isolation that accompanied their rise to international stardom: 'Limousines and laughter, parties ever after/If you play the game you pay the price/purchasing our piece of paradise'. It was a fitting valediction.

After splitting up in 1968, the quartet embarked on solo careers, with varying success. Three years later, the group briefly re-formed for *People Like Us*, but their individual contributions were taped separately and the results were disappointing. Cass enjoyed the greatest success as a solo artist but her career was tragically cut short by her sudden death in July 1974. Michelle Phillips continued to pursue an acting career, while John plummeted into serious drug addiction, near-death and arrest. He subsequently recovered and in 1982 he and Denny re-formed the Mamas And Papas. The new line-up featured Phillips' actress daughter Laura McKenzie (McKenzie Phillips) and Elaine 'Spanky' McFarlane of Spanky And Our Gang. Doherty left when the band began touring full-time, and was replaced by the aforementioned McKenzie for an attraction which steadfastly retains its popularity.
●ALBUMS: *If You Can Believe Your Eyes And Ears* (Dunhill/RCA Victor 1966)★★★★, *The Mamas And The Papas* aka *Cass, John, Michelle, Denny* (Dunhill/RCA Victor 1966)★★★★, *The Mamas And The Papas Deliver* (Dunhill/RCA Victor 1967)★★★★, *The Papas And The Mamas* (Dunhill/RCA Victor 1968)★★★, various artists *Monterey International Pop*

Festival (1971)★★★, *People Like Us* (Dunhill 1971)★.
●COMPILATIONS: *Farewell To The First Golden Era* (1967)★★★★, *Golden Era Volume 2* (1968)★★★★, *16 Of Their Greatest Hits* (1969)★★★★, *A Gathering Of Flowers* (1971)★★★★, *20 Golden Hits* (1973)★★★★, *The ABC Collection: Greatest Hits* (1976)★★★, *Creeque Alley: The History Of The Mamas And Papas* (MCA 1991)★★★★.
●FURTHER READING: *Papa John*, John Phillips with Jim Jerome. *California Dreamin' - The True Story Of The Mamas And Papas*, Michelle Phillips.

MANCINI, HENRY

b. Enrico Mancini, 16 April 1924, Cleveland, Ohio, USA, d. 14 June 1994, Los Angeles, California, USA. Prompted by his father, a steelworker who loved music, Mancini learned to play several musical instruments while still a small child. As a teenager he developed an interest in jazz and especially music of the big bands. He wrote some arrangements and sent them to Benny Goodman, from whom he received some encouragement. In 1942, he became a student at the Juilliard School of Music, but his career was interrupted by military service during World War II. Immediately following the war he was hired as pianist and arranger by Tex Beneke, who was then leading the Glenn Miller orchestra. Later in the 40s Mancini began writing arrangements for studios, prompted initially by a contract to score for a recording date secured by his wife, singer Ginny O'Connor (of the Mel-Tones). He was also hired to work on films (the first of which was the Abbott and Costello comedy *Lost In Alaska*), and it was here that his interest in big band music paid off. He wrote the scores for two major Hollywood bio-pics, *The Glenn Miller Story* (1954) and *The Benny Goodman Story* (1956), as well as Orson Welles' *Touch Of Evil* classic (1958). Mancini also contributed jazz-influenced scores for television, including those for the innovative *Peter Gunn* series and *Mr Lucky*. His film work continued with scores and songs for such films as *Breakfast At Tiffany's* (1961), from which came 'Moon River' (the Oscar winner that year), and the title songs for *Days Of Wine And Roses* (1962), which again won an Oscar, and *Charade* (1963). His other film compositions included 'Baby Elephant Walk' from *Hatari!* (1962), the theme from *The Pink Panther* (1964), 'Sweetheart Tree' from *The Great Race* (1965), and scores for *Man's Favourite Sport?*, *Dear Heart*, *Wait Until Dark*, *Darling Lili*, *Mommie Dearest*, *Victor/Victoria* (1982), for which he won an Oscar for 'Original Song Score' with Leslie Bricusse, *That's Dancing*, *Without A Clue*, *Physical Evidence*, *Blind Date*, *That's Life*, *The Glass Menagerie*, *Sunset*, *Fear*, *Switch*, and *Tom And Jerry: The Movie*, on which he again teamed with Leslie Bricusse. One of the most respected film and television composers - and the winner of 20 Grammy Awards - Mancini acknowledged his greatest legacy to be '. . . my use of jazz - incorporating various popular idioms into the mainstream of film scoring. If that's a contribution, then that's mine'. In addi-

tion he also regularly conducted orchestras in the USA and UK in concerts of his music, most of which stood comfortably on its own merits outside the context for which it was originally conceived. In the months prior to his death from cancer, Mancini was working with Leslie Bricusse on the score for the stage adaption of *Victor/Victoria*.
●ALBUMS: *The Versatile Henry Mancini* (Liberty 1959)★★★, *March Step In Stereo And Hi-Fi* (Warners 1959)★★★, *The Music From Peter Gunn* (RCA Victor 1959)★★★, *The Blues And The Beat* (RCA Victor 1960)★★★, *The Mancini Touch* (RCA Victor 1960)★★★, *Music From Mr Lucky* (RCA Victor 1960)★★★, *The Original Peter Gunn* (RCA Victor 1960)★★★, *Mr Lucky Goes Latin* (RCA Victor 1961)★★★, *Breakfast At Tiffany's* (1961)★★★, *Hatari* (1962)★★★, *Combo!* (1962)★★★, *Uniquely Mancini* (1963)★★★, *Our Man In Hollywood* (1963)★★★, *The Second Time Around* (1963)★★★, *Marches* (1963)★★★, *The Concert Sound Of Henry Mancini* (1964)★★★, with his orchestra and chorus *Dear Heart And Other Songs About Love* (1965)★★★, *The Latin Sound Of Henry Mancini* (1965)★★★, *Sounds And Voices* (1966)★★★, *Two For The Road* (1967)★★★, *Encore!* (1967)★★★, *A Warm Shade Of Ivory* (1969)★★★, *Mancini Country* (1970)★★★, *Themes From Love Story* (1971)★★★, *This Is Henry Mancini* (1971)★★★, *The Mancini Generation* (1972)★★★, with Doc Severinsen *Brass, Ivory & Strings* (1973)★★★, *The Academy Award Winning Songs* (1975)★★★, *Mancini's Angels* (1977)★★★, *Just You And Me Together Love* (1979)★★★, *Pure Gold* (1980)★★★, *Victor/Victoria* (1982)★★★, *Best Of* (1984)★★★, *A Man And His Music* (1985)★★★, with James Galway *In The Pink* (1985)★★★, *Merry Mancini Christmas* (1985)★★★, *At The Movies* (1986)★★★, with Johnny Mathis *The Hollywood Musicals* (1986)★★★, *Henry Mancini And The Royal Philharmonic Pops Orchestra* (1988)★★★, *Diamond Series* (1988)★★★, with the Royal Philharmonic Pops Orchestra *Premier Pops* (1988) and *Mancini Rocks The Pops* (1989)★★★, *Theme Scene* (1989)★★★, *Mancini In Surround Sound* (1990)★★★, and various other film and television soundtracks.
●COMPILATIONS: *In The Pink: The Ultimate Collection* (RCA Victor 1995)★★★, *Romantic Movie Themes* (Camden 1997)★★★.
●FURTHER READING: *Henry Mancini*, Gene Lees. *Did They Mention The Music?*, Henry Mancini and Gene Lees.

MANDRAKE PADDLESTEAMER

A quartet of Brian Engel (vocals), Martin Hooker (keyboards), Barry Nightingale (drums) and Paul Frolich (bass), Mandrake Paddlesteamer were responsible for recording one of the most cherished singles of the psychedelic era - 'Strange Walking Man'. Subsequently reissued by Bam Caruso in 1988, the song's popularity has continued to revive interest in the group, who were eventually featured on a compilation CD issued by Forgotten Jewels Records in 1991. Unfortunately, Mandrake Paddlesteamer never received a similar level of acclaim in their own era, and issued only one further single. 'Sunlight Guide' was released on Parlophone Records in 1969 but only for the Swedish market. The group subsequently evolved into the less celebrated Prowler, who released a single and an album, *Liverpool Echo*, for Spark Records in 1973.

●COMPILATIONS: *Mandrake Paddlesteamer* (Forgotten Jewels 1991)★★.

MANFRED MANN

During the UK beat boom of the early 60s, spearheaded by the Beatles, a number of R&B groups joined the tide with varying degrees of achievement. Of these, Manfred Mann had the most commercial success. The band was formed as the Mann-Hugg Blues Brothers by Manfred Mann (b. Manfred Lubowitz, 21 October 1940, Johannesburg, South Africa; keyboards) and Mike Hugg (b. 11 August 1942, Andover, Hampshire, England; drums/vibraphone). They became Manfred Mann shortly after adding Paul Jones (b. Paul Pond, 24 February 1942, Portsmouth, Hampshire, England; harmonica/vocals). The line-up was completed by Mike Vickers (b. 18 April 1941, Southampton, Hampshire, England; flute/guitar/saxophone) and Tom McGuinness (b. 2 December 1941, London, England; bass), following the departure of Dave Richmond. After being signed by a talent-hungry HMV Records and following one unsuccessful instrumental, they made an impression with the catchy 'Cock-A-Hoop'. The prominent use of Jones' harmonica gave them a distinct sound and they soon became one of Britain's leading groups. No less than two of their singles were used as the theme music to the pioneering British television music programme, *Ready Steady Go*. '5-4-3-2-1' provided the breakthrough Top 10 hit in early 1964. By the summer, the group registered their first UK number 1 with the catchy 'Do Wah Diddy Diddy'. Over the next two years, they charted regularly with memorable hits such as 'Sha La La', 'Come Tomorrow', 'Oh No! Not My Baby' and Bob Dylan's 'If You Got To Go, Go Now'. In May 1966, they returned to number 1 with the sublime 'Pretty Flamingo'. It was to prove the last major hit on which Jones appeared. His departure for a solo career was a potential body blow to the group at a time when personnel changes were regarded as anathema by the pop media and fans. He was replaced by Michael D'Abo recruited from A Band Of Angels, in preference to Rod Stewart, who failed the audition. Mike Vickers had previously departed for a lucrative career as a television composer. He was replaced by Jack Bruce on bass, allowing Tom McGuinness to move to lead guitar, a role with which he was happier. Additionally, Henry Lowther (trumpet) and Lyn Dobson (saxophone) enlarged the line-up for a time and Klaus Voorman replaced Bruce on bass. D'Abo's debut with the group was another hit rendering of a Dylan song, 'Just Like A Woman', their first for the Fontana label. He fitted in astonishingly well with

the group, surprising many critics, by maintaining their hit formulae despite the departure of the charismatic Jones. Both 'Semi-Detached Suburban Mr. Jones' and 'Ha! Ha! Said The Clown' were formidable Top 5 hits in the classic Mann tradition. Along with America's Byrds, the group were generally regarded as the best interpreters of Dylan material, a view endorsed by the songwriter himself. This point was punctuated in 1968 when the group registered their third number 1 with the striking reading of his 'Mighty Quinn'. They ended the 60s with a final flurry of Top 10 hits, 'My Name Is Jack', 'Fox On The Run' and 'Raggamuffin Man' before abdicating their pop crown in favour of a heavier approach. Their albums had always been meaty and showed off their considerable dexterity as musicians working with jazz and blues-based numbers. Mann went on to form the jazz/rock band Chapter Three and the highly successful Manfred Mann's Earth Band. Still highly respected, Manfred Mann remain one of the finest beat groups of the 60s.

●ALBUMS: *The Manfred Mann Album* (Ascot 1964)★★★★, *The Five Faces Of Manfred Mann* (HMV 1964)★★★★, *Mann Made* (HMV 1965)★★★★, *My Little Red Book Of Winners* (Ascot 1965)★★★★, *Mann Made Hits* (1966)★★★★, *As Is* (Fontana 1966)★★★, *Mann Made* (Ascot 1966)★★★, *Pretty Flamingo* (United Artists 1966)★★★, *Soul Of Mann* (HMV 1967)★★★, *Up The Junction* soundtrack (Fontana 1967)★★, *What A Mann* (Fontana 1968)★★★, *The Mighty Garvey* (Fontana 1968)★★★.

●COMPILATIONS: *Mann Made Hits* (HMV 1966)★★★★, *Manfred Mann's Greatest Hits* (United Artists 1966)★★★★, *What A Mann* (Fontana 1968)★★★★, *This Is Manfred Mann* (1971)★★★, *Semi-Detached Suburban* (1979)★★★, *The R&B Years* (1986)★★★★, *The Singles Plus* (1987)★★★★, *The EP Collection* (See For Miles 1989)★★★★, *The Collection* (1990)★★★, *Ages Of Mann* (1992)★★★★, *Best Of The EMI Years* (1993)★★★★, *Groovin' With The Manfreds* (EMI 1996)★★★★.

●FURTHER READING: *Mannerisms: The Five Phases Of Manfred Mann*, Greg Russo.

MANN, BARRY

b. 9 February 1939, Brooklyn, New York, USA. One of the leading pop songwriters of his generation. Although trained as an architect, Mann began his career in music following a summer singing engagement in the Catskills resort. He initially composed material for Elvis Presley's publishers Hill & Range, before briefly collaborating with Howie Greenfield. In 1961, he enjoyed a Top 10 hit in his own right with 'Who Put The Bomp?', but thereafter it was as a composer that he dominated the Hot 100. During the same year as his solo hit, Mann found a new songwriting partner in Cynthia Weil, whom he soon married. Their first success together was Tony Orlando's 'Bless You' (1961), a simple but effective love song, which endeared them to their new employer, bubblegum genius Don Kirschner, who housed a wealth of songwriting talent in the cubicles of his Brill Building offices. With intense competition from those other husband-and-wife teams Jeff Berry and Ellie Greenwich, and Gerry Goffin and Carole King, Mann and Weil responded with a wealth of classic songs which still sound fresh and impressive to this day. Like all great songwriters, they adapted well to different styles and themes, and this insured that their compositions were recorded by a broad range of artists. There was the evocative urban romanticism of the Crystals' 'Uptown' (1962) and the Drifters' 'On Broadway' (1963), novelty teen fodder such as Eydie Gorme's 'Blame It On The Bossa Nova' (1963) and Paul Petersen's 'My Dad' (1963), the desolate neuroticism of Gene Pitney's 'I'm Gonna Be Strong' (1964) and the Righteous Brothers' 'You've Lost That Lovin' Feelin'' (1964), and classic mid-60s protest songs courtesy of the Animals' 'We Gotta Get Out Of This Place', Jody Miller's 'Home Of The Brave', 'Only In America' (Jay And The Americans) and 'Kicks' (Paul Revere And The Raiders)

By the late 60s, Mann and Weil left Kirschner and moved to Hollywood. Throughout this period, they continued to enjoy hit success with Bobby Vinton's 'I Love How You Love Me' (written with Larry Kolber in 1968), Jay And The Americans' 'Walking In The Rain' (1969) and B.J. Thomas' 'I Just Can't Help Believing' (1970). Changes in the pop marketplace subsequently reduced their hit output, but there were some notable successes such as Dan Hill's 'Sometimes When We Touch' (1977). Mann himself still craved recognition as a performer and won a recording contract, but his album work, most notably 1977's aptly titled *Survivor* failed to match the sales of his and his wife's much covered golden hits. *Survivor* was produced by Bruce Johnson and Terry Melcher, and was regarded as a leading example of the 70s' singer/songwriter oeuvre.They wrote the original songs for the *Muppet Treasure Island* movie in 1996.

●ALBUMS: *Who Put The Bomp* (ABC 1963)★★, *Lay It All Out* (1971)★★, *Survivor* (1975)★★.

MANN, HERBIE

b. 16 April 1930, New York City, New York, USA. After learning to play the clarinet while still a small child, Mann took up the flute. He developed his musical experience during military service. After leaving the US army, he was active in film and television studios as both performer and composer. He played in several small jazz groups during the late 50s, including his own Afro-Jazz Sextet with which he toured internationally. Early in the 60s, his interest in Brazilian music led to a series of profitable recordings, notably 'Coming Home Baby'. Although rooted in bop and recording with leading jazzmen such as Bill Evans, by the late 60s, Mann's writing and playing had broadened to include musical influences from many lands - especially those of the Middle East. He was also open-minded about rock and by the early 70s was a leading figure in jazz-rock fusion. Indeed, his wide acceptance of areas of popular music outside jazz created some difficulties of categorization, especially when he embraced, however briefly, reggae and disco-pop. He has become one of the widest known flautists in jazz, gaining

a considerable measure of credibility for an instrument that has always had an uncertain status in jazz circles. In addition to his performing and writing, Mann has also been active as a record producer, running his own label, Embryo, under the Atlantic aegis for a decade. Subsequently, he formed his own independent label, Herbie Mann Music.

●ALBUMS: *East Coast Jazz 4* (Bethlehem 1954)★★★, *Flamingo My Goodness: Four Flutes Vol. 2* (Bethlehem 1955)★★★, *Herbie Mann Plays* (Bethlehem 1956)★★★, *Love And The Weather* (Bethlehem 1956)★★★, with Sam Most *The Herbie Mann-Sam Most Quintet* (Bethlehem 1956)★★★, *Mann In The Morning* (1956)★★★, *Salute To The Flute* (Epic 1957)★★★, *Mann Alone* (Savoy 1957)★★★, *Flute Suite* (Savoy 1957)★★★, *Sultry Serenade* (Riverside 1957)★★★, *Great Ideas Of Western Mann* (Riverside 1957)★★★, *Yardbird Suite* (Savoy 1957)★★★, with Buddy Collette *Flute Fraternity* (Mode 1957)★★★, *Flute Souffle* (Prestige 1957)★★★, *Flute Flight* (Prestige 1957)★★★, *Just Wailin'* (1958)★★★, *The Mann With The Most* (Behtlehem 1958)★★★, *Herbie Mann With The Licken Trio* (Epic 1958)★★★, *The Magic Flute Of Herbie Mann* (Verve 1958)★★★, *Just Wailin'* (New Jazz 1958)★★★, *Mann In The Morning* (Prestige 1958)★★★, *African Suite* (United Artists 1959)★★★, *Flautista! Herbie Mann Plays Afro-Cuban Jazz* (Verve 1959)★★★, *The Common Ground* (Atlantic 1960)★★★, *Flute, Brass, Vibes And Percussion* (Verve 1960)★★★, *Herbie Mann Quintet* (Jazzland 1960)★★★, *Epitome Of Jazz* (Bethlehem 1961)★★★, *The Family Of Mann* (Atlantic 1961)★★★, with Bill Evans *Brasil Bossa Nova And Blue* (United Artists 1962)★★★, *St Thomas* (United Artists 1962)★★★, *Herbie Mann At The Village Gate* (Atlantic 1962)★★★★, *Right Now* (Atlantic 1962)★★★, *Do The Bossa Nova With Herbie Mann* (Atlantic 1962)★★★, *Sound Of Herbie* (Verve 1963)★★★, with Machito *Afro-Jazziac* (Roulette 1963)★★★, *Herbie Mann Returns To The Village Gate* (Atlantic 1963)★★★, *Live At Newport* (Atlantic 1963)★★★★, *Nirvana* (Atlantic 1964)★★★, *Latin Fever* (Atlantic 1964)★★★, *My Kinda Groove* (Atlantic 1965)★★★, *The Roar Of The Greasepaint The Smell Of The Crowd* (Atlantic 1965)★★, *Latin Mann* (Columbia 1965)★★★, with Joao Gilberto *Herbie Mann And Joao Gilberto With Antonio Carlos Jobim* (Atlantic 1965)★★★, *Standing Ovation At Newport* (Atlantic 1966)★★★, *Herbie Mann Today* (Atlantic 1966)★★★, *Monday Night At The Village Gate* (Atlantic 1966)★★★★, *Our Mann Flute* (Atlantic 1966)★★★, *Bongo Conga And Flute* (Verve 1966)★★★, *Big Band Mann* (Verve 1966)★★★, *Big Band* (Surrey 1966)★★★, *New Mann At Newport* (Atlantic 1967)★★★, *Impressions Of The Middle East* (Atlantic 1967)★★★★, *The Beat Goes On* (Atlantic 1967)★★★★, *Mann And A Woman* (Atlantic 1967)★★★, *Glory Of Love* (A&M 1967)★★★, *The Herbie Mann String Album* (Atlantic 1968)★★★, *Moody Mann* (Riverside 1968)★★★, *Jazz Impressions*

Of Brazil (Solid State 1968)★★★, *Wailing Dervishes* (Atlantic 1968)★★★, *Memphis Underground* (Atlantic 1968)★★★, *Free For All* (Atlantic 1968)★★★, *Windows Open* (Atlantic 1969)★★★, *Herbie Mann In Sweden* (Prestige 1969)★★★, *Inspiration I Feel* (Atlantic 1969)★★★, *Concerto Grosso In D Blues* (Atlantic 1969)★★★, *Stone Flute* (Polydor 1970)★★★, *Memphis Two Step* (Atco 1971)★★★, *Muscle Shoals Nitty Gritty* (Atco 1971)★★★, *Push Push* (Atlantic 1972)★★★, *Mississippi Gambler* (Atlantic 1972)★★★, *London Underground* (Atlantic 1973)★★★, *Reggae* (Atlantic 1973)★★★, *Hold On I'm Coming* (Atlantic 1973)★★★, *Evolution Of Mann* (Atlantic 1973)★★★, *Turtle Bay* (Atlantic 1974)★★★, *Gagaku And Beyond* (1974)★★★, *Discotheque* (Atlantic 75)★★★, *Water Bed* (Atlantic 1975)★★★, *Surprises* (Atlantic 1976)★★★, *Brazil - Once Again* (1978)★★★, *Astral Island* (1983)★★★, *Opalescence* (Kokopelli 1989)★★★, *Caminho De Casa* (Chesky 1990)★★★, *The Jazz We Heard Last Summer* (Savoy 1993)★★★, with Bobby Jaspar *Deep Pocket* (Kokopelli 1994)★★★, *Peace Pieces* (Kokopelli 1995)★★★.
●COMPILATIONS: *Nirvana* (Atlantic 1961-62)★★★, *The Best Of Herbie Mann* (Prestige 1965)★★★, *Best Of Herbie Mann* (WEA 1993).

MAR-KEYS

Formed in Memphis, Tennessee, USA, and originally known as the Royal Spades, their line-up comprised: Steve Cropper (b. 21 October 1941, Willow Spring, Missouri, USA; guitar), Donald 'Duck' Dunn (b. 24 November 1941, Memphis, Tennessee, USA; bass), Charles 'Packy' Axton (tenor saxophone), Don Nix (b. 27 September 1941, Memphis, Tennessee, USA; baritone saxophone), Wayne Jackson (trumpet), Charlie Freeman (b. Memphis, Tennessee, USA; guitar), Jerry Lee 'Smoochy' Smith (organ) and Terry Johnson (drums). Although their rhythmic instrumental style was not unique in Memphis (Willie Mitchell followed a parallel path at Hi Records), the Mar-Keys were undoubted masters. Their debut hit, 'Last Night', reached number 3 in the US *Billboard* pop chart during the summer of 1961, establishing Satellite, its outlet, in the process. Within months, Satellite had altered its name to Stax and the Mar-Keys became the label's houseband. Initially all-white, two black musicians, Booker T. Jones (organ) and Al Jackson (drums), had replaced Smith and Johnson by 1962. The newcomers, along with Cropper and Dunn, also worked as Booker T. And The MGs. A turbulent group, the Mar-Keys underwent several changes. Freeman left prior to the recording of 'Last Night' (but would later return for live work), Nix and Axton also quit, while Joe Arnold and Bob Snyder joined on tenor and baritone saxophone. They in turn were replaced by Andrew Love and Floyd Newman, respectively. Although commercial success under their own name was limited, the group provided the backbone to sessions by Otis Redding, Sam And Dave, Wilson Pickett, Carla Thomas and many others, and were the pulsebeat to countless classic records. Axton, the son of

Stax co-founder Estelle, later fronted the Packers, who hit with 'Hole In The Wall' (1965). The single, released on Pure Soul, featured a not-inconspicuous MGs. Line-ups bearing the Mar-Keys' name continued to record despite the desertion of most of the original members. Nix later became part of the Delaney And Bonnie/Leon Russell axis while Charlie Freeman was later part of the Dixie Flyers, one of the last traditional housebands. Both he and Axton died in the early 70s, victims, respectively, of heroin and alcohol. Jackson, Love and Newman, meanwhile, continued the Mar-Keys legacy with releases on Stax and elsewhere, while simultaneously forging a parallel career as the Memphis Horns.
●ALBUMS: *Last Night* (Atlantic 1961)★★★, *Do The Popeye With The Mar-Keys* (London 1962)★★★, *The Great Memphis Sound* (Atlantic 1966)★★★, with Booker T. And The MGs *Back To Back* (Stax 1967)★★★, *Mellow Jello* (Atlantic 1968)★★★, *Damifiknow* (Stax 1969)★★, *Memphis Experience* (1971)★★.

MARCELS

The Marcels were one of several doo-wop-influenced American vocal groups to score success in the early 60s, despite the passing of the genre's golden age. Cornelius 'Nini' Harp (lead singer), Ronald 'Bingo' Mundy (tenor), Fred Johnson (bass), Gene Bricker (tenor) and Richard Knauss (baritone), all native to Pittsburg, Pennsylvania, USA, achieved fame for their distinctive version of Richard Rodgers/Lorenz Hart's classic 'Blue Moon', previously a UK Top 10 hit for Elvis Presley in 1956, which topped both the US and UK charts in 1961. Johnson's distinctive bass introduction to the song has remained one of the most enduring vocal phrases of the time. The quartet scored a further US Top 10 hit that year with 'Heartaches', but its personnel was unstable, with Allen Johnson (d. 28 September 1995) replacing Knauss, and Walt Maddox replacing Bricker. Mundy walked out on the group during this same period, which did little to prepare them for the ever-changing trends prevalent during the early 60s and eventually undermined the Marcels' long-term aspirations.
●ALBUMS: *Blue Moon* (Colpix 1961)★★★.
●COMPILATIONS: *Heartaches* (1987)★★★, *The Best Of The Marcels* (1990)★★★, *The Complete Colpix Sessions* (Sequel 1994)★★★★.

MARCH, LITTLE PEGGY

b. Margaret Battavio, 7 March 1948, Lansdale, Pennsylvania, USA. A child prodigy, at the age of five, March was a regular cast member of Rex Trailer's television show. She subsequently won a talent contest, before securing a recording deal with RCA Records. The singer secured her sole million-selling disc in 1963 when 'I Will Follow Him' topped the US charts. At the age of 15 she became the youngest person at that time to reach number 1. This memorable song had been adapted from 'Chariot', a gold disc in France for British vocalist Petula Clark the previous year. March enjoyed other minor chart entries, most notably with 'Hello Heartache,

Goodbye Love', her sole UK hit, but she is forever linked to her major success. Moving to Germany in the late 60s, she sang frequently on television shows; as a songwriter, she is credited to two European number 1 hits: 'When The Rain Begins To Fall (Jermaine Jackson and Pia Zadora) and 'Manuel Goodbye' (Audrey Landers). She returned to the USA in the 80s. She performed 'I Will Follow Him' in the 1987 John Waters film, *Hairspray*, a tongue-in-cheek homage to pre-Beatles 60s America.

●ALBUMS: *Little Peggy March* (RCA Victor 1962)★★★, *I Will Follow Him* (RCA Victor 1963)★★★, with Bennie Thomas *In Our Fashion* (RCA Victor 1965)★★, *No Foolin'* (RCA Victor 1968)★★★.

MARMALADE

Originally known as Dean Ford And The Gaylords, this Glasgow-based quintet enjoyed considerable success on the Scottish club circuit between 1961 and 1967. Eventually, they were signed by agent/manager Peter Walsh and, after moving to London, changed their name to Marmalade. The line-up then comprised: Dean Ford (b. Thomas McAleese, 5 September 1946, Coatbridge, Glasgow; lead singer), Graham Knight (b. 8 December 1946, Glasgow, Scotland; vocals/bass), Pat Fairley (b. 14 April 1946, Glasgow, Scotland; rhythm guitar), Willie Junior Campbell (b. 31 May 1947, Glasgow, Scotland; lead vocals) and Alan Whitehead (b. 24 July 1946, Oswestry, Shropshire, England; drums). Unpretentious and irresistibly commercial, the group reached the UK charts in May 1968 with 'Lovin' Things' and enjoyed a number 1 with an opportunist cover of John Lennon/Paul McCartney's 'Ob-La-Di, Ob-La-Da'. After several successes with CBS, Walsh negotiated a deal with Decca via Dick Rowe and Marmalade became the first *New Musical Express* UK chart toppers of the 70s by displacing Rolf Harris' 'Two Little Boys' with the moving 'Reflections Of My Life', a more serious work which ably displayed their underused compositional skills. In 1971, the group suffered a severe setback when Campbell, their producer and main songwriter, quit to attend the Royal College of Music. With replacement Hugh Nicolson (formerly of the Poets), they enjoyed several more hits, including 'Cousin Norman', 'Radancer' and 'Falling Apart At The Seams'. The latter proved a prophetic title, for the group were dogged by line-up changes during the 70s. Changes in the pop marketplace lessened their appeal, and a saucy 'sex on tour' story in the salacious Sunday papers caused them embarrassment. With Knight and Whitehead surviving from the original line-up, Marmalade was resuscitated for cabaret purposes later in the decade.

●ALBUMS: *There's A Lot Of It* (CBS 1969)★★★, *Reflections Of My Life* (1970)★★★, *Songs* (Decca 1971)★★★, *Our House Is Rockin'* (1974)★★, *Only Light On My Horizon* (1977)★★, *Doing It All For You* (1979)★★.

●COMPILATIONS: *The Best Of The Marmalade* (CBS 1970)★★★, *Reflections Of The Marmalade* (Decca 1970)★★★, *The Definitive Collection* (Castle 1996)★★★★.

MARTHA AND THE VANDELLAS

Martha Reeves (b. 18 July 1941, Alabama, USA), with Annette Sterling Beard, Gloria Williams and Rosalind Ashford formed the Del-Phis in 1960, one of the scores of female vocal groups then operating in Detroit, Michigan, USA. After Reeves began working as a secretary at Motown Records, they were offered a one-off single release on the label's Melody subsidiary, for which they were credited as the Vels. Gloria Williams left the group when the single flopped, but the remaining trio were allowed a second opportunity, recording 'I'll Have To Let Him Go' in late 1962, when the artist for whom it had been intended, Mary Wells, failed to turn up for the session. Renamed Martha And The Vandellas, the group divided their time between backing other Motown artists and recording in their own right. They were featured on Marvin Gaye's 1962 hit, 'Stubborn Kind Of Fellow', before the US Top 30 success of their own release, 'Come And Get These Memories', brought their career as second-string vocalists to an end. Their next single, the dynamic 'Heat Wave', was masterminded by the Holland/Dozier/Holland production team, and epitomized the confidence and verve of the Vandellas' finest work. 'Quick Sand' repeated the hit formula with a US Top 10 chart placing, while it was 'Dancing In The Street' that represented the pinnacle of their sound. The song, co-written by Marvin Gaye and William Stevenson, was an anthemic invitation to party, given added bite by the tense political situation in the black ghettos. Holland/Dozier/Holland's production exploited all the potential of the music, using clunking chains to heighten the rhythmic feel, and a majestic horn riff to pull people to their feet. 'Dancing In The Street' was the most exciting record Motown had yet made, and it was a deserved number 2 hit in America.

Nothing the Vandellas recorded thereafter reached quite the same peak of excitement, although not for want of trying. 'Nowhere To Run' in 1965 was an irresistible dance hit, which again was given political connotations in some quarters. It introduced a new group member, former Velvelette Betty Kelly, who replaced Annette Sterling Beard. This line-up scored further Top 10 hits with 'I'm Ready For Love' and the infectious 'Jimmy Mack', and celebrated Motown's decision to give Reeves individual credit in front of the group's name with another notable success, 'Honey Chile'. Reeves was taken seriously ill in 1968, and her absence forced the group to disband. By 1970, she was able to resume her career, recruiting her sister Lois and another former Velvelette, Sandra Tilley, to form a new Vandellas line-up. No major US hits were forthcoming, but in Britain they were able to capitalize on the belated 1969 success of 'Dancing In The Street', and had several Top 30 entries in the early 70s. When Motown moved their headquarters from Detroit to Hollywood in 1972, Reeves elected to stay behind. Disbanding the group once again, she fought a lengthy legal battle to have her recording contract annulled, and was eventually free to begin an abortive solo career. Her sister Lois joined Quiet Elegance, while Sandra Tilley retired from the record business, and died in 1982. Motown retained the rights to the Vandellas' name, but chose not to sully the memory of their early 60s hits by concocting a new version of the group without Martha Reeves.

●ALBUMS: *Come And Get These Memories* (Gordy 1963)★★★, *Heat Wave* (Gordy 1963)★★★, *Dance Party* (Gordy 1965)★★★, *Watchout!* (Gordy 1967)★★, *Live!* (Gordy 1967)★, *Ridin' High* (Motown 1968)★★, *Sugar 'n' Spice* (Motown 1969)★★, *Natural Resources* (1970)★★, *Black Magic* (1972)★★.

●COMPILATIONS: *Greatest Hits* (Gordy 1966)★★★★, *Anthology* (Motown 1974)★★★★, *Compact Commmand Performances* (1992)★★★, *24 Greatest Hits* (1992)★★★★, *Live Wire, 1962-1972* (Motown 1993)★★★★, *Milestones* (Motown 1995)★★★★.

MARTIN, GEORGE

b. 3 January 1926, London, England. Martin became the world's most famous record producer through his work with the Beatles. Classically trained at London's Guildhall School of Music, he joined EMI in 1950 as a junior A&R man. Five years later, Martin was given charge of the Parlophone label where he produced a wide variety of artists. Among them were ballad singers (Shirley Bassey and Matt Monro), skiffle groups (the Vipers), jazz bands (Temperance 7, Johnny Dankworth, Humphrey Lyttelton) and numerous comedy artists. Chief among these were Peter Sellers and Bernard Cribbins, whose 'Right Said Fred' and 'Hole In The Ground' were hits in 1962. By this time, Martin had signed the Beatles to Parlophone and begun a relationship which lasted until their demise in 1970. Apart from insisting that drummer Pete Best be replaced, Martin's main contribution to the group's music lay in his ability to translate their more adventurous ideas into practical terms. Thus, he added classical music touches to 'Yesterday' and 'For No One' and devised the tape loops and studio manipulations that created the stranger sounds on *Revolver* and *Sgt Pepper's Lonely Hearts Club Band*. Martin also made two orchestral albums of Beatles tunes. As Brian Epstein signed Cilla Black, Gerry And the Pacemakers and Billy J. Kramer And the Dakotas to Parlophone, Martin supervised their recordings.

In 1965, he left EMI and set up his own studios, AIR London with fellow producers Ron Richards (Hollies) and John Burgess (Manfred Mann). He continued to work with several new EMI artists, notably the Action. In the 70s he produced a series of hit albums by America. During this period he worked with Neil Sedaka, Ringo Starr, Jimmy Webb, Jeff Beck and Stackridge, while producing the soundtrack to the 1978 film of *Sgt Pepper's Lonely Hearts Club Band*. He also maintained the Beatles connection and prepared the 1977 release of the live recording *At The Hollywood Bowl* and produced two of Paul McCartney's solo efforts, *Tug Of War* (1981) and *Pipes Of Peace* (1983). He also produced the soundtrack to McCartney's film musical *Give My Regards To Broad Street*. In the late 70s, AIR was purchased by

Chrysalis and Martin became a director of the company. He opened a second studio on the Caribbean island of Montserrat, which became a favoured recording centre for artists, including McCartney, Dire Straits and the Rolling Stones, before the island was devastated by a hurricane in 1989. Those artists were among the musicians donating tracks for *After The Hurricane*, a benefit album organized by Martin. During the late 80s, he was less prolific as a producer, but created a version of Dylan Thomas' *Under Milk Wood* in 1988 and worked with ex-Dexys Midnight Runners member Andy Leek on his debut solo album. In 1990, Martin announced plans to replace AIR Studios with a 'state of the art' audio-video complex in north London. Martin's quiet and intelligent persona has masked an extraordinary talent. His work with the Beatles cannot be overstated. His punctilious attention in remastering the Beatles' entire work for compact disc is demonstrated in the quite remarkable results he achieved. In 1992, he was instrumental in producing a television documentary to mark the 25th anniversary of the Beatles' *Sgt. Pepper* album. In the mid-90s he was a major part of the Beatles Anthology series, although he was disappointed not to have been asked to produce the two new singles, 'Free As A Bird' and 'Real Love'. This task went to Jeff Lynne, who received some criticism for his production, leading to a number of 'if only George Martin had produced it' comments. Martin has no worries: his name is firmly in the history books, with an unimpeachable record. He received the Grammy Trustees Award in 1995. In addition to his chairmanship of AIR Studios he is a director of Chrysalis Group plc and is chairman of the London radio station Heart FM. Martin was rightly awarded a knighthood in 1996 for his services to music, for being such a consistent ambassador of music and for hardly ever putting a foot wrong.

●ALBUMS: *Off The Beatle Track* (Parlophone 1964)★★★, *George Martin* (United Artists 1965)★★★, *George Martin Scores Instrumental Versions Of The Hits* (1965)★★★, *Plays Help!* (Columbia 1965)★★, *Salutes The Beatle Girls* (United Artists)★★★, *And I Love Her* (Studio Two 1966)★★★, *By George!* (1967)★★★, *The Family Way* soundtrack (1967)★★★, *British Maid* (United Artists 1968)★★★, with the Beatles *Yellow Submarine* (Parlophone 1969)★★★, *Live And Let Die* (United Artists 1973)★★★, *Beatles To Bond And Bach* (Polydor 1974)★★★.

●FURTHER READING: *All You Need Is Ears*, George Martin. *Summer Of Love: The Making Of Sgt Pepper*, George Martin.

●FILMS: *Give My Regards To Broad Street* (1985).

MARTINDALE, WINK

b. Winston Martindale, 1933, Jackson, Tennessee, USA. A 1959 revival of T. Texas Tyler's 'Deck Of Cards' monologue is as synonymous with this ex-Memphis radio presenter as the pyramids are with Egypt. While studying speech and drama at the state university, he had moonlighted at a city station, working his way up from music librarian. A meeting with Dot Records executive Randy

Wood led to the release of 'Deck Of Cards' - a soldier answering a charge of playing cards in church by explaining each one's religious significance - an opus that appealed to Martindale, a former chorister and regular church-goer. Its worldwide success brought far-flung television appearances on Australia's *Bandstand* and UK's *Sunday Night At The London Palladium,* and also caused the artist to migrate to Hollywood, where he hosted the *Teenage Dance Party* television series in the early 60s. 'A Deck Of Cards' has been extraordinarily successful in the UK, re-entering the charts on several occasions in the 60s and in 1973. It peaked behind a more recently recorded rival recitation from Max Bygraves.
●ALBUMS: *Wink Martindale* (London 1960)★, Deck Of Cards (Golden Guinea 1963)★.

MARVELETTES

The Marvelettes' career epitomized the haphazard progress endured by many of the leading girl groups of the early 60s. Despite enjoying several major USA hits, they were unable to sustain a consistent line-up, and their constant shift in personnel made it difficult to overcome their rather anonymous public image. The group was formed in the late 50s by five students at Inkster High School in Michigan, USA: Gladys Horton, Georgeanna Marie Tillman, Wanda Young, Katherine Anderson and Juanita Grant. They were spotted at a school talent show by Robert Bateman of the Satintones, who introduced them to Berry Gordy, head of the fledgling Motown organization. Bateman co-produced their early releases with Brian Holland, and the partnership found immediate success with 'Please Mr Postman' - a US number 1 in 1961, and Motown's biggest-selling record up to that point. This effervescent slice of pop-R&B captivated teenage audiences in the USA, and the song was introduced to an even wider public when the Beatles recorded a faithful cover version on their second album. After a blatant attempt to repeat the winning formula with 'Twistin' Postman', the Marvelettes made the Top 20 again in 1962 with 'Playboy' and the chirpy 'Beechwood 4-5789'. The cycle of line-up changes was already underway, with Juanita Grant's departure reducing the group to a four-piece. The comparative failure of the next few singles also took its toll, and by 1965, Tillman had also left. The remaining trio, occasionally augmented by Florence Ballard of the Supremes, was paired with producer/writer Smokey Robinson. He tailored a series of ambitious hit singles for the group, the most successful of which was 'Don't Mess With Bill' in 1966 - although 'The Hunter Gets Captured By The Game' was arguably a more significant achievement. Gladys Horton, the Marvelettes' usual lead singer, left the group in 1967, to be replaced by Anne Bogan. They continued to notch up minor soul hits for the remainder of the decade, most notably 'When You're Young And In Love', before disintegrating in 1970. Wanda Young completed the group's recording commitments with an album, *The Return Of The Marvelettes*, which saw her supported by session vocalists. In 1989 original members Wanda Rogers and

Gladys Horton, plus Echo Johnson and Jean McLain, recorded for Ian Levine's Motor City label issuing the disco-sounding 'Holding On With Both Hands' and *Now*. Johnson and McLain were replaced by Jackie and Regina Holleman for subsequent releases.
●ALBUMS: *Please Mr Postman* (Tamla Motown 1961)★★★★, *The Marvelettes Sing Smash Hits Of 1962* (Tamla Motown 1962)★★★, *Playboy* (Tamla Motown 1962)★★★, *The Marvellous Marvelettes* (Tamla Motown 1963)★★★★, *Recorded Live: On Stage* (Tamla Motown 1963)★★, *The Marvelettes* (Tamla Motown 1967)★★★, *Sophisticated Soul* (Tamla Motown 1968)★★★, *In Full Bloom* (Motown 1969)★★, *The Return Of The Marvelettes* (Motown 1970)★★, *Now* (1990)★★.
●COMPILATIONS: *The Marvelettes Greatest Hits* (Tamla Motown 1963)★★★★, *Compact Command Perfomances - 23 Greatest Hits* (1992)★★★★, *Deliver The Singles 1961-1971* (Motown 1993)★★★★, *The Very Best* (Essential Gold 1996)★★★.

MAUGHAN, SUSAN

b. 1 July 1942, Newcastle-upon-Tyne, Tyne And Wear, England. A popular and vivacious singing star in the UK during the 60s, Susan Maughan began her singing career in 1958 as a member of a popular midland band led by Ronnie Hancock. Their 1961 demonstration disc alerted the Philips label to her talent, and a year in the Ray Ellington Quartet ran concurrently with a nascent recording career, which began with the timely 'Mama Do The Twist'. Maughan enjoyed chart success when the effervescent 'Bobby's Girl' reached the UK Top 3 in 1962, but although 'Hand A Handkerchief To Helen' and 'She's New To You' (both 1963) were minor hits, she was unable to repeat this early triumph. Maughan nonetheless continued to record, and albums featuring a full orchestra (*Swingin' Susan*) or a jazzband (*Hey Look Me Over*) showed her versatility. In 1965, along with a host of other pop stars such as Billy J. Kramer, the Animals, Peter and Gordon, Matt Monro, and Herman's Hermits, she appeared in the 'mock concert' film *Pop Gear*, which was hosted by Jimmy Savile. Nearly 30 years later, in 1992, Susan Maughan joined another survivor from those far off days, Jess Conrad, in the UK tour of *The Golden Sounds Of The Sixties.*
●ALBUMS: *I Wanna Be Bobby's Girl But* (Philips 1963)★★★, *Swingin' Susan* (Philips 1964)★★★, *Sentimental Susan* (Philips 1965)★★★, *Hey Look Me Over* (1966)★★★.
●COMPILATIONS: *Bobby's Girl* (Wing 1966)★★★.

MAYALL, JOHN

b. 29 November 1933, Macclesfield, Cheshire, England. The career of England's premier white blues exponent and father of British blues has now spanned five decades and much of that time has been unintentionally spent acting as a musical catalyst. Mayall formed his first band in 1955 while at college, and as the Powerhouse Four the group worked mostly locally. Soon afterwards, Mayall enlisted for National Service. He then became a commercial artist and finally moved to London to form his Blues Syndicate, the forerunner to his legendary Bluesbreakers. Along with Alexis Korner, Cyril Davies and Graham Bond, Mayall pioneered British R&B. The astonishing number of musicians who have passed through his bands reads like a who's-who. Even more remarkable is the number of names who have gone on to eclipse Mayall with either their own bands or as members of highly successful groups. Pete Frame, author of *Rock Family Trees*, has produced a detailed Mayall specimen, which is recommended. His roster of musicians included John McVie, Hughie Flint, Mick Fleetwood, Roger Dean, Davey Graham, Eric Clapton, Jack Bruce, Aynsley Dunbar, Peter Green, Dick Heckstall-Smith, Keef Hartley, Mick Taylor, Henry Lowther, Tony Reeves, Chris Mercer, Jon Hiseman, Steve Thompson, Colin Allen, Jon Mark, Johnny Almond, Harvey Mandel, Larry Taylor, and Don 'Sugercane' Harris.

His 1965 debut, *John Mayall Plays John Mayall*, was a live album which, although badly recorded, captured the tremendous atmosphere of an R&B club. His first single, 'Crawling Up A Hill', is contained on this set and it features Mayall's thin voice attempting to compete with an exciting, distorted harmonica and Hammond organ. *Bluesbreakers With Eric Clapton* is now a classic, and is highly recommended to all students of white blues. Clapton enabled his boss to reach a wider audience, as the crowds filled the clubs to get a glimpse of the guitar hero. *A Hard Road* featured some clean and sparing guitar from Peter Green, while *Crusade* offers a brassier, fuller sound. *The Blues Alone* showed a more relaxed style, and allowed Mayall to demonstrate his musical dexterity. *Diary Of A Band Vol. 1* and *Vol. 2* were released during 1968 and capture their live sound from the previous year; both feature excellent drumming from Keef Hartley, in addition to Mick Taylor on guitar. *Bare Wires*, arguably Mayall's finest work, shows a strong jazz leaning, with the addition of Jon Hiseman on drums and the experienced brass section of Lowther, Mercer and Heckstall-Smith. The album was an introspective journey and contained Mayall's most competent lyrics, notably the beautifully hymn-like 'I Know Now'. The similarly packaged *Blues From Laurel Canyon* (Mayall often produced his own artwork) was another strong album which was recorded in Los Angeles, where Mayall lived. This marked the end of the Bluesbreakers name and, following the departure of Mick Taylor to the Rolling Stones, Mayall pioneered a drumless acoustic band featuring Jon Mark on acoustic guitar, Johnny Almond on tenor saxophone and flute, and Stephen Thompson on string bass. The subsequent live album, *The Turning Point*, proved to be his biggest-selling album and almost reached the UK Top 10. Notable tracks are the furious 'Room To Move', with Mayall's finest harmonica solo, and 'Thoughts About Roxanne' with some exquisite saxophone from Almond. The same line-up plus Larry Taylor produced *Empty Rooms*, which was more refined and less exciting. The band that recorded *USA Union* consisted of

Americans Harvey Mandel, 'Sugercane' Harris and Larry Taylor. It gave Mayall yet another success, although he struggled lyrically. Following the double reunion, *Back To The Roots*, Mayall's work lost its bite, and over the next few years his output was of poor quality. The halcyon days of name stars in his band had passed and Mayall suffered record company apathy. His last album to chart was *New Year, New Band, New Company* in 1975, featuring for the first time a female vocalist, Dee McKinnie, and future Fleetwood Mac guitarist Rick Vito. Following a run of albums that had little or no exposure, Mayall stopped recording, playing only infrequently close to his base in California. He toured Europe in 1988 to small but wildly enthusiastic audiences. That same year he signed to Island Records and released *Chicago Line*. Renewed activity and interest occurred in 1990 following the release of his finest album in many years, *A Sense Of Place*. Mayall was interviewed during a short visit to Britain in 1992 and sounded positive, happy and unaffected by years in the commercial doldrums. *Wake Up Call* changed everything once more. Released in 1993, the album is one of his finest ever, and became his biggest-selling disc for over two decades. The 90s have so far been kind to Mayall; the birth of another child in 1995, and a solid new releases, *Spinning Coin*. The replacement for the departing Coco Montoya is yet another highly talented guitarist, a fortune with which Mayall is clearly blessed, Buddy Whittington is the latest, continuing a tradition that started with Clapton and Green. As the sole survivor from the four 60s UK R&B/blues catalysts, Mayall has played the blues for so long without any deviation that it is hard to think of any other white artist to compare. He has outlived his contemporaries from the early days (Korner, Bond and Davis) and recent reappraisal has put the man clearly back at the top of a genre that he can justifiably claim to have furthered more than any other Englishman.

●ALBUMS: *John Mayall Plays John Mayall* (Decca 1965)★★★★, *Bluesbreakers With Eric Clapton* (Decca 1966)★★★★★, *A Hard Road* (Decca 1967)★★★★, *Crusade* (Decca 1967)★★★, *Blues Alone* (Ace Of Clubs 1967)★★★★, *Diary Of A Band Vol. 1* (Decca 1968)★★★, *Diary Of A Band Vol. 2* (Decca 1968)★★★, *Bare Wires* (Decca 1968)★★★★★, *Blues From Laurel Canyon* (Decca 1968)★★★★, *Turning Point* (Polydor 1969)★★★★, *Empty Rooms* (Polydor 1970)★★★★, *USA Union* (Polydor 1970)★★★, *Back To The Roots* (Polydor 1971)★★★, *Beyond The Turning Point* (Polydor 1971)★★★, *Thru The Years* (Decca 1971)★★★, *Memories* (Polydor 1971)★★★, *Jazz Blues Fusion* (Polydor 1972)★★★, *Moving On* (Polydor 1973)★★, *Ten Years Are Gone* (Polydor 1973)★★, *Down The Line* (London US 1973)★★, *The Latest Edition* (Polydor 1975)★★, *New Year, New Band, New Company* (ABC 1975)★★, *Time Expired, Notice To Appear* (ABC 1975)★★, *John Mayall* (Polydor 1976)★★, *A Banquet Of Blues* (ABC 1976)★★, *Lots Of People* (ABC 1977)★★, *A Hard Core Package* (ABC 1977)★★, *Primal Solos* (London 1977)★★★, *Blues*

Roots (Decca 1978)★★, *Last Of The British Blues* (MCA 1978)★★, *Bottom Line* (DJM 1979)★★, *No More Interviews* (DJM 1979)★★, *Roadshow Blues* (DJM 1980)★★, *Last Edition* (Polydor 1983)★★, *Behind the Iron Curtain* (PRT 1986)★★, *Chicago Line* (Island 1988)★★, *A Sense Of Place* (Island 1990)★★★★, *Wake Up Call* (Silvertone 1993)★★★★, *Spinning Coin* (Silvertone 1995)★★, *Blues For The Lost Days* (Silvertone 1997)★★★★.

●COMPILATIONS: *Looking Back* (Decca 1969)★★★★, *World Of John Mayall* (Decca 1970)★★★★, *World Of John Mayall Vol. 2* (Decca 1971)★★★★, *The John Mayall Story Vol. 1* (Decca 1983)★★★, *The John Mayall Story Vol. 2* (Decca 1983)★★★, *London Blues 1964-1969* (Polygram 1992)★★★★, *Room To Move 1969-1974* (Polygram 1992)★★★★.

●VIDEOS: *John Mayall's Bluesbreakers: Blues Alive* (PVE 1995).

●FURTHER READING: *John Mayall: Blues Breaker*, Richard Newman.

MAYFIELD, CURTIS

b. 3 June 1942, Chicago, Illinois, USA. As songwriter and vocalist with the Impressions, Mayfield established an early reputation as one of soul music's most intuitive talents. In the decade between 1961 and 1971, he penned a succession of exemplary singles for his group, including 'Gypsy Woman' (1961), 'It's All Right' (1963), 'People Get Ready' (1965), 'We're A Winner' (1968) and 'Choice Of Colours' (1969), the subjects of which ranged from simple, tender love songs to broadsides demanding social and political equality. Years later Bob Marley lifted lines from the anthemic 'People Get Ready' to populate his own opus, 'One Love'. Two independent record companies, Windy C and Curtom, emphasized Mayfield's statesman-like role within black music, while his continued support for other artists - as composer, producer or session guitarist - enhanced a virtually peerless reputation. Jerry Butler, Major Lance, Gene Chandler and Walter Jackson are among the many Chicago-based singers benefiting from Mayfield's involvement. Having parted company with the Impressions in 1970, the singer began his solo career with '(Don't Worry) If There's A Hell Below We're All Going To Go', a suitably astringent protest song. The following year Mayfield enjoyed his biggest UK success when 'Move On Up' reached number 12, a compulsive dance song which surprisingly did not chart in the US. There, the artist's commercial ascendancy was maintained with 'Freddie's Dead' (US R&B number 2/number 4 pop hit) and the theme from 'Superfly' (1972), a 'blaxploitation' film which he also scored. Both singles and the attendant album achieved gold status, inspiring further excursions into motion picture soundtracks, including *Claudine*, *A Piece Of The Action*, *Sparkle* and *Short Eyes*, the last of which featured Mayfield in an acting role. However, although the singer continued to prove popular, he failed to sustain this high profile, and subsequent work, including his production of Aretha Franklin's 1978 album, *Almighty Fire*,

gained respect rather than commercial approbation. In 1981, he joined the Boardwalk label for which he recorded *Honesty*, his strongest album since the halcyon days of the early 70s. Sadly, the death of label managing director Neil Bogert left an insurmountable gap, and Mayfield's career was then blighted by music industry indifference. The singer nonetheless remained a highly popular live attraction, particularly in Britain where '(Celebrate) The Day After You', a collaboration with the Blow Monkeys, became a minor hit. In 1990, a freak accident, in which part of a public address rig collapsed on top of him during a concert, left Mayfield permanently paralyzed from the neck down. The effects, both personal and professional, proved costly, but not completely devastating in terms of his musical career . The material for *BBC Radio 1 Live In Concert* was gathered from the gig at London's Town And Country Club during Mayfield's 1990 European tour. In 1993 Warner Brothers released *A Tribute To Curtis Mayfield* with various artists; including Lenny Kravitz, Whitney Houston, Aretha Franklin, Bruce Springsteen, Rod Stewart, Elton John and Steve Winwood, as an excellent tribute to the songbook. The latter turned in the album's highlight; a sparkling version of 'It's All Right!' A year later Charly Records reissued the majority of Mayfield's 70s albums on CD as well as several compilations. The icing on the cake came in 1996 when Rhino Records collated the best package in a 3-CD box set. At the end of 1996 a new album, *New World Order*, was released to excellent reviews. After repeated plays the album stands up as a good one, but some critics may have been swayed by their affection for such an important man, together with his tragic disability. During the recording Mayfield had to lie backwards in order to give some gravitational power to his singing. His contribution to soul music has been immense: whatever the limitations of his disability, his voice, however remains perfect and unique.

●ALBUMS: *Curtis* (Buddah 1970)★★★, *Curtis Live* (Buddah 1971)★★★, *Roots* (Buddah 1971)★★★★, *Superfly* soundtrack (Buddah 1972)★★★★★, *Back To The World* (Buddah 1973)★★★★, *Curtis In Chicago* (Buddah 1973)★★★, *Sweet Exorcist* (Buddah 1974)★★★, *Got To Find A Way* (Buddah 1974)★★★, *Claudine* (Buddah 1975)★★, *Let's Do It Again* (1975)★★★, *There's No Place Like America Today* (1975)★★★, *Sparkle* (1976)★★, *Give, Get, Take And Have* (1976)★★, *Short Eyes* (1977)★★, *Never Say You Can't Survive* (1977)★★, *A Piece Of The Action* (1978)★★, *Do It All Night* (1978)★★★, *Heartbeat* (1979)★★★, with Linda Clifford *The Right Combination* (1980)★★, *Something To Believe In* (1980)★★, *Love Is The Place* (Boardwalk 1981)★★, *Honesty* (Boardwalk 1983)★★★★, *We Come In Peace With A Message Of Love* (1985)★★★, *Live In Europe* (1988)★★★, *People Get Ready* (1990)★★★, *Take It To The Streets* (1990)★★★, *BBC Radio 1 Live In Concert* (Windsong 1994)★★, *New World Order* (Warners 1996)★★★.

●COMPILATIONS: *Of All Time* (1990)★★★, *Get Down*

To The Funky Groove (1994)★★★, *Groove On Up* (1994)★★★, *Tripping Out* (Charly 1994)★★★, *A Man Like Curtis - The Best Of* (1994)★★★, *Living Legend* (Curtom Classics 1995)★★★, *People Get Ready: The Curtis Mayfield Story* 3-CD box set (Rhino 1996)★★★★.
●FILMS: *Superfly* (1973), *The Groove Tube* (1974).

MAYFIELD, PERCY

b. 12 August 1920, Minden, Louisiana, USA, d. 11 August 1984. A gifted performer, Percy Mayfield's first success came in 1950 with 'Please Send Me Someone To Love' on the Specialty label. A massive US R&B hit, it reportedly sold well in excess of one million copies and became an enduring composition through its many cover versions. Further chart entries, 'Lost Love' (1951) and 'Big Question' (1952), confirmed Mayfield's status, but it was nine years before he secured another best-seller with 'River's Invitation'. 'Hit The Road Jack' enhanced Mayfield's standing as a gifted composer when it became an international hit for Ray Charles. This influential musician recorded several of Mayfield's songs; Mayfield, in turn, pursued his career on Charles' Tangerine outlet. The talented artist remained an active performer throughout the 70s and early 80s, and his later work appeared on several different labels. His death from a heart attack in 1984 robbed R&B of one of its most individual voices. Johnny Adams released an excellent tribute album in 1989 titled *Walking On A Tightrope*.
●ALBUMS: *My Jug And I* (HMV 1962)★★★, *Percy Mayfield* (1969)★★★, *Bought Blues* (1969)★★★, *Tightrope* (1969)★★★, *Percy Mayfield Sings* (1970)★★★, *Weakness Is A Thing Called Man* (1970)★★, *Blues - And Then Some* (1971)★★, *Live* (Winner 1992)★★.
●COMPILATIONS: *The Incredible Percy Mayfield* (1972)★★★, *My Heart Is Always Singing Sad Songs* (1985)★★★, *The Voice Within* (1988)★★★, *Percy Mayfield: Poet Of The Blues* (1990)★★★, *Percy Mayfield Vol. 2: Memory Pain* (1992).
●VIDEOS: *John Lee Hooker/Lowell Fulson/Percy Mayfield* (1992).

MAYTALS

Arguably the Maytals were only ever kept from becoming 'international' artists by the runaway success of Bob Marley And The Wailers in the 70s. Rumour has it that Island Records' Chris Blackwell only originally signed the Wailers because he was unable to obtain the Maytals' signatures at the time. Frederick 'Toots' Hibbert, Nathaniel 'Jerry' Matthias/McCarthy and Henry 'Raleigh' Gordon came together in 1962 at the start of Jamaica's ska craze and began recording for Coxsone Dodd's Studio One organisation. With a hoarse vocal from Hibbert, backed by an impenetrable wall of sound, it was not long before the Maytals were the number one vocal group in Jamaica - a position they maintained throughout the 60s and on into the 70s.

They left Coxsone after some massive hits and moved on to his ex-employee and arch-rival Prince Buster, celebrating with the vengeful 'Broadway Jungle'/'Dog War': 'We were caught in the jungle . . . In the hands of a man . . .' However, their stay with Buster was also short-lived and the Maytals moved on again to Byron Lee's BMN stable. In 1965 they made Jamaican musical history when both sides of 'Daddy'/'It's You' topped both Jamaican charts, and in 1966 they won the prestigious Jamaican Festival Song Competition with 'Bam Bam'. Many of their releases in these early days were credited to 'The Vikings' or 'The Flames', for as Hibbert explained: 'Promoters in Jamaica called us all kinds of different names because they didn't want us to get our royalties'. The future was looking bright for the group, but Hibbert was imprisoned in late 1966 for possession of marijuana and was not released until 1968. The Maytals began work for Leslie Kong's Beverleys label, and their first release was a huge hit in Jamaica and the UK - '54-46 That's My Number' featured one of reggae's most enduring bass lines as Hibbert detailed his prison experiences in song. This was the beginning of a hugely successful period for the group, both artistically and financially, and they recorded many classic records for Beverleys including 'Do The Reggay' one of the first songs ever to use 'reggae' in the title, 'Monkey Man', which actually made the UK charts, and 'Sweet and Dandy', which won the Festival Song Competition again for them in 1969. They also appeared in a cameo role in the hugely popular film *The Harder They Come*, singing one of their all-time favourites, 'Pressure Drop'.

Kong's untimely death in 1971 from a heart attack robbed them of their mentor. Many believed that their best work was recorded while at Beverleys; evidence of its popularity was found in the 2-Tone craze in the late 70s when new bands took a large part of their repertoire from Hibbert's Beverleys song book. They returned to Byron Lee, now the successful owner of Dynamic Sounds, a state-of-the-art recording, mastering and record pressing complex. In 1972 the Maytals won the Festival Song Competition yet again with 'Pomps and Pride'. Through their work with Dynamic they attracted the attention of Chris Blackwell and became Toots And The Maytals. For the first time in 14 years they became widely known outside of reggae circles. Their UK and USA tours were sell-outs, and Island Records released what became their biggest selling album, *Reggae Got Soul*, which took them into the UK album charts. They made history again in 1980 when, on 29 September, they recorded a live show at London's Hammersmith Palais, which was mastered, processed, pressed and in the shops 24 hours later. Few live excursions have been able to capture the feel and spontaneity of this album, which showcases the Maytals at their best: live without any embellishments. By now they had left their Jamaican audiences far behind, but their nebulous 'pop' audience soon moved on to the next big sensation. While the Maytals continued to tour and make records in the 90s, real lasting international success always seemed to elude them. Hibbert dispensed with the services of Matthias/McCarthy and Gordon for his

1982 tour and has even experimented with non reggae line-ups. It will be interesting to see what direction he will now take to match the myriad achievements of his illustrious past.

●ALBUMS: *Presenting The Maytals* (Ska Beat 1964)★★★, *The Sensational* (Wirl 1965)★★★★, *Never Grow Old* (Studio One *c*.1966)★★★, *Original Golden Oldies (Volume Three)* (Fab Prince Buster *c*.1967)★★★, *Sweet & Dandy* (Beverley's 1969)★★★, *From The Roots* (Trojan 1970)★★★, *Monkey Man* (Trojan 1970)★★★, *Funky Kingston* (Dragon 1973)★★★, *In The Dark* (Dragon/Dynamic 1974)★★★, *Slatyam Stoot* (Dynamic)★★★, *Reggae Got Soul* (Mango/Island 1976)★★★★, *Toots Live* (Mango/Island)★★★, *Life Could Be A Dream* (Studio One 1992)★★★.

●COMPILATIONS: *Reggae Greats* (Mango/Island 1988)★★★, *Do The Reggae 1966-70* (Trojan 1988)★★★, *Sensational Ska Explosion* (Jamaica Gold 1993)★★★, *Time Tough* (Mango/Island 1996)★★★.

MC5

Formed in 1964 in Detroit, Michigan, USA, and originally known as the Motor City Five, the group was sundered the following year when its rhythm section left in protest over a new original song, 'Back To Comm'. Michael Davis (bass) and Dennis Thompson (drums) joined founder members Rob Tyner (b. Robert Derminer, 12 December 1944, Detroit, Michigan, USA, d. 18 September 1991; vocals), Wayne Kramer (guitar) and Fred 'Sonic' Smith (b. 1949, d. 4 November 1994; guitar) to pursue the radical direction this experimental composition offered. By 1967 their repertoire contained material drawn from R&B, soul and *avant garde* jazz, as well as a series of powerful original songs. Two singles, 'One Of The Guys'/'I Can Only Give You Everything' (1967) and 'Borderline'/'Looking At You' (1968), captured their nascent, high-energy sound as the group embraced the 'street' politics proselytized by mentor/manager John Sinclair. Now linked to this former DJ's Trans Love Commune and White Panther party, the MC5 became Detroit's leading underground act, and a recording deal with the Elektra label resulted in the seminal *Kick Out The Jams*. Recorded live at the city's Grande Ballroom, this turbulent set captured the quintet's extraordinary sound which, although loud, was never reckless. However, MC5 were then dropped from their label's roster following several disagreements, but later emerged anew on Atlantic. Rock journalist Jon Landau, later manager of Bruce Springsteen, was invited to produce *Back In The USA* which, if lacking the dissolute thrill of its predecessor, showed a group able to adapt to studio discipline. 'Tonight', 'Shakin' Street' and a remade 'Lookin' At You' are among the highlights of this excellent set. A third collection, *High Time*, reasserted a desire to experiment, and several local jazz musicians added punch to what nonetheless remains a curiously ill-focused album on which each member, bar Davis, contributed material. A move to Europe, where the group performed and recorded under the aegis of Rohan O'Rahilly, failed to halt dwindling commercial prospects, while the departure of Davis, then Tyner, in 1972, brought the MC5 to an end. Their reputation flourished during the punk phenomenon, during which time each former member enjoyed brief notoriety. Davis later surfaced in Destroy All Monsters, and Sonic Smith married Patti Smith (and was heavily featured on the singer/poet's 'comeback' album, *Dream Of Life*, in 1988). Both Kramer and Tyner attempted to use the MC5 name for several unrelated projects. They wisely abandoned such practices, leaving intact the legend of one of rock's most uncompromising and exciting acts. In September 1991 Tyner died of a heart attack in the seat of his parked car in his home town of Ferndale, Michigan. Smith also passed away three years later. Kramer, however, relaunched a solo career in the same year, enlisting several prominent members of the US underground/alternative scene as his new cohorts.

●ALBUMS: *Kick Out The Jams* (Elektra 1969)★★★★, *Back In The USA* (Elektra 1970)★★★, *High Time* (Elektra 1971)★★.

●COMPILATIONS: *Babes In Arms* (ROIR 1983)★★★, *Looking At You* (Receiver 1994)★★★, *Power Trip* (Alive 1994)★★★.

McCLINTON, DELBERT

b. 4 November 1940, Lubbock, Texas, USA. This white R&B artist honed his craft working in a bar band, the Straitjackets, backing visiting blues giants such as Sonny Boy Williamson, Howlin' Wolf, Lightnin' Hopkins and Jimmy Reed. McClinton made his first recordings as a member of the Ron-Dels, and was noted for his distinctive harmonica work on Bruce Channel's 'Hey Baby', a Top 3 single in the UK and number 1 in the US in 1962. Legend has it that on a tour of the UK with Channel, McClinton met a young John Lennon and advised him on his harmonica technique, resulting in the sound heard on 'Love Me Do'. Relocating to Los Angeles in the early 70s, McClinton emerged in a partnership with fellow Texan Glen Clark, performing country/soul. They achieved a degree of artistic success, releasing two albums before splitting, with McClinton embarking on a solo career. His subsequent output reflects several roadhouse influences. Three gritty releases, *Victim Of Life's Circumstances*, *Genuine Cowhide* and *Love Rustler,* offered country, R&B and southern-style funk, while a 1980 release, *Keeper Of The Flame*, contained material written by Chuck Berry and Don Covay, as well as several original songs, including loving remakes of two compositions from the Delbert And Glen period. Emmylou Harris had a C&W number 1 with McClinton's 'Two More Bottles Of Wine' in 1978, and 'B Movie Boxcar Blues' was used in the John Belushi/Dan Aykroyd film, *The Blues Brothers*. His 1980 album, *The Jealous Kind*, contained his solitary hit single, a Jerry Williams song, 'Givin' It Up For Your Love', which reached the US Top 10. After a lay-off for much of the 80s, this rootsy and largely underrated figure made a welcome return in 1989 with the fiery *Live From Austin*.

●ALBUMS: as Delbert And Glen *Delbert And Glen* (1972)★★, as Delbert And Glen *Subject To Change* (1973)★★, *Victim Of Life's Circumstances* (1975)★★★, *Genuine Cowhide* (1976)★★★, *Love Rustler* (1977)★★★, *Second Wind* (1978)★★, *Keeper Of The Flame* (1979)★★, *The Jealous Kind* (1980)★★★, *Plain' From The Heart* (1981)★★★, *Live From Austin* (1989)★★★, *I'm With You* (1990)★★★. Archive collection: *Very Early Delbert McClinton With The Ron-Dels* (1978)★★.

McCoys

Formed in Union City, Indiana, USA, in 1962, this beat group initially comprised Rick Zehringer (b. 5 August 1947, Fort Recovery, Ohio, USA; guitar), his brother Randy (b. 1951, Union City, Indiana, USA; drums) and bassist Dennis Kelly. Known variously as Rick And The Raiders or the Rick Z Combo, the group later added Ronnie Brandon (organ), becoming the McCoys soon after Randy Hobbs replaced the college-bound Kelly. The quartet became a popular attraction throughout America's midwest, and were brought to Bert Berns' Bang label by producers Feldman/Gottherer/Goldstein. The group's debut 'Hang On Sloopy' (1965), topped the US chart and reached the UK Top 5, but successive releases in a similar gutsy style fared less well; an early b-side, 'Sorrow', was later adopted by the Merseys, and in turn was covered by David Bowie on his 1973 *Pin-Ups*. The group discarded its bubblegum image with the progressive *Infinite McCoys*, and as the house band at New York's popular Scene club. Owner/entrepreneur Steve Paul later paired the group with blues protégé Johnny Winter, whose *Johnny Winter And* featured the Zehringer siblings and Randy Hobbs, with Rick, now Rick Derringer, handling production. When this group was disbanded, Derringer joined Edgar Winter before embarking on a solo career.

●ALBUMS: *Hang On Sloopy* (Bang 1965)★★★, *You Make Me Feel So Good* (Bang 1966)★★★, *Infinite McCoys* (Mercury 1968)★, *Human Ball* (Mercury 1969)★.

●COMPILATIONS: *Hang On Sloopy: The Best Of The McCoys* (Legacy 1995)★★★★.

McDaniels, Gene

b. Eugene B. McDaniels, 12 February 1935, Kansas City, Kansas, USA. A former gospel singer and bandleader, McDaniels completed studies at Omaha's Conservatory of Music before embarking on a recording career. Signed to Liberty in the late 50s, he enjoyed several local hits, including 'In Times Like These' and 'The Green Door', prior to securing two US Top 5 entries in 1961 with 'A Hundred Pounds Of Clay' and 'Tower Of Strength'. Both singles fared less well in Britain, where cover versions by Craig Douglas and Frankie Vaughan took the plaudits, but Gene's influence on British music was acknowledged by his appearance in the film *It's Trad, Dad*. McDaniels' last US chart entry came the following year with 'Point Of No Return', a smooth, jazz-based performance and arguably the singer's finest release. He sadly fell from favour when tastes changed following the rise of the Beatles and his subsequent efforts at soul, tinged with social consciousness, paled beside these early recordings.

●ALBUMS: *In Times Like These* (Liberty 1960)★★★, *Sometimes I'm Happy (Sometimes I'm Blue)* (Liberty 1960)★★★, *100 lbs Of Clay* (Liberty 1961)★★★★, *Gene McDaniels Sings Movie Memories* (Liberty 1962)★★, *Tower Of Strength* (Liberty 1962)★★★★, *Spanish Lace* (Liberty 1963)★★, *The Wonderful World Of Gene McDaniels* (Liberty 1963)★★, *Facts Of Life* (1968)★★, *Outlaw* (1970)★★, *Natural Juices* (1975)★★.

●COMPILATIONS: *Hit After Hit* (1962)★★★, *Another Tear Falls* (1986)★★★.

●FILMS: *It's Trad, Dad* aka *Ring-A-Ding Rhythm* (1962).

McGriff, Jimmy

b. James Herrell, 3 April 1936, Philadelphia, Pennsylvania, USA. Encouraged by a musical home environment (both his parents were pianists), by the time he left school, McGriff played not only piano but bass, vibes, drums and saxophone. He played with Archie Shepp, Reggie Workman, Charles Earland and Donald Bailey in his youth, but after two years as an MP in the Korean War he decided to take up law enforcement rather than music as a career. This did not satisfy him in the event, and he began moonlighting as a bassist, backing blues stars like Big Maybelle. He left the police force and studied organ at Combe College, Philadelphia, and New York's Juilliard. He also took private lessons with Jimmy Smith, Richard 'Groove' Holmes and Milt Buckner, as well as from classical organist Sonny Gatewood. His career first took off with the single 'I Got A Woman' in 1962, and he had a string of hits released through the legendary Sue label. During this decade Jimmy was arguably the crown prince of the soul jazz organ movement (the King being Jimmy Smith). His stabbing style and shrill tone was much copied, particularly in the UK with the rise of the beat R&B scene. Georgie Fame and Brian Auger were greatly influenced by McGriff. His memorable 'All About My Girl' remains one of his finest compositions, and has become a minor classic. In the late 80s he experienced a revival in his commercial success, collaborating with Hank Crawford on record and in concert. He tours for most of the year, still concentrating on Hammond organ, but also using synthesizers. A fine, bluesy player, he helped popularize a jazz-flavoured style of R&B which is still gathering adherents and is influential in London clubland's 'acid jazz' circles.

●ALBUMS: *I've Got A Woman* (Sue 1962)★, *At The Apollo* (Sue 1963)★★★, *At The Organ* (Sue 1963)★★★★, *Gospel Time* (c.1963)★★★, *Topkapi* (Sue 1964)★★★, *One Of Mine* (Sue 1964)★★★, *Blues For Mister Jimmy* (Sue 1965)★★★★, *The Big Band Of Jimmy McGriff* (Solid State 1966)★★★, *A Bag Full Of Soul* (Solid State 1966)★★★★, *Cherry* (Solid State 1967)★★★, *Honey* (Solid State 1963)★★★, *The Worm*

(Solid State 1969)★★★★, *A Thing To Come By* (Solid State 1969)★★★, *The Last Minute* (1983)★★★, *The Countdown* (Milestone 1983)★★★, *Skywalk* (1985)★★★, *State Of The Art* (Milestone 1986)★★★, with Hank Crawford *Soul Survivors* (Milestone 1986)★★★★, Fly Dude (1987)★★★, *The Starting Five* (1987)★★★, *Jimmy McGriff Featuring Hank Crawford* (LRC 1990)★★★★, *Georgia On My Mind* (LRC 1990)★★★★, *Tribute To Basie* (LRC 1991)★★★★, *Funkiest Little Band In The Land* (LRC 1992)★★★, *Electric Funk* (Blue Note 1993)★★★, with Hank Crawford *Blues Groove* (Telarc 1996)★★★.
●COMPILATIONS: *A Toast To Jimmy McGriffs Golden Classics* (Collectable 1989)★★★.

McGUIRE, BARRY

b. 15 October 1935, Oklahoma City, Oklahoma, USA. McGuire first came to prominence as a minor actor in *Route 66* before teaming up with singer Barry Kane as Barry And Barry. In 1962, he joined the New Christy Minstrels and appeared as lead singer on several of their hits, most notably, 'Green Green' and 'Saturday Night'. He also sang the lead on their comic but catchy 'Three Wheels On My Wagon'. While still a Minstrel, he composed the hit 'Greenback Dollar' for the Kingston Trio. After leaving the New Christy Minstrels, McGuire signed to Lou Adler's Dunhill Records and was assigned to staff writers P.F. Sloan and Steve Barri. At the peak of the folk-rock boom, they wrote the rabble-rousing protest 'Eve Of Destruction', which McGuire took to number 1 in the USA, surviving a blanket radio ban in the process. The anti-establishment nature of the lyric even provoked an answer record, 'Dawn Of Correction', written by John Madara and Dave White under the pseudonym the Spokesmen. Ironically, 'Eve Of Destruction' had originally been conceived as a flip-side and at one stage was offered to the Byrds, who turned it down. Coincidentally, both Barry McGuire and Byrds leader Jim (later Roger) McGuinn received a flattering namecheck on the Mamas And The Papas' hit 'Creeque Alley' ('McGuinn and McGuire were just a-getting higher in LA, you know where that's at'). McGuire, in fact, played a significant part in bringing the million-selling vocal quartet to Adler and they later offered their services as his backing singers.

McGuire unsuccessfully attempted to follow up his worldwide hit with other Sloan material, including the excellent 'Upon A Painted Ocean'. He continued to pursue the protest route on the albums *Eve Of Destruction* and *This Precious Time*, but by 1967 he was branching out into acting. A part in *The President's Analyst* led to a Broadway appearance in the musical *Hair*. After the meagre sales of *The World's Last Private Citizen*, McGuire ceased recording until 1971, when he returned with former Mamas And The Papas sideman Eric Hord on *Barry McGuire And The Doctor*. The work featured backing from the cream of the 1965 school of folk rock, including the Byrds' Chris Hillman and Michael Clarke. Soon afterwards, McGuire became a Christian evangelist and thereafter specialized in gospel albums.
●ALBUMS: *The Barry McGuire Album* (Horizon 1963)★★★, *Star Folk With Barry McGuire* (Surrey 1965)★★, *Eve Of Destruction* (1965)★★★, *This Precious Time* (Dunhill 1966)★★★, *Star Folk With Barry McGuire Vol. 2* (Surrey 1966)★★, *Star Folk With Barry McGuire Vol. 3* (Surrey 1966)★★, *Star Folk With Barry McGuire Vol. 4* (Surrey 1966)★★, *Barry McGuire Featuring Eve of Destruction* (Dunhill 1966)★★★, *The Eve Of Destruction Man* (Ember 1966)★, *The World's Last Private Citizen* (Dunhill 1968)★★, *Barry McGuire And The Doctor* (A&M 1971)★★, *Seeds* (1973)★★, *Finer Than Gold* (1981)★★, *Inside Out* (1982)★★, *To The Bride* (1982)★★, *Best Of Barry* (1982)★★.

McKENZIE, SCOTT

b. Philip Blondheim, 1 October 1944, Arlington, Virginia, USA. McKenzie began his professional career in the Journeymen, a clean-cut folk group. He later recorded some undistinguished solo material before fellow ex-member John Phillips, then enjoying success with the Mamas And The Papas, invited the singer to join him in Los Angeles. Although the folk rock-inspired 'No No No No No' failed to sell, the pairing flourished spectacularly on 'San Francisco (Be Sure To Wear Some Flowers In Your Hair)'. This altruistic hippie anthem, penned by Phillips, encapsulated the innocent wonderment felt by many onlookers of the era and the single, buoyed by an irresistible melody, reached number 4 in the US chart, but climbed to the dizzy heights of number 1 in the UK and throughout Europe. Meritorious follow-ups, 'Like An Old Time Movie' and 'Holy Man', failed to emulate such success, and although McKenzie briefly re-emerged with the low-key, country-influenced *Stained Glass Morning*, he remained out of the public eye until the 80s, when he joined Phillips in a rejuvenated Mamas And Papas.
●ALBUMS: *The Voice Of Scott McKenzie* (Ode/CBS 1967)★★, *Stained Glass Morning* (1970)★★.

McNAMARA, ROBIN

McNamara was an original member of the cast of the Broadway musical *Hair* in the 60s, before placing two singles on the charts in 1970. The same year, he signed with the New York-based Steed Records, owned by songwriter Jeff Barry, and recorded 'Lay A Little Lovin' On Me', written by the two of them plus Jim Cretecos. It reached number 11 in the US that summer, and was followed by 'Got To Believe In Love', which featured other singers from *Hair* on backing vocals. The second single did not reach number 80, however, and McNamara's recording career ended.
●ALBUMS: *Lay A Little Lovin' On Me* (1970)★★

McPHATTER, CLYDE

b. Clyde Lensley McPhatter, 15 November 1932, Durham, North Carolina, USA, d. 13 June 1972. For three years, McPhatter was the lead singer in the seminal R&B vocal group, Billy Ward And His Dominoes. He left in 1953 to form the Drifters, whose early releases were enhanced by the singer's emotional, gospel-drenched delivery. In 1954 McPhatter was drafted into the US Army, where he entertained fellow servicemen. Such work prompted a solo career, and the vibrant 'Seven Days' (1956) was followed by several other superb performances, many of which, including 'Treasure Of Love', 'Without Love (There Is Nothing)' and 'A Lover's Question', became R&B standards. A hugely influential figure, McPhatter inspired a generation of singers. His work was covered by Elvis Presley, Ry Cooder and Otis Redding, but his departure from the Atlantic label for MGM in 1959 precipitated an artistic decline. Although he scored several minor hits during the early 60s, arguably his finest work was the US Top 10 hit 'Lover Please' in 1962. The follow-up, 'Little Bitty Pretty One' became standard fodder for many UK beat groups in the early 60s (recorded by the Paramounts). The singer became increasingly overshadowed by new performers and his career started to wane in the mid-60s. Beset by personal problems, he came to Britain in 1968, but left two years later without an appreciable change in fortune. A 1970 album on Decca, *Welcome Home,* was his last recording. McPhatter, one of R&B's finest voices, died from a heart attack as a result of alcohol abuse in 1972.

●ALBUMS: *Clyde McPhatter And The Drifters* (Atlantic 1958)★★★★, *Love Ballads* (Atlantic 1958)★★★★, *Clyde* (Atlantic 1959)★★★, *Let's Start Over Again* (MGM 1959)★★★, *Ta Ta* (Mercury 1960)★★★, *Golden Blues Hits* (1962)★★★, *Lover Please* (Mercury 1962)★★★★, *May I Sing For You* (Wing 1962)★★★, *Rhythm And Soul* (Mercury 1963)★★★, *Songs Of The Big City* (Mercury 1964)★★, *Live At The Apollo* (Mercury 1964)★★, *Welcome Home* (Decca 1970)★★.

●COMPILATIONS: *Greatest Hits* (MGM 1960)★★★, *The Best Of Clyde McPhatter* (Atlantic 1963)★★★, *Greatest Recordings* (1972)★★★, *A Tribute To Clyde McPhatter* (1973)★★★, *Rock And Cry* (1984)★★★, *Rhythm And Soul* eight album set of MGM/Mercury recordings (1987)★★★★, *Deep Sea Ball - The Best Of* (1993)★★★★, *Love Ballads* (Sequel 1997)★★★.

MCWILLIAMS, DAVID

b. 4 July 1945, Cregagh, Belfast, Northern Ireland. The subject of an overpowering publicity campaign engineered by his manager Phil Solomon, McWilliams was featured on the front, inside and back covers of several consecutive issues of the *New Musical Express,* which extolled the virtues of a new talent. He was incessantly plugged on the pirate Radio Caroline. Much was made of his rebellious youth and affinity with Irish music, yet the singer's debut release, 'Days Of Pearly Spencer'/'Harlem Lady', revealed a grasp of pop's dynamics rather than those of folk. The former song was both impressive and memorable, as was the pulsating follow-up, '3 O'Clock Flamingo Street', but McWilliams was unable to shake the 'hype' tag which accompanied his launch. His manager

believed that Williams was a more promising protégé than his other star artist, Van Morrison of Them, but his faith was unrewarded. Williams disliked live performance and failed to show his true talent in front of an audience. Neither single charted and a period of reassessment followed before the artist re-emerged the following decade with a series of charming, folk-influenced collections. In April 1992 Marc Almond took 'Days Of Pearly Spencer' back into the UK charts.

●ALBUMS: *David McWilliams Sings* (Major Minor 1967)★★★, *David McWilliams Volume 2* (Major Minor 1967)★★, *Volume III* (Major Minor 1968)★★, *The Days Of David McWilliams* (Major Minor 1969)★★★, *Days Of Pearly Spencer* (1971), *Lord Offaly* (Dawn 1972)★★★, *The Beggar And The Priest* (Dawn 1973)★★★, *Living Is Just A State Of Mind* (Dawn 1974)★★★, *David McWilliams* (1977)★★, *Don't Do It For Love* (1978)★★, *Wounded* (1982)★★.

●COMPILATIONS: *Days Of Pearly Spencer* (1971)★★★.

MEAUX, HUEY P.

b. 10 March 1929, Kaplan, Louisiana, USA. Meaux is an influential figure in Texas music circles, and often acted as go-between, arranging for labels to license masters brought to him. A shrewd judge of hit potential, he also prospered as a producer with a series of excellent, contrasting acts. Barbara Lynn's 1962 hit, 'You'll Lose A Good Thing', helped finance Meaux's studios in Houston and Jackson, which in turn generated further success with B.J. Thomas ('I'm So Lonesome I Could Cry'), Roy Head ('Treat Her Right') and the Sir Douglas Quintet ('She's About A Mover'), the latter of which was released on Meaux's own Tribe label, one of several he inaugurated. A conviction in 1967 for violation of the Mann Act (escorting a female across state lines for immoral purposes), resulted in his imprisonment but he received a pardon from the then President, Jimmy Carter. It was the mid-70s before Meaux recovered momentum with Tex-Mex star Freddie Fender, who rose from regional to national acclaim with Meaux's excellent southern-style recordings. Among the many acts to use this intuitive individual's production skills are Johnny Copeland, T-Bone Walker and Johnny Winter. 'Before The Next Tear Falls' was a US number 1 single in 1975, and the producer continued this roots-based direction with several other acts, enjoying a 1985 hit with Rockin' Sydney's version of the cajun 'standard', 'My Toot Toot'. He made an appearance as a disc jockey in David Byrne's film, *True Stories,* in 1986. In 1996 he was arrested and charged with possesion of drugs and a further child pornography charge. He was found guilty and given a 15 year jail sentence in the summer of 1996.

MEEK, JOE

b. Robert George Meek, 5 April 1929, Newent, Gloucestershire, England, d. 3 February 1967, London, England. Britain's premier independent record producer of the early 60s, Meek was equally renowned for his pioneering recording techniques and eccentric personality. His career began in 1954, when he joined IBC, the leading independent recording studio of the era. Originally an engineer, he worked on a number of hits, including Lonnie Donegan's 'Cumberland Gap', Frankie Vaughan's 'Green Door', Johnny Duncan's 'Last Train To San Fernando' and Humphrey Lyttelton's 'Bad Penny Blues'. He also turned his hand to songwriting, penning Tommy Steele's 'Put A Ring On Her Finger' in 1958.

By 1960, he had set up Lansdowne Studios in west London, where he worked with producer Denis Preston on recordings by various popular jazz artists. An ill-advised expansion policy encouraged Meek to launch Triumph Records, which enjoyed a hit with Michael Cox's 'Angela Jones' before rapidly winding down its activities. Thereafter, Meek concentrated on leasing tapes to major labels, using the title RGM Sound. He worked from a converted studio situated above a shop in Holloway Road, north London, and it was here that he created the unusual sounds that were to become his hallmark. His first major hit as a producer was John Leyton's 'Johnny Remember Me', an atmospheric, eerily echo-laden affair which topped the UK charts in 1961. Leyton followed up with other Meek-produced successes, including 'Wild Wind', 'Son, This Is She' and 'Lonely City'. With Geoff Goddard composing suitably ethereal material, Meek enjoyed further vicarious chart action with Mike Berry ('Tribute To Buddy Holly') and backing group the Outlaws ('Swingin' Low' and 'Ambush'). By 1962, the increasingly inventive producer had reached his apogee on the spacy instrumental 'Telstar', which took the Tornadoes to the top of the charts on both sides of the Atlantic. He was now hailed as a genuine original, with an innovative flair unmatched by any of his rivals. The accolades were to prove short-lived.

The mid-60s beat boom spearheaded by the Beatles seriously dented Meek's credibility and commercial standing. His work was increasingly regarded as novel, rather than important, and his love for gimmicks took precedence on recordings by Screaming Lord Sutch and others. Meek responded with the much publicized Heinz, who reached the Top 10 with the Eddie Cochran tribute, 'Just Like Eddie'. The swirling 'Have I The Right' provided a 1964 UK number 1 for the Honeycombs, but this was to be Meek's last major success. By 1965, he seemed something of an anachronism, and his production techniques seemed leaden and predictable rather than startling. The departure of songwriter Geoff Goddard weakened the supply of good material, and a motley series of flop records left record companies disenchanted. Meek's tempestuous personality and often violent behaviour alienated many old friends, while his homosexuality produced feelings of self-loathing and engendered a fear of imminent scandal. His mental instability worsened with successive personal and business problems, and on 3 February 1967, he was involved in a bizarre shooting incident in which he fatally shot his landlady before turning the gun on himself. It was the end of a sometimes brilliant but frustratingly erratic career.

●ALBUMS: with the Blue Men *I Hear A New World* (1992)★★.
●COMPILATIONS: *The Joe Meek Story Volume 1* (1992)★★★, *Work In Progress* (1993)★★★, *Intergalactic Instros* (Diamond 1997)★★★.
●FURTHER READING: *The Legendary Joe Meek*, John Repsch.

MERSEYBEATS

Originally called the Mavericks, this Liverpudlian quartet comprised Tony Crane (vocals/lead guitar), Billy Kinsley (vocals/bass), David Ellis (rhythm guitar) and Frank Sloan (drums). In 1962, long before the Beatles put Liverpool on the musical map, they rechristened themselves the Merseybeats. Early line-up changes saw Ellis and Sloan replaced by Aaron Williams and John Banks. By mid-1963, Beatlemania had engulfed the UK, and A&R representatives descended upon Liverpool in search of talent. The Merseybeats were scooped up by Fontana and initially signed by Brian Epstein, but left their new mentor within weeks, following an argument over image. Burt Bacharach and Hal David's 'It's Love That Really Counts' gave them a minor hit, but it was the relatively unknown songwriter Peter Lee Stirling (see Daniel Boone) who penned their biggest hit, 'I Think Of You'. Although essentially balladeers on single, the group's EPs had a grittier edge. The *On Stage* EP, with its use of monochrome photography, was extremely progressive in design terms, as it did not feature the band on the cover, while their debut album included a variety of old musical standards. Pop star pressures prompted founding member Kinsley to leave the group briefly, but he returned in time for their third major hit, 'Wishin' And Hopin''. Other members included Bob Garner, who was himself replaced by Johnny Gustafson from the Big Three.

The eclipse of the Mersey Sound eventually took its toll on the group, although a change of management to Kit Lambert brought two more minor hits, 'I Love You, Yes I Do' and 'I Stand Accused'. In January 1966, the group split, paving the way for hit duo the Merseys. In later years, Tony Crane reactivated the group, which still performs regularly on the cabaret circuit.

●ALBUMS: *The Merseybeats* (Fontana 1964)★★★★.
●COMPILATIONS: *Greatest Hits* (Look 1977)★★★, *The Merseybeats: Beat And Ballads* (Edsel 1982)★★★★, *The Very Best Of The Merseybeats* (Spectrum 1997)★★★★.

MFQ

This folk group evolved out of the thriving coffeehouse circuit prevailing in Honolulu, Hawaii, in the early 60s. Douglas Farthing Hatelid, better-known as Chip Douglas (vocals/banjo/bass), was a member of the Wilcox Three, an act closely modelled on the Kingston Trio. Indeed, when Dave Guard left the Kingston Trio, Douglas was a possible replacement. Guard then formed the Whiskeyhill Singers, which included vocalist Cyrus Faryar. In the meantime Douglas formed a duo with Stan

White (vocals), which in turn became the Lexington Three with the arrival of Henry 'Tad' Diltz (vocals/banjo). In 1962, following the break-up of the Whiskeyhill Singers, Faryar joined the trio which became firstly the Lexington Four and then the Modern Folk Quartet. The group moved to Los Angeles in spring 1963, and played a residency at the Troubador club. White left the band following an argument with manager Herbie Cohen and was replaced by Jerry Yester, formerly of the Inn Group and New Christy Minstrels. *The Modern Folk Quartet* showcases their vigorous, close harmonies and contains their own songs as well as material written by Dino Valenti, John Stewart and Bob Gibson. The group abandoned their traditional sound upon hearing the Beatles and their November 1964 single 'The Love Of A Clown'/'If All You Think', both Yester compositions, predates the Byrds in its blend of folk music, harmonies and British Beat. Their 1965 single, 'Every Minute Of The Day', was followed by them working with producer Phil Spector. One track with Spector, 'This Could Be The Night', was completed but the finished master was shelved for 20 years. Individual MFQ members also assisted on sessions for the Ronettes and Righteous Brothers before the group, known now as the Modern Folk Quintet following the addition of drummer Eddie Hoh, resurfaced on Lou Adler's Dunhill label. Two more singles, 'Night Time Girl' and 'I Had A Dream Last Night', were released before the MFQ went their separate ways in 1967. Douglas briefly joined Gene Clark Group and the Turtles before finding fame as a producer, notably with the Monkees. Yester went solo before joining the Lovin' Spoonful. He then worked with his wife, Judy Henske, and produced and arranged for Tim Buckley and Tom Waits. Faryar undertook session work before completing two exceptional singer-songwriter albums while Diltz found fame as a photographer. The members re-formed in 1976 but outside commitments soon brought this to an end. In 1984 they re-formed again for *Moonlight Serenade*, a collection of standards issued on John Stewart's Homecoming label. Jerry's brother, Jim Yester, formerly of the Association replaced Diltz for live appearances. A single taken from *Bamboo Saloon*, 'Sister Golden Hair', reached the Japanese chart. The group still remain active in Hawaii.
●ALBUMS: *The Modern Folk Quartet* (Warners 1963)★★★, *Changes* (Warners 1964)★★★, *Moonlight Serenade* (Homecoming 1985)★★★, *The MFQ Live In Japan* (Village Green 1989)★★, *Bamboo Saloon* (1990)★★★.

MICKEY AND SYLVIA

McHouston 'Mickey' Baker (b. 15 October 1925, Louisville, Kentucky, USA) and Sylvia Vanderpool (b. 6 March 1936, New York City, New York, USA). This popular duo began recording together in 1956 and enjoyed an US R&B chart-topper that year with 'Love Is Strange', which peaked at number 11 in the US pop chart the following year. This enduring call and response song is rightly regarded as a classic of its genre, and later became

a minor UK hit when recorded by the Everly Brothers. Mickey and Sylvia had further success with 'There Oughta Be A Law' (1957) and, after a brief hiatus as a duo, 'Baby You're So Fine' (1961), but their career together was undermined by commitments elsewhere. Prolific session work for Atlantic, Savoy, King and Aladdin earned the former the epithet Mickey 'Guitar' Baker, while the latter had made her recording debut with jazz trumpeter Oran 'Hot Lips' Page as early as 1950. In 1973, she began recording as Sylvia, and later achieved notable success as an entrepreneur through her ownership of Sugar Hill Records.
●ALBUMS: *New Sounds* (Vix 1957)★★, *Love Is Strange* (Camden 1965)★★.
●COMPILATIONS: *The Willow Sessions* (Sequel 1996)★★★.

MIGIL FIVE

Red Lambert (guitar/vocals), Alan Watson (saxophone), Gil Lucas (piano), Lenny Blanche (bass) and Mike Felix (drums/lead vocals) achieved momentary fame when their 'Mockingbird Hill' single reached the UK Top 10 in 1964, on the strength of a fleeting bluebeat craze. Felix, Blanche and Lucas had previously worked as a jazz trio prior to embracing pop with the addition of Lambert. They recorded as the Migil Four before adding Watson at the suggestion of trumpeter Kenny Ball. Despite inordinate press coverage, the group was unable to repeat this success. They later became stalwarts of the cabaret circuit before disintegrating when Felix began a solo career.
●ALBUMS: *Mockingbird Hill* (Pye 1964)★★★.

MIKE STUART SPAN

The Mike Stuart Span were originally a mainstream rock/pop band formed in Brighton, Sussex, England, in the mid-60s. The prime mover behind this and all subsequent formations was vocalist Stuart Hobday. He was partnered originally by Nigel Langham (guitar), Roger McCabe (bass), Gary 'Roscoe' Murphy (drums) and Ashley Potter (organ). They drew heavily on a stylized soul and show band repertoire before coming to the attention of local promoter Mike Clayton. He encouraged them to expand their sound with the addition of brass, leading to the arrival of additional members Gary Parsley (trumpet), Dave Plumb (saxophone) and Jon Poulter (keyboards). However, their tenure as an eight-piece band was a short one, as Langham died after jumping out of an upstairs window while under the influence of LSD. The remaining members' first recording came in 1966 when they made an acetate for EMI Records comprising a cover of the Drifters' 'Follow Me' supplemented by an original Hobday composition, 'Work Out', on the b-side. EMI were sufficiently impressed to offer the group a contract and sent them back to the studio to record their debut single proper. This was headed on the a-side by another Drifters song, 'Come On Over To My Place', with another Hobday original, 'Still Nights', on the b-side. Their second single was a cover version of Cat Stevens' 'Dear', but this too failed to breach the charts. They were dropped by EMI and the original trio of Hobday, McCabe and Murphy discarded the brass section and organist Potter, and began advertising in the *Melody Maker* for a guitarist. The new recruit was Brian Bennett, who had previously recorded with Tony's Defenders. With the change in instrumentation Mike Stuart Span henceforth veered towards guitar rock, and in particular, psychedelia. In the search for a new contract the new line-up recorded a second acetate single, this time for Oak Records. An excellent original track, 'Second Production', allied with a cover of Fontella Bass' 'Rescue Me' on the b-side, failed to convince prospective backers Decca Records to invest in the group. Instead they self-funded the release of their third single proper, 'Children Of Tomorrow', released on their own Jewel Records. By now Hobday was becoming increasingly interested in other art forms. The group performed a 20-minute composition, *Cycle*, for the Brighton Arts Festival, and appeared in the film *Better A Widow*. They were also considered for the part of an aspiring pop group in a documentary filmed by the BBC. At the same time they released their final single, 'You Can Understand Me', for Fontana Records. By 1969 the group had relaunched itself as Leviathan, although a compilation album of Mike Stuart Span recordings was finally issued in 1995.

●COMPILATIONS: *Timespan* (Tenth Planet 1995)★★★.

MILLER, BOB

The instrumental group Bob Miller And The Millermen appeared regularly on UK television and radio programmes in the 50s and early 60s. After being noticed at several London gigs, including one at the Locarno Ballroom, Streatham, in London, on Coronation Day, 2 June 1953, Miller appeared on BBC Television's *Dig This*. He subsequently toured with current stars such as Cliff Richard, Bobby Darin, the Four Freshmen and Shirley Bassey. Later, on shows such as *Drumbeat* (for eight years), and the radio series, *Parade Of The Pops* ('a review of the week's popular music, and prediction of hits to come'), they backed many of the UK's top vocalists, and had their own featured spots. Their records included 'Muchacha', 'Square Bash', 'Dig This', 'The Poacher', 'Little Dipper', 'In The Mood', 'My Guy's Come Back', 'The Busker's Tune', 'Manhunt', '77 Sunset Strip' and 'Joey's Song'. For much of his life, Miller's abiding interest has been yacht racing, and in June 1972 he participated in the Transatlantic Race, providing a day-by-day radio commentary.

●ALBUMS: *The Exciting Sounds Of Bob Miller*. (60s)★★★, *Parade Of Pops* (Pye 1968)★★, *Bob Miller & M* (1978)★★.

●COMPILATIONS: *Sugar Coated Baby* (Bear Family 1997).

MILLER, MRS

Mrs Miller (b. Elva Miller, California, USA) derives her chief notoriety from her popularity among collectors of musical exotica. Her *modus operandi* involves a sea- soned although tuneless melodramatic delivery, accompanying whistles and wholly indulgent, untutored phrasing. Her versions of 'Catch A Falling Star' and 'A Hard Day's Night' reveal her as a natural precursor to the worst elements of karaoke, although she did manage chart entries for 'Downtown' and 'Lover's Concerto'.

●ALBUMS: *Greatest Hits* (Capitol 1966)★★★.

MILLER, ROGER

b. 2 January 1936, Fort Worth, Texas, USA, d. 25 October 1992, Los Angeles, California, USA. Miller was brought up in Erick, Oklahoma, and, during the late 50s, moved to Nashville, where he worked as a songwriter. His 'Invitation To The Blues' was a minor success for Ray Price, as was '(In The Summertime) You Don't Want Love' for Andy Williams. Miller himself enjoyed a hit on the country charts, with the portentously titled 'When Two Worlds Collide'. In 1962, he joined Faron Young's band as a drummer and also wrote 'Swiss Maid', a major hit for Del Shannon. By 1964, Miller was signed to Mercury's Smash label, and secured a US Top 10 hit with 'Dang Me'. The colloquial title was reinforced by some humorous, macabre lyrics ('They ought to take a rope and hang me'). The song brought Miller several Grammy awards, and the following year, he enjoyed an international Top 10 hit with 'King Of The Road'. This stoical celebration of the hobo life, with its jazz-influenced undertones, became his best-known song. The relaxed 'Engine Engine No. 9' was another US Top 10 hit during 1965, and at the end of the year, Miller once more turned his attention to the UK market with 'England Swings'. This affectionate, slightly bemused tribute to swinging London at its zenith neatly summed up the tourist brochure view of the city ('bobbies on bicycles two by two . . . the rosy red cheeks of the little children'). Another international hit, the song was forever associated with Miller. The singer's chart fortunes declined the following year, and a questionable cover of Elvis Presley's 'Heartbreak Hotel' barely reached the US Top 100. In 1968, Miller secured his last major hit with a poignant reading of Bobby Russell's 'Little Green Apples', which perfectly suited his understated vocal style. Thereafter, Miller moved increasingly towards the country market and continued performing regularly throughout America. In 1982, he appeared on the album *Old Friends* with Ray Price and Willie Nelson. Miller's vocals were featured in the Walt Disney cartoon *Robin Hood*, and in the mid-80s he wrote a Broadway musical, *Big River*, based on Mark Twain's *The Adventures Of Huckleberry Finn*.

Roger Miller finally lost his battle with cancer when, with his wife Mary and son Roger Jnr. at his bedside, he died on 25 October 1992. A most popular man with his fellow artists, he was also a great humorist and his general outlook was adequetly summed up when he once told the backing band on the *Grand Ole Opry*, 'I do this in the key of B natural, which is my philosophy in life.'

●ALBUMS: *Wild Child* (Starday 1964)★★★, *Roger And Out* (Smash 1964)★★★, *The Return Of Roger Miller* (1965)★★★ *The Country Side of Roger Miller* (Starday

1965)★★★, *The 3rd Time* (1965)★★★, *Words And Music* (1966)★★★, *Walkin' In The Sunshine* (1967)★★★, *A Tender Look At Love* (1968)★★★, *Roger Miller* (1969)★★★, *Roger Miller* (1970)★★, *Off The Wall* (1978)★★★, *Making A Name For Myself* (1980)★★, *Motive Series* (1981)★★★, *Old Friends* (1982)★★★, *The Big Industry* (1988)★★★.
●COMPILATIONS: *Little Green Apples* (1976)★★★★, *Best Of Roger Miller* (1978)★★★★, *Greatest Hits* (1985)★★★★.

MILLIE
b. Millicent Small, 6 October 1942, Clarendon, Jamaica. After leaving home at the age of 13 to further her singing career in Kingston, Millie recorded several tracks with producer Coxsone Dodd, who teamed her up with Roy Panton. As Roy And Millie, they achieved local success with 'We'll Meet' and 'Oh, Shirley' and caught the attention of entrepreneur Chris Blackwell. On 22 June 1964, Millie accompanied Blackwell to the UK and recorded Harry Edwards' 'Don't You Know', before being presented with the catchy 'My Boy Lollipop', formerly a US R&B hit for Barbie Gaye, which became a transatlantic Top 5 hit, the first crossover ska record. Such chart fame proved evanescent. A carbon copy follow-up, 'Sweet William', was only a minor hit, and 'Bloodshot Eyes' failed to reach the Top 40. Thereafter she languished in relative obscurity. Even a brief tie-up with Jackie Edwards in Jackie And Millie, and a nude spread in a men's magazine failed to revitalize her career. Ultimately handicapped by her novelty hit, Millie's more serious work, such as the self-chosen *Millie Sings Fats Domino*, was sadly ignored.
●ALBUMS: *The Best Of* (Trojan 1970)★★★.

MILLS, MRS.
Gladys Mills was a popular 50s performer when pianists of the calibre of Winifred Atwell were in vogue. The British wartime spirit of gathering around the 'ol' joanna' to sing songs was a bonding and uplifting tradition. The partygoers of the wartime generation continued the tradition into the 50s and 60s, and judging by the continuing release of albums such as this, into the 70s and 80s. Great for background music at parties, but as concentrated listening, there can be few worse trials of torture. Mills took all the popular tunes of old and ran them together in tinkly piano medleys. Never a massive success chartwise, her albums sold reasonably well in the UK, and she made countless television appearances, including several on the *Wheeltappers And Shunters Social Club* and the *Billy Cotton Band Show*. She died on 25 February 1978.
●ALBUMS: *Come To My Party* (1966)★★★, *Mrs Mills' Party Pieces* (1968)★★★, *Let's Have Another Party* (1969)★★★, *I'm Mighty Glad* (1971)★★★, *All-Time Party Dances* (1978)★★★, *Piano Party Time* (1984)★★★, *An Hour Of Mrs Mills* (1987)★★★.

MINDBENDERS
Originally a backing group for Wayne Fontana, the Mindbenders comprised Eric Stewart (b. 20 January 1945;

guitar), Bob Lang (10 January 1946; bass) and Ric Rothwell (b. 11 March 1944; drums). In October 1965, they split with their leader and early the following year enjoyed a transatlantic number 2 hit with the Carole Bayer Sager/Toni Wine composition, 'Groovy Kind Of Love'. The excellent follow-up, 'Can't Live With You, Can't Live Without You', failed to chart, while its successor 'Ashes To Ashes' was only a minor hit. A cameo appearance in the film *To Sir With Love* maintained the group's profile and they continued to record material by name writers such as Rod Argent and Robert Knight, but to no avail. A brave stab with an average cover of the Box Tops' 'The Letter' scraped into the Top 50, but shortly after the release of 'Uncle Joe The Ice Cream Man' in March 1968, the group dissolved. Eric Stewart and latter-day Mindbender Graham Gouldman went on to form Hotlegs and 10cc, while Bob Lang reappeared in Racing Cars.
●ALBUMS: *The Mindbenders* (Fontana 1966)★★★, *With Woman In Mind* (Fontana 1967)★★★.

MINGUS, CHARLES
b. 22 April 1922, Nogales, Arizona, USA, d. 5 January 1979, Cuernavaca, Mexico. Mingus was never allowed the luxury of the feeling of belonging. Reactions to his mixed ancestry (he had British-born, Chinese, Swedish and African American grandparents) produced strong feelings of anger and confirmed his sense of persecution. However, this alienation, coupled with his own deep sensitivity and tendency to dramatize his experiences, provided substantial fuel for an artistic career of heroic turmoil and brilliance. Formative musical experiences included both the strictures of European classical music and the uninhibited outpourings of the congregation of the local Holiness Church, which he attended with his stepmother. The latter included all manner of bluesy vocal techniques, moaning, audience-preacher responses, wild vibrato and melismatic improvisation, along with the accompaniment of cymbals and trombones - all of it melding into an early gospel precursor of big band that heavily influenced Mingus' mature compositional and performance style. Other influences were hearing Duke Ellington's band, and recordings of Richard Strauss' tone poems and works by Debussy, Ravel, Bach and Beethoven. Thwarted in his early attempts to learn trombone, Mingus switched from cello to double bass at high school.
He studied composition with Lloyd Reese and was encouraged by Red Callender to study bass with Herman Rheimschagen of the New York Philharmonic. He developed a virtuoso bass technique and began to think of the bass finger-board as similar to a piano keyboard. His first professional dates as a bassist included gigs with New Orleans players Kid Ory and Barney Bigard, and then stints with the Louis Armstrong Orchestra (1943-1945) and Lionel Hampton (1947), but it was with the Red Norvo Trio (1950) that he first gained national recognition for his virtuosity. Work with other great pioneers of his generation such as Charlie Parker, Miles Davis, Thelonious Monk, Bud Powell, Sonny Stitt, Stan Getz, Lee

Konitz, Dizzy Gillespie, Quincy Jones and Teddy Charles continued throughout the 50s. He joined Duke Ellington's band briefly in 1953, but a more artistically profitable association with his hero occurred with the trio album *Money Jungle*, which they made with Max Roach in 1962. Mingus was a pioneer of black management and artist-led record labels, forming Debut in 1953, and the Charles Mingus label in 1964. His early compositions were varying in success, often due to the difficulty of developing and maintaining an ensemble to realize his complex ideas.

He contributed works to the Jazz Composers' Workshop from 1953 until the foundation of his own workshop ensemble in 1955. Here, he was able to make sparing use of notation, transmitting his intentions from verbal and musical instructions sketched at the piano or on the bass. Mingus' originality as composer first began to flourish under these circumstances, and with players such as Dannie Richmond, Rahsaan Roland Kirk, Jaki Byard, Jimmy Knepper and Booker Ervin he developed a number of highly evolved works. Crucial among his many innovations in jazz was the use of non-standard chorus structures, contrasting sections of quasi-'classical' composed material with passages of freeform and group improvisations, often of varying tempos and modes, in complex pieces knitted together by subtly evolving musical motifs. He developed a 'conversational' mode of interactive improvisation, and pioneered melodic bass playing. Such pieces as *The Black Saint And The Sinner Lady* (1963) show enormous vitality and a great depth of immersion in all jazz styles, from New Orleans and gospel to bebop and free jazz. Another multi-sectional piece, 'Meditations For A Pair Of Wire Cutters', from the album *Portrait* (1964), is one of many that evolved gradually under various titles. Sections from it can be heard on *Mingus Plays Piano* (1963), there called 'Myself When I Am Real'. It was renamed 'Praying With Eric' after the tragic death of Eric Dolphy, who made magnificent contributions to many Mingus compositions, but especially to this intensely moving piece.

In the mid-60s, financial and psychological problems began to take their toll, as poignantly recorded in Thomas Reichman's 1968 film *Mingus*. He toured extensively during this period, presenting a group of ensemble works. In 1971, Mingus was much encouraged by the receipt of a Guggenheim fellowship in composition, and the publication of his astonishing autobiography, *Beneath The Underdog*. The book opens with a session conducted by a psychiatrist, and the work reveals Mingus's self-insight, intelligence, sensitivity and tendency for self-dramatization. Touring continued until the gradual paralysis brought by the incurable disease Amyotrophic Lateral Sclerosis prevented him doing anything more than presiding over recordings. His piece 'Revelations' was performed in 1978 by the New York Philharmonic under the direction of Gunther Schuller, who also resurrected *Epitaph* in 1989. Also in 1978, Mingus was honoured at the White House by Jimmy Carter and an all-star jazz concert. News of his death,

aged 56, in Mexico was marked by many tributes from artists of all fields. Posthumously, the ensemble Mingus Dynasty continued to perform his works.

Mingus summed up the preoccupations of his time in a way that transcended racial and cultural divisions, while simultaneously highlighting racial and social injustices. Introducing the first 1964 performance of *Meditations*, Mingus told the audience: 'This next composition was written when Eric Dolphy told me there was something similar to the concentration camps down South, [. . .] where they separated [. . .] the green from the red, or something like that; and the only difference between the electric barbed wire is that they don't have gas chambers and hot stoves to cook us in yet. So I wrote a piece called *Meditations* as to how to get some wire cutters before someone else gets some guns to us.' Off-mike, he can be heard saying to fellow musicians: 'They're gonna burn us; they'll try.' In the turmoil of his life and artistic achievements, and in his painful demise, Mingus became his own artistic creation. A desperate, passionate icon for the mid-20th century to which all can relate in some way, he articulated the emotional currents of his time in a way superior to that of almost any other contemporary jazz musician.

●ALBUMS: *Red Norvo Jazz Trio* (1951)★★★, with Spaulding Givens *Strings And Keys* (Decca 1951)★★★, *The Red Norvo - Charles Mingus - Tal Farlow Trio* (1951)★★★, *Autobiography In Jazz* (1953)★★★, *Strings And Keys* (Debut 1953)★★★★, with others *Quintet Of The Year/Jazz At Massey Hall* (1953)★★★, *Jazz Composers Workshop* (Savoy 1954)★★★★, *Jazz Experiments* (Jazztone 1954)★★★, *Charles Mingus And Thad Jones* (1955)★★★, *Jazzical Moods, Vol. 1* (Period 1955)★★★, *Jazzical Moods Vol. 2* (Period 1955)★★★, *Jazz Composers Workshop No 2* (Savoy 1956)★★★, *Mingus At The Bohemia* (Debut 1955)★★★, *Charlie Mingus* (Savoy 1955)★★★, with Max Roach The Charles Mingus Quintet And Max Roach (Debut 1956)★★★, *Pithecanthropus Erectus* (Atlantic 1956)★★★★, *The Clown* aka *Reincarnation Of A Lovebird* (Atlantic 1957)★★★, with Gunther Schuller, George Russell *Adventures In Sound* (1957)★★★, *Jazz Experiment* (Jazztone 1957)★★★, *Jazz Workshop Presents: Jimmy Knepper* (1957)★★★, *The Jazz Experiments Of Charles Mingus* (Jazztone 1957)★★★, *The Clown* (Atlantic 1957)★★★, *Mingus Three* (Jubilee 1957)★★★, *East Coasting* (Bethlehem 1958)★★★, *A Modern Jazz Symposium Of Music And Poetry* (Bethlehem 1958)★★★, with Langston Hughes *Weary Blues* (1958)★★★, with Billie Holiday etc *Easy To Remember* (1958)★★★, East Coasting (Bethlehem 1958)★★★, *Duke's Choice* aka *A Modern Jazz Symposium Of Music And Poetry* (Bethlehem 1958)★★★, *Wonderland* (United Artists 1959)★★★, *Jazz Portraits* (United Artists 1959)★★★, *Blues And Roots* (Atlantic 1959)★★★★, *Mingus Ah-Um* (Columbia 1959)★★★★★, *Nostalgia In Times Square* (1959)★★★, *Mingus Dynasty* (Columbia 1960)★★★, *Pre-Bird* aka *Mingus Revisited* (Emarcy 1960)★★★,

Mingus At Antibes (1960)★★★★, *Charles Mingus Presents Charles Mingus!* (Candid 1960)★★★★, *Mingus* (Candid 1960)★★★★, *The Jazz Life* (1960)★★★, *Newport Rebels* (1960)★★★, with Tubby Hayes *All Night Long* (1960)★★★★, *Oh Yeah!* (Atlantic 1961)★★★★, *Pre Bird* (Mercury 1961)★★★, *Tonight At Noon* (Atlantic 1961)★★★, *Hooray For Charles Mingus* (1962)★★★, *J-For-Jazz Presents Charles Mingus* (1962)★★★, with Duke Ellington, Max Roach *Money Jungle* (1962)★★★, *Town Hall Concert* (United Artists 1962)★★★, *Chazz!* (Fantasy 1962)★★★, *The Black Saint And The Sinner Lady* (Impulse 1963)★★★★★, *Mingus Mingus Mingus Mingus Mingus* (Impulse 1963)★★★★,*Tijuana Moods* rec. 1957 (RCA 1964)★★★, *Town Hall Concert (Portrait)* (Original Jazz Classics 1964)★★★, *Live in Oslo* rec. 1964 (60s)★★★, *Charles Mingus Sextet Live In Europe Vols. 1, 2 & 3* (1964)★★★, *The Great Concert Of Charles Mingus* (1964)★★★, *Mingus In Europe Vols. 1 & 2* (1964)★★★, *Charles Mingus In Amsterdam* (1964)★★★, *Mingus In Stuttgart* 2 vols. (1964)★★★, *Right Now! Live At The Jazz Workshop* (Fantasy 1964)★★★, *Charles Mingus In Europe* (Enja 1964)★★★, *Mingus At Monterey* (Prestige 1964)★★★, *Music Written For Monterey 1965, But Not Heard* (1965)★★★, *My Favourite Quintet* (1965)★★★, *Statements* (1970)★★★, *Charles Mingus In Paris* (DIW 1970)★★★, *Pithy Canthropus Erectus* aka *Blue Bird* (1970)★★★, *Charles Mingus In Berlin* (1970)★★★, *Charles Mingus And The New Herd* (1971)★★★, *Let My Children Hear Music* (1971)★★★, *Charles Mingus And Friends In Concert* (1972)★★★, *Jazz Jamboree* (1972)★★★, *Charles Mingus Meets Cat Anderson* (1972)★★★, *Mingus Mingus* (1973)★★★, *Mingus At Carnegie Hall* (1974)★★★, *Cumbria And Jazz Fusion* (Atlantic 1977)★★★,*Three Or Four Shades Of Blue* (1977)★★★, *Lionel Hampton Presents: The Music Of Charles Mingus* aka *His Final Works* (1977)★★★, *Me Myself An Eye* (1978)★★★, *Something Like A Bird* (1978)★★★, *The Charles Mingus Memorial Album* (1978)★★★, with Joni Mitchell *Joni Mitchell - Mingus* (Geffen 1979)★★★.
●COMPILATIONS: *The Mingus Connection* rec. 1951-53 (1957)★★★, *The Debut Recordings* (1951-57)★★★★, *Vital Savage Horizons* (1952, 1961-62)★★★, *The Atlantic Years* (1956-1978)★★★★, *Better Git It In Your Soul* (1959)★★★★, *The Complete Candid Recordings Of Charles Mingus* (1960)★★★, *Charles Mingus/Cecil Taylor: Rare Broadcast Performances* (1962, 1966)★★★, *The Impulse Years* (1963)★★★★, *Portrait* (1964)★★★, *Re-Evaluation: The Impulse Years* rec. 1963-64 (1973)★★★, *The Art Of Charles Mingus* (1974)★★★, *Passions Of A Man* rec. 1956-61, 1973, 1977 (1979)★★★, *Nostalgia In Times Square* rec. 1959 (1979)★★★, *Great Moments With Charles Mingus* rec. 1963-64 (1981)★★★, *Mingus, The Collection* rec. 50s (1985)★★★★, *Charles Mingus - New York Sketchbook* rec. 50s (1986)★★★★, *Charles Mingus - Shoes Of The Fisherman's Wife* rec. 1959, 1971 (1988)★★★★,

Abstractions rec. 1954, 1957 (1989)★★★, *Charles Mingus - Mysterious Blues* rec. 1960 (1989)★★★, *Charles Mingus 1955-1957* (1990)★★★, *Charles Mingus* (1991)★★★, *Charles Mingus - The Complete Debut Recordings* rec. 50s, 12-CD box set (Debut 1991)★★★★, *Thirteen Pictures: The Charles Mingus Anthology* rec. 1956-77 (Rhino 1993)★★★★★, *Meditations On Integration* rec. 1964 (1992)★★★.
●VIDEOS: *Charles Mingus Sextet 1964* (1994).
●FURTHER READING: *Beneath The Underdog*, Charles Mingus. *Mingus: A Critical Biography*, Brian Priestley. *Revelations*, Charles Mingus. *Charles Mingus, Sein Leben, Seine Musik, Seine Schallplatten*, Horst Weber. *Mingus/Mingus*, Janet Coleman.

MINIT RECORDS
Synonymous with both the New Orleans soul scene and the outstanding producer, writer and musician Allen Toussaint had on the development of black American music, Minit Records took its name from the original intention to supply disc jockeys with short (i.e. Minit) records which maximised the possibility to play advertisements in-between. In fact, Toussaint was not present at the label's inception in 1959, when Joe Banashak and Larry McKinley formed the company. The first release was 'Bad Luck And Trouble', by Boogie Jake. However, Boogie's moniker drew resistance from radio stations, insuring that its local popularity did not translate to national acclaim, despite Chess Records licensing it for that purpose. Chess then reneged on its future options, although neither Boogie's follow-up (this time released under his real name, Matthew Jacobs) or a further single by Noland Pitts provided success. At this stage a twist in fortunes helped shape Minit's future. Regular A&R representative Harold Batiste temporarily left, leaving Banashak and McKinley to recruit Toussaint, who had already successfully auditioned as a musician. When Batiste failed to return, the post became Toussaint's on a permanent footing. Toussaint went on to define the Minit sound - writing much of the artistic repertoire, as well as arranging, producing and playing on the sessions. Minit's first hit, however, arrived with a rare artist's-own composition - Jessie Hill's 'Ooh Poo Pah Doo'. Reaching number 28 in the *Billboard* charts and number 3 in its R&B division, it was followed by a second, lesser hit, 'Whip It On Me'. Meanwhile, Toussaint had begun to shape the careers of Minit's roster. Ernie K-Doe was a veteran of the Blue Diamonds, and later recorded for Specialty and Ember Records as a solo artist. K-Doe broke through with his third release for the label, a Toussaint composition entitled 'Mother-In-Law'. This rose to number 1 in the main *Billboard* charts and gave New Orleans its first ever such success. Follow-ups included 'Te-Ta-Te-Ta-Ta' and 'I Cried My Last Tear'. The latter was a double a-side featuring another Toussaint composition, 'A Certain Girl', which was later covered by the Yardbirds. Benny Speelman, who had provided additional vocals on K-Doe's 'Mother-In-Law' hit, was also a fellow Minit intern. He found fame under his own name with the 1962 double a-

side, 'Lipstick Traces (On A Cigarette)'/'Fortune Teller'. The first-named title was later revived by both the O'Jays and Ringo Starr. More enduringly, Aaron Neville also began his career at Minit, beginning with 1960's 'Over You'. One of many songs Toussaint composed in tandem with Allen Orange (who also recorded solo for the label), it was a precursor to the artist's major breakthrough six years later with 'Tell It Like It Is'. Another staple of the early catalogue was the subsequently popular Irma Thomas, while the Showmen scored a 1961 hit for the label with 'It Will Stand'. Leader General Johnson found subsequent success with Chairman Of The Board. However, by the time the Showmen's '30-21-46 (You)' had become another hit in 1963, Minit Records was in trouble. This coincided with Toussaint being drafted into the services, as well as the sale of Imperial Records (who distributed Minit) to Liberty Records. Minit was thus inactive until 1966, at which time Imperial revived the label, using it as a more generic soul outlet, meaning the subsidiary was now no longer dealing with exclusively New Orleans-based acts. The new roster included the Players, Jimmy Holiday, Jimmy McCracklin, Vernon Greene And The Medallions and the O'Jays, who moved over from Imperial. Ike And Tina Turner were also drafted from the parent label, and enjoyed their biggest success with Minit via the Beatles' cover, 'Come Together'. Another important name, that of Bobby Womack, also added to the discography in his guise as lead singer of the Valentinos, before staying with the label when he became a solo artist. Minit's death came in 1971, when Liberty merged with United Artists and all subsidiary labels surrendered their artist rosters to the new conglomeration. A beautifully designed package was issued in 1994 with a full history.

● COMPILATIONS: *The Mint Records Story* (EMI 1994)★★★★.

MIRACLES

Of all the R&B vocal groups formed in Detroit, Michigan, USA, in the mid-50s, the Miracles proved to be the most successful. They were founded at the city's Northern High School in 1955 by Smokey Robinson (b. William Robinson, 19 February 1940, Detroit, Michigan, USA), Emerson Rogers, Bobby Rogers (b. 19 February 1940, Detroit, Michigan, USA), Ronnie White (b. 5 April 1939, Detroit, Michigan, USA, d. 26 August 1995) and Warren 'Pete' Moore (b. 19 November 1939, Detroit, Michigan, USA). Emerson Rogers left the following year, and was replaced by his sister Claudette, who married Smokey Robinson in 1959. Known initially as the Matadors, the group became the Miracles in 1958, when they made their initial recordings with producer Berry Gordy.

He leased their debut, 'Got A Job' (an answer record to the Silhouettes' major hit 'Get A Job'), to End Records, produced a duet by Ron (White) And Bill (Robinson) for Argo, and licensed the classic doo-wop novelty, 'Bad Girl', to Chess in 1959. The following year, Gordy signed the Miracles directly to his fledgling Motown label. Recognizing the youthful composing talents of Smokey

Robinson, he allowed the group virtual free rein in the studio, and was repaid when they issued 'Way Over There', a substantial local hit, and then 'Shop Around', which broke both the Miracles and Motown to a national audience. The song demonstrated the increasing sophistication of Robinson's writing, which provided an unbroken series of hits for the group over the next few years. Their raw, doo-wop sound was further refined on the Top 10 hit 'You Really Got A Hold On Me' in 1962, a soulful ballad which became a worldwide standard after the Beatles covered it in 1963. Robinson was now in demand by other Motown artists: Gordy used him as a one-man hit factory, to mastermind releases by the Temptations and Mary Wells, and the Miracles' own career suffered slightly as a result.

They continued to enjoy success in a variety of different styles, mixing dance-floor hits like 'Mickey's Monkey' and 'Going To A Go-Go' with some of Robinson's most durable ballads, like 'Oooh Baby Baby' and 'The Tracks Of My Tears'. Although Robinson sang lead on almost all the group's recordings, the rest of the group provided a unique harmony blend behind him, while guitarist Marv Tarplin - who co-wrote several of their hits - was incorporated as an unofficial Miracle from the mid-60s onwards. Claudette Robinson stopped touring with the group after 1965, although she was still featured on many of their subsequent releases. Exhausted by several years of constant work, Robinson scaled down his writing commitments for the group in the mid-60s, when they briefly worked with Holland/Dozier/Holland and other Motown producers. Robinson wrote their most ambitious and lasting songs, however, including 'The Tears Of A Clown' in 1966 (a belated hit in the UK and USA in 1970), and 'The Love I Saw In You Was Just A Mirage' and 'I Second That Emotion' in 1967. These tracks epitomized the strengths of Robinson's compositions, with witty, metaphor-filled lyrics tied to aching melody lines and catchy guitar figures, the latter often provided by Tarplin. Like many of the veteran Motown acts, the Miracles went into a sales slump after 1967 - the year when Robinson was given individual credit on the group's records. Their slide was less noticeable in Britain, where Motown gained a Top 10 hit in 1969 with a reissue of 'The Tracks Of My Tears', which most listeners imagined was a contemporary record. The success of 'The Tears Of A Clown' prompted a revival in fortune after 1970. 'I'm The One You Need' became another reissue hit in Britain the following year, while 'I Don't Blame You At All', one of their strongest releases to date, scored chart success on both sides of the Atlantic.

In 1971, Robinson announced his intention of leaving the Miracles to concentrate on his position as vice-president of Motown Records. His decision belied the title of his final hit with the group, 'We've Come Too Far To End It Now' in 1972, and left the Miracles in the unenviable position of having to replace one of the most distinctive voices in popular music. Their choice was William 'Bill' Griffin (b. 15 August 1950, Detroit, Michigan, USA), who was introduced by Robinson to the group's audiences during a 1972 USA tour. The new line-up took time to settle, while Smokey Robinson launched a solo career to great acclaim in 1973. The group responded with *Renaissance*, which saw them working with Motown luminaries like Marvin Gaye and Willie Hutch. The following year, they re-established the Miracles as a hit-making force with 'Do It Baby' and 'Don'tcha Love It', dance-orientated singles which appealed strongly to the group's black audience. In 1975, 'Love Machine' became the Miracles' first US chart-topper, while the concept album *City Of Angels* was acclaimed as one of Motown's most progressive releases. This twin success proved to be the Miracles' last commercial gasp. Switching to Columbia Records in 1977, they lost Billy Griffin, who set out on a little-noticed solo career. Donald Griffin briefly joined the group in his place, but the Miracles ceased recording in 1978. Thereafter, Ronnie White and Bill Rogers steered the outfit into the new decade as a touring band, before the Miracles disbanded without any fanfares. Bobby Rogers re-formed the group in 1982, enlisting Dave Finlay and Carl Cotton. Former members Billy Griffin and Claudette Robinson (ex-wife of Smokey) recorded solo tracks for Ian Levine's Motor City label during 1988-91. Griffin issued *Technicolour* in 1992. Another re-formed group comprising Griffin, Robinson, Rogers, Donald Griffin, Cotton and Finlay also recorded for Levine remaking 'Love Machine' in 1990. White died in 1995 after losing the battle with leukaemia.

●ALBUMS: *Hi, We're The Miracles* (Tamla 1961)★★★, *Cookin' With The Miracles* (Tamla 1962)★★★★, *I'll Try Something New* (Tamla 1962)★★★, *The Fabulous Miracles* (Tamla 1963)★★★, *Recorded Live: On Stage* (Tamla 1963)★★, *Christmas With The Miracles* (Tamla 1963)★★, *The Miracles Doin' 'Mickey's Monkey'* (Tamla 1963)★★★, *Going To A Go-Go* (Tamla 1965)★★★★, *I Like It Like That* (Tamla Motown 1965)★★★, *Away We-A-Go-Go* (Tamla 1966)★★★, *Make It Happen* (Tamla 1967)★★★, *Special Occasion* (Tamla Motown 1968)★★★, *Live* (Tamla Motown 1968)★★, *Time Out For Smokey Robinson And The Miracles* (Tamla Motown 1969)★★★, *Four In Blue* (Tamla Motown 1969)★★★, *What Love Has Joined Together* (Tamla Motown 1970)★★★, *A Pocketful Of Miracles* (Tamla Motown 1970)★★★, *The Season For Miracles* (1970)★★★, *One Dozen Roses* (1971)★★★, *Flying High Together* (1972)★★★, *Renaissance* (1973)★★★, *Do It Baby* (1974)★★★, *Don'tcha Love It* (1975)★★, *City Of Angels* (1975)★★, *The Power Of Music* (1976)★★, *Love Crazy* (1977)★★, *The Miracles* (1978)★★, *Technicolour* (1992)★★.

●COMPILATIONS: *Greatest Hits From The Beginning* (Tamla 1965)★★★★, *Greatest Hits Vol. 2* (Tamla 1968)★★★★, *1957-72* (1972)★★★★, *Anthology 1957-1972* (Tamla Motown 1973)★★★★, *35th Anniversary Box* (Motown 1994)★★★★.

MISUNDERSTOOD

One of psychedelia's finest groups, the Misunderstood originated in Riverside, California, USA, and evolved from a local surfing group, the Blue Notes. Their first line-up - Greg Treadway (guitar), George Phelps (guitar) and Rick Moe (drums) - was augmented by Rick Brown (vocals) and Steve Whiting (bass), before adopting their new name in 1965. Phelps was then replaced by Glenn Ross 'Fernando' Campbell who played steel guitar. The quintet completed a single, 'You Don't Have To Go'/'Who's Been Talking?', before leaving for the UK on the suggestion of disc jockey John (Peel) Ravenscroft, then working in San Bernadino. Tredway was subsequently drafted, and his place was taken by Tony Hill (b. South Shields, Co. Durham, England). The group completed six masters during their London sojourn. 'I Can Take You To The Sun', a hypnotic, atmospheric and ambitious performance, was their only contemporary release although the rousing 'Children Of The Sun' was issued, after their break-up, in 1968. Campbell later re-established the name with several British musicians. Their two blues-cum-progressive singles shared little with the early, trail-blazing unit, and the latterday version then evolved into Juicy Lucy.

●COMPILATIONS: *Before The Dream Faded* (1982)★★, *Golden Glass* (1984)★★.

MITCHELL, CHAD, TRIO

Chad Mitchell, Mike Kobluk and Mike Pugh were students at Gonzaga University in Spokane, Washington, USA, when they formed this influential folk group in 1958. They then crossed America, performing when able, before arriving in New York to secure a recording deal. The following year, Pugh dropped out in favour of Joe Frazier, while the Trio's accompanist, Dennis Collins, was replaced by guitarist Roger McGuinn, who later found fame with the Byrds. The group then embarked on their most successful era, when they became renowned for songs of a satirical or socially-conscious nature. Chad Mitchell left for a solo career in 1965. He was replaced by aspiring songwriter John Denver, but the restructured act, now known as the Mitchell Trio, found it difficult to sustain momentum. Frazier and Kobluk also left the group, which was then sued by its former leader for continuing to use the 'original' name. The trio then became known as Denver, Boise And Johnson, but split up in 1969 when first Johnson, then Denver, left to pursue independent projects.

●ALBUMS: *The Chad Mitchell Trio Arrives* (1960)★★★, *A Mighty Day On Campus* (Kapp 1961)★★★★, *The Chad Mitchell Trio At The Bitter End* (Kapp 1962)★★★, *The Chad Mitchell Trio In Action aka Blowin' In The Wind* (Kapp 1962)★★★, *Hootenanny Number 3* (Kapp 1963)★★★, *Singin' Our Minds* (1963)★★★, *The Chad Mitchell Trio In Concert* (Colpix 1964)★★★, *Reflecting* (1964)★★★, *The Slightly Irreverent Mitchell Trio* (1964)★★★, *Typical American Boys* (1965)★★★, *That's The Way It's Gotta Be* (1965)★★★, *Violets Of Dawn* (1966)★★★, *Alive* (1967)★★★.

●COMPILATIONS: *The Best Of The Chad Mitchell Trio* (Kapp 1963)★★★, *The Chad Mitchell Trio And The*

Gatemen In Concert (1964)★★★, *Beginnings: The Chad Mitchell Trio Featuring John Denver* (1973)★★★.

MOBLEY, HANK

b. Henry Mobley, 7 July 1930, Eastman, Georgia, USA, d. 30 May 1986. Tenor saxophonist Mobley began his professional career with an R&B band in 1950. The following year, he was attracting the attention of such important beboppers as Max Roach and Dizzy Gillespie, and by 1954 his stature was such that he was invited to become a founder member of Horace Silver's Jazz Messengers. When Silver re-formed a band under his own name, bequeathing the Messengers to Art Blakey, Mobley went along, too. In the late 50s he was briefly with Blakey, then worked with Dizzy Reece and, in 1961, spent a short but memorable time with Miles Davis. Throughout the 60s, Mobley worked with many distinguished musicians, among them Lee Morgan, Barry Harris and Billy Higgins, often leading the bands, and recording several outstanding sessions for Blue Note. In the 70s, Mobley was dogged by poor health, but he worked sporadically, including a stint as co-leader of a group with Cedar Walton. Mobley played even less frequently in the 80s, but shortly before his death in 1986, he worked with Duke Jordan. The seemingly casual ease with which Mobley performed, comfortably encompassing complex rhythmical innovations, and the long period spent on the sidelines have tended to obscure the fact that his was a remarkable talent. Also militating against widespread appeal was his sometimes dry and intimate sound, which contrasted sharply with the more aggressively robust style adopted by many of his contemporaries.

●ALBUMS: with Art Blakey *The Jazz Messengers At The Cafe Bohemia* (1955)★★★★, *The Hank Mobley Quartet* (Blue Note 1955)★★★, *The Jazz Message Of Hank Mobley* (Savoy 1956)★★★★, *Mobley's Message* (1956)★★★★, *Mobley's Second Message* (Savoy 1956)★★★, *The Hank Mobley Sextet* (1956)★★★, *Hank Mobley-Lee Morgan: Hank's Shout* (1956)★★★, *Hank Mobley And His All Stars* (Blue Note 1957)★★★, *Hank Mobley With Donald Byrd And Lee Morgan* (Blue Note 1957)★★★, *The Hank Mobley Quintet* (1957)★★★★, *Hank* (1957)★★★, *Hank Mobley* (Blue Note 1957)★★★, *Poppin'* (1957)★★★, *Peckin' Time* (Blue Note 1958)★★★, *Monday Night At Birdland* (1958)★★★, *Soul Station* (Blue Note 1960)★★★★, *Roll Call* (Blue Note 1960)★★★, with Miles Davis *Carnegie Hall 1961* (1961)★★★, with Davis *At The Blackhawk* (1961)★★★★, *Workout* (Blue Note 1961)★★★★, *Another Workout* (1961)★★★, *Straight No Filter* (Blue Note 1963-65)★★★, *No Room For Squares* (Blue Note 1963)★★★, *52nd Street Theme* (New Jazz 1963)★★★, *The Turnaround* (1965)★★★, *Dippin'* (Blue Note 1965)★★★, *A Caddy For Daddy* (Blue Note 1965)★★★, *A Slice Of The Top* (1966)★★★, *Third Season* (1967)★★★, *Hi Voltage* (1967)★★★, *Far Away Lands* (Blue Note 1967)★★★, *Reach Out* (1968)★★★, *The Flip* (1969)★★★, *Thinking Of Home* (1970)★★★.

MOBY GRAPE

The legend that continues to grow around this late 60s San Francisco group is mainly based on their magnificent debut album, which fans vainly willed them to repeat. This iconoclastic band was formed in September 1966, with the seminal line-up of Alexander 'Skip' Spence (b. 18 April 1946, Windsor, Ontario, Canada; guitar/vocals), Jerry Miller (b. 10 July 1943, Tacoma, Washington, USA; guitar/vocals), Bob Mosley (b. 4 December 1942, Paradise Valley, California, USA; bass/vocals), Don Stevenson (b. 15 October 1942, Seattle, Washington, USA; drums) and Peter Lewis (b. 15 July 1945, Los Angeles, California, USA; guitar/vocals). With record companies queueing up to sign them, they decided to go with CBS Records and became marketing guinea pigs for an unprecedented campaign, whereupon 10 tracks (five singles plus b-sides) were released simultaneously. Not even the Beatles could have lived up to that kind of launch. Only one of the records dented the US chart: 'Omaha' reached a dismal number 88. Had the singles been released in normal sequence, they might all have been hits, as the quality of each song was outstanding. The band fell into immediate disarray, unable to cope with the pressure and hype. The resulting debut, *Moby Grape*, contained all these 10 tracks plus an additional three, and it deservedly reached the US Top 30 album charts. It is now recognized as a classic. The short, brilliantly structured, guitar-based rock songs with fine harmonies still sound fresh in the 90s.

Their follow-up was a similar success (yet a lesser work), and made the US Top 20 album chart. As with their debut, CBS continued with their ruthless marketing campaign, determined to see a return on their investment, as the band had originally held out for a considerable advance. *Wow* sported a beautiful surrealistic painting/collage by Bob Cato, depicting a huge bunch of grapes mixed with an eighteenth-century beach scene, that came with a free album, *Grape Jam*. Additionally, one of the tracks was recorded at 78 rpm, forcing the listener to get up and change the speed only to hear a spoof item played by Lou Waxman And His Orchestra. Amidst this spurious package were some of their finest songs, including Spence's 'Motorcycle Irene', Miller's 'Miller's Blues', Mosley's 'Murder In My Heart For The Judge' and arguably their best track, 'Can't Be So Bad'. Penned by Miller and featuring his stinging guitar solo, this furiously paced heavy rock item is suddenly slowed down and sweetened by an outstanding five-part Mamas And The Papas-style harmony. The song failed to chart anywhere. Spence had departed with drug and mental problems by the release of *Moby Grape '69*, although his ethereal composition 'Seeing' is one of the highlights of this apologetic and occasionally brilliant album (the hype of the past is disclaimed by the 'sincere' sleeve notes). Other notable tracks included Lewis' hymn-like 'I Am Not Willing' and the straightforward rocker 'Truck Driving Man'. A disastrous European tour was arranged, during which the band was constantly overshadowed by the support act Group Therapy. Mosley left on their return to the USA, and allegedly joined the marines, leaving the rest to fulfil their contract by making a fourth album. He also made a solo album, as did Spence. The latter, who today lives in a men's hostal as a ward of the county, released an extraordinary album. *Oar* has become a cult classic since its release in 1968. It is painfully dark ('Diana') yet hopelessly light ('Lawrence Of Euphoria'). It does at least reflect Spence's condition as a paranoid schizophrenic.

The poor-selling and lacklustre *Truly Fine Citizen* was badly received; the critics had already given up on them. The band then disintegrated, unable to use the name which was and still is owned by their manager, Matthew Katz. The remaining members have appeared as Maby Grope, Mosley Grape, Grape Escape, Fine Wine, the Melvills, the Grape, the Hermans and the Legendary Grape. During one of their many attempts at re-formation, Mosley and Miller actually released a record as Fine Wine. The original five reunited for one more undistinguished album in 1971, *20 Granite Creek*. Out of the mire, only Mosley's 'Gypsy Wedding' showed some promise. Skip Spence delivered the quirky 'Chinese Song,' played on a koto, and the silk-voiced Lewis produced 'Horse Out In The Rain' with its unusual timing and extraordinary booming bass. A live album in 1978 delighted fans, and rumours constantly abound about various re-formation plans. Some of the band still play together in small clubs and bars, but the magical reunion of the five (just like the five Byrds) can never be. Spence, sadly, is in no fit state and, unbelievably, Mosley was also diagnosed as a schizophrenic and lives rough on the streets in San Diego. The myth surrounding the band continues to grow as more (outrageous) stories come to light. The debut album is one of the true rock/pop classics of the past 30 years (along with Love's *Forever Changes*). Their influence is immense and they still have many followers (including long-standing fan Robert Plant). The 'grape sound' has shown up in many groups over the past 20 years including the Doobie Brothers, R.E.M., the Smithereens, Teenage Fanclub and Weezer. They were, more than any other band from the Bay Area in 1967/68, the true embodiment of the music (but not the culture).

●ALBUMS: *Moby Grape* (Columbia 1967)★★★★★, *Wow* (Columbia 1967)★★★, *Grape Jam* (Columbia 1967)★★, *Moby Grape '69* (Columbia 1969)★★★★, *Truly Fine Citizen* (Columbia 1969)★★, *20 Granite Creek* (Reprise 1971)★★★, *Live Grape* (1978)★★. As Fine Wine *Fine Wine* (1976)★★★. Solo: Bob Mosley *Bob Mosley* (Warners 1972)★★. Peter Lewis *Peter Lewis* (Taxim 1996)

●COMPILATIONS: *Great Grape* (Columbia 1973)★★★, *Vintage* 2-CD box set with unreleased material and alternate takes (Columbia/Legacy 1993)★★★★★.

MOJO MEN

This San Francisco-based group - Jimmy Alaimo (vocals/guitar), Paul Curcio (guitar), Don Metchick (organ) and Dennis DeCarr (drums) - was signed to Autumn, the city's leading independent label, in 1965. Here they enjoyed a fruitful artistic relationship with pro-

ducer Sly Stone, which spawned a minor US hit in 'Dance With Me'. Jan Errico, from stablemates the Vejtables, replaced DeCarr in 1966 as the quartet switched outlets to Reprise Records. The following year they secured a US Top 40 hit with a charming version of Buffalo Springfield's 'Sit Down I Think I Love You', which was engineered and arranged by Van Dyke Parks. The group truncated its name to Mojo in 1968 and, now trimmed to a trio on Metchick's departure, completed the Mojo Magic album before breaking up. Paul Curcio meanwhile founded the Pacific Recording Studio in San Mateo, where Santana recorded their early releases.

●ALBUMS: *Mojo Magic* (Autumn 1968)★★.
●COMPILATIONS: *Why's Ain't Supposed To Be* (Sundazed 1996)★★, *Sit Down, It's The Mojo Men* (Sundazed 1996)★★.

MOJOS

Originally known as the Nomads, this Liverpool beat group was formed in 1962 by Stu James (vocals), Adrian Wilkinson (guitar), Keith Karlson (bass) and John Konrad (drums). They secured early minor fame by winning a songwriting contest that resulted in a recording deal. Pianist Terry O'Toole was added to the line-up prior to the release of the Mojos' debut single, and Nicky Crouch replaced Wilkinson before a follow-up, 'Everything's Alright', was recorded. This energetic 1964 single became a UK Top 10 hit, and the crafted excitement maintained throughout the performance assured its classic status. The group's later releases failed to match this quality, and although a revitalized line-up, consisting of James, Crouch, Lewis Collins (bass) and Aynsley Dunbar (drums) continued as Stu James and the Mojos, they broke up in December 1966. The singer then pursued a career in music publishing, while Dunbar joined John Mayall's Bluesbreakers and Collins pursued a acting career, later starring in the popular UK television series, *The Professionals*.

●COMPILATIONS: *Working* (1982)★★★.

MONEY, ZOOT

b. George Bruno Money, 17 July 1942, Bournemouth, Dorset, England. A veteran of his hometown's thriving music circuit, Money played in several local rock 'n' roll groups before forming the Big Roll Band in 1961. Its original line-up comprised Roger Collis (guitar), Kevin Drake (tenor saxophone), Johnny King (bass), Peter Brooks (drums) and Zoot on piano and vocals. By 1963, the singer was fronting an all-new line-up of Andy Somers aka Andy Summers (guitar), Nick Newall (saxophone) and Colin Allen (drums), but he left the group for a temporary spot in Alexis Korner's Blues Incorporated. Zoot remained in London when his tenure ended, and his band subsequently joined him there. The Big Roll Band secured a residency at London's prestigious Flamingo Club, and added two new members, Paul Williams (bass/vocals) and Clive Burrows (saxophone), before recording their debut single, 'The Uncle Willie'. In 1965, the group released its first album, *It Should've Been Me*, a compendium of soul and R&B material that enhanced the band's growing reputation. A second album, *Zoot!*, recorded live at Klook's Kleek, introduced newcomer Johnny Almond, who replaced Burrows. This exciting set included a superb James Brown medley and confirmed the group's undoubted strength. However, a devil-may-care attitude undermined their potential, and only one of their excellent singles, 'Big Time Operator' (1966), broached the UK Top 30. Money became famed as much for dropping his trousers onstage as for his undoubted vocal talent, and several of the line-up were notorious imbibers. Yet this lifestyle was reversed in 1967, when Money, Somers and Alan embraced the emergent 'flower-power' movement with Dantalian's Chariot. However, by the following year Zoot had resumed his erstwhile direction with *Transition*, a disappointing release which was pieced together from several sessions.

In 1968, both Money and Somers joined Eric Burdon in his American-based New Animals. Zoot's vocals were heard on a number of tracks with Burdon, notably a lengthy reworking of his Dantallion's Chariot showpiece, 'Madman'. Additionally, his spoken dialogue was featured on some of Burdon's more self-indulgent efforts on *Everyone Of Us*. The singer completed *Welcome To My Head* on the group's demise before returning to London for *Zoot Money*. He continued an itinerant path with Centipede, Grimms and Ellis, before joining Somers in the Kevin Coyne and Kevin Ayers bands. In 1980, Zoot released the low-key *Mr. Money*, since which he has played on numerous sessions and enjoyed a new career as a character actor in television drama and comedy. In the early 90s he was music controller for Melody Radio, but was back on the road by 1995.

●ALBUMS: *It Should've Been Me* (Columbia 1965)★★★, *Zoot! Live At Klooks Kleek* (Columbia 1966)★★★, *Transition* (Direction 1968)★★, *Welcome To My Head* (1969)★★, *Zoot Money* (Polydor 1970)★★, *Mr. Money* (Magic Moon 1980)★★, with Chris Farlowe *Alexis Korner Memorial Concert Volume 2* (Indigo 1995)★★★.

MONK, THELONIOUS

b. 11 October 1917, Rocky Mount, North Carolina, USA, d. 17 February 1982. Monk's family moved to New York when he was five years old. He started playing piano a year later, receiving formal tuition from the age of 11 onwards. At Stuyvesant High School he excelled at physics and maths, and also found time to play organ in church. In the late 30s he toured with a gospel group, then began playing in the clubs and became pianist in Kenny Clarke's house band at Minton's Playhouse between 1941 and 1942. He played with Lucky Millinder's orchestra in 1942, the Coleman Hawkins Sextet between 1943 and 1945, the Dizzy Gillespie Big Band in 1946 and started leading his own outfits from 1947. It was Hawkins who provided him with his recording debut, and enthusiasts noted a fine solo on 'Flyin' Hawk' (October 1944). However, it was the Blue Note sessions of 1947 (subsequently issued on album and CD as *Genius Of Modern Music*) that established him as a major figure. With Art Blakey on drums, these recordings have operated as capsule lessons in music for subsequent generations of musicians. An infectious groove makes complex harmonic puzzles sound attractive, with Monk's unique dissonances and rhythmic sense adding to their charm. They were actually a distillation of a decade's work. "Round Midnight' immediately became a popular tune and others - 'Ruby My Dear', 'Well You Needn't', 'In Walked Bud' - have become jazz standards since. In his book, *Bebop*, Leonard Feather recognized Monk's genius at composition, but claimed his playing lacked technique (a slight for which he later apologized). Monk certainly played with flat fingers (anathema to academy pianists), but actually his bare-bones style was the result of a modern sensibility rather than an inability to achieve the torrents of Art Tatum or Oscar Peterson. For Monk, the blues had enough romance without an influx of European romanticism, and enough emotion without the sometimes overheated blowing of bebop. His own improvisations are at once witty, terse and thought-provoking.

A trumped-up charge for possession of drugs deprived Monk of his New York performer's licence in 1951, and a subsequent six-year ban from playing live in the city damaged his career. He played in Paris in June 1954 (recorded by Vogue Records). Riverside Records was supportive, and he found sympathetic musicians with whom to record - both under his own name and guesting with players such as Miles Davis, Sonny Rollins and Clark Terry. *Plays Duke Ellington* (1955) was a fascinating look at Duke Ellington's compositions, with a non-pareil rhythm section in bassist Oscar Pettiford and drummer Clarke. *Brilliant Corners* in 1956 showcased some dazzling new compositions and featured Sonny Rollins on tenor saxophone. Regaining his work permit in 1957, Monk assembled a mighty quintet for a residency at the Five Spot club: Shadow Wilson (drums), Wilbur Ware (bass) and John Coltrane (tenor). Coltrane always spoke of what an education he received during his brief stay with the ban although the group was never recorded live, the studio albums that resulted (*Thelonious Monk With John Coltrane*, *Monk's Music*) were classics. Monk repaid Coleman Hawkins' earlier compliment, and featured the tenorman on these records: history and the future shook hands over Monk's keyboard. Previously considered too 'way out' for mass consumption, Monk's career finally began to blossom. In 1957, he recorded with Gerry Mulligan, which helped to expose him to a wider audience, and worked with classical composer Hall Overton to present his music orchestrally (*At Town Hall*, 1959). He toured Europe for the first time (1961) and also Japan (1964). He formed a stable quartet in the early 60s with Charlie Rouse on tenor, John Ore (later Butch Warren or Larry Gales) on bass and Frankie Dunlop (later Ben Riley) on drums. Critics tend to prefer his work with other saxophonists, such as Harold Land or Johnny Griffin, but overlook the fact that Rouse really understood Monk's tunes and his raw, angular tone fitted the compositions like a glove.

In the early 70s, Monk played with Pat Patrick (Sun Ra's alto player), using son T.S. Monk on drums. Illness increasingly restricted his activity, but he toured with the Giants Of Jazz (1971-72) and presented a big band at the Newport Festival in 1974. Two albums recorded for the English Black Lion label in 1971 - *Something In Blue* and *The Man I Love* - presented him in a trio context with Al McKibbon on bass and Blakey on drums: these were stunning examples of the empathy between drummer and pianist - two of Monk's best records. When he died from a stroke in 1982, at Englewood, New Jersey, leaving his wife (for whom he had written 'Crepuscule With Nellie') and son, he had not performed in public for six years. Monk's influence, if anything, increased during the 80s. Buell Neidlinger formed a band, String Jazz, to play only Monk and Ellington tunes; Steve Lacy, who in the early 60s had spent a period playing exclusively Monk tunes, recorded two solo discs of his music; and tribute albums by Arthur Blythe (*Light Blue*, 1983), Anthony Braxton (*Six Monk's Compositions*, 1987), Paul Motian (*Monk In Motian*, 1988) and Hal Wilner (*That's The Way I Feel Now*, 1984, in which artists as diverse as the Fowler Brothers, John Zorn, Dr. John, Eugene Chadbourne, and Peter Frampton celebrated his tunes) prove that Monk's compositions are still teaching everyone new tricks. His son, T.S. Monk, is a gifted drummer who continues a tradition by encouraging young musicians through membership of his band. One of the most brilliant and original performers in jazz, Thelonious Monk was also one of the century's outstanding composers. "Round Midnight' is probably the most recorded jazz song of all time. His unique ability to weld intricate, surprising harmonic shifts and rhythmic quirks into appealing, funky riffs means that something special happens when they are played: his compositions exact more incisive improvising than anybody else's. In terms of jazz, that is the highest praise of all.

●ALBUMS: *Genius Of Modern Music, Volume 1* (Blue Note 1951)★★★★★, *Genius Of Modern Music Volume 2* (Blue Note 1952)★★★★★, *Thelonious Monk Trio* (Prestige 1953)★★★, *And Sonny Rollins* (Prestige 1954)★★★★, *Thelonious Monk Quintet* (Prestige 1954), *Pure Monk* (1954)★★★★, *Solo Monk 1954* (Vogue 1955)★★★★, *Plays Duke Ellington* (Riverside 1955)★★★, *The Unique* (Riverside 1956)★★★★, *Brilliant Corners* (Riverside 1957)★★★★, *Thelonious Himself* (Riverside 1957)★★★, *With John Coltrane* (Jazzland 1957)★★★★, with Gerry Mulligan *Mulligan Meets Monk* (Riverside 1957)★★★★, *Art Blakey/Thelonious Monk* (1958)★★★, *Monk's Music* (Riverside 1958)★★★★, *Thelonious In Action* (Riverside 1958)★★★★, *Misterioso* (Riverside 1958)★★★★★, *The Thelonious Monk Orchestra At Town Hall* (Riverside 1959)★★★, *Five By Monk By Five* (Riverside 1959)★★★, *Thelonious Alone In San Francisco* (Riverside 1960)★★★★, *At The Blackhawk* (Riverside 1960)★★★★, *Two Hours With Thelonious* (1961)★★★, *Criss Cross* (Columbia 1963)★★★, *Monk's Dream* (Columbia 1963)★★★, *April In Paris* (Riverside 1963)★★★★, *Thelonoious Monk In Italy* (Riverside 1963), *Big Band And Quartet In Concert* (1964)★★★, with Miles Davis *Miles & Monk At Newport* (1964)★★★, *It's Monk's Time* (Columbia 1964)★★★, *Monk* (Columbia 1965)★★★, *Solo Monk* (Columbia 1965)★★★, *The Thelonious Monk Story Vol. 1* (Riverside 1965)★★★, *The Thelonious Monk Story Vol. 2* (Riverside 1965)★★★, *Monk in France* (Riverside 1965)★★★, *Straight No Chaser* (Columbia 1966)★★★★, *Monk's Blues* (Columbia 1968)★★★, *Underground* (Columbia 1968)★★★, *Epistrophy* (1971)★★★, *Something In Blue* (1972)★★★, *The Man I Love* (1972)★★★, *Sphere* (1979)★★★, *April In Paris/Live* (1981)★★★, *Live At The It Club* rec. 1964 (Columbia 1982,)★★★, *Live At The Jazz Workshop* rec. 1964 (Columbia 1982)★★★, *Tokyo Concerts* rec. 1963 (1983)★★★, *The Great Canadian Concert Of Thelonious Monk* rec. 1965 (1984)★★★, *1963 - In Japan* (1984)★★★, *Live In Stockholm 1961* (1987)★★★, *Solo 1954* (1993)★★★, *The Nonet Live* rec. 1967 (Charly 1993)★★★

●COMPILATIONS: *Thelonious Monk's Greatest Hits* (Riverside 1962)★★★★, *Mighty Monk* (Riverside 1967)★★★, *Best Of Thelonious Monk* (Riverside 1969)★★★, *Always Know* rec. 1962-68 (1979)★★★, *Memorial Album* rec. 1954-60 (1982)★★★★, *The Complete Blue Note Recordings Of Thelonious Monk* rec. 1947-52, 4-LP box set (1983)★★★★★, *The Complete Black Lion And Vogue Recordings Of Thelonious Monk* 4-LP box set (1986)★★★★, *The Composer* (Giants Of Jazz 1987)★★★.

●VIDEOS: *American Composer* (1993), *Thelonious Monk: Live In Oslo* (1993).

●FURTHER READING: *Monk On Records: A Discography Of Thelonious Monk*, L. Bijl and F. Canté.

MONKEES

Inspired by the burgeoning pop phenomena and armed with an advance from Columbia's Screen Gems subsidiary, US television producers Bob Rafelson and Bert Schneider began auditions for a show about a struggling pop group in 1965. When extant acts, including the Lovin' Spoonful, proved inappropriate, an advertisement in the *Daily Variety* solicited 437 applications, including Stephen Stills, Danny Hutton (later Three Dog Night) and Paul Williams. Following suitably off-beat auditions, the final choice paired two musicians - Michael Nesmith (b. Robert Michael Nesmith, 30 December 1942, Houston, Texas, USA; guitar/vocals) and folk singer Peter Tork (b. Peter Halsten Thorkelson, 13 February 1942, Washington, DC, USA; bass/vocals) - with two budding actors and former child stars - Davy Jones (b. 30 December 1945, Manchester, England; vocals) and ex-*Circus Boy* star Mickey Dolenz (b. George Michael Dolenz, 8 March 1945, Los Angeles, California, USA; drums/vocals). On 12 September 1966, the first episode of *The Monkees* was aired by NBC-TV and, despite low initial ratings, the show quickly became hugely popular, a feat mirrored when it was launched in the UK. Attendant singles 'Last Train To

Clarksville' (US number 1) and 'I'm A Believer' (US and UK number 1), and a million-selling debut album confirmed the group as the latest teenage phenomenon, drawing inevitable comparisons with the Beatles. However, news that the quartet did not play on their records fuelled an already simmering internal controversy. Early sessions had been completed by Tommy Boyce And Bobby Hart, authors of 'Last Train To Clarksville', and their backing group, the Candy Store Prophets, with the Monkees simply overdubbing vocals. Musical supervision was later handed to Screen Gems executive Don Kirshner, who in turn called in staff songwriters Gerry Goffin and Carole King, Neil Diamond and Jeff Barry to contribute material for the show. This infuriated the Monkees' two musicians, in particular Nesmith, who described the piecemeal *More Of The Monkees* as 'the worst album in the history of the world'. Sales in excess of five million copies exacerbated tension, but the group won tacit approval from Schneider to complete several tracks under their own devices. An undeterred Kirshner coaxed Jones to sing on the already-completed backing track to 'A Little Bit Me, A Little Bit You' which was issued, without group approval, as their third single. The ensuing altercation saw Kirshner ousted, with the quartet gaining complete artistic freedom. Although not issued as a single in the USA, 'Alternate Title' (aka 'Randy Scouse Git'), Dolenz's ambitious paean to London, reached number 2 in Britain, while two further 1967 singles, 'Pleasant Valley Sunday' and 'Daydream Believer' (composed by John Stewart), achieved gold record status. *Headquarters*, the first Monkees album on which the group played, was a commercial and artistic success, consisting largely of self-penned material ranging from country-rock to vaudevillian pop. *Pisces, Aquarius, Capricorn And Jones Ltd* featured material drawn from associates Michael Murphy, Harry Nilsson and Chip Martin as the unyielding call on the group's talents continued. This creative drain was reflected in the disappointing *The Birds, The Bees And The Monkees* and its accompanying single, 'Valleri'. The track itself had been recorded in 1966, and was only issued when 'pirate' recordings, dubbed off-air from the television series, attracted considerable airplay. 'The Monkees are dead!', declared an enraged Nesmith, yet the song sold over a million copies, the group's last such success. The appeal of their series had waned as plots grew increasingly loose, and the final episode was screened in the USA on 25 March 1968. The quartet had meanwhile embarked on a feature film, *Head*, which contained many in-jokes about their artistic predicaments. Although baffling their one-time teenage audience, it failed to find favour with the underground circuit who still viewed the Monkees as bubblegum. However, *Head* has since been rightly lauded for its imagination and innovation. A dispirited Peter Tork left following its release, but although the remaining trio continued without him, their commercial decline was as spectacular as its ascendancy. Nesmith left for a solo career in 1969. and the following year the Monkees' name was dissolved in the wake of

Dolenz/Jones recording *Changes*. However, in 1975, the latter-day duo joined their erstwhile songwriting team in *Dolenz, Jones, Boyce And Hart* which toured under the banner 'The Great Golden Hits Of The Monkees Show'. The project drew cursory interest, but the group's reputation was bolstered considerably during the 80s, when the independent Rhino Records label reissued the entire Monkees back catalogue and the entire series was rescreened on MTV. Although Nesmith demured, Dolenz, Jones and Tork embarked on a highly successful, 20th anniversary world tour which engendered a live album and a new studio set, *Pool It*. The group has since disbanded as members pursued contrasting interests, while attempts to create the New Monkees around Marty Roos, Larry Saltis, Jared Chandler and Dino Kovas in 1987 were aborted. Although reviled by many contemporary critics, the original group's work is now regarded as among the best American pop of its era. Rhino Records released an ambitious 21-volume video collection in 1995 containing all 58 episodes of their television series. *Justus* was the first recording of the original band (including Nesmith) for over 20 years.

●ALBUMS: *The Monkees* (Colgems 1966)★★★, *More Of The Monkees* (Colgems 1967)★★★★, *Headquarters* (Colgems 1967)★★★, *Pisces, Aquarius, Capricorn And Jones Ltd* (Colgems 1967)★★, *The Birds, The Bees And The Monkees* (Colgems 1968)★★, *Head* soundtrack (Colgems 1968)★★, *Instant Replay* (Colgems 1969)★★★, *The Monkees Present ...* (Colgems 1969)★★★, *Changes* (Colgems 1970)★★★, *Pool It* (1986)★★, *20th Anniversary Concert Tour 1986* (1986)★★, *Justus* (Rhino 1996)★★.

●COMPILATIONS: *The Monkees Greatest Hits* (Colgems 1969)★★★★, *A Barrel Full Of Monkees* (Colgems 1971)★★★★, *The Monkees Golden Hits* (RCA Victor 1972)★★★★, *Refocus* (Bell 1973)★★★, *Monkeemania* (1979)★★★, *The Monkees* (1981)★★★, *Monkee Business* (1982)★★★, *Monkee Flips* (1984)★★★, *The And Now ... The Best Of The Monkees* (1986)★★★★, *Missing Links* (1987)★★★, *The Monkees Live - 1967* (1987)★★, *Hey! Hey! It's The Monkees Greatest Hits* (Platinum/K-Tel 1989)★★★★, *Missing Links Volume 2* (Rhino 1990)★★, *Missing Links Vol. 3* (Rhino 1996)★★.

●VIDEOS: *The Monkees Collection* (Rhino 1995), *33 1/3 Revoloutions Per Monkee* (Rhino Home Video 1996).

●FURTHER READING: *Love Letters To The Monkees*, Bill Adler. *The Monkees Tale*, Eric Lefcowitz. *The Monkees Scrapbook*, Ed Finn and T. Bone. *Monkeemania*, Glenn A. Baker. *The Monkees: A Manufactured Image*, Ed Reilly, Maggie McMannus and Bill Chadwick. *I'm A Believer-My Life Of Monkees, Music And Madness*, Mickey Dolenz and Mark Bego.

●FILMS: *Head* (1968).

MONRO, MATT

b. Terry Parsons, 1 December 1932, London, England, d. 7 February 1985, Ealing, London, England. This velvet-voiced balladeer first played in bands under the pseudonym Al Jordan before adopting the name Monro, allegedly borrowed from Winifred Atwell's father. Between stints as a bus driver and singer on the UK Camay soap commercial, he recorded for a number of labels, but his choice of material was generally too predictable. His interpretation of 'Garden Of Eden', for example, had to compete with four other versions by hit artists Frankie Vaughan, Gary Miller, Dick James and Joe Valino. Monro's luck changed when producer George Martin asked him to contribute a pseudo-Frank Sinatra version of 'You Keep Me Swingin'' to a Peter Sellers comedy album. This led to a contract with Parlophone Records and a Top 3 hit with 'Portrait Of My Love' (1960). For the next five years, Matt was a regular chart entrant with his classic up-tempo version of 'My Kind Of Girl', along with ballads such 'Why Not Now/Can This Be Love', 'Gonna Build A Mountain', 'Softly As I Leave You', and 'When Love Comes Along'. A cover of the James Bond movie theme 'From Russia With Love' and the emotive 'Walk Away' proved particularly successful, and the speedy release of a slick adaptation of the Beatles' 'Yesterday' underlined the sagacity of covering a song before your competitors. His 1962 album of Hoagy Carmichael songs, with arrangements by his regular musical director Johnny Spence, was right out of the top drawer.

A move to the USA in 1965 brought a decline in Monro's chart fortunes in the UK, but he sustained his career as an in-demand nightclub performer. The enduring commercial quality of his voice was recognized by Capitol Records with the Christmas release and television promotion of the compilation album, *Heartbreakers*, in 1980. Ill-health dogged the singer in the early 80s, and he died from cancer in 1985. Ten years later, his son Matt Jnr, who had carved out a career for himself as a golf professional, 'duetted' with his father on an album of some of Matt Snr.'s favourite songs. Since his death, the tag that he was merely a Sinatra copyist has completely reversed, especially in America. Monro's appeal continues and the rich patina of his voice is now seen as original rather than derivative.

●ALBUMS: *Blue And Sentimental* (Decca 1957)★★★, *Portrait* (Ace Of Clubs 1961)★★★, *Love Is The Same Anywhere* (Parlophone 1961)★★★, *My Kind Of Girl* (1961)★★★★, *Matt Monro Sings Hoagy Carmichael* (Parlophone 1962)★★★★, *I Have Dreamed* (Parlophone 1965)★★★, *Matt Monro And Don Rennie* (1965)★★★, *Walk Away* (1965, USA)★★★★, *Hits Of Yesterday* (Parlophone 1965)★★★★, *This Is The Life!* (Capitol 1966)★★★★, *Here's To My Lady* (Capitol 1967)★★★★, *Invitation To The Movies* (Capitol 1967)★★★, *These Years* (Capitol 1967)★★★, *The Late Late Show* (Capitol 1968)★★★★, *Invitation To Broadway* (Capitol 1968)★★★, *Here And Now* (1969)★★★, *The Southern Star* soundtrack (RCA Victor 1969), *We're Gonna Change The World* (Capitol 1970)★★★, *Let's Face The Music And Dance* (1972)★★★, *For The Present* (Columbia 1973)★★★,

The Other Side Of The Stars (Columbia 1975)★★★, *The Long And Winding Road* (1975)★★★, *If I Never Hear Another Song* (1979)★★★, *Heartbreakers* (1980)★★★, with Matt Monro Jnr. *Matt Sings Monro* (EMI 1995)★★★.
●COMPILATIONS: *Matt Monro* 3-CD box set (EMI 1995)★★★★, *Complete Heartbreakers* (EMI 1996)★★★.

MONTENEGRO, HUGO

b. 1925, New York City, New York, USA, d. 6 February 1981. An accomplished and prolific composer, arranger and orchestral conductor for film music. After two years in the US Navy where he arranged for Service bands, Montenegro graduated from Manhattan College and entered the record industry in 1955. He served as staff manager to André Kostelanetz, and was conductor-arranger for several artists, including Harry Belafonte. Montenegro also made his own orchestral albums such as *Arriba!*, *Bongos And Brass*, *Boogie Woogie And Bongos*, *Montenegro And Mayhem*, *Pizzicato Strings*, *Black Velvet* and *American Musical Theatre 1-4*. After moving to California he wrote the score for Otto Preminger's 1967 film *Hurry Sundown*, a racial melodrama starring Jane Fonda and Michael Caine. In 1968, with his orchestra and chorus, he recorded Ennio Morricone's theme from the Italian film *The Good, The Bad And The Ugly*. The record went to number 2 in the US, topped the chart in the UK, and sold well over a million copies. The instrumental contrasted with Montenegro's big, romantic string sound, and the effects were startling. From the haunting introduction featuring Arthur Smith on the ocarina, the unusual instruments used included an electric violin, electric harmonica and a piccolo trumpet, aided by a vocal group which featured the whistling of Muzzy Marcellino reinforced by grunting vocals. In 1969 Montenegro had a minor UK hit with the theme from *Hang 'Em High*, the film with which Hollywood attempted to match the brutal style of the 'spaghetti' originals, partly by using the same star, Clint Eastwood. The soundtrack album, *Music From 'A Fistful Of Dollars' & 'For A Few Dollars More' & 'The Good, The Bad And The Ugly'* made the US Top 10. There was a refreshing change from the usual film themes on *Broadway Melodies*, where the material included standards such as 'Varsity Drag', 'Thou Swell', 'Tea For Two' and 'I Got Rhythm'. Throughout the late 60s and 70s he continued to provide music for films such as *The Ambushers* (1968) and *The Wrecking Crew* (1969), both Matt Helm adventures starring Dean Martin; *Lady In Cement*, featuring Frank Sinatra as private eye Tony Rome; *Charro!* (1969), an Elvis Presley western; *The Undefeated* (1969), starring John Wayne; *Viva Max!* (1969); *Tomorrow* (1972); and *The Farmer* (1977).
●ALBUMS: *Original Music From 'The Man From UNCLE'* (RCA Victor 1966)★★★, *More Music From 'The Man From UNCLE'* (RCA Victor 1966)★★★, *Hurry Sundown* soundtrack (RCA Victor 1967)★★★, *Music From 'A Fistful Of Dollars' & 'For A Few Dollars*

More' & 'The Good, The Bad And The Ugly' (RCA Victior 1968)★★★, *Hang 'Em High* (1968)★★★, *Moog Power* (RCA Victor 1969)★★★, *Lady In Cement* (Stateside 1969)★★★ *Arriba!* (70s/80s)★★★, *Bongos And Brass* (70s/80s)★★★, *Boogie Woogie And Bongos* (70s/80s)★★★, *Montenegro And Mayhem* (80s)★★★, *Pizzicato Strings* (80s)★★★, *Black Velvet* (80s)★★★, *American Musical Theatre 1-4* (80s)★★★, *Plays For Lovers* (1981)★★★.
●COMPILATIONS: *The Best Of Broadway* (1977)★★★, *The Best Of Hugh Montenegro* (1980)★★★.

MONTEREY POP FESTIVAL

16-18 June 1967. The burgeoning west coast American music scene was effectively launched at Monterey, California, USA, in 1967. In a transition from 'pop music', performers and bands suddenly found that they were preaching their new music to a like-minded mass audience. The sounds became more adventurous as they explored other musical routes. Blues, jazz and folk became tinged with Eastern and African influences. This galvanization in turn made people more aware and tolerant of these ambitious and different styles. Nevertheless, the music was still labelled 'progressive pop' rather than rock. The festival was the brainchild of John Phillips, Alan Pariser, Paul Simon and Lou Adler, who assembled a board of artists to help stage the event. Derek Taylor, the skilful former press officer of the Beatles and the Byrds, was enrolled. Brian Wilson of the Beach Boys pulled out prior to the event. The Beatles were notably missing. The Rolling Stones, although absent, were there in spirit, with Brian Jones on the advisory board seen wandering in the crowd throughout the proceedings.

The three-day festival was a forerunner to Woodstock, and history has subsequently shown that Monterey was more 'musically' important, although by today's standards it was a comparatively small affair with only 35,000 people present at any one time. The festival gave birth to a movement and introduced major new artists to the general public. It was at Monterey that Jimi Hendrix first attracted mass attention with the public burning of his guitar. Likewise it was Janis Joplin with her band, Big Brother And The Holding Company, who grabbed the audience's imagination with her orgasmic and electrifying performance, as did a quasi-live album by the Mama And Papas. Otis Redding's accomplishment was memorable in that he brought together black soul and white rock music and became accepted by a predominantly white pop audience. His thrilling and frantic performance broke down all barriers, even although he wore a conservative blue suit instead of the regulation kaftan, beads and flowers. The first major pop music revolution since the Beatles was born at Monterey.

Among other artists who paraded their music at the festival were the Grateful Dead, Electric Flag (featuring the brilliant young Mike Bloomfield), Canned Heat, Buffalo Springfield, the Byrds, the Mamas And The Papas, Eric Burdon And The Animals, Hugh Masekela, Jefferson Airplane, Ravi Shankar, Booker T. And The MGs, the Who, Moby Grape, the Steve Miller Band, Country Joe And The Fish, Simon And Garfunkel, Beverly (Martyn), the Paupers, Lou Rawls, the Association, Johnny Rivers, Quicksilver Messenger Service, Laura Nyro, and the Blues Project. D.A. Pennebaker's 80 minute film *Monterey Pop* captured the event. No official album was ever released although a Jimi Hendrix/Otis Redding album included highlights of their performance. However, the show was broadcast on radio almost in its entirety in 1989 and further extracts from the festival have since been issued on CD.
●ALBUMS: *Monterey International Pop Festival* 4-CD box set (Castle 1992)★★★.

MONTEZ, CHRIS

b. Christopher Montanez, 17 January 1943, Los Angeles, California, USA. Teenage vocalist Montez was discovered by impresario Jim Lee in 1961, and having joined the latter's Monogram label, enjoyed an international hit the following year with 'Let's Dance'. This exciting, Lee-penned single, redolent of the Hispanic 'latino-rock' style of Ritchie Valens sold over one million copies and climbed to number 2 in the UK. A follow-up, 'Some Kinda Fun', reached the UK Top 10 in 1963, but a three-year hiatus ensued before the singer resurfaced on A&M in the US with a version of the much-covered 'Call Me'. The charmingly simple 'The More I See You' gave Montez a second UK Top 3 entry, while minor US successes followed with 'There Will Never Be Another You' and 'Time After Time'. Re-released in the UK in 1972, 'Let's Dance' confirmed its timeless appeal by reaching the UK Top 10.
●ALBUMS: *Let's Dance And Have Some Kinda Fun!!!* (Monogram 1963)★★★, *The More I See You/Call Me* (A&M 1966)★★★, *Time After Time* (Pye 1966)★★★, *Foolin' Around* (A&M 1967)★★, *Watch What Happens* (A&M 1968)★★.

MONTGOMERY, MARIAN

b. 17 November 1934, Natchez, Mississippi, USA. Montgomery quit school to sing on television in Atlanta, Georgia. After working in advertising and publishing, performing in plays and singing in strip joints and jazz clubs, she became an established cabaret performer. She moved to the UK in 1965 to sing at a new London club, the Cool Elephant, with the John Dankworth Band. That same year she married composer and musical director Laurie Holloway. Possessing a voice which has been likened to 'having a long, cool glass of mint julep on a Savannah balcony', she expanded her career with a starring role in the 1969 West End revival of *Anything Goes*, and frequent appearances on radio and television, as well as concerts and cabaret in the UK and abroad. Her one-woman show was televised by the BBC in 1975. Besides her musical association with Holloway, she successfully collaborated with classical composer/pianist Richard Rodney Bennett on several projects, including *Puttin' On The Ritz*, *Surprise Surprise* and *Town And Country*. With an instantly recognizable, relaxed and intimate

style, she has become one of a handful of American artists to take up permanent residence in the UK.
●ALBUMS: *Swings For Winners And Losers* (Capitol 1963)★★★, *Let There Be Marian Montgomery* (Capitol 1963)★★★, *What's New* (Decca 1965)★★★, *Lovin' Is Livin'* (1965)★★★, *Marian Montgomery On Stage* (1979)★★★, with Richard Rodney Bennett *Town And Country* (1978)★★★, with Bennett *Surprise Surprise* (1981)★★★, with Bennett *Puttin' On The Ritz* (1984)★★★, *I Gotta Right To Sing* (1988)★★★, *Sometimes In The Night* (1989)★★★, *Nice And Easy* (1989)★★★.

MONTGOMERY, WES

b. John Leslie Montgomery, 6 March 1923, Indianapolis, Indiana, USA, d. 15 June 1968. Montgomery was inspired to take up the guitar after hearing records by Charlie Christian. Nearly 20 years old at the time, he taught himself to play by adapting what he heard on records to what he could accomplish himself. Guided in part by Christian's example, but also by the need to find a way of playing which did not alienate his neighbours, he evolved a uniquely quiet style. Using the soft part of his thumb instead of a plectrum or the fingers, and playing the melody line simultaneously in two registers, Montgomery was already a distinctive stylist by the time he began to work with local bands. In 1948 he joined Lionel Hampton, touring and recording. In the early 50s he returned to Indianapolis and began playing with his brothers Buddy and Monk Montgomery in the Montgomery-Johnson Quintet (the other members being Alonzo and Robert Johnson). During an after-hours session at a local club, the visiting Cannonball Adderley asked him if he would like a record date. On Adderley's recommendation, Montgomery was recorded by Riverside in a series of trio albums which featured artists such as Hank Jones and Ron Carter. These albums attracted considerable attention and Montgomery quickly became one of the most talked about and respected guitarists in jazz. In the early 60s he worked with his brothers in Northern California and also played with John Coltrane. Further recordings, this time with a large string orchestra, broadened Montgomery's horizons and appealed to the non-jazz public. However, despite such commercially successful albums as *Movin' Wes*, *Bumpin'*, *Goin' Out Of My Head* and *A Day In The Life*, he continued to play jazz in small groups with his brothers and with Wynton Kelly, Herb Alpert, Harold Mabern and others. In 1965 he visited Europe, playing club and festival dates in England, Spain and elsewhere. An outstanding guitarist with an enormous influence upon his contemporaries and countless successors, Montgomery's highly personal style was developed deliberately from Christian, and unwittingly shadowed earlier conceptions by musicians such as Django Reinhardt. In Montgomery's case he stumbled upon these methods not with deliberate intent but through what jazz writer Alun Morgan has described as 'a combination of naïvety and good neighbourliness'.

●ALBUMS: *New Concepts In Jazz Guitar* (Riverside 1959)★★★★, *Far Wes* (1958-59)★★★★, *The Wes Montgomery Trio/A Dynamic New Sound* (Riverside 1959)★★★, *Movin' Along* (Riverside 1960)★★★★, *The Incredible Jazz Guitar Of Wes Montgomery* (Riverside 1960)★★★★, *So Much Guitar* (Riverside 1961)★★★, *Far Wes* (Pacific 1961)★★★, *Full House* (Riverside 1962)★★★, *Fusion* (Riverside 1963)★★★, *Portrait Of Wes* (Riverside 1963)★★★, *The Alternative Wes Montgomery* (Milestone 1960-63 recordings)★★★, *Boss Guitar* (Riverside 1963)★★★★, *Guitar On The Go* (Riverside 1965)★★★, *Goin' Out Of My Head* (Verve 1965)★★★, *Bumpin'* (Verve 1965)★★★, *'Round Midnight* (1965)★★★, *Straight No Chaser* (1965)★★★, *Movin' Wes* (Verve 1965)★★★, *Live In Paris* (1965)★★★, *Smokin' At The Half Note* (1965)★★★, *Tequila* (Verve 1966)★★★, *California Dreaming* (Verve 1966)★★★, *Easy Groove* (Pacific Jazz 1966)★★★, *In The Wee Small Hours* (Riverside 1967)★★★, *A Day In The Life* (A&M 1967)★★★, *Road Song* (1968)★★★, *Kismet* (Pacific Jazz 1968)★★★, *Down Here On The Ground* (A&M 1968)★★★, *Willow Weep For Me* (Verve 1969)★★★, *Eulogy* (Verve 1969)★★★, *Mood I'm In* (Sunset 1969).
●COMPILATIONS: *The Best Of Wes Montgomery* (Verve 1967)★★★★, *March 6 1925-June 15 1968* (Riverside 1968)★★★★, *Portrait* (Pacific Jazz 1968)★★★★, *Panorama* (Riverside 1969)★★★★, *The Best Of Wes Montgomery Vol. 2* (Verve 1969)★★★★, *The Silver Collection* (Polygram 1984)★★★★, *Wes Montgomery Plays The Blues* (Verve 1988)★★★, *Verve Jazz Masters Wes Montgomery* (Verve 1990)★★★★, *Classics* (A&M 1991)★★★.
●FURTHER READING: *Wes Montgomery*, Adrian Ingram.

MOODY BLUES

The lengthy career of the Moody Blues has come in two distinct phases. The first from 1963-67, when they were a tough R&B-influenced unit, and the second from 1967 to the present, where they are now regarded as rock dinosaurs performing a blend of melodic pop utilizing symphonic themes that has been given many labels, among them pomp-rock, classical-rock and art-rock. The original band was formed in 1964 by Denny Laine (b. Brian Hines, 29 October 1944, Jersey; vocals, harmonica, guitar), Mike Pinder (b. 12 December 1942, Birmingham, England; piano, keyboards), Ray Thomas (b. 29 December 1942, Stourport on Severn, England; flute, vocals, harmonica), Graeme Edge (b. 30 March 1941, Rochester, Staffordshire, England; drums) and Clint Warwick (b. 25 June 1940, Birmingham, England; bass). During their formative months they established a strong London club following, and soon received their big break, as so many others did, performing live on the influential UK television show *Ready Steady Go*. A few months later their Bessie Banks cover, 'Go Now', topped the UK charts, complete with its striking piano introduction and solo. Although the single made the US Top 10, their commercial fortunes were on an immediate decline, although their following releases were impeccable.

Their excellent debut *The Magnificent Moodies* was a mature effort combining traditional white R&B standards with originals. In addition to 'Go Now' they tackled James Brown's 'I'll Go Crazy' and delivered a frenetic version of Sonny Boy Williamson's 'Bye Bye Bird'. Laine and Pinder contributed among others 'Stop' and 'Let Me Go'. Warwick and Laine departed in 1966 to be replaced by Justin Hayward (b. 14 October 1946, Swindon, Wiltshire, England) and John Lodge (b. 20 July 1945, Birmingham, England). So began phase two, which debuted with Hayward's classic, 'Nights In White Satin'. The accompanying *Days Of Future Passed* was an ambitious orchestral project with Peter Knight conducting the London Festival Orchestra and Tony Clark producing. The album was a massive success and started a run that continued through a further five albums, all involving Knight and Clark. The increased use of the mellotron gave an orchestrated feel to much of their work, and while they became phenomenally popular, they also received a great deal of criticism. During this period they founded Threshold Records, their own record label based from their home territory in Cobham, Surrey. In 1973 they reached the UK Top 10 with a re-entry for 'Nights In White Satin'. (A further reissue made it a hit again in 1979).

The band parted company in 1974 to allow each member to indulge in spin-off projects. Hayward and Lodge became the Blue Jays, with great success, Thomas released *From Mighty Oaks* and Edge teamed with Adrian Gurvitz for *Kick Off Your Muddy Boots*. The group reunited for *Octave*, which became another huge hit, although shortly after its release Pinder decided to quit the business; he had been the only band member not to release a solo project. Further discontent ensued when Clark resigned. Patrick Moraz from Yes and Refugee joined the band as Hayward's 'Forever Autumn' hit the charts. This track was taken from the Jeff Wayne epic, *The War Of The Worlds*. Each subsequent release has met with predictable glory both in Europe and America. The Moodies march on with the comforting knowledge that they have the ability to fill concert halls and continue with a back catalogue that will sell until the days of future have passed.

●ALBUMS: *The Magnificent Moodies* (Decca 1965)★★★★, *Days Of Future Past* (Deram 1967)★★★★, *In Search Of The Lost Chord* (Deram 1968)★★★★, *On The Threshold Of A Dream* (Deram 1969)★★★, *To Our Children's Children* (Threshold 1969)★★★★, *A Question Of Balance* (Threshold 1970)★★★, *Every Good Boy Deserves Favour* (Threshold 1971)★★★, *Seventh Sojourn* (Threshold 1972)★★★, *Caught Live + 5* (1977)★★★, *Octave* (Threshold 1978)★★★, *Long Distance Voyager* (Threshold 1981)★★★★, *The Present* (1983)★★, *The Other Side Of Life* (Polydor 1986)★★, *Sur La Mer* (1988)★★, *Keys Of The Kingdom* (Polydor 1991)★★, *A Night At Red Rocks With The Colorado Symphony Orchestra* (Polydor/Threshold 1993)★★★. Solo: Justin

Hayward *Songwriter* (1977), *Night Flight* (1980), *Moving Mountains* (1985), with John Lodge *Blue Jays* (1975)★★★, *Night Flight* (1980)★★, *Moving Mountains* (Towerbell 1985)★★, with Mike Batt *Classic Blue* (1985)★★. Ray Thomas *From Mighty Oaks* (1975)★★★, *Hope Wishes And Dreams* (1976)★★. Mike Pinder *The Promise* (1976)★★, *Among The Stars* (One Step 1995)★★. John Lodge *Natural Avenue* (1977)★★. Graeme Edge Band *Kick Off Your Muddy Boots* (1975)★★, *Paradise Ballroom* (1977)★★.

●COMPILATIONS: *This Is The Moody Blues* (1974)★★★, *Out Of This World* (1979)★★★, *Voices In The Sky - The Best Of The Moody Blues* (1985)★★★, *Greatest Hits* (1989)★★★★, *Time Traveller* 5-CD set (Polydor 1994)★★★★, *The Very Best Of* (Polygram 1996)★★★.

●VIDEOS: *Cover Story* (1990), *Star Portrait* (1991), *Legend Of A Band* (1991), *Live At Red Rocks* (1993).

MOORE, DUDLEY

b. 19 April 1935, Dagenham, Essex, England. Although severely hampered by having a deformed foot and spending a great deal of his time in hospital as a child, this did not deter Moore from becoming passionately interested in music from an early age. The young Dudley played piano in a local youth club and organ at his church. He wore an old brown boot strapped over his normal shoe to give his bad foot extra length to touch the pedals easily. As a young teenager Moore played semi-professionally in various jazz clubs. He studied music at Oxford University, graduating in the late 50s and thereafter playing with Vic Lewis. Early in the following decade he worked with John Dankworth before forming his own trio with Pete McGurk (bass) and Chris Karan (drums). For a while he successfully performed jazz while concurrently appearing in *Beyond The Fringe* in London and New York. During this time he forged a partnership with comedian Peter Cook. With the trio, he also made records and appeared on television with the seminal *Not Only But Also* (with Cook). By the mid-60s Moore's acting career had begun to take precedence over his jazz work and he later moved to Hollywood. His musical interests continued with the writing of scores for feature films including *The Wrong Box* (1966), *30 Is A Dangerous Age Cynthia* (1967), *Inadmissible Evidence* (1968), *Bedazzled* (1968) and *Staircase* (1969), and also for stage shows, plays and the ballet. His own acting career took off to such an extent that 'Cuddly Dudley' became a huge Hollywood star in such films as *10* (1979), *Wholly Moses* (1980), *Arthur* (1981), *Six Weeks* (1982), *Lovesick* (1983), *Best Defence* (1984), *Micki And Maude* (1984) and *Santa Claus* (1985). Additionally, he made three hilarious albums with Cook of pure filth and bad language as Derek And Clive. Moore has cited Erroll Garner and Oscar Peterson as two of his main influences. His jazz playing is notable for its lightness of touch and deft right-hand filigrees although his eclecticism, allied to his absorption with other interests, has inhibited the development of a truly identifiable personal style. In recent years, having seemingly achieved everything as a 'movie star' Moore has returned to recording and performing, and has resurrected the definitive Dudley Moore Trio. In a revealing biography published in 1997 Moore disclosed a troubled soul who has seemingly succeeded at everything, but remains deeply unfulfilled. Leaving behind him a trail of broken marriages and a number of critically slammed films during the 80s and 90s, Moore has always returned to music in times of stress. His brilliance as both jazz and classical pianist has been constantly undermined by his personal life.

●ALBUMS: *Beyond The Fringe* (Parlophone 1961)★★★, *Theme From Beyond The Fringe And All That Jazz* (Atlantic 1962)★★★, *Beyond The Fringe; Original Broadway Cast* (Capitol 1962)★★★, *The Other Side Of The Dudley Moore Trio* (Decca 1965)★★★★, *Genuine Dud* (Decca 1966)★★★★, *Bedazzled* soundtrack (Decca 1968)★★★, *The Dudley Moore Trio* (Decca 1968)★★★★, *The Music Of Dudley Moore* (Decca 1969)★★★, *Today With the Dudley Moore Trio* (Atlantic 1971)★★★, *Dudley Moore At The Wavendon Festival* (Black Lion 1976)★★★, *The Dudley Moore Trio* (Warners 1978)★★★, *Dudley Down Under* (1978)★★★, *Smilin' Through* (Finesse 1982)★★★, *Orchestra* (Decca 1991)★★★, *Songs Without Words* (GRP 1991)★★★, *Concerto!* (RCA Victor 1992)★★★, *Grieg Piano Concerto In A Minor* (EMI 1995)★★★.

●FURTHER READING: *Dudley*, Paul Donovan. *Off Beat: Dudley Moore's Book Of Musical Anecdotes*, Dudley Moore. *Dudley Moore: The Authorized Biography*, Barbara Paskin.

MORGAN, LEE

b. 10 July 1938, Philadelphia, Pennsylvania, USA, d. 19 February 1972. Prodigiously talented, Morgan played trumpet professionally at the age of 15 and three years later joined Dizzy Gillespie's big band. During this same period he recorded with John Coltrane, Hank Mobley and others. In 1958 the Gillespie band folded and Morgan joined Art Blakey's Jazz Messengers where he made a tremendous impact not only nationally but around the world, thanks to the group's recordings. In the early 60s Morgan returned to his home town, where he played in comparative obscurity, but by 1963 he was back in New York, leading his own groups and also working for a while with Blakey in 1964. Morgan's popularity was enhanced by the success of a recording of his own composition, the irresistibly catchy 'The Sidewinder' which helped to spark a jazz/funk mini-boom and has remained a dance floor favourite ever since. Morgan's trumpet style was marked by his full-blooded vitality aided by the richness of his tone. Playing with the strictly-controlled Blakey band impacted his natural enthusiasm and the resulting tensions created some of the best hard-bop trumpet playing of the period. Indeed, despite the passage of time and the many fine trumpeters to have entered jazz in his wake, only a handful have attained Morgan's remarkable standards of emotional virtuosity. In the late 60s,

Morgan's career was damaged for a while by personal problems, but a female friend helped him recover. Unfortunately, this same woman became jealous of a new relationship he had formed and on 19 February 1972 she shot and killed him at the New York nightclub, where his quintet were performing.

●ALBUMS: *Introducing Lee Morgan* (Savoy 1956)★★★, *Lee Morgan Indeed* (Blue Note 1956)★★★, *Lee Morgan Vol. 2* (Blue Note 1957)★★★, with Hank Mobley *Hank's Shout* (1956)★★★★, *City Lights* (Blue Note 1957)★★★, *Lee Morgan Vol. 3* (Blue Note 1957)★★★, with John Coltrane *Blue Train* (1957)★★★★, *The Cooker* (Blue Note 1958)★★★★, *Peckin' Time* (1958)★★★, *Candy* (Blue Note 1959)★★★, with Thad Jones *Minor Strain* (1960)★★★, *Lee-Way* (Blue Note 1960)★★★, *Heres Lee Morgan* (Vee Jay 1960)★★★, *Expoobident* (Vee Jay 1960)★★★, *Indestructible Lee* (Affinity 1960)★★★, with Art Blakey *The Freedom Rider* (1961)★★★, *Take Twelve* (Jazzland 1962)★★★, *The Sidewinder* (Blue Note 1963)★★★★★, *Search For The New Land* (Blue Note 1964)★★★, *Tom Cat* (Blue Note 1964)★★★, *Cornbread* (Blue Note 1965)★★★★, *The Rumproller* (Blue Note 1965)★★★★, *Lee Morgan Quintet* (Vee Jay 1965), *Infinity* (1965)★★★★, with Mobley *Dippin'* (1965)★★★, *The Cat* (1965)★★★, *Delightfulee Morgan* (Blue Note 1966)★★★, *Charisma* (Blue Note 1966)★★★, *The Rajah* (Blue Note 1966)★★★, *The Procrastinator* (1967)★★★, *Caramba* (1968)★★★, *The Sixth Sense* (Blue Note 1969), *Live At The Lighthouse* (Fresh Sound 1970)★★★, *Capra Beach* (1971)★★★, *We Remember You* (Fresh Sound 1972)★★★.

MOTHER EARTH (60s)

Formed in Texas in 1966, Mother Earth was one of several American groups to move to the more liberal San Francisco during the west coast beat boom of the late 60s. The original line-up featured three former members of the Wigs, John 'Toad' Andrews (guitar), Bob Arthur (bass) and George Rains (drums), as well as songwriter R. Powell St. John, who composed several songs for the 13th Floor Elevators. Blues singer Tracy Nelson (b. 27 December 1944, Madison, Wisconsin, USA), was Mother Earth's featured vocalist, while the group was latterly augmented by Mark Naftalin (keyboards) and Martin Fierro (horns). The ensemble made its tentative debut on the soundtrack of the film *Revolution*, before completing a promising debut album in 1968. Nelson's powerful voice enhanced its blues-based foundation, while admirable cameos from guitarist Mike Bloomfield and fiddler Spencer Perkin. The following year Mother Earth moved to a farm on the outskirts of Nashville. Their music became increasingly country-orientated and by the release of a fourth album, *Satisfied*, only Nelson and Andrews remained from the group's first release. In 1973 they took the name Tracy Nelson/Mother Earth, but the group was dissolved when the singer's self-titled solo album won critical and commercial plaudits.

●ALBUMS: *Living With The Animals* (Mercury 1968)★★★, *Make A Joyful Noise* (Mercury 1969)★★★, *Presents Tracy Nelson Country* (Mercury 1969)★★, *Satisfied* (Mercury 1970)★★, *Bring Me Home* (Reprise 1971)★★, *Mother Earth* (1972)★★, *Poor Man's Paradise* (1973)★★★.

MOTHERS OF INVENTION

This celebrated group was formed in 1965 when guitarist Frank Zappa (b. 21 December 1940, Baltimore, Maryland, USA, d. 4 December 1993) replaced Ray Hunt in the Soul Giants, a struggling R&B-based bar band. Ray Collins (vocals), Dave Coronado (saxophone), Roy Estrada (bass) and Jimmy Carl Black (drums) completed their early line-up, but Coronado abandoned the group when the newcomer unveiled his musical strategy. Now renamed the Mothers, the quartet was relocated from Orange County to Los Angeles where they were briefly augmented by several individuals, including Alice Stuart, James Guercio and Henry Vestine, later guitarist in Canned Heat. These temporary additions found Zappa's vision daunting as the Mothers embarked on a disarming mélange of 50s pop, Chicago R&B and *avant garde* music. They were embraced by the city's nascent Underground before an appearance at the famed Whiskey A Go-Go resulted in a recording deal when producer Tom Wilson caught the end of one of their sets.

Now dubbed the Mothers Of Invention, owing to pressure from the record company, the group added guitarist Elliott Ingber (Winged Eel Fingerling) before commencing *Freak Out*, rock music's first double album. This revolutionary set featured several exceptional pieces including 'Trouble Every Day', 'Hungry Freaks, Daddy' and 'The Return Of The Son Of Monster Magnet', each of which showed different facets of Zappa's evolving tableau. The Mothers second album, *Absolutely Free*, featured a radically reshaped line-up. Ingber was fired at the end of 1966 while Zappa added a second drummer, Billy Mundi, plus Don Preston (b. 21 September 1932; keyboards), Bunk Gardner (horns) and Jim 'Motorhead' Sherwood (saxophone) to the original group nucleus. A six-month residency at New York's Garrick Theater combined spirited interplay with excellent material and the set showed growing confidence. Satire flourished on 'Plastic People', 'America Drinks & Goes Home' and 'Brown Shoes Don't Make It', much of which was inspired by the 'cocktail-bar' drudgery the group suffered in its earliest incarnation. However, Zappa's ire was more fully flexed on *We're Only In It For The Money*, which featured several barbed attacks on the trappings of 'flower-power'. Housed in a sleeve which cleverly mocked the Beatles' *Sgt. Pepper's Lonely Hearts Club Band*, the set included 'The Idiot Bastard Son' ('The father's a Nazi in Congress today, the mother's a hooker somewhere in LA') and 'Who Needs The Peace Corps' ('I'll stay a week and get the crabs and take a bus back home') and indicated Zappa's growing fascination with technology. The album also introduced new member Ian Underwood (saxophone/keyboards), who became an integral part of the group's future work. *Cruising With Ruben And The Jets* was, to quote the liner notes, 'an album of greasy love songs and cretin simplicity'. Despite such cynicism, the group displayed an obvious affection for the 50s doo-wop material on offer, all of which was self-penned and included re-recordings of three songs, 'How Could I Be Such A Fool', 'Any Way The Wind Blows' and 'You Didn't Try To Call Me', first aired on *Freak Out*. However, the album was the last wholly new set committed by the 'original' line-up. Later releases, *Uncle Meat* (a soundtrack to the then unmade film), *Burnt Weeny Sandwich* and *Weasels Ripped My Flesh*, were all compiled from existing live and studio tapes as tension within the group pulled it apart. The musicians enjoyed mixed fortunes; Estrada joined newcomer Lowell George in Little Feat, third drummer Arthur Dyre Tripp III switched allegiance to Captain Beefheart, while Jimmy Carl Black formed Geronimo Black with brothers Buzz and Bunk Gardner.

A new Mothers was formed in 1970 from the musicians contributing to Zappa's third solo album, *Chunga's Revenge*, and the scatalogical 'on the road' documentary, *200 Motels*. Three former Turtles, Mark Volman, Howard Kaylan (both vocals) and Jim Pons (bass) joined Aynsley Dunbar (drums) and long-standing affiliates Ian Underwood and Don Preston in the group responsible for *Fillmore East - June 1971*. Here, however, the early potpourri of Stravinsky, John Coltrane, doo-wop and 'Louie Louie' gave way to condescending innuendo as Zappa threatened to become the person once the subject of his ire. Paradoxically, it became the group's best-selling album to date, setting the tone for future releases and reinforcing the guitarist's jaundiced view of his audience. This period was brought to a sudden end at London's Rainbow Theatre. A 'jealous' member of the audience attacked the hapless Zappa onstage, pushing him into the orchestra pit where he sustained multiple back injuries and a compound leg fracture. His slow recuperation was undermined when the entire new Mothers, bar Underwood, quit *en masse* to form what became known as Flo And Eddie. Confined to the studio, Zappa compiled *Just Another Band From L.A.* and used the Mothers epithet for the jazz big band on *The Grand Wazoo*. Reverting to rock music, the Mothers' name was re-established with a new, tighter line-up in 1973. However subsequent albums, *Over-Nite Sensation*, *Roxy And Elsewhere* and *One Size Fits All*, are indistinguishable from projects bearing Zappa's name and this now superfluous title was abandoned in 1975, following the release *Bongo Fury*, a collaboration with Captain Beefheart. Since Zappa's death a number of biographies have appeared; Neil Slaven's Electric Don Quixote is particularly noteworthy. Zappa's entire catalogue has been expertly remastered and reissued with the advent of the compact disc. Rykodisk are to be congratulated for their programme, having purchased the whole work from Gail Zappa for a large undisclosed sum. The quality of those early Mothers Of Invention recordings are by today's standards quite outstanding.

●ALBUMS: *Freak Out* (Verve 1966)★★★★★,

Absolutely Free (Verve 1967)★★★★, *We're Only In It For The Money* (Verve 1968)★★★★, *Cruising With Ruben And The Jets* (Verve 1968)★★★, *Uncle Meat* (Bizarre 1969)★★★, *Burnt Weeny Sandwich* (Bizarre 1969)★★★, *Weasels Ripped My Flesh* (Bizarre 1970)★★★, *Fillmore East - June 1971* (1971)★★★, *200 Motels* (United Artists 1971)★★, *Just Another Band From L.A.* (Bizarre 1972)★★★, *The Grand Wazoo* (Bizarre 1972)★★★, *Over-Nite Sensation* (DiscReet 1973)★★★, *Roxy And Elsewhere* (Ryko 1974)★★★, *One Size Fits All* (Ryko 1975)★★★, with Captain Beefheart *Bongo Fury* (Ryko 1975)★★★.
●COMPILATIONS: *Mothermania* (Verve 1969)★★★★, *The Worst Of The Mothers* (MGM 1971)★★★.
●FURTHER READING: *Electric Don Quixote: The Story Of Frank Zappa*, Neil Slaven.
●FILMS: *200 Motels* (1970).

MOTOR TOWN REVUE

The celebrated Motor Town Revue was instigated by Motown Records founder Berry Gordy as an adjunct to his activities as label boss, manager (through International Talent Management) and publishing (Jobete) of his many talented artists. Indeed, some have suggested that this was an attempt to bring every aspect of their performance under his personal remit. The idea for the revue came as a result of discussions between Gordy, Thomas 'Bean' Bowles and Esther Gordy Edwards. The first show was scheduled for 2 November 1962 at the Boston Arena, before sweeping across the USA mainland playing 19 further major cities in 23 days. Promoted by Henry Wynne's Supersonic Attractions, the Motor Town Revue gave the lie to the carefully projected impression of a 'happy family' at Motown. In the touring buses musicians were separated from artists. With musicians at the back and artists at the front, the sections of the bus were analogized as 'Broadway' (front) and 'Harlem' (back) by some of the incredulous travellers. Artists including the Supremes, Stevie Wonder, the Temptations, the Marvelettes, Martha And The Vandellas were among those taking part, but they encountered significant resistance when they travelled through America's Deep South. The artists found themselves playing in the firmament of the civil rights movement, and they were often refused entry to 'white only' restaurants as they travelled. Bowles' task as road manager became increasingly frenetic, and on Thanksgiving Day 1962 he was seriously injured in a car crash that killed driver Ed McFarland Jnr. Luckily, the tour proceeds he was carrying, some $12,000, still found its way back to Motown headquarters. With Bowles confined to hospital, it then looked likely that the tour would collapse, but Esther Gordy Edwards immediately took over his responsibilities to stabilise the situation. The tour finally finished in triumph with 11 dates at Harlem's Apollo Theatre. Motown learned the lessons of the tour well, making sure that subsequent revues were better orchestrated and regulated, and that the artists concerned were tightly disciplined on stage. A UK Motor Town Revue of 1965 (with Georgie Fame as

special 'guest star') also proved problematic, although it too was a relative success and helped to develop a major international fan base for Motown's galaxy of stars.

MOTOWN RECORDS

The history of Motown Records remains a paradigm of success for independent record labels, and for black-owned industry in the USA. The corporation was formed in 1959 by Berry Gordy, a successful R&B songwriter who required an outlet for his initial forays into production. He used an $800 loan to finance the release of singles by Marv Johnson and Eddie Holland on his Tamla label, one of a series of individual trademarks that he eventually included under the Motown umbrella. Enjoying limited local success, Gordy widened his roster, signing acts like the Temptations and Marvelettes in 1960. That year, the Miracles' 'Shop Around' gave the company its first major US. hit, followed in 1961 by their first number 1, the Marvelettes' 'Please Mr Postman'. Gordy coined the phrase 'The Sound Of Young America' to describe Motown's output, and the apparent arrogance of his claim quickly proved well founded. By 1964, Motown were enjoying regular hits via the Supremes and the Four Tops, while Mary Wells' 'My Guy' helped the label become established outside the USA. The label's vibrant brand of soul music, marked by a pounding rhythm and a lightness of touch which appealed to both pop and R&B fans, provided America's strongest response to the massive impact of the British beat group invasion in 1964 and 1965. At the same time, Gordy realized the importance of widening his commercial bases; in 1965, he overtly wooed the middle-of-the-road audience by giving the Supremes a residency at the plush Copa nightclub in New York - the first of many such ventures into traditional showbiz territory. The distance between Motown's original fans and their new surroundings led to accusations that the company had betrayed its black heritage, although consistent chart success helped cushion the blow.

In 1966, Motown took three steps to widen its empire, snapping up groups like the Isley Brothers and Gladys Knight And The Pips from rival labels, opening a Hollywood office to double its promotional capabilities, and snuffing out its strongest opposition in Detroit by buying the Golden World and Ric-Tic group of R&B companies. Throughout these years, Gordy maintained a vice-like grip over Motown's affairs; even the most successful staff writers and producers had to submit their work to a weekly quality control meeting, and faced the threat of having their latest creations summarily rejected. Gradually dissent rose within the ranks, and in 1967 Gordy lost the services of his A&R controller, Mickey Stevenson, and his premier writing/production team, Holland/Dozier/Holland. Two years of comparative failure followed before Motown regained its supremacy in the pop market by launching the career of the phenomenally successful Jackson Five in 1969. Gordy made a bold but ultimately unsuccessful attempt to break into the rock market in 1970, with his Rare Earth label, one of a variety of spin-off companies launched in the early part of the decade. This was a period of some uncertainty for the company: several major acts either split up or chose to seek artistic freedom elsewhere, and the decision to concentrate the company's activities in its California office in 1973 represented a dramatic break from its roots. At the same time, Gordy masterminded the birth of Motown's film division, with the award-winning bio-pic about Billie Holiday, *Lady Sings The Blues*. The burgeoning artistic and commercial success of Stevie Wonder kept the record division on course, although outsiders noted a distinct lack of young talent to replace the company's original stalwarts.

The mid-70s proved to be Motown's least successful period for over a decade; only the emergence of the Commodores maintained the label as a contemporary musical force. Motown increasingly relied on the strength of its back catalogue, with only occasional releases, like the Commodores' 'Three Times A Lady' and Smokey Robinson's 'Being With You', rivalling the triumphs of old. The departure of Marvin Gaye and Diana Ross in the early 80s proved a massive psychological blow, as, despite the prominence of Commodores leader Lionel Richie, the company failed to keep pace with the fast-moving developments in black music. From 1986, there were increasing rumours that Berry Gordy was ready to sell the label: these were confirmed in 1988, when Motown was bought by MCA, with Gordy retaining some measure of artistic control over subsequent releases. After more than a decade of disappointing financial returns, Motown remains a record industry legend on the strength of its remarkable hit-making capacities in the 60s. Some realignment was tackled in the 90s by the new label chief Andre Harrell; his brief was to make Motown the leading black music label once again. New releases from Horace Brown, Johnny Gill, the Whitehead Brothers and Queen Latifah started the rebirth.

●COMPILATIONS: *Hitsville USA: The Motown Singles Collection 1959 - 1971* 4-CD box set (Motown 1993)★★★★★.

●VIDEOS: *The Sounds Of Motown* (1985), *The Sixties* (1987), *Time Capsule Of The 70s* (1987), *Motown 25th: Yesterday, Today, Forever* (1988).

MOVE

Formed in late 1965 from the ashes of several Birmingham groups, the original Move comprised Roy Wood (vocals/guitar), Carl Wayne (vocals), Chris 'Ace' Kefford (bass), Trevor Burton (guitar) and Bev Bevan (drums). Under the guidance of Tony Secunda, they moved to London, signed to Decca's hit subsidiary Deram, and rapidly established themselves as one of the most inventive and accomplished pop groups on the live circuit. Their first two hit singles, the classically inspired 'Night Of Fear' and upbeat psychedelic 'I Can Hear The Grass Grow' sounded fresh and abrasive and benefitted from a series of publicity stunts masterminded by Secunda. Like the Who, the Move specialized in 'auto-destruction', smashing television sets and cars onstage

and burning effigies of Adolf Hitler, Ian Smith and Dr Veerwoord. In 1967, they signed to the reactivated Regal Zonophone label which was launched with the fashionably titled 'Flowers In The Rain', the first record played on BBC Radio 1. The mischievous Secunda attempted to promote the disc with a saucy postcard depicting Harold Wilson. The Prime Minister promptly sued for libel, thereby diverting Roy Wood's royalties to charity.

In February 1968, the group returned as strong as ever with the high energy, 50s inspired, 'Fire Brigade'. Soon afterwards, Ace Kefford suffered a nervous breakdown and left the group which continued as a quartet, with Burton switching to bass. The catchy but chaotic 'Wild Tiger Woman' fared less well than expected, as did their bizarrely eclectic EP *Something Else*. Management switches from Tony Secunda to Don Arden and Peter Walsh brought further complications, but the maestro Wood responded well with the evocative 'Blackberry Way', a number 1 in some UK charts. A softening of their once violent image with 'Curly' coincided with Burton's departure and saw Carl Wayne recklessly steering them on to the cabaret circuit. Increasing friction within their ranks culminated in Wayne's departure for a solo career, leaving the Move to carry on as a trio. The heavy rock sound of 'Brontosaurus' and 'When Alice Comes Down To The Farm' supplemented their diverse hit repertoire, and further changes were ahead. The recruitment of Jeff Lynne from the Idle Race encouraged them to experiment with cellos and oboes while simultaneously pursuing their career as an increasingly straightforward pop act. The final flurry of Move hits ('Tonight', 'Chinatown' and 'California Man') were bereft of the old invention, which was henceforth to be discovered in their grand offshoots, the Electric Light Orchestra (ELO) and Wizzard.

●ALBUMS: *The Move* (Regal Zonophone 1968)★★★, *Shazam* (Regal Zonophone 1970)★★★, *Looking On* (Fly 1970)★★★, *Message From The Country* (Harvest 1971)★★★, *California Man* (Harvest 1974)★★★.

●COMPILATIONS: *The Collection* (Castle 1986)★★★, *The Early Years* (Dojo 1992)★★★, *The BBC Sessions* (Band Of Joy 1995)★★.

MUGWUMPS

Formed in New York, USA, in 1964, the Mugwumps consisted of Zalman 'Zally' Yanovsky, Denny Docherty, 'Mama' Cass Elliot and Jim Hendricks. Yanovsky and Docherty were previously members of the Halifax Three while Elliot and Hendricks, at that time husband and wife, worked as a folk duo. The quartet issued two singles, 'I Don't Wanna Know' and 'Searchin'', before breaking up a few months after their formation. Elliot and Docherty were later reunited in the Mamas And The Papas, Hendricks formed the Lamp Of Childhood and Yanovsky joined John Sebastian in the Lovin' Spoonful. *An Historic Recording* shows an act blending folk, rock 'n' roll and British Beat.

●ALBUMS: *An Historic Recording* (Warners 1967)★★.

MULDAUR, GEOFF

b. *c*.1940, Pelham, New York, USA. Muldaur began performing at the folk haunts of Cambridge, Massachusetts, while a student at Boston University. He worked as a soloist at the *Club 47*, as well as becoming a featured member of the Jim Kweskin Jug Band. Muldaur's debut, *Sleepy Man Blues*, boasted support from Dave Van Ronk and Eric Von Schmidt, and offered sterling interpretations of material drawn from country-blues singers Bukka White, Sleepy John Estes and Blind Willie Johnson. Despite this recording, the artist remained with Kweskin until the Jug Band splintered at the end of the 60s. He then completed two albums, *Pottery Pie* (1970) and *Sweet Potatoes* (1972) with his wife, Maria Muldaur, before joining Paul Butterfield's 70s venture, Better Days. The singer resumed his solo career upon the break-up of both the band and his marriage. The Joe Boyd-produced *Geoff Muldaur Is Having A Wonderful Time* showed the artist's unflinching eclecticism, a facet prevailing on all his releases. A longstanding professional relationship with guitarist and fellow Woodstock resident Amos Garrett resulted in *Geoff Muldaur And Amos Garrett*, on which the former's penchant for self-indulgence was pared to a minimum. Despite this trait, Muldaur's entire catalogue is worthy of investigation and deserves respect for its attention to music's ephemera.

●ALBUMS: *Sleepy Man Blues* (Folklore 1963)★★★, *Geoff Muldaur Is Having A Wonderful Time* (1975)★★★, *Motion* (1976)★★, *Geoff Muldaur And Amos Garrett* (1978)★★★, *Blues Boy* (1979)★★★.

MYSTERY TREND

An early but minor group in the San Francisco scene of the 60s, the Mystery Trend took its name after misunderstanding a line in Bob Dylan's 'Like A Rolling Stone' which referred to a 'mystery tramp'. The group consisted of Ron Nagle (vocals), Bob Cuff (guitar), Larry Bennett (bass), Larry West (lead guitar) and John Luby (drums). They performed many concerts in the San Francisco ballrooms of the era, but released only one single, 'Johnny Was A Good Boy'/'A House On The Hill' on Verve, in early 1967, at which time West departed. Cuff left the band in the summer of 1967 and was replaced by John Gregory, who went on to join Seatrain. The Mystery Trend split up in 1968. Nagle recorded a solo album, *Bad Rice*, in 1970 and produced albums by Paul Kantner (of Jefferson Airplane) and John Hiatt. Nagle also formed a unit called Durocs during the 70s.

NASHVILLE TEENS

Formed in Weybridge, Surrey, England, in 1962, the Nashville Teens initially comprised vocalists Arthur 'Art' Sharp (b. 26 May 1941, Woking, Surrey, England) and Ray Phillips (b. Ramon John Phillips, 16 January 1944, Tiger Bay, Cardiff, Wales), Michael Dunford (guitar), John Hawken (b. 9 May 1940, Bournemouth, Dorset, England; piano), Pete Shannon (b. Peter Shannon Harris, 23 August 1941, Antrim, Northern Ireland; bass) and Roger Groom (drums). Dunford and Groom left the line-up the following year and the group was completed by John Allen (b. John Samuel Allen, 23 April, 1945, St. Albans, Hertfordshire, England; guitar), Barrie Jenkins (b. 22 December 1944, Leicester, England; drums) and third vocalist Terry Crow for a protracted tenure in Hamburg, Germany. This period is chronicled on *Jerry Lee Lewis; Live At The Star Club* on which the septet backed the veteran rock 'n' roll star. In 1964, and with Crow now absent, the Teens were aligned with producer Mickie Most for a pounding version of 'Tobacco Road', which deservedly climbed to number 6 in the UK. The similarly-styled 'Google Eye' also proved popular, reaching the Top 10, but a split with Most ended this brief ascendancy. Collaborations with Andrew Loog Oldham ('This Little Bird') and Shel Talmy ('The Hard Way') were minor hits, but at the expense of the unit's undeniable grasp of R&B. Groom rejoined the line-up in 1966 when Jenkins left for the Animals, but despite excellent versions of Randy Newman's 'The Biggest Night Of Her Life' and Bob Dylan's 'All Along The Watchtower', the Nashville Teens were unable to rekindle former success. A spate of defections - John Hawken later found fame with Renaissance - left Phillips the sole remaining original member. He continues to front this act and concurrently performs with the British Invasion All-Stars, which features musicians drawn from the Downliners Sect, Creation and the Pretty Things.

●ALBUMS: *The Nashville Teens* (New World 1975)★★, *Live At The Red House* (1984)★★.
●COMPILATIONS: *The Best Of* (1993)★★★.
●FILMS: *Be My Guest* (1965).

NATURALS

Formed in Harlow, Essex, the Naturals - Ricki Potter (b. 1945, England; vocals), Curt Cresswell (b. 1948, England; lead guitar), Bob O'Neale (b. 1942, England; harmonica), Mike Wakelin (b. 1942, England; bass), Douglas Ellis (b. 1942, England; guitar) and Roy Heather (Hoath) (b. 1947, England; drums) - were originally known as the Blue

Beats and had recorded several singles under this early appellation. The quintet made their debut as the Naturals in 1964, scoring their only hit in the UK singles chart that same year with a version of the Beatles' song, 'I Should Have Known Better'. Suspicions that the song had been the success, rather than the performers, was confirmed when subsequent, inferior singles failed to make an impression.

NEIL, FRED

b. 1937, St. Petersburg, Florida, USA. An important figure in America's folk renaissance, Neil's talent first emerged in 1956 when he co-wrote an early Buddy Holly single, 'Modern Don Juan'. By the following decade he was a fixture of the Greenwich Village circuit, both as a solo act and in partnership with fellow singer Vince Martin. The duo embarked on separate careers following the release of *Tear Down The Walls*. Neil's subsequent solo *Bleecker And MacDougal* was an influential collection and contained the original version of 'The Other Side Of This Life', later covered by the Youngbloods, Lovin' Spoonful and the Jefferson Airplane. The singer's deep, resonant voice was equally effective, inspiring the languid tones of Tim Buckley and Tim Hardin. A reticent individual, Neil waited two years before completing *Fred Neil*, a compulsive selection that featured two of the artist's most famous compositions, 'The Dolphins' and 'Everybody's Talkin''. The latter was adopted as the theme song to *Midnight Cowboy*, a highly-successful film, although it was a version by Harry Nilsson which became the hit single. Such temporary trappings were of little note to Neil, who preferred the anonymity of his secluded Florida base, from where he rarely ventured. An appearance at the Los Angeles club, the Bitter End, provided the material for *The Other Side Of This Life*, Neil's last album to date and an effective resume of his career. This informal performance also contained other favoured material, including 'You Don't Miss Your Water', which featured assistance from country singer Gram Parsons. A major, if self-effacing talent, Fred Neil has virtually withdrawn from music altogether. He refuses to record or be interviewed and rare live appearances are constrained to benefit events for his charity, Dolphin Project, which he established with marine biologist Richard O'Berry in 1970.
● ALBUMS: *Hootenanny Live At The Bitter End* (1964)★★★, *World Of Folk Music* (1964)★★★, with Vince Martin *Tear Down The Walls* (1964)★★★, *Bleecker And MacDougal* aka *Little Bit Of Rain* (Elektra 1965)★★★★, *Fred Neil* aka *Everybody's Talkin'* (Capitol 1966)★★★★, *Sessions* (Capitol 1968)★★★, *The Other Side Of This Life* (1971)★★★.
● COMPILATIONS: *The Very Best Of Fred Neil* (1986)★★★★.

NELSON, RICKY

b. Eric Hilliard Nelson, 8 May 1940, Teaneck, New Jersey, USA, d. 31 December 1985, De Kalb, Texas, USA. Nelson came from a showbusiness family and his parents had sung in bands during the 30s and 40s. They had their own US radio show, *The Adventures Of Ozzie And Harriet*, soon transferred to television, in which Ricky and his brother David appeared. By 1957 Nelson embarked on a recording career, with the million-selling, double-sided 'I'm Walkin''/'A Teenager's Romance'. A third hit soon followed with 'You're My One And Only Love'. A switch from the label Verve to Imperial saw Nelson enjoy further success with the rockabilly 'Be-Bop Baby'. In 1958 Nelson formed a full-time group for live work and recordings, which included James Burton (guitar), James Kirkland (later replaced by Joe Osborn) (bass), Gene Garf (piano) and Richie Frost (drums). Early that year Nelson enjoyed his first transatlantic hit with 'Stood Up' and registered his first US chart topper with 'Poor Little Fool'. His early broadcasting experience was put to useful effect when he starred in the Howard Hawks movie western, *Rio Bravo* (1959), alongside John Wayne and Dean Martin. Nelson's singles continued to chart regularly and it says much for the quality of his work that the b-sides were often as well known as the a-sides. Songs such as 'Believe What You Say', 'Never Be Anyone Else But You', 'It's Late', 'Sweeter Than You', 'Just A Little Too Much' and 'I Wanna Be Loved' showed that Nelson was equally adept at singing ballads and uptempo material. One of his greatest moments as a pop singer occurred in the spring of 1961 when he issued the million-selling 'Travelin' Man' backed with the exuberant Gene Pitney composition 'Hello Mary Lou'. Shortly after the single topped the US charts, Nelson celebrated his 21st birthday and announced that he was changing his performing name from Ricky to Rick.

Several more pop hits followed, most notably 'Young World', 'Teenage Idol', 'It's Up To You', 'String Along' (his first for his new label, Decca), 'Fools Rush In' and 'For You'. With the emergence of the beat boom, Nelson's clean-cut pop was less in demand and in 1966 he switched to country music. His early albums in this vein featured compositions from such artists as Willie Nelson, Glen Campbell, Tim Hardin, Harry Nilsson and Randy Newman.

In 1969 Nelson formed a new outfit the Stone Canyon Band featuring former Poco member Randy Meisner (bass), Allen Kemp (guitar), Tom Brumley (steel guitar) and Pat Shanahan (drums). A version of Bob Dylan's 'She Belongs To Me' brought Nelson back into the US charts and a series of strong, often underrated albums followed. A performance at Madison Square Garden in late 1971 underlined Nelson's difficulties at the time. Although he had recently issued the accomplished *Rick Sings Nelson*, on which he wrote every track, the audience were clearly more interested in hearing his early 60s hits. Nelson responded by composing the sarcastic 'Garden Party', which reaffirmed his determination to go his own way. The single, ironically, went on to sell a million and was his last hit record. After parting with the Stone Canyon Band in 1974, Nelson's recorded output declined, but he continued to tour extensively. On 31 December 1985, a chartered plane carrying him to a concert date in Dallas caught fire and crashed near De Kalb, Texas. Nelson's work deserves a place in rock history as he was one of the few 'good looking kids' from the early 60s who had a strong voice which, coupled with exemplary material, remains durable.

●ALBUMS: with various artists *Teen Time* (Verve 1957)★★, *Ricky* (Imperial 1957)★★, *Ricky Nelson* (Imperial 1958)★★, *Ricky Sings Again* (Imperial 1959)★★, *Songs By Ricky* (Imperial 1959)★★, *More Songs By Ricky* (Imperial 1960)★★, *Rick Is 21* (Imperial 1961)★★, *Album Seven By Rick* (Imperial 1962)★★, *Best Sellers By Rick Nelson* (Imperial 1962)★★, *It's Up To You* (Imperial 1962)★★★, *A Long Vacation* (Imperial 1963)★★, *Million Sellers By Rick Nelson* (Imperial 1963)★★★, *For Your Sweet Love* (1963)★★, *Rick Nelson Sings For You* (Decca 1963)★★★, *Rick Nelson Sings 'For You'* (Decca 1963)★★★, *The Very Thought Of You* (Decca 1964)★★, *Spotlight On Rick* (Decca 1964)★★★, *Best Always* (Decca 1965)★★, *Love And Kisses* (Decca 1965)★★, *Bright Lights And Country Music* (Decca 1966)★★, *On The Flip-Side* film soundtrack (Decca 1966)★, *Country Fever* (Decca 1967)★★, *Another Side Of Rick* (Decca 1968)★★, *Perspective* (Decca 1968)★★, *In Concert* (1970)★★★, *Rick Sings Nelson* (1970)★★★, *Rudy The Fifth* (1971)★★★, *Garden Party* (1972)★★★, *Windfall* (1974)★★, *Intakes* (1977)★★, *Playing To Win* (1981)★★★, *Memphis Sessions* (1985)★★★, *Live 1983-1985* (1988).

●COMPILATIONS: *It's Up To You* (1963)★★★★, *Million Sellers* (1964)★★★★, *The Very Best Of Rick Nelson* (1970)★★★★, *Legendary Masters* (United Artists 1972)★★★★, *The Singles Album 1963-1976* (1977)★★★★, *The Singles Album 1957-63* (1979)★★★★, *Rockin' With Ricky* (1984)★★★★, *String Along With Rick* (1984)★★★, *The Best Of Ricky Nelson* (1985)★★★★, *All My Best* (1985)★★★★, *1969-1976* (Edsel 1995)★★★.

●FURTHER READING: *Ricky Nelson: Idol For A Generation*, Joel Selvin. *The Ricky Nelson Story*, John Stafford and Iain Young. *Ricky Nelson: Teenage Idol, Travelin' Man*, Philip Bashe.

NELSON, SANDY

b. Sander L. Nelson, 1 December 1938, Santa Monica, California, USA. Drummer Nelson began his career as a member of the Kip Tyler Band. Appearances in live rock 'n' roll shows led to his becoming an in-demand session musician, where he joined an *ad hoc* group of young aspirants including Bruce Johnston and Phil Spector. Nelson played on 'To Know Him Is To Love Him', a million-selling single written and produced by the latter for his vocal group, the Teddy Bears. Johnston, meanwhile, assisted the drummer on an early demo of 'Teen Beat', a powerful instrumental which achieved gold status in 1959 on reaching the Top 10 in both the US and UK. Two years later, Nelson secured another gold disc for 'Let There Be Drums', co-composed with Richie Podolor, who became a successful producer with Three Dog Night and

Steppenwolf. The pattern was now set for a bevvy of releases on Imperial, each of which combined a simple guitar melody with Nelson's explosive percussion breaks, a style echoing that of the concurrent surf craze. Its appeal quickly waned and 'Teen Beat '65' (1964) - recorded in the artist's garage studio - was his last chart entry. Guitarists Glen Campbell and Jerry McGee, later of the Ventures, as well as bassist Carol Kaye were among the musicians contributing to his sessions, but these lessened dramatically towards the end of the decade. During the 70s Nelson was featured in one of impresario Richard Nader's *Rock 'N' Roll Revival* shows, but he retired following the disappointing disco-influenced *Bang Bang Rhythm*. Despite being tempted into occasional, informal recordings, Nelson has remained largely inactive in professional music since 1978, although instrumental aficionados still marvel at the drummer's extensive catalogue.

●ALBUMS: *Teen Beat* (Imperial 1960)★★★, *He's A Drummer Boy* aka *Happy Drums* (Imperial 1960)★★★, *Let There Be Drums* (Imperial 1961)★★★, *Drums Are My Beat!* (Imperial 1962)★★★, *Drummin' Up A Storm* (Imperial 1962)★★★, *Golden Hits* (retitled *Sandy Nelson Plays Fats Domino*) (Imperial 1962)★★, *On The Wild Side* aka *Country Style* (Imperial 1962)★★, *Compelling Percussion* aka *And Then There Were Drums* (Imperial/London 1962)★★★, *Teenage House Party* (Imperial 1963)★★★, *The Best Of The Beats* (1963)★★, *Be True To Your School* (1963)★★, *Live! In Las Vegas* (1964)★★, *Teen Beat '65* (1965)★★★, *Drum Discotheque* (1965)★★, *Drums A Go-Go* (1965)★★, *Boss Beat* (1966)★★, *'In' Beat* (1966)★★, *Superdrums* (Liberty 1966)★★, *Beat That #!!&** Drum* (1966)★★, *Cheetah Beat* (1967)★★, *The Beat Goes On* (Liberty 1967)★★, *Souldrums* (Liberty 1968)★★, *Boogaloo Beat* (Liberty 1968)★★, *Rock 'N' Roll Revival* (Liberty 1968)★★, *Golden Pops* (1968)★★, *Rebirth Of The Beat* (1969)★★, *Manhattan Spiritual* (1969)★★, *Groovy!* (Liberty 1969)★★, *Rock Drum Golden Disc* (1972)★★, *Keep On Rockin'* (1972)★★, *Roll Over Beethoven* aka *Hocus Pocus* (1973)★★, *Let The Good Times Rock* (1974)★★, *Bang Bang Rhythm* (1975)★.

●COMPILATIONS: *Beat That Drum* (1963)★★★, *Sandy Nelson Plays* (1963)★★★, *The Very Best Of Sandy Nelson* (1978)★★★, *20 Rock 'N' Roll Hits: Sandy Nelson* (1983)★★★, *King Of Drums: His Greatest Hits* (See For Miles 1995)★★★, *Golden Hits/Best Of The Beats* (See For Miles 1997)★★★.

NEW CHRISTY MINSTRELS

Randy Sparks (b. 29 July 1933, Leavenworth, Kansas, USA), formed this commercialized folk group in 1961. Determined to create a unit that was 'a compromise between the Norman Luboff Choir and the Kingston Trio', he added a popular Oregon quartet, the Fairmount Singers, to his own Randy Sparks Three. A third unit, the Inn Group, which featured Jerry Yester, was absorbed into the line-up, while other Los Angeles-based performers embellished these core acts. Fourteen singers made up the original New Christy Minstrels but although the ensemble was viewed as supplementary to the participants' other careers, interest in the group's debut *Presenting The New Christy Minstrels*, led to it becoming a full-time venture. Most of these early recruits, including the entire Inn Group, abandoned Sparks' creation at this point, creating the need for further, wholesale changes. New recruits, including Barry McGuire, Barry Kane and Larry Ramos, joined the Minstrels whose next release, *In Person*, documented a successful appearance at the famed Troubador club. The following year (1963) the group secured its first hit single with 'Green Green' which established the ensemble as a leading popular attraction. The group, however, remained volatile as members continued to come and go. Gene Clark disbanded his Kansas-based trio, the Surf Riders, in order to join the Minstrels, but left after a matter of months, frustrated at the rather conservative material the ensemble recorded. He later formed the Byrds with (Jim) Roger McGuinn and David Crosby. Randy Sparks ended his relationship with the Minstrels in the summer of 1964. Maligned for creating their MOR image, his departure did not result in the more daring direction several members wished to pursue. McGuire, who was increasingly unhappy with such material as 'Three Wheels On My Wagon' and 'Chim Chim Cheree', left the group after seeing several British groups perform during the Minstrels European tour that year. His gravelly rasp was soon heard on his solo international protest hit, 'Eve Of Destruction'. In 1966 Larry Ramos accepted an invitation to join the Association and although several excellent new vocalists, including Kim Carnes and Kenny Rogers, had been absorbed into the Minstrels, their influential days were over. Longstanding members Mike Settle and Terry Williams left when their new ideas were constantly rejected. They formed the First Edition with the equally ambitious Rodgers, and subsequently enjoyed the kind of success the parent group previously experienced. Although the New Christy Minstrels continued to exist in some form into the 80s, singing early hits, show tunes and standards, their halcyon days ended during the mid-60s.

●ALBUMS: *Presenting The New Christy Minstrels* (1962)★★, *The New Christy Minstrels In Person* (Columbia 1962)★★★, *The New Christy Minstrels Tell Tall Tales, Legends And Nonsense* (Columbia 1963)★★★, *Ramblin' (Featuring Green, Green)* (Columbia 1963)★★★★, *Merry Christmas!* (1963)★★★, *Today* (1964)★★★, *Land Of Giants* (1964)★★★, *The Quiet Side Of The New Christy Minstrels* (1964)★★★, *The New Christy Minstrels Sing And Play Cowboys And Indians* (Columbia 1965)★★★, *The Academy Award Winner - Chim Chim Cheree* (1965)★★, *The Wandering Minstrels* (1965)★★, *In Italy...In Italian* (1966)★★, *New Kick!* (1966)★★, *Christmas With The Christies* (1966)★★, *On Tour Through Motortown* (Columbia 1968)★★, *Big Hits From Chitty Chitty Bang Bang* (1968)★★, *You Need Someone To Love* (1970)★★, *The Great Soap Opera Themes* (1976)★★.

●COMPILATIONS: *Greatest Hits* (Columbia 1966)★★★.

NEW VAUDEVILLE BAND

This parodic ensemble initially comprised studio musicians gathered to record a Geoff Stephens composition, 'Winchester Cathedral', a tale of lost love in deepest Hampshire, England, sung in the style of a Bertie Wooster character complete with megaphone vocals. The need for a permanent line-up arose when in 1966 this contagious single became an international success, to the bizarre extent of winning a Grammy for 'Best Rock And Roll Record'. Having failed to tempt the nascent Bonzo Dog Doo-Dah Band into accepting the role, a group was assembled late in 1966 around Alan Klein aka Tristram, Seventh Earl of Cricklewood (b. 29 June 1942; vocals), Henri Harrison (b. 6 June 1943, Watford, Hertfordshire, England; drums), Stan Haywood (b. 23 August 1947, Dagenham, Essex, England; keyboards), Neil Korner (b. 6 August 1942, Ashford, Kent, England; bass), Mick Wilsher (b. 21 December 1945, Sutton, Surrey, England; guitar), Hugh 'Shuggy' Watts (b. 25 July 1941, Watford, Hertfordshire, England; trombone), Chris Eddy (b. 4 March 1942; bass), and the line-up was completed by Bob Kerr (b. 14 February 1943, London, England; trombone/saxophone), a refugee from the aforementioned Bonzos. The septet continued the 20s style of that debut release and had a second UK Top 10 hit with 'Peek-A-Boo' in 1967. That same year, 'Finchley Central' and 'Green Street Green' also charted in the Top 40, but very soon their novelty appeal waned and the group underwent a gradual process of disintegration while playing out their days on the Las Vegas and English cabaret circuit. Kerr pursued the madcap angle with his new unit, Bob Kerr's Whoopee Band.

●ALBUMS: *Winchester Cathedral* (Fontana 1966)★★★, *Finchley Central* (Fontana 1967)★★.

NEWBEATS

This distinctive pop trio featured falsetto Larry Henley (b. 30 June 1941, Arp, Texas, USA) with brothers Marcus 'Marc' Mathis (b. 9 February 1942; bass) and Lewis 'Dean' Mathis (b. 17 March 1939, Hahira, Georgia, USA). Dean had joined Paul Howard's Western Swing Band in 1956 as a pianist and later moved to Dale Hopkin's Band, with Marc joining shortly afterwards. The Mathis brothers then performed and recorded as Dean And Marc; their version of 'Tell Him No' narrowly missed the US Top 40 in 1959. Henley briefly joined the act before they went their separate ways. After recording as the Brothers on Checker and Argo they also had releases on Check Mate and May before joining Hickory Records, where Henley had been recording fruitlessly as a soloist. Since neither act was successful they decided to record together as the Newbeats. Their first single, 'Bread And Butter', became their biggest hit, shooting to number 2 in the US charts and into the UK Top 20 in 1964. In the USA the shrill-

sounding trio kept the Top 40 hits rolling with 'Everything's Alright' in 1964, 'Break Away (From That Boy)' and 'Run Baby Run' (a belated UK Top 10 hit in 1971), the last two in 1965. After a decade on Hickory the trio went to Buddah Records in 1973 and then in 1974 to Playboy. The trio split up that year, with Henley then recording without chart success for Capricorn and later for Atco and Epic. He then turned his attention to songwriting, and has been very successful since. His best known song was Bette Midler's version of a 1983 country hit 'Wind Beneath My Wings'.
●ALBUMS: *Bread & Butter* (Hickory 1964)★★★, *Big Beat Sounds By The Newbeats* (Hickory 1965)★★, *Run Baby Run* (Hickory 1966)★★.
●COMPILATIONS: *The Best Of* (1992)★★★.

NICE

Originally the back-up band to soul singer P.P. Arnold, the Nice became one of the true originators of what has variously been described as pomp-rock, art-rock and classical-rock. The band comprised Keith Emerson (b. 1 November 1944, Todmorden, Yorkshire, England; keyboards), Brian 'Blinky' Davison (b. 25 May 1942, Leicester, England; drums), Lee Jackson (b. 8 January 1943, Newcastle-Upon-Tyne, England; bass/vocals) and David O'List (b. 13 December 1948, Chiswick, London, England; guitar). After leaving Arnold in October 1967 the Nice quickly built a reputation as one of the most visually exciting bands. Emerson's stage act involved, in true circus style, throwing knives into his Hammond Organ, which would emit outrageous sounds, much to the delight of the audience. Their debut, *The Thoughts Of Emerlist Davjack*, while competent, came nowhere near reproducing their exciting live sound. By the time of the release of its follow-up, *Ars Longa Vita Brevis*, O'List had departed, being unable to compete with Emerson's showmanship and subsequently joined Roxy Music. The album contained their notorious single, 'America', from *West Side Story*. During one performance at London's Royal Albert Hall, they burnt the American flag on stage and were severely lambasted, not only by the Albert Hall authorities, but also by the song's composer, Leonard Bernstein. The band continued their remaining life as a trio, producing their most satisfying and successful work. Both *Nice* and *Five Bridges Suite* narrowly missed the top of the UK charts, although they were unable to break through in the USA. The former contained an excellent reading of Tim Hardin's 'Hang On To A Dream', with exquisite piano from Emerson. The latter was a bold semi-orchestral suite about working-class life in Newcastle-upon-Tyne. One of their other showpieces was an elongated version of Bob Dylan's 'She Belongs To Me'. *Five Bridges* also contained versions of 'Intermezzo From The Karelia Suite' by Sibelius and Tchaikovsky's 'Pathetique'. Their brave attempt at fusing classical music and rock together with the Sinfonia of London was admirable, and much of what Emerson later achieved with the huge success of Emerson, Lake And Palmer should be credited to the brief but valuable career

of the Nice. With Emerson's departure, Jackson floundered with Jackson Heights, while Davison was unsuccessful with his own band, Every Which Way. Jackson and Davison teamed up again in 1974 to form the ill-fated Refugee.
●ALBUMS: *The Thoughts Of Emerlist Davjack* (Immediate 1967)★★★, *Ars Longa Vita Brevis* (Immediate 1968)★★★, *Nice* (Immediate 1969)★★★, *Five Bridges* (Charisma 1970)★★★★, *Elegy* (Charisma 1971)★★.
●COMPILATIONS: *Autumn 76 - Spring 68* (1972)★★★, *20th Anniversary Release* (1987)★★★.

NINA AND FREDERICK

This Danish singing duo was popular in the late 50s and early 60s. Nina Möller had married the wealthy Danish aristocrat Baron Frederik Jan Gustav Floris van Pallandt (b. 14 May 1934, Copenhagen, Denmark, d. 15 May 1994, Puerto Talera, Philippines) in 1954, and teamed up with her husband to record a string of duo hits, including 'Mary's Boy Child' (1959), 'Little Donkey' (1960) and 'Sucu Sucu' (1961). After having three children, they separated in 1969 largely because he wanted to retire and she did not (the marriage was dissolved in 1976). The Baron, a descendant of a Dutch ambassador to Denmark, became a virtual recluse on a farm in Ibiza (briefly purchasing the publishing rights to Burke's Peerage), then Mindoro in the Phillipines. Nina, meanwhile, ventured into cabaret and acting, making her film debut in Robert Altman's *The Long Goodbye* in 1973, co-starring with Elliot Gould. She was later implicated in a minor scandal in the early 70s when she went on holiday with Clifford Irving, the fraudulent biographer of Howard Hughes, who was later jailed. In 1980 she appeared briefly in *American Gigolo*, later adding a second Altman movie to her resume. Although they were divorced in 1976, Nina flew out to the Philippines to bring Frederick's body back to Europe after he became the victim of a 'mysterious professional killing', along with his girlfriend Susannah, in 1994.
●ALBUMS: *Nina And Frederick* i (Pye 1960)★★★, *Nina And Frederick* ii (Pye 1961)★★★, *An Evening With Nina And Frederick At The Royal Albert Hall* (Pye 1966)★★★, *Dawn* (1967)★★★.
●COMPILATIONS: Nina Möller*Golden Hour Presents Nina* (1978)★★.

1910 FRUITGUM COMPANY

The aptly named Fruitgum Company were at the forefront of a brief wave of bubblegum-pop in the late 60s. Bubblegum was a form that offered solid dance beats, infantile lyrics and catchy choruses built around instantly hummable melody lines. The Super K production team of Jeff Katz and Jerry Kasenetz were masters of the form and specialized in studio in-house creations such as the Fruitgum Company. Writer Joey Levine was the voice behind the hits which began with the nursery game anthem 'Simon Says' in 1968 and continued with '1, 2, 3, Red Light', 'Goody Goody Gumdrops', 'Indian Giver' and

'Special Delivery'. A touring troupe headed by Levine was hastily assembled and kept this manufactured group alive until they became expendable at the end of the decade.
●ALBUMS: *Simon Says* (1968)★★, *1, 2, 3, Red Light* (1968)★★, *Indian Giver* (1969)★★, *1910 Fruitgum Company And Ohio Express* (1969)★★★.

NIRVANA (UK)
Songwriters Patrick Campbell-Lyons (b. Dublin, Eire) and George Alex Spyropoulus (b. Athens, Greece) met in La Gioconda, a legendary coffee bar in Denmark Street, London. Prior to that Campbell-Lyons had been a member of the Teenbeats and had covered the familiar territory of seedy clubs in Holland and Germany. Spyropoulus was working at Kassners music publishers, also in Denmark Street. Having established an instant rapport, the duo formed a group, adding Ray Singer (guitar), Brian Henderson (bass), Michael Coe (viola/french horn) and Sylvia Schuster (cello). The quintet, dubbed Nirvana, secured a recording deal with Island Records after impressing producer Jimmy Miller who in turn influenced Chris Blackwell. They made their official debut in 1967, supporting Traffic, Jackie Edwards and Spooky Tooth at the Saville Theatre, London (owned at that time by Brian Epstein). Their exotic debut, *The Story Of Simon Simopath*, was an episodic fairy tale. It emerged in a startlingly colourful cover, featuring a winged child and miniature goddess and centaur, sur-rounded by stars, planets and three-dimensional block typography. A kitsch concept album that billed itself as a 'science-fiction pantomime', the mock libretto told of the hero's journey from a six-dimensional city to a nirvana filled with sirens. Although the songs generally lacked the weight of their epochal singles, there were some charming moments. It contained the haunting 'Pentecost Hotel', a fragile, orchestrated ballad which brought the group critical approval and was a hit in Europe. The clas-sical gentle mood was perfect for the times.

The Alan Bown Set covered the singalong 'We Can Help You', which received considerable airplay, but narrowly failed to chart. Nirvana themselves were plugged by sev-eral discriminating disc jockeys but in spite of the innov-ative qualities of their singles, the group fell tantalizingly short of a major breakthrough. Campbell-Lyons and Spyropoulus then disbanded the group format and com-pleted a second set as a duo. This melodic collection fea-tured several of Nirvana's finest songs, including 'Tiny Goddess' and 'Rainbow Chaser'. The latter was a power-house phased-production, typical of Nirvana's grandiose majesty, and became a minor UK hit in 1968. That same year a strong album followed with *All Of Us,* but soon after the group left Island and their following albums, *Black Flower* and *To Markos III* were considerably low-key. The group's career had already begun to falter when their label rejected *To Markos III*. The selection was placed with an American company which then went into liquidation. Spyropoulus dropped out of the partnership and moved into film work, leaving his colleague with the rights to the Nirvana trademark. Having completed a fourth album, *Local Anaesthetic*, Campbell-Lyons became a producer with the Vertigo label, while recording *Songs Of Love And Praise*, a compendium of new songs and re-recorded Nirvana favourites. This release was the last to bear the group's name. Campbell-Lyons subsequently issued two solo albums before reuniting with Spyropoulus for a projected musical, *Blood*. In the 90s the band are very much a cult item, their original vinyl albums fetch high prices and the CDs have been reissued by Edsel with fascinating sleeve notes from Campbell-Lyons, which are largely drawn from his forthcoming autobiography.
●ALBUMS: *The Story Of Simon Simopath* (Island 1967)★★★, *All Of Us* (Island 1968)★★, *To Markos 3* (Pye 1969)★★, *Local Anaesthetic* (Vertigo 1971)★★★, *Songs Of Love And Praise* (Philips 1972)★★. Solo: Patrick Campbell Lyons *Me And My Friend* (1973)★★, *The Electric Plough* (1981)★★, *The Hero I Might Have Been* (1982)★★.
Compilations *Black Flower* (1987)★★★, *Secret Theatre* (Edsel 1987)★★★, *Orange And Blue* (Demon 1996)★★★.

NYRO, LAURA
b. Laura Nigro, 18 October 1947, The Bronx, New York City, New York, USA, d. 9 April 1997, Danbury, Connecticut, USA. The daughter of an accomplished jazz trumpeter, Nyro was introduced to music at an early age, reputedly completing her first composition when she was only eight years old. Her main influences ranged from Bob Dylan to John Coltrane, but the artist's debut *More Than A New Discovery* (aka *The First Songs*) revealed a talent akin to Brill Building songwriters Carole King and Ellie Greenwich. Nyro's empathy for soul and R&B enhanced her individuality, although she later disowned the set, claiming its stilted arrangements were completed against her wishes. The set nonetheless contained sev-eral songs adapted by other artists, notably 'Stoney End' (Barbra Streisand), 'And When I Die' (Blood, Sweat And Tears) and 'Wedding Bell Blues' (Fifth Dimension). *Eli And The Thirteenth Confession* complied more closely to Nyro's wishes; while containing the highly popular 'Stone Souled Picnic', it revealed the growing sense of introspection that flourished on the following year's *New York Tendaberry*. Here the singer's dramatic intonation, capable of sweeping from a whisper to anguished vibrato within a phrase, emphasized a bare emotional nerve exposed on 'You Don't Love Me When I Cry' and 'Sweet Lovin' Baby'. Her frequent jumps in tempo irked certain critics, but the majority applauded its audacious ambition and peerless fusion of gospel and white soul. The extra-ordinary *Christmas And The Beads Of Sweat*, which included the startling 'Christmas Is My Soul', offered a similar passion while *Gonna Take A Miracle*, a collabo-ration with producers Kenny Gamble and Leon Huff, acknowledged the music which provided much of the artist's inspiration. Backed by the Sigma Sound Studio houseband and singing trio Labelle, Nyro completed enthralling versions of uptown R&B and Motown

favourites. She then retired from music altogether, but re-emerged in 1975 upon the disintegration of her marriage. *Smile* showed the singer's talent had remained intact and included the powerful 'I Am The Blues', while an attendant promotional tour spawned *Season Of Lights*. *Nested* was, however, less impressive and a further domestically inspired hiatus followed. *Mother's Spiritual* reflected Nyro's reactions to both parenthood and ageing; her comeback was confirmed in 1988 when she embarked on her first concert tour in over a decade. *Walk The Dog And Light The Light* was her only new release of the 90s. *Stoned Soul Picnic* was a fitting 34-song retrospective, but only weeks after its release Nyro succumbed to cancer. Laura Nyro will be remembered as a mature songwriter and a singularly impressive performer, her intonation proving influential on several other female singers, notably Rickie Lee Jones.

●ALBUMS: *More Than A New Discovery* aka *The First Songs* (Verve/Forecast 1967)★★★, *Eli And The Thirteenth Confession* (Columbia 1968)★★★★, *New York Tendaberry* (Columbia 1969)★★★★, *Christmas And The Beads Of Sweat* (Columbia 1970)★★★, *Gonna Take A Miracle* (Columbia 1971)★★★, *Smile* (Columbia 1976)★★★, *Season Of Lights* (Columbia 1977)★★★, *Nested* (Columbia 1979)★★, *Mother's Spiritual* (Columbia 1985)★★, *Live At The Bottom Line* (Columbia 1990)★★, *Walk The Dog And Light The Light* (Columbia 1993)★★.

●COMPILATIONS: *Impressions* (Columbia 1980)★★★★, *Stoned Soul Picnic: The Best Of ...* (Columbia/Legacy 1997)★★★★.

OCHS, PHIL

b. 19 December 1940, El Paso, Texas, d. 7 April 1976. A superior singer/songwriter, particularly adept at the topical song, Phil Ochs began his career at Ohio State University. He initially performed in a folksinging duo, the Sundowners, before moving to New York, where he joined the radical Greenwich Village enclave. Ochs' early work was inspired by Woody Guthrie, Bob Gibson and Tom Paxton, and its political nature led to his involvement with the *Broadside* magazine movement. The singer was signed to the prestigious Elektra Records label, and through his initial work was hailed as a major new talent. He achieved popular acclaim when Joan Baez took one of his compositions, 'There But For Fortune', into the pop charts. Ochs' own version later appeared on his *In Concert*, the artist's best-selling set which also featured the evocative 'When I'm Gone' and the wry 'Love Me I'm A Liberal'. Ochs' move to A&M Records in 1967 signalled a new phase in his career. *Pleasures Of The Harbour*, which included the ambitious 'Crucifixion', emphasized a greater use of orchestration, as well as an increasingly rock-based perspective. He remained a lyrical songwriter; his sense of melody was undiminished, but as the decade's causes grew increasingly blurred, so the singer became disillusioned. Although *Rehearsals For Retirement* documented the political travails of a bitter 1968, the sardonically titled *Phil Ochs Greatest Hits* showed an imaginative performer bereft of focus. He donned a gold lamé suit in a misguided effort to 'wed Elvis Presley to the politics of Che Guevara', but his in-concert rock 'n' roll medleys were roundly booed by an audience expecting overt social comment. This period is documented on the controversial *Gunfight At Carnegie Hall*. Ochs' later years were marked by tragedy. He was attacked during a tour of Africa and an attempted strangulation permanently impaired his singing voice. Beset by a chronic songwriting block, Ochs sought solace in alcohol and although a rally/concert in aid of Chile, *An Evening With Salvador Allende*, succeeded through his considerable entreaties, he later succumbed to schizophrenia. Phil Ochs was found hanged at his sister's home on 7 April 1976. One of the finest performers of his generation, he was considered, at least for a short time, Bob Dylan's greatest rival.

●ALBUMS: *All The News That's Fit To Sing* (Elektra 1964)★★★★, *I Ain't Marching Anymore* (Elektra 1965)★★★★, *Phil Ochs In Concert* (Elektra 1966)★★★, *The Pleasures Of The Harbour* (1967)★★★, *Tape From California* (1968)★★★,

Rehearsals For Retirement (1968)★★★, *Gunfight At Carnegie Hall* (1975)★★.

●COMPILATIONS: *Phil Ochs Greatest Hits* (1970)★★★, *Phil Ochs - Chords Of Fame* (1976)★★★★, *Phil Ochs - Songs For Broadside* (1976)★★★, *Broadside Tapes* (1976)★★★, *A Toast To Those Who Are Gone* (1987)★★★, *There But For Fortune* (1989)★★★, *The Broadside Tapes 1* (Smithsonian Folkways 1995)★★★.

●FURTHER READING: *Phil Ochs: Death Of A Rebel*, Marc Elliott.

OHIO EXPRESS

Key players in the bubblegum trend of the late 60s, the Ohio Express evolved from the Mansfield, Ohio, USA-based group Rare Breed in 1967. The group consisted of Joey Levine (lead vocals), Dale Powers (lead guitar), Doug Grassel (rhythm guitar), Jim Pflayer (keyboards), Dean Krastan (bass) and Tim Corwin (drums). Their first single, 'Beg, Borrow And Steal', had originally been recorded by the group under its old moniker in 1966 before it was reissued the following year by Cameo Records. There the group teamed up with producers Jerry Kasenetz and Jeff Katz, and reached number 29 in the autumn of 1967. A second Cameo single to chart was 'Try It', a song penned by Levine that was later covered by the Standells. In 1968 the Ohio Express signed with Neil Bogart's Buddah Records and released the bubblegum 'Yummy Yummy Yummy', which became their biggest hit, reaching the Top 5 on both sides of the Atlantic. By the end of 1969 they had charted on six more occasions, the final time with 'Sausalito (Is The Place To Go)', sung by Graham Gouldman, later of 10cc fame. The Ohio Express released six albums, of which only *Ohio Express* and *Chewy Chewy* made any real impact on the US charts. The group carried on until 1972; Levine formed Reunion in 1974.

●ALBUMS: *Beg, Borrow And Steal* (Cameo 1968)★★, *Ohio Express* (Pye 1968)★★★, *Salt Water Taffy* (1968)★★, *Chewy Chewy* (Buddah 1969)★★★, *Mercy* (1969)★★.

●COMPILATIONS: *Very Best Of The Ohio Express* (1970)★★★.

OLDHAM, SPOONER

b. Lindon Dewey Oldham. Oldham first came to prominence as an in-house pianist at the Fame recording studio. Here he met Dan Penn and the resultant songwriting partnership was responsible for scores of southern soul compositions, including hits for James And Bobby Purify ('I'm Your Puppet'). Clarence Carter ('She Ain't Gonna Do Right') and Percy Sledge ('Out Of Left Field'). Oldham later moved out to California where he became a fixture as a session musician, appearing on albums by Jackson Browne, Maria Muldaur, Linda Ronstadt and the Flying Burrito Brothers. He also maintained his relationship with Penn and the duo subsequently formed an independent production company. During the 70s/80s Oldham appeared with Neil Young as

a member of the Gone With The Wind Orchestra and the International Harvesters.

OLIVER! (STAGE MUSICAL)

As soon as it opened at the New Theatre in London on 30 June 1960, *Oliver!* was an instant success, winning rave reviews and ecstatic audiences. With book, music and lyrics by Lionel Bart, the show's storyline was reasonably faithful to *Oliver Twist*, the Charles Dickens novel upon which it was based. Filled with memorable songs, from sweet ballads to comic masterpieces, the show had the benefit of a strong cast and one performance that ranks among the genre's finest. Ron Moody's Fagin alone was worth the price of admission. Well supported by Georgia Brown, as Nancy, and with a succession of good Olivers and Artful Dodgers, *Oliver!* was excellent entertainment. Bart's songs included 'As Long As He Needs Me', 'Where Is Love?', 'Food, Glorious Food', 'Consider Yourself', 'You've Got To Pick A Pocket Or Two', 'Come Back Soon', 'I Shall Scream', 'Who Will Buy?', 'Oom-Pah-Pah', 'I'd Do Anything' and 'Reviewing The Situation'. The show also had the benefit of extraordinary sets by Sean Kenny, much-admired to the point of outright copying in later years. *Oliver!* ran for 2,618 performances in London, and Georgia Brown reprised her role, with Clive Revill as Fagin, for the 1963 New York production, which ran for nearly two years. The show won Tony Awards for composer and lyricist (Bart), scenic designer (Kenny), and musical director-conductor (Donald Pippin). The 1968 film version dropped a song or two, inexplicably replaced Brown with Shani Wallis, but fortunately preserved Moody's performance for all time. There were also good child actors in Mark Lester as Oliver and, particularly, Jack Wild as the Artful Dodger. Other young stars in the role have included Phil Collins and Steve Marriott. Not surprisingly, *Oliver!* has been revived many times over the years by amateur and professional companies alike, most recently in Cameron Mackintosh's major new production at the London Palladium which opened in December 1994 with a £7 million box office advance. Directed by Sam Mendes, it starred Jonathan Pryce as Fagin, Sally Dexter as Nancy, and featured Adam Searles as the Artful Dodger who almost stole the show. The lavish £3.5 million presentation was generally enthusiastically received by the critics - and Lionel Bart - who, courtesy of Cameron Mackintosh, recouped a portion of the show's rights which he sold many years ago. Subsequent cast changes included Claire Moore, Ruthie Henshall, and Sonia Swaby (the first time a black actress has played the role in the West End) as Nancy, and in the part of Fagin - George Layton, Jim Dale, Russ Abbott, and Robert Lindsay, who won a Laurence Olivier Award for his outstanding performance.

OLYMPICS

Originally known as the Challengers, this adaptable vocal group, Walter Ward (b. 1940, Jackson, Mississippi, USA; lead), Eddie Lewis (b. 1937, Houston, Texas, USA; tenor), Charles Fizer (b. 1940, Shreveport, Louisiana, USA; baritone) and Walter Hammond (baritone) was formed in Compton, California, in 1954. The Olympics' finest moment came with 'Western Movies' (1958), a humorous, novelty disc in the vein of the Coasters and the Clovers, which reached the Top 10 in the US and Top 20 in the UK. The song was produced and co-written by Fred Smith, who later worked with Bob And Earl. The same was true of 'Private Eye', another laconic tribute to 50s pulp-fiction culture, but it was 1960 before the group claimed another US hit with 'Big Boy Pete', by which time Melvin King (b. 1940, Shreveport, Louisiana, USA), had replaced Walter Hammond. Meanwhile, the sacked lead vocalist Fizer, whose troubled life had already resulted in a prison sentence for drugs possession, was shot by the National Guard during the Watts riots in 1965. A reshaped Olympics later went on to have hits with such dancefloor favourites as 'The Bounce' (1963), 'Good Lovin'' (1965 - later successfully covered by the Young Rascals) and 'Baby Do The Philly Dog' (1966), before being drawn towards the 'oldies' circuit.

●ALBUMS: *Doin' The Hully Gully* (Arvee 1960)★★★, *Dance By The Light Of The Moon* (Arvee 1961)★★, *Party Time* (Arvee 1961)★★, *Do The Bounce* (Tri-Disc 1963)★★, *Something Old Something New* (Mirwood 1966)★★, *Soul Music* (1968)★★

●COMPILATIONS: *Greatest Hits* (1971)★★★, *The Official Record Album Of The Olympics* (1984)★★★.

ORBISON, ROY

b. 23 April 1936, Vernon, Texas, USA, d. 6 December 1988. Critical acclaim came too late for one of the leading singers of the 60s. He became the master of the epic ballad of doom-laden despair. Orbison possessed a voice of remarkable range and power, often finding it more comfortable to stay in the high register. The former reluctant rockabilly singer, who worked with Norman Petty and Sam Phillips in the 50s, moved to Nashville and became a staff writer for Acuff-Rose Music. He used his royalties from the success of 'Claudette', recorded by the Everly Brothers, and written for his first wife, to buy himself out of his contract with Sun Records. He signed with the small Monument label. Although his main intention was to be a songwriter, Orbison found himself glancing the US chart with 'Up Town' in 1960. A few months later his song 'Only The Lonely' was rejected by Elvis Presley and the Everly Brothers. Orbison then decided to record it himself. The result was a sensation. The song topped the UK charts and narrowly missed the top spot in the USA. The trite opening of 'dum dum dum dummy doo wah, yea yea yea yea yeah', leads into one of the most distinctive pop songs ever recorded. It climaxes with a glass-shattering falsetto, and is destined to remain a modern classic.

The shy and quiet-spoken Orbison donned a pair of dark-tinted glasses to cover up his chronic astigmatism, although early publicity photos had already sneaked out. Over the next five years he enjoyed unprecedented success in Britain and America, repeating his formula with further stylish but doom-laden ballads, including 'Blue

Angel', 'Running Scared', 'Crying', 'Dream Baby', 'Blue Bayou' and 'In Dreams'. Even during the take-over of America by the Beatles (with whom he became a good friend), Roy was one of the few American artists to retain his ground commercially. During the Beatles' peak chart year he had two UK number 1 singles, the powerful 'It's Over' and the hypnotic 'Oh Pretty Woman'. The latter has an incredibly simple instrumental introduction with acoustic guitar and snare drum, and it is recognized today by millions. It was subsequently used for the blockbuster film *Pretty Woman*. Such was the art of Orbison, having the advantage of crafting his own songs to suit his voice and temperament. Although he continued to have hits throughout the 60s, none except 'It's Too Soon To Know' reached former heights; he regularly toured Britain, which he regarded as his second home. He experienced appalling tragedy when in 1966 his wife, Claudette, was killed as she fell from the back of his motorcycle, and in 1968 a fire destroyed his home, also taking the lives of his two sons. In 1967 he starred as a singing cowboy in *The Fastest Guitar Alive*, but demonstrated that he was no actor. By the end of the decade Roy's musical direction had faltered and he resorted to writing average MOR songs like the unremarkable 'Penny Arcade'.

The 70s were barren times for his career, although a 1976 compilation topped the UK charts. By the end of the decade he underwent open heart surgery. He bounced back in 1980, winning a Grammy for his duet with Emmylou Harris on 'That Lovin' You Feelin' Again' from the film *Roadie*. David Lynch used 'In Dreams' to haunting effect in his chilling film *Blue Velvet* in 1986. The following year Orbison was inducted into the Rock 'n' Roll Hall of Fame; at the ceremony he sang 'Oh Pretty Woman' with Bruce Springsteen. With Orbison once again in favour, Virgin Records signed him, and he recorded an album of his old songs using today's hi-tech production techniques. The result was predictably disappointing; it was the sound and production of those classics that had made them great. The video *A Black And White Night*, showed Roy being courted by numerous stars, including Tom Waits, Springsteen and Elvis Costello. This high profile led him to join George Harrison, Bob Dylan, Tom Petty and Jeff Lynne as the Traveling Wilburys. Their splendid debut album owed much to Orbison's major input. Less than a month after its critically acclaimed release, Roy suffered a fatal heart attack in Nashville. The posthumously released *Mystery Girl* in 1989 was the most successful album of his entire career, and not merely because of morbid sympathy. The record contained a collection of songs that indicated a man feeling happy and relaxed; his voice had never sounded better. The uplifting 'You Got It' and the mellow 'She's A Mystery To Me' were impressive epitaphs to the legendary Big 'O'.

●ALBUMS: *Lonely And Blue* (Monument 1961)★★, *Exciting Sounds Of Roy Orbison (Roy Orbison At The Rockhouse)* (Sun 1961)★★, *Crying* (Monument 1962)★★★, *In Dreams* (Monument 1963)★★★, *Oh Pretty Woman* (1964)★★★★, *Early Orbison*

(Monument 1964)★★, *There Is Only One Roy Orbison* (MGM 1965)★★, *Orbisongs* (Monument 1965)★★, *The Orbison Way* (MGM 1965)★★, *The Classic Roy Orbison* (1966)★★, *Roy Orbison Sings Don Gibson* (MGM 1966)★★, *Cry Softly, Lonely One* (MGM 1967)★★, *The Fastest Guitar Alive* (MGM 1968)★, *Roy Orbison's Many Moods* (1969)★★, *The Big O* (1970)★★, *Hank Williams: The Roy Orbison Way* (1971)★★, *Roy Orbison Sings* (1972)★★, *Memphis* (1973)★★, *Milestones* (1974)★★, *I'm Still In Love With You* (1976)★★, *Regeneration* (1977)★★, *Laminar Flow* (1979)★★, *Big O Country* (1983)★★, *Problem Child* (1984)★★, *In Dreams* (1987)★★★, *For The Lonely* (1988)★★★, *Mystery Girl* (Virgin 1989)★★★★, *Best Love Standards* (1989)★★★, *Our Love Song* (1989)★★★, *Rare Orbison* (1989)★★★, *A Black And White Night Live* (Virgin 1989)★★, *King Of Hearts* (Virgin 1992)★★★★

●COMPILATIONS: *Roy Orbison's Greatest Hits* (Monument 1962)★★★★, *More Of Roy Orbisons Greatest Hits* (Monument 1964)★★★, *The Very Best Of Roy Orbison* (Monument 1966)★★★★, *The Great Songs Of Roy Orbison* (1970)★★★★, *The Monumental Roy Orbison* (1975)★★★, *Golden Days* (1981)★★★, *My Spell On You* (Hits Unlimited 1982)★★★, *In Dreams: The Greatest Hits* (Virgin 1987)★★★★, *The Legendary Roy Orbison* (1988)★★★, *For The Lonely: A Roy Orbison Anthology 1956-1965* (Rhino 1988)★★★★, *The Greatest Hits* (1988)★★★★, *Best Love Standards* (1989)★★★, *The Sun Years* (Bear Family 1980)★★★, *Best Loved Moments* (1993)★★★, *The Very Best Of Roy Orbison* (Virgin 1996)★★★★

●FURTHER READING: *Dark Star*, Ellis Amburn. *Only The Lonely*, Alan Clayson.
●FILMS: *The Fastest Guitar Alive* (1966).

ORIOLES

This R&B vocal group was formed in 1947 in Baltimore, Maryland, USA. Along with the Ravens, the Orioles were considered the pioneers of rhythm and blues vocal harmony. All born in Baltimore, the group consisted of Sonny Til (b. Earlington Carl Tilghman, 18 August 1928; lead), Alexander Sharp (tenor), George Nelson (baritone), Johnny Reed (bass) and guitarist Tommy Gaither. Gaither died in a car accident in 1950 and was replaced by Ralph Williams, and Nelson left in 1953 and was succeeded by Gregory Carroll. The Orioles launched their career with the quiet languorous ballad, 'It's Too Soon To Know', which went to number 1 in the R&B charts (number 13 pop) in 1948. The song was written by Deborah Chessler, the group's manager, and she wrote many of their subsequent hits. Most Orioles hits followed the same formula of Til's impassioned tenor lead with sleepy vocal support and almost invisible instrumental accompaniment in which the music was felt rather than heard. These included the US R&B hits '(It's Gonna Be A) Lonely Christmas' (number 8, 1948), 'Tell Me So' (number 1, 1949), 'Forgive And Forget' (number 5, 1949), 'Crying In

The Chapel' (number 1 - and a pop number 11, 1953), and their last R&B chart record, 'In The Mission Of St. Augustine' (number 7, 1953). In 1955 the Orioles broke up with Sharp and Reed joining various Ink Spots groups. Til formed a new Orioles group from members of another group, the Regals, but could not revive the fortunes of the Orioles. George Nelson died around 1959, Alexander Sharp some time in the 60s, and Sonny Til on 9 December 1981.

●ALBUMS: *The Cadillacs Meet The Orioles* (1961)★★, *Modern Sounds Of The Orioles Greatest Hits* (1962)★★★, *Sonny Til Returns* (1970)★★★, *Old Gold/New Gold* (1971)★★★, *Visit Manhattan Circa 1950's* (1981)★★★.
●COMPILATIONS: *The Orioles Sing: Their Greatest Hits, 1948-1954* (1988)★★★, *Hold Me, Thrill Me, Kiss Me* (1991)★★, *Greatest Hits* (1991)★★★, *The Jubilee Recordings* 7-CD box set (Bear Family 1993)★★★★.

ORLONS

A mixture of school friends and neighbours, this Philadelphia-based group was formed by Shirley Brickley (b. 9 December 1944), Steve Caldwell (b. 22 November 1942), Rosetta Hightower (b. 23 June 1944) and Marlena Davis (b. 4 October 1944). Introduced to Cameo Records by the lead singer of the Dovells, Len Barry, the Orlons' first hits, 'The Wah Watusi', 'Don't Hang Up' and 'South Street', cleverly exploited the male/female aspect of the group. Each of these releases reached the US Top 5, but their potential was undermined when 'Cross Fire!' (1963) and 'Rules Of Love' (1964) were only minor hits. Any lingering impetus was lost when Davis and Caldwell left the line-up, but although Audrey Brickley took their place, the Orlons broke up in 1968 when Rosetta Hightower moved to the UK to become a session singer.

●ALBUMS: *The Wah-Watusi* (Cameo 1962)★★, *All The Hits* (Cameo 1963)★★, *South Street* (Cameo 1963)★★★, *Not Me* (Cameo 1964)★★, *Down Memory Lane* (Cameo 1964)★★★.
●COMPILATIONS: *Biggest Hits* (1963)★★, *Golden Hits Of The Orlons And The Dovells* (1963)★★, *Cameo Parkway Sessions* (London 1978)★★.

ORNADEL, CYRIL

b. 2 December 1924, London, England. A composer, arranger and conductor for the theatre and films, Ornadel studied piano, double bass, and composition at the Royal College of Music. He was with ENSA for a while, and later toured Europe with the popular singer Dorothy Carless. He led his own all-female band at Murray's Club in London, and later worked as a concert party pianist. After providing some musical and vocal arangements for the Players' Theatre, he was appointed musical director of the touring show *Hello Beautiful*, which led to his first London assignment as the conductor of a pantomime at the People's Palace in the Mile End Road. In 1950, he became the West End's youngest pit conductor when he took over the baton for the musical revue *Take It From Us* at the Adelphi Theatre. During the remainder of the

50s he conducted for the London productions of several successful American musicals, such as *Kiss Me, Kate, Call Me Madam, Paint Your Wagon, Wish You Were Here, Pal Joey, Wonderful Town, Kismet, Plain And Fancy*, and *My Fair Lady*. Ornadel also collaborated with David Croft on the scores for regional productions of *Star Maker, The Pied Piper*, and the London Palladium's 1956 pantomime, *The Wonderful Lamp* (with Phil Park). For much of the 50s he was the resident musical director for the top-rated television programme, *Sunday Night At The London Palladium*. In 1960, he and lyricist Norman Newell won Ivor Novello Awards for their delightful ballad, 'Portrait Of My Love', which gave Matt Monro his first UK chart hit. Ornadel's other 'Ivors' (to date) came in 1963 for 'If I Ruled The World' (lyric by Leslie Bricusse), the hit song from his score for the immensely successful musical, *Pickwick*, starring Harry Secombe; and the scores for two 'Best British Musicals', *Treasure Island* (1973) and *Great Expectations* (1975), both with Hal Shaper. After playing its initial UK dates and in several Canadian cities, Ornadel and Shaper rewrote the score for *Great Expectations*, and the revised version was presented at the Liverpool Playhouse (1989) and in Sydney, Australia (1991). Ornadel's other stage musicals have included *Ann Veronica* (1969, with Croft), *Once More, Darling* (1978, with Newell), *Winnie* (1988, additional songs with Arnold Sundgaard), *Cyrano: The Musical* (with Shaper), and *The Last Flower On Earth* (1991, with Kelvin Reynolds). Over the years, Ornadel has also conducted and/or composed and orchestrated the music for numerous radio, film and television productions, including *Some May Live, Subterfuge, The Waitors, I Can't, I Can't, Wedding Night, Man Of Violence, Europa Express, Cool It Carol, Die Screaming Marianne, Yesterday, The Flesh And The Blood Show, The Strauss Family* (series), *Edward VII* (series), *Christina, Brief Encounter* (1974 remake), and many more. His albums, especially those on which his Starlight Symphony Orchestra celebrated the great popular composers, have been extremely successful, especially in America. He also composed a series of children's records for EMI, and was the musical supervisor for the *Living Bible* records with Sir Laurence Olivier, and created the 'Stereoaction Orchestra' for RCA Records. A genial, and much-liked man, in the early 90s Cyril Ornadel was living and working in Israel.

●ALBUMS: *Musical World Of Lerner And Loewe, Opening Night-Broadway Overtures, Bewitched, Camelot, Carnival, Dearly Beloved, Enchanted Evening, Gone With The Wind, Musical World Of Jerome Kern, Musical World Of Cole Porter, Musical World Of Rodgers And Hammerstein, So Nice To Come Home To, The Music Man* (all 60s).

OUTLAWS (UK)

Although officially formed in December 1960, the origins of this group date to the preceding May when Billy Grey (vocals), Billy Kuy (lead guitar), Reg Hawkins (rhythm guitar), Chas Hodges (bass) and Bobby Graham (drums)

put together Billy Grey And The Stormers to play at Filey holiday camp. When Grey opted to leave music, the remaining four musicians stayed together as the Outlaws. In 1961 they were signed by producer Joe Meek who employed the group to support vocalist Mike Berry, notably on 'Don't You Think Its Time' and 'Tribute To Buddy Holly'. The Outlaws also recorded instrumentals, most of which were composed by Meek and revolved around cowboy themes. Two 1961 singles, 'Swingin' Low' and 'Ambush', reached the Top 50 of the UK charts, which in turn inspired the release of *Dream Of The West*. By 1962 only Hodges remained from the founding line-up and a reshaped Outlaws was completed by Roger Mingay (lead guitar, ex-Savages), Ken Lundgren (rhythm guitar) and Don Groom (drums). Three further singles, 'Valley Of The Sioux', 'Ku Pow' and 'Sioux Serande', followed before further changes in personnel. However, by September 1962 the Outlaws had a settled line-up of Hodges, Lundren, Ritchie Blackmore (lead guitar, ex-Savages) and Mick Underwood (drums). They remained a crucial part of Joe Meek's productions, appearing on sessions by John Leyton, Heinz and Glenda Collins, as well as numerous package tours. The Outlaws continued to record under their own name and the introduction of Blackmore brought more fire to their releases. 'Return Of The Outlaws', 'That Set The West Free' and 'Law And Order' are vibrant singles, but the rise of Merseybeat made Meek's work sound increasingly old-fashioned. The Outlaws' recording career ended with a vocal track, 'Keep A Knockin'', in 1964. Following this Blackmore left to join Heinz's Wild Boys, then Neil Christian's Crusaders. He was replaced by Harvey Hinsley, but in June 1965 the Outlaws split up. Hodges joined Cliff Bennett And The Rebel Rousers, while Underwood joined the embryonic Herd before opting for Episode Six. Lundren emigrated to Canada and Hinsley joined Hot Chocolate.

●ALBUMS: *Dream Of The West* (HMV 1961)★★.

●COMPILATIONS: *The Outlaws Ride Again (The Singles As And Bs)* (See For Miles 1990)★★★.

OVERLANDERS

This UK vocal trio - Paul Arnold (aka Paul Friswell), Laurie Mason and Peter Bartholemew - initially pursued a folk-based career, but scored a surprise, if minor, US hit in 1964 with their version of 'Yesterday's Gone'. Buoyed by the addition of Terry Widlake (bass) and David Walsh (drums), they enjoyed a UK number 1 the following year with an opportunistic version of the Beatles' 'Michelle', but the reshaped group was unable to shake off a somewhat anachronistic image. A strong follow-up to their chart-topper, 'My Life', unfortunately failed to chart. Arnold left for a solo career in 1966, but despite the arrival of Ian Griffiths, the Overlanders failed to reap reward from their early success.

●ALBUMS: *Michelle* (Pye 1966)★★★.

OWENS, BUCK

b. Alvis Edgar Owens Jnr., 12 August 1929, Sherman, Texas, USA. Buck Owens became one of the leading country music stars of the 60s and 70s, along with Merle Haggard, the leading exponent of the 'west coast sound'. Owens gave himself the nickname Buck at the age of three, after a favourite horse. When he was 10, his family moved to Mesa, Arizona, where Owens picked cotton, and at 13 years of age he began playing the mandolin. He soon learned guitar, horns and drums. Owens performed music professionally at the age of 16, starring, along with partner Ray Britten, in his own radio programme. He also worked with the group Mac's Skillet Lickers, and at 17 married their singer, Bonnie Campbell, who later launched her own career as Bonnie Owens. The couple bore a son, who also had a country music career as Buddy Alan. In 1951 Owens and his family moved to Bakersfield, California, at the suggestion of an uncle who said work was plentiful for good musicians. Owens joined the Orange Blossom Playboys, with whom he both sang and played guitar for the first time, and then formed his own band, the Schoolhouse Playboys. Owens made ends meet by taking on work as a session guitarist in Los Angeles, appearing on recordings by Sonny James, Wanda Jackson, Tommy Sands and Gene Vincent. When the Playboys disbanded in the mid-50s Owens joined country artist Tommy Collins as singer and guitarist, recording a few tracks with him.

In 1955-56 Owens recorded his first singles under his own name, for Pep Records, using the name Corky Jones for rockabilly and his own name for country recordings. Owens signed to Capitol Records in March 1957. It was not until his fourth release, 'Second Fiddle', that he made any mark, reaching number 24 on *Billboard*'s country chart. His next, 'Under Your Spell Again', made number 4, paving the way for over 75 country hits, more than 40 of which made that chart's Top 10. Among the biggest and best were 'Act Naturally' (1963), later covered by the Beatles, 'Love's Gonna Live Here' (1963), 'My Heart Skips A Beat' (1964), 'Together Again' (1964), 'I've Got A Tiger By The Tail' (1965), 'Before You Go' (1965), 'Waitin' In Your Welfare Line' (1966), 'Think Of Me' (1966), 'Open Up Your Heart' (1966) and a cover of Chuck Berry's 'Johnny B. Goode' (1969), all of which were number 1 country singles. Owens recorded a number of duets with singer Susan Raye, and also with his son Buddy Alan. He also released more than 100 albums during his career. In addition, his compositions were hits by other artists, notably Emmylou Harris ('Together Again') and Ray Charles ('Crying Time'). Owens' band, the Buckaroos (guitarist Don Rich, bassist Doyle Holly, steel guitarist Tom Brumley and drummer Willie Cantu), was also highly regarded. Their down-to-basics, honky-tonk instrumental style helped define the Bakersfield sound - Owens' recordings never relied on strings or commercialized, sweetened pop arrangements. The Buckaroos also released several albums on their own. In 1969, Owens joined as co-host the country music television variety programme *Hee Haw*, which combined comedy sketches and live performances by country stars. He stayed with the show until the mid-80s, long after his Capitol contract expired, and he had signed with Warner

Brothers Records (1976). Although Owens continued to place singles in the country charts with Warners, his reign as a top country artist had faltered in the mid-70s and he retired from recording and performing to run a number of business interests, including a radio station and recording studio in Bakersfield. In 1988, country newcomer Dwight Yoakam convinced Owens to join him in recording a remake of Owens' song 'Streets Of Bakersfield'. It reached number 1 in the country chart and brought new attention to Owens. He signed with Capitol again late in 1988 and recorded a new album, *Hot Dog*, featuring re-recordings of old Owens songs and cover songs of material by Chuck Berry, Eddie Cochran and others. Although Owens had not recaptured his earlier status by the early 90s, he had become active again, recording and touring, including one tour as a guest of Yoakam.

●ALBUMS: *Buck Owens* (LaBrea 1961)★★★, *Buck Owens Sings Harlan Howard* (Capitol 1961)★★★, *Under Your Spell Again* (Capitol 1961)★★★, *The Fabulous Country Music Sound Of Buck Owens* (Starday 1962)★★★, *You're For Me* (Capitol 1962)★★★, *On The Bandstand* (Capitol 1963)★★★, *Sings Tommy Collins* (Capitol 1963), *Together Again/My Heart Skips A Beat* (Capitol 1964)★★★, *I Don't Care* (Capitol 1964)★★★, *The Instrumental Hits Of Buck Owens And The Buckaroos* (Capitol 1965)★★★, *I've Got A Tiger By The Tail* (Capitol 1965)★★★, *Before You Go/No One But You* (Capitol 1965)★★★, *Christmas With* (Capitol 1965)★★★, *Carnegie Hall Concert* (Capitol 1966)★★★, *Roll Out The Red Carpet* (Capitol 1966)★★★, *Dust On Mother's Bible* (Capitol 1966)★★★, *Open Up Your Heart* (Capitol 1967)★★★, *Buck Owens And His Buckaroos In Japan* (Capitol 1967)★★★, *Your Tender Loving Care* (Capitol 1967)★★★, *It Takes People Like You To Make People Like Me* (Capitol 1968)★★★, *A Night On The Town* (Capitol 1968)★★★, *Sweet Rosie Jones* (Capitol 1968)★★★, *Christmas Shopping* (Capitol 1968)★★★, *Buck Owens The Guitar Player* (Player 1968)★★★, *Buck Owens In London* (1969)★★★, *Big In Vegas* (1970)★★★, with Susan Raye *We're Gonna Get Together* (1970)★★★, *A Merry Hee Haw Christmas* (Capitol 1970)★★★, *I Wouldn't Live In New York City* (1971)★★★, *The Songs Of Merle Haggard* (1972)★★★, *Hot Dog* (1988)★★★, *Act Naturally* (1989)★★★, *Blue Love* (1993)★★★.

●COMPILATIONS: *The Best Of Buck Owens* (Capitol 1964)★★★★, *The Best Of Buck Owens, Volume 2* (Capitol 1968)★★★★, *The Buck Owens Story Vol. 1 (1956-64)* (Personality 1994) ★★★★, *Vol. 2 (1964-68)* (Personality 1994) ★★★★, *Vol. 3 (1969-89)* (Personality 1994)★★★★.

PACIFIC GAS AND ELECTRIC

Formed in Los Angeles, California, USA, in 1968, Pacific Gas And Electric was a quintet that merged blues, gospel, soul, jazz and rock. The members were Charlie Allen (vocals), Glenn Schwartz (lead guitar), Thomas Marshall (rhythm guitar), Brent Black (bass) and Frank Cook (drums), the latter an alumnus of Canned Heat. The group's first album, *Get It On*, was initially issued on the small Bright Orange label and then reissued on the band's own Power Records, scraping into the charts at number 159. An appearance at the Miami Pop Festival in December 1968 was considered a highlight of that event and the group came to the attention of Columbia Records, who subsequently signed them. A self-titled album was released on Columbia in August 1969 and fared somewhat better, reaching number 91. The group's third album, *Are You Ready*, did not fare as well, reaching only number 101, but it did yield their only hit single in the title track, a gospel-influenced rocker that climbed to number 14 in mid-1970. One other album and a couple of further singles were issued but by 1971 the group was in disarray. Various personnel changes, including the addition of a horn section, left Allen the only original member by 1973, when the group's final album was issued on Dunhill Records.
●ALBUMS: *Get It On* (Bright Orange/B&C 1968)★★★, *Pacific Gas And Electric* (CBS 1969)★★★, *Are You Ready* (CBS 1970)★★, *Hard Burn* (CBS 1971)★★, *PG&E* (1971)★★, *Pacific Gas And Electric, Starring Charlie Allen* (1973)★★.
●COMPILATIONS: *The Best Of* (1985)★★★.

PAGE, JIMMY

b. James Patrick Page, 9 January 1944, Heston, Middlesex, England. One of rock's most gifted and distinctive guitarists, Page began his professional career during the pre-beat era of the early 60s. He was a member of several groups, including Neil Christian's Crusaders and Carter Lewis And The Southerners, the last of which was led by the popular songwriting team, Carter And Lewis. Page played rousing solos on several releases by Carter/Lewis protégés, notably the McKinleys' 'Sweet And Tender Romance', and the guitarist quickly became a respected session musician. He appeared on releases by Lulu, Them, Tom Jones and Dave Berry, as well as scores of less renowned acts, but his best-known work was undertaken for producer Shel Talmy. Page appeared on sessions for the Kinks and the Who, joining an elite band of young studio musicians

who included Nicky Hopkins, John Paul Jones and Bobby Graham. The guitarist completed a solo single, 'She Just Satisfies', in 1965, and although it suggested a frustration with his journeyman role, he later took up an A&R position with Immediate Records, where he produced singles for Nico and John Mayall. Having refused initial entreaties, Page finally agreed to join the Yardbirds in 1966 and he remained with this groundbreaking attraction until its demise two years later. The guitarist then formed Led Zeppelin, with whom he forged his reputation. His propulsive riffs established the framework for a myriad of tracks - 'Whole Lotta Love', 'Rock 'N' Roll', 'Black Dog', 'When The Levee Breaks' and 'Achilles Last Stand' - now established as rock classics, while his solos have set benchmarks for a new generation of guitarists. His acoustic technique, featured on 'Black Mountain Side' and 'Tangerine', is also notable, while his work with Roy Harper, in particular on *Stormcock* (1971), was also among the finest of his career. Page's recordings since Led Zeppelin's dissolution have been ill-focused. He contributed the soundtrack to Michael Winner's film *Death Wish II*, while the Firm, a collaboration with Paul Rodgers, formerly of Free and Bad Company, was equally disappointing. However, a 1988 release, *Outrider*, did much to re-establish his reputation with contributions from Robert Plant, Chris Farlowe and Jason Bonham, the son of Zeppelin's late drummer, John. The guitarist then put considerable effort into remastering that group's revered back catalogue. *Coverdale/Page* was a successful but fleeting partnership with the former Whitesnake singer in 1993, but it was his reunion with Robert Plant for the ironically titled *Unledded* project that really captured the public's imagination.
●ALBUMS: *Death Wish II* soundtrack (Swan Song 1982)★★, with Roy Harper *Whatever Happened To Jugula* (Beggars Banquet 1985)★★★, *Outrider* (Geffen 1988)★★, with David Coverdale *Coverdale/Page* (EMI 1993)★★★, with Robert Plant *Unledded/No Quarter* (Fontana 1994)★★★.
●COMPILATIONS: *Jam Session* (Charly 1982)★★, *No Introduction Necessary* (Thunderbolt 1984)★★, *Smoke And Fire* (Thunderbolt 1985)★★.
●FURTHER READING: *Mangled Mind Archive: Jimmy Page*, Adrian T'Vell.

PAGE, LARRY

b. Leonard Davies, c.1938, Hayes, Middlesex, England. While working as a packer at the nearby EMI Records factory, Davies auditioned for his record company and was duly signed. After changing his name to Larry Page in honour of Larry Parks, the star of *The Jolson Story*, the teenager began a brief recording career. Dubbed 'the Teenage Rage' by showbusiness columnist Jack Bentley, Page lived up to his sobriquet with a series of exploits, including a whirlwind romance with a fan leading to a much publicized marriage. With his sharp suits, blue-tinted hair and monotone croon, Page was an unlikely pop star but became one of the first UK performers to cover a Buddy Holly song with 'That'll Be The Day'. After retiring from performance at the end of the 50s, Page joined Mecca Enterprises as a consultant manager and ran the Orchid ballroom in Coventry. He met Eddie Kassner and formed Denmark Productions. With a deal whereby he could select and manage acts, Page launched a selection of minor talent, including Johnny B. Great, the Orchids, Little Lenny Davis and Shel Naylor.

In 1964 Page was approached by two society gentlemen, Robert Wace and Grenville Collins, and offered the chance to co-manage a north London group known as the Ravens. Page rechristened them the Kinks, helped fashion their image and prevented their imminent dissolution following a notorious quarrel between Dave Davies and Mick Avory, in which the former was hospitalized. An unsatisfactory US tour culminated in a dispute between Page and Ray Davies that festered into a High Court action. Recovering his poise, he promoted a couple of other groups, the Pickwicks and the Riot Squad, before finding another hit artist in the Troggs. On this occasion, Page not only signed the group to a management deal but produced their records and made them the leading lights of Page One (the record company he had formed with publisher Dick James). Remarkably, his association with the Troggs ended in another High Court action yet, in spite of his litigious history, Page was never regarded as one of the unscrupulous managers of the 60s. His name was well-known during this period, not only because of frequent appearances in print but the instrumental albums his label released under the self-referential title the Larry Page Orchestra. When Page One ceased operating in the early 70s, Dick James went on to found DJM Records while Larry formed the inauspicious Penny Farthing label. Page rewrote history to some extent in the 70s/80s when he briefly regained managerial control of both the Troggs and the Kinks.

● ALBUMS: *Kinky Music* (Decca 1965)★★★, *Executive Suite* (Page One 1968)★★, *From Larry With Love* (Page One 1968)★★, *Larry Page Orchestra* (Page One 1969)★★, *Rampage* (1978)★★.
● COMPILATIONS: *This Is Larry Page* (1974)★★.

PARAMOUNTS

Formed in Southend, Essex, England, in 1961, the Paramounts evolved out of local beat attraction the Raiders. Comprising Gary Brooker (b. 29 May 1945, Southend, Essex, England; keyboards/vocals), Robin Trower (b. 9 March 1945, Southend, Essex, England; guitar), Chris Copping (b. 29 August 1945, Southend, Essex, England; bass) and Mick Brownlee (drums), the latter replaced by Barrie (B.J.) Wilson (b. 18 March 1947, Southend, Essex, England) in 1963. The group became one of the region's most popular R&B acts and by 1963 had secured a prestigious deal with EMI Records. Diz Derrick replaced the college-bound Copping prior to recording their debut single 'Poison Ivy', and sole UK Top 40 entry. Subsequent releases included material drawn from the Coasters, Jackie DeShannon and P.F. Sloan, but despite considerable acclaim, the Paramounts failed to achieve due commercial success. Later reduced to

backing Sandie Shaw and Chris Andrews, they split up in October 1966. Brooker then formed a songwriting team with lyricist Keith Reid which in turn inspired the formation of Procol Harum. By 1969, and in the wake of numerous defections, this attraction contained the same line-up as that of the original Paramounts. Trower and Brooker pursued subsequent solo careers, while the latter also worked with Joe Cocker and Eric Clapton.
● COMPILATIONS: *Whiter Shades Of R&B* (1983)★★.

PARKER, ROBERT

b. 14 October 1930, New Orleans, Louisiana, USA. An accomplished saxophonist, this versatile musician was first heard on numerous recordings by pianist Professor Longhair. Parker also appeared on sessions for Irma Thomas, Ernie K-Doe and Joe Tex while at the same time embarking on a singing career. His early releases were largely unsuccessful until 'Barefootin'', an irresistible dance record, became a hit in the US and the UK during 1966. The singer continued this instinctive blend of soul and New Orleans R&B on several further releases, but 'Tip Toe' (1967) was his only further chart entry.
● ALBUMS: *Barefootin'* (Island 1966)★★.
● COMPILATIONS: *Get Ta Steppin'* (1987)★★.

PARKER, TOM, 'COLONEL'

b. Andreas Cornelius van Kuijk, 26 June 1909, Breda, The Netherlands, d. 21 Janaury 1997. There remains bitter division about Parker. Was he Sam Katzman's 'biggest con artist in the world' or merely an unsophisticated fairground barker sucked into a vortex of circumstances he was unwilling to resist? Arguments supporting either might be construed from the icy ruthlessness formidable to those accustomed to Tin Pan Alley's glib bonhomie, and his blunt stance in negotiation on behalf of Elvis Presley, his most famous managerial client. 'Don't criticize what you can't understand, son,' Elvis said in the Colonel's defence. 'You never walked in that man's shoes.' Parker was an illegal immigrant, without passport or papers, who settled into carnival life in the 20s. Over the next decade, he evolved into a cigar-chewing huckster of spectacular amorality - exemplified by his practice of snaring sparrows, painting them yellow and selling them as canaries. With duties that included palm reading, he served the Royal American, the Union's top travelling show, for a while before a seemingly steady job as promoter for a charity organization in Tampa, Florida. Extremely potent fund-raisers, he discovered, were shows headlined by a popular C&W artist and so it was that Parker came to commit himself full-time to the genre by moving to Nashville where he became Eddy Arnold's personal manager. Once, when this vocalist was indisposed, an unruffled Parker allegedly offered a substitute attraction in two unhappy 'dancing chickens' who highstepped around a cage to ease feet scorched by an electric hot plate hidden under their straw.

After Arnold left him, the Colonel (an honorary title conferred by the Tennessee Militia in 1953) took on Hank Snow - and it was in a support spot on a Snow tour of the deep south that 19-year-old Presley was noticed by his future svengali. Via connections nurtured during proceedings concerning Arnold and Snow, Parker persuaded RCA to contract his new find. A few months later in March 1956, the boy committed himself formally to Parker for life - and beyond. From that month, 'Elvis has required every minute of my time, and I think he would have suffered had I signed anyone else'. While facilitating Presley's captivation of a global 'youth market', the Colonel's instinct for the commercial and economic machinations of the record industry obliged RCA to accede to his every desire, such as the pressing of one million copies of every Elvis release, regardless of positioning research. Moreover, to the team fell an average of eight per cent of approved merchandise associated with Presley - and, when the time came for the King to act in films, producer Hal Wallis grew to 'rather try and close a deal with the Devil' than Parker. To publicize one Presley movie, Tom was not above hiring dwarfs to parade through Hollywood as 'The Elvis Presley Midget Fan Club'. He was also behind the taming of Elvis via the stressing of a cheerful diligence while on national service; the post-army chart potboilers; the overall projection of Presley as an 'all-round entertainer', and, arguably, the moulding of his reactionary leanings. Nor did Parker object to Katzman dashing off a Presley vehicle in less than a month, each one a quasi-musical of cheery unreality usually more vacuous and streamlined than the one before. This was almost all fans saw of the myth-shrouded Elvis until his impatient return to the stage in 1968, whether the Colonel liked it or not.

After Presley's death in 1977, there were rumours that Parker would be devoting himself professionally to Rick Nelson but only Elvis' posthumous career interrupted a virtual retirement in Palm Springs. Parker was a consummate showman and media manipulator, who clearly enjoyed turning down million of dollars whenever his charge was asked to headline some grand concert package. His handling of merchandising rights during the early part of Presley's career has been compared favourably to the business dealings of later starmakers such as Brian Epstein. The obsession with commerce and disavowal of artistry dominated the Colonel's thinking, however, which mainly explains the singer's appalling film-related output during the early/mid-60s. After Presley's death, Parker's business empire was threatened by the star's estate - in the form of Elvis's ex-wife Priscilla and daughter Lisa Marie. Parker fought tenaciously to protect his empire before settling in June 1983. Thereafter, he surrendered claims to all future Elvis income, but received two million dollars from RCA, and 50% of all Presley's record royalties prior to September 1982. In January 1993, Parker made one of his rare public appearances, signing autographs to promote the newly issued Elvis Presley postage stamp. He spent the last years of his life in his beloved Las Vegas, where he could feed his gambling addiction.

●FURTHER READING: *Elvis*, Albert Grossman. *Elvis And The Colonel*, Dirk Vallenga and Mick Farren.

PARNES, LARRY

b. Laurence Maurice Parnes, 1930, Willesden, London, England, d. 4 August 1989, London, England. Parnes was the most famous British pop manager and impresario of the 50s, and one of the greatest of all time. After briefly working in the family clothing business, he took over a bar in London's West End called La Caverne. The establishment was frequented by many theatrical agents and producers and, before long, Parnes was inveigled into investing in a play entitled *Women Of The Streets*. One night at a coffee bar he met publicist John Kennedy, who was then overseeing the affairs of singer Tommy Hicks. After seeing the boy perform at Lionel Bart's suggestion Parnes was impressed and went into partnership with Kennedy. Hicks was rechristened Tommy Steele and became Britain's first rock 'n' roll celebrity. He later emerged as an all-round entertainer and star of several musicals. Parnes specialized in discovering young boys, who would be systematically groomed, launched on the rock 'n' roll circuit, and finally assimilated into traditional showbusiness areas. The technique was habitual. Parnes played the part of the svengali, carefully renaming his acts with some exotically powerful surname that suggested power, virility or glamour. His second discovery proved another winner. Reg Smith was quickly snapped up by the starmaker, rechristened Marty Wilde and soon enjoyed a string of UK hits, before 'retiring' from rock 'n' roll at the close of the 50s.

By this time, Parnes had a network of contacts, including A&R managers like Hugh Mendl, Dick Rowe and Jack Baverstock, who would always take notice of a Parnes act. The bombastic television producer Jack Good also realized that supporting Parnes ensured a steady flow of teenage talent. Finally, there were the songwriters like Lionel Bart, who could provide original material, although cover versions of US hits were always popular. Parnes' third great discovery of the 50s was Billy Fury, one of the most important figures to emerge from British rock 'n' roll. Significantly, Parnes remained with the star for a considerable time and was still handling his business affairs during the late 60s. The irrepressible Joe Brown was another major find for Parnes, although their association was often stormy. Brown was an exceptional guitarist and was frequently used to back other Parnes acts. For every star he unearthed, however, there were a series of lesser talents or unlucky singers who failed to find chart success. Among the famous Parnes 'stable of stars' were Dickie Pride, Duffy Power, Johnny Gentle, Sally Kelly, Terry Dene, Nelson Keene and Peter Wynne. Larry was also briefly associated with Georgie Fame and the Tornados. Beyond his management interests, Parnes was a great provider of package shows with grandiloquent titles such as 'The Big New Rock 'n' Roll Trad Show' and the 'Star Spangled Nights'. Parnes' influence effectively ended during the early to mid-60s when new managers and entrepreneurs such as Brian Epstein and Andrew Oldham took centre stage. Ironically, Parnes had two chances to sign the Beatles but passed up the opportunity. Like his stars, he seemed intent on abdicating his position in rock 'n' roll and increasingly moved into more conservative areas of British showbusiness and theatre. During the 60s, he was involved in such musicals as *Charlie Girl* and *Chicago*. During the 70s, he returned to management in a different sphere, administering the business affairs of ice-skater John Currie. He subsequently fell ill with meningitis and effectively retired. His public image remained contradictory and subject to caricature. As the prototype British pop svengali, he was used as the inspiration for the vapid, camp starmaker in the movie *Absolute Beginners*. Ever self-protective and litigious, his wrath descended upon the BBC, among others, when he won a substantial out-of-court settlement for an alleged libel by Paul McCartney on a most unlikely programme, *Desert Island Discs*.

●FURTHER READING: *Starmakers & Svengalis: The History Of British Pop Management*, Johnny Rogan.

PARTRIDGE, DON

b. 1945, Bournemouth, Dorset, England. Self-styled 'King of the Street Singers', Partridge was discovered busking in London's Berwick Street market by former Viscount Don Paul, who in turn became his manager. 'Rosie', the singer's self-penned debut single, was reputedly recorded for the sum of £8, but became a surprise UK Top 5 hit in 1968. The artist's unconventional lifestyle and penchant for straight-talking resulted in good copy, and engendered greater publicity than his novelty status might otherwise suggest. 'Blue Eyes', Partridge's follow-up single, reached number 3, yet the song is less well recalled than its ebullient predecessor. The singer later supervised *The Buskers*, a various-artists compilation, and enjoyed one further chart entry with 'Breakfast On Pluto' in 1969. After this brief flirtation with fame, Partridge returned to busking roots and continued to perform into the 90s.

●ALBUMS: *Don Partridge* (Columbia 1968)★★.

PATTO

Patto was formed in 1969 when four members of Timebox - Michael Patrick 'Patto' McGrath (vocals), Peter 'Ollie' Halsall (guitar/vibes), Clive Griffiths (bass) and John Halsey (drums) - abandoned commercial constraints and embarked on a more progressive direction. Their debut, *Patto*, featured several of the group's most lasting performances. Although producer Muff Winwood opted for a rather rudimentary sound, the set contained a series of impressive songs, featuring complex signatures, excellent vocals and Halsall's superb guitar work. Sometimes frenzied, at other times restrained, his contributions enhanced an already outstanding collection. A second release, *Hold Your Fire*, exaggerated their jazz-rock persuasions, but retained the urgency and fire of their debut. Judicious overdubs ensured a fuller sound, yet Patto's interplay and empathy remained intact. Faced by commercial indifference, the group embarked on a third collection vowing to capture the irreverent side of their music. *Roll 'Em, Smoke 'Em, Put Another Line Out* was only partially successful with 'Singing The Blues On Reds' and the compulsive 'Loud Green Song' being the

stand-out tracks. The project fared no better than its predecessors and Patto broke up in 1973 when their label rejected a completed fourth album, *Monkey's Bum*. Mike Patto joined Spooky Tooth, appearing on their final album, *The Mirror*, in 1974. Halsall resurfaced in Tempest before forging a partnership with Kevin Ayers. He was reunited with Patto in 1975 as a member of Boxer, and subsequently worked alongside John Halsey in the Beatles spoof, the Rutles. The latter joined Patto in the ad hoc 'supergroup' Hinkley's Heroes, but the career of this expressive vocalist was cut short in March 1979 when he succumbed to throat cancer. Halsall remained an in-demand session guitarist until his death in 1993. Halsey bcame Barry Wom in the Rutles, for whom Halsall also played guitar, before taking over the managership of a Suffolk pub. After playing in sundry outfits Griffiths was permanently hospitalized following a road accident. Halsall became the third former member to meet misfortune when he died in 1992. Three years later the group's original producer, Muff Winwood, compiled a re-mastered, double CD anthology of their best work.

●ALBUMS: *Patto* (Vertigo 1970)★★★, *Hold Your Fire* (Vertigo 1971)★★★, *Roll 'Em, Smoke 'Em, Put Another Line Out* (Vertigo 1972)★★★.

●COMPILATIONS: *A Sense Of The Absurd* 2-CD set of first two albums (Mercury 1995)★★★.

PATTON, 'BIG' JOHN

b. 12 July 1935, Kansas City, Missouri, USA. Unusually for a Hammond organ supremo, Patton does not come from Philadelphia. His mother played piano in church, and Patton took it up in 1948. He played in the Lloyd Price band from 1954-59, quitting just as Price topped his 1952 hit 'Lawdy Miss Clawdy' with a string of three million-sellers. Patton moved to New York and switched to organ. He was signed to Blue Note Records on the recommendation of Lou Donaldson, debuting with *Along Came John* in 1963, which featured Grant Green on guitar. In the late 60s he worked with tenor saxophonist Clifford Jordon and guitarist James 'Blood' Ulmer, as well as sitting in with Sun Ra's musicians. In the 70s he moved to East Orange, New Jersey. John Zorn's use of him on a track of *The Big Gundown* in 1985 rekindled interest in his career, and in the 90s when the Hammond B3 was experiencing another comeback, Patton's work was rightly compared to the leaders of the genre, Jimmy Smith and Jimmy McGriff.

●ALBUMS: *Along Came John* (Blue Note 1963)★★★★, *The Way I Feel* (1964)★★★, *Blue John* (Blue Note 1964)★★★★, *Oh Baby!* (Blue Note 1964)★★★★, *Got A Good Thing Goin'* (1965)★★★, *Let 'Em Roll* (Blue Note 1966)★★★★, *That Certain Feeling* (Blue Note 1968)★★★, *Understanding* (Blue Note 1968)★★★, *Accent On The Blues* (Blue Note 1969), *Soul Connection* (Nilva 1984)★★★, *Blue Planet Man* (Paddlewheel 1993)★★★, *Memphis To New York Spirit* (Blue Note 1996)★★★.

●COMPILATIONS: *The Organization!: The Best Of Big John Patton* (Blue Note 1994)★★★★.

PAUL AND PAULA

Paul (b. Ray Hildebrand, 21 December 1940, Joshua, Texas, USA) and Paula (b. Jill Jackson, 20 May 1942, McCaney, Texas, USA) were college students prior to singing together on a local radio's cancer fund appeal. In November 1962 they auditioned a Hildebrand composition, 'Hey Paula', for Fort Worth producer Major Bill Smith, and within weeks the song topped the US chart. 'Hey Paula' captured a 'puppy-love' naïvety beloved by middle-America in the immediate pre-Beatles era. 'Hey, hey, hey Paula, I wanna marry you', and the continuing simplistic call and answer lyric found a receptive audience. 'Young Lovers', which recounted the eve of the duo's wedding, provided another hit, but although subsequent releases, including 'Our First Quarrel', continued the storyline, Paul And Paula were unable to repeat the success of their million-selling debut and ended up sounding overly cloying.
●ALBUMS: *Paul And Paula Sing For Young Lovers* (Philips 1963)★★, *We Go Together* (Philips 1963)★, *Holiday For Teens* (Philips 1963)★.

PAUPERS

Formed in Toronto, Ontario, Canada, in 1965, the Paupers have been described by former band leader Skip Prokop as 'heavy-duty folk-rock psychedelic'. Including Prokop (drums/vocals), Bill Marion (rhythm guitar/drums/lead vocals; replaced by Adam Mitchell in late 1966), Chuck Beal (lead guitar/mandolin) and Denny Gerard (bass/vocals; replaced by ex-Last Words' Brad Campbell prior to *Ellis Island*), the Paupers first released singles locally on Canadian labels Red Leaf and Roman before signing a management contract with Albert Grossman, the manager of Bob Dylan at the time. They were signed to the Verve/Forecast label in the USA, and released six singles and two albums between 1966 and 1968. The debut, *Magic People*, received much airplay on FM rock stations but only managed a number 178 placing on the US album charts. The group built a steady following on the road, and played the Monterey Pop Festival in June 1967. The Paupers disbanded in 1970. Prokop and Campbell guested on *Richard P. Havens 1983*. Following the Paupers' break-up, Campbell joined Janis Joplin in her Kozmic Blues Band and the Full-Tilt Boogie Band. Prokop played with Al Kooper and Michael Bloomfield on their 1968 *Super Session* album and went on to form Lighthouse in 1969. He recorded solo in the 70s, hosted a Christian radio programme and then retired from the music business.
●ALBUMS: *Magic People* (Verve/Forecast 1967)★★, *Ellis Island* (Verve/Forecast 1968)★★.

PAXTON, TOM

b. 31 October 1937, Chicago, Illinois, USA. Paxton's interest in folk music developed as a student at the University of Oklahoma. In 1960 he moved to New York and became one of several aspiring performers to frequent the city's Greenwich Village coffeehouse circuit. Paxton made his professional debut at the Gaslight, the renowned folk haunt that also issued the singer's first album. Two topical song publications, *Sing Out!* and *Broadside*, began publishing his original compositions which bore a debt to the traditional approach of Pete Seeger and Bob Gibson. Tom also auditioned to join the Chad Mitchell Trio, but although he failed, the group enjoyed a 1963 hit with 'The Marvellous Toy', one of his early songs. The following year Paxton was signed to the Elektra label for whom he recorded his best known work. *Ramblin' Boy* indicated the diversity which marked his recorded career and contained several highly popular performances including 'The Last Thing On My Mind', 'Goin' To The Zoo' and 'I Can't Help But Wonder Where I'm Bound'. Subsequent releases continued this mixture of romanticism, protest and children's songs, while 'Lyndon Johnson Told The Nation' (*Ain't That News*) and 'Talkin' Vietnam Pot Luck Blues' (*Morning Again*) revealed a talent for satire and social comment. *The Things I Notice Now* and *Tom Paxton 6* enhanced Paxton's reputation as a mature and complex songwriter, yet he remained better known for such simpler compositions as 'Jennifer's Rabbit' and 'Leaving London'. Paxton left Elektra during the early 70s and although subsequent recordings proved less popular, he commanded a loyal following, particularly in the UK, where he was briefly domiciled. *How Come The Sun* (1971) was the first of three albums recorded during this period and although his work became less prolific, Paxton was still capable of incisive, evocative songwriting, such as 'The Hostage', which chronicled the massacre at Attica State Prison. This powerful composition was also recorded by Judy Collins. Although Paxton was never fêted in the manner of his early contemporaries his work reveals a thoughtful, perceptive craftsmanship.
●ALBUMS: *Live At The Gaslight* (Gaslight 1962)★★, *Ramblin' Boy* (Elektra 1964)★★★★, *Ain't That News* (Elektra 1965)★★★, *Outward Bound* (Elektra 1966)★★★, *Morning Again* (Elektra 1968)★★★, *The Things I Notice Now* (Elektra 1969)★★★★, *Tom Paxton 6* (Elektra 1970)★★★, *How Come The Sun* (Reprise 1971)★★★, *Peace Will Come* (1972)★★★, *New Songs Old Friends* (1973)★★★, *Children's Song Book* (1974)★★, *Something In My Life* (1975)★★★, *Saturday Night* (1976)★★★, *New Songs From The Briar Patch* (1977)★★, *Heroes* (1978)★★★, *Up And Up* (1980)★★★, *The Paxton Report* (1981)★★★, *The Marvellous Toy And Other Gallimaufry* (1984)★★, *In The Orchard* (1985)★★★, *One Million Lawyers And Other Disasters* (1985)★★★, *Even A Gray Day* (1986)★★★, *The Marvellous Toy* (1980)★★, *And Loving You* (1988)★★★, *Politics-Live* (1989)★★, *A Car Full Of Songs* (1990)★★★, *Suzy Is A Rocker* (1992)★★★, *Wearing The Time* (Sugar Hill 1995).
●COMPILATIONS: *The Compleat Tom Paxton* (Elektra 1971)★★★, *The Very Best Of Tom Paxton* (1988)★★★, *Storyteller* (1989)★★★.
●FURTHER READING: *Englebert The Elephant*, Tom Paxton and Steven Kellogg. *Belling The Cat And Other Aesop's Fables*, Tom Paxton and Robert Rayevsky.

PEACHES AND HERB

Herb Fame (b. Herbert Feemster, 1 October 1942) and Francine Barker (b. Francine Hurd, 1947). These two Washington-based singers were signed separately to the same record label, Date, and met on a promotional tour. Producer Dave Kapralik put the couple together, and their easy, if unexceptional, voices took 'Close Your Eyes' into the US Top 10 in 1967. The duo continued to figure in the charts as 'United' (1968) and 'When He Touches Me (Nothing Else Matters)' (1969). However, although Barker was featured on these records, she had been replaced for live performances by former session singer Marlene Mack, (b. 1945, Virginia, USA). The 'sweethearts of soul' were ostensibly disbanded in July 1970 when a disillusioned Fame left music in favour of the Police Department, although a 'bogus' duo hurriedly stepped in to fill the gap. Herb resumed recording in 1976 with a new 'Peaches', Linda Greene (b. Washington, DC, USA). Following a brief spell at MCA Records, the reconstituted couple moved to Polydor where they scored a major hit with 'Shake Your Groove Thing' (1978). The following year 'Reunited' reached number 1 in the US and number 4 in the UK. They continued to enjoy success into the 80s, but such releases lacked the charm of their early work.

●ALBUMS: *Let's Fall In Love* (Date 1967)★★★, *For Your Love* (Date 1967)★★★, *Golden Duets* (1967)★★★, *Peaches And Herb* (1977)★★, *2 Hot!* (1978)★★, *Twice The Fire* (1979)★★, *Worth The Wait* (1980)★★, *Sayin' Something* (1981)★★, *Remember* (1983).★★

●COMPILATIONS: *Peaches And Herb's Greatest Hits* (1968)★★★.

PEANUT BUTTER CONSPIRACY

Originally known as the Ashes, this Los Angeles quintet assumed the above name in 1966. The group, comprising Sandi Robinson (vocals), John Merrill (guitar), Lance Fent (guitar), Al Brackett (bass) and Jim Voigt (drums) made their debut with 'Time Is After You' for the locally based Vault label, before securing a major deal with Columbia/CBS the following year. Here they were united with producer Gary Usher, who sculpted a harmonious sound redolent of the Mamas And The Papas, Jefferson Airplane and Spanky And Our Gang. *The Peanut Butter Conspiracy Is Spreading* included their anthem-like single, 'It's A Happening Thing' and the haunting 'Then Came Love', but the album failed to make a significant commercial breakthrough. Fent was replaced by Bill Wolff for *The Great Conspiracy* wherein the group showed a greater emphasis on instrumental prowess. 'Turn On A Friend' and 'Time Is After You' confirmed the unit's undoubted potential, but they were dropped from the label following the failure of 'I'm A Fool'/'It's So Hard', a non-album single. A reshaped line-up emerged to complete *For Children Of All Ages* on the Challenge label, but this lacklustre set was a great disappointment and the group then folded. Lance Fent subsequently worked with Randy Meisner, while late-period member

Ralph Shuckett (ex-Clear Light) reappeared in Jo Mama.

●ALBUMS: *The Peanut Butter Conspiracy Is Spreading* (Columbia 1967)★★, *The Great Conspiracy* (Columbia 1968)★★★, *For Children Of All Ages* (Columbia 1968)★★.

●COMPILATIONS: *Turn On A Friend* (1989)★★★.

PEARLS BEFORE SWINE

Formed in Florida, USA, in 1965, Pearls Before Swine comprised Tom Rapp (vocals, guitar), Wayne Harley (autoharp, banjo, mandolin, vibraphone), Lane Lederer (bass, guitar, horns) and Roger Crissinger (keyboards). The latter was replaced by Jim Bohannon in 1967. The group pursued a recording deal with the *avant garde* ESP label, opining that the home of the Fugs would welcome their surrealist folk-rock. The quartet's debut, *One Nation Underground*, was an enticing mixture of intimate ballads and Bob Dylan-influenced ire, while Rapp's lisping delivery gave the group its distinctiveness. *Balaclava* followed a similar path, but enhanced the air of mystery with a succession of sound effects, string arrangements and contributions from jazz musician Joe Farrell. Although the Pearls' original members were now dropping out of the group, Rapp continued to forge an idiosyncratic path. *The Use Of Ashes* included 'Rocket Man', the artist's interpretation of a Ray Bradbury short story, which inspired the Elton John song of the same title. Rapp's later work, although still inventive, embraced more conventional styles and showed a marked interest in country styles. Such releases bore either his own name or that of the group at the whim of the relevant record company. Having achieved all he felt possible, Rapp retired from music in 1975 and has since become a successful lawyer.

●ALBUMS: *One Nation Underground* (ESP 1967)★★★, *Balaclava* (ESP 1968)★★★, *These Things Too* (Reprise 1969)★★, *The Use Of Ashes* (Reprise 1970)★★★, *City Of Gold* (Reprise 1971)★★, *Beautiful Lies You Could Live* (Reprise 1971)★★, *Familiar Songs* (1972)★★, *Stardancer* (1973)★★, *Sunforest* (1973)★★.

PEDDLERS

Though short of 'teen appeal', this seated, short-haired jazz-styled combo was appreciated by other artists for their stylistic tenacity and exacting technical standards. For much of 1964, the polished jazz-pop concoctions of ex-Tornado Tab Martin (b. 24 December 1944, Liverpool, England; bass), ex-Faron's Flamingo Trevor Morais (b. 16 October 1943, Liverpool, England; drums) and the Dowlands' former backing guitarist Roy Phillips (b. 5 May 1943, Parkstone, Poole, Dorset, England; Hammond organ/vocals) were heard nightly at London's exclusive Scotch of St. James's club - and, the following January, their arrangement of Teddy Randazzo's 'Let The Sunshine In', delivered by Phillips in a blues-tinged snort, slipped fleetingly into the UK Top 50. It took over four years for the three to come up trumps again when an invigorating CBS contract launched *Freewheelers* into the album chart. This was the harbinger of a Top 10 strike with the self-penned 'Birth', a stunningly innovative composition. The follow-up, 'Girlie', was a minor success and the Peddlers fared well in the album lists with *Birthday*. The long-term benefits of this commercial Indian summer included the broadening of the group's work spectrum - notably in providing musical interludes for television chat-shows - and the command of larger fees for their stock-in-trade cabaret bookings. When the trio split in the mid-70s, Martin found employment as a session player, Phillips emigrated to Australasia and Morais joined Quantum Jump.

●ALBUMS: *The Fantastic Peddlers* (1966)★★★, *Live At The Pickwick* (Philips 1967)★★★, *Freewheelers* (CBS 1968)★★★, *Three in A Cell* (CBS)★★★, *Birthday* (CBS 1970)★★★, *Three For All* (Philips 1970)★★★, *Georgia On My Mind* (Philips 1971)★★★, *Suite London* (Philips 1972)★★.

●COMPILATIONS: *The Best Of The Peddlers* (1974)★★★.

PENN, DAN

b. Wallace Daniel Pennington, 16 November 1941, Vernon, Alabama, USA. His reputation as a songwriter was secured when one of his early compositions, 'Is A Bluebird Blue?', was a hit for Conway Twitty in 1960. Penn also led a local group, the Mark V, which included David Briggs (piano), Norbert Putnam (bass) and Jerry Carrigan (drums). Also known as Dan Penn And The Pallbearers, these musicians later formed the core of the first Fame studio house band. Their subsequent departure for a more lucrative career in Nashville left room for a second session group, among whose number was pianist Spooner Oldham. Over the next few years, Penn's partnership with this newcomer produced scores of excellent southern soul compositions, including 'Out Of Left Field', 'It Tears Me Up' (Percy Sledge), 'Slippin' Around' (Clarence Carter) and 'Let's Do It Over' (Joe Simon) and 'Dark End Of The Street', a classic guilt-laced 'cheating' ballad, first recorded by James Carr. Penn subsequently left Fame to work at the rival American Sound studio where he joined studio-owner Chips Morman, with whom he had also struck up a songwriting partnership (their 'Do Right Woman - Do Right Man' was the b-side of Aretha Franklin's first hit single for Atlantic Records). Later at American Studios Penn would also be responsible for producing hit group the Box Tops, but in 1969 he broke away to form his own studio, Beautiful Sounds. The 70s, however, were much less prolific. However, having flirted with a singing career with several one-off releases, he finally produced a fine solo album, *Nobody's Fool*, which included the first version of 'I Hate You', later covered by Bobby Bland. Penn also maintained his friendship with Oldham, but by the time the duo formed their own independent production company, the changing face of popular music rendered their talents anachronistic. However, in 1991 Oldham and Penn reunited to appear at the New York Bottom Line's In Their Own Words songwriter series. This live performance of self-penned songs was so successful that it inspired Penn to

record a new album of his own work, both old and new, the critically acclaimed *Do Right Man*. To promote the album he played a further series of live dates including the 1994 Porretta Terme Soul Festival in Italy, and then at London's South Bank Centre as part of a salute to southern songwriters under the banner The American South, which also included Allen Toussaint and Joe South.

●ALBUMS: *Nobody's Fool* (1973)★★★, *Do Right Man* (Sire/Warners Brothers 1994)★★★★.

PENTANGLE

Formed in 1967, Pentangle was inspired by *Bert And John*, a collaborative album by folk musicians Bert Jansch (b. 3 November 1943, Glasgow, Scotland) and John Renbourn. Vocalist Jacqui McShee (b. *c*.1946, Catford, south London, England) an established figure on the traditional circuit, joined Danny Thompson (b. April 1939, London, England; bass) and Terry Cox (drums), both of Alexis Korner's Blues Incorporated, in a quintet which also embraced blues and jazz forms. Their respective talents were expertly captured on *The Pentangle*, where the delicate acoustic interplay between Jansch and Renbourn was brilliantly underscored by Thompson's sympathetic support and McShee's soaring intonation. Stylish original material balanced songs pulled from folk's heritage ('Let No Man Steal Your Thyme', 'Brunton Town'), while the inclusion of the Staple Singers' 'Hear My Call' confirmed the group's eclecticism. This feature was expanded on the double-set *Sweet Child*, which included two compositions by jazz bassist Charles Mingus, 'Haitian Fight Song' and 'Goodbye Pork Pie Hat'. The group enjoyed considerable commercial success with *Basket Of Light*, which included 'Light Flight', the theme song to the UK television series, *Take Three Girls*. However, despite an undoubted dexterity and the introduction of muted electric instruments, subsequent releases were marred by a sense of sterility, and lacked the passion of concurrent releases undertaken by the two guitarists. Pentangle was disbanded in 1972, following which Thompson began a partnership with John Martyn. Cox undertook a lucrative session career before backing French singer Charles Aznavour, and while Jansch continued his solo career, McShee fronted the John Renbourn Band between 1974 and 1981. The original Pentangle reconvened the following year for a European tour and *Open The Door*, although defections owing to outside commitments led to considerable changes. McShee, Cox and Jansch were joined by Nigel Portman-Smith (bass) and Mike Piggott for 1986's *In The Round*. Cox was then replaced by Gerry Conway and Piggott by Rod Clemens (ex-Lindisfarne) for *So Early In The Spring* (1988). *Think Of Tomorrow*, released three years later, saw Clements make way for guitarist Peter Kirtley. The same line-up also completed 1993's *One More Road* and 1994's *Live*. At this time Jansch once more became distracted by solo projects and the group's later shows saw him replaced by former Cat Stevens' guitarist Alun Davies. By 1995 McShee had released her debut solo album (with Conway and Spencer Cozens), and intimated that the Pentangle story might now be drawing to a close. 'It feels like it's the end to me at the moment, but it wouldn't surprise me if Bert said that he fancied doing some more gigs.' Renbourne and McShee celebrated 30 years of playing together with a series of concerts in the spring of 1996.

●ALBUMS: *The Pentangle* (Transatlantic 1968)★★★★, *Sweet Child* (Transatlantic 1968)★★★★, *Basket Of Light* (Transatlantic 1969)★★★★, *Cruel Sister* (Transatlantic 1970)★★★, *Solomon's Seal* (Reprise 1972)★★★, *Open The Door* (Making Waves 1982)★★★, *In The Round* (Making Waves 1988)★★★, *So Early In The Spring* (1988)★★★, *Think Of Tomorrow* (1991)★★★, *One More Road* (1993)★★★, *Live At The BBC* (Strange Fruit 1994)★★★★, *Live 1994* (Hypertension 1995).

●COMPILATIONS: *Reflections* (Transatlantic 1971)★★★★, *History Book* (Transatlantic 1971)★★★★, *Pentangling* (Transatlantic 1973)★★★★, *The Pentangle Collection* (1975)★★★★, *Anthology* (1978)★★★★, *The Essential Pentangle Volume 1* (Transatlantic 1987)★★★★, *The Essential Pentangle Volume 2* (Transatlantic 1987)★★★, *People On The Highway 1968 - 1971* (Demon 1993)★★★★.

PERRY, LEE

b. Rainford Hugh Perry, 28 March 1936, Hanover, Jamaica, West Indies, aka Scratch and the Upsetter. Small in stature, but larger than life, 'Little' Lee Perry began his musical career working for seminal producer Coxsone Dodd during the late 50s and early 60s, acting as a record scout, organising recording sessions, and later supervising auditions at Dodd's record shop in Orange Street, Kingston. By 1963, as well as handling production and songwriting for Delroy Wilson ('Joe Liges', 'Spit In The Sky') and the Maytals, Perry had released the first of his own vocal records through Dodd. Featuring a bluesy, declamatory vocal style over superb backing from the legendary Skatalites, these tracks set a pattern from which Perry, throughout his career, rarely deviated. Social and personal justice, bawdy, sometimes lewd sexual commentary, and, like the material he wrote for Delroy Wilson, stinging attacks on musical rivals - mainly former Coxsone employee Prince Buster - are all prefigured on these early tracks such as 'Prince In The Pack', 'Trial And Crosses', 'Help The Weak', 'Give Me Justice', 'Chicken Scratch' (from which he acquired his nickname), 'Doctor Dick' with Rita Marley and the Soulettes on backing vocals, and 'Madhead', recorded between 1963 and 1966. Incidentally, there was obviously no acrimony between Buster and Perry, as the latter often appeared on Buster's records, including 'Ghost Dance' and 'Judge Dread'. Also during his sojourn with Dodd he began an association with the Wailers that had further repercussions later in the decade.

In 1966 Perry fell out with Coxsone and began working with other producers including JJ Johnson, Clancy Eccles and, in 1968, Joe Gibbs, for whom he wrote songs and produced artists such as Errol Dunkley, and the Pioneers. With Gibbs, he also voiced a bitter snipe directed at Dodd entitled 'The Upsetter' from which he gained his next apt epithet. On parting with Gibbs, Perry recorded several fine titles, including the big local hit, 'People Funny Boy' (1968), a vicious record, featuring a chugging rhythm in the new reggae style given to him by Clancy Eccles, wherein Perry took his former employer to task for allegedly ignoring his role in Gibbs' success, the slight made all the more pointed by employing the melody he had used for the Pioneers' hit 'Longshot'. In 1968 he the set up his own Upsetter label in Jamaica, again with help from Clancy Eccles. Right away he began having hits with David Isaacs ('Place In The Sun') and the Untouchables ('Tighten Up', which lent its title to the classic series of early 70s reggae compilations on Trojan Records), and, in common with other early reggae producers, secured a deal with Trojan whereby his records were released under his imprint in the UK.

Perry experienced his first taste of UK chart success with tenor saxophonist Val Bennett's spaghetti western-inspired title, 'Return Of Django', which spent three weeks at number 5 in the UK charts during October 1969. At the same time he began producing the Wailers on a series of records including 'Small Axe', 'Duppy Conqueror', and 'Soul Rebel', mostly available on a number of recent compilations, and which are now considered to be among that group's finest work. Just over 100 singles were released on Upsetter between 1969 and 1974 by artists such as Dave Barker (Dave And Ansell Collins) ('Shocks Of Mighty', 'Upsetting Station'), Dennis Alcapone ('Alpha & Omega'), the Stingers ('Give Me Power'), the Bleechers ('Come Into My Parlour', 'Check Him Out'), Neville Hinds ('Blackmans Time'), Leo Graham ('Newsflash'), Big Youth ('Mooving (sic) Version'), and the legendary Junior Byles ('Beat Down Babylon', 'Place Called Africa'). He also unleashed a welter of intense, energetic, and just plain barmy instrumentals: 'Night Doctor', 'Live Injection', 'Cold Sweat', 'Django Shoots First', 'The Vampire' and 'Drugs & Poison'. Other productions such as 'Selassie' by the Reggae Boys, the instrumentals 'Dry Acid', 'Return Of The Ugly', 'Clint Eastwood', and many more, appeared on other B&C and Pama labels.

From 1972-74 Perry slowed the rhythm down and consolidated his position as one of the leading innovators in Jamaican music. He released instrumentals like 'French Connection', 'Black Ipa', and DJ tracks by artists such as U-Roy (who had recorded two of his earliest records, 'Earths Rightful Ruler' and the demented 'OK Corral', for Perry in the late 60s), Dillinger, Dr. Alimantado, I Roy and Charlie Ace (on the unique and bizarre cut-and-mix extravaganza, 'Cow Thief Skak'). Perry was also one of the first producers to utilize the talents of King Tubby, then just starting his own operations, and released important early dub albums like *Rhythm Shower* (1972) and the glorious *Blackboard Jungle Dub* (1973). Perry's productions from this period: the Gatherers' monolithic 'Words Of My Mouth', Milton Henry's 'This World' - whose rhythm also served Junior Byles' reading of Little Willie John's 'Fever' and Augustus Pablo's melodic workout 'Hot & Cold', Perry's own 'Jungle Lion', the Classics' 'Civilisation', and many others, are among the heaviest and most exciting reggae records of their day.

In 1974 Perry opened his own studio, dubbed the Black Ark, situated in his back yard at Washington Gardens, Kingston. Almost immediately he scored a big Jamaican hit with Junior Byles' hugely influential 'Curly Locks'. In 1975 his production of Susan Cadogan's seminal lovers rock tune 'Hurt So Good' reached number 4 in the UK charts. He also released the overlooked but innovative dub album *Revolution Dub* (1975), featuring some of his heaviest contemporary productions like Bunny And Rickey's 'Bushweed Corntrash', Junior Byles' 'The Long Way', and Jimmy Riley's 'Womans Gotta Have It', all garnished with Perry's crazy sing-along rhymes and bursts of dialogue 'sampled' from the television. From 1975 he began to employ studio technology, notably phase shifters and rudimentary drum machines, to produce a dense, multi-layered mixing style that is instantly recognizable, and eminently inimitable. It is all the more remarkable for the fact that all this was achieved in a four-track studio. By 1976 Island Records had begun to release the fruits of this latest phase, including music by the Heptones (*Party Time*), Max Romeo (*War Inna Babylon*), Bob Marley And The Wailers ('Jah Live', 'Punky Reggae Party'), George Faith (*To Be A Lover*), Junior Murvin (*Police & Thieves*, the single of the same title being very popular in Jamaica at the time, and becoming a belated chart hit in the UK in May 1980), Prince Jazzbo (*Natty Passing Through*, released on Black Wax), and the Upsetters (the classic *Super Ape*). However, Island rejected his own vocal album *Roast Fish, Collie Weed & Corn Bread* (1978), and missed out on the Congos classic, *Heart Of The Congos*, which finally gained a UK release some years later on the Beat's Go Feet label.

With commercial success now coming infrequently the frustrations and personal problems began to increase. He was still making wonderful records; 'Mr Money Man' by Danny Hensworth, 'Open The Gate' by Watty Burnett, 'Garden Of Life' by Leroy Sibbles, and many others, but his style was now so far removed from the reggae mainstream that they met with little success in Jamaica or abroad. Perry's behaviour became increasingly strange and bewildering, and in 1980 he destroyed his studio and left for Britain, where he conducted a number of puzzling interviews that seemed to add credence to reports of his mental decline. Since then he has made a long series of eccentric, often self-indulgent solo albums with a variety of different collaborators including Adrian Sherwood, Lloyd Barnes, and Mad Professor, totally outside the mainstream of Jamaican music. Simultaneously, his earlier work began to receive significant critical and cult attention as well as commanding high prices in the collector's market. After living in the Netherlands in the mid-80s he moved back to London, occasionally performing live. In 1990 he went to Switzerland, worked with

a new management team, and reputedly married a Swiss millionairess. He also returned to Jamaica with the intention of rebuilding the trashed and burnt out Black Ark, although sadly this plan does not yet seem to have come to fruition. Whatever the future holds, Lee 'Scratch' Perry, the Upsetter, the man Bob Marley once described as a 'genius', has already made one of the most individual contributions to the development of Jamaican music, both as producer/arranger/writer, and simply as a singularly powerful guiding force during several crucial phases.

●ALBUMS: As Lee Perry/Lee Perry And The Upsetters: *The Upsetter* (Trojan 1969)★★★★, *Many Moods Of The Upsetter* (1970)★★★, *Scratch The Upsetter Again* (1970)★★★★, with Dave Barker *Prisoner Of Love: Dave Barker Meets The Upsetters* (Trojan 1970), *Africa's Blood* (1972)★★★, *Battle Axe* (1972)★★★, *Cloak & Dagger* (Rhino 1972)★★★, *Double Seven* (Trojan 1973)★★★, *Rhythm Shower* (Upsetter 1973)★★★, *Blackboard Jungle* 1974)★★★★, *Kung Fu Meets The Dragon* (D.I.P. 1974)★★★, *D.I.P. Presents The Upsetter* (D.I.P. 1974)★★★, *Revolution Dub* (Cactus 1975)★★★★, *The Super Ape* (Mango/Island 1976)★★★, with Jah Lion, as producer *Colombia Colly* (Mango/Island 1976)★★★, with Prince Jazzbo *Natty Passing Through* (Black Wax 1976) aka *Ital Corner* (Clocktower 1980), *Return Of The Super Ape* (Lion Of Judah/Mango 1977)★★★, *Roast Fish, Collie Weed & Corn Bread* (Lion Of Judah 1978)★★★, *Scratch On The Wire* (Island 1979)★★★, *Scratch And Company: Chapter 1* (Clocktower 1980)★★★, *Return Of Pipecock Jackson* (Black Star 1981)★★★, *Mystic Miracle Star* (Heartbeat 1982)★★★, *History Mystery & Prophecy* (Mango/Island 1984)★★★, *Black Ark Vol. 1 & 2* (Black Ark 1984)★★★, *Black Ark In Dub* (Black Ark 1985)★★★, *Battle Of Armagideon: Millionaire Liquidator* (Trojan 1986)★★★, with Dub Syndicate: *Time Boom X De Devil Dead* (On-U-Sound 1987)★★★, *Satan Kicked The Bucket* (Wackies 1988)★★★, *Scratch Attack* (RAS 1988)★★★, *Chicken Scratch* (Heartbeat 1989)★★★, *Turn And Fire* (Anachron 1989)★★★, with Bullwackie *Lee 'Scratch' Perry Meets Bullwackie - Satan's Dub* (ROIR 1990)★★★, *Build The Ark* (Trojan 1990)★★★, *From The Secret Laboratory* (Mango/Island 1990)★★★, *Message From Yard* (Rohit 1990)★★★, *Blood Vapour* (La/Unicorn 1990)★★★, with Mad Professor *Lee Scratch Perry Meets The Mad Professor, Volumes 1 & 2* (Ariwa 1990)★★★, *Spiritual Healing* (Black Cat 1991)★★★, *God Muzick* (Network/Kook Kat 1991)★★★, *The Upsetter And The Beat* (Heartbeat 1992)★★★, *Soundz From The Hot Line* (Heartbeat 1993)★★★, *Magnetic Mirror Master Mix* (Anachron 1990)★★★, with Mad Professor *Lee 'Scratch' Perry Meets The Mad Professor In Dub, Volumes 1 & 2* (Angella 1991)★★★.

●COMPILATIONS: *The Upsetter Collection* (Trojan 1981)★★★★, *Reggae Greats* (Island 1984)★★★, *Best Of* (Pama 1984)★★★★, *The Upsetter Box Set* (Trojan

1985)★★★, *Some Of The Best* (Heartbeat 1986)★★★, *The Upsetter Compact Set* (1988)★★★★, *All The Hits* (Rohit 1989)★★★★, *Larks From The Ark* (Nectar Masters 1995)★★★, *Voodooism* (Pressure Sounds 1996)★★★. As Lee Perry And Friends *Give Me Power* (Trojan 1988)★★★, *Open The Gate* (Trojan 1989)★★★, *Shocks Of Mighty 1969-1974* (Attack 1989)★★★, *Public Jestering* (Attack 1990). As the Upsetters *Version Like Rain* (Trojan 1990). Various: *Heart Of The Ark, Volume 1* (Seven Leaves 1982)★★★, *Heart Of The Ark, Volume 2* (Seven Leaves 1983)★★★, *Turn & Fire: Upsetter Disco Dub* (1989)★★★, *Megaton Dub* (Seven Leaves 1983)★★★, *Megaton Dub 2* (Seven Leaves 1983)★★★.
●VIDEOS: *The Ultimate Destruction* (1992).

PETER AND GORDON

Both the sons of doctors and former pupils of the prestigious English public school Westminster Boys, this privileged pair were signed by producer Norman Newell, following a residency at London's Piccadilly Club. Peter Asher (b. 2 June 1944, London, England) and Gordon Waller (b. 4 June 1945, Braemar, Grampian, Scotland), had a crucial advantage over their contemporaries - the priceless patronage of Paul McCartney, who was then dating Peter's sister, Jane. The perfectly enunciated 'A World Without Love' quickly became a transatlantic chart topper and two more 1964 McCartney compositions, 'Nobody I Know' and 'I Don't Want To See You Again', brought further success. The Beatle connection was again evident on 'Woman', which McCartney composed under the pseudonym Bernard Webb. In the meantime, the duo had switched to successful revivals of 50s material, including Buddy Holly's 'True Love Ways' and the Teddy Bears' retitled 'To Know You Is To Love You'. Peter And Gordon's wholesome image was somewhat belied by Waller's appearances in the salacious British Sunday press, but this did little to affect their popularity in the USA. Although the partnership was strained by late 1966, the saucy 'Lady Godiva' provided a new direction and was followed by the similarly- uaint novelty numbers 'Knight In Rusty Armour' and 'Sunday For Tea'. One year later, they split. Waller subsequently pursued an unsuccessful solo career while Asher emerged as a formidable producer and manager.
●ALBUMS: *Peter And Gordon* (Columbia 1964)★★★, *A World Without Love* (Capitol 1964)★★★, *In Touch With Peter And Gordon* (Columbia 1964)★★★, *I Don't Want To See You Again* (Capitol 1965)★★★, *I Go To Pieces* (Columbia 1965)★★★, *True Love Ways* (Capitol 1965)★★★, *Hurtin' 'N' Lovin'* (Columbia 1965)★★★, *Sing The Hits Of Nashville* (Capitol 1966)★★, *Woman* (Columbia 1966)★★★, *Somewhere* (Columbia 1966)★★★, *Lady Godiva* (Columbia 1967)★★, *A Knight In Rusty Armour* (Capitol 1967)★★, *In London For Tea* (Capitol 1967)★★, *Hot, Cold And Custard* (Capitol 1968)★★.
●COMPILATIONS: *Peter And Gordon's Greatest Hits* (Columbia 1966)★★★, *The Best Of Peter And Gordon*

(1983)★★★, *Hits And More* (1986)★★★, *The EP Collection* (See For Miles 1996)★★★.

PETER, PAUL AND MARY

Peter Yarrow (b. 31 May 1938, New York City, New York, USA), Noel Paul Stookey (b. Paul Stookey, 30 November 1937, Baltimore, Maryland, USA) and Mary Allin Travers (b. 7 November 1937, Louisville, Kentucky, USA) began performing together in the spring of 1961. They were brought together by Albert Grossman, one of folk music's successful entrepreneurs, in an attempt to create a contemporary Kingston Trio. The three singers were already acquainted through the close-knit coffeehouse circuit, although Dave Van Ronk was briefly considered as a possible member. The group popularized several topical songs, including 'If I Had A Hammer' and were notable early interpreters of Bob Dylan compositions. In 1963 their version of 'Blowin' In The Wind' reached number 2 in the US chart while a follow-up reading of 'Don't Think Twice, It's Alright' also broached the Top 10. They were also renowned for singing children's songs, the most memorable of which was the timeless 'Puff The Magic Dragon'. The trio became synonymous with folk's liberal traditions, but were increasingly perceived as old-fashioned as the 60s progressed. Nonetheless a 1966 selection, *Album*, included material by Laura Nyro and featured assistance from Paul Butterfield, Mike Bloomfield and Al Kooper, while the following year's 'I Dig Rock 'N' Roll Music' became their fifth US Top 10 hit. Peter, Paul And Mary enjoyed their greatest success in 1969 with 'Leaving On A Jet Plane'. This melodramatic John Denver song reached number 1 in the US and number 2 in the UK, but by then the individual members were branching out in different directions. Yarrow had been the primary force behind *You Are What You Eat*, an eccentric hippie film which also featured Tiny Tim and John Simon, and in 1970 he, Travers and Stookey announced their formal dissolution. The three performers embarked on solo careers but were ultimately unable to escape the legacy of their former group. They reunited briefly in 1972 for a George McGovern Democratic Party rally, and again in 1978. They have since continued to perform material reminiscent of their golden era. Although criticized for a smooth and wholesome delivery, Peter, Paul and Mary was one of the era's most distinctive acts and played a crucial bridging role between two contrasting generations of folk music.
●ALBUMS: *Peter, Paul And Mary* (Warners 1962)★★★★, *Peter, Paul And Mary - Moving* (Warners 1963)★★★★, *In The Wind* (Warners 1963)★★★★, *Peter, Paul And Mary In Concert* (Warners 1964)★★★★, *A Song Will Rise* (Warners 1965)★★★, *See What Tomorrow Brings* (Warners 1965)★★★, *Peter, Paul And Mary Album* (Warners 1966)★★★★, *Album 1700* (1967)★★★, *Late Again* (Warners 1968)★★★, *Peter, Paul And Mommy* (1969)★★, *Reunion* (1978)★★★, *Such Is Love* (1982)★★, *No Easy Walk To Freedom* (1988)★★, *LifeLines Live* (Warners 1996)★★.
Solo: Peter Yarrow *Peter* (1972)★★, *That's Enough For*

Me (1973)★★, Hard Times (1975). Paul Stookey Paul And (1971)★★, Band And Body Works (1980). Mary Travers Mary (1971)★★, Morning Glory (1972)★★, All My Choices (1973)★★, Circles (1974)★★, It's In Everyone Of Us (1978)★★.

●COMPILATIONS: 10 Years Together/The Best Of Peter, Paul And Mary (1970)★★★★, Most Beautiful Songs (1973)★★★, Collection (1982)★★★.

●VIDEOS: Lifelines (Warner Reprise 1996).

PETERSON, OSCAR

b. Oscar Emmanuel Peterson, 15 August 1925, Montreal, Canada. Blessed with an attractive stage personality, this behemoth of mainstream jazz's fluid technique was influenced by Art Tatum, Errol Garner and, later, George Shearing. After studying trumpet, illness redirected him to the piano. His enthusiasm resulted in endless hours of practic e which helped mould his remarkable technique. In his mid-teens, after winning a local talent contest in 1940, Peterson was heard regularly on radio in Canada and beyond. By 1944, he was the featured pianist with the nationally famous Johnny Holmes Orchestra before leading his own trio. Peterson was unusual in not serving an apprenticeship as an older player's sideman. Although early recordings were disappointing, he received lucrative offers to appear in the USA but these were resisted until a debut at New York's Carnegie Hall with Norman Granz's Jazz At The Philharmonic in September 1949. Louis Armstrong, Billie Holiday, Count Basie, Dizzy Gillespie, Zoot Sims, Ella Fitzgerald and Stan Getz have been among Peterson's collaborators during a career that has encompassed hundreds of studio and concert recordings. With 1963's Affinity as his biggest seller, Peterson's output has ranged from albums drawn from the songbooks of Cole Porter and Duke Ellington, to a Verve single of Jimmy Forrest's perennial 'Night Train', and 1964's self-written Canadiana Suite. Although he introduced a modicum of Nat 'King' Cole-type vocals into his repertoire in the mid-50s, he has maintained a certain steady consistency of style that has withstood the buffeting of fashion.

Since 1970, he has worked with no fixed group, often performing alone, although at the end of the 70s Peterson had a long stint with bass player Neils-Henning Ørsted Pedersen which continued well into the 80s. The soundtrack to the movie Play It Again Sam, the hosting of a television chat show, a 1974 tour of Soviet Russia, and 1981's A Royal Wedding Suite (conducted by Russ Garcia) have been more recent commercial high points of a fulfilling and distinguished professional life. While musicians as diverse as Steve Winwood, Dudley Moore and Weather Report's Joe Zawinul absorbed much from Peterson discs, younger admirers have been advantaged by his subsequent publication of primers such as Jazz Exercises And Pieces and Peterson's New Piano Solos. Peterson's dazzling technique and unflagging swing have helped make him one of the most highly regarded and instantly identifiable pianists in jazz. Although the technical qualities of his work have sometimes cooled the

emotional heart of his material, Peterson's commitment to jazz is undeniable. The high standard of his work over the years is testimony to his dedication and to the care which he and his mentor, Granz, have exercised over the pianist's career. Throughout this time, Peterson has displayed through his eclecticism an acute awareness of the history of jazz piano, ranging from stride to bop, from James P. Johnson to Bill Evans, but always with Art Tatum as an abiding influence. However, this influence is one that Peterson has been careful to control. Tatum may colour Peterson's work but he has never shaped it. Thus, for all his influences, Peterson is very much his own man. Yet, for all the admiration he draws from other pianists, there is little evidence that he has many followers. He may well prove to be the end of the line of master musicians in the history of jazz piano.

●ALBUMS: Oscar Peterson Piano Solos (Mercury 1950)★★★, Oscar Peterson At Carnegie Hall (Mercury 1951)★★★★, Oscar Peterson Collates (Mercury 1952)★★★, The Oscar Peterson Quartet (Mercury 1952)★★★, Oscar Peterson Plays Pretty (Mercury 1952)★★★, This Is Oscar Peterson (RCA Victor 1952)★★★, In Concert (1952)★★★, Jazz At The Philharmonic, Hartford 1953 (Pablo 1953 recording)★★★, Oscar Peterson Plays Cole Porter (Mercury 1953)★★★, Oscar Peterson Plays Irving Berlin (Mercury 1953)★★★, Oscar Peterson Plays George Gershwin (Mercury 1953)★★★, Oscar Peterson Plays Duke Ellington (Mercury 1953)★★★, Oscar Peterson Collates No. 2 (Clef 1953)★★★, 1953 Live (Jazz Band Records)★★★, Oscar Peterson Plays Pretty No. 2 (Clef 1954)★★★, The Oscar Peterson Quartet No. 2 (Clef 1954)★★★, Oscar Peterson Plays Jerome Kern (Clef 1954)★★★, Oscar Peterson Plays Richard Rogers (Clef 1954)★★★, Oscar Peterson Plays Vincent Youmans (Clef 1954)★★★, Verve Jazz Masters (Verve 1953-1962 recordings)★★★, At Zardi's (Pablo 1955 recording)★★★, Oscar Peterson Plays Harry Warren (Clef 1955)★★★, Oscar Peterson Plays Harold Arlen (Clef 1955)★★★, Oscar Peterson Plays Jimmy McHugh (Clef 1955)★★★, Recital By Oscar Peterson (Clef 1956)★★★, Nostalgic Memories By Oscar Peterson (Clef 1956)★★★, An Evening With Oscar Peterson Duo/Quartet (Clef 1956)★★★, Oscar Peterson Plays Count Basie (Clef 1956)★★★, In A Romantic Mood - Oscar Peterson With Strings (Verve 1956)★★★, Pastel Moods By Oscar Peterson (Verve 1956)★★★, Romance - The Vocal Styling Of Oscar Peterson (Verve 1956)★★★, Soft Sands (Verve 1957)★★★, The Oscar Peterson Trio At The Stratford Shakesperean Festival (Verve 1957)★★★★, Keyboard Music By Oscar Peterson (Verve 1957)★★★, Oscar Peterson Trio With Sonny Stitt, Roy Eldridge And Jo Jo Jones At Newport (Verve 1958)★★★★, Oscar Peterson Trio At The Concertgebouw (Verve 1958)★★★, Oscar Peterson Trio With The Modern Jazz Quartet At The Opera House (Verve 1958)★★★, A Night On The Town (Verve 1958)★★★, Oscar Peterson Plays My Fair Lady (Verve 1958)★★★, The Oscar Peterson Trio With

David Rose (Verve 1958)★★★, The Silver Collection (Verve 1959-63 recordings)★★★, Songs For A Swingin' Affair - A Jazz Portrait Of Frank Sinatra (Verve 1959)★★, The Jazz And Soul Of Oscar Peterson (Verve 1959)★★★, Swinging Brass With The Oscar Peterson Trio (Verve 1959)★★★, Plays The Cole Porter Songbook (Verve 1960)★★★★, Plays Porgy And Bess (Verve 1960)★★★, The Music From Fiorello (Verve 1960)★★★, The Oscar Peterson Trio At J.A.T.P. (Verve 1960)★★★, with Louis Armstrong Louis Armstrong Meets Oscar Peterson (Verve 1961)★★★, The Trio Live From Chicago (Verve 1961)★★★, Very Tall (Verve 1962)★★★, West Side Story (Verve 1962)★★, Bursting Out With The All Star Big Band! (Verve 1962)★★★, The Sound Of The Trio (Verve 1962)★★★, Night Train (Verve 1963)★★★★, Affinity (Verve 1963)★★★, with Nelson Riddle The Oscar Peterson Trio With Nelson Riddle (Verve 1963)★★★, with Gerry Mulligan The Oscar Peterson Trio And The Gerry Mulligan Four At Newport (Verve 1963)★★★, Exclusively For My Friends (1964)★★★, Oscar Peterson Trio + One (Mercury 1964)★★★, Canadian Suite (Limelight 1964)★★★, We Get Requests (Verve 1965)★★, Eloquence (Limelight 1965)★★★, With Respect To Nat (Limelight 1965)★★★, Blues Etude (Limelight 1966)★★★, Put On A Happy Face (Verve 1966)★★★, Something Warm (Verve 1966)★★★, Stage Right (Verve 1966)★★★, Thoroughly Modern 20s (Verve 1967)★★, Night Train Vol 2 (Verve 1967)★★★, Soul-O! (Prestige 1968)★★★, My Favourite Instrument (1968)★★★, The Vienna Concert (Philology 1969)★★★, Oscar's Oscar Peterson Plays The Academy Awards (Verve 1969)★★★, Motion's And Emotions (MPS 1969)★★★, Hello Herbie (MPS 1969)★★★, The Great Oscar Peterson On Prestige (Prestige 1969)★★★, Oscar Peterson Plays For Lovers (Prestige 1969)★★★, Easy Walker (Prestige 1969)★★★, Tristeza On Piano (MPS 1970)★★★, Three Originals (MPS 1970)★★★, Tracks (1970)★★★, Reunion Blues (MPS 1972)★★★, Terry's Tune (1974)★★★, The Trio (Pablo 1975)★★★, The Good Life (Original Jazz Classics 1975)★★★, with Sonny Stitt Sittin' In (1975)★★★, with Dizzy Gillespie Oscar Peterson And Dizzy Gillespie (Pablo 1975)★★★, with Roy Eldridge Oscar Peterson And Roy Eldridge (Original Jazz Classics 1975)★★★, At The Montreaux Jazz Festival 1975 (Pablo 1976)★★★, Again (1977)★★★, Oscar Peterson Jam (1977)★★★, The Vocal Styling Of Oscar Peterson (1977)★★★, Montreaux '77 i (Original Jazz Classics 1978)★★★, Montreaux '77 ii (Original Jazz Classics 1978)★★★, The Silent Partner (1979)★★★, The Paris Concert (Pablo 1979)★★★, Skol (Original Jazz Classics 1980)★★★, The Personal Touch (Pablo 1981)★★★, A Royal Wedding Suite (Pablo 1981)★★, Live At The Northsea Jazz Festival (Pablo 1981)★★, Nigerian Marketplace (Pablo 1982)★★★, Romance (1982)★★★, with Stéphane Grappelli, Joe Pass, Mickey Roker, Niels-Henning Ørsted Pedersen Skol (1982)★★★, In Russia (Pablo 1982)★★★, Oscar Peterson & Harry Edison (Pablo 1982)★★★, Carioca (Happy Bird 1983)★★★, A Tribute To My Friends (Pablo 1984)★★★, Time After Time (Pablo 1984)★★★, If You Could See Me Now (Pablo 1984)★★★, Live! (Pablo 1987)★★★, Live At the Blue Note (Telarc 1991)★★★, Saturday Night At The Blue Note (Telarc 1991)★★★, Last Call At The Blue Note (Telarc 1992)★★★, The More I See You (Telarc 1995)★★★, Christmas (Telarc 1995)★★, ... Meets Roy Hargrove And Ralph Moore (Telarc 1996)★★★, The London House Sessions 5-CD box set (Verve 1996)★★★★.

●COMPILATIONS: History Of An Artist (Pablo 1982)★★★, History Of An Artist, Volume 2 (Pablo 1987)★★★, Compact Jazz: Oscar Peterson And Friends (Verve 1988)★★★★, Compact Jazz: Plays Jazz Standards (Verve 1988)★★★★, Exclusively For My Friends Vols. 1-4 (1992)★★★.

●VIDEOS: Music In The Key Of Oscar (View Video 1995).

●FURTHER READING: Oscar Peterson Highlights Jazz Piano, Oscar Peterson. Oscar Peterson: The Will To Swing, Gene Lees.

PHILLIPS, ESTHER

b. Esther Mae Jones, 23 December 1935, Galveston, Texas, USA, d. 7 August 1984, Carson, California, USA. This distinctive vocalist was discovered by bandleader Johnny Otis. She joined his revue in 1949 where, as 'Little Esther', the teenage singer recorded two number 1 R&B singles, 'Double Crossing Blues' and 'Mistrustin' Blues'. She then worked solo following the band's collapse, but by the middle of the decade Phillips was chronically addicted to drugs. In 1954 she retired to Houston to recuperate and did not fully resume recording until 1962. Phillips' version of 'Release Me', a country standard which was later a hit for Engelbert Humperdinck, mirrored the blend of black and white music found, contemporaneously, in Ray Charles and Solomon Burke. An album, Release Me! - Reflections Of Country And Western Greats, consolidated this style, but when Phillips moved to the Atlantic label, her recordings assumed a broader aspect. Polished interpretations of show tunes and standards contrasted a soul-based perspective shown in her retitled version of the John Lennon/Paul McCartney song, 'And I Love Him', a performance showcased on the syndicated television show, Around The Beatles. Her unique, nasal intonation was perfect for her 1966 hit, 'When A Woman Loves A Man', while her several collaborations with the Dixie Flyers, the highly respected Criteria studio houseband, were artistically successful. The singer moved to Kudu Records in 1972 where she recorded the distinctly biographical 'Home Is Where The Hatred Is', an uncompromising Gil Scott-Heron composition. The same label provided 'What A Diff'rence A Day Makes' (1975), which reached the US Top 20 and the UK Top 10. She also completed two exceptional albums at this time, From A Whisper To A Scream and Alone Again Naturally, but was increasingly pushed towards a specialist rather than popular audience. Ill health sadly undermined this artist's undoubted potential, and in August 1984, Phillips died of liver and kidney failure.

●ALBUMS: *Memory Lane* (1956)★★★, *Down Memory Lane With Little Esther* (King 1959)★★★, *Release Me! - Reflections Of Country And Western Greats* (Lenox 1963)★★, *And I Love Him* (Atlantic 1965)★★★★, *Esther* (Atlantic 1966)★★★, *The Country Side Of Esther Phillips* (Atlantic 1966)★★, *Burnin' - Live At Freddie Jett's Pied Piper LA* (1970)★★★, *From A Whisper To A Scream* (Kudu 1972)★★★★, *Alone Again Naturally* (1972)★★★★, *Black-Eyed Blues* (1973)★★, *Performance* (Kudu 1974)★★★, *What A Difference A Day Makes* (1975)★★★, *Confessin' The Blues* (Atlantic 1975)★★★, with guitarist Joe Beck *Esther Phillips With Beck* (1975)★★★, *For All We Know* (1976)★★★, *Capricorn Princess* (1976)★★★, *You've Come A Long Way Baby* (1977)★★★, *All About Esther* (1978)★★, *Here's Esther ... Are You Ready* (1979)★★, *A Good Black Is Hard To Crack* (1981)★★.

●COMPILATIONS: *Little Esther Phillips - The Complete Savoy Recordings* rec. 1949-1959 (1984)★★★★.

PICKETT, BOBBY 'BORIS'

b. 11 February 1940, Somerville, Massachusetts, USA. Bobby 'Boris' Pickett (And The Crypt-Kickers) recorded the US number 1 'Monster Mash' in 1962, a song which has remained alive for decades due to perennial radio airplay each Halloween. Pickett moved to Los Angeles in 1961, upon his release from military service, hoping to become an actor. Instead, he joined a singing group called the Cordials. Pickett, an avowed fan of actor Boris Karloff, worked an impression of the horror film star into some of the group's songs and he and the Cordials' Leonard Capizzi wrote 'Monster Mash' to cash in on the dance craze launched by Dee Dee Sharp's 'Mashed Potato Time' hit of 1962. Pickett was signed to Gary S. Paxton's Garpax label and 'Monster Mash' worked its way to the top of the charts in time for Halloween 1962. The record later returned to the US charts twice, this time on Parrot Records, reaching number 91 in 1970 and then hitting the Top 10 for a second time three years later. It was not until 1973 that the song made any significant impact upon the UK chart, when it reached number 3 in September. It was also successfully covered by the UK group the Bonzo Bog Doo-Dah Band. Pickett had two other minor US chart singles in 1962-63, including the Top 30 'Monster's Holiday', but he is indelibly linked with the classic novelty number.

●ALBUMS: *The Original Monster Mash* (Garpax 1962)★★.

PICKETT, WILSON

b. 18 March 1941, Prattville, Alabama, USA. Raised in Detroit, Pickett sang in several of the city's R&B groups. He later joined the Falcons, an act already established by

the million-selling 'You're So Fine'. Pickett wrote and sang lead on their 1962 hit, 'I Found A Love', after which he launched his solo career. A false start at Correctone was overturned by two powerful singles, 'If You Need Me' and 'It's Too Late', recorded for Lloyd Price's Double L outlet. The former track's potential was undermined by Solomon Burke's opportunistic cover version on Atlantic Records, the irony of which was compounded when Pickett moved to that same label in 1964. An inspired partnership with guitarist Steve Cropper produced the classic standard, 'In The Midnight Hour', as well as, 'Don't Fight It' (both 1965), '634-5789 (Soulsville, USA)', 'Land Of A 1,000 Dances' (written by Chris Kenner), 'Mustang Sally' (all 1966) and 'Funky Broadway' (1967). The singer's other collaborators included erstwhile Falcon Eddie Floyd and former Valentino, Bobby Womack. The latter partnership proved increasingly important as the 60s progressed. A 1968 album, *The Midnight Mover*, contained six songs featuring Womack's involvement. Deprived of the Stax house band due to their break with Atlantic, Pickett next recorded at Fame's Muscle Shoals studio. A remarkable version of 'Hey Jude', with Duane Allman on guitar, was the highlight of this period. A further experiment, this time with producers Gamble And Huff, resulted in two hits, 'Engine Number 9' (1970) and 'Don't Let The Green Grass Fool You' (1971), while a trip to Miami provided 'Don't Knock My Love', his last Top 20 hit for Atlantic. Wilson switched to RCA in 1972, but the previous success was hard to regain. A mercurial talent, Pickett returned to Muscle Shoals for *Funky Situation* (1978), issued on his own Wicked label. More recently he worked alongside Joe Tex, Don Covay, Ben E. King and Solomon Burke in a revamped Soul Clan. Pickett was the invisible figure and role model in the award-winning soul music film *The Commitments* in 1991. Since then Pickett has found life a struggle and has been arrested and charged with various drug offences.

●ALBUMS: *It's Too Late* (Double-L 1963)★★, *In The Midnight Hour* (Atlantic 1965)★★★★, *The Exciting Wilson Pickett* (Atlantic 1966)★★★★, *The Wicked Pickett* (Atlantic 1966)★★★★, *The Sound Of Wilson Pickett* (Atlantic 1967)★★★★, *I'm In Love* (Atlantic 1968)★★★, *The Midnight Mover* (Atlantic 1968)★★★, *Hey Jude* (Atlantic 1969)★★★, *Right On* (Atlantic 1970)★★★, *Wilson Pickett In Philadelphia* (Atlantic 1971)★★, *If You Need Me* (Joy 1970)★★, *Don't Knock My Love* (Atlantic 1971)★★, *Mr. Magic Man* (RCA 1973)★★, *Miz Lena's Boy* (RCA 1973)★★, *Tonight I'm My Biggest Audience* (1974)★★, *Live In Japan* (1974)★★, *Pickett In Pocket* (1974)★★, *Join Me & Let's Be Free* (1975)★★, *Chocolate Mountain* (Wicked 1976)★★, *A Funky Situation* (Wicked 1978)★★, *I Want You* (1979)★★, *The Right Track* (1981)★★, *American Soul Man* (1987)★★.

●COMPILATIONS: *The Best Of Wilson Pickett* (Atlantic 1967)★★★★, *The Best Of Wilson Pickett Vol. 2* (1971)★★★★, *Greatest Hits* i (1987)★★★★, *Greatest Hits* ii (1989)★★★★, *A Man And A Half*

(1992)★★★★, *The Very Best Of Wilson Pickett* (Rhino 1993)★★★★★.

PINKERTON'S ASSORTED COLOURS

Originally known as the Liberators, this Rugby, Warwickshire-based quintet comprised: Samuel 'Pinkerton' Kemp (vocals/autoharp), Tony Newman (guitar), Tom Long (guitar), Barrie Bernard (bass) and Dave Holland (drums). One of the lesser known UK pop groups of the period, they came under the wing of Fortunes manager Reg Calvert, who encouraged them to change their name and to each don a different pastel shade suit. This unusual stress on colour was reflected in various publicity stunts such as polluting the fountains of Trafalgar Square with red dye. The gimmicky use of a kazoo and autoharp, aided by extensive plugging on the pirate radio stations Radio City and Radio Caroline, proved sufficient to break their Decca debut single, 'Mirror Mirror'. A minor dispute between their manager and rival Phil Solomon over the ownership of various group names brought them even more publicity than their next single, 'Don't Stop Loving Me Baby', which barely scraped into the Top 50. Stuart Colman replaced Bernard in the line-up, but by that time the group were losing momentum and their prospects were further blighted by the tragic death of their manager. After a lean patch, the group abbreviated their name to Pinkerton's Colours, then Pinkerton and finally evolved into the Flying Machine. That last incarnation brought a happier ending for: in the summer of 1969, the spin-off group achieved a US Top 5 hit with 'Smile A Little Smile For Me'.

PIONEERS

The original Pioneers, formed in 1962, consisted of the brothers Sidney and Derrick Crooks, and Glen Adams. The latter later enjoyed a career as vocalist and studio musician, playing organ as a member of Lee Perry's Upsetters. The Pioneers' debut, 'Sometime', was recorded for Leslie Kong's Beverleys label during 1965. By late 1967 they were recording for the Caltone label, owned by Ken Lack, former road manager of the Skatalites. In 1968, Sidney teamed up with Jackie Robinson to record a series of local hits for producer Joe Gibbs, hitting number 1 in the Jamaican chart with their first attempt, 'Gimme Little Loving'. They followed up with another number 1, 'Long Shot', a song celebrating the victories of a famous Jamaican racehorse. Further successes for Gibbs included 'Dem A Laugh', 'No Dope Me Pony', 'Me Nah Go A Bellevue', 'Catch The Beat', and 'Mama Look Deh', which the Maytals used as the basis for their huge local hit of 1968, 'Monkey Man'. Sidney and Robinson then teamed up with Desmond Dekker's brother George, and returned to record for Leslie Kong, initially releasing another local hit, 'Nana', under the group name the Slickers. Subsequent records for Kong were recorded under the name of the Pioneers, including their famous continuation of the racehorse saga, 'Long Shot Kick De Bucket', which tells how Long Shot and a horse named Combat died in a race at Caymanas Park track in Kingston. Other local hits for Kong included the Jamaican chart-topper, 'Easy Come Easy Go' (a return volley against rival group the Royals), the frenetic 'Samfie Man', about a confidence trickster, and 'Mother Rittie'. After their sojourn at Beverleys, they took up residence in England, where 'Long Shot Kick De Bucket' had reached the UK chart, peaking at number 21 in early 1970. They toured Egypt and the Lebanon later that year, returning in 1971 to record in a much more lightweight 'pop' reggae style. Their greatest success came with the Jimmy Cliff-penned 'Let Your Yeah Be Yeah' which reached number 5 in the autumn of 1971. Smaller success came with the cover versions '100 lbs Of Clay' and 'A Little Bit Of Soap'. Since 1973, Dekker has pursued a singing and composing career, Robinson has been a solo vocalist, while Sidney Crooks has concentrated on production, since the late 80s operating his own studio in Luton, Bedfordshire, England. Their best records remain those they recorded for Joe Gibbs and Leslie Kong during 1968-70.
●ALBUMS: *Greetings From The Pioneers* (Amalgam 1968)★★★, *Long Shot* (Trojan 1969)★★★★, *Battle Of The Giants* (Trojan 1970)★★★, *Let Your Yeah Be Yeah* (Trojan 1972)★★★, *I Believe In Love* (1973)★★, *Freedom Feeling* (1973)★★, *Roll On Muddy River* (1974)★★, *I'm Gonna Knock On Your Door* (1974)★★, *Pusher Man* (1974)★★.
●COMPILATIONS: *Greatest Hits* (1975)★★★.

PITNEY, GENE

b. 17 February 1941, Hartford, Connecticut, USA. Although Pitney began recording in 1959 ('Classical Rock 'N' Roll' was recorded with Ginny Mazarro as Jamie And Jane), his initial success came as a songwriter, providing the Kalin Twins with 'Loneliness', Roy Orbison with 'Today's Teardrops' and Bobby Vee with 'Rubber Ball'. His solo recording career took off in 1961 with the multi-tracked 'I Wanna Love My Life Away' and the dramatic film themes 'Town Without Pity' and 'The Man Who Shot Liberty Valance'. Throughout this period, he was still writing for other artists, creating big hits for Ricky Nelson ('Hello Mary Lou') and the Crystals ('He's A Rebel'). In 1963, Pitney toured Britain where his 'Twenty Four Hours From Tulsa' reached the Top 10. After meeting the Rolling Stones, he recorded Mick Jagger and Keith Richards' 'That Girl Belongs To Yesterday'. Despite the onslaught of the beat groups, Pitney's extraordinarily impassioned big ballads remained popular in the USA and especially in the UK. Among his hits from this era were Barry Mann and Cynthia Weill's 'I'm Gonna Be Strong' (1964), 'I Must Be Seeing Things' (1965), 'Looking Through The Eyes Of Love' (1965), 'Princess In Rags' (1965), 'Backstage' (1966), Randy Newman's 'Nobody Needs Your Love' (1966), 'Just One Smile' (1966) and 'Something's Gotten Hold Of My Heart' (1967). The controversial 'Somewhere In The Country' (about an unmarried mother) was less successful. In addition, Pitney recorded albums in Italian and Spanish, with one of his songs, 'Nessuno Mi Puo Guidicare' coming second in the 1966 San Remo Song

Festival. There were also country music albums with George Jones and Melba Montgomery. By the late 60s, his popularity in America had waned but he continued to tour in Europe, having the occasional hit like 'Maria Elena' (1969), 'Shady Lady' (1970) and 'Blue Angel' (1974). In 1988 he had unexpected success when he sang on a revival of 'Something's Gotten Hold Of My Heart' with Marc Almond, which topped the UK charts. Pitney will be remembered for his impassioned vocals and his almost faultless choice of material.

●ALBUMS: *The Many Sides Of Gene Pitney* (Musicor 1962)★★★, *Only Love Can Break A Heart* (Musicor 1962)★★★, *Gene Pitney Sings Just For You* (Musicor 1963)★★★, *Gene Pitney Sings World-Wide Winners* (Musicor 1963)★★★, *Blue Gene* (Musicor 1963)★★★★, *Gene Pitney Meets The Fair Young Ladies Of Folkland* (Musicor 1964)★★, *Gene Italiano* (Musicor 1964)★★, *It Hurts To Be In Love* (Musicor 1964)★★★★, *For The First Time Ever! Two Great Singers* (with George Jones, Musicor 1965)★, *I Must Be Seeing Things* (Musicor 1965)★★★★, *It's Country Time Again!* (Musicor 1965)★, *Looking Through The Eyes Of Love* (Musicor 1965)★★★★, *Espanol* (Musicor 1965)★★, *Being Together* (Musicor 1965)★★, *Famous Country Duets* (Musicor 1965)★, *Backstage (I'm Lonely)* (Musicor 1966)★★★, *Messumo Mi Puo Guidicare* (Musicor 1966)★, *The Gene Pitney Show* (Musicor 1966)★★★, *The Country Side Of Gene Pitney* (Musicor 1966)★, *Young And Warm And Wonderful* (Musicor 1966)★★★★, *Just One Smile* (Musicor 1967)★★★★, *Sings Burt Bacharach* (Musicor 1968)★★, *She's A Heartbreaker* (Musicor 1968)★★, *This Is Gene Pitney* (Musicor 1970)★★, *Ten Years After* (Musicor 1971)★★, *Pitney Today* (1968)★★, *Pitney '75* (1975)★★, *Walkin' In The Sun* (1979)★★.

●COMPILATIONS: *Big Sixteen* (Musicor 1964)★★★★, *More Big Sixteen, Volume 2* (Musicor 1965)★★★, *Big Sixteen, Volume 3* (Musicor 1966)★★★, *Greatest Hits Of All Time* (Musicor 1966)★★★, *Golden Greats* (Musicor 1967)★★★, *Spotlight On Gene Pitney* (Design 1967)★★★, *The Gene Pitney Story* double album (Musicor 1968)★★★, *The Greatest Hits Of Gene Pitney* (Musicor 1969)★★★★, *The Man Who Shot Liberty Valance* (Music Disc 1969)★★★, *Town Without Pity* (Music Disc 1969)★★★, *Twenty Four Hours From Tulsa* (Music Disc 1969)★★★, *Baby I Need Your Lovin'* (Music Disc 1969)★★★, *The Golden Hits Of Gene Pitney* (Musicor 1971)★★★, *The Fabulous Gene Pitney* double album (Columbia 1972)★★★, *The Pick Of Gene Pitney* (West-52 1979)★★★, *Anthology 1961-68* (Rhino 1987)★★★, *Best Of* (K-Tel 1988)★★★, *All The Hits* (Jet 1990)★★★, *Greatest Hits* (Pickwick 1991)★★★, *The Original Hits 1961-70* (Jet 1991)★★★, *The EP Collection* (See For Miles 1991)★★★, *The Heartbreaker* (Repertoire 1994)★★★, *More Greatest Hits* (Varese Sarabande 1995)★★★, *The Gold Collection: 15 Classic Hits* (Summit 1996)★★★, *The Great Recordings* (Tomato 1996)★★★, *The Definitive Collection* (Charly 1997)★★★.

PLASTIC PENNY

This immensely talented UK quartet came together in 1968 when three former members of the Universals, Brian Keith (vocals), Paul Raymond (keyboards) and Tony Murray (bass), joined Mick Grabham (lead guitar) and Nigel Olsson (drums) to record for Larry Page's recently launched Page One record label. Their debut was the refreshing and melodic 'Everything I Am', originally recorded by the Box Tops. It became a UK Top 10 hit, but after the failure of the Bill Martin/Phil Coulter composition 'Nobody Knows If', the group drifted into other recording ventures. Singer Brian Keith was the first to quit, leaving before the completion of the group's sole album. One-hit-wonders on paper, Plastic Penny nevertheless established themselves as an excellent musicians' training ground. Grabham founded Cochise and later joined Procol Harum, Murray teamed up with the Troggs, Paul Raymond had spells with Chicken Shack and Savoy Brown, and Olsson collaborated with the Spencer Davis Group and Elton John.

●ALBUMS: *Two Sides Of A Penny* (Page One 1968)★★★, *Currency* (Page One 1969)★★, *Heads You Win Tails I Lose* (Page One 1970)★★.

POETS

Formed in Glasgow, Scotland in 1961, the Poets were one of Britain's more adventurous acts. Although obliged to play contemporary hits, the group - George Gallagher (vocals), Hume Paton (guitar), Tony Myles (guitar), John Dawson (bass) and Alan Weir (drums) - brought original songs and R&B favourites into their early sets. By 1964 they had become a leading attraction, resplendent in frilled shirts and matching velvet suits. Rolling Stones' manager Andrew Loog Oldham signed the quintet to his management and production company, attracted by their image and self-composed material. The Poets' debut single 'Now We're Thru', reached number 31 in the UK charts. Its ethereal drone and echoed 12-string guitars enhanced Gallagher's nasal delivery and the performance was the template for subsequent releases. Although the group did not secure another hit, their versatile recordings included ballads and uptempo R&B, imbued with their unique approach. The Poets' line-up fragmented and by 1967 none of the original group remained. Andi Mulvey (vocals), Fraser Watson (guitar), Ian McMillan (guitar), Norrie Maclean (bass) and Raymond Duffy (drums - on loan from Dean Ford And The Gaylords) completed 'Wooden Spoon', the unit's last official single. Further fragmentation ensued, but the name was retained until the early 70s. The core of the group subsequently joined Longdancer, while McMillan formed Blue with late-period member Hughie Nicholson.

POMUS, DOC

b. Jerome Felder, 27 June 1925, Brooklyn, New York, USA, d. 14 March 1991, New York, USA. Doc Pomus wrote the lyrics for several great rock 'n' roll songs of the 60s. With Mort Shuman, who composed the music, Pomus's credits included the Drifters' 'Save The Last Dance For

Me', 'This Magic Moment', 'Sweets For My Sweet' and 'I Count The Tears'; Elvis Presley's 'Little Sister', '(Marie's The Name) His Latest Flame', 'Viva Las Vegas', 'Surrender' and others; and Dion's 'A Teenager In Love'. Pomus developed polio at the age of nine and used crutches to walk. (A fall in his adult life left him confined to a wheelchair.) At the age of 15, already playing saxophone and singing at jazz and blues clubs, he changed his name to avoid alerting his parents of his activities - they found out two years later. Pomus recorded a number of blues-influenced singles for independent companies beginning in his late teens, none of which were hits. At that time he also began writing. The first major placement for one of his compositions was 'Boogie Woogie Country Girl', the b-side of Big Joe Turner's 'Corrina, Corrina', in 1956. That same year he wrote 'Lonely Avenue', recorded by Ray Charles. In 1957 Pomus teamed up with writers/producers Leiber And Stoller to pen 'Young Blood', a hit for the Coasters, as well as 'She's Not You', a hit for Presley. Pomus and Shuman (who had played piano on some of Pomus' recordings), officially teamed in 1958 and signed to the Hill & Range publishing company in New York. Although Pomus' first love was blues, he became an adept rock lyricist, and among his earliest hits were such pop songs as Fabian's 'Turn Me Loose', 'I'm A Man' and 'Hound Dog Man'. Pomus and Shuman also wrote the Mystics' 'Hushabye', Bobby Darin's 'Plain Jane', Gary 'U.S.' Bonds' 'Seven Day Weekend', Gene McDaniels' 'Spanish Lace', Terry Stafford's 'Suspicion', Andy Williams' 'Wrong For Each Other' and 'Can't Get Used To Losing You' (later covered by the Beat), and Jimmy Clanton's 'Go, Jimmy, Go'. Presley recorded over 20 of their songs, 'Kiss Me Quick' and 'A Mess Of Blues' being among the other noteworthy titles. Pomus estimated he wrote over one thousand songs during his career. The Pomus-Shuman team separated in 1965 and Pomus kept a low profile throughout much of the late 60s and 70s. In the late 70s he was instrumental in helping assemble the Blues Brothers band and then began writing prolifically again. He co-wrote an album with Mink DeVille's *Willy DeVille*, two with Dr. John and one with B.B. King, the Grammy-winning *There Must Be A Better World Somewhere*. Later Pomus co-compositions appeared in the films *Cry Baby* and *Dick Tracy*.

He remained a champion of the blues and blues musicians until his death and was an often-seen figure at New York clubs where both older and younger blues artists performed. In 1991 Pomus received the Rhythm and Blues Foundation's Pioneer Award, the first white to be so honoured. Pomus died of lung cancer at the age of 65 later that year. He was inducted into the Rock and Roll Hall of Fame in January 1992.

POOLE, BRIAN, AND THE TREMELOES

Formed in the late 50s and fronted by vocalist Brian Poole (b. 2 November 1941, Barking, Essex, England), this UK pop group were initially known as Brian Poole and the Tremelos when they made their debut at the Ilford Palais in 1960. Poole was originally known as a Buddy Holly imitator and even went as far as wearing spectacles filled with plain glass. After his backing musicians reverted to the title Tremeloes, the entire ensemble successfully auditioned for Decca Records on 1 January 1962 and were signed in favour of the Beatles. A cover of the Isley Brothers' 'Twist And Shout' brought them a UK Top 10 hit the following year. The follow-up, a reading of the Contours' 'Do You Love Me?', hit number 1 in the UK and 15 other countries. American success, however, remained frustratingly elusive. Appropriately, the group's manager Peter Walsh recruited Buddy Holly's former mentor Norman Petty to play piano on two further UK smashes, the wistful 'Someone Someone' and mawkish 'The Three Bells'. Thereafter, the group's popularity waned and they seemed increasingly dated in comparison to the more aggressive R&B-based UK pop outfits that emerged in 1964-65. Sensing a crisis, Poole elected to leave the group and branch out into the world of big ballads. He subsequently moved into cabaret, retired to the family butcher business, and later resurfaced with a record and publishing company. Against the odds, it was his backing group, the Tremeloes, that went on to achieve enormous chart success under their own name. In the 90s Poole and most of his original Tremeloes are back ploughing the rich vein of 60s nostalgia tours. In 1996 Poole proved he was no literary slouch with the publication of *Talkback: An Easy Guide To British Slang*. His two daughters Karen and Shelly have found commercial success in the 90s as Alisha's Attic.

●ALBUMS: *Twist And Shout With Brian Poole And The Tremeloes* (Decca 1963)★★★★, *Big Hits Of '62* (Ace of Clubs 1963)★, *It's About Time* (Decca 1965)★★★.

●COMPILATIONS: *Remembering Brian Poole And The Tremeloes* (Decca 1977)★★★★, *Twist And Shout* (Decca 1982)★★★, *Do You Love Me* (Deram 1991)★★★.

●FURTHER READING: *Talkback: An Easy Guide To British Slang*, Brian Poole.

PORTER, DAVID

b. 21 November 1941, Memphis, Tennessee, USA. Although better recalled for a partnership with Isaac Hayes, Porter had been an active, if unsuccessful, performer prior to their meeting, recording for several labels including Savoy and Hi Records. The singer was also present on several early Stax sessions. Porter first encountered his future colleague when he tried to sell Hayes life insurance, but the pair soon combined in one of the 60s soul era's most electric songwriting teams. Rightly applauded for their songs for Sam And Dave, including 'Hold On I'm Comin'', 'Soul Man' and 'When Something Is Wrong With My Baby', the duo also provided hits for Carla Thomas ('B-A-B-Y') and Johnnie Taylor ('I Had A Dream'). Their friendship was strained when Hayes secured an international best-seller with his *Hot Buttered Soul*. Porter then re-embarked on a solo career

and in 1970 scored a Top 30 US R&B hit with 'Can't See You When I Want To'. His only other chart entry came in 1972 when 'Ain't That Loving You (For More Reasons Than One)' was a minor success. Credited to 'Isaac Hayes And David Porter', it ostensibly marked the end of their collaboration.
●ALBUMS: *Gritty, Groovy And Gettin' It* (Stax 1970)★★, *David Porter: Into A Real Thing* (Stax 1971)★★, *Victim Of The Joke* (1974)★★.

POTTINGER, SONIA

b. *c*.1943, Jamaica, West Indies. In the mid-60s Pottinger opened her Tip Top Record Shop on Orange Street, Kingston, and in 1966, launched her career as a record producer with 'Every Night' by Joe White And Chuck with the Baba Brooks Band, recorded at Federal Recording Studios. This sentimental C&W ballad with an R&B beat became a massive hit and stayed high in the Jamaican charts for months. As the music changed to rocksteady, she recorded a string of sweet-sounding hits such as 'The Whip' by the Ethiopians (1967), 'That's Life' by Delano Stewart (1968), and 'Swing And Dine' by the Melodians (1968), all released on her Gayfeet and High Note labels. In 1974, after Duke Reid's death, she took over his business and reissued and repackaged the Treasure Isle catalogue. In the late 70s, she issued several best-selling albums by Bob Andy, Marcia Griffiths and Culture. She retired from the recording business in 1985.
●ALBUMS: Various: *Put On Your Best Dress* 1967-68 recordings (Trojan 1990)★★★, *Musical Feast* 1967-70 recordings (Heartbeat 1990)★★★.

POWELL, KEITH

b. Birmingham, England. Vocalist Powell came to prominence during the early 60s beat boom with his group, Keith Powell And The Valets. Columbia Records signed the band in 1963. They made their debut with 'The Answer Is No', which was succeeded by 'Tore Up' and 'I Should Know Better (But I Don't)' (both 1964). Having switched to Piccadilly Records in 1965, Powell embarked on a solo career with an excellent version of the Impressions' 'People Get Ready'. Two strong soul-styled releases ensued, 'Come Home Baby' and 'Goodbye Girl', before Powell began recording concurrently with Billie Davis. Credited to Keith And Billie, their first offering was 'When You Move, You Lose', a vibrant, dance-based number which later became a favourite on the northern soul circuit. The pair's rousing rendition of Sam And Dave's 'You Don't Know Like I Know' followed, after which Powell resumed solo work with 'Victory'. He and Davis were reunited for 'Swingin' Tight', after which their partnership was sundered. Powell's own career ended in 1966 with 'It Keeps Rainin''. He later retired from music altogether without achieving the recognition his superb voice deserved.
●COMPILATIONS: *The Keith Powell Story* (Sequel 1994)★★★.

POWER, DUFFY

Power was one of several British vocalists, including Marty Wilde, Billy Fury and Dickie Pride, signed to the Larry Parnes stable. Having completed a series of pop singles, including 'Dream Lover' and 'Ain't She Sweet', the singer embraced R&B in 1963 with a pulsating version of the Beatles' 'I Saw Her Standing There' on which he was backed by the Graham Bond Quartet. Power's later singles included 'Tired, Broke and Busted', which featured support from the Paramounts, but he later supplemented his solo career by joining Alexis Korner's Blues Incorporated. The singer appeared on *Red Hot From Alex* (1964), *Sky High* (1966) and *Blues Incorporated* (1967), during which time group members Jack Bruce (bass), Danny Thompson (bass) and Terry Cox (drums) assisted on several informal sessions later compiled on Power's *Innovations* set. Guitarist John McLaughlin also contributed to the album, before joining the vocalist's next project, Duffy's Nucleus. Power resumed his solo career late in 1967 when this short-lived attraction disbanded, but an ensuing fitful recording schedule did little justice to this underrated artist's potential.
●ALBUMS: *Innovations* aka *Mary Open The Door* (Transatlantic 1970)★★★, *Little Boy Blue* (1971)★★, *Duffy Power* (Spark 1973)★★, *Powerhouse* (Buk 1976)★★.
●COMPILATIONS: *Blues Power* (1992)★★★.

PRESLEY, ELVIS

b. Elvis Aaron Presley, 8 January 1935, Tupelo, Mississippi, USA, d. 16 August 1977, Memphis, Tennessee. The most celebrated popular music phenomenon of his era and, for many, the purest embodiment of rock 'n' roll, Elvis Presley's life and career have become part of rock legend. The elder of twins, his younger brother, Jesse Garon, was stillborn, a tragedy which partly contributed to the maternal solicitude that affected his childhood and teenage years. Presley's first significant step towards a musical career took place at the age of eight when he won $5 in a local song contest performing the lachrymose Red Foley ballad, 'Old Shep'. His earliest musical influence came from attending the Pentecostal Church and listening to the psalms and gospel songs. He also had a strong grounding in country and blues and it was the combination of these different styles that was to provide his unique musical identity.

By the age of 13, Presley had moved with his family to Memphis and during his later school years began cultivating an outsider image with long hair, spidery sideburns and ostentatious clothes. After leaving school he took a job as a truck driver, a role in keeping with his unconventional appearance. In spite of his rebel posturing, Elvis remained studiously polite to his elders and was devoted to his mother. Indeed, it was his filial affection that first prompted him to visit Sun Records, whose studios offered the sophisticated equivalent of a fairground recording booth service. As a birthday present to his mother, Gladys, Elvis cut a version of the Ink Spots'

'My Happiness', backed with the Raskin/Brown/Fisher standard 'That's When Your Heartaches Begin'. The studio manager, Marion Keisker, noted Presley's unusual but distinctive vocal style and informed Sun's owner/producer Sam Phillips of his potential. Phillips nurtured the boy for almost a year before putting him together with country guitarist Scotty Moore and bassist Bill Black. Their early sessions showed considerable promise, especially when Presley began alternating his unorthodox low-key delivery with a high-pitched whine. The amplified guitars of Moore and Black contributed strongly to the effect and convinced Phillips that the singer was startlingly original. In Presley, Phillips saw something that he had long dreamed of discovering: a white boy who sang like a negro.

Presley's debut disc on Sun was the extraordinary 'That's All Right (Mama)', a showcase for his rich, multi-textured vocal dexterity, with sharp, solid backing from his compatriots. The b-side, 'Blue Moon Of Kentucky', was a country song but the arrangement showed that Presley was threatening to slip into an entirely different genre, closer to R&B. Local response to these strange-sounding performances was encouraging and Phillips eventually shifted 20,000 copies of the disc. For his second single, Presley recorded Roy Brown's 'Good Rockin' Tonight' backed by the zingy 'I Don't Care If The Sun Don't Shine'. The more roots-influenced 'Milkcow Blues Boogie' followed, while the b-side 'You're A Heartbreaker' had some strong tempo changes that neatly complemented Presley's quirky vocal. 'Baby Let's Play House'/'I'm Left, You're Right, She's Gone' continued the momentum and led to Presley performing on the *Grand Old Opry* and *Louisiana Hayride* radio programmes. A series of live dates commenced in 1955 with drummer D.J. Fontana added to the ranks. Presley toured clubs in Arkansas, Louisiana and Texas billed as 'The King Of Western Bop' and 'The Hillbilly Cat'. Audience reaction verged on the fanatical, which was hardly surprising given Presley's semi-erotic performances. His hip-swivelling routine, in which he cascaded across the stage and plunged to his knees at dramatic moments in a song, was remarkable for the period and prompted near-riotous fan mania. The final Sun single, a cover of Junior Parker's 'Mystery Train', was later acclaimed by many as the definitive rock 'n' roll single with its chugging rhythm, soaring vocal and enticing lead guitar breaks. It established Presley as an artist worthy of national attention and ushered in the next phase of his career, which was dominated by the imposing figure of Colonel Tom Parker.

The Colonel was a former fairground huckster who managed several country artists including Hank Snow and Eddy Arnold. After relieving disc jockey Bob Neal of Presley's managership, Parker persuaded Sam Phillips that his financial interests would be better served by releasing the boy to a major label. RCA Records had already noted the commercial potential of the phenomenon under offer and agreed to pay Sun Records a release fee of $35,000, an incredible sum for the period. The sheer diversity of Presley's musical heritage and his remarkable ability as a vocalist and interpreter of material enabled him to escape the cultural parochialism of his R&B-influenced predecessors. The attendant rock 'n' roll explosion, in which Presley was both a creator and participant, insured that he could reach a mass audience, many of them newly affluent teenagers.

It was on 10 January 1956, a mere two days after his 21st birthday, that Elvis entered RCA's studios in Nashville to record his first tracks for a major label. His debut session produced the epochal 'Heartbreak Hotel', one of the most striking pop records ever released. Co-composed by Hoyt Axton's mother Mae, the song evoked nothing less than a vision of absolute funereal despair. There was nothing in the pop charts of the period that even hinted at the degree of desolation described in the song. Presley's reading was extraordinarily mature and moving, with a determined avoidance of any histrionics in favour of a pained and resigned acceptance of loneliness as death. The economical yet acutely emphatic piano work of Floyd Cramer enhanced the stark mood of the piece, which was frozen in a suitably minimalist production. The startling originality and intensity of 'Heartbreak Hotel' entranced the American public and pushed the single to number 1 for an astonishing eight weeks. Whatever else he achieved, Presley was already assured a place in pop history for one of the greatest major label debut records ever released. During the same month that 'Heartbreak Hotel' was recorded, Presley made his national television debut displaying his sexually enticing gyrations before a bewildered adult audience whose alleged outrage subsequently persuaded producers to film the star exclusively from the waist upwards. Having outsold his former Sun colleague Carl Perkins with 'Blue Suede Shoes', Presley released a debut album that contained several of the songs he had previously recorded with Sam Phillips, including Little Richard's 'Tutti Fruitti', the R&B classic 'I Got A Woman' and an eerie, wailing version of Richard Rodgers/Lorenz Hart's 'Blue Moon', which emphasized his remarkable vocal range.

Since hitting number 2 in the UK lists with 'Heartbreak Hotel', Presley had been virtually guaranteed European success and his profile was increased via a regular series of releases as RCA took full advantage of their bulging back catalogue. Although there was a danger of overkill, Presley's talent, reputation and immensely strong fan base vindicated the intense release schedule and the quality of the material ensured that the public was not disappointed. After hitting number 1 for the second time with the slight ballad 'I Want You, I Need You, I Love You', Presley released what was to become the most commercially successful double-sided single in pop history, 'Hound Dog'/'Don't Be Cruel'. The former was composed by the immortal rock 'n' roll songwriting team of Leiber And Stoller, and presented Presley at his upbeat best with a novel lyric, complete with a striking guitar solo and spirited handclapping from his backing group the Jordanaires. Otis Blackwell's 'Don't Be Cruel' was equally effective with a striking melody line and some clever and amusing vocal gymnastics from the hiccupping King of

Western Bop, who also received a co-writing credit. The single remained at number 1 in the USA for a staggering 11 weeks and both sides of the record were massive hits in the UK.

Celluloid fame for Presley next beckoned with *Love Me Tender*, produced by David Weisbert, who had previously worked on James Dean's *Rebel Without A Cause*. Presley's movie debut received mixed reviews but was a box office smash, while the smouldering, perfectly enunciated title track topped the US charts for five weeks. The spate of Presley singles continued in earnest through 1957 and one of the biggest was another Otis Blackwell composition, 'All Shook Up', which the singer used as a cheekily oblique comment on his by now legendary dance movements. By late 1956 it was rumoured that Presley would be drafted into the US Army and, as if to compensate for that irksome eventuality, RCA, Twentieth Century Fox and the Colonel stepped up the work-rate and release schedules. Incredibly, three major films were completed in the next two-and-a-half years. *Loving You* boasted a quasi-autobiographical script with Presley playing a truck driver who becomes a pop star. The title track became the b-side of '(Let Me Be Your) Teddy Bear' which reigned at number 1 for seven weeks. The third movie, *Jailhouse Rock*, was Presley's most successful to date with an excellent soundtrack and some inspired choreography. The Leiber and Stoller title track was an instant classic which again topped the US charts for seven weeks and made pop history by entering the UK listings at number 1. The fourth celluloid outing, *King Creole* (adapted from the Harold Robbins novel, *A Stone For Danny Fisher*) is regarded by many as Presley's finest film of all and a firm indicator of his sadly unfulfilled potential as a serious actor. Once more the soundtrack album featured some surprisingly strong material such as the haunting 'Crawfish' and the vibrant 'Dixieland Rock'. By the time *King Creole* was released in 1958, Elvis had already been inducted into the US Forces. A publicity photograph of the singer having his hair shorn symbolically commented on his approaching musical emasculation. Although rock 'n' roll purists mourned the passing of the old Elvis, it seemed inevitable in the context of the 50s that he would move towards a broader base appeal and tone down his rebellious image. From 1958-60, Presley served in the US Armed Forces, spending much of his time in Germany where he was regarded as a model soldier. It was during this period that he first met 14-year-old Priscilla Beaulieu, whom he later married in 1967. Back in America, the Colonel kept his absent star's reputation intact via a series of films, record releases and extensive merchandising. Hits such as 'Wear My Ring Around Your Neck', 'Hard Headed Woman', 'One Night', 'I Got Stung', 'A Fool Such As I' and 'A Big Hunk O' Love' filled the long two-year gap and by the time Elvis reappeared, he was ready to assume the mantle of an all-round entertainer. The change was immediately evident in the series of number 1 hits that he enjoyed in the early 60s. The enormously successful 'It's Now Or Never', based on the Italian melody 'O Sole Mio', revealed the King as an operatic crooner, far removed from his earlier raucous recordings. 'Are You Lonesome Tonight?', originally recorded by Al Jolson as early as 1927, allowed Presley to quote some Shakespeare in the spoken-word middle section as well as showing his ham-acting ability with an overwrought vocal. The new clean-cut Presley was presented on celluloid in *GI Blues*. The movie played upon his recent Army exploits and saw him serenading a puppet on the charming chart-topper 'Wooden Heart', which also allowed Elvis to show off his knowledge of German. The grandiose 'Surrender' completed this phase of big ballads in the old-fashioned style. For the next few years Presley concentrated on an undemanding spree of films including *Flaming Star, Wild In The Country, Blue Hawaii, Kid Galahad, Girls! Girls! Girls!, Follow That Dream, Fun In Acapulco, It Happened At The World's Fair, Kissin' Cousins, Viva Las Vegas, Roustabout, Girl Happy, Tickle Me, Harem Scarem, Frankie And Johnny, Paradise Hawaiian Style* and *Spinout*. Not surprisingly, most of his album recordings were hastily completed soundtracks with unadventurous commissioned songs. For his singles he relied increasingly on the formidable Doc Pomus/Mort Shuman team who composed such hits as 'Mess Of Blues', 'Little Sister' and 'His Latest Flame'. More and more, however, the hits were adapted from films and their chart positions suffered accordingly. After the 1963 number 1 'Devil In Disguise', a bleak period followed in which such minor songs as 'Bossa Nova Baby', 'Kiss Me Quick', 'Ain't That Lovin' You Baby' and 'Blue Christmas' became the rule rather than the exception. Significantly, his biggest success of the mid-60s, 'Crying In The Chapel', had been recorded five years before, and part of its appeal came from the realization that it represented something ineffably lost.

In the wake of the Beatles' rise to fame and the beat boom explosion Presley seemed a figure out of time. Yet, in spite of the dated nature of many of his recordings, he could still invest power and emotion into classic songs. The sassy 'Frankie And Johnny' was expertly sung by Elvis as was his moving reading of Ketty Lester's 'Love Letters'. His other significant 1966 release, 'If Everyday Was Like Christmas', was a beautiful festive song unlike anything else in the charts of the period. By 1967, however, it was clear to critics and even a large proportion of his devoted following that Presley had seriously lost his way. He continued to grind out pointless movies such as *Double Trouble, Speedway, Clambake* and *Live A Little, Love A Little*, even although the box office returns were increasingly poor. His capacity to register instant hits, irrespective of the material was also wearing thin as such lowly-placed singles as 'You Gotta Stop' and 'Long Legged Woman' demonstrated all too alarmingly. However, just as Elvis's career had reached its all-time nadir he seemed to wake up, take stock, and break free from the artistic malaise in which he found himself.

Two songs written by country guitarist Jerry Reed, 'Guitar Man' and 'US Male', proved a spectacular return to form for Elvis in 1968, such was Presley's conviction that the compositions almost seemed to be written specifically for him. During the same year Colonel Tom Parker had approached NBC-TV about the possibility of recording a Presley Christmas special in which the singer would perform a selection of religious songs similar in feel to his early 60s album *His Hand In Mine*. However, the executive producers of the show vetoed that concept in favour of a one-hour spectacular designed to capture Elvis at his rock 'n' rollin' best. It was a remarkable challenge for the singer, seemingly in the autumn of his career, and he responded to the idea with unexpected enthusiasm. The *Elvis TV Special* was broadcast in America on 3 December 1968 and has since gone down as one of the most celebrated moments in pop broadcasting history. The show was not merely good but an absolute revelation, with the King emerging as if he had been frozen in time for 10 years. His determination to recapture past glories oozed from every movement and was discernible in every aside. With his leather jacket and acoustic guitar strung casually round his neck, he resembled nothing less than the consummate pop idol of the 50s who had entranced a generation. To add authenticity to the proceedings he was accompanied by his old sidekicks Scotty Moore and D.J. Fontana. There was no sense of self-parody in the show as Presley joked about his famous surly curled-lip movement and even heaped passing ridicule on his endless stream of bad movies. The music concentrated heavily on his 50s classics but, significantly, there was a startling finale courtesy of the passionate 'If I Can Dream' in which he seemed to sum up the frustration of a decade in a few short lines.

The critical plaudits heaped upon Elvis in the wake of his television special prompted the singer to undertake his most significant recordings in years. With producer Chips Moman overseeing the sessions in January 1969, Presley recorded enough material to cover two highly praised albums, *From Elvis In Memphis* and *From Memphis To Vegas/From Vegas To Memphis*. The former was particularly strong with such distinctive tracks as the eerie 'Long Black Limousine' and the engagingly melodic 'Any Day Now'. On the singles front, Presley was back in top form and finally coming to terms with contemporary issues, most notably on the socially aware 'In The Ghetto' which hit number 2 in the UK and number 3 in the USA. The glorious 'Suspicious Minds', a wonderful song of marital jealously with cascading tempo changes and an exceptional vocal arrangement, gave him his first US chart-topper since 'Good Luck Charm' back in 1962. Subsequent hits such as the maudlin 'Don't Cry Daddy', which dealt with the death of a marriage, ably demonstrated Elvis's ability to read a song. Even his final few films seemed less disastrous than expected. In 1969's *Charro*, he grew a beard for the first time in his portrayal of a moody cowboy, while *A Change Of Habit* dealt with more serious matter than usual. More importantly, Presley returned as a live performer at Las Vegas with a strong backing group including guitarist James Burton and pianist Glen D. Hardin. In common with John Lennon, who also returned to the stage that same year

with the Plastic Ono Band, Presley opened his set with Carl Perkins' 'Blue Suede Shoes'. His comeback was well-received and one of the live songs, 'The Wonder Of You', stayed at number 1 in Britain for six weeks during the summer of 1970. There was also a revealing documentary film of the tour Elvis - *That's The Way It Is* and a companion album which included contemporary cover songs such as Tony Joe White's 'Polk Salad Annie', Creedence Clearwater Revival's 'Proud Mary' and Neil Diamond's 'Sweet Caroline'.

During the early 70s Presley continued his live performances, but soon fell victim to the same artistic atrophy that had bedevilled his celluloid career. Rather than re-entering the studio to record fresh material he relied on a slew of patchy live albums that saturated the marketplace. What had been innovative and exciting in 1969 swiftly became a tedious routine and an exercise in misdirected potential. The backdrop to Presley's final years was a sordid slump into drug dependency, reinforced by the pervasive unreality of a pampered lifestyle in his fantasy home, Gracelands. The dissolution of his marriage in 1973 coincided with a further decline and an alarming tendency to put on weight. Remarkably, he continued to undertake live appearances, covering up his bloated frame with brightly coloured jump suits and an enormous, ostentatiously-jewelled belt. He collapsed onstage on a couple of occasions and finally on 16 August 1977 his tired, burnt-out body expired. The official cause of death was a heart attack, no doubt brought on by barbiturate usage over a long period. In the weeks following his demise, his record sales predictably rocketed and 'Way Down' proved a fittingly final UK number 1.

The importance of Presley in the history of rock 'n' roll and popular music remains incalculable. In spite of his iconographic status, the Elvis image was never captured in a single moment of time like that of Bill Haley, Buddy Holly or even Chuck Berry. Presley, in spite of his apparent creative inertia, was not a one-dimensional artist clinging to history but a multi-faceted performer whose career spanned several decades and phases. For purists and rockabilly enthusiasts it is the early Elvis who remains of greatest importance and there is no doubting that his personal fusion of black and white musical influences, incorporating R&B and country, produced some of the finest and most durable recordings of the century. Beyond Elvis 'The Hillbilly Cat', however, there was the face that launched a thousand imitators, that black-haired, smiling or smouldering presence who stared from the front covers of numerous EPs, albums and film posters of the late 50s and early 60s. It was that well-groomed, immaculate pop star who inspired a generation of performers and second-rate imitators in the 60s. There was also Elvis the Las Vegas performer, vibrant and vulgar, yet still distant and increasingly appealing to a later generation brought up on the excesses of 70s rock and glam ephemera. Finally, there was the bloated Presley who bestrode the stage in the last months of his career. For many, he has come to symbolize the decadence and loss of dignity that is all too often heir to pop idolatry. It is no wonder that Presley's remarkable career so sharply divides those who testify to his ultimate greatness and those who bemoan the gifts that he seemingly squandered along the way. In a sense, the contrasting images of Elvis have come to represent everything positive and everything destructive about the music industry.

● ALBUMS: *Elvis Presley* (RCA Victor 1956)★★★★, *Elvis* (RCA Victor 1956)★★★★★, *Rock 'N' Roll* (1956)★★★★, *Rock 'N' Roll No. 2* (1957)★★★★, *Loving You* soundtrack (RCA Victor 1957)★★★★, *Elvis' Christmas Album* (RCA Victor 1957)★★★, *King Creole* (RCA Victor 1958)★★★★, *Elvis' Golden Records* (RCA Victor 1958)★★★★★, *For LP Fans Only* (RCA Victor 1959)★★★★, *A Date With Elvis* (RCA Victor 1959)★★★★, *Elvis' Golden Records, Volume 2* (RCA Victor 1960)★★★★★, *Elvis Is Back!* (RCA Victor 1960)★★★★, *G.I. Blues* (RCA Victor 1960)★★★, *His Hand In Mine* (RCA Victor 1961)★★★, *Something For Everybody* (RCA Victor 1961)★★★, *Blue Hawaii* (RCA Victor 1961)★★★, *Pot Luck* (RCA Victor 1962)★★★, *Girls! Girls! Girls!* (RCA Victor 1963)★★★, *It Happened At The World's Fair* (RCA Victor 1963)★★, *Fun In Acapulco* (RCA Victor 1963)★★, *Elvis' Golden Records, Volume 3* (1964)★★★★, *Kissin' Cousins* (RCA Victor 1964)★★, *Roustabout* (RCA Victor 1964)★★, *Girl Happy* (RCA Victor 1965)★★, *Flaming Star And Summer Kisses* (1965)★★, *Elvis For Everyone* (RCA Victor 1965)★★★, *Harem Holiday* (RCA Victor 1965)★★, *Frankie And Johnny* (RCA Victor 1966)★★, *Paradise, Hawaiian Style* (RCA Victor 1966)★★, *California Holiday* (RCA Victor 1966)★★, *How Great Thou Art* (RCA Victor 1967)★★★, *Double Trouble* (RCA Victor 1967)★★, *Clambake* (RCA Victor 1968)★★, *Elvis' Golden Records, Volume 4* (RCA Victor 1968)★★★★, *Speedway* (RCA Victor 1968)★★, *Elvis - TV Special* (1968)★★★, *From Elvis In Memphis* (1970)★★★★, *On Stage February 1970* (1970)★★★★, *That's The Way It Is* (1971)★★★, *I'm 10,000 Years Old - Elvis Country* (1971)★★★, *Love Letters From Elvis* (1971)★★★, *Elvis Sings The Wonderful World Of Christmas* (1971)★★★, *Elvis Now* (1972)★★★, *He Touched Me* (1972)★★★, *Elvis As Recorded At Madison Square Garden* (1972)★★★, *Aloha From Hawaii Via Satellite* (1973)★★★, *Elvis* (1973)★★★, *Raised On Rock* (1973)★★★, *A Legendary Performer, Volume 1* (1974)★★★★, *Good Times* (1974)★★★, *Elvis Recorded On Stage In Memphis* (1974)★★★★, *Hits Of The 70s* (1974)★★★, *Promised Land* (1975)★★★, *Having Fun With Elvis On Stage* (1975)★★, *Today* (1975)★★★, *The Elvis Presley Sun Collection* (1975)★★★★★, *From Elvis Presley Boulevard, Memphis, Tennessee* (1976)★★★, *Welcome To My World* (1977)★★★, *A Legendary Performer* (1977)★★★★, *He Walks Beside Me* (1978)★★★, *The '56 Sessions, Vol. 1* (1978)★★★★, *Elvis's 40 Greatest* (1978)★★★★★, *Elvis - A Legendary Performer, Volume 3* (1979)★★★★, *Our Memories Of Elvis* (1979)★★★, *The '56 Sessions, Vol. 2* (1979)★★★★, *Elvis Presley Sings Leiber And Stoller* (1980)★★★★, *Elvis Aaron Presley* (1979)★★★, *Elvis Sings The Wonderful World Of Christmas* (1979)★★★, *The First Year* (1979)★★★, *The King...Elvis* (1980)★★★, *This Is Elvis* (1981)★★★, *Guitar Man* (1981)★★★, *Elvis Answers Back* (1981)★★★, *The Ultimate Performance* (1981)★★★, *Personally Elvis* (1982)★★★, *The Sound Of Your Cry* (1982)★★★, *Jailhouse Rock/Love In Las Vegas* (1983)★★★, *The First Live Recordings* (1984)★★★, *A Golden Celebration* (1984)★★★, *Rare Elvis* (1985)★★★, *Essential Elvis* (1986)★★★★, *Elvis From Nashville To Memphis: The Essential '60s Masters* 5-CD box set (RCA 1993)★★★★★, *Elvis Gospel: 1957-1971* (RCA 1994)★★★, *Walk A Mile In My Shoes: The Essential 70s Masters* 5-CD box set (RCA 1995)★★★★, *Elvis 56* (RCA 1996)★★★★★, *A Hundred Years From Now* (RCA 1996)★★★, *Presley - The All Time Greats* (RCA 1996)★★★★, *Great Country Songs* (RCA 1996)★★★, *Great Country Songs* (RCA 1997)★★★.

● VIDEOS: *One Night With You* (1986), *Elvis Presley In Concert* (1986), *68 Comeback Special* (1986), *Memories* (1987), *This Is Elvis* (1988), *Graceland* (1988), *Great Performances Vol 2* (1990), *Great Vocal Performances Vol. 1* (1990), *Young Elvis* (1991), *Sun Days With Elvis* (1991), *Elvis On Tour* (1991), *Elvis; A Portrait By His Friends* (1991), *56 In the Beginning* (1991), *Private Elvis* (1993), *Elvis In Hollywood* (1993).

● FURTHER READING: *I Called Him Babe: Elvis Presley's Nurse Remembers*, Marian J. Cocke. *The Three Loves Of Elvis Presley: The True Story Of The Presley Legend*, Robert Holmes. *A Century Of Elvis*, Albert Hand. *The Elvis They Dig*, Albert Hand. *Operation Elvis*, Alan Levy. *The Elvis Presley Pocket Handbook*, Albert Hand. *All Elvis: An Unofficial Biography Of The 'King Of Discs'*, Philip Buckle. *The Elvis Presley Encyclopedia*, Roy Barlow. *Elvis: A Biography*, Jerry Hopkins. *Meet Elvis Presley*, Favius Friedman. *Elvis Presley*, Paula Taylor. *Elvis*, Jerry Hopkins. *The Elvis Presley Scrapbook 1935-1977*, James Robert Paris. *Elvis And The Colonel*, May Mann. *Recording Sessions 1954-1974*, Torben Holum, Ernst Jorgensen and Erik Rasmussen. *Elvis Presley: An Illustrated Biography*, W.A. Harbinson. *Elvis: The Films And Career Of Elvis Presley*, Steven and Boris Zmijewsky. *Presley Nation*, Spencer Leigh. *Elvis*, Peter Jones. *Presley: Entertainer Of The Century*, Antony James. *Elvis And His Secret*, Maria Gripe. *On Stage, Elvis Presley*, Kathleen Bowman. *The Elvis Presley American Discography*, Ron Barry. *Elvis: What Happened*, Red West, Sonny West and Dave Hebler. *Elvis: Tribute To The King Of Rock*, Dick Tatham. *Elvis Presley*, Todd Slaughter. *Elvis: Recording Sessions*, Ernst Jorgensen, Erick Rasmussen and Johnny Mikkelsen. *The Life And Death Of Elvis Presley*, W.A. Harbinson. *Elvis: Lonely Star At The Top*, David Hanna. *Elvis In His Own Words*, Mick Farren and Pearce Marchbank. *Twenty Years Of Elvis: The Session File*, Colin Escott and Martin Hawkins. *Starring Elvis*, James W. Bowser. *My Life With Elvis*, Becky Yancey and Cliff Lindecker.

The Real Elvis: A Good Old Boy, Vince Staten. The Elvis Presley Trivia Quiz Book, Helen Rosenbaum. A Presley Speaks, Vester Presley. The Graceland Gates, Harold Lloyd. The Boy Who Dared To Rock: The Definitive Elvis, Paul Lichter. Eine Illustrierte Dokumentation, Bernd King and Heinz Plehn. Elvis Presley Speaks, Hans Holzer. Elvis: The Legend Lives! One Year Later, Martin A. Grove. Private Elvis, Diego Cortez. Bill Adler's Love Letters To Elvis, Bill Adler. Elvis: His Life And Times In Poetry And Lines, Joan Buchanan West. Elvis '56: In The Beginning, Alfred Wertheimer. Elvis Presley: An Illustrated Biography, Rainer Wallraf and Heinz Plehn. Even Elvis, Mary Ann Thornton. Elvis: Images & Fancies, Jac L. Tharpe. Elvis In Concert, John Reggero. Elvis Presley: A Study In Music, Robert Matthew-Walker. Elvis; Portrait Of A Friend, Marty Lacker, Patsy Lacker and Leslie E. Smith. Elvis Is That You?, Holly Hatcher. Elvis: Newly Discovered Drawings Of Elvis Presley, Betty Harper. Trying To Get To You: The Story Of Elvis Presley, Valerie Harms. Love Of Elvis, Bruce Hamilton and Michael L. Liben. To Elvis With Love, Lena Canada. The Truth About Elvis, Jess Stearn. Elvis: We Love You Tender, Dee Presley; Billy, Rick and David Stanley. Presleyana, Jerry Osborne and Bruce Hamilton. Elvis: The Final Years, Jerry Hopkins. When Elvis Died, Nancy and Joseph Gregory. All About Elvis, Fred L. Worth and Steve D. Tamerius. Elvis Presley: A Reference Guide And Discography, John A. Whisler. The Illustrated Discography, Martin Hawkins and Colin Escott. Elvis: Legend Of Love, Marie Greenfield. Elvis Presley: King Of Rock 'N' Roll, Richard Wooton. The Complete Elvis, Martin Torgoff. Elvis Special 1982, Todd Slaughter. Elvis, Dave Marsh. Up And Down With Elvis Presley, Marge Crumbaker with Gabe Tucker. Elvis For The Record, Maureen Covey. Elvis: The Complete Illustrated Record, Roy Carr and Mick Farren. Elvis Collectables, Rosalind Cranor. Jailhouse Rock: The Bootleg Records Of Elvis Presley 1970, Lee Cotten and Howard A. DeWitt. Elvis The Soldier, Rex and Elisabeth Mansfield. All Shook Up: Elvis Day-By-Day, 1954-1977, Lee Cotten. Elvis, John Townson, Gordon Minto and George Richardson. Priscilla, Elvis & Me, Michael Edwards. Elvis On The Road To Stardom: 1955-1956, Jim Black. Return To Sender, Howard F. Banney. Elvis: His Life From A To Z, Fred L. Worth and Steve D. Tamerius. Elvis And The Colonel, Dirk Vallenga with Mick Farren. Elvis: My Brother, Bill Stanley with George Erikson. Long Lonely Highway: 1950's Elvis Scrapbook, Ger J. Rijff. Elvis In Hollywood, Gerry McLafferty. Reconsider Baby: Definitive Elvis Sessionography, Jorgensen, E., Elvis '69, The Return, Joseph Tunzi. The Death Of Elvis: What Really Happened, Charles C. Thompson and James P., Cole. Elvis For Beginners, Jill Pearlman. Elvis, The Cool King, Bob Moreland and Jan Van Gestel. The Elvis Presley Scrapbooks 1955-1965, Peter Haining (ed.). The Boy Who Would Be King. An Intimate Portrait Of Elvis Presley By His Cousin, Earl Greenwood and Kathleen Tracy. Elvis: The Last 24 Hours, Albert Goldman. The Elvis Files, Gail Brewer-Giorgio. Elvis, My Dad, David Adler and Ernest Andrews. The Elvis Reader: Texts And Sources On The King Of Rock 'n' Roll, Kevin Quain (ed.). Elvis Bootlegs Buyer's Guide, Pts 1& 2, Tommy Robinson. Elvis: The Music Lives On-The Recording Sessions 1954-1976, Richard Peters. The King Forever, no author listed. Dead Elvis: A Chronicle Of A Cultural Obession, Greil Marcus. Elvis People: Cult Of The King, Ted Harrison. In Search Of The King, Craig Gelfand, Lynn Blocker-Krantz and Rogerio Noguera. Aren Med Elvis, Roger Ersson and Lennart Svedberg. Elvis And Gladys, Elaine Dundy. King And I: Little Gallery of Elvis Impersonators, Kent Barker and Karin Pritikin. Elvis Sessions: The Recorded Music Of Elvis Aron Presley 1953-1977, Joseph Tunzi. Elvis: The Sun Years, Howard A. DeWitt. Elvis In Germany: The Missing Years, Andreas Schroer. Graceland: The Living Legend Of Elvis Presley, Chet Flippo. Elvis: The Secret Files, John Parker. The Life And Cuisine Of Elvis Presley, David Adler. Last Train To Memphis: The Rise Of Elvis Presley, Peter Guralnick. In His Own Words, Mick Farren. Elvis: Murdered By The Mob, John Parker. The Complete Guide To The Music Of …, John Robertson. Elvis's Man Friday, Gene Smith. The Hitchhiker's Guide To Elvis, Mick Farren. Elvis, The Lost Photographs 1948-1969, Tunzi and O'Neal Joseph. Elvis Aaron Presley: Revelations From The Memphis Mafia, Alanna Nash. The Elvis Encyclopaedia, David E. Stanley. E: Reflections On The Birth Of The Elvis Faith, John, E. Strausbaugh. Elvis Meets The Beatles: The Untold Story Of Their Entangled Lives, Chris Hutchins and Peter Thompson. Elvis, Highway 51 South, Memphis, Tennessee, Joseph A. Tunzi. Elvis In The Army, William J. Taylor Jnr. Everything Elvis, Pauline Bartel. Elvis In Wonderland, Bob Jope. Elvis: Memories And Memorabilia, Richard Bushkin.

●FILMS: Love Me Tender (1956), Loving You (1957), Jailhouse Rock (1957), King Creole (1958), G.I. Blues (1960), Flaming Star (1960), Wild In The Country (1961), Blue Hawaii (1961), Kid Galahad (1962), Girls Girls Girls (1962), Follow That Dream (1962), It Happened At The World's Fair (1963), Fun In Acapulco (1963), Roustabout (1964), Viva Las Vegas (1964), Kissin' Cousins (1964), Tickle Me (1965), Harum Scarum aka Harem Holiday (1965), Girl Happy (1965), Spinout (1966), Paradise Hawaiin Style (1966), Frankie And Johnny (1966), Easy Come Easy Go (1967), Clambake (1967), Live A Little Love A Little (1968), Speedway (1968), Stay Away Joe (1968), Double Trouble (1968), The Trouble With Girls (1969), Charro! (1969), Change Of Habit (1969), This Is Elvis compilation (1981).

PRESTON, JOHNNY

b. John Preston Courville, 18 August 1939, Port Arthur, Texas, USA. This pop ballad and rock singer first performed in the Lamar University (Beaumont, Texas) group the Shades, in 1957, and was brought to the attention of

Mercury Records by disc jockey and singer, the Big Bopper (Jape Richardson). Among the tracks Richardson wrote and produced for him was the novelty 'Running Bear', a sad tale of Red Indian love gone wrong. The record took four months to chart Stateside but it then went on to became a chart-topper in the US and UK during 1959/60 (after Richardson's tragic death in the plane crash with Buddy Holly). Despite a disastrous UK tour (cut three weeks short due to poor houses), he had transatlantic Top 20 successes with the follow-ups 'Cradle Of Love' and a revival of Shirley And Lee's 'Feel So Fine'. He later recorded for Imperial, TCF Hall (including 'Running Bear '65'), ABC and Hallway, but never graced the charts again.

●ALBUMS: *Running Bear* (Mercury 1960)★★★, *Come Rock With Me* (Mercury 1961)★★, *Johnny Preston Sings* (1960)★★★.

PRETTY THINGS

One of England's seminal R&B bands, the Pretty Things were formed at Sidcup Art College, Kent, England, in September 1963. The original line-up featured a founder-member of the Rolling Stones, Dick Taylor (b. 28 January 1943, Dartford, Kent, England; guitar), plus Phil May (b. 9 November 1944, Dartford, Kent, England; vocals), Brian Pendleton (b. 13 April 1944, Wolverhampton, West Midlands, England; rhythm guitar), John Stax (b. 6 April 1944, Crayford, Kent, England; bass) and Peter Kitley (drums), although the latter was quickly replaced by Viv Andrews. The group secured a recording deal within months of their inception. Their label then insisted that the luckless Andrews be removed in favour of Viv Prince, an experienced musician and ex-member of Carter-Lewis And The Southerners. The Pretty Things' debut single, 'Rosalyn', scraped into the UK Top 50, but its unfettered power, coupled with the group's controversial, unkempt appearance, ensured maximum publicity. Their brash, almost destructive, approach to R&B flourished with two exciting UK Top 20 singles, 'Don't Bring Me Down' and 'Honey I Need'. The unit's exuberant first album offered much of the same. Skip Alan (b. Alan Skipper, 11 June 1948, London, England) replaced the erratic Prince in November 1965. Although the Pretty Things' commercial standing had declined, subsequent singles, 'Midnight To Six Man' and 'Come See Me', were arguably their finest works, combining power with purpose. However, first Pendleton, then Stax, abandoned the groups and sessions for a third album, *Emotions*, were completed with two former members of the Fenmen, Wally Allen (bass/vocals) and John Povey (b. 20 August 1944, London, England; keyboards/vocals). Initially hired on a temporary basis, the duo proved crucial to the Pretty Things' subsequent development.

By late 1967 the quintet was immersed in the emergent underground scene. Their music combined harmonies with experimentation, and two exceptional singles, 'Defecting Grey' and 'Talking About The Good Times', are definitive examples of English 'flower-power' pop. The group's newfound confidence flourished on *S.F. Sorrow*,

an ambitious concept album that reportedly influenced the Who's *Tommy*. The set was not a commercial success, and a recurring instability - Skip Alan was replaced by former Tomorrow drummer John 'Twink' Alder - only to rejoin again, also proved detrimental. Dick Taylor's departure in November 1969 was highly damaging, and although the group's subsequent album, *Parachute*, was lauded in *Rolling Stone* magazine, his distinctive guitar sound was notably absent. The Pretty Things collapsed in 1971, but re-formed under a core of May, Povey and Skip Alan to complete *Freeway Madness*. This trio remained central through the group's subsequent changes until May embarked on a solo career in 1976. Two years later the *Emotions* line-up - May, Taylor, Povey, Allen and Alan - was reunited. The same quintet, plus guitarist Peter Tolson (b. 10 September 1951, Bishops Stortford, Hertfordshire, England), completed a studio album, *Cross Talk* in 1980, and since then the group has been revived on numerous occasions, notably with May and Taylor at the helm. In 1990 a revitalized unit released a rousing version of Barry McGuire's 1965 US number 1 'Eve Of Destruction'. By the mid-90s the band were still gigging, now under the watchful eye of manager Mark St. John. He had successfully won them back rights to songs and royalties. In 1996 after dozens of changes of personnel and image the line-up was the same as the unit that recorded the stunning 'Come See Me'; May, Taylor, Alan, Allan and Povey.

●ALBUMS: *The Pretty Things* (Fontana 1965)★★★★, *Get The Picture* (Fontana 1965)★★★★, *Emotions* (Fontana 1967)★★★, *S.F. Sorrow* (EMI 1968)★★★, *Parachute* (Harvest 1970)★★★★, *Freeway Madness* (Warners 1972)★★★, *Silk Torpedo* (Swan Song 1974)★★★, *Savage Eye* (Swan Song 1976)★★★, *Live '78* (Jade 1978)★★, *Cross Talk* (Warners 1980)★★, *Live At The Heartbreak Hotel* (Ace 1984)★★, *Out Of The Island* (Inak 1988)★★, *On Air* (Band Of Joy 1992)★★. The group also completed several albums of background music suitable for films: *Electric Banana* (De Wolfe 1967)★★, *More Electric Banana* (De Wolfe 1968)★★, *Even More Electric Banana* (De Wolfe 1969)★★, *Hot Licks* (De Wolfe 1973)★★, *Return Of The Electric Banana* (De Wolfe 1978)★★.

●COMPILATIONS: *We'll Be Together* (1966)★★★, *Greatest Hits 64-67* (Philips 1975)★★★★, *The Vintage Years* (Sire 1976)★★★★, *Attention* (1976)★★★, *Attention Volume 2* (1976)★★★, *Singles A's And B's* (Harvest 1977)★★★, *Electric Banana: The Seventies* (Butt 1979)★★, *Electric Banana: The Sixties* (Butt 1980)★★, *The Pretty Things 1967-1971* (See For Miles 1982)★★★★, *Cries From The Midnight Circus: The Best Of The Pretty Things 1968-1971* (Harvest 1986)★★★, *Let Me Hear The Choir Sing* (Edsel 1986)★★★, *Closed Restaurant Blues* (Bam Caruso 1987)★★★, *Unrepentant* 2-CD box set (Fragile 1995)★★★.

●FURTHER READING: *The Pretty Things: Their Own Story And The Downliners Sect Story*, Mike Stax.

PRIMETTES

This US vocal group comprised Diana Ross (b. 26 March 1944), Mary Wilson (b. 4 March 1944), Florence Ballard (b. 30 June 1943) and Betty Travis (b. *c*.1944), and was formed in Detroit in 1959 as a sister group to the Primes (who subsequently merged with the Distants to become the Temptations). They auditioned for Berry Gordy at Motown in 1960, but he declined to sign them. Instead, they made a series of recordings for the Lu-Pine label in Detroit, most of which remained unissued until 1968. They also appeared as backing vocalists on records by Eddie Floyd, Don Revel and Gene Martin. Betty Travis was replaced in 1960 by Barbara Martin, and this line-up requested a second chance from Gordy. They were finally signed to Motown in 1961, whereupon they were renamed the Supremes.

●ALBUMS: with Eddie Floyd *Looking Back With The Primettes* (Ember 1968)★★, *The Roots Of Diana Ross* (1973)★★.

PRINCE BUSTER

b. Cecil Bustamante Campbell, 28 May 1938, Kingston, Jamaica, West Indies. Buster was named after Alexandra Bustamante, the leader of the Jamaican Labour Party, and began his career as a boxer, but soon found his pugilistic talents being put to use as a bouncer/strong arm man and minder for Coxsone Dodd's Down Beat sound system. Competition was fierce in those early days, with fights often breaking out between the supporters of rival sounds with wires (and people) being cut regularly, and Buster still carries the scars (literally). He claims, like so many others, to have personally invented the ska sound, and he was certainly involved from the very early stages - at first with his work for Coxsone and after they had parted company with his own Voice Of The People sound system, record label and shop. His very first recording session produced one of the all-time classics of Jamaican music, 'Oh Carolina', with vocals by the Folks Brothers and musical accompaniment from Count Ossie. Inventive and innovative at the time, the record still sounds every bit as exciting now as it did then. Buster released countless records both by himself and other top acts on his Wild Bells, Voice Of The People and Buster's Record Shack labels, which were subsequently released in the UK on the Blue Beat imprint. They proved as popular there as they had been in Jamaica, firstly with the Jamaican community and secondly with the mods, who took the Prince to their hearts with songs such as 'Al Capone' and 'Madness'. He toured the UK in the mid-60s to ecstatic crowds and appeared on the hugely popular *Ready, Steady, Go* television show.

He recorded in many different styles but his talking records were the most popular, including the hilarious 'Judge Dread' where he admonishes rude boys and sentences them to 400 years; the wildly misogynistic 'Ten Commandments'; the evocative 'Ghost Dance' - a look back at his early Kingston dancehall days; the confused and confusing 'Johnny Cool'; and the not so well-known but equally wonderful 'Shepherd Beng Beng'. He also claims to have taught Georgie Fame to do the ska and he influenced other white pop acts - Madness named themselves after his song (debuting with a tribute, 'The Prince') and inspired doorman/bouncer Alex Hughes to adopt the name Judge Dread and have UK chart hits with variations on Prince Buster's lewd original 'Big Five'. Buster had tended towards 'slack' or rude records towards the end of the 60s which were only mildly risqué compared with what was to follow but caused a sensation at the time. He wisely invested his money in record shops and juke box operations throughout the Caribbean and, in the early 70s, took to recording many of the current top names including Big Youth, Dennis Alcapone, John Holt, Dennis Brown and Alton Ellis with varying degrees of success. He soon realized that his older recordings would outsell his newer efforts every time and he turned to re-pressing his extensive back catalogue on single and releasing his old albums both in Jamaica and the UK. He also put together some brilliant compilations where the superb sleevenotes, written by the Prince himself, attack in no uncertain terms the music of the day: 'They have used guns to spoil the fun and force tasteless and meaningless music upon the land.'

Throughout the rest of the 70s and on into the 80s he lived on his shops, his juke boxes and his past glories but he returned to live work in the latter half of the 80s. He has become a crowd puller again for, as he says: 'The people know my songs and loved them.' He even started, for the first time in years, to record new music again (1992). While it is impossible to forecast whether this will prove successful, one cannot ever take away the fact that Prince Buster's music has already inspired generations of performers. He is respected abroad - probably more than in his native Jamaica - but he will always have his place as one of the few Jamaican artists to reach directly to the international audience. Many more have played their part indirectly but his name was known both through his own recordings ('Al Capone' reached the lower regions of the UK national charts) and his work with other people. It is unlikely that any other Jamaican artist (apart from Bob Marley) still has his records so regularly played in clubs and dances throughout the world.

●ALBUMS: *Judge Dread Rock Steady* (Blue Beat 1967)★★★, *I Feel The Spirit* (1968)★★★, *Wreck A Pum Pum* (Blue Beat 1968)★★★★, *She Was A Rough Rider* (Melodisc 1969)★★★★, *Big Five* (Melodisc 1972)★★★, *On Tour* (1966)★★★, *Judge Dread* (1968), *Tutti Fruitti* (Melodisc)★★★. Various: *Pain In My Belly* (Islam/Blue Beat 1966)★★★.

●COMPILATIONS: *Prince Buster's Fabulous Greatest Hits* (Fab 1968)★★★★, *Original Golden Oldies Vol.s 1 & 2* (Prince Buster 1989)★★★★.

PROBY, P.J.

b. James Marcus Smith, 6 November 1938, Houston, Texas, USA. This iconoclastic singer spent his early career in Hollywood, recording demos for song publishing houses. Several low-key singles ensued, credited to Jett Powers and a number of bit parts as an actor ensued, before the Proby appellation surfaced on 'So Do I' (1963). 'Powers' had already demonstrated a songwriting talent, his most notable composition being 'Clown Shoes' for Johnny Burnette in 1962. The artist came to Britain the following year, at the behest of producer Jack Good, to appear on the *Around The Beatles* television special. An ebullient revival of 'Hold Me', originally a gentle ballad, brought Proby a UK Top 3 hit, while the similarly raucous 'Together' reached number 8. Proby completely changed direction following a move to Liberty Records and, again, reached the UK Top 10 with a memorable version of 'Somewhere' from *West Side Story*. This record started a series of epic ballads featuring Proby's strong but affected vocal. Both 'I Apologise' (complete with Billy Eckstine paraphrasing) and 'Maria' (again from *West Side Story*) became big hits. Proby's biggest hit, however, was with the popular UK press. Following a 'split trousers' incident, Proby was accused of obscenity. He then made an act of regularly splitting his crushed blue velvet jumpsuit. He completed his attire during the mid-60s with a Tom Jones wig and black bow tie and baggy nightshirts. Prior to 'Maria' (4 months earlier) his chart career suddenly floundered with John Lennon and Paul McCartney's 'That Means A Lot', and although further immaculate productions followed after 'Maria' with 'To Make A Big Man Cry' and the Righteous Brothers-sounding 'I Can't Make It Alone', Proby was relegated to the cabaret circuit. Although he continued to record, the press were more interested in his tax problems and subsequent bankruptcy. *Three Week Hero* won retrospective acclaim when the singer's backing group achieved fame as Led Zeppelin. In 1970, Proby took the role of Iago in *Catch My Soul*, former mentor Good's rock adaptation of *Othello*. Proby's subsequent work was more sporadic; he appeared on the UK nightclub circuit, played Elvis Presley in the stage production *Elvis On Stage* until he was sacked, and continued to court publicity for erratic behaviour. In 1985 he completed two suitably eccentric versions of 'Tainted Love', previously a hit for Soft Cell, which became the first of a series of contentious singles for a Manchester-based independent label. Recreations of songs by Joy Division ('Love Will Tear Us Apart') and David Bowie ('Heroes') followed, but further releases were marred by poor production and the artist's often incoherent intonation. Although years of apparent self-abuse has robbed the singer of his powers of old, he retains the ability to enthral and infuriate. In 1993 Proby made an unannounced appearance in Jack Good's *Good Rockin' Tonite* at the Liverpool Empire. Further Proby sightings were made in June 1995 when he began a 15 minute spot during each performance of the London production of the Roy Orbison musical *Only The Lonely*. In late 1996, with a major interview in *Q Magazine*, Proby once again squared up for another comeback. This came in muted form with a minor hit collaboration with Marc Almond and a recording of Cupid's Inspiration's 'Yesterday Has Gone'.

●ALBUMS: *I Am P.J. Proby* (Liberty 1964)★★★★, *P.J. Proby* (Liberty 1965)★★★★, *P.J. Proby In Town* (Liberty 1965)★★★, *Enigma* (Liberty 1966)★★★, *Phenomenon* (Liberty 1967)★★, *Believe It Or Not* (Liberty 1968)★★, *Three Week Hero* (Liberty 1969)★★, *I'm Yours* (Ember 1973)★★, *The Hero* (Palm 1981)★★, *Clown Shoes* (1987)★★, *The Savoy Sessions* (Savoy 1995)★★, *Legend* (EMI 1996)★★★.

●COMPILATIONS: as Jet Powers *California License* (1969)★, *Somewhere* (1975)★★★, *The Legendary P.J. Proby At His Very Best* (1986)★★★★, *The Legendary P.J. Proby At His Very Best, Volume 2* (1987)★★★★, *Rough Velvet* (1992)★★★★, *The EP Collection* (See For Miles 1996)★★★★.

PROCOL HARUM

This UK group was formed in Essex, England following the demise of the R&B pop unit, the Paramounts, Procol Harum comprised: Gary Brooker (b. 29 May 1945, Southend, Essex, England; piano/vocals), Matthew Fisher (b. 7 March 1946, London, England; organ), Bobby Harrison (b. 28 June 1943, East Ham, London, England; drums), Ray Royer (b. 8 October 1945; guitar) and Dave Knights (b. 28 June 1945, Islington, London, England; bass). Their debut with the ethereal 'A Whiter Shade Of Pale' made them one of the biggest successes of 1967. The record has now achieved classic status with continuing sales, which now run to many millions. The long haunting Bach-influenced introduction takes the listener through a sequence of completely surreal lyrics, which epitomized the 'Summer Of Love'. 'We skipped the light fandango, turned cart-wheels across the floor, I was feeling kind of seasick, the crowd called out for more'. It was followed by the impressive Top 10 hit 'Homburg'. By the time of the hastily thrown together album (only recorded in mono), the band were falling apart. Harrison and Royer departed to be replaced with Brooker's former colleagues Barrie 'B.J.' Wilson (b. 18 March 1947, Southend, Essex, England) and Robin Trower (b. 9 March 1945, London, England), respectively. The other unofficial member of the band was lyricist Keith Reid (b. 10 October 1946), whose penchant for imaginary tales of seafaring appeared on numerous albums. The particularly strong *A Salty Dog*, with its classic John Player cigarette pack cover, was released to critical acclaim. The title track and 'The Devil Came From Kansas' were two of their finest songs.

Fisher and Knights departed and the circle was completed when Chris Copping (b. 29 August 1945, Southend, Essex, England; organ/bass) became the last remaining ex-Paramount to join. On *Broken Barricades*, in particular, Trower's Jimi Hendrix-influenced guitar patterns began to give the band a heavier image which was not compatible with Reid's introspective fantasy sagas. This was resolved by Trower's departure, to join Frankie Miller in Jude, and following the recruitment of Dave Ball (b. 30 March 1950) and the addition of Alan Cartwright (bass), the band pursued a more symphonic direction. The success of *Live In Concert With The Edmonton Symphony Orchestra* was unexpected. It marked a surge in popularity, not seen since the early days. The album contained strong versions of 'Conquistador' and 'A Salty Dog', and was a Top 5, million-selling album in the USA. Further line-up changes ensued with Ball departing and Mick Grabham (ex-Plastic Penny; Cochise) joining in 1972. This line-up became their most stable and they enjoyed a successful and busy four years during which time they released three albums. *Grand Hotel* was the most rewarding, although both the following had strong moments. 'Nothing But The Truth' and 'The Idol' were high points of *Exotic Birds And Fruit*; the latter showed traces of Keith Reid's epic work. 'Pandora's Box' was the jewel in *Procol's Ninth*, giving them another surprise hit single. By the time their final album was released in 1977 the musical climate had dramatically changed and Procol Harum were one of the first casualties of the punk and new wave movement. Having had a successful innings Gary Brooker initiated a farewell tour and Procol quietly disappeared. In the words of Keith Reid; 'they fired the gun and burnt the mast'. During 1991 the band re formed, and unlike many re-formed 'dinosaurs' the result was a well-received album *The Prodigal Stranger*, which received minimal sales. The band have continued to tour sporadically ever since with the most recent line-up of Brooker, Fisher, Matt Pegg (bass), Geoff Whitehorn (guitar) and Graham Broad (drums).

●ALBUMS: *Procol Harum* (Regal Zonophone 1967)★★★, *Shine On Brightly* (Regal Zonophone 1968)★★★, *A Salty Dog* (Regal Zonophone 1969)★★★★, *Home* (Regal Zonophone 1970)★★★, *Broken Barricades* (Chrysalis 1971)★★★, *In Concert With The Edmonton Symphony Orchestra* (Chrysalis 1972)★★★★, *Grand Hotel* (Chrysalis 1973)★★★, *Exotic Birds And Fruit* (Chrysalis 1974)★★★, *Procol's Ninth* (Chrysalis 1975)★★★, *Something Magic* (1977)★★, *The Prodigal Stranger* (1991)★★, Procol Harum with various artists *The Long Goodbye: Symphonic Music Of ...* (BMG/RCA 1995)★★.

●COMPILATIONS: *The Best Of Procol Harum* (1973)★★★★, *Platinum Collection* (1981)★★★★, *Collection: Procol Harum* (Castle 1986)★★★★, *The Early Years* (1993)★★★, *Homburg And Other Hats: Procol Harum's Best* (Essential 1995)★★★★.

PUCKETT, GARY, AND THE UNION GAP

Originally known as the Outcasts, a San Diego act renowned for cover versions, this popular group took the name Union Gap in January 1967. Although burdened by a passé image - they dressed in American Civil War uniforms - 'General' Gary Puckett (b. 17 October 1942, Hibbing, Minnesota, USA; vocals), 'Sergeant' Dwight Benett (b. December 1945, San Diego, California, USA; tenor saxophone), 'Corporal' Kerry Chater (b. 7 August 1945, Vancouver, British Columbia, Canada; bass), 'Private' Gary 'Mutha' Withem (b. 22 August 1946, San Diego, California, USA; woodwind/piano) and 'Private' Paul Whitbread (b. 8 February 1946, San Diego, California, USA; drums) enjoyed considerable success through their relationship with songwriter/producer

Jerry Fuller. 'Woman Woman' achieved gold status in 1967, and the following year the quintet scored three more million-sellers with 'Young Girl', a chart-topper in the US and UK, 'Lady Willpower' and 'Over You', each of which were marked by Puckett's soaring vocal line. However, the formula appeal of their highly polished sound gradually waned and the group disbanded in 1971. Puckett continues as a solo artist endlessly recycling his past hits. In 1996 *As It Stands* was issued and featured some re-recordings of 'Lady Willpower', 'Young Girl' and others, together with new songs such as 'As It Stands' and 'I Ain't Got Noth'n But The Blues'.

●ALBUMS: *Woman Woman* (Columbia 1968)★★★, *Young Girl* (Columbia 1968)★★★, *Incredible* (Columbia 1968)★★★, *The New Gary Puckett And The Union Gap Album* (1970)★★. Solo: Gary Puckett *The Gary Puckett Album* (1971)★★, *As It Stands* (Juslor 1996)★★.

●COMPILATIONS: *Gary Puckett And The Union Gap's Greatest Hits* (Columbia 1970)★★★, *Looking Glass* (Columbia 1995)★★★.

PUKWANA, DUDU

b. Mtutuzel Pukwana, 2 September 1941, Port Elizabeth, South Africa, d. 29 June 1990, London, England. Although for the majority of his career Pukwana specialized in the alto saxophone, playing a wild, passionate style influenced by South African township mbaqanga, sax jive, Charlie Parker and King Curtis, the first instrument he played was the piano which he learned as a 10-year-old from his father. Moving to Cape Town, and still playing piano, he joined his first band, Tete Mbambisa's Four Yanks, in 1957. It was around this time that he began playing saxophone, learning the rudiments from friend and fellow sideman Nick Moyake, and spending a lot of time listening to imported records by King Curtis, Charlie Parker, Louis Jordan, Sonny Rollins and Ben Webster. In Cape Town, he became friends with the white jazz pianist and bandleader Chris McGregor, who in 1960 invited Pukwana to join his Blue Notes band as saxophonist. He spent the next three years touring South Africa with the Blue Notes, under increasingly difficult conditions, until apartheid legislation made it practically impossible for a mixed race band to appear in public. The group's opportunity to leave the country came in 1963, when they were invited to appear at the annual jazz festival held in Antibes, France. Once the festival was over, the band spent a few months working in Switzerland, until, with the help of London musician and club owner Ronnie Scott, they were able to acquire work permits and entry visas for the UK. Pukwana remained with McGregor until 1969 (by which time the Blue Notes had been renamed the Brotherhood Of Breath), when he took up an offer to join Hugh Masekela's fledgling Union Of South Africa in the USA. When that band fell apart in 1970, he returned to London and formed his own band, Spear, shortly afterwards renamed Assegai. Pukwana also performed and recorded with, variously, Keith Tippett's Centipede, Jonas Gwangwa, Traffic, the Incredible String Band,

Gwigwi Mrwebi, Sebothane Bahula's Jabula, Harry Miller's Isipingo and the Louis Moholo Unit. He made memorable contributions to John and Beverly Martyn's *Road To Ruin* in 1970, and the same year co-led a sax jive/kwela album, *Kwela*, with fellow South African saxophonist Gwigwi Mrwebi. With Assegai, he recorded two albums - *Assegai* and *Assegai Zimbabwe* - before launching the second Spear in 1972. That year, he was also a featured artist on Masekela's London-recorded album *Home Is Where The Music Is*. The new Spear included in its line-up fellow ex-Blue Notes Mongezi Feza (trumpet) and Louis Moholo (drums), along with South Africans Harry Miller (bass) and Bixo Mngqikana (tenor saxophone). Their first album was the superb *In The Townships*, in 1973, which like its follow-up, *Flute Music*, took the mbaqanga/sax jive/jazz fusion into previously uncharted depths of emotional and creative intensity. In 1978, Pukwana disbanded Spear to form the larger band Zila, a horns and percussion dominated outfit whose album debut was *Diamond Express*. He continued leading Zila, recording the occasional album and working the UK and European jazz club and festival circuit, until his death from liver failure in 1990 deprived the jazz and African music scene of one of its most consistently inventive players.

●ALBUMS: *Spear: In The Townships* (Virgin 1971)★★★★, *Flute Music* (1974)★★★★, with Assegai *Zimbabwe* (1974)★★★, *Blue Notes For Mongezi* (1976)★★★, *Diamond Express* (1977)★★, *Blue Notes In Concert* (1978)★★★, with Zila *Sounds - Live At The 100 Club* (Jika 1981)★★★, with Zila *Live At Bracknell & Willisau* (Jika 1984)★★★, *Zila '86* (Jika 1986)★★, with John Stevens *Radebe - They Shoot To Kill* (Affinity 1987)★★★, *Blue Notes For Johnny* (1987)★★★, with Zila *Cosmics Chapter 90* (Ah-Um 1990)★★★.

PURIFY, JAMES AND BOBBY

Formed in 1965, this high-powered soul duo consisted of James Purify (b. 12 May 1944, Pensacola, Florida, USA) and Robert Lee Dickey (b. 2 September 1939, Tallahassee, Florida, USA). Unfairly tarnished as a surrogate Sam And Dave, the duo's less frenetic style was nonetheless captivating. During the early 60s Dickey worked as a singer/guitarist in the Dothan Sextet, a group fronted by Mighty Sam McClain. When Florida disc jockey 'Papa' Don Schroeder offered Sam a solo career, Dickey introduced his cousin, James Purify, as a replacement. Their onstage duets became so popular that Schroeder added them to his fast-growing roster. Their first single, 'I'm Your Puppet', was recorded at Fame in Muscle Shoals and released on Bell. Written by Dan Penn and Spooner Oldham, this simple, poignant ballad became the duo's only US Top 10 hit in September 1966. Rather than follow their own path, the cousins were tempted towards cover versions including 'Shake A Tail Feather' and 'I Take What I Want'. In spite of the undoubted quality of these releases, many critics dubbed them 'contrived'. In 1967 'Let Love Come Between Us' became their last US Top 30 hit, although several strong records followed. When

Dickey retired in 1970 James found another 'Bobby' in Ben Moore and it was this new combination which secured a 1976 British hit with a remake of 'I'm Your Puppet'. Unable to sustain this rejuvenation, the duo parted, although Moore resurfaced in 1979 with a solo album, *Purified*. The pick of the original duo's Bell recordings can be found on *100% Purified Soul*.

●ALBUMS: *James And Bobby Purify* (Bell 1967)★★★, *The Pure Sound Of The Purifys* (Bell 1968)★★★, *You And Me Together Forever* (Casablanca 1978)★★.

●COMPILATIONS: *100% Purified Soul* (1988)★★★★.

PURPLE GANG

Formed in Manchester, England, the original line-up consisted of Lucifer (b. Peter Walker; vocals/kazoo), Deejay Robinson (harmonica/mandolin), Ank Langley (jug), Geoff Bourjer (piano/washboard) and James 'Joe' Beard (guitar). All were students at Stockport College of Art. The Purple Gang achieved notoriety when 'Granny Takes A Trip', their debut single, was adopted by the English 'underground' as an unofficial anthem. Although a gentle, happy, jugband song, the 'trip' reference was taken to be about LSD, despite fervent claims by the group that this was not their intention. Joe Beard (12-string guitar), Gerry Robinson (mandolin), Geoff Bowyer (keyboards) and Lucifer completed an attendant album in the space of two days, but had split up by the time of its release. Continued interest in their anthemic single inspired a re-formation in 1969, but with George Janken (bass) and Irish Alex (washboard/drums) replacing Lucifer. However, the heavy style embraced by the new unit lacked the charm of earlier acoustic, goodtime music and failed to generate interest.

●ALBUMS: *The Purple Gang Strikes* (Transatlantic 1968)★★★.

PYRAMIDS

The Pyramids were a seven-piece, UK-based ska/rocksteady band, although they began their career as a straight 'pop' group, consisting of Josh Roberts, Ray Knight, Roy Barrington, Monty Naismith, Ray Ellis, Mick Thomas and Frank Pitter. A popular live attraction in Britain in the late 60s, they hit with 'Train Tour To Rainbow City', an appropriately chugging piece written and produced by Eddy Grant, which ran through many of the period's most popular records and bore a close resemblance to Prince Buster's 'Train To Girls Town'. As rock steady gave way to reggae, elements of the band, including Ellis, Naismith and Thomas, resurfaced in 1969 as Symarip with 'Skinhead Moon Stomp', based on Derrick Morgan's 'Moon Hop' hit, which was one of the anthems of the skinhead era but which had to wait until its 1980 re issue to gain a chart placing.

●ALBUMS: *Pyramids* (President 1968)★★★, as Symarip *Skinhead Moon Stomp* (Trojan 1970)★★★.

●FILMS: *Bikini Beach* (1964).

? AND THE MYSTERIANS

Formed in 1963 in Texas, USA, as XYZ, ? and the Mysterians entered rock 'n' roll immortality as the band that first popularized the punk-rock classic '96 Tears' in 1966 (number 1 USA, number 37 UK). ? (Question Mark) was vocalist Rudy Martinez (b. 1945, Mexico) and, after numerous line-up changes, the Mysterians became Frankie Rodriguez, Jnr. (b. 9 March 1951, Crystal City, Texas, USA; keyboards), Robert Lee 'Bobby' Balderrama (b. 1950, Mexico; lead guitar), Francisco Hernandez 'Frank' Lugo (b. 15 March 1947, Welasco, Texas, USA; bass) and Eduardo Delgardo 'Eddie' Serrato (b. 1947, Mexico; drums). '96 Tears' was initially intended as the b-side of their debut single, first issued on the tiny Pa-Go-Go label. However, disc jockeys in Michigan, where the group had now settled, turned it over and began playing the three-chord rocker with the now infamous lead organ line (played on a Vox, not Farfisa as legend dictates). The record was sold to the Cameo label and re-released, whereupon it became a number 1 single. The group's name invited further publicity, with ? (Martinez had changed his name legally) refusing to divulge his true identity and opaque sunglasses shielding him from recognition. The group charted with three more Cameo singles of which only 'I Need Somebody', in 1966, made any significant impact, reaching number 22 in the US charts. That single is notable in that the b-side, '8-Teen' was later a hit for Alice Cooper in 1971 after undergoing a slight title change to 'Eighteen'. Despite success with their singles and their first album, ? And The Mysterians never again came close to recapturing their brief moment of fame. '96 Tears' was incorporated into the live sets of countless 'garage bands' during the 60s, and was later revived by such artists as Eddie And The Hot Rods (1976), Garland Jeffreys (1981) and the Stranglers (1990).

● ALBUMS: *96 Tears* (Cameo 1966)★★★, *Action* (Cameo 1967)★★.

● COMPILATIONS: *96 Tears Forever* (1985)★★★.

QUICKLY, TOMMY

b. 7 July c.1943, Liverpool, England. A popular singer in his native Liverpool, Quickly started performing in the Challengers, a band formed with his sister. He joined Brian Epstein's management stable in 1963. A highly publicized launch ensued, including a prestigious slot on the Beatles concurrent package tour, while his debut single, 'Tip Of My Tongue', was an exclusive, if undistinguished, John Lennon/Paul McCartney song. Quickly was subse-

quently teamed with the Remo Four, but although 'Kiss Me Now' echoed the chirpy pop of Gerry And The Pacemakers, the singer was unable to repeat their success. A 1964 release, 'The Wild Side Of Life', reached the Top 40, but the artist's recording career was brought to an end when the follow-up, 'Humpty Dumpty', failed to chart. During the mid-60s he became involved in drugs and developed a strong dependency. Some years ago Quickly fell from a ladder and suffered serious head injuries, causing brain damage which has severely restricted his life.

QUICKSILVER MESSENGER SERVICE

Of all the bands that came out of the San Francisco area during the late 60s Quicksilver typified most the style, the attitude and the sound of that era. The original band in 1964 comprised: Dino Valenti (vocals), John Cipollina (guitar), David Freiberg (b. 24 August 1938, Boston, Massachusetts, USA; bass/vocals), Jim Murray (vocals/harmonica), Casey Sonoban (drums) and, very briefly, Alexander 'Skip' Spence (b. 18 April 1946, Windsor, Ontario, Canada; guitar/vocals), before being whisked off to join the Jefferson Airplane as drummer. Another problem that later proved to be significant in Quicksilver's development was the almost immediate arrest and imprisonment of Valenti for a drugs offence. He did not rejoin the band until late 1969. In 1965 the line-up was strengthened by the arrival of Gary Duncan (b. Gary Grubb, 4 September 1946, San Diego, California, USA; guitar) and, replacing Sonoban, Greg Elmore (b. 4 September 1946, San Diego, California, USA). Murray departed soon after their well-received appearance at the Monterey Pop Festival in 1967. The quartet of Cipollina, Duncan, Elmore and Freiberg recorded the first two albums; both are important in the development of San Francisco rock music, as the twin lead guitars of Cipollina and Duncan made them almost unique. The second collection *Happy Trails* is now regarded as a classic. George Hunter and his Globe Propaganda company were responsible for some of the finest album covers of the 60s and *Happy Trails* is probably their greatest work. Likewise the live music within showed a spontaneity that the band were never able to recapture on subsequent recordings. The side-long suite of Bo Diddley's 'Who Do You Love' has some incredible dynamics and extraordinary interplay between the twin guitarists. Duncan departed soon after and was replaced by UK session pianist and ex-Steve Miller Band member, Nicky Hopkins. His contributions breathed some life into the disappointing *Shady Grove*, notably with the frantic 'Edward, The Mad Shirt Grinder'. *Just For Love* shows a further decline, with Valenti, now back with the band, becoming overpowering and self-indulgent. 'Fresh Air' gave them a Top 50 US hit in 1970. Cipollina departed, as did Freiberg following his arrest in 1971 for drug possession (he found a lucrative career later with Jefferson Starship). Various incarnations have appeared over the years with little or no success. As recently as 1987, Gary Duncan recorded an album carrying the Quicksilver name, but by then old Quicksilver fans were more content to purchase copies of the first two albums on compact disc.

●ALBUMS: *Quicksilver Messenger Service* (Capitol 1968)★★★, *Happy Trails* (Capitol 1969)★★★★★, *Shady Grove* (Capitol 1969)★★, *Just For Love* (Capitol 1970)★★, *What About Me* (Capitol 1971)★★, *Quicksilver* (Capitol 1971)★★, *Comin' Thru* (Capitol 1972)★★, *Solid Silver* (Capitol 1975)★★, *Maiden Of The Cancer Moon* (1983)★★, *Peace By Piece* (1987)★★.

●COMPILATIONS: *Anthology* (Capitol 1973)★★★, *Sons Of Mercury* (Rhino 1991)★★★★.

QUOTATIONS

Formed in Brooklyn, New York, USA, in 1958, the Quotations featured Larry Kaye (aka Larry Kassman; lead), Richie Shwartz (first tenor), Lou Arno (second tenor) and Harvey Hershkowitz (baritone). MGM Records' songwriter Helen Miller agreed to take over their management, and after bringing them to Verve Records she suggested they make their debut with a cover version of Johnny Burke's 'Imagination'. Released in January 1962, the record reached number 105. They followed up early the next year with 'This Love Of Mine', but both this and their revision of the Tempos' 'See You In September' later in the year failed to build on the debut. After joining Kapp Records in 1963 the Quotations released 'Is It True What They Say About Barbara', co-written with Charles Koppelman, later co-chairman of SBK/EMI Music Publishing. However, the group were not credited as the Quotations, with the record ascribed instead to its lead vocalist, Mike Regal, formerly of the Chord-A-Boys. The group continued to perform locally but had lost momentum and identity. It came as no surprise when they broke up in 1963, although a single recorded in 1962, 'In The Night', was released later by Admiral Records.

RADIO LUXEMBOURG

The Compagnie Luxembourgeoise de Radiodiffusion was set up in 1931 to broadcast in German and French and two years later began Sunday broadcasts in English on 208 metres medium wave. Until 1939, programmes of dance music were punctuated with commercials. Sponsored shows included *The Palmolive Hour* and *The Ovaltineys*. After World War II, the English service was broadcast daily and most of its programming consisted of records, although the station broadcast a Top 20 compiled from sheet music sales until 1959. Until the arrival of pirate radio ships in 1964, Radio Luxembourg's evening shows were the most important source of pop music broadcasting for British listeners. While the BBC Light Programme devoted only a few hours a week to record shows, Luxembourg played new releases for six hours a night. Beginning with Teddy Johnson (1948) and Pete Murray (1950), virtually every disc jockey from that era had a show on Radio Luxembourg. Among those who made their broadcasting debut there were Jimmy Young, Alan Freeman and Jimmy Saville, who made his first broadcast in 1957 and hosted the *Teen And Twenty Disc Club*. For a period, a *Fab 208* magazine was also published. From 1946-68, record companies paid for 15-minute shows on the station, plugging their latest releases. These were pre-recorded in London by name disc jockeys such as Young, Kent Walton, Barry Aldis, Ray Orchard and Saville. In 1968, Radio Luxembourg abolished these slots in favour of 'mixed' programmes and the sponsored plays were spread throughout the schedule. In 1971, the station became 'all live' with every show presented by disc jockeys based in Luxembourg itself. By now, strong competition from BBC Radio 1, and after 1973, from Capital Radio and other UK-based commercial stations was affecting Luxembourg's listening figures. At the end of 1991, the English-language service was moved from 208 metres to a satellite waveband and was reorganized. By then, however, the company had set up Atlantic 252, a highly successful long-wave pop station based in Ireland but transmitting to the western side of Britain. 'Lux', as it was known, had a massive part to play in every UK 60s pop fan's life, even with the maddening fade-in and fade-out, owing to poor reception and the disc jockey's habit of often only playing part of the record (presumably due to the programme's sponsor).

RAELETTES

This vocal group was formed in the USA around Margie Hendrix, and was previously known as the Cookies, whose R&B backing voices appeared on numerous 50s sessions and inspired the new group's inception. Founded to provide responsive vocals for singer Ray Charles, this female trio provided the launching pad for several careers. Merry Clayton, Mable John, Minnie Riperton, Clydie King and Estella Yarbrough were all members at some point, although Hendrix has provided a long-serving consistency. The Raelettes did have several minor hits via Charles' Tangerine label, but their constantly changing personnel denied them a more constructive recording career. Hendrix, though, who had had early solo exposure on the Lamp label, also recorded on her own in the 60s, for Tangerine, Mercury and Sound Stage 7.

●ALBUMS: *Souled Out* (late 60s)★★★, *Yesterday, Today And Tomorrow* (1972)★★.
●FILMS: *Blues for Lovers* aka *Ballad In Blue* (1964).

RAGOVOY, JERRY

b. 4 September 1930, Philadelphia, Pennsylvania, USA. Ragovoy's career as a songwriter and producer began in the doo-wop era of the early 50s. His first successful act was the Castelles, who had a hit with 'My Girl Awaits Me' in 1953. In 1959 he began a partnership with entrepreneur Bill Fox which resulted in several collaborations with the Majors, one of the latter's successful acts. Ragovoy produced several of the group's releases, including the US Top 30 hit 'A Wonderful Dream', co-writing them under the pseudonym 'Norman Meade'. This appellation also appeared on 'Time Is On My Side', recorded by Irma Thomas in 1964 and later revived successfully by the Rolling Stones. Ragovoy also enjoyed a fruitful partnership with fellow black music producer Bert Berns and together the duo guided the career of deep soul singer Garnet Mimms. In 1966 Ragovoy wrote and produced 'Stay With Me Baby' for Lorraine Ellison, one of the decade's most compulsive vocal performances, before supervising a series of excellent releases by Howard Tate. His anthem-like recording, 'Get It While You Can', was later adopted by Janis Joplin, who covered several Ragovoy compositions including 'Piece Of My Heart', originally written for Erma Franklin. In the mid-60s he also became east coast A&R chief for Warner Brothers' then recently formed soul subsidiary, Loma, where he wrote songs for and produced artists including the Olympics, the Enchanters (ex-Garnet Mimms), Carl Hall, Lonnie Youngblood, Roy Redmond, Ben Aiken and (once again) Lorraine Ellison. Then in 1973 Ragovoy formed his own Rags production company and leased product to Epic, most notably that by Howard Tate and Lou Courtney, the latter's *I'm In Need Of Love*. In the late 70s/early 80s, Ragovoy began writing for and producing artists as diverse as Bonnie Raitt, Dionne Warwick, Essra Mohawk, Major Harris and Peggi Blu. In 1988 he produced some songs for Irma Thomas' album that year for Rounder and his name still apears occasionally on the credits of songs performed by many different artists. In his book, *Off The Record*, Joe Smith (ex-Warner President and then President of Capitol/EMI) gave Ragovoy's major contribution to soul music long overdue recognition when he said: 'You might not know him but he produced and wrote some of the best rhythm and blues of the sixties - and he's not black - he's a man with a sense of soul.'

RANDOLPH, 'BOOTS'

b. Homer Louis Randholph III, 3 June 1925, Paducah, Kentucky, USA. Known as 'Mr. Saxophone', he was of that self-contained caste that improvised the orthodox 'Nashville sound' from a notation peculiar to city studios, and thus had first refusal on countless daily record dates in 'Music City USA' until well into the 60s. Although the 'Western Swing' element of C&W had always admitted woodwinds, his employment was vital in widening the genre's range of instrumentation as the country capital beckoned purveyors of more generalized pop. Indeed, as a solo star, Randolph entered the US pop charts himself with 1963's 'Yakety Sax' *tour de force*. As well as refashioning on disc the diverse likes of 'Tequila', 'Hi Heel Sneakers', 'Willie And The Hand Jive' and 'Bridge Over Troubled Waters', he also ventured into the soul field with a version of Phil Upchurch Combo's 'You Can't Sit Down'. Although 'Yakety Sax' resurfaced as the traditional closing theme to UK television's Benny Hill Show, Randolph will be remembered chiefly as an accompanist heading horn sections for artists of such immeasurable fame as Elvis Presley - notably on 1960's *Elvis Is Back* - and Roy Orbison for whom he became a 'good luck charm. I'd pay him even if he didn't play'.

●ALBUMS: *Yakety Sax* (RCA Victor 1960)★★★, *Boots Randolph's Yakety Sax* (Monument/London 1963)★★★, *Boots Randolph Plays More Yakety Sax* (Monument/London 1965)★★, *Boots With Strings* (Monument 1967)★★, *Hip Boots* (Monument 1967)★★, *Boots Randolph With The Knightsbridge Strings And Voices* (1968)★★, *Sunday Sax* (1968)★★, *Fantastic Boots Randolph* (Monument 1968)★★, *The Sound Of Boots* (Monumernt 1968)★★, *... With Love; The Seductive Sax Of Boots Randolph* (1969)★★, *Saxsational* (Monument 1969)★★, *Yakety Revisited* (Monument 1970)★★, *Hit Boots 1970* (1970)★★, *Boots With Brass* (1971)★★, *Homer Louis Randolph III* (1971)★★, *The World Of Boots Randolph* (1971)★★, *Boots Randolph Plays The Great Hits Of Today* (1972)★★.
●COMPILATIONS: *Yakety Sax* (1989)★★★.

RATTLES

Guided by the late Manfred Weissleder, proprietor of the city's Star Club, Hamburg teenagers Achim Reichel (guitar/vocals), Hajo Kreutzfeldt (guitar), Herbert Hildebrandt (bass/vocals) and Reinhard Tarrach (drums) modelled their group on the British beat image in 1962. Among their first recordings was a version of 'The Hippy Hippy Shake', and they often shared bills with Tony Sheridan, Cliff Bennett, the Beatles and Kingsize Taylor. Later, morale was boosted by a successful fortnight's residency in Liverpool's Cavern Club, and appearances on

British television. However, shortly after a domestic chartbuster with 'The Witch' (written by Hilderbrandt) in 1968, the quartet was halted by compulsory army service and other external factors. Hilderbrandt rallied by taking a back seat as producer, composer and general *eminence grise* to a new Rattles enlisted in Italy and consisting of Frank Mille (guitar), Zappo Luengen (bass), Herbert Bornhold (drums) and a personable Israeli singer with the stage name 'Edna'. 'The Witch' was remade with English lyrics to fly into the UK Top 10. The Rattles also became the first German group to enter the US Hot 100. They were, however, unable to secure a lasting place in foreign hearts, and soon returned to the German orbit of engagements where they are remembered as one of the leading beat groups of the era.

●ALBUMS: *Twist At The Star-Club Show* (Philips 1964)★★★, *Hurra Die Rattles Kommen* soundtrack (1965)★★, *The Rattles* (Decca 1971)★★★, .

●COMPILATIONS: *Greatest Hits* (Mercury 1967)★★★, *Greatest Hits - New Recording* (Repertoire 1994)★★.

RAY, DAVE

As a member of Koerner, Ray And Glover, with 'Spider' John Koerner and Tony Glover, Dave 'Snaker' Ray was in the vanguard of the folk revival of the 60s. An accomplished 6- and 12-string guitarist, the artist pursued a concurrent solo career with two compulsive country blues albums. The first included interpretations of material by, among others, Muddy Waters, Robert Johnson and Lead Belly, while the follow-up featured a greater emphasis on original material. The rise of electric styles obscured Ray's progress and it was 1969 before he re-emerged in Bamboo, a country-based duo he had formed with pianist Will Donight. Their eccentric album made little impression and Ray's subsequent profile was distinctly low-key. However, in 1990 Ray and Glover teamed up to record *Ashes In My Whiskey* for the Rough Trade label, winning critical acclaim.

●ALBUMS: *Fine Soft Land* (1967)★★★. As Koerner, Ray And Glover *Blues, Rags And Hollers* (1963)★★★, *More Blues, Rags And Hollers* (1964)★★★, *The Return Of Koerner, Ray And Glover* (1965)★★★, *Live At St. Olaf Festival* (60s/70s)★★, *Some American Folk Songs Like They Used To Be* (1974)★★, with Tony Glover *Ashes In My Whiskey* (1990)★★★, with Glover *Picture Has Faded* (Tim/Kerr 1994)★★★.

RAYBER VOICES

This early Motown backing vocal group came from Detroit, Michigan, USA. The ensemble was established in 1958 and directed by Berry Gordy's second wife, Raynoma Gordy (b. Raynoma Mayberry, 8 March 1937, Detroit, Michigan, USA). There was no established line-up, but the most common participants were Robert Bateman (bass), Sonny Sanders (b. William Sanders, 6 August 1939, Chicago Heights, Illinois, USA; tenor), Brian Holland (b. 15 February 1941, Detroit, Michigan, USA; baritone) and Raynoma Gordy (soprano). The group made their debut on Herman Griffin's 'I Need You'

(1958), and toured with Marv Johnson the following year after his 'Come To Me' achieved a modicum of success. Joining the voices at this time was Gwendolyn Murray. As Gordy's Motown empire grew the Rayber Voices eventually included members of the Temptations, Martha And The Vandellas, and the Miracles. However, the days of using *ad hoc* ensembles soon ended and by the early 60s the Rayber Voices was replaced by a full-time back-up group, the Andantes.

READY, STEADY, GO!

While it is customary to cite *Ready, Steady, Go!* as the blueprint for UK pop music television, it is important also to acknowledge the immense excitement its original Friday transmissions in the 60s caused. With the beat boom sweeping music away from the mannered solo singers of the dancehall, television had never before embraced pop as legitimate entertainment currency. As Richard Mabey later recalled in *The Pop Process*, '. . . for those who found live musical performances as exciting to watch as to listen to, RSG was a visual goldmine: cameras swooping back and forth like robot jivers, tangled black leads from the guitars, and Pop Art Décor. Admittedly, all of these served to exaggerate the excitement of the music. But they are more an integral part of pop than the equivalent accoutrements at a serious concert are of classical music.'

The show was founded in 1964 by the ATV company, the brainchild of television producer Vicki Wickham. She found presenters Keith Fordyce from the BBC Light Programme and Cathy McGowan, who quickly became an icon of the 60s with her pop culture address of what was 'in' or 'out' that week. These two main presenters were joined by Michael Aldred and dancer Patrick Kerr. *Ready, Steady, Go!* became the first ever pop programme to introduce teenagers to the concept of 'the weekend starts here'. It also served as a watershed between generations - hosting music dismissed by parents as unseemly noise yet wholeheartedly devoured by teenagers. *Ready, Steady, Go!*'s main strengths were its live performances and carefully selected teenage audiences - in order to gain entrance, they had to pass a short dancing audition. During an incredibly fertile period for 'beat' music, the show booked all the top acts, including the Beatles, Rolling Stones, Hollies, Yardbirds, John Mayall, Graham Bond, the Kinks and the Animals. Additionally it pioneered the introduction of US R&B, blues and Tamla Motown/soul, with early British television appearances for artists including Martha And The Vandellas, the Supremes, John Lee Hooker and Wilson Pickett. The Beach Boys, Donovan, Paul Simon and a young Van Morrison, with Them, also made their television debuts. Such was the show's power that records having a first airing live on the programme were invariably hits. Good examples included the Pretty Things performing 'Rosalyn' live, and the most famous debut of all - a stunning performance of the Kinks' 'You Really Got Me'. No television audience had ever experienced such a brilliantly raucous act. There was also a memorable recording of Bob Dylan's anti-war song, 'With God On Our Side', banned by the BBC, and sung by Paul Jones of Manfred Mann.

In the 70s, long after the show's run had ended (in 1967), the entire rights for the programme were purchased by an astute Dave Clark (of the Dave Clark Five). From the 80s onwards the realized value of these re-run assets has made him a multi-millionaire. Much of today's live television uses *Ready, Steady, Go!* as its template - indeed the long running BBC series *Top Of The Pops* was originally designed to win some of its audience. Malcolm Gerrie, the producer of Channel Four's *The Tube* and *The White Room*, openly acknowledges the debt, as do many others working in the field.

RED CRAYOLA

Despite several contrasting line-ups, Red Crayola remains the vision of Mayo Thompson. He formed the Houston, Texas-based group in July 1966 with drummer Rick Barthelme, although several other individuals, including future country star Guy Clark, were temporary members until Steve Cunningham (bass) joined two months later. The group's set initially featured cover versions, but these were soon supplanted by their own remarkable original compositions. In addition the Crayola were renowned for free-form pieces, during which they were augmented by an assortment of friends known as the Familiar Ugly. This improvisatory unit was featured on the trio's debut *The Parable Of Arable Land*, where their erratic contributions punctuated the main body of work. Tommy Smith replaced Barthelme for *God Bless Red Krayola And All Who Sail With It*, the altered spelling in deference to objections from the US crayon company. Shorn of the Familiar Ugly, the album displayed an impressive discipline while maintaining a desire to challenge. Thompson disbanded the Crayola when 'obscurity hit us with great force'. He completed the solo *Corky's Cigar* aka *Corky's Debt To His Father*, before engaging in several projects including Art And Language, an *ad hoc* gathering responsible for a 1976 release, *Corrected Slogans*. Mayo then moved to the UK where he re-established Red Crayola in the light of the musical freedom afforded by punk. *Soldier Talk* featured assistance from several members of Pere Ubu, a group Thompson subsequently joined. He continued to pursue his own direction with *Kangaroo*, which also featured a billing for Art And Language, and despite a somewhat lower profile, Mayo Thompson remains a most imaginative and challenging figure.

●ALBUMS: *The Parable Of Arable Land* (International Artists 1967)★★, *God Bless Red Krayola And All Who Sail With It* (International Artists 1968)★★, *Soldier Talk* (1979), *Kangaroo* (1981)★★, *Black Snakes* (1983)★★★, *Malefactor, Ade* (1989)★★.

REDDING, OTIS

b. 9 September 1941, Dawson, Georgia, USA, d. 10 December 1967. The son of a Baptist minister, Redding assimilated gospel music during his childhood and soon became interested in jump blues and R&B. After resettling in Macon, he became infatuated with local luminary, Little Richard, and began singing on a full-time basis. A high school friend and booking agent, Phil Walden, then became his manager. Through Walden's contacts Redding joined Johnny Jenkins And The Pinetoppers as a sometime singer and occasional driver. Redding also began recording for sundry local independents and his debut single, 'She's Alright', credited to Otis And The Shooters, was quickly followed by 'Shout Ba Malama'. Both performances were firmly in the Little Richard mould. The singer's fortunes blossomed when one of his own songs, 'These Arms Of Mine', was picked up for the Stax subsidiary, Volt. Recorded at the tail end of a Johnny Jenkins session, this aching ballad crept into the American Hot 100 in May 1963. Further poignant releases, 'Pain In My Heart', 'That's How Strong My Love Is' and 'I've Been Loving You Too Long', were balanced by brassy, uptempo performances including 'Mr. Pitiful', 'Respect' and 'Fa Fa Fa Fa Fa Fa (Sad Song)'. He remained something of a cult figure until 1965 and the release of the magnificent *Otis Blue* in which original material nestled beside the Rolling Stones' 'Satisfaction' and two songs by a further mentor, Sam Cooke. Redding's version of the Temptations' 'My Girl' then became a UK hit, while the singer's popularity was further enhanced by the visit of the *Hit The Road Stax* revue in 1967. 'Tramp', a duet with Carla Thomas, also provided success while Redding's production company, Jotis, was responsible for launching Arthur Conley. A triumphant appearance at the Monterey Pop Festival suggested that Redding was about to attract an even wider following but tragedy struck on 10 December 1967. The light aircraft in which he was travelling plunged into Lake Monona, Madison, Wisconsin, killing the singer, his valet, the pilot and four members of the Bar-Kays. The wistful '(Sittin' On) The Dock Of The Bay', a song Redding recorded just three days earlier, became his only million-seller and US pop number 1. The single's seeming serenity, as well as several posthumous album tracks, suggested a sadly unfulfilled maturity. Although many now point to Redding's limited range, his emotional drive remains compelling, while the songs he wrote, often with guitarist Steve Cropper, stand among soul's most lasting moments. Redding is rightly regarded as a giant of soul music.

●ALBUMS: *Pain In My Heart* (Atlantic 1964)★★★★, *The Great Otis Redding Sings Soul Ballads* (Atlantic 1965)★★★★, *Otis Blue/Otis Redding Sings Soul* (Atlantic 1965)★★★★★, *The Soul Album* (Atlantic 1966)★★★★, *Complete And Unbelievable ... The Otis Redding Dictionary Of Soul* (Atlantic 1966)★★★★, *Live In Europe* (1967)★★★★, with Carla Thomas *The King & Queen* (Atlantic 1967)★★★★, *Here Comes Some Soul From Otis Redding And Little Joe Curtis* rec. pre-1962 (Marble Arch 1967)★, *The Dock Of The Bay* (Stax 1968)★★★, *The Immortal Otis Redding* (Atlantic 1968)★★★, *Otis Redding In Person At The Whiskey A Go Go* (Atlantic 1968)★★★, *Love Man* (Atco 1969)★★★, *Tell The Truth* (Atco 1970)★★★, shared

with Jimi Hendrix *Monterey International Pop Festival* (1970)★★★★, *Live Otis Redding* (Atlantic 1982)★★★, *Remember Me* (1992)★★★, *Good To Me* (1993)★★★.
●COMPILATIONS: *The History Of Otis Redding* (Volt 1967)★★★★, *The Best Of Otis Redding* (Atlantic 1972)★★★★, *Pure Otis* (Atlantic 1979)★★★, *Come To Me* (Charly 1984)★★, *Dock Of The Bay - The Definitive Collection* (Atlantic 1987)★★★★, *The Otis Redding Story* 4-LP box set (Atlantic 1989)★★★★, *Remember Me* US title *It's Not Just Sentimental* UK title (Stax 1992)★★★, *Otis!: The Definitive Otis Redding* 4-CD boxed set (Rhino 1993)★★★★★.
●VIDEOS: *Remembering Otis* (Virgin 1990).
●FURTHER READING: *The Otis Redding Story*, Jane Schiesel.

REED, LES

b. 24 July 1935, Woking, Surrey, England. A pianist, conductor, arranger, musical director, and highly succesful composer, particularly in the 60s and 70s. Reed's father, a semi-professional mouth-organist with a local troupe, the Westfield Kids, was eager to formalize his son's interest in music. Keyboard lessons from the age of six, and a spell as the Kids' accordionist prefaced a Royal College of Music scholarship and National Service in the Royal East Kent Regiment. As well as learning clarinet, he also played piano in a mess dance band that included saxophonist Tony Coe who, years later assisted Reed and Robert Farnon on *Pop Makes Progress*. On demobilization in 1956, Reed became a freelance session player, then joined the John Barry Seven who, as well as playing in concerts and on records in their own right, backed other artists - notably those appearing on Jack Good's *Oh Boy!* television series. Among them was Adam Faith, for whom Reed wrote a b-side. From this small beginning as a pop composer, Reed's 60 or more major hits since have earned numerous gold discs, Ivor Novello awards and, in 1982, the British Academy Gold Badge Of Merit. In the mid-60s, it was unusual for a British singles chart not to list a Les Reed song (usually with collaborators like Gordon Mills, Geoff Stephens or Barry Mason). Among numerous Top 30 acts indebted to Reed as writer and arranger are the Applejacks ('Tell Me When'), Tom Jones ('It's Not Unusual', 'Delilah'), P.J. Proby, Mirielle Mathieu, Englebert Humperdinck ('The Last Waltz'), Des O'Connor ('I Pretend') and the Dave Clark Five ('Everybody Knows', 1967). In 1969, towards the end of their regular partnership, Reed and Mason wrote 'Love Is All', a powerful ballad with which Malcolm Roberts triumphed at the San Remo Song Festival. Reed subsequently became one of the best-known faces at annual song festivals all over the world, and his contributions as a conductor, arranger and soloist were recognized in 1977 when he accepted an invitation to become President of The International Federation of Festivals (FIDOF) for one year, and then served as its Ambassador. His work in the late 60s included two songs with Robin Conrad, 'Don't Bring Me Your Heartaches', a hit for Paul and Barry Ryan, and 'Leave A Little Love', which received a compelling treat-

ment from Lulu. Reed also collaborated with comedian Jackie Rae for 'When There's No You', another of Humperdinck's US hits, and 'Please Don't Go', which provided veteran singer Donald Peers with his first chart entry. Both songs were adapted from classical pieces. Reed's renewed working association with Geoff Stephens in the late 60s and early 70s resulted in 'There's A Kind Of Hush' for Herman's Hermits, 'Daughter Of Darkness' for Tom Jones, and a Leeds United football song. 'There's a Kind Of Hush' was successfully revived by the Carpenters in 1976. Reed and Stephens also won the Silver Prize at the 1973 Tokyo Music Festival for their composition 'Sandy Sandy' which was sung by Frankie Stephens. Four years later, Reed and Tony Macaulay won the International Song Contest at Mallorca with 'You And I'. And in 1980, together with lyricist Roger Greenaway and singer Marilyn Miller, Reed carried off the Grand Prix Award in Seoul for 'Everytime You Go'. Other artists who have recorded Reed's songs over the years have included Elvis Presley ('Girl Of Mine'), Shirley Bassey ('Does Anybody Miss Me') and Bing Crosby ('That's What Life Is All About', said to be the last recording he made before his death in 1977). Reed has also composed several film scores including *Crossplot*, *Girl On A Motor Cycle*, *One More Time*, *My Mother's Lovers*, *Bush Baby*, and *Creepshow 2*, and has written for stage musicals such as *The Magic Show*, *American Heroes* and *And Then I Wrote*. When Reed celebrated 30 years in the music business in 1989, he was estimated to have written more than 2,000 songs. In the summer of 1994 he produced a CD with Max Bygraves and the Children of Arnhem that they hoped would raise money for the old Veterans who were returning to Arnhem in September. The titles included his 1973 composition 'Lest We Forget'. All his artist's royalties from this piece are donated in perpetuity to the 'Lest We Forget' Association. In the same year he was made a Freeman of the City of London for his 'contribution to the music industry'. Still resident in Surrey, Reed has executive interests in a Guildford radio station (County Sound) and his daughter Donna's publishing company, Rebecca Music Ltd.
●ALBUMS: *Fly Me To The Sun* (Deram 60s)★★★, *New Dimensions* (Deram 60s)★★★, *Man Of Action* (Chapter One 1970)★★★, *The New World Of Les Reed* (Chapter One)★★★, *Focus On* (Decca 70s)★★★, *The Hit Making World Of Les Reed* (Decca)★★★.

REESE, DELLA

b. Dellareese Taliaferro, 6 July 1932, Detroit, Michigan, USA. Reese is a renowned gospel singer, working with Mahalia Jackson and Clara Ward before becoming lead singer with the Meditation Singers. Her place was taken by Laura Lee when she left to join the Erskine Hawkins orchestra in 1956. Reese began a solo recording career with Jubilee in 1957, releasing the Top 20 hit 'And That Reminds Me' and a version of Cole Porter's 'In The Still Of The Night'. Now established as a gospel-influenced ballad singer, she signed to RCA in 1959 where Hugo And Luigi produced 'Don't You Know', based on an aria from

Puccini's opera *La Bohème*. It reached number 2 and was followed by the Top 20 single 'Not One Minute More'. Later RCA singles included revivals of 'Someday (You'll Want Me To Want You)' (1960) from 1946 and the 20s standard 'Bill Bailey' (1961). During the 60s and 70s, she worked frequently in cabaret, recording for ABC and Avco, where she had a small disco hit with 'If It Feels Good Do It' in 1972. In 1980, Reese returned to RCA to record an album of songs adapted from the classics.

● ALBUMS: *The History Of The Blues* (London 1959)★★★, *Della* (RCA 1960)★★★★, *Della Della Cha-Cha-Cha* (RCA 1960)★★★★, *Special Delivery* (RCA 1961)★★★, *The Classic Della* (1962)★★★, *Della On Stage* (RCA 1962)★★★, *Waltz With Me Della* (RCA 1964)★★★, *At Basin Street East* (RCA)★★★, *Moody* (RCA 1965)★★★, *C'mon And Hear It* (HMV 1965)★★★, *I Like It Like Dat* (HMV 1966)★★★, *Della Reese Live* (HMV 1966)★★, *One More Time* (HMV 1967)★★★, *Let Me Into Your Life* (1975)★★★, *The Classical Della* (1980)★★, *Della By Starlight* (1982)★★★, *Sure Like Lovin' You* (1985)★★★.

● COMPILATIONS: *The Best Of* (1973)★★★, *And That Reminds Me: The Jubilee Years* (Collectors Choice 1996)★★★.

REEVES, JIM

b. James Travis Reeves, 20 August 1923, Galloway, Texas, USA, d. 31 July 1964. (Reeves' plaque in the Country Music Hall Of Fame mistakenly gives his date of birth as 1924.) Reeves' father died when he was 10 months old and his mother was left to raise nine children on the family farm. Although only aged five, Reeves was entranced when a brother brought home a gramophone and a Jimmie Rodgers record, 'Blue Yodel No. 5'. When aged nine, he traded stolen pears for an old guitar he saw in a neighbour's yard. A cook for an oil company showed him the basic chords and when aged 12, he appeared on a radio show in Shreveport, Louisiana. Because of his athletic abilities, he won a scholarship to the University of Texas. However, he was shy, largely because of a stammer, which he managed to correct while at university. (Reeves' records are known for perfect diction and delivery.) His first singing work was with Moon Mullican's band in Beaumont, Texas, and he worked as an announcer and singing disc jockey at KGRI in Henderson for several years. (Reeves bought the station in 1959.) He recorded two singles for a chain store's label in 1949. In November 1952 Reeves moved to KWKH in Shreveport, where his duties included hosting the *Louisiana Hayride*. He stood in as a performer when Hank Williams failed to show and was signed immediately to Abbott Records. In 1953, Reeves received gold discs for two high-voiced, country novelties, 'Mexican Joe' and 'Bimbo'. In 1955 he joined the *Grand Ole Opry* and started recording for RCA in Nashville, having his first hit with a song based on the 'railroad, steamboat' game, 'Yonder Comes A Sucker'. Chet Atkins considered 'Four Walls' a 'girl's song', but Reeves persisted and used the song to change his approach to singing. He pitched his

voice lower and sang close to the microphone, thus creating a warm ballad style which was far removed from his hillbilly recordings. 'Four Walls' became an enormous US success in 1957, crossing over to the pop market and becoming a template for his future work. From then on, Atkins recorded Reeves as a mellow balladeer, giving him some pop standards and replacing fiddles and steel guitar by piano and strings. (Exceptions include an album of narrations, *Tall Tales And Short Tempers*.)

Reeves had already swapped his western outfit for a suit and tie, and, in keeping with his hit 'Blue Boy', his group, the Wagonmasters, became the Blue Boys. He always included a religious section in his stage show and also sang 'Danny Boy' to acknowledge his Irish ancestry. 'He'll Have To Go', topped the US country charts for 14 weeks and made number 2 in the US pop charts. In this memorable song Reeves conveyed an implausible lyric with conviction, and it has now become a country standard. A gooey novelty, 'But You Love Me Daddy', recorded at the same session with Steve, the nine-year-old son of bass player Bob Moore, was a UK Top 20 hit 10 years later. Having established a commercial format, 'Gentleman Jim' had success with 'You're The Only Good Thing', 'Adios Amigo', 'Welcome To My World' (UK number 6) and 'Guilty', which features French horns and oboes. His records often had exceptional longevity; 'I Love You Because' (number 5) and 'I Won't Forget You' (number 3) were on the UK charts for 39 and 25 weeks, respectively. He became enormously popular in South Africa, recording in Afrikaans, and making a light-hearted film there, *Kimberley Jim*, which became a local success. Reeves did not like flying but after being a passenger in a South African plane which developed engine trouble, he obtained his own daytime pilot's licence. On 31 July 1964 pilot Reeves and his pianist/manager, Dean Manuel, died when their single-engine plane ran into difficulties during a storm and crashed into dense woods outside Nashville. The bodies were not found until 2 August despite 500 people, including fellow country singers, being involved in the search. Reeves was buried in a specially-landscaped area by the side of Highway 79 in Texas, and his collie, Cheyenne, was buried at his feet in 1967. Reeves continued to have hits with such ironic titles as 'This World Is Not My Home' and the self-penned 'Is It Really Over?'. Although Reeves had not recorded 'Distant Drums' officially - the song had gone to Roy Orbison - he had made a demo for songwriter Cindy Walker. Accompaniment was added and, in 1966, 'Distant Drums' became Reeves' first UK number 1. He had around 80 unreleased tracks and his widow followed a brilliant, if uncharitable, marketing policy whereby unheard material would be placed alongside previously issued tracks to make a new album. Sometimes existing tracks were remastered and duets were constructed with Deborah Allen and the late Patsy Cline. Reeves became a best-selling album artist to such an extent that *40 Golden Greats* topped the album charts in 1975. Both the Blue Boys and his nephew John Rex Reeves have toured with tribute concerts. Although much of Jim Reeves' catalogue is available, surprisingly there is still no biography of Reeves, who was the first crossover star. Reeves' relaxed style has influenced Don Williams and Daniel O'Donnell but the combination of pop balladry and country music is more demanding than it appears, and Reeves remains its father figure.

● ALBUMS: *Jim Reeves Sings* (Abbott 1956)★★, *Singing Down The Lane* (RCA Victor 1956)★★★, *Bimbo* (RCA Victor 1957)★★★, *Jim Reeves* (RCA Victor 1957)★★★, *Girls I Have Known* (RCA Victor 1958)★★★, *God Be With You* (RCA Victor 1958)★★★, *Songs To Warm The Heart* (RCA Victor 1959)★★★, *He'll Have To Go* (RCA Victor 1960)★★★★, *According To My Heart* (RCA Victor 1960)★★★, *The Intimate Jim Reeves* (RCA Victor 1960)★★★★, *Talking To Your Heart* (RCA Victor 1961)★★★, *Tall Tales And Short Tempers* (RCA Victor 1961)★★★, *The Country Side Of Jim Reeves* (RCA Victor 1962)★★★, *A Touch Of Velvet* (RCA Victor 1962)★★★, *We Thank Thee* (RCA Victor 1962)★★★, *Good 'N' Country* (RCA Victor 1963)★★★★, *Gentleman Jim* (RCA Victor 1963)★★★★, *The International Jim Reeves* (RCA Victor 1963)★★★, *Twelve Songs Of Christmas* (RCA Victor 1963)★★★, *Have I Told You Lately That I Love You?* (RCA Victor 1964)★★★, *Moonlight And Roses* (RCA Victor 1964)★★★★, *Kimberley Jim* (RCA Victor 1964)★★, *The Jim Reeves Way* (RCA Victor 1965)★★★, *Distant Drums* (RCA Victor 1966)★★★★, *Yours Sincerely* (RCA Victor 1966)★★★, *Blue Side Of Lonesome* (RCA Victor 1967)★★★, *My Cathedral* (RCA Victor 1967)★★★, *A Touch of Sadness* (RCA Victor 1968)★★★, *Jim Reeves On Stage* (RCA Victor 1968)★★★, *Jim Reeves - And Some Friends* (RCA Victor 1969)★★★, *Jim Reeves Writes You A Record* (RCA Victor 1971)★★★, *Young And Country* (RCA Victor 1971)★★★, *My Friend* (RCA Victor 1972)★★★, *Missing You* (RCA Victor 1972)★★★, with Deborah Allen *Don't Let Me Cross Over* (RCA Victor 1979)★★★, *Abbott Recordings, Volume 1* (1982)★★, *Abbott Recordings, Volume 2* (1982)★★, *Live At The Opry* (1987)★★★, *The Definitive Jim Reeves* (1992)★★★, *Dear Hearts & Gentle People* (1992)★★★, *Country Clasics* (1993)★★★, *Jim Reeves* (Summit 1995).

● COMPILATIONS: *Welcome To My World* 16-CD box set (Bear Family 1994)★★★★, *The Essential Jim Reeves* (RCA 1996)★★★★, *The Ultimate Collection* (RCA 1996)★★★★.

● FURTHER READING: *The Saga Of Jim Reeves: Country And Western Singer And Musician*, Pansy Cook.

REID, DUKE

b. *c*.1915, Jamaica, West Indies, d. 1974. Perhaps the single biggest influence on reggae music after his close rival, Coxsone Dodd, Duke Reid's marvellous productions were, at their best, reggae at its absolute peak. Reid spent 10 years as a Kingston policeman, a sometimes dangerous profession that enabled him to develop the no-nonsense style he displayed while conducting business

negotiations in later life. He and his wife Lucille bought the Treasure Isle Liquor Store in the 50s, and in a sponsorship deal Reid hosted his own radio show, *Treasure Isle Time*, airing US R&B: his theme song was Tab Smith's 'My Mother's Eyes'. Reid also ran his own sound system, Duke Reid The Trojan, for which he visited America to find obscure R&B tunes with which to baffle rivals like Coxsone Dodd's Downbeat sound system. After flirting with the record business for three years, recording tunes such as 'Duke's Cookies', 'What Makes Honey' and 'Joker', he took up record production seriously in 1962, scoring ska hits galore with Stranger Cole, the Techniques, Justin Hinds And The Dominoes and Alton Ellis And The Flames, issuing them on three labels: Treasure Isle, Duke Reid, and Dutchess. Reid did not exactly dominate the music business, but his was a formidable presence: he was notorious for carrying a loaded gun and letting his ammunition belt be clearly visible. However, he was more than mere muscle and had an astute musical sensibility, as the fast approaching rocksteady era proved beyond doubt.

By 1966 ska was evolving into a slower, more stately beat, and with help from guitarist Ernest Ranglin and the band of sax player Tommy McCook & the Supersonics, Reid's productions at his own Treasure Isle Studio epitomised the absolute peak of the style. Hits such as the Paragons 'Ali Baba' and 'Wear You To the Ball', Alton Ellis' 'Cry Tough', 'Breaking Up', 'Rock Steady' and 'Ain't That Loving You', the Melodians' 'You Don't Need Me', 'I Will Get Along', 'I Caught You' and 'Last Train To Expo '67', the Jamaicans' 'Things You Say You Love' and the Techniques' 'Queen Majesty' were only the tip of an impressive iceberg. All are tasteful, irresistibly danceable, soul-soaked rocksteady classics, released on Reid's own labels in Jamaica and on Trojan (the label was named after his sound) or its imprints in the UK. By 1969 rocksteady had died, and Reid was apparently struggling, stuck in a musical revolution he had created. However, in 1970 he did it again, taking a sparsely recorded toaster named U-Roy, and single-handedly founded the modern DJ era. At one point U-Roy held four out of the top five Jamaican chart positions and both he and Reid were watching them swap places over a period of months: 'Wake The Town', 'Wear You To the Ball', 'Everybody Bawlin'', 'Version Galore'. Reid simply dropped the chatter over his old rocksteady hits to start a whole new genre of reggae music. He also had hits with other DJs, such as Dennis Alcapone and Lizzy. Reid's legend in the reggae pantheon was assured. By 1973 Reid's fortunes had again begun to wane, perhaps because he was notorious for not wanting to record rasta lyrics in an era dominated by roots themes, and was considered to be an establishment figure as the senior reggae producer in Jamaica. He died in 1974, his extensive back catalogue going on to sell thousands of singles and albums through a variety of licensees, his name on a record virtually a guarantee of sheer joy for the duration of its playing time.

● ALBUMS: Various: *Golden Hits* rec. 1966-69 (Trojan 1969)★★★★, *The Birth Of Ska* rec. 1962-65 (Trojan

1972)★★★★, *Hottest Hits* rec. 1966-69 (Front Line)★★★★, *Hottest Hits Volume Two* rec. 1966-69 (Front Line 1979)★★★, *Ba Ba Boom Time* rec. 1967-68 (Trojan 1988). The Skatalites: *Tribute To The Skatalites* (1991)★★★. Alton Ellis: *Greatest Hits* (1977)★★★★. Paragons: *On The Beach* (Treasure Isle 1968)★★★. Justin Hinds And The Dominoes: *From Jamaica With Reggae* (High Note 1984)★★★, *Early Recordings* (Esoldun/Treasure Isle 1991)★★★. U-Roy: *Version Galore* (Trojan 1971)★★★★.

REMAINS

This Boston, USA-based garage band was formed in 1964 by guitarist/vocalist Barry Tashian. Inspired by a trip to London, where he heard British groups playing material he loved - Jimmy Reed, Little Walter, Chuck Berry and John Lee Hooker - Tashian put together the Remains with Bill Briggs (keyboards), Vern Miller (bass) and Chip Damiani (drums). They made their debut in 1965 with 'Why Do I Cry', a melodic slice of R&B. It was succeeded by the equally persuasive 'I Can't Get Away' and an assured reading of 'Diddy Wah Diddy', but the Remains' crowning moment came with their fourth single, 'Don't Look Back'. This engaging slice of riff-laden pop was later immortalized on Lenny Kaye's seminal 60s punk compilation, *Nuggets*. The Remains moved from Boston to New York in 1966, shedding Damiani in the process. Tashian now feels this undermined the dynamics of the group. N.D. Smart joined the line-up which enjoyed a support slot on the final Beatles tour before breaking up later that year. *The Remains* was compiled and issued following the break. Tashian and Briggs then forged the original Flying Burrito Brothers, a name later appropriated by his friend, Gram Parsons. Barry accompanied the latter on his classic *GP* and *Grievous Angel* albums - N.D. Smart also surfaced in Parsons' 'road' band - and subsequently performed with Gram's erstwhile partner, Emmylou Harris. He now works with his wife in a country duo, Barry And Holly Tashian.
●ALBUMS: *The Remains* (Epic 1966)★★★.
●COMPILATIONS: *The Remains* (Columbia Legacy 1991)★★★.

REMO FOUR

The Remo Four evolved out of the skiffle circuit active in Liverpool, England, during the 50s. Their founding line-up featured Colin Manley (lead guitar), Keith Stokes (rhythm guitar), Don Andrews (bass) and Harry Prytcherch (drums). In 1961 Phil Roger (guitar) and Roy Dyke (drums) replaced Stokes and Prytcherch. The group was already renowned as accomplished musicians, and when vocalist Johnny Sandon parted company with the Searchers, the singer hired the Remo Four as his backing act. They played on both of Sandon's 1962 singles, 'Lies' (a Manley composition) and 'Yes', but the partnership was then sundered. Tony Ashton (organ) then replaced Andrews, with Roger switching to bass. In 1963 Beatles' manager Brian Epstein paired the Remo Four with new protégé Tommy Quickly. The group backed the singer on

six singles, including 'Tip Of My Tongue', 'Kiss Me Now' and 'The Wild Side Of Life', which was a minor UK hit (number 33) in 1964. However, these failed to do the Remo Four justice and their merits were heard better on recordings in their own right, notably 'Peter Gunn', the b-side of their debut single, 'I Wish I Could Shimmy Like My Sister Kate'. The Remo Four spent a considerable spell resident in Germany, where they appeared at Hamburg's fabled Star Club. They also made several recordings at this time that captured their blend of R&B and jazz to full effect. Only one single, 'Live Like A Lady' (1965) was issued, but other tracks were belatedly collected on *Smile*. Having backed another Liverpudlian aspirant, Gregory Phillips, on 'Everybody Knows' (1965), the Remo Four returned to Germany, where they remained until 1967. George Harrison then invited the group to contribute music to the film soundtrack *Wonderwall* (1968), after which they split up. Ashton and Dyke then formed Ashton, Gardner and Dyke with Kim Gardner (ex-Birds; Creation).
●ALBUMS: *Smile* (Star Club 1967)★★.

REPARATA AND THE DELRONS

Schoolfriends Mary Aiese, Nanette Licari, Anne Fitzgerald and Regina Gallagher began performing together in 1962. Dubbed the Del-Rons in honour of the Dell-Vikings and Del-Satins, they appeared at dances in their Brooklyn neighbourhood before Mary realigned the group around Carol Drobinicki, Sheila Reille, Kathy Romeo and Margi McGuire. The last was asked to leave when the group acquired a recording deal which in turn engendered 'Whenever A Teenager Cries'. This light, but plaintive offering topped the local New York chart, but although it only rose to number 60 nationally, the single - credited to Reparata And The Delrons - nonetheless secured the trio's reputation. With Mary taking the lead spot, the group underwent further alterations when original member Licari and newcomer Lorraine Mazzola replaced Reille and Romeo. Although commercial success eluded them, the revitalized trio recorded a series of excellent singles, including the Jeff Barry-penned 'I'm Nobody's Baby Now' and 'I Can Hear The Rain', which featured Melba Moore on backing vocals. Despite continued apathy at home the trio enjoyed a major UK hit when the excellent 'Captain Of Your Ship' reached number 13 in 1968. Paradoxically the vocal line featured Mazzola, who assumed the name Reparata when Mary Aiese retired in 1970. Mazzola, Licari and newcomer Cookie Sirico completed the concept album, *1970 Rock 'N' Roll Revolution*, which contained various 'girl-group' classics, before disbanding in 1973. Mazzola later appeared in Lady Flash, the backing group to Barry Manilow, but her continued use of the name Reparata was challenged by Aiese who reclaimed the appellation for a series of solo singles, of which 'Shoes' reached the UK Top 50 in 1975.
●ALBUMS: *Whenever A Teenager Cries* (World Artists 1965)★★, *1970 Rock 'N' Roll Revolution* (1970)★★.

REVERE, PAUL, AND THE RAIDERS

Formed in Portland, Oregon, USA, in 1961, when pianist Revere added Mark Lindsay (b. 9 March 1942, Cambridge, Idaho, USA; vocals/saxophone) to the line-up of his club band, the Downbeats. Drake Levin (guitar), Mike Holliday (bass) and Michael Smith (drums) completed a group later known as Paul Revere And The Nightriders, before settling on their Raiders appellation. Several locally issued singles ensued, including 'Beatnik Sticks' and 'Like Long Hair', the latter of which rose into the US Top 40. Group manager and disc jockey Roger Hart then financed a demonstration tape which in turn engendered a prestigious recording deal with CBS/Columbia. Their version of bar band favourite 'Louie Louie' was issued in 1963, but although highly successful regionally, was out-sold by local rivals the Kingsmen who secured the national hit. A year passed before the Raiders recorded a new single, during which time Phil Volk had replaced Holliday. 'Louie Go Home' showed their confidence remained undiminished, but it was 1965 before the Raiders hit their commercial stride with the punky 'Steppin' Out'. By this point the group was the resident act on *Where The Action Is*, Dick Clark's networked, daily television show. The attendant exposure resulted in a series of classic pop singles, including 'Just Like Me' (1965) 'Kicks', 'Hungry', 'Good Things' (all 1966) and 'Him Or Me - What's It Gonna Be' (1967), each of which were impeccably produced by Terry Melcher. However, the Raiders' slick stage routines and Revolutionary War garb - replete with thigh-boots, tights, frilled shirts and three-cornered hats - was frowned upon by the emergent underground audience. The departures of Smith, Levin and Volk made little difference to the Raiders' overall sound, enhancing suspicion that session musicians were responsible for the excellent studio sound. Later members Freddie Weller (guitar), Keith Allison (bass) and Joe (Correro) Jnr. (drums) were nonetheless accomplished musicians, and thus enhanced the professional approach marking *Hard & Heavy (With Marshmallow)* and *Collage*. Despite inconsistent chart places, the group maintained a high television profile as hosts of *Happening 68*. In 1969 Lindsay embarked on a concurrent solo career, but although 'Arizona' sold over one million copies, later releases proved less successful. Two years later the Raiders scored an unexpected US chart-topper with 'Indian Reservation', previously a UK hit for Don Fardon, but it proved their final Top 20 hit. Although Weller forged a new career in country music, Revere and Lindsay struggled to keep the group afloat, particularly when dropped by their longstanding label. The former eventually became the act's custodian, presiding over occasional releases for independent outlets. The Raiders flourished briefly during the US Bicentennial celebrations, before emerging again in 1983 mixing old favourites and new songs on their Raiders America label. This regeneration proved short-lived, although Revere still fronts a version of the group for the nostalgia circuit.
●ALBUMS: *Like, Long Hair* (Gardena 1961)★★★, *Paul Revere And The Raiders* aka *In The Beginning* (Jerden 1961)★★, *Here They Come* (Columbia 1965)★★★, *Just Like Us* (Columbia 1965)★★★, *Midnight Ride* (Columbia 1966)★★★, *The Spirit Of 67* aka *Good Thing* (Columbia 1967)★★★, *Revolution* (1967)★★★, *A Christmas Present ... And Past* (1967)★★★, *Goin' To Memphis* (1968)★★★, *Something Happening* (1968)★★★, *Hard And Heavy (With Marshmallow)* (Columbia 1969)★★, *Alias Pink Puzz* (1969)★★, *Collage* (1970)★★★, *Indian Reservation* (1971)★★★, *Country Wine* (1972)★★, *We Gotta All Get Together* (Realm 1976)★★, *Featuring Mark Lindsay's Arizona* (Realm 1976)★★.
●COMPILATIONS: *Greatest Hits* (Columbia 1967)★★★, *Greatest Hits Volume 2* (60s)★★★, *All-Time Greatest Hits* (70s)★★★, *Kicks* (1982)★★★, *The Essential Ride 1963-67* (Columbia/Legacy 1995)★★★★.

RHINOCEROS

A rock band that promised more than it was able to deliver, Rhinoceros was an Elektra Records signing of the late 60s. The group looked a formidable line-up on paper with Michael Fonfara, ex-Electric Flag (keyboards), Billy Mundi, ex-Mothers Of Invention (drums), Doug Hastings, ex-Buffalo Springfield (guitar), Danny Weis, ex-Iron Butterfly (guitar) and John Finlay (vocals). The spectacular fold out cover artwork on their debut by G. Sazaferin showed a brightly colourful, beaded Rhinoceros. Unfortunately the music was disappointing, only the Buddy Miles-influenced 'You're My Girl (I Don't Want To Discuss It)' and their 'greatest hit' the instrumental 'Apricot Brandy' stood out. The BBC adopted the latter as a Radio 1 theme. Two more albums followed, but by now the ponderous Rhinoceros had turned into a dodo.
●ALBUMS: *Rhinoceros* (Elektra 1968)★★★, *Satin Chickens* (Elektra 1969)★★, *Better Times Are Coming* (Elektra 1970)★.

RICHARD, CLIFF

b. Harry Roger Webb, 14 October 1940, Lucklow, India. One of the most popular and enduring talents in the history of UK showbusiness, Richard began his career as a rock 'n' roll performer in 1957. His fascination for Elvis Presley encouraged him to join a skiffle group and several months later he teamed up with drummer Terry Smart and guitarist Ken Payne to form the Drifters. They played at various clubs in the Cheshunt/Hoddesdon area of Hertfordshire before descending on the famous 2Is coffee bar in London's Old Compton Street. There they were approached by lead guitarist Ian Samwell and developed their act as a quartet. In 1958, they secured their big break in the unlikely setting of a Saturday morning talent show at the Gaumont cinema in Shepherd's Bush. It was there that the senatorial theatrical agent George Ganyou recognized Cliff's sexual appeal and singing abilities and duly financed the recording of a demonstration tape of 'Breathless' and 'Lawdy Miss Clawdy'. A copy reached the hands of EMI producer Norrie Paramor who was impressed enough to grant the ensemble an audition. Initially, he intended to record Richard as a solo artist backed by an orchestra, but the persuasive performer insisted upon retaining his own backing group. With the assistance of a couple of session musicians, the unit recorded the American teen ballad 'Schoolboy Crush' as a projected first single. An acetate of the recording was paraded around Tin Pan Alley and came to the attention of the influential television producer Jack Good. It was not the juvenile 'Schoolboy Crush' which captured his attention, however, but the Ian Samwell b-side 'Move It'. Good reacted with characteristically manic enthusiasm when he heard the disc, rightly recognizing that it sounded like nothing else in the history of UK pop. The distinctive riff and unaffected vocal seemed authentically American, completely at odds with the mannered material that usually emanated from British recording studios. With Good's ceaseless promotion, which included a full-page review in the music paper *Disc*, Richard's debut was eagerly anticipated and swiftly rose to number 2 in the UK charts. Meanwhile, the star made his debut on Good's television showcase *Oh Boy!*, and rapidly replaced Marty Wilde as Britain's premier rock 'n' roll talent. The low-key role offered to the Drifters persuaded Samwell to leave the group to become a professional songwriter, and by the end of 1958 a new line-up emerged featuring Hank B. Marvin and Bruce Welch. Before long, they changed their name to the Shadows, in order to avoid confusion with the black American R&B group, the Drifters.

Meanwhile, Richard consolidated his position in the rock 'n' roll pantheon, even outraging critics in true Elvis Presley fashion. The *New Musical Express* denounced his 'violent, hip-swinging' and 'crude exhibitionism' and pontificated: 'Tommy Steele became Britain's teenage idol without resorting to this form of indecent, short-sighted vulgarity'. Critical mortification had little effect on the screaming female fans who responded to the singer's boyish sexuality with increasing intensity.

1959 was a decisive year for Richard and a firm indicator of his longevity as a performer. With management shake-ups, shifts in national musical taste and some distinctly average singles his career could easily have been curtailed, but instead he matured and transcended his Presley-like beginnings. A recording of Lionel Bart's 'Living Doll' provided him with a massive UK number 1 and three months later he returned to the top with the plaintive 'Travellin' Light'. He also starred in two films, within 12 months. *Serious Charge*, a non-musical drama, was banned in some areas as it dealt with the controversial subject of homosexual blackmail. The Wolf Mankowitz-directed *Expresso Bongo*, in which Richard played the delightfully named Bongo Herbert, was a cinematic pop landmark, brilliantly evoking the rapacious world of Tin Pan Alley. It remains one of the most revealing and humorous films ever made on the music business and proved an interesting vehicle for Richard's varied talents.

From 1960 onwards Richard's career progressed along more traditional lines leading to acceptance as a middle-of-the-road entertainer. Varied hits such as the breezy, chart-topping 'Please Don't Tease', the rock 'n' rolling 'Nine Times Out Of Ten' and reflective 'Theme For A Dream' demonstrated his range, and in 1962 he hit a new peak with 'The Young Ones'. A glorious pop anthem to youth, with some striking guitar work from Hank Marvin, the song proved one of his most memorable number 1 hits. The film of the same name was a charming period piece, with a strong cast and fine score. It broke box office records and spawned a series of similar movies from its star, who was clearly following Elvis Presley's cinematic excursions as a means of extending his audience. Unlike the King, however, Richard supplemented his frequent movie commitments with tours, summer seasons, regular television slots and even pantomime appearances. The run of UK Top 10 hits continued uninterrupted until as late as mid-1965. Although the showbiz glitz had brought a certain aural homogeneity to the material, the catchiness of songs like 'Bachelor Boy', 'Summer Holiday', 'On The Beach' and 'I Could Easily Fall' was undeniable. These were neatly, if predictably, complemented by ballad releases such as 'Constantly', 'The Twelfth Of Never' and 'The Minute You're Gone'.

The formula looked likely to be rendered redundant by the British beat boom, but Richard expertly rode that wave, even improving his selection of material along the way. He bravely, although relatively unsuccessfully, covered a Rolling Stones song, 'Blue Turns To Grey', before again hitting top form with the beautifully melodic 'Visions'. During 1966, he had almost retired after converting to fundamentalist Christianity, but elected to use his singing career as a positive expression of his faith. The sparkling 'In The Country' and gorgeously evocative 'The Day I Met Marie' displayed the old strengths to the full, but in the swiftly changing cultural climate of the late 60s, Richard's hold on the pop charts could no longer be guaranteed. The 1968 Eurovision Song Contest offered him a chance of further glory, but the jury placed him a close second with the 'oom-pah-pah'-sounding 'Congratulations'. The song was nevertheless a consummate Eurovision performance and proved one of the biggest UK number 1s of the year. Immediately thereafter, Cliff's chart progress declined and his choice of material proved at best desultory. Although there were a couple of solid entries, Raymond Froggatt's 'Big Ship' and a superb duet with Hank Marvin 'Throw Down A Line', Richard seemed a likely contender for Variety as the decade closed.

The first half of the 70s saw him in a musical rut. The chirpy but insubstantial 'Goodbye Sam, Hello Samantha' was a Top 10 hit in 1970 and heralded a notable decline. A second shot at the Eurovision Song Contest with 'Power To All Our Friends' brought his only other Top 10 success of the period and it was widely assumed that his chart career was spent. However, in 1976 there was a surprise resurgence in his career when Bruce Welch of the Shadows was assigned to produce his colleague. The sessions resulted in the best-selling album *I'm Nearly Famous*, which included two major hits 'Miss You Nights' and 'Devil Woman'. The latter was notable for its decidedly un-Christian imagery and the fact that it gave Richard a rare US chart success. Although Welch remained at the controls for two more albums, time again looked as although it would kill off Richard's perennial chart success. A string of meagre singles culminated in the dull 'Green Light' which stalled at number 57, his lowest chart placing since he started singing. Coincidentally, his backing musicians, Terry Britten and Alan Tarney, had moved into songwriting and production at this point and encouraged him to adopt a more contemporary sound on the album *Rock 'N' Roll Juvenile*. The most startling breakthrough, however, was the attendant single 'We Don't Talk Anymore', written by Tarney and produced by Welch. An exceptional pop record, the song gave Richard his first UK number 1 hit in over a decade and also reached the Top 10 in the US. The 'new' Richard sound, so refreshing after some of his staid offerings in the late 70s, brought further well-arranged hits, such as 'Carrie' and 'Wired For Sound', and ensured that he was a chart regular throughout the 80s.

Although he resisted the temptation to try anything radical, there were subtle changes in his musical approach. One feature of his talent that emerged during the 80s was a remarkable facility as a duettist. Collaborations with Olivia Newton-John, Phil Everly, Sarah Brightman, Sheila Walsh, Elton John and Van Morrison added a completely new dimension to his career. It was something of a belated shock to realize that Richard may be one of the finest harmony singers working in the field of popular music. His perfectly enunciated vocals and the smooth texture of his voice have the power to complement work that he might not usually tackle alone.

The possibility of his collaborating with an artist even further from his sphere than Van Morrison remains a tantalizing challenge. Throughout his four decades in the pop charts, Cliff has displayed a valiant longevity. He parodied one of his earliest hits with comedy quartet the Young Ones and registered yet another number 1; he appeared in the stage musical *Time*; he sang religious songs on gospel tours; he sued the *New Musical Express* for an appallingly libellous review, far more vicious than their acerbic comments back in 1958; he was decorated by the Queen; and he celebrated his 50th birthday with a move into social commentary with the anti-war hit 'From A Distance'. Richard was nominated to appear at the celebrations in 1995 for VE day appearing with Vera Lynn, and has now been adopted as her male equivalent. It was no surprise to find that he was knighted for his services to popular music in May 1995. *Songs From Heathcliff* is the album from the John Farrar and Tim Rice production of *Heathcliff*. And so he goes on. Sir Cliff Richard has outlasted every musical trend of the past four decades with a sincerity and commitment that may well be unmatched in his field. He is British pop's most celebrated survivor.

●ALBUMS: *Cliff* (Columbia 1959)★★★, *Cliff Sings* (Columbia 1959)★★★★, *Me And My Shadows* (Columbia 1960)★★★★, *Listen To Cliff* (Columbia 1961)★★★, *21 Today* (Columbia 1961)★★★, *The* *Young Ones* (Columbia 1961)★★★, *32 Minutes And 17 Seconds With Cliff Richard* (Columbia 1962)★★★★, *Summer Holiday* (Columbia 1963)★★★, *Cliff's Hit Album* (Columbia 1963)★★★★, *When In Spain* (Columbia 1963)★★★, *Wonderful Life* (Columbia 1964)★★★, *Aladdin And His Wonderful Lamp* (Columbia 1964)★★★, *Cliff Richard* (Columbia 1965)★★★, *More Hits By Cliff* (Columbia 1965)★★★, *When In Rome* (Columbia 1965)★★, *Love Is Forever* (Columbia 1965)★★★, *Kinda Latin* (Columbia 1966)★★★, *Finders Keepers* (Columbia 1966)★★, *Cinderella* (Columbia 1967)★★, *Don't Stop Me Now* (Columbia 1967)★★★, *Good News* (Columbia 1967)★★★, *Cliff In Japan* (Columbia 1968)★★★, *Two A Penny* (Columbia 1968)★★★, *Established 1958* (Columbia 1968)★★★, *Sincerely Cliff* (Columbia 1969)★★★, *It'll Be Me* (Columbia 1969)★★★, *Cliff 'Live' At The Talk Of The Town* (1970)★★★, *All My Love* (1970)★★★, *About That Man* (1970)★★★, *Tracks 'N' Grooves* (Columbia 1970)★★★, *His Land* (Columbia 1970)★★★, *Cliff's Hit Album* (EMI 1971)★★★, *The Cliff Richard Story* (EMI 1972)★★★, *Take Me High* (EMI 1973)★★★, *Help It Along* (EMI 1974)★★★, *The 31st Of February Street* (EMI 1974)★★★, *Everybody Needs Somebody* (EMI 1975)★★★, *I'm Nearly Famous* (EMI 1976)★★★, *Cliff Live* (EMI 1976)★★★, *Every Face Tells A Story* (EMI 1977)★★★, *Small Corners* (EMI 1977)★★★, *Green Light* (EMI 1978)★★★, *Thank You Very Much* (EMI 1979)★★★, *Rock 'N' Roll Juvenile* (EMI 1979)★★★, *Rock On With Cliff* (EMI 1980)★★★, *The Cliff Richard Songbook* (EMI 1980)★★★, *Listen To Cliff* (EMI 1980)★★★, *I'm No Hero* (EMI 1980)★★★, *Love Songs* (EMI 1981)★★★, *Wired For Sound* (EMI 1981)★★★, *Now You See Me, Now You Don't* (EMI 1982)★★★, *Dressed For The Occasion* (EMI 1983)★★★, *Silver* (EMI 1983)★★★, *Cliff In The 60s* (EMI 1984)★★★, *Cliff And The Shadows* EMI 1984)★★★, *Walking In The Light* (EMI 1984)★★★, *The Rock Connection* (EMI 1984)★★★, *Time* (1986)★★★, *Hymns And Inspirational Songs* (EMI 1986)★★★, *Always Guaranteed* (EMI 1987)★★★, *Private Collection* (EMI 1988)★★★, *Stronger* (EMI 1989)★★★, *From A Distance ...The Event* (EMI 1990)★★★, *Together With Cliff* (EMI 1991)★★★, *The Album* (EMI 1993)★★★, *Songs From Heathcliff* (EMI 1995).

●COMPILATIONS: *The Best Of Cliff* (Columbia 1969)★★★★, *The Best Of Cliff Volume 2* (Columbia 1972)★★★★, *40 Golden Greats* (EMI 1979)★★★★, *The Hit List* (EMI 1994)★★★★, *At The Movies 1959-1974* (EMI 1996)★★★, *The Rock 'N' Roll Years 1958-1963* (EMI 1997)★★★.

●VIDEOS: *Two A Penny* (1978), *The Video Connection* (1983), *Together* (1984), *Rock In Australia* (1985), *Thank You Very Much* (1986), *We Don't Talk Anymore* (1987), *Video EP* (1988), *The Young Ones* (1988), *Summer Holiday* (1988), *Wonderful Life* (1988), *Take Me High* (1988), *Private Collection* (1988), *Always Guaranteed* (1988), *Live And Guaranteed* (1989), *From*

A Distance ... The Event Vols 1and 2 (1990), *Together With Cliff Richard* (1991), *Expresso Bongo* (1992), *Cliff-When The Music Stops* (1993), *Access All Areas* (1993), *The Story So Far* (1993), *The Hit List* (PMI 1995), *The Hit List Live* (PMI 1995), *Finders Keepers* (1996), *Cliff At The Movies* (1996).

●FURTHER READING: *Driftin' With Cliff Richard: The Inside Story Of What Really Happens On Tour*, Jet Harris and Royston Ellis. *Cliff, The Baron Of Beat*, Jack Sutter. *It's Great To Be Young*, Cliff Richard. *Me And My Shadows*, Cliff Richard. *Top Pops*, Cliff Richard. *Cliff Around The Clock*, Bob Ferrier. *The Wonderful World Of Cliff Richard*, Bob Ferrier. *Questions: Cliff Answering Reader And Fan Queries*, Cliff Richard. *The Way I See It*, Cliff Richard. *The Cliff Richard Story*, George Tremlett. *New Singer, New Song: The Cliff Richard Story*, David Winter. *Which One's Cliff?*, Cliff Richard with Bill Latham. *Happy Christmas From Cliff*, Cliff Richard. *Cliff In His Own Words*, Kevin St. John. *Cliff*, Patrick Doncaster and Tony Jasper. *Cliff Richard*, John Tobler. *Silver Cliff: A 25 Year Journal 1958-1983*, Tony Jasper. *Cliff Richard: The Complete Recording Sessions, 1958-1990*, Peter Lewry and Nigel Goodall. *Cliff: A Biography*, Tony Jasper. *Cliff Richard, The Complete Chronicle*, Mike Read, Nigel Goodhall and Peter Lewry. *Cliff Richard: The Autobiography*, Steve Turner.

●FILMS: *Serious Charge* (1959), *Expresso Bongo* (1960), *The Young Ones* (1961), *Summer Holiday* (1962), *Wonderful Life* (1964), *Thunderbirds Are Go!* (1966), *Finders Keepers* (1966), *Two A Penny* (1968), *Take Me High* (1973).

RIGHTEOUS BROTHERS

Despite their professional appellation, Bill Medley (b. 19 September 1940, Santa Ana, California, USA) and Bobby Hatfield (b. 10 August 1940, Beaver Dam, Wisconsin, USA) were not related. They met in 1962 at California's Black Derby club, where they won the approbation of its mixed-race clientele. By blending Medley's sonorous baritone to Hatfield's soaring high tenor, this white duo's vocal style invoked that of classic R&B, and a series of excellent singles, notably 'Little Latin Lupe Lu', followed. They achieved national fame in 1964 following several appearances on US television's highly-popular *Shindig*. Renowned producer Phil Spector then signed the act to his Philles label and proceeded to mould his 'Wagerian' sound to their dramatic intonation. 'You've Lost That Lovin' Feelin' justifiably topped the US and UK charts and is rightly lauded as one the greatest pop singles of all time. A similar passion was extolled on 'Just Once In My Life' and 'Ebb Tide', but the relationship between performer and mentor rapidly soured. The Righteous Brothers moved outlets in 1966, but despite gaining a gold disc for '(You're My) Soul And Inspiration', a performance modelled on their work with Spector, the duo was unable to sustain the same success. They split in 1968, with Medley beginning a solo career and Hatfield retaining the name with new partner Jimmy Walker, formerly of the Knickerbockers. This short-lived collaboration ended soon afterwards, but the original pair were reunited in 1974 for an appearance on *The Sonny And Cher Comedy Hour*. They scored a US Top 3 hit that year with the maudlin 'Rock 'n' Roll Heaven', but were unable to regain former glories and have subsequently separated and re-formed on several occasions. In 1987 Medley enjoyed an international smash with '(I've Had) The Time Of My Life', a duet with Jennifer Warnes taken from the film *Dirty Dancing*, while a reissue of 'Unchained Melody', a hit for the Righteous Brothers in 1965, topped the UK chart in 1990 after it featured in the film *Ghost*.

●ALBUMS: *The Righteous Brothers - Right Now* (Moonglow 1963)★★, *Blue-Eyed Soul* (Moonglow 1965)★★, *This Is New* (Moonglow 1965)★★, *You've Lost That Lovin' Feelin'* (Philles 1965)★★★★, *Just Once In My Life* (Philles 1965)★★★★, *In Action* (Sue 1966)★★, *Back To Back* (Philles 1966)★★★★, *Go Ahead And Cry* (Verve 1966)★★★, *Soul And Inspiration* (Verve 1966)★★★★, *Sayin' Somethin'* (Verve 1967)★★★, *Souled Out* (1967)★★★, *Standards* (Verve 1967)★★★, *One For The Road* (Verve 1968)★★★, *Rebirth* (Verve 1970)★★, *Kingston Rock* (1974)★★, *Give It To The People* (1974)★★, *Sons Of Mrs Righteous* (1975)★★.

●COMPILATIONS: *The Best Of The Righteous Brothers* (Moonglow 1965)★★, *Greatest Hits* (Verve 1967)★★★★, *Greatest Hits Volume 2* (70s)★★★, *2 By 2* (1973)★★★, *Best Of The Righteous Brothers* (1987)★★★★.

●VIDEOS: *21st Anniversary Celebration* (Old Gold 1990).

●FILMS: *Beach Ball* (1964).

RIOT SQUAD

A group of young UK session musicians formed by producer Larry Page, the Riot Squad consisted of Graham Bonney (vocals), Ron Ryan (lead guitar), Bob Evans (saxophone), Mark Stevens (organ), Mike Martin (bass) and John 'Mitch' Mitchell (drums). They made their recording debut in January 1965 with the gritty 'Anytime', while subsequent releases explored contrasting strands of R&B. The group completed seven singles over the ensuing two years, but was plagued by internal dissent. Bonney subsequently enjoyed momentary success with his second solo release, 'Supergirl', but it was Mitchell who gained the highest profile, first with Georgie Fame, then with the Jimi Hendrix Experience. By that point Joe Meek had assumed the Riot Squad reins from Page, but this made little difference to their fortunes. A group bearing their name struggled on into 1968, but by this point none of the original line-up remained.

●ALBUMS: *Anytime* (1988)★★.

RISING SONS

One of the most legendary unrecorded groups, the Rising Sons consisted of Taj Mahal (vocals/guitar), Ry Cooder (vocals/guitar), Gary Marker (bass), Ed Cassidy (drums) and Jesse Lee Kincaid (vocals/guitar). Kevin Kelley also deputized on drums during their brief recording period when Cassidy injured his wrist playing a frenetic version of 'Blind' Willie McTell's 'Statesboro Blues'. Formed in Los Angeles, California, USA, in 1965, the group was signed to Columbia Records but their album was never issued. One single, 'Candy Man'/'The Devil's Got My Woman', did surface, but the group had by then disbanded. Mahal son became a prominent blues/folk performer, Cooder made his name playing sessions and later recorded successfully under his own name. Kelley briefly joined the Byrds and Cassidy became a mainstay in Spirit. Maker became a renowned journalist. Sessions from the album, produced by Byrds/Paul Revere associate Terry Melcher, became widely bootlegged due to interest in the various participants, and nearly two decades later they were given an official release by Columbia Records. Mahal contributed three new vocal takes for this project, but its patchwork quality finally laid to rest one of the great mysteries of the 60s.

●ALBUMS: *Rising Sons Featuring Taj Mahal And Ry Cooder* (Columbia/Legacy 1993)★★★.

RIVERS, JOHNNY

b. John Ramistella, 7 November 1942, New York City, New York, USA. Johnny Rivers scored a long streak of pop hits in the 60s and 70s, initially by remaking earlier R&B songs and eventually with his own compositions. His singles were spirited creations, some recorded live in front of an enthusiastic, hip Los Angeles audience. His father moved the family to Baton Rouge, Louisiana, in 1945, where Rivers began playing guitar at the age of eight. By the age of 13, having become enamoured of the local rock 'n' roll and R&B artists, he was fronting his own group. In 1958 he ventured to New York to make his first recording. Top disc jockey Alan Freed met the singer and gave him his new name, Johnny Rivers, and also recommended to the local Gone Records label that they sign Rivers. They did, and his first single, 'Baby Come Back', was issued that year. At 17 Rivers moved to Nashville, where he wrote songs with another aspiring singer, Roger Miller, and recorded demo records for Elvis Presley, Johnny Cash and others, including Ricky Nelson, who recorded Rivers' 'Make Believe' in 1960. Rivers relocated to Los Angeles at that time. Between 1959 and his 1964 signing to Imperial Records he recorded singles for such small labels as Guyden, Cub and Dee Dee, as well as the larger Chancellor, Capitol Records, MGM Records, Coral Records and United Artists Records, none with any chart success.

In late 1963 Rivers began performing a three-night stand at the LA club Gazzari's, which was so successful it was extended for weeks. He then took up residency at the popular discotheque the Whisky A-Go-Go, where his fans began to include such stars as Johnny Carson, Steve McQueen and Rita Hayworth. His first album for Imperial, *Johnny Rivers At The Whisky A Go Go*, was released in the summer of 1964 and yielded his first hit, Chuck Berry's 'Memphis', which reached number 2.

Further hits during 1964-65 included Berry's 'Maybelline', Harold Dorman's 'Mountain Of Love', the traditional folk song 'Midnight Special', Willie Dixon's 'Seventh Son' and Pete Seeger's 'Where Have All The Flowers Gone', each delivered in a rousing, loose interpretation that featured Rivers' nasal vocal, his concise, soulful guitar-playing and sharp backing musicians. Relentlessly rhythmic, the tracks were produced by Lou Adler, working his way toward becoming one of the city's most formidable hit-makers. Rivers started 1966 with 'Secret Agent Man', the theme song from a popular television spy thriller. Later that year he achieved his only number 1 record with his own 'Poor Side Of Town' (co-written with Adler), an uncharacteristic ballad using top studio musicians such as Hal Blaine, James Burton and Larry Knechtel. Rivers also launched his own Soul City record label in 1966, signing the popular Fifth Dimension, who went on to have four Top 10 singles on the label. Retreating from the party atmosphere of his earlier recordings for Imperial, Rivers had hits in 1967 with two Motown covers, the Four Tops' 'Baby I Need Your Lovin'' and Smokey Robinson's 'The Tracks Of My Tears'. Following an appearance at the Monterey Pop Festival, another soulful ballad, the James Hendricks-penned 'Summer Rain', became Rivers' last major hit of the 60s. The latter also appeared on Rivers' best-selling album, the *Realization*. Early 70s albums such as *Slim Slo Slider*, *Home Grown* and *LA Reggae* were critically lauded but not commercially successful, although the latter gave Rivers a Top 10 single with Huey 'Piano' Smith's 'Rockin' Pneumonia - Boogie Woogie Flu'. A version of the Beach Boys' 'Help Me Rhonda' (with backing vocal by Brian Wilson) was a minor success in 1975, and two years later Rivers landed his final Top 10 single, 'Swayin' To The Music (Slow Dancin')'. Rivers recorded a handful of albums in the 80s, including a live one featuring the old hits, but none reached the charts.

●ALBUMS: *Johnny Rivers At The Whisky A Go Go* (Liberty 1964)★★★★, *The Sensational Johnny Rivers* (Capitol 1964)★★★★, *Go, Johnny, Go* (1964)★★★, *Here We A-Go-Go Again* (Liberty 1964)★★★, *Johnny Rivers In Action!* (Imperial 1965)★★★, *Meanwhile Back At The Whisky A Go Go* (Liberty 1965)★★★★, *Johnny Rivers Rocks The Folk* (Liberty 1965)★★, *... And I Know You Wanna Dance* (Imperial 1966)★★★, *Changes* (Liberty 1966)★★★, *Rewind* (Liberty 1967)★★★, *Realization* (Liberty 1968)★★★, *Johnny Rivers* (Sunset 1968)★★★, *A Touch Of Gold* (Liberty 1969)★★★, *Slim Slo Slider* (Liberty 1970)★★★, *Rockin' With Johnny Rivers* (Sunset 1971)★★★, *Non-Stop Dancing At The Whisky A Go Go* (United Artists 1971)★★★, *Home Grown* (United Artists 1972)★★★, *L.A. Reggae* (United Artists 1972)★★★, *Johnny Rivers* (1972)★★★, *Blue Suede Shoes* (United Artists 1973)★★★, *Last Boogie In Paris* (Atlantic 1974)★★★, *Rockin' Rivers* (1974)★★★, *Road* (Atlantic 1975)★★★, *New Lovers And Old Friends* (1975)★★★, *Help Me Rhonda* (Epic 1975)★★★, *Wild Night* (United Artists 1976)★★★, *Outside Help* (Polydor 1978)★★, *Borrowed Time* (RSO 1980)★★, *The Johnny Rivers Story*

(1982)★★★, *Portrait Of* (1982)★★★, *Not A Through Street* (Priority 1983)★★.
●COMPILATIONS: *Golden Hits* (Imperial 1966)★★★, *The History Of Johnny Rivers* (Liberty 1971)★★★, *Go Johnnny Go* (Hallmark 1971)★★★, *Greatest Hits* re-recordings (MCA 1985)★★, *The Best Of Johnny Rivers* (EMI America 1987)★★★, *Anthology 1964-1977* (Rhino 1991)★★★★.

RIVIERAS (R&B)

This R&B vocal group came from Englewood, New Jersey, USA. The members were Homer Dunn (lead), Charles Allen (bass), Ronald Cook (tenor) and Andrew Jones (baritone). The group specialized in singing doo-wop versions of old big band hits, especially those of Glenn Miller. Dunn formed his first group, the Bob-O-Links, in 1952 in Hackensack, New Jersey. Moving to Englewood, New Jersey, Dunn formed the Rivieras in 1955, and they managed to stay together for three years playing local gigs before being eventually signed to the Coed label. The Rivieras' principal hits were 'Count Every Star' (1958), which was previously a 1950 hit for Ray Anthony, and 'Moonlight Seranade' (1959), a Miller hit in 1939. Other outstanding releases put out before the group disbanded in 1961 were 'Our Love' (1959) and 'Moonlight Cocktail' (1960), previously hits for Tommy Dorsey and Miller, respectively.
●ALBUMS: with the Duprees *Jerry Blavat Presents Drive-In Sounds* (Lost Nite mid-60s), *The Rivieras Sing* (Post early 70s).
●COMPILATIONS: *Moonlight Cocktails* (Relic 1992)★★★.

ROBINSON, SMOKEY

b. William Robinson, 19 February 1940, Detroit, USA. A founding member of the Miracles at Northern High School, Detroit, in 1955, Robinson became one of the leading figures in the local music scene by the end of the decade. His flexible tenor voice, which swooped easily into falsetto, made him the group's obvious lead vocalist, and by 1957 he was composing his own variations on the R&B hits of the day. That year he met Berry Gordy, who was writing songs for R&B star Jackie Wilson, and looking for local acts to produce. Vastly impressed by Robinson's affable personality and promising writing talent, Gordy took the teenager under his wing. He produced a series of Miracles singles in 1958 and 1959, all of which featured Robinson as composer and lead singer, and leased them to prominent R&B labels. In 1960 he signed the Miracles to his Motown stable, and began to groom Robinson as his second-in-command. In Motown's early days, Robinson was involved in every facet of the company's operations, writing, producing and making his own records, helping in the business of promotion and auditioning many of the scores of young hopefuls who were attracted by Gordy's growing reputation as an entre-preneur. Robinson had begun his career as a producer by overseeing the recording of the Miracles' 'Way Over There', and soon afterwards he was charged with devel-

oping the talents of Mary Wells and the Supremes. Wells soon became Robinson's most successful protégée: Smokey wrote and produced a sophisticated series of hit singles for her between 1962 and 1964. These records, like 'You Beat Me To The Punch', 'Two Lovers' and 'My Guy', demonstrated his growing confidence as a writer, able to use paradox and metaphor to transcend the usual banalities of the teenage popular song. A measure of Robinson's influence over Wells' career is the fact that she was unable to repeat her chart success after she elected to leave Motown, and Robinson, in 1964.

Although Robinson was unable to turn the Supremes into a hit-making act, he experienced no such failure in his relationship with Motown's leading male group of the mid-60s, the Temptations. Between 1964 and 1965, Smokey was responsible for the records that established their reputation, writing lyrical and rhythmic songs of a calibre which few writers in pop music have equalled since. 'The Way You Do The Things You Do' set the hit sequence in motion, followed by the classic ballad 'My Girl' (later equally popular in the hands of Otis Redding), the dance number 'Get Ready', 'Since I Lost My Baby' and the remarkable 'It's Growing', which boasted a complex lyric hinged around a series of metaphorical images. During the same period, Robinson helped to create two of Marvin Gaye's most enduring early hits, 'Ain't That Peculiar' and 'I'll Be Doggone'. Throughout the 60s, Smokey Robinson combined this production and A&R work with his own career as leader of the Miracles. He married fellow group member Claudette Rogers in 1959, and she provided the inspiration for Miracles hits like 'You've Really Got A Hold On Me' and 'Oooh Baby Baby'. During the mid-60s, Robinson was apparently able to turn out high-quality songs to order, working with a variety of collaborators including fellow Miracle Ronnie White, and Motown guitarist Marv Tarplin. As the decade progressed, Bob Dylan referred to Robinson apparently without irony, as 'America's greatest living poet': as if to justify this assertion, Robinson's lyric writing scaled new heights on complex ballads like 'The Love I Saw In You Was Just A Mirage' and 'I Second That Emotion'. From 1967 onwards, Robinson was given individual credit on the Miracles' releases. For the next two years, their commer-cial fortunes went into a slide, which was righted when their 1965 recording of 'The Tracks Of My Tears' became a major hit in Britain in 1969, and the four-year-old 'The Tears Of A Clown' achieved similar success on both sides of the Atlantic in 1970. At the end of the decade, Smokey briefly resumed his career as a producer and writer for other acts, collaborating with the Marvelettes on 'The Hunter Gets Captured By The Game', and the Four Tops on 'Still Water'. Business concerns were occupying an increasing proportion of his time, however, and in 1971 he announced that he would be leaving the Miracles the following year, to concentrate on his role as Vice-President of the Motown corporation. A year after the split, Robinson launched his solo career, enjoying a hit single with 'Sweet Harmony', an affectionate tribute to his former group, and issuing the excellent *Smokey*. The album included the epic 'Just My Soul Responding', a biting piece of social comment about the USA's treatment of blacks and American Indians.

Robinson maintained a regular release schedule through the mid-70s, with one new album arriving every year. Low-key and for the most part lushly produced, they made little impact, although Robinson's songwriting was just as consistent as it had been in the 60s. He continued to break new lyrical ground, striking the banner for non-macho male behaviour on 1974's 'Virgin Man', and giving name to a new style of soft soul on 1975's *A Quiet Storm*. Singles like 'Baby That's Backatcha' and 'The Agony And The Ecstasy' sold well on the black market, but failed to achieve national airplay in the States, while in Britain Robinson was regarded as a remnant from the classic era of Motown. His first film soundtrack project, *Big Time* in 1977, won little praise, and it appeared as if his creative peak was past. Instead, he hit back in 1979 with 'Cruisin', his biggest chart success since 'The Tears Of A Clown' nine years earlier. A sensuous ballad in the musical tradition of his 60s work, the record introduced a new eroticism into his writing, and restored faith in his stature as a contemporary performer. Two years later, he scored his first UK number 1 with 'Being With You', a touching love song which came close to equalling that achievement in the USA. 'Tell Me Tomorrow' enjoyed more Stateside success in 1982, and Robinson settled into another relaxed release schedule, which saw him ride out the 80s on a pattern of regular small hits and consistent album sales. Robinson was contributing significantly less new material, however, and his 1988 autobiography, *Smokey*, revealed that he had been battling against cocaine addiction for much of the decade. Although his marriage to Claudette failed, he returned to full health and creativity, and enjoyed two big hits in 1987, 'Just To See Her' and 'One Heartbeat'. Voted into the Rock And Roll Hall Of Fame in 1988, Smokey Robinson is now one of the senior figures in popular music, a writer and producer still best remembered for his outstanding work in the 60s.

●ALBUMS: *Smokey* (Motown 1973)★★★, *Pure Smokey* (Motown 1974)★★★, *A Quiet Storm* (Motown 1975)★★★, *Smokey's Family Robinson* (Motown 1976)★★★, *Deep In My Soul* (Motown 1977)★★★, *Big Time* (Motown 1977)★★★, *Love Breeze* (Motown 1978)★★★, *Smokin'* (Motown 1978)★★★, *Where There's Smoke?* (Motown 1979)★★★, *Warm Thoughts* (Motown 1980)★★★★, *Being With You* (Motown 1981)★★★★, *Yes It's You Lady* (Motown 1982)★★★, *Touch The Sky* (Motown 1983)★★★, *Blame It On Love* (Motown 1984)★★★, *Essar* (Motown 1984)★★★, *Smoke Signals* (Motown 1985)★★★, *One Heartbeat* (Motown 1987)★★★, *Love, Smokey* (Motown 1990), *Double Good Everything* (SBK 1991)★★.

●COMPILATIONS: with the Miracles *The Greatest Hits* (1992)★★★★, *The 35th Anniversry Collection* (Motown Masters 1994)★★★★, *Early Classics* (Spectrum 1996)★★★★.

●FURTHER READING: *Smokey: Inside My Life*, Smokey Robinson and David Ritz.

ROCKIN' BERRIES

This early 60s UK pop quintet comprised Clive Lea (b. 16 February 1942, Birmingham, England; vocals), Geoffrey Turton (b. 11 March 1944, Birmingham, England; guitar), Bryan Charles 'Chuck' Botfield (b. 14 November 1943, Birmingham, England; guitar), Roy Austin (b. 27 December 1943, Birmingham, England; guitar) and Terry Bond (b. 22 March 1943, Birmingham, England; drums). After beginning as an R&B cover group, they fell under the spell of visiting American Kim Fowley, who suggested they cover the Tokens' US hit 'He's In Town'. The song hit the Top 5 in late 1964 and was followed by two other hits, 'What In The World's Come Over You' (not to be confused with the Jack Scott million-seller of the same name) and an excellent reading of the Reflections' 'Poor Man's Son', with Lea and Turton on counter vocals. Like several of their contemporaries, the Berries quickly laid the foundations for a career in cabaret by including comedy sketches and parodic impressions of other artists into their act. A minor hit with 'The Water Is Over My Head' in July 1966 concluded their chart run. By 1968 Turton had embarked on a solo career as Jefferson, while the group continued on the timeless supper-club circuit.

●ALBUMS: *In Town* (Piccadilly 1964)★★★, *Life is Just A Bowl Of Berries* (Piccadilly 1964)★★★, *Black Gold* (Satril 1976)★★.

●COMPILATIONS: *Bowl Of The Rockin' Berries* (1988)★★★.

ROE, TOMMY

b. 9 May 1942, Atlanta, Georgia, USA. Vocalist Roe began his career with high school act, the Satins. The group performed several of his compositions, notably 'Sheila', which they recorded in 1960. The single was unsuccessful, but Roe revived the song two years later upon securing a solo deal. This Buddy Holly-influenced rocker topped the US chart, and reached the Top 3 in Britain where the artist enjoyed considerable popularity. Roe scored two Top 10 hits in 1963 with 'The Folk Singer' and 'Everybody' and, although not a major chart entry, 'Sweet Pea' garnered considerable airplay through the auspices of pirate radio. The song reached the US Top 10, as did its follow-up, 'Hooray For Hazel', but Roe's biggest hit came in 1969 when 'Dizzy' topped the charts on both sides of the Atlantic. The singer enjoyed further success with 'Heather Honey' and 'Jam Up Jelly Tight', but for much of the 70s he opted to pursue a low-key career in his home state. Roe did attempt a 'comeback' with *Energy* and *Full Bloom*, but subsequently plied the nostalgia circuit. 'Dizzy' returned to the top of the UK charts in 1992 in a version by the Wonder Stuff and Vic Reeves.

●ALBUMS: *Sheila* (ABC 1962)★★★, *Something For Everybody* (ABC 1964)★★★, *Everybody Likes Tommy Roe* (HMV 1964)★★★, *Ballads And Beat* (HMV 1965)★★★, *Sweet Pea* (ABC 1966)★★★, *It's Now A Winter's Day* (ABC 1967)★★, *Phantasia* (1967)★★, *Dizzy* (Stateside 1969)★★★, *We Can Make Music* (Probe 1970)★★, *Beginnings* (Probe 1971)★★, *Energy* (1976)★★, *Full Bloom* (1977)★★.

●COMPILATIONS: *12 In A Roe* (1970)★★★, *Greatest Hits* (Stateside 1970)★★★, *Beginnings* (1971)★★★, *16 Greatest Hits* (1976)★★★, *16 Greatest Songs* (1993)★★★.

ROGERS, JULIE

b. Julie Rolls, 6 April 1943, London, England. She left her Bermondsey secondary school in 1959 for a long working holiday as a dancer in Spain. Next, she worked as a secretary and then a ship's stewardess before becoming singer with a middle-of-the-road band led by Teddy Foster with whom she later functioned in a cabaret duo, and, under a new stage surname, made a radio debut in 1962 on the BBC Light Programme's *Music With A Beat*. Following an audition for Philips A & R manager Johnny Franz, she recorded her first single 'It's Magic', in 1963. Her recording career touched its zenith the following year when 'The Wedding' - an orchestrated translation of a song (by Argentinian Joaquin Prieto) which she had first heard in Spain - rose to a UK number 3, triggered by an initial plug on the ITV television regional magazine, *Day By Day*. As well as generating huge sheet music sales, it also disturbed the US Top Ten, despite two previous hit versions in 1961 by Anita Bryant and Malcolm Vaughan. The yuletide follow-up, 'Like A Child' and 1965's 'Hawaiian Wedding Song' were only minor hits, but Rogers remained in demand on the variety circuit for the rest of the decade.
●ALBUMS: *The Sound Of Julie* (Mercury 1965)★★★, *Contrasts* (Mercury 1966)★★, *Songs Of Inspiration* (Mercury 1967)★★★.

ROLLING STONES

Originally billed as the Rollin' Stones, the first line-up of this immemorial English 60s group was a nucleus of Mick Jagger (b. Michael Philip Jagger, 26 July 1943, Dartford, Kent, England; vocals), Keith Richard (b. Keith Richards, 18 December 1943, Dartford, Kent, England; guitar), Brian Jones (b. Lewis Brian Hopkin-Jones, 26 February 1942, Cheltenham, Gloucestershire, England, d. 3 July 1969; rhythm guitar) and Ian Stewart (b. 1938, d. 12 December 1985; piano). Jagger and Richard were primary school friends who resumed their camaraderie in their closing teenage years after finding they had a mutual love for R&B and particularly the music of Chuck Berry, Muddy Waters and Bo Diddley. Initially, they were teamed with bassist Dick Taylor (later of the Pretty Things) and before long their ranks extended to include Jones, Stewart and occasional drummer Tony Chapman. Their patron at this point was the renowned musician Alexis Korner, who had arranged their debut gig at London's Marquee club on 21 July 1962. In their first few months the group met some opposition from jazz and blues aficionados for their alleged lack of musical 'purity' and the line-up remained unsettled for several months.
In late 1962 bassist Bill Wyman (b. William Perks, 24 October 1936, Plumstead, London, England) replaced Dick Taylor while drummers came and went including Carlo Little (from Screaming Lord Sutch's Savages) and

Mick Avory (later of the Kinks, who was billed as appearing at their debut gig, but didn't play). It was not until as late as January 1963 that drummer Charlie Watts (b. 2 June 1941, London, England) reluctantly surrendered his day job and committed himself to the group. After securing a residency at Giorgio Gomelsky's Crawdaddy Club in Richmond, the Stones' live reputation spread rapidly through London's hip cognoscenti. One evening, the flamboyant Andrew Loog Oldham appeared at the club and was so entranced by the commercial prospects of Jagger's sexuality that he wrested them away from Gomelsky and, backed by the financial and business clout of agent Eric Easton, became their manager. Within weeks, Oldham had produced their first couple of official recordings at IBC Studios. By this time, record company scouts were on the prowl with Decca's Dick Rowe leading the march and successfully signing the group. After re-purchasing the IBC demos, Oldham selected Chuck Berry's 'Come On' as their debut. The record was promoted on the prestigious UK television pop programme *Thank Your Lucky Stars* and the Stones were featured sporting matching hounds-tooth jackets with velvet collars. This was to be one of Oldham's few concessions to propriety for he would soon be pushing the boys as unregenerate rebels. Unfortunately, pianist Ian Stewart was not deemed sufficiently pop star-like for Oldham's purpose and was unceremoniously removed from the line-up, although he remained road manager and occasional pianist. After supporting the Everly Brothers, Little Richard, Gene Vincent and Bo Diddley on a Don Arden UK package tour, the Stones released their second single, a gift from John Lennon and Paul McCartney entitled 'I Wanna Be Your Man'. The disc fared better than its predecessor climbing into the Top 10 in January 1964. That same month the group enjoyed their first bill-topping tour supported by the Ronettes.
The early months of 1964 saw the Stones catapulted to fame amid outrage and controversy about the surliness of their demeanour and the length of their hair. This was still a world in which the older members of the community were barely coming to terms with the Beatles neatly groomed mop tops. While newspapers asked 'Would you let your daughter marry a Rolling Stone?', the quintet engaged in a flurry of recording activity which saw the release of an EP and an album, both titled *The Rolling Stones*. The discs consisted almost exclusively of extraneous material and captured the group at their most derivative stage. Already, however, there were strong signs of an ability to combine different styles. The third single, 'Not Fade Away', saw them fuse Buddy Holly's quaint original with a chunky Bo Diddley beat that highlighted Jagger's vocal to considerable effect. The presence of Phil Spector and Gene Pitney at these sessions underlined how hip the Stones had already become in the music business after such a short time. With the momentum increasing by the month, Oldham characteristically over-reached himself by organizing a US tour which proved premature and disappointing. After returning to the UK, the Stones released a decisive cover

of the Valentinos' 'It's All Over Now', which gave them their first number 1. A best-selling EP, *Five By Five*, cemented their growing reputation, while a national tour escalated into a series of near riots with scenes of hysteria wherever they played. There was an ugly strain to the Stones' appeal which easily translated into violence. At the Winter Gardens, Blackpool, the group hosted the most astonishing rock riot yet witnessed on British soil. Frenzied fans displayed their feelings for the group by smashing chandeliers and demolishing a Steinway grand piano. By the end of the evening over 50 people were escorted to hospital for treatment. Other concerts were terminated within minutes of the group appearing on-stage and the hysteria continued throughout Europe. A return to the USA saw them disrupt the stagey *Ed Sullivan Show* prompting the presenter to ban rock 'n' roll groups in temporary retaliation. In spite of all the chaos at home and abroad, America remained resistant to their appeal, although that situation would change dramatically in the New Year.

In November 1964, 'Little Red Rooster' was released and entered the *New Musical Express* chart at number 1, a feat more usually associated with the Beatles and, previously, Elvis Presley. The Stones now had a formidable fan base and their records were becoming more accomplished and ambitious with each successive release. Jagger's accentuated phrasing and posturing stage persona made 'Little Red Rooster' sound surprisingly fresh while Brian Jones's use of slide guitar was imperative to the single's success. Up until this point, the group had recorded cover versions as a-sides, but manager Andrew Oldham was determined that they should emulate the example of Lennon/McCartney and locked them in a room until they emerged with satisfactory material. Their early efforts, 'It Should Have Been You' and 'Will You Be My Lover Tonight?' (both recorded by the late George Bean) were bland, but Gene Pitney scored a hit with the emphatic 'That Girl Belongs To Yesterday' and Jagger's girlfriend Marianne Faithfull became a teenage recording star with the moving 'As Tears Go By'. 1965 proved the year of the international breakthrough and three extraordinary self-penned number 1 singles. 'The Last Time' saw them emerge with their own distinctive rhythmic style and underlined an ability to fuse R&B and pop in an enticing fashion. America finally succumbed to their spell with '(I Can't Get No) Satisfaction', a quintessential pop lyric with the still youthful Jagger sounding like a jaundiced roué. Released in the UK during the 'summer of protest songs', the single encapsulated the restless weariness of a group already old before its time. The distinctive riff, which Keith Richard invented with almost casual dismissal, became one of the most famous hook lines in the entire glossary of pop and was picked up and imitated by a generation of garage groups thereafter. The 1965 trilogy of hits was completed with the engagingly surreal 'Get Off Of My Cloud' in which Jagger's surly persona seemed at its most pronounced to date. As well as the number 1 hits of 1965, there was also a celebrated live EP, *Got Live If You Want It* which

reached the Top 10 and, *The Rolling Stones No. 2* that continued the innovative idea of not including the group's name on the front of the sleeve. There was also some well documented bad boy controversy when Jagger, Jones and Wyman were arrested and charged with urinating on the wall of an East London petrol station. Such scandalous behaviour merely reinforced the public's already ingrained view of the Stones as juvenile degenerates.

With the notorious Allen Klein replacing Eric Easton as Oldham's co-manager, the Stones consolidated their success by renegotiating their Decca contract. Their single output in the USA simultaneously increased with the release of a couple of tracks unavailable in single form in the UK. The sardonic put-down of suburban valium abuse, 'Mother's Little Helper' and the Elizabethan-styled 'Lady Jane', complete with atmospheric dulcimer, displayed their contrasting styles to considerable effect. Both these songs were included on their fourth album, *Aftermath*. A breakthrough work in a crucial year, the recording revealed the Stones as accomplished rockers and balladeers, while their writing potential was emphasized by Chris Farlowe's chart-topping cover of 'Out Of Time'. There were also signs of the Stones' inveterate misogyny particularly on the cocky 'Under My Thumb' and an acerbic 'Stupid Girl'. Back in the singles chart, the group's triumphant run continued with the startlingly chaotic '19th Nervous Breakdown' in which frustration, impatience and chauvinism were brilliantly mixed with scale-sliding descending guitar lines. 'Paint It Black' was even stronger, a raga-influenced piece with a lyric so doom-laden and defeatist in its imagery that it is a wonder that the angry performance sounded so passionate and urgent. The Stones' nihilism reached its peak on the extraordinary 'Have You Seen Your Mother Baby, Standing In The Shadow?', a scabrous-sounding solicitation taken at breathtaking pace with Jagger spitting out a diatribe of barely coherent abuse. It was probably the group's most adventurous production to date, but its acerbic sound, lengthy title and obscure theme contributed to rob the song of sufficient commercial potential to continue the chart-topping run. Ever outrageous, the group promoted the record with a photo session in which they appeared in drag, thereby adding a clever, sexual ambivalence to their already iconoclastic public image.

1967 saw the Stones' anti-climactic escapades confront an establishment crackdown. The year began with an accomplished double a-sided single, 'Let's Spend The Night Together'/'Ruby Tuesday' which, like the Beatles' 'Penny Lane'/'Strawberry Fields Forever', narrowly failed to reach number 1 in their home country. The accompanying album, *Between The Buttons*, trod water and also represented Oldham's final production. Increasingly alienated by the Stones' bohemianism, he moved further away from them in the following months and surrendered the management reins to his partner Klein later in the year. On 12 February, Jagger and Richard were arrested at the latter's West Wittering home 'Redlands' and charged with drugs offences. Three months later, increasingly unstable Brian Jones was raided and charged with similar offences. The Jagger/Richard trial in June was a cause célèbre which culminated in the notorious duo receiving heavy fines and a salutary prison sentence. Judicial outrage was tempered by public clemency, most effectively voiced by *The Times*' editor William Rees-Mogg who, borrowing a phrase from Pope, offered an eloquent plea in their defence under the leader title, 'Who Breaks A Butterfly On A Wheel?' Another unexpected ally was rival group the Who, who rallied to the Stones' cause by releasing a single coupling 'Under My Thumb' and 'The Last Time'. The sentences were duly quashed on appeal in July, with Jagger receiving a conditional discharge for possession of amphetamines. Three months later, Brian Jones tasted judicial wrath with a nine-month sentence and suffered a nervous breakdown before seeing his imprisonment rescinded at the end of the year. The flurry of drug busts, court cases, appeals and constant media attention had a marked effect on the Stones' recording career which was severely curtailed. During their summer of impending imprisonment, they released the fey 'We Love You', complete with slamming prison cell doors in the background. It was a weak, flaccid statement rather than a rebellious rallying cry. The image of the cultural anarchists cowering in defeat was not particularly palatable to their fans and even with all the publicity, the single barely scraped into the Top 10. The eventful year ended with the Stones' apparent answer to *Sgt Pepper's Lonely Hearts Club Band* - the extravagantly-titled *Their Satanic Majesties Request*. Beneath the exotic 3-D cover was an album of psychedelic/cosmic experimentation bereft of the R&B grit that had previously been synonymous with the Stones' sound. Although the album had some strong moments, it had the same inexplicably placid inertia of 'We Love You', minus notable melodies or a convincing direction. The overall impression conveyed was that in trying to compete with the Beatles' experimentation, the Stones had somehow lost the plot. Their drug use had channelled them into laudable experimentation but simultaneously left them open to accusations of having 'gone soft'. The revitalization of the Stones was demonstrated in the early summer of 1968 with 'Jumpin' Jack Flash', a single that rivalled the best of their previous output. The succeeding album, *Beggars Banquet*, produced by Jimmy Miller, was also a return to strength and included the socio-political 'Street Fighting Man' and the brilliantly macabre 'Sympathy For The Devil', in which Jagger's seductive vocal was backed by hypnotic Afro-rhythms and dervish yelps.

While the Stones were re-establishing themselves, Brian Jones was falling deeper into drug abuse. A conviction in late 1968 prompted doubts about his availability for US tours and in the succeeding months he contributed less and less to recordings and became increasingly jealous of Jagger's leading role in the group. Richard's wooing and impregnation of Jones' girlfriend Anita Pallenberg merely increased the tension. Matters reached a crisis point in June 1969 when Jones officially left the group.

The following month he was found dead in the swimming pool of the Sussex house that had once belonged to writer A.A. Milne. The official verdict was 'death by misadventure'. A free concert at London's Hyde Park two days after his death was attended by a crowd of 250,000 and became a symbolic wake for the tragic youth. Jagger released thousands of butterflies and narrated a poem by Shelley. Three days later, Jagger's former love Marianne Faithfull attempted suicide. This was truly the end of the first era of the Rolling Stones.

The group played out the last months of the 60s with a mixture of vinyl triumph and further tragedy. The sublime 'Honky Tonk Women' kept them at number 1 for most of the summer and few would have guessed that this was to be their last UK chart topper. The new album, *Let It Bleed* (a parody of the Beatles' *Let It Be*) was an exceptional work spearheaded by the anthemic 'Gimme Shelter' and revealing strong country influences ('Country Honk'), startling orchestration ('You Can't Always Get What You Want') and menacing blues ('Midnight Rambler'). It was a promising debut from John Mayall's former guitarist Mick Taylor (b. 17 January 1948, Hertfordshire, England) who had replaced Jones only a matter of weeks before his death. Even while *Let It Bleed* was heading for the top of the album charts, however, the Stones were singing out the 60s to the backdrop of a Hells Angels killing of a black man at the Altamont Festival in California. The tragedy was captured on film in the grisly *Gimme Shelter* movie released the following year. After the events of 1969, it was not surprising that the group had a relatively quiet 1970. Jagger's contrasting thespian outings reached the screen in the form of *Performance* and *Ned Kelly* while Jean-Luc Goddard's tedious portrait of the group in the studio was delivered on *One Plus One*. For a group who had once claimed to make more challenging and gripping films than the Beatles and yet combine artistic credibility with mass appeal, it all seemed a long time coming.

After concluding their Decca contract with a bootleg-deterring live album, *Get Yer Ya-Ya's Out*, the Stones established their own self-titled label. The first release was a three track single, 'Brown Sugar'/'Bitch'/'Let It Rock', which contained some of their best work but narrowly failed to reach number 1 in the UK. The lead track contained a quintessential Stones riff: insistent, undemonstrative and stunning, with the emphatic brass work of Bobby Keyes embellishing Jagger's vocal power. The new album, *Sticky Fingers* was as consistent as it was accomplished, encompassing the bluesy 'You Gotta Move', the thrilling 'Moonlight Mile', the wistful 'Wild Horses' and the chilling 'Sister Morphine', one the most despairing drug songs ever written. The entire album was permeated by images of sex and death, yet the tone of the work was neither self-indulgent nor maudlin. The group's playful fascination with sex was further demonstrated on the elaborately designed Andy Warhol sleeve which featured a waist-view shot of a figure clad in denim, with a real zip fastener which opened to display the lips and tongue motif that was shortly to become their corporate image. Within a year of *Sticky Fingers*, the group returned with a double album, *Exile On Main Street*. With Keith Richard firmly in control, the group were rocking out on a series of quick-fire songs. The album was severely criticized at the time of its release for its uneven quality but was subsequently re-evaluated favourably, particularly in contrast to their later work.

The Stones' soporific slide into the 70s mainstream probably began during 1973 when their jet-setting was threatening to upstage their musical endeavours. Jagger's marriage and Richard's confrontations with the law took centre stage while increasingly average albums came and went. *Goat's Head Soup* was decidedly patchy but offered some strong moments and brought a deserved US number 1 with the imploring 'Angie'. 1974's 'It's Only Rock 'n' Roll' proved a better song title than a single, while the undistinguished album of the same name saw the group reverting to Tamla/Motown for the Temptations' 'Ain't Too Proud To Beg'.

The departure of Mick Taylor at the end of 1974 was followed by a protracted period in which the group sought a suitable replacement. By the time of their next release, *Black And Blue*, former *Faces* guitarist Ron Wood (b. 1 June 1947, London, England) was confirmed as Taylor's successor. The album showed the group seeking a possible new direction playing variants on white reggae, but the results were less than impressive.

By the second half of the 70s the gaps in the Stones' recording and touring schedules were becoming wider. The days when they specially recorded for the singles market were long past and considerable impetus had been lost. Even big rallying points, such as the celebrated concert at Knebworth in 1976, lacked a major album to promote the show and served mainly as a greatest hits package.

By 1977, the British music press had taken punk to its heart and the Stones were dismissed as champagne-swilling old men, who had completely lost touch with their audience. The Clash effectively summed up the mood of the time with their slogan 'No Elvis, Beatles, Stones' in '1977'.

Against the odds, the Stones responded to the challenge of their younger critics with a comeback album of remarkable power. *Some Girls* was their most consistent work in years, with some exceptional high-energy workouts, not least the breathtaking 'Shattered'. The disco groove of 'Miss You' brought them another US number 1 and showed that they could invigorate their repertoire with new ideas that worked. Jagger's wonderful pastiche of an American preacher on the mock country 'Far Away Eyes' was another unexpected highlight. There was even an attendant controversy thanks to some multi-racist chauvinism on the title track, not to mention 'When The Whip Comes Down' and 'Beast Of Burden'. Even the cover jacket had to be re-shot because it featured unauthorized photos of the famous, most notably actresses Lucille Ball, Farrah Fawcett and Raquel Welch. To conclude a remarkable year, Keith Richard escaped what seemed an almost certain jail sentence in Toronto for drugs offences and

was merely fined and ordered to play a couple of charity concerts. As if in celebration of his release and reconciliation with his father, he reverted to his original family name Richards. In the wake of Richards' reformation and Jagger's much-publicized and extremely expensive divorce from his model wife Bianca, the Stones reconvened in 1980 for *Emotional Rescue*, a rather lightweight album dominated by Jagger's falsetto and over-use of disco rhythms. Nevertheless, the album gave the Stones their first UK number 1 since 1973 and the title track was a Top 10 hit on both sides of the Atlantic. Early the following year a major US tour (highlights of which were included on *Still Life*) garnered enthusiastic reviews, while a host of repackaged albums reinforced the group's legacy. 1981's *Tattoo You* was essentially a crop of old outtakes but the material was anything but stale. On the contrary, the album was surprisingly strong and the concomitant single 'Start Me Up' was a reminder of the Stones at their 60s best, a time when they were capable of producing classic singles at will. One of the Stones' cleverest devices throughout the 80s was their ability to compensate for average work by occasional flashes of excellence. The workmanlike *Undercover*, for example, not only boasted a brilliantly menacing title track ('Undercover Of The Night') but one of the best promotional videos of the period. While critics continually questioned the group's relevance, the Stones were still releasing worthwhile work, albeit in smaller doses.

A three-year silence on record was broken by *Dirty Work* in 1986, which saw the Stones sign to CBS Records and team up with producer Steve Lillywhite. Surprisingly, it was not a Stones original that produced the expected offshoot single hit, but a cover of Bob And Earl's 'Harlem Shuffle'. A major record label signing often coincides with a flurry of new work, but the Stones were clearly moving away from each other creatively and concentrating more and more on individual projects. Wyman had already tasted some chart success in 1983 with the biggest solo success from a Stones' number, 'Je Suis Un Rock Star' and it came as little surprise when Jagger issued his own solo album, *She's The Boss*, in 1985. A much-publicized feud with Keith Richards led to speculation that the Rolling Stones story had come to an anti-climactic end, a view reinforced by the appearance of a second Jagger album, *Primitive Cool*, in 1987. When Richards himself released the first solo work of his career in 1988, the Stones' obituary had virtually been written. As if to confound the obituarists, however, the Stones reconvened in 1989 and announced that they would be working on a new album and commencing a world tour. Later that year the hastily recorded *Steel Wheels* appeared and the critical reception was generally good. 'Mixed Emotions' and 'Rock And A Hard Place' were radio hits, while 'Continental Drift' included contributions from the master musicians of Joujouka, previously immortalized on vinyl by the late Brian Jones. After nearly 30 years in existence, the Rolling Stones began the 90s with the biggest-grossing international tour of all time, and ended speculation about their future by reiterating their intention of playing on indefinitely. *Voodoo Lounge* in 1994 was one of their finest recordings, both lyrically daring and musically fresh. They sounded charged up and raring to go for the 1995 US tour. Monies taken at each gig could almost finance the national debt, and the tour confirmed (as if it were needed) that they are still the world's greatest rock band, a title that is likely to stick, even although Bill Wyman officially resigned in 1993. Riding a crest after an extraordinarily active 1995, *Stripped* was a dynamic semi-plugged album. Fresh-sounding and energetic acoustic versions of 'Street Fighting Man', 'Wild Horses' and 'Let It Bleed', among others, emphasized just how great the Jagger/Richards songwriting team is. The year was marred, however, by some outspoken comments by Keith Richards on R.E.M. and Nirvana. These clumsy comments are unlikely to endear the grand old man of rock to a younger audience; this was all the more surprising as the Stones had so far, appeared in touch with today's rock music. Citing R.E.M. as 'wimpy cult stuff' and Kurt Cobain as 'some prissy little spoiled kid' were comments that were, at best, ill-chosen.

●ALBUMS: *The Rolling Stones* (London/Decca 1964)★★★, *12X5* (London 1964)★★★★, *The Rolling Stones No 2* (London/Decca 1965)★★★★, *The Rolling Stones Now!* (London 1965)★★★★, *December's Children (And Everybody's* (London 1965)★★★★, *Out Of Our Heads* (Decca/London 1965)★★★★, *Aftermath* (Decca/London 1966)★★★★, *Got Live If You Want It* (London 1966)★★★, *Between The Buttons* (London/Decca 1967)★★★, *Their Satanic Majesties Request* (Decca/London 1967)★★★, *Flowers* (London 1967)★★★★, *Beggars Banquet* (1968)★★★★, *Let It Bleed* (London/Decca 1969)★★★★★, *Get Yer Ya-Ya's Out!* (Decca/London1970)★★★, *Sticky Fingers* (Rolling Stones 1971)★★★★★, *Exile On Main Street* (1972)★★★★★, *Goat's Head Soup* (Rolling Stones 1973)★★★, *It's Only Rock 'N' Roll* (Rolling Stones 1974)★★★, *Black And Blue* (Rolling Stones 1976)★★★, *Love You Live* (Rolling Stones 1977)★★★, *Some Girls* (Rolling Stones 1978)★★★★, *Emotional Rescue* (Rolling Stones 1980)★★★, *Tattoo You* (Rolling Stones 1981)★★★, *Still Life (American Concerts 1981)* (Rolling Stones 1982)★★★, *Undercover* (Rolling Stones 1983)★★★, *Dirty Work* (Rolling Stones 1986)★★★, *Steel Wheels* (Rolling Stones 1989)★★★, *Voodoo Lounge* (Virgin 1994)★★★★, *Stripped* (Virgin 1995)★★★★.

●COMPILATIONS: *Big Hits (High Tide And Green Grass* (London 1966)★★★★★, *Through The Past, Darkly* (London 1969)★★★, *Hot Rocks 1964-1971* (London 1972)★★★★★, *More Hot Rocks (Big Hits And Fazed Cookies)* (London 1972)★★★★★, *The Rolling Stones Singles Collection: The London Years* 3-CD box set (Abko/London 1989)★★★★★.

●VIDEOS: *The Stones In The Park* (BMG 1993), *Gimme Shelter* (1993), *Live At The Max* (Polygram 1994), *25 x 5 The Continuing Adventures Of The Rolling Stones* (1994), *Sympathy For The Devil* (BMG 1995), *Voodoo Lounge* (Game Entertainment 1995).

●FURTHER READING: *The Rolling Stones File*, Tim Hewat. *The Stones*, Philip Carmelo Luce. *Uptight With The Rolling Stones*, Richard Elman. *Rolling Stones: An Unauthorized Biography In Words, Photographs And Music*, David Dalton. *Mick Jagger: The Singer Not The Song*, J. Marks. *Mick Jagger: Everybody's Lucifer*, Anthony Scaduto. *STP: A Journey Through America With The Rolling Stones*, Robert Greenfield. *Les Rolling Stones*, Philippe Contantin. *The Rolling Stones Story*, George Tremlett. *The Rolling Stones*, Cindy Ehrlich. *The Rolling Stones: A Celebration*, Nik Cohn. *The Rolling Stones*, Tony Jasper. *The Rolling Stones: An Illustrated Record*, Roy Carr. *The Rolling Stones*, Jeremy Pascall. *The Rolling Stones On Tour*, Annie Leibowitz. *Up And Down With The Rolling Stones*, Tony Sanchez with John Blake. *The Rolling Stones: An Annotated Bibliography*, Mary Laverne Dimmick. *Keith Richards*, Barbara Charone. *Rolling Stones In Their Own Words*, Rolling Stones. *The Rolling Stones: An Illustrated Discography*, Miles. *The Rolling Stones In Their Own Words*, David Dalton and Mick Farren. *The Rolling Stones: The First Twenty Years*, David Dalton. *Mick Jagger In His Own Words*, Miles. *The Rolling Stones In Concert*, Linda Martin. *The Rolling Stones: Live In America*, Philip Kamin and Peter Goddard. *Death Of A Rolling Stone: The Brian Jones Story*, Mandy Aftel. *Jagger*, Carey Schofield. *The Rolling Stones A To Z*, Sue Weiner and Lisa Howard. *The Rolling Stones*, Robert Palmer. *The Stones*, Philip Norman. *Satisfaction: The Rolling Stones*, Gered Mankowitz. *The Rolling Stones*, Dezo Hoffman. *On The Road With The Rolling Stones*, Chet Flippo. *The True Adventures Of The Rolling Stones*, Stanley Booth. *Heart Of Stone: The Definitive Rolling Stones Discography*, Felix Aeppli. *Yesterday's Papers: The Rolling Stones In Print*, Jessica MacPhail. *The Life And Good Times Of The Rolling Stones*, Philip Norman. *Stone Alone*, Bill Wyman and Ray Coleman. *The Rolling Stones 25th Anniversary Tour*, Greg Quill. *Blown Away: The Rolling Stones And The Death Of The Sixties*, A.E. Hotchner. *The Rolling Stones: Complete Recording Sessions 1963-1989*, Martin Elliott. *The Rolling Stones Story*, Robert Draper. *The Rolling Stones Chronicle: The First Thirty Years*, Massimo Bonanno. *Rolling Stones: Images Of The World Tour 1989-1990*, David Fricke and Robert Sandall. *The Rolling Stones' Rock 'N' Roll Circus*, no author listed. *The Rolling Stones: Behind The Buttons (Limited Edition)*, Gered Mankowitz and Robert Whitaker (Photographers). *Golden Stone: The Untold Life And Mysterious Death Of Brian Jones*, Laura Jackson. *Rolling Stones: Das Weissbuch*, Dieter Hoffmann. *Not Fade Away: Rolling Stones Collection*, Geoffrey Giuliano. *Keith Richards: The Unauthorised Biography*, Victor Bockris. *The Rolling Stones: The Complete Works Vol. 1 1962-75*, Nico Zentgraf. *Street Fighting Years*, Stephen Barnard. *Paint It Black: The Murder Of Brian Jones*, Geoffrey Giuliano. *Brian Jones: The Inside Story Of The Original Rolling Stone*, Nicholas Fitzgerald. *Who Killed Christopher Robin*,

Terry Rawlings. *A Visual Documentary*, Miles. *Not Fade Away*, Chris Eborn. *Complete Guide To The Music Of*, James Hector. *The Rolling Stones Chronicle*, Massimo Bonanno.

RONETTES

Veronica 'Ronnie' Bennett (b. 10 August 1943, New York, USA), her sister Estelle (b. 22 July 1944, New York, USA) and cousin Nedra Talley (b. 17 January 1946, New York, USA) began their career as a dance act the Dolly Sisters. By 1961 they had become the resident dance troupe at the famed Peppermint Lounge, home of the twist craze, and having taken tuition in harmony singing, later secured a recording deal. The trio's first single, 'I Want A Boy', was credited to Ronnie And The Relatives, but when 'Silhouettes' followed in 1962, the Ronettes appellation was in place. They recorded four singles for the Colpix/May group and appeared on disc jockey Murray The K's *Live From The Brooklyn Fox* before a chance telephone call resulted in their signing with producer Phil Spector. Their first collaboration, the majestic 'Be My Baby' defined the girl-group sound as Spector constructed a cavernous accompaniment around Ronnie's plaintive, nasal voice. The single reached the Top 5 in the US and UK before being succeeded by the equally worthwhile 'Baby I Love You', another Top 20 entrant in both countries. The producer's infatuation with Ronnie - the couple were later married - resulted in some of his finest work being reserved for her and although ensuing singles, including 'The Best Part of Breaking Up', 'Walking In The Rain' (both 1964) and 'Is This What I Get For Loving You' (1965), failed to emulate the Ronettes' early success, they are among the finest pop singles of all time. The group's career was shelved during Spector's mid-60s 'retirement', but they re-emerged in 1969 with 'You Came, You Saw You Conquered'. Credited to 'The Ronettes Featuring The Voice Of Veronica', this excellent single was nonetheless commercially moribund and Ronnie's aspirations were again sublimated. She separated from Spector in 1973 and joined Buddah Records, founding a new group with vocalists Denise Edwards and Chip Fields. Ronnie And The Ronettes made their debut that year with 'Lover Lover', before changing their name to Ronnie Spector and the Ronettes for 'I Wish I Never Saw The Sunshine', an impassioned remake of a song recorded by the original line-up, but which remained unissued until 1976. The group's name was then dropped as its lead singer pursued her solo ambitions.

●ALBUMS: *The Ronettes Featuring Veronica* (Colpix 1965)★★★, *Presenting The Fabulous Ronettes* (Philes 1965)★★★.

●COMPILATIONS: *The Ronettes Sing Their Greatest Hits* (1975)★★★, *Their Greatest Hits - Vol. II* (1981)★★, *The Colpix Years 1961-63* (1987)★★★, *The Best Of* (ABKCO 1992).

RONNY AND THE DAYTONAS

Ronny Dayton (b. 26 April 1946, Tulsa, Oklahoma, USA; guitar) formed this group with close friends Jimmy Johnson (guitar), Van Evans (bass) and Lynn Williams (drums). Avid fans of surf and hot rod music, the quartet succeeded with the latter genre when 'G.T.O.' reached the US Top 5 in 1964. This homage to a beloved stock car eventually sold in excess of 1 million, but the group was unable to repeat this success. They did enjoy minor hits with 'California Bound', 'Bucket T' (later covered by the Who), and 'Sandy', but had become too closely associated with a passing trend to enjoy a long career.

●ALBUMS: *GTO* (Mala 1964)★★, *Sandy* (Mala 1965)★★.

●COMPILATIONS: *The Best Of The Mala Recordings* (Sundazed 1997)★★.

ROOFTOP SINGERS

Cashing in on the folk music revival of the early 60s, the Rooftop Singers were a trio specifically assembled for the purpose of recording a single song, 'Walk Right In', originally recorded in 1930 by Gus Cannon And The Jugstompers. The Rooftop Singers consisted of Erik Darling (b. 25 September 1933, Baltimore, Maryland, USA), Bill Svanoe and former Benny Goodman band vocalist, Lynne Taylor. Darling had played in folk groups called the Tune Tellers and the Tarriers, the latter including future actor Alan Arkin, and replaced Pete Seeger in the Weavers in 1958, remaining with them for four years. In 1962 he heard 'Walk Right In' and adapted the lyrics for a more modern sound, utilizing two 12-string guitars and an irresistible rhythm; he then assembled the trio and signed with Vanguard Records. 'Walk Right In' became that label's, and the group's, only number 1 record. The Rooftop Singers placed one album and two other folk songs in the US charts: 'Tom Cat' and 'Mama Don't Allow'. The group disbanded in 1967 and Taylor died the same year; Darling and Svanoe subsequently retired from the music business.

●ALBUMS: *Walk Right In!* (Vanguard 1963)★★★★, *Goodtime* (1964)★★★, *Rainy River* (1965)★★★.

ROSE, TIM

b. 23 September 1940. A one-time student priest and navigator for the USAF Strategic Air Command, Rose began his professional music career playing guitar with the Journeymen, a folk group active in the early 60s which featured John Phillips and Scott McKenzie. He subsequently joined Cass Elliot and James Hendricks in another formative attraction, the Big Three. Although initially based in Chicago, the trio later moved to New York, where Rose forged a career as a solo singer on the group's disintegration in 1964. A gruff stylist and individual, he was turned down by Elektra and Mercury before securing a contract with Columbia Records. A series of majestic singles then followed, including 'Hey Joe' (1966) and 'Morning Dew' (1967). Rose's slow, brooding version of the former was the inspiration for that of Jimi Hendrix, while the latter, written by Rose and folksinger Bonnie Dobson, was the subject of cover versions by, among others, Jeff Beck and the Grateful Dead.

Tim Rose was assembled from several different sessions,

but the presence of several crack session musicians - Felix Pappalardi (bass/piano), Bernard Purdie (drums) and Hugh McCracken (guitar) - provided a continuity. The set included a dramatic reading of 'I'm Gonna Be Strong', previously associated with Gene Pitney, and the haunting anti-war anthem 'Come Away Melinda', already recorded by the Big Three, on which Rose's blues-soaked, gritty voice was particularly effective. The singer's next release, 'Long Haired Boys', was recorded in the UK under the aegis of producer Al Kooper, before Rose returned to the USA to complete *Through Rose Coloured Glasses* (1969). This disappointing album lacked the strength of its predecessor and the artist was never again to scale the heights of his early work. He switched outlets to Capitol for *Love, A Kind Of Hate Story*, before the disillusioned performer abandoned major outlets in favour of the Playboy label where his manager's brother was employed. The promise of artistic freedom was fulfilled when Gary Wright of Spooky Tooth, a group Rose revered, produced the ensuing sessions. The album, also entitled *Tim Rose*, contained a version of the Beatles' 'You've Got To Hide Your Love Away' performed at a snail's pace. It was not a commercial success and the singer again left for the UK where he believed audiences were more receptive. Resident in London, Rose undertook a series of live concerts with fellow exile Tim Hardin, but this ill-fated partnership quickly collapsed. *The Musician*, released in 1975, revealed a voice which retained its distinctive power, but an artist without definite direction. In 1976 Rose was recording a new album with help from Andy Summers, Snowy White, Raphael Ravenscroft, B.J. Cole and Michael D'Alberquerque. This country-tinged album was finally released on President in 1991 as *The Gambler*. Rose moved back to New York in the late 70s. Little has been heard from him for several years.

●ALBUMS: *Tim Rose* (Columbia 1967)★★★★, *Through Rose Coloured Glasses* (Columbia 1969)★★★, *Love, A Kind Of Hate Story* (Capitol 1970)★★, *Tim Rose* (Dawn 1972)★★, *The Musician* (Atlantic 1975),★★ *The Gambler* (President 1991)★★.

ROSS, ANNIE

b. Annabelle Short Lynch, 25 July 1930, Mitcham, Surrey, England. After working as a child actress in Hollywood, she then toured internationally as a singer. She sang with both Tony Crombie and Jack Parnell during the 50s. Ross had recorded successful wordless jazz vocals before becoming a member of the famous vocalese trio, Lambert, Hendricks And Ross from 1958-62. Her song 'Twisted', written with Wardell Gray, was expertly covered by Joni Mitchell, among others. In the mid-60s Ross operated Annie's Room, a jazz club in London, and in later years worked in films and television as both actress and singer, at one point being briefly reunited with Jon Hendricks. Personal problems affected the continuity of Ross's career but despite the resulting irregularity of her public performances she maintained an enviably high standard of singing. Her scat singing was some of the finest ever heard. In the early 80s she found a compatible musical partner in Georgie Fame with whom she toured and recorded.

●ALBUMS: *Annie Ross Sings* (Original Jazz Classics 1953)★★★★, *Annie By Candlelight* (Pye 1956)★★★★, with Gerry Mulligan *Annie Ross Sings A Song With Mulligan* (World Pacific 1958)★★★★, *Gypsy* (World Pacific 1959)★★★, with Zoot Sims *A Gasser* (Pacific Jazz 1959)★★★★, *You And Me Baby* (c.1964)★★★, *Annie Ross And Pony Poindexter With The Berlin All Stars* (1966)★★★, with Tony Kinsey *With The Tony Kinsey Quartet* (Extra 1966)★★★★, *Fill My Heart With Song* (Decca 1967)★★★, with Georgie Fame *In Hoagland '81* (Bald Eagle 1981)★★★★, *Sings A Handful Of Songs* (Fresh Sounds 1988)★★★.

ROTHCHILD, PAUL A.

b. 18 April 1935, Brooklyn, New York, USA, d. 30 March 1995. A subtle, sympathetic producer, Rothchild first garnered attention for his work on the Prestige label. Here he oversaw sessions by folksingers Tom Rush and Eric Von Schmidt, before moving to a rival outlet, Elektra, in 1964. There he continued his association with Rush, while supervising other acoustic acts, including Fred Neil, Tom Paxton, Phil Ochs and Koerner, Ray And Glover. Rothchild eased the label's transition from folk to rock via work with their first electric signing, the Paul Butterfield Blues Band. His production skills were a crucial element in several of Elektra's most innovative releases, including Love's *Da Capo* and Tim Buckley's impressive debut album. However, it was Rothchild's relationship with the Doors, the company's premier act, which proved most fruitful. He produced the group's entire output, save their final selection, *LA Woman*. Paradoxically the finished album was a major success in the wake of singer Jim Morrison's death. Rothchild was also responsible for recordings by Clear Light and Rhinoceros, an in-house 'supergroup' he had instigated, but left the label in 1970 to pursue an independent career. His freelance productions included Janis Joplin's final collection, *Pearl*, several of John Sebastian's solo releases and Bonnie Raitt's excellent *Home Plate*, but his wider ambitions were thwarted when his ill-fated Buffalo label collapsed. In 1978, Rothchild resumed his association with the Doors when the three surviving members re grouped to provide backing on *An American Prayer*, a collection of Morrison's poetry readings initially recorded during the *LA Woman* sessions. This reconstituted partnership resulted in post-production work for other resurrected performances including *Alive She Cried* and *The Doors Live At Hollywood Bowl*. He was later involved in the music production for the 1991 Oliver Stone film, *The Doors*. In recent years he worked on a number of film soundtracks and with Holzman on some jazz recordings including *Body Heat - Jazz At The Movies* and more recently the *Lost Elektra Paul Butterfield Tapes*. He died after a long battle against cancer in a career that had his professional involvement in over 150 albums.

ROULETTES

Formed in London, England in 1962, the Roulettes made their recording debut that year with 'Hully Gully Slip And Slide', released on Pye Records. The single was not a success but the group was saved from obscurity in 1963 when they were invited to back singer Adam Faith. By this point their line-up comprised of Russ Ballard (lead guitar), Peter Salt (rhythm guitar), John Rodgers (bass) and Bob Henrit (drums). Ballard and Henrit had previously worked together as members of the Daybreakers. The Roulettes were featured on all of Faith's singles until May 1965, including the hits 'The First Time' and 'We Are In Love'. They also played on his 1964 album *On The Move*. The Roulettes rekindled their own recording career in 1963 with 'Soon You'll Be Leaving Me'. It was the first of a series of superior beat singles they recorded for Parlophone Records including 'Bad Time', 'I'll Remember Tonight' (both 1964) and the excellent 'The Long Cigarette' (1965). By that point John 'Mod' Rogan had replaced John Rodgers, who died in a car crash in 1964. The Roulettes momentum faltered upon breaking from Faith. They split up in 1967, having completed two memorable singles, 'Rhyme Boy Rhyme' and 'Help Me To Help Myself', for Fontana Records. Ballard and Henrit switched to Unit Four Plus Two with whom they already enjoyed a close association, as leader 'Buster' Meilke had also been a member of the Daybreakers. Indeed Ballard played guitar on Unit Four Plue Two's 1965 hit, 'Concrete And Clay' and both musicians were featured on several subsequent recordings. Following a period of inactivity after Unit Four Plus Two's demise, Ballard and Henrit returned in Argent
●ALBUMS: *Stakes And Chips* (Parlophone 1965)★★★.

ROUTERS

A US instrumental group formed in the early 60s in the Los Angeles area, the original Routers were not the same musicians that eventually secured the group's only hit in 1962 with 'Let's Go (Pony)'. The original group consisted of musicians Mike Gordon, Al Kait, Bill Moody, Lynn Frazier and a fifth musician (unknown). Signed to Warner Brothers Records, the group was assigned to producer Joe Saraceno, who then proceeded to use studio musicians and not the actual group on the recording of 'Let's Go (Pony)'. The single reached the US charts at number 19 and *Let's Go With The Routers*, was released, but it too was apparently recorded by session musicians such as Hal Blaine and Plas Johnson. Probably unknown to the band and the composers of the song 'Let's Go' was that this chorus was adopted by UK football fans in the mid-60s. The handclapping is followed by the chant of the 'let's go' lyric, which is replaced by the name of the team in question. Football historians have deemed that West Ham supporters were the first to use it, later imitated by other London clubs. It is now a universal chant. If the composers were entitled to a performing royalty they would be billionaires many times over. Warner Brothers continued to issue singles under the name Routers, one of which, 'Sting Ray', reached the charts in 1963. There were three other Warner albums, followed by later Routers singles on RCA and Mercury Records (which also released an album) as late as 1973, after which the name was apparently shelved and the remaining members disbanded.
●ALBUMS: *Let's Go With The Routers* (Warners 1963)★★★, *The Routers Play 1963's Great Instrumental Hits* (Warners 1963)★★, *Charge!* (Warners 1964)★★, *Go Go Go With The Chuck Berry Songbook* (Warners 1965)★★.

ROYAL GUARDSMEN

As if to prove just about any topic could become a hit song, the Royal Guardsmen made a career in the mid-60s out of writing about Snoopy, the dog in the *Peanuts* comic strip. The group formed in 1966 in Ocala, Florida, USA, and consisted of Chris Nunley (vocals), Tom Richards (lead guitar), Barry Winslow (rhythm guitar/vocals), Bill Balogh (guitar), Billy Taylor (organ) and John Burdette (drums). That same year, under the management of Phil Gernhard, the group signed to Laurie Records and recorded a novelty tune, 'Snoopy Vs. The Red Baron', which ultimately peaked at number 2 in the US chart in January 1967 and eventually reached number 8 in the UK chart that same year. Capitalizing on the debut's success, they recorded further Snoopy songs - 'The Return Of The Red Baron', 'Snoopy's Christmas' and 'Snoopy For President' - as well as other novelty songs. One 1967 single, 'Airplane Song (My Airplane)', was written by Michael Martin Murphey, who had his own US number 3 hit in 1975 with 'Wildfire'. The Royal Guardsmen disbanded in 1968.
●ALBUMS: *Snoopy Vs. The Red Baron* (Laurie 1967)★★, *Return Of The Red Baron* (Laurie 1967)★, *Snoopy And His Friends* (Laurie 1967)★, *Snoopy For President* (Laurie 1968)★.

ROYAL SHOWBAND

The most popular Irish showband of the 60s, the Royal originally formed in 1957 and turned fully professional two years later, with a line-up comprising Michael Coppinger (saxophone/accordion), Brendan Bowyer (vocals/trombone), Gerry Cullen (piano), Jim Conlan (guitar), Eddie Sullivan (saxophone), Charlie Matthews (drums) and Tom Dunphy (bass). After coming under the management of the astute T.J. Byrne, the Royal were poised to emerge as the biggest act in Eire, playing almost every night to audiences in excess of 2,000. Ballroom gods, they ushered in the era of the showband and in Brendan Bowyer boasted the genre's most potent sex symbol. In 1961, they toured the UK, were supported by the Beatles in Liverpool and received the Carl Alan Award for their prodigious box-office success. At some halls firemen were called upon to hose unruly crowds as the group's popularity reached unforeseen proportions. Back in Ireland, they were the first showband to record a single, with Tom Dunphy singing lead on the infectious, quasi-traditional 'Come Down The Mountain Katie Daly'. That was just the start. The Royal soon notched up four successive number 1 hit singles: 'Kiss Me Quick', 'No More', 'Bless You' and 'The Hucklebuck'. The latter became one of the best-selling dance records in Irish chart history. Dunphy and Bowyer continued the chart-topping spree with 'If I Didn't Have A Dime' and the cash-in 'Don't Lose Your Hucklebuck Shoes', respectively. Having conquered Eire, the band switched their attention to Las Vegas where they became a regular attraction from the late 60s onwards. In 1971, Bowyer and Dunphy rocked the Irish music world by leaving Eire's most famous septet to form the showband supergroup, the Big 8. Although the star duo were briefly replaced by vocalists Lee Lynch and Billy Hopkins, the Royal collapsed within a year. Their founding member Tom Dunphy died tragically in a car accident on 29 July 1975. The abrupt dissolution of the Royal at the beginning of the 70s symbolically ended the showband domination of the previous era, to which they had made an incalculable contribution.

●ALBUMS: *The One Nighters* (HMV 1964)★★★.

RUBY AND THE ROMANTICS

Edward Roberts (first tenor), George Lee (second tenor), Ronald Mosley (baritone) and Leroy Fann (bass) had been working as the Supremes prior to the arrival of Ruby Nash Curtis (b. 12 November 1939, New York City, New York, USA) in 1962. Ruby had met the group in Akron, Ohio and took on the role as their lead singer. They subsequently secured a contract with the New York label Kapp and at the suggestion of the company, changed their name to Ruby And The Romantics. By the following year they had taken the evocative 'Our Day Will Come' to the top of the US pop chart, earning them a gold disc. Over the next 12 months the group scored a further six hits including the original version of 'Hey There Lonely Boy' which, with a change of gender, was later revived by Eddie Holman. After three years at Kapp, the group signed to the ABC label. In 1965 'Does He Really Care For Me', the Romantics' last chart entry, preceded a whole-sale line-up change. Ruby brought in a new backing group: Richard Pryor, Vincent McLeod, Robert Lewis, Ronald Jackson and Bill Evans, but in 1968 the forthright Curtis replaced this version with Denise Lewis and Cheryl Thomas.

●ALBUMS: *Our Day Will Come* (Kapp 1963)★★★, *Till Then* (Kapp 1963)★★★, *Ruby And The Romantics* (Kapp 1967)★★, *More Than Yesterday* (1968)★★.

●COMPILATIONS: *Greatest Hits Album* (Kapp 1966)★★★, *The Very Best Of ...* (Target 1995)★★★.

RUSH, TOM

b. 8 February, 1941, Portsmouth, New Hampshire, USA. Tom Rush began performing in 1961 while a student at Harvard University. Although he appeared at clubs in New York and Philadelphia, he became a pivotal figure of the Boston/New England circuit and such haunts as the Cafe Yana and the Club 47. *Live At The Unicorn*, culled from two sets recorded at another of the region's fabled coffeehouses, was poorly distributed but its competent mixture of traditional songs, blues and Woody Guthrie compositions was sufficient to interest the renowned Prestige label. *Got A Mind To Ramble* and *Blues Songs And Ballads*, completed over three days, showcased an intuitive interpreter. Rush's exemplary versions of 'Barb'ry Allen' and 'Alabama Bound' were enough to confirm his place alongside Dave Van Ronk and Eric Von Schmidt, the latter of whom was an important influence on the younger musician. *Tom Rush*, his first release on the Elektra label, was one of the era's finest folk/blues sets. The artist had developed an accomplished bottleneck guitar style that was portrayed to perfection on 'Panama Limited', an 8-minute compendium comprising several different songs by Bukka White. *Take A Little Walk With Me* contained the similarly excellent 'Galveston Flood', but its high points were six electric selections drawn from songs by Bo Diddley, Chuck Berry and Buddy Holly. Arranged by Al Kooper, these performances featured musicians from Bob Dylan's ground-breaking sessions and helped transform Rush from traditional to popular performer. This change culminated in *The Circle Game*, which contained material by Joni Mitchell, James Taylor and Jackson Browne, each of whom had yet to record in their own right. The recording also included the poignant 'No Regrets', the singer's own composition, which has since become a pop classic through hit versions by the Walker Brothers (1976) and Midge Ure (1982).

Tom Rush, the artist's first release for Columbia/CBS, introduced his long-standing partnership with guitarist Trevor Veitch. Once again material by Jackson Browne and James Taylor was to the fore, but the album also contained compositions by Fred Neil and Murray McLaughlin's beautiful song of leaving home, 'Child's Song', confirming Rush as having immaculate taste in choice of material. However, two subsequent releases, *Wrong End Of The Rainbow* and *Merrimack County*, saw an increased emphasis on material Rush either wrote alone, or with Veitch. By contrast a new version of 'No Regrets' was the sole original on *Ladies Love Outlaws*, a collection which marked a pause in Rush's recording career. It was 1982 before a new set, *New Year*, was released. Recorded live, it celebrated the artist's 20th anniversary while a second live album, *Late Night Radio*, featured cameos from Steve Goodman and Mimi Farina. Both were issued on Rush's Night Light label on which he also repackaged his 1962 debut. In 1990 his New Hampshire home and recording studio were totally destroyed by fire, and this cultured artist has since moved to Wyoming. Little has been heard of Rush in the 90s, and it is many years since he released an album. It is a pity that the owner of such an expressive voice is not recording, even if his own songwriting has seemingly been exhausted.

●ALBUMS: *Live At The Unicorn* (1962)★★, *I Got A Mind To Ramble* later known as *Mind Rambling* (Folklore 1963)★★, *Blues Songs And Ballads* (Prestige 1964)★★, *Tom Rush* (Elektra 1965)★★★★, *Take A Little Walk With Me* aka *The New Album* (Elektra

1966)★★★, *The Circle Game* (Elektra 1968)★★★, *Tom Rush* (CBS 1970)★★★★, *Wrong End Of The Rainbow* (CBS 1970)★★★, *Merrimack County* (CBS 1972)★★★, *Ladies Love Outlaws* (1974)★★★, *New Year* (1982)★★, *Late Night Radio* (1984)★★.
●COMPILATIONS: *Classic Rush* (Elektra 1970)★★★★, *The Best Of Tom Rush* (Columbia 1975)★★★★.

RYAN, PAUL AND BARRY

b. Paul and Barry Sapherson, 24 October 1948, Leeds, England. Paul, d. 29 November 1992. The twin sons of popular singer Marion Ryan, Paul and Barry were launched as a clean-cut act to attendant showbusiness publicity. Their debut single, 'Don't Bring Me Your Heartaches' reached the UK Top 20 in 1965, and over the ensuing months the siblings enjoyed respectable, if unspectacular, chart placings with 'Have Pity On The Boy' and 'I Love Her'. The Ryans shifted away from their tailored image with 'Have You Ever Loved Somebody' (1966) and 'Keep It Out Of Sight' (1967), penned, respectively, by the Hollies and Cat Stevens, but such releases were less successful. They split amicably in 1968 with Paul embarking on a songwriting career while Barry recorded as a solo act. Together they created 'Eloise', the latter's impressive number 2 hit and subsequent million seller, but ensuing singles failed to emulate its popularity. Paul's compositions included 'I Will Drink The Wine', which was recorded by Frank Sinatra, but neither brother was able to sustain initial impetus. During 1969 Barry had an accident which caused serious burns to his face. In the 70s Paul moved to the USA, but later left the music business and opened a chain of hairdressing salons.
●ALBUMS: *The Ryans Two Of A Kind* (Decca 1967)★★★, *Paul And Barry Ryan* (MGM 1968)★★★. Solo: Barry Ryan *Barry Ryan Sings Paul Ryan* (1968)★★★. Paul Ryan *Scorpio Rising* (1976)★★★.

RYDELL, BOBBY

b. Robert Ridarelli, 26 April 1942, Philadelphia, Pennsylvania, USA. Probably the most musically talented of the late 50s Philadelphia school of clean-cut teen-idols, Rydell first performed in public as a drummer at the age of seven. At nine he debuted on Paul Whiteman's *Teen Club* amateur television show and was the show's regular drummer for three years. He attended the same boys club as Fabian and Frankie Avalon, formed a duo with Avalon in 1954 and shortly afterwards, they both joined local group Rocco And The Saints. After several rejections from labels, he recorded his first solo single 'Fatty Fatty' for his manager's Veko label. In 1958 he joined Cameo and his fourth release for that label, 'Kissin' Time' (which owed something to 'Sweet Little Sixteen'), became the first of his 18 US Top 40 hits over the next four years. The photogenic pop/rock singer's best-known transatlantic hits are 'Wild One', 'Sway' and 'Volare' (only two years after the song first topped the charts) all in 1960 and 'Forget Him', a song written and produced in Britain

by Tony Hatch in 1963. Rydell, whose ambition was always to be an all-round entertainer, starred in the movie *Bye Bye Birdie* and quickly, and initially successfully, moved into the cabaret circuit. The arrival of the British groups in 1964 was the final nail in his chart coffin. He later recorded without success for Capitol, Reprise, RCA, Perception and Pickwick International. Rydell has continued to work the club and oldies circuit and had some recognition for his role in rock when the high school in the hit 70s musical *Grease* was named after him. He returned to the studio in 1995 to re-record all his greatest hits as *The Best Of Bobby Rydell*.
●ALBUMS: *We Got Love* (Cameo 1959)★★★, *Bobby Sings* (Cameo 1960)★★, *Bobby Rydell Salutes The Great Ones* (Cameo 1961)★★, *Bobby's Biggest Hits* (1961)★★★, *Rydell At The Copa* (Cameo 1961)★★, *Rydell/Chubby Checker* (1961)★★★, *Biggest Hits Vol. 2* (1962)★★, *All The Hits* (1962)★★★, *Bye Bye Birdie* (Cameo 1963)★★, *Wild Wood Days* (Cameo 1963)★★, *Top Hits Of 1963* (Cameo 1964)★★, *Forget Him* (Cameo 1964)★★.
●COMPILATIONS: *16 Golden Hits* (Cameo 1965)★★, *Greatest Hits* (1993)★★, *Best Of Bobby Rydell* (K-Tel 1995)★★.
●FILMS: *Because They're Young* (1960).

RYDER, MITCH, AND THE DETROIT WHEELS

b. William Levise Jnr., 26 February 1945, Detroit, Michigan, USA. An impassioned singer, bearing an aural debt to Little Richard, Mitch Ryder spent his formative years frequenting the clubs on Woodward Avenue, watching many of Tamla/Motown's star attractions. Having outgrown two high school bands, Levise formed Billy Lee And The Rivieras in 1963. Jim McCarty (lead guitar - later of Buddy Miles Express and Cactus), Joe Cubert (rhythm guitar), Earl Elliott (bass) and 'Little' John Badanjek (drums) completed the group's early line-up, which recorded two singles for local labels prior to their 'discovery' by producer Bob Crewe. The quintet was then given a sharper name - Mitch Ryder And The Detroit Wheels - and in 1965 secured their biggest hit with the frenzied 'Jenny Take A Ride', a raw and earthy performance which set new standards in 'blue-eyed' soul. Uninhibited at a time of increasing sophistication, Ryder successfully captured the power of his black inspirations. Subsequent releases showed a similar verve, but the group reached its zenith with the exceptional medley of 'Devil With A Blue Dress On' and 'Good Golly Miss Molly'. From there, however, the formula became predictable and more studied recreations failed to emulate its fire. The Wheels were summarily fired in 1967 as the singer was coaxed towards safer fare. He and Crewe split up in rancorous circumstances but a union with guitarist Steve Cropper resulted in the excellent *Detroit/Memphis Experiment*.
In 1971 Levise formed Detroit, a hard-edged rock band of great promise which disintegrated prematurely. The

singer then abandoned music, nursing a throat ailment that threatened his one-time livelihood. He resumed performing in the late 70s and although later releases lack the overall passion of those initial recordings, there are moments when that erstwhile strength occurs. In the 90s Mitch Ryder is still a major concert attraction. A primary influence on Bruce Springsteen, the architect of Detroit's 'high-energy' performers, the MC5 and the Stooges, Ryder's talent should not be under-estimated.

●ALBUMS: with the Detroit Wheels *Take A Ride* (New Voice 1966)★★★★, *Breakout ...!!!* (New Voice 1966)★★★, *Sock It To Me!* (New Voice 1967)★★★, Mitch Ryder solo *What Now My Love* (Stateside 1967)★★, *All The Heavy Hits* (1967)★★★, *Mitch Ryder Sings The Hits* (1968)★★, *The Detroit-Memphis Experiment* (1969)★★★, *How I Spent My Vacation* (1978)★★★, *Naked But Not Dead* (1979)★★★, *Got Change For A Million* (1981)★★★, *Live Talkies* (1982)★★★, *Smart Ass* (1982)★★★, *Never Kick A Sleeping Dog* (1983)★★★, *In The China Shop* (1986)★★★, *Red Blood And White Mink* (1989)★★★, *La Gash* (1992)★★.

●COMPILATIONS: *All Mitch Ryder Hits!* (New Voice/Bell 1967)★★★, *Mitch Ryder And The Detroit Wheels' Greatest Hits* (1972)★★★, *Wheels Of Steel* (1983)★★★, *Rev Up* (1990)★★, *The Beautiful Toulang Sunset* (1992)★★, *Document Series Presents ...* (1992)★★★.

SAINTE-MARIE, BUFFY

b. 20 February 1941, Piapot Reserve, Saskatchewan, Canada. An honours graduate from the University of Massachusetts, Sainte-Marie eschewed a teaching career in favour of a folksinger. She was signed to the Vanguard label in 1964, following her successful performances at Gerde's Folk City. Her debut, *It's My Way*, introduced a remarkable compositional and performing talent. Sainte-Marie's impassioned plea for Indian rights, 'Now That The Buffalo's Gone', reflected her native-American parentage and was one of several stand out tracks, along with 'Cod'ine' and 'The Universal Soldier'. The latter was recorded, successfully, by Donovan, which helped introduce her to a wider audience. Her second selection included 'Until It's Time For You To Go', a haunting love song that was later recorded by Elvis Presley. However, Sainte-Marie was also a capable interpreter of other writers' material, as her versions of songs by Bukka White, Joni Mitchell and Leonard Cohen showed. Her versatility was also apparent on *I'm Gonna Be A Country Girl Again*, and *Illuminations*. A campaigner for American Indian rights, Sainte-Marie secured an international hit in 1971 with the theme song to the film, *Soldier Blue*, but subsequent releases failed to capitalize on this success. Temporarily bereft of direction, Sainte-Marie returned to the Indian theme with *Sweet America*, but with the collapse of the ABC labels, she retired to raise her family and concentrate on her work for children's foundations. She composed the 1982 Joe Cocker/Jennifer Warnes' hit, 'Up Where We Belong' with lyricist Will Jennings, which featured in the film *An Officer And A Gentleman*. Her welcome return in 1991, following her signing with Chrysalis Records, produced *Coincidence And Likely Stories*, which displayed her interest in computer technology. She is married to record producer Jack Nitzsche.

●ALBUMS: *It's My Way* (Vanguard 1964)★★★, *Many A Mile* (Vanguard 1965)★★★, *Little Wheel Spin And Spin* (Vanguard 1966)★★★, *Fire, Fleet And Candlelight* (Vanguard 1967)★★★, *I'm Gonna Be A Country Girl Again* (1968)★★, *Illuminations* (Illuminations 1970)★★★, *She Used To Wanna Be A Ballerina* (Vanguard 1971)★★★★, *Moonshot* (Vanguard 1972)★★★, *Quiet Places* (Vanguard 1973)★★, *Buffy* (MCA 1974), *Changing Woman* (MCA 1975)★★, *Sweet America* (ABC 1976)★★, *Coincidence And Likely Stories* (1992)★★, *Up Where We Belong* (EMI 1996)★★.

●COMPILATIONS: *The Best Of Buffy Sainte-Marie*

(Vanguard 1970)★★★★, *Native North American Child: An Odyssey* (1974)★★★, *The Best Of Buffy Sainte-Marie, Volume 2* (Vanguard 1974)★★★.

SAM AND DAVE

Samuel David Moore (b. 12 October 1935, Miami, Florida, USA) and David Prater (b. 9 May 1937, Ocilla, Georgia, USA, d. 11 April 1988). Sam And Dave first performed together in 1961 at Miami's King Of Hearts club. Moore originally sang in his father's Baptist church before joining the Melonaires, while Prater, who had worked with the Sensational Hummingbirds, was also gospel-trained. Club-owner John Lomelo became the duo's manager and was instrumental in securing their contract with Roulette. Five singles and one album subsequently appeared between 1962-64, produced by R&B veteran Henry Glover, but it was not until Jerry Wexler signed Sam And Dave to Atlantic Records that their true potential blossomed. For political reasons their records appeared on Stax; they used the Memphis-based house-band while many of their strongest moments came from the Isaac Hayes/David Porter staff writing team. 'You Don't Know Like I Know', 'Hold On I'm Comin' (both 1966), 'Soul Man' (1967) and 'I Thank You' (1968), featuring Prater's gritty delivery and Moore's higher inter-jections, were among the genre's finest. When Stax and Atlantic separated in 1968, Sam And Dave reverted to the parent company, but a disintegrating personal relationship seemed to mirror their now decaying fortune. The amazing 'Soul Sister, Brown Sugar' (1969) delayed the slide, but the duo split briefly the next year when Sam Moore began his own career. Three solo singles followed, but the pair were reunited by a deal with United Artists. A renewed profile, on the strength of the Blues Brothers' success with 'Soul Man', faltered when the gulf between the two men proved irreconcilable. By 1981, Moore was again pursuing an independent direction, but his sole chart success came when he was joined by Lou Reed for a remake of 'Soul Man' six years later. Prater found a new foil in the 'Sam' of Sam & Bill, but before they were able to consolidate this new partnership, Prater died in a car crash on 11 April 1988. Arguably soul's definitive duo, Sam And Dave released records that combined urgency with an unbridled passion.

●ALBUMS: *Sam And Dave* i (Roulette/King 1966)★★, *Hold On, I'm Comin'* (Stax 1966)★★★★, *Double Dynamite* (Stax 1967)★★★★, *Soul Men* (Stax 1967)★★★★, *I Thank You* (Atlantic 1968)★★★, *Double Trouble* (Stax 1969)★★★, *Back At 'Cha* (United Artists 1976)★★, *Sam And Dave* ii rec. 1962-63 (Edsel 1994)★★.

●COMPILATIONS: *The Best Of Sam And Dave* (Atlantic 1969)★★★★, *Can't Stand Up For Falling Down* (1984)★★★, *Wonderful World* (1987)★★★, *Sweet Funky Gold* (1988)★★★, *Sam & Dave Anthology* (1993)★★★★, *The Very Best Of ...* (Rhino 1995)★★★★.

SAM GOPAL

This late 60s UK psychedelic group were named after their tabla player and percussionist, Sam Gopal. With Roger D'Elia (guitars), Phil Duke (bass) and Ian 'Lemmy' Willis (b. Ian Kilminster; vocals/guitar), they made their debut in 1969 with *Escalator* for Stable Records. Produced by Trevor Walters, it included a version of 'Season Of The Witch' as well as group originals from Willis. Gopal himself made his greatest contribution on the eastern-flavoured 'Yesterlove'. However, commercial rewards eluded the group, but Lemmy found much greater success as a member of Hawkwind and founder of Motörhead. Largely as a result, Sam Gopal's sole album, EP (also titled *Escalator*) and single ('Horse'/'Back Door Man') have become interesting historical footnotes and prized collector's items.

●ALBUMS: *Escalator* (Stable 1969)★★.

SAM THE SHAM AND THE PHARAOHS

b. Domingo Samudio aka Sam Samudio, Dallas, Texas, USA. Although drawing inspiration from the Tex-Mex tradition, Sam's initial releases were made for Memphis-based outlets. Backed by the Pharaohs, which comprised Ray Stinnet (guitar), Butch Gibson (saxophone), David Martin (bass) and Jerry Patterson (drums) - he had a US chart-topper in 1965 with 'Wooly Bully', a pulsating novelty dance song which achieved immortality as a staple part of aspiring bar band repertoires. The single became the act's sole UK Top 20 hit, but they enjoyed further success in the USA with 'Lil' Red Riding Hood', which reached number 2 the following year. The group later mutated into the Sam The Sham Revue, but the singer dissolved the venture in 1970 to embark on a solo career under his own name. Although *Hard And Heavy* featured support from guitarist Duane Allman, the set was marred by inconsistency and failed to establish its proponent's talent. Domingo subsequently contributed to the soundtrack of the motion picture *The Border* (1982) and remains a popular talent in his native state.

●ALBUMS: *Sam The Sham And Wooly Bully* (MGM 1965)★★★, *Their Second Album* (MGM 1965)★★, *When The Boys Meet The Girls* soundtrack (1965)★★, *Sam The Sham And The Pharaohs On Tour* (MGM 1966)★★, *Lil' Red Riding Hood* (MGM 1966)★★, *The Sam The Sham Revue/Nefertiti* (MGM 1967)★★, *Ten Of Pentacles* (MGM 1968)★★.

●COMPILATIONS: *The Best Of Sam The Sham And The Pharaohs* (MGM 1967)★★★. As Sam Domingo *Hard And Heavy* (1970)★★.

●FILMS: *The Fastest Guitar Alive* (1966).

SAMMES, MIKE

b. 19 February 1928, Reigate, Surrey, England. The son of a photographic equipment dealer, Sammes attended the local grammar school and played cello in its orchestra. However, his greater interest in vocal music led to the formation of the Michael (later, Mike) Sammes Singers in 1957, while he was working for a London publishing firm.

The mixed choir's professional debut was at the London Palladium where they appeared frequently as accompanists to solo stars like Judy Garland. As well as being the name most readily mentioned whenever a BBC Light Entertainment producer requires a polished vocal group (and having their own Radio 2 series, *Sammes Songs*, the Singers have been employed on innumerable studio sessions for Cliff Richard, Michael Holliday, Tommy Steele, Val Doonican, Engelbert Humperdinck, Tom Jones, Matt Monro, Julie Andrews, Cilla Black, and even the Beatles. They have also recorded in their own right for HMV Records, and had a UK hit in 1966 with 'Somewhere My Love' ('Lara's Theme' from the film *Doctor Zhivago*) - which peaked at number 14 after overtaking a rival version by Manuel And His Music Of The Mountains.

● ALBUMS: *Sammes Session* (World Record Club 1965)★★★, *Sounds Sensational* (Columbia 1965)★★★, *Colour It Folksy* (EMI 1965)★★★, *Love Is A Happy Thing* (EMI 1968)★★★, *Songs That Live Forever* (1973)★★★, *Cole* (1974)★★★, *Sammes Songs* (1976)★★★, *Double Take, Volumes 1 & 2* (1986)★★★, *Just For You* (1987)★★★, *The Songs We Love* (1988)★★★.

● COMPILATIONS: *The Very Best Of* (1992)★★★.

● FURTHER READING: *Backing Into The Limelight*, Mike Sammes.

SANDPIPERS

Richard Shoff, Mike Piano and Jim Brady were members of the California-based Mitchell Boys Choir prior to forming a harmonic singing group known initially as the Four Seasons. When a New York attraction also laid claim to the name, the trio became the Grads and as such recorded several singles before securing a successful residency at a Lake Tahoe nightclub. A mutual friend introduced the act to Herb Alpert, owner of A&M Records, but several unsuccessful releases, under both the Grads and Sandpipers appellations, followed before producer Tommy LiPuma suggested they record 'Guantanamera'. The Sandpipers' 1966 rendition of this South American folk song reached the Top 10 in both the USA and UK, and set a pattern for several lesser hits, including similarly sweet interpretations of 'Louie Louie' (1966), 'Quando M'Innamoro (A Man Without Love)' (1968), 'Kumbaya' (1969) and the posthumous 'Hang On Sloopy' (1976). Such MOR recordings, coupled with the trio's clean-cut image, has tended to obscure their undoubted vocal skill.

● ALBUMS: *Guantanamera* (1966)★★★, *The Sandpipers* (1967)★★★, *Misty Roses* (1967)★★★, *Softly* (1968)★★★, *The Wonder Of You* (1969)★★★, *Come Saturday Morning* (1970)★★★, *Second Spanish Album* (1974)★★, *Overdue* (1977)★★★.

● COMPILATIONS: *Greatest Hits* (1970)★★★.

SANTO AND JOHNNY

Santo Farina (b. 24 October 1937, Brooklyn, New York, USA; steel guitar) and Johnny Farina (b. 30 October 1941, Brooklyn, New York, USA; rhythm guitar/steel guitar). Santo and Johnny's father, a serviceman, had found the steel guitar on C&W records very soothing when he was overseas. He encouraged his children to learn the instrument and was impressed when they wrote an instrumental, 'Sleep Walk', which was released on the Canadian-American label. (The record label and the publicity referred to a third composer, Ann Farina, who was supposedly a sister. This was a mistake - they did not even have a sister.) Although the haunting sound could easily be duplicated today, it was highly original for 1959. The record topped the US charts, selling over two million copies, but only made number 22 in the UK. Since then, the tune has become a standard and there are versions by the Ventures, the Shadows and, with words, Caterina Valente. Santo And Johnny had moderate success with 'Tear Drop' and the albums, *Sleep Walk* and *Encore*. They often recorded in an Hawaiian setting and some of their later titles are 'Goldfinger', 'Spanish Harlem' and 'Last Tango In Paris'. In their later years together, they tried to shake their 'easy listening' tag by adding fuzz guitar and doing songs by Deep Purple and Led Zeppelin. They also recorded many Italian tunes as they established a huge following there, being awarded 33 gold discs. The duo split in the 70s and both have released their own albums - Johnny's label Aniraf is his surname backwards. The eerie 'Sleep Walk' was the theme of the Stephen King film, *The Sleepwalkers*.

● ALBUMS: *Santo & Johnny* (Canadian American 1959)★★★★, *Sleep Walk* (Canadian-American 1960)★★★★, *Encore* (Canadian-American 1960)★★★, *Come On In* (Canadian-American 1961)★★★★, *Around The World* (Canadian-American 1961)★★★, *Offshore* (Canadian-American 1961)★★★, *In The Still Of The Night* (Canadian-American 1962)★★★★, *Santo And Johnny Wish You Love* (Canadian-American 1962)★★, *Santo And Johnny Play The Beatles Greatest Hits* (Canadian-American 1964)★★★, *The Brilliant Guitar Sound Of Santo And Johnny* (Canadian-American 1964)★★★, *Mucho* (Canadian American 1965), *Golden Guitars* (Imperial 1965)★★★, *On The Road Again* (Imperial 1966)★★★★, *Best That Could Happen* (Imperial 1966)★★, *Hawaii* (Stateside 1963)★★, *Mona Lisa* (Philips 1966)★★, *Pulcinella* (Philips 1966)★★, *Io Per Lei* (Produttoriassociati 1970)★★★, *Adagio* (Produttoriassociati 1971)★★★, *Classics* (Produttoriassociati 1972)★★★★, *Santo And Johnny* (Produttoriassociati 1973)★★★, *Dance, Dance, Dance* (Produttoriassociati 1974)★★★, *Film Sounds* (Discricordi 1974)★★★, *Gold Disc* (Produttoriassociati 1975)★★★, *Santo And Johnny* (Produttoriassociati 1976)★★★, *Santo And Johnny Play The Beatles* (Epic 1977)★★★. Solo: Santo Farina *The Lonely Santo* (Laboratorio 1979)★★★, *The Many Tastes Of Santo* (Cicogna 1980)★★★. Johnny Farina *Pure Steel, Volume 1* (Aniraf 1994)★★★.

SARSTEDT, PETER

Brother of 60s pop idol Eden Kane, this singer/songwriter was a denizen of the British folk scene when the hunt was on for a native riposte to Bob Dylan. Sarstedt was not chosen but, growing a luxuriant black moustache, he cultivated the image of a suave wanderer of global bohemia. Recording for United Artists, his 'I Am A Cathedral' was an airplay hit on pirate radio and university juke-boxes, but it was not until 1969 that he restored family fortunes with a UK number 1, 'Where Do You Go To My Lovely', which has since attained status as a pop classic and is a perennial on 'gold' format radio stations. That year, both an album and another single ('Frozen Orange Juice') also sold well throughout Europe. Yet, although a forerunner of the early 70s 'self-rock' school, his style was not solemn enough for its collegian consumers. In 1973, he teamed up on *Worlds Apart Together* with Kane and another sibling, Robin Sarstedt. Then came the resumption of his solo career with the issue of further albums, which was accompanied by the unexpected BBC airplay for 'Beirut' from *PS ...*, and 'Love Among The Ruins' almost charting in 1982. Based in Copenhagan for several years, he settled down with his American wife, Joanna, on a Wiltshire farm. In the early 90s, he was seen on 60s nostalgia shows, often supporting Gerry And The Pacemakers.

●ALBUMS: *Peter Sarstedt* (United Artists 1969)★★, *As Though It Were A Movie* (United Artists 1969)★★, *Every Word You Say* (United Artists 1971)★★★, *PS ...* (1979)★★★, *Up Date* (1981)★★★, *Asia Minor* (1987)★★★, *Never Say Goodbye* (1987)★★★.
●COMPILATIONS: *The Very Best Of Peter Sarstedt* (1987)★★★.

SAXON, SKY

b. Richard Marsh. Saxon emerged from the nascent Los Angeles music circle during the early 60s. He recorded 'Goodbye' as Little Richie Marsh, before taking his above sobriquet as the frontperson of two groups, the Soul Rockers and the Electra Fires. In 1965 he formed the Seeds, arguably the city's finest punk/garage group, which later evolved into a psychedelic/flower-power attraction. Although the quartet broke up officially in 1969, Saxon retained the name for a series of increasingly deranged singles, including 'Love In A Summer Basket' and 'Shucking And Jiving'. The singer, who variously dubbed himself Sky Sunlight, Sunstar, or Sky Sunlight Saxon, subsequently founded several groups, known either as the Universal Stars Band or Star's New Seeds Band. A series of self-mythologizing, yet engaging, releases ensued, many of which featured cohort guitarist Rainbow. *Firewall* was a collaboration with Mars Bonfire, who wrote Steppenwolf's million-seller, 'Born To Be Wild'. It featured cameos from several luminaries from the 'new psychedelic' movement, including members of the Dream Syndicate, Yard Trauma and the Plimsouls, in turn confirming Sky's revered status among this particular group of musicians. Now domiciled in Hawaii, Saxon remains an idiosyncratic figure, yet one who, in common with Roky Erickson, still commands a considerable cult following.
●ALBUMS: *Sunlight And The New Seeds* (1976)★★★, *In Love With Life* (1978)★★★, *Heavenly Earth - Live* (1978)★★, *Starry Ride* (1983)★★★, *Masters Of Psychedelia* (1984), *A Groovy Thing* (1986), *Firewall* (1986)★★★, as Sky Sunlight Saxon And Firewall *In Search Of Brighter Colours* (1988)★★★.
●COMPILATIONS: *Retrospective* (1986)★★★.

SCAFFOLD

Formed in Liverpool, England, in 1962, the Scaffold was the unlikely confluence of two concurrent 'booms' - satire and Merseybeat. Poet Roger McGough (b. 9 November 1937) and humorist John Gorman (b. 4 January 1937) joined Mike McGear (b. Michael McCartney, 7 January 1944), younger brother of Paul McCartney, to create an act not solely reliant on pop for success. They contributed material to *Gazteet*, a late-night programme on ABC-Television and following an acclaimed residency at London's Establishment club, took their 'Birds, Marriages and Deaths' revue to the 1964 Edinburgh Festival, where they later returned on several occasions. Although the trio enjoyed major hits with 'Thank U Very Much' (1967) and 'Lily The Pink' (1968) - the latter of which was a massive Christmas UK number 1 - these tongue-in-cheek releases contrasted the group's in-concert revues and albums. Here McGough's poetry and Gorman's comedy routines were of equal importance and their versatility was confirmed on *The Scaffold* and *L The P*. The schoolboy-ish 'Gin Gan Goolie' gave the group a minor chart entry in 1969, before the unit was absorbed by Grimms, a larger, if similarly constituted, act which also featured members of the Liverpool Scene. On its demise McGear recorded *Woman*, before agreeing to resurrect Scaffold for *Fresh Liver* on which Zoot Money (keyboards) and Ollie Halsall (guitar) joined the Average White Band horn section to help bring a rock-based perspective to the trio's work. The haunting 'Liverpool Lou' provided another UK Top 10 hit in 1974, but the founder members embarked on separate paths following *Sold Out*. McGear resumed his solo career, and became a credible photographer, while McGough returned to writing poetry. Gorman pursued a career in television, principally on the cult UK television children's show *Tiswas* and was back in the UK charts alongside Sally James, Chris Tarrant and Lenny Henry as the Four Bucketeers with 'The Bucket Of Water Song' in 1980.
●ALBUMS: *The Scaffold* (1967)★★★, *L The P* (1968)★★★, *An Evening With* (Parlophone 1968)★★, *Fresh Liver* (Island 1973)★★, *Sold Out* (1974)★★.
●COMPILATIONS: *The Singles A's And B's* (1984)★★★.

SCHIFRIN, LALO

b. 21 June 1932, Buenos Aires, Argentina. Schifrin was taught classical piano from the age of six but later studied sociology and law at university. He won a scholarship to the Paris Conservatoire where he studied with Olivier Messiaen. In 1955 he represented Argentina in the Third International Jazz Festival in Paris. He met Dizzy Gillespie first in 1956 when the trumpeter was touring South America. Schifrin had founded the first Argentine

big band in the Count Basie tradition and in 1957 wrote his first film music. He moved to New York in 1958 and toured Europe in 1960 with a Jazz At The Philharmonic ensemble, which included Gillespie, with whom he played between 1960 and 1962. He had become increasingly interested in large-scale compositions and wrote two suites for Gillespie - *Gillespiana* and *New Continent*. He worked with Quincy Jones when he left Gillespie, but became more and more involved in scoring for television and feature films including *The Cincinatti Kid* (1965), *Bullitt* (1968) and *Dirty Harry* (1971). His more than 150 scores over a period of nearly 30 years have also included *The Liquidator, Cool Hand Luke, The Fox, Coogan's Bluff, Kelly's Heros, Hit!, Magnum Force, Voyage Of The Damned, The Eagle Has Landed, Rollercoaster, The Amityville Horror, The Competition, The Sting II, Hollywood Wives* (television mini-series), *The Fourth Protocol, F/X2 - The Deadly Art Of Illusion, The Dead Pool, Return From The River Kwai, A Woman Called Jackie* (1992 television series), and *The Beverly Hillbillies* (1993). He lectured in composition at the University of California, Los Angeles (1968-71), and has spent a good deal of his career searching for common ground between jazz and classical music. In 1995, he conducted the London Philharmonic Orchestra at London's Festival Hall, in *Jazz Meets The Symphony*, 'an evening of jazz-symphonic fusion'.
●ALBUMS: *Bossa Nova - New Brazilian Jazz* (Audio Fidelity 1962)★★★, *New Fantasy* (Verve 1966)★★★, *The Dissection And Reconstruction Of Music From The Past As Performed By The Inmates Of Lalo Schiffrin's Demented Ensemble As A Tribute To The Memory Of The Marquis De Sade* (Verve 1966)★★★, *Music From 'Mission: Impossible'* (1967)★★★, *Insensatez* (Verve 1968)★★★, *Towering Toccata* (1977)★★, *Black Widow* (1976)★★, *Free Ride* (1979)★★, *Guitar Concerto* (1985)★★, *Anno Domini* (1986)★★, with Jimmy Smith *The Cat Strikes Again* (Verve 1986)★★★, *Firebird* (Four Winds 1996)★★★.

SCHROEDER, JOHN

b. 1935, London, England. Schroeder became assistant to EMI's Columbia label chief Norrie Paramor in 1958. His first production was 'Sing Little Birdie' by Pearl Carr And Teddy Johnson, which finished second in the Eurovision Song Contest in the following year. Subsequently Schroeder supervised recording sessions by numerous Columbia artists including Cliff Richard and the Shadows. In 1961, he discovered the 14-year-old Helen Shapiro and when Paramor could find no suitable material for her, Schroeder wrote his first song and her first hit, 'Please Don't Treat Me Like A Child'. A subsequent Shapiro song, 'Walking Back To Happiness' won the Ivor Novello award for Schroeder and co-writer Mike Hawker. He next spent two years as label manager for Oriole, the UK's only significant independent record company. There he produced hits by Marion Evans, Clinton Ford and Swedish instrumental group the Spotniks. Oriole was also the first British label to issue material from Berry Gordy's Tamla

Motown labels. Schroeder left Oriole shortly before it was purchased by CBS to become head of Pye Records' Piccadilly label. There, he had immediate success with the Rockin' Berries, the Ivy League and Sounds Orchestral, an instrumental studio group he formed with keyboards player Johnny Pearson who had a major success in 1965 with the lilting 'Cast Your Fate To The Wind'. Schroeder and Pearson went on to record 14 Sounds Orchestral albums and were planning to revive the group in the early 90s. During a seven year tenure with Pye, he wrote for and produced artists as diverse as Status Quo, Geno Washington and Shapiro. For a period during the 70s, Schroeder ran his own Alaska Records whose roster included Afro-rock band Cymande, rock 'n' roll revivalists Flying Saucers and Joy Sarney, whose 'Naughty Naughty Naughty' was a minor hit in 1977. Schroeder was also a pioneer in the video business before moving to Vancouver, Canada in 1978 where he was active throughout the 80s as an independent producer.
●ALBUMS: *Workin In The Soul Mine* (Piccadilly 1966)★★★, *The Dolly Catcher* (Pye 1967)★★★, *Witchi Tai To* (Pye 1971)★★★, *Dylan Vibrations* (Polydor 1971)★, *TV Vibrations* (Polydor 1972)★★★.

SCOTT, RONNIE

b. 28 January 1927, London, England, d. 24 December 1996. Scott began playing on the soprano saxophone but switched to tenor in his early teens. After playing informally in clubs he joined the Johnny Claes band in 1944, before spells with Ted Heath, Bert Ambrose and other popular British dance bands. Scott also played on transatlantic liners in order to visit the USA and hear bebop at first hand. By the late 40s he was a key figure in the London bop scene, playing at the Club Eleven, of which he was a co-founder. During the 50s he led his own band and was also co-leader with Tubby Hayes of the Jazz Couriers. In 1959, he opened his own club in Gerrard Street, London, later moving to Frith Street. During the 60s he divided his time between leading his own small group and running the club, but also found time to play with the Clarke-Boland Big Band. The decade of the 60s was a milestone for popular music; for quality jazz there was only one place in London to visit - Ronnies. In the 70s and 80s he continued to lead small bands, usually a quartet, occasionally touring but most often playing as the interval band between sessions by the modern American jazz musicians he brought to the club. As a player, Scott comfortably straddles the mainstream and modern aspects of jazz. His big tone lends itself to a slightly aggressive approach, although in his ballad playing he displays the warmth that characterized the work of Zoot Sims and late-period Stan Getz, musicians he admires, but does not imitate. Although a gifted player, Scott's greatest contribution to jazz was in his tireless promotion of fine British musicians and in his establishment of his club, booking the best American talent. His venue has become renowned throughout the world for the excellence of its setting and the artists on display. In 1981, Scott was awarded an OBE in recognition of his services to music. Following a bout of depression he was found dead at his home in December 1996.

●ALBUMS: *Battle Royal* (Esquire 1951)★★★, *The Ronnie Scott Jazz Group* i (Esquire 1952)★★★, *The Ronnie Scott Jazz Group* ii (Esquire 1953)★★★, *The Ronnie Scott Jazz Group* iii (Esquire 1954)★★★, *The Ronnie Scott Jazz Group* iv (Esquire 1954)★★★, *At The Royal Festival Hall* (Decca 1956)★★★, *Presenting The Ronnie Scott Sextet* (Philips 1957)★★★, *The Jazz Couriers In Concert* (1958)★★★, *The Last Word* (1959)★★★, *The Night Is Scott And You're So Swingable* (Fontana 1966)★★★, *Live At Ronnie's* (1968)★★★, *Scott At Ronnie's* (1973)★★★, *Serious Gold* (1977)★★★, *Great Scott* (1979)★★★, with various artists *Ronnie Scott's 20th Anniversary Album* (1979)★★★, *Never Pat A Burning Dog* (Jazz House 1990)★★★.

●FURTHER READING: *Jazz At Ronnie Scott's*, Kitty Grime (ed.). *Let's Join Hands And Contact The Living* , John Fordham. *Jazz Man: The Amazing Story Of Ronnie Scott And His Club*, John Fordham.

SCOTT, SHIRLEY

b. 14 March 1934, Philadelphia, Pennsylvania, USA. Although she had studied both piano and trumpet as a child, Scott's breakthrough occurred when she switched to organ in the mid-50s. Mostly working in small groups with a saxophone leader and a drummer, she became very popular. Her musical associates have included such outstanding jazzmen as Eddie 'Lockjaw' Davis, Stanley Turrentine (to whom she was married for a while), Jimmy Forrest and Dexter Gordon. A gifted player with an eclectic style that encompasses the blues and bebop, Scott is one of only a handful of organists to satisfactorily fit a potentially unsuitable instrument into a jazz setting. Her career received a boost in the 90s when the Hammond organ became fashionable once more.

●ALBUMS: *Great Scott* (Prestige 1958)★★★, *Shirley's Sounds* (Prestige 1958)★★★, *The Eddie Lockjaw Davis Cookbook* (1958)★★★, *Great Scott!* (1958)★★★, *Scottie* (Prestige 1959)★★★, *Shirley Scott Plays Duke* (Prestige 1959)★★★, *Soul Searching* (Prestige 1959)★★★, *The Shirley Scott Trio* i (Prestige 1960)★★★, *Mucho Mucho* (Prestige 1960)★★★, *Like Cozy* (Moodsville 1960)★★★, *Satin Doll* (Prestige 1961)★★★, *Hip Soul* (Prestige 1961)★★★, *Shirley Scott Plays Horace Silver* (Prestige 1961)★★★, *Hip Twist* (Prestige 1961)★★★, with Stanley Turrentine *Dearly Beloved* (1961)★★★, *Happy Talk* (Prestige 1962)★★★, *The Soul Is Willing* (Prestige 1963)★★★, *Drag 'Em Out* (Prestige 1963)★★★, *For Members Only* (Impulse 1963)★★★, *Soul Shoutin'* (Prestige 1963)★★★, *Travellin' Light* (Prestige 1964)★★★, *Blue Flames* (Prestige 1964)★★★, *Shirley Scott And Her Orchestra* i (1964)★★★, *The Great Live Sessions* (1964)★★★, *Great Scott!* (Impulse 1964)★★★, *Everybody Loves A Lover* (Impulse 1964)★★★, *The Shirley Scott Sextet* (1965)★★★, *Sweet Soul* (Prestige 1965)★★★, *Soul Seven* (Prestige 1965)★★★, *Soul Sisters* (Prestige 1965)★★★, *Queen Of The Organ* (Impulse 1965)★★★, *Latin Shadows* (Impulse 1965)★★★, *The Shirley Scott Trio* ii (1966)★★★, *The Shirley Scott Trio* iii (1966)★★★, *The Night Is Scott And You're So Swingable* (Fontana 1966)★★★, *Roll Em* (Impulse 1966)★★★, *Workin'* (Prestige 1966)★★★, *Now's The Time* (Prestige 1966)★★★, with Clark Terry *Soul Duo* (Impulse 1967)★★★, *Shirley Scott And Her Orchestra* ii (1966)★★★, *Stompin'* (Prestige 1961)★★★, *Soul Song* (Atlantic 1969)★★★, *The Shirley Scott Quintet* (1972)★★★, *One For Me* (1974)★★★, *Oasis* (Muse 1990)★★★, *Blues Everywhere* (Candid 1993)★★★, *A Walking Thing* (Candid 1996)★★★.

●COMPILATIONS: *The Best Of Shirley Scott And Stanley Turrentine* (Prestige 1969)★★★.

SEARCHERS

One of the premier groups from the mid-60s Merseybeat explosion, the Searchers comprised: Chris Curtis (b. Christopher Crummey, 26 August 1941, Oldham, Lancashire, England; drums), Mike Pender (b. Michael John Prendergast, 3 March 1942, Liverpool, England; lead guitar), Tony Jackson (b. 16 July 1940, Liverpool, England; vocals/bass) and John McNally (b. 30 August 1941, Liverpool, England; rhythm guitar). Having previously backed Liverpool singer Johnny Sandon, they broke away and took their new name from the 1956 John Ford western, *The Searchers*. During 1962, they appeared in Hamburg and after sending a demo tape to A&R representative Tony Hatch were signed to Pye Records the following year. Their Doc Pomus/Mort Shuman debut 'Sweets For My Sweet' was a memorable tune with strong harmonies and a professional production. By the summer of 1963, it climbed to number 1 establishing the Searchers as rivals to Brian Epstein's celebrated stable of Liverpool groups. *Meet The Searchers*, was swiftly issued and revealed the group's R&B pedigree on such standards as 'Farmer John' and 'Love Potion Number 9'. Meanwhile, Tony Hatch composed a catchy follow-up single, 'Sugar And Spice', which just failed to reach number 1. It was their third single, however, that won them international acclaim. The Jack Nitzsche/Sonny Bono composition 'Needles And Pins' was a superb melody, brilliantly arranged by the group and a striking chart-topper of its era. It also broke the group in the USA, reaching the Top 20 in March 1964. It was followed that same year with further US successes, including 'Ain't That Just Like Me' (US number 61), 'Sugar And Spice' (US number 44), and 'Some Day We're Gonna Love Again' (US number 34).

Earlier that year the band released their superbly atmospheric cover of the Orlons' 'Don't Throw Your Love Away', which justifiably gave the group their third UK number 1 single. The pop world was shocked by the abrupt departure of bassist Tony Jackson whose falsetto vocals had contributed much to the group's early sound and identity. He was replaced in the autumn by Frank Allen (b. Francis Renaud McNeice, 14 December 1943,

Hayes, Middlesex, England), a former member of Cliff Bennett And The Rebel Rousers and close friend of Chris Curtis. A strident reading of Jackie DeShannon's 'When You Walk In The Room' was another highlight of 1964 which showed their rich Rickenbacker guitar work to notable effect. The Malvina Reynolds protest song, 'What Have They Done To The Rain?', indicated their folk-rock potential, but its melancholic tune and slower pace was reflected in a lower chart placing. A return to the 'old' Searchers sound with the plaintive 'Goodbye My Love', took them back into the UK Top 5 in early 1965, but the number 1 days were over. For a time, it seemed that the Searchers might not slide as inexorably as rivals Billy J. Kramer And The Dakotas and Gerry And The Pacemakers. They enjoyed further US success when their cover of the Clovers' 'Love Potion Number 9' was a Top 10 hit at the end of 1964 and on into 1965. This continued with 'Bumble Bee (US number 21), 'Goodbye My Lover Goodbye' (US number 52). The Curtis/Pender hit, 'He's Got No Love' (US number 79, UK number 12) showed that they could write their own hit material but this run could not be sustained. The release of P.F. Sloan's 'Take Me For What I'm Worth' (US number 76, UK number 20) suggested that they might become linked with the Bob Dylan-inspired folk-rock boom. Instead, their commercial fortunes rapidly declined and after Curtis left in 1966, they were finally dropped by Pye. Their last UK hit was a version of Paul And Barry Ryan's 'Have You Ever Loved Somebody'; this proved to be their penultimate success in the USA which ended with 'Desdemona' (number 94) in 1971. Cabaret stints followed but the Searchers continued playing and in the circumstances underwent minimal line-up changes. They threatened a serious resurgence in 1979 when Sire issued a promising comeback album. The attempt to reach a new wave audience was ultimately unsuccessful, however, and after the less well received *Play For Today* (titled *Love's Melodies* in the USA), the group stoically returned to the cabaret circuit. To their credit, their act does not only dwell on 60s hits and they remain one of the most musically competent and finest surviving performing bands from the 60s' golden age. Ex-member Jackson was imprisoned in 1997 for making threats with an offensive weapon.

●ALBUMS: *Meet The Searchers* (Pye 1963)★★★★, *Sugar And Spice* (Pye 1963)★★★, *Hear! Hear!* (Mercury 1964)★★★, *It's The Searchers* (Pye 1964)★★★, *This Is Us* (Kapp 1964)★★★, *The New Searchers LP* (Kapp 1965), *The Searchers No. 4* (Kapp 1965), *Sounds Like The Searchers* (Pye 1965)★★★, *Take Me For What I'm Worth* (Pye/Kapp 1965)★★★, *Second Take* (RCA 1972)★★, *Needles And Pins* (1974)★★★, *The Searchers* (Sire 1979)★★★, *Play For Today* (1981)★★.

●COMPILATIONS: *100 Minutes Of The Searchers* (1982)★★★★, *The Searchers Hit Collection* (1987)★★★★, *The EP Collection* (1989)★★★★, *30th Anniversary Collection* (1992)★★★★, *The EP Collection Vol. 2* (1992)★★★, *Rare Recordings* (1993)★★★.

SEDAKA, NEIL

b. 13 March 1939, Brooklyn, New York, USA. Pianist Sedaka began his songwriting career with lyricist Howard Greenfield in the early 50s. During this high school period, Sedaka dated Carol Klein (later known as Carole King). For a brief period, Sedaka joined the Tokens, then won a scholarship to New York's Juilliard School of Music. In 1958, the pianist joined Don Kirshner's Brill Building school of instant songwriters. Sedaka's first major hit success came with 'Stupid Cupid', which was an international smash for Connie Francis. The following year, Sedaka signed to RCA as a recording artist and enjoyed a minor US hit with 'The Diary'. The frantic follow-up, 'I Go Ape', was a strong novelty record, which helped establish Sedaka. This was followed by one of his most famous songs, 'Oh Carol', a lament directed at his former girlfriend Carole King, who replied in kind with the less successful 'Oh Neil'. Sedaka's solid voice and memorable melodies resulted in a string of early 60s hits, including 'Stairway To Heaven', 'Calendar Girl', 'Little Devil', 'King Of Clowns', 'Happy Birthday Sweet Sixteen' and 'Breaking Up Is Hard To Do'. These songs summed up the nature of Sedaka's lyrical appeal. The material subtly dramatized the trials and rewards of teenage life and the emotional upheavals resulting from birthdays, break-ups and incessant speculation on the qualities of a loved one. Such songs of neurotic love had their distinct time in the early 60s, and with the decline of the clean-cut teen balladeer and the emergence of groups, there was an inevitable lull in Sedaka's fortunes. He abandoned the pop star role but continued writing a fair share of hits over the next 10 years, including 'Venus In Blue Jeans' (Jimmy Clanton/Mark Wynter), 'Working On A Groovy Thing' (Fifth Dimension), 'Puppet Man' (Tom Jones) and 'Is This The Way To Amarillo?' (Tony Christie). In 1972, Sedaka effectively relaunched his solo career with *Emergence* and relocated to the UK. By 1973, he was back in the British charts with 'That's When The Music Takes Me' from *Solitaire*. The third album of the comeback, *The Tra La Days Are Over*, was highly regarded and included 'Our Last Song Together', dedicated to Howard Greenfield. With *Laughter In The Rain*, Sedaka extended his appeal to his homeland. The title track topped the US charts in 1975, completing a remarkable international comeback. That same year, the Captain And Tennille took Sedaka's 'Love Will Keep Us Together' to the US number 1 spot and the songwriter followed suit soon after with 'Bad Blood'. The year ended with an excellent reworking of 'Breaking Up Is Hard To Do' in a completely different arrangement which provided another worldwide smash. He enjoyed his last major hit during 1980 in the company of his daughter Dara on 'Should've Never Let You Go'. Sedaka continues to tour regularly.

●ALBUMS: *Neil Sedaka* (RCA Victor 1959)★★★★, *Rock With Sedaka* (1959)★★★, *Circulate* (RCA Victor 1960)★★★, *Smile* (RCA Victor 1966)★★★, *Emergence* (1972)★★★, *Solitaire* (1972)★★★, *The Tra-La Days Are Over* (1973)★★★, *Laughter In The Rain* (1974)★★★, *Live At The Royal Festival Hall*

(1974)★★★, *Overnight Success* (1975)★★, *The Hungry Years* (1975)★★, *Steppin' Out* (1976)★★, *A Song* (1977)★★, *In The Pocket* (1980)★★, *Come See About Me* (1984)★★, *Love Will Keep Us Together: The Singer And His Songs* (1992)★★★, *Classically Sedaka* (Vision 1995).★★★

●COMPILATIONS: *Little Devil And His Other Hits* (RCA Victor 1961)★★★★, *Neil Sedaka Sings His Greatest Hits* (RCA Victor 1962)★★★★, *Sedaka's Back* (1975)★★★, *Laughter And Tears: The Best Of Neil Sedaka Today* (1976)★★★, *Neil Sedaka's Greatest Hits* (1977)★★★, *Timeless* (1991)★★★, *Originals: The Greatest Hits* (1992)★★★, *Laughter In The Rain: The Best Of ... 1974-1980* (Varese Sarabande 1995)★★★★.

●FURTHER READING: *Breaking Up Is Hard To Do*, Neil Sedaka.

SEEDS

Formed in 1965, the Seeds provided a pivotal link between garage/punk rock and the emergent underground styles. They were led by Sky Saxon (b. Richard Marsh), a charismatic figure already established on the fringes of a budding Los Angeles scene through a handful of low-key releases. Jan Savage (guitar), Darryl Hooper (keyboards) and Rick Andridge (drums) completed his newest venture that had a US hit the following year with the compulsive 'Pushin' Too Hard'. Its raw, simple riff and Saxon's howling, half-spoken intonation established a pattern that remained almost unchanged throughout the group's career. The Seeds enjoyed minor chart success with 'Mr. Farmer' and 'Can't Seem To Make You Mine', while their first two albums, *The Seeds* and *A Web Of Sound*, were also well received. The latter featured the 14-minute 'Up In Her Room', in which Saxon's free-spirited improvisations were allowed to run riot. The quartet embraced 'flower-power' with *Future*. Flutes, tablas, cellos and tubas were added to the basic Seeds riffs while such titles as 'March Of The Flower Children' and 'Flower Lady And Her Assistant' left little doubt as to where Saxon's sympathies lay. This release was followed by a curious interlude wherein the group, now dubbed the Sky Saxon Blues Band, recorded *A Full Spoon Of Seedy Blues*. This erratic and rather unsatisfactory departure came replete with a testimonial from Muddy Waters, but it later transpired that the project was a failed ploy by the group to escape their recording contract. Their last official album, *Raw And Alive At Merlin's Music Box*, marked a return to form. Subsequent singles charted a collapsing unit and psyche, although Saxon later re-emerged as Sky Sunlight, fronting several aggregations known variously as Stars New Seeds or the Universal Stars Band. Jan Savage, meanwhile, joined the Los Angeles Police Department.

●ALBUMS: *The Seeds* (Crescendo 1966)★★★, *A Web Of Sound* (Crescendo 1966)★★★, *Future* (Crescendo 1967)★★, *A Full Spoon Of Seedy Blues* (Crescendo 1967)★★, *Raw And Alive At Merlin's Music Box* (Crescendo 1967)★★★, *Flower Punk* reissue (Drop Out/Demon 1996)★★★.

●COMPILATIONS: *Fallin' Off The Edge* (1977)★★★, *Evil Hoodoo* (1988)★★★, *A Faded Picture* (1991)★★★.

SEEGER, MIKE

b. 15 August 1933, New York City, New York, USA. Mike is the son of well-known musicologist Charles Seeger, and Ruth Crawford Seeger, composer and author. From his youngest days he was surrounded by traditional music, and learned to play the autoharp at the age of 12. A few years later, he started to play guitar, mandolin, fiddle, dulcimer, mouth harp, and dobro. Together with his sister Peggy Seeger, he played with local square dance bands in the Washington area. His first involvement with country music came about while serving 'time' for conscientious objection, working in a hospital, when he teamed up with Hazel Dickens and Bob Baker. Mike formed the New Lost City Ramblers in 1958, with John Cohen and Tom Paley. That year, Seeger won the Galax Old Time Fiddlers Convention in Virginia for banjo work. It was during the late 50s that Mike started the first of his many recordings of other singers, including Elizabeth 'Libba' Cotten, and Dock Boggs. With changes in the personnel of the New Lost City Ramblers, Mike worked a great deal more in a solo capacity, but still recorded with the New Lost City Ramblers for the Folkways label. Among other projects, Mike was involved with the Newport Folk Festival in Rhode Island, and was a director of the Smithsonian Folklife Company from 1970. By the late 60s, he had formed the Strange Creek Singers with Alice L. Gerrard, Lamar Grier and Hazel Dickens. On 16 August 1970 he married Gerrard, but they were later divorced. Mike has recorded numerous albums with the various line-ups, with sister Peggy, and solo, and has continued to perform at festivals in the same capacity at home and throughout the world. His earlier work as a collector has also helped to keep alive a great deal of Southern traditional music.

●ALBUMS: *Oldtime Country Music* (Folkways 1962)★★★, *Mike Seeger* (Vanguard 1964)★★★, *Tipple, Loom And Rail: Songs Of The Industrialization Of The South* (Folkways 1965)★★★, *Mike And Peggy Seeger* (Argo 1966)★★★, *Strange Creek Singers* (1968)★★★, with Peggy Seeger *American Folksongs For Children* (1970)★★★, *Mike And Alice Seeger In Concert* (1970)★★★, *Music From True Vine* (Mercury 1971)★★★, *Second Annual Farewell Reunion* (Mercury 1973)★★★, *Alice And Mike* (Greenhays 1980)★★★, as A. Roebic And The Exertions *Old Time Music Dance Party* (Flying Fish 1986)★★★, *Fresh Old Time-String Band Music* (Rounder 1988)★★★, with Peggy and Penny Seeger and members of their families *American Folksongs For Christmas* (Rounder 1989)★★★, *Solo-Oldtime Country Music* (Rounder 1990)★★★, *Third Annual Farewell Reunion* (Rounder 1995)★★★.

SEEGER, PEGGY

b. Margaret Seeger, 17 June 1935, New York City, New York, USA. Seeger was accomplished on guitar, banjo, Appalachian dulcimer, autoharp and concertina. Her parents, Ruth Crawford and Charles Seeger were both professional musicians and teachers. They insisted that their daughter receive a formal musical education from the age of seven years. At the same time they encouraged her interest in folk music and, at the age of 10 Peggy started to learn guitar. A few years later she began to play 5-string banjo. After majoring in music at college, she started singing folksongs professionally. In 1955, Seeger relocated to Holland and studied Russian at university. Peggy first came to the UK in 1956 as an actress, to take part in a television film, *Dark Side Of The Moon*, and also joined the Ramblers, a group that included Ewan MacColl, Alan Lomax and Shirley Collins. In 1957, together with MacColl and Charles Parker, she worked on a series of documentaries for the BBC which are now commonly known as *The Radio Ballads*. These programmes were highly innovative and, together with music, brought the thoughts and views of a whole range of workers to a large listening public. In 1959, Peggy became a British subject, since she has been in much demand at folk clubs and festivals. In addition, she holds workshops and seminars, both at home and abroad. Along with Frankie Armstrong, Seeger has long championed women's rights through many of her songs. One such song, 'Gonna Be An Engineer' is possibly her best-known on the subject of equal rights for women. Due to her knowledge of folk music, Peggy was a leading light in the English folk song revival. After MacColl died in 1989, Peggy again launched a solo career, touring both the USA and Australia. Her collaboration with MacColl produced hundreds of songs and she has recorded a substantial number of albums in her own right, as well as with Mike and Penny Seeger. *The New Briton Gazette No.3* and *Fields Of Vietnam*, both recorded on Folkways in the USA, with Ewan MacColl and the Critics Group, were never released.

●ALBUMS: with Ewan MacColl *Two Way Trip* (1961)★★★, with MacColl *The Amorous Muse* (1966)★★★, with MacColl *The Long Harvest, Vol. 1* (1966)★★★, with MacColl *The Long Harvest, Vol. 2* (1967)★★★, with MacColl *The Long Harvest, Vol. 3* (1968)★★★, with MacColl *The Angry Muse* (1968)★★★, with Sandra Kerr, Frankie Armstrong *The Female Frolic* (1968)★★★, with MacColl *The Long Harvest, Vol. 4* (1969)★★★, with MacColl *The Long Harvest, Vol. 5* (1970)★★★, with Mike Seeger *American Folksongs For Children* (1970)★★★, with MacColl *The Long Harvest, Vol. 6* (1971)★★★, with MacColl *The Long Harvest, Vol. 7* (1972)★★★, with MacColl *The Long Harvest, Vol. 8* (1973)★★★, with MacColl *The Long Harvest, Vol. 9* (1974)★★★, with MacColl *The Long Harvest, Vol. 10* (1975)★★★, with MacColl *Penelope Isn't Waiting Anymore* (1977)★★★, with MacColl *Saturday Night At The Bull And Mouth* (1977)★★★, *Cold Snap* (1977)★★, *Hot Blast* (1978)★★, *Different Therefore Equal* (1979)★★★, with Ewan MacColl *Kilroy Was Here* (1980)★★★, *From Where I Stand* (1982)★★★, *Familiar Faces* (1988), with Seeger, MacColl families *American Folksongs For*

Christmas (Rounder 1989))★★★, with Ewan MacColl *Naming Of Names* (1990)★★★, with Irene Scott *Almost Commercially Viable* (1993).

●COMPILATIONS: *The Best Of Peggy Seeger* (1962)★★★★, *The World Of Ewan MacColl And Peggy Seeger* (1970)★★★★, *The World Of Ewan MacColl And Peggy Seeger, Vol. 2* (1972)★★★, *The Folkways Years 1955-92 - Songs Of Love And Politics* (1992)★★★★.

●FURTHER READING: *Who's Going To Shoe Your Pretty Little Foot, Who's Going To Glove Your Hand?*, Peggy Seeger with Tom Paley. *Folk Songs Of Peggy Seeger*, Peggy Seeger. *Travellers Songs Of England And Scotland*, Peggy Seeger and Ewan MacColl. *Doomsday In The Afternoon*, Peggy Seeger and Ewan MacColl.

SEEKERS

Founded in Australia in 1963, the original Seekers comprised Athol Guy (b. 5 January 1940, Victoria, Australia; vocals/double bass), Keith Potger (b. 2 March 1941, Columbo, Sri Lanka; vocals/guitar), Bruce Woodley (b. 25 July 1942, Melbourne, Australia; vocals/guitar) and Ken Ray (lead vocals/guitar). After a year with the above line-up, Athol Guy recruited Judith Durham (b. 3 July 1943, Melbourne, Australia) as the new lead singer and it was this formation which won international success. Following a visit to London in 1964, the group were signed to the Grade Agency and secured a prestigious guest spot on the televised *Sunday Night At The London Palladium*. Tom Springfield, of the recently defunct Springfields, soon realized that the Seekers could fill the gap left by his former group and offered his services as songwriter/producer. Although 1965 was one of the most competitive years in pop, the Seekers strongly challenged the Beatles and the Rolling Stones as the top chart act of the year. A trilogy of folk/pop smashes: 'I'll Never Find Another You', 'A World Of Our Own' and 'The Carnival Is Over' widened their appeal, leading to lucrative supper-club dates and frequent television appearances. Apart from Tom Springfield's compositions, such as 'Walk With Me', they also scored a massive chart hit with Malvina Reynolds' 'Morningtown Ride' and gave Paul Simon his first UK success with a bouncy adaptation of 'Someday One Day'. Meanwhile, Bruce Woodley teamed up with Simon to write some songs, including the Cyrkle hit 'Red Rubber Ball'. In early 1967, the breezy 'Georgy Girl' (written by Tom Springfield and Jim Dale) was a transatlantic Top 10 hit but thereafter, apart from 'When Will The Good Apples Fall' and 'Emerald City', the group were no longer chart regulars. Two years later they bowed out in a televised farewell performance, and went their separate ways. Keith Potger oversaw the formation of the New Seekers before moving into record production; Bruce Woodley became a highly successful writer of television jingles; Athol Guy spent several years as a Liberal representative in the Victoria parliament; and Judith Durham pursued a solo singing career. She had a minor UK hit in 1967 with 'Olive Tree', and her 1973 album *Here I Am* contained songs by Rod McKuen, Nilsson and Elton

John, as well as some folksy and jazz material. In 1975, the Seekers briefly re-formed with teenage Dutch singer Louisa Wisseling replacing Judith Durham. They enjoyed one moment of chart glory when 'The Sparrow Song' topped the Australian charts. In 1990 Judith Durham was involved in a serious car crash and spent six months recovering. The experience is said to have inspired her to reunite the original Seekers, and they played a series of 100 dates across Australia and New Zealand, before appearing in several 1994 Silver Jubilee Reunion Concerts in the UK at venues that included London's Royal Albert Hall and Wembley Arena.

●ALBUMS: *The Seekers* (1965)★★★, *A World Of Our Own* (1965)★★★, *The New Seekers* (1965)★★★, *Come The Day* (1966)★★★, *Seen In Green* (1967)★★★, *Georgy Girl* (1967)★★★, *Live At The Talk Of The Town* (1968)★★, *Four And Only Seekers* (1969)★★, *The Seekers* (1975)★★.

●COMPILATIONS: *The Sound Of The Seekers* (1967)★★★, *Love Is Kind* (1967)★★★, *Seekers Golden Collection* (1969)★★★, *A World Of Their Own* (1969)★★★, *The Very Best Of The Seekers* (1974)★★★, *An Hour Of The Seekers* (1988)★★★, *The Seekers Greatest Hits* (1988)★★★, *A Carnival Of Hits* (1994)★★★.

●FURTHER READING: *Colours Of My Life*, Judith Durham.

SHADES OF BLUE

Vocal group from Detroit, Michigan, USA. Shades Of Blue are known for just one hit, 'Oh How Happy', which with its singalong simplicity and good cheer raced up the chart in 1966 reaching number 12. Members of the group were Nick Marinelli, Linda Allan, Bob Kerr and Ernie Dernai. They were discovered and produced by soul singer Edwin Starr, who was looking for a white group to record 'Oh How Happy', a song he had written years earlier. After the group were turned down by another Detroit company, Starr took them to Harry Balk's small Impact operation, and with 'Oh How Happy' Impact achieved its only national hit. The group could not give Balk another big record, as their two subsequent records in 1966 - 'Lonely Summer' and 'Happiness' - stalled on the lower reaches of charts.

●ALBUMS: *Happiness Is The Shades of Blue* (Impact 1966)★★.

SHADOWS

The UK's premier instrumental group, the Shadows evolved from the Five Chestnuts to become Cliff Richard's backing group, the Drifters. By late 1958 the line-up had settled and under their new name the Shadows, the group comprised: Hank B Marvin (b. Brian Robson Rankin, 28 October 1941, Newcastle-upon-Tyne, England; lead guitar), Bruce Welch (b. 2 November 1941, Bognor Regis, Sussex, England; rhythm guitar), Jet Harris (b. Terence Hawkins, 6 July 1939, London, England; bass) and Tony Meehan (b. Daniel Meehan, 2 March 1943, London, England; drums). Soon after backing Cliff

Richard on his first single, they were signed as a group by EMI Columbia's A&R manager Norrie Paramor. After two singles under their old name, the Drifters, they issued the vocal 'Saturday Dance', which failed to sell. An abrupt change of fortune came in 1960 when they met singer/songwriter Jerry Lordan, who presented them with 'Apache'. Their instrumental was one of the finest of its era and dominated the UK number 1 position for six weeks, as well as being voted single of the year in several music papers. It was duly noted that they had knocked their singer's 'Please Don't Tease' off the top of the charts and, in doing so, firmly established themselves as important artists in their own right. The Shadows' influence on the new generation of groups that followed was immense. Marvin was revered as a guitarist, and although the group were firmly part of the British showbusiness establishment, their musical credibility was beyond question. A wealth of evocative instrumentals followed, including 'FBI', 'The Frightened City', 'The Savage' and 'Guitar Tango'. These Top 10 singles were interspersed with four formidable UK number 1 hits: 'Kon Tiki', 'Wonderful Land', 'Dance On' and 'Foot Tapper'. Despite such successes, the group underwent personnel shifts. Both Tony Meehan and Jet Harris left the group to be replaced by drummer Brian Bennett (b. 9 February 1940, London, England) and bassist Brian Locking. Ironically, the Shadows soon found themselves competing against the combined forces of Jet Harris And Tony Meehan, who recorded some startling instrumentals in their own right, including the chart-topping 'Diamonds'.

The Shadows continued to chart consistently during 1963-64 with 'Atlantis', 'Shindig', 'Geronimo', 'Theme For Young Lovers' and 'The Rise And Fall Of Flingel Bunt', but it was clear that the Mersey beat boom had lessened their appeal. Throughout this period, they continued to appear in films with Cliff Richard and undertook acting and musical roles in *Aladdin And His Wonderful Lamp* at the London Palladium, which spawned the hit 'Genie With The Light Brown Lamp'. An attempted change of direction was notable in 1965 with the minor vocal hits, 'The Next Time I See Mary Ann' and 'Don't Make My Baby Blue'. Further movie and pantomime appearances followed, amid a decline in chart fortunes. At the end of 1968, the group announced that they intended to split up. In late 1969, a streamlined Shadows featuring Marvin, Rostill, Bennett and pianist Alan Hawkshaw toured Japan. Marvin then pursued some solo activities before reuniting with Welch for the Crosby, Stills & Nash-influenced Marvin, Welch & Farrar. The early 70s coincided with numerous personal dramas. Marvin became a Jehovah's Witness, Welch had a tempestuous relationship with singer Olivia Newton-John and Rostill was fatally electrocuted while playing his guitar. In 1974, the Shadows reconvened for *Rockin' With Curly Leads*, on which they were joined by bassist/producer Alan Tarney. Several live performances followed and the group were then offered the opportunity to represent the United Kingdom in the Eurovision Song Contest. They achieved second place with 'Let Me Be The One', which also provided them with their first UK Top 20 hit in 10 years. The stupendous success of an accompanying *20 Golden Greats* compilation effectively revitalized their career. By 1978, they were back in the UK Top 10 for the first time since 1965 with an instrumental reading of 'Don't Cry For Me Argentina'. That feat was repeated several months later with 'Theme From The Deer Hunter (Cavatina)'. Regular tours and compilations followed and in 1983, the group received an Ivor Novello Award from the British Academy of Songwriters, Composers and Authors to celebrate their 25th anniversary. Long regarded as one of the great institutions of UK pop music, the Shadows have survived a generation of musical and cultural changes in fashion yet continue to please audiences with their instrumental abilities. It is, however, for their massive influence of five decades over budding young guitarists that they will be remembered. No UK 'beat combo' has ever been or is ever likely to be more popular.

●ALBUMS: *The Shadows* (Columbia 1961)★★★★, *Out Of The Shadows* (Columbia 1962)★★★★, *Dance With The Shadows* (Columbia 1964)★★★★, *The Sound Of The Shadows* (Columbia 1965)★★★★, *Shadow Music* (Columbia 1966)★★★, *Jigsaw* (Columbia 1967)★★★, *From Hank, Bruce, Brian And John* (Columbia 1967)★★★, with Cliff Richard *Established 1958* (1968)★★★, *Shades Of Rock* (Columbia 1970)★★★, *Rockin' With Curly Leads* (EMI 1974)★★★, *Specs Appeal* (EMI 1975)★★★, *Live At The Paris Olympia* (1975)★★, *Tasty* (1977)★★★, *Thank You Very Much* (1978)★★★, *Change Of Address* (1980)★★, *Hits Right Up Your Street* (1981)★★, *Life In The Jungle/Live At Abbey Road* (1982)★★, *XXV* (1983)★★★, *Guardian Angel* (1984)★★, *Moonlight Shadows* (1986)★★★, *Simply Shadows* (1987)★★★, *Stepping To The Shadows* (1989)★★★, *Reflections* (1991)★★★.

●COMPILATIONS: *The Shadows Greatest Hits* (Columbia 1963)★★★★, *More Hits* (Columbia 1965)★★★★, *Somethin' Else* (1969)★★★, *20 Golden Greats* (EMI 1977)★★★★, *String Of Hits* (1980)★★★★, *Another String Of Hot Hits* (1980)★★★, *At Their Very Best* (1989)★★★★, *Themes And Dreams* (1991)★★★, *The Early Years 1959-1966* 6-CD box set (EMI 1991)★★★★, *The First 20 Years At The Top* (EMI 1995)★★★★.

●FURTHER READING: *The Shadows By Themselves*, Shadows. *Foot Tapping: The Shadows 1958-1978*, George Thomson Geddes. *The Shadows: A History And Discography*, George Thomson Geddes. *The Story Of The Shadows: An Autobiography*, Shadows as told to Mike Reed. *Rock 'N' Roll: I Gave You The Best Years Of My Life: A Life In The Shadows*, Bruce Welch. *Funny Old World: The Life And Times Of John Henry Rostill*, Rob Bradford.

●FILMS: *Carnival Rock* (1957), *Expresso Bongo* (1960), *Finders Keepers* (1966).

SHADOWS OF KNIGHT

Formed in Chicago in 1965, the original line-up comprised Jim Sohns (vocals), Warren Rogers (lead guitar),

Jerry McGeorge (rhythm guitar), Norm Gotsch (bass) and Tom Schiffour (drums). As the house band at the city's Cellar club, the Shadows were already highly popular when they secured a recording contract. Their debut single, a cover version of the classic Them track, 'Gloria', was the climax to the quintet's stage act, but when the group toned down its mildly risqué lyric, they were rewarded with a US Top 10 hit. By this point Gotsch had been replaced, with Rogers switching to lead to accommodate new guitarist Joe Kelly. Their best-known line-up now established, the Shadows Of Knight enjoyed another minor chart entry with 'Oh Yeah', before completing their debut album. *Gloria* consisted of several Chicago R&B standards which, paradoxically, were patterned on British interpretations of the same material. Two excellent group originals, 'Light Bulb Blues' and 'It Happens That Way', revealed an emergent, but sadly under used, talent. *Back Door Men* offered a slightly wider perspective with versions of 'Hey Joe' and 'Tomorrow's Gonna Be Another Day' (also recorded by the Monkees), but the highlight was an inspired interpretation of 'Bad Little Woman', originally recorded by Irish group the Wheels. Dave 'The Hawk' Wolinski replaced Warren Rogers when the latter was drafted in late 1966. This was the prelude to wholesale changes when, on 4 July 1967, Sohns fired the entire group. The singer subsequently reappeared fronting a new line-up - John Fisher, Dan Baughman, Woody Woodfuff and Kenny Turkin - and a new recording deal with the bubblegum Super K label. 'Shake' gave the group a final US Top 50 entry, but its unashamed pop approach owed little to the heritage of the 'old'. Further releases for the same outlet proved equally disappointing, while an attempt at recreating the past with 'Gloria 69' was unsuccessful. Sohns has led several versions of his group over the ensuing years, McGeorge found fleeting notoriety as a member of H.P. Lovecraft, while Wolinski found fame as a member of Rufus and his work with Michael Jackson.

●ALBUMS: *Gloria* (Dunwich 1966)★★★, *Back Door Men* (Dunwich 1967)★★★, *The Shadows Of Knight* (Super-K 1969)★★★.

●COMPILATIONS: *Gloria* (1979)★★★, *Gee-El-O-Are-I-Ay* (1985)★★★, *Raw And Alive At The Cellar: 1966* (1992)★★.

SHANGRI-LAS

Late entrants in the early 60s school of 'girl groups', the Shangri-Las comprised two pairs of sisters, Mary-Ann (b. *c*.1948) and Margie Ganser (b. *c*.1947, d. August 1996) and Betty (b. *c*.1948) and Mary Weiss (b. *c*.1947). During 1963 they were discovered by George 'Shadow' Morton and recorded two singles under the name Bon Bons before signing to the newly formed Red Bird label. Relaunched as the Shangri-Las, they secured a worldwide hit with 'Remember (Walkin' In The Sand)', a delightful arrangement complete with the sound of crashing waves and crying seagulls. It was the sound-effect of a reving motorbike engine which opened their distinctive follow-up, 'Leader Of The Pack', which was even more successful and a prime candidate for the 'death disc' genre with its narrative of teenage love cut short because of a motorcycle accident. By 1966, Margie Ganser had left the group, although this had little effect on their popularity or output. They had already found a perfect niche, specializing in the doomed romanticism of American teenage life and unfolding a landscape filled with misunderstood adolescents, rebel boyfriends, disapproving parents, the foreboding threat of pregnancy and, inevitably, tragic death. This hit formula occasionally wore thin but Shadow Morton could always be relied upon to engineer a gripping production. During their closing hit phase in 1966/67, the group recorded two songs, 'I Can Never Go Home Anymore' and 'Past Present And Future', which saw the old teenage angst transmogrified into an almost tragic, sexual neuroticism. The enduring commercial quality of their best work was underlined by consistent repackaging and the successive chart reappearances of the biker anthem, 'Leader Of The Pack'.

●ALBUMS: *Leader Of The Pack* (Red Bird 1965)★★★, *'65* (Red Bird 1965)★★★.

●COMPILATIONS: *Golden Hits* (Mercury 1966)★★★, *The Best Of the Shangri-La's* (Bac-Trac 1985)★★★, *16 Greatest Hits* (1993)★★★, *Myrmidons Of Melodrama* (RPM 1995)★★★.

●FURTHER READING: *Girl Groups: The Story Of A Sound*, Alan Betrock.

SHANNON, DEL

b. Charles Westover, 30 December 1934, Coopersville, Michigan, USA, d. 8 February 1990. From the plethora of clean, American, post doo-wop male vocalists to find enormous success in the early 60s, only a small handful retained musical credibility. Shannon was undoubtedly from this pedigree. More than 30 years after his chart debut, Shannon's work is still regularly played. His early musical interests took him under the country influence of the legendary Hank Williams. Shannon's first record release, however, was pure gutsy pop; the infectious melody was written by accident while rehearsing in the local Hi-Lo club with keyboard player Max Crook (Maximillian). The song was 'Runaway', a spectacular debut that reached the top of the charts in the USA and UK, and was subsequently recorded by dozens of admiring artists. The single, with its shrill sounding Musitron (an instrument created by Crook) together with Shannon's falsetto, was irresistible. Johnny Bienstock, who was running Big Top Records in New York, received a telephone order following a Miami radio station's playing of the track. The order was for an unprecedented 39,000 copies. At that stage Bienstock knew he had unleashed a major star. What is not generally known is that Shannon sang flat on all the recordings of the song. Bienstock and a colleague went into the studio overnight, and sped up and redubbed the master tape so that Shannon's voice was correct. The record was released a full 10 seconds shorter, and nobody, including Shannon, ever noticed. He succeeded, however, where others failed, due to his talent as a composer and his apparent

maturity, appealing to the public with a clear youthful strident voice. This paradox was cleared up many years later, when it was discovered that he was five years older than stated. Had this come out in 1961, it is debatable whether he would have competed successfully alongside his fresh-faced contemporaries. His teenage tales of loneliness, despair, broken hearts, failed relationships, infidelity and ultimate doom, found a receptive audience; Shannon rarely used the word 'love' in his lyrics. Even the plaintive, almost happy, 1962 hit 'Swiss Maid' combined his trademark falsetto with yodelling, ending with the heroine dying, forlorn and unhappy. Over the next three years Shannon continued to produce and write his own material with great success, especially in Britain, where his run of 10 consecutive hits ended with 'Sue's Gotta Be Mine' in October 1963. In the interim, he had produced several memorable Top 10 successes, including the bitingly acerbic 'Hats Off To Larry' and 'Little Town Flirt', which betrayed an almost misogynistic contempt. The reworked themes of his songs were now beginning to pale, and together with the growth of Merseybeat, Shannon's former regular appearances in the charts became sporadic, even although he was the first US artist to record a Beatles song, 'From Me To You'.

Shannon worked steadily for the next 25 years, enjoying a few more hit singles including a cover version of Bobby Freeman's 'Do You Wanna Dance', followed by 'Handy Man', formerly a hit for Jimmy Jones, from whom he 'borrowed' his famous falsetto. In 1965 'Keep Searchin'' was Shannon's last major success. The song had an elegiac feel, recalling an era of innocence already passed. Throughout the 60s and 70s Shannon was a regular visitor to Britain where he found a smaller but more appreciative audience. He acquired many professional admirers over the years including Jeff Lynne, Tom Petty and Dave Edmunds, who variously helped him rise above his sad decline into a nether world of alcohol and pills. The 1981 Petty-produced *Drop Down And Get Me* was critically well-received but sold poorly. Ironically, he received a belated hit in America with 'Sea Of Love', which found favour in 1982. This led to a brief renaissance for him in the USA. Although Shannon was financially secure through wise property investment, he still performed regularly. Ultimately, however, he was branded to rock 'n' roll revival tours that finally took their toll on 8 February 1990, when a severely depressed Shannon pointed a .22 calibre rifle to his head and pulled the trigger, ending the misery echoed in his catalogue of hits.

●ALBUMS: *Runaway With Del Shannon* (Big Top/London 1961)★★★★, *Hats Off To Del Shannon* (London 1963)★★★★, *Little Town Flirt* (Big Top 1963)★★★★, *Handy Man* (Amy 1964)★★★★, *Del Shannon Sings Hank Williams* (Amy 1965)★★, *1,661 Seconds With Del Shannon* (Amy 1965)★★★, *This Is My Bag* (Liberty 1966)★★, *Total Commitment* (Liberty 1966)★★, *The Further Adventures Of Charles Westover* (Liberty 1968)★★, *Live In England* (United Artists 1972)★★, *Drop Down And Get Me* (1981)★★★, *Rock On* (1991)★★.

●COMPILATIONS:*The Best Of Del Shannon* (Dot 1967)★★★★, *The Vintage Years* (Sire 1975)★★★★, *The Del Shannon Collection* (Line 1987)★★★★, *Runaway Hits* (Edsel 1990)★★★★, *I Go To Pieces* (Edsel 1990)★★★★, *Looking Back, His Biggest Hits* (1991)★★★★, *Greatest Hits* (Charly 1993)★★★★.
●FILMS: *It's Trad, Dad* aka *Ring-A-Ding Rhythm* (1962).

SHAPIRO, HELEN

b. 28 September 1946, Bethnal Green, London, England. Helen Shapiro drew considerable attention when, as a 14-year-old schoolgirl, she scored a UK Top 3 hit with 'Don't Treat Me Like A Child'. A deep intonation belied her youth, and by the end of 1961 the singer had scored two chart-topping singles with 'You Don't Know' and 'Walkin' Back To Happiness'. This success was maintained the following year with 'Tell Me What He Said' (number 2) and 'Little Miss Lonely' (number 8), as Helen won concurrent polls as 'Best British Female Singer' and was voted 'Best Newcomer' by the Variety Club of Great Britain. However, having recorded the original version of 'It's My Party' during an artistically fruitful session in Nashville, Helen was disappointed when an acetate reached Lesley Gore, who enjoyed a massive international hit using a similar arrangement. Shapiro's producer, Norrie Paramor, also vetoed the opportunity to record 'Misery', composed with Helen in mind by John Lennon and Paul McCartney. Indeed the advent of the Beatles helped undermine the singer's career. Despite being younger than many beat group members, Shapiro was perceived as belonging to a now outmoded era and despite a series of excellent singles, was eclipsed by 'newcomers' Cilla Black and Dusty Springfield. The late 60s proved more fallow still and, barring one pseudonymous release, Helen did not record at all between 1970-75. A Russ Ballard song, 'Can't Break The Habit' became a minor hit in Europe during 1977 and in turn engendered *All For The Love Of The Music*, a set sadly denied a UK release. Six years later Shapiro resurfaced on writer Charlie Gillett's Oval label. *Straighten Up And Fly Right* showed the singer had lost none of her early power and this excellent collection of standards was rightly acclaimed. An equally confident collaboration with jazz musician Humphrey Lyttelton ensued, since which Helen Shapiro has maintained a high profile through radio, television and live appearances, singing jazz-influenced big band material and gospel songs. She also made an impressive London cabaret debut at the Café Royal in 1995.
●ALBUMS: *Tops With Me* (Columbia 1962)★★★★, *Helen's Sixteen* (Columbia 1963)★★★★, *Helen In Nashville* (Columbia 1963)★★, *Helen Hits Out* (Columbia 1964)★★★, *All For The Love Of The Music* (1977)★★★, *Straighten Up And Fly Right* (1983)★★★, *Echoes Of The Duke* (1985)★★★, *The Quality Of Mercer* (1987)★★★★, *Nothing But The Best* (1995)★★★.
●COMPILATIONS: *Twelve Hits And A Miss Shapiro* (Encore 1967)★★★, *The Very Best Of Helen Shapiro* (Columbia 1974)★★★★, *The 25th Anniversary Album* (1986)★★★★, *The EP Collection* (1989)★★★★, *Sensational! The Uncollected Helen Shapiro* (RPM 1995)★★★.
●FURTHER READING: *Walking Back To Happiness*, Helen Shapiro, *Helen Shapiro: Pop Princess*, John S. Janson.
●FILMS: *It's Trad, Dad* aka *Ring-A-Ding Rhythm* (1962).

SHARP, DEE DEE

b. Dione LaRue, 9 September 1945, Philadelphia, Pennsylvania, USA. A backing vocalist for the Cameo-Parkway labels, Dee Dee Sharp was the uncredited voice on Chubby Checker's 'Slow Twistin'' single. Her own debut, 'Mashed Potato Time', was recorded at the same session and thanks to the power of Dick Clark's *American Bandstand* television show this energetic, excited song became an immediate success. Cameo sadly chose to milk its dance-based appeal and releases such as 'Gravy (For My Mashed Potatoes)' and 'Do The Bird' packaged her as a temporary novelty act at the expense of an untapped potential. Dee Dee resurfaced in the 70s on the TSOP/Philadelphia International labels. Married to producer Kenny Gamble, she scored two minor soul hits with 'I'm Not In Love' (1976 - a cover of the 10cc hit) and 'I Love You Anyway' (1981).
●ALBUMS: *It's Mashed Potato Time* (Cameo 1962)★★★, *Songs Of Faith* (Cameo 1962)★★, with Chubby Checker *Down To Earth* (Cameo 1962)★★, *Do The Bird* (Cameo 1963)★★★, *All The Hits* (Cameo 1963)★★, *Down Memory Lane* (Cameo 1963)★★, *What Color Is Love* (1978)★★★.
●COMPILATIONS: *Biggest Hits* (Cameo 1963)★★★, *18 Golden Hits* (Cameo 1964)★★★.
●FILMS: *Don't Knock The Twist* (1962).

SHAW, SANDIE

b. Sandra Goodrich, 26 February 1947, Dagenham, Essex, England. Discovered by singer Adam Faith, Shaw was taken under the imperious wing of his manager Eve Taylor and launched as a teenage pop star in 1964. Her first single, 'As Long As You're Happy', proved unsuccessful but the follow-up, an excellent reading of Burt Bacharach and Hal David's '(There's) Always Something There To Remind Me' reached number 1 in the UK. A striking performer, known for her imposing height, model looks and bare feet, Shaw's star shone for the next three years with a series of hits, mainly composed by her songwriter/producer Chris Andrews. His style, specializing in abrupt, jerky, oom-pah rhythms and plaintive ballads, served Sandie well, especially on the calypso-inspired 'Long Live Love', which provided her second UK number 1 in 1965. By the following year, Shaw's chart placings were slipping and Taylor was keen to influence her towards cabaret. Chosen to represent Britain in the 1967 Eurovision Song Contest, Shaw emerged triumphant with the Bill Martin/Phil Coulter-composed 'Puppet On A String', which gave her a third UK number 1. After one further Martin/Coulter hit, 'Tonight In Tokyo', she returned to Andrews with only limited success. By 1969 she was back on the novelty trail with Peter Callender's translation of the French 'Monsieur Dupont'. Attempts to launch Shaw as a family entertainer were hampered by salacious newspaper reports and during the 70s, troubled by a failed marriage to fashion entrepreneur Jeff Banks, she effectively retired. In the early 80s she was rediscovered by Heaven 17 offshoots BEF, and recorded a middling version of 'Anyone Who Had A Heart', previously a number 1 for her old rival Cilla Black. The Shaw resurgence was completed when she was heavily promoted by Smiths vocalist Morrissey, one of whose compositions, 'Heaven Knows I'm Miserable Now' was clearly inspired by the title of Shaw's failed 60s single, 'Heaven Knows I'm Missing You Now'. With instrumental backing from the Smiths, Shaw enjoyed a brief chart comeback with 'Hand In Glove' in 1984. In 1986, she reached the lower regions of the UK chart with a cover of Lloyd Cole's 'Are You Ready To Be Heartbroken?' Her comeback album, on Rough Trade, featured songs by Morrissey, the Smiths and Jesus And Mary Chain.

●ALBUMS: *Sandie Shaw* (Pye 1965)★★★, *Me* (Pye 1965)★★★, *Puppet On A String* (Pye 1967)★★, *Love Me, Please Love Me* (Pye 1967)★★, *The Sandie Shaw Supplement* (Pye 1968)★★, *Reviewing The Situation* (Pye 1969)★★, *Hello Angel* (1988)★★.

●COMPILATIONS: *Golden Hits Of Sandie Shaw* (Golden Guinea 1965)★★★★, *Sandie Sings* (Golden Guinea 1967)★★★★, *The Golden Hits Of Sandie Shaw* (Marble Arch 1968)★★★★, *A Golden Hour Of Sandie Shaw - Greatest Hits* (1974)★★★★ *20 Golden Pieces* (1986)★★★★ *The Sandie Shaw Golden CD Collection* (1989)★★★★ *The EP Collection* (1991)★★★★ *The 64/67 Complete Sandie Shaw Set* (1993)★★★★ *Nothing Less Than Brilliant: The Best Of Sandie Shaw* (Virgin 1994)★★★★ *Cover To Cover* (Emporio 1995)★★★.

●FURTHER READING: *The World At My Feet*, Sandie Shaw.

SHEARING, GEORGE

b. 13 August 1919, London, England. Shearing was born blind but started to learn piano at the age of three. After limited training and extensive listening to recorded jazz, he began playing at hotels, clubs and pubs in the London area, sometimes as a single, occasionally with dance bands. In 1940 he joined Harry Parry's popular band and also played with Stéphane Grappelli. Shortly after visiting the USA in 1946, Shearing decided to settle there. Although at this time in his career he was influenced by bop pianists, notably Bud Powell, it was a complete break with this style that launched his career as a major star. Developing the locked-hands technique of playing block-chords, and accompanied by a discreet rhythm section of guitar, bass, drums and vibraphone, he had a succession of hugely popular records including 'September In The Rain' and his own composition, 'Lullaby Of Birdland'. With shifting personnel, which over the years included

Cal Tjader, Margie Hyams, Denzil Best, Israel Crosby, Joe Pass and Gary Burton, the Shearing quintet remained popular until 1967. Later, Shearing played with a trio, as a solo and increasingly in duo. Among his collaborations have been sets with the Montgomery Brothers, Marian McPartland, Brian Torff, Jim Hall, Hank Jones and Kenny Davern (on a rather polite dixieland selection). Over the years he has worked fruitfully with singers, including Peggy Lee, Ernestine Anderson, Carmen McRae, and, especially, Mel Tormé, with whom he performed frequently in the late 80s and early 90s at festivals, on radio and record dates. Shearing's interest in classical music resulted in some performances with concert orchestras in the 50s and 60s, and his solos frequently touch upon the musical patterns of Claude Debussy and, particularly, Erik Satie. Indeed, Shearing's delicate touch and whimsical nature should make him an ideal interpreter of Satie's work. As a jazz player Shearing has sometimes been the victim of critical indifference and even hostility. Mostly, reactions such as these centre upon the long period when he led his quintet. It might well be that the quality of the music was often rather lightweight but a second factor was the inability of some commentators on the jazz scene to accept an artist who had achieved wide public acceptance and financial success. That critical disregard should follow Shearing into his post-quintet years is inexplicable and unforgivable. Many of his late performances, especially his solo albums and those with Torff, bassist Neil Swainson, and Tormé, are superb examples of a pianist at the height of his powers. Inventive and melodic, his improvisations are unblushingly romantic but there is usually a hint of whimsy which happily reflects the warmth and offbeat humour of the man himself.

●ALBUMS: *George Shearing Quintet* (Discovery 1949)★★★, *Piano Solo* (Savoy 1950)★★★, *Souvenirs* (London 1951)★★★, *You're Hearing The George Shearing Quartet* (MGM 1950)★★★, *Touch Of Genius* (MGM 1951)★★★, *I Hear Music* (MGM 1952)★★★, *When Lights Are Low* (MGM 1953)★★★, *An Evening With George Shearing* (MGM 1954)★★★, *Shearing In Hi-Fi* (MGM 1955)★★★★, *The Shearing Spell* (Capitol 1955)★★★, *By Request* (London 1956)★★★, *Latin Escapade* (Capitol 1956)★★★, *Velvet Carpet* (Capitol 1956)★★★, *Black Satin* (Capitol 1957)★★★, *Shearing Piano* (Capitol 1957)★★★, *Burnished Brass* (Capitol 1958)★★★, *Latin Lace* (Capitol 1958)★★★, with Peggy Lee *Americana Hotel* (1959)★★★★, *Blue Chiffon* (Capitol 1959)★★★, *Shearing On Stage* (Capitol 1959)★★★, *Latin Affair* (Capitol 1959)★★★, *White Satin* (Capitol 1960)★★★, *On The Sunny Side Of The Strip* (Capitol 1960)★★★, *San Francisco Scene* (Capitol 1960)★★★, *The Shearing Touch* (Capitol 1960)★★★, with the Montgomery Brothers *Love Walked In* (Jazzland 1961)★★★, *Mood Latino* (Capitol 1961)★★★, *Satin Affair* (Capitol 1961)★★★, *Nat 'King Cole' Sings/George Shearing Plays* (1962)★★★★★, *Soft And Silky* (MGM 1962)★★★, *Jazz Moments* (Capitol 1963)★★★, *Jazz Concert* (1963)★★★, *Bossa Nova*

(Capitol 1963)★★★, *Deep Velvet* (Capitol 1964)★★★, *Rare Form* (Capitol 1965)★★★, *Out Of The Woods* (Capitol 1965)★★★, *Classic Shearing* (Verve 1966)★★★, *That Fresh Feeling* (Capitol 1966)★★★, *George Shearing Today* (Capitol 1968)★★★, *Fool On The Hill* (Capitol 1969)★★★, *My Ship* (1974)★★★, *Light, Airy And Swinging* (1974)★★★, *The Way We Are* (1974)★★★, *Continental Experience* (1975)★★★, with Stéphane Grappelli *The Reunion* (1976)★★★, *The Many Facets Of George Shearing* (1976)★★★, *500 Miles High* (MPS 1977)★★★, *Windows* (1977)★★★, *On Target* (1979)★★, with Brian Torff *Blues Alley Jazz* (Concord 1979)★★★, *Getting In The Swing Of Things* (1979)★★★, *On A Clear Day* (1980)★★★, with Carmen McRae *Two For The Road* (Concord 1980)★★★, with Marian McPartland *Alone Together* (Concord 1981)★★★, with Jim Hall *First Edition* (Concord 1981)★★★, *An Evening With Mel Tormé And George Shearing* (1982)★★★, with Mel Tormé *Top Drawer* (1983)★★★, *Bright Dimensions* (1984)★★★, *Live At The Cafe Carlyle* (Concord 1984)★★★, *Grand Piano* (Concord 1985)★★★, with Tormé *An Elegant Evening* (1985)★★★, *George Shearing And Barry Treadwell Play The Music Of Cole Porter* (Concord 1986)★★★, *More Grand Piano* (Concord 1986)★★★, *Breakin' Out* (Concord 1987)★★★, *Dexterity* (Concord 1987)★★★, *A Vintage Year* (1987)★★★, with Ernestine Anderson *A Perfect Match* (Concord 1988)★★★, with Hank Jones *The Spirit Of '76* (Concord 1988)★★★, *Piano* (Concord 1989)★★★, *George Shearing In Dixieland* (Concord 1989)★★, with Tormé *Mel And George 'Do' World War II* (1990)★★★, *I Hear A Rhapsody* (Telarc 1992)★★★, *Walkin'* (Telarc 1995)★★★.
●COMPILATIONS: *The Young George Shearing (1939-44)* (1961)★★★, *The Best Of George Shearing* (MFP 1983)★★★, *White Satin - Black Satin* (Capitol 1991)★★★, *The Capitol Years* (Capitol 1991)★★★★.
●FILMS: *The Big Beat* (1957).

SHERIDAN, MIKE, AND THE NIGHTRIDERS

Remembered as one of the finest Birmingham groups of the beat era, Mike Sheridan And The Nightriders formed in the early 60s around a line-up of Sheridan (vocals), Dave Pritchard (guitar), Roger Spencer (drums) and Greg Masters (bass). Signing to Columbia Records, their debut single was 'Tell Me Watcha Gonna Do' in 1963. In the same year they also released a version of 'Please Mr. Postman'. By 1964 and their third single, 'What A Sweet Thing That Was', they had been joined by Roy Wood as additional guitarist. One final single, 'Here I Stand', emerged, but no chart success resulted. Staying with Columbia, the group changed its suffix in 1965 to become Mike Sheridan's Lot. However, neither 'Take My Hand' nor 'Don't Turn Your Back On Me, Babe' resulted in chart success, and Sheridan left to pursue a solo career in 1966 (releasing the first single on the Gemini label, 'Follow Me Follow'). The remaining members of the Nightriders/Lot

released one further single before Wood formed the Move. With the addition of Jeff Lynne, the remainder of the Nightriders eventually became the Idle Race. A compilation documenting all the single releases by both versions of this band was released in 1984. *Birmingham Beat* was most notable for the inclusion of 'Make Them Understand', Roy Wood's first published composition. Sheridan later worked with Rick Price in the Sheridan-Price duo, who recorded an album for Gemini Records in 1970.
●COMPILATIONS: *Birmingham Beat* (Edsel 1984)★★★.

SHERIDAN, TONY

b. Anthony Sheridan McGinnity, 21 May 1940, Norwich, Norfolk, England. Sheridan formed his first band, the Saints, in 1955, before moving to London. There he joined Vince Taylor And The Playboys in early 1959, with whom he played a residency in Hamburg, Germany. A popular attraction at clubs such as the Kaiserkeller with the Jets, that group soon evolved into the Beat Brothers with a line-up of Sheridan (vocals/guitar), Ken Packwood (guitar), Rick Richards (guitar), Colin Melander (bass), Ian Hines (keyboards) and Jimmy Doyle (drums), although their various formations changed almost constantly. Some of the more interesting personnel to pass through the Beat Brothers in these nebulous days at the Kaiserkeller were John Lennon, Paul McCartney, George Harrison, Stuart Sutcliffe and Pete Best. This line-up recorded with producer Bert Kaempfert at the controls, although by later in 1962 the Beat Brothers had been joined by Ringo Starr, Roy Young (keyboards) and Rikky Barnes (saxophone). Sheridan's first appearance at the infamous Star Club arrived on 12 May 1962, fronting the Tony Sheridan Quartet, who were later retitled the Star Combo. By 1964 he had teamed up with Glaswegian expatriates Bobb Patrick Big Six. However, with the Hamburg beat boom all but over by 1964, Sheridan travelled to Vietnam to play US army bases, accompanied by Volker Tonndorf (bass), Jimmy Doyle (drums) and vocalist Barbara Evers. He eventually returned to Hamburg to turn solo in 1968, where his cult status had not diminished - a reputation that endures to this day. Sheridan then converted to the Sannyasin religion, renamed himself Swami Probhu Sharan, living with his family in Wuppertal, Germany.
●ALBUMS: *My Bonnie* (Polydor 1962)★★, *The Beatles' First Featuring Tony Sheridan* (Polydor 1964)★★, *Just A Little Bit Of Tony Sheridan* (1964)★★, *The Best Of Tony Sheridan* (1964)★★, *Meet The Beat* (1965)★★, *Rocks On* (1974)★★, *On My Mind* (1976)★★, *Worlds Apart* (1978)★★.

SHERRILL, BILLY

b. Philip Campbell, 5 November 1936, Winston, Alabama, USA. Sherrill's father was a travelling evangelist - he is shown on horseback on the cover of Charlie Rich's album *Silver Linings* - and Sherrill played piano at his meetings. He also played saxophone in a local rock 'n' roll

band, Benny Cagle and the Rhythm Swingsters. In 1956 he left to work with Rick Hall in the R&B-styled Fairlanes. His 1958 Mercury single, 'Like Making Love', was covered for the UK market by Marty Wilde, and he had some success in Alabama with an instrumental, 'Tipsy', in 1960. He worked for Sun Records' new Nashville studios from 1961 to 1964; in particular, he brought out Charlie Rich's talent as a blues singer. He and Rick Hall then established the Fame studios in Nashville. In 1964 he started working for Columbia Records and he produced R&B records by Ted Taylor and the Staple Singers as well as an album by Elvis Presley's guitarist, Scotty Moore, *The Guitar That Changed The World*. He co-wrote and produced David Houston's US number 1 country hit, 'Almost Persuaded', and his subsequent hits with Houston include a duet with Tammy Wynette, 'My Elusive Dreams'. It was Sherrill who discovered Wynette and in 1968 they wrote 'Stand By Your Man' in half an hour and recorded it immediately. Although Sherrill's records crossed over to the pop market, he did not avoid country music instruments such as the steel guitar, although he did favour lavish orchestrations. He also discovered Tanya Tucker, Janie Frickie and Lacy J. Dalton, and has made successful records with Charlie Rich ('Behind Closed Doors', 'The Most Beautiful Girl'), George Jones, Marty Robbins and Barbara Mandrell. He became a freelance producer in 1980 but he continued to work with many of the same artists. He has produced over 10 albums apiece for David Allan Coe, George Jones and Tammy Wynette; other credits include *The Baron* for Johnny Cash and the soundtrack for the film, *Take This Job And Shove It*. His best works include two all-star country albums, *My Very Special Guests* with George Jones, and *Friendship* with Ray Charles. The friction between him and Elvis Costello while making the album, *Almost Blue*, was shown on a UK television documentary, but the album did very well and yielded a Top 10 hit, 'A Good Year For The Roses'.
● ALBUMS: *Classical Country* (1967)★★.

SHIRELLES

Formed in Passaic, New Jersey, USA, the Shirelles are arguably the archetypal 'girl-group'; Shirley Owens (b. 10 June 1941), Beverly Lee (b. 3 August 1941), Doris Kenner (b. 2 August 1941) and Addie 'Micki' Harris (b. 22 January 1940, d. 10 June 1982) were initially known as the uncomfortably named Poquellos. School friends for whom singing was simply a pastime, the quartet embarked on professional career when a classmate, Mary Jane Greenberg, recommended them to her mother. Florence Greenberg, an aspiring entrepreneur, signed them to her Tiara label, on which the resultant single, 'I Met Him On A Sunday', was a minor hit. This inspired the inauguration of a second outlet, Scepter, where the Shirelles secured pop immortality with 'Will You Love Me Tomorrow'. Here Alston's tender, aching vocal not only posed the ultimate question, but implied she already had decided 'yes' to her personal dilemma. One of pop's most treasured recordings, it was followed by a series of excep-

tional singles, 'Mama Said' (1961), 'Baby It's You' (1962) and 'Foolish Little Girl' (1963), which confirmed their exemplary position. The Shirelles' effect on other groups, including those in Britain, is incalculable, and the Beatles, the Merseybeats, and Manfred Mann are among those who covered their work. The quartet's progress was dealt a crucial setback when producer and arranger Luther Dixon left to take up another post. Newer Scepter acts, including Dionne Warwick, assumed the quartet's one-time prime position while a punitive record contract kept the group tied to the label. By the time the Shirelles were free to move elsewhere, it was too late to enjoy a contemporary career and the group was confined to the 'oldies' circuit. By combining sweetening strings with elements of church music and R&B, the group exerted an unconscious pivotal influence on all female vocal groups.
● ALBUMS: *Tonight's The Night* (Scepter 1961)★★★, *The Shirelles Sing To Trumpets And Strings* (Scepter/Top Rank 1961)★★★, *Baby It's You* (Scepter/Stateside 1962)★★★★, *Twist Party* (Scepter 1962)★★★, *Foolish Little Girl* (Scepter 1963)★★★, *It's A Mad Mad Mad Mad World* (Scepter 1963)★★, *The Shirelles Sing The Golden Oldies* (Scepter 1964)★, *Spontaneous Combustion* (Scepter 1997)★★, with King Curtis *Eternally Soul* (Wand 1970)★★★, *Tonight's The Night* (Wand 1971)★★★. Solo: Shirley Alston (Owens) *With A Little Help From My Friends* (1975)★★, *Lady Rose* (1977)★★.
● COMPILATIONS: *The Shirelles Hits* (Scepter/Stateside 1963)★★★★, *The Shirelles Greatest Hits Vol. 2* (Scepter 1967)★★★, *Remember When Vol. 1* (Wand 1972)★★★, *Remember When Vol 2* (Wand 1972)★★★, *Soulfully Yours* (1985)★★★, *Sha La La* (1985)★★★, *Lost And Found* (1987)★★★, *Greatest Hits* (1987)★★★★, *The Collection* (1990)★★★★, *The Best Of* (1992)★★★★, *16 Greatest Hits* (1993)★★★★, *Lost And Found: Rare And Unissued* (1994)★★★, *The Very Best Of ...* (Rhino 1994)★★★★, *The World's Greatest Girls Group* (Tomato/Rhino 1995)★★★★.
● FURTHER READING: *Girl Groups: The Story Of A Sound*, Alan Betrock.

SHORTER, WAYNE

b. 25 August 1933, Newark, New Jersey, USA. Shorter first played clarinet, taking up the tenor saxophone during his late teens. He studied music at New York University during the mid-50s before serving in the US army for two years. During his student days he had played with various bands, including that led by Horace Silver, and on his discharge encountered John Coltrane, with whom he developed many theoretical views on music. He was also briefly with Maynard Ferguson. In 1959 he became a member of Art Blakey's Jazz Messengers, remaining with the band until 1963. The following year he joined Miles Davis, staying until 1970. Late that year he teamed up with Joe Zawinul, whom he had first met in the Ferguson band, to form Weather Report. During his stints with Blakey and Davis Shorter had written extensively and his compositions had also formed the basis of several increasingly experimental record sessions under his own name for the Blue Note label. He continued to write for the new band and also for further dates under his own name and with V.S.O.P., with whom he worked in the mid- and late 70s. In the mid-80s he was leading his own band and also recording and touring with other musicians, thus reducing his activities with Weather Report. As a player, Shorter developed through his period with Blakey into a leading proponent of hard bop. His fiery, tough-toned and dramatically angular playing was well-suited to the aggressive nature of the Blakey band. During his time with Davis another side to his musical personality emerged, in which a more tender approach greatly enhanced his playing. This side had made its appearance earlier, on *Wayning Moments*, but was given greater scope with Davis. On Davis's *Bitches Brew*, Shorter also played soprano saxophone: two weeks later he employed this instrument throughout on his own *Super Nova*, playing with exotic enthusiasm. The years with Zawinul broadened his range still further, highlighting his appreciation of freer forms and giving rein to his delight in musical exotica. Although laying ground rules for many later fusion bands, Weather Report's distinction lay in the way the group allowed the two principals to retain their powerful musical personalities. Later, as the band began to sound more like other fusion bands, Shorter's exploratory nature found greater scope in the bands he formed away from Weather Report. As a composer, Shorter was responsible for some of the best work of the Blakey band of his era and also for many of Davis's stronger pieces of the late 60s. A major innovator and influence on hard boppers and fusionists alike, Shorter remains one of the most imaginative musicians in jazz, constantly seeking new horizons but retaining identifiable links with the past.

● ALBUMS: *The Vee Jay Years* (Affinity 1959)★★★★, *Introducing Wayne Shorter* (Vee Jay 1960)★★★★, *Wayne Shorter* (1959-62)★★★★, *Wayning Moments* (Vee Jay 1962)★★★, *Second Genesis* (Vee Jay 1963)★★★, *Night Dreamer* (Blue Note 1964)★★★★, *Juju* (Blue Note 1964)★★★★, *Speak No Evil* (Blue Note 1964)★★★★, *Night Dreamer* (Blue Note 1964)★★★, *The Best Of Wayne Shorter* (1964-67)★★★, *The Soothsayer* (1965)★★★, *The All-Seeing Eye* (Blue Note 1965)★★★★, *Etcetera* (1965)★★★, *Adam's Apple* (Blue Note 1966)★★★, *Schizophrenia* (Blue Note 1967)★★★, *Super Nova* (Blue Note 1969)★★★★, *Odyssey Of Iska* (1970)★★★, *Moto Grosso Feio* (c.1971)★★★, *Native Dancer* (Columbia 1974)★★★, *Atlantis* (CBS 1985)★★★, *Endangered Species* (1985)★★, *Phantom Navigator* (CBS 1987)★★, *Joy Ryder* (CBS 1987)★★★, with Herbie Hancock, Ron Carter, Wallace Roney, Tony Williams *A Tribute To Miles* (QWest/Reprise 1994)★★★, *All Seeing Eye* (Connoisseur 1994)★★★, *High Life* (Verve 1995)★★★.

SHUMAN, MORT

b. 12 November 1936, Brooklyn, New York, USA, d. 2 November 1991, London, England. After studying music, Shuman began writing songs with blues singer Doc Pomus in 1958. Early in 1959 two of their songs were Top 40 hits: 'Plain Jane' for Bobby Darin, and Fabian's 'I'm A Man'. During the next six years, their catalogue was estimated at over 500 songs, in a mixture of styles for a variety of artists. They included 'Surrender', 'Viva Las Vegas', 'Little Sister' and 'Kiss Me Quick' (Elvis Presley), 'Save The Last Dance For Me', 'Sweets For My Sweet' and 'This Magic Moment' (the Drifters), 'Teenager In Love' (Dion And The Belmonts), 'Can't Get Used To Losing You' (Andy Williams), 'Suspicion' (Terry Stafford), 'Seven Day Weekend' (Gary 'U.S.' Bonds) and 'Spanish Lace' (Gene McDaniels). Around the time of the team's break-up in 1965, Shuman collaborated with several other writers. These included John McFarland for Billy J. Kramer's UK number 1, 'Little Children', Clive Westlake for 'Here I Go Again' (the Hollies), ex-pop star Kenny Lynch, for 'Sha-La-La-La-Lee' (Small Faces), 'Love's Just A Broken Heart' (Cilla Black), producer Jerry Ragovoy for 'Get It While You Can' and 'Look At Granny Run, Run' (Howard Tate). Subsequently, Shuman moved to Paris, where he occasionally performed his own one-man show, and issued solo albums such as *Amerika* and *Imagine* ..., as well as writing several songs for Johnny Hallyday. In 1968 Shuman translated the lyrics of French composer Jacques Brel; these were recorded by many artists including Dusty Springfield, Scott Walker and Rod McKuen. Together with Eric Blau, he devised, adapted and wrote lyrics for the revue *Jacques Brel Is Alive And Well And Living In Paris*. Shuman also starred in the piece, which became a world-wide success. In October 1989, *Budgie*, a musical set in London's Soho district, with Shuman's music and Don Black's lyrics, opened in the West End. It starred former pop star, turned actor and entrepreneur, Adam Faith, and UK soap opera actress, Anita Dobson. The show closed after only three months, losing more than £1,000,000. Shuman wrote several other shows, including *Amadeo, Or How To Get Rid Of It*, based on an Ionesco play, a Hong Kong portrayal of *Madame Butterfly* and a reworking of Bertolt Brecht and Kurt Weill's opera *Aufstieg Und Fall Der Stadt Mahogonny*. None has yet reached the commercial theatre. After undergoing a liver operation in the spring of 1991, he died in London.

SILVER, HORACE

b. 2 September 1928, Norwalk, Connecticut, USA. Silver studied piano and tenor saxophone at school, settling on the former instrument for his professional career. Early influences included Portuguese folk music (from his father), blues and bop. He formed a trio for local gigs which included backing visiting musicians. One such visitor, Stan Getz, was sufficiently impressed to take the trio on the road with him in 1950. The following year Silver settled in New York, playing regularly at Birdland and other leading venues. In 1952 he began a long-lasting association with Blue Note, recording under his own name and with other leaders. In 1953 he formed a band named the Jazz Messengers with Art Blakey, who ater adopted the name for all his own groups. By 1956 Silver was leading his own quintet, exploring the reaches of bop and becoming a founding father of the hard bop movement. Silver's line-up - trumpet, tenor saxophone, piano, bass and drums - was subject to many changes over the years, but the calibre of musicians he hired was always very high. Among his sidemen were Donald Byrd, Art Farmer, Michael and Randy Brecker, Woody Shaw, Blue Mitchell, Hank Mobley and Joe Henderson. He continued to lead fine bands, touring and recording extensively during the following decades, and in the late 80s and early 90s could still be heard at concerts around the world performing to an impressively high standard. As a pianist Silver is a powerful, thrusting player with an urgent rhythmic pulse. As a composer, his early musical interests have constantly reappeared in his work and his incorporation into hard bop of elements of gospel and R&B have ensured that for all the overall complexities of sound his music remains highly accessible. Several of his pieces have become modern standards, among them 'Opus de Funk', 'Doodlin'', 'Nica's Dream' and 'The Preacher'. The introduction on Steely Dan's 'Ricki Don't Lose That Number' was strongly influenced by Silver's memorable 'Song For My Father'. During the 70s Silver experimented with compositions and recordings that set his piano-playing and the standard quintet against larger orchestral backing, often achieving far more success than others who have written and performed in this way.

●ALBUMS: *Introducing The Horace Silver Trio* (Blue Note 1953)★★, *Horace Silver Trio* (Blue Note 1954)★★★, *Horace Silver And The Jazz Messengers* i (Blue Note 1954)★★★★, *Horace Silver Quintet Vols. 1 & 2* (Blue Note 1955)★★★, *Horace Silver And The Jazz Messengers* ii (Blue Note 1955)★★★, *Six Pieces Of Silver* (Blue Note 1956)★★★★, *Silver's Blue* (Epic 1956)★★★, *The Stylings Of Silver* (Blue Note 1957)★★★, *Further Explorations* (Blue Note 1958)★★★, *Finger Poppin'* (Blue Note 1959)★★★★, *Blowin' The Blues Away* (Blue Note 1959)★★★, *Horace-Scope* (Blue Note 1960)★★★, *Doin The Thing At The Village Gate* (Blue Note 1961)★★★★, *The Tokyo Blues* (Blue Note 1962)★★★, *Silver's Serenade* (Blue Note 1963)★★★★, *Song For My Father* (Blue Note 1964)★★★★★, *Live 1964* (1964)★★★, *Cape Verdean Blues* (Blue Note 1965)★★★★, *The Jody Grind* (Blue Note 1966)★★★★★, *Serenade To A Soul Sister* (Blue Note 1968)★★★, *You Gotta Take A Little Love* (Blue Note 1969)★★★, *That Healin' Feelin'* (The United States Of Mind, Phase I) (1970)★★, *Total Response (Phase II)* (c.1971)★★, *All (Phase III)* (c.1973)★★★, *Silver 'N' Brass* (1975)★★, *Silver 'N' Wood* (1976)★★, *Silver 'N' Voices* (1976)★★, *Silver 'N' Percussion* (1977)★★, *Silver 'N' Strings Play The Music Of The Spheres* (1978)★★, *Guides To Growing Up* (1981)★★, *Spiritualizing The Senses* (1983)★★, *There's No Need To Struggle* (1983)★★, *It's Got To Be Funky* (Columbia 1993)★★, *Pencil Packin' Papa* (1994)★★★, *The Hardbop Grandpop* (Impulse 1996)★★★.

●COMPILATIONS: *The Best Of Horace Silver* (Blue Note 1969)★★★, *The Best Of Horace Silver - The Blue Note Years* (Blue Note 1988).

SILVERSTEIN, SHEL

b. Shelby Silverstein, 1932, Chicago, Illinois, USA. A former artist with *Stars And Stripes* magazine, Silverstein joined the staff of *Playboy* at its inception during the early 50s and for almost two decades his cartoons were a regular feature of the publication. He later became a successful illustrator and author of children's books, including *Uncle Shelby's ABZ Book*, *Uncle Shelby's Zoo* and *Giraffe And A Half*. Silverstein was also drawn to the folk scene emanating from Chicago's Gate Of Horn and New York's Bitter End, latterly becoming a respected composer and performer of the genre. Early 60s collaborations with Bob Gibson were particularly memorable and in 1961 Silverstein completed *Inside Folk Songs* which included the original versions of 'The Unicorn' and '25 Minutes To Go', later popularized, respectively, by the Irish Rovers and Brothers Four. Silverstein provided 'novelty' hits for Johnny Cash ('A Boy Named Sue') and Loretta Lynn, ('One's On The Way'), but an association with Dr. Hook proved to be the most fruitful. A series of successful singles ensued, notably 'Sylvia's Mother' and 'The Cover Of *Rolling Stone*', and a grateful group reciprocated by supplying the backing on *Freakin' At The Freaker's Ball*. This ribald set included many of Silverstein's best-known compositions from this period, including 'Polly In A Porny', 'I Got Stoned And I Missed It' and 'Don't Give A Dose To The One You Love Most', the last of which was adopted in several anti-venereal disease campaigns. *The Great Conch Robbery*, released on the traditional music outlet Flying Fish, was less scatological in tone, since which Silverstein has adopted a less public profile.

●ALBUMS: *Hairy Jazz* (Elektra 1959)★★★, *Inside Folk Songs* (Atlantic 1961)★★★, *I'm So Good I Don't Have To Brag* (Cadet 1965)★★★, *Drain My Brain* (Cadet 1966)★★★, *A Boy Named Sue* (RCA Victor 1968)★★★, *Freakin' At The Freaker's Ball* (1969)★★★, *Songs And Stories* (1972)★★, *The Great Conch Train Robbery* (1979)★★.

SIMON AND GARFUNKEL

This highly successful vocal duo first played together during their early years in New York. Paul Simon (b. 13 October 1941, Newark, New Jersey, USA) and Art Garfunkel (b. Arthur Garfunkel, 5 November 1941, Queens, New York City, USA) were initially inspired by the Everly Brothers and under the name Tom And Jerry enjoyed a US hit with the rock 'n' roll-styled 'Hey Schoolgirl'. They also completed an album that was later reissued after their rise to international prominence in the 60s. Garfunkel subsequently returned to college and Simon pursued a solo career before the duo reunited in 1964 for *Wednesday Morning 3AM*. A strong, harmonic work, which included an acoustic reading of 'The Sound Of Silence', the album did not sell well enough to encourage the group to stay together. While Simon was in England the folk rock-boom was in the ascendant and producer Tom Wilson made the presumptuous but prescient decision to overdub 'Sound Of Silence' with electric instrumentation. Within weeks, the song was number 1 in the US charts, and Simon and Garfunkel were hastily reunited. An album titled after their million-selling single was rush-released early in 1966 and proved a commendable work. Among its major achievements was 'Homeward Bound', an evocative and moving portrayal of life on the road, which went on to become a transatlantic hit. The solipsistic 'I Am A Rock' was another international success with such angst-ridden lines as, 'I have no need of friendship, friendship causes pain'. In keeping with the social commentary that permeated their mid-60s work, the group included two songs whose theme was suicide: 'A Most Peculiar Man' and 'Richard Cory'. Embraced by a vast following, especially among the student population, the duo certainly looked the part with their college scarves, duffle coats and cerebral demeanour. Their next single, 'The Dangling Conversation', was their most ambitious lyric to date and far too esoteric for the Top 20. Nevertheless, the work testified to their artistic courage and boded well for the release of a second album within a year: *Parsley, Sage, Rosemary And Thyme*. The album took its title from a repeated line in 'Scarborough Fair', which was their excellent harmonic weaving of that traditional song and another, 'Canticle'. An accomplished work, the album had a varied mood from the grandly serious 'For Emily, Whenever I May Find Her' to the bouncy '59th Street Bridge Song (Feelin' Groovy)' (subsequently a hit for Harpers Bizarre). After two strong but uncommercial singles, 'At The Zoo' and 'Fakin' It', the duo contributed to the soundtrack of the 1968 film, *The Graduate*. The key song in the film was 'Mrs Robinson' which provided the group with one of their biggest international sellers. That same year saw the release of *Bookends*, a superbly crafted work, ranging from the serene 'Save The Life Of My Child' to the personal odyssey 'America' and the vivid imagery of 'Old Friends'. *Bookends* is still felt by many to be their finest work.

In 1969 the duo released 'The Boxer', a long single that nevertheless found commercial success on both sides of the Atlantic. This classic single reappeared on the group's next album, the celebrated *Bridge Over Troubled Water*. One of the best-selling albums of all time (303 weeks on the UK chart), the work's title track became a standard with its lush, orchestral arrangement and contrasting tempo. Heavily gospel-influenced, the album included several well-covered songs such as 'Keep The Customer Satisfied', 'Cecilia' and 'El Condor Pasa'. While at the peak of their commercial success, with an album that dominated the top of the chart listings for months, the duo became irascible and their partnership abruptly ceased. The release of a *Greatest Hits* package in 1972 included four previously unissued live tracks and during the same year the duo performed together at a benefit concert for Senator George McGovern. In 1981 they were again

reunited. The results were captured in 1981 on *The Concert In Central Park*. After a long break, a further duet occurred on the hit single 'My Little Town' in 1975. Although another studio album was undertaken, the sessions broke down and Simon transferred the planned material to his 1983 solo *Hearts And Bones*. In the autumn of 1993 Paul Simon and Art Garfunkel settled their differences long enough to complete 21 sell-out dates in New York.

● ALBUMS: *The Sound Of Silence* (Columbia 1966)★★★, *Parsley, Sage, Rosemary And Thyme* (Columbia 1966)★★★★, *The Graduate* soundtrack (Columbia 1968)★★★, *Wednesday Morning 3AM* (Columbia 1968)★★, *Bookends* (Columbia 1968)★★★★★, *Bridge Over Troubled Water* (Columbia 1970)★★★★, *The Concert In Central Park* (Geffen 1981)★★★.

● COMPILATIONS: *Simon And Garfunkel's Greatest Hits* (Columbia 1972)★★★★, *The Simon And Garfunkel Collection* (1981)★★★★★, *The Definitive Simon And Garfunkel* (1992)★★★★.

● FURTHER READING: *Simon & Garfunkel: A Biography In Words & Pictures*, Michael S. Cohen. *Paul Simon: Now And Then*, Spencer Leigh. *Paul Simon*, Dave Marsh. *Simon And Garfunkel*, Robert Matthew-Walker. *Bookends: The Simon And Garfunkel Story*, Patrick Humphries. *The Boy In The Bubble: A Biography Of Paul Simon*, Patrick Humphries. *Simon And Garfunkel: Old Friends*, Joseph Morella and Patricia Barey.

SIMONE, NINA

b. Eunice Waymon, 21 February 1933, Tyron, North Carolina, USA. An accomplished pianist as a child, Nina later studied at New York's Juilliard School Of Music. Her jazz credentials were established in 1959 where she secured a hit with an emotive interpretation of George Gershwin's 'I Loves You Porgy'. Her influential 60s work included 'Gin House Blues', 'Forbidden Fruit' and 'I Put A Spell On You', while another of her singles, 'Don't Let Me Be Misunderstood', was later covered by the Animals. The singer's popular fortune flourished upon her signing with RCA. 'Ain't Got No - I Got Life', a song lifted from the mock-hippie musical, *Hair*, was a UK number 2, while her searing version of the Bee Gees' 'To Love Somebody' reached number 5. In America, her own composition, 'To Be Young, Gifted And Black', dedicated to her late friend and playwright, Lorraine Hansberry, reflected Nina's growing militancy. Releases then grew infrequent as her political activism increased. A commanding, if taciturn live performer, Simone's appearances were increasingly focused on benefits and rallies, although a fluke UK hit, 'My Baby Just Cares For Me', a resurrected 50s master, pushed the singer, momentarily, into the commercial spotlight when it reached number 5 in 1987. Tired of an America she perceived as uncaring, Simone has settled in France. An uncompromising personality, Simone's interpretations of soul, jazz, blues and standards are both compulsive and unique.

●ALBUMS: *Little Girl Blue* (Bethlehem 1959)★★, *Nina Simone And Her Friends* (Bethlehem 1959)★★, *The Amazing Nina Simone* (Colpix 1959)★★★, *Nina Simone At The Town Hall* (Colpix 1959)★★★, *Nina Simone At Newport* (Colpix 1960)★★★, *Forbidden Fruit* (Colpix 1961)★★★, *Nina Simone At The Village Gate* (Colpix 1961)★★★, *Nina Simone Sings Ellington* (Colpix 1962)★★★, *Nina's Choice* (Colpix 1963)★★★, *Nina Simone At Carnegie Hall* (Colpix 1963)★★★★, *Folksy Nina* (Colpix 1964)★★★, *Nina Simone In Concert* (Philips 1964)★★★, *Broadway ... Blues ... Ballads* (Philips 1964)★★★, *I Put A Spell On You* (Philips 1965)★★★, *Tell Me More* (1965)★★★, *Pastel Blues* (Philips 1965)★★★, *Let It All Out* (Philips 1966)★★★, *Wild Is The Wind* (Philips 1966)★★★, *Nina With Strings* (Colpix 1966)★★★, *This Is* (1966)★★★, *Nina Simone Sings The Blues* (RCA Victor 1967)★★★★, *High Priestess Of Soul* (Philips 1967)★★★, *Sweet 'N' Swinging* (1967)★★★, *Silk And Soul* (RCA Victor 1967)★★★, *'Nuff Said* (RCA Victor 1968)★★★, *And Piano!* (1969)★★★, *To Love Somebody* (1969)★★★, *Black Gold* (RCA 1970)★★★, *Here Comes The Sun* (RCA 1971)★★★, *Heart And Soul* (1971)★★★, *Emergency Ward* (RCA 1972)★★★, *It Is Finished* (1972)★★★, *Gifted And Black* (Mojo 1974)★★★, *I Loves You Porgy* (1977)★★★, *Baltimore* (CTI 1978)★★★, *Cry Before I Go* (1980)★★★, *Nina Simone* (1982)★★★, *Fodder On My Wings* (1982)★★★, *Live At Vine Street* (1987)★★★, *Live At Ronnie Scott's* (1988)★★★, *Nina's Back* (1989)★★★, *Live* (Zeta 1990)★★, *In Concert* (1992)★★★, *A Single Woman* (1993)★★, *The Great Show Of Nina Simone: Live In Paris* (Accord 1996)★★.

●COMPILATIONS: *The Best Of Nina Simone* (Philips 1966)★★★★, *Fine And Mellow* (1975)★★★, *The Artistry Of Nina Simone* (1982)★★★, *Music For The Millions* (1983)★★★, *My Baby Just Cares For Me* (1984)★★★★, *Lady Midnight* (1987)★★★, *The Nina Simone Collection* (1988)★★★★, *The Nina Simone Story* (1989)★★★, *16 Greatest Hits* (1993)★★★★, *Anthology: The Colpix Years* (Rhino 1997)★★★★.

●FURTHER READING: *I Put A Spell On You: The Autobiography Of Nina Simone*, Nina Simone with Stephen Cleary.

SINATRA, NANCY

b. 8 June 1940, Jersey City, New Jersey, USA. Determined not to rest on the laurels of famous father, Frank Sinatra, Nancy spent several years taking lessons in music, dance and drama. She made an impressive appearance on the Frank Sinatra/Elvis Presley television special (1959), and two years later made her recording debut with 'Cuff Links And A Tie Clip'. From 1960-65, she was married to pop singer Tommy Sands. Further releases were combined with a budding acting career until 1966 when, having teamed with producer/song-writer Lee Hazelwood, Nancy enjoyed an international smash with the sultry number 1 'These Boots Are Made For Walkin''. It's descending bass line on every verse

made it one of the most recognisable hits of 1966. 'How Does That Grab You Darlin'', 'Friday's Child', and 'Sugar Town', all entered the US Top 40, before 'Somethin' Stupid', a duet with her father, gave the singer a second UK and US chart topper. Her other mostly country-styled record hits during the 60s included 'Love Eyes', 'Jackson' and 'Lightning's Girl' (both with Hazelwood), 'Lady Bird', 'Highway Song', and 'Some Velvet Morning'. In 1971, she joined Hazelwood again for the slightly risqué 'Did You Ever'. She also made nightclub appearances, and starred in television specials and feature films such as *Get Yourself A College Girl*, *The Wild Angels* and Elvis Presley's *Speedway*, and sang the theme song to the *James Bond* film *You Only Live Twice*. After spending some years away from the limelight, in 1985 she published a biography entitled *Frank Sinatra: My Father*. A decade later she embarked on a major comeback, releasing her first solo album for more than 15 years, and posing *au naturel* for a six-page pictorial in *Playboy* magazine.

●ALBUMS: *Boots* (Reprise 1966)★★★, *How Does That Grab You Darlin'* (Reprise 1966)★★★, *Nancy In London* (Reprise 1966)★★, *Sugar* (Reprise 1967)★★★, *Country My Way* (Reprise 1967)★★★, *Movin' With Nancy* (Reprise 1968)★★★, with Lee Hazelwood *Nancy And Lee* (Reprise 1968)★★★, *Nancy* (Reprise 1969)★★, *Woman* (Reprise 1970)★★★, *This Is Nancy Sinatra* (RCA 1971)★★, with Hazelwood *Did You Ever* (RCA 1972)★★.

●COMPILATIONS: *Nancy's Greatest Hits* (Reprise 1970)★★★, *All-Time Hits* (1988)★★★, *Lightning's Girl* (80s)★★★, with Mel Tillis *Mel And Nancy* (Elektra 80s)★★★, *The Very Best Of Nancy Sinatra* (1988)★★★, *One More Time* (Cougar 1995)★★★.

●FILMS: *Get Yourself A College Girl* (1964), *The Ghost In The Invisible Bikini* (1966).

SIR DOUGLAS QUINTET

Formed in 1964, the quintet was fashioned by a Houston-based producer, Huey P. Meaux, and former teenage prodigy, Doug Sahm (b. 6 November 1941, San Antonio, Texas, USA). The name, Sir Douglas Quintet, first used on 'Sugar Bee' (1964), was fashioned to suggest Anglo credentials in the midst of the British Invasion, but Sahm's southern accent soon belied the attempted deception. Augie Meyers (b. 31 May 1940; organ), Francisco (Frank) Morin (b. 13 August 1946; horns), Harvey Kagan (b. 18 April 1946; bass) and John Perez (b. 8 November 1942; drums) completed the line-up which had an international hit with 'She's About A Mover', an infectious blend of Texas pop and the Beatles' 'She's A Woman', underscored by Meyers' simple, insistent keyboards. This charming style continued on several further singles and the band's debut album, prematurely entitled *The Best Of The Sir Douglas Quintet*. In keeping with several Texans, including Janis Joplin and the Thirteenth Floor Elevators, the Quintet sought the relaxed clime of San Francisco following an arrest on drugs charges in 1966. However, it was two years before the band resumed recording with *Honky Blues*, although only Sahm and Morin were retained from the earlier unit which was bolstered by other Lone Star state exiles Wayne Talbert (piano), Martin Fierro (horns) and George Rains (drums). The original Quintet was reconstituted for *Mendocino*. This superb selection remains their finest offering and includes the atmospheric 'At The Crossroads', a fiery remake of 'She's About A Mover' and the compulsive title track, which became the group's sole million-seller when released as a single. This commercial peak was not sustained and despite delivering several other excellent albums, the unit broke up in 1972 when Sahm embarked on a solo career. It was, however, a temporary respite and since re-forming in 1976 the group has been resurrected on several occasions, in part to tour and capitalize on a continued European popularity.

●ALBUMS: *The Best Of The Sir Douglas Quintet* (Tribe 1965)★★★, *Sir Douglas Quintet + 2 - Honkey Blues* (Smash 1968)★★★, *Mendocino* (Smash 1969)★★★★, *Together After Five* (Mercury 1969)★★, *1 + 1 + 1 = 4* (Philips 1970)★★, *The Return Of Doug Salanda* (Philips 1971)★★, *Rough Edges* (Mercury 1973)★★, *Quintessence* (1982)★★, *Border Wave* (1983)★★, *Rio Medina* (1984)★★, *Very Much Alive/Love Ya, Europe* (1988)★★, *Midnight Sun* (1988)★★, *Day Dreaming At Midnight* (Elektra 1994)★★.

●COMPILATIONS: *The Sir Douglas Quintet Collection* (1986)★★★★, *Sir Doug's Recording Trip* (1988)★★★.

SIREN

This folk rock group were formed in Bradford, Yorkshire, England, in the late 60s. The line-up of Kevin Coyne (guitar/vocals), John Chichester (lead guitar), Dave Clague (bass), Nick Codworth (piano), Tat Meager (drums) and Colin Wood (keyboards/flute) then relocated to London where they found a waiting contract with John Peel's Dandelion Records. *Siren* was typical of much of the material released on the label in that it sold in minute quantities despite Peel's patronage. Nevertheless, a follow-up collection was assembled. By the time *Strange Locomotion* was released in 1971, Chichester and Wood had departed, with Mick Gratton joining on guitar. There was also a single of the same title released, but this too failed to sell. The group disintegrated thereafter, although they did record two singles on the same day for Dandelion under the name Clague. Coyne recorded a solo set for Dandelion before establishing himself as one of the early 70s premier songwriters with a contract with Virgin Records.

●ALBUMS: *Siren* (Dandelion 1969)★★, *Strange Locomotion* (Dandelion 1971)★★.

SKATALITES

The Skatalites were formed in June 1964, drawing from the ranks of session musicians then recording in the studios of Kingston, Jamaica. The personnel included Don Drummond (trombone), Roland Alphonso (tenor saxophone), Tommy McCook (tenor saxophone), Johnny 'Dizzy' Moore (trumpet), Lester Sterling (alto saxophone), Jerome 'Jah Jerry Hines (guitar), Jackie Mittoo (piano), Lloyd Brevett (bass) and Lloyd Knibbs (drums). The band name was a Tommy McCook pun on the Soviet space satellite of 1963. The Skatalites' music, reputedly named after the characteristic 'ska' sound made by the guitar when playing the 'after beat', was a powerful synthesis, combining elements of R&B and swing jazz in arrangements and solos, underpinned by the uniquely Jamaican-stressed 'after beat', as opposed to the 'down beat' of R&B. Many of the musicians had learned music at Alpha Boys' School in Kingston, then honing their talent in the Jamaican swing bands of the 40s and early 50s, and in numerous 'hotel bands' playing for the tourist trade. Most of the musicians thereby developed recognizable individual styles. Repertoire was drawn from many sources, including adaptations of Latin tunes, movie themes and updated mento, a Jamaican folk song form. Perhaps their most famous and identifiable tune is 'Guns Of Navarone' recorded in 1965 and a big club hit in the UK in the mid-60s. They recorded hundreds of superb instrumentals for various producers, either under the group name or as bands led by the particular musician who had arranged the session. Under the Skatalite name they made important music for Coxsone Dodd and Duke Reid, as well as for Justin and Philip Yap's Top Deck record label. They stayed together for just over two years until August 1965, when a combination of financial, organizational and personal problems caused the break-up of the band after their last gig, a police dance at the Runaway Bay Hotel. Of the main protagonists, Jackie Mittoo and Roland Alphonso were persuaded by Coxsone Dodd to form the Soul Brothers band, who make made instrumentals and supplied backing tracks at Studio One until 1967. McCook worked principally for Duke Reid, where he formed the studio band known as the Supersonics, and was musical co-director for Reid's Treasure Isle label with alto saxophonist Herman Marques. The tragically wayward Don Drummond suffered from severe depression and died on 6 May 1969 in Bellevue Asylum, Kingston. The Skatalites had backed virtually every singer of note in the studios, at the same time laying the musical foundation for subsequent developments in Jamaican music. They released a reunion album in 1975; not ska, but high quality instrumental reggae. In 1984 the band played the Jamaican and London 'Sunsplash' concerts to rapturous acclaim. The re-formed group also toured Japan and recorded with vocalists Prince Buster and Lord Tanamo in 1989.

●ALBUMS: *Ska Authentic* (Studio One 1967)★★★, *Ska Boo Da Ba* (Top Deck/Doctor Bird 60s)★★★, *The Skatalites* (Treasure Isle 1975)★★★, *Return Of The Big Guns* (Island 1984)★★★, *Live At Reggae Sunsplash* (Synergy 1986)★★★★, *Stretching Out* (ROIR 1987)★★★, *Celebration Time* (Studio One 1988)★★★.

●COMPILATIONS: *Best Of The Skatalites* (Studio One 1974)★★★, *Scattered Lights* (Top Deck 1984)★★★.

SKIP BIFFERTY

John Turnbull (guitar/vocals), Mickey Gallagher (keyboards), Colin Gibson (bass) and Tommy Jackman

(drums) were all members of the Chosen Few, a popular beat group initially based in Newcastle-upon-Tyne, England. Vocalist Graham Bell was added to the line-up which assumed the name Skip Bifferty in the spring of 1966. The quintet made their energetic debut in August the following year with the excellent 'On Love', a song from their previous incarnation's repertoire. It was followed by two memorable examples of pop psychedelia, the last of which, 'Man In Black', was produced by the Small Faces team of Steve Marriott and Ronnie Lane. Skip Bifferty's first album continued the melodic craftsmanship of those singles. Bell's assured voice soared over a rich tapestry of sound, resulting in one of the late 60s' most rewarding collections. The group's potential withered under business entanglements and an astonishing conflict with their proprietorial manager Don Arden. Although they tried to forge an alternative career as Heavy Jelly, litigation over the rights to the name brought about their demise. Bell, Turnbull and Gallagher were later reunited in Bell And Arc, but while the singer then embarked on an ill-fated solo career, his former colleagues found success in Ian Dury's Blockheads. The band have subsequently become a cult item for UK record collectors.
●ALBUMS: *Skip Bifferty* (RCA 1968)★★★.

SLEDGE, PERCY

b. 25 November 1941, Leighton, Alabama, USA. An informal, intimate singer, Sledge led a popular campus attraction, the Esquires Combo, prior to his recording debut. Recommended to Quin Ivy, owner of the Norala Sound studio, Sledge arrived with a rudimentary draft of 'When A Man Loves A Woman'. A timeless single, its simple arrangement hinged on Spooner Oldham's organ sound and the singer's homely, nasal intonation. Released in 1966, it was a huge international hit, setting the tone for Percy's subsequent path. A series of emotional, poignant ballads followed, poised between country and soul, but none achieved the same commercial profile. 'It Tears Me Up', 'Out Of Left Field' (both 1967) and 'Take Time To Know Her' (1968) nonetheless stand among southern soul's finest achievements. Having left Atlantic Records, Sledge re-emerged on Capricorn in 1974 with *I'll Be Your Everything*. Two 80s collections, *Percy* and *Wanted Again*, confirm the singer's intimate yet unassuming delivery. Released in Britain following the runaway success of a resurrected 'When A Man Loves A Woman', they are not diminished by comparison. In 1994 Sledge recorded his first all-new set for some time, the excellent *Blue Night* on Sky Ranch/Virgin, which majored on the Sledge 'strong suit', the slow-burning countrified soul-ballad, even although the sessions were recorded in Los Angeles. The appearance of musicians such as Steve Cropper and Bobby Womack helped insure the success of the album.
●ALBUMS: *When A Man Loves A Woman* (Atlantic 1966)★★★★, *Warm And Tender Soul* (Atlantic 1966)★★★★, *The Percy Sledge Way* (Atlantic 1967)★★★, *Take Time To Know Her* (Atlantic

1968)★★★, *I'll Be Your Everything* (Capricorn 1974)★★★, *If Loving You Is Wrong* (Charly 1986)★★★, *Percy* (Capricorn 1987)★★★, *Wanted Again* (1989)★★, *Blue Night* (Sky Ranch 1994)★★★★. Compilations *The Best Of Percy Sledge* (Atlantic 1969)★★★★, *Any Day Now* (Charly 1984)★★★, *When A Man Loves A Woman (The Ultimate Collection)* (Atlantic 1987)★★★★, *It Tears Me Up: The Best Of ...* (Rhino 1992)★★★★, *Greatest Hits* (1993)★★★★.

SLIM HARPO

b. James Moore, 11 January 1924, Lobdel, Louisiana, USA, d. 31 January 1970. The eldest of an orphaned family, Moore worked as a longshoreman and building worker during the late 30s and early 40s. One of the foremost proponents of post-war rural blues, he began performing in Baton Rouge bars under the name Harmonica Slim. He later accompanied Lightnin' Slim, his brother-in-law, both live and in the studio, before commencing his own recording career in 1957. Christened 'Slim Harpo' by producer Jay Miller, the artist's solo debut coupled 'I'm A King Bee' with 'I Got Love If You Want It'. Influenced by Jimmy Reed, he began recording for Excello and enjoyed a string of popular R&B singles which combined a drawling vocal with incisive harmonica passages. Among them were 'Raining In My Heart' (1961), 'I Love The Life I Live', 'Buzzin'' (instrumental) and 'Little Queen Bee' (1964). These relaxed, almost lazy, performances, which featured an understated electric backing, set the tone for Moore's subsequent work. His warm, languid voice enhanced the sexual metaphor of 'I'm A King Bee', which was later recorded by the Rolling Stones. The same group also covered the pulsating 'Shake Your Hips', which Harpo first issued in 1966, while the Pretty Things, the Yardbirds and Them featured versions of his songs in their early repertoires.
Harpo scored a notable US Top 20 pop hit in 1966 with 'Baby Scratch My Back' (also a number 1 R&B hit), which revitalized his career. Never a full-time musician, Harpo had his own trucking business during the 60s although he was a popular figure during the late 60s blues revival, with appearances at several renowned venues including the Electric Circus and the Fillmore East, but suffered a fatal heart attack on 31 January 1970.
●ALBUMS: *Rainin' In My Heart* (Excello 1961)★★★, *Baby Scratch My Back* (1966)★★★, *Tip On In* (Excello 1968)★★.
●COMPILATIONS: *The Best Of Slim Harpo* (Excello 1969)★★★★, *He Knew The Blues* (Excello 1970)★★★, *Blues Hangover* (1976)★★, *Got Love If You Want It* (1980)★★★, *Shake Your Hips* (Ace 1986)★★★★, *I'm A King Bee* (Ace 1989)★★★★.

SLOAN, P.F.

b. Phillip Gary Schlein, 1944, New York City, New York, USA. Sloan moved to Los Angeles as a teenager and in 1959 recorded his first single, 'All I Want Is Loving', for the ailing Aladdin label. When a second release, 'If You Believe In Me' failed to sell, Sloan began a career as a contract songwriter. In 1964 he joined Lou Adler's Trousdale Music where he was teamed with fellow aspirant Steve Barri. Together they wrote singles for Shelly Fabares, Bruce And Terry and Terry Black, as well as Adler protégés, Jan And Dean. Sloan and Barri composed several of the duo's hits and contributed backing harmonies under a pseudonym, the Fantastic Baggys. The pair recorded a much-prized surf album under this sobriquet. The emergence of folk rock had a profound influence on Sloan. By 1965 he was writing increasingly introspective material. The Turtles recorded three of his songs, 'You Baby', 'Let Me Be' and 'Can I Get To Know You Better', but passed on 'Eve Of Destruction', which became a US number 1 for the gruff-voiced Barry McGuire, despite an extensive radio ban. Folk purists balked at Sloan's perceived opportunism, but he was embraced by many as the voice of youth and a spokesman for a generation. The singer rekindled his own recording career with 'The Sins Of A Family' and the brilliant *Songs Of Our Times*. His poetic lyrics and love of simile provoked comparisons with Bob Dylan, but Sloan's gift for pop melody was equally apparent. The set included 'Take Me For What I Am Worth', later a hit for the Searchers. *Twelve More Times* featured a much fuller sound and featured two of Sloan's most poignant compositions, 'This Precious Time' and 'I Found a Girl'. He also enjoyed success, with Barri, as part of another 'backroom' group, the Grass Roots. When 'Where Were You When I Needed You' reached the US Top 30 in 1966, the pair put an official band together to carry on the name. By this point the more altruistic Sloan was growing estranged from his commercially minded partner and they drifted apart the following year. 'Karma (A Study Of Divination's)', credited to Philip Sloan, showed an artist embracing the trinkets of 1967, although the subsequent *Measure Of Pleasure* was rather bland. A lengthy break ensued, broken only by the singer/songwriter-styled *Raised On Records*, Sloan's last recording to date. Without a contract, he wound down music business commitments, prompting no less a personage than Jim Webb to mourn his absence with the moving tribute 'P.F. Sloan' from *El Mirage*.

Sloan re-emerged from seclusion in 1985 with an appearance at New York's Bottom Line club. Here he was supported by Don Ciccone (ex-Critters; Four Seasons) and future Smithereens' member Dennis Dikem. In 1990 the singer re-wrote 'Eve Of Destruction' as 'Eve Of Destruction, 1990 (The Environment)', which was recorded by the equally reclusive Barry McGuire. In November that year Sloan played, and received a standing ovation, at the annual National Academy Of Songwriters' convention.

●ALBUMS: *Songs Of Our Times* (Dunhill 1965)★★★, *Twelve More Times* (Dunhill 1966)★★★, *Measure Of Pleasure* (Atco 1968)★★, *Raised On Records* (Mums 1972)★★.

●COMPILATIONS: with the Grass Roots *Songs Of Other Times* (1988)★★★.

SLY AND THE FAMILY STONE

This US group was formed in San Francisco, California, in 1967 and comprised: Sly Stone (b. Sylvester Stewart, 15 March 1944, Dallas, Texas, USA), Freddie Stone (b. 5 June 1946, Dallas, Texas, USA; guitar), Rosie Stone (b. 21 March 1945, Vallejo, California, USA; piano), Cynthia Robinson (b. 12 January 1946, Sacramento, California, USA; trumpet), Jerry Martini (b. 1 October 1943, Colorado, USA; saxophone), Larry Graham (b. 14 August 1946, Beaumont, Texas, USA; bass) and Greg Errico (b. 1 September 1946, San Francisco, California, USA; drums). Sly Stone's recording career began in 1948. A child prodigy, he drummed and added guitar to 'On The Battlefield For My Lord', a single released by his family's group, the Stewart Four. At high school he sang harmony with the Vicanes, but by the early 60s he was working the bars and clubs on San Francisco's North Beach enclave. Sly learned his trade with several bands, including Joe Piazza And The Continentals, but he occasionally fronted his own. 'Long Time Away', a single credited to Sylvester Stewart, dates from this period. He also worked as a disc jockey at stations KSOL and KDIA. Sly joined Autumn Records as a songwriter/house-producer, and secured a 1964 success with Bobby Freeman's 'C'mon And Swim'. His own opportunistic single, 'I Just Learned How To Swim', was less fortunate, a fate that also befell 'Buttermilk Pts 1 & 2'. Stone's production work, however, was exemplary; the Beau Brummels, the Tikis and the Mojo Men enjoyed a polished, individual sound. In 1966 Sly formed the Stoners, a short-lived group which included Cynthia Robinson. The following year Sly And The Family Stone made its debut on the local Loadstone label with 'I Ain't Got Nobody'. The group was then signed to Epic, where their first album proclaimed itself *A Whole New Thing*. However, it was 1968 before 'Dance To The Music' became a Top 10 single in the US and UK. 'Everyday People' topped the US chart early the following year, but Sly's talent was not fully established until a fourth album, *Stand!*, was released. Two million copies were sold, while tracks including the title song, 'I Want To Take You Higher' and 'Sex Machine', transformed black music forever. Rhythmically inventive, the whole band pulsated with a crazed enthusiasm that pitted doo-wop, soul, the San Francisco sound, and more, one upon the other. Contemporaries, from Miles Davis to George Clinton and the Temptations, showed traces of Sly's remarkable vision.

A sensational appearance at the Woodstock Festival reinforced his popularity. The new decade began with a double-sided hit, 'Thank You (Falettinme Be Mice Elf Agin)'/'Everybody Is A Star', an R&B and pop number 1, but the optimism suddenly clouded. Sly began missing concerts; those he did perform were often disappointing and when *There's A Riot Goin' On* did appear in 1971, it was dark, mysterious and brooding. This introverted set nevertheless reached number 1 in the US chart, and provided three successful singles, 'Family Affair' (another US R&B and pop number 1), 'Running Away' and 'Smilin'', but the joyful noise of the 60s was now over. *Fresh* (1973) lacked Sly's erstwhile focus while successive releases, *Small Talk* and *High On You*, reflected a waning power. The Family Stone was also crumbling, Larry Graham left to form Graham Central Station, while Andy Newmark replaced Greg Errico. Yet the real undermining factor was the leader's drug dependency, a constant stumbling block to Sly's recurrent 'comebacks'. A 1979 release, *Back On The Right Track*, featured several original members, but later tours were dogged by Stone's addiction problem. Jailed for possession of cocaine in 1987, this innovative artist closed the decade fighting further extradition charges.

●ALBUMS: *A Whole New Thing* (Direction/Epic 1967)★★★, *Dance To The Music* (Direction/Epic 1968)★★★★, *Life* (Epic 1968)★★★★, *M'Lady* (Direction 1968), *Stand!* (Epic 1969)★★★★, *There's A Riot Going On* (Epic 1971)★★★★, *Fresh* (Epic 1973)★★★, *Dance To The Music* (Embassy 1973)★★★, *Small Talk* (Epic 1974)★★★, *High Energy* (Epic 1975)★★, *High On You* (Epic 1975)★★, *Heard Ya Missed Me, Well I'm Back* (Epic 1976)★★, *Back On The Right Track* (Warners 1979), *Ain't But The One Way* (Warners 1983).

●COMPILATIONS: *Greatest Hits* (Epic 1970)★★★★, *Ten Years Too Soon* (Epic 1979)★★★, *Anthology* (Epic 1981)★★★★, *The Best Of* (1992)★★★★, *Precious Stone: In The Studio With Sly Stone 1963-1965* (Ace 1994)★★.

SMALL FACES

Formed in London during 1965, this mod-influenced group initially comprised: Steve Marriott (b. 30 January 1947, Bow, London, England, d. 20 April 1991; vocals/guitar), Ronnie Lane (b. 1 April 1946, Plaistow, London, England, d. 4 June 1997, Trinidad, Colorado, USA; bass), Jimmy Winston (b. James Langwith, 20 April 1945, Stratford, London, England; organ) and Kenny Jones (b. 16 September 1948, Stepney, London, England; drums). Fronted by former child actor Marriott, the group were signed to Don Arden's Contemporary Records management and production and their product was licensed to Decca. Their debut, 'Whatcha Gonna Do About It', an in-house composition/production by Ian Samwell (formerly of Cliff Richard's Drifters) was a vibrant piece of Solomon Burke-influenced R&B that brought them into the UK Top 20. Within weeks of their chart entry, organist Smith was replaced by Ian McLagan (b. 12 May 1945, London, England), a former member of Boz And The Boz People. While their first release had been heavily hyped, the second, 'I Got Mine', failed to chart. Arden responded to this setback by recruiting hit songwriters Kenny Lynch and Mort Shuman, whose catchy 'Sha-La-La-La-Lee' gave the group a UK Top 3 hit. The Marriott/Lane-composed 'Hey Girl' reinforced their chart credibility, which reached its apogee with the striking Arden-produced 'All Or Nothing'. The latter was their most raucous single to date; its strident chords and impassioned vocal ensuring the disc classic status in the annals of mid-60s UK white soul. The festive 'My Mind's Eye' brought a change of style, which coincided with disagreements with their record company.

By early 1967, the group were in litigation with their manager and found themselves banned from the prestigious television programme *Top Of The Pops* after Marriott insulted its producer. A final two singles for Decca, 'I Can't Make It' and 'Patterns', proved unsuccessful. Meanwhile, the group underwent a series of short term management agreements with Harold Davison, Robert Wace and Andrew Oldham. The Rolling Stones' manager signed them to his label Immediate and this coincided with their metamorphosis into a quasi-psychedelic ensemble. The drug-influenced 'Here Comes The Nice' was followed by the experimental and slightly parodic 'Itchycoo Park'. With their Top 10 status reaffirmed, the group returned to their blues style with the powerful 'Tin Soldier', which featured P.P. Arnold on backing vocals. For 'Lazy Sunday' the group combined their cockney charm with an alluring paean to hippie indolence; it was a strange combination of magnificent music-hall wit and drug-influenced mind expansion. Those same uneasy elements were at work on their chart-topping *Ogden's Nut Gone Flake*, which won several design awards for its innovative round cover in the shape of a tobacco tin. For their final single, the group bowed out with the chaotic 'The Universal' and the posthumous hit 'Afterglow Of Your Love'. By February 1969, Marriott decided to join Peter Frampton of the Herd in a new group, which emerged as Humble Pie. The Small Faces then disbanded only to re-emerge as the Faces. Successful reissues of 'Itchycoo Park' and 'Lazy Sunday' in the mid-70s persuaded Marriott, Jones, McLagan and new boy Rick Wills to revive the Small Faces name for a series of albums, none of which were well received. Subsequently, Jones joined the Who, Wills teamed up with Foreigner, McLagan played live with the Rolling Stones and Marriott reverted to playing small pubs in London. In 1989, Marriott recorded *30 Seconds To Midnight*, but was unable to forge a fully successful solo career. He perished in a fire in his Essex home in 1991. Lane was slowly deteriorating with multiple sclerosis from his base in the USA. Over the past three decades, the Small Faces, probably more than any other band, have been victims of ruthless reissues. Using inferior master tapes, reduced in quality by generation upon generation of duplicating, a superb catalogue of songs (that the band does not own) has been passed like a hot potato between just about every mid-price record company in existance. During the 'Britpop' explosion of the mid-90s, the band were favourably reappraised. Much of the chirpy exuberance of bands such as Blur, Supergrass, Cast and the Candyskins is indebted to the Small Faces. In 1995 Jones started litigation, attempting to recover substantial missing and unpaid royalties from the previous 25 years. The same year, a UK television documentary and a box set, *The Immediate Years*, were produced. Now that the public have been made aware of their plight through naïvety, a wealthy major record company should step in once and for all, seek out and buy the master tapes, financially reimburse the remaining band members and produce a glorious box set of the entire catalogue. It is the least that should be done for this criminally underrated and influential beat group. Bowing to public (or at least music business) opinion, Castle Communications paid a six figure sum to the members of the band in 1996, together with a future royalty stream.

●ALBUMS: *The Small Faces* (Decca 1966)★★★, *Small Faces* (Immediate 1967)★★★, *There Are But Four Faces* (1968)★★★, *Ogden's Nut Gone Flake* (Immediate 1968)★★★★.

●COMPILATIONS: *From The Beginning* (Decca 1967)★★★, *The Autumn Stone* (Immediate 1969)★★★★, *In Memoriam* (Immediate 1969)★★★, *Archetypes* (MGM 1970)★★★, *Wham Bam* (Immediate 1970)★★★, *Early Faces* (Pride 1972)★★★, *The History Of The Small Faces* ((Pride 1972)★★★, *In Memorium, Small Faces Live* (Immediate 1975)★★★, *Rock Roots, The Decca Singles* (Decca 1977)★★★, *Playmates* (1977)★★★, *78 In The Shade* (1978)★★★, *Profile* (Teldec 1979)★★★, *Small Faces, Big Hits* (Virgin 1980)★★★, *For Your Delight, The Darlings Of Wapping Wharf Launderette* (Virgin 1980)★★★, *For Your Delight* (1980)★★★, *Sha La La La Lee* (Decca 1981)★★★, *Historia De La Musica Rock* (Decca Spain 1981)★★★, *By Apppointment* (Accord 1982)★★★, *Golden Hits* (Astan 1984)★★★, *Sorry She's Mine* (Platinum 1985)★★★, *The Collection* (Castle 1985)★★★, *Quite Naturally* (Castle 1986)★★★, *The Small Faces* (London 1988)★★★, *20 Greatest Hits* (Big Time 1988)★★★, *Nightriding: Small Faces* (Knight 1988)★★★, *The Ultimate Collection* (Castle 1990)★★★, *Singles A's And B's* (See For Miles 1990)★★★, *Lazy Sunday* (Success 1990)★★★, *Green Circles* (Sequel 1991)★★★, *Quite Naturally Rare* (Dojo 1991)★★★, *The Complete Collection* (Castle 1991)★★★, *25 Greatest Hits* (Repertoire 1992)★★★, *It's All Or Nothing* (Spectrum 1993)★★★, *Itchycoo Park* (Laserlight 1993)★★★, *Here Comes The Nice* (Laserlight 1994)★★★, *The Small Faces Boxed: The Definitive Anthology* (Repertoire 1994)★★★★, *The Immediate Years* 4-CD box set (Charly 1995)★★★★.

●VIDEOS: *Big Hits* (Castle 1991).

●FURTHER READING: *The Young Mods' Forgotten Story*, Paolo Hewitt.

●FILMS: *Dateline Diamonds* (1965).

SMITH, 'WHISTLING' JACK

b. William Moeller, 2 February 1946, Liverpool, Merseyside, England. Moeller, whose brother Tommy was the vocalist with Unit Four Plus Two, scored a substantial novelty pop hit with the release of 'I Was Kaiser Bill's Batman' in 1967. Despite press coverage at the time, the whistling on the record was actually performed by producer Ivor Raymonde rather than 'Whistling' Jack Smith himself. In fact, 'I Was Kaiser Bill's Batman' was a studio production by the Mike Sammes Singers, written by Cook And Greenaway. Moeller was hired to tour under the name 'Whistling' Jack Smith to capitalize on the song's

popularity. The song reached number 5 in the UK charts and number 20 in the US in 1967. However, it did not prove to be the launching pad for a sustained musical career. None of the subsequent singles credited to the same artist, which included 'Hey There Little Miss Mary', 'Ja Da', 'Only When I Larf' and 'Battle Of Waterloo Love Theme', made the charts. Moeller also recorded under a further pseudonym, Coby Wells.

●ALBUMS: *Around The World With Whistling Jack Smith* (Deram 1967)★.

SMITH, JIMMY

b. James Oscar Smith, 8 December 1925, Norristown, Pennsylvania, USA. The sound of the Hammond Organ in jazz was popularized by Smith, often using the prefix 'the incredible' or 'the amazing'. Smith has become the most famous jazz organist of all times and arguably the most influential. Brought up by musical parents he was formally trained on piano and bass and combined the two skills with the Hammond while leading his own trio. He was heavily influenced by Wild Bill Davis. By the mid-50s Smith had refined his own brand of smoky soul jazz which epitomized laid-back 'late night' blues-based music. His vast output for the 'soul jazz' era of Blue Note Records led the genre and resulted in a number of other Hammond B3 maestros' appearing, notably, Jimmy McGriff, 'Brother' Jack McDuff, 'Big' John Patten, Richard 'Groove' Holmes and 'Baby Face' Willette. Smith was superbly complemented by outstanding musicians. Although Art Blakey played with Smith, Donald Bailey remains the definitive Smith drummer, while Smith tackled the bass notes on the Hammond. The guitar was featured prominently throughout the Blue Note years and Smith used the talents of Eddie McFadden, Quentin Warren and Kenny Burrell. Further immaculate playing came from Stanley Turrentine (tenor saxophone), Lee Morgan (trumpet) and Lou Donaldson (alto saxophone). Two classic albums from the late 50s were *The Sermon* and *Houseparty*. On the title track of the former, Smith and his musicians stretch out with majestic 'cool' over 20 minutes, allowing each soloist ample time. In 1962 Jimmy moved to Verve Records where he became the undisputed king, regularly crossing over into the pop best-sellers and the singles charts with memorable titles such as 'Walk On The Wild Side', 'Hobo Flats' and 'Who's Afraid Of Virginia Woolf'. These hits were notable for their superb orchestral arrangements by Oliver Nelson, although they tended to bury Smith's sound. However, the public continued putting him in the charts with 'The Cat', 'The Organ Grinder's Swing' and, with Smith on growling vocals 'Got My Mojo Working'.

His albums at this time also made the best-sellers, and between 1963 and 1966 Smith was virtually ever-present in the album charts with a total of 12 albums, many making the US Top 20. Smith's popularity had much to do with the R&B boom in Britain during the early 60s. His strong influence was found in the early work of Steve Winwood, Georgie Fame, Zoot Money, Graham Bond and John Mayall. Smith's two albums with Wes Montgomery were also well received; both allowed each other creative space with no ego involved. As the 60s ended Smith's music became more MOR and he pursued a soul/funk path during the 70s, using a synthesizer on occasion. Organ jazz was in the doldrums for many years and although Smith remained its leading exponent, he was leader of an unfashionable style. During the 80s after a series of low-key and largely unremarkable recordings Smith delivered the underrated *Off The Top* in 1982. Later in the decade the Hammond organ began to come back in favour in the UK with the James Taylor Quartet and the Tommy Chase Band and in Germany with Barbara Dennerlein. Much of Smith's seminal work has been re-mastered and reissued on compact disc since the end of the 80s, almost as vindication for a genre that went so far out of fashion, it disappeared. A reunion with Kenny Burrell produced a fine live album, *The Master*, featuring reworkings of classic trio tracks; further renewed interest in his career came in 1995 when he returned to Verve for *Damn!*, the home of of his most commercial work. On this album he was joined by some of the finest young jazz players, many were barely born when Smith was having his heyday in the 60s. The stellar line-up on this, one of the finest albums of his career, comprises Roy Hargrove (b. 16 October 1969, Waco, Texas, USA; trumpet), Mark Turner (b. 10 November 1965, Wright Patterson Air Force Base, Ohio, USA; saxophone), Ron Blake (b. 7 September 1965, St. Thomas, Virgin Islands; saxophone), Nicholas Payton (b. 26 September 1973, New Orleans, Louisiana, USA; trumpet), Abraham Burton (17 March 1971, New York City, New York, USA; saxophone), Art Taylor (b. 6 April 1929, New York City, New York, USA, d. 6 February 1995; drums), Tim Warfield (b. 2 July 1965, York, Pennsylvania, USA; saxophone), Mark Whitfield (b. 6 October 1966, Lindehurst, New York, USA; guitar), Bernard Purdie (b. 11 June 1939, Elkton, Maryland, USA; drums), Christian McBride (b. 31 May 1972, Philadelphia, Pennsylvania, USA; bass).

●ALBUMS: *Jimmy Smith At The Organ Vol. 1* (Blue Note 1956)★★★★, *Jimmy Smith At The Organ Vol. 2* (Blue Note 1956)★★★★, *The Incredible Jimmy Smith At The Organ Vol. 3* (Blue Note 1956)★★★, *The Incredible Jimmy Smith At Club Baby Grand Vol. 1* (Blue Note 1956)★★★, *The Incredible Jimmy Smith At Club Baby Grand Vol. 2* (Blue Note 1956)★★★, *The Champ* (Blue Note 1956)★★★, *A Date With Jimmy Smith Vol. 1* (Blue Note 1957)★★★, *A Date With Jimmy Smith Vol. 2* (Blue Note 1957)★★★, *The Sounds Of Jimmy Smith* (Blue Note 1957)★★★, *Plays Pretty Just For You* (Blue Note 1957)★★★, *Groovin' At Small's Paradise Vol. 1* (Blue Note 1958)★★★, *Groovin' At Small's Paradise Vol. 2* (Blue Note 1958)★★★, *The Sermon* (Blue Note 1958)★★★★, *House Party* (Blue Note 1958)★★★★, *Cool Blues* (Blue Note 1958)★★★★, *Home Cookin'* (1958)★★★★, *Crazy Baby* (Blue Note 1960)★★★★, *Midnight Special* (Blue Note 1960)★★★★, *Open House* (Blue Note 1960)★★★★, *Back At The Chicken Shack* (Blue Note 1960)★★★★, *Peter And The Wolf* (1960)★★★, *Plays Fats Waller*

(Blue Note 1962)★★★, *Bashin'* (Verve 1962)★★★★, *Hobo Flats* (Verve 1963)★★★, *I'm Movin' On* (Blue Note 1963)★★★★, *Any Number Can Win* (Verve 1963)★★★, *Rockin' The Boat* (Blue Note 1963)★★★, with Kenny Burrell *Blue Bash!* (1963)★★★, *Prayer Meetin'* (Blue Note 1964)★★★★, *Christmas '64* (Blue Note 1964)★★★, *Who's Afraid Of Virginia Woolf* (Verve 1964)★★★★, *The Cat* (Verve 1964)★★★★, *Organ Grinder's Swing* (Verve 1965)★★★★★, *Softly As A Summer Breeze* (Blue Note 1965)★★★, *Monster* (Verve 1965)★★★, *'Bucket'!* (Blue Note 1966)★★★★, *Peter And The Wolf* (Verve 1966)★★★, *Get My Mojo Workin'* (Verve 1966)★★★, *Christmas Cookin'* (Verve 1966)★★★, *Hoochie Coochie Man* (Verve 1966)★★★★, with Wes Montgomery, *Jimmy & Wes The Dynamic Duo* (Verve 1966)★★★★, with Montgomery *Further Adventures Of Jimmy And Wes* (Verve 1966)★★★★, *Respect* (Verve 1967)★★★, *Stay Loose* (Verve 1968)★★★, *Livin' It Up* (Verve 1968)★★★, featuring George Benson *The Boss* (Verve 1969)★★★, *Groove Drops* (Verve 1969)★★★, *Mr Jim* (Manhattan 1981)★★, *Off The Top* (Elektra 1982)★★★, *Keep On Comin'* (1983)★★★, *Go For Whatcha Know* (Blue Note 1986)★★★, *Jimmy Smith At The Organ* (1988)★★★, *The Cat Strikes Again* (Laserlight 1989)★★★, *Prime Time* (Milestone 1991)★★★, *Fourmost* (Milestone 1991)★★★, *Sum Serious Blues* (Milestone 1993)★★★, *The Master* (Blue Note 1994)★★★, *Damn!* (Verve 1995)★★★★, with Eddie Harris *All The Way Live* (Milestone 1996)★★★, *Angel Eyes - Ballads And Slow Jams* Verve 1996)★★★★.

●COMPILATIONS: *Jimmy Smith's Greatest Hits* (1968)★★★, *Compact Jazz: The Best Of Jimmy Smith* (Verve 1988)★★★★, *Compact Jazz: Jimmy Smith Plays the Blues* (Verve 1988)★★★★.

SMOKE

Mick Rowley (vocals), Mal Luker (lead guitar), Phil Peacock (rhythm guitar), John 'Zeke' Lund (bass) and Geoff Gill (drums) were initially known as the Shots. This Yorkshire, England, group was groomed for success by Alan Brush, a gravel pit owner and self-made millionaire who harboured dreams of pop management. His ambitions faltered when the Shots' lone single, 'Keep A Hold Of What You Got', failed to sell. Phil Peacock then dropped out of the line-up, but within months the remaining quartet approached producer Monty Babson with several new demos. The most promising song, 'My Friend Jack', was released in February 1967 under the group's new name, the Smoke. Although irresistibly commercial, problems arose when the line 'my friend Jack eats sugar lumps' was construed as celebrating drug abuse. The record was banned in Britain, but became a massive hit on the continent and on the pirate radio ships, inspiring a release for the group's only album, *It's Smoke Time*. Later singles continued their quirky-styled pop, but they failed to garner a significant breakthrough. Having toyed with yet another appellation, Chords Five, Lund, Luker and Gill began work as resident musicians at

Babson's Morgan Sound studios. Several more singles, credited to the Smoke, appeared on various labels during the late 60s/early 70s. These often throwaway efforts featured sundry variations on the above triumvirate, accompanied by any other backroom staff present.

●ALBUMS: *It's Smoke Time* (1967)★★★.
●COMPILATIONS: *My Friend Jack* (1988)★★★.

SNOBS

A quartet comprising John Boulden, Eddie Gilbert, Colin Sandland and Peter Yerral, this UK pop band were most notable for their extravagant dress sense. Their 1965 debut single for Decca Records, 'Buckle Shoe Stomp', was promoted via visual apparel which included powdered wigs as well as the footwear described in its title. However, they proved more popular in Scandinavia than the UK, and eventually relocated to Sweden where they recorded a further single, 'Ding Dong', backed by a version of 'Heartbreak Hotel'. That was to be their final release, although both sides of their two singles have resurfaced regularly on 60s beat compilations such as *Search In The Wilderness*, *English Freakbeat Vol. 4* and *Sixties Lost And Found*.

SOFT MACHINE

Founded in 1966, the original line-up was Robert Wyatt (b. 28 January 1945, Bristol, Avon, England; drums/vocals), Kevin Ayers (b. 16 August 1945, Herne bay, Kent, England; vocals), Daevid Allen, Mike Ratledge and, very briefly, guitarist Larry Nolan. By autumn 1967 the classic line-up of the Soft Machine's art-rock period (Ayers, Wyatt and Ratledge) had settled in. They toured with Jimi Hendrix, who, along with his producer, ex-Animals member Chas Chandler, encouraged them and facilitated the recording of their first album. (There had been earlier demos for Giorgio Gomelsky's Marmalade label, but these were not issued until later, and then kept reappearing in different configurations under various titles.) From the end of 1968, when Ayers left, until February 1970, the personnel was in a state of flux (Lyn Dobson, Marc Charig and Nick Evans were members for a while), and the music was evolving into a distinctive brand jazz-rock. Arguably, *Volume Two* and *Third* contain their most intriguing and exciting performances. Highlighted by Wyatt's very English spoken/sung vocals, the group had still managed to inject some humour into their work. The finest example is Wyatt's mercurial 'Moon In June'. By mid-1970 the second definitive line-up (Ratledge, Wyatt, Hugh Hopper and Elton Dean) was finally in place. It was this band that Tim Souster showcased when he was allowed a free hand to organize a late-night Promenade Concert in August 1970. In autumn 1971, Wyatt left to form Matching Mole (a clever pun on the French translation of Soft Machine; Machine Molle), and Phil Howard came in on drums until John Marshall became the permanent drummer. For the next few years, through a number of personnel changes (farewell Dean and Hopper, welcome Roy Babbington, Karl Jenkins) the Soft Machine were, for many listeners, the standard against which all jazz-rock fusions, including most of the big American names, had to be measured. However, with Ratledge's departure in January 1976 the group began to sound like a legion of other guitar-led fusion bands, competent and craftsmanlike, but, despite the virtuosity of Allan Holdsworth and John Etheridge, without the edge of earlier incarnations, and certainly without the dadaist elements of Wyatt's time. In 1984, Jenkins and Marshall brought together a new edition of the band (featuring Dave Macrae, Ray Warleigh and a number of new Jenkins compositions) for a season at Ronnie Scott's club. Jenkins moved into a highly successful career composing some prestigeous advertising jingles, including work for Renault, Levi's and Jaguar cars. His composition for Delta Airlines 'Adiemus' was released as a single and became a hit in Germany. It is their first three albums that contain the best of their work and that clearly show they were one of the most adventurous and important progressive bands of the late 60s, one that gently led their followers to understand and appreciate jazz.

●ALBUMS: *Soft Machine* (Probe 1968)★★★, *Soft Machine Volume Two* (Probe 1969)★★★★, *Third* (CBS 1970)★★★★, *Fourth* (CBS 1971)★★★, *Fifth* (CBS 1972)★★★, *Six* (CBS 1973)★★, *Seven* (CBS 1973)★★, *Bundles* (Harvest 1975)★★★, *Softs* (Harvest 1976)★★, *Triple Echo* (Harvest 1977)★★, *Alive And Well* (Harvest 1978)★★, *Live At The Proms 1970* (1988)★★, *The Peel Sessions* (Strange Fruit 1990)★★★★, *The Untouchable* (1990)★★★, *As If ...* (1991)★★, *Rubber Riff* (Voiceprint 1995)★★, *Spaced* rec. 1968 (Cuneiform 1996)★★★.

●FURTHER READING: *Gong Dreaming*, Daevid Allen.

SOFTLEY, MICK

b. Michael Softley, England. A UK protest folk singer who modelled himself closely on Bob Dylan, Mick Softley made his debut for Immediate Records in 1965 with 'I'm So Confused'. However, long-playing records suited him better, and the attendant debut album, released on Columbia Records, included some notable self-compositions. Tracks such as 'All I Want Is A Chance', 'After The Third World War Is Over (Or How I Learned To Live With Myself)' and particularly 'The War Drags On' revealed a songwriter of considerable potential. The latter track was later reprised by Donovan, who shared the same management team, on his *Universal Soldier* EP. As a testament to the enduring influence of Dylan, *Songs For Swingin' Survivors* also included a version of his 'The Bells Of Rhymney', as well as Woody Guthrie's 'Plains Of The Buffalo'. His subsequent releases for CBS, which included three albums in addition to singles such as 'Can You Hear Me Now?' and 'Lady Willow', saw him move to a more electric folk sound. None brought him mainstream attention, however, and by the mid-70s he had ceased recording.

●ALBUMS: *Songs For Swingin' Survivors* (Columbia 1965)★★★, *Sunrise* (CBS 1970)★★, *Street Singer* (CBS 1971)★★, *Any Mother Doesn't Grumble* (CBS 1972)★★.

SONNY AND CHER

Although touted as the misunderstood young lovers of 1965 folk rock Sonny Bono and Cher were not as fresh and naïve as their image suggested. Salvatore Bono (b. 16 February 1935, Detroit, Michigan) already had a chequered history in the music business stretching back to the late 50s when he wrote and produced records by such artists as Larry Williams, Wynona Carr and Don And Dewey. Bono also recorded for several small labels under an array of aliases such as Don Christy, Sonny Christy and Ronny Sommers. With arranger Jack Nitzsche, he co-wrote 'Needles And Pins', a UK number 1 for the Searchers in 1964. That same year, Sonny married Cherilyn Sarkasian La Pier (b. 20 May 1946, El Centro, California) whom he had met while recording with the renowned producer Phil Spector. Although the duo recorded a couple of singles under the exotic name Caeser And Cleo, it was as Sonny and Cher that they found fame with the transatlantic number 1, 'I Got You Babe'. Arranged by the underrated Harold Battiste, the single was a majestic example of romanticized folk rock and one of the best-produced discs of its time. Bono's carefree, bohemian image obscured the workings of a music business veteran and it was no coincidence that he took full advantage of the pair's high profile. During late 1965, they dominated the charts as both a duo and soloists with such hits was 'Baby Don't Go', 'All I Really Want To Do', 'Laugh At Me', 'Just You' and 'But You're Mine'. Although their excessive output resulted in diminishing returns, their lean periods were still punctuated by further hits, most notably 'Little Man' and 'The Beat Goes On'. By the late 60s, they had fallen from critical grace, but starred in a couple of low budget movies, *Good Times* and *Chastity*. A brief resurgence as MOR entertainers in the 70s brought them their own television series, although by that time they had divorced. Eventually, extra-curricular acting activities ended their long-standing musical partnership.

While Cher went on to achieve a phenomenally successful acting and singing career, Bono also continued to work as an actor, but adopted a completely different role in 1988 when he was voted mayor of Palm Springs.

●ALBUMS: *Look At Us* (Atco 1965)★★, *The Wondrous World Of Sonny And Cher* (Atco 1966)★★, *In Case You're In Love* (Atco 1967)★★, *Good Times* (1967)★★, *Sonny And Cher Live* (1971)★, *All I Ever Need Is You* (1972)★★, *Mama Was A Rock And Roll Singer - Papa Used To Write All Her Songs* (1974)★, *Live In Las Vegas, Vol. 2* (1974)★.

●COMPILATIONS: *Baby Don't Go* (1965)★★, *The Best Of Sonny And Cher* (1967)★★★, *Greatest Hits* (1974)★★★, *The Sonny And Cher Collection: An Anthology Of Their Hits Alone And Together* (1991)★★★, *All I Ever Need: The Kapp/MCA Anthology* (MCA 1996)★★★.

●FURTHER READING: *Sonny And Cher*, Thomas Braun.

●FILMS: *Good Times* (1967).

SONS OF CHAMPLIN

Bill Champlin (vocals/trumpet) and Tim Caine (saxophone) formed this enigmatic white-soul aggregation in 1965. They were initially joined by Terry Haggerty (lead guitar), Al Strong (bass) and Jim Myers (drums), but when a horn player, Geoff Palmer, was added, Champlin switched to guitar. Draft victim Myers was then replaced by Bill Bowen. Originally dubbed the Masterbeats, then, the Sons Of Father Champlin, the group adopted their more familiar name in 1966. A confident debut single, 'Sing Me A Rainbow', preceded their transformation from besuited aspirants to chemical proselytizers. Now established on the San Francisco scene, a sprawling double album, *Loosen Up Naturally*, encapsulated their unique blend of love, peace, happiness and funk.

A second album, named after the group's now truncated title, the Sons, refined a similar mixture before they embarked on one of their periodic implosions, during which time various members joined, and left such ensembles as the Rhythm Dukes and the Nu-Boogaloo Express. A reconstituted line-up, shorn of its horn-section, reappeared on *Follow Your Heart*. Champlin, Haggerty and Palmer were joined by David Shallock (guitar) and Bill Vitt (drums) in a new venture, Yogi Phlegm, but this unfortunate/wonderful appellation was then abandoned. The quintet later reclaimed the Sons Of Champlin name, but although they secured some commercial success, it was tempered by mis management and misfortune. Bill Champlin embarked on a solo career during the late 70s. He appeared as a backing singer on a score of releases and co-wrote 'After The Love Is Gone' for Earth, Wind And Fire. Having completed two solo albums, *Single* and *Runaway*, this expressive vocalist joined Chicago in 1982.

●ALBUMS: *Loosen Up Naturally* (Capitol 1969)★★★, *The Sons* (1969)★★, *The Sons Minus Seeds And Stems* (1970)★★, *Follow Your Heart* (1971)★★★, *Welcome To The Dance* (Columbia 1973)★★, *The Sons Of Champlin* (1975)★★, *A Circle Filled With Love* (1976)★★, *Loving Is Why* (1977)★★.

●COMPILATIONS: *Marin County Sunshine* (1988)★★★.

SOPWITH CAMEL

Formed in San Francisco, California in 1965, Sopwith Camel originally consisted of Peter Kraemer (guitar/vocals), Terry McNeil (guitar/keyboards), Rod Albin (bass) and Fritz Kasten (drums). This embryonic line-up faltered with the loss of its rhythm section, but the arrival of William Sievers (guitar), Martin Beard (bass) and former Mike Bloomfield drummer Norman Mayell heralded the beginning of the group's most successful era. Their debut single, 'Hello Hello', reached the US Top 30 in January 1967, and its charming simplicity recalled the good-time music of the Lovin' Spoonful. The two groups shared the same label and Sopwith Camel were promoted as a surrogate, denying them the guitar-based direction their live show offered. *Sopwith Camel* was, nonetheless, a fine collection, highlighted by the enthralling 'Frantic Desolation'. The group broke up, however, when the record was not as successful as they had hoped. However, in 1972 the 'hit' line-up, bar Sievers, was reunited for *The Miraculous Hump Returns From The Moon*. This showcased a jazz-based emphasis, but failed to rekindle past glories and in 1974 the band split again. Kraemer did attempt to resurrect the name three years later, but when a van containing all of their equipment was destroyed by fire, Sopwith Camel was officially grounded.

● ALBUMS: *Sopwith Camel* reissued in 1986 with one extra track as *Frantic Desolation* (Kama Sutra 1967)★★★, *The Miraculous Hump Returns From The Moon* (Reprise 1972)★★★.

SORROWS

Formed in Coventry, England, in 1963, the Sorrows consisted of Don Maughn (vocals), Pip Whitcher (lead guitar), Wez Price (rhythm guitar), Philip Packham (bass) and Bruce Finley (drums). They achieved minor fame with 'Take A Heart', a pulsating, brooding performance wherein a rolling drum pattern and throbbing bass created a truly atmospheric single. Their fusion of R&B and mod-pop continued on several ensuing releases, but the quintet was unable to secure consistent success. Maughn, who was later known as Don Fardon, left the group for a solo career in 1967. A restructured Sorrows, Price, Packham, Finley and Chris Fryers (vocals/organ/guitar), then moved to Italy where 'Take A Heart' had become a substantial hit. The group completed several further recordings exclusive to that country, before breaking up at the end of the decade.

● ALBUMS: *Take A Heart* (Piccadilly 1965)★★★, *Old Songs New Songs* (1968)★★.
● COMPILATIONS: *Pink Purple Yellow And Red* (1987)★★★.

SOUL, JIMMY

b. James McCleese, 24 August 1942, Weldon, North Carolina, USA, d. 25 June 1988. A former boy preacher, McCleese acquired his 'Soul' epithet from his congregations. He subsequently toured southern US states as a member of several gospel groups, including the famed Nightingales, wherein Soul was billed as 'The Wonder Boy', before discovering a forte for pop and R&B. He became a popular attraction around the Norfolk area of Virginia where he was introduced to songwriter/producer Frank Guida, who guided the career of Gary 'U.S.' Bonds. Soul joined Guida's S.P.Q.R label and enjoyed a Top 20 US R&B hit with his debut single, 'Twistin' Matilda', before striking gold with his second release, 'If You Wanna Be Happy', which topped the US pop chart in 1963. Both songs were remakes of popular calypso tunes, reflecting Guida's passion for West Indian music. The song also became a minor hit in Britain, and was latterly covered by the Peter B's, a group that included Peter Bardens, Peter Green and Mick Fleetwood. It sadly proved Soul's final chart entry although he nonetheless remained a popular entertainer. Soul died in June 1988.

● ALBUMS: *If You Wanna Be Happy* (SPQR 1963)★★★, *Jimmy Soul And The Belmonts* (1963)★★★.
● COMPILATIONS: *If You Wanna Be Happy: The Very Best Of* (Ace 1996)★★★.

SOUNDS NICE

When Decca Records' A&R representative Tony Hall heard Jane Birkin and Serge Gainsbourg's 'Je T'Aime ... Moi Non Plus' at the Antibes festival in the South of France, he immediately recognized the potential of an instrumental version. When the song was duly banned in Britain in 1969 this newly formed and as yet unnamed group recorded a non-sexy version retitled 'Love At First Sight' which later became a Top 20 hit. After the recording session, Hall played a finished tape to Paul McCartney who casually remarked, 'sounds nice', thereby giving the group a name. Although the hit duo never charted again, their line-up was particularly interesting. Tim Mycroft, after stints with the Freewheelers, the Third Ear Band and Gun, had decided to concentrate on writing and collaborated with arranger Paul Buckmaster. The third man behind the hit was producer Gus Dudgeon, who had recently enjoyed hits with David Bowie, Locomotive and the Bonzo Dog Doo-Dah Band. Following their pledge to create 'instrumentals with a difference' Buckmaster and Dudgeon went on to work successfully with Elton John.

● ALBUMS: *Love At First Sight* (Parlophone 1969)★★★.

SOUNDS ORCHESTRAL

Led by pianist John Pearson (b. 18 June 1925, London, England), Sounds Orchestral was a conglomeration of session musicians who included in their ranks Kenny Clare (ex-drummer with Johnny Dankworth) and bass player/producer Tony Reeves (ex-Colosseum). The orchestral concept was conceived by renowned producer John Schroeder. 'People are looking for a change from the incessant beat and I intend Sounds to fulfil that demand', he told the pop press in early 1965. The group went some way towards fulfilling that ambition with their cover of the Vince Guaraldi Trio's 1960 recording 'Cast Your Fate To The Wind'. With its melodic arrangement and subtle jazz rhythm, the song took the UK charts by storm in January 1965, climbing into the Top 3. Surprisingly, this unlikely pop hit also reached the US Top 10, paving the way for a number of instrumental hits during 1965, courtesy of artists ranging from Horst Jankowski to Marcello Minerebi and Nini Rosso.

● ALBUMS: *Thunderball, Sounds Orchestral Meet James Bond* (Pye 1965)★★★, *Cast Your Fate To The Wind* (Pye 1970)★★★, *Dreams* (1983)★★★, *Sleepy Shores* (1985)★★★.
● COMPILATIONS: *Golden Hour Of Sounds Orchestral* (Pye 1973)★★★.

SOUTHLANDERS

This male vocal quartet, which claims to be the longest-lasting vocal group in British pop music history, was formed by Vernon Nesbeth (b. c.1933, Jamaica, West Indies) in 1954. Nesbeth had won an *Opportunity Knocks* contest in his native country, and travelled to England in 1950 intent on making a career as a singer. He studied at the Royal College of Music, London, and took lessons from the renowned black actor, singer and teacher, Edric Connor. When Connor needed some backing singers for two Caribbean albums, Nesbeth recruited Frank Mannah, and brothers Alan and Harry Wilmot. Harry was the father of the popular contemporary UK entertainer Gary Wilmot. After changing their name from the Caribbeans to the Southlanders, the group was signed by the Grade Organization, and toured the UK variety circuit. On a broadcast with Geraldo, they sang 'Earth Angel', and this song became their first record release in 1956. It was produced by George Martin, several years before he came to prominence with Peter Sellers' comedy albums and the Beatles' recordings. The Southlanders' other sides through to 1961 included 'The Crazy Otto Rag', 'Ain't That A Shame', 'Have You Ever Been Lonely', 'Hush-A-By-Rock', 'The Wedding Of The Lucky Black Cat', 'Swedish Polka', 'I Never Dreamed', 'Peanuts', 'Penny Loafers And Bobby Socks', 'Put A Light In The Window', 'Down Deep', 'Wishing For Your Love', 'I Wanna Jive Tonight', 'Torero', 'Coo-Choo-Choo Cha-Cha-Cha', 'Roma Rockarolla', 'Down Deep', 'Charlie', and 'Imitation Of Love'. They had their biggest hit in 1957 with the beautiful 'Alone', which is said to have sold 750,000 copies in the first few weeks of release, but the group is most identified with the novelty, 'Mole In A Hole' ('I am a mole and I live in a hole'), which they are required to include in every performance (they can even sing a version in Japanese). In the late 50s and early 60s the Southlanders were regulars on top-rated television programmes such as *6.5 Special* and *Crackerjack*, and had their own show with Emile Ford And The Checkmates. They were among the first entertainers to join Jimmy Saville's Mecca dance hall shows, which were the cradle of what became the disco boom. Since then, they have appeared in concerts and cabaret throughout the world, with a classy, highly entertaining act that combines their record hits with a weave of traditional calypso, spiritual rhythms and soul classics. Harry Wilmot died in 1961, and Alan retired in 1974; Frank Mannah died three years later. Nesbeth is still the lead singer and focal point in the 1995 line-up of baritone Randolph Patterson, bass Julian John Lewis, and tenor Joseph Servie. Over more than 40 years of the group's existence, he has also done some solo work. In 1975, he appeared with Michael Denison in *The Black Mikado* at London's Cambridge Theatre, and in 1982 he sang in the opera, *A Great Day In The Morning*, with Jesse Norman and Robert Wilson, in Paris.

SPANKY AND OUR GANG

The original line-up of this engaging US harmony group - Elaine 'Spanky' McFarlane (tambourine/washboard), Nigel Pickering (12-string guitar) and Oz Bach (stand-up bass/kazoo) - began performing together in Chicago's folk clubs. Within months they were joined by Malcolm Hale (guitar/vocals) and John George Seiter (drums) and this restructured line-up shad a US Top 10 hit with its debut release, 'Sunday Will Never Be The Same'. This evocative song bore traces of the Mamas And The Papas and the more conservative Seekers, a style maintained on its follow-up, 'Lazy Day'. Bach was then replaced by Geoffrey Myers, who in turn made way for Kenny Hodges. Sixth member Lefty Baker (vocals/guitar) expanded the group's harmonic range, but while the haunting 'Like To Get To Know You' suggested a more mature direction, Spanky And Our Gang seemed more content with a bubbly, good-time, but rather lightweight approach. The premature death of Hale in 1968 undermined the group's inner confidence, and any lingering momentum faltered when 'Give A Damn', a campaign song for the Urban Coalition League, incurred an airplay ban in several states. The remaining quintet broke up in 1969 although McFarlane and Pickering retained the name for the country-influenced *Change*. In 1981 the former joined a rejuvenated Mamas And The Papas, before touring with an all-new Spanky And Our Gang.

● ALBUMS: *Spanky And Our Gang* (Mercury 1967)★★★, *Like To Get To Know You* (Mercury 1968)★★★, *Anything You Choose/Without Rhyme Or Reason* (Mercury 1969)★★, *Spanky And Our Gang Live* (1970)★★, *Change* (1975)★★.
● COMPILATIONS: *Spanky's Greatest Hits* (1969)★★★, *The Best Of Spanky And Our Gang* (Rhino 1986)★★★.

SPECTOR, PHIL

b. Harvey Phillip Spector, 26 December 1940, Bronx, New York, USA. Arguably pop's most distinctive record producer. Spector became involved in music upon moving to Fairfax, California, in 1953. While there, he joined a loosely knit community of young aspirants, including Lou Adler, Bruce Johnson and Sandy Nelson, the last of whom played drums on Spector's debut recording, 'To Know Him Is To Love Him'. This million-selling single for the Teddy Bears - Spector, Annette Kleibard and Marshall Leib - topped the US chart in 1958, but further releases by the group proved less successful. The artist's next project, the Spectors Three, was undertaken under the aegis of local entrepreneurs Lee Hazelwood and Lester Sill, but when it, too, reaped little commercial reward, the latter recommended Phil's talents to New York production team Leiber And Stoller. In later years Spector made extravagant claims about his work from this period which have been rebuffed equally forcibly by his one-time mentors. He did contribute greatly as a composer, co-writing 'Spanish Harlem' and 'Young Boy Blues' for Ben E. King, while adding a notable guitar obligato to the Drifters' 'On Broadway'. His productions, although less conspicuous, included releases by LaVern Baker, Ruth Brown and Billy Storm, as well as the Top Notes' original version of the seminal 'Twist And Shout'. Spector's first major success as a producer came with Ray Petersen's version of 'Corrina Corrina', a US Top 10 in 1960, and Curtis Lee's 'Pretty Little Angel Eyes', which reached number 7 the following year. Work for the Paris Sisters not only engendered a Top 5 hit, ('I Love How You Love Me') but rekindled an association with Lester Sill, with whom Spector formed Philles Records in 1961.

Within months he bought his partner out to become sole owner; this autocratic behaviour marked all subsequent endeavours. It nonetheless resulted in a string of classic recordings for the Crystals and Ronettes including 'He's A Rebel' (1962), 'Then He Kissed Me', 'Be My Baby' and 'Baby I Love You' (all 1963), which were not only substantial international hits, but defined the entire 'girl-group' genre. Imitative releases supervised by David Gates, Bob Crewe and Sonny Bono, although excellent in their own right, failed to recapture Spector's dense production technique, later dubbed the 'wall of sound', which relied on lavish orchestration, layers of percussion and swathes of echo. Recordings were undertaken at the Gold Star studio in Los Angeles where arranger Jack Nitzsche and engineer Larry Levine worked with a team of exemplary session musicians, including Tommy Tedeso (guitar), Larry Knechtal (piano/bass), Harold Battiste, Leon Russell (keyboards) and Hal Blaine (drums). Although ostensibly geared to producing singles, Phil did undertake the ambitious *A Christmas Gift To You*, on which his label's premier acts performed old and new seasonal favourites. Although not a contemporary success - its bonhomie was made redundant following the assassination of President Kennedy - the set is now rightly regarded as a classic. Spector's releases also featured some of the era's finest songwriting teams - Goffin And King, Barry And Greenwich and Barry Mann and Cynthia Weil - the last of which composed 'You've Lost That Lovin' Feelin'' for the Righteous Brothers, the producer's stylistic apogee. Several critics also cite 'River Deep Mountain High', a 1966 single by Ike And Tina Turner as Spector's greatest moment. It represented Spector's most ambitious production, but although his efforts were rewarded with a UK Top 3 hit, this impressive release barely scraped the US Hot 100 and a dispirited Spector folded his label and retired from music for several years.

He re-emerged in 1969 with a series of releases for A&M which included 'Black Pearl', a US Top 20 hit entry for Sonny Charles And The Checkmates. Controversy then dogged his contribution to the Beatles' *Let It Be* album. Spector assembled the set from incomplete tapes, but his use of melancholic orchestration on 'The Long And Winding Road' infuriated the song's composer, Paul McCartney, who cited this intrusion during the group's rancorous break-up. Spector nonetheless became installed at their Apple label, where he produced albums by John Lennon (*The Plastic Ono Band, Imagine, Sometime In New York City*), George Harrison (*All Things Must Pass* and the commemorative *Concert For Bangla Desh*). However, his behaviour grew increasingly erratic following the break-up of his marriage to former Ronette Ronnie Spector, and his relationship with Lennon was severed during sessions for the nostalgic *Rock 'N' Roll* album (1974). In the meantime Spector had estab-

lished the Warner-Spector outlet which undertook new recordings with, among others, Cher and Nilsson, as well as several judicious re-releases. A similar relationship with UK Polydor led to the formation of Phil Spector International, on which contemporary singles by Dion, Darlene Love and Jerri Bo Keno vied with 60s recordings and archive material. As the 70s progressed so Spector became a recluse, although he emerged to produce albums by Leonard Cohen (*Death Of Ladies Man* - 1977) and the Ramones (*End Of The Century* - 1980), the latter of which included a revival of 'Baby I Love You', the group's sole UK Top 10 hit. Despite undertaking abortive sessions with the Flamin' Groovies, Spector remained largely detached from music throughout the 80s, although litigation against Leiber and Stoller and biographer Mark Ribowsky kept his name in the news. Spector was inducted into the Rock 'n' Roll Hall Of Fame in 1989, and having adopted Allen Klein as representative, completed negotiations with EMI for the rights to his extensive catalogue. The interest generated by this acquisition is a tribute to the respect afforded this producer whose major achievements were contained within a brief three-year period.

●COMPILATIONS: *Today's Hits* (Philles 1963)★★★, *A Christmas Gift To You* (Philles 1963)★★★★, *Phil Spector Wall Of Sound, Volume 1: The Ronettes* (1975)★★★★, *Phil Spector Wall Of Sound, Volume 2: Bob B. Soxx And The Blue Jeans* (1975)★★★★, *Phil Spector Wall Of Sound, Volume 3: The Crystals* (1975)★★★★, *Phil Spector Wall Of Sound, Volume 4: Yesterday's Hits Today* (1976)★★★★, *Phil Spector Wall Of Sound, Volume 5: Rare Masters* (1976)★★★, *Phil Spector Wall Of Sound, Volume 6: Rare Masters Volume 2* (1976)★★★, *The Phil Spector Story* (1976)★★★, *Echoes Of The Sixties* (1977)★★★, *Phil Spector 1974-1979* (1979)★★★, *Wall Of Sound* (1981)★★★, *Phil Spector: The Early Productions 1958-1961* (1984)★★★, *Twist And Shout: Twelve Atlantic Tracks Produced By Phil Spector* (1989)★★★, *Back To Mono* box set (Rhino 1991)★★★★★

●FURTHER READING: *The Phil Spector Story: Out Of His Head*, Richard Williams. *The Phil Spector Story*, Rob Finnis. *He's A Rebel*, Mark Ribowskys. *Collecting Phil Spector: The Man, The Legend, The Music*, Jack Fitzpatrick and James E. Fogerty.

SPINNERS (UK)

This popular folk group was formed in 1958 with the following line-up: Tony Davis (b. 24 August 1930, Blackburn Lancashire, England; banjo/tin whistle/guitar/kazoo), Mick Groves (b. 29 September 1936, Salford, Lancashire, England; guitar), Hughie Jones (b. Hugh E. Jones, 21 July 1936, Liverpool, England; guitar/harmonica/banjo) and Cliff Hall (b. 11 September 1925, Oriente Pourice, Cuba; guitar/harmonica). Hall was born to Jamaican parents who returned to Jamaica in 1939. He came to England after joining the Royal Air Force in 1942. The group was often augmented in concert by 'Count' John McCormick (double bass), who is generally regarded as the fifth

'Spinner'. Occasionally rebuked by folk 'purists' as bland and middle-of-the-road, the Spinners nevertheless introduced many people to folk music. The regular sell-out attendances at their concerts are a testimony to this. Songs that are now covered by other performers and often mistakenly referred to as 'traditional' are in fact Hughie Jones originals: 'The Ellan Vannin Tragedy', 'The Marco Polo' and 'The Fairlie Duplex Engine'. In 1990, Jones produced *Hughie's Ditty-Bag*, a book of songs and stories. He is still performing occasionally as a soloist. After a 30 year career, the Spinners decided to call it a day, and released the double album *Final Fling*. Since retiring, the group have made a number of reunion tours, proving that both their interest, and the public's enthusiasm, have not waned.

●ALBUMS: *Quayside Songs Old And New* (1962)★★★, *The Spinners* (Fontana 1964)★★★, *Folk At The Phil* (1964)★★★, *More Folk At The Phil* (1965)★★★, *The Family Of Man* (1966)★★★, *Another LP By The Spinners* (1967)★★★, *The Spinners Clockwork Storybook* (1969)★★★, *Not Quite Folk* (1969)★★★, *The Spinners Are In Town* (1970)★★★, *Love Is Teasing* (1972)★★★, *Sing Out, Shout With Joy* (1972)★★★, *By Arrangement* (1973)★★★, *The Spinners At The London Palladium* (1974)★★★, *The Spinners English Collection* (1976)★★★, *All Day Singing* (1977)★★★, *Songs Of The Tall Ships* (1978)★★★, *Your 20 Favourite Christmas Carols* (1978)★★★, *Around The World And Back Again* (1981)★★★, *Here's To You...From The Spinners* (1982)★★★, *Final Fling* (1988)★★★, *Hughie's Ditty Bag* (1991)★★★.

●COMPILATIONS: *Meet The Spinners* (1981)★★★, *18 Golden Favourites* (1982)★★★, *This Is The Spinners* (1982)★★★, *20 Golden Folk Songs* (1984)★★★, *The Singing City* (1984)★★★.

●FURTHER READING: *The Spinners*, David Stuckey.

SPIRIT

'Out of Topanga Canyon, from the Time Coast' stated the CBS publicity blurb for one of their finest acts of the late 60s. The rock band with a hint of jazz arrived with their self-titled debut album. Formerly Spirits Rebellious, the new band comprised: Randy California (b. Randolph Wolfe, 20 February 1951, Los Angeles, California, USA, d. 2 January 1997; guitar), Ed 'Mr Skin' Cassidy (b. 4 May 1931, Chicago, Illinois, USA; drums), John Locke (b. 25 September 1943, Los Angeles, California, USA; keyboards), Jay Ferguson (b. 10 May 1947, Burbank, California, USA; vocals) and Mark Andes (b. 19 February 1948, Philadelphia, Pennsylvania, USA; bass). Media interest was assured when it was found out that not only had the band a shaven-headed drummer who had played with many jazz giants including Gerry Mulligan, Cannonball Adderley and Thelonious Monk, but that he was also the guitarist's father (later amended to stepfather). The quality of the music, however, needed no hype. The album's tasteful use of strings mixed with Locke's stunning electric piano blended well with

California's mature hard-edged guitar. Ferguson's lyrics were quirky and brilliant. 'Fresh Garbage', for example, contained the lines: 'Well look beneath your lid some morning, see the things you didn't quite consume, the world's a can for your fresh garbage.' The album reached number 31 in the US chart and stayed for over seven months. The following year's *The Family That Plays Together* in 1969, was a greater success and spawned a US Top 30 hit single, 'I Got A Line On You'. Ferguson had to share the songwriting credits with the fast-developing California. The Lou Adler-produced set flowed with perfect continuity and almost 30 years later, the album sounds fresh. *Clear Spirit* contained Locke's instrumental music for the film *The Model Shop*, including the beautifully atmospheric 'Ice'. As a touring band they were most impressive, with Cassidy's massive drum kit sometimes dwarfing the stage. California would often use a clear perspex Stratocaster, while tinkering with his echoplex device which emitted the most colourful sound. The band's fourth collection, *The Twelve Dreams Of Dr Sardonicus*, was arguably their finest work, with Ferguson and California's songwriting reaching a peak. Although it was their lowest charting album to date (failing to make the Top 50 in the USA), it has subsequently and deservedly become their best-selling record. Randy's awareness for environmental and ecological issues was cleverly linked into his song 'Nature's Way', while Ferguson put in strong contributions including 'Animal Zoo'. At this time Spirit had their legendary album *Potatoland* rejected (it was eventually released after active petitioning from the UK rock magazine, *Dark Star*). The tensions within the band were mounting and Ferguson and Andes left to form Jo Jo Gunne. Surprisingly, California also departed to be replaced by Al and Christian Staehely. The John Locke-dominated *Feedback* was not a commercial or critical success. The remains of Spirit disintegrated, while Jo Jo Gunne prospered and Randy attempted a solo career.

In 1976 Spirit returned with a new recording contract and a rejuvenated California. During the recent past it was found that California had jumped off London's Waterloo Bridge into the polluted River Thames and was miraculously rescued. The new nucleus of California, Cassidy and bassist Larry Knight toured regularly and built up a loyal following in Britain and Germany. The albums, while delighting the fans, sold poorly and the band became despondent. Nevertheless, there were some spectacular highlights, most notably the stunning yet perplexing double album *Spirit Of '76* (still not reissued on CD). While Ferguson was enjoying great success as a solo artist, Mark Andes was with Firefall. A depressed California, interviewed in London in 1978-79, stated that Spirit would not rise and that he would *never* play with Ed Cassidy again. Fortunately California was wrong, as the original five were back together in 1984 for *The Thirteenth Dream*. They attempted reworkings of vintage Spirit numbers and sadly the album failed. California still attempts to keep the Spirit name alive with various assorted line-ups, usually together with the fatherly hand of Ed Cassidy. Both *Rapture In the Chambers* and *Tent Of Miracles* were disappointing works. The Staehely brothers continue to work in the business, Christian as a session musician and Al has become one of the leading music business lawyers in the USA. Cassidy and California have since continued into the 90s using the Spirit moniker with varied line-ups. At the time of California's tragic death the band were about to release *California Blues* prior to a lengthy tour of Europe, where they retained a strong following. On 2 January 1997 California and his 12-year-old son were swimming in Hawaii when a freak wave engulfed them. California was able to push his son to safety but was dragged back by the undertow. His body was never found. Ironically, it is only California who could have continued as the moral owner of the name, as he is and has always been the true spirit of the band.

●ALBUMS: *Spirit* (Ode/Columbia 1968)★★★, *The Family That Plays Together* (Ode/Columbia 1969)★★★★, *Clear Spirit* (Columbia 1969)★★★, *The Twelve Dreams Of Dr. Sardonicus* (Epic 1970)★★★★★, *Feedback* (Epic 1972)★★, *Spirit Of '76* (Mercury 1975)★★★★, *Son Of Spirit* (Mercury 1976)★★★, *Farther Along* (Mercury 1976)★★★, *Future Games (A Magical Kahuana Dream)* (Mercury 1977)★★★, *Live* (Illegal 1978), *Journey To Potatoland* (Rhino/Beggars Banquet 1981)★★★, (1984), *The Thirteenth Dream (Spirit Of '84)* (Mercury 1984)★★, *Rapture In The Chamber* (IRS 1989)★★, *Tent Of Miracles* (1990)★★, *Live At La Paloma 1993* (C.R.E.W. 1995)★★★.

●COMPILATIONS: *The Best Of Spirit* (Epic 1973)★★★, *Chronicles* (C.R.E.W. 1991)★★★★, *Time Circle* (Epic/Legacy 1991)★★★★, *Spirit - The Collection* (1991)★★★, *The Mercury Years* (Mercury 1997)★★★★.

SPOOKY TOOTH

Formed in 1967 as a blues group, they quickly moved into progressive rock during the heady days of the late 60s. Formerly named Art, they released a ponderous version of Buffalo Springfield's 'For What It's Worth' as 'What's That Sound'. The original band comprised Gary Wright (b. 26 April 1945, Englewood, New Jersey, USA; keyboards/vocals), Mike Kellie (b. 24 March 1947, Birmingham, England; drums), Luther Grosvenor (b. 23 December 1949, Worcester, England; guitar), Mike Harrison (b. 3 September 1945, Carlisle, Cumberland, England; vocals) and Greg Ridley (b. 23 October 1947, Cumberland, England; bass). Their hard work on the English club scene won through, although their only commercial success was in the USA. They combined hard-edged imaginative versions of non-originals with their own considerable writing abilities. *Its All About* was a fine debut; although not a strong seller it contained their reading of 'Tobacco Road', always a club favourite, and their debut single 'Sunshine Help Me', which sounded uncannily similar to early Traffic. It was *Spooky Two*, however, that put them on the map; eight powerful

songs with a considerable degree of melody, this album remains as one of the era's finest heavy rock albums. Their self-indulgent excursion with Pierre Henry on *Ceremony* was a change of direction that found few takers, save for the superb cover painting by British artist John Holmes. *The Last Puff* saw a number of personnel changes: Ridley had departed for Humble Pie, Gary Wright left to form Wonderwheel and Grosvenor later emerged as 'Ariel Bender' in Stealers Wheel and Mott The Hoople. Three members of the Grease Band joined; Henry McCullough, Chris Stainton and Alan Spenner. The album contained a number of non-originals, notably David Ackles' 'Down River' and a superb version of Elton John's 'Son Of Your Father'. The band broke up shortly after its release, although various members, including Foreigner's Mick Jones, Bryson Graham (drums), Mike Patto and Ian Herbert (bass) eventually regrouped for three further albums which, while competent, showed no progression and were all written to a now dated formula. Judas Priest recorded 'Better By You, Better Than Me', which resulted in a court case following the deaths of two fans. The band were accused of inciting violence, causing the two fans to shoot themselves.

●ALBUMS: *It's All About* (Island 1968)★★★, *Spooky Two* (Island 1969)★★★★, *Ceremony* (Island 1970)★★, *The Last Puff* (Island 1970)★★★★, *You Broke My Heart So I Busted Your Jaw* (Island 1973)★★, *Witness* (Island 1973)★★, *The Mirror* (Island 1974)★★. Solo: Luthor Grosvenor *Under Open Skies* (Island 1971)★★★. Mike Harrison *Mike Harrison* (Island 1971)★★★, *Smokestack Lightning* (Island 1972)★★, *Rainbow Rider* (Good Ear 1975)★★.

●COMPILATIONS: *That Was Only Yesterday* (1976)★★★, *The Best Of Spooky Tooth* (Island 1976)★★★★.

SPOTNICKS

A Swedish instrumental group of the late 50s and early 60s, their career actually continued well into the 80s. Originally they consisted of Bo Winberg (b. 27 March 1939, Gothenburg, Sweden), Bob Lander (b. Bo Starander, 11 March 1942, Sweden), Bjorn Thelin (b. 11 June 1942, Sweden) and Ole Johannsson (b. Sweden). They were assembled by Winberg in 1957 as the Frazers, with Lander on guitar and vocals, Thelin on bass, Johannsson on drums, with Winberg himself playing lead guitar and building most of the band's equipment; including a guitar transmitter that allowed primitive flex-free playing. Spotted by Roland F. Fernedorg in 1960 they became the Spotnicks in 1961 and had several hit singles in their homeland. They were signed to Oriole in the UK in 1962 and toured the country, gaining instant notoriety for their gimmick of wearing spacesuits on stage. They played a mixture of instrumentals and Lander vocals, and first hit with 'Orange Blossom Special' in 1962. That same year they toured Russia and were introduced to cosmonaut Yuri Gagarin.

They had further UK hits with 'Rocket Man', 'Hava Nagila' and 'Just Listen To My Heart' during 1962-63. In

1963 they made their cinematic debut in the pop film *Just For Fun*. A cover of the Tornados' 'Telstar' was released in Sweden under the pseudonym the Shy Ones. Johansson left in 1963 to become a priest and was replaced by Derek Skinner (b. 5 March 1944, London, England). In 1965 they added organist Peter Winsens to the line-up and in September Skinner left to be replaced by Jimmy Nicol. Nicol was the drummer famed for having deputized for Ringo Starr on a 1964 Beatles World Tour, when he was hospitalized after having collapsed with tonsillitis. Nicol had also played with the Blue Flames and his own band the Shubdubs. After much touring Nicol left in early 1967 and was replaced by Tommy Tausis (b. 22 March 1946). In October Thelin was called up for National Service and replaced by Magnus Hellsberg. Several further line-up changes occurred over the following years as the band continued to tour and record prolifically in Europe. Winberg was the only constant member although Lander was normally in the band until he left to form the Viking Truckers. The band were still active as of the mid-80s.

●ALBUMS: *Out-A-Space* (1963)★★★, *The Spotnicks In Paris* (1964)★★, *The Spotnicks In Spain* (Oriole 1964)★★, *The Spotnicks In Berlin* (Oriole 1965)★★, *In The Middle Of The Universe* (1984)★★, *Music For The Millions* (1985)★★, *Highway Boogie* (1986)★★, *Love Is Blue* (1988)★★.

●COMPILATIONS: *The Very Best of The Spotnicks* (Air 1981)★★★.

●FILMS: *Just For Fun* (1963).

SPRINGFIELD, DUSTY

b. Mary Isabel Catherine Bernadette O'Brien, 16 April 1939, Hampstead, London, England. A long-standing critical favourite but sadly neglected by the mass public from the early 70s until the end of the 80s. The career of Britain's greatest ever white soul/pop singer has been a turbulent one. Formerly referred to as 'the White Negress', Dusty began as a member of the cloying pop trio the Lana Sisters in the 50s, and moved with her brother Tom (Dion O'Brien) and Tim Field into the Springfields, one of Britain's top pop/folk acts of the early 60s. During the Merseybeat boom she made a bold move and went solo. Her debut in late 1963 with 'I Only Want To Be With You' (the ever first song performed on the long-running UK television programme, *Top Of The Pops*), removed any doubts the previously shy convent girl may have had; this jaunty, endearing song is now a classic of 60s pop. She joined the swinging London club scene and became a familiar icon for teenage girls with her famous beehive blonde hairstyle and her dark 'panda' eye make-up. Over the next three years Springfield was constantly in the best-selling singles chart with a string of unforgettable hits and consistently won the top female singer award in the UK, beating off stiff opposition from Lulu, Cilla Black and Sandie Shaw. During this time she campaigned unselfishly on behalf of the then little-known black American soul, R&B and Motown artists; her mature taste in music differentiated her from many of her contemporaries. Her commitment to black music carried over into her tour of South Africa in 1964: she played in front of a mixed audience and she was immediately deported.

Dusty's early albums were strong sellers, although they now appear to have been rushed works. Her pioneering choice of material by great songwriters such as Burt Bacharach, Hal David, Randy Newman and Carole King was exemplary. The orchestral arrangements of Ivor Raymonde and Johnny Franz, however, often drowned Dusty's voice, and her vocals appeared thin and strained due to insensitive production. She made superb cover versions of classics such as 'Mockingbird', 'Anyone Who Had A Heart', 'Wishin' And Hopin'', 'La Bamba', and 'Who Can I Turn To'. Her worldwide success came when her friend Vicki Wickham, and Simon Napier-Bell added English words to the Italian hit 'Io Che Non Vivo (Senzate)' and thus created 'You Don't Have To Say You Love Me'. This million-selling opus proved her sole UK chart-topper in 1966. At the end of a turbulent year she had an altercation with jazz drummer Buddy Rich, with whom she was sheduled to play at New York's prestigious Basin Street East club. The music press reported that she had pushed a pie in his face. Years later, in an interview in *Q Magazine*, she told the real story. The often outspoken Rich was allegedly resentful at not receiving top billing and made things difficult for her when she asked to rehearse her show with the (his) band. Rich was heard to respond 'you fucking broad, who do you think you fucking are, bitch?' Dusty retaliated by punching him in the face. By the end of the following year (1967), she was becoming disillusioned with the showbusiness carousel on which she found herself trapped. She appeared out of step with the summer of love and its attendant psychedelic music. Her BBC television series may have been a success with healthy viewing figures, but it was an anathema to the sudden change in the pop scene. The comparatively progressive and prophetically titled *Where Am I Going?* attempted to redress this. Containing a jazzy orchestrated version of Bobby Hebb's 'Sunny' and Jacques Brel's 'If You Go Away' (UK lyrics by Rod McKuen). It was an artistic success but it flopped (or as biographer Lucy O'Brien expertly put it, 'released to stunning indifference'). The following year a similar fate awaited the excellent *Dusty ... Definitely*. On this she surpassed herself with her choice of material, from the rolling 'Ain't No Sunshine Since You've Been Gone' to the aching emotion of Randy Newman's 'I Think It's Gonna Rain Today', but her continuing good choice of songs was no longer getting through to the fans.

In 1968, as Britain was swamped by the progressive music revolution, the uncomfortable split between what was underground and hip, and what was pop and unhip, became prominent. Dusty, well aware that she could be doomed to the variety club chicken-in-a-basket circuit in the UK, departed for Memphis, Tennessee, one of the music capitals of the world, and immediately succeeded in recording a stunning album and her finest work, *Dusty In Memphis*. The expert production team of Tom

Dowd, Jerry Wexler and Arif Mardin were the first people to recognize and allow her natural soul voice to be placed up-front, rather than competing with full and overpowering string arrangements. The album remains a classic and one of the finest records of the 60s. The single 'Son Of A Preacher Man' became a major hit, but the album failed in the UK and only reached a derisory number 99 in the US chart. Following this bitter blow Dusty retreated and kept a lower profile, although her second album for Atlantic, *A Brand New Me*, was a moderate success. Released in the UK as *From Dusty With Love*, the Thom Bell/Kenny Gamble-credited production boosted her failing popularity in her homeland, where she still resided, although she spent much of her time in the USA. *Cameo*, from 1973, exuded class and featured a superlative cover of Van Morrison's 'Tupelo Honey', but sold little and produced no hit singles.

Dusty had now disappeared from the charts, and following a veiled admission in an interview with Ray Coleman for the London *Evening Standard* in 1975 that she was bisexual, moved to Los Angeles. For the next few years she recorded sporadically, preferring to spend her time with tennis players like Billie Jean King and to campaign for animal rights (she is an obsessive cat lover). Additionally she succumbed to pills and booze and even attempted suicide. Following the release of the inappropriately titled *It Begins Again* some five years after her last relase, she was propelled towards a comeback, which failed, although the album did garner respectable sales. Notable tracks were the Carole Bayer Sager gem, 'I'd Rather Leave While I'm In Love', and a Barry Manilow song, 'Sandra', a lyric addressing chillingly similar events in her life over the past few years. The follow-up, *Living Without Your Love*, was poorly received; it contained an indifferent version of the Miracles' 'You Really Got A Hold On Me'. 'Baby Blue' became a minor hit in 1979 but the comeback was over. Dusty went to ground again, even although one flop single in 1980, 'Your Love Still Brings Me To My Knees', remains an undiscovered nugget.

In the early 80s she relocated to Toronto and resurfaced in 1982 with the energetic disco-influenced *White Heat*. Featuring ex-Hookfoot guitarist Caleb Quaye and Nathan East (bass), it was her best album during these musically barren years yet it failed to gain a release outside the USA. Two years later she duetted with her old friend from the 60s beat group era, Spencer Davis. The choice of song: Judy Clay and William Bell's 'Private Number' was excellent, but the choice of Davis as a partner highlighted his limited vocal range. A further attempt to put her in the public eye was orchestrated by club owner Peter Stringfellow in 1985. He booked her at his Hippodrome and contracted her to his similarly-named record label. After one single 'Just Like Butterflies' she fluttered out of sight again.

Her phoenix-like return towards the end of the 80s was due entirely to Neil Tennant and Chris Lowe of the Pet Shop Boys, who persuaded her to duet with them on their hit single 'What Have I Done To Deserve This?' in 1987.

They then wrote the theme for the film *Scandal*, which Dusty took into the best-sellers. That song 'Nothing Has Been Proved' was ideal for her, as the lyrics cleverly documented an era that she knew only too well. She followed this with another of their compositions 'In Private', which although a lesser song lyrically, became a bigger hit. The subsequent album, *Reputation*, became her most successful album for over 20 years. In the early 90s she moved back from America and for a time resided in The Netherlands, surrounded by her beloved cats.

At present she is recording and living once again in Britain, and is less insecure, older and wiser but still plagued by ill luck. In 1994 she underwent chemotherapy for breast cancer. This delayed the release and promotion of her long-awaited new album with Columbia Records. In the spring of 1995 it was announced that the treatment had been carried out successfully and she was in remission. The album *A Very Fine Love* arrived in the wake of the single 'Wherever Would I Be'. This Diane Warren big production ballad featured a duet with Daryl Hall. The rest of the album showed that Springfield still retained a singing voice that could chill the spine and warm the heart, and with modern recording techniques she could make any song sound good. Her greatest asset, in addition to her voice, is her remarkable ability of spotting a good songwriter; her choice of material over the years has been consistently good. A diva who is able to cross over into every gender genre, adored by gays and straights, no British female singer has ever commanded such love and respect.

● ALBUMS: *A Girl Called Dusty* (Philips 1964)★★★★, *Ev'rything's Coming Up Dusty* (Philips 1965)★★★★, *Where Am I Going* (Philips 1967)★★★★, *Dusty ... Definitely* (Philips 1968)★★★★, *Dusty In Memphis* (Philips 1969)★★★★★, *A Brand New Me (From Dusty With Love)* (Philips 1970)★★★★, *See All Her Faces* (Philips 1972)★★★, *Cameo* (1973)★★★, *Dusty Sings Burt Bacharach And Carole King* (Philips 1975)★★★, *It Begins Again* (Mercury 1978)★★★, *Living Without Your Love* (Mercury 1979)★★★, *White Heat* (Casablanca 1982)★★★, *Reputation* (Parlophone 1990)★★★, *A Very Fine Love* (Columbia 1995)★★.

● COMPILATIONS: *Golden Hits* (Philips 1966)★★★★, *Stay Awhile* (Wing 1968)★★★★, *This Is Dusty Springfield Vol. 2: The Magic Garden* (Philips 1973)★★★★, *Greatest Hits* (1981)★★★★ *Dusty: Love Songs* (Philips 1983)★★★★, *The Silver Collection* (Philips 1988),★★★★★ *Dusty's Sounds Of The 60's* (Pickwick 1989)★★★★, *Love Songs* (Pickwick 1989)★★★★, *Dusty Springfield Songbook* (Pickwick 1990)★★★★, *Blue For You* (1993)★★★★, *Goin' Back: The Very Best Of Dusty Springfield* (Philips 1994)★★★★★, *Dusty* 4-CD box set (Phonogram 1994)★★★★, *The Legend Of Dusty Springfield* 4-CD box set (Philips 1994)★★★★, *Something Special* (Mercury 1996)★★★★.

● FURTHER READING: *Dusty*, Lucy O'Brien.

SPRINGFIELDS

Formed in 1960, this popular UK folk-based attraction was based around singer/songwriter Dion O'Brien (b. 2 July 1934, Hampstead, London, England) and his sister Mary Isabel Catherine Bernadette (b. 16 April 1939, Hampstead, London, England), who accompanied him on guitar. Better known as Tom and Dusty Springfield, the duo was later joined by the former's partner, Tim Field, and the following year the revitalized unit became one of Britain's top vocal groups. The trio enjoyed UK Top 5 singles with 'Island Of Dreams' (1962) and 'Say I Won't Be There' (1963), by which time Field had been replaced by Mike Longhurst-Pickworth, who took the less cumbersome professional name Mike Hurst. The Springfields enjoyed success in America with 'Silver Threads And Golden Needles', a country standard that paradoxically failed to chart in Britain. However, although the single went on to sell in excess of one million copies, it was the group's only substantial US hit. The group split up in 1963 with each member then pursuing solo ventures. Dusty Springfield became one of Britain's leading female singers, brother Tom continued his songwriting career, while Hurst established himself as a leading pop producer through his work with Cat Stevens.

●ALBUMS: *Kinda Folksy* (Philips 1963)★★★, *Silver Threads And Golden Needles* (1962)★★★, *Folk Songs From The Hills* (Philips 1963)★★.

●COMPILATIONS: *The Springfields Story* (Philips 1964)★★★, *Sing Again* (Fontana 1969)★★★, *Island Of Dreams* (Contour 1971)★★★.

●FILMS: *It's All Over Town* (1964).

ST. LOUIS UNION

Initially based in Manchester, England, the St. Louis Union - Tony Cassiday (vocals), Keith Miller (guitar), Alex Kirby (tenor saxophone), David Tomlinson (organ), John Nichols (bass) and Dave Webb (drums) - attracted attention as winners of the 1965 *Melody Maker* beat group contest. Their prize was a recording contract with Decca Records, the first fruits of which was a version of 'Girl', plucked from the Beatles' album *Rubber Soul*. The sextet took the song into the UK Top 30, despite competition from the Truth. They later enjoyed a role in *The Ghost Goes Gear*, a film that also featured the Spencer Davis Group. However, the chart failure of subsequent singles, 'Behind The Door' and 'East Side Story', brought their brief career to an end.

●FILMS: *The Ghost Goes Gear* (1965).

ST. PETERS, CRISPIAN

b. Robin Peter Smith, 5 April 1943, Swanley, Kent, England. Originally a member of UK pop group the Beat Formula Three, Smith was plucked from obscurity by manager Dave Nicolson, rechristened Crispian St. Peters and signed to a 10-year management and production contract. After two unsuccessful singles for Decca ('At This Moment' and 'No No No') Nicolson persuaded him to cover We Five's US hit 'You Were On My Mind'. Although the single was almost buried in the pre-Christmas sales rush of 1965, it continued to sell into the New Year and took Crispian into the UK Top 10. Under Nicolson's tutelage, the shy star was momentarily transformed into arrogance incarnate and astonished the conservative music press of the period by his suggestion that he had written 80 songs of better quality than those of the Beatles. Other stars were also waved aside as Crispian announced that he was better than Elvis Presley: 'I'm going to make Presley look like the Statue of Liberty . . . I am sexier than Dave Berry and more exciting than Tom Jones . . . and the Beatles are past it'. Outraged readers denounced him in letters columns, but St. Peters returned stronger than ever with the sprightly 'Pied Piper', a Top 10 hit on both sides of the Atlantic. Thereafter he was remembered more for his idle boasts than his music. After successive chart failures, he switched to country, a form that better suited his singing style. Serious psychological problems hampered his remote chances of a comeback and he fell into obscurity, reappearing irregularly on the flickering revivalist circuit.

●ALBUMS: *Simply ... Crispian St Peters* (1970)★★.

●COMPILATIONS: *The Anthology* (Repertoire 1997)★★.

STAFFORD, TERRY

b. Hollis, Oklahoma, USA, d. 17 March 1996. This tall, local sports champion was also a fan of Elvis Presley and Buddy Holly, artists into whose repertoires he would dip when singing with his school group. With his parents' blessing, he began a showbusiness career in Hollywood where, after two years as a nightclub entertainer, he was spotted by John Fisher and Les Worden who had just founded Crusader Records. His first record, 'Suspicion' - later a hit for Presley - was issued in February 1964 and, despite the onset of Beatlemania, scrambled to number 3 in the US chart, and beat a cover by Millicent Martin to UK's Top 40. Further hits proved harder to come by, and a transfer to MGM Records in 1971 did not improve his fortunes.

●ALBUMS: *Suspicion!* (Crusader 1964)★★, *Dr. Goldfoot And The Girl Bombs* film soundtrack (1966)★, *Born Losers* film soundtrack (1966)★.

●FILMS: *Dr Goldfoot And The Girl Bombs* (1966)★★.

STANDELLS

Tony Valentino (guitar/vocals) and Larry Tamblyn (organ) formed the Standells in 1962. The early line-up included drummer Gary Leeds, who later found fame in the Walker Brothers, Gary Lane (bass) and former Mouseketeer Dick Dodd (drums). The quartet became a leading teen-based attraction in plush Los Angeles nightspots. This conformist image was shattered on their association with producer Ed Cobb, who fashioned a series of angst-cum-protest punk anthems in 'Sometimes Good Guys Don't Wear White', 'Why Pick On Me' and the exceptional 'Dirty Water', a US number 11 hit in 1966. In 1966 Gary Lane left the group during a tour of Florida. He was initially succeeded by Dave Burke, who in turn was replaced the following year by John Fleck (né

Fleckenstein). The latter, who co-wrote 'Can't Explain' on Love's debut album, has since become a leading cinematographer. The Standells also appeared in the exploitation film, *Riot On Sunset Strip* (1967), but by this time their career was waning. Unfashionable in the face of San Francisco's acid-rock, the group's career was confined to the cabaret circuit as original members drifted away. Lowell George, later of Frank Zappa's Mothers Of Invention and Little Feat, briefly joined their ranks, but by 1970 the Standells had become an oldies attraction.

●ALBUMS: *The Standells Live At PJs* (Liberty 1964)★★★, *Live And Out Of Sight* (Sunset 1966)★★★, *Dirty Water* (Tower 1966)★★★, *Why Pick On Me* (Tower 1966)★★, *The Hot Ones* (Tower 1966)★★, *Try It* (Tower 1967)★★.

●COMPILATIONS: *The Best Of The Standells* (1984)★★★.

●FILMS: *Get Yourself A College Girl* (1964).

STAPLE SINGERS

This well-known US family gospel group consisted of Roebuck 'Pops' Staples (b. 28 December 1915, Winona, Mississippi, USA) and four of his children, Mavis Staples (b. 1940, Chicago, Illinois, USA), Pervis Staples (b. 1935), Cleotha Staples (b. 1934) and Yvonne Staples (b. 1939). The quintet fused an original presentation of sacred music, offsetting Mavis Staples' striking voice against her father's lighter tenor, rather than follow the accustomed 'jubilee' or 'quartet' formations, prevalent in the genre. Pops' striking guitar work, reminiscent of delta-blues, added to their inherent individuality. Singles such as 'Uncloudy Day', 'Will The Circle Be Unbroken' and 'I'm Coming Home', proved especially popular, while an original song, 'This May Be The Last Time' provided the inspiration for the Rolling Stones' hit 'The Last Time'.

During the early half of the 60s, the group tried to broaden its scope. Two singles produced by Larry Williams, 'Why (Am I Treated So Bad)' and 'For What It's Worth', a Stephen Stills composition, anticipated the direction the Staples would take on signing with Stax in 1967. Here they began recording material contributed by the label's established songwriters, including Homer Banks and Bettye Crutcher, which embraced a moral focus, rather than a specifically religious one. Reduced to a quartet following the departure of Pervis, a bubbling version of Bobby Bloom's 'Heavy Makes You Happy' (1970) gave the group their first R&B hit. This newfound appeal flourished with 'Respect Yourself' (1971) and 'I'll Take You There' (1972 - a US pop number 1), both of which expressed the group's growing confidence. Their popularity was confirmed with 'If You're Ready (Come Go With Me)' (1973), 'City In The Sky' (1974), and by appearances in two films, *Wattstax* and *Soul To Soul*. The Staple Singers later moved to the Curtom label where they had an immediate success with two songs from a Curtis Mayfield-penned film soundtrack, 'Let's Do It Again' (another US pop number 1) and 'New Orleans'. These recordings were the group's last major hits although a series of minor R&B chart places between

1984 and 1985 continued the Staples' long-established ability to be both populist and inspirational.

●ALBUMS: *Uncloudy Day* (Vee Jay 1959)★★, *Swing Low* (Vee Jay 1961)★★, *Gospel Program* (1961)★★, *Hammers And Nails* (1962)★★, *Great Day* (1963)★★, *25th Day Of December* (1963)★★★, *Spirituals* (1965)★★, *Amen* (1965)★★, *Freedom Highway* (1965)★★, *Why* (Epic 1966)★★, *This Little Light* (1966)★★, *For What It's Worth* (1967)★★★, *Amen* (Epic 1967)★★★, *Staple Singers* (1968)★★★, *Pray On* (1968)★★★, *Soul Folk In Action* (Stax 1968)★★★, *We'll Get Over* (Stax 1970)★★★, *I Had A Dream* (1970)★★★, *Heavy Makes You Happy* (1971)★★★, *The Staple Swingers* (Stax 1971)★★★★, *Beatitude: Respect Yourself* (Stax 1972)★★★★, *Be What You Are* (Stax 1973)★★★, *Use What You Got* (1973)★★★, *City In The Sky* (1974)★★★, *Let's Do It Again* (1975)★★★, *Pass It On* (1976)★★★, *Family Tree* (1977)★★, *Unlock Your Mind* (1978)★★, *Hold On To Your Dream* (1981)★★, *Turning Point* (Private 1984)★★★, *Are You Ready*. (Private 1985)★★★.

●COMPILATIONS: *Tell It Like It Is* (1972)★★★, *The Best Of The Staple Singers* (Stax 1975)★★★★, *Great Day* (Milestone 1975,)★★★, *Stand By Me* (1977)★★★, *Respect Yourself: The Best Of The Staple Singers* (1988)★★★★, *Freedom Highway* (Legacy 1991)★★★★, *Staple Swingers* (1991)★★★, *Soul Folk In Action/We'll Get Over* (1994)★★★.

STARR, EDWIN

b. Charles Hatcher, 21 January 1942, Nashville, Tennessee, USA. The brother of soul singers Roger and Willie Hatcher, Edwin Starr was raised in Cleveland, where he formed the Future Tones vocal group in 1957. They recorded one single for Tress, before Starr was drafted into the US Army for three years. After completing his service, he toured for two years with the Bill Doggett Combo, and was then offered a solo contract with the Ric Tic label in 1965. His first single, 'Agent Double-O-Soul', was a US Top 30 hit and Starr exploited its popularity by appearing in a short promotional film with actor Sean Connery, best known for his role as James Bond. 'Stop Her On Sight (SOS)' repeated this success, and brought Starr a cult following in Britain, where his strident, gutsy style proved popular in specialist soul clubs. When Motown Records took over the Ric Tic catalogue in 1967, Starr was initially overlooked by the label's hierarchy. He re-emerged in 1969 with '25 Miles', a Top 10 hit which owed much to the dominant soul style of the Stax label. An album of duets with Blinky brought some critical acclaim, before Starr resumed his solo career with the strident, politically outspoken, 'War', a US number 1 in 1970. Teamed with writer/producer Norman Whitfield, Starr was allowed to record material which had been earmarked for the Temptations, who covered both of his subsequent Motown hits, 'Stop The War Now' and 'Funky Music Sho Nuff Turns Me On'.

Starr's own credentials as a writer had been demonstrated on 'Oh How Happy', which had become a soul standard since he first recorded it in the late 60s. He was given room to blossom on the 1974 soundtrack *Hell Up In Harlem*, which fitted into the 'blaxploitation' mould established by Curtis Mayfield and Isaac Hayes. Tantalized by this breath of artistic freedom, Starr left the confines of Motown in 1975, recording for small labels in Britain and America before striking a new commercial seam in 1979 with two major disco hits, 'Contact' and 'HAPPY Radio'. In the 80s, Starr was based in the UK, where he collaborated with the Style Council on a record in support of striking coalminers, and enjoyed a run of club hits on the Hippodrome label, most notably 'It Ain't Fair' in 1985. Between 1989 and 1991 Starr worked with Ian Levine's Motor City Records, recording a re make of '25 Miles' in a modern style and releasing *Where Is The Sound*.

●ALBUMS: *Soul Master* (Tamla Motown 1968)★★★, *25 Miles* (Tamla Motown 1969)★★★, with Blinky *Just We Two* (Tamla Motown 1969)★★★, *War And Peace* (1970)★★★, *Involved* (Tamla Motown 1971)★★★, *Hell Up In Harlem* (Tamla Motown 1974)★★★, *Free To Be Myself* (1975)★★★, *Edwin Starr* (1977)★★, *Afternoon Sunshine* (1977)★★★, *Clean* (1978)★★, *HAPPY Radio* (1979)★★★, *Stronger Than You Think I Am* (1980)★★, *Where Is The Sound* (1991)★★.

●COMPILATIONS: *The Hits of Edwin Starr* (Tamla Motown 1972)★★★, *20 Greatest Motown Hits* (1986)★★★, *Early Classics* (Spectrum 1996)★★★.

STAX RECORDS

Stax Records was founded in Memphis, Tennessee, USA, by brother and sister Jim (St) Stewart (b. 1930) and Estelle (ax) Axton (1918). Stewart, an aspiring fiddler, began recording local C&W artists in 1957, using a relative's garage as an improvised studio. The following year Estelle funded the purchase of an Ampex recorder and the siblings, newly named company, Satellite, was relocated in the nearby town of Brunswick. By 1960, however, they had returned to Memphis and established themselves in a disused theatre on McLemore Avenue. Local talent was attracted to the fledgling label and national hits for Carla Thomas and the Mar-Keys followed before the Satellite name was dropped in favour of Stax to avoid confusion with another company. These early successes were distributed by Atlantic Records, a relationship that soon proved mutually beneficial.

'Green Onions', the hypnotic instrumental by Booker T. And The MGs, was another best-seller and defined the sound that established the studio's reputation. A subsidiary outlet, Volt, secured success with Otis Redding and the Stax empire flourished with releases by Eddie Floyd, Johnnie Taylor and Rufus Thomas. However, relations between the company and Atlantic became strained and the sessions that produced Wilson Pickett's 'In The Midnight Hour' were the last recorded at Stax to bear Atlantic's imprint. Future releases bore the studio's distinctive logo (the Clicking Fingers), the most notable songs of which were those by Sam And Dave.

The two sides began renegotiations in 1967. The sale of Atlantic to Warner Brothers and the premature death of Otis Redding undermined Stewart's confidence, but a final twist proved irrevocable. Under the terms of the parties' original agreement, Atlantic owned every Stax master, released or unreleased, leaving the latter with a name and roster, but no back catalogue. In 1968 Stax signed a distribution deal with the Gulf/Western corporation, although it resulted in Estelle Axton's departure and the promotion of former disc jockey Al Bell to company vice-president. Although the immediate period was fruitful - releases by Johnnie Taylor, Booker T. Jones. and Judy Clay and William Bell were major hits - an ill-advised move into the album market proved over-ambitious. Nonetheless, Stax enjoyed considerable success with Isaac Hayes and in 1970 Stewart and Al Bell brought it back into private ownership through the financial assistance of the European classical label, Deutsche Grammophon. Within a year Stewart relinquished control to Bell, who then secured a lucrative distribution deal with Columbia. Despite a series of successful releases during the early 70s, including 'If Loving You Is Wrong (I Don't Want To Be Right)' (Luther Ingram) and 'Woman To Woman' (Shirley Brown), Stax grew increasingly troubled. Audits from the Internal Revenue Service and the Union Planters band revealed serious discrepancies and resulted in the indictment of several employees. In 1973, Columbia was granted an injunction preventing Stax from breaking its distribution arrangement; two years later the company was unable to meet its January payroll. Artists began seeking other outlets, Isaac Hayes sued for non-payment of royalties and despite Stewart's best efforts, Stax was closed down on 12 January 1976 on the order of the bankruptcy court judge. The feelings of the musicians at the label was summed up later when Donald 'Duck' Dunn, the label's longstanding session bassist commented, 'I knew it was over when they signed Lena Zavaroni.'

Although the bank attempted to salvage the situation, the label was sold to Fantasy Records in June the following year. Since then the new owners have judiciously repackaged the company's heritage and during the late 80s, secured the rights to all unreleased material from the Atlantic era.

●COMPILATIONS: *The Stax Story Volume 1* (Stax 1975)★★★★, *The Stax Story Volume 2* (Stax 1975)★★★★, *Stax Blues Masters* (1978)★★★, *Stax Gold* (1979)★★★, *Stax Greatest Hits* (1987), *Stax Sirens And Volt Vamps* (1988)★★★, *The Complete Stax/Volt Singles, 1959-1968* 9-CD box set (Stax 1991)★★★★★, *The Complete Stax/Volt Singles 1968-1971* 9-CD box set (Stax 1993)★★★★, *The Complete Stax/Volt Soul Singles, 1972-1975* 9-CD box set (Stax 1994)★★★.

STEAM PACKET

The idea for this 60s revue-styled package, encompassing R&B, soul, jazz and instrumentals, came from Giorgio Gomelsky, impresario and manager to several of Britain's leading beat groups. Determined to find a strong vocalist for one of his acts, Brian Auger And The Trinity,

Gomelsky adopted three: Long John Baldry, Rod Stewart and Julie Driscoll. Auger (organ), Vic Briggs (guitar), Rick Brown (bass) and Mickey Waller (drums) provided the instrumental muscle, while each singer was apportioned a slot in a show which culminated in a rousing, gospel-like fervour. Indeed, Steam Packet's live appearances were received with great enthusiasm, but their progress was hampered by inter-management bickering. Stewart was fired in March 1966, and Baldry walked out some months later, leaving Auger and Driscoll to pursue a career which reaped due commercial rewards later in the decade. The Steam Packet's sole recorded legacy was recorded one morning in December 1965. It was intended solely as a demonstration tape, but the results were released in the wake of the participants' subsequent success.

●ALBUMS: *First Of The Supergroups* (1977)★★★.

STEAMHAMMER

Kieran White (d. December 1995; vocals/harmonica), Martin Pugh (lead guitar), Martin Quittenton (rhythm guitar), Steve Davy (bass) and Michael Rushton (drums) made their recording debut in 1969 with the excellent *Steamhammer*. The set featured an impressive group original, 'Junior's Wailing', which was later adopted by Status Quo during their transformation from pop group to boogie band. Pugh and Quittenton also contributed to Rod Stewart's first debut, *An Old Raincoat Won't Let You Down*, and the latter guitarist subsequently remained with the singer, co-writing the million-selling 'Maggie May', and adding the song's distinctive mandolin sound. Pugh, White and Davy were then joined by Steve Jollife (saxophones/flute) and Mick Bradley (drums) for *Steamhammer Mk. II* which, although offering the blues base of its predecessor, showed an increased interest in improvisation, as evidenced in the extended 'Another Travelling Tune'. This propensity for a more progressive direction was maintained on ensuing releases, the last of which was only issued in Europe, where the group had amassed a considerable following. Defections, sadly, undermined their potential and Steamhammer broke up during the mid-70s.

●ALBUMS: *Steamhammer* (CBS 1969)★★★★, *Steamhammer Mk. II* (CBS 1970)★★★, *Mountains* (B&C 1970)★★★, *Speech* (1972)★★.

●COMPILATIONS: *This Is Steamhammer* (1972)★★★.

STEPHENS, LEIGH

Guitarist/vocalist Leigh Stephens was a founder member of infamous US power trio Blue Cheer. His impulsive, but heavy, style of playing is featured on this group's seminal releases, *Vincebus Eruptum* and *Outsideinside* (both 1968). In 1969 Stephens left San Francisco, California, USA, and settled in Britain, where he recorded *Red Weather*. On this he was supported by British musicians including Nicky Hopkins (piano) and Mickey Waller (drums). Although of merit, the album lacked the fire of Stephens' erstwhile group. Waller then joined Stephens and British bassist Pete Sears in the short-lived Silver

Metre, after which Stephens completed ... *And A Cast Of Thousands*. Ashton, Gardner And Dyke, Dick Morrissey, plus members of Brinsley Schwarz and Jethro Tull provided support, but the album was a marked disappointment. Stephens then returned to the USA where he formed Pilot with Waller.

●ALBUMS: *Red Weather* (Phillips 1969)★★, *Leigh Stephens ... And A Cast Of Thousands* (Charisma 1971)★.

STEPPENWOLF

Although based in southern California, Steppenwolf evolved out of a Toronto act, the Sparrow(s). John Kay (b. Joachim F. Krauledat, 12 April 1944, Tilsit, Germany; vocals), Michael Monarch (b. 5 July 1950, Los Angeles, California, USA; lead guitar), Goldy McJohn (b. 2 May 1945; keyboards), Rushton Moreve (bass) and Jerry Edmonton (b. 24 October 1946, Canada; drums) assumed their new name in 1967, inspired by the novel of cult author Herman Hesse. John Morgan replaced Moreve prior to recording. The group's exemplary debut album included 'Born To Be Wild' which reached number 2 in the US charts. This rebellious anthem was written by Dennis Edmonton (Mars Bonfire), guitarist in Sparrow and brother of drummer Jerry. It was featured in the famous opening sequence of the film *Easy Rider*, and has since acquired classic status. Steppenwolf actively cultivated a menacing, hard rock image, and successive collections mixed this heavy style with blues. 'Magic Carpet Ride' and 'Rock Me' were also US Top 10 singles yet the group deflected the criticism attracted by such temporal success by addressing contemporary issues such as politics, drugs and racial prejudice. Newcomers Larry Byrom (guitar) and Nick St. Nicholas (b. 28 September 1943, Hamburg, Germany; bass), former members of Time, were featured on *Monster*, Steppenwolf's most cohesive set. A concept album based on Kay's jaundiced view of contemporary (1970) America, it was a benchmark in the fortunes of the group. Continued personnel changes undermined their stability, and later versions of the band seemed content to further a spurious biker image, rather than enlarge on earlier achievements. John Kay dissolved the band in 1972, but his solo career proved inconclusive and within two years he was leading a reconstituted Steppenwolf. The singer has left and re-formed his creation several times over the ensuing years, but has been unable to repeat former glories.

●ALBUMS: *Steppenwolf* (Dunhill 1968)★★★, *The Second* (Dunhill 1968)★★★, *Steppenwolf At Your Birthday Party* (Dunhill 1969)★★★, *Early Steppenwolf* (Dunhill 1969)★★, *Monster* (Dunhill 1969)★★★★, *Steppenwolf 'Live'* (Dunhill 1970)★★, *Steppenwolf 7* (Dunhill 1970)★★, *For Ladies Only* (Dunhill 1971)★★★, *Slow Flux* (Mums 1974)★★, *Hour Of The Wolf* (Epic 1975)★★, *Skullduggery* (Epic 1976)★★, *Live In London* (Attic 1982)★★, *Wolf Tracks* (Attic 1982)★★, *Rock & Roll Rebels* (Qwil 1987)★★, *Rise And Shine* (IRS 1990).

●COMPILATIONS: *Steppenwolf Gold* (Dunhill 1971)★★★★, *Rest In Peace* (Dunhill 1972)★★★, *16 Greatest Hits* (Dunhill 1973)★★★★, *Masters Of Rock* (Dunhill 1975)★★★★, *Golden Greats: Steppenwolf* (MCA 1985)★★★★.

STEVENS, GUY

b. c.1940, d. 29 August 1981. This enigmatic figure first came to prominence during the early 60s as a disc jockey at London's influential Scene club. His collection of soul and R&B releases was one of the finest in Britain and compilation tapes culled from this remarkable archive supplied several groups, including the Who and the Small Faces, with their early live repertoires. Having helped assemble several anthologies culled from the Chess label, Stevens joined Island Records in order to mastermind their Sue subsidiary. He also began work as a producer, and following a successful debut with *Larry Williams On Stage*, he took control of the VIPs, a new signing to the parent company. This Carlisle-based group accompanied Stevens on a 1967 album, *Hapshash And The Coloured Coat*, which also featured designers Michael English and Nigel Weymouth. The VIPs later evolved into Spooky Tooth. Stevens' best-known collaboration came with Mott The Hoople. He produced their first four albums but, more crucially, shaped the sound and attitude of this early work. Free, Traffic and Mighty Baby also benefited from Steven's involvement, but by the early 70s, his persona had become too erratic. Chronic alcoholism debilitated his abilities and few now considered using his talents. Stevens did produce some early demos for the Clash and in 1979 they invited him to work on what became *London Calling*. Arguably the group's definitive release, its success should have engendered a renewed career for its producer, but considerable resistance still remained. On 29 August 1981, Guy Stevens was found dead in his south London home, the victim of a heart attack. His influence on music, although not of the highest profile, remains incalculable.

STEVENS, RAY

b. Ray Ragsdale, 24 January 1941, Clarksdale, Georgia, USA. A prolific country-pop writer and performer, Stevens' novelty hits of the 70s and 80s form a history of the fads and crazes of the era. He became a disc jockey on a local station at 15 and the following year recorded 'Five More Steps' on the Prep label. Stevens' first nonsense song, 'Chickie Chickie Wah Wah' was written in 1958 but it was not until 1961, with Mercury Records that he had a Top 40 hit with the tongue-twisting 'Jeremiah Peabody's Poly Unsaturated Quick Dissolving Fast Acting Pleasant Tasting Green And Purple Pills'. This was followed by 'Ahab The Arab' (1962) and 'Harry The Hairy Ape' (1963). Stevens also had a penchant for social comment which emerged in songs such as 'Mr Businessman' (1968), 'America Communicate With Me' and the first recording of Kris Kristofferson's 'Sunday Morning Coming Down'. However, the zany songs were the most successful and in 1969 he sold a million copies of

'Gitarzan' and followed with a version of Leiber And Stoller's Coasters' hit 'Along Came Jones' and 'Bridget The Midget (The Queen Of The Blues)'. His first number 1 was the simple melodic ballad 'Everything Is Beautiful' in 1970. All of these, however, were outsold by 'The Streak', which topped the charts on both sides of the Atlantic in 1974. Stevens' softer side was evident in his version of Erroll Garner's 'Misty' which won a Grammy in 1976 for its bluegrass-styled arrangement. Later novelty efforts, aimed principally at country audiences, included 'Shriner's Convention' (1980), 'It's Me Again Margaret' (1985), 'I Saw Elvis In A UFO' (1989) and 'Power Tools'.
●ALBUMS: *1,837 Seconds Of Humor* (Mercury 1962)★★★, *Ahab The Arab* (1962)★★★, *This Is Ray Stevens* (Mercury 1963)★★★, *Gitarzan* (Monument 1969)★★★, *Unreal!!!* (Barnaby 1970)★★★, *Everything Is Beautiful* (Barnaby 1970)★★★, *Turn Your Radio On* (Barnaby 1972)★★★, *Boogity Boogity* (Barnaby 1974)★★★, *Misty* (Barnaby 1975)★★★, *Just For The Record* (1975)★★★, *Feel The Music* (1976)★★★, *Shriner's Convention* (RCA 1980)★★★, *Don't Laugh Now* (1982)★★★, *Me* (1983)★★★, *He Thinks He's Ray Stevens* (RCA 1985)★★★, *Surely You Joust* (1988)★★★, *I Have Returned* (1988)★★★, *Beside Myself* (1989).
●COMPILATIONS: *Ray Stevens' Greatest Hits* (Barnaby 1971)★★★, *The Very Best Of Ray Stevens* (Barnaby 1975)★★★, *Both Sides Of Ray Stevens* (1986)★★★, *Greatest Hits* (1987)★★★, *The Best Of Ray Stevens* (More Music 1995)★★★, *Everything Is Beautiful* (Rhino 1996)★★★.
●VIDEOS: *Comedy Video Classics* (1993), *Live* (Club Video 1994), *Get Serious* (MCA Music Video 1996).

STORM, RORY

b. Alan Caldwell, 1940, Liverpool, England, d. 28 September 1972. Vocalist Caldwell began performing as a member of the Texan Skiffle Group, before forming one of the city's first beat groups with Johnny Byrne (alias Johnny Guitar), Lou Walters, Ty Brian and Ritchie Starkey, later known as Ringo Starr. The quintet employed several names - the Raving Texans, Al Caldwell And His Jazzmen - before becoming Rory Storm And The Hurricanes in 1960, with Caldwell assuming the lead persona. They enjoyed a fervent local popularity, in part because of the singer's showmanship, and were placed third behind the Beatles and Gerry And The Pacemakers in a poll undertaken by the *Mersey Beat* newspaper in 1962. Starr's switch to the Beatles in August that year precipitated a recurrent drumming problem, and a stand-in was required on the Hurricanes' contributions to *This Is Merseybeat*. Spirited but unoriginal, the three tracks they completed revealed a barely adequate vocalist, while a later version of 'America', produced by Brian Epstein, failed to capture an in-concert fire. The premature death of Ty Brian and the departure of Lou Walters ended any lingering potential, and the Hurricanes were disbanded in 1966 following their appearance at the last night of the famed Cavern club. Rory then pursued a career as a disc jockey but, increasingly prone to ill-heath, he died following an accidental overdose of alcohol and medication. His grief-stricken mother committed suicide on discovering his body.

STRANGELOVES

Formed in 1964 in New York City, USA, the Strangeloves consisted of songwriters and record producers Bob Feldman, Jerry Goldstein and Richard Gottehrer. Although they left their mark under the name Strangeloves with only four singles and one album, their fascinating story extends both before and beyond the group's brief tenure. Feldman and Goldstein had been childhood friends in Brooklyn, New York, and sang in street corner doo-wop groups. They began writing songs together and had their first success with 'Big Beat', which disc jockey Alan Freed used as the theme song of his television show. By 1960 they had recorded some unsuccessful singles as Bob And Jerry when they met Bronx native Gottehrer, who was also writing songs. Before long the trio's compositions were being recorded by such major artists as Dion, Pat Boone, Freddy Cannon, Bobby Vee and the Jive Five. Their greatest success came in 1963 when Feldman, Goldstein and Gottehrer wrote and produced 'My Boyfriend's Back', which became a number 1 hit for the Angels. By the following year, however, the landscape of pop music had changed with the arrival of the Beatles, and the trio had to rethink its approach. They created the Strangeloves (taking their name from the Stanley Kubrick/Peter Sellers film, *Dr. Strangelove*) and a mythical story to go with them. Wearing bizarre costumes, they said they were from the Australian outback and put on phony accents. Their names became Niles, Miles and Giles Strange.

In 1965, they released their debut, 'Love Love Love', on Swan Records, which failed to chart. They then signed to Bang Records and released 'I Want Candy', a Bo Diddley-like rocker that reached number 11. Three further singles charted: 'Cara-Lin' (number 39 in 1965), 'Night Time' (number 30 in 1966) and 'Hand Jive' (number 100 in 1966). Their only album also made the charts.

In addition to their recordings as the Strangeloves, Goldstein And Feldman recorded as the Kittens, as Rome And Paris, as Bobby And the Beaus and as Ezra And The Iveys. The trio produced the McCoys' hit 'Hang On Sloopy' and recorded as the Sheep.

Following the break-up of the Strangeloves, Goldstein worked for Uni Records, and later produced the group War. Feldman continued to write music and produce, working with artists such as Jay And The Americans, Johnny Mathis, Freddy Cannon and Link Wray. Gottehrer became a partner in Sire Records and a successful record producer during the punk era, producing the first two albums by the Go-Go's, the debut album by Blondie and many others. Feldman recently formed a new Strangeloves group.

●ALBUMS: *I Want Candy* (Bang 1965)★★★.
●COMPILATIONS: *I Want Candy: The Best Of The Strangeloves* (Epic/Legacy 1995)★★★.

STRAWBERRY ALARM CLOCK

Based in California and originally known as the Sixpence, the Strawberry Alarm Clock enjoyed a US number 1 in 1967 with the memorable 'Incense And Peppermints'. This euphoric slice of 'flower-power' bubblegum was initially intended as a b-side and the featured voice was that of a friend on hand during the session, rather than an official member. The group - Mark Weitz (organ), Ed King (lead guitar), Lee Freeman (rhythm guitar), Gary Lovetro (bass) and Randy Seol (drums) - added a second bassist, George Bunnell, prior to recording a debut album. The new arrival was also an accomplished songwriter, and his contributions enhanced a set that coupled hippie trappings with enchanting melodies and some imaginative instrumentation. Such features were maintained on successive Strawberry Alarm Clock albums, while 'Tomorrow' and 'Sit With The Guru' continued their reign as chart contenders. The group supplied much of the music for the film *Psyche-Out*, in which they also appeared. Gary Lovetro left the line-up prior to *Wake Up It's Tomorrow*, and several subsequent changes undermined the band's direction. *Good Morning Starshine*, released in 1969, introduced a reshaped band where Jimmy Pitman (guitar) and Gene Gunnels (drums) joined Weitz and King, the latter of whom was relegated to bass. They remained together until 1971, but the Strawberry Alarm Clock was unable to regain its early profile. Ed King later joined Lynyrd Skynyrd, while several of his erstwhile colleagues were reunited during the 80s for a succession of 'summer of love revisited' tours.
●ALBUMS: *Incense And Peppermints* (Uni 1967)★★★, *Wake Up It's Tomorrow* (Uni 1967)★★, *The World In A Seashell* (Uni 1968)★★, *Good Morning Starshine* (Uni 1969)★★.
●COMPILATIONS: *The Best Of The Strawberry Alarm Clock* (Uni 1970)★★★, *Changes* (Vocalion 1971)★★, *Strawberries Mean Love* (1987)★★★.

STRAY

Formed in 1969, UK hard rock act Stray comprised, Del Bromham (guitar/vocals/keyboards) Steve Gadd (guitar/harmonica/vocals), Gary Giles (bass) and Ritchie Cole (drums). They were signed by Transatlantic Records as the label sought to expand its previously folk-based roster. *Stray* captured the group at the height of its powers, notably on the exciting 'All In Your Mind' and 'Taken All The Good Things'. Subsequent albums followed in a similar vein but, despite a prolific output, Stray were unable to break free from the shackles of their rather limited style. They did, however, achieve momentary notoriety when briefly managed by Charlie Kray, brother of the notorious Kray twins. Peter Dyer (guitar/vocals) replaced Gadd prior to recording *Houdini*, but this made little impact on Stray's dwindling fortunes. They split up in 1977, after which Bromham embarked on a short-lived solo career, recording for Gull Records, among others. Bromham resurrected the band in the mid-90s.
●ALBUMS: *Stray* (Transatlantic 1970)★★★, *Suicide*

(Transatlantic 1971)★★, *Saturday Moving Pictures* (Transatlantic 1972)★★, *Mundaz* (Transatlantic 1973)★★, *Move It* (Transatlantic 1974)★★, *Tracks* (Transatlantic 1975)★★, *Stand Up And Be Counted* (Dawn 1975)★★, *Houdini* (Pye 1976)★★, *Hearts Of Fire* (Pye 1976)★★, *Live At The Marquee* (Mystic 1996)★★, as Del Bromham's Stray *Alive And Gigging* (Mystic 1997)★★.

STRONG, BARRETT

b. 5 February 1941, Westpoint, Mississippi, USA. The cousin of two members of the R&B vocal group the Diablos, Barrett Strong launched his own singing career with Berry Gordy's fledgling Tamla label in 1959. At the end of that year, he recorded the original version of Gordy's song 'Money', a major US hit which became a rock standard after it was covered by the Beatles and the Rolling Stones. Strong also wrote Eddie Holland's US hit 'Jamie' in 1961. Later that year, he briefly joined Vee Jay Records, but he returned to the Motown stable in the early 60s to work as a writer and producer. He established a partnership with Norman Whitfield from 1966-73; together, the pair masterminded a series of hits by the Temptations, with Strong contributing the powerful lyrics to classics like 'Cloud Nine', 'Just My Imagination' and 'Papa Was A Rolling Stone'. Strong left Motown in 1973 to resume his recording career, finding some success with 'Stand Up And Cheer For The Preacher' on Epic, and 'Is It True' on Capitol in 1975. He lacked the distinctive talent of the great soul vocalists, however, and seems destined to be remembered for his behind-the-scenes work at Motown rather than his own sporadic releases.

●ALBUMS: *Stronghold* (Capitol 1975)★★★, *Live And Love* (Capitol 1976)★★, *Love Is You* (1988)★★.

SUE RECORDS

Former real estate entrepreneur Henry 'Juggy Murray' Jones established the Sue label in New York City on 2 January 1957. Initially sited on West 125th Street, close to the fabled Apollo Theatre, the company was well placed to sign aspiring R&B talent. Sue achieved its first hit single the following year with its seventh release, Bobby Hendricks' 'Itchy Twitchy Feeling', which reached the US Top 30. This exciting performance featured the Coasters on backing vocals and helped establish the label as one of the earliest successful black-owned companies, pre-empting Tamla/Motown's first hit by some six months. By 1960 Murray had relocated to West 54th Street, near to Bell Sound Studios where many of the label's recording sessions were undertaken. His early signings included Don Covay, but it was with Ike and Tina Turner that Juggy found consistent success. Two of the duo's finest singles, 'A Fool In Love' and 'It's Gonna Work Out Fine', were released on Sue and their success allowed Murray to expand his company. Soul and R&B remained at its core, but the label also featured several jazz-based acts, including Jimmy McGriff, Bill Doggett and Hank Jacobs. Subsidiary companies were also established, including Symbol, the roster of which included Inez and Charlie

Foxx, who enjoyed considerable success with 'Mockingbird' (number 2 R&B) and 'Hurt By Love'. Famed R&B songwriter Bert Berns also recorded for this outlet under the pseudonym 'Russell Byrd'. A.F.O. provided a short-lived association with a New Orleans-based collective headed by producer Harold Battiste. 'I Know' (Barbara George) and 'She Put The Hurt On Me' (Prince La La) were issued on this outlet, while the Crackerjack imprint included Derek Martin's 'Daddy Rollin' Stone', cited by George Harrison as one of his favourites of the era and later covered by the Who.

A handful of Sue recordings were initially issued in Britain on Decca's London/American outlet, but in 1964 Murray struck a licensing deal with Island's Chris Blackwell. Responsibility for the British Sue label was passed to disc jockey/producer Guy Stevens who, after 17 singles, decided to use it for product leased from other sources. Murray felt this diminished Sue's individual identity, withdrew from the arrangement and reverted to London/American for future releases. Stevens retained the Sue name, and thereafter the path of both companies was entirely different. In Britain, the label issued material by, among others, James Brown, Freddy King, B.B. King and Elmore James. It proved instrumental in introducing acts to a UK audience and many musicians, including Stevie Winwood, Steve Marriott and Eric Clapton, expressed a debt to Stevens' interest. British Sue folded in February 1967 as the Island label switched priorities from black music to white rock. The entire catalogue was deleted in 1969, but was briefly revived in 1983 with a series of commemorative EPs; *Sue Instrumentals*, *Sue Soul Brothers* and *Sue Soul Sisters* (all ★★★).

Juggy Murray continued to administer Sue but failed to address the changes evolving during the mid-60s. He claims to have signed Jimi Hendrix prior to the guitarist's departure for England, although no tracks were recorded. A proposed distribution deal with Stax Records fell through, the latter company eventually opting for Atlantic Records. In 1968 Murray sold his remaining masters and publishing to United Artists. He produced several former Sue acts for their Veep and Minit subsidiaries including the Soul Sisters, Baby Washington and Tina Britt. Murray retained the rights to the Sue name, reactivating it on occasions over the ensuing years. He enjoyed a 'comeback' hit in 1969 when one-man band Wilbert Harrison re-recorded his own 'Let's Stick Together' as 'Let's Work Together'. The latter was then popularized by Canned Heat. Murray then founded another short-lived outlet, Juggernaught, before moving to Los Angeles to launch Jupiter Records. It was here he found belated success as an artist. 'Inside America', credited to Juggy Murray Jones, issued in Britain via the Contempo label, climbed to 39 in 1976. It is, however, for his pioneering Sue label that he will be best remembered. An indispensible box set was compiled by Alan Warner in 1994.

●COMPILATIONS: *The Sue Story: Volumes One To Three* (1966)★★★, *The Sue Story* (Line 1984)★★, *The Beat Is On* (Stateside 1987)★★, *The Sue Records Story: The Sound Of Soul* 4-CD box set (EMI 1994)★★★★.

SULLIVAN, BIG JIM

b. c.1940, London, England, he worked in a sheet-metal factory before joining a skiffle group as a guitarist. Sullivan was soon hired by Marty Wilde as a member of his backing group, the Wildcats. In 1959, the group backed Eddie Cochran on his final UK tour, and later recorded the instrumentals 'Trambone' and 'Samovar' as the Krew Kats. After that group disbanded, Sullivan became a session musician and teacher, giving lessons to young hopefuls like Ritchie Blackmore and Jimmy Page. During the 60s he played on thousands of recordings, backing such artists as Michael Cox, the Kinks, Small Faces, Jonathan King, Donovan, the Rolling Stones, Nancy Wilson and Sarah Vaughan. In 1969 he accompanied Tom Jones on a world tour. Sullivan made occasional records under his own name at this time. 'You Don't Know What You've Got' (1961) was a cover version of Ral Donner's hit while 'She Walks Through The Fair' was a traditional Irish tune. Sullivan also studied Indian music with Ustad Vilayat Khan and in 1968 made a sitar album for Mercury. Two years later, he played with Blackmore and Albert Lee as Green Bullfrog, a studio group reproduced by Derek Lawrence. In 1974 he made a rare vocal album for Lawrence's Retreat label, following this by forming Tiger with Dave Macrae (keyboards), Phil Curtis (bass) and Billy Rankin (drums). The band made albums for Retreat and EMI (*Going Down Laughing*, 1976). During the 80s, Sullivan remained in demand for session work and made more solo recordings, among which was *Test Of Time* produced by Mike Vernon.
●ALBUMS: *Sitar A Go-Go* (Mercury 1967)★★, *Sitar Beat* (1968)★★, *Jim Sullivan* (1972)★★, *Big Jim's Back* (Retreat 1974)★★, *Sullivan Plays O'Sullivan* (1977)★★, *Rock 'N' Roll Wrecks* (1983)★★ *Test Of Time* (1983)★★.

SUMMER HOLIDAY (1962)

Cliff Richard's second 'teenage' feature, released in 1962, maintained the light-hearted nature of its successful predecessor, *The Young Ones*. *Summer Holiday* revolves around four London Transport mechanics who borrow a double-decker bus and embark for the Continent. Pursuit, love, capture and an inevitable happy ending ensue, but Peter Yates' snappy direction and location shots result in a film no less slight than much British light comedy of its time. Indeed, the appearance of the singer's backing group, the Shadows, in various different guises, was one of the films endearing features. However, the presence of established stalwarts Ron Moody and David Kossoff alongside Richard, Una Stubbs and Mervyn Hayes help place the musical within the framework of all-round entertainment. Winter season pantomime was the next logical step. *Summer Holiday* contained some of the singer's most enduring hit singles, including the double-sided chart topper, 'Bachelor Boy'/'The Next Time' and the title track itself, which also reached number one in the UK. Cliff Richard (and the Shadows), were arguably at the peak of their collective popularity at this point. In February 1963 the *Summer Holiday* album took over the number 1 spot on the album list from *Out Of The Shadows*. It reigned there for 14 unbroken weeks, until being replaced, prophetically, by the Beatles' *Please Please Me*.

SUNRAYS

In 1965 Murray Wilson was fired as manager of the Beach Boys and sought a new US surf act. Carl Wilson, Murray's son, had already introduced his father to Rick Henn, a talented singer, songwriter and drummer. Murray then persuaded Eddie Medora (lead guitar), Byron Case (rhythm guitar) and Marty Di Giovanni (piano) to join, each of whom were ex-members of the Snowmen, who had had a local hit in 1963 with 'Ski Storm'. Bassist Vince Hozier was added to complete the line-up. Wilson secured a recording/production deal with the Los Angeles-based Tower label and was rewarded in the summer of 1965 when the Sunrays' debut single, 'I Live For The Sun', reached the US Top 50. The song, which Henn wrote, gave Vanity Fare a UK Top 20 hit three years later. Two follow-up Sunrays singles, 'Car Party' and 'Outta Gas', were not successful, but 'Andrea' took them back into the US chart in 1966. It showed a marked Four Seasons influence. The quintet's final hit was 'Still', after which Wilson lost interest in the group, preferring instead to record in his own right. The Sunrays split up soon afterwards.
●ALBUMS: *Andrea* (Tower 1966)★★★.
●COMPILATIONS: *Vintage Rays* 3-CD box set (Collectables 1996)★★★.

SUPREMES

America's most successful female vocal group of all time was formed by four Detroit schoolgirls in the late 50s. Diana Ross (b. 26 March 1944, Detroit, USA), Betty Hutton, Florence Ballard (b. 30 June 1943, Detroit, USA) and Mary Wilson (b. 4 March 1944, Greenville, Mississippi, USA) named themselves the Primettes in tribute to the local male group, the Primes - who themselves found fame in the 60s as the Temptations. Having issued a solitary single on a small local label, the Primettes were signed to Berry Gordy's Motown stable, where they initially found public acceptance hard to find. For more than two years, they issued a succession of flop singles, despite the best efforts of top Motown writer/producer Smokey Robinson to find them a suitable vehicle for their unsophisticated talents. Only when Diana Ross supplanted Florence Ballard as the group's regular lead vocalist, at Gordy's suggestion, did the Supremes break into the US charts. The dynamic 'When The Lovelight Starts Shining In His Eyes', modelled on the production style of Phil Spector, was the group's first hit in 1963. The follow-up single flopped, so Gordy handed the group over to the newly formed Holland/Dozier/Holland writing and production team. They concocted the slight, but effervescent, 'Where Did Our Love Go' for the Supremes, which topped the US charts and was also a major hit in Britain.

This achievement inaugurated a remarkable run of success for the group and their producers, as their next four releases - 'Baby Love', 'Come See About Me', 'Stop! In The Name Of Love' and 'Back In My Arms Again' - all topped the US singles charts, while 'Baby Love' became the only record by an American group to reach number 1 in Britain during the beat-dominated year of 1964. All these singles were hinged around insistent, very danceable rhythms with repetitive lyrics and melodies, which placed no great strain on Ross's fragile voice. With their girl-next-door looks and endearingly unsophisticated demeanour, the Supremes became role models for young black Americans and their name was used to promote a range of merchandising, even (ironically) a brand of white bread.

The rather perfunctory 'Nothing But Heartaches' broke the chart-topping sequence, which was immediately restored by the more ambitious 'I Hear A Symphony'. As Holland/Dozier/Holland moved into their prime, and Ross increased in confidence, the group's repertoire grew more mature. They recorded albums of Broadway standards, played residencies at expensive night-clubs, and were expertly groomed by Motown staff as all-round entertainers. Meanwhile, the hits kept coming, with four more US number 1 hits in the shape of 'You Can't Hurry Love', 'You Keep Me Hanging On', 'Love Is Here And Now You're Gone' and 'The Happening' - the last of which was a blatant attempt to cash in on the psychedelic movement. Behind the scenes, the group's future was in some jeopardy: Florence Ballard had grown increasingly unhappy in the supporting role into which Berry Gordy had forced her, and her occasionally erratic and troublesome behaviour was ultimately used as an excuse to force her out of the group. Without fanfare, Ballard was ousted in mid-1967, and replaced by Cindy Birdsong; most fans simply did not notice. At the same time, Ross's prime position in the group's hierarchy was confirmed in public, when she was given individual credit on the group's records, a move which prompted a flurry of similar demands from the lead singers of other Motown groups.

'Reflections', an eerie, gripping song that was one of Motown's most adventurous productions to date, introduced the new era. Motown's loss of Holland/Dozier/Holland slowed the group's progress in 1968, before they bounced back with two controversial slices of overt social commentary, 'Love Child' and 'I'm Livin' In Shame', the first of which was yet another US number 1. The Supremes also formed a successful recording partnership with the Temptations, exemplified by the hit single 'I'm Gonna Make You Love Me'.

During 1969, there were persistent rumours that Berry Gordy was about to launch Diana Ross on a solo career. These were confirmed at the end of the year, when the Supremes staged a farewell performance, and Ross bade goodbye to the group with the elegiac 'Someday We'll Be Together' - a US chart-topper on which, ironically, she was the only member of the Supremes to appear. Ross was replaced by Jean Terrell, sister of heavyweight boxer Ernie Terrell. The new line-up, with Terrell and Mary Wilson alternating lead vocal duties, found immediate success with 'Up The Ladder To The Roof' in early 1970, while 'Stoned Love', the group's biggest UK hit for four years, revived memories of their early successes with its rhythmic base and repetitive hook. The Supremes also tried to revive the atmosphere of their earlier recordings with the Temptations on a series of albums with the Four Tops. Gradually, their momentum was lost, and as Motown shifted its centre of activity from Detroit to California, the Supremes were left behind. Lynda Laurence replaced Cindy Birdsong in the line-up in 1972; Birdsong returned in 1974 when Laurence became pregnant. The latter move coincided with the departure of Jean Terrell, whose place was taken by Scherrie Payne. With the group recording only rarely, Birdsong quit again, leaving Mary Wilson - at last established as the unchallenged leader - to recruit Susaye Greene in her place. This trio recorded the self-explanatory *Mary, Scherrie And Susaye* in 1976, before disbanding the following year. Mary Wilson attempted to assemble a new set of Supremes for recording purposes, and actually toured Britain in 1978 with Karen Rowland and Karen Jackson in the line-up. The termination of her Motown contract stymied this move, however, and since then the use of the Supremes' name has legally resided with Motown. They have chosen not to sully the memory of their most famous group by concocting an ersatz Supremes to cash in on their heritage. Jean Terrell, Scherrie Payne and Lynda Laurence won the rights to use the Supremes' name in the UK. Payne began recording disco material with producer Ian Levine in 1989, for the Nightmare and Motor City labels. Levine also signed Laurence, Wilson and ex-Supreme Susaye Greene to solo deals and recorded Terrell, Lawrence and Greene for a remake of 'Stoned Love'. The career of Mary Wilson has also continued with a starring role in the Toronto, Canada, production of the stage musical *The Beehive* in 1989 and the publication of the second volume of her autobiography in 1990.

●ALBUMS: *Meet The Supremes* (Motown 1963)★★★, *Where Did Our Love Go?* (Motown 1964)★★★, *A Bit Of Liverpool* (Motown 1964)★★, *The Supremes Sing Country, Western And Pop* (Motown 1964)★, *We Remember Sam Cooke* (Motown 1965)★★★, *More Hits By The Supremes* (Motown 1965)★★★, *Merry Christmas* (Motown 1965)★★★, *The Supremes At The Copa* (Motown 1965)★★★, *I Hear A Symphony* (Motown 1966)★★★, *Supremes A-Go-Go* (Motown 1966)★★★, *The Supremes Sing Holland, Dozier, Holland* (Motown 1967)★★★★, *Right On* (Motown 1970)★★★, with the Four Tops *The Magnificent Seven* (Motown 1970)★★★★, *New Ways But Love Stays* (Motown 1970)★★, with the Four Tops *The Return Of The Magnificent Seven* (Motown 1971)★★, *Touch* (Motown 1971)★★, with the Four Tops *Dynamite* (Motown 1971)★★★, *Floy Joy* (Motown 1972)★★★, *The Supremes* (Motown 1975)★★, *High Energy* (1976)★★, *Mary, Scherrie And Susaye* (1976)★★★. as Diana Ross And The Supremes *Diana Ross And The Supremes Sing Rodgers And Hart* (Motown 1967)★★,

Reflections (Motown 1968)★★★, *Diana Ross And The Supremes Sing And Perform 'Funny Girl'* (Motown 1968)★, *Diana Ross And The Supremes Live At London's Talk Of The Town* (Motown 1968)★★, with the Temptations *Diana Ross And The Supremes Join The Temptations* (Motown 1968)★★★, *Love Child* (Motown 1968)★★★, with the Temptations *TCB* (Motown 1968)★★★, *Let The Sunshine In* (Motown 1969)★★, with the Temptations *Together* (Motown 1969)★★★, *Cream Of The Crop* (Motown 1969)★★, *Diana Ross And The Supremes On Broadway* (Motown 1969)★★, *Farewell* (Motown 1970)★★.

●COMPILATIONS: *The Supremes Greatest Hits* (Motown 1967)★★★★, *Anthology 1962-69* (Motown 1984)★★★★, *Early Classics* (Spectrum 1996)★★★.

●FURTHER READING: *Reflections*, Johnny Bond. *Dreamgirl: My Life As A Supreme*, Mary Wilson. *Supreme Faith: Someday We'll Be Together*, Mary Wilson with Patricia Romanowski. *All That Glittered: My Life With The Supremes*, Tony Turner and Barbara Aria.

●FILMS: *Beach Ball* (1964).

SURFARIS

Formed in Glendale, California, in 1962, the Surfaris - Jim Fuller (b. 1947; lead guitar), Jim Pash (b. 1949; guitar), Bob Berryhill (b. 1947; guitar), Pat Connolly (b. 1947; bass) and Ron Wilson (b. 1945; drums) - achieved international success the following year with 'Wipe Out'. This frantic yet simplistic instrumental, originally envisaged as a throwaway b-side, is recognized as one of the definitive surfing anthems, although some of its lustre has been removed in the wake of a protracted allegation of plagiarism. Merrell Fankhauser, former guitarist with the Impacts, successfully claimed the piece infringed his composition of the same title. Further controversy arose when the Surfaris discovered that the music gracing their debut album was, in fact, played by a rival group, the Challengers. However, despite their understandable anger, such backroom machinations remained rife throughout the quintet's career. Their third album, *Hit City '64*, introduced a partnership with producer Gary Usher, who employed a team of experienced session musicians on ensuing Surfaris' releases.

In 1965 the group abandoned beach and hot-rod themes for folk rock. Wilson had developed into an accomplished lead singer and with Ken Forssi replacing Connolly on bass, the Surfaris completed the promising *It Ain't Me Babe*. However, Usher then severed his relationship with the band and they broke up when the last remaining original member, Jim Pash, left the line-up. Wilson died in 1989 from a brain haemorrhage. Newcomer Forssi then joined Love, and although no other member achieved similar success, Berryhill resurrected the Surfaris' name in 1981.

●ALBUMS: *Wipe Out* (Dot 1963)★★★, *The Surfaris Play Wipe Out And Others* (Decca 1963)★★★, *Hit City '64* (Decca 1964)★★★, *Fun City, USA* (Decca 1964)★★, *Hit City '65* (Decca 1965)★★, *It Ain't Me Babe* (Decca 1965)★★★, *Surfaris Live* (1983)★★.

●COMPILATIONS: *Yesterday's Pop Scene* (1973)★★★, *Surfers Rule* (1976)★★★, *Gone With The Wave* (1977)★★★, *Wipe Out! The Best Of ...* (Varese Sarabande 1994)★★★, *Surfaris Stomp* (Varese Sarabande 1995)★★★.

SUTCH, SCREAMING LORD

b. David Sutch, 10 November 1940, Middlesex, England. Sutch rose to prominence in 1960 as the first long-haired pop star, with tresses in excess of 18 inches. His recording career peaked with such early releases as 'Til The Following Night', 'Jack The Ripper' and 'I'm A Hog For You Baby', all produced by the late Joe Meek. Although never registering a chart entry, Sutch boasted one of the most accomplished live acts of the era in the Savages, whose ranks included such luminaries as Ritchie Blackmore, Nicky Hopkins and Paul Nicholas. For 30 years, Sutch has sustained his flagging recording career with a plethora of publicity stunts ranging from dramatic marriage proposals to standing for Parliament and founding his own radio station. In 1970, he enjoyed some minor success in the US album charts with *Lord Sutch And Heavy Friends*, which featured Blackmore, Jimmy Page, Jeff Beck, Keith Moon, Nicky Hopkins, Noel Redding and John Bonham. He now combines regular club work with the presidency of the Monster Raving Loony Party.

●ALBUMS: *Lord Sutch And Heavy Friends* (Atlantic 1970)★, *Hands Of Jack The Ripper* (Atlantic 1972)★, *Rock And Horror* (1982)★, *Alive And Well* (1982)★.

●FURTHER READING: *Life As Sutch: The Official Autobiography Of Monster Raving Looney*, Lord David Sutch with Peter Chippindale.

SWEET INSPIRATIONS

The Sweet Inspirations' career reached back into the Drinkards, a formative gospel group whose fluid line-up included Dionne Warwick and Cissy Houston. The group dropped this name on pursuing a secular path as session singers. Houston remained at the helm during several subsequent changes, (Doris Troy and Judy Clay were among the former members), and the group emerged from its backroom role with a recording deal of its own. Now dubbed the Sweet Inspirations by Atlantic Records producer Jerry Wexler, the line-up of Cissy Houston, Sylvia Shemwell, Myrna Smith and Estelle Brown secured a minor hit with 'Why (Am I Treated So Bad)' (1967), but it was a self-titled composition, 'Sweet Inspiration' which gave the group its best-remembered single, reaching the US Top 20 in 1968. When Cissy Houston left for a belated solo career in 1970, the remaining trio, Myrna Smith, Estelle Brown and Sylvia Shemwell, joined Elvis Presley's concert retinue, and recorded a further album on their own, a good 1973 outing for Stax. After a hiatus from the recording scene, Smith and Shemwell were joined by Gloria Brown in place of Estelle Brown who had quit earlier, and a final album appeared on RSO in 1979, although Brown herself was replaced on the actual recording by Pat Terry. In 1994 Estelle, Sylvia and Myrna reunited for a special series of shows, including a tribute to Presley.

●ALBUMS: *The Sweet Inspirations* (Atlantic 1967)★★★, *Songs Of Faith And Inspiration* (Atlantic 1968)★★★, *What The World Needs Now Is Love* (Atlantic 1968)★★, *Sweets For My Sweet* (Atlantic 1969)★★★, *Sweet, Sweet Soul* (Atlantic 1970)★★★, *Estelle, Myrna And Sylvia* (Stax 1973)★★★, *Hot Butterfly* (1979)★★.

●COMPILATIONS: *Estelle, Myrna And Sylvia* (1991)★★★, *The Best Of ...* (1994)★★★.

SWINGING BLUE JEANS

Determined to concentrate on rock 'n roll, several leading figures in Liverpool's skiffle scene founded the Bluegenes in 1958. They were singer and lead guitarist Ray Ennis (b. 26 May 1942), rhythm guitarist Ray Ellis (b. 8 March 1942), bass player Les Braid (b. 15 September 1941), drummer Norman Kuhlke (b. 17 June 1942) and Paul Moss (banjo), all born in Liverpool. Minus Moss, the group became one of the leading attractions in the Merseyside beat group scene and also played in Hamburg. Following the Beatles' first successes, the Swinging Blue Jeans (as they had been renamed) signed a recording deal with EMI's HMV label. The Beatles-sounding 'It's Too Late Now', was a minor hit the following year, but it was the group's third single, 'Hippy Hippy Shake', that provided their biggest success when it reached number 2. This rasping rendition of a Chan Romero song remains one of the era's finest performances, invoking a power the Blue Jeans never quite recaptured. Their version of 'Good Golly Miss Molly' nonetheless peaked at number 11, while the reflective rendition of Betty Everett's soul ballad 'You're No Good' reached number 3. An excellent reading of Dionne Warwick's hit 'Don't Make Me Over' stalled outside the Top 30. It was, however, the quartet's last substantial hit despite a series of highly polished singles, including 'Promise You'll Tell Her' (1964), 'Crazy 'Bout My Baby' (1965). The Blue Jeans were unfairly dubbed anachronistic. Several personnel changes also ensued, including the induction of two former Escorts, Terry Sylvester and Mike Gregory, but neither this, nor a brief change of name to Music Motor, made any difference to their fortunes. In 1968, the band was briefly renamed Ray Ennis And The Blue Jeans but when Sylvester was chosen to replace Graham Nash in the Hollies, the remaining members decided to split up. However, the revival of interest in 60s music persuaded Ennis to re-form the Swinging Blue Jeans in 1973. He re-recorded 'Hippy Hippy Shake' for an album on Dart Records and continued leading the band on the UK scampi-and-chips revival circuit for the next two decades. A 1992 reissue album included nine previously unreleased tracks; among them were versions of Little Richard's 'Ready Teddy' and 'Three Little Fishes', the novelty song first recorded in 1939 by US bandleader Kay Kyser.

●ALBUMS: *Blue Jeans A' Swinging* aka *Swinging Blue Jeans* aka *Tutti Frutti* (HMV 1964)★★★, *The Swinging Blue Jeans: La Voce Del Padrone* (1966)★★★, *Hippy Hippy Shake* (1973)★★★, *Brand New And Faded* (Dart 1974)★★, *Dancin'* (1985)★★.

●COMPILATIONS: *Hippy Hippy Shake* (1964)★★★, *Shake: The Best Of The Swinging Blue Jeans* (1986)★★★.

SWINGLE SINGERS

The commercial success of this French choir undermined many engrained prejudices by pop consumers against serious music, preparing them for Walter Carlos' *Switched-On Bach*, Deep Purple's *Concerto For Group And Orchestra* and the promotion of the Portsmouth Sinfonia as a pop act. In 1963, the Singers were assembled by Ward Lamar Swingle (b. 21 September 1927, Mobile, Alabama, USA), a former conductor of Les Ballets De Paris. Addressing themselves to jazzy arrangements of the classics - particularly Bach - their wordless style had the novel effect of predetermined mass scat-singing. After *Jazz Sebastian Bach* and *Bach's Greatest Hits* made respective inroads into the UK and US Top 20, the outfit was catapulted into an arduous schedule of television and radio appearances during back-to-back world tours that embraced over 2,000 concerts by 1991. While the main choir continued to earn Grammy awards for 1965's *Going Baroque* and similar variations on his original concept, Swingle formed a smaller unit (Swingles II) for more contemporary challenges such as Luciano Berio's *Sinfonia* which was premiered in New York in 1973 - and for *Cries, A-Ronne* and other increasingly more complex works by the same composer.

●ALBUMS: *Bach's Greatest Hits* (1963)★★★, *Jazz Sebastian Bach* (1963)★★★★, *Going Baroque* (1964)★★★, *Anyone For Mozart?* (Philips 1965)★★★, *Place Vendome* (Philips 1966)★★★, *Folio* (1980)★★★, *Swingle Singers Christmas Album* (1980)★★★★, *Anyone For Mozart, Bach, Handel, Vivaldi?* (1986)★★★.

●COMPILATIONS: *Compact Jazz: Best Of The Swingle Singers* (Verve 1987)★★★★.

SYMBOLS

This Essex, England-based beat group of the late 60s originally operated under the title Johnny Milton And The Condors, although they did not record as such. Comprising Mick Clarke (bass/vocals), Clive Graham (drums), Johnny Milton (vocals) and Rikki Smith (lead guitar), they made their debut as the Symbols in 1965 with a single, 'One Fine Girl', for Columbia Records, which was produced by Mickie Most. However, they experienced several line-up shuffles during their four-year existence, with Joe Baccini (bass), Sean Corrigan (guitar) and Chris (Chas) Wade (drums) also playing with the group at various times. After a cover version of 'Why Do Fools Fall In Love' failed to procure mainstream success, the group switched to President Records in 1966. The best of the seven singles they recorded between then and 1968 was a cover of the Ronettes' 'Best Part Of

Breaking Up', which became their second chart hit at number 25 in January 1968. They had first reached the charts a year previously with 'Bye Bye Baby', this time a cover version of a Four Seasons song. Both boasted the group's distinctive close harmony sound, but any impetus they gained from the success of these singles was not carried forward to their sole album, which members of the group publicly disowned in the press. After the group's dissolution, Clarke joined the Rubettes. Wade and Milton played with the pub-rock band JJ Foote in the mid-70s.
●ALBUMS: *The Best Part Of The Symbols* (President 1968)★★★.

SYNDICATE OF SOUND

Formed in San Jose, California, USA, in 1964, the Syndicate Of Sound were known for one classic garage band/punk single, 'Little Girl', a US Top 10 hit on Bell Records in 1966. The group consisted of Don Baskin (b. 9 October 1946, Honolulu, Hawaii, USA; vocals/saxophone), John Sharkey (b. 8 June 1946, Los Angeles, California, USA; guitar/keyboards), Jim Sawyers (lead guitar), Bob Gonzales (bass) and John Duckworth (b. 18 November 1946, Springfield, Missouri, USA; drums). After an unsuccessful single for the Scarlet label, they recorded 'Little Girl' for the local Hush Records. It was a regional hit and picked up for national distribution by Bell, for which the group also recorded an album. The group placed two other minor singles on the charts, one later that year for Bell and another in 1970 on Buddah. They also recorded unsuccessfully for Capitol and disbanded in 1970.
●ALBUMS: *Little Girl* (Bell 1966)★★.

TAMS

This US group was formed in 1952 as the Four Dots in Atlanta, Georgia, USA. Their line-up featured Joseph Pope (b. 6 November 1933, d. 16 March 1996), Charles Pope (b. 7 August 1936), Robert Lee Smith (b. 18 March 1936) and Horace Kay (b. 13 April 1934). Although such an early origin suggests longevity, it was not until 1960 that the group emerged with a single on Swan. Now dubbed the Tams (derived by their wearing of Tam O'Shanter hats on stage), they added a further member, Floyd Ashton (b. 15 August 1933), prior to signing with Bill Lowery, an Atlanta song publisher and entrepreneur. Among those already on his books were Joe South and Ray Whitley, two musicians who would work closely with the group. 'Untie Me', a South composition, was recorded at Fame and leased to Philadelphia's Arlen Records. The song became a Top 20 US R&B hit, but follow-up releases failed until 1963 when Lowery secured a new deal with ABC Paramount. The Tams' first single there, 'What Kind Of Fool (Do You Think I Am)', reached the US Top 10 and established a series of Whitley-penned successes. His compositions included 'You Lied To Your Daddy' and 'Hey Girl Don't Bother Me', ideal material for Joe Pope's ragged lead and the group's unpolished harmonies. After 1964, the group preferred Atlanta's Master Sound studio, by which time Albert Cottle (b. 1941, Washington, DC, USA) had replaced Ashton. South and Whitley continued their involvement, writing, playing on and producing various sessions, but the Tams had only one further US hit in 1968 with the bubbling 'Be Young, Be Foolish, Be Happy', which peaked on the *Billboard* R&B chart at 26 and reached the UK Top 40 in 1970. By the end of the 60s their mentors had moved elsewhere while the Master Sound house band was breaking up. Dropped by ABC, the Tams unsuccessfully moved to 1-2-3 and Capitol Records until a chance reissue of 'Hey Girl Don't Bother Me' became a surprise UK number 1 in 1971. They were not to chart again until 16 years later when their association with the Shag, a dance craze and subsequent 80s film, secured a further lifeline to this remarkable group, giving the group a UK Top 30 with 'There Ain't Nothing Like Shaggin''.
●ALBUMS: *Presenting The Tams* (ABC 1964)★★★, *Hey Girl Don't Bother Me* (ABC 1964)★★★★, *Time For The Tams* (ABC 1967)★★★, *A Portrait Of The Tams* (ABC 1969)★★, *Be Young, Be Foolish, Be Happy* (Stateside 1970)★★.
●COMPILATIONS: *A Little More Soul* (ABC 1968)★★★★, *The Best Of The Tams* (Capitol 1971)★★★, *The Mighty Mighty Tams* (Sounds South

1978)★★★, *Greatest Hits - Beach Party Vol. 1* (Carousel South 1981)★★★, *Atlanta Soul Connection* (Charly 1983)★★★, *Beach Music From The Tams* (Compleat 1983)★★★, *Reminiscing* (Wonder 1982)★★★, *There Ain't Nothing Like ... The Tams* (Virgin 1987)★★★.

TAYLOR, CHIP
b. James Wesley Voight, 1940, Yonkers, New York, USA. The younger brother of actor Jon Voight, Taylor began his recording career during the late 50s with several rockabilly-styled recordings. He subsequently formed Just Us with songwriting partner Al Gorgoni and produced material for local act the Flying Machine, which featured James Taylor and guitarist Danny Kortchmar. However Taylor became better known as the composer of 'Wild Thing', a risqué pop song popularized by the Troggs and, later, Jimi Hendrix. Other credits included 'Anyway That You Want Me', a follow-up hit for the former group, 'I Can't Let Go' (the Hollies), 'Angel Of The Morning' (Merilee Rush/Juice Newton) and 'Storybook Children' (Billy Vera/Judy Clay), many of which he shared with either Gorgoni, Trade Martin, or both. During the late 60s the trio began recording as Gorgoni, Martin And Taylor, but in 1971 the latter embarked on a solo career with *Gasoline*. *Chip Taylor's Last Chance* was the subject of effusive critical acclaim but poor sales, although the artist's unerring grasp of country styles was maintained on *Some Of Us*. Waylon Jennings, Bobby Bare and Tammy Wynette were among those recording his songs, although a fourth collection, *This Side Of The Big River*, was less strong. Taylor's last solo release, *Saint Sebastian*, maintained the high quality of his recorded output. The continued popularity of his best-known work is a testament to his importance as a singer/songwriter.
●ALBUMS: *Gasoline* (Buddah 1971)★★, *Chip Taylor's Last Chance* (Warners 1973)★★★, *Some Of Us* (1974)★★★, *This Side Of The Big River* (1975)★★, *Somebody Shot Out Of The Jukebox* (1976)★★★, *Saint Sebastian* (1979)★★★.

TAYLOR, DEREK
b. Liverpool, England. As a London *Daily Express* show-business correspondent, he was briefed to do a 'hatchet job' on the Beatles' agreement to appear on 1963's Royal Variety Show but he could only praise them. Another *Express* commission to collate George Harrison's weekly ruminations for 12 Fridays (Harrison was paid £150 for each one) was the foundation of a lasting friendship with the guitarist, strengthened when Taylor was put on the group's payroll as Brian Epstein's personal assistant and ghost writer of his *Cellarful Of Noise* autobiography. In October 1964, he became the Beatles' press officer after his predecessor's outraged resignation. Conflicts with Epstein hastened Taylor's own exit in 1965. Emigrating to California, he gained employment as publicist for the Byrds, the Beach Boys, the Mamas And The Papas, Buffalo Springfield and other acts, and was on the steering committee of the celebrated Monterey Pop

Festival in 1967. The following year found him back in London as the obvious choice to organize the Beatles' Apple Corps publicity department, his urbane, sympathetic manner winning many important contacts. While at Apple, he attempted to compose a stage musical with Harrison, but a more tangible legacy was his *As Time Goes By* memoir of two years 'in a bizarre royal court in a strange fairy tale'. Following Apple's collapse Taylor moved to Los Angeles as Head of Special Projects for Warner-Reprise Records (later WEA) before transfer to Europe as the label's general manager. Further musical chairs ensued and then promotion to Vice-President of Creative Services back in Hollywood, where he was honoured with a *This Is Your Life*-type citation, with Harrison and Ringo Starr among other leading entertainers walking on to tell some funny story from the past. By autumn 1979, the mercurial Taylor had gravitated back to England after Harrison's HandMade film company cried out for his unique skills. Extra-mural duties included penning scene-setting commentaries to the ex-Beatle's taped reminiscences for publication as *I Me Mine*. Happy with the result, Harrison interceded on his hireling's behalf to convince Genesis Publications that Taylor's idiosyncratic account of his own life would be viable. In 1985, therefore, 2,000 hand-tooled copies of Taylor's witty yarn, *Fifty Years Adrift*, went on sale at £148 each. His sparkling book, *It Was Twenty Years Ago Today* was accompanied by a television film. They brilliantly encapsulated the essence of the 'summer of love'. Among Taylor's recent projects is the narrative to a collection of the late Michael Cooper's photographs. He also works occasionally for British regional television - and on Apple Records' 1991 reissue programme. Taylor is a gentle soul who is crucial to any student of the Beatles and the 60s.
●FURTHER READING: *As Time Goes By*, Derek Taylor. *Fifty Years Adrift (In An Open-Necked Shirt)*, Derek Taylor. *It Was Twenty Years Ago Today*, Derek Taylor.

TAYLOR, JOHNNIE
b. 5 May 1938, Crawfordsville, Arkansas, USA. Having left home at the age of 15, Taylor surfaced as part of several gospel groups, including the Five Echoes and the Highway QCs. From there he joined the Soul Stirrers, replacing Sam Cooke on the latter's recommendation. Taylor switched to secular music in 1961; releases on Cooke's Sar and Derby labels betrayed his mentor's obvious influence. In 1965 he signed with Stax Records and had several R&B hits before 'Who's Making Love' (1968) crossed over into *Billboard*'s pop Top 5. Further releases, including 'Take Care Of Your Homework' (1969), 'I Believe In You (You Believe In Me)' and 'Cheaper To Keep Her' (both 1973), continued this success. Taylor maintained his momentum on a move to Columbia. The felicitous 'Disco Lady' (1976) was the first single to be certified platinum by the RIAA, but although subsequent releases reached the R&B chart they fared less well with the wider audience. Following a short spell with Beverley Glenn, the singer found an ideal niche on Malaco

Records, a bastion for traditional southern soul. Taylor's first album there, *This Is The Night* (1984), reaffirmed his gritty, blues-edged approach, a feature consolidated on *Wall To Wall*, *Lover Boy* and *Crazy 'Bout You*. It is *Wanted: One Soul Singer*, *Who's Making Love* and *Taylored In Silk* that best encapsulate his lengthy period at Stax. Taylor had one of the great voices of the era: expressive graceful and smooth, and yet it is a mystery why he failed to reach the heights of the likes of Otis Redding, Marvin Gaye and Wilson Pickett. *Somebody's Gettin' It* compiles several Columbia recordings while Taylor's early work on Sar is found on *The Roots Of Johnnie Taylor*.

●ALBUMS: *Wanted One Soul Singer* (Stax 1967)★★★★, *Who's Making Love?* (Stax 1968)★★★★, *Looking For Johnny Taylor* (Stax 1969)★★★★, *The Johnnie Taylor Philosophy Continues* (Stax 1969)★★★, *Rare Stamps* (Stax 1970)★★★, *One Step Beyond* (Stax 1970)★★★, *Taylored In Silk* (Stax 1973)★★★, *Super Taylor* (Stax 1974)★★★, *Eargasm* (1976)★★★, *Rated Extraordinaire* (1977)★★★, *Disco 9000* (1977)★★★, *Ever Ready* (1978)★★, *Reflections* (197)★★, *She's Killing Me* (1979)★★, *A New Day* (1980)★★, *Just Ain't Good Enough* (1982)★★, *This Is Your Night* (Malaco 1984)★★★, *Best Of The Old And The New* (1984)★★★, *Wall To Wall* (Malaco 1985)★★★, *Lover Boy* (Malaco 1987)★★★, *In Control* (1988)★★, *Crazy 'Bout You* (Malaco 1989)★★★, *Little Bluebird* (Stax 1991)★★★, *Just Can't Do Right* (90s)★★★, *Real Love* (90s)★★★, *Good Love!* (Malaco 1996)★★★.

●COMPILATIONS: *The Roots Of Johnnie Taylor* (Star1969)★★★, *The Johnnie Taylor Chronicle (1968-1972)* (Stax 1978)★★★★, *The Johnnie Taylor Chronicle (1972-1974)* (Stax 1978)★★★, *Somebody's Getting It* (1989)★★★, *Raw Blues/Little Bluebird* (1992)★★★, *The Best Of ... On Malaco Vol. 1* (1994)★★★.

TEMPERANCE 7

Formed in 1955 to play 20s-style jazz, the Temperance 7 consisted at various times of Whispering Paul McDowell (vocals), Captain Cephas Howard (trumpet/euphonium and various instruments), Joe Clark (clarinet), Alan Swainston-Cooper (pedal clarinet/swanee whistle), Philip 'Finger' Harrison (banjo/alto and baritone sax), Canon Colin Bowles (piano/harmonica), Clifford Beban (tuba), Brian Innes (drums), Dr. John Grieves-Watson (banjo), Sheik Haroun el John R.T. Davies (trombone/alto sax) and Frank Paverty (sousaphone). Their debut single, 'You're Driving Me Crazy' (producer George Martin's first number 1), was followed by three more hits in 1961, 'Pasadena', 'Hard Hearted Hannah'/'Chili Bom Bom', and 'Charleston'. In 1963 they appeared in the play *The Bed Sitting Room* written by John Antrobus and Spike Milligan. They split in the mid 60s, but their spirit resurfaced in groups like the Bonzo Dog Doo-Dah Band and the New Vaudeville Band. The Temperance 7 were re-formed in the 70s by Ted Wood, brother of the Rolling Stones' Ronnie Wood. At the time of

writing in 1995, Colin Bowles is reported to have died several years ago, but the other members are said to be pursuing a variety of interests, including publishing, sound retreval, film set and graphic designing, acting and antiques.

●ALBUMS: *Temperance 7* (Parlophone 1961)★★★★, *Temperance 7 Plus One* (Argo 1961)★★★, *Hot Temperance 7* (1987)★★★, *Tea For Eight* (1990)★★★, *33 Not Out* (1990)★★★.

TEMPO, NINO, AND APRIL STEVENS

Nino Tempo, (b. 6 January 1935, Niagara Falls, New York, USA) forged a career as session musician and arranger/composer for Rosemary Clooney and Steve Lawrence, before forming a duo with sister April Stevens (b. 29 April, Niagara Falls, New York, USA). The latter had already enjoyed minor success as a solo act with 'Teach Me Tiger', but the siblings scored a major hit in 1963 when their revival of 'Deep Purple', which topped the US charts and secured a Grammy award as that year's 'Best Rock 'N' Roll Recording'. They also held the record for many years with the longest title; the b-side of 'Deep Purple' was 'I've Been Carrying A Torch For You For So Long That It's Burned A Great Big Hole In My Heart'. Reworkings of 'Whispering' and 'Stardust' also reached the best-sellers but Tempo achieved a more contemporary outlook following backroom and compositional work with Phil Spector. He and Stevens embraced a folk-rock/girl group direction with 'All Strung Out' and 'I Can't Go On Living (Without You Baby)' which the former co-wrote with Jerry Riopelle. An excellent attendant album contained compositions by David Gates and Warren Zevon, but the couple's passé image hindered potential interest. They later embarked on separate paths with Tempo resuming his association with Spector during the 70s, particularly with new protégé Jerri Bo Keno.

●ALBUMS: *Deep Purple* (Atco 1963)★★★, *Nino & April Sing The Great Songs* (Atlantic 1964)★★★, *Hey Baby* (Atco 1966)★★★, *Nino Tempo, April Stevens Programme* (60s), *All Strung Out* (White Whale 1967)★★.

●COMPILATIONS: *Sweet And Lovely: The Best Of ...* (Varese Sarabande 1996)★★★.

TEMPTATIONS

The most successful group in black music history was formed in 1961 in Detroit, Michigan, USA, by former members of two local R&B outfits. Eddie Kendricks (b. 17 December 1939, Union Springs, Alabama, USA) and Paul Williams (b. 2 July 1939, Birmingham, Alabama, USA, d. 17 August 1973) both sang with the Primes; Melvin Franklin (b. David English, 12 October 1942, Montgomery, Alabama, USA, d. 23 February 1995, Los Angeles, California, USA), Eldridge Bryant and Otis Williams (b. Otis Miles 30 October 1941, Texarkana, Texas, USA) came from the Distants. Initially known as the Elgins, the quintet were renamed the Temptations by Berry Gordy when he signed them to Motown in 1961.

After issuing three singles on the Motown subsidiary Miracle Records, one of them under the pseudonym of the Pirates, the group moved to the Gordy label. 'Dream Come Home' provided their first brief taste of chart status in 1962, although it was only when they were teamed with writer/producer/performer Smokey Robinson that the Temptations achieved consistent success. The group's classic line-up was established in 1963, when Eldridge Bryant was replaced by David Ruffin (b. 18 January 1941, Meridian, Mississippi, USA). His gruff baritone provided the perfect counterpoint to Kendricks' wispy tenor and falsetto, a contrast that Smokey Robinson exploited to the full. Over the next two years, he fashioned a series of hits in both ballad and dance styles, carefully arranging complex vocal harmonies that hinted at the group's doo-wop heritage. 'The Way You Do The Things You Do' was the Temptations' first major hit, a stunningly simple rhythm number featuring a typically cunning series of lyrical images. 'My Girl' in 1965, the group's first US number 1, demonstrated Robinson's graceful command of the ballad idiom, and brought Ruffin's vocals to the fore for the first time. This track, featured in the movie 'My Girl', was reissued in 1992 and was once again a hit.

'It's Growing', 'Since I Lost My Baby', 'My Baby' and 'Get Ready' continued the run of success into 1966, establishing the Temptations as the leaders of the Motown sound. 'It's Growing' brought a fresh layer of subtlety into Robinson's lyric writing, while 'Get Ready' embodied all the excitement of the Motown rhythm factory, blending an irresistible melody with a stunning vocal arrangement. Norman Whitfield succeeded Robinson as the Temptations' producer in 1966 - a role he continued to occupy for almost a decade. He introduced a new rawness into their sound, spotlighting David Ruffin as an impassioned lead vocalist, and creating a series of R&B records that rivalled the output of Stax and Atlantic for toughness and power. 'Ain't Too Proud To Beg' introduced the Whitfield approach, and while the Top 3 hit 'Beauty Is Only Skin Deep' represented a throwback to the Robinson era, 'I'm Losing You' and 'You're My Everything' confirmed the new direction.

The peak of Whitfield's initial phase with the group was 'I Wish It Would Rain', a dramatic ballad that the producer heightened with delicate use of sound effects. The record was another major hit, and gave the Temptations their sixth R&B number 1 in three years. It also marked the end of an era, as David Ruffin first requested individual credit before the group's name, and when this was refused, elected to leave for a solo career. He was replaced by ex-Contour Dennis Edwards, whose strident vocals fitted perfectly into the Temptations' harmonic blend. Whitfield chose this moment to inaugurate a new production style. Conscious of the psychedelic shift in the rock mainstream, and the inventive soul music being created by Sly And The Family Stone, he joined forces with lyricist Barrett Strong to pull Motown brutally into the modern world. The result was 'Cloud Nine', a record that reflected the increasing use of illegal drugs among young people, and shocked some listeners with its lyrical ambiguity. Whitfield created the music to match, breaking down the traditional barriers between lead and backing singers and giving each of the Temptations a recognizable role in the group. Over the next four years, Whitfield and the Temptations pioneered the concept of psychedelic soul, stretching the Motown formula to the limit, introducing a new vein of social and political comment, and utilizing many of rock's experimental production techniques to hammer home the message. 'Runaway Child, Running Wild' examined the problems of teenage rebellion; 'I Can't Get Next To You' reflected the fragmentation of personal relationships (and topped the US charts with the group's second number 1 hit); and 'Ball Of Confusion' bemoaned the disintegrating fabric of American society. These lyrical tracts were set to harsh, uncompromising rhythm tracks, seeped in wah-wah guitar and soaked in layers of harmony and counterpoint. The Temptations were greeted as representatives of the counter-culture, a trend that climaxed when they recorded Whitfield's outspoken protest against the Vietnam War, 'Stop The War Now'. The new direction alarmed Eddie Kendricks, who felt more at home on the series of collaborations with the Supremes that the group also taped in the late 60s. He left for a solo career in 1971, after recording another US number 1, the evocative ballad 'Just My Imagination'. He was replaced first by Richard Owens, then later in 1971 by Damon Harris. This line-up recorded the 1972 number 1, 'Papa Was A Rolling Stone', a production *tour de force* which remains one of Motown's finest achievements, belatedly winning the label its first Grammy award. After that, everything was an anti-climax. Paul Williams left the group in 1971, to be replaced by another former Distant member, Richard Street; Williams shot himself in 1973, after years of depression and drug abuse. Whitfield's partnership with Strong was broken the same year, and although he continued to rework the 'Papa Was A Rolling Stone' formula, the commercial and artistic returns were smaller. The Temptations still had hits, and 'Masterpiece', 'Let Your Hair Down' (both 1973) and 'Happy People' (1975) all topped the soul charts, but they were no longer a leading force in black music.

Whitfield left Motown in 1975; at the same time, Glenn Leonard replaced Damon Harris in the group. After struggling on for another year, the Temptations moved to Atlantic Records for two albums, which saw Louis Price taking the place of Dennis Edwards. When the Atlantic partnership brought no change of fortunes, the group returned to Motown, and to Dennis Edwards. 'Power' in 1980 restored them to the charts, before Rick James engineered a brief reunion with David Ruffin and Eddie Kendricks for a tour, an album, and a hit single, 'Standing On The Top'. Ruffin and Kendricks then left to form a duo, Ron Tyson replaced Glenn Leonard, and Ali-Ollie Woodson took over the role of lead vocalist from Edwards. Woodson brought with him a song called 'Treat Her Like A Lady', which became their biggest UK hit in a decade. Subsequent releases confirmed the quality of the current line-up, although without a strong guiding hand they are unlikely to rival the achievements of the late 60s and early 70's line-ups, the culmination of Motown's classic era.

●ALBUMS: *Meet The Temptations* (Gordy 1964)★★★★, *The Temptations Sing Smokey* (Gordy 1965)★★★★, *The Temptin' Temptations* (Gordy/Tamla Motown 1965)★★★★, *Gettin' Ready* (Gordy 1966)★★★★, *Live!* (Gordy 1967)★★, *With A Lot O' Soul* (Gordy 1967)★★★, *In A Mellow Mood* (Gordy 1967)★★★, *Wish It Would Rain* (Gordy 1968)★★★★, *Diana Ross And The Supremes Join The Temptations* (Tamla Motown 1968)★★★, with Diana Ross And The Supremes *TCB* (1968)★★★, *Live At The Copa* (Tamla Motown 1968)★★, *Cloud Nine* (Tamla Motown 1969)★★★★, *The Temptations' Show* (Tamla Motown 1969)★★★, *Puzzle People* (Tamla Motown 1969)★★★, with Diana Ross And The Supremes *Together* (Tamla Motown 1969)★★★, with Diana Ross And The Supremes *On Broadway* (Tamla Motown 1969)★★★, *Psychedelic Shack* (Tamla Motown 1970)★★★★, *Live At London's Talk Of The Town* (Tamla Motown 1970)★★★, *Christmas Card* (Tamla Motown 1970)★, *Sky's The Limit* (Tamla Motown 1971)★★★, *Solid Rock* (Tamla Motown 1972)★★★, *All Directions* (Tamla Motown 1972)★★★, *Masterpiece* (Tamla Motown 1973)★★★, *1990* (Tamla Motown 1973)★★★, *A Song For You* (Tamla Motown 1975)★★★, *House Party* (Tamla Motown 1975)★★, *Wings Of Love* (Tamla Motown 1976)★★, *The Temptations Do The Temptations* (Tamla Motown 1976)★★, *Hear To Tempt You* (Tamla Motown 1977)★★, *Bare Back* (Tamla Motown 1978)★★, *Power* (Tamla Motown 1980)★★, *The Temptations* (1981)★★, with Jimmy Ruffin and Eddie Kendricks *Reunion* (1982)★★★, *Surface Thrills* (1983)★★, *Back To Basics* (1984)★★★, *Truly For You* (1984)★★, *Touch Me* (1985)★★, *To Be Continued ...* (1986)★★★, *Together Again* (1987)★★★, *Special* (1989)★★★, *Milestone* (1991)★★.

●COMPILATIONS: *Greatest Hits* (Tamla Motown 1966)★★★★, *Greatest Hits, Volume 2* (Tamla Motown 1970)★★★★, *Anthology* (Tamla Motown 1973)★★★★★, *25 Anniversary* (Motown 1986)★★★★, *Compact Command Performances* (1989)★★★, *Hum Along And Dance: More Of The Best 1963-1974* (Rhino 1993)★★★, *The Original Lead Singers Of The Temptations* (1993)★★★, *Emperors Of Soul* 5-CD set (Motown 1994)★★★★, *Early Classics* (Spectrum 1996)★★★.

●VIDEOS: *Live In Concert* (Old Gold 1990).

●FURTHER READING: *Temptations*, Otis Williams with Patricia Romanowski.

TEN YEARS AFTER

Formed in Nottingham, England, as the Jaybirds in 1965, they abandoned their pedestrian title for a name that slotted in with the booming underground progressive music scene. The quartet of Alvin Lee (b. 19 December 1944, Nottingham, England; guitar/vocals), Chick Churchill (b. 2 January 1949, Mold, Flint/Clywd, Wales; keyboards), Ric Lee (b. 20 October 1945, Cannock, Staffordshire, England; drums) and Leo Lyons (b. 30 November 1943, Bedford, England; bass) played a mixture of rock 'n' roll and blues that distinguished them from the mainstream blues *cognoscenti* of Fleetwood Mac, Chicken Shack and Savoy Brown. Their debut album was largely ignored and it took months of gruelling club work to establish their claim. The superb live *Undead*, recorded at Klooks Kleek club, spread the word that Lee was not only an outstanding guitarist, but he was the fastest by a mile. Unfortunately for the other three members, Lee overshadowed them to the extent that they became merely backing musicians in what was described as the Alvin Lee show. The band began a series of US tours which gave them the record of more US tours than any other UK band. Lee's furious performance of 'Goin' Home' at the Woodstock Festival was one of the highlights, although that song became a millstone for them. Over the next two years they delivered four solid albums, which all charted in the UK and the USA. *Ssssh*, with its Graham Nash cover photography, was the strongest. 'Stoned Woman' epitomized their sound and style, although it was 'Love Like A Man' from *Cricklewood Green* that gave them their only UK hit. *A Space In Time* saw them briefly relinquish guitar-based pieces in favour of electronics. By the time of *Rock 'N' Roll To The World* the band were jaded and they rested from touring to work on solo projects. This resulted in Lee's *On The Road To Freedom* with gospel singer Mylon Le Fevre and a dull album from Chick Churchill, *You And Me*. When they reconvened, their spark and will had all but gone and remaining albums were poor. After months of rumour, Lee admitted that the band had broken up. In 1978 Lee formed the trio Ten Years Later, with little reaction, and in 1989 the original band re-formed and released *About Time,* but only their most loyal fans were interested. The band was still active in the early 90s.

●ALBUMS: *Ten Years After* (Deram 1967)★★★, *Undead* (Deram 1968)★★★★, *Stonedhenge* (Deram 1969)★★★, *Ssssh* (Deram 1969)★★★★, *Cricklewood Green* (Deram 1970)★★★★, *Watt* (Deram 1970)★★★, *A Space In Time* (Chrysalis 1971)★★★, *Rock 'N' Roll Music To The World* (Chrysalis 1972)★★, *Recorded Live* (Chrysalis 1973)★★, *Positive Vibrations* (Chrysalis 1974)★★, *About Time* (Chrysalis 1989)★★.

●COMPILATIONS: *Alvin Lee & Company* (Deram 1972)★★★, *Goin' Home! - Their Greatest Hits* (Deram 1975)★★★, *Original Recordings Vol. 1* (1987)★★★, *The Essential* (Chrysalis 1992)★★★★.

TERRELL, TAMMI

b. Thomasina Montgomery, 29 April 1945, Philadelphia, Pennsylvania, USA, d. 16 March 1970. Tammi Terrell began recording for Scepter/Wand Records at the age of 15, before touring with the James Brown Revue for a year. In 1965, she married heavyweight boxer Ernie Terrell, the brother of future Supreme Jean Terrell. Tammi's warm, sensuous vocals won her a contract with Motown later that year, and in 1966 she enjoyed a series of R&B hits, among them a soulful rendition of 'This Old Heart Of Mine'. In 1967, she was selected to replace Kim Weston as Marvin Gaye's recording partner. This inspired teaming produced Gaye's most successful duets, and the pair issued a stream of hit singles between 1967 and 1969. 'Ain't No Mountain High Enough' and 'You're All I Need To Get By' epitomized their style, as Marvin and Tammi weaved around each other's voices, creating an aura of romance and eroticism that led to persistent rumours that they were lovers.

From the beginning, their partnership was tinged with unhappiness, Terrell collapsing in Gaye's arms during a performance in 1967. She was diagnosed as suffering from a brain tumour, and despite a series of major operations over the next three years, her health steadily weakened. By 1969, she was unable to perform in public, and on several of the duo's final recordings, their producer, Valerie Simpson, controversially claims to have taken her place. Ironically, one of these tracks, 'The Onion Song', proved to be the most successful of the Gaye/Terrell singles in the UK. Tammi Terrell died on 16 March 1970, her burial service attracting thousands of mourners, including many of her Motown colleagues. Her death has been the subject of much speculation, centred on rumours that her brain disorders were triggered by alleged beatings administered by a member of the Motown hierarchy. These accusations were given voice in *Number One With A Bullet*, a novel by former Gaye aide Elaine Jesmer, which included a character clearly based on Terrell.

●ALBUMS: with Marvin Gaye *United* (Motown 1968)★★★★, with Gaye *You're All I Need* (Motown 1968)★★★, with Gaye *Easy* (1969)★★★, *Early Show* (1969)★★★, *Irresistible Tammy* (Motown 1969)★★★ .

TEX, JOE

b. Joseph Arrington Jnr., 8 August 1933, Rogers, Texas, USA, d. 13 August 1982. The professional career of this popular singer began onstage at the Apollo. He won first place in a 1954 talent contest and duly secured a record deal. Releases on King, Ace and the Anna labels were derivative and disappointing, but Tex meanwhile honed his songwriting talent. James Brown's version of 'Baby You're Right' (1962) became a US R&B number 2, after which Tex was signed by Buddy Killen, a Nashville song publisher, who in turn established Dial as a recording outlet. Although early releases showed promise, it was not until 1965 that Tex prospered. Recorded at Fame and distributed by Atlantic, 'Hold On To What You've Got' was a US Top 5 hit. The first of several preaching singles, its homely values were maintained on 'A Woman Can Change A Man' and 'The Love You Save (May Be Your Own)'. However, Joe was equally comfortable on uptempo songs, as 'S.Y.S.L.J.F.M. (The Letter Song)' (1966) and 'Show Me' (1967) proved. Later releases were less successful and although 'Skinny Legs And All' and 'Men Are Gettin' Scarce' showed him still capable of major hits, the singer seemed unsure of his direction. A fallow period ended with 'I Gotcha' (1972), an irresistibly

cheeky song, but Tex chose this moment to retire. A convert to the Muslim faith since 1966, he changed his name to Yusuf Hazziez, and toured as a spiritual lecturer. He returned to music in 1975. Two years later he enjoyed a 'comeback' hit with the irrepressible 'Ain't Gonna Bump No More (With No Big Fat Woman)'. By the 80s, however, Joe had withdrawn again from full-time performing. He devoted himself to Islam, his Texas ranch and the Houston Oilers football team. He was tempted into a Soul Clan reunion in 1981, but in August 1982 he died following a heart attack.

●ALBUMS: *Hold On* (Checker 1964)★★★, *Hold What You've Got* (Atlantic 1965)★★★, *The New Boss* (Atlantic 1965)★★★★, *The Love You Save* (Atlantic 1966)★★★, *I've Got To Do A Little Better* (Atlantic 1966)★★★★, *Live And Lively* (Atlantic 1968)★★, *Soul Country* (Atlantic 1968)★★★, *Happy Soul* (1969)★★★, *You Better Believe It* (Atlantic 1969)★★★, *Buying A Book* (Atlantic 1969)★★★, *With Strings And Things* (1970)★★★, *From The Roots Came The Rapper* (1972)★★, *I Gotcha* (1972)★★, *Joe Tex Spills The Beans* (1973)★★, *Another Man's Woman* (1974)★★, *Bumps And Bruises* (1977)★★, *Rub Down* (1978)★★, *He Who Is Without Funk Cast The First Stone* (1979)★★.

●COMPILATIONS: *The Best Of Joe Tex* (King 1965)★★★, *The Very Best Of Joe Tex* (Atlantic 1967)★★★★, *Greatest Hits* (Atlantic 1967)★★★★, *The Very Best Of Joe Tex - Real Country Soul ... Scarce As Hen's Teeth* (1988)★★★, *I Believe I'm Gonna Make It: The Best Of Joe Tex 1964-1972* (Rhino 1988)★★★★, *Different Strokes* (1989)★★★, *Stone Soul Country* (1989)★★★, *Ain't Gonna Bump No More* (1993)★★★, *I Gotcha (His Greatest Hits)* (1993)★★★, *Skinny Legs And All: The Classic Early Dial Sides* (Kent 1994)★★★, *You're Right Joe Tex!* (Kent 1995)★★★.

THEM

Formed in Belfast, Northern Ireland, in 1963, Them's tempestuous career spawned some of the finest records of their era. The original line-up - Van Morrison (b. 31 August 1945, Belfast, Northern Ireland; vocals/harmonica), Billy Harrison (guitar), Eric Wrixen (keyboards), Alan Henderson (bass) and Ronnie Millings (drums) - were stalwarts of the city's Maritime Hotel, where they forged a fiery, uncompromising brand of R&B. A demo tape featuring a lengthy version of 'Lovelight' engendered a management deal with the imposing Phil Solomon, who persuaded Dick Rowe to sign the group to Decca Records. The group then moved to London and issued their debut single, 'Don't Start Crying Now' which flopped. Brothers Patrick and Jackie McAuley had replaced Wrixen and Millings by the time Them's second single, 'Baby Please Don't Go', was released. Although aided by session musicians, the quintet's performance was remarkable, and this urgent, exciting single - which briefly served as the theme song to the influential UK television pop programme *Ready Steady Go* - deservedly reached the UK Top 10. It was backed by the Morrison-penned 'Gloria', a paean to teenage lust hinged to a hypnotic riff, later adopted by aspiring bar bands. The follow-up 'Here Comes The Night', was written and produced by R&B veteran Bert Berns. It peaked at number 2, and although it suggested a long career, Them's internal disharmony undermined progress. Peter Bardens replaced Jackie McAuley for the group's debut album, which matched brooding original songs, notably the frantic 'Mystic Eyes' and 'You Just Can't Win', with sympathetic cover versions. Further defections ensued when subsequent singles failed to emulate early success and by the release of *Them Again*, the unit had been recast around Morrison, Henderson, Jim Armstrong (guitar), Ray Elliott (saxophone/keyboards) and John Wilson (drums). This piecemeal set nonetheless boasted several highlights, including the vocalist's impassioned reading of the Bob Dylan composition, 'It's All Over Now, Baby Blue'. Dave Harvey then replaced Wilson, but this version of Them disintegrated in 1966 following a gruelling US tour and dispute with Solomon. Posthumous releases included the extraordinary 'The Story Of Them', documenting the group's early days at the Maritime in Belfast. Morrison then began a highly prolific solo career, leaving behind a period of confusion that saw the McAuley brothers re-emerge with a rival unit known variously as 'Them', 'Them Belfast Gypsies', the 'Freaks Of Nature', or simply the 'Belfast Gypsies'. Meanwhile ex-Mad Lads singer Kenny McDowell joined Henderson, Armstrong, Elliott and Harvey in a reconstituted Them who moved to Los Angeles following the intervention of producer Ray Ruff. *Now And Them* combined garage R&B with the *de rigueur* west coast sound exemplified by the lengthy 'Square Room', but the new line-up found it hard to escape the legacy of its predecessors. Elliott left the group in 1967, but the remaining quartet completed the psychedelic *Time Out, Time In For Them* as a quartet before McDowell and Armstrong returned to Belfast to form Sk'Boo. Henderson then maintained the Them name for two disappointing albums, on which he was supported by anonymous session musicians, before joining Ruff for a religious rock-opera, *Truth Of Truths*. He subsequently retired from music altogether, but renewed interest in his old group's heritage prompted a reunion of sorts in 1979 when the bassist recruited Billy Harrison, Eric Wrixen, Mel Austin (vocals) and Billy Bell (drums) for *Shut Your Mouth*. True to form both Harrison and Wrixen were fired prior to a tour of Germany, after which the Them appellation was again laid to rest.

●ALBUMS: *Them aka The Angry Young Them* (Decca 1965)★★★★, *Them Again* (Decca 1966)★★★★, *Now And Them* (Tower 1967)★★★, *Time Out, Time In For Them* (Tower 1968)★★★, *Them* (1970)★★★, *In Reality* (Happy Tiger 1971)★★★, *Belfast Gypsies* (Sonet 1978)★, *Shut Your Mouth* (1979)★★★.

●COMPILATIONS: *Here Comes The Night* (1965)★★★★, *The World Of Them* (Decca 1969)★★★★★, *Them Featuring Van Morrison Lead Singer* (Deram 1973)★★★, *Backtrackin' With Them* (70s)★★★, *Rock Roots: Them* (Decca 1976)★★★★, *Collection: Them* (1986)★★★, *The Singles* (1987)★★★★.

●FURTHER READING: *Van Morrison: A Portrait Of The Artist*, Johnny Rogan.

THIRD EAR BAND

Described by founder Glenn Sweeny as 'electric-acid-raga', the music of the UK Third Ear Band employed the drone-like figures and improvisatory techniques beloved by fellow pioneers the Soft Machine and Terry Riley. However, the esoteric, almost preternatural sweep of their work gave the group its originality as they studiously invoked an aura of ley-lines, druids and cosmology. Sweeny (drums/percussion) had been part of London's free-jazz circle prior to forming two *avant garde* ensembles, the Sun Trolly and the Hydrogen Jukebox. Paul Minns (oboe) and Richard Koss (violin) completed the early Third Ear Band line-up, although cellist Mel Davis augmented the group on their debut *Alchemy*. The unit was later commissioned to compose a soundtrack to Roman Polanski's film, *Macbeth*. However, although their ethereal music provided the ideal accompaniment to this remarkable project, the group's highly stylized approach proved too specialized for mainstream acceptance. Despite record company indifference, Sweeny has pursued his vision into the 90s, while a late-period member, Paul Buckmaster, has become a successful arranger.

●ALBUMS: *Alchemy* (Harvest 1969)★★★★, *Third Ear Band* (Harvest 1970)★★★, *Music From Macbeth* (Harvest 1972)★★, *Magic Music* (1990)★★.

●COMPILATIONS: *Experiences* (Harvest 1976)★★★.

THIRTEENTH FLOOR ELEVATORS

Formed in Austin, Texas, USA, in 1965, this influential group evolved from the nucleus of the Lingsmen, a popular local attraction. The original line-up included Stacy Sutherland (guitar), Bennie Thurman (bass), John Ike Walton (drums) and Max Rainey (vocals), but the latter was replaced by Roky Erickson (vocals/guitar). The quartet retained their anachronistic name until adding lyricist and jug player Tommy Hall, whose wife Clementine, suggested their more intriguing appellation. The Elevators made their recording debut with 'You're Gonna Miss Me'. Erickson had recorded this acerbic composition with an earlier group, the Spades, but his new colleagues added an emphatic enthusiasm missing from the original version. Hall's quivering jug interjections, unlikely in a rock setting, suggested a taste for the unusual enhanced by the group's mystical air.

Their debut, *The Psychedelic Sounds Of ...*, combined this off-beat spiritualism with R&B to create some of the era's most compulsive music. However the group's overt drug culture proselytization led to inevitable confrontations with the conservative Texan authorities. Several arrests ensued, the group's live appearances were monitored by the state police, while a management dispute led to the departure of Walton and new bassist Ronnie

Leatherman. The Elevators broke up briefly during the summer of 1967, but Hall, Erickson and Sutherland regrouped around a new rhythm section of Danny Galindo and Danny Thomas. A second album, *Easter Everywhere*, maintained the high quality of its predecessor, but external pressures proved too strong to repel. Studio out-takes were overdubbed with fake applause to create the implausible *Live*, while a final collection, *Bull Of The Woods*, coupled partially-completed performances with older, unissued masters. Despite an occasional reunion, the Elevators disintegrated when Erickson was committed to a mental institution and Sutherland was imprisoned. Reissues and archive compilations have furthered their reputation, but the group's personal tragedies culminated in 1978 when Sutherland was shot dead by his wife.

●ALBUMS: *The Psychedelic Sounds Of The Thirteenth Floor Elevators* (International 1966)★★★★, *Easter Everywhere* (International 1967)★★★, *Live* (International 1968)★, *Bull Of The Woods* (International 1968)★★.

●COMPILATIONS: *Fire In My Bones* (Texas 1985)★★, *Elevator Tracks* (Texas 1987)★, *Original Sound* (13th Hour 1988)★, *I've Seen Your Face Before* (1988)★★★, *The Collection* (1991)★★★, *Out Of Order* (1993)★★★, *The Best Of ...* (Eva 1994)★★★★, *The Interpreter* (Thunderbolt 1996)★★★.

THOMAS, CARLA

b. 21 December 1942, Memphis, Tennessee, USA. The daughter of Rufus Thomas, Carla first performed with the Teen Town Singers. "Cause I Love You', a duet with her father, was released on Satellite (later Stax) in 1960, but the following year she established herself as a solo act with 'Gee Whiz (Look At His Eyes)'. Leased to Atlantic, the song became a US Top 10 hit. 'I'll Bring It On Home To You' (1962 - an answer to Sam Cooke), 'What A Fool I've Been' (1963) and 'Let Me Be Good To You' (1965) then followed. 'B-A-B-Y', written by Isaac Hayes and David Porter, reached the US R&B Top 3, before a series of duets with Otis Redding proclaimed her 'Queen of Soul'. An excellent version of Lowell Fulson's 'Tramp' introduced the partnership. 'Knock On Wood' and 'Lovey Dovey' followed before Redding's premature death. Thomas' own career was eclipsed as Aretha Franklin assumed her regal mantle. Singles with William Bell and Johnnie Taylor failed to recapture past glories, although the singer stayed with Stax until its bankruptcy in 1975. Since then Thomas has not recorded, although she does tour occasionally with the Stax revival shows, and she appeared, along with her father, at the Porretta Terme Soul Festival in 1991.

●ALBUMS: *Gee Whiz* (Atlantic 1961)★★★, *Comfort Me* (Stax 1966)★★★★, *Carla* (Stax 1966)★★★★, with Otis Redding *King And Queen* (Stax 1967)★★★★, *The Queen Alone* (Stax 1967)★★★★, *Memphis Queen* (Stax 1969)★★★, *Love Means Carla Thomas* (Stax 1971)★★.

●COMPILATIONS: *The Best Of Carla Thomas* (Atlantic 1969)★★★★, *Hidden Gems* (1992)★★★, *The Best Of -*

The Singles Plus 1968-73 (1993)★★★★, *Sugar* (1994)★★★, *Gee Whiz: The Best Of Carla Thomas* (Rhino 1994)★★★★.

THOMAS, IRMA

b. Irma Lee, 18 February 1941, Ponchatoula, Louisiana, USA. The 'Soul Queen Of New Orleans' was discovered in 1958 by bandleader Tommy Ridgley. Her early records were popular locally, but an R&B hit came in 1960 with '(You Can Have My Husband But Please) Don't Mess With My Man'. The following year Thomas rejoined producer/writer Allen Toussaint, with whom she had worked on her first recordings. This reunion resulted in two of Irma's finest singles, 'It's Raining' and 'Ruler Of My Heart' (1962), the latter a prototype for Otis Redding's 'Pain In My Heart'. After signing with the Imperial label in 1963 she recorded 'Wish Someone Would Care' (1964), which reached the US Top 20, while the follow-up, 'Anyone Who Knows What Love Is (Will Understand)', also entered the national chart. This single is better recalled for its b-side, 'Time Is On My Side', which was successfully covered by the Rolling Stones. Thomas continued to record excellent singles without achieving due commercial success. Her final hit was a magnificent interpretation of 'Good To Me' (1968), recorded at Muscle Shoals and issued on Chess. She then moved to Canyon, Roker and Cotillion, before appearing on Swamp Dogg's short-lived Fungus label with *In Between Tears* (1973). Irma has continued to record fine albums and remains a highly popular live attraction. Her career continues into the 90s with new albums and a planned biography.

●ALBUMS: *Wish Someone Would Care* (Imperial 1964)★★★★, *Take A Look* (Imperial 1968)★★★★, *In Between Tears* (Fugus 1973)★★★, *Irma Thomas Live* (Island 1977)★★, *Soul Queen Of New Orleans* (1978)★★★, *Safe With Me* (1979)★★★, *Hip Shakin' Mama* (1981)★★, *The New Rules* (1986)★★, *The Way I Feel* (1988)★★★, *Simply The Best* (1991)★★★, *True Believer* (1992)★★★, *Walk Around Heaven: New Orleans Gospel Soul* (Rounder 1994)★★, *The Story Of My Life* (Rounder 1997)★★.

●COMPILATIONS: *Irma Thomas Sings* (70s)★★★, *Time Is On My Side* (1983), *Down At Muscle Shoals i* (1984)★★★, *Best Of: Breakaway* (1986)★★★, *Something Good: The Muscle Shoals Sessions* (1989)★★★, *Down At Muscle Schoals ii* (1989), *Ruler Of Hearts* (1989), *Down At Muscle Schoals iii* (1991)★★★, *Wish Someone Would Care* (1991)★★★, *Safe With Me/Irma Thomas Live* (1991)★★, *Time Is On My Side: The Best Of Vol. 1* (1992)★★★★, *The Soul Queen Of New Orleans* (1993)★★★, *Time Is On My Side* (Kent 1996)★★★★, *The Irma Thomas Collection* (Razor & Tie 1997)★★★★.

THOMAS, RUFUS

b. 26 March 1917, Cayce, Mississippi, USA. A singer, dancer and entertainer, Thomas learned his trade as a member of the Rabbit's Foot Minstrels, a Vaudeville-inspired touring group. By the late 40s he was performing in several Memphis nightclubs and organizing local talent shows. B.B. King, Bobby Bland and Little Junior Parker were discovered in this way. When King's career subsequently blossomed, Thomas replaced him as a disc jockey at WDIA and remained there until 1974. He also began recording and several releases appeared on Star Talent, Chess and Meteor before 'Bear Cat' became a Top 3 US R&B hit. An answer to Willie Mae Thornton's 'Hound Dog', it was released on Sun in 1953. Rufus remained a local celebrity until 1960 when he recorded with his daughter, Carla Thomas. Their duet, "Cause I Love You' was issued on the fledgling Satellite (later Stax) label where it became a regional hit. Thomas secured his reputation with a series of infectious singles. 'Walking The Dog' (1963) was a US Top 10 entry while several of his other recordings, notably 'Jump Back' and 'All Night Worker' (both in 1964) were beloved by aspiring British groups. His later success with novelty numbers – 'Do The Funky Chicken' (1970), '(Do The) Push And Pull, Part 1' (1970) and 'Do The Funky Penguin' (1971) – has obscured the merits of less brazen recordings. 'Sophisticated Sissy' (1967) and 'Memphis Train' (1968) are prime 60s R&B. Rufus stayed with Stax until its 1975 collapse, from where he moved to AVI. His releases there included *If There Were No Music* and *I Ain't Getting Older, I'm Gettin' Better*. In 1980 Thomas re-recorded several of his older songs for a self-named collection on Gusto. In the 80s he discarded R&B and recorded some rap with *Rappin' Rufus*, on the Inchiban label, and tackled blues with *That Woman Is Poison*, on the Alligator label. Bob Fisher's Sequel Records released a new album from Thomas in 1996. *Blues Thang* proved to be an unexpected treat from a man celebrating his 79th birthday at the time of release. He continues to perform regularly.

●ALBUMS: *Walking The Dog* (Stax 1963)★★★★, *Do The Funky Chicken* (Stax 1970)★★★★, *Doing The Push And Pull Live At PJs* (Stax 1971)★★★, *Did You Heard Me?* (Stax 1973)★★★, *Crown Prince Of Dance* (Stax 1973)★★★, *Blues In The Basement* (1975)★★★, *If There Were No Music* (AVI 1977)★★★, *I Ain't Gettin' Older, I'm Gettin' Better* (AVI 1977)★★★, *Rufus Thomas* (Gusto 1980)★★, *Rappin' Rufus* (Ichiban 1986)★★, *That Woman Is Poison* (Alligator 1989)★★, *Timeless Funk* (1992)★★, *Blues Thang* (Sequel 1996)★★★.

●COMPILATIONS: *Jump Back - A 1963-67 Retrospective* (1984)★★★, *Can't Get Away From This Dog* (1991)★★★, *The Best Of - The Singles* (Ace/Stax 1993)★★★★.

THUNDER, JOHNNY

b. Gil Hamilton, 15 August 1941, Leesburg, Florida, USA. Adopting the name Johnny Thunder, the singer first worked with street-corner groups in the late 50s. He worked briefly as a member of the Drifters in 1959 and recorded a few singles under his real name before meeting producer Teddy Vann. They co-wrote the dance song 'Loop De Loop', which was issued on the Diamond label and reached number 4 in the US pop charts in 1963.

Finding himself typecast as a performer of novelty dance records ('Ring Around The Rosey' and 'Everybody Do The Sloppy'), Thunder was unable to duplicate his initial success, although he continued recording for Diamond, Calla and United Artists. He was still performing into the late 80s.

●ALBUMS: *Loop De Loop* (Diamond 1963)★★★.

THUNDERCLAP NEWMAN

Although singer/composer Speedy Keen (b. John Keen, 29 March 1945, Ealing, London, England) wrote much of this short-lived group's material, its impact was derived from the quirky, old-fashioned image of pianist Andy Newman. Guitarist Jimmy McCulloch completed the original line-up responsible for 'Something In The Air', a soaring, optimistic song which was a dramatic UK number 1 hit in the summer of 1969. The song was produced by Pete Townshend. *Hollywood Dream* bode well for the future, highlighting Keen's surreal vision and Newman's barrelhouse piano fills, but a long delay in selecting a follow-up single undermined the band's standing. The eventual choice, 'Accidents', was another excellent composition, but lacked the immediacy of its predecessor. Despite the addition of two new members - Jim Pitman-Avory (bass) and Jack McCulloch (drums) - Thunderclap Newman were unable to achieve a satisfactory live sound and, bereft of chart success, broke up. Speedy Keen and Andy Newman began solo careers, while Jimmy McCulloch joined Stone The Crows and, later, Wings.

●ALBUMS: *Hollywood Dream* (Track 1970)★★★.

TIMMONS, BOBBY

b. 19 December 1935, Philadelphia, Pennsylvania, USA, d. 1 March 1974. Timmons studied with an uncle who was a musician, and then attended the Philadelphia Academy for a year. After playing piano around his home town he joined Kenny Dorham's Jazz Prophets in February 1956. He next played with Chet Baker (April 1956 to January 1957), Sonny Stitt (February to August 1957), Maynard Ferguson (August 1957 to March 1958) and Art Blakey's Jazz Messengers (July 1958 to September 1959). Although this last stint was no longer than the others, it was with the Messengers that he made his name. He replaced Sam Dockery to become part of a classic line-up, with Wayne Shorter on tenor and Lee Morgan on trumpet, and recorded *Like Someone In Love*. His composition 'Moanin'' became a signature for the Messengers, and has remained a definitive example of gospel inflected hard bop ever since. In October 1959 he joined Cannonball Adderley, for whom he wrote 'This Here' and 'Dat Dere'. He rejoined Blakey briefly in 1961, touring Japan in January (a broadcast was subsequently released as *A Day With Art Blakey* by Eastwind) and recording on some of *Roots & Herbs*. From the early 60s Timmons led his own trios and appeared regularly in Washington, DC. In Spring 1966 he had a residency at the Village Gate in New York and played throughout Greenwich Village in the early 70s. He died of cirrhosis of the liver in 1974. Timmons was a seminal figure in the soul-jazz movement, which did so much to instil jazz with the vitality of gospel. Although best known as a pianist and composer, he also played vibes during the last years of his life.

●ALBUMS: *This Here Is Bobby Timmons* (Riverside 1956)★★★★, with John Jenkins, Clifford Jordan *Jenkins, Jordan & Timmons* (1957)★★★, *Soul Time* (Riverside 1960)★★★, *Easy Does It* (Riverside 1961)★★★, *The Bobby Timmons Trio In Person At The Village Vanguard* (Riverside 1961)★★★★, *Sweet And Soulful Sounds* (Riverside 1962)★★★, *Born To Be Blue* Riverside 1963)★★★★, *From The Bottom* (1964)★★★, *Workin' Out* (1964)★★★, *Holiday Soul* (1964)★★★, *Chun-king* (Prestige 1964)★★★, *Little Barefoot Soul* (Prestige 1964)★★★, *Chicken And Dumplin's* (Prestige 1965)★★★, *Soul Food* (Prestige 1966)★★★★, *The Soul Man* (Prestige 1966)★★★★, *Got To Get It* (Milestone 1968)★★★, *Do You Know The Way* (Milestone 1968)★★★, *Live At The Connecticut Jazz Party* (Early Bird 1981)★★★, *This Here* (Riverside 1984)★★★.

●COMPILATIONS: *Moanin'* (Milestone 1963)★★★★.

TINTERN ABBEY

Tintern Abbey were formed in London, England, by John Dalton (drums), Stuart MacKay (bass), David MacTavish (vocals) and Dan Smith (lead guitar) in the mid-60s. Although rooted in the nascent UK psychedelic tradition their sole single, 'Beeside'/'Vacuum Cleaner', released on Deram Records in 1967, was notable for its excellent layered fuzz guitar. It did not bring them mainstream success, however, although it has since become one of the most collectable records of the period. Smith, arguably the group's main talent, was replaced by Paul Brett, formerly a collaborator with Arthur Brown, in January 1968. However, no further studio recordings emerged, with MacTavish leaving to join Big Bertha.

TINY TIM

b. Herbert Khaury, 12 April 1930, New York, USA, d. 30 November 1996. Eccentric entertainer Tiny Tim played regularly on the New York Greenwich Village circuit during the early/mid-60s. With his warbling voice, long scraggly hair and camp mannerisms, he specialized in show tunes dating back to the musicals of the 20s. Following an appearance in the film *You Are What You Eat*, he secured a regular spot on the highly rated *Rowan And Martin's Laugh-In* comedy series. The comic incongruity of this middle-aged man, who sang in a cracked falsetto and played the ukulele proved novel enough to warrant a Top 20 US hit in 1968 with 'Tiptoe Through The Tulips With Me'. Several albums and tours followed and at the height of his media fame he attracted a mass audience for his live television marriage on Johnny Carson's *The Tonight Show* to the young girl he called 'Miss Vicky' (Victoria May Budinger). His professed celibacy and highly moral sexual standpoint created instant copy and the controversial marriage was well

chronicled, from the birth of baby Tulip, to the divorce court. By the early 70s the Tiny Tim fad had passed, and having lost his contract with Reprise Records he continued to issue singles on small independent labels, to little success. In the late 80s Tim completed a cassette-only release, *The World's Longest Non-Stop Singing Record*, which was recorded live in Brighton, England. He subsequently moved to Australia where he became acquainted with graphic artist Martin Sharp, who designed Cream's distinctive *Wheels Of Fire* sleeve as well as several covers of *Oz* magazine. Sharp's work graced *Tiny Tim Rocks*, a disappointing mélange of the singer's high falsetto and ill-fitting hard rock. In 1989 his version of AC/DC's 'Highway To Hell' was released to modest sales. During the 90s known as Mr. Tim, the singer returned to the USA to live in Des Moines, Iowa, 'because it's clean.' In 1993 he married for a third time, he and 'Miss Sue' lived in Minneapolis until his death in 1996.

●ALBUMS: *God Bless Tiny Tim* (Reprise 1968)★★★, *Tiny Tim's Second Album* (Reprise 1969)★★★, *For All My Little Friends* (Reprise 1969)★★, *With Love And Kisses: A Concert from Fairyland* (Bouquet 1968)★★, *Tiny Tim, Michelle Ramos And Bruce Haack* (Ra-Jo International 1986)★★, *Rock* (Regular 1993)★★, *I Love Me* (Seeland 1995)★★, *Live In Chicago* (Bughouse 1995)★★, *Songs Of An Impotent Troubadour* (Durtro 1995)★★, *Tiny Tim's Christmas Album* (Durtro 1995)★★★, *Unplugged* (Tomanna 1996)★★, with Brave Combo *Girl* (Rounder 1996)★★.

●FURTHER READING: *Tiny Tim*, Harry Stein.

TOKENS

Formed in 1955 in Brooklyn, New York, USA, the Tokens were one of the most successful white harmony groups of the early 60s, best known for their 1961 number 1 single 'The Lion Sleeps Tonight' (number 11 in the UK). The group was originally called the Linc-Tones (taken from Lincoln High School, which the original members all attended) and consisted of tenor vocalist Hank Medress (b. 19 November 1938, Brooklyn), Neil Sedaka (b. 13 March 1939, Brooklyn), Eddie Rabkin and Cynthia Zolitin. The following year Rabkin left and was replaced by Jay Siegel (b. 20 October 1939, Brooklyn). With that line-up the group recorded 'I Love My Baby' for the Melba label, with no success. The next change came in 1958 when Sedaka departed for a hugely successful solo career as a performer and songwriter. Zolitin also left in 1958 and the remaining duo carried on for a year with other singers as Darrell And The Oxfords, recording two singles for Roulette Records.

Twelve-year-old Mitch Margo (b. 25 May 1947, Brooklyn) and his brother Phil (b. 1 April 1942, Brooklyn) joined Medress and Siegel in December 1959 and the group changed its name to the Tokens. This was the most successful and stable line-up of the Tokens. Their first recording as such was the 1961 self-penned 'Tonight I Fell In Love', which the Tokens sold to the small Warwick Records. Following the record's rise to number 15 in the

USA, the Tokens forged a creative partnership with producers and songwriters Hugo Peretti and Luigi Creatore at RCA Records.

That pair, along with songwriter George Weiss, reworked the folk song 'Wimoweh', itself reworked by the folk group the Weavers from a 30s South African song called 'Mbube', into 'The Lion Sleeps Tonight'. After the single peaked at the top of the US charts (number 11 in the UK), the quartet took on another vocalist, Joseph Venneri, for live performances (he later appeared on recordings, and was replaced in the mid-60s by Brute Force, (real name Stephen Friedland), who went on to record two solo albums under the Brute Force pseudonym after leaving the Tokens in 1970). In early 1962 the Tokens branched out from recording under their own name by signing a production deal with Capitol Records and establishing Big Time Productions in New York. During 1962, they attempted to repeat the success of their number 1 record by reworking other songs, including another African folk song, 'B'wa Nina (Pretty Girl)', and the Ritchie Valens hit 'La Bomba' (with a slight spelling change), itself an old Mexican folk song. The Tokens never recaptured the success they enjoyed with 'The Lion Sleeps Tonight', although they appeared on the US singles chart regularly until the beginning of the 70s on a succession of record labels, including their own B.T. Puppy Records, which they formed in 1964 (the label's greatest success was with the group the Happenings, who released two Top 5 singles on the label, produced by the Tokens). Among their other notable releases were 'He's In Town' in 1964, 'I Hear Trumpets Blow' in 1966 and 'Portrait Of My Love' in 1967.

Meanwhile, their production career took off in 1963 with the success of 'He's So Fine', a number 1 single by the girl group the Chiffons. Members of the Tokens also sang on many sessions for other artists at this time, including Bob Dylan (*Highway 61 Revisited*) and the Blues Project. In 1967 the Tokens signed with Warner Brothers Records (which refused to release a concept album they had recorded entitled *Intercourse,* which the group released itself in 1971) and two years later switched over to Buddah Records. By then their reign as hitmakers was long over, and the group began splintering. Mitch Margo spent 1969-71 in the Army and Medress departed the group in October 1970 to produce. His most successful venture was as co-producer of Tony Orlando and Dawn, one of the best-selling pop groups of the 70s. Medress also produced a 1972 remake of 'The Lion Sleeps Tonight' by Robert John, which reached number 3 in the USA, and produced records by singer Dan Hill and New York rocker/cabaret singer Buster Poindexter, a pseudonym for ex-New York Dolls singer David Johansen. The Tokens carried on without Medress until 1973, when the remaining trio changed its name to Cross Country and signed to Atco Records. As such, they placed one single on the US chart, a remake of the Wilson Pickett hit 'In The Midnight Hour' which reached number 30 in 1973. The group finally split in 1974, although they cut a single together, 'A Tribute To The Beach Boys '76', in 1976. A reunion concert in New York in 1981 featured the Margo brothers, Siegel and Medress. Some of the group members, particularly Mitch Margo, attempted to keep the Tokens name alive by forming new groups into the 80s, and one even re-recorded 'The Lion Sleeps Tonight' in 1988 for the small Downtown label. Phil Margo went on to become a manager of rock bands. Jay Siegel became owner/manager of a recording studio in New York.

● ALBUMS: *The Lion Sleeps Tonight* (RCA Victor 1961)★★★★, *We, The Tokens, Sing Folk* (RCA Victor 1962)★★★★, *Wheels* (RCA Victor 1964)★★★, *Again* (RCA Victor 1966)★★★, *King Of The Hot Rods* (Diplomat 1966)★★★, *I Hear Trumpets Blow* (BT Puppy 1966)★★, with the Happenings *Back To Back* (1967)★★, *It's A Happening World* (Warners 1967)★★, *Life Is Groovy* (1970)★★, *Tokens Of Gold* (BT Puppy 1969)★★★, *December 5th* (BT Puppy 1971)★★, *Both Sides Now* (1971)★★, *Intercourse* (BT Puppy 1971)★★, *Cross Country* (1973)★★.

● COMPILATIONS: *Greatest Moments* (BT Puppy 1970)★★★, *Very Best Of The Tokens* (Buddah 1971)★★★.

TOM AND JERRY

This singing duo consisted of Paul Simon (b. 13 October 1941, Newark, New Jersey, USA) and Art Garfunkel (b. Arthur Garfunkel, 5 November 1941, Queens, New York City, USA) . They met while attending high school and began recording home demos together in 1957. They were 'discovered' by Sid Prosen of Big Records during a session at Manhattan's Sanders Studio. The duo's names were changed to Tom Graph (Garfunkel) and Jerry Landis (Simon) and, as Tom And Jerry, the pair scored a minor US hit with an original composition, 'Hey! Schoolgirl'. Drawing influence from Buddy Holly and the Everly Brothers, Tom And Jerry completed another three singles, 'Our Song', 'That's My Story' (both 1958) and 'Looking At You' (1959), before parting company. Garfunkel then recorded 'Dream Alone' and 'Forgive' Me' as Artie Garr, while Simon undertook several different projects. He recorded under the names True Taylor and Tico And The Triumphs, as well as issuing four singles between 1959 and 1962 as Jerry Landis. He wrote and produced releases by Ritchie Cordell (later songwriter for Tommy James And The Shondells) and in 1963 recorded 'Carlos Dominguez'/'He Was My Brother' as Paul Kane.

By this point he had become part of the Greenwich Village folk circuit, both as a solo act and in partnership with Garfunkel. As Simon And Garfunkel the duo became one of the most successful acts of the 60s. This inspired the release of *Simon And Garfunkel*, a deliberately mistitled compendium of Tom And Jerry recordings, the True Taylor single and instrumental filler. The album was withdrawn following court action by Simon.

● ALBUMS: *Simon And Garfunkel* (Pickwick 1966)★★.

TONEY, OSCAR, JNR.

b. 26 May 1939, Selma, Alabama, USA. Oscar Toney developed his early craft singing gospel with the Sensational

Melodies Of Joy. A spell with a secular group, the Searchers, preceded two solo singles for King, but several years would pass before he recorded again. Toney's debut for the Bell label, 'For Your Precious Love' (1967), revived the Jerry Butler/Impressions song, but he prefaced this impassioned reading with a spoken sermon. Further singles, including 'You Can Lead A Woman To The Altar' and 'Never Get Enough Of Your Love', failed to recapture its impact. In 1971, the singer moved outlets to Capricorn before switching to a British outlet, Contempo. Six singles and an album followed, much of which was recorded in Britain where Toney had temporarily settled. He returned to the USA in 1976, but plans to revive his career there failed.

●ALBUMS: *For Your Precious Love* (Bell 1967)★★, *I've Been Loving You Too Long* (1974)★★.
●COMPILATIONS: *Papa Don's Preacher* (1988)★★★.

TORNADOS

The only serious challengers to the Shadows as Britain's top instrumental unit, the Tornados merely lasted as long as their console svengali, independent record producer Joe Meek. In 1961, he assembled the quintet initially as house band at his Holloway, London studio, to back solo performers such as Don Charles, John Leyton and Billy Fury, who was namechecked in the title of their debut, 'Love And Fury'. From Colin Hicks and his Cabin Boys, Meek had drawn Alan Caddy (b. 2 February 1940, London, England; guitar) and drummer Clem Cattini (b. 28 August 1939, London, England). Guitarist George Bellamy (b. 8 October 1941, Sunderland, England; guitar) and Roger Lavern (b. Roger Jackson, 11 November 1938, Kidderminster, England; keyboards) were session players while Heinz Burt (b. 24 July 1942, Germany) on bass was one of Meek's own protégés.

In their own right, the Tornados made the big time with a second single, the otherworldly 'Telstar'. Composed by Meek with his creative confrère Geoff Goddard deputizing for Lavern on clavioline, this quintessential 60s instrumental anticipated many of the electronic ventures of a subsequent and less innocent pop generation. Moreover, in 1962 it topped the domestic hit parade and unbelievably did likewise in the USA, where no UK group, not even the Shadows, had made much headway. Although a capitalizing tour of North America was unwisely cancelled, Meek's boys played 'Eric the Red' to Britain's invasion of US charts two years later. 1963 was another good year for the Tornados with 'Globetrotter', 'Robot' and 'The Ice Cream Man' - all with catchy juxtapositions of outer space aetheria and funfair vulgarity - cracking the UK Top 20. Flattering too were those myriad copyist combos in their artistic debt, notably the Volcanos with 'Polaris'. Danger, however, became apparent in the comparative failure of 'Dragonfly' shortly after the exit of Burt. The absence of his blond Norse radiance onstage, coupled with the levelling blow of the beat boom and its emphasis on vocals had rendered the Tornados passé. Worse, new ideas were thin on the ground. The 'Robot' b-side, 'Life On Venus', for instance, almost repeated the

'Telstar' melody while 'Early Bird' and 1965's 'Stingray' harked back to its million-selling sound. Following the departure of Cattini, the last original Tornado, there came further desperate strategies until the penniless Meek's 1967 suicide and the outfit's interrelated disbandment. In the mid-70s, Bellamy, Burt, Cattini and Lavern - as 'The Original Tornados' - managed some nostalgia revues and a remake of 'Telstar' before going their separate ways. Nevertheless, with a new Tornados, Cattini tried again in 1989. While this line-up features a female singer, the loudest cheers are reserved for the ancient instrumentals, especially Meek's eerie US number 1.

●ALBUMS: *Away From It All* (1964)★★★.
●COMPILATIONS: *The World Of The Tornados* (Decca 1972)★★★, *Remembering* (Decca 1976)★★★, *The Original 60s Hits* (Music Club 1994)★★★, *The EP Collection* (See For Miles 1996)★★★★.

TRAFFIC

Formed in 1967, this stellar UK group comprised Steve Winwood (b. 12 May 1948, Birmingham, England; keyboards/guitar/ bass/vocals), Chris Wood (b. 24 June 1944, Birmingham, England, d. 12 July 1983; saxophone/flute), Jim Capaldi (b. 24 August 1944, Evesham, Worcestershire, England; drums/percussion/vocals) and Dave Mason (b. 10 May 1947, Worcester, England; guitar/vocals). Winwood had conceived, plotted and formed Traffic just prior to his departure from the Spencer Davis Group. Traffic were archetypes of psychedelic Britain in 1967 in dress, attitude and music. They were the originators of the 'getting it together in the country cottage' syndrome, which found so many followers. Their pot-pourri of musical styles was innovative and daring, created in the communal atmosphere of their cottage in Berkshire. Their first single, 'Paper Sun', with its infectious sitar opening was an instant hit, closely followed by 'Hole In My Shoe' (parodied in a 1984 number 2 UK hit by Neil the hippie, from BBC Television's *The Young Ones*) and the film theme 'Here We Go Round The Mulberry Bush'. Mason left at the end of an eventful year, just as the first album, *Mr Fantasy* was released. From then on Traffic ceased to be a singles band, and built up a large following, especially in the USA. Their second album, *Traffic*, showed refinement and progression. Dave Mason had returned briefly and two of his songs were particularly memorable, 'You Can All Join In' and 'Feelin' Alright' (later covered by Joe Cocker). In 'Who Knows What Tomorrow Might Bring?', Winwood sings, 'We are not like all the rest, you can see us any day of the week, come around, sit down, take a sniff, fall asleep, baby you don't have to speak'. This lyric perfectly encapsulated the hippie lifestyle of the late 60s. Another outstanding song, 'Forty Thousand Headmen' combined a lyrical tale of pure fantasy with lilting flute and jazz tempo.

Last Exit was a fragmented affair and during its recording Mason departed once more. The second side consisted of just two tracks recorded live with the band as a trio. Winwood bravely attempted to hold the ensemble together by singing and playing Hammond organ in addition to using the bass pedals to compensate for the lack of a bass guitar. At this point the band disintegrated leaving Winwood to wander into Blind Faith. The others teamed up once again with Dave Mason to form the short-lived Mason, Capaldi, Wood and Frog. The Frog was Mick Weaver (aka Wynder K. Frog). Neither band lasted; the former made one highly successful album and the latter were never committed to vinyl.

Following a brief spell as a member of Ginger Baker's Airforce, Winwood embarked on a solo project, to be called Mad Shadows. He enlisted the help of Wood and Capaldi, and to the delight of the music press this became Traffic once again. The resulting album was the well-received *John Barleycorn Must Die*. Rick Grech, formerly of Family, Blind Faith and Airforce, also joined the band. In 1971 *Welcome To The Canteen* appeared with Dave Mason rejoining for a third time. This disappointing live album contained an overlong version of 'Gimme Some Lovin'' from Winwood's days in the Spencer Davis Group. Ironically it was Mason who shone, with two tracks from his superb *Alone Together* album.

Drummer Jim Gordon (from Derek And The Dominos) and Reebop Kwaku Baah joined in 1971, allowing Capaldi to take the role as frontman. The excellent *Low Spark Of The High Heeled Boys* (1971) was followed by *Shoot Out At The Fantasy Factory* in 1973. The latter saw the substitution of David Hood and Roger Hawkins for Grech and Gordon. Both albums achieved gold status in the USA. Throughout their turbulent career Traffic were never able to reproduce their inventive arrangements on stage. Witnesses would concur that Traffic were erratic when playing live. This trait was highlighted on their penultimate album, *On The Road*.

The final record was *When The Eagle Flies* in 1974, another fine collection with Rosko Gee on bass and 'Gentleman' Jim Capaldi back behind the drum kit. Traffic did not so much break up as fizzle out, although they did record together again when Capaldi became involved on Winwood's later solo work. Traffic had already left an indelible mark as creators of inventive and sometimes glorious music and it was a delight that 20 years after they dissolved, the name was born again with Capaldi and Winwood attempting to re-create their unique sound. The album *Far From Home* was warmly rather than ecstatically received and they followed it with a major tour of the USA supporting the Grateful Dead and then a short European tour. The album was a true joint effort, but the strong structured soul sound of the record erred towards a Winwood solo outing rather than the wandering and ethereal beauty of Traffic. Outstanding tracks include the funky 'Here Comes The Man', and 'Some Kinda Woman' and the almost Traffic-like 'State Of Grace', with its spiritual feel complemented by the rousing gospel piano introduction for the glorious 'Every Night, Every Day'.

●ALBUMS: *Mr Fantasy* (Island 1967)★★★★, *Traffic* (Island 1968)★★★★, *Last Exit* (Island 1969)★★, *John Barleycorn Must Die* (Island 1970)★★★★, *Welcome To The Canteen* (Island 1971)★★, *Low Spark Of The High Heeled Boys* (Island 1971)★★★★, *Shoot Out At The Fantasy Factory* (Island 1973)★★★, *On The Road* (Island 1973)★★, *When The Eagle Flies* (Island 1974)★★★, *Far From Home* (Virgin 1994)★★★.

●COMPILATIONS: *Best Of Traffic* (Island 1970)★★★★, *Heavy Traffic* (Island 1975)★★★★, *More Heavy Traffic* (Island 1975)★★★, *Smiling Phases* 2-CD set (Island 1991)★★★★★.

●FURTHER READING: *Keep On Running: The Steve Winwood Story*, Chris Welch. *Back In The High Life: A Biography Of Steve Winwood*, Alan Clayson.

TRAMLINE

A quartet of John McCoy (vocals/harmonica), Micky Moody (guitar), Terry Popple (drums) and Terry Sidgwick (bass/vocals), Tramline were a typical if not particularly inspiring example of the UK blues boom of the late 60s. Signed by Island Records, Chris Blackwell himself produced their debut album, although it revealed little to distinguish itself from the herd. As with their subsequent album, it relied almost exclusively on Moody's expressive guitar lines. However, Guy Stevens' production of their second collection, *Moves Of Vegetable Centuries*, proved as ponderous as the title. Nothing it contained was as fluid as their best known song, the Steve Winwood/Jim Capaldi composition, 'Pearly Queen', which had been included on the influential *You Can All Join In* blues boom compilation. Facing a round of austere reviews the group broke up, with Moody subsequently joining Whitesnake in the 70s.

●ALBUMS: *Somewhere Down The Line* (Island 1968)★★, *Moves Of Vegetable Centuries* (Island 1969)★.

TREMELOES

When UK chart-toppers Brian Poole And The Tremeloes parted company in 1966 few would have wagered that the backing group would outdo the lead singer. Remarkably, however, the relaunched Tremeloes went on to eclipse not only Poole, but the original hit-making group. At the time of their reconvening in 1966, the line-up comprised Rick West (b. Richard Westwood, 7 May 1943, Dagenham, Essex, England; guitar), Alan Blakely (b. 1 April 1942, Dagenham, Essex, England; rhythm guitar), Dave Munden (b. 2 December 1943, Dagenham, Essex, England; drums) and Alan Howard (b. 17 October 1941, Dagenham, Essex, England; bass). In May of 1966 Howard was replaced by Mike Clark; however, a mere three months later his spot was taken by Len 'Chip' Hawkes (b. 11 November 1946, London, England), whose lead vocals and boyish looks gave the group a stronger visual identity. In order to keep up with the times, the group abandoned their stage suits in favour of Carnaby Street garb and fashionably longer hair. Their second generation debut was a cover of Paul Simon's 'Blessed', which proved unsuccessful. Seeking more commercial material they next covered 'Good Day Sunshine' from the Beatles' *Revolver*. In spite of radio play it too failed to chart, but their third release 'Here Comes My Baby' (a Cat Stevens composition) smashed into the Top 10 on both sides of the Atlantic. An astute follow-up with 'Silence Is Golden', previously the flip-side of the Four Seasons' 'Rag Doll', proved a perfect vehicle for the Tremeloes' soft harmonic style and gave them their only number 1. Having established themselves as a hit act, they notched up an impressive run of hits during the late 60s including 'Even The Bad Times Are Good', 'Suddenly You Love Me', 'Helule Helule' and 'My Little Lady'. At the end of the decade, the group seemed weary of their role in the pop world and broke away from their usual Tin Pan Alley songsmiths to write their own material. Their first attempt, '(Call Me) Number One', was an impressive achievement, arguably superior to the material that they had recorded since 1967. When it reached number 2 in the charts, the group convinced themselves that a more ambitious approach would bring even greater rewards. Overreacting to their dream start as hit writers, they announced that they were 'going heavy' and suicidally alienated their pop audience by dismissing their earlier record-buying fans as 'morons'. Their brief progressive phase was encapsulated in the album *Master*, which won no new fans but provided a final Top 20 single, 'Me And My Life'. Thereafter, they turned increasingly to cabaret where their strong live performances were well appreciated. In 1974 Chip Hawkes went to Nashville, USA, to pursue an ultimately unsuccessful solo career.

●ALBUMS: *Here Comes The Tremeloes* (CBS 1967)★★★★, *The Tremeloes: Chip, Rick, Alan And Dave* (CBS 1967)★★★, *Here Comes My Baby* (USA 1967)★★★★, *1958/68 World Explosion* (1968)★★★, *The Tremeloes 'Live' In Cabaret* (CBS 1969)★★, *Master* (CBS 1970)★★, *Shiner* (1974)★★, *Don't Let The Music Die* (1976)★★.

●COMPILATIONS: *Suddenly You Love Me* (1993)★★★, *Silence Is Golden* (Spectrum 1995)★★★.

TROGGS

The original Troggs were an ill-starred early 60s group from Andover, Hampshire, England, who suddenly found themselves reduced to two members: vocalist Dave Wright and bassist Reginald Ball (b. 12 June 1943, Andover, England). Another local group, Ten Foot Five, were suffering similar personnel upheavals with bassist Peter Staples (b. 3 May 1944, Andover, England) and guitarist Chris Britton (b. 21 January 1945, Watford, Hertfordshire, England) surviving the purge. At the suggestion of their respective managers, the two groups amalgamated, with Ball surprisingly emerging as the new lead vocalist. On the advice of *New Musical Express* journalist Keith Altham, Ball later changed his name to Reg Presley in the hope of attracting some attention from Elvis fans. Wright, meanwhile, had moved on to another Hampshire group, the Loot, while the revitalized Troggs found a drummer, Ronnie Bond (b. Ronald Bullis, 4 May 1943, Andover, England, d. 13 November 1992). After signing with producer/manager Larry Page, the group recorded a one-off single for CBS, 'Lost Girl'. Their debut flopped but after switching to Larry's new label Page One

(distributed by Fontana), they found success with a cover of Chip Taylor's 'Wild Thing', which reached number 2 in the UK in May 1966. The follow-up, 'With A Girl Like You', went one better, establishing the Troggs as one of the most popular groups in the country. Stateside success was equally impressive with 'Wild Thing' topping the charts. Unfortunately, due to a misunderstanding with Sonny And Cher's managers Charlie Greene and Brian Stone (who had organized a re-recording of the disc), 'Wild Thing' was released on two different labels, Atco and Mercury. To make matters worse, the flip-side of the Atco version was the scheduled follow-up, 'With A Girl Like You'.

While their prospects in America waned, the group enjoyed an affectionate notoriety at home where their provincial politeness and inane naïvete contrasted markedly with the forced sexiness of songs such as 'I Can't Control Myself' and 'Anyway That You Want Me'. Although the group boasted three songwriters and potential solo artists whose work was covered by others, they were never taken seriously by the press or pop élite. While clearly at home with basic rockers like 'Give It To Me', the group also tinkered with counter-culture subject matter on 'Night Of The Long Grass' and 'Love Is All Around', and their albums also occasionally veered towards the psychedelic market.

Any hopes of sustaining their hit career were lost when they fell out with Larry Page in a High Court action that made case law. Thereafter they became predominantly a touring group, with Presley infrequently abetted by Britton, Bond and Tony Murray (from Plastic Penny). During the 70s they achieved a certain cult status thanks to the hilarious 'Troggs Tapes', a notorious bootleg recording of an abortive session, consisting mainly of a stream of swear words. Later that decade they reunited with Page for an odd reworking of the Beach Boys' 'Good Vibrations' and recorded a live album at Max's Kansas City. Two-and-a-half decades on, the band still perform with their credibility growing rather than shrinking. Their R.E.M.-linked *Athens Andover* took people by surprise. The band had utilized Presley songs (and one from Chip Taylor), and blended the raw Troggs sound with R.E.M.'s Peter Buck and Mike Mills. The album was a clear indication that after being the butt of jokes for many years the Troggs are one of the finest ever 60s pop bands, a fact that was confirmed when Wet Wet Wet's version of 'Love Is All Around' took up residence at the head of the UK listings for over three months in 1994. Reg Presley, now an enthusiastic crop-circle investigator and UFO watcher, could at last look forward to a long and financially comfortable retirement.

●ALBUMS: *From Nowhere The Troggs* (Fontana 1966)★★★★, *Trogglodynamite* (Page One 1967)★★★★, *Cellophane* (Page One 1967)★★★★, *Mixed Bag* (Page One 1968)★★★, *Trogglomania* (Page One 1969)★★★, *Contrasts* (DJM 1976)★★, *With A Girl Like You* (DJM 1976)★★, *The Original Troggs Tapes* (DJM 1976)★, *Live At Max's Kansas City* (President 1981)★, *Black Bottom* (New Rose 1982)★★, *Rock It*

Baby (Action Replay 1984)★★, *Wild Things* (Konnexion 1987)★★, *Au* (New Rose 1990)★★, *Athens Andover* (Essential/Page One 1992)★★★.
●COMPILATIONS: *Best Of The Troggs* (Page One 1968)★★★★, *Best Of The Troggs Volume 2* (Page One 1968)★★★, *14 Greatest Hits* (Spectrum 1988)★★★★, *Archaeology 1966 - 1976* (1993), *Greatest Hits* (Polygram 1994)★★★★, *The EP Collection* (See For Miles 1996)★★★★.

TROY, DORIS

b. Doris Higginsen, 6 January 1937, New York City, USA. The daughter of a Baptist preacher, Doris abandoned her gospel beginnings in favour of a jazz group, the Halos. She recorded as half of Jay And Dee and soon also began making her mark as a songwriter, using her grandmother's name of Payne as a *nom de plume*. In 1960 Dee Clark recorded her song 'How About That' for Vee Jay, while Troy cut a lone single for Everest before concentrating on background singing, with ex-Drinkard Singers Dionne and Dee Dee Warwick and their aunt Cissy Houston, behind many acts including the Drifters, Solomon Burke and Chuck Jackson. Then in 1963 Troy co-penned 'Just One Look', and when Juggy Murray of Sue Records 'sat on' a demo of it, she took a copy to Jerry Wexler at Atlantic Records, who promptly released it exactly as recorded and watched it become a US Top 10 hit. It was covered the following year by the Hollies, and reached the UK number 2 slot. Other releases included the equally insistent 'What'cha Gonna Do About It?', which reached the UK Top 40 in 1964, but failed to succeed in her home country. Later singles for Capitol and Calla were equally underrated. After settling in London in 1969, she recorded a self-titled album for the Beatles' label Apple, with the help of George Harrison and Eric Clapton. Troy also recorded for People and Polydor and later worked as a session singer, contributing to a number of albums including Pink Floyd's *Dark Side Of The Moon*. From the mid-80s to 1991 Troy performed in an off-Broadway musical about her life, *Mama, I Want To Sing*, and again when it opened in London in February 1995.
●ALBUMS: *Just One Look* (Atlantic 1963)★★★, *Doris Troy* (Apple 1970)★★★, *Rainbow Testament* (1972)★★, *Stretching Out* (1974)★★★, *Mama, I Want To Sing* (1986)★★★.
●COMPILATIONS: *Just One Look: The Best Of ...* (Ichiban 1994)★★★★.

TUCKER, TOMMY

b. Robert Higginbotham, 5 March 1933, Springfield, Ohio, USA, d. 22 January 1982. Renowned as an R&B performer, Tucker began his career as a jazz musician playing piano and clarinet for the Bob Woods Orchestra. He led his own group, the Dusters, recorded under the name Tee Tucker for Atco in 1961 and worked with saxophonist Roland Kirk prior to recording 'Hi-Heel Sneakers' in 1964. This simple, but compulsive 12-bar blues song established the singer's reputation when it was consis-

tently covered by other acts. This one song contained a pot-pourri of references, the bizarre 'hi-heel sneakers' and 'wig hats on her head.' The casually understated delivery of the line: 'You better wear some boxing gloves, in case some fool might want to fight', gave the song great subtle humour. Further excellent singles in a similar style, including 'Long Tall Shorty', were less successful and forced Tucker to revert to club work. He visited Britain during the 70s as part of the *Blues Legends* package and, inspired by an enthusiastic response, began recording again. This irrepressible performer, sadly, died from poisoning in January 1982.
●ALBUMS: *Greatest Twist Hits (Rock And Roll Machine)* (Atlantic 1961)★★★, *Hi-Heel Sneakers & Long Tall Shorty* (Checker 1964)★★★★, *Mother Tucker* (1974),★★★ *Rocks Is My Pillow, Cold Ground Is My Bed* (1982)★★, *Memphis Badboy* (1987)★★★, *1933 Tommy Tucker* (1988)★★, *1942 Tommy Tucker* (1988)★★★.

TURNER, IKE AND TINA

Ike Turner (b. 5 November 1931, Clarkdale, Mississippi, USA) and Tina Turner (b. Annie Mae Bullock, 26 November 1938, Brownsville, Tennessee, USA). The commercial rebirth of singer Tina Turner, coupled with revelations about her ex-husband's unsavoury private life, has obscured the important role Ike Turner played in the development of R&B. A former piano-player with Sonny Boy Williamson and Robert Nighthawk, Turner formed his Kings Of Rhythm during the late 40s. This influential group was responsible for 'Rocket 88', a 1950 release often named as the first rock 'n' roll recording but confusingly credited to its vocalist, Jackie Brenston. Turner then became a talent scout for Modern Records where he helped develop the careers of Bobby Bland, B.B. King and Howlin' Wolf. Now based in St. Louis, his Kings Of Rhythm were later augmented by a former gospel singer, Annie Mae Bullock. Originally billed as 'Little Ann', she gradually became the core of the act, particularly following her marriage to Ike in 1958. Their debut release as Ike And Tina Turner came two years later. 'A Fool In Love', a tough, uncompromising release featuring Tina's already powerful delivery, preceded several excellent singles, the most successful of which was 'It's Gonna Work Out Fine' (1961). Highlighted by Ike's wry interjections, this superior performance defined the duo's early recordings.
Although their revue was one of the leading black music touring shows, the Turners were curiously unable to translate this popularity into record sales. They recorded for several labels, including Sue, Kent and Loma, but a brief spell with Philles was to prove the most controversial. Here producer Phil Spector constructed his 'wall-of-sound' around Tina's impassioned voice but the resultant single, 'River Deep Mountain High', was an unaccountable miss in the US, although in the UK charts it soared to the Top 3. Its failure was to have a devastating effect on Spector. Ike, unhappy at relinquishing the reins, took the duo elsewhere when further releases were less suc-

cessful. A support slot on the Rolling Stones' 1969 North American tour introduced the Turners to a wider, generally white, audience. Their version of John Fogerty's 'Proud Mary' was a gold disc in 1971, while the autobiographical 'Nutbush City Limits' (1973) was also an international hit. The group continued to be a major in-concert attraction, although Tina's brazen sexuality and the show's tried formula ultimately paled. The Turners became increasingly estranged as Ike's character darkened; Tina left the group in the middle of a tour and the couple were finally divorced in 1976. Beset by problems, chemical or otherwise, Ike spent some 18 months in prison, a stark contrast to his ex-wife's very public profile. In *What's Love Got To Do With It?* (1993), a film biograpahy of Tina Turner, Ike was portrayed as a 'vicious, womanising Svengali'. Since his return Turner has attempted to redress the balance of his past with little success. Other than 'Rocket 88' there is little in the Ike Turner solo catalogue to excite about. An embarrassing 'I Like Ike' campaign was undertaken by the UK purist fanzine *Juke Blues*, which also failed to convince the outside world that Ike had anything to offer musically.

●ALBUMS: *The Soul Of Ike And Tina Turner* (Sue 1960)★★, *Dance With The Kings Of Rhythm* (Sue 1960)★★★, *The Sound Of Ike And Tina Turner* (1961)★★★, *Dance With Ike And Tina Turner* (1962)★★★, *Festival Of Live Performances* (1962)★★, *Dynamite* (Sue 1963)★★★★, *Don't Play Me Cheap* (Sue 1963)★★★, *It's Gonna Work Out Fine* (Sue 1963)★★★★, *Please Please Please* (Kent 1964)★★★, *The Soul Of Ike And Tina Turner* (Kent 1964)★★★, *The Ike And Tina Turner Show Live* (Warners 1965)★★★★, *Ike And Tina Turner Revue Live* (Kent 1965)★★★★, *River Deep - Mountain High* (London 1966)★★★★, *So Fine* (Pompeii 1968)★★★★, *In Person* (Minit 1968)★★★★, *Cussin', Cryin' And Carrying On* (Pompeii 1969)★★★, *Get It Together!* (Pompeii 1969)★★★, *River Deep - Mountain High* (A&M/London 1969)★★★★, *Her Man, His Woman* (Capitol 1969)★★★, *A Black Man's Soul* (1969)★★★, *Outta Season* (Liberty 1969)★★★, *Come Together* (Liberty 1970)★★★, *The Hunter* (Harvest 1970)★★★★, *Live In Paris* (Liberty 1971)★★★★, *Workin' Together* (Liberty 1971)★★★, *Live At Carnegie Hall - What You Hear Is What You Get* (Liberty 1971)★★★, *Bad Dreams* (1971)★★, *'Nuff Said* (1971)★★, *Feel Good* (1972)★★, *Let Me Touch Your Mind* (1973)★★, *Nutbush City Limits* (1973)★★★★, *Strange Fruit* (1974)★★★, *Sweet Island Rhode Red* (1974)★★, *Delilah's Power* (1977)★★, *Airwaves* (1978)★★, *Love Explosion* (1978)★★. Solo: Ike Turner *Blues Roots* (1972)★★, *I'm Tore Up* (1978)★★. His early work with the Kings Of Rhythm and as a talent scout is represented on *Hey Hey* (1984)★★★, *Rockin' Blues* (1986)★★★, *Ike Turner And His Kings Of Rhythm Volumes 1 & 2* (1988)★★★, *Talent Scout Blues* (Ace 1988)★★★, *Rhythm Rockin' Blues* (Ace 1995)★★★.

●COMPILATIONS: *Ike And Tina Turner's Greatest Hits* (Sue 1965)★★★, *Ike And Tina Turner's Greatest Hits* (Warners 1969)★★★★, *Tough Enough* (1984)★★★, *The Ike And Tina Turner Sessions* (1987)★★★, *The Best Of Ike And Tina Turner* (1987)★★★★, *Fingerpoppin' -The Warner Brothers Years* (1988)★★★, *Best Of Ike And Tina Turner* (1991)★★★★, *Live!!!* (1993)★★★.

●FURTHER READING: *I Tina*, Tina Turner with Kurt Loder.

TURTLES

Having begun their career playing in college-based surf instrumental groups, the Nightriders and the Crossfires, this Los Angeles sextet abruptly switched to beat music during 1964 in imitation of the Beatles. The line-up consisted of Howard Kaylan (b. Howard Kaplan, 22 June 1947, New York, USA; vocals/saxophone) and Mark Volman (b. 19 April 1947, Los Angeles, California, USA; vocals/saxophone), backed by Al Nichol (b. 31 March 1945, North Carolina, USA; piano/guitar), Jim Tucker (b. 17 October 1946, Los Angeles, California, USA; guitar), Chuck Portz (b. 28 March 1945, Santa Monica, California, USA; bass) and Don Murray (b. 8 November 1945, Los Angeles, California, USA, d. 22 March 1996; drums). By the summer of l965 they found themselves caught up in the folk rock boom and, impressed by the success of local rivals the Byrds, elected to call themselves the Tyrtles. That idea was soon dropped, but as the Turtles they slavishly followed the Byrds blueprint, covering a Bob Dylan song, 'It Ain't Me Babe' to considerable effect. After rejecting 'Eve Of Destruction' as a possible follow-up, they used the services of its composer, the new 'king of protest' P.F. Sloan. His pen provided a further two major US hits, 'Let Me Be' and 'You Baby' before their commercial appeal wilted. The psychedelic boom of 1967 saw a change in the group's image and coincided with line-up fluctuations resulting in the induction of drummer John Barbata and successive bassists Chip Douglas and Jim Pons.

The exuberant 'Happy Together' revitalized their chart fortunes, reaching number 1 in the US and also charting in the UK. That song has now achieved classic status and is a perennial turntable hit. The follow-up 'She'd Rather Be With Me' was another zestful singalong establishing the group as expert pop craftsmen. The mid-tempo 'You Know What I Mean' and 'Elenore' were also impressive, with the usual sprinkling of affectionate parody that worked against the odds. The Turtles hardly looked like pop stars but sang delightfully anachronistic teen ballads and ended their hit career by returning to their folk-rock roots, courtesy of 'You Showed Me', first recorded by the Byrds in 1964. With a final touch of irony their record company issued the once rejected 'Eve Of Destruction' as the group's final single. After the group dissolved, Kaylan and Volman (with Pons) joined Frank Zappa and his Mothers Of Invention and later emerged as Flo And Eddie, offering their services as producers and backing singers to a number of prominent artists. Don Murray died following complications during surgery in 1996.

●ALBUMS: *It Ain't Me Babe* (White Whale 1965)★★★, *You Baby* (White Whale 1966)★★★, *Happy Together* (White Whale 1967)★★★, *The Battle Of The Bands* (White Whale 1968)★★, *Turtle Soup* (1969)★★, *Wooden Head* (White Whale 1971)★★, *Happy Together Again* (Sire 1974)★★.

●COMPILATIONS: *Happy Together* (Rhino 1983)★★★, *20 Greatest Hits: Turtles* (Rhino 1986)★★★, *20 Golden Classics* (Mainline 1990)★★★, *Happy Together: The Very Best Of The Turtles* (Music Club 1991)★★★, *25 Classic Hits* (1993)★★★, *Love Songs* (Rhino 1995)★★★.

TWINKLE

b. Lynn Annette Ripley, 15 July 1947, Surbiton, Surrey, England. Unlike her mid-60s female contemporaries, Twinkle actually wrote her own hits, a feat that should not be underestimated. After traipsing around Denmark Street, the Tin Pan Alley of British pop, the 17-year-old was auditioned by producer Tommy Scott and placed in the hands of manager Phil Solomon. Like most of the Solomon stable she was signed to Decca by Dick Rowe and her records were arranged by Phil Coulter. 'Terry', a biker anthem similar in theme to the contemporaneous Shangri-Las' hit 'Leader Of The Pack', was a Top 3 smash in early 1965. The teenager soon made her first public appearance supporting Jerry Lee Lewis at Brighton and prepared her next release, the charming 'Golden Lights', which proved only a minor hit. Although she wrote several other songs, including 'Boy That I Once Knew', 'Saturday Nights' and 'Unhappy Boy', no further success was forthcoming. Her main frailty was a lack of vocal power which prevented her building a following on the live circuit. After retiring to become a housewife, marrying the actor spotlighted in the 'And all because the lady loves Milk Tray' advertising campaign, she returned briefly in 1972 with a cover of the Monkees' 'I'm A Believer'. More recently, her work was introduced to a younger audience thanks to the Smiths' cover of 'Golden Lights'.

●ALBUMS. *Golden Lights - The Twinkle Story* (1993)★★.

TWITTY, CONWAY

b. Harold Lloyd Jenkins, 1 September 1933, Friars Point, Mississippi, USA, d. 5 June 1993, Springfield, Missouri, USA. His father, a riverboat pilot, named him after a silent film comedian and gave him a guitar when he was five years old. The boat travelled between Mississippi and Arkansas, and the family moved to Helena, Arkansas. Twitty's schoolboy friends - Jack Nance, Joe E. Lewis and John Hughey - have played in his professional bands. In 1946, he recorded a demo, 'Cry Baby Heart', at a local radio station, although he was convinced that his real calling was to be a preacher. He was drafted into the US army in 1954 and worked the Far East service bases with a country band, the Cimarrons. He hoped for a baseball career, but when he returned to the USA in 1956 and heard Elvis Presley's 'Mystery Train', he opted for a career in music. Like Presley, he was signed by Sam Phillips to Sun Records, although his only significant contribution was writing 'Rockhouse', a minor US hit for Roy Orbison. His various Sun demos are included, along with later recordings for Mercury and MGM, in the eight-album, Bear Family set, *Conway Twitty - The Rock 'n' Roll Years*.

In 1957, while touring with a rockabilly package, he and his manager stuck pins in a map and the combination of a town in Arkansas with another in Texas led to Conway Twitty, a name as memorable as Elvis Presley. Twitty then moved to Mercury where 'I Need Your Lovin'' made number 93 in the US pop charts. He had written 'It's Only Make Believe' with his drummer Jack Nance in-between sets at the Flamingo Lounge, Toronto, and he recorded it for MGM with the Jordanaires, a croaky vocal and a huge crescendo. The record became a transatlantic number 1, and subsequent UK Top 10 versions of 'It's Only Make Believe' appeared by Billy Fury (1964), Glen Campbell (1970) and Child (1978). Twitty's record sounded like an Elvis Presley parody so it was ironic that Peter Sellers should lampoon him as Twit Conway and that he became the model for Conrad Birdie in the musical, *Bye Bye Birdie*. Twitty, unwisely but understandably, followed 'It's Only Make Believe' with more of the same in 'The Story Of My Love', while the b-side, the harsh and sexy 'Make Me Know You're Mine', remains one of the 'great unknowns'. His debut, *Conway Twitty Sings*, includes a beat treatment of 'You'll Never Walk Alone', which was undoubtedly heard by Gerry And The Pacemakers.

Twitty came to the UK for ITV's pioneering *Oh Boy!* and his presence eased his rock 'n' roll version of Nat 'King' Cole's 'Mona Lisa' into the Top 10. His US Top 10 recording of a song, 'Lonely Blue Boy', which had been left out of Elvis Presley's film *King Creole*, led to him naming his band the Lonely Blue Boys, although they subsequently became the Twitty Birds. Another US hit, 'Danny Boy' could not be released in the UK because the lyric was still in copyright, this did not apply to its melody, 'The Londonderry Air', so Twitty recorded a revised version, 'Rosaleena'. While at MGM, he appeared in such unremarkable movies as *Platinum High School* and *Sex Kittens Go To College*, which also featured Brigitte Bardot's sister. Twitty continued croaking his way through 'What Am I Living For?' and 'Is A Bluebird Blue?', but was also recording such country favourites as 'Faded Love' and 'You Win Again'. After being dropped by MGM and having a brief spell with ABC-Paramount, Twitty concentrated on placing his country songs with other artists including 'Walk Me To The Door' for Ray Price. He began recording his own country records for producer Owen Bradley and US Decca Records in Nashville, saying, 'After nine years in rock 'n' roll, I had been cheated and hurt enough to sing country and mean it.' In March 1966 Twitty appeared in the US country charts for the first time with 'Guess My Eyes Were Bigger Than My Heart'. His first US country number 1 was with 'Next In Line' in 1968 and this was followed by 'I Love You More Today' and 'To See An Angel Cry'.

He became the most consistent country chartmaker of all time, although none of his country records made the UK charts. His most successful country record on the US pop charts is 'You've Never Been This Far Before', which made number 22 in 1973. 'Hello Darlin'' was heard around the world when he recorded a Russian version for the astronauts on a USA/USSR space venture in 1975. His records, often middle-of-the-road ballads, include 'I See The Want To In Your Eyes', 'I'll Never Make It Home Tonight', 'I Can't Believe She Gives It All To Me', 'I'd Love To Lay You Down' and 'You Were Named Co-Respondent'. He has recorded several successful duet albums with Loretta Lynn, and also recorded with Dean Martin and his own daughter, Joni Lee ('Don't Cry, Joni'). His son, who began recording as Conway Twitty Jnr., changed to Mike Twitty, while another daughter, Kathy Twitty, had minor country hits both as herself ('Green Eyes') and as Jesseca James ('Johnny One Time'). Through the 70s, Twitty expanded into property, banking and fast food, although his Twittyburgers came to a greasy end. His wife Mickey, whom he married and divorced twice, published *What's Cooking At Twitty City?*, in 1985, and his tacky museum and theme park, Twitty City, was up for sale. Despite new successes, the focal point of his stage act was still 'It's Only Make Believe', right up until his death in June 1993, by which time his tally of chart-toppers stood at 41 - higher than any other artist in any genre.

●ALBUMS: *Conway Twitty Sings* (MGM 1959)★★★, *Saturday Night With Conway Twitty* (MGM 1959)★★★, *Lonely Blue Boy* (MGM 1960)★★★, *The Rock 'N' Roll Story* (MGM 1961)★★★, *The Conway Twitty Touch* (MGM 1961)★★★, *Conway Twitty Sings 'Portrait Of A Fool' And Others* (MGM 1962)★★★, *R&B '63* (MGM 1963)★★★, *Hit The Road* (MGM 1964)★★★, *Conway Twitty Sings* (Decca 1966)★★★, *Look Into My Teardrops* (Decca 1966)★★★, *Country* (Decca 1967)★★★, *Here's Conway Twitty And His Lonely Blue Boys* (Decca 1968)★★★, *Next In Line* (Decca 1968)★★★, *I Love You More Today* (Decca 1969)★★★, *You Can't Take The Country Out Of Conway* (MGM 1969)★★★, *Darling, You Know I Wouldn't Lie* (Decca 1969)★★★, *Hello Darling* (Decca 1970)★★★, *Fifteen Years Ago* (Decca 1970)★★★, *To See My Angel Cry* (Decca 1970)★★★, *How Much More Can She Stand?* (Decca 1971)★★★, with Loretta Lynn *We Only Make Believe* (Decca 1971)★★★, with Lynn *Lead Me On* (Decca 1971)★★★, *Conway Twitty* (Decca 1972)★★★, *I Wonder What She'll Think About Me Leaving* (Decca 1971)★★★, *Conway Twitty Sings The Blues* (MGM 1972)★★★, *Shake It Up* (Pickwick 1972)★★★, *I Can't See Me Without You* (Decca 1972)★★★, *I Can't Stop Loving You* (Decca 1972)★★★, *You've Never Been This Far Before* (MCA 1973)★★★, with Lynn *Louisiana Woman, Mississippi Man* (MCA 1973)★★★, *Clinging To A Saving Hand/Steal Away* (MCA 1973)★★★, *She Needs Someone To Hold Her* (MCA 1973)★★★, *Honky Tonk Angel* (MCA 1974)★★★, *I'm Not Through Loving You Yet* (MCA 1974)★★★, with Lynn *Country Partners*

(MCA 1974)★★★, *Linda On My Mind* (MCA 1975)★★★, *The High Priest Of Country Music* (MCA 1975)★★★, with Lynn *Feelin's* (MCA 1975)★★★, *Twitty* (MCA 1975)★★★, *Now And Then* (MCA 1976)★★★, with Lynn *United Talent* (MCA 1976)★★★, with Lynn *Loretta And Conway Sing The Great Country Hits* (TVP 1976, double album)★★★, *Play, Guitar, Play* (MCA 1977)★★★, with Lynn *Dynamic Duo* (MCA 1977)★★★, *I've Already Loved You In My Mind* (MCA 1977)★★★, *Georgia Keeps Pulling On My Ring* (MCA 1978)★★★, *Conway* (MCA 1978)★★★, with Lynn *Honky Tonk Heroes* (MCA 1978)★★★, *Cross Winds* (MCA 1979)★★★, *Country-Rock* (MCA 1979)★★★, *Boogie Grass Band* (MCA 1979)★★★, with Lynn *Diamond Duet* (MCA 1979)★★★, *Heart And Soul* (MCA 1980)★★★, *Rest Your Love On Me* (MCA 1980)★★★, *Mr.T.* (MCA 1981)★★★, with Lynn *Two's A Party* (MCA 1981)★★★, *Southern Comfort* (Elektra 1982)★★★, *Dream Maker* (Elektra 1982)★★★, *Classic Conway* (MCA 1983)★★★, *Merry Twismas From Conway Twitty And His Little Friends* (Warners 1983)★★★, *Lost In The Feeling* (Warners 1983)★★★, *Shake It Up Baby* rec. 1956-57 (Bulldog 1983)★★★, *By Heart* (Warners 1984)★★★, *Don't Call Him A Cowboy* (Warners 1985)★★★, *Chasin' Rainbows* (Warners 1985)★★★, *Fallin' For You For Years* (Warners 1986)★★★, *Live At Castaway Lounge* (Demand 1987)★★★, *Borderline* (MCA 1987)★★★, *Still In Your Dreams* (MCA 1988)★★★, with Lynn *Making Believe* (1988)★★★, *House On Old Lonesome Road* (MCA 1989)★★★, *Crazy In Love* (MCA 1990)★★★, *Even Now* (MCA 1991)★★★, *Final Touches* (MCA 1993)★★★.

●COMPILATIONS: *Number Ones* (MCA 1982)★★★★, *Conway's #1 Classics Volume 1* (Elektra 1982)★★★★, *Conway's #1 Classics Volume 2* (Elektra 1983)★★★★, *The Rock 'N' Roll Years* 8-LP box set (Bear Family 1985)★★★★, *The Beat Goes On* rec. 1958-1962 (Charly 1986)★★★★, *The Final Recordings Of His Greatest Hits* (Pickwick 1995)★★★.

●VIDEOS: *Golden Country Greats* (1993).
●FURTHER READING: *The Conway Twitty Story - An Authorised Biography*, Wilbur Cross and Michael Kosser.
●FILMS: *College Confidential* (1959).

TYRANNOSAURUS REX

Formed in 1967 by singer/guitarist Marc Bolan, Tyrannosaurus Rex was originally envisioned as an electric sextet until a hire purchase company repossessed their equipment. Bolan was then joined by percussionist Steve 'Peregrine' Took (b. 28 July 1949, Eltham, South London, England, d. 27 October 1980) in an acoustic-based venture that combined his love of classic rock 'n' roll with an affection for faerie mythology. Marc's unusual quivering vocal style rendered most of his lyrics incomprehensible, but the effect was genuinely enchanting and the duo were quickly adopted by the emergent 'underground'. BBC disc jockey John Peel became a tireless promoter of the group, which shared billings on his roadshow and was featured heavily on his radio programme *Top Gear*. Tyrannosaurus Rex enjoyed three minor hit singles with 'Debora', 'One Inch Rock' and 'King Of The Rumbling Spires', and achieved notable success with their albums, of which *My People Were Fair And Had Sky In Their Hair But Now They're Content To Wear Stars On Their Brows* and *Unicorn* reached the UK Top 20. The latter set showed a marked departure from previous stark accompaniment, adding harmonium, bass and piano to their lexicon. Their partnership was sundered in 1969 following an acrimonious US tour and Bolan was joined by Mickey Finn, late of Hapshash And The Coloured Coat for *A Beard Of Stars*. Here the unit's transformation was complete and this electric set, although still encompassing chimerical fables, was the natural stepping-stone for Bolan's transformation into a fully fledged pop idol with T. Rex.

●ALBUMS: *My People Were Fair And Had Sky In Their Hair But Now They're Content To Wear Stars On Their Brows* (Regal Zonophone 1968)★★★★, *Prophets, Seers, Sages, The Angels Of The Ages* (Regal Zonophone 1968)★★★★, *Unicorn* (Regal Zonophone 1969)★★★, *A Beard Of Stars* (Regal Zonophone 1970)★★★.

●COMPILATIONS: *The Best Of T.Rex* (Fly 1971)★★★★, *The Definitive Tyrannosaurus Rex* (Sequel 1993)★★★★, *BBC Radio 1 Live In Concert* (Windsong 1993)★★★★, *A BBC History* (Band Of Joy 1996)★★★★.

ULTIMATE SPINACH

One of three bands from Boston, Massachusetts, USA, signed to MGM Records in an attempt to create a 'Bosstown Sound' to rival San Francisco's music scene (the others were Orpheus and Beacon Street Union), Ultimate Spinach recorded three albums in a two-year period before fading away. The band, originally called Underground Cinema, comprised Ian Bruce-Douglas (vocals/keyboards - also the group's songwriter/arranger), Keith Lahteinen (vocals/drums), Geoffrey Winthrop (lead guitar/sitar/vocals), Barbara Hudson (vocals/guitar) and Richard Ness (bass). The group's self-titled 1968 album was the highest-charting of any of the 'Bosstown' albums, reaching number 34 in the USA. The record was typically pseudo-psychedelic for the period, both lyrically and musically. It was followed later that year with *Behold & See* and in 1969 by a third release, also self-titled, sporting an entirely new line-up save for Hudson. Among the new members in that second line-up was Jeff 'Skunk' Baxter on guitar, later of Steely Dan and the Doobie Brothers.

●ALBUMS: *Ultimate Spinach* (MGM 1968)★★, *Behold & See* (MGM 1968)★, *Ultimate Spinach* (MGM 1969)★, *III* (Big Beat 1996)★★.

UNDERTAKERS

Formed in Wallasey, Merseyside, in 1961, the Undertakers were initially known as the Vegas Five, but assumed their new sobriquet when a printer's error advertised them as such in a local newspaper. Their original line-up featured Jimmy McManus (vocals), Chris Huston (lead guitar), Geoff Nugent (guitar/vocals), Brian 'Boots' Jones (saxophone/vocals), Dave 'Mushy' Cooper (bass) and Bob Evans (drums), but within 18 months the core of Jones, Huston and Nugent had been joined by Jackie Lomax (bass/vocals) and Bugs Pemberton (drums). The quintet completed four singles between 1963 and 1964, including versions of material by the Shirelles ('Everybody Loves A Lover'), Solomon Burke ('Stupidity') and Roscoe Gordon ('Just A Little Bit'). Adequate rather than urgent, these releases lacked the passion of corresponding live performances where, bedecked in black frock coats, the Undertakers added a strong visual approach to their brand of driving R&B. An album entitled *Undertakers* was recorded for Pye in 1964, but was not released until the mid-90s. The group attempted to update their image by truncating their name to the 'Takers, but split up in 1965 following a chaotic spell domiciled in New York. Jackie Lomax then pursed an intermittently successful career both as a solo and as a session vocalist.

●COMPILATIONS: *Unearthed* (Big Beat 1996)★★.

UNIT FOUR PLUS TWO

Formed in Hertfordshire, England, this aptly named 60s pop sextet comprised: Buster Meikle (b. David Meikle, 1 March 1942, vocals/guitar), Tommy Moeller (b. 23 February 1945; vocals/tambourine/piano/guitar), Peter Moules (b. 14 October 1944; vocals/autoharp/guitar/banjo), Rodney Garwood (b. 27 March 1944; bass) and Hugh Halliday (b. 12 December 1944; drums). Originally Unit Four, a folk quartet, they extended their ranks to six in January 1962. The folk element remained in their repertoire with such standards as 'Cottonfields' and 'La Bamba', while their first two Decca singles, 'Green Fields' and 'Sorrow And Rain', were out of keeping with the prevalent beat scene. With the assistance of Russ Ballard and Bob Henrit of the Roulettes (who later joined the group), they recorded the rhythmic 'Concrete And Clay', which brought them to number 1 in the UK in 1965. The follow-up, 'You've Never Been In Love Like This Before', reached the Top 20, but after a couple of further minor hits with 'Baby Never Say Goodbye' and 'Hark!', their lightweight pop style proved insufficient for chart success. In 1969, with the beat boom long forgotten, they disbanded.

●ALBUMS: *Unit Four Plus Two - First Album* (Decca/London 1965)★★, *Unit Four Plus Two* (Fontana 1969)★★.

●COMPILATIONS: *Remembering* (1977)★★.

UNITED STATES OF AMERICA

Formed in 1967 by New York-born electronics composer, Joseph Byrd. The rest of the line-up comprised University of California Los Angeles students Dorothy Moskowitz (vocals), Gordon Marron (electric violin), Rand Forbes (bass) and Craig Woodson (drums). The quintet's lone, self-titled album, a biting satire on contemporary America, featured several haunting compositions including 'Love Song For The Dead Che' and 'The Garden Of Earthly Delights'. The humorous 'I Won't Leave My Wooden Wife For You Sugar' received most airplay as disc jockey's found thenm hard to categorize. At times reminiscent of Jefferson Airplane, the innovative use of electronic effects gave the collection its chilling factor and it remains one of the era's more lasting works. Byrd was also responsible for arranging Phil Ochs' powerful composition 'Pleasures Of The Harbour' and later formed a new group, the Field Hippies. However, the resultant *The American Metaphysical Circus*, lacked the discipline of his first release. Moscovitz subsequently re-emerged in Country Joe McDonald's All Star Band while Byrd produced Ry Cooder's 1978 release, *Jazz*, and recording two quirky synthesizer solo albums.

●ALBUMS: *The United States Of America* (Columbia 1968)★★★. Solo: Joseph Byrd *Joe Byrd And The Field Hippies* (1969)★★, *Yankee Trancendoodle* (1975)★★, *Xmas Yet To Come* (1980)★★.

UPCHURCH, PHIL

b. 19 July 1941, Chicago, Illinois, USA. Although this excellent guitarist later became a respected session musician, his name is synonymous with 'You Can't Sit Down', a propulsive two-part instrumental recorded with his group, the Phil Upchurch Combo. The band, with Upchurch on guitar, comprised Cornell Muldrow (organ), David Brooks (saxophone), Mac Johnson (trumpet) and Joe Hoddrick (drums). Muldrow wrote the tune and had recorded an earlier version. 'You Can't Sit Down' reached the US Top 30 in 1961 and the UK Top 40 on its reissue five years later. However, its influence was felt far beyond such placings, as the tune became a staple part of almost every budding US fraternity or bar band. Upchurch began playing in R&B backing bands, including those of the Kool Gents, the Dells, the Spaniels and for Dee Clark, who used 'You Can't Sit Down' as a theme song. He later appeared on releases by Bo Diddley, Muddy Waters, Jimmy Reed and Howlin' Wolf, and in the 70s guested on sessions for several fusion artists including Grover Washington, George Benson (*Breezin'* and *In Flight*) and the Crusaders. His own work was rather overshadowed by this workload while the artist's inventive style was marred by an anonymity resulting from his many of supporting roles. His most successful collaboration was with fellow Chicagoan, Tennyson Stephens, a keyboardist whose vocals were important to the duo's success in the R&B market in the mid-70s.

●ALBUMS: as the Phil Upchurch Combo *You Can't Sit Down* (Boyd 1961)★★★, *You Can't Sit Down, Part Two* (United Artists 1961)★★★, *Twist The Big Hit Dances* (United Artists 1961)★★, *Feeling Blue* (Milestone 1968)★★★, *The Way I Feel* (1969)★★, *Darkness Darkness* (Blue Thumb 1972)★★★, *Lovin' Feelin'* (1973)★★★, with Tennyson Stephens *Upchurch Tennyson* (1975)★★★, *Phil Upchurch* (1978)★★★, *Companions* (1985)★★★.

VAGRANTS

Formed in 1964, the Vagrants were one of the most popular acts in the New York/Long Island/New Jersey area. Leslie West (guitar/vocals), Pete Sabatino (vocals), Jerry Storch (organ/vocals), Larry West (bass/vocals) and Roger Masour (drums) played a driving, pop-edged R&B similar to contemporaries the (Young) Rascals, but they were unable to attain the same commercial success. The Vagrants' debut single, 'I Can't Make A Friend', appeared on Vanguard Records in 1966 before the groups switched to Atco Records. Three more singles ensued, produced respectively by Dave Brigati, Felix Pappalardi and Shadow Morton. These included a pounding version of Otis Redding's 'Respect', later immortalized on Lenny Kaye's seminal garage-band compilation, *Nuggets*. The Vagrants disbanded in 1968, having supported the Doors at New York's Village Gate. West then recorded a solo album which Pappalardi produced. The pair then formed a new group using its title, Mountain.
●COMPILATIONS: *The Great Lost Album* (Arista 1987)★★.

VALANCE, RICKY

b. David Spencer, *c*.1939, Ynytsdou, South Wales. After singing in local clubs for a couple of years, Valance was discovered by an A&R representative from EMI Records and placed in the hands of producer Norrie Paramor. At the first recording session, Valance was given the chance of covering Ray Peterson's US hit, 'Tell Laura I Love Her'. A wonderfully enunciated reading was rewarded with a number 1 hit in September 1960, thanks to airplay on Radio Luxembourg, but none of Valance's follow-ups including 'Movin' Away', 'Jimmy's Girl', 'Bobby', or 'Try To Forget Her' created any interest, and even with a move to Decca Records the dismal 'Six Boys' flopped. He continues playing clubs and the revival circuit.

VALENS, RITCHIE

b. Richard Steve Valenzuela, 13 May 1941, Los Angeles, California, USA, d. 3 February 1959, Iowa, USA. Valens was the first major Hispanic-American rock star, the artist who popularized the classic 50s hit 'La Bamba'. He grew up in the city of Pacoima, California, and was raised in poverty. His parents separated when he was a child and Valens lived with his father until the latter's death in 1951. Afterwards he lived with his mother and brothers and sisters. Occasionally they stayed with other relatives, who introduced him to traditional Mexican music. He also enjoyed cowboy songs by Roy Rogers and Gene Autry and began playing in junior high school. While attending Pacoima Junior High School Valens was exposed to R&B music and rock 'n' roll. In 1956 Valens joined the Silhouettes (not the group that recorded 'Get A Job'), who performed at record hops in the San Fernando Valley area. Valens also performed solo and was heard by Bob Keane of Del-Fi Records, who took him into Gold Star Studios to record several songs. (Keane also shortened the singer's name from Valenzuela to Valens and added the 't' to Richie.) A session band including Earl Palmer (drums), Carol Kaye (guitar), Red Collendar (stand-up bass), Ernie Freeman (piano) and Rene Hall (guitar) played behind Valens (who also played guitar). One of the songs they recorded for that first album was 'La Bamba', a traditional Mexican folk song. Their first single release, 'Come On, Let's Go', which Valens wrote, reached number 42 in the USA. Valens went on an 11-city US tour after its release. In October 1958 the single 'Donna'/'La Bamba' was issued. It was actually the ballad 'Donna', written by Valens about his high school friend Donna Ludwig, that was, contrary to popular belief, the side of the record that was the bigger hit, reaching number 2. 'La Bamba', the b-side, only reached number 22 in the USA but is the more fondly remembered song.

'La Bamba' was a traditional huapango song from the Vera Cruz region of eastern Mexico, performed as early as World War II, and sung at weddings. (A huapango is a Mexican song consisting of nonsense verses, the meaning of the lyrics often known only to the composer.) Valens was reportedly reluctant to record the song, fearing its Spanish lyrics would not catch on with American record buyers. Following the record's release, Valens again went on tour, performing in California, Hawaii and on the *American Bandstand* show in Philadelphia.

It was during the winter part of the tour that Valens and his fellow performers met their fate, choosing to charter a small aeroplane rather than ride to the next concert site in a bus whose heater had broken. It was on 3 February 1959 when he, Buddy Holly and the Big Bopper were killed in an aeroplane crash following a concert in Clear Lake, Iowa. In the wake of Valens' death, several further singles were issued, only two of which - 'That's My Little Suzie' and 'Little Girl' - were minor chart hits. Three albums - *Ritchie Valens, Ritchie* and *Ritchie Valens In Concert At Pacoima Junior High* - were released from sessions recorded for Del-Fi and at a performance for Valens' classmates. Valens' status grew in the years following his death, culminating in the 1987 film *La Bamba*, a dramatized version of Valens' brief life and stardom. His songs have been covered by several artists, including the Hispanic-American group Los Lobos, who supervised the film's music and recorded 'La Bamba'. Their version, ironically, went to number 1 in 1987, out-performing Valens' original chart position.
●ALBUMS: *Ritchie Valens* (Del Fi/London 1959)★★★★, *Ritchie* (Del Fi/London 1959)★★★★, *Ritchie Valens In Concert At Pacoima Jnr High* (Del Fi 1960)★★★.
●COMPILATIONS: *His Greatest Hits* (Del Fi

1963)★★★★, *His Greatest Hits Vol 2* (Del Fi 1965)★★, *I Remember Ritchie Valens* (President 1967)★★★, *A History Of ...* (1985)★★★, *Greatest Hits* (1987)★★★, *The Ritchie Valens Story* (Ace 1993)★★★★, *The Very Best Of ...* (Music Club 1995)★★★.

●FURTHER READING: *Ritchie Valens: The First Latino Rocker*, Beverly Mendheim. *Ritchie Valens 1941-1959: 30th Anniversary Memorial Series No 2*, Alan Clark.

●FILMS: *Go Johnny Go* (1958).

VALENTINOS

Formed in the 1950s and originally known as the Womack Brothers, the group's line-up featured Bobby Womack (b. 4 March 1944, Cleveland, Ohio, USA), Friendly Womack Jnr. (b. 1941, Cleveland, Ohio, USA), Harry Womack (b. 1946, Cleveland, Ohio, USA), Curtis Womack (b. 1943, Cleveland, Ohio, USA), Cecil Womack (b. 1941, Cleveland, Ohio, USA). They were also known briefly as the Lovers. Part of a large religious family, their father, Friendly Snr., led his own gospel group, the Voices Of Love. The Womack Brothers also sang spiritual material and were signed to singer Sam Cooke's Sar label following a Cleveland concert. They were later renamed the Valentinos. One of Bobby's songs, 'Couldn't Hear Nobody Pray', was reshaped by Cooke's manager into the secular 'Looking For A Love', a Top 10 R&B single in 1962. Another original, 'Somewhere There's A God', became 'Somewhere There's A Girl', but the Valentinos' next chart entry came in 1964 with the bubbling 'It's All Over Now'. Their own version was overshadowed by that of the Rolling Stones; their fate was impeded further by Cooke's death. The group subsequently recorded for several labels, including Checker, although little was ever released. Disillusioned, the brothers drifted apart and Bobby Womack began his solo career. However, the Valentinos did briefly reunite for two 70s singles, 'I Can Understand It' and 'Raise Your Hand In Anger'. The family's personal history has been remarkably complex. Cecil married and managed singer Mary Wells, but the couple were later divorced. Mary then married Curtis Womack. Cecil meanwhile married Sam Cooke's daughter, Linda, inaugurating the successful Womack And Womack duo. In 1986 Friendly Jnr and Curtis formed the Brothers Womack with singer Lewis Williams. The remaining brother, Harry, was stabbed to death by his wife. *Double Barrelled Soul* (1968) offers six Valentinos Sar masters alongside six by the Simms twins. *Bobby Womack And The Valentinos* (1984) divides itself between group recordings and solo material recorded for Checker.

●ALBUMS: one side only *Double Barrelled Soul* (1968)★★, *Bobby Womack And The Valentinos* (1984)★★.

VANILLA FUDGE

This US rock group were formed in December 1966 and comprised Mark Stein (b. 11 March 1947, New Jersey, USA; organ), Vince Martell (b. 11 November 1945, New York City, New York, USA; guitar), Tim Bogert (b. 27 August 1944, Richfield, New Jersey, USA; bass) and Joey Brennan (drums). All were previously members of the Pigeons, a New York-based group modelled on the (Young) Rascals. Brennan was latterly replaced by Carmine Appice (b. 15 December 1946, New York, USA), and having established a style in which contemporary songs were imaginatively rearranged, the unit was introduced to producer Shadow Morton, who had a reputation for melodramatic pop with the Shangri-Las. Dubbed Vanilla Fudge by their record label, the quartet scored an immediate success with an atmospheric revival of the Supremes' hit, 'You Keep Me Hanging On'. The slowed tempo, studious playing and mock-gospel harmonies set a precedent for the group's debut album, which featured similarly operatic versions of the Impressions' 'People Get Ready', Sonny And Cher's 'Bang Bang' and the Beatles' 'Eleanor Rigby' and 'Ticket To Ride'. The audacity of this first selection was impossible to repeat. A flawed concept album, *The Beat Goes On*, proved overambitious, while further selections showed a group unable to create original material of the calibre of the first album. Subsequent records relied on simpler, hard-edged rock. When Vanilla Fudge split in 1970, the bassist and drummer remained together in Cactus before abandoning their creation in favour of Beck, Bogert And Appice. Stein worked with Tommy Bolin and Alice Cooper before forging a new career composing advertising jingles, while Martell later appeared in the Good Rats, a popular Long Island bar-band. The group briefly re-formed in 1983 and released *Mystery*.

●ALBUMS: *Vanilla Fudge* (Atco 1967)★★★, *The Beat Goes On* (Atco 1968)★★, *Renaissance* (Atco 1968)★★, *Near The Beginning* (Atco 1969)★★, *Rock And Roll* (Atco 1970)★★, *Mystery* (Atco 1984)★★.

●COMPILATIONS: *The Best Of The Vanilla Fudge* (Atco 1982)★★, *Psychedelic Sundae - The Best Of* (Rhino 1993)★★★.

VANITY FARE

This late 60s British pop quintet, which took its name (respelled) from Thackeray's famous novel, comprised: Dick Allix (b. 3 May 1945, Gravesend, Kent, England; drums), Trevor Brice (b. 12 February 1945, Rochester, Kent, England; vocals), Tony Goulden (b. 21 November 1944, Rochester, Kent, England; guitar), Tony Jarrett (b. 4 September 1944; double bass, guitar) and Barry Landeman (b. 25 October 1947, Woodbridge, Suffolk, England; keyboards). Managed by Roger Easterby and signed to Larry Page's Page One label, the clean-cut Vanity Fare hit the UK Top 20 in the summer of 1968 with 'I Live For The Sun'. It was almost a year and another summer before they returned to the charts with 'Early In The Morning', this time leaving their suits behind in favour of neckerchiefs and Carnaby Street garb. Although they claimed they could only chart in the warm season, their final hit 'Hitchin' A Ride' was a surprise festive hit.

●ALBUMS: *The Sun, The Wind And Other Things* (Page One 1969)★★.

VAUGHAN, FRANKIE

b. Frank Abelson, 3 February 1928, Liverpool, England. While studying at Leeds College of Art, Vaughan's vocal performance at a college revue earned him a week's trial at the Kingston Empire music hall. Warmly received, he went on to play the UK variety circuit, developing a stylish act with trademarks which included a top hat and cane, a particularly athletic side kick, and his theme song 'Give Me The Moonlight' (Albert Von Tilzer-Lew Brown). His Russian-born maternal grandmother inspired his stage name by always referring to him as her 'Number Vorn' grandchild. After registering strongly in pre-chart days with 'That Old Piano Roll Blues', 'Daddy's Little Girl', 'Look At That Girl', and 'Hey, Joe', during the mid-late 50s Vaughan was consistently in the UK Top 30 with hits such as 'Istanbul (Not Constantinople)', 'Happy Days And Lonely Nights', 'Tweedle Dee', 'Seventeen', 'My Boy Flat Top', 'Green Door', 'Garden Of Eden' (number 1), 'Man On Fire'/'Wanderin' Eyes', 'Gotta Have Something In the Bank Frank' (with the Kaye Sisters), 'Kisses Sweeter Than Wine', 'Can't Get Along Without You'/'We Are Not Alone', 'Kewpie Doll', 'Wonderful Things', 'Am I Wasting My Time On You', 'That's My Doll', 'Come Softly To Me' (with the Kaye Sisters), 'The Heart Of A Man', and 'Walkin' Tall'. In spite of the burgeoning beat boom, he continued to flourish in the 60s with 'What More Do You Want', 'Kookie Little Paradise', 'Milord', 'Tower Of Strength' (number 1), 'Don't Stop Twist', 'Loop-De-Loop', 'Hey Mama', 'Hello Dolly', 'There Must Be A Way', 'So Tired', and 'Nevertheless' (1968). With his matinée idol looks he seemed a natural for films, and made his debut in 1956 in the Arthur Askey comedy *Ramsbottom Rides Again*. This was followed by a highly acclaimed straight role in *These Dangerous Years*, and a musical frolic with the normally staid Anna Neagle in *The Lady Is A Square*. Other screen appearances included *Wonderful Things! Heart Of A Man* with Anne Heywood, Tony Britton and Anthony Newley, and *It's All Over Town*, a pop extravaganza in which he was joined by current favourites such as Acker Bilk, the Bachelors, the Springfields, and the Hollies. In the early 60s, Vaughan began to experience real success in America, in night-clubs and on television. He was playing his second season in Las Vegas when he was chosen to star with Marilyn Monroe and Yves Montand in the 20th Century-Fox picture *Let's Make Love*. Although he gave a creditable performance, especially when he duetted with Monroe on Sammy Cahn and Jimmy Van Heusen's 'Incurably Romantic', his disaffection with Hollywood ensured that a US film career was not pursued. At home, however, he had become an extremely well-established performer, headlining at the London Palladium and enjoying lucrative summer season work, appealing consistently to mainly family audiences. In 1985, he was an unexpected choice to replace James Laurenson as the belligerent Broadway producer Julian Marsh, in the West End hit musical *42nd Street*. A one-year run in the show ended with ill health and some acrimony. His career-long efforts for the benefit of young people, partly through the assignment of record royalties to bodies such as the National Association of Boys' Clubs, was recognized with an OBE in 1965. He was honoured further in 1993, when the Queen appointed him as the Deputy Lord Lieutenant of Buckinghamshire. In the preceding year he had undergone a life-saving operation to replace a ruptured main artery in his heart. However, in 1994, when he was in cabaret at London's Café Royal, the legendary side-kick was still (gingerly) in evidence.

● ALBUMS: *Happy Go Lucky* (Philips 1957)★★★, *Showcase* (Philips 1958)★★★, *At The London Palladium* (Philips 1959)★★★, *Let Me Sing And I'm Happy* (Philips 1961)★★★, *Warm Feeling* (Philips 1961)★★★, *Songbook* (1967)★★★, *There Must Be A Way* (1967)★★★, *Double Exposure* (1971)★★★, *Frankie* (1973)★★★, *Frankie Vaughan's Sing Song* (1973)★★★, *Sincerely Yours, Frankie Vaughan* (1975)★★★, *Sings* (1975)★★★, *Seasons For Lovers* (1977)★★★, *Time After Time* (1986).

● COMPILATIONS: *Spotlight On Frankie Vaughan* (1975)★★★, *100 Golden Greats* (1977)★★★, *Golden Hour Presents* (1978)★★★, *Greatest Hits* (1983)★★★, *Love Hits And High Kicks* (1985)★★★, *Music Maestro Please* (1986)★★★, *The Best Of* (1990)★★★, *The Essential Recordings 1955-65* (1993)★★★.

VEE, BOBBY

b. Robert Thomas Velline, 30 April 1943, Fargo, North Dakota, USA. Vee's first exposure to the rock 'n' roll scene occurred in macabre circumstances when his group, the Shadows, were deputized for Buddy Holly after the singer was killed in an air crash. Soon after, Vee's group were discovered by famed producer Tommy 'Snuff' Garrett and saw their record 'Suzie Baby' released on a major label, Liberty. Vee rapidly became a solo artist in his own right. One of his first recordings was a cover of Adam Faith's 'What Do You Want', which failed to emulate the British artist's UK chart-topping success. Vee was subsequently groomed as a soloist; his college-boy looks and boy-next-door persona combined cleverly with a canon of teenage anthems provided by Brill Building songwriters. After charting with a revival of the Clovers' 1956 hit 'Devil Or Angel', Vee found transatlantic success via the infectious, if lyrically innocuous 'Rubber Ball'. Between 1961 and 1962, he peaked with a series of infectious hits including 'More Than I Can Say', 'How Many Tears', 'Take Good Care Of My Baby' (a US number 1), 'Run To Him', 'Please Don't Ask About Barbara', 'Sharing You' and 'A Forever Kind Of Love'. The imaginatively-titled 'The Night Has A Thousand Eyes' proved his most enduring song. Like many American teen-orientated artists, Vee's appeal waned following the arrival of the Beatles and the beat group explosion.

He did manage a couple of film appearances (*Play It Cool* and *Just For Fun*) before the hit bubble burst. While Beatlemania raged, he reverted to the work of his original inspiration, Buddy Holly. Both *Bobby Vee Meets The Crickets* and *Bobby Vee Meets The Ventures* were promoted by touring. In 1967 Vee returned to the US Top 10 with 'Come Back When You Grow Up'. An attempt to fashion a more serious image prompted Vee to revert to his real name for *Nothing Like A Sunny Day*. The experiment was short-lived, however, and Vee later contented himself with regular appearances at rock 'n' roll revival shows.

●ALBUMS: *Bobby Vee Sings Your Favorites* (Liberty 1960)★★, *Bobby Vee* (Liberty 1961)★★★, *Bobby Vee With Strings And Things* (Liberty 1961)★★★, *Bobby Vee Sings Hits Of The Rockin' '50s* (Liberty 1961)★★★, *Take Good Care Of My Baby* (Liberty 1961)★★★★, *Bobby Vee Meets The Crickets* (Liberty 1962)★★★★, *A Bobby Vee Recording Session* (Liberty 1962)★★★★, *Merry Christmas From Bobby Vee* (Liberty 1962)★★, *The Night Has A Thousand Eyes* (Liberty 1963)★★★, *Bobby Vee Meets The Ventures* (Liberty 1963)★★★, *I Remember Buddy Holly* (Liberty 1963)★★★, *Bobby Vee Sings The New Sound From England!* (Liberty 1964)★★, *30 Big Hits From The 60s* (Liberty 1964)★★★, *Bobby Vee Live On Tour* (Liberty 1965)★, *C'Mon Let's Live A Little* film soundtrack (1966)★★, *Look At Me Girl* (Liberty 1966)★★, *Come Back When You Grow Up* (Liberty 1967)★★, *Just Today* (Liberty 1968)★★, *Do What You Gotta Do* (Liberty 1968)★★, *Gates, Grills And Railings* (1969)★★, *Nothing Like A Sunny Day* (1972)★★, with the Shadows *The Early Rockin' Years* (K-Tel 1995)★★.

●COMPILATIONS: *Bobby Vee's Golden Greats* (Liberty 1962)★★★★, *Bobby Vee's Golden Greats, Volume Two* (Liberty 1966)★★★, *A Forever Kind of Love* (Sunset 1969)★★★, *Legendary Masters* (United Artists 1973)★★★★, *The Bobby Vee Singles Album* (1980)★★★★, *The EP Collection* (See For Miles 1991)★★★★, *The Very Best Of* (1993)★★★★.

●FILMS: *C'mon Let's Live A Little* (1967).

VEJTABLES

Although popular in the San Francisco Bay Area in the mid-60s, the Vejtables never managed to break out nationally. Signed to the Tower label subsidiary Uptown Records in 1965, the group consisted of Jan Ashton, Bob Bailey, Ned Hollis, Reese Sheets and Frank Smith. Their first single, 'Feel The Music' garnered attention locally and the group then signed with Autumn Records, best known as the home of the Beau Brummels. The Vejtables' 'I Still Love You', sung by female drummer Ashton, became their only minor hit record, reaching number 84. The group broke up in 1966; Ashton joined labelmates the Mojo Men and sang on their only hit, a cover of Buffalo Springfield's 'Sit Down I Think I Love You'.

●COMPILATIONS: *Feel ...* (Sundazed 1996)★★★.

VELVELETTES

Two pairs of sisters, Millie and Cal Gill, and Bertha and Norma Barbee, formed the original Velvelettes line-up in 1961 at Western Michigan State University. After recording a one-off single, 'There He Goes', for IPG Records in 1963, they were signed to Motown, where they were placed in the hands of fledgling producer Norman Whitfield. This partnership spawned three classic singles, 'Needle In A Haystack', 'He Was Really Sayin' Something' and 'These Things Will Keep Me Lovin' You', which epitomized Motown's approach to the all girl-group sound. A flurry of personnel changes effectively halted the Velvelettes' progress in 1965: Millie Gill and the Barbee sisters left, to be replaced briefly by two future members of Martha And The Vandellas, Sandra Tilley and Betty Kelly, and Annette McMullen. This line-up also dissolved after a few months. In 1970, 'These Things Will Keep Me Loving You' became a belated UK hit, confirming the Velvelettes' cult status among British soul fans. The original line-up re-grouped in 1984 to play revival shows, and re-recorded their hits for Nightmare Records. The original line-up of Carolyn Gill-Street, Bertha Barbee-McNeal, Norma Barbee-Fairhurst and Millie Gill-Arbour recorded a disco version of 'Needle In A Haystack' for Ian Levine's label in 1987 and continue recording to the present time. *One Door Closes* contained half of old hits and half of new material, recorded in an updated Motown style.

●ALBUMS: *One Door Closes* (1990)★★.

VELVET OPERA

This popular UK act, which adeptly mixed soul and psychedelic/progressive styles, evolved from Jaymes Fenda And The Vulcans, one of several groups to secure a recording deal following their appearance in the televised contest, *Ready Steady Win*. Former Vulcan songwriter John Ford (b. 1 July 1948, Fulham, London, England; bass) was subsequently joined by Elmer Gantry (vocals), Colin Forster (guitar) and Richard Hudson (b. Richard William Stafford Hudson, 9 May 1948, London, England; drums) in a group initially dubbed Elmer Gantry's Velvet Opera. Their excellent debut album included the pulsating 'Flames' which, despite regular appearances on BBC Radio 1's *Top Gear*, failed to become a hit. In 1968 Forster was replaced by Paul Brett who then left to join Fire. Gantry also abandoned the group, which then truncated their name to Velvet Opera. Colin Forster rejoined Ford, Hudson and new vocalist John Joyce for *Ride A Hustler's Dream*, but this lacked the purpose of its predecessor save for the excellent 'Anna Dance Square'. The quartet fell apart when Hudson and Ford joined the Strawbs, with whom they remained until 1973. Having written several of the group's most commercial offerings, the duo then left to pursue their own career as Hudson-Ford. By 1974, Gantry was fronting a band which, until checked by litigation, accepted illicit bookings as 'Fleetwood Mac' while the genuine article were off the road. A year later, Gantry emerged once more as singer on Stretch's solitary UK chart entry, 'Why Did You Do It'.

●ALBUMS: *Elmer Gantry's Velvet Opera* (CBS 1967)★★★, *Ride A Hustler's Dream* (CBS 1969)★★★.

●COMPILATIONS: *The Very Best Of Elmer Gantry* (See For Miles 1996)★★★.

VELVET UNDERGROUND

The antithesis of late-60s west coast love and peace, New York's Velvet Underground portrayed a darker side to that era's hedonism. Their pulsating drive married with intellectual precision and resulted in one of rock's most innovative and lasting catalogues. Lou Reed (b. 2 March 1942, Freeport, Long Island, New York, USA; guitar/vocal) and John Cale (b. 9 March 1940, Crynant, West Glamorgan, Wales; viola/bass/organ) provided a contrast in personality and approach which ensured the group's early notoriety. Reed was a contract songwriter/performer at Pickwick Records, responsible for a series of budget-priced recordings issued under several names, the best known of which was the Primitives. Cale, a classically trained child prodigy, had secured a scholarship to study in America, but was drawn into the group's nascent circle when he contributed a viola passage to Reed's anti-dance composition, 'The Ostrich'. A third Primitive, Walter De Maria, was quickly replaced by Sterling Morrison (b. 29 August 1942, East Meadow, Long Island, New York, USA, d. 30 August 1995, Poughkeepsie, New York, USA; guitar), who had studied creative writing with Reed at Syracuse University. The reshaped unit was completed by drummer Angus MacLise who suggested they adopt the name 'Velvet Underground', the title of a contemporary pulp paperback. MacLise was also instrumental in securing the group's first gigs at multi-media events and happenings, but left when the Velvets began accepting fees. He was replaced by Maureen 'Mo' Tucker (b. 1945, New Jersey, USA), sister to a friend of Sterling Morrison. The group met pop-art celebrity Andy Warhol in 1965 following an appearance at the Cafe Bizarre. He invited them to join the Exploding Plastic Inevitable, a theatrical mixture of music, films, light-shows and dancing, and also suggested adding actress/singer Nico (b. Christa Paffgen, 16 October 1938, Cologne, Germany, d. 18 July 1988) to the Velvets' line-up.

The group recorded their debut album in the spring of 1966 but the completed master was rejected by several major companies, fearful of both its controversial content and lengthy tracks. *The Velvet Underground And Nico* was eventually issued by MGM/Verve the following year. Infamous for Warhol's prominent involvement - he designed the distinctive peel-off banana screenprint featured on its sleeve and is credited as producer - this powerful collection introduced Reed's decidedly urban infatuations, a fascination for street culture and amorality bordering on voyeurism. Reed's talent, however, was greater than mere opportunism. His finely honed understanding of R&B enhanced a graphic lyricism whereby songs about drugs ('I'm Waiting For The Man'/'Heroin'), sado-masochism ('Venus In Furs') or sublimation ('I'll Be Your Mirror') were not only memorable for their subjects, but also as vibrant pop compositions. Such skills were intensified by Cale's haunting, graphic viola work, Nico's gothic intonation and the group's combined sense of dynamism that blended Tucker's relentless pulse with some of rock's most inspired sonic experimentation. Now rightly regarded as a musical milestone, *The Velvet Underground And Nico* was generally reviled on release. Contemporary radio shunned its stark ugliness and subject matter, while the disparate counter-cultures

of Los Angeles and San Francisco abhorred the dank underbelly this uncompromising group posed to challenge their floral dreams.

Nico left for a solo career in 1967 and the remaining quartet then parted from Warhol's patronage. Sessions for a second album, *White Light/White Heat*, exacerbated other internal conflicts and its six compositions were marked by a raging intensity. While the title track and the relentless 'I Heard Her Call My Name' suggested an affinity to 'I'm Waiting For The Man', two extended pieces, 'The Gift' and 'Sister Ray', caught the group at its most radical. The latter performance, a grinding, remorseless, sexual cacophony, was recorded live in the studio at maximum volume, and although Reed later suggested he was trying to approximate the free-jazz of Ornette Coleman, this 17-minute *tour de force* offers some of John Cale's most inspired atonal instrumental work. This pivotal figure was then removed from the group and replaced by an orthodox bassist, former Grass Menagerie member, Doug Yule. A third album, entitled simply *The Velvet Underground*, unveiled a pastoral approach, gentler and more subtle, retaining the chilling, disquieting aura of previous releases. Now firmly within Reed's grasp, the quartet were implicit rather than direct, although moments of their previous fury were apparent on several interludes.

Loaded, an album of considerable commercial promise, emphasized their newfound perspective. Released in 1970, this unfettered collection contained one of Reed's most popular compositions, 'Sweet Jane', and in celebrating pop's rich heritage, offered an optimism rarely heard in previous work. Paradoxically, by the time *Loaded* was issued, Lou Reed had abandoned the group he had created and Doug Yule, who had encouraged the commercial aspect of the album, now took control, leading several variations on the Velvet Underground name. A poorly received album, *Squeeze*, confirmed that the definitive unit ended with Reed's departure, so much so that the album is not generally perceived to be part of the Velvets' discography.

Despite the tribulations endured during its brief lifespan, the Velvets have since become one of rock's most influential groups, particularly during the 80s when a new generation of performers, from Joy Division to Jesus And Mary Chain, declared their indebtedness. A series of archive releases, including *1969 - The Velvet Underground Live*, *VU* and *Another View*, add further fuel to the talent and insight which lay within the Velvet Underground and enhance their legendary status. A rumour, followed by an announcement in 1993 that the band without Doug Yule, had re-formed for a major tour, was greeted with anxious excitement. The subsequent performances delighted thousands of fans, with a vast percentage barely born when the Velvets last performed. Old wounds were opened between Cale and Reed and no further plans were imminent other than a one-off appearance together following their induction to the Rock And Roll Hall Of Fame in 1996. Sadly, Sterling Morrison missed the event having died a few months earlier.

●ALBUMS: *The Velvet Underground and Nico* (Verve 1967)★★★★★, *White Light/White Heat* (Verve 1967)★★★★, *The Velvet Underground* (Verve 1969)★★★★, *Loaded* (Atlantic 1970)★★★, *Live At Max's Kansas City* (Atlantic 1972)★, *Squeeze* (Polydor 1973)★★, *1969 - The Velvet Underground Live* (Mercury 1974)★★★, *VU* (Verve 1985)★★★, *Another View* (Polydor 1986)★★, *Live MCMXCIII* (1993)★★★, *Loaded (Fully Loaded)* (Atlantic 1997)★★★★.
●COMPILATIONS: *Andy Warhol's Velvet Underground* (1971)★★★, *Velvet Underground* 5 album box set (1986)★★★, *The Best Of The Velvet Underground* (Verve 1989)★★★★, *Peel Slowly And See* 5-CD box set (Polydor 1995)★★★★.
●VIDEOS: *Velvet Redux - Live MCMXCII* (1993).
●FURTHER READING: *Beyond The Velvet Underground*, Dave Thompson. *Uptight: The Velvet Underground Story*, Victor Bockris and G. Malanga. *Velvet Underground: A Complete Mediography*, Michael C. Kostek. *The Velvet Underground Handbook*, Michael C. Kostek.
●FILMS: *Hedy* (1965).

VELVETT FOGG

This UK, Midlands-based attraction was one of several acts launched by the Pye label in 1969 during a belated attempt to enter the progressive rock market. *Velvett Fogg*, replete with BBC disc jockey John Peel's glowing testimony, revealed an organ-based sound redolent of the Nice and Spooky Tooth. 'Come Away Melinda', popularized by Tim Rose and the Bee Gees' 'New York Mining Disaster 1941', contrasted several original songs, the most interesting of which, 'Lady Caroline' and 'Wizard Of Gobsolod', were penned by guitarist Paul Eastment. The group also completed a non-album single, 'Telstar '69', in which they reconstructed the famed Joe Meek/Tornadoes' classic. Velvett Fogg disbanded soon afterwards, although Eastment quickly reappeared in cult favourites, the Ghost.
●ALBUMS: *Velvett Fogg* (Pye 1969)★★★.
●COMPILATIONS: *Velvett Fogg ... Plus* (1989)★★★.

VENTURES

This pivotal instrumental group was formed in Tacoma, Washington, USA, in 1959 when workmates Don Wilson (rhythm guitar) and Bob Bogle (lead guitar) discovered a mutual interest in music. They began performing together as the Impacts, using a pick-up rhythm section, before Nokie Edwards (bass) and Skip Moore (drums) completed a line-up redubbed the Ventures. The quartet made its debut with 'Cookies And Coke', released on their own Blue Horizon label, before discovering 'Walk Don't Run' on Chet Atkins' *HiFi In Focus* album. Initially a jazz instrumental, it nonetheless lent itself to a simplified chord structure and by emphasizing its beat, the Ventures constructed a powerful, compulsive sound that not only became their trademark, but was echoed in the concurrent surfing style. The single reached number 2 in the US charts (number 8 UK) with sales in excess of one million copies, a distinction matched by its follow-up, 'Perfidia'. At this point Moore had been replaced by Howie Johnson, who in turn retired following a major car accident. Drummer Mel Taylor (b. 1934, New York City, New York, USA, d. 11 August 1996, Los Angeles, California, USA) was then added to the group.

Other notable Ventures singles included '2000 Pound Bee' (1962), which featured the then revolutionary fuzz-guitar, 'The Savage' (1963), originally recorded by the Shadows, and 'Diamond Head' (1965), later immortalized by the Beach Boys. The Ventures' continued appeal lay in an ability to embrace contemporary fashion, as evinced on *The Ventures (Batman)* (1966), *Super Psychedelics* (1967) or *Underground Fire* (1968), without straying too far from their established format. They also survived several personnel changes; Nokie traded roles with Bogle in 1963 before leaving altogether four years later. He was replaced by session guitarist Jerry McGee, whose numerous credits include Elvis Presley, the Monkees and Kris Kristofferson, and organist Sandy Lee, although the latter was in turn supplanted by Johnny Durrill, formerly of the Five Americans. In 1969 the Ventures had their last major US hit when 'Hawaii Five-O', the theme tune to a popular detective series, reached number 4. They remained a popular attraction, particularly in Japan, where the group were the subject of almost fanatical reverence. Annual tours throughout the 70s were supplemented by many exclusive recordings, and several tracks were hits twice: once as instrumentals and again with lyrics courtesy of local composers and singers. The group withstood the loss of Taylor, McGee and Durrill; the remaining trio added new drummer Jo Barile, and with a succession of keyboard players and vocalists, they continued their career. Musically, the Ventures continued to court contemporary trends, including disco and reggae, while assuming greater artistic control with the founding of their Tridex label. Mel Taylor rejoined Bogle, Wilson and Edwards in 1979 as the unit attempted to rekindle their reputation at home. The Ventures remain one of the world's most respected instrumental units.
●ALBUMS: *Walk Don't Run* (Dolton 1960)★★★★, *The Ventures* (Dolton 1961)★★★★, *Another Smash!!!* (Dolton 1961)★★★, *The Colorful Ventures* (Dolton 1961)★★★, *Twist With The Ventures* aka *The Ventures - Dance* (Dolton 1962)★★★, *The Ventures' Twist Party* aka *Dance With The Ventures* (Dolton 1962)★★★, *Mashed Potatoes And Gravy* aka *The Ventures' Beach Party* (Dolton 1962)★★★, *Going To The Ventures' Dance Party* (Dolton 1962)★★★★, *The Ventures Play Telstar, The Lonely Bull* (Dolton 1963)★★, *The Ventures Surfing* (Dolton 1963)★★★, *Bobby Vee Meets The Ventures* (Dolton 1963)★★★, *The Ventures Play The Country Classics* aka *I Walk The Line* (Dolton 1963)★★, *Let's Go!* (Dolton 1963)★★★★, *The Ventures In Space* (Dolton 1964)★★, *Walk Don't Run Volume Two* (Dolton 1964)★★★, *The Ventures Knock Me Out* (Dolton 1965)★★★, *Play Guitar With The Ventures* (Dolton 1965)★★★, *The Ventures In Japan* (Dolton 1965)★★★, *The Ventures On Stage* (Dolton

1965)★★★, *The Ventures A-Go-Go* (Dolton 1965)★★★, *The Ventures Christmas Album* (Dolton 1965)★★★, *Where The Action Is* (Dolton 1966)★★★, *All About The Ventures* (Dolton 1966)★★★, *The Ventures (Batman)* (Dolton 1966)★★★, *Go With The Ventures* (Dolton 1966)★★★, *Wild Things* (Dolton 1966)★★★, *Guitar Freakout* aka *Revolving Sounds* (Dolton 1967)★★★, *The Ventures On Stage Encore* (Liberty 1967)★★★, *Super Psychedelics* aka *Changing Times* (Liberty 1967)★★★, *$1,000,000 Weekend* (Liberty 1967)★★, *Flights Of Fantasy* (Liberty 1968)★★★, *The Ventures Live Again* (Liberty 1968)★★★, *Pops In Japan* (1968)★★★, *The Horse* aka *The Ventures On The Scene* (Liberty 1968)★★★, *The Ventures In Tokyo '68* (1968)★★★, *Underground Fire* (Liberty 1968)★★★, *Hawaii Five-O* (1969)★★, *Swamp Rock* (1969)★★★, *The Ventures 10th Anniversary Album* (1970)★★★, *Live! The Ventures* (1970)★★★, *Golden Pops* (1970)★★★, *New Testament* (1971)★★★, *Theme From Shaft* (United Artists 1971)★★, *Pops In Japan '71* (1971)★★★, *Joy - The Ventures Play The Classics* (United Artists 1972)★★★, *Rock 'N' Roll Forever* (1972)★★★, *The Ventures On Stage '72* (1972)★★★, *The Ventures On Stage '73* (1973)★★★, *Pops In Japan '73* (1973)★★★, *The Ventures On Stage '74* (1974)★★★, *The Jim Croce Songbook* (1974)★★, *The Ventures Play The Carpenters* (1974)★★, *Hollywood Yuya Meets The Ventures* (1976)★★★, *The Ventures On Stage '76* (1976)★★★, *Rocky Road* (1976)★★, *TV Themes* (1977)★★, *Live In Japan '77* (1977)★★★, *The Ventures On Stage '78* (1978)★★★, *Latin Album* (1978)★★, *The Ventures Original Four* (1980)★★★, *Chameleon* (1980)★★, *Super Live '80* (1980)★★★, *The Ventures* (1981)★★★, *60's Pops* (1981)★★★, *Tokyo Callin' 60s Pops Of Japan* (1981)★★★, *Pops In Japan '81* (1981)★★★, *St Louis Memory* (1982)★★, *The Ventures Today* (Valentine 1983)★★★.

●COMPILATIONS: *Running Strong* (1966)★★★, *The Versatile Ventures* (1966)★★★, *Golden Greats By The Ventures* (1967)★★★, *Supergroup* (1969)★★★, *More Golden Greats* (1970)★★★, *A Decade With The Ventures* (1971)★★★, *Only Hits* (1973)★★★, *Legendary Masters* (1974)★★★, *15th Anniversary* ●ALBUMS: *15 Years Of Japanese Pops* (1975)★★★, *The Very Best Of The Ventures* (1975)★★★, *Now Playing* (1975)★★★, *The Early Sounds Of The Ventures* (1976)★★★, *Ventures' Rare Collections For Great Collectors Only* (1980)★★★, *Best 10 Volume Two* (1980)★★★, *The Ventures Greatest Hits* (1981)★★★, *The Last Album On Liberty* (1982)★★★, *Twenty Rock 'N' Roll Hits: The Ventures* (1983)★★★, *Collection: The Ventures* (1986)★★★, *The Best Of The Ventures* (1987)★★★, *Walk Don't Run - The Best Of The Ventures* (1990)★★★, *The EP Collection Vol. 2* (See For Miles 1993).

VERNONS GIRLS

The group sponsored by UK's Vernon's football pools started with 70 members singing songs like 'Nymphs And Shepherds'. This choir was reduced to 16 by the late 50s and was regularly seen on pop television shows like *Oh Boy*. They recorded for Parlophone without success between 1958 and 1961. Their only hits appeared on Decca when they were reduced to the trio of Maureen Kennedy, Jean Owen and Frances Lee. Their first and biggest hit was a cover of Clyde McPhatter's 'Lover Please', which reached the UK Top 20 in 1962. The b-side, the Liverpudlian-sung 'You Know What I Mean', also hit the charts as did covers of 'Loco-Motion' and 'Do The Bird' and their original song 'Funny All Over'. The Vernons Girls group of the 50s also spawned solo hit maker Lyn Cornell and groups the Ladybirds, the Breakaways and the Two-Tones. With frequently changing personnel, the group continued for many more years, playing the UK cabaret circuit and recording (sometimes simply as the Vernons) on labels like Pye and Galaxy. One member, Joyce Baker, later married singer Marty Wilde. Members of the original television group have been frequently seen backing artists on UK television and stage and been heard singing backing vocals on countless hit records.

●ALBUMS: *The Vernons Girl* (Parlophone 1958)★★★.

VICKERS, MIKE

b. 18 April 1941, Southampton, Hampshire, England. Vickers first came to prominence as a founder member of the Mann Hugg Blues Brothers, later highly successful as Manfred Mann. His skills on a multitude of instruments - guitar, saxophone and vibes - allowed the group to bring new textures to their R&B palate, and his skills as an arranger helped enliven already well-known material. Vickers left Manfred Mann in 1965 to further such diverse talents. His debut, 'On The Brink' (1965), credited to Mike Vickers And Orchestra, was an ambitious instrumental with overtones of big band jazz, a musical style he subsequently pursued. In 1966 Vickers composed the soundtrack to the film *Morgan - A Suitable Case For Treatment*. The main theme was issued as a single prior to an imaginative version of 'Air On A G String' (1967). These were succeeded by theme song to the children's television show 'Captain Scarlet And The Mysterions' (1968). *I Wish I Were A Group Again* fully captures Vickers' talents as a composer and arranger with material ranging from easy listening to soul. He has subsequently continued to write for films and television.

●ALBUMS: *I Wish I Were A Group Again* (Columbia 1968)★★★.

VINTON, BOBBY

b. Stanley Robert Vinton, 16 April 1935, Canonsburg, Pennsylvania, USA. Born of Polish extraction, Vinton was one of the more enduring boy-next-door pop idols who sprang up in the early 60s. He began as a trumpeter before agreeing to front his high school band as featured vocalist. A tape of one such performance reached Epic Records which signed him in 1960. Composed by Al Byron and Paul Evans, 'Roses Are Red' was Vinton's first national smash but it was overtaken in Britain by Ronnie

Carroll's Top 10 cover. Despite a much-publicized arrival in London for his cameo in the teen-exploitation film, *Just For Fun*, a second US number 1, 'Blue Velvet', was initially ignored in the UK, although another American smash, a revival of Vaughn Monroe's 'There I've Said It Again', made number 34 in 1963. Vinton continued playing in supper clubs until 1968, when a policy of revamping hits by old rivals put his arrangements of Jimmy Crawford's 'I Love How You Love Me', Bobby Vee's 'Take Good Care Of My Baby and the Teddy Bears' retitled 'To Know Her Is To Love Her' high up the Hot 100. This formula worked again in 1972 with Brian Hyland's 'Sealed With A Kiss' but it was 1974's 'My Melody Of Love', a new song co-written by Vinton himself, that gave him one more US chart-topper. His version of 'Blue Moon' was heard on the soundtrack of *An American Werewolf In London* in 1981 but it was the use of 'Blue Velvet' in both the 1989 film of the same name and a television commercial that brought about a huge 1991 windfall in Britain, where the pragmatic Vinton became omnipresent until its fall from the chart and the failure of 'Roses Are Red', which was reissued as the follow-up.

●ALBUMS: *Dancing At The Hop* (Epic 1961)★★★, *Young Man With A Big Band* (Epic 1961)★★★, *Roses Are Red* (Epic 1962)★★★, *Bobby Vinton Sings The Big Ones* (Epic 1962)★★★, *The Greatest Hits Of The Greatest Groups* (Epic 1963)★★, *Blue On Blue* (Epic 1963)★★★, *Blue Velvet* (Epic 1963)★★★, *There! I've Said It Again* (Epic 1964)★★★, *My Heart Belongs To Only You* (Epic/Columbia 1964)★★★, *Tell Me Why* (Epic/Columbia 1964)★★★, *Mr. Lonely* (Epic/Columbia 1964)★★★, *Bobby Vinton Sings For Lonely Nights* (1965)★★★, *Laughing On The Outside (Crying On The Inside)* (1965)★★★, *Great Motion Picture Themes* (1966)★★, *Satin Pillows And Careless* (1966)★★★, *Please Love Me Forever* (1967)★★★, *Take Good Care Of My Baby* (1968)★★★, *I Love How You Love Me* (1968)★★★, *Vinton* (1969)★★★, *My Elusive Dreams* (1970)★★★, *Ev'ry Day Of My Life* (1972)★★★, *Sealed With A Kiss* (1972)★★★, *Melodies Of Love* (1974)★★★, *With Love* (1974)★★★, *Heart Of Hearts* (1975)★★★, *The Bobby Vinton Show* (1975)★★★, *The Name Is Love* (1977)★★★, *Kissin' Christmas* (Epic 1995)★★.

●COMPILATIONS: *Bobby Vinton's Greatest Hits* (Epic 1964)★★★, *Bobby Vinton's Greatest Hits Of Love* (1969)★★★, *Bobby Vinton's All-Time Greatest Hits* (1972)★★★, *With Love* (1974)★★★, *Bobby Vinton Sings The Golden Decade Of Love - Songs Of The 50s* (1975)★★★, *16 Most Requested Songs* (Columbia 1993)★★★.

●FURTHER READING: *The Polish Prince*, Bobby Vinton.

VOGUES

This US vocal group were formed in Turtle Creek, near Pittsburgh, Pennsylvania, by schoolfriends Bill Burkette (lead baritone), Don Miller (baritone), Hugh Geyer (first tenor) and Chuck Blasko (second tenor). They began singing as the Val-Aires in 1960, but took the above name prior to signing with the tiny Co & Ce label. In 1965 the Vogues scored two US Top 5 singles with 'You're The One' and 'Five O'Clock World', the latter of which was a majestic slice of east coast harmony pop, reminiscent of Jay And The Americans or the Four Seasons at their best. The quartet continued to enjoy minor success, but it was not until they joined Reprise Records that the group enjoyed another significant hit. 'Turn Around, Look At Me' was the Vogues' only million-selling release and the prelude to a decidedly MOR direction when they took the 1957 Bobby Helms hit, 'My Special Angel', to the Top 10. Their later work lacked the earthy enthusiasm of those early offerings, although its professionalism secured a place with adult audiences.

●ALBUMS: *Meet The Vogues* (Co&Ce 1965)★★★, *You're The One* (Ling 1966)★★★, *Five O'Clock World* (Co&Ce 1966)★★★, *Turn Around, Look At Me* (Reprise 1968)★★★, *Till* (Reprise 1969)★★, *Memories* (1969)★★.

●COMPILATIONS: *The Vogues' Greatest Hits* (1969)★★★, *You're The One: The Best Of ... The Co & Ce Sessions* (Varese Vintage 1996)★★★.

WALKER BROTHERS

Hailing from America but transposed to England in the mid-60s, this hit trio comprised Scott Walker (b. Noel Scott Engel, 9 January 1944, Hamilton, Ohio; USA), John Walker (b. John Maus, 12 November 1943, New York; USA) and Gary Walker (b. Gary Leeds, 3 September 1944, Glendale, California; USA). Leeds, an ex-member of the Standells, had discovered former Routers bassist Engel appearing with Maus in an ensemble called the Dalton Brothers. In 1964, the trio changed their name to the Walker Brothers and following a false start at home decided to relocate to the UK. After arriving in February 1965, they fell into the hands of manager Maurice King and were soon signed to Philips Records. Their debut, 'Pretty Girls Everywhere', featured Maus as lead vocalist, but it was the Engel-voiced follow-up, 'Love Her', which cracked the UK Top 20 in May 1965. By this time, Scott was the chosen 'a-side' main vocalist, with Maus providing the strong high harmony. The group neatly slotted into the gap left by Phil Spector's protégés the Righteous Brothers, who had topped the charts earlier in the year but failed to sustain their impact in the UK. As well as emulating their rivals' vocal power, the Walkers boasted film star looks and swiftly emerged as pin-up idols with a huge teenage following. On album, the trio played a contrasting selection of ballads, soul standards and occasional upbeat pop, but for the singles they specialized in high melodrama, brilliantly augmented by the string arrangements of Johnny Franz, with accompaniment directed by either Ivor Raymonde or Reg Guest.

The lachrymose Burt Bacharach/Hal David ballad 'Make It Easy On Yourself' (originally a US hit for Jerry Butler) gave them a UK chart number 1, while the similarly paced 'My Ship Is Coming In' reached the Top 3. Their neurotic romanticism reached its apogee on the Bob Crewe/Bob Gaudio composition, 'The Sun Ain't Gonna Shine Anymore', in which Scott's deep baritone was wonderfully balanced by John's Four Seasons-styled soaring harmony. The song topped the UK listings for a month and gave them their second and last US Top 20 hit. Thereafter, there was immense friction in the Walkers' camp and their second EP *Solo Scott, Solo John* (1967) neatly summarized their future intentions.

Although they continued to chart in the UK between 1965 and 1967, the quality of their material was generally less impressive. Pete Autell's '(Baby) You Don't Have To Tell Me' seemed a weak follow-up to their grandiose number 1 and commenced their gradual commercial decline. Another Bacharach/David composition, 'Another Tear

Falls', fared little better at number 12, while the film theme, 'Deadlier Than The Male' could only scrape the Top 30. The much-covered Bert Berns composition 'Stay With Me Baby' retained the melodrama, but there was no emphatic comeback and in early 1967 the group elected to break up. The emotional impact of the break-up on their loyal fan base should have pushed their farewell single, 'Walking In The Rain', to the upper echelons of the chart but as the *New Musical Express* reviewer Derek Johnson sadly noted: 'Walkers Last Not So Great'.

As soloists, the Walkers suffered mixed fortunes, but it was still a surprise when the trio reunited in 1975. Their comeback album, *No Regrets*, consisted largely of extraneous material, but the classy Tom Rush title track returned the group to the Top 10 for the first time since 'The Sun Ain't Gonna Shine Anymore', released nearly a decade before. A follow-up album, *Lines*, was similar in style to its predecessor, but for their swansong, the self-penned *Nite Flights*, the trio produced a brave, experimental work, with oblique, foreboding lyrics and unusual arrangements. The album was a commercial failure, but by the time the initial sales figures had been computed, Scott, John and Gary had returned to their individual ventures and concomitant obscurity.

● ALBUMS: *Take It Easy With The Walker Brothers* (Philips 1965)★★★, *Portrait* (Philips 1966)★★★, *Images* (Philips 1967)★★, *No Regrets* (GTO 1975)★★★, *Lines* (GTO 1977)★★, *Nite Flights* (GTO 1978)★★★★, *The Walker Brothers In Japan* 1968 recording (Bam Caruso 1987)★★.

● COMPILATIONS: *After The Lights Go Out - The Best Of 1965-1967* (Fontana 1990)★★★★, *No Regrets - The Best Of The Walker Brothers* (1991)★★★★, *The Collection* (Spectrum 1996)★★★★.

● FILMS: *Beach Ball* (1964).

WALKER, JUNIOR, AND THE ALL STARS

b. Autry DeWalt II, 1931, Blythesville, Arkansas, USA, d. 23 November 1995. His record label, Motown, stated that he was born in 1942. Walker was inspired to take up the saxophone by the jump blues and R&B bands he heard in the early 50s. In his mid-teens, he formed his first instrumental group, the Jumping Jacks, adopting the stage name Junior Walker after a childhood nickname. By 1961 he had achieved a prominent local reputation, which reached the ear of label owner and former Moonglow, Harvey Fuqua. He signed Walker to his Harvey label, allowing him free rein to record a series of raw saxophone led instrumentals. In 1964 Walker followed Fuqua to Motown, where he perfected a blend of raunchy R&B and Detroit soul typified by his 1965 hit, 'Shotgun'. With its repeated saxophone riffs and call-and-response vocals, it established Walker as the label's prime exponent of traditional R&B, a reputation that was confirmed by later hits like 'Shake And Fingerpop' and 'Road Runner'. The latter was produced by Holland/Dozier/Holland, who also encouraged Walker to record instrumental versions of hits they had written for other Motown artists.

Walker's style became progressively more lyrical in the late 60s, a development that reached its peak on the 1969 US Top 5 hit, 'What Does It Take (To Win Your Love)?' This also marked the pinnacle of his commercial success, as subsequent attempts to repeat the winning formula were met with growing public indifference, and from 1972 onwards the All Stars recorded only sporadically. *Hot Shot* in 1976, produced by Brian Holland, marked a move towards the burgeoning disco market, which was confirmed on two further albums that year, Walker's first as a solo artist. In 1979, he was one of several Motown artists to move to Whitfield Records. Finding his career deadlocked, Walker returned to Motown in 1983, issuing *Blow The House Down*, an exercise in reclaiming lost ground. The novelty single 'Sex Pot' rekindled memories of his classic hits, although Walker's greatest commercial success in the 80s came when he guested with Foreigner and played the magnificent saxophone solo on their hit single 'Urgent'. He lost a two-year battle with cancer in November 1995.

●ALBUMS: *Shotgun* (Soul/Tamla Motown 1965)★★★★, *Soul Session* (Tamla Motown 1966)★★★★, *Road Runner* (Tamla Motown 1966)★★★★, *Live!* (Tamla Motown 1967)★★★, *Home Cookin'* (Tamla Motown 1969)★★★, *Gotta Hold On To This Feeling* (Soul 1969)★★★, *What Does It Take To Win Your Love?* (Soul 1969)★★★, *Live* (1970)★★★, *A Gassssssss* (Soul 1970)★★★, *Rainbow Funk* (Soul 1971)★★★, *Moody Jr.* (Soul 1971)★★★, *Peace And Understanding Is Hard To Find* (Soul 1973)★★, *Hot Shot* (Soul 1976)★★, *Sax Appeal* (Soul 1976)★★★, *Whopper Bopper Show Stopper* (Soul 1976)★★, ... *Smooth* (Soul 1978)★★, *Back Street Boogie* (Whitfield 1979)★★, *Blow The House Down* (Motown 1983)★★.

●COMPILATIONS: *Greatest Hits* (Soul 1969)★★★★, *Anthology* (Motown 1981)★★★★, *Junior Walker's Greatest Hits* (1982)★★★★, *19 Greatest Hits* (1987)★★★★, *Shake And Fingerpop* (Blue Moon 1989)★★★, *Compact Command Performance - 19 Greatest Hits* (1992)★★★★.

WALKER, SCOTT

b. Noel Scott Engel, 9 January 1944, Hamilton, Ohio, USA. After relocating to New York during childhood, this precocious talent initially pursued a career as an actor, and also briefly recorded under the name Scotty Engel. Moving to Hollywood, he worked on sessions with arranger Jack Nitzsche before joining the Routers as a bassist. He next teamed up with singer John Maus as the Dalton Brothers, which gradually evolved into the Walker Brothers with the addition of drummer Gary Leeds. The trio moved to England and found themselves fêted as teen-idols, with a string of hits that established them as one of the most successful UK-based groups of the mid-60s. The group broke up in May 1967 at a time when Scott was still regarded as a sex symbol and potential solo superstar. Yet there was something contradictory about the singer's image. Ridden with angst during the Walkers' teen-idol peak, he was known for his moody reclusive-

ness, tendency to wear dark glasses and stay in curtain-closed rooms during daylight hours. The classic pop existentialist, Walker was trapped in a system that regarded him as a contradiction. His manager Maurice King encouraged a straightforward showbusiness career involving regular television appearances and even cabaret. Walker, meanwhile, had become a devotee of French composer Jacques Brel and included several of his songs on his debut solo album, *Scott*. There is no finer example of the contradiction that Walker faced than the incongruous image of the singer performing 'My Death' on BBC television's chirpy *Billy Cotton Band Show*.

Walker's solo albums were equally quirky and stylistically diverse, fusing the brutal visions of Brel alongside contemporary MOR standards such as Tony Bennett's 'When Joanna Loved Me'. Walker was also displaying immense talent as a songwriter in his own right with poetic, brooding songs, such as 'Such A Small Love' and 'Always Coming Back To You'. Eschewing young, modern producers, Walker stuck with the lush, orchestral arrangements of Johnny Franz, Reg Guest, Peter Knight and Wally Stott. The resulting concoction was rendered unique by Walker's distinctive, deep, crooning tone and strong vibrato. On the strength of the Walker Brothers' dedicated audience, Scott's solo albums were chart successes in the UK, but as an artist he remained the great contradiction. Singer/songwriter, MOR entertainer, Brel interpreter and television personality, his entire career dramatized a constant clash between pop star trappings and artistic endeavour. Even his similarly titled hit singles emphasized the grand contradiction: 'Jackie' was a racy Brel song that mentioned 'authentic queers' and was banned by the BBC; 'Joanna' was pure schmaltz, written by the Tin Pan Alley husband and wife team Tony Hatch and Jackie Trent. Walker's uneasiness about his career was emphasized in a number of confusing decisions and record releases. At one point, he reverted to his real surname Engel, and announced that he would no longer be issuing singles.

While the brilliant *Scott 4* at last contained solely original material and might have heralded the re-evaluation of Walker as a serious songwriter, the BBC chose that very same period to issue the MOR *Scott Sings Songs From His Television Series*. Undervalued and apparently uncertain about his direction, Walker's muse grew increasingly weary after the 60s. Reissued in 1996, *'Til The Band Comes In*, his 1970 collaboration with songwriter Ady Semeland however, is a joy of discovery. Released a year after the Woodstock festival, Walker could not have been more out of step with musical fashion, yet more than 25 years later the quality of the songs stands up, and above all they feature a voice to weep to. By 1972 he seemed to bow to popular demand by recording an album of cover versions, *The Moviegoer*. A shift towards country music followed before Scott reunited with Maus and Leeds for a series of Walker Brothers albums. Thereafter, Scott retreated from the music business returning only for the critically acclaimed *Climate Of Hunter* in 1984. His enigmatic career, remarkable voice and intense songwriting have inspired a wealth of performers including Julian Cope (who compiled a Walker album), Marc Almond (who provided sleeve notes for a compilation) and a number of deep, crooning vocalists, who have attempted to recapture that unique Scott vibrato. It was reported in 1992 that Walker had signed a major recording contract and three years later he delivered a new album. *Tilt* was the most ear-challenging work he has so far recorded. The record found two distinct camps: one that criticized him for not delivering the smooth ballad of old and the other (a much younger audience) who found this difficult work intriguing. The record company showed a great sense of humour when they released the title track as a single. Radio play was not forthcoming.

●ALBUMS: *Scott* (Philips 1967)★★★, *Scott 2* (Philips 1968)★★★★, *Scott 3* (Philips 1969)★★★★, *Scott 4* (Philips 1969)★★★★, *Scott Sings Songs From His Television Series* (Philips 1969)★★, *'Til The Band Comes In* (Philips 1970)★★★, *The Moviegoer* (Philips 1972)★★, *Any Day Now* (Philips 1973)★★, *Stretch* (Columbia 1973), *We Had It All* (Columbia 1974)★★, *Climate Of Hunter* (Virgin 1984)★★★★, *Tilt* (Fontana 1995)★★★.

●COMPILATIONS: *Looking Back With Scott Walker* (Ember 1968)★★★, *Best Of Scott Walker* (Philips 1970)★★★, *This Is Scott Walker* (Philips 1971)★★★★, *This Is Scott Walker - Volume II* (Philips 1972)★★★, *Spotlight On Scott Walker* (Philips 1976)★★★, *Fire Escape In The Sky - The Godlike Genius Of Scott Walker* (Zoo 1981)★★★★, *Scott Walker Sings Jacques Brel* (Philips 1981)★★★, *Boy Child - The Best Of 1967-1970* (1990)★★★★.

●FURTHER READING: *A Deep Shade Of Blue*, Mike Watkinson and Pete Anderson.

WARM SOUNDS

In 1965, Denver Gerrard (b. 1945, Johannesburg, South Africa) and Barry (Young) Husband (formerly of Tuesday's Children) were two young UK-based songwriters in search of a hit. After traipsing around London's Tin Pan Alley they decided to pool their resources and briefly switch to recording their own work. Producer Mike Hurst recognized their potential and in 1967 they signed to the highly fashionable Deram Records label under the name Warm Sounds. The line-up was completed by John Carr. They enjoyed a Top 40 hit that year with the harmonious 'Birds And Bees', which astonishingly reached number 1 on UK pirate radio ship Radio London's often spurious Fab 40. Subsequent releases, 'Nite Is A-Comin'' and 'Sticks And Stones' (the latter on Andrew Loog Oldham's label, Immediate Records), sold poorly. The team soon split and Gerrard went on to record a commercially unsuccessful album, *Sinister Morning*. Gerrard and Carr later worked together in Hapshash And The Coloured Coat and Open Road.

●ALBUMS: Denver Gerrard solo *Sinister Morning* (Nova 1969)★★.

WARWICK, DEE DEE

b. 1945, New Jersey, USA. Warwick has always sung in the shadow of her older sister, Dionne Warwick, but she has created a body of work that holds up well decades later. Her first record on the Jubilee label, 'You're No Good', was superseded by the much superior production done in Chicago by Vee Jay on Betty Everett. In 1964 Warwick signed with Mercury's Blue Rock subsidiary and, with production handled by Ed Townsend, recorded a spate of finely crafted songs, notably 'We're Doing Fine' (number 28 R&B). After switching to the parent label in 1966 she reached the charts with 'I Want To Be With You' (number 9 R&B, number 41 pop), which was taken from the Broadway musical *Golden Boy*, and 'I'm Gonna Make You Love Me' (number 13 R&B, number 88 pop), which was remade the following year with much greater success in the pop market by Madelaine Bell and much later by a united Supremes/Temptations group. Warwick moved to Atco in 1970 and was produced in Miami by Dave Crawford, achieving chart success with 'She Didn't Know (She Kept On Talking)' (number 9 R&B, number 70 pop) and a remake of 'Suspicious Minds' (number 24 R&B, number 80 pop). 'Get Out Of My Life' was her last chart record in 1975.

●ALBUMS: *I Want To Be With You/I'm Gonna Make You Love Me* (Mercury 1967)★★★, *Foolish Fool* (Mercury 1969)★★, *Turning Around* (Atco 1970)★★.

WARWICK, DIONNE

b. Marie Dionne Warrick, 12 December 1940, East Orange, New Jersey, USA. One of soul music's truly sophisticated voices, Warwick first sang in Newark's New Hope Baptist Church choir. She played piano with the Drinkard Singers, a gospel group her mother managed, and studied at Connecticut's Hart School of Music. During the same period, Warwick also formed the Gospelaires with her sister, Dee Dee and aunt Cissy Houston. Increasingly employed as backing singers, the trio's voices appeared on records by the Drifters and Garnet Mimms. Through such work Warwick came into contact with songwriters Burt Bacharach and Hal David. Her first solo single, on the Scepter label, 'Don't Make Me Over' (1963), was a fragile slice of 'uptown R&B' and set the tone for such classic collaborations as 'Anyone Who Had A Heart' and 'Walk On By'. Bacharach's sculpted, almost grandiose compositions were the perfect setting for Warwick's light yet perfect phrasing, delicate almost to the point of vulnerability. 'You'll Never Get To Heaven (If You Break My Heart)', 'Reach Out For Me' (both 1964) and 'Are You There (With Another Girl)' (1966) epitomized the style. Although many of her singles charted, few were Top 10 hits, and the soulful edge, prevalent for the first two years, was gradually worn away. As her songwriters moved ever closer to the mainstream, so Dionne too embraced a safer, albeit classier, approach with such successes as the uplifting 'I Say A Little Prayer' (1967) and 'Do You Know The Way To San Jose?' (1968).

In 1971 Warwick abandoned both her label and mentors for Warner Brothers Records, but despite several promising releases, the relationship floundered. Around this time she also added an extra 'e' to the end of her name, on advice given to her by an astrologer. Her biggest hit came with the (Detroit) Spinners on the Thom Bell-produced 'Then Came You' (1974). Warwick moved to Arista Records in 1979 where work with Barry Manilow rekindled her commercial standing. *Heartbreaker*, her collaboration with the Bee Gees, resulted in several hit singles while a pairing with Luther Vandross on 'How Many Times Can We Say Goodbye?' was also a success. 'That's What Friends Are For' pitted Dionne with Elton John, Gladys Knight and Stevie Wonder, and became a number 1 in both the US R&B and pop charts. Duets with Jeffrey Osborne, Kashif and Howard Hewitt, of Shalamar, maintained this newly-rediscovered profile in the 80s.

●ALBUMS: *Presenting Dionne Warwick* (Scepter 1963)★★★, *Anyone Who Had A Heart* (1964)★★★★, *Make Way For Dionne Warwick* (Scepter 1964)★★★★, *The Sensitive Sound Of Dionne Warwick* (Scepter 1965)★★★★, *Here I Am* (Scepter 1966)★★★★, *Dionne Warwick In Paris* (Scepter 1966)★★★, *Here Where There Is Love* (Scepter 1967)★★★, *Dionne Warwick Onstage And In The Movies* (Scepter 1967)★★★, *The Windows Of The World* (Scepter 1968)★★★, *Dionne In The Valley Of The Dolls* (Scepter 1968)★★★★, *Magic Of Believing* (1968)★★★, *Promises Promises* (Scepter 1968)★★★★, *Soulful* (Scepter 1969)★★★, *Dionne Warwick's Greatest Motion Picture Hits* (Scepter 1969)★★★, *I'll Never Fall In Love Again* (Scepter 1970)★★★, *Very Dionne* (Scepter 1970)★★, *The Love Machine* (1971)★★★, *The Dionne Warwick Story - Live* (Scepter 1971)★★, *From Within* (Scepter 1972)★★, *Dionne* (Warners 1972)★★, *Just Being Myself* (Warners 1973)★★, *Then Came You* (Warners 1975)★★★, *Track Of The Cat* (Warners 1975)★★★, with Isaac Hayes *A Man And A Woman* (1977)★★★, *Only Love Can Break A Heart* (Musicor 1977)★★★, *Love At First Sight* (1979)★★, *Dionne* (Arista 1979)★★★★, *No Night So Long* (Arista 1980)★★, *Hot! Live And Otherwise* (Mobile Fidelity 1981)★★★, *Friends In Love* (Arista 1982)★★★, *Heartbreaker* (Arista 1982)★★★, *How Many Times Can We Say Goodbye* (Arista 1983)★★, *So Amazing* (1983)★★★, *Friends* (Arista 1985)★★★, *Finder Of Lost Loves* (Arista 1985)★★★, *Without Your Love* (Arista 1985)★★★, *Reservations For Two* (Arista 1988)★★★, *Dionne Warwick Sings Cole Porter* (Arista 1989)★★★, *Friends Can Be Lovers* (Arista 1993)★★★, *Aquarela Do Brazil* (Arista 1995).

●COMPILATIONS: *Dionne Warwick's Golden Hits, Part 1* (Scepter 1967)★★★★, *Dionne Warwick's Golden Hits, Part 2* (Scepter 1969)★★★★, *The Best Of Dionne Warwick* (1983)★★★★, *The Original Soul Of Dionne Warwick* (1987)★★★, *The Love Songs* (1989)★★★★, *Greatest Hits 1979-1990* (Arista 1989)★★★★, *The Essential Collection* (Global 1996)★★★★.

WASHINGTON, BABY

b. Justine Washington, 13 November 1940, Bamberg, South Carolina, USA. Washington's (aka Jeanette Washington) tremendously moving voice, earthy but sophisticated, perfectly epitomized uptown soul. Yet unlike her southern counterparts she has never experienced great crossover recognition, although once cited by Dusty Springfield as her all-time favourite singer. Washington was raised in Harlem, singing first in a vocal group, the Hearts, in 1956 and becoming a solo artist the following year. She built a career with 16 chart entries during a decade and a half, most of them during the 60s, recording in New York first for Donald Shaw's Neptune label and then for Juggy Murray's Sue label. She established herself as a major soul singer recording 'The Time' (US R&B Top 30) and 'The Bells' (US R&B Top 20), both in 1959, and 'Nobody Cares' (US R&B Top 20) in 1961. Moving to Sue Records in 1962, Washington hit the US national Top 40 with the sublime 'That's How Heartaches Are Made' (1963) and the US R&B Top 10 with 'Only Those In Love' (1965). Washington revived her career in the early 70s, recording in Philadelphia a duet with Don Gardner, a revival of the Marvelettes' 'Forever', (number 30 R&B), a solo release 'I've Got To Break Away' (number 73 R&B), and a well-received album. The coming of disco in the mid-70s effectively killed her career, as it did those of many soul artists.

●ALBUMS: *That's How Heartaches Are Made* (Sue 1963)★★★★, *Only Those In Love* (Sue 1965)★★★, *With You In Mind* (Veep 1968)★★, with Don Gardner *Lay A Little Lovin' On Me* (1973)★★★, *I Wanna Dance* (1978)★★★.

●COMPILATIONS: *Great Oldies* (70s)★★★, *The One And Only* (1971)★★★, *The Best Of Baby Washington* (1987)★★★, *Only Those In Love* (1988)★★★, *That's How Heartaches Are Made* (c.1989)★★★, *Only Those In Love* (c.1989)★★★, *The Best Of ...* (1989)★★★, *The Sue Singles* (Kent 1996)★★★★.

WASHINGTON, GENO (AND THE RAM JAM BAND)

Born in Indiana, USA, Washington was in the US Air Force, stationed in East Anglia, England, when he initiated his singing career by climbing onstage to join a local band for an impromptu performance. On leaving the services, he remained in Britain and headed for London where he fronted the Ram Jam Band which comprised Pete Gage (guitar), Lionel Kingham (tenor saxophone), Buddy Beadle (baritone saxophone), Jeff Wright (organ), John Roberts (bass) and Herb Prestige (drums). The group adopted a fast-paced, almost frantic style which pitched one soul favourite after another, deliberately leaving the audience with little time to breathe, or to question the ensemble's lack of subtlety. Although none of Washington's singles reached the UK Top 30, his fervent in-concert popularity ensured that the first two albums charted, both reaching the UK Top 10. The formula was repeated on later collections, but by 1968 the mixture was growing ever more anachronistic as progressions elsewhere in music left the Ram Jam Band behind. Peter Gage went on to join Vinegar Joe. They disbanded by the end of the decade and Geno's several comebacks notwithstanding, the group remained fixed to a particular mid-60s era. Although immortalized in the 1980 UK number 1 hit, 'Geno' by Dexys Midnight Runners, Washington was more of a footnote than innovator. He continues to record sporadically, and performs the occasional London club date and tour. Part of his current act incorporates, with audience participation, Washington's musical talents with hypnotism. In the mid-90s he had seemingly reinvented himself as a blues singer.

●ALBUMS: with the Ram Jam Band *Hand Clappin' - Foot Stompin' - Funky Butt - Live!* (Piccadilly 1966)★★★, *Hipsters, Flipsters, Finger Poppin' Daddies* (Piccadilly 1967)★★, *Shake A Tail Feather* (Piccadilly 1968)★★, *Running Wild - Live* (Pye 1969)★★, *Up Tight* (1969)★★. Solo: Geno Washington *Geno's Back* (1976)★★, *Live* (1976)★★, *That's Why Hollywood Loves Me* (1979)★★, *Put Out The Cat* (1981)★★, *Live Sideways* (1986★★, *Take That Job And Stuff It* (1987)★★, *Loose Lips* (Uncensored 1995)★★.

WATSON, JOHNNY 'GUITAR'

b. 3 February 1935, Houston, Texas, USA, d. 17 May 1996, Yokohama, Japan. Before Watson made a name for himself in the 70s playing funk R&B, he had a long career going back to the early 50s. Watson's father played piano, which also became Watson's first instrument. On seeing Clarence 'Gatemouth' Brown perform, he convinced himself that he had to play guitar. He inherited a guitar from his grandfather, a sanctified preacher, on the condition that he did not play the blues on it - 'that was the first thing I played', Watson later said. In the early 50s his family moved to Los Angeles, where he started playing piano in the Chuck Higgins band and was billed as 'Young John Watson'. Switching to guitar, he was signed to Federal and recorded 'Space Guitar', an instrumental way ahead of its time in the use of reverberation and feedback. He also played 'Motorhead Baby' with an enthusiasm that was to become his trademark. He recorded the same track for Federal with the Amos Milburn band in tow. Watson became in demand as a guitarist and in the late 50s toured and recorded with the Olympics, Don And Dewey and Little Richard. Johnny 'Guitar' Watson was from the same mould of flamboyance that motivated another of Little Richard's guitarists: Jimi Hendrix. Watson later stated: 'I used to play the guitar standing on my hands, I had a 150 foot cord and I could get on top of the auditorium - those things Jimi Hendrix was doing, I *started* that shit!'.

Moving to the Modern label in 1955, he had immediate success with a bluesy ballad, 'Those Lonely, Lonely Nights' (US R&B Top 10), but failed to follow up on the label. In 1957 the novelty tune 'Gangster Of Love' (later adopted by Steve Miller) gave him a minor hit on the west coast. A partnership with Larry Williams was particularly successful and in 1965 they toured England and

recorded an album for Decca. Watson did not return to the charts until 1962, when on the King label he hit with 'Cuttin' In' (US R&B number 6), which was recorded with strings accompaniment. The following year he recorded *I Cried For You*, a 'cocktail-lounge' album with hip renditions of 'Polkadots And Moonbeams' and 'Witchcraft'. The Beatles invasion signified hard times for the inventors of rock 'n roll. Watson cut two soulful funk albums for the Fantasy label (*Listen* and *I Don't Want To Be Alone, Stranger*) with keyboardist Andre Lewis (who later toured with Frank Zappa). As if to repay his enthusiasm for Watson's guitar playing, of which Zappa had often said was among his favourite, Watson was recruited for Zappa's *One Size Fits All* in 1975. In 1976 Watson released *Ain't That A Bitch* on DJM Records, a brilliant marriage of 50s rockin' R&B, Hollywood schmaltz and futuristic funk. Watson produced, played bass, keyboards and drums. It went gold, and a further six albums appeared on DJM to the same formula. In 1981 he quit the label for A&M, but the production diluted Watson's unique sound and the record was a failure. One positive side-effect was a characteristic solo on Herb Alpert's *Beyond*. Watson retired to lick his wounds, emerging with *Strike On Computers* at the end of the 80s and an appearance at London's Town & Country Club in 1987.

●ALBUMS: *Gangster Of Love* (King 1958)★★★★, *Johnny Guitar Watson* (King 1963)★★★, *The Blues Soul Of Johnny Guitar Watson* (Chess 1964)★★★★, *Bad* (Chess 1966)★★★★, with Larry Williams *Two For The Price Of One* (1967)★★★★, *Johnny Watson Plays Fats Waller In The Fats Bag* (OKeh 1968)★★★, *Listen* (Fantasy 1974)★★★, *I Don't Want To Be Alone, Stranger* (Fantasy 1975)★★★, *Captured Live* (1976)★★★, *Ain't That A Bitch* (DJM 1976)★★★, *A Real Mother For Ya* (DJM 1977)★★, *Funk Beyond The Call Of Duty* (DJM 1977)★★, *Gangster Of Love* (1977)★★★, with the Watsonian Institute *Master Funk* (1978)★★, *Giant* (DJM 1978)★★, with Papa John Creach *Inphasion* (1978)★★, with the Watsonian Institute *Extra Disco Perception* (1979)★★, *Whut The Hell Is This?* (DJM 1979)★★, *Love Jones* (DJM 1980)★★, *Johnny 'Guitar' Watson And The Family Clone* (DJM 1981)★★, *That's What Time It Is* (A&M 1981)★★, *Strike On Computers* (Valley Vue 1984)★★, *Bow Wow* (M-Head 1996)★★.

●COMPILATIONS: *I Heard That!* (Chess 1985)★★★★, *Hit The Highway* (Ace 1985)★★★★, *Gettin' Down With Johnny 'Guitar' Watson* (Chess 1987)★★★, *Three Hours Past Midnight* (Flair 1991)★★★, *Gangster Of Love* (Charly 1991)★★★★★, *Listen/I Don't Want To Be Alone, Stranger* (1992)★★★, *Bow Wow* (Wilma/Bellmark 1994)★★★, *Gangster Of Love: The Best Of Johnny 'Guitar' Watson* (Castle 1995)★★★★, *Hot Just Like TNT* (Ace 1996)★★★★.

WATTS 103RD STREET RHYTHM BAND

Originally conceived as an instrumental group, Bernard Blackman (guitar), Raymond Jackson (trombone), John

Rayford (b. 1943; tenor saxophone), Melvin Dunlap (bass) and James Gadson (drums), were still known by their former name, the Soul Runners, when a 1967 release, 'Grits And Cornbread', reached the US R&B Top 30. Having changed their name in deference to the Watts district of Los Angeles, they enjoyed further success with 'Spreadin Honey' the same year. The group also backed comedian Bill Cosby, whose influence helped secure a deal with Warner Brothers Records. The new signings then acquired a featured vocalist, Charles Wright (b. 1942, Clarkdale, Mississippi, USA), and following two 1969 singles, 'Do Your Thing' and 'Till You Get Enough', the band's name was changed to Charles Wright And The Watts 103rd Street Band. Subsequent singles 'Express Yourself' (1970) and 'Your Love (Means Everything To Me)' (1971) both reached the soul Top 10, but their unstable personnel constantly undermined the group's potential. Wright later left the group for a solo career.

●ALBUMS: *Cornbread And Grits* (1967)★★★, *Together* (Warners1968)★★, *In The Jungle, Babe* (Warners 1969)★★, *Express Yourself* (Warners 1970)★★★, *You're So Beautiful* (1971)★★.

WEEDON, BERT

b. 10 May 1920, London, England. Weedon may be one of the most omnipotent of British electric guitarists, given that fretboard heroes including Jeff Beck and George Harrison, began by positioning as yet uncalloused fingers on taut strings while poring over exercises prescribed in Weedon's best-selling *Play In A Day* and *Play Every Day* manuals. This self-taught guitarist started learning flamenco guitar at the age of 12 before playing in London dance bands. During World War II, he strummed chords in the touring groups of Django Reinhardt and Stéphane Grappelli. With such prestigious experience, he became the featured soloist with Mantovani, Ted Heath and, by the early 50s, Cyril Stapleton's BBC Show Band.

By 1956, he was leading his own quartet and had released a debut single, 'Stranger Than Fiction', but only his theme to television's *$64,000 Question* sold even moderately before 1959. That year, his cover of the Virtues' 'Guitar Boogie Shuffle' made the UK Top 10. Subsequent hit parade entries, however, proved less lucrative than countless record dates for bigger stars. Although he accompanied visiting Americans such as Frank Sinatra, Rosemary Clooney and Nat 'King' Cole - later, the subject of a Weedon tribute album - his bread-and-butter was sessions for domestic artists from Dickie Valentine and Alma Cogan to the new breed of Elvis Presley-inspired teen-idols - Tommy Steele, Cliff Richard, Billy Fury *et al*. Steele won music press popularity polls as Best Guitarist, but the accolade belonged morally to his middle-aged hireling.

In the early 60s, Weedon's singles hovered around the lower middle of the Top 40. The most notable of these was 1960's 'Apache' which was eclipsed by the Shadows' version. Although the group was dismissive of his 'Apache', they acknowledged an artistic debt to Weedon by penning 'Mr. Guitar', his last singles chart entry to

date. Nevertheless, he remained in the public eye through a residency on the ITV children's series *Five O' Clock Club* - as well as a remarkable 1964 spot on *Sunday Night At The London Palladium*, on which he showed that he could rock out on his Hofner 'cutaway' as well as anyone. Indeed, it was as a rock 'n' roller that Weedon succeeded seven years later - with *Rockin' At The Roundhouse*, a budget-price album much at odds with the easy listening efforts that sustained him during the 70s. A renewal of interest in guitar instrumentals suddenly placed him at the top of the album chart in 1976 with *22 Golden Guitar Greats*. Nothing since has been as successful - and 1977's *Blue Echoes* was criticized severely in the journal *Guitar*, but - hit or miss - Bert Weedon, ever the professional, continued to record production-line albums throughout his sixth decade. In 1991, Weedon made history by becoming the first instrumentalist to be elected King Rat, the top post in the best known show business charity organization, the Grand Order of Water Rats.

●ALBUMS: *King Size Guitar* (Top Rank 1960)★★★, *Honky Tonk Guitar* (Top Rank 1961)★★★, *The Romantic Guitar Of Bert Weedon* (Fontana 1970)★★★, *Rockin At The Roundhouse* (Fontana 1971)★★★, *Sweet Sounds* (Contour 1971)★★★, *Bert Weedon Remembers Jim Reeves* (Contour 1973)★★, *The Gentle Guitar Of Bert Weedon* (Contour 1975)★★, *Bert Weedon Remembers Nat 'King' Cole* (Contour 1975)★★, *22 Golden Guitar Greats* (Warwick 1976)★★★, *Let The Good Times Roll* (Warwick 1977)★★★, *Blue Echoes* (Polydor 1977)★★★, *Honky Tonk Guitar Party* (EMI 1977)★★★, *16 Country Guitar Greats* (Polydor 1978)★★★, *40 Guitar Greats* (Pickwick 1979)★★★, *Heart Strings* (Celebrity 1980)★★★, *Dancing Guitars* (1982)★★★, *Guitar Favourites* (Ditto 1983)★★★, *Love Letters* (Everest 1983)★★★, *Mr Guitar* (MFP 1984)★★★, *An Hour Of Bert Weedon* (EMI 1987)★★★, *Once More With Feeling* (Pickwick 1988)★★★.

●COMPILATIONS: *Guitar Gold - 20 Greatest Hits* (Pickwick 1978)★★★.

WELLS, MARY

b. 13 May 1943, Detroit, Michigan, USA, d. 26 July 1992. At the age of 17, Mary Wells composed 'Bye Bye Baby', a song which she offered to R&B star Jackie Wilson. His producer, Berry Gordy, was sufficiently impressed to offer her a contract with the newly formed Motown label, and Wells' rendition of her song became one of the company's first Top 50 hits in 1960. Gordy entrusted her career to Smokey Robinson, who masterminded all her subsequent Motown releases. Robinson composed a remarkable series of clever, witty soul songs, full of puns and unexpected twists, and set to irresistible melody lines. Wells responded with the fluency of the natural vocalist and the results were Motown's most mature and adventurous records of the early 60s. 'The One Who Really Loves You' set the pattern as a Top 10 hit in 1962, while 'You Beat Me To The Punch' and 'Two Lovers' matched that success and offered two of Robinson's more subtle lyrics. 'What's Easy For Two Is So Hard For One' was Wells' answer to the predominant New York girl-group sound, and another Top 30 hit in 1964. The pinnacle of the Robinson/Wells partnership, however, was 'My Guy', a US number 1 and UK Top 5 in 1964. Sophisticated and assured it marked out Wells as America's most promising soul vocalist. At the same time, Berry Gordy encouraged her to record an album of duets with Motown's top male star, Marvin Gaye, from which 'Once Upon A Time' was pulled as another major hit single. Just as Well's career reached its peak, she chose to leave Motown, tempted by an offer from 20th Century Fox that included the promise of film work. Without the guidance of Smokey Robinson, she was unable to capture her hit form, and she left the label the following year. In 1966, she married Cecil Womack of the Valentinos, and moved to Atco Records, where she had three minor hits with 'Dear Lover', 'Such A Sweet Thing' and 'The Doctor'. That marked the end of her chart career: subsequent sessions for a variety of US labels proved less than successful, and after a long period without a contract she was reduced to re-recording her Motown hits for Allegiance in the early 80s. Despite being diagnosed as having throat cancer she continued touring during the late 80s. Wells signed to Ian Levine's Motor City label in 1987 and released *Keeping My Mind On Love* in 1990. She lost her battle against her illness on 26 July 1992.

●ALBUMS: *Bye Bye Baby, I Don't Want To Take A Chance* (Motown 1961)★★★, *The One Who Really Loves You* (Motown 1962)★★★, *Two Lovers And Other Great Hits* (Motown 1963)★★★, *Recorded Live On Stage* (Motown 1963)★★★, *Second Time Around* (Motown 1963)★★★, with Marvin Gaye *Together* (Motown 1964)★★★, *Mary Wells Sings My Guy* (Motown 1964)★★★, *Mary Wells* (20th Century 1965)★★★, *Mary Wells Sings Love Songs To The Beatles* (20th Century 1965)★★★, *Vintage Stock* (Motown 1966)★★★, *The Two Sides Of Mary Wells* (Atco 1966)★★★, *Ooh!* (Movietone 1966)★★★, *Servin' Up Some Soul* (Jubilee 1968)★★, *In And Out Of Love* (1981)★★, *Keeping My Mind On Love* (1990)★★.
●COMPILATIONS: *Greatest Hits* (Motown 1964)★★★, *The Old, New And Best Of Mary Wells* (1984)★★★, *The Best Of* (1993)★★★, *Compact Command Performances* (early 90s)★★★, *The Complete Jubilee Sessions* (Sequel 1993)★★★, *Ain't It The Truth: The Best Of 1964-82* (c.1993)★★★, *Looking Back 1961-64* (c.1993)★★★, *My Guy* (1994)★★★, *Dear Lover - the Atco Years* (1994)★★★, *Early Classics* (Spectrum 1996)★★★, *Never, Never Leave Me: The 20th Century Sides* (Ichiban 1997)★★★.
●FILMS: *Catalina Caper* (1967).

WEST COAST POP ART EXPERIMENTAL BAND

This perplexing and inscrutable group made its recording debut in 1966 when Michael Lloyd (vocals/guitar),

Dennis Lambert (rhythm guitar), Shaun Harris (bass), Bob Markley (tambourine/bongos) and Danny Belsky (drums) completed a rudimentary album of contemporary hits and original compositions. Despite their comparative youth, Lloyd, Harris and Markley had already pursued careers in music. Their new venture was quickly accepted into the emergent Los Angeles 'underground' rock scene and despite a paucity of concert appearances during their later incarnation, the early group were a popular live attraction. Lambert and Belsky were replaced by Danny Harris (guitar) and John Ware (drums) before the band began work on their first album for a major company. *Part 1* offered a similarly styled mixture to that of its predecessor, although the cover versions, of Frank Zappa ('Help, I'm A Rock'), P.F. Sloan ('Here's Where You Belong') and Van Dyke Parks ('High Coin'), were far more daring. By *Volume 2* the group had been reduced to a trio of Markley and the Harris brothers, a line-up sustained until the band's demise. The former tambourine player was now firmly in command, taking most of the vocals and writing almost all of the material. The trio reached a creative peak with *A Child's Guide To Good And Evil*, which offered an enthralling patchwork of material ranging from sumptuous harmony pop ('Eighteen Is Over The Hill') to off-the-wall eccentricity ('Our Drummer Always Plays In The Nude'). The West Coast Pop Art Experimental Band was dissolved following the release of *Where's My Daddy?* but the same trio participated on Markley's solo album, *A Group*. Also present was the prodigal Lloyd who had established himself as a leading pop entrepreneur, producing and writing for a variety of different groups.
●ALBUMS: *The West Coast Pop Art Experimental Band* (Fifo 1966)★★, *The West Coast Pop Art Experimental Band - Part 1* (Reprise 1967)★★, *Breaking Through ... The West Coast Pop Art Experimental Band (Volume 2)* (Reprise 1967)★★, *A Child's Guide To Good And Evil* (Reprise 1968)★★★, *Where's My Daddy?* (Amos 1969)★★.

WEST, KEITH

b. Keith Hopkins, 6 December 1943, Dagenham, Essex, England. Lead vocalist with the In Crowd and Tomorrow, West embarked on a concurrent solo career while still a member of the latter group. His debut single written with Mark Wirtz, 'Excerpt From A Teenage Opera (Grocer Jack)', was a UK Top 10 hit in 1967, but when 'Sam', another song from the same project, failed to emulate its predecessor, West withdrew from further involvement. Tomorrow broke up in 1968 and West temporarily abandoned performing when 'On A Saturday' failed to chart. He resumed recording in 1973 with two low-key singles, before founding Moonrider with ex-Animals guitarist John Weider. In the 90s West can fondly hark back to the ambitions of record producer Wirtz and the potentially endless stream of material for various Teenage Operas. West is now a director of Burns Guitars.
●ALBUMS: with Mark Wirtz *A Teenage Opera* (RPM 1996)★★.

WESTON, KIM

b. Agatha Natalie Weston, 20 December 1939, Detroit, Michigan, USA. Kim Weston received her musical education with the Wright Specials gospel group, an influence that survived throughout her subsequent career. Torn between pursuing music or acting, she was persuaded to join the Motown label in the early 60s by Johnny Thornton, the cousin of two of the label's top producers, Eddie and Brian Holland. After a minor hit with 'Love Me All The Way' in 1963, Weston joined Marvin Gaye's soul revue, forming a partnership that was captured on record in 1964 and again in 1967. In the interim, Weston was produced by Holland/Dozier/Holland on a series of classic dance records that highlighted her versatile, gospel-tinged vocals. 'Take Me In Your Arms' was a substantial soul hit in 1965, followed the next year by the equally fluent 'Helpless'. In 1967, she and Gaye recorded 'It Takes Two', one of the finest of Motown's love duets. That same year, Weston married Motown producer Mickey Stevenson, who encouraged her to join him in a new venture at MGM Records. The move proved a commercial disappointment, and later releases on People and Pride failed to restore Weston to the charts. In the 70s, she devoted much time to community projects and art groups, besides finding time to record an album of jazz standards with the Hastings Street Jazz Experience. More recently, she was one of several Motown artists to re-record her hits on Ian Levine's Nightmare label. In 1987 she became the first ex-Motown artist to work with producer Ian Levine, who proceeded to sign virtually every Motown act during the next three years. Weston teamed up with Marvin Gaye's brother Frankie for a remake of 'It Takes Two' in 1989. She has so far released two new albums which mix new material with fresh versions of 60s Motown hits.
●ALBUMS: with Marvin Gaye *Take Two* (1966)★★★, *For The First Time* (MGM 1967)★★★, *This Is America* (MGM 1968)★★★, *Kim Kim Kim* (Volt 1970)★★, *Investigate* (1990)★★, *Talking Loud* (1992)★★.
●COMPILATIONS: *Greatest Hits And Rare Classics* (1991)★★★, *The Very Best* (Essential Gold 1996)★★★.

WEXLER, JERRY

b. 10 January 1917, New York City, USA. A high school graduate at age 15, Wexler completed a degree in journalism following his spell in the US Army. Having initially worked at BMI, writing biographies of contemporary stars, he joined the staff of *Billboard* magazine, but left, having refused to compile a dossier on the Weavers during the height of the McCarthy era. In 1952 Wexler was invited to run the publishing arm of Atlantic Records, but demurred, only joining the company as a partner and shareholder the following year when an opportunity in record promotion arose. He entered production with LaVern Baker's 'Soul On Fire', which he co-wrote with Ertegun and Jesse Stone. Weeks later he produced the Drifters' single, 'Money Honey', one of the biggest R&B hits of 1953, and was instrumental in insisting on the high quality which marked Atlantic's subsequent releases, notably those of Ray Charles. This was reinforced by Herb Abramson and Ahmet Ertegun. The following decade he produced several hits for Solomon Burke and became a pivotal figure in the company's distribution and recording deal with Stax Records. The arrangement breathed new life into Atlantic, giving it access to southern soul artists and musicians. Wexler brought Aretha Franklin to the label, and their collaborations, including 'I Never Loved A Man (The Way I Love You)' and 'Respect', resulted in some of the era's finest recordings which in turn won him industry awards as best producer in 1967 and 1968. He retained an interest in 'roots' music through work with Delaney And Bonnie, Dr. John and Jesse Davis. However, Wexler gradually distanced his commitment to Atlantic following its absorption into the WEA Records group and resigned in 1975. He undertook 'outside' production, notably with Bob Dylan (*Slow Train Coming*) and Dire Straits (*Communique*), and remains one of the most respected professionals of post-war music.
●FURTHER READING: *Rhythm And The Blues: A Life In American Music*, Jerry Wexler with David Ritz. *Making Tracks*, Charlie Gillett.

WHO

Formed in Shepherd's Bush, London, in 1964, the Who evolved out of local youth club band the Detours. Pete Townshend (b. 19 May 1945, Chiswick, London, England; guitar/vocals), Roger Daltrey (b. 1 March 1944, Hammersmith, London, England; vocals) and John Entwistle (b. John Alec Entwistle, 9 October 1944, Chiswick, London, England; bass) founded this attraction, and having jettisoned Colin Dawson (vocals) and Doug Sanden (drums), recruited Keith Moon (b. 23 August 1947, Wembley, London, England, d. 7 September 1978) as a replacement for the latter in a unit now bearing their more dynamic appellation. The restructured quartet was adopted by manager/publicist Peter Meadon, who changed the group's name to the High Numbers, dressed them in stylish clothes and determinedly courted a mod audience. Their sole single, 'I'm The Face', proclaimed this allegiance although Meadon shamelessly purloined its melody from Slim Harpo's 'Got Love If You Want It'. Two budding film directors, Kit Lambert and Chris Stamp, then assumed management responsibilities and having reverted to their Who sobriquet, the group assiduously began courting controversial publicity.
Townshend's guitar pyrotechnics were especially noteworthy; the instrument was used as an object of rage as he smashed it against floors and amplifiers in simulation of painter Gustav Metzke's auto-destructive art, although the origins of the act derived from when Townshend accidentally broke the neck of his guitar in a low-ceilinged club to the perverse delight of the crowd. Their in-person violence matched an anti-social attitude and despite a highly successful residency at the famed Marquee club, the Who were shunned by major labels. They eventually secured a deal through Shel Talmy, an independent pro-

ducer who placed the group with American Decca. Their recordings were then sub-contracted through UK subsidiary, Brunswick, a perilous arrangement bearing later repercussions. 'I Can't Explain', released in January 1965, rose to the UK Top 10 on the strength of appearances on television's *Ready Steady Go* and *Top Of The Pops*, the latter transpiring when another act dropped out. Written by Townshend - already the group's established composer - but modelled on the Kinks, the song's formal nature surprised those expecting a more explosive performance. Such hopes were answered by the innovative 'Anyway, Anyhow, Anywhere' and 'My Generation', the latter of which encapsulated the frustrations of an amphetamine-charged adolescent, both in its stuttered intonation and smash-and-grab instrumental section. This pivotal release - one of the benchmarks of British 60s pop - served as the title track to the Who's debut album, the release of which was delayed to accommodate new Townshend originals at the expense of now *passé* cover versions. 'The Kids Are Alright' and 'Out In The Street' articulated a sense of cultural affinity and if the songwriter's attachment to the mod phenomenon was undoubtedly expedient, the cult held a lasting fascination for him.

However, despite artistic and commercial success, the Who wished to sever their punitive contract with Talmy. When he refused to renegotiate their terms of contract, the group simply refused to honour it, completing a fourth single, 'Substitute', for a new label and production company. The ensuing wrangle was settled out of court, but although the unit achieved their freedom, Talmy retained 5% royalty rights on all recordings made until the end of the decade. The Who continued to enjoy chart success, adeptly switching subject matter from a parochial clique to eccentric characterizations involving transvestism ('I'm A Boy') and masturbation ('Pictures Of Lily'). Townshend's decidedly English perceptions initially precluded a sustained international success. *A Quick One* and *The Who Sell Out*, the latter of which was, in part, programmed as a homage to pirate radio, thus proved more acceptable to the UK audience. The Who's popularity in the USA flourished only in the wake of their appearance at the 1967 Monterey Pop Festival.

They returned to the UK Top 10 in the winter of 1967 with the powerful 'I Can See For Miles'. Despite their strength as singles artists, however, the group failed to achieve a number 1 hit on either side of the Atlantic. The group embraced the album market fully with *Tommy*, an extravagant rock opera which became a staple part of their increasingly in-demand live appearances. The set spawned a major hit in 'Pinball Wizard' but, more crucially, established the group as a serious act courting critical respectability. *Tommy* was later the subject of a film, directed by the suitably eccentric Ken Russell, as well as an orchestral interpretation, recorded under the aegis of impresario Lou Reizner. This over-exposure undermined the power of the original, and fixed a musical albatross around its creator's neck. The propulsive *Live At Leeds* was a sturdy concert souvenir (regarded by many

as one the best live albums ever recorded), while Townshend created his next project, *Lighthouse*, but this ambitious work was later aborted, with several of its songs incorporated into *Who's Next*. Here the Who asserted their position as one of rock's leading attractions by producing an album that contained 'Baba O'Reilly' and 'Won't Get Fooled Again', two songs destined to form an integral part of the group's 70s lexicon. The latter reached the UK Top 10 and was the prelude to a series of specifically created singles - 'Let's See Action' (1971), 'Join Together' (1972), 'Relay' (1973) - which marked time as Townshend completed work on *Quadrophenia*. This complex concept album was a homage to the mod subculture which provided the artist with his first inspiration. Although compared unfavourably with *Tommy*, the set's plot and musical content - while stylistically the antithesis of the group's early outburst - has shown a greater longevity and was the subject of a commercially successful film, featuring future stars Toyah and Sting. Commitments to solo careers undermined the parent unit's progress and *The Who By Numbers*, although a relevant study of the ageing rock star, was deemed low-key in comparison with earlier efforts. Another hiatus ensued, during which the ever self-critical Townshend reassessed his progress in the light of punk.

The quartet re-emerged with the confident *Who Are You*, but its release was sadly overshadowed when, on 23 August 1978, Keith Moon died following an overdose of medication taken to alleviate alcohol addiction. His madcap behaviour and idiosyncratic, exciting drumming had been an integral part of the Who fabric and rumours of a permanent split abounded. A retrospective film, *The Kids Are Alright*, enhanced a sense of finality, but the group resumed recording in 1979 having added former Small Faces/Faces drummer Kenny Jones (b. 16 September 1948, Stepney, London, England) to the line-up. However, any newfound optimism was undermined that year when 11 fans were killed prior to a concert at the Cincinnati Riverfront Colosseum in Ohio during a rush to secure prime vantage points, and neither *Face Dances* nor *It's Hard* recaptured previous artistic heights, although the former contained the fiery 'You Better You Bet', which restored them to the UK Top 10. A farewell tour was undertaken in 1982-83 and although the group did reunite for an appearance at Live Aid, they remained estranged until the end of the decade. Townshend's reluctance to tour - he now suffered from tinnitus - and his much-publicized period of heroin addiction, were major stumbling blocks, but in 1989 he agreed to undertake a series of US dates to celebrate the group's 25th anniversary (with Simon Phillips; drums). Townshend, Daltrey and Entwistle were augmented by a large ensemble of supporting musicians for a set indebted to nostalgia, which culminated in Hollywood with an all-star gala rendition of *Tommy*. As such, the tour confirmed the guitarist's fears - a request to include material from his concurrent solo album *The Iron Man* was vetoed. His desire to progress and challenge preconceptions has marked the very best of the Who's extensive and timeless catalogue. In 1993, over 25 years after its original release as an album, a production of *Tommy*, retitled *The Who's Tommy*, was staged on Broadway, and won five Tony Awards. The Who's star continued to rise in 1994 with the sympathetically packaged *30 Years Of Maximum R&B* CD box set, and was maintained with the reissued *Live At Leeds* with many extra tracks added from that memorable gig. The recording recalls a period that showed Townshend's playing at its most fluid and Daltrey's vocals strong and effortless. Further reissues in 1995 included *The Who Sell Out*, *Who's Next* and *A Quick One*. Both are expertly remastered and contain many extra tracks, including the legendary *Ready Steady Who* EP. From these albums it is clear from where bands such as Dodgy, Blur, Afghan Whigs and Swervedriver derive their 'Cockney' rock. In June 1996 the band performed at London's Hyde Park performing *Quadrophenia* in front of 200,000 people. Further performances were given in the USA and the UK later that year. The drummer for this latest re-formation was Zak Starkey, son of the famous Beatle. Released three decades too late for most Who fans, the *Live At The Isle Of Wight* set demonstrates (as did *Live At Leeds*) what an astonishing live band they were. The quality of the Isle Of Wight concert recording is remarkably good, and is a welcome windfall to their (still) considerable following. Unquestionably one of the finest groups of our generation, they continue to be one of the most influential.

●ALBUMS: *My Generation* (Brunswick 1965)★★★★, *The Who Sings My Generation* (Decca 1966), *A Quick One* (Reaction 1966)★★★★, *The Who Sell Out* (Track 1967)★★★★, *Happy Jack* (Decca 1967)★★★, *Magic Bus-The Who On Tour* (Decca 1968)★★★, *Tommy* (Track 1969)★★★★, *Live At Leeds* (Track 1970)★★★★★, *Who's Next* (Track 1971)★★★★★, *Quadrophenia* (MCA 1973)★★★★, *The Who By Numbers* (Polydor 1975)★★★, *Who Are You* (Polydor 1978)★★, *The Kids Are Alright* soundtrack (Polydor 1979)★★★, *Face Dances* (Polydor 1981)★★, *It's Hard* (Polydor 1982)★★, *Join Together* (Virgin 1990)★★★, *Live At The Isle Of Wight Festival 1970* (Essential 1996)★★★★.

●COMPILATIONS: *Magic Bus* (1967)★★★, *Direct Hits* (1968)★★★, *Meaty Beaty Big And Bouncy* (Polydor 1971)★★★★★, *Odds And Sods* (Track 1974)★★★, *The Story Of The Who* (Polydor 1976)★★★, *Hooligans* (MCA 1981)★★★, *Rarities Volume 1 (1966-1968)* (Polydor 1983)★★★, *Rarities Volume 2 (1970-1973)* (Polydor 1983)★★★, *Once Upon A Time* (Polydor 1983)★★★, *The Singles* (Polydor 1984)★★★, *Who's Last* (MCA 1984)★★, *Who's Missing* (MCA 1985)★★, *Who's Better Who's Best* (Polydor 1988)★★★★, *The Who Collection* (Stylus 1988)★★★, *30 Years Of Maximum R&B* 4-CD box set (Polydor 1994)★★★★★, *My Generation: The Very Best Of ...* (Polydor 1996)★★★★★.

●VIDEOS: *The Kids Are Alright* (1990), *Thirty Years Of Maximum R&B Live* (Polygram 1994), *The Who Live At The Isle Of Wight Festival 1970* (Warner Music Vision 1996), *Live, Featuring The Rock Opera Tommy* (SMV Enterprises 1996).

●FURTHER READING: *The Who*, Gary Herman. *The Who*, Jeff Stein and Chris Johnston. *The Who ... Through The Eyes Of Pete Townshend*, Conner McKnight and Caroline Silver. *The Who*, George Tremlett. *The Who: Ten Great Years*, Cindy Ehrlich. *The Who Generation*, Nik Cohn. *A Decade Of The Who: An Authorized History In Music, Paintings, Words And Photo*, Steve Turner. *The Story Of Tommy*, Richard Barnes and Pete Townshend. *Whose Who? A Who Retrospective*, Brian Ashley and Steve Monnery. *Keith Moon: The Life And Death Of A Rock Legend*, Ivan Waterman. *The Who: Britain's Greatest Rock Group*, John Swenson. *The Who File*, Pearce Marchbank. *Quadrophenia*, Alan Fletcher. *The Who In Their Own Words*, Steve Clarke. *Mods!*, Richard Barnes. *The Who*, Paul Sahner and Thomas Veszelits. *The Who* , Giacomo Mazzone. *The Who: An Illustrated Discography*, Ed Hanel. *Moon The Loon: The Amazing Rock And Roll Life Of Keith Moon*, Dougal Butler with Chris Trengove and Peter Lawrence. *The Who: The Illustrated Biography*, Chris Charlesworth. *Full Moon: The Amazing Rock & Roll Life Of Keith Moon, Late Of The Who*, Dougal Butler. *The Who Maximum R & B: An Illustrated Biography*, Richard Barnes. *Before I Get Old: The Story Of The Who*, Dave Marsh. *The Who: The Farewell Tour*, Philip Kamin and Peter Goddard. *The Complete Guide To The Music Of ...*, Chris Charlesworth. *The Who In Sweden*, Ollie Lunden (ed.).

●FILMS: *Tommy* (1975), *Quadrophenia* (1979).

WILLIAMS, ANDY

b. Howard Andrew Williams, 3 December 1928, Wall Lake, Iowa, USA. Williams began his singing career in the local church choir with his three brothers. The quartet became popular on their own radio shows from Cincinnati, Des Moines and Chicago. They backed Bing Crosby on his Oscar-winning 'Swinging On A Star', from the 1944 movie *Going My Way*, and in the same year appeared in the minor musical film *Kansas City Kitty*. In the following year, Andy Williams dubbed Lauren Bacall's singing voice in her first film with Humphrey Bogart, *To Have And Have Not*. From 1947-48 the Williams Brothers worked with top pianist/singer Kay Thompson in nightclubs and on television. Williams went solo in 1952, and featured regularly on Steve Allen's *Tonight Show* for over two years. Signed to the Cadence label, Williams had his first success in 1956 with 'Canadian Sunset', which was followed by a string of Top 20 entries, including 'Butterfly' (number 1), 'I Like Your Kind Of Love' (a duet with Peggy Powers), 'Lips Of Wine', 'Are You Sincere?', 'Promise Me, Love', 'The Hawaiian Wedding Song', 'Lonely Street' and 'The Village Of St. Bernadette'. In 1961, Williams moved to Columbia Records, and had his first big hit for the label with the Doc Pomus/Mort Shuman composition, 'Can't Get Used To Losing You', which went to number 2 in the US charts in

1963. From then, until 1971 when the singles hits dried up, he was in the US Top 20 with 'Hopeless', 'A Fool Never Learns', and '(Where Do I Begin) Love Story'. Williams reached number 4 in the UK in 1973 with Neil Sedaka's 'Solitaire', but it was in the album charts that he found greater success.

By the early 70s it was estimated that he had received 13 worldwide gold disc awards for chart albums such as *Moon River & Other Great Movie Themes, Days Of Wine And Roses* (a US number 1), *The Wonderful World Of Andy Williams, Dear Heart, Born Free, Love Andy* (a UK number 1), *Honey, Happy Heart, Home Loving Man* (another UK number 1), and *Love Story*. The enormous sales were no doubt assisted by his extremely successful weekly variety showcase which ran from 1962-71, and won an Emmy for 'Best Variety Show'. It also gave the Osmond Brothers consistent nationwide exposure. In 1964, Williams made his film debut in *I'd Rather Be Rich*, which starred Maurice Chevalier, Robert Goulet, Sandra Dee, and Hermione Gingold. It was a remake of the 1941 comedy *It Started With Eve*, and Williams sang the Jerry Keller/Gloria Shayne number, 'Almost There', which just failed to reach the top of the UK chart in 1965. Despite the lack of consistent television exposure in the late 70s, Williams still sold a remarkable number of albums, particularly in the UK where his *Solitaire, The Way We Were*, and *Reflections*, all made the Top 10. In 1984, the album *Greatest Love Classics* featured Williams singing contemporary lyrics to classical themes, accompanied by the Royal Philharmonic Orchestra. In the early 90s, Williams became the first non-country entertainer to build his own theatre along Highway 76's music-theatre-strip in Branson, Missouri. The $8 million 2,000-seater Andy Williams Moon River Theatre is part of a complex which includes a 250-room hotel and restaurant. Williams headlines there himself, and remains one of America's most popular singers, renowned for his smooth vocal texture and relaxed approach. As a stylist, he is the equal of any popular singer from his era.

●ALBUMS. *Andy Williams Sings Steve Allen* (Cadence 1957)★★, *Andy Williams* (Cadence 1958)★★, *Sings Rogers And Hammerstein* (Cadence 1959)★★★, *Lonely Street* (Cadence 1959)★★★, *The Village Of St Bernadette* (Cadence 1960)★★, *Two Time Winners* (Cadence 1960)★★★, *To You Sweetheart Aloha* (Cadence 1960)★★, *Under Paris Skies* (Cadence 1961)★★★, *'Danny Boy' And Other Songs I Like To Sing* (Columbia 1962)★★★, *Moon River & Other Great Movie Themes* (Columbia 1962)★★★★, *Warm And Willing* (Columbia 1962)★★★, *Days Of Wine And Roses* (Columbia 1963)★★★★, *Million Seller Songs* (Cadence 1963)★★★, *The Andy Williams Christmas Album* (Columbia 1963)★★★, *The Wonderful World Of Andy Williams* (Columbia 1964)★★★, *The Academy Award Winning 'Call Me Irresponsible'* (Columbia 1964)★★★, *The Great Songs From 'My Fair Lady' And Other Broadway Hits* (Columbia 1964)★★★★, *Dear Heart* (Columbia 1965)★★★★,

Almost There (Columbia 1965)★★★★, *Can't Get Used To Losing You* (Columbia 1965)★★★★, *Hawaiian Wedding Song* (Columbia 1965)★★, *Canadian Sunset* (Columbia 1965)★★★, *Merry Christmas* (Columbia 1965)★★★, *The Shadow Of Your Smile* (Columbia 1966)★★★, *May Each Day* (Columbia 1966)★★★, *In The Arms Of Love* (Columbia 1967)★★★, *Born Free* (Columbia 1967)★★★★, *Love, Andy* (Columbia 1967)★★★★, *Honey* (Columbia 1968)★★★★, *Happy Heart* (Columbia 1969)★★★★, with the Osmonds *Get Together With Andy Williams* (Columbia 1969)★★, *Can't Help Falling In Love* (Columbia 1970)★★★★, *Raindrops Keep Falling On My Head* (Columbia 1970)★★★, *The Andy Williams' Show* (Columbia 1970)★★★, *Home Loving Man* (Columbia 1971)★★★★, *Love Story* (Columbia 1971)★★★, *You've Got A Friend* (Columbia 1971)★★★, *The Impossible Dream* (Columbia 1972)★★★★, *Love Theme From 'The Godfather'* (Columbia 1972)★★★, *A Song For You* (Columbia 1972)★★★, *Alone Again (Naturally)* (Columbia 1972)★★★, *The First Time Ever I Saw Your Face* (Columbia 1973)★★★, *Solitaire* (Columbia 1973)★★★, *You Lay Easy On My Mind* (Columbia 1974)★★★, *The Way We Were* (Columbia 1974)★★★, *An Evening With Andy Williams, Live In Japan* (1975)★★★, *The Other Side Of Me* (1975)★★★, *Showstoppers* (1977)★★★, *Let's Love While We Can* (1980)★★★, with the Royal Philharmonic Orchestra *Greatest Love Classics* (1984)★★★, *Close Enough For Love* (1986).

●COMPILATIONS: *Andy Williams' Best* (Cadence 1962)★★★, *Andy Williams' Newest Hits* (1966)★★★, *The Andy Williams Sound Of Music* (1969)★★★, *Andy Williams' Greatest Hits* (Columbia 1970)★★★, *Andy Williams' Greatest Hits, Volume Two* (Columbia 1973)★★★, *Reflections* (1978)★★★, *Great Songs Of The Seventies* (1979)★★★, *Great Songs Of The Sixties* (1980)★★★, *Portrait Of A Song Stylist* (1989)★★★, *16 Most Requested Songs* (1993)★★★, *The Best Of ...* (Columbia 1996).

WILLIAMS, MASON

b. 24 July 1936, Abilene, Texas, USA. This Oklahoma City University mathematics student was a self-taught guitarist who, after moonlighting in local venues, toured North America with the Wayfarers Trio before enlistment in the US Navy. On demobilization, he peddled topical tunes on the Los Angeles folk club circuit where he met the Limeliters' Glenn Yarbrough who introduced him to the Smothers Brothers. When this comedy duo began performing his compositions on their nationally broadcast television series, other acts - among them the Kingston Trio and Petula Clark - began recording his material. His most lucrative song was the 1968 novelty UK number 1 'Cinderella Rockefella', (with Nancy Ames) for Esther And Abi Ofarim. That year, he enjoyed a million-seller in his own right with the Grammy-winning 'Classical Gas', an orchestrated instrumental (from The Mason Williams Phonograph Record song cycle). A one-hit-wonder, he, nevertheless, protracted a prolific recording career into the 70s with accompaniment by such LA session colleagues as Hal Blaine, Ron Tutt, Milt Holland and Al Casey. He also achieved success as a poet, author, cabaret entertainer and concept artist with one of his exhibitions at Pasadena Arts Museum the subject of a feature in *Life* magazine. A reissue of 'Classical Gas' in 1978 met with further success.

●ALBUMS: *Them Poems And Things* (Vee Jay 1968)★★★, *The Mason Williams Phonograph Record* (1968)★★★, *The Mason Williams Ear Show* (1968)★★★, *Music By Mason Williams* (1969)★★★, *Hand Made* (1970)★★, *Improved* (1971)★★★.

WILLIAMS, MAURICE, AND THE ZODIACS

This R&B vocal group from Lancaster, South Carolina, USA, was led by Maurice Williams (pianist/songwriter). The hit record 'Stay', which went to number 3 R&B and number 1 pop in 1960, immortalized the Zodiacs as a one-hit-wonder group. (In the UK 'Stay' went to number 14 in 1961.) Williams, however, had a long history before and after the hit, forming his first group, the Gladiolas, in 1955. Besides Williams (b. 26 April 1938, Lancaster, South Carolina, USA), the group consisted of Earl Gainey (tenor), William Massey (tenor/baritone), Willie Jones (baritone), and Norman Wade (bass). Their one hit for the Nashville-based Excello label was 'Little Darlin'', which went to number 11 R&B and number 41 pop in 1957. The record was covered with greater success by the Canadian group, the Diamonds. In 1960 Williams formed the Zodiacs, consisting of Wiley Bennett (tenor), Henry Gaston (tenor), Charles Thomas (baritone), Albert Hill (double bass), and Little Willie Morrow (drums). After the unforgettable 'Stay' the group honoured themselves with many outstanding compositions, most notably 'I Remember' (number 86 pop in 1961), 'Come Along' (number 83 pop in 1961), and 'May I' (1966), but nothing close to a hit resulted. The latter song was re-recorded in 1969 by Bill Deal And The Rhondels who had a Top 40 national hit with it. The most frequently remade Williams song was 'Stay', which the Hollies in the UK (1963), the Four Seasons (1964), and Jackson Browne (1978) all placed on the charts. Its timeless lyric of teenage lust and angst has been passed through the decades: 'Well your mama don't mind, well your papa don't mind', leading to the punch line, 'Oh won't you stay, just a little bit longer'. During the 70s and 80s Williams sustained a career with a new group of Zodiacs playing their classic catalogueto the Beach Music club circuit in the Carolinas.

●ALBUMS: *Stay* (Herald 1961)★★★★, *At The Beach* (early 60s)★★★ *Maurice Williams And The Zodiacs* (1988)★★★.

●COMPILATIONS: *Best Of Maurice Williams & the Zodiacs* (1989)★★★★, *Little Darlin'* (1991)★★★, *Best Of Maurice Williams & The Zodiacs* (1991)★★★★.

WILSON, JACKIE

b. 9 June 1934, Detroit, Michigan, USA, d. 21 January 1984, New Jersey, USA. When parental pressure thwarted his boxing ambitions, Wilson took to singing in small local clubs. He sang with the Thrillers (a predecessor group to the Royals) and recorded some solo tracks for Dizzy Gillespie's Dee Gee label as Sonny Wilson, before replacing Clyde McPhatter in Billy Ward And The Dominoes. Wilson joined this notable group in 1953, but embarked on a solo career four years later with Brunswick Records. His first single for that label was the exuberant 'Reet Petite', a comparative failure in the USA where it crept to a lowly pop position and missed the R&B lists altogether. In the UK, however, it soared to number 6 thereby establishing Wilson in the minds of the British pop purchasing audience. 'Reet Petite' had been written by Berry Gordy and Tyran Carlo (Roquel 'Billy' Davis), who went on to compose several of Wilson's subsequent releases, including the hits 'Lonely Teardrops' (1958), 'That's Why (I Love You So)' (1959) and 'I'll Be Satisfied' (1959).

In 1960, Wilson enjoyed two R&B number 1 hits with 'Doggin' Around' and 'A Woman, A Lover, A Friend'. His musical direction then grew increasingly erratic, veering from mainstream to pseudo-opera. There were still obvious highlights such as 'Baby Workout' (1963), 'Squeeze Her Please Her' (1964), 'No Pity (In The Naked City)' (1965), but all too often his wonderfully fluid voice was wasted on cursory, quickly dated material. The artist's live appearances, however, remained both exciting and dramatic, capable of inspiring the ecstasy his sometimes facile recordings belied. Wilson's career was rejuvenated in 1966. Abandoning his New York recording base, he moved to Chicago where he worked with producer Carl Davis. Here, at last, was a more consistent empathy and 'Whispers (Gettin' Louder)' (1966), '(Your Love Keeps Lifting Me) Higher And Higher' (1967) and the sublime 'I Get The Sweetest Feeling' (1968), stand among his finest recordings. It did not last. 'This Love Is Real (I Can Feel Those Vibrations)' (1970) proved to be Wilson's last Top 10 R&B entry, by which time his work was influenced by trends rather than setting them. In September 1975, while touring with the Dick Clark revue, Wilson suffered a near fatal heart attack onstage at New Jersey's Latin Casino. He struck his head on falling and the resulting brain damage left him comatose. He remained hospitalized until his death on 21 January 1984. Wilson's career remains a puzzle; he never did join Berry Gordy's Motown empire, despite their early collaboration and friendship. Instead the singer's legacy was flawed; dazzling in places, disappointing in others. Immortalized in the Van Morrison song, 'Jackie Wilson Said', which was also a UK Top 5 hit for Dexys Midnight Runners in 1982, his name has remained in the public's eye. Fate left its final twist for in 1987, when an imaginative video (which some claimed belittled the singer's memory) using plasticine animation, propelled 'Reet Petite' to number 1 in the UK charts.

●ALBUMS: *He's So Fine* (Brunswick 1958)★★★,

Lonely Teardrops (Brunswick 1959)★★★, *Doggin' Around* (1959)★★★, *So Much* (Brunswick 1960)★★★, *Night* (1960)★★★, *Jackie Wilson Sings The Blues* (Brunswick 1960)★★★★, *A Woman A Lover A Friend* (Brunswick 1961)★★★★, *Try A Little Tenderness* (1961)★★★, *You Ain't Heard Nothing Yet* (Brunswick 1961)★★★, *By Special Request* (Brunswick 1961)★★★, *Body And Soul* (Brunswick 1962)★★★, *Jackie Wilson At The Copa* (Brunswick 1962)★★★, *Jackie Wilson Sings The World's Greatest Melodies* (Brunswick 1962)★★★, *Baby Workout* (Brunswick 1963)★★★★, *Merry Christmas* (Brunswick 1963)★★, with Linda Hopkins *Shake A Hand* (Brunswick 1963)★★, *Somethin' Else* (Brunswick 1964)★★★★, *Soul Time* (Brunswick 1965)★★★★, *Spotlight On Jackie Wilson* (Brunswick 1965)★★★, *Soul Galore* (Brunswick 1966)★★★, *Whispers* (Brunswick 1967)★★★, *Higher And Higher* (Brunswick 1967)★★★★, with Count Basie *Manufacturers Of Soul* (1968)★★★, with Basie *Too Much* (1968)★★★, *I Get The Sweetest Feeling* (1968)★★★★, *Do Your Thing* (1970)★★★, *This Love Is Real* (1970)★★★, *You Got Me Walking* (1971)★★, *Beautiful Day* (1973)★★, *Nowstalgia* (1974)★★, *Nobody But You* (1976)★★.

●COMPILATIONS: *My Golden Favourites* (Brunswick 1960)★★★, *My Golden Favourites - Volume 2* (Brunswick 1964)★★★, *Jackie Wilson's Greatest Hits* (1969)★★★, *It's All Part Of Love* (1969)★★★, *Jackie Wilson: S.R.O.* (1982)★★★, *Classic Jackie Wilson* (1984)★★★, *Reet Petite* (1985)★★★★, *The Soul Years* (1985)★★★★, *The Soul Years Volume 2* (1986)★★★, *Higher And Higher* i (1986)★★★, *The Very Best Of Jackie Wilson* (1987)★★★, *Mr Excitement* 3-CD (1992)★★★★, *Higher And Higher* ii (1993)★★★, *The Dynamic Jackie Wilson* (1993)★★★★, *The Chicago Years Vol. 1* (c.1993)★★★★, *Original Hits* (1993)★★★★, *The Jackie Wilson Hit Story Vol. 1* (1993)★★★★, *The Jackie Wilson Hit Story Vol. 2* (1993)★★★, *The Very Best Of ...* (Rhino 1994)★★★★, *A Portrait Of ...* (Essential Gold/Pickwick 1995)★★★★, *Higher And Higher* (Rhino 1995)★★★★.

●FILMS: *Go Johnny Go* (1958).

WILSON, NANCY

b. 20 February 1937, Chillicothe, Ohio, USA. Wilson began singing in clubs in and around Columbus, Ohio. She attracted attention among jazz musicians, made her first records in 1956, and in the late 50s toured with a band led by Rusty Bryant. At the end of the decade she sang with George Shearing, with whom she recorded, and Cannonball Adderley. It was at Adderley's insistence that she went to New York, where she was soon signed by Capitol. During the next few years Wilson made numerous albums, toured extensively, and built a substantial following among the popular audience but always retained a connection, if sometimes tenuously so, with jazz. In the early 80s she was again working more closely with jazz musicians, including Hank Jones, Art Farmer, Benny Golson and Ramsey Lewis. Later in the decade she

was active around the world, performing at major concert venues and singing in a style that revealed that the long years in the more flamboyant atmosphere of popular music had given her a taste for slightly over-dramatizing songs. Nevertheless, when backed by top-flight musicians she could still deliver a rhythmic and entertaining performance.

●ALBUMS: *Like Love* (Capitol 1959)★★★★, *Something Wonderful* (Capitol 1960)★★★★, *Nancy Wilson With Billy May's Orchestra* (1959)★★★★, *Nancy Wilson* (1960)★★★★, with George Shearing *The Swingin's Mutual* (Capitol 1961)★★★★, *Nancy Wilson With Gerald Wilson's Orchestra* (1961)★★★, *Nancy Wilson/Cannonball Adderley* (Capitol 1962)★★★, *Hello Young Lovers* (Capitol 1962)★★★★, *Broadway - My Way* (Capitol 1963)★★★★, *Hollywood - My Way* (Capitol 1963)★★★, *Nancy Wilson With Jimmy Jones's Orchestra* (1963)★★★★, *Yesterday's Love Songs, Today's Blues* (Capitol 1963)★★★★, *Today, Tomorrow, Forever* (Capitol 1964)★★★, *Nancy Wilson With Kenny Dennis's Group* (Capitol 1964)★★★, *How Glad I Am* (Capitol 1964)★★★, *The Nancy Wilson Show!* (Capitol 1965)★★★★, *Today - My Way* (Capitol 1965)★★★, *Gentle Is My Love* (Capitol 1965)★★★, *From Broadway With Love* (Capitol 1966)★★★★, *A Touch Of Today* (Capitol 1966)★★★, *Tender Loving Care* (Capitol 1966)★★★, *Nancy Wilson With Oliver Nelson's Orchestra* (Capitol 1967)★★★★, *Nancy - Naturally* (Capitol 1967)★★★, *Just For Now* (1967)★★★, *Nancy Wilson With H. B. Barnum's Orchestra* (Capitol 1967)★★★, *Lush Life* aka *The Right To Love* (Capitol 1967)★★★★, *Welcome To My Love* (Capitol 1968)★★★★, *Easy* (Capitol 1968)★★★, *The Sound Of Nancy Wilson* (Capitol 1968)★★★★, *Nancy Wilson With The Hank Jones Quartet* (Capitol 1969)★★★, *Nancy* (Capitol 1969)★★★, *Son Of A Preacher Man* (Capitol 1969)★★★, *Hurt So Bad* (Capitol 1969)★★★, *Can't Take My Eyes Off You* (Capitol 1970)★★★★, *Now I'm A Woman* (Capitol 1970)★★★, *But Beautiful* (Capitol 1971)★★★, *Kaleidoscope* (Capitol 1971)★★★, *All In Love Is Fair* (Capitol 1974)★★★, *Come Get To This* (Capitol 1975)★★★, *This Mother's Daughters* (Capitol 1976)★★★, *I've Never Been To Me* (Capitol 1977)★★★, *What's New?* (1982)★★★, *Nancy Wilson In Performance At The Playboy Jazz Festival* (1982)★★★, with Ramsey Lewis *The Two Of Us* (Capitol 1984)★★★, *Godsend* (1984)★★★, *Keep You Satisfied* (1985)★★★, *Forbidden Love* (1987)★★★.

●COMPILATIONS: *The Best Of Nancy Wilson* (Capitol 1968)★★★★, *Nancy Wilson's Greatest Hits* (Capitol 1988)★★★★, *The Capitol Years* (Capitol 1992)★★★★.

WINSTON, JIMMY

b. James Langwith, 20 April 1945, Stratford, London, England. A founder member of the Small Faces, organist/vocalist Winston embarked on a solo career on being fired from the band in 1965. Credited to Jimmy Winston And His Reflections, 'Sorry She's Mine' is an excellent version of a song that also appeared on the first Small Faces album. In 1967 Winston switched instruments to guitar and formed a new group, Winston's Fumbs. Tony Kaye (keyboards), Alex Paris (bass) and Ray Stock (drums) completed the line-up. Their lone single for RCA Records coupled the eccentric 'Real Crazy Apartment' with the psychedelic 'Snow White'. Winston's Fumbs split up when Kaye joined Yes. Winston then took a role in the rock musical, *Hair*, and in 1976 released a third single, 'Sun In The Morning', for NEMS Records. He has since ceased recording.

●ALBUMS: *Mood Mosaics* (RPM 1996)★★★, *A Teenage Opera* (RPM 1996)★★★.

WONDER WHO

At the 1966 apogee of their chart career, Nick Massi was replaced by Joe Long in the Four Seasons. Included in the new line-up's year of hits was a curious joke adaptation of Bob Dylan's 'Don't Think Twice It's All Right' under the *nom de turntable*, Wonder Who. The song itself mattered less than lead vocalist Frankie Valli's 'baby' falsetto - supposedly his impersonation of jazz singer Rose Murphy. Although it reached the US Top 5, the group did intend to seriously pursue this vocational tangent beyond a couple more singles, having made the point to their record company that the number *per se* was commercial enough without buyers knowing it was by the Four Seasons.

WONDER, STEVIE

b. Steveland Judkins, 13 May 1950, Saginaw, Michigan, USA. Born Judkins, Wonder now prefers to be known as Steveland Morris after his mother's married name. Placed in an incubator immediately after his birth, baby Steveland was given too much oxygen, causing Steveland to suffer permanent blindness. Despite this handicap, Wonder began to learn the piano at the age of seven, and had also mastered drums and harmonica by the age of nine. After his family moved to Detroit in 1954, Steveland joined a church choir, the gospel influence on his music balanced by the R&B of Ray Charles and Sam Cooke being played on his transistor radio. In 1961, he was discovered by Ronnie White of the Miracles, who arranged an audition at Motown Records. Berry Gordy immediately signed Steveland to the label, renaming him Little Stevie Wonder (the 'Little' was dropped in 1964). Wonder was placed in the care of writer/producer Clarence Paul, who supervised his early recordings. These accentuated his prodigal talents as a multi-instrumentalist, but did not represent a clear musical direction. In 1963, however, the release of the ebullient live recording 'Fingertips (Part 2)' established his commercial success, and Motown quickly marketed him on a series of albums as 'the 12-year-old genius' in an attempt to link him with the popularity of 'the genius', Ray Charles. Attempts to repeat the success of 'Fingertips' proved abortive, and Wonder's career was placed on hold during 1964 while his voice was breaking. He re-emerged in 1965 with a sound that was much closer to the Motown mainstream, scoring a worldwide hit with the dance-orientated 'Uptight (Everything's

Alright)', which he co-wrote with Henry Cosby and Sylvia Moy. This began a run of US Top 40 hits that continued unbroken (apart from seasonal Christmas releases) for over six years.

From 1965-70, Stevie Wonder was marketed like the other major Motown stars, recording material that was chosen for him by the label's executives, and issuing albums that mixed conventional soul compositions with pop standards. His strong humanitarian principles were allowed expression on his version of Bob Dylan's 'Blowin' In The Wind' and Ron Miller's 'A Place In The Sun' in 1966. He co-wrote almost all of his singles from 1967 onwards, and also began to collaborate on releases by other Motown artists, most notably co-writing Smokey Robinson And The Miracles' hit 'The Tears Of A Clown', and writing and producing the (Detroit) Spinners' 'It's A Shame'.

His contract with Motown expired in 1971; rather than resigning immediately, as the label expected, Wonder financed the recording of two albums of his own material, playing almost all the instruments himself, and experimenting for the first time with more ambitious musical forms. He pioneered the use of the synthesizer in black music, and also widened his lyrical concerns to take in racial problems and spiritual questions. Wonder then used these recordings as a lever to persuade Motown to offer a more open contract, which gave him total artistic control over his music, plus the opportunity to hold the rights to the music publishing in his own company, Black Bull Music. He celebrated the signing of the deal with the release of the solo recordings, *Where I'm Coming From* and *Music Of My Mind*, which despite lukewarm critical reaction quickly established him at the forefront of black music.

Talking Book in 1972 combined the artistic advances of recent albums with major commercial success, producing glorious hit singles with the poly-rhythmic funk of 'Superstition' and the crafted ballad, 'You Are The Sunshine Of My Life'. Wonder married fellow Motown artist Syreeta on 14 September 1970; he premiered many of his new production techniques on *Syreeta* (1972) and *Stevie Wonder Presents Syreeta* (1974), for which he also wrote most of the material. *Innervisions* (1973) consolidated his growth and success with *Talking Book*, bringing further hit singles with the socially aware 'Living For The City' and 'Higher Ground'. Later that year, Wonder was seriously injured in a car accident; his subsequent work was tinged with the awareness of mortality, fired by his spiritual beliefs. The release of *Fulfillingness' First Finale* in 1974 epitomized this more austere approach. The double album *Songs In The Key Of Life* (1976) was widely greeted as his most ambitious and satisfying work to date. It showed a mastery and variety of musical forms and instruments, offering a joyous tribute to Duke Ellington on 'Sir Duke', and heralding a pantheon of major black figures on 'Black Man'. This confirmed Wonder's status as one of the most admired musicians and songwriters in contemporary music.

Surprisingly, after this enormous success, no new recordings surfaced for over three years, as Wonder concentrated on perfecting the soundtrack music to the documentary film, *The Secret Life Of Plants*. This primarily instrumental double album was greeted with disappointing reviews and sales. Wonder quickly delivered the highly successful *Hotter Than July* in 1980, which included a tribute song for the late Dr. Martin Luther King, 'Happy Birthday', and a notable essay in reggae form on 'Masterblaster (Jamming)'.

The failure of his film project brought an air of caution into Wonder's work, and delays and postponements were now a consistent factor in his recording process. After compiling the retrospective double album *Stevie Wonder's Original Musiquarium I* in 1982, which included four new recordings alongside the cream of his post-1971 work, Wonder scheduled an album entitled *People Move Human Play* in 1983. This never appeared; instead, he composed the soundtrack music for the film *The Woman In Red*, which included his biggest-selling single to date, the sentimental ballad 'I Just Called To Say I Loved You'.

The album on which he had been working since 1980 eventually appeared in 1985 as *In Square Circle*. Like his next project, *Characters* in 1987, it heralded a return to the accessible, melodic music of the previous decade. The unadventurous nature of both projects, and the heavy expectations engendered by the delay in their release, led to a disappointing reception from critics and public alike.

Wonder's status as an elder statesman of black music, and a champion of black rights, was boosted by his campaign in the early 80s to have the birthday of Dr. Martin Luther King celebrated as a national holiday in the USA. This request was granted by President Reagan, and the first Martin Luther King Day was celebrated on 15 January 1986 with a concert at which Wonder topped the bill. Besides his own recordings, Wonder has been generous in offering his services as a writer, producer, singer or musician to other performers. His most public collaborations included work with Paul McCartney, which produced a cloying but enormous hit, 'Ebony And Ivory', Gary Byrd, Michael Jackson, and Eurythmics, and on the benefit records by USA For Africa and Dionne Warwick & Friends. *Conversation Peace* in 1995 was an average album with no outstanding songs, but our expectation of Wonder is different to that of most other artists. He could release ten indifferent, poor, weak or spectacular records over the next 20 years and nothing would change our fixed perception of him and of the body of outstanding music he has produced since 1963.

●ALBUMS: *Tribute To Uncle Ray* (Tamla 1962)★★★, *The Jazz Soul Of Little Stevie* (Tamla 1962)★★★, *The 12-Year-Old Genius Recorded Live* (Tamla 1963)★★★, *With A Song In My Heart* (Tamla 1963)★★, *Stevie At The Beach* (Tamla 1964)★★, *Up-Tight (Everything's Alright)* (Tamla 1966)★★★, *Down To Earth* (Tamla 1966)★★★, *I Was Made To Love Her* (Tamla 1967)★★★★, *Someday At Christmas* (Tamla 1967)★★, *For Once In My Life* (Tamla 1968)★★★★, *My Cherie Amour* (Tamla 1969)★★★★, *Stevie Wonder Live* (Tamla 1970)★★, *Stevie Wonder Live At The Talk Of The Town* (Tamla 1970)★★★, *Signed, Sealed And Delivered* (Tamla 1970)★★★★, *Where I'm Coming From* (Tamla 1971)★★★, *Music Of My Mind* (Tamla 1972)★★★, *Talking Book* (Tamla Motown 1972)★★★★★, *Innervisions* (Tamla Motown 1973)★★★★★, *Fulfillingness' First Finale* (Tamla Motown 1974)★★★, *Songs In The Key Of Life* (Motown 1976)★★★★, *Stevie Wonder's Journey Through The Secret Life Of Plants* (Motown 1979)★★, *Hotter Than July* (Motown 1980)★★★, *The Woman In Red* soundtrack (Motown 1984)★★, *In Square Circle* (Motown 1985)★★, *Characters* (Motown 1987)★★, *Conversation Peace* (Motown 1995)★★, *Natural Wonder* (Motown 1995)★★.

●COMPILATIONS: *Greatest Hits* (Tamla 1968) ★★★★, *Greatest Hits, Volume Two* (Tamla 1971)★★★★, *Anthology* aka *Looking Back* rec. 1962-71(Motown 1977)★★★★, *Stevie Wonder's Original Musiquarium I* (Motown 1982)★★★, *Song Review* (Motown 1996)★★★.

●FURTHER READING: *Stevie Wonder*, Sam Hasegawa. *The Story Of Stevie Wonder*, Jim Haskins. *Stevie Wonder*, Ray Fox-Cumming. *Stevie Wonder*, Constanze Elsner. *The Picture Life Of Stevie Wonder*, Audrey Edwards, *Stevie Wonder*, C. Dragonwagon. *Stevie Wonder*, Beth P. Wilson. *The Stevie Wonder Scrapbook*, Jim Haskins with Kathleen Benson. *Stevie Wonder*, Rick Taylor.

●FILMS: *Bikini Beach* (1964).

WOOD, BRENTON

b. Alfred Jesse Smith, 26 July 1941, Shreveport, Louisiana, USA. Smith was a veteran of several vocal groups, including the Dootones, the Quotations and Little Freddie And The Rockets, before assuming the name Brenton Wood in deference to his home district in Los Angeles. As a solo act he enjoyed fame with 'The Oogum Boogum Song' (1967), a nonsense novelty record. The follow-up, 'Gimme Little Sign' (although not a novelty), was in a similar style, but its more lasting appeal was confirmed when the single reached the UK and US Top 10. Further releases, 'Baby You Got It' (1967) and 'Some Got It, Some Don't' (1968), diluted the pattern and were less successful. Wood later recorded a duet with Shirley Goodman, before making a belated return to the US R&B chart in 1977 with 'Come Softly To Me'.

●ALBUMS: *Gimme Little Sign* (Liberty 1967)★★★, *The Oogum Boogum Man* (Double Shot 1967)★★★, *Baby You Got It* (1967)★★★.

●COMPILATIONS: *Brenton Wood's 18 Best* (1991)★★★.

WOODSTOCK FESTIVAL

The original Woodstock Art and Music Fair was forcibly moved from its planned location after protest from local townsfolk of Wallkill, New York State, USA. Their opposition to 'long-haired weirdos' was indigenous to 1969. The new location was 40 miles away at a 600-acre dairy farm in Bethel owned by Max Yasgur. If the Monterey Pop Festival in 1967 was the birth of the new music revolution, Woodstock was its coming of age.

A steady trail of spectators arrived up to a week before the event, which took place on 15, 16 and 17 August 1969, to make sure they had a reasonable chance to catch a glimpse of at least one of the dozens of stars scheduled to appear. The line-up was intimidating in its scale: the Who, Jimi Hendrix, Crosby, Stills, Nash And Young, John Sebastian, Jefferson Airplane, Grateful Dead, Santana, Joe Cocker, Sly And The Family Stone, Country Joe And The Fish, Ten Years After, the Band, Johnny Winter, Blood, Sweat And Tears, the Paul Butterfield Blues Band, Sha Na Na, Janis Joplin, Ravi Shankar, the Keef Hartley Band, the Incredible String Band, Canned Heat, Melanie, Sweetwater, Tim Hardin, Joan Baez, Arlo Guthrie, Richie Havens and Creedence Clearwater Revival. Estimates vary but it was generally felt that no less than 300,000 spectators were present at any one time, sharing 600 portable lavatories and inadequate water facilities. Nobody was prepared for the wave of bodies that formed, choking the highways from all directions. The world press which had previously scorned the popular hippie movement and the power of their musical message, were at last speaking favourably, as one. It was possible for vast amounts of youngsters to congregate for a musical celebration, without violence and regimented supervision. Joni Mitchell (who was not present) was one of the artists who eulogized the event in her song 'Woodstock': 'I'm going down to Yasgur's Farm, I'm gonna join in a rock 'n' roll band, I'm gonna camp out on the land and set my soul free'.

The subsequent film and live albums have insured Woodstock's immortality, and although there are some critics of the 'love generation' few can deny that Woodstock was a milestone in musical history. It is no exaggeration to claim that the festival totally changed the world's attitude towards popular music.

●ALBUMS: *Woodstock* (Atco 1969)★★★★, *Woodstock II* (Atco 1970)★★★, *Woodstock: Three Days Of Peace And Music - The 25th Anniversary Collection* (Atlantic 1994)★★★, *Woodstock '94* (A&M 1994)★★★.

●VIDEOS: *Woodstock 94* (Polygram 1994).

●FURTHER READING: *Woodstock: Festival Remembered*, Jean Young. *Woodstock Festival Remembered*, Michael Lang. *Woodstock Vision*, Elliott Landy. *Woodstock: An Oral History*, Joel Makowers.

WRIGHT, O.V.

b. Overton Vertis Wright, 9 October 1939, Memphis, Tennessee, USA, d. 16 November 1980. One of deep soul's most impressive stylists, O.V. Wright's first recordings were in the gospel tradition and it was while a member of the Harmony Echoes that he became acquainted with Roosevelt Jamison. This aspiring songwriter penned the singer's secular debut, 'That's How Strong My Love Is', an impassioned ballad later covered by Otis Redding and the Rolling Stones. Wright's plaintive delivery excelled on slow material, as two imploring R&B hits, 'You're Gonna

Make Me Cry' (1965) and 'Eight Men, Four Women' (1967), testified. Wright's next single, 'Heartaches-Heartaches' (1967), confirmed a working relationship with producer Willie Mitchell, but despite excellent collaborations in 'Ace Of Spades' (1970), 'A Nickel And A Nail' (1971) and 'I'd Rather Be (Blind, Crippled And Crazy)' (1973), the singer was unable to reach a wider audience. Imprisoned for narcotics offences during the mid-70s, he re-emerged on the Hi Records in 1975, but intense recordings here, including 'Rhymes' (1976) and 'I Feel Love Growin'' (1978), met a similar fate. Hard living and a continuing drug problem weakened his health and in 1980, O.V. Wright died from a heart attack. For many he remains one of southern soul's most authoritative and individual artists.

●ALBUMS: *If It's Only For Tonight* (Back Beat 1965)★★★, *8 Men And 4 Women* (Back Beat 1967)★★★, *Nucleus Of Soul* (Back Beat 1968)★★★, *A Nickel And A Nail And Ace Of Spades* (Back Beat 1971)★★★, *Memphis Unlimited* (Back Beat 1973)★★, *Into Something I Can't Shake Loose* (1977)★★, *The Wright Stuff* (1977)★★★, *The Bottom Line* (Hi 1978)★★★, *Live* (1979)★★, *We're Still Together* (Hi 1979)★★★.

●COMPILATIONS: *Gone For Good* (1984)★★★, *The Wright Stuff* (1987)★★★, *Here's Another Thing* (1989)★★★, *That's How Strong Love Is* (1991)★★★, *The Soul Of O.V. Wright* (1993)★★★.

WRITING ON THE WALL

Originally formed as the Jury in 1966 in Penicuik, Scotland, the nucleus of this tough, soul-based band comprised Willie Finlayson (guitar/vocals), Jimmy Hush (drums), Jake Scott (bass/vocals) and Bill Scott (keyboards). Linnie Patterson, a former member of the Boston Dexters and Three's A Crowd (which included the future Rainbow guitarist Jimmy Bain), subsequently joined as vocalist and by 1967 the Jury were a leading attraction under the managerial hand of Tam Paton. A new name, Writing On The Wall, was assumed when the quintet abandoned soul for a more progressive style. They then became highly popular on London's underground circuit, but their lone album on the Middle Earth label was marred by an amateurish production which negated any power the group could muster. Bound by contractual obligations, they were unable to move to another label and although a new guitarist, Robert 'Smiggy' Smith (b. 30 March 1946, Kiel, Germany; guitar), also an ex-member of Three's A Crowd, had replaced Finlayson, the enthusiasm he brought with him rapidly disappeared. He and Patterson left the line-up, and although Finlayson returned for a final single, the group split in 1973. Most of the ex-members retained an interest in music. Finlayson worked with several bands, including Meal Ticket while Smiggy joined Blue. Paterson sang with a later version of the group Beggar's Opera, but failed to achieve due recognition. He completed a solo single, which featured several luminaries from the Edinburgh beat scene, prior to his premature death from asbestosis in 1990.

●ALBUMS: *The Power Of The Picts* (Middle Earth 1970)★★.

●COMPILATIONS: *Rarities From The Middle Earth* (Pie & Mash 1995)★★, *Crack In The Illusion Of Life* (Tenth Planet 1995)★★, *Burghley Road: The Basement Sessions* (Tenth Planet 1996)★★.

WYNDER K. FROG

b. Michael Weaver, *c*.1947, Colchester, Essex, England. A pseudonym for the highly talented session organist/pianist (see Mick Weaver) who released three albums including the exceptional *Out Of The Frying Pan* in 1968. Dubbed the Booker T. of Bolton, Weaver enlisted a stellar team of musicians including Dick Heckstall-Smith, Chris Mercer, Alan Spenner (bass), Neil Hubbard (guitar), Bruce Rowland (drums).

●ALBUMS: *Sunshine Superfrog* (Island 1967)★★, *Out Of The Frying Pan* (Island 1968)★★★, *Into The Fire* (United Artists 1970)★★.

YANOVSKY, ZALMAN 'ZALLY'

b. 19 December 1944, Toronto, Canada. A former member of the Halifax Three and the Mugwumps, Yanovsky founded the Lovin' Spoonful with songwriter John Sebastian. Yanovsky's extrovert behaviour provided the group's visual identity while his exceptional and under-rated guitar playing was a vital fixture of their overall sound. He left the band in 1967. Arrested on a drugs charge in San Francisco, he incriminated his supplier rather than face deportation. The guitarist then formed a fruitful partnership with Jerry Yester who, paradoxically, had replaced him in the Spoonful. The duo produced Tim Buckley's *Happy Sad* as well as Yester's collaboration with Judy Henske, *Farewell Alderbaran* and Yanovsky's own eccentric offering, *Alive And Well In Argentina*. Its irreverent mixture of cover versions and new songs proved a commercial disaster and the artist's career withered in its wake. Although he made several unannounced guest appearances during John Sebastian concerts, Yanovsky gradually withdrew from music altogether. Sebastian reported during an interview that Yanovsky was now a restaurateur.

●ALBUMS: *Zalman Yanovsky Is Alive And Well In Argentina* (Buddah 1968)★.

YARDBIRDS

This UK R&B group was formed in London in 1963 when Keith Relf (b. 22 March 1944, Richmond, Surrey, England, d. 14 May 1976; vocals/harmonica) and Paul Samwell-Smith (b. 8 May 1943; bass), both members of semi-acoustic act the Metropolis Blues Quartet, joined forces with Chris Dreja (b. 11 November 1944, Surbiton, Surrey, England; rhythm guitar), Tony 'Top' Topham (guitar) and Jim McCarty (b. 25 July 1944, Liverpool, England; drums). Within months Topham had opted to continue academic studies and was replaced by Eric Clapton (b. Eric Clapp, 30 March 1945, Ripley, Surrey, England). The reconstituted line-up forged a style based on classic Chicago R&B and quickly amassed a following in the nascent blues circuit. They succeeded the Rolling Stones as the resident band at Richmond's popular Crawdaddy club, whose owner, Giorgio Gomelsky, then assumed the role of group manager. Two enthusiastic, if low-key singles, 'I Wish You Would' and 'Good Morning Little Schoolgirl', attracted critical interest, but the quintet's fortunes flourished with the release of *Five Live Yardbirds*. Recorded during their tenure at the Marquee club, the set captured an in-person excitement and was marked by a rendition of Howlin' Wolf's 'Smokestack Lightning'.

Clapton emerged as the unit's focal point, but a desire for musical purity led to his departure in 1965 in the wake of a magnificent third single, 'For Your Love'. Penned by Graham Gouldman, the song's commerciality proved unacceptable to the guitarist despite its innovative sound. Clapton later resurfaced in John Mayall's Bluebreakers. Jeff Beck (b. 24 June 1944, Surrey, England), formerly of the Tridents, joined the Yardbirds as the single rose to number 1 in the UK's New Musical Express chart. Gouldman provided further hits in 'Heartful Of Soul' and 'Evil Hearted You', the latter of which was a double-sided chart entry with the group-penned 'Still I'm Sad'. Based on a Gregorian chant, the song indicated a desire for experimentation prevailing in the rage-rock 'Shapes Of Things', the chaotic 'Over Under Sideways Down' and the excellent Yardbirds. By this point Simon Napier-Bell had assumed management duties, while disaffection with touring, and the unit's sometimes irreverent attitude, led to the departure of Samwell-Smith in June 1966. Respected session guitarist Jimmy Page (b. 9 January 1944, London, England) was brought into a line-up which, with Dreja switching to bass, now adopted a potentially devastating twin-lead guitar format. The experimental 'Happenings Ten Years Time Ago' confirmed such hopes, but within six months Beck had departed during a gruelling USA tour.

The Yardbirds remained a quartet but, despite a growing reputation on the American 'underground' circuit, their appeal as a pop attraction waned. Despite late-period collaborations with the commercially minded Mickie Most, singles, including 'Little Games' (1967) and 'Goodnight Sweet Josephine' (1968), failed to chart. The disappointing Little Games was denied a UK release but found success in the USA. They followed with two bizarre minor successes in America: 'Ha Ha Said The Clown' and Harry Nilsson's 'Ten Little Indians'. When Relf and McCarty announced a desire to pursue a folk-based direction, the group folded in June 1968. Page subsequently founded Led Zeppelin, Dreja became a highly successful photographer while the remaining duo forged a new career, firstly as Together, then Renaissance. Nonetheless, the legacy of the Yardbirds has refused to die, particularly in the wake of the fame enjoyed by its former guitarists. Relf was fatally electrocuted in 1976, but the following decade McCarty and Dreja joined Samwell-Smith - now a respected record producer - in Box Of Frogs. When this short-lived attraction folded, the former colleagues reverted to their corresponding careers, with McCarty remaining active in music as a member of the British Invasion All-Stars. The allure of his first group still flourishes and they remain acclaimed as early practitioners of technical effects and psychedelic styles. The 'blueswailing' Yardbirds have maintained enormous credibility as true pioneers of British R&B, classic experimental pop and early exponents of heavy rock.
●ALBUMS: Five Live Yardbirds (Columbia 1964)★★★★, For Your Love (Epic 1965)★★★, Having A Rave Up With The Yardbirds (Epic 1966)★★, Over Under Sideways Down (Epic 1966)★★★, Yardbirds aka Roger The Engineer (Columbia 1966)★★★, Blow Up soundtrack (MGM 1967)★★, Little Games (Epic 1968)★★★.
●COMPILATIONS: The Yardbirds With Sonny Boy Williamson (Fontana 1966)★★★, Greatest Hits (Epic 1967)★★, Remember The Yardbirds (Regal 1971)★★★★, Live Yardbirds (Epic 1971)★★★, Yardbirds Featuring Eric Clapton (Charly 1977)★★★, Yardbirds Featuring Jeff Beck (Charly 1977)★★★, Shapes Of Things (Collection 1964-1966) (Charly 1978)★★★, The First Recordings (Charly 1982)★★★, Shapes Of Things box set (Charly 1984)★★★, The Studio Sessions (Charly 1989)★★★, Yardbirds ... On Air (Band Of Joy 1991)★★, Greatest Hits (1993)★★★, Train Kept A Rollin': The Complete Giorgio Gomelsky Recordings 4-CD box set (Charly 1993)★★★★, Honey In Your Hips rec. 1963-66 (Charly 1994)★★★, The Best Of ... (Rhino 1994)★★★, Good Morning Little Schoolgirl (Essential Gold 1995)★★★.
●FURTHER READING: Blues In The Night: The Yardbirds' Story, James White. Yardbirds, John Platt. Yardbirds World, Richard Mackay and Michael Ober.

YELLOW SUBMARINE

Released in 1968, and named and inspired by one of the Beatles' most enduring pop songs, Yellow Submarine was a full-length animated feature that deftly combined comic-book imagery with psychedelia. Any lingering disappointment that the Beatles did not provide the voices for their characters vanished in a sea of colour and surrealism. Creations such as the anti-music Blue Meanies and their herald, Glove, were particularly memorable and if several songs were already established Beatles favourites, the quartet did contribute some excellent new compositions, including John Lennon's acerbic 'Hey Bulldog', George Harrison's anthemic 'It's All Too Much' and Paul McCartney's naggingly memorable 'All Together Now'. The group do briefly appear at the close singing the last-named song, but the film's strength lies in its brilliant combination of sound and visuals.

YOUNG ONES, THE

Cliff Richard had already appeared in two films, Expresso Bongo and Serious Charge, prior to starring in this unashamedly teen-orientated vehicle. It combined many of the genre's sub-plots - unsympathetic adults, romance and an inevitable, jejune show which is finally performed despite adversity. Unashamedly light and frothy, The Young Ones (titled Wonderful To Be Young in the USA) also boasted a highly popular soundtrack album. The memorable title track, a number 1 single in its own right, defines the innocence of Britain's pre-Beatles 60s, while 'When The Girl In Your Arms Is The Girl In Your Heart' remains one of the singer's most affecting ballads. The Young Ones confirmed Richard's status as one of the most popular entertainers of his era. The film was released in 1962 and was directed by Sidney J. Furie. The musical interludes other than those by Cliff and the Shadows were composed by Stanley Black.

YOUNG RASCALS

This expressive act, one of America's finest pop/soul ensembles, made its debut in a New Jersey club, the Choo Choo in February 1965. Felix Cavaliere (b. 29 November 1943, Pelham, New York, USA; organ/vocals), Eddie Brigati (b. 22 October 1946, New York City, USA; vocals/percussion) and Dino Danelli (b. 23 July 1945, New York City, USA; drums) were each established musicians on the city's R&B circuit, serving time in several popular attractions, including Joey Dee And The Starlighters. It was here the trio encountered Gene Cornish (b. 14 May 1946, Ottawa, Canada; vocals/guitar), who became the fourth member of a breakaway group, initially dubbed Felix And The Escorts, but later known as the Young Rascals. The quartet enjoyed a minor hit with 'I Ain't Gonna Eat Out My Heart Anymore' before securing a US number 1 with the energetic 'Good Lovin''. Despite a somewhat encumbering early image - knicker-bockers and choir boy shirts - the group's soulful performances endeared them to critics and peers, earning them a 'group's group' sobriquet. Now established as one of the east coast's most influential attractions, spawning a host of imitators from the Vagrants to Vanilla Fudge, the Young Rascals secured their biggest hit with 'Groovin''. This became an international hit, signalling a lighter, more introspective approach, and although Brigati was featured on the haunting 'How Can I Be Sure', a US Top 5 entry, Cavaliere gradually became the group's focal point. In 1968 the group dropped its 'Young' prefix and enjoyed a third US number 1 with 'People Got To Be Free'. An announcement that every Rascals' live appearance must also include a black act enforced the group's commitment to civil rights, but effectively banned them from southern states. The quartet later began exploring jazz-based compositions, and although remaining respected, lost much of their commercial momentum. Brigati and Cornish left the group in 1971, and although newcomers Buzzy Feiten (guitar), Ann Sutton (vocals) and Robert Popwell (drums) contributed to final albums, *Peaceful World* and *Island Of Real*, the Rascals were clearly losing momentum and broke up the following year. Felix Cavaliere then enjoyed a moderate solo career while Danelli and Cornish formed Bulldog and Fotomaker. The three musicians were reunited in 1988 for an extensive US tour.

●ALBUMS: *The Young Rascals* (Atlantic 1966)★★★, *Collections* (Atlantic 1966)★★★, *Groovin'* (Atlantic 1967)★★★★, *Once Upon A Dream* (Atlantic 1968)★★★, *Freedom Suite* (Atlantic 1969)★★★, *Search And Nearness* (Atlantic 1969)★★, *See* (Atlantic 1970)★★, *Peaceful World* (Columbia 1971)★★, *The Island Of Real* (Columbia 1972)★★.

●COMPILATIONS: *Timepeace - The Rascals' Greatest Hits* (Atlantic 1968)★★★★, *Star Collection* (1973)★★★, *Searching For Ecstasy - The Rest Of The Rascals 1969-1972* (1988)★★★★.

YOUNG TRADITION

One of the leading practitioners of the English folk revival, the Young Tradition was formed in 1964 by Heather Wood (b. 1945; vocals), Royston Wood (b. 1935, d. 8 April 1990; vocals/tambourine) and Peter Bellamy (b. 8 September 1944, Bournemouth, Dorset, England, d. September 1991; guitar/concertina/vocals). The trio continued the oral harmony tradition of the influential Copper Family, while simultaneously enjoying the patronage of the Soho circuit and the emergent 'underground' audience. Their choice of material and powerful harmonies captured what was regarded as the essence of rural folk music. The group completed three albums during their brief sojourn. Their debut included guest performances from Dave Swarbrick and Dolly Collins and their much heralded *Galleries* highlighted the divergent interests that eventually pulled them apart. Several selections featured support from David Munrow's Early Music Ensemble, a trend towards medieval perspectives that Bellamy considered unwelcome. Unable to make a commercial breakthrough, the Young Tradition broke up in 1969, although Heather and Royston Wood remained together to record *No Relation*. The latter musician enjoyed a brief association with the Albion Country Band, before forming Swan Arcade. He died in April 1990, following a three-week coma after being run over by a car in the USA. Heather Wood teamed up with Andy Wallace to form the duo, Crossover. Pete Bellamy, meanwhile, enjoyed a successful solo career. This was abruptly cut short in 1991 when Bellamy committed suicide.

●ALBUMS: *The Young Tradition* (Transatlantic 1966)★★★★, *So Cheerfully Round* (Transatlantic 1967)★★★★, *Galleries* (Transatlantic 1968)★★, with Shirley And Dolly Collins *The Holly Bears The Crown* rec. 1969 (Fledg'ling 1995)★★★.

●COMPILATIONS: *The Young Tradition Sampler* (Transatlantic 1969)★★★★, *The Young Tradition* (1989)★★★.

YOUNG, FARON

b. 25 February 1932, Shreveport, Louisiana, USA, d. 10 December 1996, Nashville, Tennessee. Young was raised on the farm his father bought just outside Shreveport and learned to play the guitar and sing country songs as a boy. Greatly influenced by Hank Williams (in his early days he was something of a sound-alike) and while still at school, he formed a country band and began to establish a local reputation as an entertainer. In 1950, he gave up his college studies to accept an offer of a professional career and joined radio station KWKH, where he soon became a member of the prestigious *Louisiana Hayride* show and found other work in the nightclubs and honky tonks. He became friends with Webb Pierce and for a time toured with him as a vocalist with Pierce's band. In 1951, he made his first recordings for the Gotham label with Tillman Franks and his band and achieved minor success with 'Have I Waited Too Long' and 'Tattle Tale Eyes' before he joined Capitol Records. In the summer of 1952, Faron was dating a girl called Billie Jean Jones, when she attracted the attention of Hank Williams. He persuaded Faron to arrange a double date, which resulted in Hank threatening him with a pistol and claiming Jones for his own. Young backed off and Billie Jean became the second Mrs Hank Williams. In 1953, Young formed his own band, moved to Nashville, where he became a member of the *Grand Ole Opry* and gained his first US country chart hit with a self-penned song called 'Goin' Steady'. His career was interrupted when, because of the Korean War, he was drafted into the army. Although interrupted by this, his career certainly benefited from the exposure he received after winning an army talent competition. This led to him touring the world entertaining US forces, as well as appearing on recruiting shows that were networked to hundreds of radio stations. Young returned to Nashville in November 1954 and resumed his career, gaining his first US country number 1 the following year with 'Live Fast, Love Hard, Die Young'.

This established him beyond any doubt as a major recording star, and between 1955 and 1969 he amassed a total of 63 US country chart hits of which 46 made the Top 20. He developed the knack of picking the best material by other writers and had a number 2 hit with Don Gibson's 'Sweet Dreams' and further number 1s with Roy Drusky's songs 'Alone With You' and 'Country Girl'. In 1961, he recorded 'Hello Walls' thus making the song one of the first Willie Nelson compositions to be recorded by a major artist. It reached number 1 in the US country charts, also became a Top 20 US pop hit and was Young's first million-seller. In 1956, his popularity as a singer earned him a role in the film *Hidden Guns*. This led to his own nickname of The Young Sheriff and his band being called the Country Deputies. (At one time Roger Miller was a member of the band.) In later years he became the Singing Sheriff before, as he once suggested, someone queried his age and started asking 'What's he trying to prove?' After the initial success with this easily forgettable b-western, he made further film appearances over the years including *Daniel Boone, Stampede, Raiders Of Old California, Country Music Holiday, A Gun And A Gavel, Road To Nashville* and *That's Country*. He left Capitol for Mercury in 1962, immediately charting with 'The Yellow Bandanna', 'You'll Drive Me Back' and a fine duet recording with Margie Singleton of 'Keeping Up With The Joneses'.

In 1965, he had a US country Top 10 hit with 'Walk Tall', a song that had been a UK pop hit for Val Doonican the previous year. Young quit the *Opry* in the mid-60s, finding, like several other artists, that it was not only difficult keeping up the expected number of Saturday night appearances but also that he lost a lot of lucrative bookings. After the success of 'Hello Walls', he perhaps unintentionally tended to look for further pop chart hits, and in consequence his recordings, at times, became less country in their arrangements. He soon returned to his country roots, usually choosing his favourite twin fiddle backings. Young easily maintained his popularity throughout the 60s and 70s and toured extensively in the USA and made several visits to Europe, where he performed in the UK, France and Germany. He appeared on all the major network television shows but seemed to have little interest in having his own regular series. At times he has not endeared himself to some of his fellow performers with his imitations of their acts.

In the 70s he was still a major star with a series of Top 10 US country hits including 'Step Aside', 'Leavin' And Saying Goodbye', 'This Little Girl Of Mine' and 'Just What I Had In Mind' . 'It's Four In The Morning', another country number 1, had crossover success and also gave him a second million-seller. It also became his only UK pop chart success, peaking at number 3 during a 23 week chart run. He left Mercury Records in 1979 and briefly joined MCA. In 1988, he joined Step One Records and 'Stop And Take The Time', a minor hit, became country chart entry number 85. Over the years he became involved in several business interests and apart from losing heavily in the 60s, in respect of investments to convert an old baseball stadium into a stock car racing track in Nashville, he was very successful. Young became involved in publishing companies, a recording studio, and a booking agency plus co-ownership of *Music City News* newspaper. He was always noted for very plain speaking and has incurred the wrath of the establishment on several occasions for his outspoken views. A suggested association with Patsy Cline led to various stories of his dalliances and whether correct or not, it may well be that he revelled in the publicity they caused.

In September 1972, he gained unwanted publicity by his reaction to an incident at a show. At a time when 'This Little Girl Of Mine' was a hit for him, he invited six-year-old Nora Jo Catlett to join him on stage in Clarksville, West Virginia. She refused, whereupon Young swore at the audience, stormed off stage, grabbed the child and spanked her repeatedly. (The child collected autographs and had been told by her mother not to approach the stage but to wait near the front until Young finished his act.) The child's father swore out a warrant for his arrest and after pleading guilty to a charge of assault, he was fined $35. The following year a civil action claiming $200,000 was filed. In his defence, Young claimed the child spat in his face. Eventually, almost two years later, the Catlett family were awarded only $3400. He has been involved in various actions, once stating, 'I am not an alcoholic, I'm a drunk', and on one occasion, he shot out the light fittings of a Nashville bar. He is reputed to have had affairs with many women while remaining supposedly happily married. In 1987, after 34 years of marriage, his wife finally obtained a divorce on the grounds of physical abuse. She claimed that he had also threatened her and their 16-year-old daughter with a gun and often shot holes in the kitchen ceiling. It may perhaps be more accurate to describe him as the singing outlaw rather than the singing sheriff! Perhaps a fair summary would be to quote the heading from an article written in 1980 by Bob Allen, who parodied Young's hit song by writing 'Live Fast, Love Hard And Keep On Cussin'. Faron Young is one of country music's greatest legends, while remaining relatively unknown to many. Paddy MacAloon of Prefab Sprout paid tribute to him when he wrote the beautiful 'Faron Young' on the group's *Steve McQueen* album. Until his death in 1996 he was semi-retired but still made concert performances as well as guest appearances on the *Opry*.

●ALBUMS: *Sweethearts Or Strangers* (Capitol 1957)★★★, *The Object Of My Affection* (Capitol 1958)★★★, *My Garden Of Prayer* (Capitol 1959)★★★, *This Is Faron Young* (Capitol 1959)★★★, *Talk About Hits* (Capitol 1959)★★★, *Sings The Best Of Faron Young* (Capitol 1960)★★★, *Hello Walls* (Capitol 1961)★★★, *The Young Approach* (Capitol 1961)★★★, *All-Time Great Hits* (Capitol 1963)★★★, *This Is Faron* (Mercury 1963)★★★, *Aims At The West* (Mercury 1963)★★★, *Memory Lane* (Mercury 1964)★★★, *Country Dance Favorites* (Mercury 1964)★★★, *Songs For Country Folks* (Mercury 1964)★★★, *Story Songs Of Mountains And Valleys* (Mercury 1964)★★★, *Falling In Love* (Mercury 1965)★★★, *Pen And Paper* (Mercury 1965)★★★, *Faron Young* (Mercury 1966)★★★, *Sings The Best Of Jim Reeves* (Mercury 1966)★★★, *If You Ain' t Lovin', You Ain't Livin'* (Mercury 1966)★★★, *It's A Great Life* (Mercury 1966)★★★, *Unmitigated Gall* (Mercury 1967)★★★, *Here's Faron Young* (Mercury 1968)★★★, *I' ll Be Yours* (Mercury 1968)★★★, *This Is Faron Young* (Merc ury 1968)★★★, *Just Out Of Reach* (Mercury 1968)★★★, *The World Of Faron Young* (Mercury 1968)★★★, *I' ve Got Precious Memories* (Mercury 1969)★★★, *Wine Me Up* (Mercury 1969)★★★, *20 Hits Over The Years* (Mercury 1969)★★★, *Occasional Wife/If I Ever Fall In Love With A Honky Tonk Girl* (Mercury 1970)★★★, *Leavin' And Sayin' Goodbye* (Mercury 1971)★★★, *Step Aside* (Mercury 1971)★★★, *It's Four In The Morning* (Mercury 1972)★★★, *This Little Girl Of Mine* (Mercury 1972)★★★, *This Time The Hurtin's On Me* (Mercury 1973)★★★, *Just What I Had In Mind* (Mercury 1973)★★★, *Some Kind Of Woman* (Mercury 1974)★★★, *A Man And His Music* (1975)★★★, *I'd Just Be Fool Enough* (1976)★★★, *That Young Feelin'* (1977)★★★, *Chapter Two* (1979)★★★, *Free And Easy* (1980)★★★, *The Young Sheriff (1955-1956 Radio Broadcasts)* (1981)★★★, *The Sheriff* (1984)★★★, with Jerry Lee Lewis, Webb Pierce, Mel Tillis *Four Legends* (1985)★★★, *Here's To You* (1988)★★★, *Country Christmas* (1990)★★★, *The Classic Years* 5-CD set (1992)★★★★, with Ray Price *Memories That Last* (1992).

●COMPILATIONS: *Greatest Hits Volumes 1, 2 & 3* (1988)★★★★, *The Classic Years 1952 - 1962* (1992)★★★★, *Live Fast, Love Hard: Original Capitol Recordings, 1952-1962* (CMF 1995)★★★★, *All American Country* (Spectrum 1997)★★★★.

YOUNGBLOODS

Formed in 1965 in Boston, Massachusetts, the Youngbloods evolved from the city's thriving traditional music circuit. The group was formed by folk singers Jesse Colin Young (b. Perry Miller, 11 November 1944, New York City, New York, USA) and Jerry Corbitt (b. Tifton, Georgia, USA) who together completed a single, 'My Babe', prior to the arrival of aspiring jazz drummer Joe

Bauer (b. 26 September 1941, Memphis, Tennessee, USA) and guitarist/pianist Lowell Levinger III, better known simply as Banana (b. 1946, Cambridge, Massachusetts, USA). Young began playing bass when several candidates, including Felix Pappalardi and Harvey Brooks, proved incompatible, and the quartet took the name 'Youngbloods' from the singer's second solo album. Having secured a residency at New York's famed Cafe Au Go Go, the group established itself as a leading folk rock cum good-time attraction. Their debut, *The Youngbloods*, captures this formative era and mixes excellent original songs, including the ebullient 'Grizzly Bear', with several choice cover versions. The group's reading of Dino Valenti's 'Get Together' subsequently became a hit in California where it was adopted as a counter-culture anthem. The lyric: 'Come on now people, smile on your brother, everybody get together, try and love one another right now', perfectly captured the mood of late-60s Californian rock music.

The Youngbloods then settled on the west coast. *Elephant Mountain*, their most popular album, reflected a new-found peace of mind and included several of the group's best-known songs, including 'Darkness Darkness' and 'Sunlight'. Jerry Corbitt had left the line-up during the early stages of recording allowing Bauer and Banana space to indulge in improvisational interludes. The Youngbloods gained complete artistic freedom with their own label, Racoon. However releases by Bauer, Banana and Young dissipated the strengths of the parent unit whose final releases were marred by inconsistency. A friend from the Boston days, Michael Kane, joined the band in the spring of 1971, but they split the following year when Young resumed his solo career. Banana, Bauer and Kane continued as Banana And The Bunch, but this occasional venture subsequently folded. In 1984 Levinger reappeared in the Bandits, before retiring from music to run a hang-gliding shop.

●ALBUMS: *The Youngbloods* (RCA Victor 1967)★★★, *Earth Music* (RCA Victor 1967)★★★, *Elephant Mountain* (RCA 1969)★★★★, *Rock Festival* (1970)★★, *Ride The Wind* (1971)★★, *Good 'N' Dusty* (1971)★★, *High On A Ridgetop* (1972)★★.

●COMPILATIONS: one side only *Two Trips* (Mercury 1970)★★, *The Best Of The Youngbloods* (RCA 1970)★★★, *Sunlight* (1971)★★, *Get Together* (1971)★★, *This Is The Youngbloods* (RCA 1972)★★★, *Point Reyes Station* (1987)★★, *From The Gaslight To The Avalon* (1988)★★.

YURO, TIMI

b. Rosemarie Yuro, 4 August 1940, Chicago, Illinois, USA. Yuro moved to Los Angeles as a child, and by the late 50s was singing in her mother's Italian restaurant. She was signed to Liberty by the head of the company, Al Bennett, and recorded her most famous track, 'Hurt' in 1961. Produced by Clyde Otis, who had supervised many of Dinah Washington's hits, the dramatic ballad was a revival of Roy Hamilton's 1954 R&B hit. Yuro's searing white soul rendering entered the Top 10 in 1961 and inspired numerous artists to cover the song, notably Elvis Presley, whose version was a Top 30 hit in 1976. The follow-ups 'I Apologise' and 'Smile' made less impact, but in 1962, 'What's A Matter Baby?' reached the Top 20. Yuro had minor hits with 'Make The World Go Away' (a greater success the following year for Eddy Arnold) and the country song 'Gotta Travel On'. Her Liberty albums contained a mix of standard ballads such as Mitchell Parish and Hoagy Carmichael's 'Stardust' and soul songs ('Hallelujah I Love Him So'), but mid-60s records for Mercury found Yuro veering towards a more mainstream cabaret repertoire. There were later records for Playboy (1975), and in 1981 a reissued 'Hurt' was a big hit in The Netherlands. This led to a new recording deal with Polydor. During the late 80s Yuro recorded an album of songs by Willie Nelson, but soon afterwards her performing career was curtailed by serious illness.

●ALBUMS: *Hurt* (Liberty 1961)★★★★, *Let Me Call You Sweetheart* (1962)★★★, *Soul* (Liberty 1962)★★★, *What's A Matter Baby?* (1963)★★★, *Make The World Go Away* (1963)★★★, *Amazing* (1964)★★★, *All Alone Am I* (1981)★★★, *Today* (1982)★★.

●COMPILATIONS: *Very Best Of Timi Yuro* (1980)★★★, *18 Greatest Hits* (1988)★★★, *The Lost Voice Of Soul* (RPM 1993)★★★.

ZACHARIAS, HELMUT

b. 27 January 1920, Germany. A violinist, arranger, composer, and bandleader. At the age of three Zacharias was given a toy violin by his father, himself a professional violinist. The gift was soon replaced by the real thing, and when Zacharias was 17, he bought himself a Hammig instrument with the proceeds of a Fritz Kreisler Award. He formed his own orchestra which became popular throughout Europe. One of his biggest hits, 'When The White Lilacs Bloom Again', was also released in the USA in 1956, and almost made the Top 10. In the late 1950s Zacharias settled in Ascona, the Italian part of Switzerland, and, soon afterwards, in the early 60s, began to make an impact in the UK with several successful albums. Some of them were credited 'with Orchestra', and others 'with Magic Violins'. One of the latter was 'Love Is Like A Violin', which was enormously successful for Zacharias on the Continent, but was kept out of the UK chart by a version from singing comedian Ken Dodd in 1960. Four years later, Zacharias made the British Top 10, unopposed, with 'Tokyo Melody', which he wrote with Heinz Hellmer and Lionel Bart. It was the theme tune for the 1964 Olympic Games, the first occasion they had been held in Asia. Zacharias continued to prosper with his mixture of contemporary pops and light classics, played in a relaxed, swinging style, with the ever-present fiddle. His *Greatest Hits* contained numbers such as 'Cherry Pink And Apple Blossom White', 'Under The Linden Tree', and one of his own most attractive compositions, 'Blue Blues'.

●ALBUMS: *Rendezvous For Strings, Pop Goes Baroque, A Violin Sings, Super Twist, Crazy Party, Dance With My Fair Lady, Teatime In Tokyo, Romantically Yours, Violins Victorious, Happy Strings Of, This Is My Song, Plays The Hits, For Lovers-With Love, Strauss Waltzes, Golden Award Songs, On Lovers Road, Candlelight Serenade, The Best Of Everything, Hi-Fi Fiddle* (all 60s), *Light My Fire* (Sounds Superb 1971)★★★, *Greatest Hits* (1973)★★★.

ZAGER AND EVANS

One of the biggest-selling hits of 1969 was the pessimistic look into the future, 'In The Year 2525 (Exordium & Terminus)' by Zager And Evans. The duo was Denny Zager (b. 1944, Wymore, Nebraska, USA) and Rick Evans (b. 1943, Lincoln, Nebraska, USA), who had met in 1962 and joined a band called the Eccentrics. Evans left that band in 1965 but the pair teamed up again at the end of the decade. Zager had written 'In The Year 2525' five

years earlier, and they recorded it in Texas in 1968. It was released on the local Truth label and picked up the following year by RCA Records, climbing to number 1, where it remained for six weeks in the US charts and three weeks in the UK, ultimately selling a reported five million copies. Unable to follow this success, Zager quit in 1970; neither he nor Evans were heard of again, although RCA continued to release their recordings for some time in attempts to make lightning strike twice.
●ALBUMS: *2525 (Exordium & Terminus)* (RCA 1969)★★, *Zager And Evans* (RCA 1970)★, *Food For The Mind* (RCA 1971)★.

ZOMBIES

Rod Argent (b. 14 June 1945, St. Albans, Hertfordshire, England; piano), Colin Blunstone (b. 24 June 1945, St. Albans, Hertfordshire, England; vocals), Paul Atkinson (b. 19 March 1946, Cuffley, Hertfordshire, England; guitar), Paul Arnold (bass) and Hugh Grundy (b. 6 March 1945, Winchester, Hampshire, England; drums) formed the Zombies in 1963, although Chris White (b. 7 March 1943, Barnet, Hertfordshire) replaced Arnold within weeks of their inception. This St. Albans-based quintet won the local Herts Beat competition, the prize for which was a recording deal with Decca Records. The Zombies' debut single, 'She's Not There', rose to number 12 in the UK, but proved more popular still in America, where it reached number 2. Blunstone's breathy voice and Argent's imaginative keyboard arrangement provided the song's distinctive features and the group's crafted, adventurous style was then maintained over a series of excellent singles. Sadly, this diligence was not reflected in success, and although 'Tell Her No' was another US Top 10 entrant, it fared much less well at home while later releases, including 'Whenever You're Ready' and 'Is This The Dream' unaccountably missed out altogether.

The group, not unnaturally, grew frustrated and broke up in 1967 on completion of *Odyssey And Oracle*. The promise of those previous releases culminated in this magnificent collection which adroitly combined innovation, melody and crafted harmonies. Its closing track, 'Time Of The Season', became a massive US hit, but despite several overtures, the original line-up steadfastly refused to reunite. Argent and Grundy were subsequently joined by ex Mike Cotton bassist Jim Rodford (b. 7 July 1941, St. Albans, Hertfordshire, England) and Rick Birkett (guitar) and this reshaped ensemble was responsible for the Zombies' final single, 'Imagine The Swan'. Despite the label credit, this release was ostensibly the first recording by the keyboard player's new venture, Argent. Colin Blunstone, meanwhile embarked on a stop-start solo career. The band reconvened to record *New World* in 1991, which on release received respectable reviews.
●ALBUMS: *Begin Here* (Decca 1965)★★★, *Odessey And Oracle* (CBS 1968)★★★★, *Early Days* (London 1969),★★ *The Zombies Live On The BBC 1965-1967* (Rhino 1985)★★★, *Meet The Zombies* (Razor 1989)★★★, *Five Live Zombies* (Razor 1989)★★★, *New World* (JSE 1991)★★.
●COMPILATIONS: *The World Of The Zombies* (Decca 1970)★★★, *Time Of The Zombies* (Epic 1973)★★★, *Rock Roots* (Decca 1976)★★★, *The Best And The Rest Of The Zombies* (Back Trac 1984)★★★, *Greatest Hits* (DCC 1990)★★★, *Best Of The Zombies* (Music Club 1991)★★★, *The EP Collection* (See For Miles 1992)★★★★, *The Zombies 1964-67* (More Music 1995)★★★.

INDEX

A

A Band Of Angels, 5, 138, 290
A Cappella, 42
A Man Called Adam, 145-146
A Witness, 235
A&M Records, 11, 25, 94, 152, 330, 391
A.B. Skhy, 5, 201
Abba, 59, 90
Abbot, Gary, 266
Abbott Records, 369
Abbott, George, 50
Abbott, Russ, 331
ABC Records, 8, 62, 67, 106, 184
Abelson, Frank, 457
Above All, 181, 464
Abrahams, Mick, 112
Abramson, Herb, 20, 470
Abshire, Nathan, 28-29
Absolute Beginners, 143, 339
Abyssinians, 5
AC/DC, 174, 444
Academy, 6 and passim
Ace Records, 28, 95, 206
Ace, Charlie, 343
Ace, Johnny, 62
Acid House, 117
Acid Jazz, 300
Ackles, David, 177, 239, 421
Acklin, Barbara, 6, 105
Ackroyd, Dan, 135
Action, 6 and passim
Acuff, Roy, 118
Acuff-Rose Music, 332
Ad Libs, 6
Adam, Mike And Tim, 6
Adams Singers, 7, 274
Adams, Cliff, 7, 274
Adams, Derroll, 156
Adams, Glen, 349
Adams, Johnny, 298
Adams, Lee, 145, 230
Adams, Pete, 178
Adams, Ray, 22
Adams, Roy, 103
Adderley, Cannonball, 7-8, 143, 155, 183, 318, 420, 443, 475
Adderley, Nat, 7-8
Addie, 404
Adler, Lou, 8, 11, 60, 165, 187, 250, 288, 301, 304, 317, 376, 411, 418
Adler, Luther, 194
Admiral Records, 364
Admirations, 263
Adnopoz, Elliott Charles, 178
Adolescents, 400
Afghan Whigs, 472
After Hours, 107, 238
After Tea, 9, 146
Afterglow, 412
Aftermath, 380, 383
Aggression, 183
Aguilar, Dave, 112
Aiese, Mary, 371
Air Supply, 18

Airey, Don, 121
Airforce, 27, 69, 273, 447
Aitken, Bobby, 9
Aitken, Laurel, 9
Akens, Jewel, 10
Alaimo, Jimmy, 312
Alan Brown, 73
Alan, Buddy, 335
Alan, Carl, 29, 386
Alaska Records, 393
Albin, Peter, 55, 129
Albin, Rod, 416
Albion Band, 481
Albion Country Band, 481
Albuagh, Bill, 277
Alcapone, Dennis, 343, 359, 370
Alcatraz, 49
Alder, John 'Twink', 358
Aldis, Barry, 364
Aldridge, Alan, 43
Alex, George, 329
Alexander, Arthur, 10
Alexander, Bill, 162
Alexander, Denny, 117
Alexander, Gary, 19
Alexander, James, 30
Alford, John, 11
Alfredo, Giovanni, 112
Ali, Rashied, 122
Alice Cooper, 247, 363, 456
Alice's Restaurant, 10
Alisha's Attic, 351
Allan, David, 404
Allan, Jan, 251
Allbut, Jiggs, 14-15
Allegro, 183
Allen, Barbara, 6
Allen, Bob, 482
Allen, Charles, 377
Allen, Charlie, 336
Allen, Colin, 140, 296, 312
Allen, Daevid, 415
Allen, Deborah, 369-370
Allen, Don, 370
Allen, Frank, 46, 394
Allen, Jack, 169
Allen, Jeff, 44, 173
Allen, John, 324
Allen, Mark, 296
Allen, Mick, 169, 415
Allen, Mike, 415
Allen, Nat, 269
Allen, Paul, 233
Allen, Peter, 25
Allen, Rick, 73
Allen, Robert, 166
Allen, Rod, 197
Allen, Rodney, 197
Allen, Steve, 275, 472-473
Allen, Wally, 178, 358
Allen, Woody, 285
Allen, Yvonne, 11
Alligator Records, 5
Allin, Mary, 345
Allison, Bob, 11
Allison, Jerry, 134

Allison, Keith, 372
Allison, Mose, 10-11, 65, 190
Allisons, 11
Allix, Dick, 456
Allman Brothers Band, 241
Allman, Duane, 213, 240, 265, 348, 390
Allman, Gregg, 240
Allman, Kurt, 50
Almer, Tandyn, 19
Almighty, 205, 297
Almond, Johnny, 225, 296, 313
Almond, Marc, 302, 350, 360, 465
Alpert, Herb, 8, 11, 19, 24-25, 60-61, 318, 391, 467
Alphonso, Roland, 409
Alston, Barbara, 136
Alston, Shirley, 404
Altham, Keith, 448
Altman, Robert, 328
Ambient Sound Records, 94
Amboy Dukes, 12, 205
Ambrose, 112, 268-270, 393
Amburn, Ellis, 258, 333
Amen Corner, 12-13, 17, 149, 245
American Breed, 13
American Hot Wax, 52
Ames Brothers, 13, 24, 199
Ames, Ed, 13
Ames, Nancy, 473
Amey, Ian, 141
Ammons, Albert, 66
Amorphous, 218
Amory Kane, 190
Ampex, 161, 194, 426
Amsterdam, Morey, 38
Amy Records, 261
Anders And Poncia, 64, 81, 134, 261-262
Andersen, Eric, 120
Andersen, Terry, 5
Anderson, Cat, 308
Anderson, Edward, 51
Anderson, Ernestine, 402-403
Anderson, Gary, 69
Anderson, Katherine, 295
Anderson, Miller, 146, 225-226
Anderson, Pete, 32, 465
Anderson, Terry, 24
Andersson, Benny, 59
Andes, Mark, 420
Andrew, Archie, 13
Andrew, John, 258
Andrew, Sam, 55, 66, 257
Andrews, Bob, 268, 320
Andrews, Chris, 13, 188, 224, 337, 401
Andrews, Don, 371
Andrews, Ernie, 8
Andrews, James, 14
Andrews, Julie, 13-14, 76, 91, 391
Andrews, Viv, 358
Andridge, Rick, 396
Andrijasevich, Gary, 112
Andromeda, 14
Andwella's Dream, 14

Andy, Bob, 352
Angel, Johnny, 187
Angels (USA), 14
Animal Tracks, 15
Animals, 15-17, 41, 54, 75, 82, 102, 104, 109, 126, 128, 140, 145, 152, 167, 212-213, 231, 264, 291, 295, 313, 317, 321, 324, 366, 407
Anka, Paul, 116, 203
Annette, 16, 22, 38, 165, 293, 418, 451, 458
Anthony, Clay, 16
Anthony, John, 73
Anthony, Mike, 245
Anthony, Paul, 153
Anthony, Ray, 22, 96, 377
Anthony, Richard, 16, 222
Anthrax, 66
Antonioni, Michelangelo, 65
Aorta, 16
Aphrodite, 38
Aplan, Richard, 261
Apocalypse, 159
Apollo, 70, 77-79, 82-83, 300, 302, 322, 430, 440
Appice, Carmine, 65, 456
Applause, 255, 278, 442
Apple Records, 247, 436
Applejacks (UK), 16
Appletree Theatre, 17
Aquarian Age, 233
Arama, Greg, 12
Arbus, Dave, 173
Arby, 146
ARC, 410
Arcade, 332, 481
Arcadium, 17
Archies, 17, 32, 137, 151, 200
Arden, Don, 12, 17, 21, 323, 379, 410, 412
Arden, Eve, 230
Argent, 128, 306, 386, 485
Argent, Rod, 306, 485
Arista Records, 204, 267, 466
Arkin, Alan, 384
Arlen Records, 435
Arlen, Harold, 47, 346
Arlin, Bobby, 275
Armageddon, 282
Armstrong, Bob, 100
Armstrong, Frankie, 397
Armstrong, Jim, 441
Armstrong, Louis, 29, 111, 230, 306, 346-347
Arnaz, Alberto, IV, 153
Arnaz, Desi, 153
Arno, Lou, 364
Arnold, Billy Boy, 152
Arnold, Bob, 292
Arnold, Eddy, 284, 337, 353, 484
Arnold, Jerry, 57
Arnold, Joe, 292
Arnold, P.P., 18, 328, 412
Arnold, Patricia, 18
Arnold, Paul, 334, 485
Arntz, James, 14

Aronson, Boris, 89
Arrington, Joseph, Jnr., 440
Arrow, 67, 82
Arrows, 30
Ars Nova, 18
Art, 18 and *passim*
Art Ensemble Of Chicago, 34
Art Of Noise, 175, 257
Artery, 457
Arthur, Art, 19, 61, 324
Arthur, Beatrice, 194
Arthur, Bob, 320
Arthur, J., 116
Arthur, Jean, 50
Arthur, Robert, 91, 97
Artwoods, 18-19, 225
Arvee Records, 45
Asher, John, 132
Asher, John Symon, 132
Asher, Peter, 345
Ashes, 240, 306, 323, 341, 366
Ashford And Simpson, 208
Ashford, Rosalind, 293
Ashley, Steve, 472
Ashton, Arthur, 243
Ashton, Floyd, 435
Ashton, Gardner And Dyke, 57, 371, 427
Ashton, Jan, 458
Ashton, Tony, 243, 371
Asia, 392, 484
Askew, John, 210
Askey, Arthur, 457
Aspects Of Love, 59
Aspinall, Neil, 19
Assegai, 361-362
Assembly, 214
Association, 19 and *passim*
Astaire, Fred, 116
Asylum Choir, 19
Asylum Records, 88, 169, 239
At The Gates, 31
Atco Records, 55, 196, 445, 455, 469
Atkins, Chet, 19-20, 131, 229, 369, 460
Atkins, Jim, 19
Atkinson, Bill, 211
Atkinson, Craig, 129
Atkinson, Paul, 485
Atlanta Rhythm Section, 117
Atlantic Records, 16, 20-21, 48, 55, 82, 95, 106, 122, 127, 135, 161-162, 204, 227-228, 247, 286-287, 342, 348, 390, 410, 426, 430, 433, 438, 449, 470
Atomic Rooster, 14, 27, 77, 192
Atrophy, 181, 355
Attack, 21 and *passim*
Attwool, Hugh, 179
Attwell, Winifred, 306, 316
Au Go-Go Singers, 19, 81
Auger, Brian, 28, 164, 213, 300, 426
Austin, Danny, 6
Austin, Mel, 441
Austin, Peter, 114
Austin, Roy, 378
Austin, Tony, 83
Autell, Pete, 463
Autosalvage, 21
Autry, Gene, 119, 269, 455
Autumn Records, 21-22, 44, 156, 160, 219, 411, 458
Avallone, Francis, 22
Avalon, 16, 22, 38, 116, 187, 388, 483
Avalon, Frankie, 16, 22, 38, 116, 187, 388
Average White Band, 265-266, 392
Avery, Bob, 132
Aviator, 264, 272
Avon Sisters, 22
Avons, 22
Avory, Mick, 266-267, 337, 379
Axe, 343-344
Axelrod, David, 177, 262

Axiom, 27
Axis, 232-233, 292
Axton, Estelle, 426
Axton, Hoyt, 353
Ayers, Kevin, 313, 339, 415
Aykroyd, Dan, 299
Azevedo, Walter, 90
Aznavour, Charles, 22-23, 58, 342

B

B Records, 404, 438
B-Movie, 24
B. Bumble And The Stingers, 24, 201
B., Anthony, 16, 46-47, 138, 225, 280, 403
B., Derek, 165, 205, 234, 422, 436
B., Stevie, 476
B.B. Blunder, 65, 164
B.T. Puppy Records, 148, 445
Babbington, Roy, 415
Babes In Arms, 299
Babes In Toyland, 16
Babineaux, Sidney, 109
Babylon, Bobby, 114
Bacall, Lauren, 472
Baccini, Joe, 434
Bach, Sebastian, 284, 434
Bacharach, Burt, 11, 24-25, 52, 54, 58, 74, 150, 204, 210, 248, 256, 284, 303, 350, 401, 422-423, 463, 465
Bachelors, 25-26, 457
Back Door, 133, 158, 263, 271, 390, 399
Backbeat, 39, 43, 61, 113, 282
Bacon, Francis, 95
Bacon, Maurice, 285
Bad Boy, 380
Bad Dreams, 450
Bad News, 39, 284
Badanjek, John, 388
Badfinger, 42, 248
Baez, Joan, 26-27, 156, 167, 169, 191, 211, 257, 330, 478
Bagdasarian, Ross, 111
Baggott, Martin, 16
Bags, 123, 144
Bahula, Sebothane, 362
Bailey, Bill, 140, 369
Bailey, Bob, 458
Bailey, Donald, 300, 413
Bailey, Pearl, 47, 230
Bailey, Pete, 35
Bain, Jimmy, 478
Bairstow, Michael, 251
Daja Marimba Band, 149
Baker Gurvitz Army, 27, 221
Baker Street, 41
Baker, Arthur, 170
Baker, Bob, 396
Baker, Butch, 32
Baker, Chet, 127, 443
Baker, David, 5
Baker, Ginger, 27-28, 63, 69, 132, 213, 221, 271, 273, 447
Baker, Jack, 69
Baker, John, 5, 32
Baker, Joyce, 461
Baker, Keith, 28
Baker, Kenny, 29, 228
Baker, LaVern, 418, 470
Baker, Lloyd, 253
Baker, Maury, 18
Baker, Mickey, 304
Baker, Peter, 27, 132
Bakerloo, 28
Bakker, Tammy Faye, 238
Baldry, Long John, 28, 142, 164, 271, 427
Balfa Brothers, 28-29
Balfa, Dewey, 28-29
Balin, Marty, 12, 253
Balk, Harry, 398

Ball, Dave, 360
Ball, Kenny, 29, 56, 304
Ball, Lucille, 153, 382
Ball, Michael, 59
Ball, Reginald, 448
Ballad In Blue, 107, 365
Ballard, Florence, 29, 295, 359, 431-432
Ballard, Hank, 108, 249
Ballard, Hank, And The Midnighters, 108
Ballard, Russ, 188, 386, 401, 454
Ballinger, Dave, 32
Balogh, Bill, 386
Banana And The Bunch, 483
Banashak, Joe, 160, 308
Bancroft, Anne, 215
Band Of Gypsies, 232-233
Bang Records, 182, 429
Banished, 136
Banks, Bessie, 127, 318
Banks, Homer, 30, 425
Bar None Records, 182
Bar-Kays, 30, 367
Barab, Seymour, 148
Barbarians, 30-31
Barbata, John, 450
Barbee, Norma, 458
Barber, Adrian, 55
Barber, Chris, 29, 56, 271
Barclay James Harvest, 53
Barclay Records, 146
Barclay, Michael, 262
Barclay, Nicole, 146
Bardens, Peter, 110, 417, 441
Bardot, Brigitte, 451
Bare, Bobby, 256, 436
Bargeron, Dave, 64
Barile, Jo, 460
Barker, Dave, 343-344
Barker, Francine, 341
Barnes And Barnes, 344, 403, 472
Barnes, Ken, 38
Barnes, Lloyd, 344
Barnes, Richard, 472
Barnes, Ricky, 226
Barnett, Grace, 219, 253
Barnett, Tommy, 84
Barnum, 475
Barnum, H.B., 475
Barrett, Richie, 105
Barrett, Ritchie, 55
Barrett, Roger, 31
Barrett, Roger Keith, 31
Barrett, Syd, 31-32, 285
Barri, Steve, 8, 165, 190, 217, 301, 411
Barrie, J.J., 50, 337, 360
Barrie, J.M., 50
Barrington, Roy, 362
Barris, Chuck, 93
Barron Knights, 32, 284
Barron, Kenny, 66
Barry And The Tamerlanes, 32
Barry, Jeff, 17, 32, 36, 54, 64, 76, 154, 200, 220, 301, 315
Barry, John, 58-59, 73, 75, 188, 197, 368
Barry, Len, 32, 160-161, 276, 333
Barry, Paul, 368, 387-388, 395
Barry, Sandra, 6
Barry, Tony, 175
Bart, Lionel, 33-34, 63, 189, 331, 338, 373, 484
Barthelme, Rick, 367
Barthol, Bruce, 129
Bartholomew, Dave, 52
Bartlett, Bill, 277
Bartlett, Henry, 190
Bartoli, Frank, 245
Barton, Gordon, 14
Basie, Count, 47, 145-147, 346, 393, 475
Baskin, Don, 435
Bass, Billy, 232, 431

Bass, Colin, 140, 403, 409
Bass, Fontella, 33-34, 150, 305
Bass, Ralph, 77, 110
Bassey, Shirley, 33-35, 58, 63, 75, 294, 305, 368
Bateman, Robert, 30, 295, 366
Bates, Django, 143
Bates, Elias, 152
Batiste, Harold, 308
Batt, Mike, 223, 319
Battavio, Margaret, 292
Battered Ornaments, 35, 80
Battin, Skip, 88, 201
Battiste, Harold, 416, 419, 430
Bauer, Joe, 483
Baughman, Dan, 399
Baughn, David, 163
Bauldie, John, 172
Baverstock, Jack, 11, 141, 190, 196, 262, 338
Baxter, Les, 149
Bay City Rollers, 90, 101
Bayntun, Amanda, 63
Beach Boys, 16, 35-38, 41, 51, 53, 61, 90, 93, 136-137, 139, 153, 199, 211, 224, 237, 239, 251, 263, 283, 317, 366, 376, 431, 436, 445, 448, 460
Beach Party, 16, 22, 38, 108, 139, 152, 239, 251, 274, 436, 460
Beach, Alan, 129
Beacon Street Union, 38, 72-73, 453
Beadle, Len, 276
Bean, George, 380
Bear Family Records, 99, 261
Beard, Joe, 362
Beard, Martin, 416
Beat, 152, 197, 213, 290, 302, 399
Beat Club, 18, 38-39, 243
Beat Unlimited, 478
Beatles, 6, 10, 12, 15, 19-21, 32-33, 35-36, 39-46, 49, 51, 53, 55, 58, 65, 68, 70-71, 76, 82, 86-87, 90, 93, 101-105, 107, 111-116, 127, 132, 137, 142, 149-150, 156, 166-167, 175, 179-181, 186, 188, 194, 199, 205, 210-212, 214, 217, 223-224, 227, 230, 234, 236-238, 242-244, 260-261, 267-269, 271-272, 274, 277, 279, 282, 290, 294-295, 300, 303-304, 309, 311, 315-317, 321, 325, 332, 334-335, 338-339, 347, 351-352, 354, 357, 360, 363, 365-366, 371, 379-382, 385-386, 391, 397, 400-401, 403-404, 408, 418-419, 422, 424, 428-431, 434, 436, 447, 449-450, 456-457, 467, 469, 480
Beatmasters, 18
Beatstalkers, 44
Beau Brummels, 21, 44-45, 156, 225, 411, 458
Beaumont, Robin, 75
Bechet, Sidney, 66, 111
Beck, Bogert And Appice, 456
Beck, Don, 152
Beck, Jeff, 21, 57, 65, 157, 221, 233, 294, 384, 433, 468, 480
Beck, Joe, 348
Beck, John, 275
Becker, Walter, 252
Beckett, Barry, 170
Beckett, Harry, 225
Bedrocks, 45
Bee Gees, 55, 207, 286, 407, 460, 466
Beefeater, 60
Been, Michael, 16, 222
BEF, 402
Beggars Opera, 45
Begleiter, Lionel, 33
Behan, Dominic, 164
Bel Canto, 268
Bel-Airs, 45
Belafonte, Harry, 45, 116, 166, 316
Belfast Gypsies, 201, 441
Bell And Arc, 410

Bell Records, 83, 90, 131, 151, 435
Bell, Al, 426
Bell, Alec, 286
Bell, Billy, 441
Bell, Graham, 410
Bell, Jimmy, 286
Bell, Johnnie, 442
Bell, Madeline, 142
Bell, Richard, 258
Bell, Sam, 179
Bell, Thom, 423
Bell, William, 196, 423, 426, 442
Bellamy, George, 446
Bellamy, Pete, 481
Belle, 178, 206
Belle Stars, 178
Belley, Richard, 241
Belmonts, 93, 148, 153-154, 405, 417
Belshaw, Brian, 65
Belsky, Danny, 469
Belsky, Harold Simon, 61
Beltone Records, 248
Belushi, John, 135, 299
Bender, Ariel, 421
Beneke, Tex, 289
Benett, Dwight, 361
Benjamin, Louis, 240
Bennett, Al, 483
Bennett, Alan, 54
Bennett, Anthony, 46
Bennett, Brian, 305, 398
Bennett, Cliff, 46, 138, 334, 365, 395
Bennett, Don, 112
Bennett, Duster, 46
Bennett, John, 29
Bennett, Larry, 324
Bennett, Patricia, 111
Bennett, R., 186
Bennett, Richard Rodney, 317-318
Bennett, Ronnie, 384
Bennett, Tony, 47-48, 75, 122, 182, 184, 464
Bennett, Val, 343
Bennett, Veronica, 384
Bennett, Wiley, 474
Benno, Marc, 19
Benny, Jack, 145
Benoit, David, 221
Benson, Bruce, 30
Benson, George, 414, 454
Benson, John, 29
Benson, Kathleen, 477
Benson, Renaldo, 199-200
Benson, Robby, 210
Benton, Brook, 48
Berigan, Bunny, 124
Berio, Luciano, 434
Berlin, Irving, 50, 72, 241, 346
Berline, Byron, 153
Bernard, Barrie, 349
Bernard, Rob, 109
Bernardi, Herschel, 194
Bernhardt, Warren, 18
Bernhart, Milt, 49
Berns, Bert, 48, 83, 163, 186, 197, 265, 300, 365, 430, 441, 463
Bernstein, Elmer, 49-50, 58, 60
Bernstein, Leonard, 50-51, 328
Bernstein, Louis, 50
Berry, Chuck, 15, 37, 40-42, 51-52, 57, 109, 152, 191, 228, 274, 299, 335, 355, 371, 376, 379, 386-387
Berry, Dave, 52-53, 102, 336, 424
Berry, Jan, 250-251
Berry, Jeff, 291
Berry, John, 371
Berry, Mike, 53, 101, 303, 334
Berry, Richard, 53, 266, 325
Berryhill, Bob, 433
Berryman, Pete, 190
Bertrand, Eddie, 45
Best, George, 191, 403
Best, Graham, 17

Best, John, 28, 188, 279, 284
Best, Johnny, 83, 98, 100, 264, 377, 467
Best, Pat, 72
Best, Pete, 19, 39, 43, 53, 102, 180, 284, 294, 403
Best, Tony, 48, 403
Betesh, Danny, 52-53
Bethel, John, 243
Betrock, Alan, 400, 404
Betsy, 192
Bettis, John, 25
Beveridge, Alistair, 288
Beverley's, 149, 299
Beverly Hillbillies, 393
Bickerton, Wayne, 53
Bidwell, Dave, 110
Bienstock, Freddy, 54
Bienstock, Johnny, 54, 400
Bifferty, Skip, 18, 229, 409-410
Big 8, 93, 386
Big Audio Dynamite, 33
Big Bertha, 444
Big Bopper, 80, 358, 455
Big Brother And The Holding Company, 55, 129, 215, 257, 317
Big Country, 333
Big Daddy, 156
Big Fun, 144
Big House, 168
Big Joe, 351
Big Maybelle, 300
Big Records, 55, 400, 445
Big River, 97, 305, 436
Big Star, 73, 347
Big Three, 55-56, 102, 178, 180, 192, 303, 384-385
Big Top Records, 55, 400
Big Two, 32, 378
Big Youth, 5, 343, 359
Bigard, Barney, 306
Bigsby, Paul, 193
Bikel, Theodore, 239
Bilk, Acker, 27, 29, 56, 102, 148, 457
Bill And Joe, 143
Bill Deal And The Rhondels, 474
Billings, Vic, 56, 262
Billingslea, Joe, 125
Billy Liar, 59
Billy The Kid, 169
Bilsbury, Jimmy, 287
Birch, Bob, 166
Birdie, Conrad, 451
Birds, 10, 57, 81, 149, 265, 315, 361, 392, 451, 465
Birdsong, Cindy, 432
Birkett, Rick, 485
Birkin, Jane, 417
Birrell, Pete, 205
Birth Of The Blues, 145
Birthday Party, 188, 244, 271, 427
Bishop, Elvin, 5, 86
Bishop, Sid, 151
Bjorn, Frank, 48
Black Cat Bones, 57
Black Flag, 182
Black Grape, 157
Black Lace, 57
Black Pearl, 31, 419
Black Sabbath, 18
Black Slacks, 74
Black Velvet Band, 164
Black Velvet Flag, 182
Black Widow, 393
Black, Bill, 57, 353
Black, Brent, 336
Black, Cilla, 24, 40, 58, 74, 102, 137, 142, 180, 283, 294, 391, 401-402, 405, 422
Black, David, 252
Black, Don, 49, 58-60, 405
Black, Jay, 252
Black, Jimmy Carl, 77, 321
Black, Johnny, 100

Black, Roy, 38, 60
Black, Stanley, 7, 480
Black, Ted, 7
Black, Terry, 411
Blackburn, Kenneth, 60
Blackburn, Tony, 60
Blackfoot, 30
Blackford, Andy, 16, 82, 104
Blackhawk, 144, 311, 314
Blackman, Bernard, 467
Blackmore, Ritchie, 53, 72, 112, 120, 130, 230, 334, 431, 433
Blackwell, Chris, 9, 127, 146, 175, 298, 306, 329, 430, 447
Blackwell, Otis, 198, 353-354
Blackwell, Robert 'Bumps', 60
Blackwood, Lloyd, 130
Blaikley, Alan, 141, 234, 240
Blaikley, Howard, 141, 234, 240
Blaine, Hal, 61, 262, 376, 386, 419, 474
Blair, William, 122
Blake, John, 43, 383
Blake, Ron, 414
Blake, William, 158, 206
Blakely, Alan, 447
Blakely, Paul, 94
Blakey, Art, 61-62, 66, 156, 311, 313-314, 320, 404-405, 413, 443
Blakey, Arthur, 61
Blakley, Ronee, 169
Blanchard, Terence, 61
Bland, Bobby 'Blue', 62
Blasko, Chuck, 462
Blau, Eric, 405
Blavat, Jerry, 377
Bley, Carla, 85
Bley, Paul, 85, 183
Blind Faith, 27, 63, 134, 146, 447
Blitz, May, 28, 33
Blitzkrieg, 66
Blonde On Blonde, 63, 167-169, 171
Blondheim, Philip, 301
Blondie, 36, 429
Blood Brothers, 117
Blood, Sweat And Tears, 37, 63-64, 68, 98-99, 212, 226, 238, 256, 329, 478
Bloom, Bobby, 64, 262, 425
Bloomfield, Mike, 64-65, 86, 138, 176, 213, 257, 317, 320, 345, 416
Blossom Time, 147
Blossom Toes, 65, 164, 213
Blossom White, 484
Blossoms, 68, 146
Blow Monkeys, 297
Blow Up, 65, 480
Blow, Will, 265
Blue Angel, 147, 181, 225, 332, 350
Blue Angels, 14
Blue Blue World, 11
Blue Boys, 369, 451-452
Blue Cheer, 65-66, 109, 427
Blue Hawaii, 66, 354, 356-357
Blue Jays, 53, 67, 201, 319
Blue Magic, 21
Blue Mink, 142
Blue Note Records, 7, 66-67, 339, 413
Blue Skies, 244
Blue Stars, 147, 183, 311
Blue Velvets, 133
Blue, David, 67
Blue, Desmond, 151
Blue, Jimmy, 114, 395, 414
Bluejays, 67
Blues Band, 57, 64, 68, 86, 130, 136, 152-153, 165, 167, 176-177, 213, 239, 254, 257-258, 260, 287, 340, 351, 385, 396, 478
Blues Brothers, 71, 78-79, 107, 135, 204-205, 290, 299, 351, 390, 461
Blues In The Night, 63, 249, 480
Blues Machine, 84
Blues Magoos, 67-68, 247

Blues Project, 64, 68, 280, 317, 445
Bluesbreakers, 46, 132, 212, 225, 296-297, 312
Blumenfeld, Roy, 68
Blunder, B.B., 65, 164
Blunstone, Colin, 224, 273, 485
Blur, 33, 268, 412, 472
Blythe, Arthur, 314
Bo Street Runners, 68, 110, 254
Boat People, 26
Bob And Earl, 68, 332, 382
Bob B. Soxx And The Blue Jeans, 68, 419
Bock, Jerry, 145, 194
Bockner, Rick, 287
Bockris, Victor, 383, 460
Boettcher, Curt, 19
Bogart, Humphrey, 472
Bogart, Neil, 81, 331
Bogert, Tim, 456
Boggs, Dock, 396
Bogguss, Suzy, 20
Bogle, Bob, 460
Bohannon, Jim, 341
Boisot, Louise, 127
Bolan, Marc, 255, 452
Bolin, Tommy, 456
Bolton, Pete, 100
Bond, Graham, 15, 27, 35, 69, 80, 132, 142, 186, 213, 271, 279, 296, 352, 366, 413
Bond, James, 34, 58, 75, 90, 99, 256, 316, 408, 417, 425
Bond, Johnny, 433
Bond, Ronnie, 448
Bond, Terry, 378
Bonds, Gary 'U.S.', 69-70, 248, 351, 405, 417
Boney M, 288
Bonfire, Mars, 392, 427
Bonham, 336, 433
Bonham, Jason, 336
Bonham, John, 433
Bonney, Graham, 375
Bono, 70, 394, 416, 419
Bono, Sonny, 70, 394, 416, 419
Bonzo Dog Doo-Dah Band, 70, 327, 417, 437
Boogie Jake, 308
Bookbinder, Anthony, 138
Booker T. And The MGs, 30, 71, 135, 196, 273, 292, 317, 426
Boone, Daniel, 13, 303, 482
Boone, Debby, 71
Boone, Pat, 31, 71-72, 263, 275, 429
Boone, Skip, 21
Boone, Steve, 21, 285-286
Boones, 71
Boot, Adrian, 233
Booth, Stanley, 383
Booth, Tim, 162
Borisoff, Leonard, 160
Bornhold, Herbert, 366
Bosstown Sound, 38, 72-73, 453
Bostic, Earl, 122
Boston Dexters, 478
Boston, Mark, 94
Boulden, John, 415
Bound For Glory, 166
Bourgeois, Les, 74
Bourjer, Geoff, 362
Bourke, Ciaran, 164
Bow Wow Wow, 467
Bowden, Ron, 29
Bowen, Bill, 416
Bowie, David, 44-45, 74, 149, 207, 240, 286, 300, 360, 417
Bowie, Lester, 34
Bowles, Thomas 'Bean', 322
Bown, Alan, 73, 329
Bown, Andy, 234
Bowyer, Brendan, 386
Bowyer, Geoff, 362
Box Of Frogs, 480
Box Tops, 70, 73, 306, 342, 350

Boxcar Willie, 284
Boyce And Hart, 73-74, 315
Boyce, Tommy, 73-74, 315
Boyd, Craig, 275
Boyd, Eddie, 109, 136
Boyd, Eva Narcissus, 281
Boyd, Jenny, 157
Boyd, Joe, 162
Boylan, Jeffrey, 222
Boylan, Terry, 17
Boyle, Denny, 269
Brackeen, Joanne, 61
Brackett, Al, 341
Bradbury, Ray, 341
Bradley, Billy, 255
Bradley, Mick, 427
Bradley, Owen, 119, 276, 451
Brady, Jim, 391
Brady, Phil, 103
Braff, Ruby, 47
Brambell, Wilfred, 223
Brand, Rick, 277
Brando, Marlon, 50, 116
Brandon, Ronnie, 300
Brassens, Georges, 141
Bratton, Creed, 217
Brautigan, Richard, 287
Brave Combo, 444
Braxton, Anthony, 314
Brayley, Rex, 285
Bread, 121, 125, 177, 191, 239-240,
267, 281, 327-328, 344, 432
Breakaways, 74, 461
Breakfast At Tiffany, 289
Breathless, 372
Brecht, Bertolt, 121, 140, 158, 405
Brecht, Kurt, 121, 140, 158, 405
Brecker, Michael, 85, 123
Brecker, Randy, 64, 406
Breitenberger, Edward, 88
Breitenfeld, Paul, 150
Brel, Jacques, 74, 121, 405, 422,
464-465
Brenda And The Rattlesnake, 221
Brenda And The Tabulations, 74-75
Brennan, Eileen, 230
Brennan, Joey, 456
Brenston, Jackie, 449
Brent Records, 238
Bretone, Ronnie, 132
Brett, Paul, 444, 458
Brevett, Lloyd, 409
Brewer And Shipley, 81, 262
Brewer, Teresa, 269
Brian, Eddie, 470
Brian, Lewis, 379
Brian, Ty, 428
Brice, Trevor, 456
Bricker, Gene, 292
Brickley, Audrey, 333
Brickley, Shirley, 333
Brickman, Marshall, 258
Bricusse, Leslie, 75, 145, 270, 289,
334
Bridgeman, Dan, 260
Brigati, Dave, 455
Brigati, Eddie, 147, 481
Briggs, Bill, 371
Briggs, David, 342
Briggs, Vic, 15, 427
Bright, Ronnie, 137
Brightman, Sarah, 59, 374
Brill Building, 54-55, 76, 136, 151,
262, 290, 329, 395, 457
Brilliant Corners, 313-314
Brinsley Schwarz, 176, 268, 427
Britt, Elton, 235
Britt, Mai, 145
Britt, Tina, 430
Britten, Ray, 335
Britten, Terry, 374
Britton, 173, 448, 457
Britton, Chris, 448
Britton, Geoff, 173
Britton, Tony, 457

Broken Arrow, 82
Broken English, 189
Bromham, Del, 429-430
Bronco, 73
Brood, Herman, 136-137
Brook Brothers, 76
Brook, Geoffrey, 76
Brook, Ricky, 76
Brooker, Gary, 337, 360-361
Brookmeyer, Bob, 182
Brooks, Arthur, 245
Brooks, Baba, 352
Brooks, Danny, 160
Brooks, David, 454
Brooks, Derek, 57
Brooks, Harvey, 167, 176, 257, 483
Brooks, Peter, 176, 312
Brooks, Richard, 245
Brooks, Stuart, 57
Broonzy, 'Big' Bill, 220
Brotherhood Of Breath, 361
Brotherhood Of Man, 175
Brothers Four, 76, 104, 406
Brothers Johnson, 386
Brotman, Stuart, 260
Broussard, Austin, 28
Broussard, Grace, 138
Brown Brothers, 79
Brown, Alan, 73
Brown, Andy, 197
Brown, Arthur, 77, 223, 273, 444
Brown, Billy, 418
Brown, Bobby, 77
Brown, Charlie, 221
Brown, Clarence 'Gatemouth', 92,
467
Brown, Clifford, 66, 156
Brown, Dave, 179
Brown, Dennis, 359
Brown, Estelle, 433
Brown, Georgia, 54, 331
Brown, Gloria, 433
Brown, Horace, 323
Brown, James, 71, 77-79, 150, 204,
313, 319, 430, 439-440
Brown, Joe, 20, 74, 79, 108, 207,
228, 259, 338
Brown, John, 71, 122
Brown, Kenny, 84
Brown, Lee, 66
Brown, Marion, 122
Brown, Maxine, 79-80, 205, 212,
248
Brown, Michael, 277
Brown, Pete, 35, 69, 80, 132, 186
Brown, Peter, 43
Brown, Polly, 13
Brown, Ray, 8, 221
Brown, Rick, 310, 427
Brown, Roy, 353
Brown, Ruth, 20, 161, 418
Brown, Sally, 9
Brown, Sam, 18, 79
Brown, Sandy, 112
Brown, Shirley, 30, 426
Brown, Tom, 264
Brown, Tony, 233
Brown, Vikki, 74
Brown, Vincent, 77
Browne, Ivan, 277
Browne, Jackson, 17, 26, 240, 331,
387, 4/4
Brownlee, Mick, 337
Browns, 79, 284
Brox, Annette, 165
Brox, Victor, 165
Broyles, Ben, 104
Brubeck, Dave, 150-151
Bruce And Terry, 291, 411
Bruce, Jack, 27-28, 69, 80, 132, 165,
213, 271, 290, 296, 352
Bruce, Tommy, 80, 274
Bruce-Douglas, Ian, 453
Brumley, Tom, 325, 335
Brunswick Records, 6, 140, 201, 474

Brush, Alan, 414
Bryan, Dora, 108
Bryan, Mark, 108
Bryant, Anita, 80, 379
Bryant, Boudleaux, 184
Bryant, Eldridge, 437-438
Bryant, Rusty, 475
Buchanan, Bob, 247
Buchanan, Roy, 193
Buchwald, Martyn Jerel, 253
Buck, Alan, 198
Buck, Mike, 448
Buck, Peter, 448
Buckinghams, 81
Buckley, Lord, 231
Buckley, Tim, 177, 239, 282, 304,
325, 385, 479
Buckmaster, Paul, 417, 441
Buckner, Milt, 300
Buda, Max, 260
Budd, Eric, 195
Buddah Records, 10, 76, 81, 113,
262, 328, 331, 384, 445
Budgie, 59, 188, 405
Buffalo Springfield, 21, 55, 81-82,
85, 135, 138, 312, 317, 421, 436, 458
Bullet, Jim, 19
Bunn, Alan, 113
Bunnell, George, 429
Burdon, Eric, 15-16, 82, 107, 140,
232, 313, 317
Burgess, John, 294
Burke, Dave, 424
Burke, Johnny, 364
Burke, Pat, 198
Burke, Solomon, 49, 82-83, 102,
130, 347-348, 449, 453, 470
Burke, Sonny, 102
Burkette, Bill, 462
Burnett, Carol, 14
Burnett, Ranie, 84
Burnett, Watty, 344
Burnette, Dorsey, 32, 83
Burnette, Johnny, 83, 360
Burnette, Rocky, 83
Burns, David, 230
Burns, Eddie, 31
Burns, Paddy, 90
Burns, Tito, 11, 83
Burnside, R.L., 84
Burrell, Kenny, 66, 84, 123, 413-414
Burrows, Clive, 113, 312
Burrows, Tony, 175, 196, 248
Burt, David, 204
Burt, Heinz, 230, 446
Burton, Abraham, 414
Burton, Gary, 84-85, 402
Burton, James, 85-86, 193, 325,
355, 376
Burton, Richard, 13, 91
Burton, Trevor, 323
Bush, Richard, 16
Bushnell, Yvonne, 253
Bushy, Ron, 247
Bussch, Hans, 259
Bustamante, Alexandra, 359
Butala, Tony, 277
Butler, Chris, 472
Butler, Jerry, 105, 184, 227, 241,
245, 297, 446, 463
Butler, Joe, 285-286
Butterfield Blues Band, 64, 86, 167,
176-177, 239, 385, 478
Butterfield, Billy, 124
Butterfield, Paul, 64, 86, 167, 176-
177, 220, 324, 345, 385, 478
Butts Band, 159
Byard, Jaki, 307
Bye Bye Birdie, 141, 388, 451
BYG Records, 213
Bygraves, Max, 56, 75, 295, 368
Byrd, Bobby, 66, 77
Byrd, Charlie, 254
Byrd, Donald, 311, 406
Byrd, Gary, 477

Byrd, Joseph, 454
Byrd, Russell, 48, 430
Byrds, 19, 40, 42, 57, 61, 81, 86-88,
120, 123, 135-136, 150, 152, 167,
173, 201, 211-212, 239, 247, 254,
275, 290, 301, 304, 310, 312, 317,
327, 376, 436, 450
Byrne, David, 302
Byrne, Johnny, 428
Byrne, Sean, 129
Byrne, T.J., 386
Byrnes, Edd, 89
Byrom, Larry, 427
Bystanders, 89, 101

C

C Records, 391
C, Roy, 49, 89
Cacophony, 459
Cactus, 119, 344, 388, 456
Caddy, Alan, 264, 446
Cadence Records, 20
Cadets, 35, 90, 253
Cadillacs, 131, 333
Cadogan, Susan, 344
Caesar, Julius, 264
Cagle, Benny, 404
Cahill, Patricia, 26
Cahn, Sammy, 457
Caine, Michael, 316
Caine, Tim, 416
Caiola, Al, 90
Calder, Tony, 90, 245
Caldwell, Al, 428
Caldwell, Alan, 428
Caldwell, Ronnie, 30
Caldwell, Steve, 333
Cale, J.J., 85, 127
Cale, John, 161, 221, 459
California, Randy, 231, 420
Callender, Peter, 402
Callender, Red, 306
Calling, Carroll, 96
Calloway, Cab, 277
Calvert, Bernie, 237
Calvert, Reg, 197, 349
Camel, 154, 177, 228, 261, 416-417
Cameo Records, 160, 331, 333
Cameo-Parkway Records, 81, 162
Cameron, Dave, 68, 178
Cameron, George, 277
Camp, Bob, 211
Camp, Hamilton, 211
Campbell, Alan, 44
Campbell, Barbara, 8
Campbell, Bonnie, 335
Campbell, Brad, 257-258, 340
Campbell, Eddie, 44
Campbell, Glen, 32, 36, 210, 262,
325-326, 451
Campbell, Ian, 91
Campbell, Ian, Folk Group, 91
Campbell, James, 281
Campbell, James Milton, Jnr., 281
Campbell, John, 91
Campbell, Junior, 197, 293
Campbell, Lorna, 91
Campbell, Milton, 281
Campbell, Philip, 403
Campbell, Rick, 76
Campbell, Tommy, 262
Campbell, William, 197
Campbell, Willie Junior, 293
Campbell-Lyons, Patrick, 329
Candide, 50
Candoli, Conte, 221
Candoli, Pete, 49
Candy Flip, 78
Candy Man, 75, 145, 376
Cane, Ray, 239
Canetti, Jacques, 74
Canned Heat, 92, 106, 187, 317,
321, 336, 430, 478

Cannibal And The Headhunters, 92, 264
Cannon, Ace, 57
Cannon, Freddy, 93, 429
Cannon, Gus, 384
Cannonball, Wabash, 29
Cantrall, Bobby, 255
Capaldi And Frog, 447
Capaldi, Jim, 148, 201, 229, 446-447
Capitol (Eire), 93-94 and passim
Capitol Records, 6, 35, 139, 147, 210, 258, 265, 275, 278, 280, 282, 316, 335, 376, 435, 445, 481
Capitols, 94
Capizzi, Leonard, 348
Capone, Al, 359
Capris, 94
Captain And Tennille, 61, 395
Captain Beefheart, 81, 84, 94-95, 205, 262, 321-322
Caravan, 62, 116, 156, 263
Caravelles, 95
Cardiac Arrest, 30
Carefree, 108, 129, 416
Cargman, Jerry, 190
Carisi, John, 183
Carless, Dorothy, 333
Carless, Mick, 224
Carlisle, Bill, 19
Carlos, Don, 131
Carlton And His Shoes, 5
Carlton, Larry, 143
Carman, 105
Carman, Brian, 105
Carmen Jones, 45
Carmichael, Hoagy, 189, 316, 484
Carnegie, Dale, 97
Carnes, Kim, 150, 327
Carolina Moon, 202
Carpenter, Mary-Chapin, 27
Carpenters, 11, 25, 61, 125, 270, 368, 461
Carr, Ian, 143-144
Carr, James, 95, 342
Carr, Jesse Willard, 241
Carr, Pearl, 95, 393
Carr, Pearl, And Teddy Johnson, 95, 393
Carr, Roy, 43, 357, 383
Carr, Teddy, 393
Carr, Tony, 43
Carr, Vikki, 74, 96
Carr, Wynona, 60, 416
Carreras, José, 50
Carrie, 374
Carrigan, Jerry, 342
Carrington, Jack, 154
Carroll, Bernadette, 15
Carroll, Dave, 244
Carroll, Diahann, 264
Carroll, Gregory, 333
Carroll, Hattie, 167
Carroll, Ronnie, 96
Carson, Johnny, 147, 376, 444
Carson, Terry, 149
Carter And Lewis, 96-97, 196, 336
Carter Family, 20, 98-99
Carter, Benny, 7, 112, 142
Carter, Betty, 107
Carter, Carlene, 99
Carter, Clarence, 331, 342
Carter, Jimmy, 302, 307
Carter, John, 96, 98, 142, 243, 248
Carter, June, 98-100
Carter, Maybelle, 20
Carter, Peter, 197
Carter, Ray, 107
Carter, Ron, 143, 155, 318, 405
Carthy, Martin, 91, 167
Cartwright, Alan, 360
Casablanca Records, 81, 200
Casady, Jack, 232, 253
Cascades, 32, 97, 278
Case, Byron, 431
Casey, Al, 474

Cash, Alvin, 97
Cash, Fred, 245
Cash, Jack, 97
Cash, John R., 100
Cash, Johnny, 97-100, 168, 178, 247, 284, 376, 404, 406
Cash, Philip, 16
Cash, Rosanne, 97, 99
Casinos, 100, 284
Cass And The Cassanovas, 55, 210
Cassavetes, John, 49
Cassiday, Tony, 424
Cassidy, David, 130, 137
Cassidy, Ed, 375, 420-421
Castelles, 101, 365
Castells, 100
Castle, Bill, 224
Castro, Peppy, 67
Casual, 35, 65, 311, 380
Casuals, 88, 101
Caswell, Dave, 226
Catch My Soul, 18, 214, 227, 360
Catchpole, Tony, 73
Cathedral, Grace, 221
Catlett, Nora Jo, 482
Cato, Bob, 311
Cattini, Clem, 101, 264, 446
Cauchi, Les, 76
Cauley, Ben, 30
Causi, Jerry, 30
Cavaliere, Felix, 147, 481
Cavallari, Tony, 222
Caveman, 33
Cavern, The, 39, 55, 101-103, 149, 180, 212, 271, 428
CBS Records, 44, 73, 86, 146, 169, 285, 311, 382
CCS, 271
Cennamo, Louis, 254
Centipede, 164, 313, 361
Chad And Jeremy, 103
Chadbourne, Eugene, 314
Chairmen Of The Board, 162, 236
Challenger, 45
Challenger, Reg, 45
Challengers, 331, 363, 433, 446
Chamberlain, Richard, 104
Chambers Brothers, 104, 214
Chambers, Joe, 143
Chambers, Paddy, 56, 181, 192
Chambers, Paul, 7, 143, 263
Chameleons, 140
Champagne, 270
Champion, Gower, 230
Champions, 217
Champlin, Bill, 416
Chan, Jackie, 166
Chance, Larry, 172
Chancellor Records, 22, 187, 376
Chandler, Bodie, 92
Chandler, Bryan James, 15, 104
Chandler, Chas, 15, 104, 176, 231-232, 415
Chandler, Gene, 6, 104-105, 156, 297
Chaney, Roy, 129
Channel, Bruce, 105, 299
Channing, Carol, 230
Chantays, 105, 139
Chantels, 105
Chants, 188
Chapin, Harry, 177
Chaplin, Blondie, 36
Chaplin, Charles, 116
Chaplin, Ed, 231, 270
Chapman, Michael, 226
Chapman, Mike, 28
Chapman, Philip, 217
Chapman, Roger, 191
Chapman, Tony, 234, 379
Charig, Marc, 415
Chariot, 140, 292, 313
Charisse, Cyd, 108
Charlatans, 22, 105-106, 156

Charlatans (USA), 105
Charles, Bobby, 109, 233
Charles, Bryan, 378
Charles, David, 107
Charles, Don, 446
Charles, Jimmy, 177
Charles, Ray, 15, 20, 47, 60, 106-107, 127, 140, 161, 178, 214, 226, 298, 335, 347, 351, 365, 404, 470, 476
Charles, Sonny, 419
Charles, Teddy, 307
Charly Records, 297
Charms, 72
Charro, 316, 355, 357
Chas And Dave, 53
Chase, Tommy, 69, 414
Chater, Kerry, 361
Checker Records, 176
Checker, Chubby, 70, 108, 116, 130, 147, 155, 162, 197, 222, 388, 401
Checkmates, 197, 418-419
Cheech And Chong, 8, 11
Cheetah, 326
Chelsea, 147, 246, 270
Chenier, C.J., 109
Chenier, Clifton, 109
Cher, 21, 61, 67, 70, 86, 184, 214, 230, 280, 375, 416, 419, 448, 456
Cherokees, 109
Cherry, Don, 123-124
Chess Records, 51, 83, 109-110, 128, 191, 308
Chess, Leonard, 110
Chess, Philip, 109
Chessler, Deborah, 333
Chessmen, 21
Chevalier, Maurice, 473
Cheynes, 110, 277
Chi-Lites, 6
Chicago Line Blues Band, 68, 254
Chicago Loop, 213
Chichester, John, 409
Chicken Shack, 110-111, 249, 350, 414, 439
Chiffons, 111, 212, 445
Chilliwack, 120
Chilton, Alex, 73
Chilton, John, 111
Chimes, 111, 167
Chimes (USA), 111
Chinatown, 323
Chinn And Chapman, 60
Chipmunks, 111-112
Chisholm, George, 29, 112
Chocolate Watch Band, 76, 112
Chodorov, Jerome, 50
Chosen Few, 410
Christian, Charlie, 51, 84, 219, 318
Christian, Neil, 17, 112, 334, 336
Christian, Roger, 38
Christie, 53, 112-113, 267, 395
Christie, Julie, 267
Christie, Lou, 112-113
Christie, Tony, 53, 395
Christy Minstrels, 21, 301, 304, 326-327
Christy, Don, 70, 416
Christy, Sonny, 70, 416
Chrome, 63
Chrysalis Records, 389
Chung, Geoffrey, 5
Churchill, Chick, 439
Ciconne, Don, 134
Ciner, Al, 13
Cipollina, John, 363
Cipriani, John, 200
Circle Game, 91, 387
Circus, 113 and passim
Citizen Kane, 201, 262
City Of Angels, 310
City Records, 114, 426
Claes, Johnny, 393
Clague, Dave, 70, 409

Clancy, 113, 164, 343
Clancy Brothers, 113, 164
Clancy Brothers And Tommy Makem, 113, 164
Clancy, Tom, 113
Clane, George, 130
Clanton, Jimmy, 113-114, 351, 395
Clapton, Eric, 27, 41, 55, 63, 132, 161, 193, 231, 233, 271, 282, 296, 337, 430, 449, 479-480
Clare, Kenny, 417
Clarendonians, 114
Clark And Hillman, 88
Clark, Alan, 437, 456
Clark, Andy, 234
Clark, B., 86, 114-116, 152, 181
Clark, Brian, 91
Clark, Chris, 114
Clark, Christine, 114
Clark, Dave, 32, 114-115, 125, 367-368
Clark, Dave, Five, 32, 114-115, 125, 367-368
Clark, Dee, 115, 449, 454
Clark, Delecta, 115
Clark, Dick, 31, 93, 108, 115-116, 187, 372, 401, 474
Clark, Gene, 86-88, 152, 275, 304, 327
Clark, Glen, 299
Clark, Guy, 99, 367
Clark, Harold Eugene, 86, 152
Clark, Joe, 437
Clark, Mike, 447
Clark, Pete, 181
Clark, Petula, 102, 116-117, 160, 270, 283, 292, 473
Clark, Sonny, 279
Clark, Terry, 85, 156, 234, 279, 313, 394
Clark, Tony, 319
Clarke, Allan, 236-237
Clarke, Eddie, 270
Clarke, Gussie, 131
Clarke, Mark, 121
Clarke, Michael, 86-88, 301
Clarke, Mick, 434
Clarke, Ross, 160
Clarke, Steve, 260, 472
Clarke-Boland Big Band, 393
Clash, 152, 160, 207, 382, 428, 464
Class, Barry, 198
Classics IV, 117
Claunch, Quinton, 95
Clay, Judy, 423, 426, 433, 436
Clayderman, Richard, 274
Clayson, Alan, 43, 74, 146, 333, 447
Clayton Squares, 117
Clayton, John, 365
Clayton, Merry, 365
Clayton, Mike, 304
Clayton-Thomas, David, 64, 256
Clearlight, 118
Clefs, 278
Cleghorn, Ronald, 96
Clement, Jack, 97
Clements, Terry, 257
Clempson, Dave, 28, 121
Cliff, Tony, 46, 365, 375
Clifford, Buzz, 118
Clifford, Doug, 133
Clifford, John, 444
Clifford, Linda, 297
Clifford, Reese Francis, III, 118
Clifton, Cisco, 97
Climax, 135, 148, 399
Cline, Gerald, 118
Cline, Patsy, 118-120, 369, 482
Clinton, Bill, 103
Clinton, George, 78, 411
Clique, 118
Clock Records, 128
Clooney, Dave, 128
Clooney, Rosemary, 124, 437, 468

Cloud Nine, 259, 430, 438-439
Clouds, 120
Clover, 250
Clovers, 20, 332, 395, 457
Clowney, David Cortez, 128
Cluskey, Conleth, 25
Clutch, 168
Clyde, Jeremy, 103
Coasters, 20, 161, 236, 265, 272, 332, 337, 351, 428, 430
Coates, Maurice, 74
COB, 190
Cobain, Kurt, 383
Cobb, Ed, 112, 424
Cobb, James, 117
Cobb, Jimmy, 143, 263
Cobby, Richard, 6
Cobham, Billy, 143
Cobra, 184
Coburn, James, 118
Cocco, Lenny, 111
Cochise, 350, 361
Cochran, Eddie, 65, 230, 263, 284, 303, 335, 431
Cochran, Hank, 119
Cocker, Joe, 11, 101, 107, 127, 262, 337, 389, 446, 478
Cockney Rebel, 65
Codworth, Nick, 409
Coe, Allan, 404
Coe, David Allan, 404
Coe, George, 404
Coe, Michael, 329
Coe, Tony, 368
Cogan, Alma, 24, 33, 468
Cohen, David, 67, 74, 129, 219
Cohen, Ellen Naiomi, 177
Cohen, Herbie, 304
Cohen, John, 396
Cohen, Leonard, 74, 121, 153, 193, 389, 419
Cohen, Paul, 407
Cohen, S. David, 67
Cohen, Stuart David, 67
Cohn, Al, 144
Cohn, Nik, 49, 383, 472
Colbert, Charles, 13
Cold Sweat, 77-78, 343
Cole, B.J., 385
Cole, Bill, 123
Cole, Gary, 76
Cole, George, 402
Cole, Lloyd, 402
Cole, Nat 'King', 48, 51, 96, 106, 208-209, 262, 402, 451, 468
Cole, Paddy, 93
Cole, Ritchie, 429
Cole, Stranger, 370
Coleman, Cy, 47, 145
Coleman, George, 263
Coleman, Ornette, 7, 66, 94, 155, 459
Coleman, Ray, 43, 181, 211, 383, 423
Coleman, Shepard, 230
Coles, Brian, 19
Collectors, 120 and passim
Collette, Buddy, 291
Collier, Mike, 268, 287
Collins, Ansell, 343
Collins, Bernard, 5
Collins, Bootsy, 78
Collins, Clarence, 280
Collins, Dave, 321
Collins, Dennis, 310
Collins, Dolly, 481
Collins, Frances, 136
Collins, Glenda, 120, 334
Collins, Grenville, 266, 337
Collins, Joan, 211
Collins, John, 85, 113
Collins, Judy, 82, 85, 120-121, 177, 211, 219, 239, 246, 257, 340
Collins, Larry, 266
Collins, Lewis, 312

Collins, Mel, 113
Collins, Phil, 331
Collins, Ray, 321
Collins, Shirley, 216, 397
Collins, Shirley And Dolly, 481
Collins, Tom, 177, 239
Collins, Tommy, 335
Collis, Roger, 312
Collum, Roy, 244
Colman, Stuart, 349
Colomby, Bobby, 64
Colon, August, 149
Colorado, 280, 283, 319, 411-412
Colosseum, 28, 69, 121-122, 192, 213, 225, 471
Colours, 98, 121, 148, 157, 285, 297, 349, 392, 398
Colpix Records, 187
Colquhoun, Andy, 192
Coltrane, John, 7, 61, 84, 122-123, 143-144, 155, 183, 313-314, 318, 320-321, 329, 404
Columbia Records, 6, 20, 47, 55, 64, 68, 80, 98, 118, 124, 148, 166, 197, 200, 212, 234, 239, 244, 250, 263, 271, 282, 286, 310, 336, 352, 376, 384, 403-404, 415, 423, 434, 472
Colville, Chris, 255
Colyer, Ken, 56
Combustible Edison, 182
Comden, Betty, 50
Comerford, Paul, 181
Commodores, 131, 323
Common Ground, 84, 227, 291, 393
Common, Bob, 40
Como, Perry, 20, 24, 137, 172, 262
Concert For Bangla Desh, The, 419
Concords, 123-124
Condron, Jim, 226
Coney Island, 11
Conflict, 36, 87, 209, 216, 410
Congos, 285, 344
Congregation, 306
Conka, Don, 284
Conlan, Jim, 386
Conley, Arthur, 124, 367
Conly, Paul, 283
Connery, Sean, 425
Conniff, Ray, 124-125, 251
Connolly, Billy, 242
Connor, Edric, 418
Connor, Jack, 108
Connor, Kay, 108
Conrad, Jess, 125, 295
Conroy, Dennis, 136
Constanten, Tom, 218
Contemporary Records, 17, 412
Conti, Bill, 25
Contours, 114, 125, 148, 214, 351
Conversation Piece, 50
Convy, Bert, 194
Conway, Gerry, 174, 342
Conway, Russ, 125-126
Cooder, Ry, 84, 94, 175, 302, 375-376, 454
Cook And Greenaway, 142, 163, 190, 278, 413
Cook, Barbara, 50
Cook, Dale, 126
Cook, Frank, 92, 336
Cook, Peter, 54, 319
Cook, Roger, 142, 163, 190
Cook, Ronald, 377
Cook, Stu, 133
Cooke, Sam, 8, 11, 15, 60-61, 108, 124, 126-127, 160, 196, 204, 231, 234, 265, 269, 367, 432, 436, 442, 456, 476
Cookies, 127, 364, 370, 383, 460
Coonce, Erik Michael, 217
Coonce, Rick, 217
Cooney, Ray, 108
Cooper, Andy, 29
Cooper, Dave, 453
Cooper, Michael, 436

Cooper, Mike, 165
Cooper, Mushy, 192, 453
Copas, Cowboy, 119
Cope, Julian, 465
Copeland, Johnny, 302
Copland, Aaron, 50
Copper Family, 481
Copping, Chris, 337, 360
Coppinger, Michael, 386
Coppola, Francis Ford, 159, 285
Coral Records, 148, 275, 376
Corbitt, Jerry, 483
Cord, Joe, 137
Cordell, Denny, 127, 149
Cordell, Ritchie, 132, 250, 445
Cordell-Laverack, Dennis, 127
Cordet, Helene, 127
Cordet, Louise, 127, 283-284
Corea, Chick, 85, 143, 183
Corneal, Jon, 153, 247
Cornelius, Andreas, 337
Cornell, Lynn, 127
Cornish, Gene, 147, 481
Coronado, Dave, 321
Corrigan, Sean, 434
Corsairs, 128
Cortez, Dave 'Baby', 128
Corvettes, 128
Cory, Richard, 407
Coryell, Larry, 17, 85
Cosby, Bill, 468
Cosby, Henry, 476
Costa, Don, 282
Costell, David, 278
Costello, Elvis, 25, 47, 84, 332, 404
Cotillion Records, 48
Cotten, Elizabeth 'Libba', 396
Cottle, Albert, 435
Cotton Pickers, 111
Cotton, Billy, 126, 306, 464
Cotton, Jeff, 94
Cotton, Mike, 15, 128, 267, 485
Cotton, Paul, 245
Cottrell, John, 14
Coulter, Phil, 93, 350, 451
Council, Floyd, 31
Count Belcher, 84
Count Bishops, 161
Count Five, 129
Count Ossie, 196, 359
Count Talent And The Originals, 65
Country Classics, 131, 274, 460
Country Current, 111
Country Folk, 44, 87-88, 129, 161, 184, 229, 243, 280
Country Jim, 370
Country Joe And The Fish, 55, 129, 219, 287, 317, 478
Countrymen, 129
County, Lee, 104
Courtney, Lou, 365
Covay, Don, 129-130, 135, 208, 299, 348, 430
Coverdale Page, 336
Coverdale, David, 336
Coverdale, Larry, 250
Cowan, Dennis, 70
Cowan, Tommy, 5
Cowap, Peter, 234
Coward, Noël, 155, 203, 270
Cowboy, Copas, 119
Cowsills, 130
Cox, Billy, 231-232
Cox, John, 342
Cox, Michael, 56, 130, 284, 303, 431
Cox, Mike, 176
Cox, Neil, 91
Cox, Terry, 252, 271, 342, 352
Coxsone, Lloyd, 130-131
Coyne, Kevin, 313, 409
Cozens, Spencer, 343
Craig, Judy, 111
Craine, Don, 161
Cramer, Floyd, 20, 131, 353

Cranberries, 127
Crane, Tony, 303
Crane, Vincent, 77
Craswell, Denny, 100
Crawford, Dave, 465
Crawford, Hank, 300-301
Crawford, Jack, 49
Crawford, Jimmy, 462
Crawford, Joan, 49
Crawford, Michael, 59, 230
Crawford, Randy, 130
Cray, Robert, 130
Crazy Elephant, 131-132, 213
Creach, 'Papa' John, 254, 467
Cream, 6, 11, 21, 27-28, 35, 55, 69, 80, 95, 132, 213, 254, 271, 301, 306, 433, 444, 446, 477
Creation, 132-133 and passim
Creatore, Luigi, 445
Creatures, 149, 159
Creed, 150, 217
Creedence Clearwater Revival, 133, 355, 478
Creek, 10, 257, 312, 396, 462
Cregan, Jim, 65
Creme, Lol, 287
Cresswell, Curt, 324
Crests, 76
Crewe, Bob, 93, 198, 388, 419, 463
Crewsdon, Roy, 205
Cribbins, Bernard, 294
Crickets, 85, 134, 207, 211, 282, 457-458
Crill, Connie, 260
Crime, 275
Criss Cross, 314
Criss, Sonny, 221
Crissinger, Roger, 341
Critters, 134, 150, 262
Croce, Jim, 461
Croce, Joe, 111
Crocitto, Margo, 213
Crocker, Johnny, 128
Croft, David, 334
Crombie, Tony, 385
Crome Cyrcus, 134
Cromey, Felix, 67
Crooks, Derrick, 349
Crooks, Sidney, 349
Cropper, Steve, 71, 130, 134, 193, 259, 292, 348, 367, 388, 410
Crosby And Nash, 21, 82, 87, 135-136, 216, 218, 237, 256
Crosby, Bing, 29, 96, 185, 187, 247, 368, 472
Crosby, Bob, 111, 124
Crosby, David, 12, 81-82, 86-87, 135, 254, 256, 327
Crosby, Israel, 402
Crosby, Stills And Nash, 12, 21, 82, 87-88, 118, 135-136, 216, 218, 237, 256, 478
Crosby, Stills, Nash And Young, 12, 21, 81, 88, 118, 135, 216, 218, 478
Cross Country, 445
Cross, Christopher, 25
Crossfire, 115, 255
Crossfires, 450
Crouch, Nicky, 192, 312
Crow, Terry, 324
Crowell, Rodney, 85, 99
Crowl, Charles, 253
Crown Prince, 300, 443
Crows, 140, 213, 226, 443
Cruickshank, Pete, 234
Crumb, Ann, 59
Crummey, Christopher, 394
Crusader Records, 424
Crusaders, 112, 165, 241, 334, 336, 454
Crush, 373
Crutcher, Bettye, 30, 425
Cruz, Vera, 455
Cruzados, 170
Cry Of Love, 232-233

Cryan' Shames, 136
Crystal Ball Records, 223
Crystals, 136 and passim
Cubert, Joe, 388
Cuby And The Blizzards, 136-137
Cuckoo Patrol, 206
Cuff Links, 137, 408
Cuff, Bob, 324
Cuffley, John, 197
Cullen, Gerry, 386
Culture Shock, 87
Cummings, Robert, 38
Cunha, Rick, 229
Cunningham, Billy, 73
Cunningham, Carl, 30
Cunningham, Steve, 367
Cupid's Inspiration, 137, 360
Curbishley, Bill, 273
Curcio, Paul, 312
Curd, John, 229
Cure, 233
Curtis, Adrian, 221
Curtis, Chris, 394-395
Curtis, Lee, 53, 102, 192, 418
Curtis, Lee, And The All-Stars, 53
Curtis, Paul, 221
Curtis, Phil, 431
Curtis, Sam, 221
Curtis, Sonny, 134
Cuscuna, Michael, 66
Cymande, 393
Cymbal, Johnny, 137
Cyrkle, 137, 263, 397

D

D'Abo, Michael, 138, 198, 290
D'Angelo, 153
D'Arby, Terence Trent, 146
D'Elia, Roger, 390
DAF, 147
Daffodil Records, 147
Daily Flash, 138
Daisley, Bob, 110
Dakar Records, 273
Daking, Geoff, 67
Dakota, 65, 238, 457
Dakotas, 25, 138, 180, 264, 272, 294, 395
Dale And Grace, 138
Dale, Allan, 198
Dale, Dick, 38, 138-140
Dale, Glen, 197-198
Dale, Jim, 331, 397
Daley, Lloyd, 5
Dalton, David, 189, 219, 258, 383
Dalton, Jack, 263
Dalton, John, 132, 267, 444
Dalton, Lacy J., 404
Dalton, Les, 141
Daltrey, Peter, 260
Daltrey, Roger, 188, 470
Dalziel, Denis, 240
Dameron, Tadd, 66
Dames, 74
Damned, 33, 393
Damon, Stuart, 108
Damone, Vic, 24
Dancho, Dante, 253
Dandelion Records, 409
Dane, Barbara, 104
Daneman, Paul, 91
Dangerous Birds, 57
Daniels, Billy, 145, 230
Daniels, Charlie, 262
Daniels, Eddie, 10
Daniels, Maxine, 286
Daniels, Mike, 111
Danko, Rick, 167, 228
Dankworth, John, 102, 317, 319
Danneman, Monika, 232
Dante, Ron, 17, 137, 151
Danus, Vicens, 283
Darin, Bobby, 20, 55, 102, 116, 140-

141, 162, 219, 224, 269, 305, 351, 405
Darion, Joe, 264
Darling, Erik, 384
Darrell And The Oxfords, 444
Darren, James, 141
Darrow, Chris, 128, 260-261
Dart Records, 434
Darts, 73, 165
Darway, Chris, 134
Dash, Leslie, 230
Dassin, Joe, 141
Dassin, Jules, 141
Daughtry, Dean, 117
Dave And Ansell Collins, 343
Dave Dee, Dozy, Beaky, Mick And Tich, 38, 141-142, 190
Davenport, Darius LaNoue, 21
Davenport, Lester, 152
Davern, Kenny, 402
David And Jonathan, 142, 278
David, C., 455
David, Charles, 107
David, Hal, 24-25, 204, 210, 256, 284, 303, 401, 422, 463, 465
David, Jay, 252
David, Kal, 244
David, Mack, 24, 49
Davidson, Jim, 125, 162
Davidson, Lenny, 114
Davidson, Leonard, 67
Davies, Alun, 342
Davies, Billie, 268
Davies, Cyril, 28, 69, 86, 142, 271, 296
Davies, Dave, 266-268, 337
Davies, Graham, 63, 296
Davies, Hunter, 43
Davies, Irving, 125
Davies, John R.T., 437
Davies, Leonard, 74, 336
Davies, Mansell, 91
Davies, Megan, 17
Davies, Ray, 17, 52, 54, 74, 98, 159, 266-268, 337
Davies, Trevor, 141
Davis Records, 7
Davis, 'Billy' Roquel, 474
Davis, Bette, 150
Davis, Bill, 413
Davis, Billie, 142, 186, 352
Davis, Billy, 195, 474
Davis, Billy, Jnr., 195
Davis, Carl, 6, 474
Davis, Charles, 125
Davis, Danny, 20
Davis, Eddie, 93, 263, 394
Davis, Eddie 'Lockjaw', 263, 394
Davis, Hal, 238
Davis, Jesse, 470
Davis, Joe, 253
Davis, John, 123
Davis, Johnny, 210
Davis, Kim, 150
Davis, Larry, 147
Davis, Marlena, 333
Davis, Mary, 253
Davis, Mel, 441
Davis, Michael, 299
Davis, Miles, 7, 61, 122-123, 142-144, 182-183, 216, 251, 263, 306, 311, 313-314, 404, 411
Davis, Nathan, 8
Davis, Newman, 190
Davis, Richard, 104, 144
Davis, Sammy, Jnr., 75, 145, 270
Davis, Skeeter, 284
Davis, Spencer, 9, 30, 38, 146, 175, 238, 350, 423-424, 446-447
Davis, Spencer, Group, 9, 30, 38, 146, 175, 238, 350, 423-424, 446-447
Davis, Tim, 5
Davis, Wild Bill, 413
Davis, Willie, 147
Davison, Harold, 412

Davison, Wild Bill, 112
Davy, Steve, 427
Dawes, Tom, 137
Dawson, Colin, 470
Dawson, Dave, 229
Dawson, John, 350
Dawson, Johnny, 177
Day, Bob, 11
Day, Bobby, 68
Day, Bruce, 397
Day, Doris, 269
Day, Francis, 59
Day, Jimmy, 90
Day, Mark, 43
Day, Richard, 191
Day, Wyatt, 18
Daybreakers, 386
Days, Holly, 273
Dayton, Ronny, 384
De Angelis, Peter, 187
De Cocq, Jim, 190
De La Barreda, Antonio, 92
De La Parra, Adolfo, 92
De La Parra, Fito, 92
De Maria, Sugar Pie, 34, 150
De Paris, Wilbur, 161
De Paul, Lynsey, 18
De Veuve, Doreen, 190
De Vore, Darrell, 106
De Wilde, Brandon, 247
de Young, Cliff, 118
Deacon Blue, 25
Dead Elvis, 357
Dean, Elton, 415
Dean, Hazell, 57
Dean, James, 117, 166, 354
Dean, Johnny, 165
Dean, Paul, 153
Dean, Roger, 14, 296
Deane, Sandy, 252
Dearie, Blossom, 146-147
Death In June, 452
Death Row, 228
Debussy, Claude, 402
DeCarr, Dennis, 312
Decca Records, 6, 32, 44, 52-53, 68, 79, 90, 102, 117, 120, 125, 127, 134, 145, 149, 179-180, 213, 242-243, 261, 269, 305, 351, 415, 417, 424, 440, 451, 455, 485
Decker, Jack, 134
Dee, Alan, 110
Dee, Dave, 38, 141-142, 190
Dee, David, 141
Dee, Jay, 68, 449
Dee, Joey, And The Starliters, 137, 147
Dee, Kiki, 57
Dee, Sandra, 140, 473
Deene, Carol, 147
Deep Feeling, 146, 201
Deep Purple, 19, 179, 196, 225, 264, 391, 434, 437
Deinum, Herman, 136
DeJohnette, Jack, 143
Dekker, Desmond, 349
Del Din, Robert, 172
Del Giudice, Peter, 148
Del-Fi Records, 455
Del-Satins, 76, 148, 371
Delaney And Bonnie, 292, 470
Delaney, Eric, 29
Delaney, Paddy, 102
Delfonics, 280
Dell, Lenny, 148
Dell-Vikings, 248, 371
Dello, Pete, 239
Dells, 148, 454
Delmark Records, 281
Delvy, Richard, 45
Demensions, 148
Demon, 79, 169, 329, 343, 396
Dench, Judi, 89
Dene, Terry, 338
Denim, 381

Denison, Michael, 418
Dennerlein, Barbara, 414
Dennis, Denny, 127
Dennis, Mike, 160
Dennisons, 102, 148-149
Dennistoun, 226
Denny And The Diplomats, 273
Denny, David, 206
Denny, Jim, 118
Denny, John, 149, 288
Denny, Martin, 149
Denny, Sandy, 203
Densmore, John, 158, 160
Denton, Mickey, 100
Denver, John, 61, 310-311, 345
Denver, Karl, 149
DePrisco, Pat, 111
Deram Records, 149, 186, 239, 444, 465
Derek And The Dominos, 55, 447
Derek B, 165, 205, 234, 422, 436
Derrick, Diz, 337
Derringer, Rick, 300
Des Barres, Michael, 221
DeSanto, Sugar Pie, 34, 150
DeShannon, Jackie, 24, 70, 134, 150, 189, 337, 395
Desi And Billy, 153
Desmond, Paul, 150-151
Destiny, 117, 141
Destroy All Monsters, 299
Detective, 460
Detergents, 151
Detroit Spinners, 21, 466, 476
Deuce, 38
Devey, Willie, 90
Deviants, 151, 192
DeVille, Willy, 351
DeVito, Nick, 198
DeVito, Ralph, 223
DeVito, Tommy, 198-199
Devotions, 151
Dewar, Jim, 286
Dewey, Greg, 129, 287
Dexter, Sally, 331
Dexys Midnight Runners, 467, 474
Dey, Tony, 138
Di Benedetto, Joe, 200
Di Giovanni, Marty, 431
Diablos, 430
Diamond Head, 460
Diamond, Max, 162
Diamond, Neil, 25, 32, 61, 220, 252, 286, 315, 355
Diamonde, Dick, 173
Diaz, Herman, 182
Dick And Dee Dee, 151
Dick, Charlie, 119
Dick, Michael, 86
Dickens, Charles, 331
Dickens, Hazel, 396
Dickey, Robert Lee, 362
Dickinson, Angie, 25
Dickon, Richie, 67
Dickson, Jim, 86
Diddley, Bo, 52, 99, 109, 152, 208, 228, 363, 379, 387, 454
Dietrich, Marlene, 24
Dillard And Clark, 88, 152-153, 229
Dillard, Doug, 152
Dillards, 152
Dillinger, 5, 343
Dillon, Paul, 173
Diltz, Henry 'Tad', 304
Dimino, Rick, 137
DiMucci, Dion, 153-154
Dines, Peter, 225
Dinning, Mark, 284
Dino, Desi And Billy, 153
Dion And The Belmonts, 153-154, 405
Diplomats, 250, 273
Dire Straits, 170, 285, 294, 470
DiScuillo, Hank, 172
Dixie Cups, 32, 154

Dixie Flyers, 292, 347
Dixon, Eugene, 104
Dixon, Luther, 404
Dixon, Willie, 158, 376
Django Reinhardt, 318, 468
DJM Records, 337, 467
Dmochowski, Alex, 112, 165, 229
DNA, 192
Dobson, Anita, 59, 405
Dobson, Bonnie, 384
Dobson, Lyn, 290, 415
Docherty, Denny, 323
Docherty, Tony, 264
Dockery, Sam, 443
Doctor Bird, 409
Doctor Dolittle, 75
Doctor West's Medicine Show And
Jug Band, 154
Doctor Zhivago, 124, 391
Dodd, Coxsone, 5, 114, 298, 306,
343, 359, 370, 409
Dodd, Dick, 45, 424
Dodd, Ken, 154-155, 484
Dodson, Brian, 281
Dodson, Larry, 30
Dog Soldier, 226
Doggett, Bill, 425, 430
Doherty, Denny, 178, 288
Dolan, Michael, 223
Dolan, Steve, 224
Dolenz, Mickey, 73-74, 314-315
Dolinger, Jim, 222
Doll By Doll, 49
Dollar, 98, 168, 238, 280, 301
Dolphy, Eric, 122-123, 155, 307
Dominguez, Carlos, 129, 445
Domino, Fats, 71, 93, 108, 205, 263,
306, 326
Dominoes, 226, 302, 370-371, 474
Don And Dewey, 138, 416, 467
Don And The Goodtimes, 266
Don't Knock The Rock, 155
Don, Johnny, 253
Don, Ricki, 406
Donahue, Tom, 21, 44, 156, 219,
227
Donaldson, Lou, 66, 156, 339, 413
Donaldson, Pat, 140
Doncaster, Patrick, 43, 53, 375
Donegan, Lonnie, 29, 102, 109, 140,
188, 303
Donegan, Norman, 6
Donen, Stanley, 50
Donight, Will, 366
Donlinger, Jim, 16
Donlinger, Tom, 16
Donna, Jim, 100
Donnellan, Jay, 284
Donner, Ral, 431
Donovan, 26, 156-157, 189, 229,
240, 243, 251, 269, 320, 366, 389,
415, 431
Donovan, Terence, 65
Doobie Brothers, 312, 453
Doonican, Val, 157-158, 391, 482
Doors, 158-160 and *passim*
Dootones, 477
Dorados, El, 71
Dorham, Kenny, 443
Dorman, Harold, 376
Dorman, Lee, 247
Dorsey, Irving Lee, 160
Dorsey, Lee, 160
Dorsey, Tommy, 140, 377
Dot Records, 71-72, 118, 195, 270,
294
Dothan Sextet, 362
Dott, Gerald, 246
Doubleday, Marcus, 176, 257
Douglas, Alan, 233
Douglas, Chip, 303, 450
Douglas, Craig, 160, 300
Douglas, Josephine, 214
Douglas, Kirk, 99
Douglas, Paul, 45

Douglas, Steve, 174
Dovells, 32, 160-162, 333
Dowd, Tom, 55, 161
Dowell, Joe, 260
Dower, David, 109
Down South, 307
Downbeats, 177, 372
Downes, Bob, 14, 101
Downliners, 161, 324, 358
Downliners Sect, 161, 324, 358
Doyle, Jimmy, 403
Dozier, Lamont, 161, 235-236
Dr. Feelgood, 161
Dr. Hook, 406
Dr. John, 18, 64-65, 314, 351, 437,
470
Dr. Strangely Strange, 162
Drachen Theaker, 77
Dragon, Daryl, 36
Drain, 315, 406
Drake, Charlie, 125, 140, 162
Drake, Jay, 255
Drake, John, 12
Drake, Kevin, 312
Draper, Robert, 383
Dream Syndicate, 392
Dreamlovers, 162
Dreja, Chris, 479
Drew, Ronnie, 164
Drifters, 20, 24, 46, 49, 148, 161-
163, 212, 216, 252, 259, 265, 291,
302, 304, 350, 372-373, 398, 405,
412, 418, 443, 449, 465, 470
Driscoll, Julie, 28, 163-164, 213,
427
Driven, 251
Drobinicki, Carol, 371
Druckman, Joel, 70
Druian, Greg, 287
Drummond, Don, 409
Drummond, Tim, 143
Drusky, Roy, 482
Dry City Scat Band, 260
Dryden, Spencer, 253
Dub Syndicate, 344
Dubliners, 91, 164
DuCann, John, 14
Duckworth, John, 435
Duddy, Lyn, 187
Dudgeon, Gus, 417
Duffy's Nucleus, 352
Duffy, Raymond, 197, 350
Duffy, Thomas, 174
Duke, George, 7
Duke, Patty, 164
Duke, Phil, 390
Dulcimer, 21, 380, 396
Dulfer, Candy, 143
Dummer, John, 165
Dunbar, Aynsley, 112, 165, 229,
264, 296, 312, 321
Duncan, Gary, 76, 363
Duncan, Johnny, 303
Duncan, Kirk, 79
Dundas, David, 59
Dundy, Elaine, 357
Dunford, Michael, 324
Dunkerley, John, 91
Dunkley, Errol, 343
Dunlop, Frankie, 313
Dunlop, Ian, 246
Dunn, Duck, 71, 292, 426
Dunn, Harold, 241
Dunn, Homer, 377
Dunn, James, 162
Dunn, James Ray, 162
Dunn, Pete, 117
Dunphy, Tom, 386-387
Dupree, Champion Jack, 46, 57
Dupree, Cornell, 265
Dupree, Jack, 46, 57
Dupree, Simon, 165-166
Dupree, Simon, And The Big

Sound, 165
Duprees, 200, 377
Durante, Jimmy, 145
Dure, Mike, 190
Durham, Judith, 397-398
Durocs, 324
Durrill, Johnny, 460
Dury, Ian, 410
Dwyer, Bernie, 205
Dyer, Peter, 429
Dyke, Roy, 371
Dylan, Bob, 19, 26-27, 40, 42, 61,
64, 67-68, 76, 83, 86-87, 91, 98, 120,
138, 153, 156-157, 164, 166-173,
175, 178, 191, 199-200, 211, 213,
216, 218-220, 224, 227-228, 232, 241,
280, 290, 324-325, 328-330, 332,
340, 345, 367, 377, 387, 391, 411,
415, 441, 445, 450, 470, 476
Dymond, John, 141
Dyre, Arthur, 321

E

E Street Band, 69
Eagles, 17, 67, 85, 148, 153
Earl Of Wharncliffe, 101
Earl Sixteen, 131
Earl, James, 104
Earl, Robert, 172
Earl-Jean, 127, 212
Earland, Charles, 300
Earls, 172-173
Early B, 106, 189, 255
Earth Band, 290
Earth Opera, 73, 173, 177
Earth, Wind And Fire, 279, 416
East Of Eden, 44, 173
East Orange, 339, 465
East, Nathan, 423
Easterby, Roger, 268, 456
Eastman, Lee, 269
Easton, Eric, 216, 269, 379-380
Eastwood, Clint, 316, 343
Easybeats, 38, 173-174, 217, 283
Eaton, Roger, 67
Eaton, Sally, 222
Eaton, Wally, 117
Ebb, Fred, 89
Eccles, Clancy, 343
Echoes, 174 and *passim*
Echols, John, 284
Eckstine, Billy, 17, 61, 96, 142, 148,
360
Eclection, 174, 231
Eddie And The Hot Rods, 363
Eddy, Chris, 327
Eddy, Duane, 46, 174-175, 259
Edge, Graeme, 250, 318-319
Edison Lighthouse, 175
Edmonton Symphony Orchestra,
360-361
Edmonton, Dennis, 427
Edmonton, Jerry, 427
Edmund, John, 258
Edmunds, Dave, 285, 400
Edsels, 175
Edward, Charles, 51
Edward, Jim, 159
Edwards, Blake, 13
Edwards, Bobby, 262
Edwards, Denise, 384
Edwards, Dennis, 125, 438
Edwards, Don, 306
Edwards, Earl, 104
Edwards, Esther Gordy, 322
Edwards, George, 222
Edwards, Harry, 306
Edwards, Ian, 243
Edwards, Jackie, 9, 175, 197, 306,
329
Edwards, Millard, 181
Edwards, Nokie, 460
Edwards, Tommy, 200

Edwards, Vincent, 262
Edwards, Wilfred, 175
EG Records, 5
Eire Apparent, 176
El Dorados, 71
Elbert, Donnie, 176
Eldridge, Roy, 346-347
Electric Flag, 64, 176, 213, 257, 317
Electric Indian, 93
Electric Light Orchestra, 18, 244,
323
Electric Prunes, 173, 176-177
Elektra Records, 18, 86, 120, 158,
177, 229, 239, 284, 330, 372
Elena, Maria, 350
Eley, Brian, 164
Elgins, 177, 437
Eliot, T.S., 209
Ellington, Duke, 10, 122-123, 146,
306-308, 313-314, 346, 476
Ellington, Ray, 295
Elliot, 'Mama' Cass, 177, 323
Elliot, Mike, 198
Elliott, Bern, And The Fenmen,
178
Elliott, Earl, 388
Elliott, Garth, 234
Elliott, Jack, 28, 169, 178
Elliott, Marc, 331
Elliott, Ramblin' Jack, 28, 178
Elliott, Ron, 44
Ellis, Alfred, 77
Ellis, Alton, 359, 370-371
Ellis, David, 303
Ellis, Glyn, 196
Ellis, Herb, 84
Ellis, Ian, 120
Ellis, Keith, 271
Ellis, Ray, 362, 434
Ellis, Shirley, 178, 197
Ellis, Steve, 285
Ellis, Vivian, 60
Ellison, Andy, 179, 255
Ellison, Lorraine, 49, 179, 365
Ellwood, Alan, 17
Ellwood, Robert, 17
Elmore, Greg, 76, 363
Elsdon, Alan, 29
Elson, Derek, 148
Elson, Steve, 274
Elvis On Tour, 356
Ely, Jack, 266
Ember Records, 308
Emblow, Jack, 7
Embrace, 87, 135, 460
Embryo, 291
Emergency, 408
Emerson, Keith, 18, 328
Emerson, Lake And Palmer, 328
EMI Records, 286, 304, 309, 334,
336-337, 455
End Records, 148, 162, 309
Endino, Jack, 66
Enemy, 78
Engber, Evan, 154
Engel, Brian, 289
Engel, Scott, 463-464
Engemann, Bob, 277
England, John, 15, 109, 240, 319,
444
England, Paul, 387, 485
Engle, Butch, And The Styx, 44
Engler, Rick, 195
English, B., 437
English, Michael, 18, 223, 428
Englishman, 296
Enigma, 360
Ennis, Ray, 434
Eno, Brian, 5
Enthoven, David, 5
Entner, Warren, 217
Entwistle, John, 470
Epic Records, 124, 461
Episode Six, 179, 334
Epp, Fenrus, 260

Epstein, Brian, 33, 39, 41, 43, 46, 55, 58, 102, 137, 179-181, 201, 210, 214, 223, 269, 272, 294, 303, 329, 338, 363, 371, 394, 428, 436
Equals, 103, 181, 262
Era Records, 100, 315
Ercolani, James, 141
Erickson, Roky, 392, 441
Errico, Greg, 411-412
Errico, Jan, 312
Erskine, Marshall, 45
Erskine, Peter, 85
Ertegun, Ahmet, 20, 81, 135, 161, 470
Ervin, Booker, 307
Ervin, DiFosco, 247
Erwin, Alda Denise, 246
Escorts (UK), 181
Escott, Colin, 356-357
Eskerson, Dave, 55
Esposito, Mike, 67
Esquires, 181, 410
Esquivel, 149, 181-182
Estes, Sleepy John, 324
Estrada, Roy, 321
Eternal, 188
Etheridge, John, 415
Etheridge, Melissa, 127
Ethiopians, 352
Ethos, 260
Ethridge, Chris, 247
Eubanks, Kevin, 85
Euphoria, 312
Eurythmics, 477
Evans, Bill (pianist), 182
Evans, Bill (saxophonist), 143
Evans, Bob, 375, 453
Evans, Ernest, 108
Evans, Gil, 84, 142-144, 155
Evans, Jack, 261
Evans, John, 73
Evans, Mal, 19
Evans, Marion, 393
Evans, Mark, 375
Evans, Maureen, 184
Evans, Mike, 6, 117, 247, 281
Evans, Nick, 415
Evans, Paul, 22, 79, 261, 461
Evans, Rick, 484
Evans, Tom, 247
Evans, Tornado, 112
Even Dozen Jug Band, 173
Event Records, 253
Everett, Betty, 184, 434, 465
Everett, Kenny, 260
Everett, Rupert, 170
Everett, Tanya, 194
Evergreen, 56, 278
Evergreens, 54, 125
Everly Brothers, 11, 16, 20, 44, 76, 99, 101, 184-186, 210, 284, 304, 332, 379, 406, 445
Everly, Don, 184-185
Everly, Phil, 85, 101, 175, 185, 374
Evers, Barbara, 403
Everything But The Girl, 211
Evita, 59
Exciters, 32, 142, 186, 220
Exiles, 409
Expanding Headband, 283
Explorers, 217
Expresso Bongo, 373, 375, 399, 480
Eyes Of Blue, 149, 186, 247
Eyre, Mickey, 194
Eyre, Tommy, 165

F

F.M., 440
Fabares, Michelle, 187
Fabares, Shelley, 187
Fabian, 22, 116, 187, 351, 388, 405
Fabray, Nanette, 187
Fabric, Bent, 48

Fabulous Rhinestones, 245
Face The Music, 34, 316
Factory Records, 336
Fagen, Donald, 252
Fahey, John, 187-188
Fairburn, Werly, 67
Fairfield Parlour, 260
Fairley, Pat, 197, 293
Fairport Convention, 91, 203, 251
Fairs, Jim, 136
Fairweather, 12, 29
Fairweather-Low, Andy, 12, 234
Fairytale, 17, 157
Faith, Adam, 13, 59, 188, 224, 284, 368, 386, 401, 405, 457
Faith, George, 344
Faith, Percy, 47, 90
Faithfull, Marianne, 90, 101, 127, 150, 156, 189, 284, 380-381
Faithless, 189
Falcons, 196, 348
Falk, Peter, 38
Fame, Georgie, 10, 127, 160, 189-190, 197, 230-231, 300, 322, 338, 359, 375, 385, 413
Fame, Herb, 341
Family Dogg, 190, 288
Family Tree, 76, 190, 425
Famous Jug Band, 190
Fandango, 11, 360
Fankhauser, Merrell, 433
Fann, Leroy, 387
Fantastic Baggys, 190, 411
Fantasy Records, 184, 206, 426
Fardon, Don, 191, 284, 372, 417
Fargo, 457
Farina, Ann, 391
Farina, Dick, 191
Farina, Johnny, 391
Farina, Mimi, 191, 387
Farina, Richard, 26, 67, 120, 191
Farina, Santo, 391
Farinas, 191, 201
Farley, Frank, 138, 264
Farlow, Tal, 307
Farlowe, Chris, 57, 68, 77, 121, 191-192, 245, 254, 271, 313, 336, 380
Farmer, Art, 406, 475
Farmer, Michael, 406
Farmer, Steve, 12
Farnham, John, 108
Farnon, Robert, 47, 368
Faron's Flamingos, 125, 192
Farrar, John, 374
Farrell, Brian, 221
Farrell, Joe, 341
Farrell, Louie, 221
Farren, Mick, 151, 192, 338, 356-357, 383
Farrow, Mia, 75
Faryar, Cyrus, 211, 303
Fat Boys, 37, 108
Fat City, 84
Fat Mattress, 196, 232
Favio, Tony, 151
Fawkes, Wally, 111
Fayad, Frank, 284
FBI, 398
Feather, Leonard, 313
Federal Records, 5
Feelies, 192
Feemster, Herbert, 341
Feiten, Buzzy, 481
Felder, Jerome, 350
Feldman, Bob, 429
Feldthouse, Solomon, 260
Felix, Julie, 193
Felix, Mike, 304
Fell, Simon, 203
Fenda, Jaymes, And The Vulcans, 458
Fender, B., 193
Fender, Leo, 139, 193
Fendermen, 193
Fenner, John, 29

Fenton, Shane, 194, 236, 283
Fentones, 194, 236
Fenwick, Ray, 9, 146
Ferguson, Jay, 420
Ferguson, Maynard, 404, 443
Ferguson, Michael, 106
Ferguson, Tony, 224
Ferrara, Fred, 76, 148
Feza, Mongezi, 362
Fielder, Jim, 64, 81
Fifth Dimension, 61, 87-88, 195, 222, 329, 376, 395
Fifth Estate, 195
Figueiredo, Larry, 172
Final Solution, 219
Finlay, Dave, 310
Finlay, John, 372
Finlayson, Willie, 478
Finley, Bruce, 417
Finn, Mickey, 453
Finnegan, John, 67
Finnegan, Mike, 55
Finnis, Rob, 419
Fireballs, 195-196
Firefall, 420
Fireworks, 108
First Call, 321, 448
First Choice, 256
First Class, 63, 97
Fisher, Bob, 443
Fisher, Carl, 253
Fisher, Eddie, 17, 59
Fisher, John, 399, 424
Fisher, Martin, 173
Fisher, Matthew, 14, 161, 360
Fisher, Morgan, 285
Fitzgerald, Anne, 371
Fitzgerald, Ella, 122, 251, 346
Fitzpatrick, James, 419
Five Americans, 460
Five Crowns, 163, 265
Five Dutones, 6
Five Satins, 148
Five Stairsteps, 81
Five Star, 227
Flack, Roberta, 21, 25, 227
Flamin' Groovies, 419
Flaming Star, 354, 356-357
Flamingos, 56, 71, 125, 192
Flanagan, Kevin, 161
Flanagan, Ralph, 90
Flanagan, Tommy, 122, 183
Flanders, Tommy, 68
Flatt And Scruggs, 98
Fleck, John, 424
Fleckenstein, Johnny, 284
Fleetwood Mac, 37, 46, 110, 208, 245, 296, 439, 458
Fleetwood, Mick, 68, 110, 296, 417
Fleming, Robert, 177
Flint, Hughie, 296
Flippo, Chet, 357, 383
Flirtations, 53
Flo And Eddie, 214, 275, 321, 450
Flophouse, 137
Flowerpot Men, 97, 149, 196, 248
Floy Joy, 432
Floyd, Eddie, 135, 196, 348, 359, 426
Fluke, 104, 407
Flying Burrito Brothers, 11-12, 87-88, 128, 153, 221, 247, 331, 371
Flying High, 30, 310
Flying Machine, 349, 436
Flynn, Charlie, 243
FM, 155, 194, 294, 340
Fogerty, John, 83, 133, 450
Fogerty, Tom, 133
Foley, Ellen, 220
Foley, Red, 71, 275, 352
Folks Brothers, 196, 359
Folschow, Bob, 100
Folwell, Bill, 18
Fonda, Jane, 77, 316

Fonda, Peter, 173
Fonfara, Mike, 176
Fontana Records, 11, 57, 141, 191, 196, 243, 260, 305, 386
Fontana, D.J., 57, 196, 353, 355
Fontana, Wayne, 53, 196-197, 306
Fontenot, Hadley, 28
Forbes, Rand, 454
Forbidden, 149, 407-408, 475
Ford, Aiden, 91
Ford, Clinton, 102, 393
Ford, Dean, 197, 293, 350
Ford, Emile, 197, 258, 283, 418
Ford, Ernie, 276
Ford, John, 208, 394, 458
Ford, Mary, 197
Ford, Perry, 97, 248
Ford, Richard, 189
Ford, Robben, 189
Ford, Russell, 283
Ford, Tennessee Ernie, 276
Fordham, John, 394
Fordyce, Keith, 366
Foreigner, 412, 421, 464
Formations, 304, 403, 425
Formby, George, 201
Forrest, Jimmy, 219, 346, 394
Forssi, Ken, 284, 433
Forster, Colin, 458
Forsyth, Bruce, 75
Fortune, Lance, 197
Fortune, Nick, 81
Fortunes, 197-198 and *passim*
Foster, Colin, 208
Foster, John, 181
Foster, Julia, 198
Foster, Stephen, 86
Foster, Teddy, 274, 379
Fotheringay, 140, 174
Foul Play, 181
Foundations, 7, 107, 138, 198, 378, 389
Fountain, Pete, 276
Four Bucketeers, 392
Four Freshmen, 35, 248, 305
Four Lovers, 198
Four Pennies, 32, 198
Four Preps, 32
Four Seasons, 134, 137, 198-199, 217, 248, 270, 391, 411, 431, 435, 448, 462, 474, 476
Four Tops, 125, 161, 199-200, 224, 236, 263, 277, 322, 376-377, 432
Four Tunes, 10
Four-Evers, 200
Four-Star Records, 119
Fourmost, 40, 102, 180, 201, 414
Fowler, Mick, 217
Fowler, Wally, 118
Fowley, Kim, 5, 24, 191, 201, 238, 378
Fox, Bill, 365
Foxx, Inez And Charlie, 201-202, 430
Frame, Pete, 103, 296
Frampton, Peter, 234, 314, 412
Francis, Connie, 58, 116, 140, 202-203, 234, 395
Francis, John, 129
Francis, Ritchie, 186
Franco, 214
Franco, Joe, 214
Francois, Claude, 203
Frank, C., 193, 203
Frank, Jackson C., 193, 203
Frank, Joe, 151
Frankie And Johnny, 56, 354, 356-357
Franklin, Aretha, 21, 55, 79, 126, 130, 161-162, 203-205, 212, 227, 265, 297, 342, 442, 470
Franklin, Bruce, 297
Franklin, Erma, 49, 271, 365
Franklin, Mark, 205

Franklin, Melvin, 437
Franks, Tillman, 481
Franz, Johnny, 96, 379, 422, 463-464
Fraser, Ian, 76
Fraternity Of Man, 173, 205
Fraternity Records, 100
Fratto, Russ, 51
Frazier, Dallas, 238
Frazier, Joe, 310
Frazier, Lynn, 386
Fred, John, 205
Freda', 160, 162, 236
Freda, Michael, 160
Freddie And The Dreamers, 53, 90, 102, 190, 205-206
Free I, 132
Freed, Alan, 51, 83, 148, 280, 376, 429
Freeman, Alan, 364
Freeman, Bobby, 21, 156, 400, 411
Freeman, Charlie, 292
Freeman, Ernie, 24, 259, 455
Freeman, Gerry, 17
Freeman, Lee, 429
Freiberg, David, 363
French, John, 94
Freshmen, 35, 248, 305
Frey, Glenn, 85
Fricke, David, 383
Frickie, Janie, 404
Friedland, Stephen, 445
Friedman, Myra, 258
Friend, Simon, 203
Frisell, Bill, 27
Frishberg, Dave, 147
Friswell, Paul, 334
Froggatt, Raymond, 373
Frogman, 233
Frolich, Paul, 289
Frost, Max, 16
Frost, Richie, 325
Frumious Bandersnatch, 206
Fry, Royston, 68
Fryer, Fritz, 198
Fryers, Chris, 417
Fugs, 151, 206, 239, 341
Full Tilt Boogie Band, 258
Fuller, Bobby, 206-207
Fuller, Jerry, 361
Fuller, Jim, 207, 433
Fullilove, Arthur, 255
Fulson, Lowell, 109, 298, 442
Fungus, 442
Funicello, Annette, 16, 38
Funkadelic, 78
Funny Girl, 59, 433
Fuqua, Harvey, 208, 249, 463
Furay, Richie, 21, 81
Furniture, 28, 166
Fury Records, 160
Fury, Billy, 194, 207, 214, 259, 338, 352, 446, 451, 468
Fuse, 45, 379-380
Fuzzy, 14, 128
Fuzzy Duck, 14

G

G-Clefs, 93
Gabler, Milt, 260
Gadd, Steve, 189, 429
Gadenwitz, Peter, 51
Gadson, James, 468
Gaff, Billy, 234
Gage, Pete, 466
Gaines, Ron, 173
Gaines, Steven, 38, 43
Gainey, Earl, 474
Gainsbourg, Serge, 417
Gaither, Tommy, 333
Galahad, Kid, 354, 357
Gale, Eric, 17
Gales, Larry, 313

Galindo, Danny, 442
Gallagher, George, 350
Gallagher, Noel, 25
Gallagher, Regina, 371
Gallagher, Rory, 193
Gallucci, Don, 266
Galway, James, 289
Gamble And Huff, 54, 329, 348
Gamble, Kenny, 329, 401
Gamble, R.C., 24
Gamblers, 15, 207
Ganser, Margie, 399-400
Gantry, Elmer, 208, 458
Ganyou, George, 372
Ganz, Bobby, 124
Garbarek, Jan, 123
Garborit, John, 134
Garcia, Jerry, 5, 217, 254
Garcia, Juan, 181
Garcia, Russ, 346
Gardiner, Ricky, 45
Gardner, Bunk, 321
Gardner, Don, 466
Gardner, Kim, 57, 132, 282, 371
Gardner, Morris, 162
Garf, Gene, 325
Garforth, Jim, 128
Garfunkel, Art, 406-407, 445
Garland, Hank, 85
Garland, Judy, 33, 148, 235, 391
Garland, Red, 7, 143, 183
Garner, Bob, 132, 303
Garner, James, 260
Garner, Paul, 288
Garnett, David, 59
Garon, Jesse, 352
Garrett, Amos, 324
Garrett, Pat, 169
Garrett, Snuff, 282, 457
Garrett, Tommy, 457
Garrison, Jimmy, 122
Garrity, Freddie, 205-206
Garros, Christian, 284
Garwood, Rodney, 454
Gary, Bruce, 27
Gary, John, 463
Gaston, Henry, 474
Gates, David, 184, 419, 437
Gatewood, Sonny, 300
Gatlin, Larry, 98
Gaudio, Bob, 198, 200, 463
Gauvin, Mickey, 246
Gavin, Pete, 254
Gayden, Mac, 271
Gaydon, John, 5
Gaye, Barbie, 306
Gaye, Ellie, 220
Gaye, Marvin, 129, 200, 208-210, 214, 235, 293, 310, 323, 377, 437, 440, 469-470
Gayle, Crystal, 98
Gaynor, Gloria, 242
Gayten, Paul, 233
Gee, Mickey, 285
Gee, Rosko, 447
Geffen, David, 67, 169
Geils, J., Band, 93
Gelling, Eelco, 179
Gemini Records, 403
Genesis, 149, 212, 405, 436
Genies, 89
Gentle Giant, 166, 186
Gentle Soul, 436
Gentle, Johnny, 39, 101, 210, 338
Gentry, Bobbie, 210
Gentry, Ruby, 210
Gentrys, 244
George, Barbara, 124, 430
George, Lowell, 205, 218, 221, 321, 425
George, Nelson, 333
George, Samuel, 94
George, Terry, 29
Geraldo, 270, 418
Gernhard, Phil, 386

Geronimo Black, 321
Gerrard, Alice, 396
Gerrard, Denver, 465
Gerrard, Rod, 234
Gerrie, Malcolm, 367
Gerry And The Pacemakers, 102, 127, 149, 180, 210-211, 294, 363, 392, 395, 428, 451
Gershwin, George, 223, 275, 346, 407
Getz, Dave, 129
Getz, Stan, 10, 85, 122, 211, 254, 306, 346, 393, 405
Ghost Dance, 343, 359
GI Blues, 354
Gibb, Barry, 199
Gibb, Maurice, 286
Gibbins, Mike, 247
Gibbons Band, 244, 282
Gibbons, Steve, 244, 282
Gibbs, Joe, 343, 349
Gibbs, Mike, 85
Gibson, Bob, 211, 304, 330, 340, 406
Gibson, Butch, 390
Gibson, Colin, 409
Gibson, Don, 20, 99, 333, 482
Gibson, Jerry, 229
Gibson, Jill, 288
Gibson, Ray, 211
Gibson, Terry, 161
Giguere, Russ, 19
Gilbert, Carl, 246
Gilbert, Eddie, 415
Gilbert, Ronnie, 67
Gilberto, Astrud, 211, 274
Gilberto, João, 254
Giles, Gary, 429
Gill, Bob, 137
Gill, Cal, 458
Gill, Carolyn, 256
Gill, Geoff, 414
Gill, Johnny, 323
Gill, Millie, 458
Gillan, 179
Gillan, Ian, 179
Gillespie, Dizzy, 61, 84, 122, 142, 254, 263, 307, 311, 313, 320, 346-347, 392, 474
Gillett, Charlie, 265, 401, 470
Gilliam, Holly Michelle, 288
Gilmer, Jimmy, 195
Gilmore, John, 122
Gin Mill Skiffle Group, 102
Gingerbread, 90
Gingold, Hermione, 473
Ginsberg, Allen, 169
Ginsburg, Arnie, 250
Girard, Chuck, 100
Giuliano, Geoffrey, 43, 383
Glass Menagerie, 211, 289
Glassock, Brian, 212
Glassock, John, 110, 212
Gleason, Jackie, 22
Gleason, Ralph J., 254
Glitter, Gary, 57
Glover, Dave, 366
Glover, Henry, 390
Glover, Roger, 179
Glover, Tony, 366
Glynn, Ray, 79
Go-Go's, 429
Godcheaux, Donna, 218
Godchaux, Keith, 218
Goddard, Geoff, 53, 279, 303, 446
Godding, Brian, 65
Godfrey, Arthur, 71, 80, 119, 202
Godley And Creme, 53, 287
Godley, Kevin, 287
Gods, 43, 212, 386
Godspell, 125
Goffin, David, 79
Goffin, Gerry, 87, 134, 212, 281, 291, 315
Goffin/King, 40, 134, 212, 419

Going My Way, 472
Goins, Herbie, 212
Gold, Jack, 174
Goldberg, Barry, 65, 176, 213
Goldberg, Terry, 276
Golden Boy, 145, 465
Golden Earring, 136
Golden Records, 356
Golden, John, 54
Goldie And The Gingerbreads, 213
Goldman, Albert, 357
Goldman, Dickie, 123
Goldner, George, 154
Goldsboro, Bobby, 52, 79
Goldstein, Jerry, 429
Goldwax Records, 95
Golliwogs, 133
Golson, Benny, 475
Gomelsky, Giorgio, 65, 163, 213, 379, 415, 426, 479-480
Gomez, Eddie, 182
Gomez, Tony, 198
Gone Records, 376
Gonella, Nat, 22
Gong, 213, 415
Good Rats, 214, 456
Good, Jack, 18, 79, 125, 128, 130, 214, 338, 360, 368, 373
Goodall, Graeme, 9
Gooden, Sam, 245
Goodhand-Tait, Philip, 113
Goodman, Benny, 50, 84, 146, 251, 289, 384
Goodman, Shirley, 477
Goodman, Steve, 387
Goodness, 261, 291
Goodsall, John, 73
Goosly, Ronald, 253
Gopal, Sam, 390
Gordon, Billy, 125
Gordon, Dexter, 61, 66, 394
Gordon, Jim, 447
Gordon, John, 357
Gordon, Johnny, 264
Gordon, Lincoln, 181
Gordon, Mike, 386
Gordy Records, 256, 476
Gordy, Anna, 209
Gordy, Berry, 29, 161, 199, 208, 214-215, 235-236, 255, 295, 309, 322-323, 359, 366, 377, 393, 430-432, 437, 468-469, 474, 476
Gordy, Raynoma, 366
Gore, Lesley, 165, 215, 263, 401
Gorgoni, Al, 436
Gorilla, 70
Goring, Sonia, 105
Gorka, Kenny, 134
Gorman, Freddy, 235
Gorman, John, 392
Gorme, Eydie, 269, 275, 291
Gottehrer, Richard, 429
Gottlieb, Lou, 279
Gould, Don, 17
Goulden, Tony, 456
Goulding, Tim, 162
Gouldman, Graham, 197, 236-237, 306, 331, 480
Goulet, Robert, 91, 473
Gourdine, Anthony, 280
Govan, Dave, 253
Grabham, Mick, 350, 361
Grable, Betty, 230
Gracious, 156
Graham Central Station, 412
Graham, Bill, 65, 170, 215-216, 253
Graham, Bobby, 334, 336
Graham, Bryson, 421
Graham, Clive, 434
Graham, Davey, 216, 251, 296
Graham, Ernie, 176
Graham, George, 216
Graham, Larry, 411-412
Graham, Lee, 134
Graham, Leo, 343

Graham, Mike, 421
Graham, Nick, 179
Grainer, Ron, 59
Grainger, Michael, 194
Granahan, Gerry, 252
Grand Funk Railroad, 212
Grand Hotel, 67, 361
Grand Prix, 116, 368
Grant, Al, 117
Grant, Bob, 63
Grant, Eddie, 90, 181
Grant, Eddy, 362
Grant, Gogi, 244
Grant, Juanita, 295
Grant, Julie, 74, 216
Grant, Keith, 161
Grant, Marshall, 97
Granz, Norman, 147, 346
Grapefruit, 216-217
Graph, Tom, 445
Grappelli, Stéphane, 85, 347, 402-403, 468
Grateful Dead, 5, 12, 36, 156, 171, 206, 215-219, 253, 258, 317, 384, 447, 478
Gratton, Mick, 409
Gravenites, Nick, 55, 64, 86, 176, 257
Gravy Train, 156
Gray, Dobie, 279
Gray, Eddie, 250
Gray, Michael, 172
Gray, Owen, 9, 196
Gray, Roger, 137
Gray, Wardell, 385
Graybill, Teddy, 124
Graziano, Lee, 13
Grease Band, 165, 176, 189, 421
Great Guitars, 52, 152
Great White, 168
Grebb, Marty, 81, 222
Grech, Ric, 134, 191
Green Bullfrog, 431
Green Linnet Records, 195
Green River, 133
Green, Adolph, 50
Green, Al, 71, 150
Green, Bill, 233
Green, Dave, 148
Green, Dick, 296
Green, Doc, 163
Green, Doc, Jnr., 163
Green, Grant, 66, 84, 219-220, 339
Green, Jerome, 152
Green, Jerry, 125
Green, Jim, 109
Green, John, 46
Green, Johnny, 303
Green, Karl, 234
Green, Mick, 138, 264, 417
Green, Peter, 46, 165, 296, 417
Green, Richard, 148
Greenaway, Roger, 142, 163, 190, 368
Greenbaum, Norman, 154
Greenberg, Florence, 404
Greene, Charlie, 448
Greene, Linda, 341
Greene, Richard, 68, 272
Greene, Susaye, 432
Greenfield, Howard, 202, 395
Greenfield, Howie, 290
Greenfield, Robert, 216, 383
Greenslade, 121, 192
Greenslade, Dave, 121, 192
Greensleeves, 29
Greenwich, Ellie, 17, 32, 36, 54, 76, 154, 220, 291, 329
Greenwood, Nick, 77
Gregg, Brian, 264
Gregorio, Mike, 148
Gregory, John, 68, 324
Gregory, Mike, 181, 434
Grey, Billy, 334
Grey, Joel, 89-90

Gribble, Jim, 148
Grier, Lamar, 396
Grievous Angel, 371
Griffin, Billy, 310
Griffin, Colin, 179
Griffin, Donald, 310
Griffin, Herman, 366
Griffin, Johnny, 66, 147, 313
Griffin, Merv, 147
Griffiths, Andy, 352
Griffiths, Brian, 55
Griffiths, Derek, 19
Griffiths, Ian, 334
Griffiths, Marcia, 352
Griffiths, Martin, 45
Griffiths, Ron, 247
Grill, Rob, 217
Grim Reaper, 135
Grimms, 281, 313, 392
Grind, Jody, 254, 406
Grisman, David, 173
Groom, Don, 334
Groom, Roger, 324
Grooner, Louie, 255
Groovies, 419
Gross, Jerry, 160
Grossman, Albert, 55, 83, 166-167, 220, 338, 340, 345
Grosvenor, Luther, 18, 148, 421
Groundhogs, 223, 234
Group Therapy, 311
Groves, Mick, 419
Grubb, Gary, 76, 363
Grundy, David Holgate, 52
Grundy, Hugh, 485
GTOs, 220-221
Guaraldi, Vince, 221, 417
Guard, Dave, 303
Guercio, James William, 36
Guercio, Jim, 81
Guess Who, 72
Guest Stars, 124
Guest, Reg, 463-464
Guida, Frank, 69, 417
Guilino, Sam, 174
Guillory, Isaac, 136
Guinness, Alec, 116
Guitar Slim, 60, 106
Guitar, Bonnie, 154
Gull Records, 429
Gumbo, 284
Gummoe, John, 97
Gun (60s), 221
Gunn, Peter, 174-175, 289, 371
Gunne, Jo Jo, 420
Gunnell, Rik, 191
Gunnels, Gene, 429
Guns N'Roses, 72
Guralnick, Peter, 21, 124, 357
Gurley, James, 55
Guru Guru, 157, 201, 429
Gurvitz, Adrian, 221, 319
Gurvitz, Paul, 221
Gustafson, Johnny, 55, 179, 303
Guthrie, Arlo, 10, 478
Guthrie, Woody, 10, 166, 168, 178, 226, 330, 387, 415
Guy, Athol, 397
Guy, Buddy, 109, 165
Guys And Dolls, 286
Gwangwa, Jonas, 361
Gypsies, 201, 232-233, 441
Gypsy Kings, 26

H

H.P. Lovecraft, 16, 222, 399
Hackett, Bobby, 47
Hackl, Cornelius, 230
Haden, Charlie, 27
Hadley, Mike, 91
Hage, Martin, 9
Haggard, Merle, 85, 247, 335

Haggerty, Terry, 416
Hague, Ian, 192
Haines, Norman, 282
Hair, 222 and passim
Haldane, Stan, 73
Hale, Malcolm, 418
Haley, Bill, 355
Halifax Three, 323, 479
Hall, Adrian, 219
Hall, Bob, 165, 182, 218
Hall, Cliff, 419
Hall, Clifton, 197
Hall, Daryl, 423
Hall, Dave, 165
Hall, Edmond, 66
Hall, James, 66
Hall, Jane, 417
Hall, Jim, 85, 150-151, 182-183, 402-403
Hall, John, 181
Hall, Kelvin, 268
Hall, Rick, 21, 204, 404
Hall, Robert, 217
Hall, Tommy, 441
Hall, Tony, 417
Hall, Willie, 71
Hallam, Jesse, 99
Halliday, Hugh, 454
Halliday, Johnny, 16
Halligan, Dick, 64
Hallowell, John, 133
Hallyday, Johnny, 222-223, 405
Hallyday, Lee, 222
Halsall, Ollie, 339, 392
Halsey, John, 339
Ham, Pete, 247
Hamilton, Chico, 155
Hamilton, George, 284
Hamilton, George, IV, 284
Hamilton, Gil, 443
Hamilton, Roy, 48, 483
Hamilton, Tim, 178
Hamlisch, Marvin, 60
Hammersmith, 70, 298, 470
Hammerstein, Oscar, II, 116
Hammock, Cleveland, Jnr., 162
Hammond, Albert, 142, 190, 237, 288
Hammond, John, 64, 66, 166-167, 204, 220
Hammond, John Paul, 64
Hammond, John, Jnr., 167
Hammond, Laurence, 287
Hammond, Paul, 64
Hammond, Roy, 89
Hammond, Roy Charles, 89
Hammond, Walter, 332
Hampton, Carl, 30
Hampton, Christopher, 59
Hampton, Lionel, 8, 85, 265, 306, 308, 318
Hancock, Herbie, 65, 138, 143, 183, 219, 405
Hancock, Keith, 183
Hancox, Paul, 110
Handley, Jerry, 94
Hanna, Jeff, 128
Hansberry, Lorraine, 407
Happenings, 223, 445, 459, 480
Happy Mondays, 149, 157
Hapshash And The Coloured Coat, 18, 223, 428, 453, 465
Harburg, E.Y. 'Yip', 116
Hard Day's Night, A, 40, 42-43, 223, 230, 305
Hard Meat, 223-224
Hard Stuff, 164
Harder, Eddie, 172
Hardin And York, 146
Hardin, Eddie, 146
Hardin, Glen D., 85, 134, 355
Hardin, Tim, 26, 114, 140, 178, 189, 200, 211, 219, 224, 229, 325, 328, 385, 478
Hardy, Damon J., 6

Hardy, Françoise, 224
Hare, Colin, 239
Hargrove, Roy, 347, 414
Harlequin, 229
Harley, Wayne, 341
Harman, David, 141
Harman, James, 269
Harmony Grass, 224
Harnick, Sheldon, 194, 264
Harper Valley, 210
Harper, Roy, 203, 336
Harpers Bizarre, 44, 137, 225, 407
Harptones, 172
Harrell, Andre, 323
Harris, Barry, 311
Harris, Bill, 221
Harris, Bobby, 49
Harris, Damon, 438
Harris, Danny, 6, 469
Harris, David, 26
Harris, Eddie, 414
Harris, Emmylou, 85, 98-99, 153, 222, 299, 332, 335, 371
Harris, Hugh, 6
Harris, Jackie, 105
Harris, Jet, 142, 225, 283, 375, 398
Harris, Jet, And Tony Meehan, 225, 283, 398
Harris, Julie, 89
Harris, Lois, 105
Harris, Major, 365
Harris, Micki, 404
Harris, Peter, 324
Harris, Richard, 8, 45, 91, 200
Harris, Rolf, 293
Harris, Shaun, 469
Harris, Thurston, 10
Harris, Tim, 198
Harris, Wee Willie, 274
Harrison, Bobby, 360
Harrison, George, 19-20, 34, 39-40, 61, 74, 79, 102, 111, 171, 174-175, 236, 259, 269, 282, 332, 371, 403, 419, 430, 436, 449, 468, 480
Harrison, Henri, 327
Harrison, Mike, 18, 421
Harrison, Noel, 225, 280
Harrison, Rex, 13, 75, 225
Harrison, Wilbert, 92, 430
Harry, Bill, 43, 102
Harryman, Martin, 254
Hart, Bobby, 73, 315
Hart, Charles, 59
Hart, Charlie, 35
Hart, Les, 197
Hart, Lorenz, 75, 292, 353
Hart, Mickey, 219
Hart, Mike, 281
Hart, Moss, 90
Hart, Peter, 197
Hart, Roger, 372
Hartley, Keef, Band, 19, 225, 478
Hartman, Johnny, 123
Harvey, Alex, 74, 222, 226
Harvey, Bob, 253
Harvey, Laurence, 91
Harvey, Tam, 242
Haseman, Vikki, 74
Haskell, Gordon, 137
Haskins, Jim, 477
Hassilev, Alex, 280
Hastings, Doug, 138, 372
Hastings, Roy, 287
Hatch, Tony, 74, 76, 116, 259, 388, 394, 464
Hatcher, Charles, 425
Hatcher, Willie, 425
Hatfield, Bobby, 375
Hathaway, Donny, 227
Hatton, Billy, 201
Havens, Richie, 224, 227, 478
Hawken, John, 324
Hawker, James, 248
Hawker, Kenneth, 96

Hawker, Mike, 393
Hawkes, Chip, 447-448
Hawkins, Barbara Ann, 154
Hawkins, Bill, 100
Hawkins, Coleman, 61, 111-112, 142, 313
Hawkins, Dale, 85, 109, 228
Hawkins, Edwin, Singers, 81, 227-228
Hawkins, Erskine, 368
Hawkins, Hawkshaw, 119
Hawkins, Jamesetta, 249
Hawkins, Jay, 77
Hawkins, John, 61, 228
Hawkins, Martin, 356-357
Hawkins, Reg, 334
Hawkins, Roger, 447
Hawkins, Ron, 228
Hawkins, Ronnie, 85, 228
Hawkins, Rosa Lee, 154
Hawkins, Terence, 398
Hawks, Howard, 325
Hawkshaw, Alan, 197, 398
Hawksworth, Mick, 14
Hawkwind, 27, 390
Haworth, Jill, 89
Haydock, Eric, 236-237
Hayes, Brian, 228
Hayes, David, 30, 352, 390, 442
Hayes, Edward Brian, 228
Hayes, Isaac, 30, 263, 351-352, 390, 426, 442, 466
Hayes, Louis, 7
Hayes, Steve, 283
Hayes, Tony, 283
Hayes, Tubby, 228-229, 308, 393
Haymes, Dick, 277
Haynes, Roy, 85
Hayward, Justin, 319
Hayward, Lawrence, 205
Hayward, Richard, 205
Hayworth, Rita, 376
Hazell, Hy, 108
Hazelwood, Mike, 190
Hazlewood, Lee, 210, 247
Hazziez, Yusuf, 440
Head, Roy, 229, 302
Heads, Hands And Feet, 254
Heartbeats, 56, 234
Heartbreakers, 170, 316
Hearts And Flowers, 225, 229
Hearts Of Fire, 170, 227, 430
Heath, Frederick, 264
Heath, Ted, 7, 393, 468
Heathcliff, 374
Heather, Roy, 324
Heatwave, 235
Heaven 17, 402
Heavenly, 392
Heavy Jelly, 229, 282, 410
Heavy Metal Kids, 223
Hebb, Bobby, 229, 422
Hecht, Donn, 119
Heckstall-Smith, Dick, 69, 80, 121, 213, 271, 296, 479
Hedgehoppers Anonymous, 230
Hedges, Carol, 142
Heidt, Horace, 263
Heinz, 102, 230, 303, 334, 357, 446, 484
Hellman, Lillian, 50
Hellmer, Heinz, 484
Hellsberg, Magnus, 422
Helm, Levon, 167-168, 228
Helmet, 77
Helms, Bobby, 462
Help Yourself, 176, 256-257
Help!, 230-231
Hemmings, David, 65, 91
Henderson, Alan, 440
Henderson, Bill, 120
Henderson, Brian, 329
Henderson, David, 233
Henderson, Dickie, 157
Henderson, Dorris, 174, 231

Henderson, Harvey, 30
Henderson, Joe, 406
Henderson, Joe 'Mr Piano', 58
Henderson, Michael, 81, 329
Hendricks, Bobby, 430
Hendricks, James, 178, 384
Hendricks, Jim, 323
Hendricks, Jon, 128, 189, 385
Hendrickse, Margorie, 127
Hendrix, Jimi, 15, 65, 82, 104, 120, 123, 132, 143, 147, 153, 173, 176, 193, 223, 231-233, 270, 273, 275, 285, 317, 368, 375, 384, 415, 430, 436, 467, 478
Hendrix, Margie, 127, 364
Hendryx, Nona, 220
Heneker, David, 108
Henley, Larry, 327
Henn, Rick, 431
Henri, Adrian, 103, 281
Henrit, Bob, 386, 454
Henry, Chris, 421
Henry, Clarence 'Frogman', 233
Henry, Dolores, 136
Henry, Hank, 311
Henry, James, 53
Henry, John, 191, 399
Henry, Lenny, 392
Henry, Milton, 343
Henry, Pierre, 421
Henry, Thomas, 92
Henry, Tony, 296
Henshall, Ruthie, 331
Henske, Judy, 304, 479
Hensley, Ken, 212
Hensley, Patsy, 118
Hensley, Roy, 100
Hensworth, Danny, 344
Hepburn, Audrey, 13
Heptones, 344
Herald Records, 123
Herbal Mixture, 234
Herbert, Bongo, 373
Herbert, Ian, 421
Herd, 190, 234, 308, 334, 412, 447
Herman's Hermits, 53, 79, 101-102, 187, 212, 234, 295, 368
Herman, Gary, 472
Herman, Jerry, 230
Herman, William, 16
Herman, Woody, 8, 146, 221
Heron, 162, 246
Heron, Mike, 162, 246
Herrell, James, 300
Herrmann, Bernard, 50
Hershkowitz, Harvey, 364
Hesse, Herman, 427
Hester, Carolyn, 166, 191
Hewitt, Howard, 466
Hewlett, John, 255
Heywood, Anne, 457
Hi Records, 57, 292, 351, 478
Hi-Lo's, 35
Hiatt, John, 324
Hibbert, Toots, 298
Hibler, Son, 84
Hickory Records, 327
Hickory Wind, 87
Hicks, Colin, 101, 198, 446
Hicks, Dan, 106
Hicks, Leo, 63
Hicks, Tom, 100
Hicks, Tommy, 101, 338
Hicks, Tony, 236
Hideaways, 102
Higginbotham, Robert, 449
Higgins, Billy, 311
Higgins, Chuck, 467
Higgins, Eddie, 13
Higgins, Henry, 104, 180
High On Love, 30
High Spirits, 112
High Tide, 383
Hightone Records, 139
Hightower, Rosetta, 333

Hildebrand, Ray, 340
Hildebrandt, Herbert, 365
Hildred, Stafford, 257
Hill, Albert, 474
Hill, Alfred Hawthorne, 235
Hill, Andrew, 66, 155
Hill, Benny, 235, 365
Hill, Dan, 291, 445
Hill, Jessie, 308
Hill, Tony, 310
Hilliard, Bob, 24
Hillman, Chris, 81, 86, 301
Hillsiders, 284
Hinchcliffe, Tony, 194
Hincks, Mick, 282
Hinds, Justin, 370-371
Hinds, Neville, 343
Hine, Eric, 165
Hines, Brian, 273, 318
Hines, Ian, 403
Hinkley, Tim, 68, 254
Hinnen, Peter, 235
Hinsley, Harvey, 334
Hinson, Arthur, 125
Hirsh, Chicken, 129
Hiseman, Jon, 28, 69, 121, 225, 296
Hite, Bob, 92
Hixon, William, 45
HMV Records, 53, 274, 286, 290, 391
Hoagland, Dan, 16
Hoax, 177
Hobbs, Randy, 300
Hobday, Stuart, 304
Hoddrick, Joe, 454
Hodge, Keith, 14
Hodges, Chas, 53, 334
Hodges, Eddie, 76
Hodges, Johnny, 122
Hodges, Kenny, 418
Hodges, Pete, 277
Hodgkinson, Colin, 271
Hodkinson, Mark, 189
Hoellerich, Gerd, 60
Hoffman, Dustin, 215
Hogan, Carl, 51
Hogan, Don, 162
Hogan, Jimmy, 93
Hogarth, Nicky, 270
Hoggs, Billy, 125
Hoh, Eddie, 304
Holden, Randy, 66
Holdsworth, Allan, 415
Holiday, Jimmy, 309
Holland, Bernie, 254
Holland, Brian, 161-162, 235, 295, 366, 464, 470
Holland, Dave, 143, 349
Holland, Eddie, 161, 214, 235, 322, 430
Holland, Jools, 258
Holland, Milt, 474
Holland, Steve, 173
Holland/Dozier/Holland, 161-162, 177, 199-200, 235-236, 293, 309, 322, 431-432, 463, 470
Holleman, Regina, 295
Holler, Dick, 153
Holliday, Michael, 24, 391
Holliday, Mike, 372
Hollies, 40, 102, 135, 142, 179, 181, 185, 236-237, 247, 294, 366, 388, 405, 434, 436, 449, 457, 474
Hollis, Peter, 110
Holloway, Brenda, 6, 237-238
Holloway, Laurie, 317
Holloway, Stanley, 59
Holly, Buddy, 16, 40, 53, 63, 134, 193, 195, 237, 241, 265, 282, 303, 325, 334, 336, 345, 351, 355, 358, 379, 387, 424, 445, 455, 457-458
Holly, Doyle, 335
Hollywood Argyles, 201, 238
Hollywood Flames, 68
Hollywood Hotel, 258

Holman, Eddie, 387
Holmes, Christine, 108, 190
Holmes, John, 421
Holmes, Johnny, 346
Holmes, Richard 'Groove', 238, 300, 413
Holmes, Robert, 356
Holofcener, Larry, 145
Holt, Dennis, 359
Holt, John, 359
Holtzman, Jac, 158, 177
Holtzman, Vivian, 194
Holy Modal Rounders, 173, 206, 238-239
Holzman, Jac, 239
Home Of The Blues Records, 97
Homer And Jethro, 19
Hondells, 101, 239
Honeyball, Ray, 230
Honeybus, 239-240
Honeycombs, 141, 240, 303
Honeydrippers, 53
Honeys, 16
Hood, David, 447
Hood, Roger, 447
Hooker, John Lee, 84, 92, 110, 143, 152, 165-166, 298, 366, 371
Hooker, Martin, 289
Hooper, Darryl, 396
Hope, Bob, 47, 145
Hopkin, Dale, 327
Hopkin, Mary, 240, 282
Hopkins, Billy, 387
Hopkins, Jerry, 159-160, 233, 356-357
Hopkins, Keith, 469
Hopkins, Lightnin', 84, 109, 299
Hopkins, Linda, 475
Hopkins, Mike, 244
Hopkins, Nicky, 142, 179, 336, 363, 427, 433
Hopkins, Richard, 63
Hopper, Dennis, 143, 173
Hopper, Hugh, 31, 415
Hopwood, Keith, 234
Hord, Eric, 301
Horn, Jim, 174
Horn, Trevor, 257
Hornsby, Bruce, 218
Hornsby, Clive, 149
Hornsby, Paul, 240
Horton, Gladys, 295
Hot And Blue, 98-99
Hot Butter, 151
Hot Chocolate, 59, 240, 262, 334
Hot Tuna, 254
Hot Wax Records, 162
Hotchner, A.E., 383
Hotlegs, 306
Hour Glass, 240-241
Houston, Cisco, 27
Houston, Cissy, 249, 433, 449, 465
Houston, Dale, 138
Houston, David, 404
Houston, Thelma, 241
Houston, Whitney, 204, 297
Hovorka, Bob, 151
Howard And Blaikley, 141, 234, 240
Howard The Duck, 265
Howard, Alan, 141, 234, 240, 447
Howard, Harlan, 119, 335
Howard, James, 274
Howard, John, 193
Howard, Johnny, 241
Howard, Ken, 141, 234, 240
Howard, Paul, 327
Howie B., 148, 252
Howlin' Wolf, 86, 109-110, 126, 165, 214, 299, 449, 454, 479
Hozier, Vince, 431
Hubbard, Freddie, 66, 155, 182-183, 263
Hubbard, Neil, 479
Hudson, Garth, 167, 228
Hudson, Richard, 208, 228, 458

Hudson-Ford, 458
Huff, Leon, 329
Hugg, Mike, 165, 290
Hughes, Alex, 359
Hughes, Harry, 120
Hughes, Howard, 328
Hughes, Langston, 307
Hughes, Lynne, 106
Hughey, John, 451
Hullaballoos, 241
Hultgren, Georg, 174
Human Beinz, 241-242
Human Nature, 173
Human Records, 241
Humble Pie, 31, 234, 245, 412, 421
Humblebums, 242
Humes, Anita, 182
Humperdinck, Engelbert, 41, 101, 242, 257, 266, 347, 368, 391
Humphrey, Phil, 193
Humphries, John, 172
Humphries, Patrick, 172, 407
Hunt, Joe, 18
Hunt, Marsha, 222
Hunt, Ray, 321
Hunter, George, 92, 105, 363
Hunter, Ivory Joe, 71
Hunter, Meredith, 12
Hunter, Robert, 218
Hunter, Russell, 151
Hurd, Francine, 341
Hurst, Mike, 240, 424, 465
Hush Records, 435
Hustler, 208, 226, 458
Huston, Chris, 453
Hutch, Willie, 310
Hutcherson, Bobby, 155
Hutchinson, Johnny, 55
Hutchinson, Nigel, 68
Hutson, Leroy, 245
Hutton, Betty, 431
Hutton, Danny, 314
Huxley, Rick, 114
Hyams, Margie, 402
Hyland, Brian, 137, 242-243, 278, 462
Hyman, Jerry, 64
Hynde, Chrissie, 192, 267
Hynes, Dave, 79

I

I Roy, 343
Ian And The Zodiacs, 243
Ian Folk Group, 91
Ideals, 254
Idle Race, 65, 244, 323, 403
Ifield, Frank, 244
Ikettes, 18
Illinois Speed Press, 244-245
Illusion, 393, 479
Immediate Records, 90, 245, 336, 415, 465
Imperial Records, 309, 376
Imperial Teen, 326
Impressions, 245-246 and passim
Impulse! Records, 122
Incredible String Band, 162, 177, 190, 246, 361, 478
Incredibles, 246
Ingber, Elliot, 205
Ingmann, Jorgen, 283
Ingram, Adrian, 318
Ingram, Luther, 30, 426
Ink Spots, 333, 352
Inmates, 393
Inner Circle, 145
Inner City, 208
Innes, Brian, 437
Innes, Neil, 70
Innocents, 201
Instant Action Jug Band, 129
Intermezzo, 328
International Submarine Band,

246-247
Intrigue, 224
Intruders, 71
IPG Records, 458
Iron Butterfly, 21, 55, 247
Iron Curtain, 297
Irvine, Andy, 162
Irving, Bill, 197
Irving, Clifford, 328
Irving, Don, 44
Irwin, Big Dee, 247, 281
Isaacs, David, 343
Isherwood, Christopher, 89
Isley Brothers, 49, 77, 81, 108, 110, 128, 147, 226, 231, 236, 242, 286, 322, 351
Ives, Burl, 284
Iveys, 247, 429
Ivy League, 8, 97, 101, 248, 393
Ivy, Quin, 410

J

J., Harry, 5
J.J. Foote, 224
Jackie And Millie, 306
Jackman, Tommy, 409
Jackon, David, 229
Jacks, Terry, 74
Jackson Heights, 328
Jackson, Al, 17, 30, 71, 135, 273, 292
Jackson, Ben, 130
Jackson, Calvin, 84
Jackson, Carl, 30
Jackson, Charlie, 292
Jackson, Chuck, 24, 79, 130, 248-249, 449
Jackson, David, 152
Jackson, Eddie, 74
Jackson, George, 169
Jackson, Jack, 172
Jackson, Jermaine, 293
Jackson, Jill, 340
Jackson, John, 467
Jackson, Karen, 432
Jackson, Lee, 328
Jackson, Mahalia, 204, 368
Jackson, Maurice, 74
Jackson, Michael, 42, 58, 143, 399, 477
Jackson, Mick, 285
Jackson, Millie, 30
Jackson, Milt 'Bags', 123
Jackson, Pipecock, 344
Jackson, Raymond, 30, 467
Jackson, Roger, 446
Jackson, Stonewall, 284
Jackson, Tommy, 335
Jackson, Tony, 46, 394
Jackson, Walter, 297
Jackson, Wanda, 335
Jackson, Wayne, 292
Jacobs, David, 180, 258
Jacobs, Hank, 430
Jacobs, Matthew, 308
Jacobsen, Erik, 154
Jacquet, Illinois, 142
Jaeger, Rick, 5
Jagger, Mick, 12, 18, 189, 191, 245, 271, 349, 379, 383
Jah Jerry, 409
Jah Lion, 344
Jailhouse Rock, 54, 354, 356-357
Jam, 55, and passim
Jamerson, James, 263
James, Barry, 263
James, Bob, 274
James, Chris, 392
James, Curley, 5
James, David, 249
James, Dick, 39, 42, 180, 269, 316, 337
James, Eddie, 225

James, Elmore, 109, 430
James, Etta, 53, 110, 150, 249
James, Fanita, 68
James, Glyn, 243
James, Graham, 63
James, Harry, 124
James, Jesse, 9, 125
James, Jesseca, 452
James, Jimmy, 231, 300, 336, 413, 417, 475
James, John, 190
James, Joni, 387
James, Larry, 250
James, Lewis, 248, 312
James, Marcus, 359
James, Michael, 130
James, Nicky, 250
James, Ray, 162, 205
James, Richard, 74, 77
James, Rick, 438
James, Sally, 392
James, Sonny, 335
James, Stu, 312
James, Tommy, And The Shondells, 132, 220, 250, 445
James, Tony, 53
Jamison, Roosevelt, 95, 478
Jan And Arnie, 250
Jan And Dean, 8, 11, 35, 61, 165, 190, 250-251, 411
Jan Dukes De Grey, 251
Janken, George, 362
Jankowski, Horst, 251, 417
Jans, Tom, 191
Jansch, Bert, 189, 216, 251-252, 342
Jansen, Hans, 9
Jansen, Linda, 14
Jardell, Robert, 28
Jardine, Al, 35, 37
Jarmels, 259
Jarrett, Keith, 85, 143, 183
Jarrett, Tony, 456
Jaspar, Bobby, 292
Jay And The Americans, 252, 291, 429, 462
Jay And The Techniques, 252-253
Jay, David, 252
Jay, Peter, And The Jaywalkers, 253
Jayhawks (R&B), 253
Jaynetts, 253
Jazz Masters, 254, 318, 346
Jazz Messengers, 61-62, 156, 311, 320, 404-406, 443
Jefferson Airplane, 12, 22, 215-216, 219, 232, 253-254, 317, 324-325, 341, 363, 454, 478
Jefferson Starship, 254, 363
Jefferson, John, 478
Jefferson, Thomas, 274
Jeffery, Mike, 176
Jeffrey, Mike, 17
Jeffreys, Garland, 363
Jeffries, Mike, 104, 231
Jelfs, Ian, 113
Jelly Beans, 32, 220
Jellybread, 71
Jemmott, Jerry, 265
Jenkins, Barrie, 324
Jenkins, Barry, 15, 229
Jenkins, Harold, 451
Jenkins, John, 444
Jenkins, Johnny, 367
Jenkins, Jordan, 444
Jenkins, Karl, 415
Jenkins, Lyle, 226
Jenner, Martin, 148
Jennings, John, 25
Jennings, Waylon, 20, 99-100, 436
Jennings, Will, 25, 389
Jerome, Jerome, 50, 152, 195, 217, 289, 334, 346, 350, 409
Jerome, Jim, 289
Jesmer, Elaine, 440
Jesters, 93

Jesus And Mary Chain, 402, 459
Jet Records, 18
Jethro Tull, 214, 427
Jewel And Eddie, 10
Jewel Records, 305
Jewell, Jimmy, 225
Jewels, 290
Jewry, Bernard, 194
Jigsaw, 399
Jim, Country, 370
Jive Five, 114, 429
Jo Jo Gunne, 420
Jo Mama, 341
Joan Marie, 154
Jobim, Antonio, 254, 291
Jody Grind, 254, 406
Joel, Billy, 250
Johansen, David, 445
John And Johnny, 56
John's Children, 179, 255, 273
John, Chris, 191
John, Clive, 89
John, Elton, 25, 28, 71, 113, 204, 297, 341, 350, 374, 397, 417, 421, 466
John, Graham, 366
John, Little Willie, 78, 344
John, Mable, 365
John, Richard, 63, 375, 413
John, Robert, 445
Johnnie And Joe, 253
Johnny And John, 56
Johnny And The Hurricanes, 55, 255
Johnny And The Moondogs, 39
Johnson, 'Blind' Willie, 187, 216, 324
Johnson, Allen, 292
Johnson, Andy, 192
Johnson, Bill, 346
Johnson, Blind Willie, 187, 216, 324
Johnson, Bob, 270
Johnson, Bruce, 275, 291, 418
Johnson, Candy, 84
Johnson, Carol, 186
Johnson, D., 292
Johnson, Dave, 253
Johnson, Derek, 463
Johnson, Earl, 255
Johnson, Echo, 295
Johnson, Eddie, 214, 322
Johnson, Enotris, 60
Johnson, Fred, 292
Johnson, Gareth, 63
Johnson, Gene, 292
Johnson, Howie, 460
Johnson, Hubert, 125
Johnson, J.J., 8
Johnson, Jack, 14
Johnson, James, 66, 346
Johnson, Jill, 190
Johnson, Jimmy, 253, 384
Johnson, JJ, 343
Johnson, Joe, 182
Johnson, Johnnie, 51
Johnson, Johnny, And The Bandwagon, 255
Johnson, Mac, 454
Johnson, Marc, 182
Johnson, Marv, 214, 255-256, 322, 366
Johnson, Paul, 45
Johnson, Plas, 386
Johnson, Ralph, 245
Johnson, Richard, 45, 60, 63
Johnson, Robert, 231, 318, 366
Johnson, Ron, 261
Johnson, Rudolph, 182
Johnson, Syl, 71
Johnson, Teddy, 95, 364, 393
Johnson, Tommy, 92, 162
Johnson, Van, 384
Johnson, Victor, 96
Johnson, Wilko, 192
Johnson, William, 162

Johnson, Willie, 187, 216, 324
Johnston, Bruce, 36-37, 250, 326
Jollife, Steve, 427
Jolson, Al, 54, 223, 354
Jones, Allen, 12
Jones, Andrew, 377
Jones, Angela, 56, 130, 284, 303
Jones, Bill, 143
Jones, Billie Jean, 481
Jones, Billy, 192
Jones, Bob, 285
Jones, Bobby, 16, 336
Jones, Booker T., 71, 135, 292, 426
Jones, Brian, 317, 379-383, 453
Jones, Bridget, 428
Jones, Chuck, 55
Jones, Corky, 335
Jones, Davy, 73-74, 314
Jones, Dorothy, 127
Jones, Eddie, 74
Jones, Elvin, 122
Jones, Esther Mae, 347
Jones, Geoff, 117
Jones, George, 124, 175, 257, 350, 404
Jones, Graham, 421
Jones, Hank, 318, 402-403, 475
Jones, Henry 'Juggy Murray', 430
Jones, Hughie, 419-420
Jones, Jack, 23-24, 132
Jones, James Earl, 104
Jones, Jeff, 89
Jones, Jerry, 74
Jones, Jimmy, 76, 256, 400, 475
Jones, Jo, 346
Jones, Joe, 7, 143, 154, 183
Jones, John Paul, 18, 174, 336
Jones, Kenny, 402, 412, 471
Jones, Lee, 330
Jones, Malcolm, 31
Jones, Max, 111
Jones, Michael, 16, 284
Jones, Mick, 421
Jones, Mickey, 73, 89, 168
Jones, Neil, 12
Jones, Paul, 5, 18, 138, 174, 178, 271, 290, 336, 367
Jones, Percy, 281
Jones, Peter, 356
Jones, Phalin, 30
Jones, Philly Joe, 7, 143, 183
Jones, Quincy, 59-60, 144, 186, 215, 307, 393
Jones, Ray, 138, 272
Jones, Rickie Lee, 330
Jones, Ron, 318
Jones, Sam, 7
Jones, Shirley, 101
Jones, Thad, 307, 320
Jones, Willie, 474
Joneses, 482
Jook, 255
Joplin, Janis, 49, 55, 129, 179, 220, 257-258, 317, 340, 365, 385, 408, 478
Jordan, Al, 316
Jordan, Clay, 134
Jordan, Clifford, 66, 444
Jordan, Danny, 151
Jordan, Duke, 311
Jordan, John, 152
Jordan, Louis, 51, 152, 361
Jordan, Ronnie, 143
Jordan, Stanley, 66
Jordan, Tommy, 151
Jordanaires, 353, 451
Joseph, Patrick, 110
Joshua, 121, 340
Journeymen, 258, 288, 301, 384
Joy Division, 360, 459
Joy Records, 30
Joyce, James, 31
Joyce, John, 438
Joyce, Teddy, 112
Juan, Don, 208, 325

Judas Jump, 12
Judas Priest, 168, 421
Judge Dread, 343, 359
Judge, Alan, 178
Juicy Lucy, 152, 310
Juju, 405
Juke Box Jury, 258
Juke Boy, 258
Jumbo, 118
Junior, Byles, 343-344
Junior, Guitar, 137, 293
Jury, 18, 258, 373, 478
Just Records, 284
Justice, Jimmy, 74, 258-259, 284
Justis, Bill, 174, 259

K

K-Doe, Ernie, 259, 308, 337
Kador, Ernest, Jnr., 259
Kaempfert, Bert, 80, 259-260, 403
Kagan, Harvey, 408
Kahn, Steve, 105
Kait, Al, 386
Kak, 66
Kalb, Danny, 68
Kaleidoscope (UK), 260
Kalin Twins, 79, 150, 261, 349
Kalin, Harold 'Hal', 261
Kalmar, Bert, 202
Kama Sutra Records, 106, 261
Kander, John, 89
Kane, Amory, 190
Kane, Barry, 301, 327
Kane, Eden, 57, 262, 391
Kane, Howie, 252
Kane, Michael, 483
Kane, Paul, 445
Kantner, Paul, 253-254, 324
Kaplan, Howard, 450
Kaplan, Jeff, 261
Kapner, Mark, 129
Kapp Records, 137, 242, 364
Kapralik, Dave, 341
Karloff, Boris, 50, 348
Karlson, Keith, 312
Karmen, Janice, 111
Karmon, Freddy, 93
Karnilova, Maria, 194
Kasenetz, Jerry, 81, 131, 262, 328, 331
Kassner, Eddie, 262, 337
Kasten, Fritz, 416
Kat, 89, 344
Katz, Jeff, 81, 131, 262, 328, 331
Katz, Matthew, 312
Katz, Steve, 64, 68
Katzman, Sam, 234, 337
Kaukonen, Jorma, 253
Kay, Horace, 435
Kay, John, 427
Kaye Sisters, 457
Kaye, Carol, 262, 326, 455
Kaye, Danny, 75
Kaye, Larry, 364
Kaye, Lenny, 371, 455
Kaye, Tony, 255, 282, 476
Kaylan, Howard, 214, 321, 450
KC And The Sunshine Band, 262
Keane, Bob, 455
Keaton, Diane, 222
Keen Records, 60
Keen, John, 443
Keen, Speedy, 443
Keene, Nelson, 338
Keep On Rockin', 326
Kefford, Chris 'Ace', 323
Keisker, Marion, 353
Keith And Billie, 352
Keith, Bill, 272
Keith, Brian, 350
Keith, Jeff, 433
Keliehor, Jon, 138
Keller, Dennis, 194

Keller, Helen, 164
Keller, Jack, 212
Keller, Jerry, 263, 473
Kelley, Alton, 217
Kelley, Kevin, 87, 376
Kellie, Mike, 18, 421
Kellogg, Burns, 66
Kellogg, Lynn, 222
Kelly, Ann, 165
Kelly, Betty, 293, 458
Kelly, Dave, 165
Kelly, Gene, 50
Kelly, George, 263
Kelly, Jo Ann, 165
Kelly, Joe, 100, 399
Kelly, Johnny, 93
Kelly, Luke, 91, 164
Kelly, Mike, 165
Kelly, Mike, 165
Kelly, Ned, 381
Kelly, Sally, 338
Kelly, Wynton, 8, 66, 183, 263, 318
Kemp, Allen, 325
Kendall, Alan, 211
Kendricks, Eddie, 437-439
Kennedy, Jimmy, 60
Kennedy, John, 230, 338
Kennedy, John F., 230
Kennedy, Maureen, 461
Kennedy, Nigel, 233
Kenner, Chris, 93, 109, 191, 248, 263, 348
Kenner, Doris, 404
Kennibrew, Dee Dee, 136
Kenny And The Cadets, 35
Kenny, Sean, 63, 331
Keno, Jerri Bo, 419, 437
Kenton, Stan, 90, 202
Kerley, Lenny, 136
Kern, Jerome, 334, 346
Kern, Jimmy, 275
Kerr, Bob, 70, 327, 398
Kerr, Patrick, 366
Kerr, Sandra, 397
Kerr, Tim, 188, 366
Kerrison, John, 179
Kerschenbaum, Howard, 252
Kerslake, Lee, 212
Kesey, Ken, 217
Keyes, Bobby, 223, 381
Keynotes, 96
Keys, Cherry, 129
KGB, 65
Khan, 35, 431
Khan, George, 35
Khan, Ustad Vilayat, 431
Khaury, Herbert, 444
Khouri, Ken, 9
Kibbee, Martin, 205
Kid Galahad, 354, 357
Kidd, Johnny, 10, 101, 264
Kiley, Richard, 264
Kilgore, Merle, 98
Killen, Buddy, 440
Killen, Louis, 113
Kilminster, Ian, 390
Kim, Andy, 17, 32, 200
Kimbrough, Junior, 84
Kincaid, Jesse Lee, 376
Kincaid, Mark, 177
Kinds, Hans, 136
King Bee, 410
King Crimson, 5, 113, 137, 212
King Curtis, 231, 265, 279, 361, 404
King Diamond, 315
King Kasuals, 231
King Kolax, 122
King Of The Wheels, 207
King Records, 275, 282, 361
King Tubby, 131, 343
King, Alan, 6
King, Albert, 30, 135
King, B.B., 5, 24, 30, 62, 79, 85, 216, 231, 241, 265, 332, 351, 430, 443,

449
King, Ben E., 49, 102, 130, 163, 259, 265, 348, 418
King, Bill, 257
King, Billie Jean, 423
King, Bob, 357
King, Bobby, 5, 130, 443
King, Carole, 8, 11, 76, 79, 87, 118, 127, 134, 141, 207, 212, 229, 281, 291, 315, 329, 395, 422-423
King, Clydie, 365
King, Dave, 24
King, Denis, 59
King, Don, 274
King, Ed, 429
King, Freddie, 18, 110, 127, 206
King, Freddy, 430
King, Hal, 132
King, Jackson, 206
King, Jean, 423
King, Jim, 191
King, Jimmy, 24, 30, 300
King, Joe, 440
King, John, 85
King, Johnny, 312
King, Jonathan, 230, 431
King, Kim, 283
King, Martin Luther, 46, 153, 477
King, Maurice, 463-464
King, Melvin, 332
King, Mick, 46
King, Pete, 6
King, Pet
King, Reggie, 6
King, Solomon, 83, 266, 348
King, Stephen, 391
King, Steve, 8, 275
Kingdom Come, 77
Kingham, Lionel, 466
Kings Of Rhythm, 449-450
Kingsley, Ben, 14
Kingsmen, 53, 266, 372
Kingston Trio, 74, 211, 301, 303, 326, 345, 473
Kinks, 17, 53-54, 74, 98, 101, 128, 132, 152, 159, 213, 221, 237, 262, 266-268, 336-337, 366, 379, 431, 471
Kinnear, Roy, 230
Kinney Corporation, 21, 239
Kinrade, John, 181
Kinsey, Tony, 385
Kinsley, Billy, 303
Kippington Lodge, 268
Kirby, Alex, 424
Kirby, John, 109
Kirby, Kathy, 22, 268-269
Kirchherr, Astrid, 39
Kirchin, Tim, 191
Kirk, Rahsaan Roland, 307
Kirke, Simon, 57
Kirkham, Terry, 19
Kirkland, Frank, 152
Kirkland, James, 325
Kirkwood, Pat, 13
Kirshner, Don, 17, 76, 140, 212, 315, 395
Kitley, Peter, 358
Kitt, Eartha, 202
Klaus And Gibson, 181
Klein, Alan, 327
Klein, Allen, 42, 269, 380, 419
Klein, Carol, 395
Klein, Warren, 205
Knapp, John, 221
Knauss, Richard, 292
Knechtel, Larry, 174, 376
Knepper, Jimmy, 307
Knibbs, Lloyd, 409
Knickerbockers, 269-270, 375, 481
Knight, Curtis, 231, 233, 270
Knight, Gladys, 25, 81, 130, 208, 322, 466
Knight, Graham, 197, 293
Knight, Larry, 420
Knight, Peter, 270, 319, 464

Knight, Robert, 270, 285, 306
Knights, Barron, 32, 284
Knopfler, Mark, 20, 170, 193
Knox, Buddy, 269
Knust, Michael, 194
Koblin, Ken, 81
Kobluk, Mike, 310
Koerner, 'Spider' John, 366
Koerner, John, 366
Koerner, Ray And Glover, 177, 366, 385
Kogel, Mike, 283
Koko Records, 30
Kokomo, 37
Kolber, Larry, 291
Kong, Leslie, 9, 298, 349
Konikoff, Sandy, 168
Konitz, Lee, 150, 182, 184, 306
Konrad, John, 312
Koobas, 271
Kool Gents, 115, 454
Kooper, Al, 64-65, 68, 167, 169, 197, 278, 340, 345, 385, 387
Kootch, Danny, 206
Koppelman, Charles, 364
Koppycats, 243
Korner, Alexis, 27, 69, 113, 142, 192, 212, 216, 271-272, 296, 312-313, 342, 352, 379
Korner, Neil, 327
Kornfeld, Artie, 130
Kortchmar, Danny, 118, 436
Koschminder, Bruno, 39
Koss, Richard, 441
Kosser, Michael, 452
Kossoff, David, 431
Kossoff, Paul, 57
Kostelanetz, André, 316
Kotke, Lenny, 214
Kottke, Leo, 188
Koussevitzky, Serge, 50
Kovak, Laszlo, 173
Kovas, Dino, 315
Kraemer, Peter, 416
Kramer, Billy J. And The Dakotas, 25, 180, 272, 294, 395
Kramer, Eddie, 233
Kramer, John, 149
Kramer, Wayne, 299
Krastan, Dean, 331
Krauledat, Joachim F., 427
Kraus, Peter, 203
Kravitz, Lenny, 297
Kreisler, Fritz, 484
Kretmar, Don, 68
Kretzmer, Herbert, 23
Kreutzfeldt, Hajo, 365
Kreutzmann, Bill, 217
Krikorian, Steve, 134
Kristina, Sonja, 192
Kristofferson, Kris, 98-100, 228, 258, 276, 428, 460
KRLA, 207
Kubas, 271
Kubrick, Stanley, 429
Kudu Records, 347
Kulberg, Andy, 68
Kupferberg, Tuli, 206
Kuti, Fela, 27
Kuy, Billy, 334
Kweskin, Jim, 272, 324
Kyser, Kay, 434

L

(Les) Fleur De Lys, 110
La Faro, Scott, 182
La Pierre, Cherilyn, 70
La's, 369
LaBarbera, Joe, 182
LaBelle, 25, 329
Labelle, Patti, 25
Lack, Ken, 349
LaCroix, Jerry, 64

Lacy, Steve, 314
Lady Flash, 371
Lady Saw, 415
Lafaille, Hans, 136
Lagos, Paul, 260
Lagueux, Val, 174
Lahteinen, Keith, 453
Lai, Francis, 59
Laine, Cleo, 107, 283
Laine, Denny, 149, 250, 273, 318
Laine, Frankie, 244
Lake, Greg, 212
Lalor, Steve, 138
Lamb, Bob, 244, 282
Lambert, Constant, 273
Lambert, Dennis, 469
Lambert, Hendricks And Ross, 385
Lambert, Kit, 273, 303, 470
Lamour, Dorothy, 230
Lamp Of Childhood, 323
Lana Sisters, 422
Lance, Major, 196, 273-274, 297
Land, Harold, 184, 313
Landau, Jon, 299
Lander, Bob, 421
Lander, Tony, 179
Landerman, Barry, 268
Landers, Audrey, 273
Landis, Jerry, 129, 445
Landis, Karl, 253
Landon, Neil, 196
Landry, Jackie, 105
Landy, Eugene, 37
Lane, Burton, 14, 116
Lane, Gary, 424
Lane, Lois, 95
Lane, Ronnie, 410, 412
Lane, Rosemary, 252
Lang, Bob, 306
Lang, Don, 274
lang, k.d., 47, 276
Lang, Peter, 188
Langford, Peter, 32
Langham, Nigel, 304
Langhorn, Gordon, 274
Langley, Ank, 362
Langwith, James, 412, 475
Lanois, Daniel, 171
Lantree, John, 240
LaPore, Dennis, 67
Lark, Stan, 195
Larkey, Charles, 206
Larks, 345
Larson, Nicolette, 85
LaRue, Dione, 401
Lasker, Jay, 8, 165
Last Exit, 75, 446-447
Last, James, 74, 211, 251, 274
Lateef, Yusef, 7
Latimer, Carlton, 147
Latin Fever, 291
Latouche, John, 50
Laud, Alan, 230
Laufer, Larry, 132
Laundau, Bill, 100
Lauper, Cyndi, 116, 143, 220
Laurence, Lynda, 432
Laurents, Arthur, 50
Laurie Records, 30, 148, 386
Laurie, Billy, 286
Lavern, Roger, 446
Law And Order, 334
Lawmen, 250
Lawrence, Claire, 120
Lawrence, Derek, 431
Lawrence, Gertrude, 13
Lawrence, Steve, 24, 203, 212, 223, 269, 274-275, 437
Layden, Graham, 35
Lea, Clive, 378
Lead Belly, 36, 216, 366
Leadon, Bernie, 128, 152, 229
Leaf, David, 37-38
Leahy, Dick, 260
Lean, David, 54

Lease, 81, 152
Leatherwood, Stu, 271
Leave It To Me!, 5, 211
Leaves, 29, 153, 263, 275, 345
Leavill, Otis, 273
Leckenby, Lek, 234
Led Zeppelin, 18, 21, 190, 336, 360, 391, 480
Ledigo, Hugh, 29
Lee Curtis And The All-Stars, 53
Lee, Albert, 112, 134, 185, 192, 431
Lee, Alvin, 14, 439
Lee, Amy, 160
Lee, Arthur, 284-285
Lee, Barbara, 111
Lee, Barry, 160, 311
Lee, Bernie, 137
Lee, Bert, 158
Lee, Beverly, 404
Lee, Billy, And The Rivieras, 388
Lee, Brenda, 97, 150, 275-276, 284
Lee, Brian, 276
Lee, Bunny, 9
Lee, Byron, 298
Lee, Curtis, 53, 102, 192, 418
Lee, Dave, 192
Lee, Eddie, 96
Lee, Frances, 461
Lee, Frankie, 168
Lee, George, 387
Lee, Graham, 134
Lee, Irma, 442
Lee, Jackie, 68, 276
Lee, Jennie, 250
Lee, Jim, 317
Lee, Joni, 452
Lee, Larry, 232
Lee, Laura, 110, 368
Lee, Peggy, 145, 402
Lee, Peter, 303
Lee, Phil, 185
Lee, Ric, 439
Lee, Robert, 275, 362-363, 435
Lee, Roy, 100
Lee, Sammy, 75
Lee, Sandy, 460
Lee, Stan, 306
Leeds, Gary, 424, 463-464
Leeman, Mark, 110, 127, 276-277
Lees, Gene, 289, 347
Left Banke, 200, 277
Legrand, Michel, 59, 264
Leib, Marshall, 418
Leiber And Stoller, 40, 49, 54, 76, 154, 161, 163, 186, 252, 351, 353-354, 356, 418-419, 428
Leiber, Jerry, 154
Leiber, Mike, 154
Leibowitz, Stephen, 274
Leigh, Carolyn, 47
Leigh, Mitch, 264
Leigh, Spencer, 43, 103, 356, 407
Leillo, John, 67
Lejeune, Louis, 28
Leka, Paul, 277
Lemon Pipers, 81, 277
Lemon Tree, 282
Lena, Miz, 348
Lennon, John, 39, 43, 61, 86, 102-103, 105, 137, 180, 201, 217-218, 223, 228, 231, 236, 265, 267, 269, 272, 293, 299, 347, 355, 360, 363, 379, 401, 403, 419, 480
Lennox, Annie, 150, 204
Lennox, Davie, 44
Lenoir, Phil, 57
Lenya, Lotte, 89
Leonard, Chuck, 96
Leonard, Deke, 89
Leonard, Glenn, 438
Lerner, Alan Jay, 14, 50, 59, 90, 264
Lesh, Phil, 217
Lester, Eddie, 29
Lester, Ketty, 277, 354

Lester, Mark, 331
Lester, Richard, 223, 230
Lettermen, 277-278
Levi, Dolly, 230
Leviathan, 305
Levin, Drake, 372
Levine, Ian, 114, 125, 177, 238, 248, 256, 295, 310, 426, 432, 458, 469-470
Levine, Irwin, 197
Levine, Joey, 81, 132, 328, 331
Levine, Larry, 419
Levinger, Lowell, III, 483
Levise, William, Jnr., 388
Levital, Gary, 278
Levitt And McClure, 44
Levitt, Dan, 44
Levy, Harry, 17
Levy, Jacques, 169
Lewis, Barbara, 49
Lewis, Bunny, 160
Lewis, Dave, 14
Lewis, Denise, 387
Lewis, Eddie, 331
Lewis, Gary, 19, 61, 278
Lewis, Gary, And The Playboys, 19, 61, 278
Lewis, Huey, 216
Lewis, James, 248, 312
Lewis, Jerry Lee, 85, 92, 98, 100, 119, 214, 259, 324, 451, 483
Lewis, Joe E., 451
Lewis, John, 66, 96, 142, 155, 418, 451
Lewis, Julian John, 418
Lewis, Ken, 96, 248
Lewis, Meade 'Lux', 66
Lewis, Mike, 123
Lewis, Peter, 311-312
Lewis, Ramsey, 278-279, 475
Lewis, Richard, 283
Lewis, Robert, 387
Lewis, Ron, 155
Lewis, Terry, 255
Lewis, Vic, 228, 274, 319
Lewisohn, Mark, 43-44
Lexington Four, 304
Leyton, John, 279, 303, 334, 446
Libert, David, 223
Liberto, Vivian, 97
Liberty Records, 66, 96, 111, 134, 278, 280, 309, 360
Licari, Nanette, 371
Lifesong Records, 153
Lifetime, 60, 64, 75, 107-108, 154, 204, 209, 264
Liges, Joe, 343
Liggins, Joe, 53
Lightfoot, Gordon, 121, 228
Lightfoot, Terry, 27, 29, 198
Lightnin' Slim, 410
Lightnings, 179
Lili, 14, 289
Lillie, Beatrice, 75
Lillywhite, Steve, 382
Limbo, 71, 108
Limit, 95, 438-439
Lincoln, Abbey, 155
Lincoln, Abraham, 228
Lind, Bob, 239, 280
Linde, Sam, 106
Lindley, David, 260-261
Lindsay, Jimmy, 131
Lindsay, Mark, 372
Lindsay, Robert, 331
Linhart, Buzzy, 186
Lion, Alfred, 66
Lipman, Maureen, 50
Lipscomb, Mance, 109
Lipsius, Fred, 64
Lipton, Sydney, 172, 270
LiPuma, Tommy, 391
Liquid, 158, 246
Lisberg, Harvey, 234
Litherland, James, 121

Little Anthony And The Imperials, 73, 137, 280-281
Little Big Band, 226
Little Caesar, 67
Little Eva, 127, 212, 247, 281
Little Feat, 44, 205, 221, 321, 425
Little Joe, 367
Little John, 78, 344, 388
Little Me, 126, 315
Little Milton, 33, 150, 281
Little Miss Marker, 14
Little Richard, 60, 71, 77, 130, 166, 231, 353, 367, 379, 388, 434, 467
Little Sonny, 109
Little Walter, 86, 109, 371
Little, Booker, 155
Little, Carlo, 196, 229, 379
Little, Joe, 367
Little, Marie, 351
Live Aid, 170, 216, 471
Liverpool Scene, 103, 117, 281, 392
Lloyd Webber, Andrew, 18, 34, 59
Lloyd Webber, Julian, 240
Lloyd, Charles, 253
Lloyd, George, 253
Lloyd, Michael, 469
Lloyd, Patrick, 181
Locke, Alfred, 63
Locke, John, 420
Locke, Sondra, 185
Locking, Brian, 398
Lockjaw, 263, 394
Locks, Fred, 131
Locomotive, 243, 282, 417
Loder, Kurt, 450
Lodge, John, 319
Loewe, Frederick, 13-14, 90, 264
Lofgren, Nils, 18
Loft, 251
Loizzo, Gary, 13
Lomax, Alan, 231, 397
Lomax, Jackie, 229, 282, 453
London Records, 175, 268
London Town, 6, 297, 467
London, Eric, 192
London, John, 128
London, Mark, 46, 59
Londonbeat, 286
Lone Star, 409
Long And The Short, 213
Long, Don, 93
Long, Joe, 199, 476
Long, Richard, 60
Long, Shorty, 449
Long, Tom, 349
Longbranch Pennywhistle, 85
Longdancer, 350
Longhurst Pickworth, Mike, 424
Looking Glass, 76, 361
Loomis, Mark, 112
Loose Gravel, 106
Lopez, Trini, 203, 282-283
Lorber, Alan, 72
Lorber, Rick, 12
Lord Buckley, 231
Lord, Jon, 19, 196, 225
Lord, Tracy, 280
Lordan, Jerry, 127, 283, 398
Lords, 38, 159
Los Angeles Philharmonic Orchestra, 270
Los Bravos, 283
Los Lobos, 455
Lost And Found, 212, 404, 415
Lost Nite Records, 94
Lothar And The Hand People, 283
Lotis, Dennis, 125
Lou, Lilly, 187
Loudermilk, John D., 100, 130, 148, 191, 283-284
Loughman, Patrick, 93
Louisiana Red, 109
Lounsbury, Jim, 273
Loussier, Jacques, 284
Louvin Brothers, 20

Love, 284-285 and *passim*
Love Affair, 101, 107, 124, 148, 271, 285
Love Jones, 101, 467
Love Me Or Leave Me, 145
Love Sculpture, 285
Love Unlimited, 68
Love, Andrew, 292
Love, Darlene, 68, 136, 262, 419
Love, Geoff, 154
Love, John, 43, 394, 417
Love, Laura, 32, 258, 279, 455
Love, Mike, 35-37
Love, Willie, 281
Lovetro, Gary, 429
Lovin' Spoonful, 19, 21, 81, 134, 164, 239, 261-262, 272, 283, 285-286, 304, 314, 323, 325, 416, 479
Lowe, Chris, 423
Lowe, Earl, 104
Lowe, James, 104
Lowe, Jim, 176
Lowe, Mundell, 182
Lowe, Nick, 99, 268
Lowery, Bill, 117, 435
Lowther, Henry, 225, 290, 296
Loxender, Dave, 137
Luboff, Norman, 326
Luby, John, 324
Lucas, 128, 174, 304
Lucas, Gil, 304
Lucas, Trevor, 174
Lucasta, Anna, 145-146
Lucia, Peter, 250
Luciano, 434
Lucky 13, 158
Ludwig, Donna, 455
Luker, Mal, 414
Lulu, 49, 58-59, 213, 286, 336, 368, 422
Luman, Bob, 85, 284
Lund, John, 414
Lundgren, Ken, 334
Lunny, Donal, 113
Lute Records, 238
Lutton, Dave, 176
Lydon, John, 258
Lyle, Tom, 283
Lyles, Pat, 127
Lyman, Mel, 272
Lynch, Bob, 164
Lynch, David, 332
Lynch, Eddie, 110
Lynch, Kenny, 216, 286, 405, 412
Lynch, Lee, 387
Lynn, Barbara, 287, 302
Lynn, Chris, 226
Lynn, Loretta, 276, 406, 452
Lynn, Vera, 63, 262, 374
Lynne, Jeff, 42, 171, 175, 244, 257, 294, 323, 332, 400, 403
Lynyrd Skynyrd, 429
Lyons, Leo, 439
Lyttelton, Humphrey, 56, 294, 303, 401

M

M.A.F.I.A., 469
M.A.R.S., 11
Mabern, Harold, 318
Mabey, Richard, 258, 366
Macabre, 137, 256, 305, 381, 457
MacAlise, Thomas, 197
Macauley, Tony, 28, 138, 142, 163, 175, 198
Macbeth, Peter, 198
MacColl, Ewan, 397
MacColl, Kirsty, 267
MacDermot, Galt, 222
MacDonald, Ian, 43
Machinations, 73, 338, 433
Machito, 291
Mack, Bob, 250

Mack, Jimmy, 161, 235, 293
Mack, Marlene, 341
Mack, Ted, 71
Mackay, David, 444
MacKay, Stuart, 444
MacKenna, Barney, 164
Mackintosh, Cameron, 33, 59, 331
Mackintosh, Ken, 274
MacLaine, Shirley, 145
Maclean, Bryan, 284
Maclean, Norrie, 350
MacLeod, John, 198
MacLise, Angus, 459
Macrae, Dave, 415, 431
MacTavish, David, 444
Mad Professor, 344
Mad River, 129, 287
Madara, John, 301
Maddox, Walt, 292
Madge, Bill, 282
Madisons, 179
Madness, 173, 201, 222, 315, 358-359
Madonna, 116
Mae, Annie, 281, 449
Maestro, Johnny, 76, 148
Maggie May, 33, 427
Magic Carpet, 138, 427
Magic Lanterns, 190, 287-288
Magic Sam, 127
Magma, 213
Magnificent Men, 148
Magnum, 35, 52, 103, 185, 393
Magnus, Kerry, 266
Maguire, Les, 210
Maiden Voyage, 279
Main Attraction, 220
Main Source, 33, 241
Main Squeeze, 258
Mainstream Records, 194
Mair, Alan, 44
Maitland, Joan, 63
Majewski, Hank, 198
Majors, 365
Makeba, Miriam, 45
Makem, Tommy, 113, 164
Malaco Records, 62, 196, 281
Male, Kerilee, 174, 231
Mallard, 95
Mallett, Saundra, 177
Mamas And The Papas, 8, 37, 61, 165, 178, 258, 285, 288-289, 301, 317, 323, 341, 418, 436
Mamas Boys, 436
Mammoth, 267
Manassas, 88, 118, 135
Mancini, Henry, 58, 76, 289
Mandel, Harvey, 92, 296
Mandrake Paddlesteamer, 73, 289-290
Mandrell, Barbara, 124, 404
Manfred Mann, 5, 32, 79, 110, 132, 138, 152, 165, 186, 198, 212, 220, 271, 290, 294, 367, 404, 461
Manfred Mann's Earth Band, 290
Mango Records, 127
Manhattan Transfer, 6
Manigo, Alex, 67
Manilow, Barry, 151, 371, 423, 466
Manker, Sid, 259
Manley, Colin, 371
Mann, Barry, 15, 76, 141, 212, 290, 349, 419
Mann, Herbie, 265, 291-292
Mann, Kal, 108
Mann, Roberto, 149
Mannah, Frank, 418
Manne, Shelly, 49, 183
Manning, Donald, 5
Manning, Tom, 287
Mansfield, Tony, 138, 272
Manson, Charles, 36, 41, 206
Mantovani, 468
Manuel And His Music Of The Mountains, 391

Manuel, Bobby, 71
Manuel, Dean, 369
Manuel, Richard, 167, 228
Manzarek, Ray, 158
Mar-Keys, 71, 135, 196, 292, 426
Marascalco, John, 60
Marathons, 253
Marauders, 97
Marcellino, Muzzy, 316
Marcels, 175, 292
March, Little Peggy, 292-293
Marchello, Mickey, 214
Marcos, Ferdinand, 40
Marcotte, Jim, 5
Marcus, Greil, 169, 357
Mardi Gras, 133, 173
Mardin, Arif, 423
Margo, Mitch, 444-445
Margo, Phil, 445
Margouleff, Robert, 283
Marionette, 168
Mark Four, 132
Mark IV, 89
Mark, Jon, 296
Marker, Gary, 375
Markley, Bob, 469
Markowitz, Roy, 257
Marks, David, 35
Markulin, Ting, 241
Marley, Bob, 114, 297-298, 344, 359
Marley, Rita, 343
Marmalade, 41, 45, 65, 101, 197, 213, 277, 293, 415
Marquee Club, 44, 73, 226, 379, 470, 479
Marques, Herman, 409
Marriott, Steve, 18, 331, 410, 412, 430
Marron, Gordon, 454
Mars Bonfire, 392, 427
Marsalis, Wynton, 61
Marsden, Beryl, 102
Marsden, Freddie, 210
Marsden, Gerry, 108, 127, 210-211
Marsh, Dave, 357, 407, 472
Marsh, Julian, 457
Marsh, Richard, 392, 396
Marsh, Ted, 238
Marsh, Warne, 184
Marshall, Bob, 105
Marshall, Grant, 97
Marshall, Jack, 147
Marshall, John, 415
Marshall, Thomas, 336
Marshall, Tom, 224
Martell, Vince, 456
Martelli, Marisa, 148
Martha And The Vandellas, 161, 208, 235, 293, 322, 366, 458
Martin, Anthony, Jnr., 153
Martin, Barbara, 359
Martin, Bill, 350, 401
Martin, Chip, 315
Martin, David, 390
Martin, Dean, 99, 145, 153, 316, 325, 452
Martin, Derek, 430
Martin, Dewey, 81
Martin, Gene, 359
Martin, George, 6, 39, 41, 43, 58, 60, 162, 180, 240, 257, 294, 316, 418, 437
Martin, Jeff, 277
Martin, John, 153
Martin, Linda, 383
Martin, Mary, 167, 230
Martin, Michael, 386
Martin, Mike, 375
Martin, Millicent, 96, 424
Martin, Paul, 153
Martin, Steve, 277
Martin, Vince, 325
Martindale, Wink, 294-295
Martinez, Antonio, 283
Martinez, Rudy, 363

Martini, Jerry, 411
Martino, Al, 137, 259
Martyn, Beverly, 317, 362
Martyn, John, 342
Marucci, Bob, 22, 187
Marvelettes, 235, 295, 322, 377, 466
Marvelows, 181
Marvin, Hank B., 193, 373, 398
Mary Poppins, 13-14, 124
Masekela, Hugh, 11, 87, 317, 361
Mason, Barbara, 81
Mason, Barry, 6, 80, 115, 175, 368
Mason, Dave, 148, 178, 201, 218, 446-447
Mason, Laurie, 334
Mason, Wood, Capaldi And Frog, 447
Masour, Roger, 455
Massacre, 22, 340
Massey, Calvin, 122
Massey, Marian, 286
Massey, William, 474
Massi, Nick, 198-199, 476
Masterbeats, 416
Masteroff, Joe, 89
Masters, Greg, 244, 403
Mastin, Will, 145
Mastrangelo, Carlo, 153
Mastrangelo, John, 76
Matching Mole, 415
Material Issue, 393
Mathews, Tom, 100
Mathis, Johnny, 151, 289, 429
Matthau, Walter, 230
Matthews, Onzy, 238
Maughan, Susan, 262, 295
Maughn, Don, 191, 417
Mauldin, Joe B., 134
Maus, John, 463-464
Mavericks, 303
Max Frost And The Troopers, 16
Maxfield, Mike, 138, 272
May Blitz, 28, 33
May, Billy, 49, 334, 475
May, Maggie, 33, 427
May, Phil, 358
May, Simon, 59
Mayall, John, 10, 19, 46, 86, 92, 110, 121, 132, 136, 140, 156, 165, 212, 225-226, 295-297, 312, 336, 366, 381, 413, 480
Mayberry, Raynoma, 366
Mayfield, Curtis, 81, 104, 227, 245-246, 273, 297-298, 426
Mayfield, Percy, 298
Mayhem, 168, 316-317
Mayorga, Lincoln, 24
Maytals, 298-299, 343, 349
Mazarro, Ginny, 349
Mazzola, Lorraine, 371
Mazzy Star, 188
Mbambisa, Tete, 361
Mbaqanga, 361-362
MC5, 31, 177, 299, 388
MCA Records, 215, 233, 341
McAndrew, Marianne, 230
McAuley, Jackie, 440-441
McBride, Christian, 414
McCabe, Roger, 304
McCann, Jim, 164
McCann, Les, 238
McCarthy, 221, 298, 470
McCarthy, David, 221
McCartney, Michael, 43, 392
McCartney, Mike, 43
McCartney, Paul, 19, 27, 39, 46, 58, 70, 99, 134, 175, 180-181, 185, 201, 223, 231, 240, 247, 267, 269, 272-273, 282, 293-294, 339, 345, 347, 360, 363, 379, 392, 401, 403, 417, 419, 477, 480
McCarty, Jim, 388, 479
McClain, Charly, 124
McClain, Mighty Sam, 362
McClain, Sam, 362

McClane, Ian, 14
McClean, Norbert, 177
McCleese, James, 417
McClelland, Geoff, 255
McClinton, Delbert, 105, 299-300
McCloud, Brewster, 9
McClure, Bobby, 33
McCoo, Marilyn, 195
McCook, Tommy, 370, 409
McCoy, John, 447
McCoy, Van, 184
McCoys, 49, 245, 253, 300, 429
McCracken, Charlie, 65, 146
McCracken, Hugh, 385
McCracklin, Jimmy, 309
McCulloch, Danny, 15
McCulloch, Gordon, 91
McCulloch, Jack, 14, 443
McCulloch, Jimmy, 443
McCullough, Henry, 176, 421
McCurdy, Ed, 177, 239
McDaniel, Elias, 152
McDaniels, Gene, 24, 300, 351, 405
McDaniels, Pete, 57
McDermott, Jack, 93
McDermott, John, 233
McDonald, Carol, 213
McDonald, Country Joe, 129, 454
McDonald, Joe, 129, 454
McDonald, Kathi, 55
McDonald, Michael, 25
McDonald, Robin, 138, 272
McDougall, Dave, 14
McDougall, Richard, 94
McDowell, Fred, 84
McDowell, Kenny, 441
McDowell, Mississippi Fred, 84
McDuff, Brother Jack, 66, 413
McEwan, Bill, 240
McFadden, Eddie, 413
McFall, Ray, 102
McFarland, Ed, 322
McFarland, John, 272, 405
McFarland, Spanky, 211
McFerrin, Bobby, 66
McGear, Mike, 392
McGee, Alan, 133
McGee, Bobby, 178, 258
McGee, Jerry, 326, 460
McGeorge, Jerry, 222, 399
McGhee, Howard, 66
McGough, Roger, 281, 392
McGovern, George, 345, 407
McGowan, Cathy, 366
McGregor, Chris, 361
McGregor, Craig, 172
McGregor, Freddie, 114
McGriff, Jimmy, 238, 300-301, 339, 413, 430
McGuffie, Bill, 96
McGuinn, Clark And Hillman, 88
McGuinn, Jim, 86, 120, 327
McGuinn, Roger, 37, 86, 120, 169, 173, 211, 301, 310, 327
McGuinness Flint, 212
McGuinness, Tom, 290
McGuire, Barry, 8, 165, 288, 301, 327, 358, 411
McGuire, Margi, 371
McGuire, Pat, 371
McIntyre, Mac, 253
McJohn, Goldy, 427
McKay, Ken, 264
McKechnie, Licorice, 246
McKenzie, Ali, 57
McKenzie, Angus, 149
McKenzie, Laura, 288
McKenzie, Scott, 8, 165, 258, 288, 301, 384
McKernan, Ron, Pigpen, 217
McKibbon, Al, 314
McKinley, Larry, 308
McKinleys, 97, 336
McKinney's Cotton Pickers, 111
McKinney, Mabron, 240

McKinnie, Dee, 296
McKuen, Rod, 397, 405, 422
McLachlan, Craig, 152
McLagan, Ian, 170, 412
McLain, Jean, 295
McLaren, Malcolm, 224
McLaren, Steve, 148
McLaughlin, John, 69, 143, 352
McLaughlin, Murray, 387
McLaughlin, Ollie, 94
McLean, Jackie, 66
Mclean, Norman, 177
McLemore, Lamont, 195
McLeod, Alice, 122
McLeod, John, 28
McLeod, Vincent, 387
McManus, Jimmy, 453
McMillan, Ian, 350
McMullen, Annette, 458
McNally, John, 394
McNamara, Robin, 200, 301
McNeil, Terry, 416
McNeill, Noel, 93
McPartland, Marian, 402-403
McPhatter, Clyde, 48, 163, 301-302, 461, 474
McPhee, Skip, 186
McPhee, Tony, 165, 223, 234
McQueen, Steve, 376, 482
McRae, Barry, 144
McRae, Carmen, 145, 402-403
McShee, Jacqui, 252, 342
McTell, 'Blind' Willie, 171, 376
McTell, Ralph, 240
McVay, Ray, 101
McVie, Christine, 37, 110
McVie, John, 46, 296
McWhirter, Norris, 235
McWilliams, David, 302
Meade, Norman, 365
Meadon, Peter, 470
Meager, Tat, 409
Meagher, Ron, 44
Meaux, Huey P., 229, 287, 302, 408
Medallions, 309
Medicine, 154, 156, 169, 234
Medicine Ball Caravan, 156
Meditation Singers, 368
Meditations, 123, 307-308
Medley, Bill, 270, 375
Medley, John, 211
Medley, Phil, 48
Medora, Eddie, 431
Medress, Hank, 444
Meeham, Mike, 234
Meehan, Daniel, 398
Meehan, Tony, 127, 225, 283, 398
Meek, Joe, 46, 101, 120, 230, 240, 256, 279, 302-303, 334, 375, 433, 446, 460
Meek, Robert George, 302
Meeley, Jim, 160
Megaton, 345
Meikle, Buster, 454
Meikle, David, 454
Meisner, Randy, 325, 341
Mel And Kim, 276
Mel-Tones, 289
Melander, Colin, 403
Melanie, 81, 227, 478
Melcher, Terry, 86, 217, 291, 372, 376
Mellers, Wilfred, 43
Mellotron, 63, 69, 319
Melly, George, 111
Melodians, 352, 370
Melody Maker, 270, 305, 424
Melton, Barry, 129
Members, Dave, 448
Memphis Horns, 105, 292
Memphis Slim, 46, 92
Menard, D.L., 29
Mendes, Sergio, 11
Mendl, Hugh, 338
Mercer, Chris, 226, 296, 479

Mercer, Johnny, 140, 147
Mercer, Mabel, 147
Mercer, Pat, 74
Merciless, 54
Mercouri, Melina, 260
Mercury Records, 30, 51, 67, 89, 99, 105, 130, 186, 200, 239, 253, 263, 358, 386, 428, 482, 484
Mercury, Freddie, 206
Meredith, David, 148
Merger, 164
Merlin, 194, 396
Merman, Ethel, 230
Merrick, David, 230
Merrill, John, 341
Merryweather, Neil, 213
Merseybeats, 56, 102, 132, 303, 404
Merseys, 300, 303
Merseysippi Jazz Band, 101
Messiaen, Olivier, 392
Messina, Jim, 81
Metchick, Don, 312
Metheny, Pat, 85, 233
Metzke, Gustav, 470
Metzner, Doug, 129
Meyers, Augie, 408
MFQ, 303-304
MGM Band, 202-203
MGM Records, 20, 38, 72, 83, 137, 160, 202, 262, 364, 376, 424, 453, 470
Mia, Cara, 252
Mice, 62, 251, 411
Michael, George, 78, 204, 314
Michael, Peter, 43, 85
Michaels, David, 222
Michaels, Lee, 190
Michalski, John, 129
Michelot, Pierre, 284
Micki And Maude, 319
Midas Touch, 25, 54-55
Middel, Willy, 136
Middle Earth Records, 17
Midler, Bette, 328
Migenes, Julia, 194
Mighty Baby, 6, 428
Mighty Glad, 306
Mighty Sam, 362
Migil Five, 304
Mike Stuart Span, 304-305
Milano, Freddie, 153
Milburn, Amos, 467
Miles, Barry, 144
Miles, Buddy, 176, 232, 388
Miles, John, 144
Miles, Reid, 66, 84
Miles, Richard, 144
Miller, Andy, 305
Miller, Blue, 188
Miller, Bob, 286, 305
Miller, Cleo, 177
Miller, David, 286
Miller, Don, 462
Miller, Eddie, 119
Miller, Elva, 305
Miller, Frankie, 360
Miller, Gary, 24, 29, 316
Miller, Glenn, 120, 289, 377
Miller, Harry, 362
Miller, Helen, 364
Miller, Jay, 410
Miller, Jerry, 112, 311
Miller, Jimmy, 329, 381
Miller, Jody, 291
Miller, Jonathan, 50, 54
Miller, Keith, 424
Miller, Marilyn, 368
Miller, Mitch, 47, 124
Miller, Mrs, 305
Miller, Perry, 483
Miller, Peter, 253
Miller, Robert, 177
Miller, Roger, 305-306, 376, 482
Miller, Ron, 476
Miller, Ronnie, 130

Miller, Steve, 5, 51, 206, 213, 317, 467
Miller, Vern, 371
Miller, Willie, 305
Millie, 13-14, 30, 49, 176, 306, 458
Milligan, Spike, 437
Millinder, Lucky, 313
Mills Brothers, 233
Mills, Freddie, 214
Mills, Gary, 125
Mills, Gladys, 306
Mills, Gordon, 210, 242, 256, 266, 368
Mills, Leroy, 45
Mills, Marty, 263
Mills, Mike, 448
Mills, Mrs., 306
Milton, Johnny, 434
Mimms, Garnet, 49, 179, 365, 465
Mincelli, Mike, 94
Mindbenders, 53, 196-197, 306
Minerebi, Marcello, 417
Mingus, Charles, 143, 155, 182, 216, 263, 306-308, 342
Minit Records, 308-309
Minnelli, Liza, 90, 145
Minns, Paul, 441
Minogue, Kylie, 281
Minott, Sugar, 131
Minus, Rene, 105
Mira Records, 275
Miracle Records, 438
Miracles, 74, 194, 214, 236, 309-310, 322, 366, 377-378, 421, 423, 476
Mirage, 227, 250, 309, 377, 411
Miranda, Bob, 223
Miranda, Faybiene, 131
Misfits, 267-268
Mission, 333, 393
Misunderstood, 15, 82, 310, 400, 407, 416
Mitch Ryder And The Detroit Wheels, 388-389
Mitchell, Adam, 340
Mitchell, Billy, 232
Mitchell, Blue, 156, 406
Mitchell, Bob, 21, 44, 156, 266
Mitchell, Bobby, 233
Mitchell, Chad, Trio, 45, 310-311, 340
Mitchell, George, 84
Mitchell, Guy, 124
Mitchell, James, 387
Mitchell, Joni, 85, 121, 153, 228, 308, 385, 387, 389, 478
Mitchell, Leonard, 153, 389
Mitchell, Liz, 288
Mitchell, Mike, 266, 310
Mitchell, Mitch, 104, 231, 233, 375
Mitchell, Red, 182
Mitchell, Willie, 292, 478
Mitropoulos, Dimitri, 50
Mittell, Lynn, 89
Mittoo, Jackie, 409
MJQ, 151
Mobley, Hank, 66, 123, 219, 311, 320, 406
Moby Grape, 112, 221, 311-312, 317
Moch, Fred, 259
Mocking Bird, 49
Mockingbirds, 245
Models, 432
Modern Folk Quartet, 304
Modern Jazz Quartet, 150, 346
Modern Records, 449
Moe, Rick, 310
Moeller, Tommy, 454
Moeller, William, 413
Mohawk Records, 148
Moholo, Louis, 362
Moines, Des, 444, 472
Mojo Men, 21, 312, 411, 458
Mojos, 109, 312
Moles, 166

Molland, Joey, 248
Möller, Nina, 328
Moman, Chips, 355
Mona Lisa, 391, 451
Monarch, Michael, 427
Moncur, Ian, 287
Money, Zoot, 15, 140, 192, 271, 312-313, 392, 413
Monitors, 66, 170
Monk, T.S., 314
Monk, Thelonious, 10, 61-62, 66, 122-123, 144, 156, 306, 313-314, 420
Monkees, 16-17, 61, 64, 73, 92, 131, 212, 214, 232, 252, 304, 314-315, 399, 451, 460
Monro, Matt, 23, 58-59, 75, 283, 294-295, 315-316, 334, 391
Monroe, Bill, 173
Monroe, Marilyn, 71, 139, 457
Monroe, Vaughn, 462
Monster Magnet, 321
Montand, Yves, 457
Montanez, Christopher, 317
Monte Carlo, 75, 203
Monte, Vinnie, 200
Montenegro, Hugo, 316
Montez, Chris, 276, 317
Montgomery Brothers, 402
Montgomery, Bob, 134
Montgomery, John, 318
Montgomery, Marian, 317-318, 402
Montgomery, Melba, 350
Montgomery, Monk, 318
Montgomery, Thomasina, 439
Montgomery, Wes, 8, 263, 318, 413-414
Montoya, Coco, 296
Moody Blues, 63, 127, 149, 181, 200, 250, 270, 273, 318-319
Moody, Bill, 386
Moody, Micky, 447
Moody, Ron, 76, 331, 431
Moon, Charley, 75
Moon, Doug, 94
Moon, Keith, 433, 470-472
Mooney, Ralph, 85
Moonglows, 208
Moonrider, 469
Moore, Ben, 362
Moore, Bob, 369
Moore, Butch, 93
Moore, Claire, 331
Moore, David, 390
Moore, Dudley, 54, 319-320, 346
Moore, Gary, 27, 121, 162
Moore, James, 410
Moore, Johnny, 163, 409
Moore, Melba, 222, 371
Moore, Pete, 309
Moore, Ralph, 347
Moore, Sam, 390
Moore, Scotty, 57, 353, 355, 404
Moore, Stan, 61
Moorer, Alvis, 181
Moorer, Betty, 181
Moorer, Gilbert, 181
Morais, Trevor, 341
Moraz, Patrick, 319
Moreshead, John, 229
Morgan, Adrian, 129
Morgan, Alun, 318
Morgan, Barry, 311
Morgan, Derrick, 362
Morgan, John, 427
Morgan, Lee, 66, 311, 320, 413, 443
Morgan, Mark, 177
Morgan, Ron, 177
Morias, Trevor, 192
Morin, Frank, 408
Morphine, 218, 381
Morricone, Ennio, 316

Morris, Chris, 197
Morris, Jeff, 30
Morris, Keith, 271
Morris, Roy, 271
Morrison, Bob, 159
Morrison, Dorothy Combs, 227
Morrison, James, 158, 160
Morrison, Jim, 158-160, 385, 441
Morrison, Sterling, 459
Morrison, Van, 49, 53, 84, 107, 136, 189-190, 216, 257, 302, 366, 374, 423, 440-441, 474
Morrissey, 53, 174, 402, 427
Morrissey, Dick, 427
Morrissey, Tom, 174
Morrow, Little Willie, 474
Morshead, Jon, 165, 264
Morter, Al, 93
Morton, George 'Shadow', 220, 399
Morton, Rockette, 94
Mosaic Records, 150
Moshe, Murray, 123
Mosley, Bob, 311-312
Mosley, Ronald, 387
Moss, Geoff, 253
Moss, Jerry, 11
Moss, Paul, 434
Most Wanted, 229
Most, Mickie, 15, 17, 46, 109, 193, 234, 286, 324, 434, 480
Mostel, Zero, 194
Mother Earth, 257, 320-321
Mother Earth (60s), 320
Motherlode, 79
Mothers Of Invention, 77, 81, 92, 94, 201, 221, 262, 275, 321, 425, 450
Motian, Paul, 182, 314
Motor Town Revue, 322
Motörhead, 270, 390
Motown Records, 114, 125, 177, 214-215, 238, 241, 293, 309, 322, 425, 476
Mott, 285, 421, 428
Mott The Hoople, 285, 421, 428
Motta, Stanley, 9
Moules, Peter, 454
Mouse, Stanley, 217
Mouskouri, Nana, 262
Move, 323 and passim
Moy, Sylvia, 476
Moyake, Nick, 361
Moyet, Alison, 277
Mrs Miller, 305
Mud, 60, 110
Muddy Waters, 51, 84, 86, 109, 152, 216, 249, 366, 379, 396, 454
Mudlarks, 22
Mugwumps, 178, 285, 288, 323, 479
Muldaur, Geoff, 272, 324
Muldaur, Maria, 272, 324, 331
Muldoon, Clive, 151
Muldrow, Cornell, 454
Mullican, Moon, 118-119, 369
Mulligan, Declan, 44
Mulligan, Gerry, 142, 150-151, 313-314, 347, 385, 420
Mulvany, Maeve, 93
Mulvey, Andi, 350
Munden, Dave, 447
Mundi, Billy, 321, 372
Mundy, 292
Munroe, Pete, 151
Munroe, Tony, 57
Munrow, David, 481
Murdoch, Bruce, 67
Murphey, Michael Martin, 386
Murphy, Bernard, 74
Murphy, Gary 'Roscoe', 304
Murphy, Kevin, 13
Murphy, Michael, 110, 315
Murphy, Roscoe, 304
Murphy, Rose, 476
Murray Brothers, 35
Murray The K, 148, 384
Murray, Anne, 228

Murray, Arthur, 265
Murray, Charles Shaar, 233
Murray, Dee, 146
Murray, Don, 450
Murray, Gwendolyn, 366
Murray, Jim, 363
Murray, Larry, 229
Murray, Martin, 240
Murray, Mitch, 40, 55
Murray, Neil, 121, 228, 387
Murray, Peg, 89
Murray, Pete, 364
Murray, Ruby, 96
Murray, Tony, 350, 448
Murvin, Junior, 344
Muscle Shoals, 170, 204, 241, 249, 292, 348, 362, 442
Music Explosion, 262
Music Machine, 275
Muskee, Harry, 136
Musselwhite, Charlie, 213
Mycroft, Tim, 417
Mydland, Brent, 218
Myers, Jim, 416
Myers, Stanley, 59
Myles, John, 350
Myles, Tony, 350
Myman, Bob, 190
Mynah Birds, 81
Mystery Trend, 324
Mystics, 252, 351

N

Nacardo, Vinny, 94
Nader, Richard, 326
Naftalin, Mark, 86, 320
Nagle, Ron, 156, 324
Nagy, John, 173
Naiff, Lynton, 243
Naismith, Monty, 362
Naked City, 474
Naked Truth, 81
Nance, Jack, 451
Nanette, 187, 371
Napier-Bell, Simon, 255, 422, 480
Napoleon XIV, 201
Nash, Graham, 135, 138, 181, 236-237, 254, 434, 439
Nash, Johnny, 147
Nashville Teens, 15, 17, 161, 213, 284, 324
Nassour, Ellis, 120
Naturals, 324-325
Navarro, Fats, 66
Naylor, Shel, 337
Neagle, Anna, 108, 457
Neal, Bob, 353
Nefertiti, 143-144, 390
Neidlinger, Buell, 314
Neil, Barry, 76
Neil, Christopher, 112
Neil, Fred, 177, 239, 325, 385, 387
Nelson, Earl, 68, 265
Nelson, Eric Hilliard, 325
Nelson, George, 333
Nelson, Jim, 286
Nelson, John, 326
Nelson, Lee, 68
Nelson, Oliver, 155, 413, 475
Nelson, Pete, 196
Nelson, Phil, 326
Nelson, Ricky, 83, 85, 325-326, 349, 376
Nelson, Ross, 286
Nelson, Sandy, 201, 250, 326, 418
Nelson, Teri, Group, 262
Nelson, Tracy, 320-321
Nelson, Willie, 99-100, 119, 276, 305, 325, 482, 484
NEMS Records, 476
Nesbeth, Vernon, 418
Nesmith, Michael, 85, 252, 314
Ness, Richard, 453

Neville, Aaron, 309
New Breed, 78, 127, 131, 468
New Christy Minstrels, 21, 301, 304, 326-327
New Colony Six, 16
New Edition, 415
New Lost City Ramblers, 396
New Order, 42, 115, 297
New Riders Of The Purple Sage, 201
New Seekers, 142, 177, 397-398
New Vaudeville Band, 70, 327, 437
New York Dolls, 253
Newbeats, 327-328
Newell, Norman, 34, 58, 125, 154, 334, 345
Newley, Anthony, 33, 75, 116, 145, 157, 270, 283, 457
Newman, Andy, 443
Newman, David, 422
Newman, Floyd, 292
Newman, Randy, 44, 58, 107, 150, 164, 225, 324-325, 349, 422
Newman, Richard, 297
Newman, Tom, 349
Newman, Tony, 141, 349
Newmark, Andy, 412
Newton, Juice, 436
Newton, Paul, 212
Newton, Wayne, 259
Newton-John, Olivia, 374, 398
Ney, Michael, 118
Nice, 328 and *passim*
Nichol, Al, 450
Nichol, Ed, 286
Nicholas, Paul, 108, 222, 433
Nichols, John, 424
Nichols, Penny, 81
Nicholson, Geoff, 173
Nicholson, Hughie, 350
Nicholson, Jack, 173
Nico, 245, 336, 383, 459-460
Nicol, Jimmy, 422
Nicolette, 85
Nicolson, Dave, 424
Nicolson, Hugh, 293
Night And Day, 40
Nighthawk, Robert, 109, 449
Nightingale, Barry, 289
Nightingales, 121, 417
Nightmare Records, 458
Nilsson, Harry, 315, 325, 480
Nimmo, Derek, 108
Nina And Frederick, 328
Nirvana (UK), 329
Nitty Gritty Dirt Band, 128, 240, 260
Nitzsche, Jack, 70, 150, 280, 389, 394, 416, 419, 464
Nix, Don, 292
No Strings, 264
No Sweat, 64
Nolan, Larry, 415
Noon, Terry, 239
Noonan, Steve, 239
Noone, Peter, 234
Nordby, Bob, 266
Norman, Dave, 6
Norman, James, 284
Norman, Jesse, 418
Norman, Philip, 43, 383
Norvo, Red, 306-307
Novello, Ivor, 56, 58-60, 75, 108, 237, 268, 270, 334, 368, 393, 399
Noy, Derek, 251
Nuese, John, 246
Nugent, Geoff, 453
Nugent, Ted, 12
Null, Lisa, 195
Nunlee, Darrel, 125
Nunley, Chris, 386
Nyholt, Jim, 16
Nyro, Laura, 195, 317, 329-330, 345

O

O'Brien, Dion (Tom), 422
O'Brien, Lucy, 422-423
O'Brien, Tim, 422
O'Connor, Des, 368
O'Connor, Sinead, 78
O'Day, Anita, 147
O'Donnell, Daniel, 370
O'Jays, 280, 309
O'Rahilly, Ronan, 15, 54
O'Riley, Tony, 271
O'Toole, Peter, 116
Oak Records, 305
Oakley, Vic, 89
Oakman, Pete, 79
Oasis, 25, 240, 268, 394
Obispo, Luis, 176
Ochs, Phil, 26, 67, 177-178, 239, 330-331, 385, 454
Octopus, 31
Oden, Jim, 92
Odeon Records, 254
Odet, Clifford, 145
Odetta, 45, 113, 166, 220, 257
Ofarim, Esther And Abi, 473
Offitt, Lillian, 184
Offspring, 7, 221
Ogermann, Claus, 263
Ohio Express, 81, 131, 262, 329, 331
Ohio Knox, 118
OKeh Records, 273
Old Town Records, 94
Oldham, Andrew Loog, 18, 90, 189, 213, 234, 245, 269, 324, 350, 379, 465
Oldham, Spooner, 331, 342, 362, 410
Oliver, Paul, 222
Oliver, Sy, 108
Olivier, Laurence, 331, 334
Olsen, Keith, 218
Olsen, Mike, 190
Olsen, Richard, 106
Olsson, Nigel, 146, 350
Olympics, 59, 249, 331-332, 365, 467
One Records, 13, 33, 90, 94, 438, 482
Only Ones, 44
Only The Lonely, 332-333, 360
Ono, Yoko, 42, 228, 269
Onslaught, 349
Open Road, 157, 465
Oppenheimer, Ronnie, 190, 288
Oral, 478, 481
Orange Juice, 392
Orange, Allen, 309
Orbison, Roy, 98, 100-101, 171, 332-333, 349, 360, 365, 369, 451
Orchard, Ray, 364
Ore, John, 313
Oriole Records, 192, 243
Orioles, 333
Orion, 251-252
Orion, Jack, 251-252
Orlando, 207, 290, 445
Orlando, Tony, 207, 290, 445
Orlons, 160-161, 333, 394
Ornadel, Cyril, 58, 75, 333-334
Orr, Don, 24
Ørsted Pedersen, Neils-Henning, 346-347
Osborn, Joe, 219, 325
Osborne, Jeffrey, 466
Osbourne, Ozzy, 18
Oskar, Lee, 82
Osmond, Marie, 80, 138
Osmonds, 473
Other Half, 66
Other Records, 5, 23, 131
Otis And The Shooters, 367
Otis, Clyde, 48, 483
Otis, Johnny, 53, 150, 152, 249, 347

Otis, Shuggie, 249
Ott, Horace, 130
Ousley, Curtis, 265
Outcasts, 361
Outlaws (UK), 334
Outsiders, 323
Overkill, 353
Overlanders, 142, 334
Owens, Alvis Edgar, Jnr., 334
Owens, Bonnie, 335
Owens, Buck, 247, 334-335
Owens, Calvin, 80
Owens, Jimmy, 18
Owens, Richard, 438
Owens, Shirley, 404
Owsley, Stanley, 217
Ozone, 85
Ozone, Makoto, 85

P

Paar, Jack, 147
Pablo, Augustus, 344
Pace, Ronnie, 186
Pace, Sam, 181
Pachuta, Mel, 241
Pacific Gas And Electric, 336
Pacific Records, 280
Paddy, Klaus And Gibson, 181
Paffgen, Christa, 459
Pagan Baby, 133
Page, Jimmy, 65, 97, 112, 132, 150, 192, 245, 248, 336, 431, 433, 480
Page, Larry, 266, 336-337, 350, 375, 448, 456
Page, Oran 'Hot Lips', 304
Page, Patti, 61
Paige, Elaine, 59
Palance, Jack, 49
Paley, Tom, 396-397
Palmer Brothers, 9
Palmer, Alan, 73
Palmer, Bruce, 81
Palmer, Carl, 77, 192
Palmer, Clive, 190, 246
Palmer, Dave, 12
Palmer, Earl, 61, 455
Palmer, Geoff, 416
Palmer, John, 65, 148, 174
Palmer, Michael, 131
Palmer, Poli, 65, 174
Palmer, Richard, 32
Palmer, Robert, 73, 262, 383
Palumbo, Larry, 172
Pandora, 19, 361
Pandora's Box, 361
Panebianco, Ginger, 213
Panton, Roy, 306
Papalia, Giovanni, 18
Pappalardi, Felix, 385, 455, 483
Pappalardo, Fred, 245
Paradons, 201
Paramor, Norrie, 22, 80, 129, 197, 244, 372, 393, 398, 401, 455
Paramount Jazz Band, 56
Paramounts, 10, 259, 270, 302, 337, 352, 360
Parcel Of Rogues, 164
Pardo, Joe, 151
Paris Records, 174
Paris Sisters, 419
Paris, Alex, 476
Paris, Johnny, 255
Pariser, Alan, 317
Parish, Mitchell, 484
Park, Alan, 45
Parker, 'Little' Junior, 62, 443
Parker, Billy, 170
Parker, Charles, 397
Parker, Charlie, 7, 10, 61, 122, 142, 306, 361
Parker, Ian, 237
Parker, John, 17, 357
Parker, John Albert, 17

Parker, Junior, 62, 353, 443
Parker, Maceo, 78
Parker, Robert, 131, 337
Parker, Thomas, 277
Parker, Tom, 'Colonel', 54, 181, 220, 337, 353, 355
Parks, Larry, 336
Parks, Van Dyke, 36, 121, 225, 312, 469
Parkway Records, 160, 176
Parliament, 397, 433
Parlophone Records, 102, 212, 290, 316, 386
Parnell, Jack, 228, 385
Parnell, Val, 157
Parnes, Larry, 11, 39, 79-80, 101, 180, 189, 197, 207, 210, 259, 338, 352
Parrot Records, 348
Parry, Eddie, 148
Parry, Harry, 402
Parry, Steve, 148
Parsley, Gary, 304
Parsons, Gene, 87
Parsons, Gram, 85, 87-88, 153, 246, 284, 325, 371
Parsons, Nicholas, 108
Parsons, Terry, 315
Parton, Dolly, 276
Partridge Family, 61, 130
Partridge, Don, 339
Partridge, John, 61
Pash, Jim, 433
Pass, Joe, 347, 402
Pastels, 247
Pate, Johnny, 245
Paton, Hume, 350
Paton, Tam, 478
Patrick, Bill, 226
Patrick, Charles, 71
Patrick, James, 336
Patrick, John, 375
Patrick, Michael, 339
Patrick, Pat, 314
Patrick, Phil, 151
Patten, Big John, 66, 413
Patten, Brian, 281
Patten, John, 66, 413
Patterson Hensley, Virginia, 118
Patterson, Bill, 226
Patterson, Jerry, 390
Patterson, Joe, 100
Patterson, Linnie, 478
Patterson, Ottilie, 271
Patterson, Randolph, 418
Patto, 68, 264, 339, 421
Patton, 'Big' John, 339
Patton, John, 339
Paul And Paula, 340
Paul, Alan, 317
Paul, Clarence, 476
Paul, Dean, 153
Paul, Don, 339
Paul, Frankie, 131
Paul, Mike, 345
Paul, Steve, 300
Paul, Terry, 229
Paupers, 317, 340
Paverty, Frank, 437
Pawle, Ivan, 162
Paxton, Gary, 201, 238, 348
Paxton, Tom, 67, 177, 193, 196, 211, 239, 330, 340, 385
Payne, Bill, 205
Payne, Freda, 162, 236
Payne, Gordon, 134
Payne, Jim, 250
Payne, Ken, 372
Payne, Scherrie, 432
Payton, Brenda, 74
Payton, Denis, 114
Payton, Nicholas, 414
Peabody, Jeremiah, 428
Peaches And Herb, 340-341
Peacock, Phil, 414

Peacock, Roger, 110, 277
Peanut Butter Conspiracy, 118, 341
Pearls Before Swine, 341
Pearson, Duke, 66
Pearson, John, 417
Pearson, Johnny, 393
Pearson, Ken, 258
Pearson, Noel, 110
Peaston, David, 34
Peay, Benjamin Franklin, 48
Peck, Ged, 196
Peck, Gregory, 97
Peckinpah, Sam, 169
Peddlers, 192, 341-342
Peel, John, 110, 194, 208, 221, 281, 285, 310, 409, 452, 460
Peels, Leon, 67
Peer, Bill, 118
Peerce, Jan, 194
Peers, Donald, 368
Pegg, Dave, 91
Peloquin, Jerry, 253
Pelosi, Jeff, 134
Pelsia, J.W., 28
Pemberton, Bugs, 453
Pender, Mike, 394
Pendleton, Brian, 358
Penetration, 203
Penn, Arthur, 10
Penn, Dan, 73, 331, 342, 362
Penniman, Richard, 60
Pentangle, 252, 342-343
Pere Ubu, 367
Peretti, Hugo, 445
Perez, John, 408
Perfect, Christine, 110
Perkins, Carl, 40, 54, 83, 97-98, 100, 353, 355
Perkins, Luther, 97-98
Perkins, Polly, 6
Perkins, Terence, 160
Perkins, Walter, 6
Perks, William, 379
Perry, Chris, 270
Perry, Jimmy, 248
Perry, John, 216
Perry, Lee, 9, 343-345, 349
Perry, Rainford Hugh, 343
Perry, Richard, 257
Persuasions, 339
Pet Shop Boys, 423
Peter And Gordon, 40, 103, 207, 295, 345
Peter Pan, 50, 75
Peter, Paul And Mary, 16, 167, 211, 220, 282, 345-346
Peters, Bernadette, 59
Peters, Dave, 79
Peters, Jeff, 79
Peters, Richard, 357
Petersen, Dick, 266
Petersen, John, 44
Petersen, Paul, 187, 291
Petersen, Ray, 418
Peterson, Cole, 346
Peterson, Dickie, 65
Peterson, Ella, 251
Peterson, Oscar, 84, 251, 313, 319, 346-347
Peterson, Ray, 32, 455
Peterson, Sylvia, 111
Petrucciani, Michel, 183
Petters, John, 112
Pettiford, Oscar, 7, 313
Petty, Norman, 134, 195, 282, 332, 351
Petty, Tom, 127, 170-171, 332, 400
Peyser, Joan, 51
Peyton, Lawrence, 199
Pflayer, Jim, 331
Phay, Danny, 112
Phelps, George, 310
Phenomena, 89, 314
Phil The Fluter, 96
Philips Records, 250, 463

Philles Records, 419
Phillips, Andrew, 258
Phillips, Dave, 91
Phillips, Eddie, 132
Phillips, Esther, 347-348
Phillips, Gene, 347
Phillips, Gregory, 371
Phillips, Jim, 289
Phillips, John, 85, 178, 258, 288-289, 301, 317, 324, 384
Phillips, McKenzie, 288
Phillips, Michelle, 258, 288-289
Phillips, Ray, 324
Phillips, Roy, 341
Phillips, Sam, 83, 97, 259, 281, 332, 353, 451
Phillips, Shawn, 203
Phillips, Sid, 29, 46
Phillips, Simon, 471
Piaf, Edith, 23, 116
Piano Red, 7
Piano, Mike, 55, 391
Piazza, Joe, 411
Piblokto!, 35, 80
Picariello, Freddy, 93
Piccadilly Records, 5, 352, 393
Pickens, Earl, 137
Pickett, Bobby 'Boris', 238, 348
Pickett, Kenny, 132
Pickett, Wilson, 21, 71, 93, 130, 135, 196, 264-265, 292, 348-349, 366, 426, 437, 445
Pickford Hopkins, Gary, 186
Pierce, Webb, 481, 483
Pierson, Clark, 258
Pierson, Jon, 18
Piggott, Mike, 342
Pike, Jim, 277
PiL, 27, 258
Pilloud, Rod, 134
Pilot, 214, 367, 369, 427, 451
Pinder, Mike, 318-319
Pine, Courtney, 61
Pinera, Mike, 247
Pink Fairies, 31, 151, 192, 221, 241
Pink Floyd, 31-32, 449
Pinkerton's Assorted Colours, 349
Pinkney, Bill, 163
Pinky, Bill, And The Turks, 259
Pins And Needles, 70, 394-395, 416
Pinz, Shelly, 277
Pioneers, 226, 306, 333, 343, 349, 441, 480
Pipkins, 175
Pippin, 331
Pirates, 101, 138, 165, 179, 222, 264, 438
Pisces, 315
Pitman, Jimmy, 429
Pitman-Avory, Jim, 443
Pitney, Gene, 24, 136-137, 151, 291, 325, 349-350, 379-380, 385
Pitt, Ken, 44
Pitter, Frank, 362
Pitts, Noland, 308
Pixies, 177
Pizer, Robin, 221
Plain And Fancy, 334
Plainsong, 281
Plait, Jacques, 141
Planet Records, 94
Plant, Robert, 271, 312, 336
Plaster Casters, 220
Plastic Ono Band, 355, 419
Plastic Penny, 110, 350, 448
Platt, John, 233, 480
Playboy Records, 484
Player, John, 360
Playmates, 413
Plimsouls, 392
Plumb, Dave, 304
Poacher, 305
Pockriss, Lee, 137, 151, 187
Poco, 245, 325
Podolor, Richie, 326

Poets, 80, 245, 293, 350
Pogues, 164
Poindexter, Buster, 445
Poindexter, Pony, 385
Point Blank, 203
Poison, 337, 343, 443
Polanski, Roman, 270, 441
Polci, Gerry, 199
Pollack, Lew, 26
Polydor Records, 78, 211, 259, 274, 286
PolyGram Records, 176
Pomus, Doc, 54, 76, 153, 187, 265, 350, 354, 394, 405, 472
Poncia, Vinnie, 261
Pons, Jim, 275, 321, 450
Pool, Malcolm, 19
Poole, Brian, And The Tremeloes, 39, 114, 125, 192, 351, 447
Poole, Terry, 28
Pop Art, 41, 179, 366, 469
Pop Gear, 295
Pope, Charles, 435
Pope, Joe, 435
Popple, Terry, 447
Popsicle, 251
Porter, Cole, 29, 153, 225, 241, 334, 346-347, 368, 403, 466
Porter, David, 30, 351-352, 390, 442
Porter, Roy, 155
Portman-Smith, Nigel, 342
Portz, Chuck, 450
Potger, Keith, 397
Potter, Ashley, 304
Potter, Butch, 35
Potter, Dennis, 202
Potter, Ricki, 324
Pottinger, Sonia, 352
Potts, Sylvester, 125
Poulos, Jon Jon, 81
Poulter, Jon, 304
Povey, Jon, 178
Powell, Alan, 192
Powell, Bud, 66, 182-183, 306, 402
Powell, Clive, 189, 197
Powell, Dick, 28, 134
Powell, Keith, 352
Powell, Robert, 76
Powell, Roger, 6
Powell, William, 280
Power, Duffy, 194, 338, 352
Power, Vincent, 94
Powers, Dale, 331
Powers, Peggy, 472
Powers, Toni, 220
Prater, David, 390
Preager, Lou, 241
Pretab Sprout, 482
Preminger, Otto, 316
Prescod, Frank, 128
Prescott, Betty, 74
President Records, 262, 434
Presley, Elvis, 16, 20, 24, 54, 57, 61, 66, 71, 83, 85, 96, 98, 116, 131, 181, 184, 187, 196-197, 203, 214, 218, 220, 222, 228, 260, 262, 277, 290, 292, 302, 305, 316, 330, 332, 337-338, 351-357, 360, 365, 368, 372-373, 376, 380, 389, 404-405, 408, 424, 433, 451, 460, 484
Presley, Reg, 448
Pressure Drop, 298
Presti, Charles 'Chippy', 123
Preston, Billy, 42, 265
Preston, Denis, 303
Preston, Don, 321
Preston, Johnny, 270, 357-358
Preston, Mike, 283
Pretenders, 233, 256, 267
Pretty Things, 31, 136, 151-152, 156, 161, 178, 324, 358, 366, 379, 410
Previn, André, 14
Previn, Dory, 262
Price, Alan, 15, 102, 156, 189-190,

213
Price, Jim, 223
Price, John, 156
Price, Lloyd, 16, 60, 197, 339, 348
Price, Louis, 438
Price, Ray, 305, 451, 483
Price, Rick, 403
Price, Rod, 57
Pride, Charley, 20
Pride, Dickie, 101, 338, 352
Priestley, Brian, 123, 308
Prieto, Joaquin, 379
Prime Time, 414
Primes, 359, 431, 437
Primettes, 29, 359, 431
Primitives, 459
Prince Buster, 298-299, 343, 359, 362, 409
Prince Jazzbo, 344
Prince La La, 430
Prince, Hal, 50
Prince, Harold, 89
Prince, Viv, 358
Prine, John, 99
Prism, 120
Prisoners, 98, 222
Pritchard, Barry, 197
Pritchard, Dave, 244, 403
Proby, P.J., 33, 97, 101, 190, 197, 201, 214, 359-360, 368
Procol Harum, 127, 149, 161, 243, 337, 350, 360-361
Professionals, 176, 312, 470
Professor Longhair, 337
Prokop, Skip, 340
Prosen, Sid, 445
Provine, Dorothy, 38
Prowler, 290
Pryce, Jonathan, 33, 331
Pryor, Richard, 387
Prytcherch, Harry, 371
Psyche-Out, 429
Public Enemy, 78
Puckett, Gary, 117, 263, 361
Pugh, Bryan, 248
Pugh, Martin, 427
Pugh, Mike, 310
Pukwana, Dudu, 361
Pulp, 25, 38, 139, 459
Pumer, Eddie, 260
Purdie, Bernard 'Pretty', 265
Purify, James And Bobby, 331, 362
Purple Gang, 362
Putnam, Norbert, 342
Pye Records, 29, 74, 76, 90, 93, 211, 216, 240, 271, 386, 393-394
Pye, Peter, 240
Pyramids, 294, 362

Q

? And The Mysterians, 363
Quaife, Peter, 266
Quantrell, Margot, 74
Quarrymen, 39, 42
Quatermass, 56, 179
Quaye, Caleb, 423
Quebec, Ike, 66
Queen Latifah, 323
Quest, 123, 192, 239
Questions, 65, 375, 476
Quickly, Tommy, 180, 363, 371
Quicksand, 235
Quicksilver Messenger Service, 76, 106, 152, 215-216, 287, 317, 363-364
Quill, Greg, 383
Quincy, Dave, 68
Quinichette, Paul, 123
Quinn, Derek, 205
Quinn, Freddy, 274
Quintessence, 184, 409
Quirico, DeWayne, 207
Quittenton, Martin, 427
Quixote, Don, 264, 321-322

Quotations, 364, 477
Qwest, 107, 405

R

R.E.M., 25, 312, 383, 448
Rabbit Foot Minstrels, 442
Rabkin, Eddie, 444
Racing Cars, 306
Radio Luxembourg, 96, 102, 148, 364, 455
Radio Stars, 179, 255
Rado, James, 222
Rae, Jackie, 368
Raelettes, 127, 364-365
Rafelson, Bob, 314
Rafferty, Gerry, 242
Rag, Otto, 418
Ragni, Gerome, 222
Ragovoy, Jerry, 49, 179, 197, 258, 365, 405
Ragsdale, Ray, 428
Rainbow Bridge, 232-233
Rainer, 66, 357
Rainey, Chuck, 17
Rainey, Max, 441
Rains, George, 320, 409
Rainwater, Marvin, 202, 284
Raised On Records, 411
Raitt, Bonnie, 130, 365, 385
Rake, 80, 288
Ralph Records, 110
Ram Jam, 191, 277, 466-467
Rambeau, Eddie, 200
Ramistella, John, 376
Ramones, 419
Ramos, Larry, 327
Rampart Records, 93
Ramsey, Alan, 278
Randall, Eddie, 142
Randall, Freddy, 29
Randazzo, Teddy, 341
Randell, Buddy, 269
Randholph, Homer Louis, III, 365
Randolph, Boots, 365
Ranglin, Ernest, 370
Rankin, Billy, 268, 431
Rankin, Brian, 398
Ransley, Tony, 165
Rap, 37, 443
Rapp, Tom, 341
Rare Bird, 111
Rare Earth, 322
Rascals, 21, 147, 161, 332, 455-456, 481
Raskin, Gene, 240
Raskin, Jonathan, 18
Raspberry Singers, 248
Rathbone, Don, 236
Ratledge, Mike, 31, 415
Rattles, 38, 223, 365-366
Ravel, Chris, 13
Raven, Paul, 57
Ravens, 158, 192, 266, 333, 337
Ravenscroft, Raphael, 385
Rawls, Lou, 11, 317
Ray, Ada, 253
Ray, Anthony, 22, 96, 377
Ray, Dave, 366, 415
Ray, James, 162, 205
Ray, Johnnie, 59, 124, 145
Ray, Ken, 397
Ray, Paul, 340
Rayber Voices, 366
Raye, Martha, 230
Raye, Susan, 335
Raymond, Don, 155
Raymond, Paul, 110, 350
Raymonde, Ivor, 207, 413, 422, 463
RCA Records, 13-14, 17, 19, 22, 48, 97, 118, 123, 126, 182, 198, 224, 247, 263, 280, 292, 334, 353, 356, 445, 476, 485
Reading, Bertice, 270

Real Life, 85
Real World Records
Reardon, Jack, 261
Rebennack, Mac, 64
Reckless, 299
Record, Eugene, 6
Red Crayola, 367
Red Light, 328-329
Redding, Noel, 104, 231, 233, 433
Redding, Otis, 21, 30, 83, 124, 126, 135, 161, 176, 249, 265, 292, 302, 317, 367-368, 377, 426, 437, 442, 455, 478
Rede, Emma, 276
Redgrave, Vanessa, 65, 91
Reece, Dizzy, 311
Reed, Jerry, 20, 98, 354
Reed, Jimmy, 15, 161, 299, 371, 410, 454
Reed, John, 161
Reed, Johnny, 333
Reed, Les, 6, 115, 149, 256, 368
Reed, Lou, 161, 390, 459
Reed, Lulu, 368
Reed, Robert, 368
Reef, 104
Rees, Wyndham, 186
Rees-Mogg, William, 381
Reese, Della, 368-369
Reese, Jim, 207
Reese, Lloyd, 306
Reeves, Barry, 65
Reeves, Jim, 20, 90, 131, 369-370, 468, 483
Reeves, John, 369
Reeves, Martha, 293-294
Reeves, Tony, 121, 296, 417
Reeves, Vic, 378
Regal Zonophone, 27, 127, 244, 323, 361, 453
Regal, Mike, 364
Regals, 333
Regan, Joan, 125, 148
Reggae George, 344
Reichel, Achim, 365
Reichman, Thomas, 307
Reid, Duke, 9, 130, 352, 370, 409
Reid, Eileen, 90
Reid, Keith, 337, 360-361
Reid, Terry, 253
Reilly, Maggie, 315
Reiner, Fritz, 50
Reiner, Robert Lee, 275
Reinhardt, Django, 318, 468
Reins, Frank, 94
Relf, Bob, 68
Relf, Keith, 479
Remo Four, 363, 371
Renaldo And Clara, 67, 169, 228
Renbourn, John, 174, 203, 231, 251-252, 342
Rendell, Don, 69
Reparata And The Delrons, 277, 371
Reprise Records, 48, 188, 282, 312, 444, 462
Repsch, John, 303
Requiem, 77
Residents, 93, 236
Resnick, Artie, 81
Revaux, Jacques, 203
Revel, Don, 359
Revere, Paul, And The Raiders, 53, 201, 266, 291, 371-372
Revill, Clive, 331
Rey, Alvino, 146
Rey, Bobby, 238
Reynolds, Kelvin, 334
Reynolds, Malvina, 395, 397
Rheimschagen, Herman, 306
Rhino Records, 139, 266, 297, 315
Rhinoceros, 138, 177, 372, 385
Rhodes, Robert, 38
Rhythm albums, 343
Rhythm Dukes, 416

Rhythm Heritage, 32
Ribowsky, Mark, 419
Rice, Tim, 18, 374
Rich, Buddy, 422
Rich, Charlie, 98, 259, 403-404
Rich, Don, 335
Rich, Herbie, 176
Rich, S., 119, 177, 259, 403-404, 459
Richard, Cliff, 11, 31, 33, 54, 74, 76, 83, 101, 115, 185, 188, 194, 214, 223, 261, 283, 305, 372-375, 391, 393, 398-399, 412, 431, 468, 480
Richard, Ervin 'Dick', 28
Richard, Roy, 101
Richards, Billy, 152
Richards, Keith, 51-52, 152, 170, 349, 379, 382-383
Richards, Rick, 403
Richards, Tom, 386
Richardson, Jape, 358
Richardson, Joe, 128
Richardson, Van Earl, 67
Richie, Lionel, 215, 323
Richmond, Dannie, 307
Richmond, Dave, 290
Richmond, Fritz, 272
Rick And The Ravens, 158
Rickenbacker, Adolph, 193
Rickfors, Mickael, 237
Ricks, Tommy, 162
Ridarelli, Robert, 388
Riddell, Kirk, 113
Riddle, Nelson, 34, 347
Ridgley, Tommy, 442
Ridley, Greg, 18, 254
Rifkin, Joshua, 121
Riggio, Gene, 282
Right Said Fred, 294
Righteous Brothers, 58, 61, 212, 214, 229, 270, 291, 304, 375, 419, 463
Riley, Ben, 313
Riley, Jeannie C., 210
Riley, Jimmy, 344
Riley, John, 87
Riley, Terry, 441
Rimbaud, Arthur, 167
Rinehart, Bill, 275
Riopelle, Jerry, 437
Ripp, Artie, 64, 252, 341
Riot Squad, 231, 337, 375
Riperton, Minnie, 365
Rising Sons, 271, 375-376
Ritchie, Brian, 428
Ritchie, Jean, 177
Ritenour, Lee, 254
Ritter, Preston, 176
Ritter, Tex, 119
Ritz, David, 107, 210, 249, 378, 470
Rivers, Johnny, 8, 61, 165, 317, 376-377
Rivers, Sam, 66
Rivers, Tony, And The Castaways, 216, 224
Riverside Records, 7, 182, 313
Rivingtons, 201
Rizzo, Pat, 137
Roach, Max, 61, 155, 279, 307-308, 311
Roadhouse, 159, 299
Roadrunners, 102, 165
Roaring Sixties, 191
Robbins, Harold, 354
Robbins, Jerome, 50, 195
Robbins, Marty, 24, 32, 124, 404
Roberts, Andy, 117, 281
Roberts, Bobby, 8, 165
Roberts, Cliff, 243
Roberts, Doug, 195
Roberts, Jim, 45
Roberts, Josh, 362
Roberts, Malcolm, 368
Roberts, Mike, 281
Robertson, B.A., 25
Robertson, John, 44, 233, 357

Robertson, Liz, 76
Robertson, Robbie, 167, 228
Robey, Don, 62
Robic, Ivor, 259
Robin, Don, 368
Robins, 53
Robinson, Bill, 145, 309
Robinson, Bill 'Bojangles', 145
Robinson, Claudette, 309-310
Robinson, Cynthia, 411
Robinson, David, 287, 378
Robinson, Harry, 11
Robinson, Jackie, 349
Robinson, John, 341
Robinson, Peter, 179
Robinson, Sandi, 341
Robinson, Smokey, 125-126, 200, 214, 235, 295, 309-310, 323, 376-378, 431, 438, 468-469, 476
Robinson, William, 309, 377
Roche, Pierre, 23
Rock, Tommy, 472
Rockets, 213, 477
Rockin' Berries, 201, 378, 393
Rockwell, 215
Rocky Sharpe And The Replays, 175
Roden, Jess, 73
Roderick, 198
Roderick, David, 198
Rodford, Jim, 128, 485
Rodgers, Jimmie (country), 193
Rodgers, John, 386
Rodgers, Paul, 336
Rodgers, Richard, 14, 75, 116, 123, 264, 292, 353
Rodrigo, Joaquin, 143
Rodzinski, Artur, 50
Roe, Tommy, 117, 378
Rogan, Johnny, 18, 82, 88, 136, 267-268, 339, 441
Roger, Phil, 371
Rogers, Bill, 310
Rogers, Bobby, 309-310
Rogers, Claudette, 377
Rogers, Emerson, 309
Rogers, Ginger, 230
Rogers, Glouster, 280
Rogers, Jimmy, 109
Rogers, Julie, 379
Rogers, Kenny, 259, 327
Rogers, Pete, 49
Rogers, Richard, 346
Rogers, Roy, 143, 455
Rogers, Shorty, 49
Rogers, Wanda, 295
Rogers, Warren, 399
Roker, Mickey, 347
Rolling Stones, 10, 12, 15-17, 21, 31-33, 35, 40, 42, 51, 57, 70-71, 83, 87, 90, 93, 99, 109-110, 126, 152, 154, 156, 170, 176, 178, 189, 191, 213, 216, 236, 241, 245, 253, 267, 269, 271, 287, 294, 296, 317, 349-350, 358, 365-367, 373, 379-384, 397, 410, 412, 425, 430-431, 437, 442, 450, 476, 478-479
Rollins, Sonny, 85, 122, 143-144, 313-314, 361
Rolls, Julie, 379
Romanowski, Patricia, 433, 439
Romantics, 387
Rome, Tony, 316
Romeo, Kathy, 371
Romeo, Max, 344
Romero, Chan, 102, 434
Ronettes, 32, 61, 136, 154, 220, 262, 304, 379, 384, 419, 434
Roney, Wallace, 405
Ronny And The Daytonas, 384
Ronson, Mick, 169
Ronstadt, Linda, 17, 128, 331
Rooftop Singers, 384
Rooney, Herb, 186
Roos, Marty, 315

Rory Storm And The Hurricanes, 39, 102, 225, 428
Rose, Antonio, 119, 131
Rose, David, 104, 347
Rose, Fred, 20
Rose, Peter, 274
Rose, Tim, 178-179, 384-385, 460
Rosen, Mike, 174
Rosenberg, Kenny, 252
Rosenwinkel, Kurt, 85
Roskams, Alan, 276
Rosolino, Frank, 221
Ross, Adam, 100
Ross, Andy, 179
Ross, Annie, 189-190, 385
Ross, Diana, 29, 117, 209, 212, 215, 236, 323, 359, 431-433, 439
Ross, Glenn, 310
Ross, Jerry, 253, 263
Ross, Katherine, 215
Ross, Margaret, 127
Rossman, Ronnie, 250
Rosso, Nini, 417
Rostill, John, 399
Rothchild, Paul A., 385
Rothschild, Paul, 18
Rotolo, Suze, 166-167
Rough House, 156
Roughley, Bill, 192
Roulettes, 16, 188, 386, 454
Rouse, Charlie, 313
Roustabout, 354, 356-357
Routers, 386, 463-464
Routh, J.W., 99
Rowan, Peter, 173
Rowberry, Dave, 15, 128
Rowe, Barbara, 219, 254
Rowe, Dick, 26, 39, 160, 180, 256, 293, 338, 379, 440, 451
Rowland, Karen, 432
Rowland, Steve, 141, 190, 288
Rowley, Mick, 414
Roxy Music, 5, 56, 328
Royal Guardsmen, 386
Royal Showband, 93, 386
Royal Teens, 198, 269
Royal Wedding, 346-347
Royal, Billy Joe, 117
Royer, Ray, 360
RSO Records, 55
Rubettes, 53, 435
Rubin, Rick, 99
Ruby And The Romantics, 387
Ruby, Harry, 202
Rude Boy, 114
Rudolph, Paul, 151
Ruff, Ray, 441
Ruffin, David, 438
Ruffin, Jimmy, 238, 439
Rufus, 13, 71, 93, 399, 426, 442-443
Rugge-Price, James, 5
Runaways, 201
Rundgren, Todd, 130, 220-221
Running Wild, 438, 467
Rupe, Art, 60, 126
Rush, Otis, 109
Rush, Tom, 152, 177-178, 385, 387, 463
Rushton, Michael, 427
Russell, Bert, 48, 186
Russell, Bobby, 305
Russell, Brian, 120
Russell, George, 155, 182-183, 307
Russell, Ken, 77, 471
Russell, Leon, 11, 19, 107, 127, 225, 275, 278, 280, 292, 419
Russell, Rosalind, 50
Russell, Willy, 117
Rust Records, 123, 223
Rutles, 339
Ryan, Don, 134
Ryan, Eddie, 93
Ryan, Jim, 134
Ryan, Marion, 388
Ryan, Mick, 114

Ryan, Paul And Barry, 368, 388, 395
Ryan, Phil, 80, 186
Ryan, Ron, 375
Rydell, Bobby, 76, 108, 116, 200, 388
Ryder, Jean, 74
Ryder, Mitch, 213, 388-389

S

S'Express, 18, 279
S.O.S., 11, 13-14, 129, 158, 164, 405, 475
Sabatino, Pete, 455
Sad Cafe, 53
Sade, 211, 393
Sager, Carole Bayer, 25, 204, 306, 423
Sahm, Doug, 408
Sailor, 36, 103, 116, 174
Sain, Oliver, 33-34
Sainte-Marie, Buffy, 389-390
Salad, 36, 355
Salewicz, Chris, 233
Salgues, Y., 23
Salt, Peter, 386
Saltis, Larry, 315
Salty Dog, 360-361
Sam And Dave, 21, 71, 83, 292, 351-352, 362, 390, 426
Sam Gopal, 390
Sam The Man, 127
Sam The Sham And The Pharaohs, 390
Sammes, Mike, 274, 390-391, 413
Samson, 275
Samudio, Domingo, 390
Samudio, Sam, 390
Samwell, Ian, 372-373, 412
Samwell-Smith, Paul, 479
Sanborn, David, 86
Sanchez, 151, 383
Sanchez, Ray, 151
Sanchez, Tony, 383
Sanctuary, 154, 173
Sanden, Doug, 470
Sanders, Pharoah, 122
Sanders, Sonny, 366
Sanders, William, 366
Sanderson, Duncan, 151
Sandland, Colin, 415
Sandlin, Johnny, 240-241
Sandon, Johnny, 371, 394
Sandpipers, 391
Sands, Tommy, 61, 73, 335, 408
Santana, 12, 170, 216, 312, 478
Santiglia, Peggy, 14-15
Santo And Johnny, 391
Sapherson, Barry, 387
SAR Records, 127
Saraceno, Joe, 386
Sarne, Mike, 97, 142, 248
Sarstedt, Peter, 262, 391-392
Sarstedt, Richard, 262
Sarstedt, Robin, 57, 262, 392
Satan, 59, 344
Satie, Erik, 402
Satintones, 235, 295
Saunders, Marty, 252
Saunders, Mike, 6
Saunders, Red, 115
Saunders, Tim, 6
Savage, Jon, 268
Savile, Jimmy, 295
Saville, Jimmy, 364, 418
Savoy Brown, 110, 244, 350, 439
Savoy, Mark, 28
Sawyer, Phil, 110, 146
Sawyers, Jim, 435
Saxon, 58, 114, 392, 396
Saxon, Sky, 392, 396
Saxon, Stan, 114
Sayer, Leo, 188

Sayers, Pete, 284
Sazaferin, G., 372
Scaduto, Anthony, 172, 383
Scaffold, 281, 392
Scaggs, Boz, 189
Scala, Ralph, 67
Scales, Harvey, 181
Scarce, 440
Scarlet, 13, 435, 461
Scars, 100, 359
Scenic, 89, 230, 331
Scepter Records, 439
Scheck, George, 140
Scheer, 190
Scheer, Ireen, 190
Schiffour, Tom, 399
Schifrin, Lalo, 392
Schneider, Bert, 314
Schoen, Danke, 259
Schoenberg, Arnold, 280
Schoolboys, 267-268
Schroeder, John, 393, 417
Schuller, Gunther, 155, 307
Schuster, Sylvia, 329
Schwabach, Kurt, 260
Schwartz, Glenn, 336
Schwartz, Peter, 28
Schwartz, Tracy, 28-29
Schwarz, Brinsley, 176, 268, 427
Schwarzenegger, Arnold, 172
Scofield, John, 66, 85, 143
Scoppettone, Dick, 225
Scorsese, Martin, 49
Scott, Bill, 478
Scott, Bobby, 117
Scott, David, 6
Scott, Freddie, 248
Scott, Freddy, 49
Scott, Irene, 397
Scott, Jack, 378
Scott, Jake, 478
Scott, Joe, 62
Scott, John, 394, 463
Scott, Keith, 271
Scott, Noel, 463-464
Scott, Ronnie, 62, 102, 147, 189, 228, 361, 393-394, 408, 415
Scott, Shirley, 394
Scott, Tommy, 256, 451
Scott, Tony, 182
Scott-Heron, Gil, 347
Scotti Brothers, 78-79
Scotty, 57, 353, 355, 404, 464
Scotty And Bill, 57, 353
Screaming Blue Messiahs, 177
Scrooge, 76
Sea Train, 173
Seal, 53, 96, 118, 343
Seal, Bob, 118
Searchers, 32, 44, 46, 53, 70, 102, 136, 150, 163, 371, 394-395, 411, 416, 446
Sears, Pete, 427
Seatrain, 68, 324
Sebastian, John, 134, 140, 245, 285, 323, 385, 478-479
Secombe, Harry, 75-76, 270, 334
Secret Affair, 196
Secret Life, 189, 225, 477
Secrets, 31, 82, 183
Secunda, Tony, 127, 323
Sedaka, Neil, 76, 114, 127, 202, 212, 294, 395-396, 444, 473
Sedgewick, Mike, 6-7
Sedgewick, Peter 'Adam', 6
Seeds, 19, 201, 280, 301, 392, 396, 416
Seeger, Charles, 396-397
Seeger, Mike, 396-397
Seeger, Peggy, 396-397
Seeger, Penny, 396-397
Seeger, Pete, 10, 86, 193, 282, 340, 376, 384
Seeger, Ruth Crawford, 396
Seekers, 137, 142, 177, 397-398, 418

Segarini, Bob, 190
Seger, Bob, 152
Sehorn, Marshall, 160
Seider, Steve, 123
Seiter, George, 418
Seiter, John, 418
Sellar, Gordon, 45
Sellers, Peter, 294, 316, 418, 429, 451
Selvin, Joel, 326
Sensations, 11, 177
Seol, Randy, 429
September Records, 402
Sequel Records, 443
Serenaders, 255
Sergeant, 210, 361
Sergides, Miguel, 17
Serpell, Grant, 243
Servie, Joseph, 418
Settle, Mike, 327
Seville, David, 111, 274
Sewell, Marshall, 175
Sex Pistols, 52, 125, 203
Sha Na Na, 262, 478
Shades Of Blue, 93, 308, 398
Shadows, 398-399 and passim
Shadows Of Knight, 399
Shag, 435
Shakespeare, John, 96, 248
Shakespeare, William, 174
Shakin' Stevens, 146, 214
Shakin' Street, 299
Shalamar, 466
Shalett, Emile, 9
Shallock, David, 416
Shanachie, 65, 130, 188
Shanahan, Pat, 325
Shanghai, 46, 74
Shangri-Las, 32, 151, 161, 220, 399, 451, 456
Shankar, Ravi, 40, 216, 317, 478
Shannon, Del, 55, 113, 243, 256, 305, 400-401
Shannon, Pete, 324
Shaper, Hal, 334
Shapiro, Harry, 69, 233, 272
Shapiro, Helen, 150, 160, 393, 401
Shapiro, Nat, 74
Sharkey, John, 435
Sharon, Ralph, 47
Sharp, Alexander, 333
Sharp, Cecil, 164
Sharp, Dee Dee, 108, 155, 162, 348, 401
Shaw, Artie, 124
Shaw, Bernard, 264
Shaw, Chris, 337
Shaw, Donald, 466
Shaw, Robin, 196
Shaw, Sandie, 13, 24, 58, 224, 337, 401-402, 422
Shaw, Woody, 406
Shayne, Gloria, 473
Shearing, George, 85, 346, 402-403, 475
Sheeley, Sharon, 150
Sheen, Bobby, 68
Sheffler, Ted, 134
Shehan, John, 164
Sheldon, Ernie, 280
Shelter Records, 19
Shelton, Robert, 166, 172
Shemwell, Sylvia, 463
Shepard, Sam, 171-172, 239
Shepp, Archie, 122-123, 183, 300
Sheppard, Andy, 123
Sheridan, Mike, 244, 403
Sheridan, Tony, 39, 43, 132, 260, 365, 403
Sheridan-Price, 403
Sherley, Glen, 98
Sherman, Bobby, 280
Sherman, Joe, 75
Sherrill, Billy, 403
Sherwood, Adrian, 344

Shields, Harvey, 179
Shirelles, 53, 152, 212, 265, 288, 404, 453
Shirley And Lee, 358
Shirley, Jerry, 31
Shirts, 129, 350, 372, 481
Shoesmith, Peter, 287
Shoff, Richard, 391
Sholes, Steve, 20
Shore, Dinah, 90, 262
Short Lynch, Annabelle, 385
Short, Brian, 57, 242
Shorter, Davis, 404
Shorter, Wayne, 66, 143, 404-405, 443
Shotgun Express, 165
Showaddywaddy, 73, 173
Showstoppers, 473
Shriver, Dave, 282
Shuckett, Ralph, 118, 341
Shulman, Derek, 165-166
Shuman, Mort, 54, 59, 74, 76, 153, 187, 265, 272, 350, 354, 394, 405, 412, 472
Shwartz, Richie, 364
Sibbles, Leroy, 5, 344
Side Kicks, 260
Sidgwick, Terry, 447
Sidran, Ben, 5, 10, 190
Siegel, Jay, 444-445
Siegel, Peter, 173
Sievers, William, 416
Siggins, Bob, 272
Sigma, 329
Sigman, Carl, 260
Signal, 52
Signatures, 120, 150, 298, 339
Silhouettes, 234, 309, 384, 455
Silk, 358, 408, 437
Sill, Lester, 418-419
Silver Metre, 427
Silver, Cliff, 375
Silver, Horace, 66, 156, 182, 226, 254, 311, 394, 404-406
Silverhead, 221
Silverman, Charlie, 234
Silverstein, Shel, 98, 189, 406
Simmons, Gene, 57
Simms, Bobby, 456
Simon And Garfunkel, 26, 61, 91, 137, 150, 215, 225, 263, 317, 406-407, 445
Simon, Carly, 177, 239
Simon, Joe, 342
Simon, John, 345
Simon, Neil, 49
Simon, Paul, 6, 26, 129, 137, 190, 193, 203, 216, 224, 317, 366, 397, 406-407, 445, 447
Simone, Nina, 15, 407-408
Simosko, Vladimir, 155
Simper, Nick, 196, 264
Simpson, Andrea, 95
Simpson, Rae, 246
Simpson, Rose, 246
Simpson, Valerie, 440
Sims, Zoot, 182, 346, 385, 393
Sinatra, Frank, 19, 29, 49-50, 61, 140, 145, 153, 203, 219, 254, 260, 262, 275, 282, 316, 347, 388, 408, 468
Sinatra, Nancy, 61, 75, 280, 408
Sinclair, John, 299
Sinfield, Pete, 224
Singer, Ray, 329, 365
Singleton, Charles, 260
Singleton, Margie, 482
Sinks, Earl, 134
Sir Douglas Quintet, 302, 408-409
Sire Records, 429
Siren Records, 409
Sirico, Cookie, 371
Sirico, Stan, 15
6.5 Special, 160, 214, 274, 418
Skatalites, 343, 349, 371, 409

Skeletons, 219
Skellern, Peter, 240
Skhy, A.B., 5, 201
Skillet Lickers, 335
Skinner, Derek, 422
Skip And Flip, 201, 238
Skip Bifferty, 18, 229, 409-410
Skipper, Alan, 358
Sklar, Buddy, 275
Sky, Patrick, 67, 195
Skyline, 87, 98, 168, 171
Slade, 104
Slapp Happy, 101
Slater, Rodney, 70
Slaughter, 78, 356-357
Slaven, Neil, 226, 321-322
Sledge, Percy, 21, 331, 342, 410
Sleep, Wayne, 90
Slick, Grace, 22, 219, 253-254
Slide Records, 309
Slim Harpo, 410, 470
Sloan, Frank, 303
Sloan, P.F., 8, 85, 165, 190, 217, 301, 337, 395, 410-411, 450, 469
Sloan, Philip, 411
Sloman, Larry, 172
Sly And The Family Stone, 229, 411, 438, 478
Small Faces, 17-18, 21, 245, 286, 405, 410, 412-413, 428, 431, 471, 475-476
Small, Joey, 81, 262
Small, Millie, 176
Smart, Terry, 372
Smash Records, 77, 105, 200, 253
Smeenk, Paul, 136
Smet, Jean-Philippe, 222
Smiley Culture, 143
Smith, 'Whistling' Jack, 413
Smith, Alfred Jesse, 477
Smith, Andy, 91
Smith, Arlene, 105
Smith, Arthur, 316
Smith, Bessie, 257
Smith, Bill 'Major', 340
Smith, Carl, 98
Smith, Clarence 'Pine Top', 108
Smith, Dan, 444
Smith, Ernest, 253
Smith, Frank, 458
Smith, Fred, 243, 299, 332
Smith, G.E., 171
Smith, Huey 'Piano', 376
Smith, Ian, 323
Smith, Jack, 413
Smith, James B., 359, 413
Smith, James Marcus, 359
Smith, James Oscar, 413
Smith, Jean, 246
Smith, Jesse, 477
Smith, Jimmy, 19, 66, 84, 122, 238, 286, 300, 339, 393, 413-414
Smith, Joe, 365
Smith, John, 100, 413
Smith, John L., 100
Smith, Johnny, 100
Smith, Keith, 112
Smith, Kim, 276
Smith, Larry, 70
Smith, Les, 117
Smith, Mel, 276
Smith, Michael, 372
Smith, Mike, 12, 17, 114, 138
Smith, Myrna, 433
Smith, Nigel, 14
Smith, Norman, 45
Smith, Oliver, 230
Smith, Patti, 299
Smith, Ray, 259
Smith, Reg, 338
Smith, Richard, 193, 300
Smith, Rikki, 433
Smith, Robert, 435, 478
Smith, Robert B., 435, 478
Smith, Robert Lee, 435

Smith, Ronnie, 44
Smith, Sam, 259
Smith, Tab, 370
Smith, Terry, 32
Smith, Tommy, 85, 367
Smith, Tony, 286
Smith, Warren, 98
Smith, Willie, 156
Smithereens, 312, 411
Smiths, 402, 451
Smoke, 414-415 and passim
Smokie, 57
Smothers, 473
Smothers Brothers, 473
Smythe, Danny, 73
Snafu, 173
Snap!, 250, 397
Sniper, 265
Snobs, 415
Snow, C.P., 214
Snow, Hank, 20, 337, 353
Snow, Tom, 246
Snuff, 282, 457
Snyder, Bob, 292
Snyder, Dave, 97
Snyder, Eddy, 97
Snyder, Ted, 202
Soft Cell, 360
Soft Machine, 31, 164, 176, 201, 223, 415, 441
Softley, Mick, 415
Sohns, Jim, 399
Soho, 33, 59, 142, 197, 405, 481
Solley, Pete, 192
Soloff, Lew, 64
Solomon, Andy, 12
Solomon, Dorothy, 26
Solomon, King, 83, 266, 348
Solomon, Phil, 26, 93, 164, 256, 302, 349, 440, 451
Somers, Andy, 140, 312
Sommers, Joanie, 89, 148
Sommers, Ronny, 70, 416
Son House, 92
Sondheim, Stephen, 14, 50, 96, 121
Sone, Ray, 161
Sonet Records, 28
Sonia, 105, 331, 352
Sonny And Cher, 21, 70, 214, 375, 416, 448, 456
Sonoban, Casey, 363
Sons Of Champlin, 416
Sopwith Camel, 154, 261, 416-417
Sorrow, S.F., 358
Sorrows, 166, 191, 417
Soul Brothers, 107, 409, 430
Soul Children, 126
Soul Sisters, 34, 150, 394, 430
Soul Stirrers, 126-127, 436
Soul Survivors, 301
Soul, David, 34
Soul, Jimmy, 417
Sound Machine, 84
Sounds Nice, 417
Sounds Orchestral, 221, 393, 417
Souster, Tim, 415
South, Harry, 189, 362
South, Joe, 342, 435
Southern Comfort, 452
Southern Star, 316
Southern, Terry, 173
Southlanders, 417-418
Sovine, Red, 20
Spaniels, 454
Spanky And Our Gang, 288, 341, 418
Spann, Otis, 152
Spark Records, 290
Sparks, 255-256, 326-327
Sparks, Randy, 326-327
Sparrow, 398, 427
Spear, Roger Ruskin, 70
Specials, 25, 34, 214, 408, 470
Specialty Records, 60, 70
Spector, Abner, 128

Spector, Larry, 87
Spector, Phil, 19, 21, 32, 36, 42, 54, 61, 68-70, 74, 105, 136, 148, 153, 163, 173, 192, 200, 220, 262, 304, 326, 375, 379, 384, 416, 418-419, 431, 437, 449, 463
Spector, Ronnie, 384, 419
Spedding, Chris, 35, 80, 101
Speedway, 354, 356-357, 408
Speedy Gonzales, 72
Speelman, Benny, 308
Spellman, A.B., 155
Spence, Johnny, 264, 316
Spence, Skip, 253, 285, 311-312, 363
Spencer, David, 455
Spencer, Herbert, 76
Spencer, Herbert W., 76
Spencer, Jon, 84
Spencer, Mike, 244
Spencer, Paul, 407
Spencer, Roger, 244, 403
Spenner, Alan, 421, 479
Sperling, Dee Dee, 151
Spickard, Bob, 105
Spinella, Bob, 134
Spinetti, Victor, 223, 230
Spinners (UK), 419
Spinout, 187, 354, 357
Spires, 453
Spirit, 420-421 and passim
Spirits Rebellious, 420
Splodgenessabounds, 150
Spontaneous Combustion, 8, 404
Spooky Tooth, 18, 329, 339, 385, 421, 428, 460
Spoons, Sam, 70
Spotnicks, 421-422
Sprigall, Charles, 162
Springfield, Dusty, 24-25, 57-58, 74, 83, 101, 160-161, 212, 401, 405, 422-424, 466
Springfield, Tom, 397, 422
Springfields, 57, 397, 422, 424, 457
Springsteen, Bruce, 53, 69, 99, 153, 193, 297, 299, 332, 388
Squadronaires, 112, 276
Squeeze, 109, 258, 459-460, 474
Squier, Billy, 118
SRG Records, 174
St John Gostine, Dick, 151
St. Clair, Alex, 94
St. Cyr, Johnny, 279
St. John, Mark, 358
St. John, Powell, 257, 320
St. Louis Union, 424
St. Nicholas, Nick, 427
St. Peters, Crispian, 424
Staccato, Johnny, 49
Stackridge, 294
Staczek, Don, 255
Staehely, Christian, 420
Stafford, Jim, 210
Stafford, Terry, 351, 405, 424
Stained Glass, 301
Stainton, Chris, 421
Stairsteps, 81
Stallone, Sylvester, 172
Stallybrass, Will, 192
Stamp, Chris, 273, 470
Stamp, Terence, 267
Stampede, 82, 482
Stampfel, Pete, And The Bottlecaps, 239
Stampfel, Peter, 206, 238
Stamping Ground, 222
Standells, 45, 112, 331, 424-425, 463
Stanford, Trevor, 125
Stanley, George, 357
Stanshall, Vivian, 70
Staple Singers, 30, 342, 404, 425
Staples, Mavis, 425
Staples, Pervis, 425
Staples, Peter, 448
Staples, Pops, 135, 425
Staples, Yvonne, 425

Stapleton, Cyril, 7, 274, 468
Starander, Bo, 421
Starchild, 233
Stardust, Alvin, 194, 236
Starfighters, 174
Starkey, Ritchie, 428
Starkey, Zak, 472
Starlets, 14
Starr, Edwin, 398, 425-426
Starr, Kay, 72, 119
Starr, Ringo, 39, 53, 61, 102-103, 180-181, 225, 269, 282, 294, 309, 403, 422, 428, 436
Starrs, Mike, 121
Starship, 254, 363
State Fair, 72, 140
State, Wayne, 409
Statler Brothers, 98
Staton, Dakota, 238
Status Quo, 234, 393, 427
Stax Records, 30, 124, 130, 161, 426, 430, 436, 470
Stax, John, 358
Stay Away Joe, 357
Stealers Wheel, 242, 421
Steam Packet, 164, 426-427
Steamhammer, 427
Steampacket, 15, 28, 213
Steel, John, 15
Steele, Tommy, 33, 101, 116, 198, 225, 303, 338, 373, 391, 468
Steely Dan, 182, 252, 406, 453
Steelyard Blues, 65
Stein, Chris, 472
Stein, Joseph, 194
Stein, Mark, 456
Steinberg, Lewis, 71
Stephens, Bruce, 66
Stephens, Geoff, 59, 327, 368
Stephens, Leigh, 65, 427
Stephens, Tennyson, 454
Steppenwolf, 165, 173, 326, 392, 427-428
Stereolab, 182
Sterling, Annette, 293
Sterling, Lester, 409
Stevens, April, 437
Stevens, Cat, 18, 126, 149, 201, 271, 304, 342, 388, 424, 447
Stevens, Connie, 89
Stevens, Craig, 264
Stevens, Dave, 97
Stevens, Geoff, 52
Stevens, Guy, 18, 223, 428, 430, 447
Stevens, John, 362
Stevens, Mark, 375
Stevens, Ray, 428
Stevens, Shakin', 146, 214
Stevenson, Albert, 96
Stevenson, Bill, 173
Stevenson, Don, 311
Stevenson, Mickey, 322, 470
Stevenson, William, 293
Stevie B., 476
Stewart, Al, 203, 426
Stewart, Billy, 129, 150, 208
Stewart, Bob, 304
Stewart, Chad, 103
Stewart, Chaz, 45
Stewart, Chris, 176
Stewart, Delano, 352
Stewart, Diane, 69
Stewart, Eric, 306
Stewart, Ian, 271, 379
Stewart, Jim, 21, 426
Stewart, John, 85, 230, 297, 304, 315
Stewart, Michael, 230
Stewart, Rod, 28, 30, 65, 79, 126, 135, 161, 164-165, 224, 290, 297, 427
Stewart, Simon, 203
Stewart, Sylvester, 21, 44, 156, 411
Stewart, Winston, 30

Stiff Records, 192
Stigwood, Robert, 120, 142, 180, 279
Stiles, Ray, 237
Still, Bob, 359
Stills And Nash, 12, 21, 82, 87-88, 118, 135-136, 216, 218, 237, 256, 478
Stills, Stephen, 21, 64, 81, 121, 135, 314, 425
Sting, 160, 386, 393, 471
Stingray, 446
Stinnet, Ray, 390
Stipe, Michael, 25
Stirling, Peter Lee, 303
Stitt, Sonny, 279, 306, 346-347, 443
Stock, Ray, 476
Stokes, John, 25-26
Stokes, Keith, 371
Stokes, Sean James, 25
Stokes, Terry, 109
Stoller, Mike, 154
Stone Canyon Band, 325
Stone The Crows, 140, 213, 226, 443
Stone, Brian, 383, 448
Stone, Freddie, 411
Stone, Gerry, 136
Stone, Jesse, 470
Stone, Joe, 478
Stone, Martin, 6
Stone, Mary, 187
Stone, Oliver, 159, 385
Stone, Rosie, 411
Stone, Sly, 21, 44, 78, 156, 204, 312, 411-412
Stonebridge, Lou, 211
Stoneground, 44
Stooges, 177, 388
Stookey, Paul, 345-346
Stop Records, 482
Stop The World I Want To Get Off, 75, 146
Storball, Donald, 94
Storch, Jerry, 455
Storm, Billy, 418
Storm, Rory, 39, 102, 225, 428
Storyteller, 228, 340
Storyville, 111
Stott, Wally, 464
Strain, Sammy, 280
Strange Creek Singers, 396
Strange, Billy, 262
Strange, Giles, 429
Strangeloves, 49, 245, 429
Strangers, 44, 65, 260, 277, 483
Stranglers, 363
Strauss, Richard, 306
Strawberry Alarm Clock, 429
Strawbs, 12, 208, 458
Stray, 429-430
Strazza, Peter, 176
Street Rhythm Band, 467
Street, Richard, 438
Streeter, Roberta Lee, 210
Streisand, Barbra, 60-61, 230, 329
Stringfellow, Peter, 423
Strong, Al, 416
Strong, Barrett, 430, 438
Strouse, Charles, 145, 230
Structure, 77, 94, 114, 150, 460
Struthers, Dave, 14
Stuart, Alice, 321
Stuart, Barry, 10
Stuart, Mike, 304-305
Stubblefield, Clyde, 78
Stubbs, Joe, 125
Stubbs, Levi, 199
Stubbs, Una, 431
Stuckey, David, 420
Studholme, Joe, 108
Studio One, 5, 94, 114, 298-299, 409
Style Council, 211, 426
Stylistics, 280
Styne, Jule, 59
Styx, 44

Sue Records, 430, 449, 466
Suede, 54, 86, 97, 353, 355, 376
Sugerman, Danny, 159-160
Sullivan, Big Jim, 431
Sullivan, Ed, 39, 113-114, 139, 167, 380
Sullivan, Eddie, 386
Sullivan, Jim, 431
Sullivan, Nicky, 134
Sullivan, Peter, 256
Summer Holiday (1962), 374-375
Summer Stock, 275
Summers, Andy, 15, 140, 312, 385
Summers, Jerry, 160
Sun Ra, 122, 314, 339
Sun Records, 57, 83, 97-98, 332, 352-353, 404, 451
Sundays, 264
Sundgaard, Arnold, 334
Sundholm, Norm, 266
Sundowners, 330
Sundquist, Jim, 193
Sunnyland Slim, 109
Sunrays, 431
Sunset Boulevard, 59, 201
Supergrass, 268, 412
Supremes, 29-30, 61, 117, 123, 161, 176, 200, 215, 235-237, 263, 295, 322, 359, 366, 377, 387, 431-433, 438-439, 456, 465
Suranovitch, George, 284
Surfaris, 37, 433
Sutch, Screaming Lord, 303, 379, 433
Sutcliffe, Pauline, 44
Sutcliffe, Stuart, 39, 403
Sutherland, Stacy, 441
Sutra Records, 106, 261
Sutton, Johnny, 161
Svanoe, Bill, 384
Swail, John, 148
Swainson, Neil, 402
Swallow, Steve, 85
Swamp Dogg, 83, 124, 442
Swan Arcade, 481
Swan Records, 429
Swarbrick, Dave, 91, 481
Sweeney's Men, 93
Sweeney, Paul, 93
Sweeny, Glenn, 441
Sweeny, Vic, 73
Sweet Exorcist, 297
Sweet Inspirations, 433-434
Sweet Love, 89, 326
Sweetenham, Geoff, 216-217
Sweetenham, Pete, 216
Sweetman, Dave, 197
Swervedriver, 472
Swing Out Sister, 6
Swing, Will, 347
Swinging Blue Jeans, 102, 181, 434
Swingle Singers, 147, 434
Swingle, Ward, 434
Sylvester, Andy, 110
Sylvester, Mike, 434
Sylvester, Terry, 181, 237, 434
Symarip, 362
Symbols, 262, 434-435
Syndicate Of Sound, 435
Synergy, 409
Syreeta, 476
Sytner, Alan, 101
Szelest, Stan, 228

T

T Power, 438
T. Rex, 453
T.A.S.S., 32, 72, 209
T.S. Monk, 314
Tait, Rob, 35
Taj Mahal, 143, 375-376
Take That, 59, 251, 467

Takoma Records, 187
Talking Records, 359
Talley, Gary, 73
Talley, Nedra, 384
Talmy, Shel, 26, 74, 132, 149, 174, 273, 324, 336
Tamblyn, Larry, 424
Tampa Red, 10
Tams, 117, 435-436
Tangerine Dream, 260
Tangier, 216
Tanner, Dave, 128
Tarantino, Quentin, 38, 139
Tarbuck, Jimmy, 245
Tarney, Alan, 374, 398
Tarplin, Marv, 309, 377
Tarrach, Reinhard, 365
Tarrant, Chris, 392
Tartachny, Paul, 38
Tate, Howard, 179, 365, 405
Tatman, Mike, 241
Tatum, Art, 146, 313, 346
Tausis, Tommy, 422
Tavares, Leo, 193
Taylor, Alan, 101, 358
Taylor, Alistair, 43, 102
Taylor, Allan, 358
Taylor, Art, 122, 414
Taylor, Billy, 386
Taylor, Bob, 161
Taylor, Cecil, 66, 183, 308
Taylor, Chip, 18, 222, 237, 436, 448
Taylor, Clive, 12
Taylor, Creed, 150
Taylor, Dallas, 118, 136
Taylor, Derek, 43, 317, 436
Taylor, Dick, 358, 379
Taylor, Eve, 13, 401
Taylor, Gary, 120, 234
Taylor, James, 36, 118, 256, 387, 414, 436
Taylor, James, Quartet, 414
Taylor, John, 6, 108, 212
Taylor, John T., 6
Taylor, Johnnie, 30, 126, 351, 426, 436-437, 442
Taylor, Johnny, 437
Taylor, Kingsize, 226
Taylor, Larry, 92, 296
Taylor, Lynne, 384
Taylor, Martin, 436
Taylor, Mel, 460
Taylor, Mick, 170, 212, 282, 296, 381-382
Taylor, Rick, 477
Taylor, Rodney, 182
Taylor, Shawn, 181
Taylor, Ted, 404
Taylor, Terry, 179
Taylor, True, 445
Taylor, Vince, 403
Taylor, William, 357
Te Kanawa, Kiri, 50
Tea And Symphony, 244
Tea Set, 9
Teagarden, Jack, 112
Tear Gas, 226
Teardrops, 47, 148, 197, 249, 349, 452, 474-475
Tearle, Derek, 128
Tebb, Johnny, 101
Techniques, 69, 84, 161, 252-253, 303, 306, 332, 370, 423, 438, 441, 476
Teddy Bears, 326, 345, 418, 462
Tedesco, Tommy, 262
Tee, Richard, 189, 265
Teenage Fanclub, 312
Tegza, Michael, 222
Temperance 7, 294, 437
Tempest, 121, 207, 339
Temple, Jerry, 192
Temple, Nat, 172
Temple, Shirley, 118
Templeman, Ted, 225

Tempo, Nino, and April Stevens, 437

Tempos, 155, 223, 307, 364

Temptations, 125, 177, 200, 263, 309, 322, 359, 366-367, 377, 382, 411, 425, 430-433, 437-439, 465

10cc, 53, 132, 287, 306, 331, 401

10,000 Maniacs, 177

Ten Years After, 14, 26, 350, 439, 478

Tennant, Neil, 423

Tennessee Ernie Ford, 276

Tepedino, Sal, 124

Tepperman, Barry, 155

Terrell, Ernie, 432, 439

Terrell, Jean, 432, 439

Terrell, Tammi, 208-209, 439-440

Terry, Clark, 85, 156, 234, 279, 313, 394

Terry, Pat, 434

Terry, Phil, 451

Tesluk, Paul, 255

Tete, 229, 361

Tex, Joe, 130, 265, 337, 348, 440

Thain, Gary, 225

Tharp, Chuck, 195

Thaxton, Lloyd, 270

Thelin, Bjorn, 421

Them, 440-441 and passim

Thibaut, Gilles, 203

Thibodeaux, Gladius, 28

Thielemans, Toots, 184

Third Ear Band, 417, 441

Third World, 415

Thirteenth Floor Elevators, 408, 441-442

Thomas, B.J., 25, 52, 291, 302

Thomas, Carla, 21, 100, 292, 351, 367, 426, 442-443

Thomas, Charles, 474

Thomas, Charlie, 163

Thomas, Cheryl, 387

Thomas, Danny, 442

Thomas, Dave, 63

Thomas, Frank, 362

Thomas, Gary, 68

Thomas, Glyn, 68

Thomas, Henry, 92

Thomas, Irma, 110, 309, 337, 365, 442

Thomas, Leon, 216

Thomas, Mary, 6, 136

Thomas, Mary Ann, 6

Thomas, Mick, 362

Thomas, Ray, 250, 318-319

Thomas, Robert, 457

Thomas, Rufus, 71, 93, 426, 442-443

Thompson, Barbara, 121, 226

Thompson, Danny, 240, 252, 271, 342, 352

Thompson, Dave, 255, 460

Thompson, Dennis, 299

Thompson, Derek, 226

Thompson, James, 357

Thompson, Kay, 472

Thompson, Mayo, 367

Thompson, Mick, 132

Thompson, Phil, 103

Thompson, Randall, 50

Thompson, Steve, 296

Thompson, Sue, 148, 284

Thomson, Liz, 172

Thorkelson, Peter Halsten, 314

Thornbury, James, 92

Thornton, Johnny, 470

Thorup, Peter, 271

Thrasher, Andrew, 163

Three Bells, 284, 351

Three Dog Night, 165, 314, 326

Three O'Clock, 260-261

Threshold Records, 250, 319

Throbbing Gristle, 149

Thunder Alley, 16

Thunder, Johnny, 443

Thunderbeats, 271

Thunderclap Newman, 273, 443

Thurman, Bennie, 441

Thurman, John, 441

Tibbs, Gary, 192

Tickner, George, 206

Tico And The Triumphs, 445

Tidmarsh, Christopher, 112

Tierney, Tony, 286

Tiffen, Harry, 130

Tijuana Brass, 11

Till, John, 258

Tilley, Sandra, 293, 458

Tillis, Mel, 408, 483

Tillman, Georgeanna Marie, 295

Tillman, Keith, 165

Tillotson, Johnny, 276, 284, 286

Tilton, Martha, 146

Timebox, 68, 149, 339

Timmons, Bobby, 7, 443-444

Timms, Sally, 99

Tin Soldier, 18, 245, 412

Tintern Abbey, 444

Tiny Goddess, 329

Tiny Tim, 220, 345, 444

Tippett, Keith, 164, 361

Tjader, Cal, 402

TNT, 229, 467

Tobias, Oliver, 222

Tobler, John, 38, 159, 375

Toe Fat, 46, 212

Together Records, 274

Tokens, 444-445

Tolson, Peter, 358

Tom And Jerry, 289, 406, 445

Tomlinson, David, 424

Tommis, Colin, 91

Tommy And The Tornadoes, 250

Tomsco, George, 195

Toney, Oscar, Jnr., 445

Tongue And Groove, 106

Tonkin, Garfield, 137

Tonto's Expanding Headband, 283

Tony's Defenders, 305

Toots And The Maytals, 298

Top Hat, 156, 256, 457

Top Records, 55, 76, 279, 400

Topham, Tony, 479

Topham, Top, 479

Topol, 195

Torff, Brian, 402-403

Torian, Reggie, 245

Tork, Peter, 314-315

Tormé, Mel, 402-403

Tornados, 39, 101, 207, 230, 338, 422, 446

Torney, Ned, 112

Torrance, Dean, 250

Touch, Peter, 345

Tourists, 103, 108

Toussaint, Allen, 160, 233, 259, 282, 308, 342, 442

Towner, Ralph, 85

Townsend, Ed, 465

Townsend, Ron, 195

Townshend, Pete, 10, 231, 267, 273, 443, 470, 472

Townson, Chris, 255

Toyah, 274, 471

Toys, 180

Track Records, 273

Tradewinds, 262

Traffic, 446-447 and passim

Trailer, Rex, 292

Tramline, 447

Trammell, Danny, 195

Tramp, 324, 367, 442

Transatlantic Records, 91, 251, 429

Traveling Wilburys, 171, 332

Travers, Mary, 345-346

Travis, Betty, 29, 359

Travis, Merle, 20

Treadway, Greg, 310

Treadwell, George, 163

Treat Her Right, 229, 302

Tremeloes, 39, 114, 125, 192, 351, 447-448

Trent D'Arby, Terence, 146

Trent, Jackie, 116, 464

Tricky, 150

Trinity, 32, 164, 213, 426

Tristano, Lennie, 182

Troggs, 222, 337, 350, 436, 448-449

Trojan, 176, 299, 306, 343-345, 349, 352, 362, 370-371

Trovajoli, Armando, 75

Trower, Robin, 213, 337, 360

Troy, Doris, 236, 433, 449

True West, 98-99

Truffaut, François, 23

Tucker, Bob, 57

Tucker, Jim, 450

Tucker, Maureen 'Mo', 459

Tucker, Tanya, 404

Tucker, Tommy, 150, 449

Tucky Buzzard, 179

Tudanger, Steve, 200

Tufano, Dennis, 81

Tulin, Mark, 176

Turnbull, John, 409

Turner, 'Big' Joe, 351

Turner, Alan, 68

Turner, Bobby, 105

Turner, Bruce, 111

Turner, Charles, 161

Turner, Ike, 33, 281, 449-450

Turner, Ike And Tina, 18, 32, 220, 263, 309, 419, 430, 449-450

Turner, Joe, 20, 127, 161, 351

Turner, Mark, 414

Turner, Ray, 161

Turner, Rick, 21

Turner, Steve, 43, 243, 375, 472

Turner, Tina, 18, 32, 220, 263, 286, 309, 419, 430, 449-450

Turney, Ross, 120

Turrentine, Stanley, 66, 84, 219, 394, 413

Turtles, 245, 275, 280, 304, 321, 411, 450-451

Tutt, Ron, 474

Tuttle, John, 194

Twain, Mark, 46, 305

Twiggy, 129, 240

Twinkle, 451

Twisters, 108, 147, 274

Twitch, Elmer, 79, 112

Twitty, Conway, 228, 342, 451-452

Twitty, Kathy, 452

Twitty, Mike, 452

Twomey, Kay, 260

Tyler, Kip, 326

Tyler, T. Texas, 294

Tyner, McCoy, 122, 183, 219

Tyner, Rob, 299

Tyrannosaurus Rex, 255, 452-453

Tyson, Barbara, 273

Tyson, Ron, 438

U-Roy, 343, 370-371

UB40, 9

Ubu, Pere, 367

UFO, 223, 428, 448

Ulaky, Wayne, 38

Ullman, Tracey, 150, 284

Ulmer, Charles, 23

Ulmer, James 'Blood', 339

Ulrick, Ed, 13

Ultimate Spinach, 38, 72, 453

Ulvaeus, Bjorn, 59

Under The Influence, 304, 400

Undercover, 382-383

Underdog, 307-308

Undertakers, 282, 453

Undertones, 247, 305

Underwood, Ian, 321

Underwood, Mick, 179, 334

UNI Records, 194, 429

Union City, 300

Unit Four Plus Two, 68, 386, 413, 454

United Artists, 5, 22, 28, 32, 34, 62, 70-71, 82-83, 90, 92, 96, 101, 145-146, 165, 174, 186, 219-221, 252, 255-256, 275, 280, 290-291, 294, 307-309, 322, 326, 376, 390, 392, 400, 430, 443, 454, 458, 461, 479

United States Of America, 454

Upchurch, Phil, 115, 160, 365, 454

Upsetters, 130, 344-345, 349

Uptown Records, 458

Ure, Midge, 387

Uriah Heep, 28, 212

USA For Africa, 45-46, 107, 170, 477

Usher, Gary, 16, 38, 87, 103, 211, 239, 341, 433

Ussery, Bob, 100

Uzzell, Jay, 128

Uzzell, Moses, 128

V

Vadim, Roger, 77, 224

Vagrants, 455, 481

Valance, Ricky, 32, 455

Vale, Jerry, 58

Vale, Mike, 250

Valence, Ricky, 279

Valens, Ritchie, 317, 445, 455-456

Valente, Caterina, 251, 274, 391

Valenti, Dino, 156, 304, 363, 483

Valentine, Davy, 137

Valentine, Dickie, 468

Valentine, Hilton, 15

Valentines, 44, 128

Valentino, Bobby, 348

Valentino, Sal, 44, 156

Valentino, Tony, 424

Valentinos, 126, 231, 309, 380, 456, 469

Valiant Records, 97

Valino, Joe, 316

Vallee, Rudy, 154

Vallenga, Dirk, 338, 357

Valli, Frankie, 113, 198-199, 476

Vallory, Ross, 206

Van Der Graaf Generator, 271

Van Druten, John, 89

Van Heusen, Jimmy, 457

Van Kuyk, Meg, 57

Van Ronk, Dave, 67, 324, 345, 387

Van Vliet, Don, 84, 94-95

Van Vliet, Jan, 94

Vance, Kenny, 252

Vance, Paul, 137, 151

Vanda And Young, 174, 217

Vanda, Harry, 173, 217

Vandergelder, Horace, 230

Vandergelder, Peter, 219

Vanderpool, Sylvia, 304

Vandross, Luther, 204, 466

Vandyke, Les, 188

Vanguard Records, 188, 191, 384, 455

Vanilla Fudge, 21, 456, 481

Vanity Fare, 268, 431, 456

Vann, Teddy, 443

Vartan, Sylvie, 223

Vaughan, Frankie, 24, 57, 300, 303, 316, 457

Vaughan, Jimmie, 152

Vaughan, Malcolm, 172, 379

Vaughan, Ray, 139

Vaughan, Sarah, 431

Vaughan, Stevie Ray, 139

Vaughn, Billy, 259-260

Vee, Bobby, 134, 151, 212, 278, 284, 349, 429, 457-458, 460, 462

Vee Jay Records, 115, 184, 187, 198, 430

Veitch, Trevor, 387

Vejtables, 21, 312, 458

Velez, Jerry, 232
Velez, Martha, 46
Velvelettes, 256, 458
Velvet Opera, 208, 458
Velvet Underground, 161, 458-460
Velvett Fogg, 460
Venable, Kim, 117
Venet, Nik, 35
Vengerova, Isabella, 50
Venneri, Joseph, 445
Ventures, 460-461 and passim
Venus And The Razorblades, 201
Vera, Billy, 114, 130, 436
Verdon, Gwen, 264
Vermouth, Apollo C., 70
Vernieri, Larry, 147
Vernon, Mike, 46, 57, 110, 152, 431
Vernons, 74, 127, 461
Vernons Girls, 74, 127, 461
Vertigo Records, 45
Verve Records, 147, 364, 413
Vestine, Henry, 92, 187, 321
Vibrators, 192
Vickers, Howie, 120
Vickers, Mike, 290, 461
Vickers, Walter, 182
Victor Records, 356
Vidican, John, 260
Vikings, 298
Villeneuve, Craig, 250
Vincent, Gene, 17, 29, 83, 103, 197, 201, 335, 379
Vinegar Joe, 73, 467
Vinson, Eddie 'Cleanhead', 7, 122, 249
Vinton, Bobby, 269, 291, 461-462
VIPs, 18, 428
Virgin Records, 95, 332, 409
Virtues, 239, 302, 468
Visconti, Tony, 240
Viscounts, 210, 242, 256
Vito, Rick, 296
Vitt, Bill, 416
Vivid, 288, 407
Vogue Records, 313
Vogues, 462
Voice Masters, 161
Voight, Jon, 436
Voigt, Jim, 341
Volck, Betsy, 192
Volk, Phil, 372
Volman, Mark, 214, 321, 450
Von Schmidt, Eric, 15, 191, 324, 385, 387
Voorman, Klaus, 290

W

Wace, Robert, 266, 337, 412
Waddell, Bugs, 192
Waddilove, Philip, 262
Waddington, Tony, 53
Wade, Brett, 177
Wade, Charlie, 243
Wade, Chris, 434
Wade, Norman, 474
Wade, Wellington, 243
Wadey, Steve, 283
Wadsworth, Derek, 226
Wagenfeald, Eddie, 255
Wagstaff Clark, Richard, 115
Wailers, 114, 234, 266, 298, 343-344
Wainright, Nicholas, 108
Waite, David, 129
Waits, Tom, 99, 304, 332
Wakelin, Mike, 324
Wakeman, Rick, 262
Wald, Jerry, 182
Walden, Narada Michael, 25, 204
Walden, Phil, 367
Waldron, Mal, 155
Wales, Howard, 5
Walker Brothers, 24-25, 74, 237, 387, 424, 463-464

Walker, Cindy, 369
Walker, Dave, 244
Walker, David, 278
Walker, Gary, 424, 463
Walker, Jimmy, 269, 375
Walker, John, 463
Walker, Johnny, 174, 302
Walker, Junior, 463-464
Walker, Junior, And The All Stars, 214, 463
Walker, Lillian, 186
Walker, Nancy, 264
Walker, Peter, 362
Walker, Scott, 74, 224, 405, 463-465
Walker, T-Bone, 232, 281, 302
Walker, Thomas, 193
Wall Of Sound, 136, 298, 419
Wallace, Andy, 481
Wallace, Peter, 243
Wallach, Bonnie, 154
Waller, Fats, 29, 80, 112, 414, 467
Waller, Gordon, 345
Waller, Gordon, 345
Waller, Mickey, 142, 427
Wallis, Hal, 338
Wallis, Larry, 192
Wallis, Shani, 331
Walmsley, Steve, 277
Walsh, John, 253, 374
Walsh, Peter, 18, 293, 323, 351
Walsh, Sheila, 374
Walter, Dick, 6
Walters, Hank, 102
Walters, Lou, 428
Walters, Trevor, 390
Walton, Cedar, 311
Walton, Kent, 364
Wand Records, 79, 439
Wandon, Harold, 173
Ward, Alan, 240
Ward, Billy, 302, 474
Ward, Billy, And The Dominoes, 474
Ward, Clara, 204, 368
Ward, Ed, 65
Ward, Paul, 288
Ward, Walter, 331
Ware, John, 128, 469
Ware, Wilbur, 313
Warfield, Tim, 414
Warhol, Andy, 381, 459-460
Warleigh, Ray, 226, 415
Warlocks, 217
Warner Brothers Records, 10, 21-22, 44, 54, 68, 88, 95, 184, 224-225, 277, 335, 386, 445, 465, 468
Warner, Alan, 198, 430
Warner, Jimmy, 206
Warnes, Jennifer, 375, 389
Warrant, 136, 444, 482
Warren, Butch, 313
Warren, Diane, 257, 423
Warren, Harry, 346
Warren, Quentin, 413
Warwick Records, 444
Warwick, Clint, 318
Warwick, Dee Dee, 449, 465
Warwick, Dionne, 6, 24-25, 79, 365, 404, 433-434, 465-466, 477
Was, Don, 44, 112, 185, 295, 416
Washburn, Donna, 153
Washington, Baby, 48, 430, 466
Washington, Dinah, 48, 263, 483
Washington, Geno, 212, 393, 466-467
Washington, George, 454
Washington, Jeanette, 466
Washington, Justine, 466
Washington, Kenny, 84
Washington, Lamont, 222
Waterfront, 50
Waters, John, 84, 293
Waters, Roger, 31
Waters, Warren, 105
Watmough, Ralph, Jazz Band, 102

Watson, Alan, 304
Watson, Doc, 20
Watson, Fraser, 350
Watson, Johnny, 61, 152, 467
Watson, Junior, 92
Watson, Mike, 6
Watt, Norman, 6
Watt-Roy, Garth, 173
Watts 103rd Street Rhythm Band, 467
Watts, Charlie, 179, 271, 379
Watts, David, 267
Watts, George, 91
Watts, John, 467
Wattstax, 281, 425
Waxman, Lou, 311
Way, Pete, 254
Wayfarers, 473
Waymon, Eunice, 407
Wayne, Artie, 287
Wayne, Bob, 197
Wayne, Carl, 323
Wayne, Chris, 323
Wayne, Jeff, 319
Wayne, John, 187, 316, 325
Wayne, Mick, 241
We Five, 424
WEA Records, 436, 470
Weakley, Michael, 176
Weather Report, 346, 404-405
Weathers, John, 186
Weaver, Ken, 206
Weaver, Mick, 225, 447, 479
Weavers, 384, 445, 470
Webb, Bernard, 345
Webb, Dave, 424
Webb, David, 186
Webb, Gary, 238
Webb, Harry Roger, 372
Webb, Jim, 411
Webb, Jimmy, 76, 195, 211, 241, 294
Webb, Marti, 58-59
Webb, Stan, 110
Weber, Eberhard, 85
Weber, Steve, 206, 238
Webster, Ben, 238, 361
Webster, Tony, 253
Wechter, Julius, 149
Weedon, Bert, 248, 468
Weezer, 312
Weider, John, 15, 264, 469
Weill, Cynthia, 15, 76, 290, 349, 419
Weill, Kurt, 14, 121, 140, 158, 189, 405
Weir, Alan, 350
Weir, Bob, 217
Weirdos, 477
Weis, Danny, 372
Weisberg, Richard, 38
Weisbert, David, 354
Weisbrod, Bob, 151
Weisman, Ben, 260
Weiss, George, 145, 445
Weissleder, Manfred, 365
Weissman, Dick, 258
Weitz, Mark, 429
Welby, Marcus, 277
Welch, Alvin, 97
Welch, Bruce, 193, 283, 373, 398-399
Welch, Chris, 132, 146, 233, 447
Welch, Raquel, 382
Weld, Tuesday, 187
Welk, Lawrence, 251
Weller, Paul, 25
Welles, Orson, 289
Wells, Chris, 114
Wells, Coby, 413
Wells, Julia, 13
Wells, Kitty, 118, 184, 276
Wells, Mary, 208-209, 253, 293, 309, 322, 377, 456, 468-469
Welnick, Vince, 218
Welsh, Alex, 111, 198

Welsh, Bob, 105
Wenders, Wim, 67
Wertheimer, Alfred, 357
Wesley, Fred, 78
Wesley, John, 168, 171, 220
Wesselman, Tom, 223
West Coast Jazz, 61
West Coast Pop Art Experimental Band, 179, 469
West, Keith, 469
West, Larry, 324, 455
West, Leslie, 455
West, Mike, 264
West, Richard, 447
West, Rick, 447
Westlake, Clive, 405
Westlake, Kevin, 65
Weston, Bob, 158
Weston, Kim, 208-209, 236, 440, 470
Westover, Charles, 400
Westwood, Richard, 447
Wet Wet Wet, 448
Wexler, Jerry, 20, 55, 170, 204, 286, 390, 423, 433, 449, 470
Weymouth, Nigel, 18, 223, 428
Whale, Pete, 268
Whaley, Paul, 65
Wham!, 80, 125, 214, 413
Wheels, Dave, 399
Whetstone, Richard, 177
Which Witch, 22
While, Chris, 80
Whiplash, 244, 287
Whipped Cream, 11
Whirlwind, 336
Whiskeyhill Singers, 303-304
Whispers, 6, 474-475
Whitbread, Paul, 361
Whitcher, Pip, 417
White, Andrew, 123
White, Andy, 127
White, Bill, 12, 309-310
White, Buck, 71
White, Bukka, 324, 387, 389
White, Chris, 485
White, Clarence, 87-88
White, Dave, 301
White, Forrest, 193
White, George, 41, 152
White, James, 480
White, Joe, 352, 355
White, John, 123, 324, 480
White, Josh, 15, 113
White, Maurice, 279
White, Priscilla, 58, 102
White, Ray, 100
White, Roger, 186
White, Ronnie, 309-310, 377, 476
White, Snowy, 385
White, Stan, 303
White, T.H., 91
White, Ted, 204
White, Timothy, 37-38
White, Tony, 355
White, Tony Joe, 355
Whitehead, Alan, 293
Whitehorn, Geoff, 361
Whiteman, Ian, 6
Whiteman, Paul, 22, 388
Whites, 70
Whitesnake, 121, 336, 447
Whitfield, Mark, 414
Whitfield, Norman, 425, 430, 438, 458
Whiting, Steve, 310
Whitley, Ray, 435
Whitney, Charlie, 191
Whitsett, Carson, 71
Whittington, Bill, 76, 190
Whitwam, Barry, 234
Wickham, Vicki, 366, 422
Widlake, Terry, 334
Wiener, Stu, 123
Wilbur, Richard, 50

Wilcox, Jerry, 194
Wild Angels, 408
Wild Child, 305, 438
Wild Horses, 381, 383
Wild In The Country, 354, 357
Wild Man, 11, 27, 232, 383
Wild, Jack, 331
Wilde, Kim, 276
Wilde, Marty, 130, 194, 214, 242, 338, 352, 373, 404, 431, 461
Wilder, Thornton, 230
Wilhelm, Mike, 106
Wilkinson, David, 5
Wilkinson, Keith, 312
Wilkinson, Lois, 95
Williams, John, 76
Willard, 112, 241
Willard, Glen, 112
Williams Brothers, 472
Williams, Aaron, 303
Williams, Allan, 39, 43, 103
Williams, Andy, 142, 214, 263, 265, 305, 351, 405, 472-473
Williams, Anthony, 66
Williams, Don, 370
Williams, Eddie, 187
Williams, Esther, 228
Williams, Gloria, 293
Williams, Hank, 20, 99, 131, 139, 166, 187, 202, 228, 276, 284, 333, 369, 400, 481-482
Williams, Hank, Jnr., 202, 284
Williams, Jerry, 299
Williams, Joe, 147
Williams, John (guitar), 285
Williams, Kenneth, 110
Williams, Larry, 66, 70, 113, 231, 416, 425, 428, 467
Williams, Lewis, 456
Williams, Margaret, 107
Williams, Mary Lou, 61
Williams, Mason, 473-474
Williams, Maurice, 474
Williams, Maurice, And The Zodiacs, 474
Williams, Miller, 305
Williams, Otis, 72, 437, 439
Williams, Otis, And The Charms, 72
Williams, Paul, 172, 312, 314, 437-438
Williams, Phil, 419
Williams, Ralph, 333
Williams, Ray, 89, 186
Williams, Richard, 144, 419, 438
Williams, Roy, 333
Williams, Steve, 473
Williams, Terry, 285, 327, 405
Williams, Tony, 143, 405
Williamson, 'Tudge', 44
Williamson, Robin, 246
Williamson, Sonny Boy 'Rice Miller', 10, 109, 213
Williamson, Steve, 61
Willie And The Poor Boys, 133
Willis, Alan, 149
Willis, Bobby, 58
Willis, Bruce, 172
Willis, Chuck, 127
Willis, Ian, 390
Willis, Ian 'Lemmy', 390
Willmer, Eric, 178
Willow Spring, 71, 134, 292
Wills, Bob, 131
Wills, Martin, 57
Wills, Rick, 412
Willson, Meredith, 50, 264
Wilmot, Alan And Harry, 418
Wilmot, Gary, 418
Wilner, Hal, 314
Wilsh, Mike, 198
Wilsher, Mick, 327
Wilson Phillips, 224
Wilson, Al, 162
Wilson, Alan, 92

Wilson, Allan, 287
Wilson, B.J., 337, 360
Wilson, Barrie, 68
Wilson, Barry, 254
Wilson, Bob, 244
Wilson, Brian, 16, 35, 37-38, 239, 251, 285, 317, 376
Wilson, Carl, 35-37, 431
Wilson, Charlie, 65
Wilson, Delroy, 343
Wilson, Dennis, 35-37
Wilson, Don, 460
Wilson, Ernest, 114
Wilson, Frank, 200, 238
Wilson, Gerald, 155, 238, 475
Wilson, J., 337, 360
Wilson, Jackie, 6, 125, 214, 255, 377, 468, 474-475
Wilson, Jim, 65
Wilson, Jimmy, 475
Wilson, Joe, 117, 130, 343
Wilson, John, 441
Wilson, Mary, 29, 359, 431-433
Wilson, Michael, 141
Wilson, Murray, 35-37, 431
Wilson, Nancy, 8, 279, 431, 475
Wilson, Patricia, 433
Wilson, Raymond, 45
Wilson, Robert, 418
Wilson, Ron, 433
Wilson, Sandy, 13
Wilson, Smokey, 200
Wilson, Sonny, 474
Wilson, Terry, 106
Wilson, Thomas S., 14
Wilson, Tom, 167, 321, 407
Wilson, Willie, 31
Wimmer, Kevin, 28
Winberg, Bo, 421
Winchester, Jesse, 85, 220
Windeler, Robert, 14
Windsong, 246, 297, 453
Wine, Toni, 17, 306
Winfield, Chuck, 64
Winfield, Jeff, 277
Wing, Barnett, 219, 253
Winged Eel Fingerling, 205, 321
Winkelman, Bob, 206
Winn Records, 148
Winner, Michael, 336
Winsens, Peter, 422
Winslow, Barry, 386
Winston, Jimmy, 412, 475
Winter, Edgar, 64, 300
Winter, Johnny, 300, 302, 478
Winterhalter, Hugo, 90
Winters, Ricky, 46
Winters, Ted, 238
Winwood, Mervyn, 146
Winwood, Muff, 146, 339
Winwood, Steve, 27, 63, 75, 107, 146, 232, 297, 346, 413, 430, 446-447
Wirtz, Mark, 268, 469
Wisdom, Norman, 75
Wisdom, Owen, 45
Wisdom, Trevor, 45
Wise, Fred, 260
Wisseling, Louisa, 398
Withers, Pick, 170
Witherspoon, Jimmy, 82
Witnesses, 447
Wizzard, 18, 323
Wolfe, Randolph, 420
Wolfe, Tom, 217
Wolff, Bill, 341
Wolff, Francis, 66
Wolfgang Press, 257
Wolinski, Hawk, 399
Wom, Barry, 339
Womack And Womack, 286, 410, 456
Womack, Bobby, 126, 130, 286, 309, 348, 410, 456
Womack, Cecil, 456, 469

Womack, Curtis, 456
Womack, Harry, 456
Wombles, 223
Wonder Stuff, 378
Wonder, Stevie, 25, 71, 102, 107, 208, 214-215, 263, 322-323, 466, 476-477
Wonderful Life, 374-375
Wonderful Town, 50, 334
Wood, Arthur, 19, 267
Wood, Brenton, 477
Wood, Chris, 110, 229, 232, 282, 446
Wood, Colin, 409
Wood, Heather, 481
Wood, Ron, 19, 57, 132, 170, 382
Wood, Ronnie, 152, 437
Wood, Roy, 18, 46, 101, 323, 403
Wood, Royston, 481
Wood, Ted, 437
Woodfuff, Woody, 399
Woodley, Bruce, 137, 397
Woods, Bob, 449
Woodson, Craig, 454
Woodward, Mark, 257
Woody, Dan, 229, 399
Wooler, Bob, 102-103, 192
Woonton, Andrew, 241
Wooster, Bertie, 327
Wooten, George, 128
Worden, Les, 424
Words And Pictures, 159
Workman, Reggie, 122, 300
Worth, Johnny, 188, 259
Wray, John, 172
Wray, Link, 429
Wrecks, 431
Wren, Christopher S., 100
Wright, Charles, 468
Wright, Darlene, 136
Wright, Dave, 448
Wright, Ernest, Jnr., 280
Wright, Gary, 18, 223, 385, 421
Wright, Jeff, 466
Wright, John, 38, 466
Wright, John Lincoln, 38
Wright, Larry, 250
Wright, O.V., 478
Wright, Pat, 136
Wright, Rick, 31
Wright, Steve, 173
Wright, William C., 283
Writing On The Wall, 478
Wrixen, Eric, 440-441
Wyatt, Robert, 31, 415
Wyatt, Tessa, 60
Wycherley, Ronald, 207
Wyman, Bill, 179, 379, 383
Wynder K. Frog, 225, 447, 479
Wynette, Tammy, 404, 436
Wynn, Tommy, 151
Wynne, Peter, 338
Wynter, Mark, 90, 108, 114, 395

X

X, 344, 383
X-Vik Records, 22
Xanadu, 141, 263
XYZ, 363

Y

Yaguda, Sandy, 252
Yana, 387
Yanovsky, Zalman 'Zally', 323, 479
Yap, Philip, 409
Yarbrough, Estella, 365
Yarbrough, Glenn, 280, 473
Yard Trauma, 392
Yardbirds, 40, 65, 110, 152, 161, 163, 213, 241, 259, 308, 336, 366, 410, 479-480
Yarrow, Peter, 345

Yasgur, Max, 478
Yates, Peter, 431
Yello, 34
Yellow Submarine, 40-41, 43-44, 294, 480
Yerral, Peter, 415
Yester, Jerry, 19, 286, 304, 326, 479
Yester, Jim, 19, 304
Yo Yo, 93, 108, 154
Yoakam, Dwight, 335
Yoder, Gary, 66
York, George, 419
York, John, 87, 279
York, Keith, 52
York, Paul, 406
York, Pete, 146
Yost, Dennis, 117
You Are What You Eat, 345, 444
You're A Big Boy Now, 285-286
Youmans, Vincent, 346
Young At Heart, 124
Young Ones, The, 11, 373-375, 431, 446, 480
Young Rascals, 147, 161, 332, 455-456, 481
Young Tradition, 481
Young, Ally, 28
Young, Barry, 465
Young, Colin, 198, 483
Young, Dick, 28, 225
Young, Eldee, 278
Young, Faron, 119, 305, 481-483
Young, George, 173-174, 217, 403
Young, Jesse Colin, 483
Young, Jimmy, 364
Young, Kenny, 279
Young, Larry, 66
Young, Leon, 56
Young, Lester, 122, 263
Young, Neil, 67, 81-82, 135, 138, 228, 331
Young, Paul, 146
Young, Reggie, 57
Young, Richard, 112, 375
Young, Vicki, 61
Young, Wanda, 295
Young-Holt Unlimited, 279
Youngbloods, 325, 483
Your Own Thing, 48
Yule, Doug, 459
Yuma, Johnny, 99
Yuro, Timi, 483-484

Z

Zabo, Dave, 97
Zabriskie Point, 188, 261
Zacharias, Helmut, 274, 484
Zadora, Pia, 293
Zagami, Nick, 200
Zager And Evans, 484-485
Zagni, Iav, 254
Zappa, Frank, 12, 94-95, 201, 205, 220, 263, 321-322, 425, 450, 467, 469
Zavaroni, Lena, 426
Zawinul, Joe, 7, 143, 346, 404
Ze Records, 192
Zehringer, Rick, 300
Zephyrs, 152
Zevon, Warren, 201, 437
Zila, 362
Zimmer, Dave, 82, 136
Zimming, Bernie, 151
Zipprodt, Patricia, 89, 195
Ziska, Stan, 148
Zolitin, Cynthia, 444
Zombies, 485
Zorn, John, 314, 339